Holding Onto You

VOLUME 2

- PIPER RAYNE - ASHLEY JADE - SUSAN STOKER -
- KD ROBICHAUX & CC MONROE - CARRIE ANN RYAN -

The Rival Roomies

PIPER RAYNE

Chapter One

RIAN

THE SHRILL SOUND OF MY PHONE WAKES ME, AND MY BLURRY EYES FOCUS ON THE screen. Only my parents ever call me before my alarm goes off. I'd ignore the damn thing if I didn't know they'd call right back or have the National Guard come check on their precious daughter.

"It's early," I answer.

"You're not up yet?" my mom asks.

"Why are you calling me so early?" I snip.

"We were out to dinner with the Fredericksons last night," she says.

I lie back down on the bed, putting the phone on speaker and resting it on my pillow beside my head.

This is going to be a long one.

"Uh-huh," I say, trying not to let my annoyance be heard.

My mom says, "Johann is working on an equation."

Johann would be the Fredericksons' son and the person I'm constantly compared to. The one his parents named after Johann Carl Friedrich Gauss, the famous German mathematician. Imagine living in the United States with the name Johann and being the leader of the mathletes—pre bully awareness. Let's just say by the end of high school, he was walking himself into his locker and shutting the door.

I roll my eyes. "Yeah."

"Yes," my dad corrects me.

I say nothing. Obviously I've woken up on the defiant side of the bed this morning.

"It's for a contest the Mathematical Society of America is running," my mom says.

"That's great," I say with a yawn.

"They said he thinks it will take him a while to solve it." The excitement level in my mom's voice grows higher and higher while my interest wanes further and further.

"I'm sure he will. No one is better than him," I say.

"Except you, sweetheart," my dad says.

The man adds sweetheart when he wants me to do something. It's a trigger word that says this conversation will suck and I'm most likely going to commit to doing something I don't want to do. Namely this contest.

I say, "Jo is going to crush it. If he's already started it, he's as good as won."

"The contest is open, and if you win, it's worth prize money," my dad says.

"How much?" I ask.

"I didn't catch the amount. Did you, Larry?" my mom asks. "Not that it's important. You wouldn't be doing it for the money."

Uh, yeah, I would.

"You don't need money, right, sweetheart? You save a quarter of your paycheck for a rainy day like we've always taught you, right?" my dad asks.

"Of course." How many lies can you tell your parents in your lifetime? I stopped counting.

"That's my girl," he says with pride.

Mom continues. "You do it for the notoriety. Your name will grace every conversation in the industry. You could get a much better job and forget Pierson Education. They should've had you writing college-level equations by now. Fifth grade math is an insult to your intelligence."

"Mom, I don't really have the time for another—"

"Make the time. I'm emailing you all the details now. And don't tell anyone. I don't want Johann working day and night to beat you. It's about time they see how talented you are," she says.

I roll my eyes. "I'll look into it."

There's a moment of silence, and the scratching on the phone line says one of them is doing something else.

"What's going on with you, sweetheart?" my dad asks.

I glance at the phone to make sure the connection is still with my parents. Rarely do they show any interest in how I'm really doing, preferring instead to cling to the prefabricated assurances I feed them. "Good. Sierra moved out to live with her boyfriend."

"The prince," my dad says. "We saw the footage. The Fredericksons didn't know what to say when we told them that."

"That your daughter's roommate is dating a prince?"

"Is Johann's roommate dating a princess?"

"Johann doesn't have a roommate," I say.

"Exactly." My dad's tone is one of satisfaction.

Does he not realize his daughter has to live with people in order to have a nice place to live? Johann lives in New York City in a studio apartment all by himself.

"Okay, I registered you," my mom cuts in.

I sit up in bed. "What?"

"This way it's done. Taken care of."

I blow out a breath. The last thing I want to spend my free time on is a math problem, but I will say the money sounds intriguing. "Okay."

"Make sure you start on it right away. Johann already has a head start," my mom says.

"I need to get to work now," I say.

"That's fine. Your dad and I are going with a few other friends to talk to the administrators of the SAT. We think there should be different ones for gifted kids. They all shouldn't be able to score perfect."

"And that's not a knock on you, sweetheart," my dad says.

"Although you should've taken it over," my mom says.

I roll my eyes. I didn't need to take it over. I had an excellent score, she just still isn't over the fact that Johann scored better than I did. "I gotta go. Work and all."

"Bye, sweetheart," my dad says.

"Don't forget, mum's the word. No posting on social media about doing the math—"

"Got it, Mom. Bye."

"Love —"

I click off the phone, then pull up the email with all the details. The problem will be emailed to me directly by a Dr. Giroux. Once I finish, I send him my work and am only to talk to him. They don't disclose how many people are trying to solve the problem, but as soon as the right answer is given, everyone will be notified of the winner. And there's a twenty-five-thousand-dollar prize that they would prefer go to continued education but understand they cannot dictate that.

Dylan's loud voice interrupts my concentration and I rise from my bed to see what's going on. It's been only one day since my entire roommate situation took a one-eighty. I went from living with a couple to two men. One of which I still haven't really gotten to know well.

"There are rules here," Dylan says.

I press my ear against my bedroom door.

"Just relax, Phillips. I'm not looking for complications," Jax says.

None of us ever use Dylan's last name. Mostly because when Dylan introduces himself to someone, he never uses his last name. Even his business cards at Ink Envy only have Dylan in a black block font. He's always touchy about his middle name too.

"I just want to make it clear—you aren't to touch her."

Jax laughs sarcastically as my palm flattens on the door as though Dylan's recent body-guard behavior has anything to do with romantic feelings for me. *He's your friend and only moved into your apartment so you didn't have to live alone with a guy you don't know. Do not think of this as anything more.*

Jax's laugh abruptly cuts off. "Tell me, Phillips, are you touching her?"

"None of your business."

"So this is a Naomi situation all over again?"

Naomi? I mentally mark that name to ask Knox about later.

"No. Rian is just…"

"What?" Jax eggs him on.

Dylan groans. The same tone he uses when his employees call in sick and he has to go in. "Different."

"She's into girls?" Jax asks.

"No!"

"So you want to nail her and are afraid, by comparison to me, you'll come up short?"

"Fuck no!" Dylan yells.

I slowly back away from the door. I guess that answers the question I've never asked anyone but myself.

I've wanted Dylan since he moved in across the hall with Knox. They've known each other since high school. But when the question comes to his feelings for me, the answer isn't only no—it's hell no.

I sit on the edge of my bed. Someday I need to get over this crush I have on a guy who doesn't even know I exist—at least not in *that* way. Maybe I should list all the reasons why we would never work. Perhaps our differences are too big to ever allow us to meet in the middle.

It's the classic tale—good girl wants bad boy. Cliché enough to be a romance novel. Not realistic. I shouldn't want a guy who thinks of commitment as a life sentence. He sure as hell doesn't want a girl whose only experience is a handful of half adept short-term boyfriends.

God help me.

I pick up a pillow and groan. I'd scream, but they'd hear me and I'm pretending like I'm not up yet. Which shows how much Dylan knows my schedule and routine. I'm always the first one dressed and ready.

Their voices grow softer. Dylan's door next to mine shuts minutes later.

I slide my shower cap on my head. Now's my time to escape, so I open my door and tiptoe across the living area to the bathroom.

"Good morning," Dylan says.

I jump and circle back around. He's in workout clothes and has a bag hanging from his shoulder. My gaze goes to the microwave clock in the kitchen. It's only seven-thirty. The shop was open last night, and he didn't return home until after one.

Someone hit me with a sledgehammer. It's so pathetic that I know that.

"Morning." I slide my shower cap off my head. "Where are you off to?"

"The gym." He grabs a bottle of water from the fridge. "Ethan asked me to start going with him first thing in the morning rather than later. I guess love makes you eat. Seth's supposed to come too." The way his mouth scrunches to the side on the word love means he never wants to find out. More evidence to mark under commitment-phobe.

"Enjoy." I wave and keep to my mantra to take a shower and get ready for work. I miss being able to work from home but my job changed their requirements and now I have to work from the office several days a week.

"You should be fine. Jax just got home smelling like he closed the bar down. He'll probably pass out. Shouldn't bother you."

I pause by the bathroom door. Usually I'd turn around and smile and thank him. Be polite and courteous. But a bitter taste fills my mouth—because he's acting like one of Blanca's older brothers. I never asked for, nor do I need any saving from Jax.

"Have a great workout." I step into the bathroom, shut the door, and flick the lock.

Have a great workout? Way to really give him a piece of your mind, Rian.

I turn on the shower to the hottest possible temperature so that the mirror will fill with steam and I won't have to look at myself. I need a life. One where my obsession with Dylan isn't the main focus.

Screw him. I'm baking lemon cake today.

Chapter Two

DYLAN

"WE DON'T NEED TO GO BALLS TO THE WALL ON THE FIRST DAY," ETHAN says next to me, his finger hovering over the treadmill's buttons, his feet pounding on the moving belt.

"I thought you worked out?" I ask, not adjusting my speed or incline.

"I run. Occasionally. I've been blessed with a great metabolism."

I glance at him. "Until Blanca?"

He groans. "You should see what she can consume. And then there's something inside me that says I'm the man, she can't out eat me."

"Hence the gut." I pat my stomach.

He cringes. He hasn't gained enough to be that noticeable, but no harm in him thinking he has. It'll keep him coming to the gym with me and get me out of the damn apartment while Rian is getting ready for work.

Ethan looks down at his stomach and I want to bust out laughing, but I up the incline.

"Fucker," he says, clicking the button on his machine. Ethan can't back away from a challenge.

"Come on. After this, we'll do weights so you don't turn into a pansy-ass who can't lift his fiancée to fuck her against the wall."

An older woman with a displeased expression stops in front of my treadmill. I'm about to apologize before a smile forms on her lips and she looks Ethan up and down. "I bet he has no problem with it."

Winnie, my foster mom, taught me to respect my elders, so I swallow my amusement and watch Ethan smile nicely to avoid offending the woman.

She slowly walks over to the bikes and spends five minutes finding the television show she wants to watch before pedaling. Even then, she has no headphones.

I turn off my treadmill, sliding back until I can hop off.

"What the hell? We can't just stop," Ethan says.

"Why not?" I ask.

"Sir! Wipe your machine," the man who works here—and wears his shorts too tight—calls to me.

I put up my hand and grab a pair of the cheap earbuds the gym offers for free. I wink at the girl behind the counter. She's been trying to flirt with me for the last two weeks, but she's got to be only twenty-one or something. The younger they are, the more attached they become.

"Dylan!" Ethan calls, his hands up in the air, his eyes tracking my movements toward the elderly lady.

I take the headphones out of the plastic disposable bag and hand them to her, plugging the cord into the television portion of the bike. She gives me a thumbs-up and a smile.

"Sir!" the guy says again.

"Relax there. Are your shorts so tight they're cutting circulation off to your brain?" I pull a sanitary wipe from the container and head over to my machine.

Tight shorts guy huffs and stalks off.

"You left me hanging?" Ethan says, shutting off his treadmill.

"You telling me you didn't want that over with?"

Ethan says nothing. Yeah, he's happy as shit I turned off my treadmill.

"Weights then." I hold up my wipe so moose-knuckle can see me dispose of it in the trash can.

He rolls his eyes and shifts his vision away.

"What's with you today?" Ethan asks, throwing his wipe away right after and grabbing a towel.

"Nothing."

"Really? Because you're being an ass to everyone but that old lady over there. Since when are you responsible for handing out earbuds? Did you get a job here I don't know about?"

I grab two dumbbells and stand in front of the mirror as Ethan follows suit. I'm not even sure if I can trust Ethan with what's bothering me, nor do I know if I want anyone to know. It's ridiculous anyway. I do a bicep curl with one arm, then the other.

"So?" Ethan asks.

"So nothing. We don't have to be like chicks and talk while we work out."

"There's a reason you're being a dick." He does a bicep curl, his eyes boring into mine in the mirror.

Ethan knows me well. I went through a lot of phases of independence in college, especially when the guilt that Winnie was wasting her savings on me made me try to sabotage my future, and Ethan was the one who set me straight.

I sit on the bench while Ethan continues pumping his arms. "I'm pissed that Knox brought Jax back here. He knows how things are between us."

He puts the dumbbells back and stacks some weights onto the bar on the bench. "What's the deal with the two of you? You're so much alike."

From the outside, Jax and I are similar. Both wounded foster kids who opted to ink their bodies with symbols and memories of harder times.

I went to college to study art and Jax headed to Los Angeles. I sold a painting out of college that earned me enough money to start Ink Envy two years after graduation. Last I heard, Jax trained under Alex Choi, a guy who'd earned his credentials on the street. Our training and paths were different, but we're still in the same fucking spot. We're both in-demand tattoo artists. The only difference now is I'm planted in Cliffton Heights and Jax just happened to follow a wind that blew him here.

"The asshole probably expects me to give him a job." I lower my back to the bench and Ethan stands above to spot me.

"Is he that kind of guy?"

No, he's not. Jax doesn't take handouts, just like me. But why is he here in Cliffton Heights? This town is too small for a personality like his.

"He's like us. You earn it yourself or it means shit."

Ethan nods, his hands hovering under the pole just in case. He's on crack. I'd need a lot more weight than this to make me struggle. I rack the weights, sit up, and wipe the sweat off my face.

"Hey, assholes, I thought we were in this together!" Seth yells from the other side of the room.

"No yelling in the facility," moose-knuckle says.

Seth looks him up and down, concentrating on his obvious package. "I think you took your ten-year-old brother's shorts this morning."

The girl at the desk cracks up and Seth winks at her. The guy's face turns red, but he continues folding the towels. Usually we're not this big of jerks to people, so I wonder if something is bothering Seth like it is me.

Seth lays his towel on the bench and Ethan acts offended, but we both know bench pressing isn't really Ethan's thing.

"So after you dickheads deserted me—"

"We knocked five times," Ethan says.

"You have a key," Seth says, looking at me over his chest.

Ethan gets back into spotter position like he did for me.

"I overslept. It's been a shit morning all around," Seth says. "Guess who was standing on the other side of the road when I left our building?"

Neither of us answers.

"Her."

"Her who?" Ethan asks.

Seth mocks offense and stares at me like *what's with this guy*, but I'm not sure who he's talking about either. "Evan Erickson. I think she's stalking me."

Ethan smirks at me over the weight bar. "Why would she stalk you?"

"Because a few months ago, we had that altercation outside her bagel shop. Remember when Adrian worked there?"

"Yeah," I say.

"She must've liked it because after years of never running into her, she's been popping up everywhere. I found her in the gazebo with some guy last week. I mean, what would she be doing outside our apartment building that early in the morning?"

"Did you ask her?" Ethan asks.

"No!" His voice cracks like a thirteen-year-old boy's. "Why would I do that?"

Ethan shrugs. "Why wouldn't you?"

Seth pushes up his last rep and sits up, wiping his head with a towel before standing for me to take his place.

"Hello?" Ethan gives me an exasperated look and holds his hands out to the side.

"Oh, you want a piece of this?" I ask, pointing at the bench.

Ethan narrows his eyes, and Seth and I burst out laughing.

Ignoring us, Ethan lies on the bench. "Since I'm the only one who isn't hashing out imaginary problems, I think it's only fair."

"Having a stalker *is* a problem," Seth says.

"As is Knox bringing that asshole back into our lives," I argue.

I walk around the bench to act as the spotter for Ethan.

"What's your problem with Jax anyway?" Seth asks.

"He's just not someone I like to spend time with."

Seth tries to stop his smirk from forming, but I see it on his smug face anyway. Whatever is about to come out of his mouth, I'm not gonna like it.

"When I left, I heard music blaring from your apartment," Seth says. "Rian was leaving for work, and she mentioned that Jax likes to walk around naked."

I stare at him because this is Seth—he fucks around with people's heads all the time. He has to be joking.

"He-lllll… o?"

I glance down to see Ethan struggling to get the bar up. Seth hurries over to help, but between Ethan and I, we get the bar back on the hooks.

"So it's exactly what I thought then?" Seth picks up dumbbells.

"What?"

"This isn't about whatever beef happened between you and Jax years ago. This is about Rian." His cockiness grates on my nerves.

"Rian? What crack are you smoking?" I give Seth a what-the-fuck look that would make a lesser man piss himself.

"No crack. You're upset about Rian seeing Jax's schlong."

"No, I'm annoyed because I hate the asshole and I don't want to see his dick twenty-four seven."

Seth coughs out, "Bullshit."

Ethan doesn't say anything. Can he see how uncomfortable I am? That I'm trying my hardest to seem unfazed?

"Okay, so if Knox walked around naked all the time, you wouldn't have a problem with it?" I ask.

Seth huffs as he does some lateral raises. "I couldn't give a shit. Hell, I had to see his naked ass the other day when I walked in on him fucking Leilani on the couch. I just grabbed my chips from the kitchen and went to my room. The naked body isn't something to be ashamed about."

Him and his fucking mouth.

"Come on. Why the hell would you move in with them otherwise? Time to face the facts," Seth says.

I sit on the bench. "You're delusional."

"I don't think I am. We're your friends. Why would you be embarrassed to have a thing for Rian?"

The noose around my neck winds tighter and tighter, making it hard to swallow. "I wouldn't be embarrassed to have a thing for Rian—if I actually did. I love her the same as you both do. Because she's our friend and for her killer baking skills."

Seth nods like, 'yeah right.'

Ethan acts as if he's concentrating on the reps, but his glimpses at me say he's trying to decipher exactly how I feel about Rian.

"Just mind your own business and worry about your stalker," I say.

Seth throws his towel at me and we continue our workout without any more talk of stalkers or women who can bake.

Later that night, after a dead night at Ink Envy, I walk into the apartment to find a half-eaten cake. Jax comes out of the bathroom, a towel around his waist.

"Clothes aren't optional around here," I say.

He spots me eyeing the cake. "She's a great baker, huh? Lemon is my favorite."

"Lemon?" I mumble. "I fucking hate lemon."

He puts his hand on my shoulder. "Oh shit, am I already taking your place?" He chuckles and stalks off to his room.

Rian knows I hate lemon. Why would she bake that?

Chapter Three

RIAN

I SIT AT THE KITCHEN TABLE, WORKING AWAY AND WAITING FOR MY CINNAMON muffins to finish baking. The paperwork from the Mathematical Society of America sits on the counter like a puppy starved for attention.

What would I do if I won the money? I don't think I'd go back to school. My mom texted me twice this morning, asking if I've started the problem. She's fooling herself if she thinks she wants me to win for me. She wants me to win because Johann has beat me at everything our entire lives.

A key in the door startles me and I bury my head in my project. Fractions are a bitch for kids to learn and the recipients of this textbook will be lucky if I don't take out my frustration by making them harder.

"Hey, Rian," Jax says.

I blow out a relieved breath into my papers.

"Were you expecting a burglar?" His arms slide out of his jacket and he hangs it on the hook by the door.

I take a moment to soak him in, see him in my space. We only met briefly the other morning, so it still kind of feels as if a stranger lives with me. Even so, he's not the one I was worried was going to walk through that door. But I can't be honest about that with Jax.

I stand and bury my head in the fridge. "No. I was working, and you startled me when you came in."

"Grab me a beer while you're in there?" he asks. The sound of chair legs sliding along our wooden floor rings out.

I twist off the top of a beer and hand it to him.

"My own personal waitress. I could get used to this." He grins.

I sit back down. "Don't get your hopes up."

He sips his beer, his gaze on me the entire time he rests the bottle on his lips and lowers it back down. I glance up a few times.

"So what's your story?" he asks. His approach leaves something to be desired, but he seems genuinely interested in the answer, based on the fact that his eyes haven't strayed anywhere but my face.

I place my pencil down and lean back in my seat. "What do you want to know?"

"Anything you want to offer."

He sips his beer again. Most women would probably be drooling from having Jax's attention. His dark hair and five o'clock shadow, the definition of the muscles in his arms—it all works to make him more than appealing. So although it feels nice, it's obligatory. We're sharing a bathroom now.

"I write math textbooks for elementary grade levels," I say.

He nods and sips his beer. "So you're like genius level, or math just gets you all excited?"

"Definitely not genius level." My gaze veers to the stack of papers by my purse, where the contract for the contest sits.

"You probably got some perfect score on that ASS test," he says.

I giggle. "You mean SAT or ACT?"

"Whatever." He shrugs. "I never took it."

"Why not?" I relax back into my chair and push my work to the side.

He downs another gulp of his beer. "I wasn't meant for college. That shit only gave Phillips a hard-on."

I nod, not sure if I should ask more questions or not.

"Boyfriend?" he asks.

At first, I think the question is rude, but mostly because my two good friends are now in serious relationships, which makes me wonder if I'm going to end up as a cat lady cliché. But I'm allergic to cat hair, so I'd have to be a bird lady or fish woman. Which sounds even worse. I imagine myself in a tank while my fish swim around my head or having birds resting along the lengths of my arms, their tiny claws digging into my skin, and I shudder.

"No boyfriend."

"Really?" He tilts his head and one side of his lips tip up.

Heat rushes up my neck. "Yeah. Why?"

He shrugs. "I'm surprised Phillips hasn't locked you down yet."

"Locked me down? Next you'll be calling me someone's old lady." I place my pencil in the crack of the book to keep my place and close it.

He laughs and tips the mouth of his beer in my direction.

"I think you can probably think of a nicer way to say that?"

He chuckles. "You're one of those, huh?"

"So far I'd say we're not on the best of terms with your word choices." I don't mean anything horrible, I'm mostly joking, but I don't believe anyone is going to "lock me down."

"I didn't mean any offense, I'm just surprised. You're hot in that innocent schoolgirl way. Makes me want to make you all dirty."

I open my mouth, but nothing comes out. No one has ever said anything like that to me. I never thought I was the type of girl who would get turned on by it, but my core aches with his words.

"There must be something wrong with Phillips. How long have the two of you known each other?"

I shrug. "A few years."

He nods, his gaze dipping to my cleavage. I shouldn't like the way his eyes almost sear the clothes from my body. I have no doubt he's envisioning me naked right now. I shouldn't like it, but I do.

I've found myself feeling like a wanton woman about as often in my life as I've found myself the winner of the lottery. Which is to say never. I always ended up in that middle ground.

"And you guys have never…"

We both know what he's asking.

"That would be none of your business." Luckily the oven buzzer goes off, so I have a reason to excuse myself from this conversation.

"So you write math equations and bake. Those are your turn-ons?"

I pull the muffins out of the oven and place them on top of the stove. "They aren't my turn-ons. I just enjoy baking."

"Ah, but not the math? Good girl has a secret."

I whip my head in his direction. His cocky smirk says he's already figured me out.

"I think it's time we shift the focus of our conversation to you."

He twirls his beer bottle in circles on the table, following my movements as I transfer the muffins from the pan to the cooling rack.

"Name is Jax Owens. I'm a tattoo artist. Grew up in New York City. Once I turned eighteen, I aged out of the foster care system and got the fuck outta Dodge as fast as a criminal who slipped his cuffs before being thrown in jail. Right now, I need some calm from my chaotic life. So here I am."

I lean against the counter. "What's so chaotic about your life?"

"People following me on Instagram. Everyone wanting something. You're not from my world, but I'm kind of a big deal."

I laugh but stop once his eyes meet mine. "Conceited much?"

"It's not conceited when it's fact. Why do you think Phillips hates me so much?"

"I didn't know he hated you." I'm lying, but I can't help but feel like Dylan's bodyguard and I don't like people putting words in his mouth. I have no idea why Dylan dislikes Jax.

"He does. I'm everything he wanted to be, but Winnie forced him to take one of those tests and attend college."

I say nothing. The selfish part of me wants Jax to fill in all the blanks I have about Dylan's past, because Dylan always has a way of dodging personal questions.

"The bastard got lucky with that painting."

I nod because that is something I know about Dylan's past. The painting Dylan sold in order to start Ink Envy. No one except for Ethan has ever seen it. I wonder if Jax has though.

"Talent isn't luck," I say.

He smirks, his gaze falling down my body. "You don't have to stick up for him. He knows as well as I do that he got fucking lucky."

"Maybe by finding the right buyer, but someone would have purchased it eventually."

"So you've seen it?" Jax asks.

I place a cinnamon muffin on a plate and slide it over to him.

"Distraction by sweets. I'll take that as a no." He unwraps the muffin and chomps down.

"Are you two going to be able to play nice?" I ask, putting the muffin pan in the sink and turning on the water before adding soap.

"I don't play nice, but I do play fair." He winks and takes another healthy bite of the muffin.

"Just get along, respect each other's things, and we'll be good." I turn around and wash the muffin pan.

A minute later, the chair legs slide along the hardwood floor again. He throws the balled-up muffin wrapper into the garbage in the cupboard to my right. Then his hands land on either side of me, caging me to the sink. "Let me ask you something, square root girl, are you Team Phillips?"

Shivers rise up my neck. "I'm no one's team." My voice doesn't hold the conviction it should.

"I guess we'll see about that." He pushes off the counter. "You should make some pie," he says while walking toward his bedroom.

I look over my shoulder at him. "Why?"

He turns around in the middle of the room. "Because I'd love to eat your pie."

His smirk deepens and his gaze flows up and down my body once more with the scorching heat of a thousand flames. He walks into his bedroom and shuts the door just as the front door opens.

Dylan stands in the doorway like a German Shepherd who just found his scent after searching for miles. His gaze meets mine then travels to Jax's closed bedroom door and wanders back to me. "Why are you so red? Is it too hot in here?"

I swallow past the dry lump in my throat. "No. I just took muffins out of the oven."

Dylan drops his stuff by the door and beelines it to the muffins. "Hot muffins? My favorite?"

He takes one, pulling the top off first like he does with cupcakes. He eats it then goes to take off his jacket but stops with half the muffin in his mouth and one arm out of his jacket. I'm too busy processing Jax's pie comment to wonder why he stopped.

By the time Dylan clears his throat after finishing the muffin, he holds a stack of papers in his hands. "What's this?"

"Nothing." I step forward, reaching for the papers, but he puts his hand on my head like an older sibling would to their younger one keeping me at arm's length. "Dylan!" I scold, my arms frantically reaching.

"A math problem?" He continues reading. "Shit. Twenty-five K?" He stares at me without releasing my head. "You're doing this?"

"No. I don't know. My mom…" I blow out a breath and give up the fight.

He releases my head and sits at the table. "You don't know? You totally should." He flips the pages, reading through the contract. "You haven't signed yet?"

I shake my head, falling into the chair next to him.

He throws down the papers and bends down to untie his boots. "Why?"

I shrug.

"Scared?"

"No."

He cocks his eyebrow.

I sigh. "I'm not scared about whether I can do it. I'm scared about what happens if I succeed."

"That makes sense."

I look at him. How does he understand what I was saying? Surely, he's never had the pressure and expectations my parents put on me. If I succeed, they'll only expect more.

"The prize is pretty awesome though. You could do a lot with it." He stands, hooking his fingers in his boots so they hang off his fingers. "Like open a bakery or something." He raises his eyebrows and disappears into his room.

My head falls to the table and I blow out a long pent-up breath of frustration. This roommate situation is ridiculous. One guy treats me like he's my big brother and protects me, pushing me like a best friend would to do something I'm scared of. The other guy makes crude comments that make me hot and horny. The latter would be great if he was the guy I was into.

Chapter Four

DYLAN

I RETURN FROM THE GYM, MY LEGS BURNING FROM TOO MANY SQUATS. I'LL STILL BE there tomorrow though because the gym is my excuse to get out of the apartment before anyone else is awake. Rian is a creature of habit and her alarm goes off at the exact same time every day. I wake up fifteen minutes before, giving me ample time to go to the bathroom, brush my teeth, and grab my gym bag. When I return, she's already left for work. Perfect plan really.

Until today—when I walk in after my workout to find Jax at the kitchen table in his boxers, his head in a bowl of cereal. Damn it. He usually sleeps later than this.

I'm about to bypass him to hit the shower then spend the day at Ink Envy when he slides a piece of paper toward me. My footsteps stop, but I don't pick it up.

"It's from Rian," he says.

I swoop up the piece of paper, knowing he's already read it.

Roommate dinner tonight. We're all cooking something. Initial next to your item.

Rian's initials are next to dessert and Jax's are next to meat.

"I'm left with vegetables?" I ball up the note and toss it onto the table.

"Come on, Phillips, you know I've got all the meat Rian needs." He laughs as I slam my door.

I'm not in the mood to deal with his bullshit. I strip off my shirt and grab my towel, walking back out to the main living area.

Jax is walking back to his room, so we come face to face. Both of us are shirtless, leaving the compass tattoo on the left side of his chest visible. His eyes zero in on the anchor on my left pec. At sixteen, we had them done together, for each other. I was supposed to anchor down his wild streak, and he was supposed to push me to explore and take more chances. Unfortunately, no one could tame Jax, and my obligation to Winnie kept me from seeing the world. I'm happy with where life took me so far, but I wonder if Jax feels the same.

His gaze meets mine. "Maybe you should work out twice a day." He smirks and side-steps me.

"Some of us own our own business. Well, one of us anyway," I say.

He laughs and shuts his door.

I shake my head. He's not worth the aggravation. Never has been.

Lucky for me, after I shower and get dressed, Jax is nowhere in sight.

On the elevator ride down, I retrieve my phone from my pocket in order to text Rian.

Me: What's up with this roommate dinner?

The three dots appear immediately, as they usually do. She's never one to leave you hanging. It's one of the best things about her.

Rian: Because we need to set some rules in order to get along. This whole everyone ignoring everyone thing isn't going to work.

Me: I'll let the other guys know.

Rian: No you won't.

Rian: It's just us.

Rian: The three of us.

I send a gif of a man rolling on the floor in a tantrum.

Rian: Funny. But still happening. See you tonight.

I pocket my phone and walk across the street, then unlock the door of Ink Envy. My favorite part of the day is coming here in the morning when it's quiet. Sometimes I still can't believe it's mine. Walking by the stations of all the tattoo artists who want to work for me feels surreal. Heading to the back, I go to my office because I have paperwork to do that I've been putting off.

I boot up my computer then spot a note from Frankie on my desk.

I'll be out for a while. Call you when I can.

I crumple the note and toss it into the trash can. Seems I don't like any notes I receive today. I was hoping to ask Frankie for some advice about Rian.

Instead of worrying about all the bullshit that will surely go down tonight, I bury my head in the part of this business I hate—the actual business bullshit.

After an hour of recording expenses, I review last month's numbers. There's no way last month took a loss. I inch up closer as if I'm eighty and can't see the glaring red number on my computer screen that's blinking like a stoplight at two in the morning.

I knew things had been slow. Frankie was out more than usual, and let's face it, when I lost Mad Max, he took one helluva following with him to New York City. Not that I blame him for wanting to make it big. Cliffton Heights isn't where you make a name for yourself in the tattoo industry. Although I do have some clients who come from pretty far away for me and Frankie specifically, most of our customers are from neighboring towns.

Without Mad Max and Frankie working, I'm not making a cut of their jobs which has clearly hit my bottom line.

I press my palms to the edge of the desk and push myself back. The wheels of my chair slide until it hits the wall. What the fuck can I do? I need to get another artist in here.

Pulling out my phone, I scan Instagram for a newbie in the tat world who's trying to make a name for him or herself. The first artist to pop up is Jax, so I click off my phone and toss it onto the desk.

One thing's for sure—I'd better do something, otherwise I'm not making bills next month. The worst thing you can do in this industry is not have a functioning space for your artists to work in. Might as well lock your doors.

Hoobastank plays on the other side of the door, which means Jax is already home. Rian is more of a country music girl.

I put my hand on the doorknob and stand there for a second. Rian's right—we can't live like this until Jax decides Cliffton Heights isn't for him. Since high school, he usually cut ties every four months from wherever he's living at least. We don't have to be best friends, but we can keep it civil.

All the kumbaya shit in my head dies when the door opens and I find Jax licking batter off of Rian's finger.

Her head shoots my way, eyes wide like I caught her doing something wrong. Jax's Cheshire Cat grin is obvious even with his lips wrapped around her finger. My jaw aches from clenching.

"Don't let me interrupt." I hold up my hands and walk through the living room toward my bedroom.

"You're not interrupting. Jax was just joking around," Rian says, but I'm already at my bedroom door.

"Let me know when you two are done, and I'll do my vegetables."

I kick the door shut and throw my bag on the bed. When I hook my phone to my radio, Papa Roach's "Scars" plays, since that's what I was listening to at Ink Envy. For a moment, I calm myself down, pissed I showed any cards to that fucker by slamming the door. I can already picture his cocky smirk waiting for me when I open that door again.

Not much has changed since high school with Jax and me. We listen to the same music, we're almost like the same person. Hell, even down to being into the same girl.

I gotta get a grip though, because Rian isn't Naomi. She's not even close to being mine. She's a grown woman who can protect herself. My reaction is just from the stress of the store. The underlying worry that I'm going to lose everything I've worked so hard to achieve.

Might as well get this roommate dinner over with. I leave the seclusion of my bedroom and thank God that it's only Rian in the kitchen.

She turns around, her blonde hair pulled back into a messy ponytail. She's wearing the apron I got her last Christmas. I still remember the blush that crawled across her skin when she read, "Warning: spooning will lead to forking."

"You okay?" she asks.

I hate that question. I've probably been asked that same question five million times in my life. It was part of the social worker's handbook. When they come to get you because you're not wanted, they lay their hands on your shoulders as they bend over to get face to face. Always the same question—are you okay?

"I'm good. Just didn't want to interrupt." I pull out the vegetables I picked up at lunch and ran up here to put in the fridge.

"You're not interrupting. You just happened to walk in when he was trying out my batter."

"Where is he anyway?" I ask.

"He's gone up to the roof to heat the grill up."

I eye her like she can cut the bullshit. "You like him?" Grabbing the cutting board, I place it on the counter and open the drawer with the knives.

"I barely know him."

I wash the lettuce, peeling back the bad layers. "He's not the ever-after type. He's not like Adrian or Ethan."

She says nothing, and when I look up from the sink, the kindness that usually radiates off her isn't there. "Who said I want that?"

I chop the lettuce as a distraction. Rian isn't a one-night-only kinda girl. She might think she could do it, but she can't.

"Are you going to answer my question?"

I scoop up the lettuce and put it into a bowl, ready to peel the carrots, but Rian's already doing that for me. She thinks I'm incapable of doing shit, which is why she always does it for me. "Even if you want a quick fuck, do you really think your new roommate is the best choice?"

She peels the carrots more forcefully now, the scraps falling into the sink at record pace. "I'm not sure that's any of your business."

"I'm your friend. It's my business."

She hands me a carrot, and I slice it into coins.

"Friends offer advice. They don't tell someone what to do." She buries her head in the fridge, grabbing the salad dressings.

The knife drops from my hand and I lean against the counter to face her. She turns around and startles.

"You'll be wasting your time with Jax."

She shakes the salad dressing and her gaze slowly rises to meet mine. "How do you know? Maybe I'm the one who changes him. Or maybe he wants someone like me. I get that I'm not what you'd consider in your league, what with me not having any tattoos or piercings, but can you really speak for a guy you haven't talked to in almost a decade?" She puts the dressings on the table, a little harder than necessary, and grabs the salad bowl from behind me.

My shoulders slump. "You're right."

"What?" she snips.

I've never seen Rian this mad.

"Anyone would be lucky to have you. Just be careful." I grip her shoulder and take the asparagus out of the fridge. "I'm going to grill this up on the roof. I'll be back."

Leaving the apartment, I rest my back against the door for a moment before heading up to the roof. The last person I want to sit down and share a meal with is Jax. Rian's the only person I'd put myself through torture for.

Chapter Five

RIAN

"**W**HAT'S FOR DINNER?" SETH BREEZES INTO MY APARTMENT AND SITS AT the table, his thumb and forefinger descending into the salad bowl.

I snatch the bowl away before he has a chance to grab anything. "Nope. Roommates only."

He looks over one shoulder then the other shoulder at the empty apartment. "I'm a roommate."

"No, you're a neighbor."

He mocks offense. "I've always thought of us all as roommates."

"You don't pay rent for this apartment."

"Speaking of, you stole one of my roommates. Do you know how many extra boudoir sessions I've had to do in order to pay my share of the rent? I'm almost desperate enough to hold a sign out on the sidewalk and dress up in a suit with a rose between my teeth."

I stare blankly at him.

He laughs. "Thankfully, Blanca is giving me some freelance work."

"I hadn't heard anything about that?" I sit down.

Poor Seth's journey toward his dream career of photography has been hard. Not horribly difficult—the man gets to see half naked women every day—but he complains about it nonstop.

"She and Ethan are doing that blog thing or whatever. She's asked me to take some landscape shots of New York City."

I grab his hand. "That's great."

He shrugs. "It's something and keeps me from having to take over my parents' bagel shop for a little while longer."

"I haven't stopped in lately. How is Mama Andrews?" I stand and grab him a beer from the fridge, then I open a bottle of wine because as long as Jax and Dylan don't throw one another off the roof, dinner should be ready soon.

"Don't get me started." He sips his beer. "She asked me if I'd take pictures of her for my dad." His head falls to the table.

I purse my lips in an attempt not to laugh. His mom is very into having an active sex life and isn't afraid to talk to her son about it. I struggle to pull the cork from the bottle of wine. "What did you say?"

"What do you think? Hell. No. Then she asked if any of my coworkers would do it."

"Oh, that's reasonable."

Seth waves me over and I hand him the bottle. He pops the cork out with ease. "No, it's not. Why would I want my coworker to see my mom half naked, puckering her lips for the camera?"

I laugh and he can't help but laugh too.

"Yeah, my life is a fucking joke. My mom is worried about turning on my dad and my brother is AWOL again."

"Oh, Seth."

He shakes his head like he doesn't want to talk about it, but the way he pushes the half-drank beer to the middle of the table says he's worried about his brother.

I don't know much about his brother, other than that he disappears now and then. I think it has something to do with drinking or drugs. Seth only mentions it in passing and every time he does, he brushes the topic away before we can really talk about it.

The door to the apartment opens and we both look over.

"The girl put her finger in my petroleum jelly container and smeared it on her lips," Dylan says.

"Fuck, I'm guessing you gave it to her?" Jax asks.

"Yeah, but I charged her for it. I mean, use some common sense. Do you want an infection?"

I stare dumbfounded as the two of them walk in like they're best friends. Even Seth's eyes are bouncing between me and them.

"Shit, those steaks look good," Seth says, his eyes wide like one of those cartoons where the ribeye is hanging off a fork in front of the dog.

"Thanks. Want to join us? I got plenty." Jax places the plate in the middle of the table.

"Nope. Seth has to get home to Knox. This is a roommate-only dinner," I say.

Dylan slides the asparagus onto the table and picks up a stalk, chomping down. "Sorry, dude, I'll leave the scraps at your door." He winks.

Seth sighs, stands from the chair, leaving his beer behind. "No need. I'm gonna convince Knox to get his dick out of Leilani long enough to go to dinner. You realize I'm the only single one now besides all of you, right?" His shoulders slouch and he exaggerates walking to the door like a child.

Dylan and Jax glance at me. I hadn't really thought about that. Blanca and Ethan, Sierra and Adrian, Knox and Leilani. Seth shoots a pair of pathetic eyes over his shoulder one last time when he reaches the door.

"Jesus," Dylan says.

"Let the guy stay, Rian," Jax says.

"Fine. But you're not to talk."

Seth straightens and smiles, walking back over and picking his beer up off the table. "I feel like I should've contributed something." He digs his hand in his pocket and pulls out some business cards. "Here. Free bagel for everyone."

The cards are for Andrews Bagels. He passes them out like a grandpa does butterscotch candies.

"Jeez, thanks. I'll add this to the stack in my room." Dylan pockets it.

I shove mine in the drawer with the others we've gotten in the past.

Jax examines it. "This is your place?"

Seth swallows his sip of beer. "My parents."

"I was at the Bagel Place this morning. They have a hot girl working there. Is there a hot girl at Andrews Bagels? You might be able to convince me to switch."

Dylan looks over his beer bottle at me and we share a look. The Ericksons own the Bagel Place. They're pretty much the Andrews' archenemies, which means Seth Andrews can never entertain the idea of Evan Erickson. Some of us think that upsets him to a degree, but we let him pretend the only thing he feels for her is hate.

Seth cuts his steak and the knife screeches across the plate. "Long dark curly hair?"

Jax's eyes light up. "Yeah. When she bent over to get me a bagel…" He sticks his bent finger in his mouth and bites the knuckle.

Dylan and I share another look. I want him to be prepared to act in case Seth's knife dives toward Jax's throat.

"The two bagel places are competitors," I say in the hopes that Jax will read between lines.

His eyes only light up further. "Oh, I get it. So she's like an enemy of yours."

Seth shrugs, sawing into the steak again. "Andrews' bagels are better anyway."

Jax finally looks at Dylan and me and quirks an eyebrow. I don't know anything about Dylan and Jax's relationship, but they obviously have some sort of non-verbal conversation. Jax nods as if he's in the loop now.

"She's your Juliet?" Jax asks Seth.

"Owens." Dylan shakes his head.

Seth's gaze flies to Jax. "No. It's not like that."

"If you say so. You're cool if I hit on her then?" He winks at me.

Dylan growls over his forkful of salad.

"Why would I care?" Seth picks up the salad dressing and douses his salad with it. Not one piece of lettuce isn't covered with dressing.

"Cool." Jax nods, stabs the piece of meat he cut, and leans back in his chair while he chews, amused.

Dylan continues to shake his head.

"So, Jax, Knox says you're pretty famous?" Seth asks.

Dylan grunts again, stabbing at his lettuce.

"I wouldn't say famous, but I've made a name for myself."

"You're modest. Knox showed me all your Instagram followers."

"Really?" I pull out my phone and look him up on Instagram. "OMG, you're friends with all these celebrities?" I show Seth then Dylan.

Dylan never bothers to look up. Does he feel competitive with Jax? Duh, Rian. Of course he does. How do I feel about Johann? I place my phone screen-side down and pick my fork back up.

"We're acquaintances. None of them would take a bullet for me or anything." Jax eyes Dylan, who rolls his eyes.

"Super impressive," Seth says. "Maybe I'll go to you for my next piece."

He and Jax share a laugh since Dylan has yet to pick his head up from his plate. Dylan has done all three of Seth's tattoos.

"Yeah, I've always wanted to get one." I play along with the joke.

But this time, Dylan's head raises like I just announced there's a bullet coming right for him. He cocks his head to the side. "What?"

"I'll totally tattoo you. Do you have anything in mind?" Jax asks. "I've got an entire book of just chick tattoos."

"If you want a tattoo, I'll give you one," Dylan says softly, eyes focused only on me.

Jax holds his hands in the air. "Oh yeah, I'd hate to step on any toes."

"You live for stepping on fucking toes," Dylan says, looking him square in the eye.

My patience breaks. This dinner was supposed to help us figure out how to coexist, but if anything, it's made it worse.

"Okay, this entire friendship-turned-hatred thing is driving me crazy. Can you please just tell me what the hell happened between the two of you so we can clear the air?" My eyes shift from Jax to Dylan and back to Jax.

"It's Phillips's problem, not mine." Jax shrugs and continues to eat.

"It's water under the bridge," Dylan mumbles.

"Bullshit," Seth coughs out.

I'll second Seth. I cannot continue to live with all this animosity. My fork slams down on the table and all three of their heads pop up. Jax doesn't look as surprised as Dylan and Seth, but then again, Jax doesn't know me well. Which, sad to say, I kind of like.

"Talk." I lean back and cross my arms.

Dylan wipes his mouth. "It's shit from high school. I'm over it if he is."

Jax scoffs. "I came here willingly. Do you really think Knox didn't tell me you were here or that I didn't know Ink Envy was yours? Clearly, the problem isn't mine."

"It's pretty obvious you like to get under Dylan's skin," I say.

Jax laughs and rolls his eyes. "You need Rian to do your talking, Phillips?"

"Hell no, but I don't control her."

Seth looks as happy as a child watching Tom Brady and Peyton Manning throw a football back and forth.

"She's right though. You haven't been Mary fucking Poppins since you got here." Dylan pushes away from the table, rising, and grabs another beer out of the fridge.

"Why would I be nice? You act like I'm Jack the Ripper!" Jax yells.

Maybe this was a bad idea.

"I'll have a bee—" Seth raises his finger, but Dylan shuts the fridge and sits back down. "Never mind."

"Because I know how you are and things around here don't work that way." Dylan unscrews the top, flicking it into the garbage can and makes it.

"Don't act like you know me. We haven't talked in years. You have no idea who the fuck I am now."

I look at Seth. His eyes widen and he stands, holding his arms out toward both of them. Although neither of them have stood up, so they both look at him like he's a dumbass. "Let's just calm this down now."

"Sit down, Andrews," Dylan says. "I'm not going to fight him."

Could have fooled me.

Dylan stands and puts his plate in the sink, calmly finishes his beer, and tosses the bottle into the recycling container. Jax keeps one eye on Dylan the entire time. I'm so out of my league with these two. Am I going to come home one day to a crime scene?

"Thanks for trying, Rian, but our friendship died a long time ago." I open my mouth to respond, but Dylan keeps going. "And Owens, you stay out of my way and I'll stay out of yours. Got it?" Without waiting for a response, he grabs his keys and walks out the door.

"He's such an asshole." Jax heads toward his bedroom. "Thanks for planning the dinner, Rian. Sorry it's ruined." Then he shuts his bedroom door.

Seth and I look at one another. My gaze detours to the untouched chocolate-on-chocolate cake sitting on the counter. I pick it up and place it on the table between us. Seth's fork digs right in without me cutting a piece.

"Remind me to thank Knox for this," I say. Seth smiles at me over the cake. "Not." I dig my fork in the cake.

Chocolate cake always makes things better.

Chapter Six

DYLAN

I PACK A CHANGE OF CLOTHES IN MY WORKOUT BAG THIS MORNING BECAUSE I NEED to head into the city afterward. But first, I scribble a letter to Rian to apologize for last night. She started the shower already, so I can slip it under her door and hightail it out of here.

I have no idea why I allow Jax to use up my last ounce of patience. What happened between us is so far in the past.

When I walk out of my bedroom, the kitchen is spotless as usual, so I notice the math problem on the table right away. I wonder what time she woke up to start working on it. I glance at it as I grab a water, but all the numbers and symbols and letters make no sense to me. Which shows how different Rian and I are. She's uber smart. The girl teachers loved and colleges begged for an application. Me, on the other hand, not so much.

Instead of sliding my note under her door, I decide to stuff it in her book. Anyone who knows Rian knows that now that she's started, she'll be obsessing over this problem until she figures it out.

The shower turns off. That's my sign to leave, so I quietly open the apartment door and shut it behind me, turning to find Knox in the hallway.

"Shit, man." I grab my chest.

Knox is a big guy and intimidating at first glance. Plus, he holds that whole cop persona like "try me and see what happens."

He yawns. "Sorry, but I wasn't gonna miss out this time."

Like clockwork, Seth walks out of the apartment behind Knox while Ethan slowly shuts his apartment door down the hall, locking it behind him. We all look like shit—our hair up in different directions, except for Knox, who wears a baseball hat.

"Extra big bag there," Ethan says as we file into the elevator.

"I'm heading to the city after," I say.

No one says anything, but Seth shoots me a look like, "you're going to have to talk about your outburst yesterday at some point."

"Where you headed?" Knox asks after we're on the bottom level, as though his brain isn't working at full speed yet.

"The neighborhood. I need to find another artist for the shop."

We begin the short walk toward the gym, Knox and me in front with Seth and Ethan behind us.

"What about Jax? I get the history and shit, but he'd be good for Ink Envy," Knox says.

He isn't wrong. If I could tolerate Jax for more than a nanosecond, I'd ask him to come on for the short interim he'll be in Cliffton Heights. But no matter how much I love Ink Envy, I cannot work around him.

I shake my head and Knox blows out a long breath. "You gotta get over it, man."

"What exactly does he have to get over?" Seth's head pushes between our shoulders.

I turn to put my hand on his face and push him back. "Nothing."

"That's like physical abuse, dude," Seth says from behind me.

Ethan mumbles something and they both laugh. I have no interest in dealing with their shit.

"For your information, I am over it. He's the one who showed up with a chip on his shoulder."

Knox's gaze holds steady on me for a moment as he opens the door for us to enter the gym. "We both know that's not all of it. You guys were like brothers. There has to be a way to find your way back there, and I think him working at Ink Envy is a great start."

Seth and Ethan walk in, and I stop as we dig out our cards to scan in. "Hell will freeze over, pigs will fly, and Seth will nail Evan before we're ever like brothers again."

"Why are you bringing me into this?" Seth asks, handing his card to the girl at the front desk. "Just FYI, Evan is a girl," he whispers to her.

She looks at him like, "whatever, guy, keep moving." After scanning my card, she hands it to me, and I stuff it back into my wallet.

"You're being a stubborn jackass."

I ignore Knox.

I'm quiet the entire workout. Ethan and Knox talk about all the sex they're getting while Seth groans that there are no available women in Cliffton Heights. I want to call him out on his bullshit. There's just one woman in Cliffton Heights who isn't available to him and that's what he's pissed about.

But I can't very well cast stones when I'm living life in a glass house myself right now, so I keep my mouth shut.

The train is about to pull away from the station when I arrive, so I use my last reserve of energy after my workout to chase it down. Lucky for me, I catch it, but the conductor gives me a nasty look. Like I give a shit.

My footsteps halt when I enter the train cab. I was going to use this hour and a half to nap. Now that's not going to happen. Not that I'm complaining.

"Rian," I say.

She looks up from whatever she's reading, her smile immediate. No one can put me in a better mood than Rian. Maybe because she always seems happy to see me.

"What are you doing here?"

"I could ask you the same thing." I sit down in the seat across from her.

She shuts that math book, the same one I saw on the table this morning, and holds my note. "Thanks for the apology."

"I shouldn't have reacted that way," I say.

"No. I shouldn't have pushed the two of you. It's none of my business." Her smile dims.

I owe her an explanation. I get that everyone wants to know the story of me and Jax, but it's embarrassing, which is the only reason I'm not open to share.

"Do you mind?" I nod at the empty space beside her.

She slides closer to the window. "No."

I place my duffle bag between my feet on the floor. She's wearing jeans and a jacket, her gray hat with the giant pom-pom on it still on her head. Spring will hopefully arrive soon.

"Where are you getting off?" I ask, losing the nerve to tell her about all the shit with Jax.

"The city. I have a brunch with"—she lifts the math book in her lap—"Johann Frederickson."

"Sounds like quite the intellectual," I say.

She giggles. "He's the guy my parents constantly compare me to." She rolls her eyes, looks out the window for a second, then sets her gaze on me. "Whose child is smarter? That's all my parents and his parents talk about. They're not obvious about it—that would be un-couth. It's all done covertly with a comment here, a comment there. I feel bad because my parents got the short end of the stick—Johann is way smarter than me."

I pat her thigh. "Not possible."

She laughs, but it doesn't make my heart warm. There's something off. "Johann is a math professor at Columbia. He went to an Ivy League college while I was at NYU. He's already working on his doctorate and I never even considered getting mine, much to my parents' dis-appointment. He's single, but I am too, so that doesn't really hold weight in their arguments. That's why my parents want me to win this contest, because it'll prove something to them."

One thing I've always liked about Rian is her way of laying out her cards like a treasure map. There's no gold or jewels hidden layers deep in the sand. There's no game with her.

"How come I've never heard of this guy?" I ask, wondering if Johann looks like his name suggests.

"Because he's not my friend. I think he secretly likes that our parents banter back and forth about who's better. I don't much care for him. He's egotistical and a jackass, truthfully."

"Then why are you having brunch with him?"

A blush fills her cheeks. A clear sign there's more to this little brunch. "I wanted to get into his condo and see if he has any notes."

My mouth opens. "You're going to cheat?"

She's quick to shake her head. "No. I just want to see if I even stand a chance."

I tilt my head. This is so not like her. Maybe I put Rian too high up on the morals plat-form, but I'm more likely than her to be a cheater. She's pure. "Where's your phone?"

She narrows her eyes but retrieves her phone from her bag. I grab it, and she allows me to thumb through her phone to retrieve his contact.

I hand the phone back to her. "Cancel the brunch."

"What? No." She holds the phone and glances at his name.

"Rian, you won't be able to live with yourself if you go through with this plan. We both know it."

She opens her mouth but quickly shuts it.

"You know I'm right. Plus, you're the smartest person I know. You can solve this prob-lem and grab that prize well before him."

"The problem is impossible. I've tried and—"

"You wouldn't even feel good about winning if you cheated to get the right answer." I grip her thigh and shake her leg.

Her shoulders slump and she nods. "I'm just going to disappoint them."

I've met Mr. and Mrs. Wright once. They came to the apartment on a surprise visit, so Rian wasn't able to shuffle all of us away. They took one look at me, all four eyes slowly perus-ing me from head to toe, and it was clear—I wasn't what they liked for their daughter, even as an acquaintance.

"Who the hell cares? You have a job, you're self-sufficient. What do you still need from them?" My voice is angrier than normal, and Rian's wide eyes say I've surprised her.

She glances out the window, watching the landscape breeze past. "I'll never be enough."

I fucking hate that she feels that way. It makes me want to dial up Mr. and Mrs. Wright and tell them how much they've fucked up their daughter and if they can't see how damn perfect she is, then they're the ones who need to have their IQ tested.

I put my arm around her shoulders, pulling her into my chest. The smell of her sham-poo, which I've discovered since sharing a shower with her, hits my nostrils. I'm not sure if it's because we share an apartment now, but it feels like home. "You are enough. You're an amazing woman."

I pluck her phone from her hand and hammer out a text to Johann.

She sits up, seeing I canceled on her behalf. "Dylan!"

"Time for a Dylan and Rian day out, don't you think?"

Rian smiles as if I'm the keeper of her happiness. That look scares the shit out of me. I'm no one's keeper of happiness. I may hate Mr. and Mrs. Wright, but they're not wrong. I'm not who their daughter needs in her life. She can do much better than me.

Chapter Seven

RIAN

I probably need a support group. *Hello, I'm Rian, and I'm addicted to Dylan Phillips.* I'd tell my story of falling in love with a boy who will surely break my heart without ever knowing he did. The problem is that just like any addiction, there's only one thing you can do to keep clean—abstinence. The fact that I just agreed to spend the day with Dylan is the complete opposite of what I should do.

He takes me to a bagel place to kill time. It's his favorite, and I see why—though I'd never admit that to Seth.

At eleven o'clock, we approach a tattoo parlor near NYU, my old stomping grounds.

"I remember this place," I say, nostalgia hitting me. Sierra always had at least two reservations here that she canceled last minute.

"Yeah?"

"I've never been inside, but a lot of the students came here." I glance down the street at some bars that I only went to when Sierra dragged me out. Rarely did I not have my mind solely on my grades.

"I worked here," he says. "Too bad you never came in. We'd have been friends way before."

Truth is, I remember seeing the artists and customers smoking outside. I'd put my head down and walk by, trying not to be seen. At the time, those people seemed so sure of themselves and comfortable in their own skin. That quality has always scared me. Probably because I never felt the same.

I stare at Dylan, his bright smile directed at me with his hand on the door. "Yeah, too bad I didn't."

He opens the door and allows me to walk in first.

The guy behind the counter looks me up and down, raised eyebrows to why I'm standing in front of him. "Can I help you? I'm going to start my day with tattooing a fucking flower, aren't I?"

He's intimidating just like when I was in college. Tall, big, and tatted from neck to collar, short sleeves to wrist. His blue eyes are amazing though, and I lose myself for a second.

"Phillips?" he says, his smile growing wide and welcoming when he notices Dylan at my side. He comes around the counter and the two of them hug, each hitting the others back harder and harder until they back up from one another.

"What's up, Big Man?" Dylan says.

I can see how the nickname fits. The guy has a few inches on Dylan and a lot of mass.

"She yours?" Big Man eyes me, his gaze once again flowing over my body like I couldn't possibly be with Dylan.

Bingo, Big Man.

"She's my roommate. Rian, this is Big Man," he introduces me.

The guy puts his hand out in front of me and almost bows. "You can call me Brian."

"Hey, Brian."

He studies me for a second, and I shift my weight from one foot to the other, releasing his hand.

"Virgin skin, am I right?" Brian asks.

Dylan smiles at me.

"Yes," I say, forced to answer so I'm not impolite.

"And when she wants one, I'll be the one doing it," Dylan says.

Big Man holds up his hands, laughing. "No worries, I get enough virgin canvas around here."

He walks to their waiting area and sits on the couch, holding his arm out for the two of us to follow him.

"Yeah, Rian graduated from NYU," Dylan says.

"And I never converted you then?" Big Man shakes his head like I do when I'm trying to solve the damn math problem.

"Sorry." I shrug.

He laughs. "As long as Phillips got you, I'm cool. I just hate when virgin skin goes to some asshole who will tattoo their neck before their ankle or wrist or some shit."

"Truth," Dylan says.

I had no idea there were rules in tattooing.

"So what's this visit about? Especially so bright and early." Big Man puts his ankle on his knee, and leans back in his chair.

"I'm in need of a fresh artist."

Big Man tilts his head. "Cliffton Heights suffering?"

Dylan briefly glances at me, but I pretend not to notice. "Nah. Never, but Mad Max moved on and I need to replace him."

Big Man taps his Vans. "I heard a rumor that Jax is back." His eyebrows raise in question.

Dylan inhales through his nose. "You of all people know that will never work."

"He's your best bet. All I got are people who can make a college kid happy. Ink Envy is different, you know that."

"I was hoping you might know someone up and coming," Dylan says.

Brian shakes his head. "Nah, not at the moment. Most of the people I've come across are just wannabes who watched a few YouTube videos and practiced on an orange, know what I'm sayin'?"

"Yeah, I get it. Not real artists." Disappointment rings in Dylan's voice.

"Exactly."

"If anyone comes to mind, send them my way, yeah?" Dylan asks, standing.

"I don't know a lot who'd be willing to go out to the country." Brian laughs. Dylan pretends he's going to hit him, but they end up doing that man hug again. "But we both know people will go out there for Jax. You should do it even if it's temporary."

Dylan shakes it off like he doesn't agree.

Brian turns to me. "And you're welcome any time." He holds his hand out to me and I shake it. "Although I do have to refuse your virgin skin. Dylan's claimed it, I suppose." He acts as if that's a big loss.

I laugh and Dylan's hand finds mine. Even Brian looks down and a shit-eating grin appears on his face. We leave the tattoo place and walk down the road toward the subway station before he releases my hand.

"Why won't you just hire Jax?" I ask. It's the million-dollar question because it'd surely help out his business. "You love Ink Envy. Do it for the company."

"It's not that easy." He runs his hand through his dark hair.

A few college girls walk by and snicker to one another about Dylan. At least I'm not the only one who wants to climb him like a tree today.

"I just spilled all my family shit on you."

He looks at me from the corner of his eyes. "Up for a field trip?"

"I thought we were already on one?"

We continue walking as he laughs. "Today's destination is to visit the part of the city that fucked up Dylan Phillips. You in?"

Am I ever. "I'm in."

He doesn't smile—if anything, he looks nauseated—but we head to the subway, and once again, he pays for me. Which makes me get all swoony.

Come on, Rian, it's a train fare, not a romantic dinner for two.

"Just stay close to me, okay?" His voice is hard and lacking any type of affection.

We're in his old neighborhood. Needless to say, it's very different from where I grew up. The concrete buildings are all decorated with graffiti, and homeless people line the sidewalk.

"So, you and Jax and Knox all grew up here?" I ask.

"Yeah."

My heart sinks to my stomach. This wasn't an easy place to grow up. The lack of anything green and alive pulls on my heart.

We walk by a high-rise apartment. Some guys are hanging out by the doors, and others are playing a basketball game across the street.

"That's where Jax and I grew up." He turns me by putting his hands on my shoulders to face a building kitty-corner to us. "That's where Naomi Jennings lived."

I nod though I don't understand. "Who is Naomi Jennings?"

"The wedge that came between Jax and me."

He signals with his head for us to walk. "Winnie, my foster mom, took me in my freshman year and Jax our junior year. I already knew Jax before then because we went to the same school, ran in the same circle. We were both foster kids and had been thrown together a few times when we were younger."

No wonder they can still have non-verbal conversations across a table like they did last night.

"The first day Jax moved in with Winnie, I thought it would be cool to live together. I think that's a big part of the reason Winnie agreed to take him in. Jax was labeled as a troublemaker. Technically, we both were, but Winnie got me under control, so they thought they could give her the tougher cases, I suppose."

The farther we walk, the farther we move away from all the concrete. There's some grass, but most of it is still recovering from the long winter.

"Jax had a giant chip on his shoulder from day one. He constantly called me momma's boy, which pissed me off because although I loved Winnie, she wasn't my mom. And Jax knew that all I knew about my parents was that they didn't want me. He, on the other hand…" Dylan stops and looks at me. "Well, that's his story to tell."

I entwine my arm through his and lean my head on his shoulder because I feel like an idiot for complaining about my parents. Parents who only want me to succeed. They gave me shelter and food. Who cares that they gave me extra homework on top of my school requirements? I had parents who cared for me.

"Don't pity me," Dylan says in a low voice.

I remove my arm and stand up straight next to him. A rush of guilt hits me.

Dylan stops us on the street corner. "I'm sorry. I didn't mean to upset you, but I've had people pity me my whole life."

"I don't." Although I kind of do, I'll keep that to myself.

"I made a life for myself."

"You did, and you've done amazing."

He offers me a soft smile as I take the familiar role of his cheerleader. "I wouldn't have been able to get out if it wasn't for one person, and if you want to know the true reason Jax and I are where we are now, a lot of it has to do with her." He nods toward the cemetery across the street.

"Who?"

The light changes and we walk across, dodging the pedestrian traffic on the other side. When we come together again on the other side, we enter the small cemetery attached to a Catholic church. He's quiet as we walk a path through the rows of burial plots. This cemetery doesn't have huge granite headstones carved with quotes about their lives. There are no statues of angels or crosses. Everyone has a small rectangular marker with their name and birth and death dates.

He walks a path he definitely has memorized until he stops under a tree and shoves his hands into his pockets. "She's the one who helped me, and that's why Jax hates me the way he does."

My heart breaks as I read the name.

Chapter Eight

DYLAN

Bringing Rian to Winnie's burial plot isn't what I had on the agenda today. I wanted us to have a fun day. But after another asshole brought up the problems between Jax and me, I knew I owed her some answers. Especially since she opened her chest and let her heart fall out on the train ride here.

"She died our senior year. I'd already aged out of the system, but she let me stay through graduation. Hell, she would've let me stay after too. But Jax was a month shy of aging out, so he had to go to another family." My mind floats back to that time. Jax and I were best friends, along with Knox, but we fought like brothers. "She left me her savings with the stipulation that I had to use it on myself to attend school."

I look at Rian and she nods.

"Jax went to a shitty house for his last month of high school, but again, that's his story to tell." I've never told anyone Jax's story and I won't start now, even if our relationship is in disrepair.

She nods again. "I thought it was whoever that Naomi girl is who came between you?"

My head whips in her direction. "No. The Naomi situation wasn't good, but it was only a symptom of the problem."

I've told her enough at this point. Time to take a turn off memory lane. Rian's and my childhoods couldn't have been more opposite. The pity in her eyes is driving me insane, making me want to punch the trunk of that nearby oak tree.

I stare at the grave marker and read her name. Winifred Ann Carlson. Although it doesn't say mother, she was one. To so many kids, but most of all to me. Everything I've done since the day she died in that hospital bed, I've done for her.

I bend down and run my hands over the etching, removing the dead leaves from around the small stone.

"Ready?" I say to Rian when I stand again.

"Yeah." Her voice cracks.

More reason to get the hell out of here. I'm probably not going to find myself a new tattoo artist in New York City who wants to live in Cliffton Heights anyway, even if I was still in the mood to do so.

We walk out of the cemetery and stand on the street corner, waiting for the light to turn. A couple walks over to wait near us. They have a dog and Rian bends down to pet it, asking its name. They tell us how they just adopted him down the street from a shelter that didn't think it'd be able to keep their doors open.

"Oh, that's so sad." Rian looks at them with sad puppy eyes.

"There are two more there. She tried to get me to adopt all three," the man says with a nod to the woman. "We can barely put food on our table. We can't feed three dogs."

I laugh, remember Winnie saying she couldn't take any more kids because the government pays shit and if she can't feed herself, how can she feed others? But she took in Jax even after she had been laid off, and she made it work.

The woman bends down to Rian's level. "They're so cute. The people at the shelter said they aren't getting enough donations. I'm not sure how anyone with a heart can just walk by."

The light changes, so the guy tells the woman to pick up the dog so they can cross.

Rian looks at me. "Are you allergic to dogs?"

I shake my head, wishing I could lie to her. "No, but—"

"Do you know if Jax is?"

"I'd like to say yes."

She pulls out her phone and dials him up while walking in the direction the couple came from. "Hey, Jax, are you allergic to dogs?"

My blood shouldn't boil that she has his number, but I feel it heating anyway.

"You'll have to pay that ridiculously high pet deposit to the landlord," I say.

Rian turns around, putting the phone to her chest. "I have some savings."

"What's happened to you?" I ask. First, she's going to cheat on the math problem and now she suddenly wants a dog?

"Great. And you don't mind?" She smiles at whatever Jax has said. "Oh, Dylan and I are in the city and there are these dogs at this shelter that might be closing." Rian finishes her conversation and hangs up with Jax while we walk another block.

"Do you really think any of us can take care of a dog?"

She shrugs. "I don't know, but it sounds like fun and they need homes."

I put my hand on her arm to stop her and she steps out of the way of pedestrian traffic, moving to the edge of the sidewalk. "Are you doing this because I'm a foster kid?"

The excitement drains from her face. I feel like I just told a kid that Santa Claus isn't real. Fuck.

"No. That's not why."

"Okay, just making sure." I step back onto the sidewalk and she joins me, not nearly as excited as she was before. "I want to make sure you're not on some do-good kick now that I told you about Winnie. It can be contagious, you know?"

"What can?"

"You hear a story about how someone did good and you want to replicate it."

She pulls me aside by the sleeve, closer to the buildings. "That's not why. For the first time, I wasn't thinking of the consequences of something. I saw the dog. The dog was cute. I wanted the dog. That was all. But let me ask you a question…"

"Spit it out," I say.

She still hems and haws for a moment.

"Rian, I can take it."

"Well… don't you ever want to repay what Winnie did for you?"

I chuckle. Out of everyone, I never would've thought it would be Rian to call me out. But actually, paying it forward is something I feel guilty about. Like someone saved me, so shouldn't I save two more people and keep the good deeds going? I understand her bigger point, but I'm not sure this is the situation to step up.

"So because Winnie saved me, I should let a shelter dog shit and piss all over the apartment? You have the dog for its entire life, not until it reaches adulthood or its parents sort their shit out."

Rian bites her lower lip and stares at the sidewalk. "True. Maybe this is a bad idea."

Her disappointment hits me square in the chest, making it tighten. But the more I think about it, she's kind of right. Adopting a dog who's hours or days away from death sounds pretty damn appealing right now. And yes, I'm fully aware I'm probably more willing to do this because I just left Winne's grave. Plus, dogs piss off Jax. He's never liked them. Naomi had one that would always hump his leg.

"Maybe not," I say.

Rian's eyes light up. Shit, to see that excitement from her, I'd adopt ten dogs. "Really?"

"Yeah, come on." I tug her sleeve and we walk a little faster now. Our excitement escalates the farther we make it down the sidewalk.

"How far away was it?" she asks.

"I don't think they said."

"They didn't act like it was this far, did they?" She bites her lip again and her sunshine smile dims.

Finally, I see the shelter's sign on the corner, but we have to wait to cross when we're met with the big red hand. When we reach the animal shelter, a couple is walking away with a dog and Rian claps her hands in front of herself. But when we look in the little pen, all that's there is shredded newspaper with some dog shit.

"Where are the puppies?" Rian asks a woman who approaches us.

"That couple just took the last one. Thank goodness. Did you see our flyer?"

I put my arm around Rian's waist because we're not going to be dog parents today.

"They're all gone?" she asks with a strangled voice.

The woman finally understands and touches Rian's hand. "I'm sorry. They are."

Rian splashes on a fake smile, something she does often. "That's good. I'm glad they all have homes." She steps away and out of my hold.

"There are a lot of other shelters. Would you like a list?" the woman calls.

I take the piece of paper from her since Rian isn't listening anymore, then I catch up to Rian down the street.

"Hey." I duck to meet her eyes. No tears, thank fuck. I have a hard time dealing with tears.

"We should probably head back, huh?"

And just like that, the dog subject is abandoned.

We walk off the train, neither one of us accomplishing what we wanted. I've never seen Rian so depressed. Like she owned a puppy and someone ran over it.

I stop us outside our apartment building. "I've gotta go to Ink Envy, want to join me?"

"Nah. I'm going to try to work on that equation."

I nod. "Cool. I'll be home in a little bit. Let's order pizza tonight?"

A slight smile creases her lips. "Sure."

After she gets in the front door, I walk across the street. The parlor is dead. Of course, that's because neither Frankie nor I are working and we're what keep this place going.

Lyle takes his feet off the front desk and sets his sketchpad on the table. "What's up, boss?"

"You can relax," I say, beelining it to my office, but I stop midway and turn back to him. "Do you have an Instagram account?"

Lyle is my newbie. He's still trying to find clients, but you find lots of those through walk-ins. It's why he has the crappy shift. But he needs to produce on the crappy shift too.

"I don't take pretty pictures, boss," he says.

"Start taking pictures of your drawings and posting them on Instagram, tagging Ink Envy. Same if you do a piece on someone. Friend every eighteen-plus person in Cliffton Heights. Find a way to bring in some business, or you're out."

His face pales. Once I'm back in my office, I feel like a jackass. I can't pressure him like that—he'll never produce what I need him to through fear.

Rian was wrong when she suggested I'm not into repaying my debt for what Winnie did for me. I take in the artists people won't give a chance and try to teach them the way of old tattooing—not the nuevo way of get a client and do whatever the fuck they want no matter what reputation you get from it.

I'm all about the no face until chest and no hands until arms. If I don't think I can give them what they want, I send them to someone I know will. Tattooing is about the art, not the ink. And not solely the money.

I pick up the phone and buzz to the front.

"Yeah, boss?" Lyle says, his voice apprehensive.

"I'm not firing you. But I think the Instagram thing is a good idea. It might drum up clients who like your stuff."

"Okay, I just joined on my phone."

I chuckle. "Okay."

I hang up and press my fingertips to my temple. I should be worried about my bottom line, but all I see is Rian's frown.

Instead of posting my own sketches to Instagram, I start a group text.

Me: Game night tonight. We're playing Drawing Without Dignity because it's Rian's favorite and she needs cheering up.

A whole slew of messages come in.

Sierra: We got the pizza.
Blanca: Ethan says he'll get her favorite wine.
Seth: I'll pick up a dessert.

With that settled, I open up another chat box.

Me: Hey, Rian needs some cheering up, game night tonight at our apartment.

Three dots appear. Guess I shouldn't be surprised that he never changed his number.

Jax: Your dick would cheer her up. On second thought mine would do a better job.
Me: This was a peace offering so you weren't excluded. Now you can fuck off.
Jax: Aw, don't be such a sourpuss.

I toss the phone onto the desk, regretting extending him an invitation. One thing I need to figure out soon is whether Jax wants revenge or friendship. Because he's back for a reason, and I need to find out which one it is.

Chapter Nine

RIAN

I GOT ABOUT TEN PERCENT THROUGH THE PROBLEM TODAY AND I FEEL AS THOUGH I'M on the right track, but I've had enough for one day, so I shut the notebook and swing my purse over my shoulder.

Jax comes out of his bedroom in a pair of jeans and a faded T-shirt that hugs his muscled shoulders and chest. "Where are you going?"

"Grocery store," I say. "Do you need anything?"

It's been an entire week since Dylan planned a game night to cheer me up after my out-of-body experience when I couldn't get a puppy, and since then, he and Jax have been civil enough. There's no watching television at the same time or eating at the table together, but there are no more mean words being spat at one another.

I'm still embarrassed when I think about how that puppy thing threw me into a funk in front of Dylan, but it warms my heart that he planned a night with our friends to cheer me up.

"Do you mind if I go with you?" Jax asks.

"Um… no." I wouldn't mind the company. Dylan works late on Saturdays, so it'll just be Jax and me around the apartment tonight.

"You sound unsure. You worried Phillips will have a problem with it?" He grabs his phone off the charger and pockets it.

"No," I say in a tone that would only convince a senile eighty-five-year-old dementia-ridden grandma.

"Right." He opens the door and holds it, not hiding his smirk.

We walk down the hall and ride the elevator down.

"You guys don't use that roof nearly enough," he says.

"Yeah, I know. But it's just getting nice out again. We will."

I don't necessarily feel uncomfortable around Jax. He's an easy-going guy who doesn't bite his tongue. But we haven't spent that much time together since he moved in. Usually because I'll go to my bedroom if he's watching television when I come home.

"We should watch a movie tonight," he says.

I nod and rock back on my flats. "Yeah, that's a good idea."

We walk out and he's a gentleman, allowing me to go first and holding the door open for me.

"So we'll make something to eat and watch a movie on the roof?"

"Um…"

I'm not sure what has my tongue tied? Is it because part of me worries I'm going against Dylan? Like I'm picking Jax's side over Dylan's?

"I'm not asking you out, Rian. This is strictly a platonic thing."

I yank the cart at the grocery store, but the damn thing won't separate from the one in front. I move to the next row, and it's the same fucking thing.

Jax puts his hand on mine to stop me. *Stay True* is inked across his knuckles. "I've got it."

He fixes the child seatbelts so they're not interlaced with the metal openings and a cart slides out easily. Instead of handing it to me, he takes control, pushing it ahead. "What should we make tonight?"

"Um…"

"You know, for a girl, you sure don't talk a lot." He chuckles.

I giggle because I'm still tongue-tied. Jax is intimidating in the same way I found Dylan to be when he moved in with Knox across the hall.

"I'm just…" I'm what? Finish the damn sentence, Rian.

"How about we ask each other questions? You ask me one and I'll ask you one?"

I pick up a head of lettuce and put it in the cart. "Okay."

"Ladies first." He stops the cart and throws in a bag of pistachios.

"How long are you staying in Cliffton Heights?"

"Man, right for the jugular, huh? I underestimated you." His head moves side to side. "At least six months. We'll see how it goes."

"You signed a year lease…" I say. Technically it was a sublease through Sierra.

He tugs on my ponytail. "I pay all my debts. If I leave before a year, I'll pay you."

"Okay." I push away the reoccurring fear of me living alone like Ms. Merrigold on the first floor. Except for the cats, since I'm allergic.

"My turn then." He rubs his hands together and looks me over as though he's trying to think of something that will embarrass me. "Why on Earth do you write math textbooks?"

I chuckle. "That's your question?"

"Would you rather me ask how long you've had a female boner for Phillips?"

My cheeks heat.

"Relax, your secret is safe with me." He grins.

"It's not like that."

He holds up his hand as though he doesn't want to talk about it. "I simply asked you why you chose your profession."

I nod and put some apples in the cart. "I was always good at math. I don't have to interact with many people. And it pays the bills."

He nods. "But you don't love it?"

"I like that I'm good at it."

"Interesting." He grabs oranges and puts them in the cart.

"What does that mean?" I ask, pulling my list out of my purse, along with my pen.

"It means it's interesting. I always like to hear why people chose to do what they do." He pushes the cart and rides it to the deli counter, where he tosses in pita bread and pulls a number from the red ticket dispenser.

I stop since I don't have meat on my list. "Why did you become a tattoo artist?"

His smile is wicked and cocky and drop-dead gorgeous. "I love art, but I hate confinement. I love giving people ways to express their beliefs or celebrate the life of a loved ones or just make a statement. It's an honor when someone lets me put my art on them permanently."

I'm stunned silent. Those are all good reasons. I have nothing like that for being a math textbook writer. He winks when he realizes I'm second-guessing why I do what I do for money.

"I love baking," I blurt.

"I've noticed. Do you do that because you're good at it too?"

My mouth hangs open. Few people have ever talked to me like this. I guess it's his don't-give-a-shit attitude. "I enjoy tweaking recipes. I love the preciseness of it. Baking is really mathematical and scientific when you get down to it. And I love seeing people enjoy something I made."

He taps my nose with his finger. "Then why aren't you doing that?"

His number gets called and he holds up his hand without looking away from me until he absolutely has to. As he requests from the nice lady an order of every processed meat that's doing absolutely horrible things to his insides, I peruse the baked items. None of them look half as good as mine.

"Ready?" he says, and I nod. "Round two?"

"You have more questions?"

"I have lots of questions. But it's your turn."

I look him over and decide to stay away from his childhood. "Why are you here?"

"I thought I'd get some groceries to eat so that I don't die from starvation." I tilt my head, and he laughs. "My life was getting out of control. I don't like that feeling. I called Knox at the right moment to snag the opportunity for a place to stay."

"You're so honest," I say.

He looks over the meat in the coolers. "I noticed you didn't have any steak the other night. Are you only a chicken gal, or do you eat red meat? Please don't tell me you're the tofu girl." He dodges my comment, so I let it die.

"I eat all three, although if you ask my mom, I only eat red meat once every two weeks and I prefer fish over anything." I pick up some organic chicken breasts and put them in the cart.

He laughs, picking up a package of steaks. "Oh, I love you parent-pleasers. You guys amuse me."

I roll my eyes. "Steaks again?"

"If I'm cooking for you, you can't complain."

"True enough."

"And it's my turn now. You're digging deep here, so I feel like I should nail you with something you don't want to answer." He makes an exaggerated effort of hemming and hawing.

My stomach stirs. I wonder what I should tell him if he does ask me about Dylan. While I anxiously wait for what he's going to ask, we turn down the bread aisle.

"Have you always had a thing for bad boys?" he finally asks.

My entire body heats. "I don't have a thing for bad boys."

I'm such a liar. If I didn't already want Dylan, I'd probably be looking at Jax like every middle-aged woman we've passed in the store has. Like they want him to jump on the end cap and do a striptease.

"So that's how it's gonna be? We're going to lie to one another?"

I pick up English muffins and hold the package in front of my face so he can't see me blush.

"Rian?"

"I swear if you tell him, I will come into your room at night and cut off your balls."

He crosses his legs and puts his hands over his junk. "Ouch. You're not that kind of girl. Don't say things that will make me hide all the knives under my pillow at night."

I laugh and he does too as we walk down another aisle, each of us picking up things and tossing them in the cart.

"I won't say anything, but you know Phillips knows, right?" he says.

"No, he doesn't, and it's just a crush. Not like anything would come from it."

He stops the cart and backs me up to the end of the aisle, plucking my paper and pen out of my hand and tossing them behind him. I try to weave to the side to see where they went, but he moves in the same direction. "I guarantee you, Phillips knows how you feel and so far he's done nothing about it, so why don't you give this bad boy a try? I promise to check all your boxes." His hand lands on my hip.

There's nothing terribly inappropriate about what he's doing. But I can't help but notice that he smells different than Dylan. It's muskier.

"My boxes?" I roll my eyes and look away.

His forefinger lands under my chin and forces me to face him. He is gorgeous. All chiseled jaw and sharp nose. Scruff like he doesn't care, and his hair gelled into a mess of perfection. Lean muscles that could have him front and center in a Calvin Klein ad.

"Yeah, your boxes. Don't-give-a-shit attitude. Check. Fuck you in public. Check. Dirty talker. Check. Know how to make a woman orgasm five times one after the other. Check."

With the last pluck of his tongue, my lady parts are scratching their heads saying, *Phillips who?*

But that's not totally true, because all I can think about is Dylan giving me those things. Maybe Jax is *too* bad boy for me, if there's even such a thing.

"Okay, playtime is over." I push his hard chest and he backs up, laughing.

I bow my head at an elderly lady who's blatantly gawking from down the aisle.

"I thought playtime was just starting. Man, Phillips really has his grip on you." He places a box of Triscuits in the cart.

I do admire his ass as he heads down the aisle though.

"If you aren't taking me up on my offer, then you can't enjoy staring at my finer qualities," he says, turning the corner and leaving me in the cookie and cracker aisle in stunned silence once again.

I grab all the E.L.Fudge cookie variations and follow him.

We reach the frozen foods section without making another scene, although I really need to get home to make good use of my toys. I think I'll imagine Dylan caging me in in the supermarket like Jax did.

Standing in front of the ice cream, I debate between Ben and Jerry's and a gallon of store brand since they're the same price. Jax grabs a gelato pint.

"So far, your Triscuits and gelato aren't supporting your bad boy claim," I say with amusement.

"Then take a chance and go out with me. If for no reason but to drive Phillips crazy."

There's no smile or amusement in his tone. He's serious. All I can think is, does Dylan really know how I feel? Does he have any interest other than remaining friends? Because if he did have any interest in me, wouldn't he have hit on me at some point? Or asked me out?

I bite my lip. I might not have feelings for Jax like I do Dylan, but maybe it's time I put Dylan aside and see what else is out there. I don't know Jax well. Maybe I could end up liking him in that way.

"Okay," I say.

Jax's eyes widen. "I'll pick you up tomorrow night at six. Dress casual."

My heart flips-flops. Here's a guy who knows what he wants and isn't afraid to go after it. All that needs to happen now is for the universe to shift so that I want him instead of the guy who doesn't see me as anything other than a friend.

Chapter Ten

DYLAN

SATURDAY NIGHTS ARE ALWAYS LONG. NOT THAT I HAVE ANY RIGHT TO COMPLAIN. Lyle actually had two girls come in after they saw his designs on Instagram. One got a piece and the other one said maybe next week. And the line that never died down is a good thing. Most of Frankie's regulars trusted me to do theirs. Still, it was a nonstop night that required stellar concentration and my brain is fried.

As I trudge down the hall to my apartment, all I want is to strip bare and crawl into bed, but the giggling on the other side of the door when I insert my key says Jax brought someone home.

When I enter the apartment, all I see is Jax on top of someone on the couch. I'm half tempted to shut the door and crash on Seth's couch until the blonde peers up to see who it is.

My gut twists in one giant knot as Rian says, "You're home."

"You're up." I take off my jacket and hang it up on the hook.

"We couldn't sleep, so we started watching wrestling. Jax said he once wanted to be a wrestler and was showing me what his signature move would've been."

She's all happy and now I'm grumpy. Jax's arrogant smile makes my blood pressure rise, and I swear I can feel my heartbeat in my neck.

"I guess I don't have to ask how your Saturday night was?" I reach inside the fridge for a beer, torn between staying out here so that maybe Rian will feel uncomfortable letting Jax be all over her and locking myself in my room to continue to live in denial.

"Jax set up the rooftop to watch a movie, so we ate dinner and watched *The Wedding Singer*. You know, the one with Adam Sandler." Rian's giddiness grates on any nerves I had left after my last client didn't feel the need to tip me since I'm the owner.

"Yeah, I know it." I sip my beer in the kitchen. "It was a long night. I'm going to head to bed. Enjoy the night, you two."

Rian sits up and looks over the back of the couch. Surprisingly, no smartass comment comes out of Jax's mouth, and the two remain quiet as I walk through the apartment to my bedroom.

After closing the door, I sit on the edge of my bed, finishing my beer and overhearing their laughter from the other side of the wall. How the hell did I ever get here? Usually I'd be out at the bars after work. I should've accepted Lyle's offer after we closed up.

I kick off my boots and slide up to the headboard of my bed, putting in a pair of earbuds and grabbing my sketchpad. Rian's giggling can be heard over the music while I sketch the design that's occupied my mind since we were in New York last week. A peony with shedding petals—meant for Rian if she ever comes to me for ink. She needs something as beautiful as her and she's like a peony—a symbol of beauty and fragility, but also a happy life and prosperity.

While my pencil sketches the design, I imagine where I'd ink her if the choice was mine. Her right ribcage would hurt more than somewhere else, but as I curved it around and under her breast, it would be beautiful. Even if I'm only going off of the few times I've seen her wear a bikini when she and Sierra sunbathed on the roof.

As soon as that thought comes to mind, I reprimand myself for thinking about that part of her body. I need to get a grip on my feelings for her. The attraction remained in that box I kept under double locks until Jax arrived. The more he flirts with her, the more a King Kong version of me wants to kidnap her.

What bothers me is that I have no idea if this is Jax's way of reliving the past or if he truly likes her. If he does, he's more man than me to pursue her without any guilt that she's too perfect for him to mess up.

But that's Jax—he does now and thinks later. It's the greatest difference between us. Where I get lost in my head, he acts without thinking, hurting innocent people.

I can't protect Rian, but if I want her, I'd better be able to suffer the consequences.

The next morning, I'm sure that Rian won't be up. It's Sunday, and the only dumbass who will work out with me is the other single guy in our friend group, Seth. So when I come face to face with Rian as she opens the bathroom door, I'm surprised.

She doesn't see me at first, probably still half asleep. Her matching T-shirt and shorts pajama set clings to her figure. Her hair is thrown up in a messy ponytail and a chunk of strands have fallen out of it. There's even a dry line from drool off her mouth. She's adorable.

"Dylan!" She startles, her hands releasing her ponytail holder, allowing her hair to cascade down her shoulders.

"Go back to bed. I'm heading to the gym." I walk by her and grab my water from the fridge.

"So early? Take a day off." Her voice is still rough from sleep.

I say nothing, but she's waiting by her door as I shove the water into my bag. Her gaze follows me, but as soon as I look her in the eye, she stares at the floor.

"You okay?" I ask.

"Yeah. Um…"

We stand across the room from one another, me waiting for her to say what she needs to. "Is something wrong?"

She shakes her head. "I just wanted to let you know—I mean, it's not a huge deal. But with this roommate situation, you need to be in the loop. You probably don't even care—"

"Spit it out," I say.

Her eyes fix on mine. "Jax asked me out on a date. We're supposed to go tonight."

My stomach drops. He's made the first move. I'm surprised, but I'm not. This is how Jax works.

I smack on the fakest smile I can at this time in the morning. "Cool. Have fun."

Her hands twist in front of her. "You're okay with it?"

"Does it matter?"

She's quiet but observant. Her deep inhales suggest she's not sure how she should act right now.

"It's great. Have a great time. Seth's waiting for me." I thumb at the door and hightail it out of there before I climb over all the furniture to smash my own lips to hers and beg her not to go out with him. The problem with that move is, what the hell do I back it up with? Wait for me? Wait for what? For me to get my head out of my ass?

I rush out the door to find Seth sitting on the floor outside his door, waiting for me. His gray hoodie is over his head and his phone is in his hands. I glance at the screen to see an Instagram post of a curly dark-haired girl holding a tray of bagels.

"Good morning," I announce myself.

He looks up, quickly turning off his screen. "This is ridiculous. It's Sunday." He pushes up off the floor. "I was up half the night listening to Knox fuck like a damn porn star."

I laugh because back in high school, Knox earned the nickname Ron Jeremy. He's a cop now, but back then, indecent exposure wasn't something he had an issue with. He'd screw a girl on the park bench if she let him. Then again, back then he was going through as much shit as the rest of us.

"Well, get ready for a good workout. Rian just told me Jax asked her out." I step into the elevator.

Seth stands idly in the hallway, his jaw hanging open. I grab his sweatshirt strings and drag him into the elevator.

"That's low."

I press the ground floor button. "Is it really? I mean, she's not seeing anyone."

"Yeah, but anyone who's around you guys knows…"

His words drift off because this isn't something we've ever talked about. I flirt with Rian, and yeah, I've felt that maybe she might like me. But I've kept my feelings close to my chest because anyone can predict the outcome of the two of us in a relationship.

We head out of the apartment building and down the street toward the gym.

"I think it's time you're truthful with her," Seth says, repositioning his bag over his shoulder.

I want to ask him if he's ready to admit why he's following Evan Erickson or the Bagel Place on Instagram if he hates her that much. "I'm not into losing friendships at the moment."

We walk into the gym. A guy who's roughly our age takes our cards and says good morning. We return his greeting and make our way to the locker room.

"You'd rather risk the chance that she and Jax start dating? What are you gonna do? Watch them make out during *Blue Bloods?*" He strips off his track pants and sweatshirt, shoving them into the locker.

I shrug. "I'll move back in with you and Knox." Easiest solution ever.

"Sorry, man, Leilani is paying your rent now. I guess she needed a place and Knox offered her your old room."

I lock my locker, grab my towel and water, and follow Seth to the treadmills. "Why didn't I know this?"

He shrugs, positioning all his shit exactly where he wants it. He pins his key to his shorts. "Because it didn't matter. Not like you consulted us when you moved out to protect Rian from Jax. The same guy you're laying down on the pavement so he can turn you into roadkill."

I up my speed and incline. Screw warming up.

Seth's not like Ethan though, so he doesn't compete with me. The fucker takes a leisurely Sunday stroll on his machine.

"I have no right to stop her." I'm talking more to myself than Seth.

He waves to the girl who's always folding towels. "You do have a right. You're her friend. You have her best interests in mind. It's piss or get off the pot time."

I shake my head, starting to sweat. I can't admit that I'm being a pussy here. She's the only one of my friends that I've told about Winnie and my upbringing. There's a reason for that. Somehow, I know I can trust her with the information, and I know it'll never be slung back at me. To put a relationship like that in jeopardy for a few orgasms seems moronic.

"Let's talk about something else. How about the Bagel Place?"

Seth rolls his eyes, slowly walking as he waves to everyone as though he's running for office or something. "Don't turn this on me. You're the one with the girl problems. Which is funny when you think about it. When we first moved in together, I idolized you and all the women you got. Now you're wound up tight over one. I'm enjoying sitting on the sidelines." He waves and says hello to Joe, an elderly man who's here on the bicycle every morning.

I up his speed without him realizing and he fumbles to keep up, falling off the back of the treadmill.

Payback is a bitch.

Chapter Eleven

RIAN

"A DATE?" BLANCA'S EYES LIGHT UP.

"With Jax?" The disgust in Sierra's voice tells me where her allegiance lies.

"He asked." I sit in Sierra's plush living room on Sunday afternoon. I guess when you date a prince, you end up living a cushy lifestyle.

"Is that the only reason you're going out with him?" Blanca asks. She's sitting cross-legged and reading a bridal magazine. They've yet to set a date, though I know she's getting pressure from her mom about having a big Italian wedding.

"No." I fall over on the couch, clutching a pillow to my stomach. I wish Dylan was the one who had asked me out, but I have no control over him. The look on his face this morning when I told him made me think for a second that he didn't want me to go. Then he smiled and said it was cool. "He's a funny guy actually."

"I ran into him in the elevator the other day. He asked me why I would want to get married." Blanca's face shows no emotion, I'm not sure where her mind is. "I had three commitment-phobe brothers. I'm familiar with the type."

"See!" Sierra refills our glasses of wine.

Blanca raises her hand. "But I've also witnessed what happens when they find a woman who brings them to their knees, so I can say with confidence that sometimes the playboy falls."

"Hardly ever—except in a romance novel." Sierra sits next to Blanca and points at the open page of the magazine. "Beautiful."

"Too revealing." Blanca flips the page. "Shall I remind you that you're with a prince who didn't exactly keep his dick in his pants?"

Sierra smiles as if she's remembering something. It's common knowledge that she and Adrian slept together their first night together. Not that any of us care, but if he was like that with her, I'm sure there were girls before her.

"Where is he anyway?" I ask.

"Sandsal. Gets in tonight." Another million-dollar smile is on Sierra's lips. Adrian has to go back and forth to his country on occasion until everything is done and the new rules of the monarchy are official. Long story that I don't care to get into. Sierra points at another page in the magazine. "Oh, I like that one."

Blanca turns the magazine so that I can see it and we both laugh.

"What?" Sierra asks.

"That's you, not Blanca." The dress is a skintight mermaid-style design. Blanca is more a fairytale Cinderella-style dress girl. As for me, I have no idea what I would want to wear.

"Sometimes you have to go outside your comfort zone," Sierra says. "You have the body." She stands and disappears into the kitchen.

A little of the tension releases with Sierra's departure, though it's not because of her. Sierra and I met in college, and I was intimidated. She had a quick tongue, never afraid to tell people what she was thinking. Her personality was loud and boisterous. You either hated her or loved her. I guess you can be drawn to your opposite, because I never cared if I stood in her shadow or was drowned out by her ability to control everything. In some ways, I envy that side of her. If Jax had cornered her in the grocery store, she would've known exactly how to react. Whereas my comebacks come twenty minutes later.

"I'm kind of nervous," I say to Blanca.

She looks up from her magazine, shuts it, and scoots closer. "Why?"

I shrug, sipping my wine. "He's forward."

Blanca's lips turn down. "I'm not sure this is such a good idea. I mean, if you still like Dylan and you're trying to get a reaction from him, what if you don't get the one you're looking for?"

She sips her wine as I recall my day with Dylan in New York City. When he took me to his foster mom's grave. How much he divulged to me. More than he has with anyone else as far as I know. I almost understand how someone growing up like that could leave someone scared to lose anyone they care for.

"I'm not trying to get a reaction out of him." The words feel like a blatant lie coming off my tongue, but I have to save some face. "I think maybe it's time I move on."

There's a little truth to my words. I've been pining away for Dylan for years, and though I did hope for a reaction from him, maybe it really is time to accept that nothing's ever going to happen between us. I can't put my life on hold forever, hoping that will change.

Blanca nods. "True enough. See what else is out there."

I twist my hands in my lap. "But Jax doesn't bite his tongue, and you know me. I'm slow on the uptake. I'm polite to a fault."

"Oh, Rian." She puts down her wine and slides over, wrapping her arm around my shoulders. "If you're not comfortable, don't go. If you want to go, then just be straight with him. If you're uncomfortable, call me. I grew up with three brothers—I know exactly where to hurt them."

I laugh, understanding what she's saying. "It's just… what am I going to wear? A cardigan and mom jeans?"

"Dramatic much?" Blanca says.

Sierra comes out with a tray of cheese and crackers and grapes.

"We're not royalty," Blanca says, laughing and sharing a look with me. "I'd happily take chips and guacamole."

"Well, this is what I have. Believe me, if I served this to the queen, she'd probably turn her nose up at it." She falls into the couch and appraises Blanca's arm around my shoulders. Her finger waggles between us. "What's going on?"

"Rian's a little nervous."

Blanca says it nicely, but in truth, my heart has drummed all day whenever I think about the date.

"I'm not his type," I say.

"You don't even know his type," Sierra says, which I guess is technically true, but I checked his Instagram account. There's definitely a specific type of woman he hangs out with.

"I have no tattoos. There's nothing edgy or sexy about me." I could keep going, but Sierra's eyes widening with excitement stops me.

"Uh oh," Blanca says, laughing because we've seen that look on Sierra's face more than once. The last time was when she decided to enter a contest to win a date with Prince Adrian Marx. Of course, that worked out pretty well for her. "What are you thinking?"

"Makeover!" Sierra tosses the rest of the cracker into her mouth and springs up off the couch, her hand on my arm pulling me up. "Come on."

"Like what kind of makeover?" I say, allowing her to tug me off the couch.

Blanca follows us.

"Nothing crazy. We'll just show off your amazing body a little more than you usually do. Maybe some more dramatic makeup."

Before I can blink, I'm on Sierra's bed and she's lost in her closet. Blanca runs her hand down my arm, shooting me a sympathetic smile before joining Sierra in her closet.

This could go two ways. Either I'm more confident—like the time in college when Sierra dressed me for a party and the star quarterback actually cornered me to talk the majority of the night—or it goes bad. Like Halloween of our junior year, when she convinced me to dress in a slutty nurse costume and I ended up getting a taxi home midway through the night because I couldn't handle all the stares and inappropriate touches by asshole frat boys. Sometimes it's a curse we're the same size.

Sierra comes out with a stack of clothes on hangers. "Did he say what to wear?"

"Casual," I say, shaking my head at her gown. "Let's get back to reality here. I'm not dating a prince, so no need for an actual ballgown."

Sierra laughs.

"Casual, so jeans?" Blanca asks.

I nod.

"But heels," Sierra says, holding her finger up and diving back into her closet.

"I haven't worn heels since I got dragged to that frat formal in college when you made me be Trey Longfield's date because you were going with his best friend."

Sierra comes out with a pair of black suede boots with a stiletto heel that will probably snap the first time I twist my ankle.

"Why can't I wear my flats? That's casual."

Sierra blows out a breath and Blanca nibbles on the inside of her cheek.

"Come on, it will be fun to dress a little outside of your usual," Blanca says. "Sierra promises not to go too crazy, right, Sierra?"

"Definitely. You're gorgeous. We're just upping the look a little because it's a first date."

I release a breath. Maybe a new look will give me more confidence. "Fine. But no crazy makeup. I'm not Sandy from *Grease*."

They both laugh.

Sierra pretends to stomp out a cigarette and says, "Tell me about it, stud."

Then she saunters back into the closet, and I succumb to her and Blanca's suggestions.

Two hours later, I emerge from the bathroom. The girls jump off the bed.

"Are you ready?" Sierra asks.

I nod. I haven't looked at myself in the full-length mirror yet, so I turn to check myself out. I'm wearing ripped tight jeans with a tight body suit. Somehow, I'm managing to walk in Sierra's black boots that have an opening at the toes, but they make me about three inches taller.

They both look at me from behind through the mirror.

"I'm not sure. I'm super tall," I say.

"Jax is huge. You're fine," Blanca says.

My hair is curled in long tendrils and my makeup is smokier and darker than I ever wear it, but my lipstick isn't nearly as dark as I anticipated Sierra would go. All in all, I love the look. Not that I'd do this daily, which makes me feel as though I'm falsely advertising myself.

"Sierra!" Adrian's voice booms through the apartment, and her eyes go huge.

"I'll be right back," she says and rushes out of the room.

"Let's go before they start having sex while we're still here and we end up stuck in this bedroom," Blanca says, grabbing her purse off the bed.

I collect my stuff and we walk out of the bedroom. Sierra is attached to Adrian like a koala bear, casting kisses on every part of his face, his hands plastered to her ass.

He glances over her shoulder. "Ladies."

"Hey, Adrian," Blanca and I say in unison.

"We'll be leaving the two of you alone," I say.

Blanca slides by them to the front door.

"No. Wait." Sierra slides down Adrian. "What do you think? Rian's going out with Jax tonight."

Adrian's eyes roam over my body, but in a polite way, never stopping on any one part, even though my boobs are the first thing anyone would see when they look at me.

"Very nice. Jax?" he asks with a wrinkle on his forehead as he glances at Sierra.

"I'm escorting her across the street." Blanca swings her arm through mine.

"Really it's so I don't break my ankle," I say.

Blanca laughs, knowing I'm telling the truth.

"Have fun with… Jax?" Adrian says as though maybe he has the situations wrong.

"Thanks." I smile.

Adrian slides out of his jacket and puts his phone on the wireless charger by the couch. I wonder what it's like to go from country to country at least once a month.

Sierra pulls me into her body. "I want a detailed report tonight."

"No need to call tonight, Rian." All of us look at Adrian. "I've been gone for five days, babe."

Sierra blushes. I love seeing that look on her face because she's so smitten, more vulnerable and in touch with her feelings. "Oh, yeah. Tomorrow morning is fine."

Adrian comes up behind her, his arms around her waist. "After eleven though." He winks.

I smile at the two of them. So in love. Although I'm slightly jealous, I'm happy for my friends.

Blanca and I say our goodbyes and take the elevator down their expensive apartment building to the main floor. We're out on the street and about to cross to our own apartment when we spot Dylan at the door of Ink Envy. He glances over then does a double-take.

"Hey, Dylan," Blanca waves.

He stands there gawking. "Hey, you two," he says, his voice sounding distant and far away.

We cross the street and I glance over my shoulder, but he's walking into Ink Envy. I guess that's all I'll see of Dylan tonight.

Chapter Twelve

RIAN

"I heard Frankie's been gone and Dylan's had to work extra shifts," Blanca says once we're in the elevator.

I nod. Of course she knows all this because of Ethan. "Yeah."

"Okay, so let's go over some things." The elevator reaches our floor but she holds the door closed button.

"What?"

"First of all, he asked you out. Remember that. *He* wants to date *you*. Do not think he is at all above you in any way. You are at his level, got it?"

I nod.

"Good. I can't stress this enough, Rian, and I would never lie to you—he's the lucky one. Lucky to go on a date with you."

I nod again.

"And if he tries anything funny, you get ahold of his wrists." She grabs my wrists, forcing them down to my sides. "Dig your nails into the inside and thrust your knee as hard as you can into his balls."

I laugh.

"I'm serious. You never know. Then you call me, and I'll handle the rest."

I stare at her little five-foot-two body and raise my eyebrows.

"Don't underestimate me because I'm small. All my brothers are over six foot and I've had them on their knees, praying for mercy." I laugh again, and even her lips tip up. "This last piece of advice is the most important part though."

My shoulders fall. "What?"

"Have fun. Just enjoy him. Enjoy his flirting and flirt back. This is your night. Make the most of it." She hugs me and sways us back and forth. The doors slowly open.

"Thanks, Blanca."

We turn to leave, and Seth and Ethan are standing there.

"Don't mind us. Continue as you were," Seth says with a grin.

Ethan takes no time at all to corner Blanca in the elevator. "Come on, we're headed out to grab a pizza and a beer."

"We said no chicks," Seth says.

Blanca looks around the small space. "I don't hear any chirping, do you, Rian?"

I laugh, stepping out of the elevator. "No."

Seth gets in and looks me up and down. "Looking good, Rian." He nods at me as the doors slide shut between us.

I inhale a deep breath and glance at my watch to see it's five fifty-five. Using my key, I open the apartment door and find Jax in the kitchen, opening a bottle of water. He doesn't look much different than he does on any normal day. A pair of jeans and a gray T-shirt with a jacket over top. His hair is still mussed up perfection any girl would want to run her fingers through. He really is hot.

The bottle stays tipped to his lips as his gaze floats over me like a feather, pausing at my breasts, my hips, and my shoes. He's blatantly and unapologetically checking me out. All those doubts and worries vanish.

He stops drinking, securing the top of the bottle. "I thought you were standing me up." His vision won't stop dipping to my chest, and I can't deny that it feels good to be wanted. "You look fucking hot."

I laugh, which spurs his own deep chuckle.

"Let me just put this away." I head to my room and toss a bag with the clothes I was wearing onto my bed. I check that everything I need is in my purse, adding a phone charger just in case.

When I come back out of the bedroom, Dylan's sitting in a chair with a water bottle in hand. I glance around not finding Jax in the room anymore, which only makes this even more awkward.

"Hey," Dylan says. He's still wearing his boots, one ankle resting on the knee of his other leg. He takes pull after pull off his water bottle. His eyes move the way Jax's did over my body, but instead of the lust that filled Jax's eyes, distaste fills Dylan's. "Nice look."

"Is that your way of complimenting me?"

Dylan's gaze shoots up. Even I'm surprised I had the balls to ask him, but I'm stepping out into the world with the possibility of getting hurt. When's the last time he did that?

"Good luck holding a conversation with him. He'll be staring at your tits the entire night."

I say nothing, every retort running through my brain not nearly good enough.

"Is that what you want, Rian? A guy who just wants to fuck you?"

"You're being ugly tonight." I beeline across the room to the kitchen. "Have you seen Jax?"

"He got a call. In his room."

I turn around to find Dylan's gaze still on me. He can act like he doesn't like what I'm wearing, but this is the first time he hasn't been able to take his eyes off me. Our eyes lock and he quickly diverts his, raising his water bottle to his lips. Those luscious lips I dream of kissing. Ugh. Maybe going on a date with Jax is a bad idea.

Before I have a chance to really think about why I'm doing this, Jax comes out of his bedroom. "Phillips." He nods and shuts his door.

"Owens."

The two are cordial.

"Ready, angel?" Jax asks, holding out his hand for me.

I nod and slide my hand into his. I'm surprised by how smooth it is.

"See you, Phillips." Jax never turns around as he leads me to the apartment door.

"Have a great date. Just put a sock on the doorknob if you want to be alone later." Dylan waves his water bottle.

Jax laughs, opening the door and waiting for me to walk through. His hand guides me by the small of my back, and we walk down the hall in silence. The elevator arrives quickly so I don't have to force conversation, but Jax has a different idea once we're alone in the small space.

"Was that as painful as it was to watch?" he asks.

I peek up. "What do you mean?"

"You pretending that you didn't want Phillips and me to switch places?"

I smile at this man I barely know but who can somehow see through me as though I'm as transparent as a piece of glass. "I'm happy to be going out with you."

"Bullshit."

The elevator stops on the bottom floor and we file out. "I'm sorry. I'm not using you to make him jealous or anything."

He nods. "I didn't figure you were the type."

"Do you want to call this thing off?" I ask.

A wicked smile crosses his lips. "Hell no. You're looking smokin' hot and Phillips is about to rage right now. We're going out and staying out. You might not have an agenda to make him jealous, but I like to torture the shithead." He grabs my hand again and pushes through the front door of our apartment building.

"Where are we going?" I ask.

"That's for me to know and you to find out." He winks and we stop by a motorcycle. "Have you ever ridden on one?"

I shake my head.

"Never with Phillips?"

I shake my head again.

He blows out a breath. "I guess we're walking then."

I tear my hand out of his. "Wait, why? I can ride it."

He smirks and stuffs his hands into the pockets of his jeans. He looks up at the apartment then down at the bike. "Your first time on a motorcycle shouldn't be holding on to me. Everyone needs a great memory of the first time they ride, and if I allow you on my bike, you'll regret it like girls do their virginity—always wishing they'd saved it for someone else."

I step toward him, my hand on his cheek, and stare into his beautiful blue eyes. "You're sentimental?"

"No. I'm just letting Phillips pop that cherry of yours. Contrary to what he might think, I'm not a complete asshole." He removes my hand from his face and entwines our fingers.

The door of the building opens and Dylan walks out, his eyes falling to mine then to where my hand is in Jax's. He walks in the opposite direction, climbs on his bike that's a few spots down from Jax's, secures his helmet, then he's gone, turning right before the yellow turns red.

"If he's going to be a pussy, the least I can do is show you a good time."

Jax tears my attention away and we walk down the sidewalk to begin our date.

Jax takes me bowling. Which would be fine if I was wearing socks. But the gentleman he is, he buys me a pair for six dollars through the vending machine.

"What a prince you are." I rest my cheek on his chest and flutter my eyelashes at him.

He shakes his head.

It turns out that Jax isn't intimidating once we figured out nothing would happen between us. Although he is just as big a flirt.

We each get our shoes on and Jax asks the guy to put us at the far end of the lanes, away from other people. The kid tries to say he's not supposed to do that but ultimately gives Jax his way. I'm pretty sure the sixteen-year-old was intimidated by the big Jax Owens.

I slide off the heels, which is a relief. I worry for a second that I won't be able to get my feet back into them to go home. After I tie my shoes, I jump up to pick a ball. "I haven't bowled since I was, like, eight. There was a birthday party and it was boys versus girls."

Jax smiles and shakes his head as he ties his shoes. "And you kissed a boy by the bathroom?"

"No," I screech, and he laughs as though he expected that to be my answer.

"How old were you when you had your first kiss?" I ask, then wave off the question. "I don't even want to know."

He grabs a sixteen-pound ball and I grab a respectable ten. "You probably don't want to know."

I type in our names on the electronic screen while a waitress comes over. I'm happy for the distraction. Comparing sexual conquests isn't really a conversation I want to have with Jax. I'm pretty sure I know how I'll stack up against him. He orders us a pizza, a pitcher of beer and two waters, and stops her before she leaves to add on an order of wings.

When Jax slides into the chair next to me, his arm brushes mine. For a moment, I wonder what would have happened if I had met Jax before Dylan. Would I feel differently?

"Ladies first." He leans back, stretching both his arms long the back of the booth.

I stand, pick up my ball, and prepare as best I can to mimic what the couples with matching shirts a few lanes down are doing. As I walk up to the line, I pull back my hand with the ball.

"Man, you do have a great ass."

My foot slips, my fingers almost lodging in the ball as I bring it forward to release it. A terrible scene flashes through my mind of me splayed on the wooden lane with my arm outstretched and the ball still attached. But at the last minute, my thumb pops out and the ball slides straight into the gutter.

When I walk back to wait for my ball to return, Jax is standing there. "Let me give you some pointers."

"Is this your way of getting your hands on my hips?"

He smirks. "You're smarter than I give you credit for."

"Thanks?"

"I see what Phillips sees."

I turn away from him and he grabs my ball before I can, showing me where to put my fingers. He walks me up the line with one of his hands on my hip and the other on my hand holding the ball. His palm is so big, it fits over my hand.

The ball careens down the lane and six pins go down. I jump up and Jax high fives me.

"See? Only good things happen when my hands are on your hips." He winks and busies himself getting his ball while I sit back down and sip my beer.

Jax and I play two games while eating our pizza. He eats more wings than me and probably drinks more beer too. But I see why Jax and Dylan were best friends at one point. They're so similar. They each put themselves last. Jax asked me five times if I wanted the last slice before cutting it in half and demanding we split it.

I'm on Jax's back when we step out of the bowling alley because as I assumed my feet are swollen and I couldn't get the boots back on my feet.

"Shit, it's raining," Jax says, raising his hand for a cab. "Looks like I don't get the opportunity to have you on my back the whole way home."

A taxi that was waiting down the street parks along the curb and I slide in, Jax joining me. He gives the driver the address of our apartment and I pull out my phone for no reason but to look like I have something to do. I sit up straight when I see the first text in an exchange in our group.

Knox: Dylan was in an accident. He's headed to Memorial. One of you need to come because I'm still working.

A huge boulder lands in my stomach and my lungs stop working properly. I put my head through the open space in the plastic divider and the cab driver startles.

"We need to go to Memorial Hospital," I say.

Jax glances at me.

"Dylan was in an accident."

His face pales for a moment, but he quickly recovers. "That asshole will do anything to ruin my date with you." He stares out the window, leg bouncing now.

I say nothing, tapping out a text to our friends to find out who is already there, but no one answers.

Chapter Thirteen

DYLAN

"I'M FINE. LET ME GO HOME," I REPEAT TO THE NURSE WHO SAYS I NEED AN MRI of my head.

"Just relax, will you? You're making their job, like, ten times harder." Seth sits in the chair to my right, watching *The Bachelor* and eating a bag of Funyuns.

"I'll be back in a few," she says and leaves the room.

"I hate hospitals. It's bad enough I fucking broke my arm." I lift my arm that's in a temporary soft cast until some of the swelling goes down and they put on a hard cast. My *left* fucking arm. The one I write with, the one I wipe my ass with, and most importantly, the one I fucking tattoo people with. My head falls back to the bed. "I have no choice. I'm going to have to offer Jax a job."

It doesn't seem like Seth hears me when he looks away from the screen. "Do you think you could be on this show and kiss some girl one night and another one the next? Seems a little sleazy the way the guy leads them all on, no?" He chomps down on another onion ring chip. "That probably makes me sound like a pussy. It's probably most guys' wet dream."

Knox walks in. Thank fuck I get a reprieve from *Bachelor* talk for a moment. He's in full uniform, gun holstered to his hip. If someone had told me when I was sixteen that Knox Whelan would be a cop, I would've asked them when their rocket leaves for Mars.

"You're being cited." He hands me a ticket.

"You're ticketing your best friend?" Seth asks.

"No. The other officer did. I'm just delivering the ticket." Knox glances at the television, where the rose ceremony is beginning, and his eyebrows scrunch. "Failure to yield, which means this hospital bill"—he circles his finger at my arm—"is on your insurance, not the guy who hit you."

My head drops back to the bed again. What has happened to my life?

Knox pulls up a chair next to my bed.

"Hey, Knox. Do you think you could be the Bachelor?" Seth asks.

Knox glances at the television again. "Go to exotic places and have twenty gorgeous women vying for me? Yeah, I think I could." His tone says, "Is that even a fucking question?"

"So I'm the pussy." Seth brings his Coke to his lips.

Knox leaves Seth to watch television. Knox has those same eyes I got when Winnie died. The same ones he gave me when I watched Jax make stupid-ass decisions and did nothing. Strike my earlier comment—Knox Whelan was meant to be a cop.

"The witnesses said you were reckless," he says. "That with the rain, you took the corner faster than you should have."

He's telling the facts instead of asking me questions. It's his way. He wants to know what's on my mind. Out of everyone, Knox knows I don't share my problems because people try to fix them and give me those damn looks of pity. That's not changing now.

I could tell him it's about business, which isn't a complete lie. Add on this hospital stay and my insurance deductible, the fact that I'll be out of work until my arm is out of the cast, and it all leads to one word—*broke*!

But the reason I sped through that light was because Rian was stunningly beautiful when she left our apartment to go out with another guy. And not just any guy. Not the smart accountant I always envisioned her marrying. My archenemy. A guy who hates me so much, he'll do anything to hurt me. Jax is a smart guy. It probably took him five minutes in a room with Rian and me to figure out there are hidden feelings there. Jax also knows me well enough to know why I've never done anything about it.

Everyone gets dealt their hand in life. I've made the most of mine. I've been blessed in many ways I wouldn't have thought of, based on the shit hand I was dealt at birth. The one thing I love the most in my life is the friendships I've made. Friends that are like a family to me. Something I've never really had. If I start something with Rian and we can't make it work, which I've never been able to do with anyone, then we split up the group just like a divorced couple would.

I watched it with Sierra and Ethan. The jagged line that divided our close-knit group of friends. Ethan on the outskirts, forced to move out even if he says he did it by choice. It's not worth the risk. What are the chances a guy like me could make Rian happy long term?

"Dylan," Knox says, drawing me from my internal thoughts.

"Like, think about it. When you kiss someone, you're kissing everyone they've kissed." Seth shakes his head, crumpling up the Funyuns bag and tossing it in the trash can. "And how come the women don't care? Where do they find them to sign up for this? It's kind of sexist." He turns his attention to us only because the show has gone to commercial. "What?"

"Get off the *Bachelor*," Knox says.

Seth props his feet up on my bed and relaxes back into his chair with his fingers laced over his stomach. "I'm just saying—"

Knox shoots Seth the stern dad look before turning to me. "We're your friends, Dylan. You can talk to us."

I blow out a breath and stare at the ceiling.

"Just fucking tell him," Seth says.

My head shoots in his direction. Knox's attention shifts between Seth and me, obviously waiting for one of us to spill.

"Shut up," I say and kick Seth's feet off my bed.

He props them back up.

"Rian went out with Jax tonight," Seth says, smirking as he wiggles his ass to get comfortable in the chair.

"Why are you here again?" I ask him.

"Because I'm your in case of emergency. Which I should say, I feel honored about." Seth's hand covers his heart. "No offense, but mine is my mom, but you know, she'll baby me if something bad happens."

I stare blankly at him.

"I feel oddly offended I'm not your in case of emergency. As pussy as that sounds." Knox looks down as if he's examining himself for thinking that.

"You're a cop. You'll know when something happens to me. Seth's got nothing going on in his life."

"Jeez, thanks." Seth gives me the stink-eye.

"And no offense, I'm changing my in case of emergency now," I say.

He flips up his middle finger, his attention back on the television. "Man, I'm surprised there aren't any cat fights. One rose left. Even my heart is pounding."

"Is this about Rian going out with Jax?" Knox asks me.

I shake my head. "No."

He looks at me long and hard. Is this what he does with the people he pulls over?

"You're trying to intimidate me into confessing. Not ethical, man."

He chuckles.

"Shit, I hate how they drag out this last rose," Seth says.

"Do you always watch this show?" Knox asks Seth.

They might live together, but they're on opposite shifts most of the time.

Seth scoffs. "No."

Knox picks up the remote from the bed and turns off the television.

"You fucker, he had the rose in his hand!" If looks could kill, Seth just murdered Knox.

"Give me a damn break. Why do you give a shit? There will never be twenty women vying for your heart."

"That's insulting," Seth says. "I like to think I'm quite the catch. Case in point, I don't think the show is very ethical."

I let them go on as long as they want even if it's annoying the shit out of me because who the hell cares at this point? The longer they argue, the less likely the conversation will turn my way again.

Then Knox's radio squawks and his hand raises to the walkie on his shoulder. Thank goodness—he'll have to go. I'll let Seth watch *The Bachelor* and hopefully the nurse will take me for my damn MRI. After Knox is done talking, he stands.

Perfect. Just as I predicted.

"I gotta get back on the road," he says. "Seth, take him home. You can stay in Leilani's bed if you don't want to stay with Rian and Jax. She can sleep with me."

"I'll be in my bed."

"It's just an offer. You haven't driven your bike crazy since Winnie died." He pins me with a stare.

My hands clench on the sheets. Seth looks at me too. He knows about Winnie. Not everything, just that she was my foster mom who died.

My driving crazy after Winnie died was completely different. I'm actually surprised I'm still alive after all the races I took part in.

"I'm fine in my own bed," I say. "And please let's not make some big deal about this."

"Sure," Knox says.

"Of course not," Seth says.

Just as Knox is leaving the room, Rian appears in the doorway. All the rage from earlier refills the empty well inside me when I see her in that outfit and makeup again.

"They didn't want to let me in." She rushes over to the bed, taking me in as though she's examining where all my injuries might be.

"Where's your date?" I snip.

"Dylan," Knox says, sighing.

"He's in the waiting room. I told the nurse at the front that I was your sister."

"Um… Rian?" Seth asks.

She turns to him, but then looks back at me quickly, looking as if she's mentally checking off each part of my body that isn't harmed.

"Where are your shoes?" Seth asks.

I lean over the bed to see her white-sock-covered feet.

She looks down at them. "I couldn't get my shoes back on. Long story."

"So where are they now?" Seth asks.

I want to take the shortbread cookies they gave me after taking my blood and shove them down Seth's throat when I picture the boots she had on earlier on the floor of Jax's room.

Rian shrugs. "Jax has them."

Knox waves from the doorway. "I'll see you at home. Glad nothing more serious happened."

"Yeah, thanks for the ticket." I hold up the piece of paper.

Rian plucks it from my grasp.

"Hey, you do the crime, you do the time," Knox says.

"Har-har, Officer Knox," Seth says.

Knox flips him off, walking out of the hospital room.

"So is it just your arm?" Rian's hand on mine pulls my attention back to her.

I hate all the makeup Sierra and Blanca put on her. Rian doesn't need to change for Jax. She's beautiful. "Yeah, six weeks in a cast."

Her shoulders fall. "It's your left."

I nod. "Yeah, which means no tattoo unless you want to be my first right-handed attempt." I laugh.

She doesn't. "This is serious. What happened?"

She reads over the ticket, her tongue sliding out as she reads. I desperately want to tell her how cute she looks when she does that. Like when she's trying to tweak a recipe and she thinks about it for most of the day before, her tongue teases me like that the entire time.

Seth clears his throat. "I'm hungry. Anything?" He stands and points at us.

"Nah," I say.

Rian doesn't answer.

"How was your date?" I ask once we're alone so that no one is a witness to me losing my balls.

She puts down the paper. "Failure to yield? The bike is so dangerous."

I wait because I know she heard me and we're not going to play this game.

She sighs. "It was good. We went bowling."

That explains the shoe thing. I'm relieved it wasn't what I was envisioning.

"I'm not sure why you had to put on all that makeup or dress like that." My gaze falls over her body. She's so damn hot, my dick is already on board with banging her. Her tits practically beg for me to grab them, her hard nipples poking out through her bra. "It's way too much."

She stands and heaves a breath. "Thanks for the advice. Next time you can do my makeup."

Of course she takes it wrong.

I grab her hand, my thumb running along her inner wrist. She doesn't pull away, which has to be a good sign. "I've been a bastard."

"Yeah, you have." She doesn't look at me.

"Okay, you ready to ride the MRI train?" A woman I haven't seen before comes in. She smiles sweetly at both of us. "He'll be right back." She unlocks the wheels on the bed, and before I have time to say anything or stop her, I'm being taken out of the room. "You can wait here or go down to vending. We'll be about thirty or forty minutes."

Rian says nothing, and I can't see anything since the bed is already rolling.

On my way down the hall, I get a glimpse of the waiting room. I see Knox and Jax in deep conversation by a vending machine. Seth is with Ethan and Blanca. Adrian and Sierra are just walking in, both with just fucked heads of hair.

It all reconfirms not to fuck with this. It wasn't that long ago when I was laid up in the emergency room with a horrible case of the flu and there was no one to call. I waited for discharge and I left the hospital all by myself. Back when my in case of emergency was an empty box.

Chapter Fourteen

RIAN

I SIT IN THE CHAIR IN DYLAN'S HOSPITAL ROOM. I'D NEVER ADMIT TO ANYONE HOW scared I was when I saw that message from Knox. How does a police officer not tell you exactly what's wrong? If he would've said Dylan's conscious, I wouldn't have been nearly as worried that something horrible had happened.

"Oh, did they take him for his MRI?" A nurse comes in, sanitizes her hands, and stops by the door.

"Yeah."

Her smile dims into a sympathetic look. "Oh, don't worry. I'm sure he's fine. He's one of the smart ones who wears a helmet. But he'll need some help until that cast comes off."

"Of course."

"My husband slipped on the ice at his job last winter and had to have surgery on his shoulder. As you know, men can't handle things like this quite like us women can. He whined and complained his whole recovery. I chalked it up to him having the 'man flu.'" She puts man flu in quotations. "But turns out he got so depressed, we had to get antidepressants. It's hard for men like them to sit back and allow their loved ones to care for them."

She talks as though she knows Dylan. My gut twists when the question pops in my head, and I'm not even prepared to hear the answer. She's only a few years older than us and I spotted a tattoo on the inside of her wrist when she raised her hands to sanitize them. "Do you know Dylan?"

"No. I just know his type. A replica of my husband." She picks up the papers on the tray. "Mind if I go over the care instructions with you?"

I sit up straighter. Should I tell her we're not a couple? Then the haunting thought that might be going through Dylan's mind right now triggers in my own. Who will help him? He doesn't have a girlfriend to see him back to health. He's definitely too proud to ask.

"Sure," I say, knowing that Dylan's rehabilitation is up to me.

"My husband loved the sponge baths." She laughs. "But just wrap his arm in plastic and use a scrunchie to secure it at the top of the arm. If you need to, a bigger rubber band will help. He obviously can't swim in a pool. No scratching by sticking a pen or ruler or anything down there. He'll probably go through some itching as it heals, so keep an eye out for that." She shrugs. "Other than that, it's just a broken arm. He did say it's his dominant though, which means he'll have to relearn to do stuff with his right, I suppose."

She stands and tucks the doctor's chair under a table with a computer on it. She scans her badge and types away.

Seth walks in with a Snickers bar in hand. "What's up, buttercup?" The nurse looks at him and he raises his hand. "In case of emergency contact." He points at himself with a big grin then sits next to me and holds the Snickers bar in front of my face.

"No thanks."

"Oh, you look sour like Knox did earlier. All these people vying to be Dylan's in case of emergency. I know. I was shocked too."

I stare blankly at him, and even the nurse is eyeing him from the corner of her eye.

"Should I go over the care instructions with him?" she asks, closing up the computer.

"Care instructions?" he asks.

"No, I'm Dylan's roommate," I say.

"What kind of care instructions?" Seth asks again.

"Sponge bath techniques," the nurse says, picking up the papers and handing them to him.

The Snickers bar drops to his lap and he holds up his hands in front of him like a ten-year-old boy.

The nurse laughs. "I think you need to have a conversation about that in case of emergency thing. As soon as his MRI comes back clean, the doctor will be in and you guys can get home."

"Thank you," I say.

She smiles and walks out of the room.

Seth picks up his Snickers bar and blows on it. "What're your thoughts on the *Bachelor?*"

An hour later, Dylan is released and being wheeled out in a wheelchair by an orderly. Seth is on one side and I'm on the other. All our friends stand as we push through the doors of the waiting room. Each of them hugs Dylan or shakes his hand. Jax is even there, having stuck around, and the two do a handshake thing I've never seen Dylan do with anyone.

A few minutes later, we're all outside and Adrian's car pulls into the circle.

We shuffle Dylan into the car and the orderly goes back into the hospital. We all split up between Ethan, Adrian, and Seth's cars. Somehow, I end up with Blanca and Ethan.

"This is a nice car, Ethan."

"Thanks. It's nothing like Adrian's, but it gets us from A to B," he says with a big smile. It's not a brand new car, but it's his first. I know how proud he was when he purchased it last month.

We aren't even out of the circle driveway of the hospital before Blanca peers at me between the seats. "So?"

"So what?" I ask.

"How was the date?"

Ethan says nothing. I've actually known him longer than I've known Blanca, so even though it feels a little odd, talking about Jax in front of him isn't weird.

"It was good. He's a really nice guy."

"Nice?" Blanca looks at Ethan for a moment before her brown eyes land on me again. "Did anything happen?"

"Blanc," Ethan says.

"I'm just asking." She waves. "You don't have to answer if you don't want to."

"I didn't kiss him. We were just leaving the bowling alley when we got the call about Dylan," I say.

I'm not sure if I want to tell Blanca, and Ethan, that Jax saw right through me. That he knows I'm pathetic and have fallen for a man who will never feel the same about me. It's embarrassing even if Blanca knows my feelings for Dylan. But to deny the attention of another guy because of that crush feels ridiculous. Like I'm holding out for something that's never going to happen.

"Oh, I bet he knows how to kiss," she says.

"Blanca!" Ethan yells.

Blanca bites her lip. "Not as good as you, babe." She kisses his cheek before whispering something in his ear.

"Better," Ethan says.

"Do you think you'll go out with him again?" she asks.

I shrug. "I'm not sure. We're roommates, and I don't want to mess that up either."

Blanca turns back around to face forward. Ethan looks at me in the rearview mirror, and our eyes meet. I can tell by his expression that I'm not as transparent as I like to think to him either.

"Dylan's going to need some help until that cast comes off," he says, giving me an out of the conversation about Jax.

I mouth, "Thank you," and he nods.

"Yeah, we'll all have to pitch in," Blanca says.

"I'm sure I can handle most of it," I say. "Who knows? Jax stayed around the hospital, so maybe those two can kiss and make up now."

"Yeah, what's up with them?" Blanca asks.

Ethan looks at me again through the rearview mirror as if he knows everything.

"I have no idea," I lie because it's not my business to share.

Thankfully, Blanca isn't Sierra. She gives up. Sierra's like the dog that never lets go of the tug toy until you give her something bigger and better.

We pull up to the apartment building and Ethan lets us out before he goes to hunt for a parking space. Dylan and Sierra are already waiting at the doors since Adrian gets to park in the lot designated for his building across the street.

"Here, take your boots." I pass her the boots I have in my hand. "You can go, Sierra," I tell her, inserting our key into the building.

"Are you sure?" she asks.

"God yes. Please carry on with your sex fest," Dylan says, walking over with a mumbled thanks after I open the door.

"Okay, I'll come by and check on you tomorrow!" She's already about to cross the street.

"I guess we don't have to tell her twice," Blanca says, following us inside.

We ride the elevator, Blanca asking Dylan a million questions about what happened. He only offers one-word answers. She shoots me looks behind his back.

Dylan digs his keys out of the pocket of his jacket and tries to open our door with his right hand, but the tip of the key keeps missing the hole.

"Struggle to get it in? That's probably a first for you," Blanca says, laughing on her way down to her apartment.

"Here." I hold out my hand even though my keys are in my purse.

"I have to figure it out eventually."

He doesn't release them, and I watch the tip of the key keep hitting the lock. I think whatever pain killer they must've given him at the hospital is affecting him. Finally, it goes in the hole and he unlocks the deadbolt, but we still have the bottom lock. Amazingly, it only takes four tries until we're in, but by the time we enter, Jax, Seth, and Ethan are in the hallway with us.

"Just call me if you need me. Remember, I'm his in case of emergency," Seth says and Jax slams the door in his face.

"I'm going to make him a badge," Jax says, moving right to the fridge. He pulls out two beers and one water bottle, untwists the caps, and hands the water to Dylan, a beer to me, and downs a huge sip of his own beer. "Well, this sucks, huh?"

Dylan says nothing and downs his water. I take off and throw the white gym socks in the trash.

"Hey now, I paid good money for those socks!" Jax laughs, and I join in.

Dylan grunts and stands. "Listen, you guys, don't worry about me. I'll be fine."

"Let me help you get settled in bed. I have some extra pillows," I say.

But Dylan is already halfway to his room. When he gets to the door, he turns to us again. "I'm good. Promise." Then he disappears into his room.

Jax steps over to me. "He's such a martyr, I swear."

"He's too proud."

Jax rolls his eyes and puts his empty beer bottle in the recycling. "I'm going to head to bed too. It was nice going out with you tonight even if…" He leans forward and I wonder what I would do if he did try to kiss me. "It was platonic. I don't usually welcome second place, Rian."

I bite my lip, unsure what he wants me to say.

"But if you ever get lonely at night, my bed is open." He winks.

I'm not sure if he's serious or just has no idea how to handle the situation we find ourselves in.

After his door shuts, I dump my beer down the drain and add the bottle to the recycling bin, lock the apartment door, and go into my room. Once I'm completely ready for bed, I knock on Dylan's door. He mumbles a come in and I twist the doorknob.

"Just checking on…" My words trail off as my gaze falls to his bare chest.

I've seen Dylan shirtless plenty of times, but never have I seen him only in his boxer briefs. They're lime green—which seems odd to me because the majority of his wardrobe is black and gray. I would've placed money on them being a neutral color. Maybe navy blue. But never lime green.

"Eyes up here, Rian," he says.

As my vision sweeps up his hard chest to his eyes, I find his attention centered on my chest. It's then I realize I'm not wearing a bra and I'm nipping. They're like two flashlights seeking attention.

"I could say the same."

He laughs, licks his lips. "I've never seen you in that," he says, nodding toward my silk-and-lace tank-and-short pajama set.

"I change before coming out in the morning. I wasn't thinking."

"Are you telling me you're a closet lingerie wearer?" he asks, his smirk so big my stomach flip-flops nonstop.

"No, it's just not appropriate to wear…"

His gaze descends down my body one more time and I really wish I would have grabbed my cardigan. I just thought I'd pop my head in.

"You're right. I don't want Owens to see you like that."

His words warm me, and I nibble on my bottom lip. "Do you need another pillow or anything?"

"No. I'm good."

I nod with one last look at him. "Okay then. Goodnight."

"Goodnight, Rian," he says, and I shut the door.

As I hustle back to my room, I've never felt sexier. Maybe my lingerie needs to come out a little more often.

Chapter Fifteen

DYLAN

MONDAY. INK ENVY IS CLOSED, BUT THE MINUTE MY ALARM GOES OFF BECAUSE I should be getting ready to go to the gym, I groan. My permanent cast was put on yesterday and it's even more awkward and uncomfortable than the temporary one was.

Sliding my ass to the edge of my bed, I stand then open my dresser drawer and pull out a pair of track pants. Sitting back down, I open the right side to step through successfully, but opening the left is somehow impossible. After sweat beads along my hairline, I get my leg in, but now I have to pull them up.

"I look like I'm doing some kind of chicken dance at a wedding," I mumble, shimmying them up my legs.

Forget the damn T-shirt.

I walk into the living room and toward the kitchen. Rian's just getting out of bathroom. Shit, did it really take me that long to get the pants on?

"How are you this morning?" She tightens her robe.

It's not the first time I've thought about her being naked under that puffy thing. But after I tried unsuccessfully to beat off with my right hand after she came in wearing those short silk shorts and tight cami that outlined her tits last night, I have to try to ignore the thought of her naked. Going six weeks with blue balls isn't going to help my mood.

Again, her eyes fall to my chest. It makes me want to walk around without a shirt on all the time.

"I'm good. Sore." I'm not sure sore from the broken arm. The bruises and scrapes all demand more attention at the moment.

"Well, eat something before taking the pain pills." She walks across the living room.

"Got it, Mom, but I need to take a shower before I do anything."

Her feet stop and she turns around. "Your nurse told me that you have to wrap the cast up in plastic." She comes toward me. "She said we could try one of my scrunchies."

"Yeah, I read the instructions last night."

She grabs a garbage bag, not listening to me, and puts it over my arm. "Like this, I think. Maybe I should YouTube it?" She leaves the bag on my arm and turns to head back to her room.

"I got it, Rian, no worries."

"Are you sure?"

I nod.

"Okay." Her expression reminds me of the day she couldn't get the puppy. "Well, my scrunchies are in the drawer on the left."

She disappears through her bedroom door and I feel like an asshole for not allowing her to help me, but somehow, I think she's probably not surprised. I chomp down on a granola bar and take two of my painkillers before taking my garbage bag to the bathroom.

I open up the left drawer and there's a stockpile of hair stuff. I put my arm through the garbage bag and roll the scrunchie up my arm, although it feels like my circulation is cut off.

Taking a shower without the use of your dominant hand sucks. My right hand feels as if I'm a robot and it's short-circuiting every minute. By the time I'm finished, I still don't feel completely clean. And drying myself off? It's a damn joke. I can't wrap the towel around my waist with only one hand. My track pants are my only hope of walking out of here covered.

I stick one leg through the pants, though my skin is still damp because I apparently have no muscle strength in my right arm to even dry my skin. Shimmying them up my legs like I did this morning is ten times harder with wet skin, and I end up falling on my ass with a huge bang.

"Fuck!"

A knock sounds on the door immediately.

"I'm good, Rian," I say.

"Okay. I can cover my eyes if that makes you feel more comfortable." There's a long pause. "I mean, if you need help."

I look between my legs, my dick limp and flaccid. No way in hell is she coming in here.

But the track pants aren't an option either.

"I need you to close your eyes because I'm going out with only a towel covering my dick."

"Oh… okay." Then there's nothing for a second. "My eyes are closed."

I shrug off the track pants. Covering my dick with a towel, I open the door and walk out.

Rian's at the kitchen table with her hand covering her closed eyes. "I'm not looking. Swear."

"She might not be, but I am. Great bod, Phillips."

Jax shuts the fridge door with a smile. He's actually dressed in a shirt and pajama pants on for once.

"Fuck off, Owens." I slam my bedroom door like an angry teenager.

This fucking sucks. I look at the zip-up hoodie I laid on my bed. I need to cut the left sleeve to work with my cast, but I have no scissors. Not to mention if I try to cut it with my right hand, it will never work out. Having no other choice, I open my bedroom door, looking for Jax.

What I find is Rian still at the kitchen table.

"What are you doing here?"

She glances up then down then back up. I'm still shirtless. If I'm not careful, she'll become immune to the image soon.

"I'm working from home. Pierson doesn't have a problem with it."

"Why?"

"To help you." She stands from the chair. "What do you need?"

"I was going to have Jax…"

"Jax just left. Went to do his laundry."

He's never up this early. And laundry? Likely excuse. Where did he really go? If it was the city… I stop my mind from assuming anything. Jax isn't my business. He never really was, and if he wants to look up old acquaintances and get into trouble, I can't stop him.

"I just need someone to cut off my sweatshirt sleeve."

She turns and opens her junk drawer that's not really a junk drawer. It's more like an organized miscellaneous drawer. All her different types of tape are lined up according to size. Coupons stacked neatly in the corner. She turns back around with a pair of scissors. "Got it."

Before I can blink, she's in my room. Although this hasn't always been my room, I've made mine since living here and it feels weird to have her in my space.

She eyes the sweatshirt on my bed. "Do you know where I should cut it already?"

"I never put it on, so no."

She picks it up and unzips it. With her feather-light touch, she pulls it over my good arm. Her wet hair is twisted into a bun on top of her head and her face is bare of makeup. She's beautiful, pure, and natural. How does she not see that? Allowing Blanca and Sierra to give her a makeover was unnecessary.

She arranges the other side of the sweatshirt to rest on my shoulder, the sleeve hanging down empty. She reaches for my casted arm and eyeballs where she'll have to cut. Her eyes follow the track of her hands until our eyes connect.

I swallow past the dryness in my mouth. "Thanks for doing this."

She steps closer, tearing her eyes from mine and touching the part of the sweatshirt we'll be cutting off. "Do you have a pen?" She moves to my dresser where my sketchbook is and stops, staring at the picture. "Dylan…" A sigh falls from her lips. "It's beautiful. Did someone request this?"

I admire the peony tattoo I'm sketching for her. "No. I just sketched it for someone who I think it would be beautiful on."

Her ass falls to my bed and her hands run down the paper. "I love it."

"Really?" I seek out the confirmation that I really do know her as well as I think I do.

"Yeah. I never knew if I'd have the guts for a tattoo. Seeing all the girls who go into Ink Envy and pick a generic tattoo that could be on anyone else's body never appealed to me. This is unique. When you do something like this, do you ever resell the image?" She stares at the picture in her hand.

"No. Not if the client asked me to draw it."

"So you could draw something for me that's just mine and no one else would have it?"

My mind screams *tell her*. Tell her you drew the peony for her. Let her eyes soften and her lips part. Open yourself up and allow her to climb in. Rian is safe, she'd never destroy the friendship you've built.

Instead I say, "Definitely. As soon as I'm out of the cast, I can sketch something. Any ideas?"

Coward, my conscience screams.

She glances at the sketchbook. "Just something beautiful like this."

"And you'll really let me tattoo you?"

She nods and stands, abandoning the sketchbook on the bed and picking up the scissors and the pen. She marks a spot on the sleeve, and I suffer through her closeness while she helps me take off my sweatshirt. She cuts off the sleeve and puts the hoodie back on me.

"Thanks," I say.

"Zipped or unzipped?" Her fingers hold the edge of the zipper dangerously close to my dick that's at half-chub from the scent of her soap and her being so near.

I'm screwed. Why now, after all these years, is she like a drug and I'm an addict? "Zipped."

After she's done, we go out to the living room, her heading to the kitchen table and me to the couch.

"How's that problem going?" I ask, clicking on the news.

"It's okay. I think I might have part of it right, but this might be above my intelligence level. No matter what my parents believe."

I slide on the cushion so I'm turned in her direction, resting my broken arm on the back of the couch. "You're the smartest woman I know." And that's the truth.

She rolls her eyes. "Thanks."

"Does my opinion mean nothing?"

She stands from the chair and refills her coffee cup. She pulls another cup, fills it, and comes over to me. "You get a coffee for the compliment."

I sip the black coffee. "Is this how we'll work it?"

She laughs. "Sure."

"In all seriousness, you know you don't have to stay home. I'll manage."

She picks up her coffee and joins me on the couch. "I get that you're not used to having people to count on, but you have us. We all want the best for you."

"Thanks, but—"

"No, Dylan. I can do the same work here as I can at the office. After a few weeks when you're used to the cast, I'll go back, but you'll have to suck it up for now. This is the way it is." She tucks her legs under her body and sips her coffee.

My chest gets a warm funny feeling in it. "Listen, about last night..."

I want to say what I should have told her a long time ago. It's time she knows how I feel about her and why I've ignored the telltale signs that maybe she likes me more than a friend.

She glances away from the television to me. "What's up?"

I open my mouth to tell her, but the buzzer from downstairs goes off.

She places her coffee on the table, standing to answer. "I have no idea who that would be." She presses the intercom button near the door of the apartment. "Hello?"

"Hey, it's Frankie."

"Come on up." Rian presses the button to allow her in then opens our apartment door a crack. "I'm going to bake some cookies or something. I'm sure you'll have a lot of visitors today."

Just like that, I lose the nerve to say lock the door, keep Frankie out, and let me be straight with you.

Chapter Sixteen

DYLAN

Jolie's sings as she and Frankie come through the door. Rian's giddy to see the three-year-old and already cleared the table of her work. I'm fairly sure she can't bake cookies when she's at the office, but I'm not saying anything. I fear I'll need Rian's help, so her being around is probably a good thing.

"Uncle Dylan!" Jolie runs toward me but stops. She points at my arm. "Hurt?"

Frankie follows right behind, closing the door and saying hello to Rian with a hug. She's thinner than she was a week ago.

"Hey, boss," Frankie says, sitting in the chair beside the couch, Jolie's bag between her legs. Her jeans and T-shirt hang off her. She's always been thin, but she's gauntly now.

"Jolie, want to help me make monster cookies?" Rian asks.

Jolie's eyes widen and her mouth forms a small O. She stares at me as though she's wondering if she heard Rian ask that or if she's hearing things.

"Whoa, did you ever come on a good day, huh?" I say.

She unzips her coat as she circles around the room to reach Rian.

Frankie sends Rian a look of appreciation before she leans back, her eyes wide on me. "Fell off your bike, huh?"

"Yeah, I'm out for six weeks."

"I heard," she says. "And what are we going to do about it?"

I sit up, sliding down the couch toward her so we can talk with a little more privacy, although Jolie's excitement is so loud, I doubt they can hear us. Rian probably wouldn't care or judge me anyway, but the alpha in me would prefer her not to know business is bad. "Are you back now?"

She nods. "He's locked up." Her worried eyes venture to Jolie.

I touch her knee. "How long?"

Frankie lives a complicated life and I try not to pry, allowing her to dish out information as she sees fit. I guess it's because of how I grew up.

"Six months, I hope."

At least she should be in good shape to take over Ink Envy for me. "I need to find a replacement for myself. I went to the city before this happened and nothin'. Lyle is progressing, but I don't want to rush him."

She laughs. "He told me you lost your cool the other day. I thought he was going to piss his pants when he called."

Good to know my employees gossip about me.

"Yeah, not my finest moment. Neither was getting myself in this situation." I lift the cast.

"And how exactly did you do that?"

I glance over my shoulder to where Rian is tying one of her aprons on Jolie.

"Rian, it's okay if she gets dirty," Frankie says.

"Yay!" Rian looks at Jolie and they toss the apron away. "How about I sit down and just read you the directions?" Rian sits and crosses her legs, but Jolie grabs her hand to pull her back up.

"We'll talk about it later," I say and try to move my left hand up to my hair. Fuck.

"Oh, I gotcha." Frankie winks. She's been giving me hell about Rian for a while now.

We shoot the shit about nothing important. I fill her in on the shop. She asks about the arm and the accident. Jolie and Rian have fun making cookies.

I head into the kitchen to get Frankie a coffee, where I catch a glimpse of the cookies. "I thought they'd look like monsters?"

Rian pours out a container of sprinkles on top of the drops of batter she already has on the cookie sheets. Jolie watches on with wide eyes.

"No, they're just big cookies with a lot of sprinkles and candies."

She really is great with kids. Another damn checkmark for Rian.

Frankie and I chitchat the entire morning. Once Jolie gets bored baking cookies, she pours the contents of her bag on the table in front of the television. Soon the news gets replaced by a talking dog show.

Frankie and I move to the kitchen to help Rian with the cookies. Mostly Frankie though.

"So what's he paying you to nurse him back to health?" Frankie asks Rian.

"He'd prefer to be left alone. You know how he thinks he always has everything under control." Rian rolls her eyes.

"Oh, I can only imagine. What's he had you do so far?" Frankie asks.

Rian tells her about the bathroom and how she had to close her eyes after my shower, then tells her about the sweatshirt situation, not mentioning the sexual tension. Unless maybe she didn't feel the thick as smoke pull in the air.

They like to talk about me as if I'm not there. I guess Rian knows me the best out of all the girls we hang out with and Frankie is stuck with me at work, day after day. They openly complain about me when we're all around each other.

Right before Frankie packs up Jolie because she has to take a nap, Jax walks in with his laundry bag over his shoulder. Frankie eyes him as he stops just inside the door, his large duffle falling to the floor in front of him.

Jolie runs over, her feet sliding to a stop in front of him. "Who are you?"

Jax peers down at Jolie, then at us standing around the kitchen. "Did I just walk into the wrong apartment?"

Rian laughs. "Jax, this is Frankie." She places her hand on Frankie's shoulder as Frankie nods a hello. "And that's her daughter, Jolie."

"I'm Jax," he says to Jolie, picking up his duffle and swinging it over his shoulder. He walks to his room.

"Friendly guy," Frankie says.

"He really is a nice guy," Rian adds, which bothers me to a degree I'm not comfortable with.

"Oh, Rian." Frankie puts her hand on Rian's shoulder and shakes her head.

"What?" Rian asks, packing up cookies for them to take home.

"We're just different. You always see the good in people and I always see the bad." Frankie puts her purse over her shoulder.

That's all I need to hear. Rian sees the good in me, and she won't see my bad until I've already hurt her. Without even asking for it, Frankie gave me the advice I needed to hear.

"I'm going to walk them out," I say to Rian.

Frankie hugs Rian goodbye. "Don't let him talk you into any sponge baths or anything."

Rian's cheeks redden. I love that look on her. Before I was restricted to only using my right hand, I'd imagine telling her all the things I wanted to do to her and that blush hijacking her body when I beat off.

"Thanks, Rian." Jolie hugs Rian while consuming a cookie that's bigger than her face.

"Bye, Jolie." Rian hugs her tightly. "You're welcome any time you want, okay?"

Jolie nods, hugs my knees, and I tug on one of her pigtails.

Outside in the hallway, Frankie lets Jolie have her phone and sit against the wall so we can talk.

"So what's really up?" she asks.

"If I don't find anyone soon, I'm going to ask Jax"—I nod toward my apartment—"to come in on a temporary basis."

"Wait." She shakes her head. "Who is that guy?"

I blow out a breath. Frankie wouldn't be impressed by the people Jax has tattooed. She's strictly does it for love, not money. But she follows enough artists that she'll know who he is.

"Jax Owens."

Her mouth drops open. "Shut the front door!" She moves to beeline by me, but I grab her arm and pull her back. "Why didn't you introduce me to him?"

"Rian introduced you."

She cocks her hip. "No, Rian introduced me to a new *roommate* of yours named Jax."

I shrug. "Not my fault you didn't recognize him."

Technically it'd be Jax's. He's not big on his picture being on Instagram. He showcases his artwork more often than not.

"So you're going to have me manage *him*?" She points toward the door.

I nod.

"You're insane. And please tell me why you're allowing the business to suffer when the solution is right inside that apartment?"

I stare at her for a moment. "He went to high school with Knox and me. We aren't exactly on the best of terms."

She pats my shoulder. "Time to kiss some ass, Dylan. And since I was going to bring this up later anyway, you should be kissing Rian's ass too while you're at it. Literally." She glances at Jolie, who's watching something uber loud that echoes through the hall.

"My mind is so fucked up right now."

"Good." She smiles sweetly.

Frankie isn't a sweet girl. She's the girl other girls are afraid of. She's got a sharp tongue and her insults cut deep. She can come back with a snappy retort within a second and she honestly doesn't give a shit what you think of her.

That's why she says, "I'm going to be your working mind for the time being. You're going to go in there and ask Jax to come work at Ink Envy. Give him whatever the hell he wants. And then you're going to tell Rian exactly how you feel."

"What the hell are you talking about?"

"Make a good deal. Tell him you want a percentage of who he brings in. It happens all the time."

I shake my head because the Jax thing I can handle. And she's right—I'm sitting on my gold mine, fiddling with my limp dick.

"And the Rian thing." She places her hand on my heart. "It's a good thing. You're a good guy. Stop pretending you don't like her, because if I had to guess, this experiment of the two of you together day in and day out, alone? It's gonna blow up in your face if neither one of you will talk about it, and it'll kill the friendship. Be mature and talk it out."

"You seriously want me to tell her 'I like you' as though I'm some twelve-year-old adolescent boy who just got his first boner?"

She laughs and shakes her head. "You have to get out of your own head first. For now, save your company. No one wants to date an unemployed loser," Frankie playfully smacks me on my cheek. "Let's go, Jolie."

They disappear into the elevator, and I walk back into the apartment. Frankie's words aren't helping me in the slightest. When I get inside, all the baking stuff is put away, replaced with her work stuff on the kitchen table now. Rian smiles at me, and I beeline across the apartment, knocking on Jax's door before I lose my nerve.

"Come in," he says.

I open it to find that he hasn't really made the room his. It still has Sierra's cream-colored bedframe she left behind. There are no posters or pictures or anything personal, and his clothes lay in piles on the floor as though he'd just have to stack them together to pack into his bag to leave.

He tosses his book aside and pulls his Air Pods out of his ears. "What's up?"

"Ever think about taking some shifts at Ink Envy?" I should ask nicer.

He glances at me from the corner of his eye and his smirk shines bright. He knew this day was coming. "I have been kind of bored lately. Who was that girl here with the kid?"

"She works there. We can do this one of two ways. You work and she'll manage you, or you rent a chair."

"I'll rent a chair."

"Okay."

After we negotiate price, we reach that awkward point where I should probably thank him. He knows exactly why I came in here. I'm screwed and we both know it. He's my only hope of keeping Ink Envy.

He says, "I'll post on my Instagram and tell them by appointment only. Can they book through your place?"

"Yeah. Maybe I'll take over the schedules. I can at least do shit like that." I raise my arm.

"Sounds good," he says.

"Okay then. Are you starting tomorrow?"

"Yeah."

"Any days off you want?"

He shakes his head but then stops. "I'm good as long as Mondays are always off."

"Yeah, shop's closed Mondays so no worries." I'm actually impressed we're being so civil to one another.

I go to leave, and my hand is on the doorknob when I look at him over my shoulder. "Thanks," I say, not nearly loud enough.

"Happy to help your sorry ass out." He grins.

I huff. One day we'll have to converse more than we are right now, but I'm at max capacity for touchy-feely shit today.

Chapter Seventeen

RIAN

FIVE DAYS AFTER HE CAME HOME FROM THE HOSPITAL, DYLAN IS FULLY WALLOWING in his own self-pity.

"Look at you," I say, coming out of the bathroom.

Every day he comes out of his bedroom and plants his big body on the couch, where he watches daytime television. Yesterday I stole the remote when he put on the soap opera channel.

"What?"

"You should be at the shop. You're not unable to walk. It's just a broken arm. That adorable scruff you love so much is now a full-on mountain man beard. And the whole not showering thing?"

He stares at me as though he can't understand the words I'm saying.

I pick up a pillow and throw it at his head. "Hello?"

He whips it back at me as though I'm his annoying younger sister. I wouldn't be surprised if that's all he sees me as.

"Want to help me make up math word problems?" I sit in the chair by the couch, cross-legged with my computer on my lap.

"Sure. If I sleep for five hours and Rian sleeps for zero hours for the next six weeks, how many more hours of happiness do I have?"

"Now your lazy mood has affected your brain because that's a stupid word question."

He glances at me then looks back at the television. "Aren't you kind of like an educator? There are no stupid questions?"

"There are stupid questions, and I'm not an educator."

He props up his head on his good arm. "Fine. How about if I lay here for ten more hours and do the same thing for the next three days, how long until the couch smells like ass?"

"The couch already smells like ass. Plus there's not enough information to logically answer that question."

He grunts and his head falls back on the pillow. I pull the pillow out from under his head and his head crashes to the arm of the couch. I hate this whole "feel sorry for myself" version of Dylan. Not to mention being alone with him in our apartment day in and out kind of sucks. Jax is working at Ink Envy now. Other than when he pops in between clients to grab something to eat, it's just Dylan and me. Time I would have cherished before he turned into this man I don't recognize.

"Well, if I didn't have a concussion before, I have one now." He sits up and rubs the side of his head, staring at me like a confused boy.

"Why don't I start a shower for you?" I close my laptop. "We could go for a walk or go visit Ink Envy. Get lunch."

"Or I could sit here and find out if Jake really *is* the father."

I shake my head, concentrating on my computer as I try to find some other way to get to him. I'm not strong enough to get him into the shower. Even if I did manage that feat, how would I keep him there? Then there's the whole thing about wrapping his arm in plastic.

"Can I bribe you?" The words fall out of my mouth as soon as they pop into my mind.

"Bribe me? I never figured you for bartering sexual favors, but…" He laughs, hooking his thumbs into his track pants.

My eyes betray me before I can look away. Damn them. "I was thinking more with my baking. Chocolate cake with Oreo crumbs between the layers with the chocolate frosting." Surely that will make him stand and take a shower.

"Eh."

I swear I've entered another dimension. Dylan loves chocolate more than sex. I think. I'm not exactly sure, of course.

"Seriously?"

He glances up from the television. "You think you own me when it comes to your baking, don't you?"

I roll my eyes and concentrate on the same question I've been trying to form for the past hour. "No."

"You do." The familiar lilt to his voice that's been void since the accident is present and my stomach flutters.

"Well, you usually do go gaga over my chocolate desserts."

He laughs. "So all these years, you've been using them to get what you want?"

I scrunch my eyes. If I got what I want, I would have him and I would have used my naked body to persuade him to get into the shower. "You act like I've swindled money from you."

He shakes his head. "No, but remember that time we were arguing about what new series to start watching? You wanted *Blue Bloods* and I wanted *Hawaii Five-O*. What do we watch now? *Blue Bloods*."

"You're absurd. We put that to a vote."

"You made chocolate on chocolate cake that night."

"How do you even remember that?" I close my laptop because I can't concentrate right now.

He snaps his fingers and points an accusatory finger at me. "And what about that time we were talking about going on a weekend trip? And it was a split vote between skiing in Vermont or Portland, Maine?"

I bite my lip to not smile. "Those are just coincidences," I say with as straight of a face as I can manage.

"Bullshit. You use your baked goods like a pair of brand new tits."

I cough out a laugh. "You're delusional and that's disgusting. I would do no such thing."

He shakes his head in a joking manner. "To think I thought I could trust you, that you were different, but all women use tactics against men to get what they want."

The buzzing of someone calling up from downstairs interrupts us.

I place my computer on the coffee table and make my way over to the door. "You're very wrong. Cake is not the same as sex."

"Maybe to me it is. Maybe I like your chocolate cake as much as I love tits." He winks.

I pretend to roll my eyes. But the idea that Dylan thinks about my tits does weird things to my insides.

"Imagine if I licked chocolate frosting off a pair of tits. Best of both worlds."

Thank goodness I'm no longer right in front of him because my entire body feels as if an inferno is ready to engulf me in a ball of flames.

I press the intercom button and say hello.

"Hey, it's Lyle. Is Dylan there?"

I pretend to laugh. "Of course he is, but plug your nose when you come in."

I press the button to let him in downstairs, then I open the door and walk back to the chair, picking up my computer.

Dylan's hand lands on my upper thigh, way too close to the center of my legs. "Your chocolate cake doesn't control me anymore."

I stare at his hand, his warmth leaking through my leggings and spreading across my skin like a brush fire. I set my computer on the table again and lean toward him. "Okay, so if I bake one right now, you wouldn't take a shower for one slice?"

His fingertips grip my inner thigh a little tighter and all I can think about is how if they inched a little higher, they'd be exactly where I want them.

"Not on your life."

"Only one way to test the theory," I singsong.

He wraps one arm around my waist and pulls me into his lap. With only one arm, he still manages to tickle my ribcage as I squirm out of his hold.

"You're going to hurt your arm," I say.

Between his track pants and my leggings, I'm sliding around his lap. His lips are right at my ear, my body over his. It's then a hard ridge slides against the seam of my ass.

We both freeze in place.

"Is this what you guys do for fun?"

Our heads whip up to Lyle gawking over the couch. I scurry off Dylan's lap. He grabs the pillow and places it over his crotch.

"Rian," Lyle says, his eyes scanning my body as if he has X-ray vision.

"Lyle," I say, though not in the same flirtatious tone he said my name.

Not that he's a bad kid, but he's just that—a kid. Lyle's nineteen and has followed Dylan around since he was sixteen, begging for him to take him on as an apprentice. Dylan finally had a moment of weakness last year and took him under his wing.

"You two could add Jell-O or oil to your wrestling routine," Lyle says with a smirk.

"What do you want?" Dylan asks.

Lyle sits on the opposite end of the couch as I busy myself in the kitchen, trying to convince myself that my ass wiggling didn't give Dylan a hard-on.

"You gotta come down to the shop. Frankie and Jax argue nonstop. It's bringing back memories of my childhood, man." Lyle's voice cracks as if he's going to cry.

"What are they fighting over?" I ask, my interest piqued. I thought for sure they'd work well together.

"Everything. His clients. Her clients. What's for lunch. The candy Frankie brought in for clients. The magazines in the waiting area. Everything and anything. It's like they secretly enjoy it." Lyle pinches the bridge of his nose.

"And you're here why?" Dylan asks.

"Because you're the boss. Fix it. I can't be creative in that type of environment."

Dylan looks at me and I shrug.

"Jax actually says things?" Dylan asks, which would be my question.

Frankie definitely speaks her mind and I can see her going crazy about certain things. But Jax is pretty laid-back, allowing stuff to roll off his shoulders.

"He mostly grumbles and grunts. But they went in the storage room to hash it out when this group of girls came in last night. They came for Jax, but as you know, he's booked."

Dylan nods.

"He told them they could stay and observe if they wanted. Frankie lost it because she had a client booked and there was nowhere for them to sit while they waited."

As Lyle tells the story, he's so dramatic. Like they're his parents having fights all over again.

Dylan raises his hand. "Okay, I'll head over and see if I can't get this straightened out."

Lyle looks him over. "After you shower, right? Because they'll probably just team up on you if you come in looking like that. How much food has fallen into that shag carpet on your chin?"

Dylan peers down at the track pants and T-shirt I think he's been sleeping and living in, then he looks at me.

"And I didn't even have to make the chocolate cake." I smile sweetly.

He grumbles and stands, heading to his room. "Give me a half hour."

Lyle stands. "You guys are into some kinky shit." He leaves, shutting the door.

Dylan walks out of his room. "Well, lucky you. You get to shave me."

My stomach catapults like I was shot out of a cannon. "Shave you?" I follow him to the bathroom. "I said I would start a shower for you."

"I'm not going to use my right hand because I don't care for the 'I just got mugged in an alley' look." He peeks over his shoulder. "You're the only one here, so you're the lucky lady."

"But... I could call Seth or Knox. I've never shaved anyone before."

"You shave your legs?" he asks.

I nod.

"And your pussy?"

My eyes widen. "That's none of your business."

He holds out the razor. "I'll walk you through it. Just imagine my face is your pussy. Be gentle as fuck."

He grins and pats the bathroom counter, stripping off his T-shirt with his good arm. He's really getting used to the one arm thing. My eyes zero in on his tattoos. I slide up on the counter, my heart racing a million beats per second. He starts the water and pulls out the shaving cream.

His hand glides up my inner leg, spreading my thighs. My breath hitches.

"Come on, make room for me," he says and laughs.

"Are you sure?"

He locks eyes with me, and I swallow the lump in the back of my throat. He's the most gorgeous man I've ever known. "You're the only person I would trust to do this."

I slowly take the razor from his hand and nod.

So we're doing this then.

Chapter Eighteen

DYLAN

After Rian uses my trimmers to trim off the excess hair, I debate whether I should have her shave the rest completely off. I could keep the scruff I've perfected over the years, but being this close to her feels good. If I have to look like I'm fifteen all over again to prolong this feeling, so be it.

Rian's hands are soft as she puddles water in her palms and runs it through my beard. I ignore the droplets falling to my bare chest. Once what's left of the beard is wet enough, she cups her hand and dishes shaving cream in it, then uses both hands to lather it on my skin.

"It's now or never," she says, her gorgeous blue eyes shining under the lights in the bathroom.

My hands are on either side of her hips, my body between her open legs. We're so close, it's nearly impossible to ignore the pull my lips feel toward hers.

"Let's do it. Just go slow and steady," I say in a gravelly voice.

I'm a little worried about how this will turn out. But if I've figured out anything in the past five days, it's that I'm not ambidextrous. Rian had to open up the pickle jar for me yesterday. Hold on while I hang up my man card until this cast is off.

"Tell me about your tattoos," she says. "I can't do this in silence."

"Which ones?"

"All, any, whatever." Her hand shakes as she raises the razor to my face.

I grip her wrist, my thumb smoothing along the surface. "Relax. Nothing horrible is gonna happen."

She nods, but the worry is alive in her eyes, so I do as she requested. I talk about my tattoos.

"The ones on my legs, I did to myself mostly. When I was practicing."

"You did them yourself?" Her eyes are on my sideburns, watching the razor move down my face.

"Yeah." I move my jaw as little as possible when I speak so I don't mess her up. "A few of my friends, like Big Man, trusted me to tattoo them. But to get the feel of the needle to know how deep to go, you have to feel that for yourself."

"I've never really looked at your legs," she says, pulling the razor down my skin.

"Funny, I've checked out yours."

She glances at me as she washes off the razor. "I don't have any tattoos."

"Your legs, Rian. I've checked out your legs."

Her flush is the most gorgeous thing I've seen on a woman. She believes that she's not beautiful. If I confessed to her how many guys I told she wasn't available, she'd be pissed, but truth is, none of them were good enough for her. They would have broken her, and seeing Rian broken? I'd rather gouge out my eyes.

"Stop the flirting and let me concentrate. Tell me about your arms."

I want to glance down to know which specific tattoo she's asking about. "They all have different meanings. The apple is for Winnie, because she made a killer apple pie in the fall."

"Not for a teacher, huh?" She rinses the razor.

"Nope, although I did have some teachers who had an impact on my life. The phoenix on my back is self-explanatory. I think every foster kid gets one." I laugh to settle her sympathetic heart from giving me that pitying look. "The wolf is to remind me to be noble and loyal to those who are to me. A lot of the roses, stars, and other things are just filler. Things my friends thought would look killer. But all of them have a memory of some kind. Whether it's who did it or what it represents."

Her gaze skates across my chest. "What does the anchor mean?"

"Anyone tell you that you have a knack of digging crap out of people?"

She smiles softly, the razor grazing along my cheek. "I think only you. Maybe you want to tell someone. Have you ever thought of that?"

I'm not sure if she purposely doesn't look at me after that comment. She might be right. Maybe I've held all this shit in for so long, I want to purge to someone. Maybe it's a way to prove to her that I might not be good enough for her—but then look how far I've come. Maybe in my lifetime, we'll be equals.

My hands slide closer and rest beside her hips.

She wiggles, washing the razor off in the sink. "So the anchor?"

"The anchor." I nod. "Jax and I went into a tattoo place when we were sixteen. We knew a kid who was working under someone, so they didn't card. He got the compass and I got the anchor. It's not our most brilliant plan. I was supposed to see the compass on his chest and that'd tell me to explore the world. Don't stay in one spot. And if he looked at my anchor, he should remember to have a place to call home."

"So in truth, maybe you should've gotten the compass and he should have gotten the anchor?" She chuckles.

"Yeah, which is exactly why I make sure to tell my clients if their ideas are stupid. I'm blunt and have insulted more than one customer, but I won't have it on my conscience. Plus, if you knew how many calls we get days after we do a tattoo." I shake my head.

Regrets. People with regrets. I've never wanted to have them, which is probably why I've never ventured too far from where I grew up.

"And do you want to travel? Be like Jax?"

There's a hitch in her voice. She doesn't know if she wants the answer. I don't blame her, because I'm not sure I want to give it to her.

I shrug. "I don't want to be like Jax, but sometimes I wonder. Who doesn't wonder, right? Either about some old boyfriend or girlfriend. The what-ifs life leaves you with. But then I never would have come here to Cliffton Heights or moved into the Rooftop Apartments. I wouldn't have met Ethan or Sierra, or Seth, or you. You've all given me a sense of family."

She swallows, and the small room grows quiet except for the sound of the razor against skin.

"Rian?" I say, and her gaze dips up from my chin.

The tension in the room becomes a living, breathing thing.

A fake smile lands on her lips. "What?" She's trying to be flippant.

"Me and you. I can't imagine you not in my life."

Her smile turns real as her entire face beams. "You don't have to worry about that unless you're going to travel the world like Jax."

I say nothing. Jax's life isn't for me.

We go through the motions without saying much more. I'm not sure if we're both lost in thought. I hold court in my head on whether to tell her that there's a reason I never made a move on her. That fear paralyzes me. But then she'll look at me like I'm weak, which I am. She swipes up the last strip of my neck and looks over my face.

"It's coming though," she says, never making eye contact.

"What is?"

"Ethan's engaged. Sierra's not far behind. Knox and Leilani are practically moving in together. Eventually, every one of us will find someone to share our life with."

I doubt Knox and Leilani have any happy ever after in their future if the past is an indicator, but I keep my opinion to myself. "Doesn't mean we won't still be in each other's life."

She nods and wets a washcloth, wiping it down my face. "Not every day. Not like we are now. You don't hear about married couples who all live together with their kids." Her hand pauses. "But you don't plan on getting married."

She says it like a fact. I've never said that, but I guess I've never disputed it either. Mostly because I never thought marriage was for me. Not because I'm into juggling a million girls at one time. It's mostly because the girls I've dated aren't the marrying type and girls like Rian… I'm not even going there.

"True. I guess it's inevitable for me to be the fun uncle, huh?"

Her hands fall to her lap as though the washcloth is now too heavy to hold up. "Why don't you want to get serious with anyone?"

I step back, shift over, and look in the mirror, my hand sliding over the smooth skin. "Wouldn't you like to feel this along your inner thighs?" I pull her hand up to my face.

No smile creases her lips. "Don't do that." She jumps off the counter, snatching her hand back.

I follow her out of the bathroom. "What?"

She whips around. "Don't use sexual advances to keep from answering the question."

"It's not some new revelation. I've always been upfront and honest about my feelings on commitment. Plus, you like my sexual advances." I step closer, locking her to the wall. "You blush when I say them."

Her hands land on my chest and she shoves me back before stepping over and jumping off the arm of the chair to get to her room. At the last minute, she circles back around, up on the chair and back down again, poking her finger at me. "You know what I think? You're scared. The whole no commitment thing is so you can keep everyone at arm's length. I think you really want a wife and kids and the whole package, but you'd rather act like you don't than let someone in here." She places her hand over my heart.

I desperately deny the urge to cover her hand with mine.

"As far as the sexual advances. Yes, they make me blush because I want those things from you. I want to feel the smoothness of the skin I just shaved run up my thigh. I want your hands and lips to explore my body. And you can act like you don't want those things, and until recently, I believed you. I thought I was invisible to you." Tears well in her eyes and my heart splinters as if it took a blow from a sledgehammer.

She's never been invisible to me.

"Rian," I whisper.

She shakes her head, and strands of hair fall from her ponytail. The tears magically disappear, and fury transforms her blue irises. "Go ahead and deny it. Tell me you don't want me, and I'll box you up and put you on the top shelf." She pulls my good hand up to run my fingers over her lips. "Tell me you don't want to taste these?"

I stare at her lips, but I say nothing.

She tips her head back and runs my fingers down her throat and through the valley of her breasts. "How much do you want to truly feel me?"

I'm stunned into silence because I never thought there was a woman like this living inside Rian. She's putting her hand out for me to see. Everything the pansy inside of me hides.

All my muscles tense, trying to deny the urge to give into her. The thick air around us makes dragging in a breath impossible.

"It's now or never. Take me now or never." She rests my hand between her breasts, her eyes glued to mine.

When I say nothing, she shifts away, but I grab her wrist. "Do you have any idea what you're asking me to do?"

"Do you have any idea the agony you're putting me through?"

The cord of tension between us snaps like an elastic pulled to its limits, and I push aside the thought of all consequences. Whipping her around so her back is plastered to the wall, I cradle her cheek with my good hand and I lock her against it with my hips.

"Just remember you asked for this," I say and slam my lips to hers.

My entire body feels as if it's floating ad I'm having an out of body experience. That this is a dream would make sense, because Rian's never complained to anyone about anything. She's the least confrontational person I know.

But as our lips melt together and she opens for my tongue, all the worries that fill my life every day vanish and all I feel, see, and smell is her. The sweetness of her perfume, the softness of her touch, the blush that goes from her neck to cheeks. I'd die kissing her and be content. She's everything and nothing like I imagined she'd be, but one thing she is, is perfect.

Someone knocks on the door, but it doesn't stop us. I've waited too long for this, so whoever it is can go the fuck away. Rian's grip on my shoulders must mean we're in agreement.

"Holy…" Seth says from somewhere behind us.

My tongue only deepens the kiss because if Seth's smart, he'll walk back out that door. Rian's moan says she's on board with my plan.

"*Rian Isabella Wright!*"

Fuck. Our lips fly off one another's and look toward the door to find Rian's mom with her hands on her hips. Seth can't hide his amusement—laughing, stopping, then laughing again. Eventually he covers his mouth with his shirt.

"Mom!" Rian says, wiping her mouth while I back away from her.

My heart that was flying like a balloon in the blue sky with white clouds pops, landing in my stomach like a semi-truck. Time to get the hell out of Dodge.

Chapter Nineteen

RIAN

YOU'D THINK SOMEONE SCREAMED FIRE WITH THE SPEED THAT DYLAN SHAKES MY parents' hands, heads to his room for a second, says goodbye and is out the door. Seth follows him.

As soon as they leave, my mom says my name like a question, as though she doesn't need to ask me the actual question of why I was lip-locked with Dylan when she walked through the door.

"What?" I ask.

"You know exactly what. Am I to assume you finished that math equation if you have time to kiss your roommate?"

My dad sits at the kitchen table, grabbing an apple out of his pocket and biting into it. I'm not even going to ask where he got the apple.

"I haven't figured it out yet. Well, the first part I have, but that's it." I grab a water from the fridge. "Do either of you want anything?"

"Water would be great," my dad says, smiling. "You look good, sweetheart. Your cheeks are rosy like when you were a baby."

"Because she couldn't breathe with Dylan suctioned to her face like that," my mom says, sitting. "Do you have coffee? I didn't have enough this morning and I have a horrible headache."

"I can make some."

Which I will gladly do in order to not have to sit at that table. It's much easier for me to roll my eyes with my back turned to her.

As my mom rambles on about Johann, all I can think about is how I had the nerve to pressure Dylan into kissing me. I was so angry with his flirty behavior, knowing he wasn't planning to back it up with action. I also can't stop thinking about what his lips felt like on mine. The way he didn't want it to end—just like me. Although he barely touched me, it felt as if he was everywhere on my skin.

"Hanging out here isn't the type of environment you need. A tattoo artist? And then that Seth gave me a business card of what he does. Nude pictures." She purses her lips and shakes her head.

"I don't know, Barbie. Maybe we should give it a try."

I glance over my shoulder to see my mom's reaction to the thought of having her picture taken in lingerie. My dad waggles his eyebrows as my mom looks at him as if he's lost his mind.

"It's not nude, Mom," I say, turning back around.

"There's a picture on his business card."

"Let me see it," my dad says.

"I dropped it by mistake in the hallway."

I huff. Does she really think Seth won't figure out what she did?

I'm not sure what look my dad gives my mom, but she sighs. "I did. Sorry. I didn't realize you wanted to lower your IQ by looking at nude pictures. Next thing, you'll be asking me to have plastic surgery."

Mom is the most dramatic person I know. I always chalked it up to her growing up gifted with the name Barbie. Had to have been hard on her.

"Did you stop in here just to ask me about the equation?" I let the coffee pot work as I lean against the counter.

"We wanted to get out of the city for a while. Figured a day trip to check on you would be nice." My mom forces a smile.

She really wants to see where I am on solving the problem. She's not opposed to me cheating to win, I'm sure. Imagine my surprise when I turned in a paper my sophomore year in high school and my teacher pulled me aside to talk about plagiarism, only for me to find out my mom had switched her paper for mine during the night. Talk about feeling inadequate.

"I'm not showing you the problem," I say, pouring her a cup of coffee.

"Then let's take this time to talk about some of your life decisions. Like you working from home in order to care for your delinquent roommate who crashed his motorcycle, probably from driving recklessly." She sips her coffee. "This is too strong. Do you have milk?"

I stand and pull the milk from the fridge.

"Do you have almond or soy?" she asks.

"We're not Whole Foods," I say, grabbing the regular whole milk.

My mom has a specific look when I've annoyed her. So far, I've seen it three times in this short visit. I like to count because the child inside me enjoys pissing her off.

"Are you dating him?" my dad asks, which is surprising. He didn't even come out of his office when I went to prom.

"We're friends, and I'd rather not talk to you about it right now." I sip my water.

My dad pats my hand. "Okay, sweetheart, but I will agree with your mother. A man like him might be easy on the eyes, but he's going to be hard on the bank account."

I stare blankly, and he chuckles. Another stupid joke.

"He runs his own tattoo parlor," I say.

"Rian, you cannot be serious. Is this some phase you're going through? You need to be with someone with goals and dreams and... money." Mom nods the entire time like a bobblehead. Barbie the bobblehead. No one would buy one because they'd be nauseated by how much it bobbles.

"I told you I don't want to talk about it."

"That's not an option. We're your parents," my mom says.

"And I'm not twelve."

There's the look again. We're up to four times now.

"What on Earth do you talk about? Surely you have nothing in common." My dad continuing this line of conversation makes me want to bash my head on the table.

"Another topic please," I say.

My dad looks at my mom and they nod in agreement, but it won't be the last they have to say about Dylan.

But if they can't talk to me about the math problem or Dylan, there isn't a ton left.

"Looks like you haven't baked in a while?" my dad says, scanning the counters. He wants a sweet since my mom limits them as though he's a child.

"Not in a few days."

My mom exaggerates leaning over as she examines my body in the chair. "You looked thinner over there." She motions to the wall that Dylan had me pinned against.

Reliving that moment, my body warms like I've sunk into a hot bath. "Is that a compliment?"

"You're very touchy today. I think you're probably getting your period," Mom suggests. "Johann is going to beat you if you don't start making smart decisions. I feel like we raised you well."

And here we go. Same old same old.

She stares at my father with her trembling chin. He puts his hand on hers on the table, leaving the apple core in the middle.

"We did great," he says. "She has a job and supports herself. What else can we ask for? I think we knew at three there were no Nobel Prizes in our future."

Cue my mouth drop.

I must make a noise because both of them look at me as though they're surprised I'm in the room. My dad's other hand reaches for mine and I'm too dumbstruck to care.

"No offense, sweetie. It's like winning the lottery."

I stand so fast my parents' eyes widen. "Did I miss the part where the two of you won a Nobel Prize? Is it hidden in a box somewhere?" A strangled laugh erupts out of me, which is good because at least they won't see me cry. "You two get off on how smart you are. Well, I'm sorry that two smart people didn't make an uber-smart person, but I am smart. And if I choose to write textbooks for a living, then so be it. And if I run out and marry Dylan, then that's my choice." I point at myself. "Me, because I'm an adult."

"I doubt Dylan is the marrying type. And even if he did, he screams cheater." My mom rolls her eyes.

My hand flies out, pointing at the door. "*Out!*" I inhale a deep breath. "Out. Leave."

"Sweetie, you're overreacting," my dad says.

"We'll talk after you're done with your period," my mom says, standing and tucking in her chair. "You're obviously emotional."

My arm drops and my fists clench at my sides.

"It wasn't a knock on you," my dad says, but my mom pushes him toward the door.

"You're lucky to have us, and you need to realize that one of these days," my mom says. "Poor Sierra would probably love to have her mother here."

It's game over. All I see is red. Words and phrases flash in my mind. I could use the classic fuck off, or I could go into detail about how she's the worst mom ever.

"Just please leave before I say something that would hurt you like you've hurt me all these years," I say in a calm voice.

That sentence makes her stop. "Rian." She sighs.

I shake my head, swallowing the lump and pushing back the tears.

The apartment door opens, and my parents rear back, the door barely missing them. Jax slides by, nodding his hello but never stopping to converse.

"Who's this?" Mom asks, but I don't answer.

Jax looks at me standing near the kitchen table and stops on the way to his bedroom. His gaze flickers from my parents to me and back to my parents. For once not one smart comment comes out of his mouth.

"Just go, Mom," I say softly.

My mom looks at Jax. "Just another horrible decision. Let's go, Larry." She squares her shoulders and walks out the door.

"Bye, sweetie. We love you. I never meant—"

"*Larry!*" my mom screams.

"Call us after you're done menstruating."

He shuts the door and I collapse into a chair, throwing the apple core at the door. My head falls into my folded arms and I weep for everything I'm not in my parents' eyes.

"Hey," Jax says, running his hand over my back. "You okay?"

I sit up and wipe the tears from my eyes. "You know, you and Dylan think your lives are so hard because you don't have parents, but not all parents are good people."

He slides the chair beside me out from the table and lowers himself into it. "I get that."

"They expect me to be perfect. I was valedictorian." I swipe a tear. "I was dean's list every semester in college. I never did anything bad. Never got arrested or in trouble. I respect my elders. I'm polite and courteous to everyone I meet. Do you think any of that is enough for them?" I point toward the door. "No, because all they care about is whether I get some award they can brag to their friends about."

My voice shakes, and my anxiety is through the roof. The tears won't stop piling on top of one another as they spill down my cheeks.

"Hey." Jax slides his chair closer. Gripping my one arm, he pulls me to him. "It's okay. Parents suck. I mean, I don't have any, but mine would have hated me. Talk about a disappointment." He pulls me into his chest and his large hand runs down my back.

"Don't make me laugh. I want to be mad," I say.

His chest rumbles with laughter. "I'm serious though. You are what parents hope for when they decide to have kids. I'm the nightmare. If your parents don't see that, then fuck them. I'm also proof that you don't need a parent to survive."

Oddly enough, his words help me. I know my parents and I were coming to a crossroads. That eventually our relationship would change as we moved in different directions like a fork in the road. I just hoped we could be headed in the same direction.

The apartment door opens behind me, and Jax's body stiffens. I turn my head and find Dylan standing there. I sit up straighter as Jax releases me almost with a shove.

But it doesn't matter because Dylan walks right back out and slams the door.

Chapter Twenty

DYLAN

I PRESS THE ELEVATOR BUTTON, AND WHEN IT DOESN'T COME RIGHT AWAY, I RACE down the stairs. I'm pissed at myself for being a coward when Rian's parents showed up, but damn, I'm confused about that kiss and where we stand. How would I sit and talk with her parents?

How naive of me to assume whatever happened between her and Jax was over. I never asked her after my accident.

I walk into Ink Envy.

"Boss." Lyle slides off his stool.

I raise my hand as I pass him.

"We need to talk," Frankie says.

"Later," I mumble.

She's in the middle of a tattoo, so that gives me time to lock myself in the office. I slam my door, lock it, and sit in my office chair. Staring at my cast, I want to take a pair of scissors and cut it off. I want to go out there and take a client and lose myself for hours in art and ink. Get my mind off all this shit swirling around.

All I can think of is Rian's lips and the softness of her touch.

Then I picture her in Jax's arms.

He was the one consoling her after her parents said something else to hurt her. Hell, they have their opinions on me too, I'm sure. With them witnessing our first kiss, she probably took a heavy dose of disappointed looks from both of them.

That's why I stayed at Seth's, waiting for them to leave so I could go back in and apologize for running out. Joke's on me though, because once again, Jax sneaked in and got the girl.

A knock sounds on the door.

"Not now," I yell.

"Okay, boss," Lyle says.

But no less than a minute later, another knock sounds on the door. When I say nothing, a key is inserted and the door is unlocked.

Frankie stands there, dangling her keys in front of her. "Why are you locking yourself in the office? And you look like shit, by the way. Like a fifteen-year-old boy who got his heart broken. What the hell happened?"

I run my hand down my face. "Rian shaved me." Her eyes light up with intrigue, so I raise my hand to stop her mind before it gets too carried away. "Don't worry, I'm pretty sure she's into Jax."

Her eyebrows shoot up and she shuts the door before coming over to the chair on the other side of the desk.

"You're with a client," I say.

"She needed a breather. I'm giving her a five-minute break." She sits. "Talk to me. What happened?"

Before I can respond, the door busts open and Jax stands there. "You're a fucking idiot, you know that?"

I put my hand up to stop him. "Just, everyone, leave me the fuck alone."

"You need to leave," Jax says to Frankie.

Her eyebrows shoot up. "In case you missed it, I'm the second in command around here." She dangles her keys in the air.

"This has nothing to do with the business." Jax holds the door open and gestures for her to leave.

"I'm not in the mood to rehash our fucked up history right now." I boot up my computer.

"Too fucking bad. I'm done with this shit." He squares his eyes on Frankie. "Kindly leave."

Frankie straightens her back and crosses her legs, getting comfortable. "I've been here a long time and they're both my friends. I'm sure as hell not going to leave a man like you in charge of him seeing the error of his ways."

"A man like me?"

"Yeah. A man who probably thinks commitment is for the weak. A man who dates a younger version of the same woman he's always dated because he has some warped sense of self-image when in reality, people look at him like he's pathetic."

"You know nothing about me," Jax says. "You've known me less than a week."

Frankie crosses her arms. "I know your type all too well."

A hollow and bitter laugh falls from Jax. "Don't take out your heartbreaks on me. I wasn't the guy who fucked you over."

She laughs right back.

I roll my eyes. Thankfully, she doesn't say anything else. Jax bows dramatically and ushers his hand toward the door. Frankie shakes her head.

He slams the door. "Fine, you're about to find out a lot of things about your boss and me then."

"Can we please do this another time?" I ask.

Frankie looks at me with concerned eyes. That's when I make the decision that Frankie shouldn't be in the room right now. Jax is right on that. Whatever is going down behind this door, she doesn't need to know about it. No one does but us.

Jax leans against the wall with his arms folded across his chest.

"Just give us ten minutes," I say to Frankie.

She inspects my face. Oh, how she's used to being a bodyguard for everyone but herself. Standing, she touches my shoulder and walks to the door. "Don't listen to his bullshit about relationships."

Jax shakes his head, and she flips him off. Whatever is transpiring between these two isn't good. Which is weird, because if someone would've asked me to bet money on how well they'd get along, I would've said they'd be best friends within a week.

She leaves and shuts the door. Jax pushes off the wall and sits in the chair Frankie just occupied. He leans his forearms on his knees and clasps his hands together.

His head hangs low and he speaks to the floor. "I don't want her, man."

I lean back in my chair, my casted arm lying on the armrest and my other hand fiddling with a pen. "Could've fooled me."

He peeks up. "I've been an asshole. I thought it would be fun to fuck with you, but that all ended the night of your accident. That isn't to say if she wasn't so hung up on you, I wouldn't have banged her."

My jaw clenches.

"But that's all she would have been," he says. "Just like Naomi was."

There were times I wondered if Jax and I would ever mend our rift. Could there ever be a time when we could get back to being friends? What would the conversation consist of? Would we skate over the Naomi situation or dissect it? I guess by him bringing her up, he wants to get it all out in the open.

"I never wanted her. It's no excuse, but she was consoling me about Winnie and it just kind of happened," he says. "She loved you. She did."

I'm surprised he's ready to show his vulnerability. I huff. "I think she loved both of us."

He looks at me and shrugs. Naomi wanted us to be morphed into the same person. She loved my stability and the fact I was headed to college. She also loved Jax's wild streak and tendency to get into fights. To say I was surprised when I walked in on them would be a lie. Which is probably why I felt more betrayed by Jax than Naomi.

"But Rian is different, Phillips. She likes you, and for some fucked up reason, you keep pushing her away." He looks at me, expecting an answer.

"Man, you know just like I do that Rian isn't anything like Naomi."

"Which is a good thing." He leans back.

I nod. True enough. "You know her type. She's meant for an accountant who works nine to five and is home every weekend. A guy who gives her the American dream of a house and two point five kids and a dog running around the yard. A guy who gets excited for pizza nights on Friday and movies on Saturdays."

"Nah," Jax says. "She doesn't want some douche who only screws her missionary and can't work his tongue on her."

I huff out a laugh. "Her parents hate me."

"Sounds like she hates her parents." He locks his fingers together over his stomach. "Keep coming up with excuses. We both know you're more the settling down type than you want to admit."

Have I ever thought about marriage? Yeah. But did I ever think I could go through with it? I'm not sure.

"I haven't seen any other girls hanging around you," he adds.

"Are you trying to diss my game?"

He laughs. "No, I'm saying you're not interested in anyone but her."

He's got a point. Somehow when Jax moved in, my fear of losing her overruled my fear of ruining our friendship. "If you hadn't come back, I'm not sure I would've ever acted on my feelings."

A smirk crosses his lips.

Son of a bitch.

"You did it on purpose?" I ask. "You purposely asked her out just to get me to act on my feelings?"

He holds up his hands. "Truth?"

"Yeah."

"I liked her when I first moved in, but I saw how protective you were of her. You've always been transparent," he says, his smirk grows wider. "I thought I'd just give you an extra push if you were toeing the line. I didn't think you'd need a bulldozer."

"So much could go wrong."

"So much could go right," he counters.

I nod. He's right.

"You can sit here and be a pussy, all scared in your boots and worried about what-ifs, or you can go over there and own your feelings for her." I stare at him, and he sighs. "What are you worried about?"

What am I not worried about?

"Our friendship. Hers and mine. Other than Naomi, I've never had anything serious. What if I don't like it? What if I feel suffocated and screw it all up? It's not just our friendship at stake. It's all our friends. We're in an interconnected cobweb and if Rian cuts one strand, it rocks the entire group."

He nods. "You guys do have a little family here, don't you?" He nods toward the door. "Even that spark plug out there."

There's longing in his tone. I first heard it in ninth grade when Winnie would make me come home for dinner at six. Then he had to do the same once he moved in with Winnie. Maybe that's the one thing Jax hasn't gotten since he left—a sense of home, family. Which is why he thinks it's okay to throw yourself to the wild and deal with consequences later. I can't do that with Rian.

"They're all really important to me."

This is usually when Jax would cut off any sentimentality. When his jokester side would prevail, and he'd make a snide remark so the person believes he doesn't really care. But this time, he looks me square in the eye. Something he hasn't done since he returned. "Let me ask you a question."

"What?"

"Do you really think the two of you will survive being friends forever? Was it just that you didn't want to lose out to *me*? You were going to sit through that wedding to the accountant? Be the godfather of her baby? Where does it end? How long do you torture yourself?"

The things he mentions flash in my mind. Me sitting in the pew, watching her give me one more look before saying I do to some other guy. Or me coming to her house to celebrate my godchild's milestones. I'd no doubt be wondering what could have been if I hadn't been a pussy. Could it have been me she was saying I do to? My hand she held as she went through labor?

"You're a fucking asshole," I say, standing from my desk.

He smiles.

I walk to the door but turn around. "I'm sorry. I should have allowed you at Winnie's funeral."

I was so angry about him and Naomi that I forbade him from attending her service. Looking back, I think I was just angry at the world and the fact that Winnie had died more than I was at Jax. But he was as good a target as any to direct my fury at.

He shakes his head. "Forget it." He pauses as though he has something more to say, so I wait. "I shouldn't have blamed you when Winnie left you that money for your future. I understand now why she did. Anything that came my way I would've just blown through. Probably would've done more harm than good."

I nod. I figured that out a while ago. Jax was always wilder than I was. I think Winnie trusted that I would put the money to good use. Jax, not so much, as harsh as that is.

I open my arms. "Hug it out?"

"Fuck you. Go get your girl." He nods toward the door.

I laugh all the way through Ink Envy until I'm outside our apartment door.

Chapter Twenty-One

RIAN

SOME PEOPLE CLEAN. OTHERS COOK. OTHERS MIGHT EXERCISE. I EITHER DO MATH or bake when I'm upset. Today it's math. When my mind is scrambling with a million uncontrollable thoughts swarming like bees, the precision of math, the fact that there is only one correct answer, calms me.

So after Jax runs after Dylan, I take my stuff to my room and pull out the problem.

Okay, yeah, I would love to solve this problem just to prove to my parents that I'm not some stupid child. A psychologist would probably say that proving it to them is still seeking their approval. But I don't really care. To me. it's like a middle finger to them.

The apartment door opens and my math bubble pops. Suddenly, all my issues are front and center in my mind again. Either Jax or Dylan is home, and I'm not sure which one I'd rather talk to right now.

Footsteps pound across the hardwood, making my heart race as though I should be hiding under the bed. It feels as if everything stable in my life is about to crash down.

The pencil slips from my grasp with the rap of knuckles on my door, falling from the paper to my mattress and rolling to the floor. "Yeah?"

"Rian." A thud sounds on the wood.

My shoulders fall at the sound of Dylan's voice. "Yeah?"

"Can I come in?"

"Sure."

My eyes lock on the doorknob as it turns, and the door pushes open. And there he is, his cleanly shaven face making him look more innocent and youthful than normal.

He shuts the door and stands with his back pressed to it.

"I'm sor—" I say, but he holds up his hand.

"I'm the sorry one. I never should've left when your parents showed up."

I shake my head. I'm used to it. My house was never the hang-out house. I quit asking for birthday parties when I was nine years old and my parents made the girls do a hundred question multiplication sheet. Whoever completed it the fastest and most accurately won the prize—an abacus. "It's okay."

"No, it's not. Do you want to talk about what happened with them?" He pushes off the door, and I suck in a breath the closer he moves. Before I can soak in everything that's happening, he's at the edge of my bed.

"Nah. Same old."

He eyes my book and picks up the pencil from the floor, handing it to me. "I'm jealous of Jax."

"Why?" It's a stupid question. The kiss sealed the fact that whatever is lying dormant under our friendship isn't just on my end. But maybe because I've waited so long, I want to hear the words from him. How badly does he want me?

He stares at me for a moment. It's all there in his gorgeous light brown eyes. "Do I have a reason to be jealous?"

The silence is deafening, the tension wound tight. "No."

His eyes close for a second and his chest rises and falls. Leaning forward, he tucks a strand of my hair behind my ear. "Good."

It's clear that he wants to kiss me again, and after the wall incident, I know that one kiss is going to end with both of us naked in this bed, my math book forgotten. Part of me wants to tell my conscience to allow that to happen, but what if he only wants me because Jax made him jealous?

My hand presses on his chest.

His eyebrows raise in question, but Dylan's a good guy, so he backs up and my hand falls to the mattress between us. "Are you sure I shouldn't be jealous?"

"This has nothing to do with Jax, but are you sure whatever competition you have with him isn't the reason you want to be with me? Can you honestly say we would be here if Jax had never showed up?"

"We've always been friends who wanted more."

I shake my head. "You were content dating other women. Having sex with other women. Why now?"

He looks as if I slapped him, but we can't live in a bubble and not face the truth. Something bad will happen and that bubble will pop. "Jax made me realize that I could lose you."

I nod. "Because you guys compete over everything. This would be your way of winning."

He shakes his head. "No. That's not it at all."

I stand, unable to be so close to him while I put on hold something I've wanted for years. "Put yourself in my shoes."

His head falls and he stares at the floor. Slowly, he nods.

"Believe me, Dylan, I want nothing more than to strip down and beg you to take me right now. To fall under the covers with you and do all the things I've masturbated to for years, but I can't do that with the prospect of heartbreak once you win me."

He nods again. "I get what you're saying, but I'm telling you that's not it. I've always felt like I wasn't good enough for you."

He stands and I step back, which stops him from approaching. My forehead wrinkles. "Why?"

"Come on, Rian. Why do you think your parents have a problem with me? They see it. I bring you down."

I don't care what my parents think, and I've never thought that about Dylan. "That's not true."

When I don't move, he welcomes that as his opportunity to continue toward me. "But I don't care anymore. I mean, I do, but I'm not going to lose this opportunity. I was so hung up on the what-ifs, I never thought about three or five years in the future—the what-ifs I'd feel then. The regrets I'd live with if I never tried to see if we can work this out." He cages me against my dresser, our chests pressed together and his hands on my hips as though he's afraid I'm going to run. "I'm scared of losing your friendship or messing up our friends' circle, but I'll take the chance because the other alternative is too painful to bear."

I've loved him from afar for so long, I never took into consideration the impact on our group of friends. What happened to Ethan and Sierra could happen to us. But I decide right then, "I'd never let that happen—unless one of us did something stupid." Like cheat.

"I can't say I'm going to be the best boyfriend at first. There's a learning curve." I tilt my head, and he chuckles. "I'd never fuck it up by cheating. I meant other things."

I stare at him and he steps closer, his chest pushing against mine. When I woke up this morning, I never thought we'd end up here. "Why don't you take a shower? Think it over some more."

He chuckles. "I have a better idea. Why don't *we* take a bath?" His hand slides down and he links his fingers with mine. "We can talk this over while naked and wet." He winks and my heart somersaults.

Who am I kidding? I want this as much as he does, and I don't want regrets in a few years either. All I can do is trust him when he says that this isn't because of Jax and their competitive nature.

"That's tempting," I say. "One condition."

"What?" He squeezes my hand, stepping back toward the door.

"You tell me about Naomi."

His face falls, but he nods, tugging me forward so I fall into his chest. He wraps his good arm around me, stares into my eyes, and bends down for a kiss.

Just as it did hours earlier, my heartbeat skyrockets the minute his soft lips land on mine.

But he ends the kiss too quickly. "Let's get me clean so I can show you exactly how dirty I can get."

I bite my lip, and he chuckles.

"I guess it's time for me to see what I'm getting, huh?" I unzip his sweatshirt and help him pull it off his arm. My hands run along his bare chest, over all his ink. He groans as my fingers hook on either side of his track pants, pushing them down his legs until they pool at his feet. "My boyfriend doesn't wear underwear?"

"Not since the accident. Too fucking hard to put on."

He stands there and allows my gaze to drift over his body. He's not embarrassed or self-conscious, nor should he be. He's lean, muscled perfection and it makes my mouth water. His hard dick is pointed north. Nice for me. I step closer, taking his dick in my palm and rubbing.

"Whoa." His hand covers mine. "Don't I get to see my girlfriend?"

I smile and bite the corner of my mouth, sliding my tongue over my bottom lip.

"Don't be embarrassed. I can't wait to see you."

He knows me so well. Of course I'm embarrassed. The heat in my cheeks says I'm wearing that emotion like a flashing stop sign. I step back, taking the hem of my T-shirt and pulling it up over my body.

"Slowly," he says, and my eyes rise to meet his. "I want to savor this moment."

That's all it takes for my embarrassment to fade away.

I raise the shirt over my stomach and my bra until I lose sight of him as I pull it over my head. I drop the shirt onto the floor and his eyes are on my ribcage, not my breasts like I assumed. I reach back with both hands and unhook my bra, then I slide the straps off each arm.

He grunts, and his attention moves to my breasts. "Jesus, I can't wait to have both my hands on them."

A maddening look fills his face. I forgot about his arm and how trying sex is going to be.

I unbutton my jeans as his vision zeros in as though I'm giving him the code to a vault holding millions of dollars. My forefinger and thumb glide my zipper down and his breathing becomes labored. His rapt attention boosts my self-esteem. He's making this so easy for me.

"Turn around," he says.

I circle around, pushing my jeans down. As I get them halfway down my ass, he puts his hand on the side of my hip.

"Slow it down for me."

I look over my shoulder to see that he's wrapped his hand around his dick, tugging and nodding for me to continue. I shimmy instead of pushing my jeans the rest of the way down.

When I stand up straight again, he's closer to me. One hand slides around from my ass to cup a breast. His dick digs into my satin panties.

"You're so damn beautiful," he whispers. "Mouthwatering tits, and an ass I want to slap until it looks like a strawberry." His hand slides down my torso, under the hem of my panties, and cups my mound. "I'm not sure I can handle seeing this without spreading you open right here for a taste."

My entire body is Jell-O, willing to bend and shift, molding to whatever he wants to do to me. I want to experience it all with him. The screams, scrapes, and moans. The gentle graze of his knuckles along the lips of my pussy make my head fall back on his bare shoulder and his mouth casts small bites along my flesh, working his way up to my ear.

"I want you so bad," he whispers.

"Take me," I whisper back and tilt my head to the side.

He captures my mouth, his tongue diving in. His finger runs the length of my center, pressing the smallest, lightest circles along my clit, and I moan into his mouth.

"You like that?" he asks once he stops kissing me. "Let's go."

His hand slides out from between my legs and I miss it already. "Can we take a shower rather than a bath?"

"Why?"

"Faster."

His eyes light up. "I love the way you think."

He guides me across the living room, and we lock the bathroom door once we're inside. Best. Day. Ever.

Chapter Twenty-Two

DYLAN

RIAN'S BODY DESERVES A REACTION LIKE THAT CARTOON CHARACTER WHOSE JAW hangs low and drags on the floor. I've gotten glimpses throughout the years. A shirt that rode up a little high or a button that popped open. Pajama shorts where I could tell she wasn't wearing panties. All of those pieced together to give me a vision of what I thought Rian looked like naked. Turns out I was dead wrong. She's flawless and beautiful in a delicate way. Like when a tattoo is done and nothing more needs to be added. Her body is perfect.

"What about Jax?" she asks with the click of the lock.

"Don't worry, Jax isn't coming home for a while."

He understood exactly what I was going to do when I left Ink Envy, so if he's the guy I've always known, he'll crash somewhere else, at least for tonight.

My arm slides behind the shower curtain and I turn on the water.

"Oh, your arm," Rian says.

"Shit. I'll be right back."

She laughs as I slide out of the bathroom and head to the kitchen to grab a garbage bag. I'm more upset that one set of my fingers won't be able to participate today. Being restricted to only one hand is a lot to expect from a guy during his first time with a girl. She might think I'm a horrible screw.

"I got the scrunchie!" she hollers.

I grab the garbage bag and shut the cabinet right as the apartment door opens. I swear to fucking God. We have to start locking that thing.

"Oh shit, I'm blind!" Seth screams.

I scramble to escape to the bathroom, but Rian screeches and slams the bathroom door. Seth still didn't take my nakedness as his clue to leave.

"What the hell are you talking about?" Knox bumps Seth out of the way.

I slowly turn around, covering my junk. Knox nods at me and sits on the couch, pressing the power button on the controller.

"What are you guys doing?" I ask.

Seth joins Knox on the couch. "It's, like, channel five hundred or something."

When *Superbad* plays on the television, they both relax with their feet up on the table.

"Perfect," Knox says.

"Don't you two have jobs?" I ask.

"Day off," Knox says.

Seth raises his hand. "I cut out early."

The bathroom door behind me slides open. "Dylan," Rian whispers, "I have no clothes in here."

I nod. "You two need to leave."

The bathroom door shuts again.

That seems to alert Knox that something isn't normal. "Oh, I thought you were just finally showering." He nods toward the bathroom. "You got someone in there?"

Seth turns to look at me.

I didn't think I'd be telling everyone about Rian and me this soon, but they'll find out anyway. "Yeah."

"Cool. We'll just be out here. We don't have this movie channel." Knox points the remote at the television.

"Yeah, I'm not a public fucker like you, so you'll have to pay for it On Demand or something."

Knox looks offended. "I'm not a public fucker or whatever the hell that means. I'm just not ashamed of my body or my skills. If someone wants to watch because it's their kink, that's not my problem. It's not gonna stop me from doing what I want. Especially when I'm in my own apartment."

"Thanks for the Ted Talk. Now get the fuck out." I nod at the door.

Seth stands and looks around. "Where's Rian?"

She groans from the other side of the door, but neither of them hear her.

"I gotta say, the naked body is beautiful. And the shame you both have about sex makes me think you're a bunch of church ladies with nothing better to talk about," Knox continues, but Seth's clearly catching on.

"Do you two mind? I'm naked here." I knock on the door, but Rian still doesn't unlock it.

"Where's Rian?" Seth asks again, glancing around, walking toward her bedroom door with a grin on his face. "Thought she was working from home to help your sorry ass." He stops cold outside her bedroom door, probably seeing our discarded clothes on the floor. "Oh shit!"

He circles back around, and a smile as long and wide as the Brooklyn Bridge creases his lips.

"We gotta go." Seth points at the door.

"What am I missing?" Knox asks.

"Rian is the girl," Seth mouths.

"Yes, I know Rian is a girl," Knox says.

"You're really a cop, right?" I ask with a lifted brow.

Knox thinks it over, then his mouth opens in an O and he nods, looking impressed. "You could've just said that."

"Said what?" I whisper.

"'Hey, I'm fucking Rian right now. Take off.'"

I shake my head.

Knox turns off the television while Seth's nodding like a crazy man. "About fucking time. Can I say something to her?" He steps toward me.

"Fuck no. Get the hell out."

Seth nods like "yeah, that was an idiotic move" and twists on his heels to head toward the door. "Finally. I swear I think I was getting blue balls watching Dylan drag his feet."

The door shuts behind them, and I flip the lock.

"Open up for me," I say, turning to the bathroom door.

She peeks around the door, and when she hears the quiet and doesn't see the guys, she opens it all the way. "So, two down, huh?"

Rian's skin glistens in the steamy room from the humidity. I shut the door and lock it, putting my hand in the bag. She secures it with her scrunchie.

"Technically Jax too," I say.

She sighs.

"Did you want us to keep it a secret?" Maybe I pegged her all wrong. Should I have told the guys it was someone else?

"No! It'll be embarrassing the first time, but I don't want us to hide."

"Good. I think the shower's ready." My good hand snakes down her body, grabbing her ass.

"I'm ready." She takes a hair elastic from her drawer and twirls her hair into a messy ponytail on top of her head.

She steps in first and I quickly follow. My gaze follows the stream of water flowing over her body and I realize this was a big mistake.

"Let's just wash me and get the hell out of here. I cannot properly fuck you in a shower with one arm." I step under the showerhead with her, my lips falling to hers until her back hits the tile wall.

"Happy to," she says, her hands in my hair, our naked bodies pressed together. She's soft, oh so fucking soft, and she's grinding along my length.

"I can't stop touching you." Even my broken arm wants something. My fingers find their way to the seam of the bag, begging to touch any part of her.

She presses on my chest and I step back, using my time away from her to take her in. Commit the curves of her body to memory. How her tits fall like heart-shaped Hershey's kisses just waiting for my mouth to devour them.

She puddles shampoo into her hand before bringing both up to my hair. Her fingers thread through the strands and massage my scalp.

"You probably need me closer, right?" I laugh, my hands on her hips leaving us only millimeters apart.

"I really need you to dip your head. You're so damn tall."

So I do just that and take the opportunity to lick one of her breasts, sucking the nipple into my mouth. "Is this what you meant?"

She arches into me, her hands not as vigorous anymore.

"Keep washing my hair," I say, shifting my attention to her other breast.

"Trade places."

The suds from my hair drip down over her chest.

"You don't play fair," she says.

We switch so the water falls over my head. To speed up the process, I stand to my full height, dipping my head back under the showerhead to rinse my hair.

"FYI, I never play fair."

But then neither does she, because her lips attach to my nipples, her tongue running small circles around them. I grab a hold of her nipples, twisting. The harder I pull, the more she moans. I think I found a kink of Rian Wright's.

She stands up, not taking nearly enough time down there. "Conditioner."

"We can skip the conditioner."

She looks at me with mock offense. "No way. If my hands are going to thread through this hair tonight, I want it soft."

"Only if you agree to pull it." I grin. A blush travels over her whole body, and I break the distance between us. "I might just get addicted to you blushing. Tell me what you were thinking when I just said that."

She shakes her head, grabbing my bar of soap, and runs the soap over my body. "I was thinking of your head between my legs."

I put my finger under her chin and bring her face up to meet my eyes. "You better pull my hair when I'm between your legs. I plan on spending a lot of time down there."

She runs the soap over my dick, pushing her body against mine to hold me in place until she slides the soap to my back side, moving over my ass.

"You get the job of showering me every morning until this cast comes off." I kiss her nose.

She smiles. "Oh, do I? And what do I get in return?"

"You get me washing you." My hand molds around her tit, my thumb over her nipple.

"I'm not sure either one of us will make it to work." She puts the soap down and walks me back under the showerhead. "Time to rinse off, my dirty boy."

"If I'm a good boy, do I get a treat?"

She laughs without answering, and after I'm rinsed off, I turn off the water. She gets out and pulls two towels from the rack.

"I'll dry you." I take her towel. Fuck my right hand. I won't let it fuck this up because it can't coordinate itself.

She watches me run the plush towel up both of her legs, pausing an inch shy of her pussy. I dry off her arms and torso, taking my time to make sure her tits are fully dry. Sliding the towel around her back, I make sure her ass is good and dry. With her hair up, all that's left is her pussy. I put the towel there, my hand molded to her mound, and she bucks into my hand. I need to get this girl to a bed.

Opening the bathroom door, I'm happy to find the apartment empty. We tiptoe across the room as though it's not, and when we're secure in her room, I back her up to the bed until she falls on the mattress.

"Condom?" I ask.

She shakes her head. "I have an IUD. I'm clean."

My knees nudge her legs open. Fuck, she's killing me. Is she giving me permission to just slide right in? I've never done that before. I desperately want to and I'm clean, but I fear that with nothing between us, I'll be the minute man inside her.

"I'm clean too—just tested before the accident—but I'll be right back." I stand from the mattress and point at her. "Stay right where you are."

I run out of the room and over to my bedroom, grab a row of condoms, and return to her. Rian listened, lying exactly where I left her except she's taken out her ponytail so her blonde hair is strewn around her like a fucking angel's.

Fuck the condoms. I toss them aside and shimmy up on the bed with my knees. "Are you sure you're okay without a condom?"

She nods. I hold myself over her on my good arm, the tip of my dick piercing her opening.

"I trust you," she says softly.

I hope she doesn't come to regret those three words.

Chapter Twenty-Three

RIAN

DYLAN SLIDES INTO ME INCH BY INCH, FILLING ME UNTIL I GASP. HE STARES AT me—and it's then I realize we did this all wrong.

"I should be on top. Your arm," I say.

He looks at his arm as though he has no idea what I'm talking about. "Shit, you're right."

He slides out of me, and I groan from missing him so much. The shower was some hella foreplay. I need him. Maybe after the first time, my girly parts will have more patience.

"I guess you get to ride me." He smirks and lies back on my bed, his head on my pillows, one arm outstretched and reaching for me.

Suddenly, I'm self-conscious. I've never ridden anyone. I've watched porn, but the fact that's all I have to go on is pathetic and not something I'm about to share, no matter how much I trust Dylan with my secrets.

"Are you fantasizing about cowboys?" He laughs, waiting for me.

Well, if I'm not going to tell him, it's time to hop on. I swing one leg over to straddle him.

"Put me in you." His attention is focused on the space between our groins.

Just imagine your dildos, Rian. You totally have this. I grab his base, inching up and positioning him at my opening before sinking down on his hard length.

The fact that his head is arched back with his eyes shut says I'm doing something right.

"We'll definitely be doing this when I have use of both my arms." His good hand molds to my hip.

I rock a little as his fingertips push into my skin. He smiles at me and my hands land on his chest, my gaze pouring over his tattoos to get my mind off of what I'm doing.

"Just go on feeling," he whispers.

My eyes shoot to his. He knows. *Of course he does. You've lived across from him for years and he's never once seen you bring a guy home.* I rock deeper, opening my legs farther.

He groans, his fingertips tightening on my hipbone. "There you go."

His hand ventures off my hip to my breast. He squeezes it and runs his thumb over my puckered nipple. I pause for a moment without him directing me, but the more aroused I become, the more I chase my orgasm and the thoughts about whether I'm doing it right or not are thrown out the window.

His hips raise up off the mattress, pushing him deeper inside me. The way he's stretching me isn't painful; it feels sinful and I'll never tire of this feeling. I slide up and down on him, my hands digging into his chest for stability. He's perfect.

My orgasm climbs, but I push it back because I don't want this moment to end. I want to feel like this for the rest of my life. The closeness of today, his hands scanning every inch of my body, his lust-filled eyes staring at me as though I'm the only woman who could ever satisfy him. It's all too much and I'm flooded by desire ripping through my body.

"You're fucking amazing," he says, his eyes lazily closing for a moment. "I want to tear off my cast to drill inside you until I can't see straight."

He manipulates my tit, pinching my nipple, and the dam I built around my orgasm collapses. I cry out as the waves of my climax crest over me. Dylan's hand moves to my hip and he pumps inside me from below, finding his own release with a growl and my name on his lips.

I roll off him, lying on the mattress until he seeps out of me. "I'll be right back," I say and shoot out the door to the bathroom.

I'm not in there longer than a minute when Dylan knocks on the door. "You okay?"

The concern in his voice warms my heart. "Yes. Just cleaning up."

I finish, flush the toilet, and wash my hands before opening the door to a still-naked Dylan.

He walks into the bathroom, pressing me to the bathroom counter. "I would have cleaned you."

I laugh. "Well, it took me a little by surprise."

"Yeah, I forgot that it would get messy. Which means…" He kisses me briefly and moves to the tub. "We need to take that bath now. Soothe all those parts I'm not done with yet."

I smile. "I think I have some bubble bath."

A half hour later, Dylan drains some of the water and runs the tap to add more hot water to the tub. I'm across from him, our legs tangled, our hands entwined. I can't help looking at all his tattoos again.

"Have you thought of my tattoo yet?" I ask.

A mischievous smile arises on his gorgeous face. "I have."

"Can you tell me what it is?"

He shakes his head. "Nope."

"After the cast is off, you'll sketch it though?"

He shrugs. "You let me know when you're ready."

"I'm ready now."

He nods and I know he's hiding something, but I have no idea what it could be. "You've got at least five more weeks."

He stares at me so long, I look away.

"Come here," he says. I slide so that my back is to his chest and he nuzzles his face into my neck, securing the one arm he can get wet around me, the other in plastic propped up on the side of the tub. "Have you finished that math problem yet?"

"No, but I'm getting close."

"That's my girl." He kisses my ear, his tongue twirling around the lobe. "I'm not sure you're going to get to work on it for a while though."

"Why is that?" I look at him over my shoulder.

"Because I have a lot of masturbation material and I want to make live footage with you."

I turn around fully and he takes the opportunity to get me to straddle him. "You masturbated to me?"

Stop looking for affirmation.

He laughs. "Are you kidding me? I've been masturbating to you since the first day we met."

"You're lying. That's a way to save face. You probably masturbated to Blanca and Sierra too."

He says nothing for a moment. "Truth is, I never did. I can't really say why. Maybe Sierra scares me a little and by the time I met Blanca, you were a permanent part of my highlight reel."

"Now I feel giddy and it shouldn't matter, but…" I lean forward and press a kiss to his lips. "I'm flattered."

He holds me to him. "Wait to be flattered until you find out what we were doing."

"I think bath time is over." I pull the drain plug.

He chuckles, and I step out of the bath then help him. We remove the bag then dry off with the towels from earlier.

"We've gotten entirely too wet tonight. I'm turning into a prune." I walk in front of him to the bedroom.

"Oh, I haven't gotten you nearly as wet as I want you yet."

I'm not sure I'll ever grow tired of the dirty things he says to me. He's so open about how much he wants me physically. I wonder where that comes from when he's so insecure about showing any vulnerability. Maybe he views sex and relationships differently.

We get back to my bed and I pick up the condoms. "So we're just not going to use these?"

He picks them up and tosses them on the floor. I guess that answers that.

"Me on top again?" I ask.

"Yeah, but are you up for trying something?"

I nod.

He slides by me on the bed, lying in the same position he was in the first time. "Straddle me, but turn the opposite way so I'm looking at your ass."

"Reverse cowgirl?" I ask and his eyes narrow as though he's wondering who I've done it with. "I'm not some naive virgin. I watch porn."

A huge smile takes over his face. "Oh, that's our next thing. We're watching porn together."

"I have another idea first though."

"Do tell."

My cheeks heat, but I force myself to say the words. "A little sixty-nine before reverse cowgirl?"

He slides down the bed on his back a bit. "You are the girl of my dreams. By all means. I did skip dinner."

And let me say I haven't found one thing Dylan isn't good at. Even if he only has one good arm.

I spring up in bed and turn to my side. Dylan's asleep on his back, his casted arm on his side, half on his stomach, and his other arm above his head. He looks as tired as my body feels. Even with the use of only one arm, Dylan did a fabulous job of giving me multiple orgasms.

After pushing the covers off my legs, I grab a shirt and shorts, then I pull my books off my dresser. My mind is clearer than it's been in weeks. I grab my reading light and clip it to my book, putting pencil to paper, and the block lifts, the answer coming to me as if someone placed it in my mind.

Jax comes home, his footsteps moving through the apartment as he goes through his nightly routine of changing his clothes and having a late night snack and a beer while watching television. For a moment, I debate joining him and asking him what he told Dylan to spur the breakthrough of that wall he put between us. But then I turn to look at Dylan sleeping in my bed and I don't want to know. I'm just happy we crossed that line we've toed for so long.

Another wave of clarity washes over me and I work out another part of the equation. The rush of flying through the solution is addicting and I'm unable to stop my pencil from moving across the paper. Jax's footsteps on the other side of the door says he heads to his room, his door quietly shutting.

Dylan shifts in my sheets and steals my attention away for a second.

Picking up my books, I admire the man I'm way too invested in. He could break me, and I have to prepare myself for that. But he feels worth the risk.

I head out to the dark living room and sit at the kitchen table, working through the rest of the solution and feeling as though life couldn't get much better than this.

Chapter Twenty-Four

DYLAN

My hand falls beside me, expecting to feel a warm body, but it lands on a cold sheet instead.

I peek at an empty spot next to me. I rarely wake up alone after a night of sex. If anything, the girl is usually begging me for another round. My heart squeezes over the idea that maybe Rian is having second thoughts. Maybe last night was too much, too fast. Maybe my mouth was way too filthy for her or my one-handed fucking wasn't stellar.

Shaking my head, I push away that notion. She was right there with me, her body instinctively knowing what to do even though her experience is limited. I tried to guide her and not make her feel inadequate because she was anything but. Hell, the caveman alpha male in me likes that I'll get to teach her some things.

I sit up, find my track pants, and after what feels like a lifetime and I'm sweating from the effort of putting them on, I leave the sanctuary of her room—only to stop in her doorway. She's asleep at the kitchen table, her hands tucked under her head on top of the pile of papers strewn everywhere.

I slide back the veil of blonde hair covering her face and kiss her cheek. "Time to wake up, brainiac."

She stirs, swatting me away, and I laugh. My lips travel down her ear and suck her earlobe. She moans and my morning wood screams good morning once again.

"Go to the bed," I say.

When she still doesn't get up, I delve my hand under the bottom of her T-shirt and squeeze her breast, pinching her nipple.

She jolts, looks at me, and gives me one of those dick-saluting smiles. "Morning."

I chuckle and kiss her lips. "Morning."

She cuts the kiss off short and wipes her mouth.

"Should I be offended that I woke up alone?" I leave her to make coffee.

"I had a breakthrough on the problem."

"So you came out here?" I ask, shuffling between the sink and coffee maker.

Her arms reach around me as I scoop coffee grounds into the maker. "You freed my blockage," she says, her lips casting small kisses on my back.

How natural it is for us this morning. I worried we would be stoic around one another, worried what the other is thinking, but we seem to be in the same place.

I start the coffee maker and turn around, taking her in my arm. She lays her head on my chest.

"I have to go to the shop tonight," I spit out like I'm worried she's going to get upset.

She rests her chin on my chest and looks up at me. "Okay."

"You're not mad?" I expected some jealousy or disappointment over the fact that I can't spend the weekend in bed with her. I would love to, but Jax and Frankie might kill one another if I don't make an appearance.

Her hand runs up my back. "Why would I be mad?"

I shake my head. "No reason. You'll come by though?"

"If you want me to?"

I kiss the top of her head. "Definitely. I can sneak out for a late dinner."

She kisses my chest. "Deal."

We stay locked in each other's hold until the coffee maker dings. This is way too easy. I wish I could relax and enjoy it, but experience says something bad is on the horizon.

Ink Envy is buzzing when I show up at six o'clock. I meant to be here earlier, but Rian and I got waylaid trying out new positions with her on top. She's really finding what gets her off and I fucking love watching her sexual side awaken.

Lyle's on the bar stool by the welcome table. Jax is working on a customer and has another one waiting. Frankie's busy with a group of girls who seem to be all getting the same tattoo on their hipbone. Everything's running well, so I figure I'll head back to Rian—then my gaze stops on Mad Max coming out of the back area where the piercing station is. A woman follows him, her red face beaming. My guess is she either got her nips or pussy done.

"What the hell?" I put my hand out to him when he approaches.

"I heard you might need a little pick-me-up around here?"

"It's Saturday night. What about the place in the city?" That's where he should be. Where the money is for him. I was proud he got the job in the city.

"I'm needed here, man." He claps me on the shoulder. "I have a few more appointments set up, but I'll swing by your office to shoot the shit when I'm done."

I nod, hoping my eyes convey the words that can be hard for me to speak. But the fact he's here until I can get the business thriving again speaks volumes to me. I wonder who called him and let him know the state of things.

Jax nods at me then looks back down to his client. "I'm guessing all is peachy keen now? Or should I say you're the king of Rian's peach now?"

"Yeah, things are..." A montage of Rian and me in fifty million positions over the last twenty-four hours rolls through my mind. All our jagged edges fit together like puzzle pieces. "Good."

"Yeah, I know, I'm not deaf."

I chuckle and head to my office, passing Frankie's station.

"Hey, boss. I heard you got your head out of your ass."

I look over her shoulder to see a butterfly with three Greek letters underneath. The girl she's working on looks me over. A look that, once upon a time, would've had me sliding a chair next to Frankie and shooting the shit.

"I did. She'll be here shortly to give you all the details, I'm sure."

"Can't wait." Frankie chuckles. "Oh, I had no one for Jolie. She's coloring in your office. Sorry."

"My favorite girl." I wink to her to let her know it's okay.

As I walk away, I overhear the girl asking Frankie if we're a couple.

Frankie, being Frankie, says, "Hell no, he's my boss. He's taken by a gorgeous blonde who's a brilliant mathematician."

I smile all the way back to my office. Who would've thought the word taken would sound so calming? Not me.

I'm on cloud nine until I open my office door to find Jolie with a crayon on my wall.

She freezes. Then she gives me that sweet smile of hers. "Uncle Dylan!"

She runs to me, so I bend down. When she wraps her little arms around my neck, I pick her up and squeeze her.

"You're a lucky girl we're so free with art around here." Which is true. Our welcome table has drawings from all the tattoo artists who have come through here. "Do you want paper or a coloring sheet?" I put her down.

"I have a coloring book." She holds up a coloring tattoo book. Of course. She kneels on the floor and opens the book, choosing to color an angel tattoo.

"Can I join you?" I ask, sitting on the couch and grabbing her crayons.

"Want to pick?" She hands me the book.

I scroll through and pull out a heart with angel wings and a banner across the front. Holding the crayon in my right hand feels weird. The fact that I miss inking so much I've resorted to coloring says the next five weeks are going to be a struggle.

Jolie joins me on the couch and cringes. "You're outside the lines."

"I'm a lefty, so I don't do much with my right hand," I say. And I don't say that her angel is all blue and she's outside the lines too.

"Mommy says to stay in the outline if I want to be like her when I grow up."

I chuckle. "Is that what you want to be when you grow up? A tattoo artist?"

"I want to be Mommy," she says, coloring a line on my page with her blue crayon. She giggles.

I watch her concentrate on her picture, pressing too hard. She's such a sweet kid but hasn't had the easiest life so far. She's heard and seen way more than she ever should at her age.

"Your mommy is pretty cool," I remark, exchanging my red for gold.

"Rian too," she says. "You like Rian?"

"Man, news gets around quick in these parts."

She giggles and slides down to sit on her knees on the other side of the coffee table, leaning forward and staring at me.

"Yeah, I like Rian."

"She's pretty like a princess," she says.

I nod. Jolie's right. Rian is pretty like a princess, and instead of being with a prince, she's chosen me, the commoner who wants to brand her with a tattoo drawn just for her.

"Mommy's not pretty like a princess," she says.

I laugh. Maybe they should make a princess doll with tattoos and an edge that would challenge any prince that came her way.

"Mommy doesn't like princess stories. She says there's no such thing as a prince and I need to be able to save myself. Be strong."

Only Frankie would lecture her kid about fairy tales, but I can't say I blame her.

"I don't really believe in all that 'prince saving the princess' stuff either," I admit as Frankie opens the office door.

Jolie's eyes widen. "Really?"

I shake my head. "I think sometimes both the princess and the prince need saving."

Her small eyebrows crinkle.

"Someday you'll understand," I say.

"Lecturing my kid on fairytales?" Frankie walks in and sits in my office chair. "Finally being productive, huh?"

"Can you tell I'm itching to do anything with art?" I continue to color outside the lines, shading the wings.

"Not bad for your right hand," she says.

"Look, Mommy. An angel." Jolie hands her picture to Frankie.

"I love it. It's beautiful. Remember you have all those colors though. See how Dylan uses more than one? You can too."

Jolie snatches back the picture.

"Only you would criticize a kid's coloring page."

Frankie shrugs, not offended in the least. "It's merely a suggestion." She winks at Jolie, whose face lights up.

Jolie takes the gold crayon from my hand and puts a halo on the top of the angel's head. Then she puts the gold down and takes out the blue one again.

"Blue is her favorite color," I say and Frankie nods.

"How do you spell Jax?" Jolie asks me, and I side-eye Frankie.

"J.A.X." I write it on the back of my paper so she can see the letters.

When she writes them, it looks more like UAT, but she gave it a try. Her name at the bottom is more legible but spaced so far apart it takes a minute to figure out what it is.

"Can I go out there?" she asks, knowing she's not allowed to run through the tattoo stations. The waiting area and my office are the only places she has free rein.

"He just finished," Frankie says, and Jolie bolts out of the room.

"And you?" I stand.

"The girl brigade is complete. I have an appointment in ten though. I hate to ask this on a Saturday night, but would you mind watching Jolie?" She cringes the same way Jolie did when she told me I color outside the lines.

"Sure. What else do I have to do?" Other than take out my girlfriend. "Mind if Rian and I take her to dinner?"

"Not at all. She'll give you a good idea of what it'll be like when you have your own kids." She laughs, and I throw a crayon at her back as she leaves.

Jolie runs back in and Frankie swoops her up. "He loved it. He hung it on the wall."

Frankie turns to me and I can't decipher the look on her face, but it's not one of happiness. "That's nice."

Jolie does a little shimmy to get Frankie to set her down.

"Go work, I got this," I say.

"Thanks, boss."

As Frankie leaves and I watch Jolie, my mind wanders to kids. I'm sure it's something Rian wants, and I used to think about back when I was a teenager, probably because I never had my own family. But now that I'm a grown man I know that kids are a lot of responsibility and you have to be a good role model. That thought is terrifying.

So I do what I do best and push it aside to deal with another day.

Chapter Twenty-Five

RIAN

I'M GETTING READY TO HEAD OVER TO INK ENVY WHEN THE APARTMENT DOOR opens—thanks to someone who obviously still has a key.

"Hello?" I call.

"We're very disappointed that we had to hear about you and Dylan from Seth." Sierra barges into the bathroom, almost making me hit my arm against the curling iron.

"I would've told you. It *just* happened."

Sierra hops up on the counter and Blanca sits on the toilet.

"This is huge. It deserved a text at the very least," Blanca says. "Hell, maybe even a picture."

Sierra and I look at her.

"Not a sex pic or a dick pic, just a picture of him in your bed or something." When we still look confused, Blanca waves us off. "Never mind."

Sierra wiggles to get comfortable. "Give us all the deets."

My blush comes quickly, reflected back to me in the mirror. "It just kind of happened. He said he's liked me for a while but was afraid to cross the line."

Blanca slaps her thigh. "I knew it."

"And the sex?" Sierra asks.

"Sex is good. Great actually."

"I figured as much." Sierra rolls her eyes, a silent reminder that I'm far from his first conquest.

"What else?" Blanca asks.

I shrug, pulling another chunk of hair to curl. "There isn't much. I'm going over to Ink Envy and we're going to dinner. Nothing seemed awkward this morning. He's very handsy and affectionate with me. It's just so…"

"Perfect," Blanca says, her lovesick eyes rolling to the back of her head.

"Is that scary? I feel like it's scary." I lay the curling iron on the counter and shake out my curls.

"Why would it be scary?" Blanca asks.

"You're waiting for something like the shoe to drop?" Sierra understands where I'm coming from.

"Ahh," Blanca says. "I get that. But maybe this is all turning out perfect because it's meant to be."

I nod, not really convinced. Regardless, I'm ecstatic Dylan's admitted he holds the same feelings I've harbored for him. And I'll live this out until that shoe drops.

Sierra's hand runs up and down my arm. "I thought the same thing with Adrian. You're very invested in Dylan. You always have been. Although this is great and we were all waiting for this moment, it's a big chance. A big step."

"Not making me feel better." I leave the bathroom for some space.

"I don't mean it like that, but you guys have a lot to lose. At the same time, I think you guys are great friends who won't allow this to tear apart your friendship if it didn't work out."

"I'm not sure we should think about the negative right now. It's way too early," Blanca says. "Rian." She takes my hands in hers. "When is the last time you lived in the moment? Without thinking about the future?"

She's right. Never. Never except when I confronted Dylan yesterday. My life has always had a plan, whether it was my mom's or my own. I was taught that there's always somewhere or something I should be striving for. There's always more to achieve.

"You're right," I say. "My fear of the future could keep me from enjoying the here and now if I let it."

Blanca and Sierra smile.

"Exactly," Blanca says.

"It could be nothing goes wrong, or if it does, you get through it." Sierra opens up the bottle of wine they must've brought over. "Who would've ever thought Adrian would get the rules changed so he doesn't have to rule?"

She's right, but my worry isn't over something we'll have to face together. It's Dylan that feels unpredictable to me. He went from zero to one hundred in a night.

My friends stare at me as though they want to know my thoughts, but I'm going to keep these to myself.

"I'm good, guys, really."

Sierra pours the wine. "Then let's celebrate. You waited long enough, so enjoy that fine piece of ass."

We all laugh, clinking our glasses to toast the future.

I walk into Ink Envy. Jax tattoos a girl's back as she's sprawled on his table on her stomach. Frankie works on a guy's chest, and Lyle's head is buried in his sketchbook.

"What's up?" Lyle nods and starts drawing again when he sees it's me. "Dylan is letting me tattoo him."

"That's cool. Tonight?" I ask. Lyle isn't the first to apprentice under Dylan. Everyone gets to tattoo him at some point.

He looks up with a smirk. "No. He said he had plans." His gaze sweeps over me. "I assume you're his plans."

"He's got two girls tonight," Jax says.

My heart constricts so tightly, I feel as if it's going to stop beating.

Frankie gives him a death stare. "Jolie is here," she says to me. "Way to give the girl a heart attack," she says to Jax.

"I only speak the truth."

The girl on her stomach stares lovingly over her shoulder at him. How he's able to work with some girl drooling over him like that, I have no idea.

"They're in the office," Frankie says.

"Thanks." I walk to the back.

"I do expect details at some point," Frankie says, her tattoo machine moving along the skin with skilled precision.

"We'll do lunch."

"What do you really need to know? They're fucking. I can record her moans and his grunts as proof if you'd like. I think I counted ten 'oh my gods' this morning." Jax smiles at me, not seeming upset in the least. He must see something else in my eyes though. "Relax, I'm good."

I nod and disappear down the hallway.

"You can't just take the phone," Dylan says. "You have to ask. I was on a call."

"But *Paw Patrol*," Jolie whines.

It's late for her. She's probably ready for bed.

I walk through the doorway, Dylan looks up, relief clear in his demeanor and his eyes. "Heaven sent us an angel," he says, pointing at me.

"Rian!" Jolie runs at me.

I pick her up, situating her on my hip. "I heard you had a great babysitter tonight." I tap my finger on her nose.

"Uncle Dylan won't let me watch *Paw Patrol*."

Our gazes shift to him, and he blows out a breath. "I had Jax's client on the phone. He wanted to cancel for tonight. I'm arguing with him that he forfeits his deposit and she stole my phone to put on that talking dog show."

Jolie's head falls on my shoulder and her fingers play with my long hair.

Dylan points at her. "Don't let that sweetness put your guard down."

I hug her tightly. "I guess our dinner is takeout?" I sit down in the chair next to his desk, Jolie situating herself so she's straddling me with her head on my shoulder.

"I was hoping you'd be my dinner." He waggles his eyebrows.

"That's very inappropriate now, although I will take a raincheck."

He slides his chair over to me and kisses me.

"Ew." Jolie's hand moves to his face, pushing it away.

"See, she's sweet." I chuckle.

He kisses her forehead before falling back down into his chair. "Chinese, Mexican, or pizza?"

I shrug. "I'm game for whatever."

"Pick one." He's desperately trying to use his mouse with his right hand, but every time he has to click on something, he hits the wrong selection.

I stand from the chair, trying not to disturb Jolie since she's growing limp in my arms. "Sit down." I point at the chair I was just in.

"I like you bossy," he says, sitting in the chair.

I transfer Jolie to him. Her eyes open but fall closed again right away. Cradled in his good arm, she wraps her arms around his neck.

"Well, that was a bad move," I say, sitting in his office chair to take control of the order.

"Why? She's still asleep," he says, oblivious to how good he looks with a baby, especially a little girl, in his arms.

"Yeah. On you."

He looks down at her. "She's much more tolerable now."

Having been friends with Dylan for years, I can order our Chinese food by heart. I order some extra for the employees so everyone can eat since that's something he'll want.

"That's not it," I singsong, clicking the items he loves.

I sneak another peek at him. He scrunches his eyebrows. God, Dylan holding a child should be illegal. The image could cause ovaries to explode everywhere.

"It's you and her." I open my eyes wider at him. "Your attractiveness meter just went into overheating range with her asleep in your arms."

He smiles and looks at Jolie. "She's not mine."

"She doesn't have to be."

His smile grows. "So this does it for you, huh?"

I click the moo shu pork and sit back, examining them. His legs are spread open in a casual stance with his broken arm resting on the chair arm. Jolie's face is tucked into his chest.

"Pretty much." I slide the chair back to the computer.

"Make sure to get enough for everyone," he says, ignoring my confession.

I've never really thought about having a kid with Dylan. Mostly my time has been spent imagining him in bed, but not really as a boyfriend. I have no expectations of what our relationship will be like. There's only one stipulation I have and that's monogamy.

"I did. Are Seth and Knox stopping by?" I ask.

"I don't know, but I don't need to feed their asses. My credit card is on file."

"I see that." I click the final button and check out using his credit card. "You're a very generous tipper."

"Am I?" he asks. "Maybe I should give you a tip for doing the ordering?"

I flutter my eyelids. "Sounds promising."

"You should give me a peep show."

"No!" I point at Jolie. "She's right there."

He follows my vision. "She's dead asleep."

I stand in front of him and look at him one more time. "You have me at a disadvantage. I want to snap a picture just to relive you and Jolie like that."

He shakes his head, and his smile doesn't reach his eyes. In Dylan language, that means something is bothering him.

"Does that scare you?" I ask.

His lips purse and he shakes his head. Same reaction I got when I told him I was going out with Jax.

"I think it might," I say.

"No. But—"

I put up my hand. "Your hot level going up because you're holding her does not mean I want to have your baby."

"Really? Are you sure?"

I laugh. "What? Of course! Why would you ask me if I'm sure?"

He stares at Jolie and I step forward to take her, but he shakes his head. "I got her. Keep drooling."

I cross my arms and wait for him to answer my question.

He blows out a breath. "You're a girl who thinks about the future."

I laugh again and he gives me a blank stare. "Sorry, continue," I say.

"Now I seem like an arrogant prick."

I nod.

"It's just you're you. All life plans and timetables. I figure you've planned out our wedding and how many kids you want."

"Maybe I'm using you for your body," I say, raising an eyebrow.

A smirk indents his adorable face. "Nah, it's not that great." He crooks his finger for me to come to him.

"You think just because you beckon, I should answer your call?"

The office door opens, and Frankie stands there, watching us before her eyes land on Jolie. "I had a feeling she'd crash. I'm between clients."

She swoops up Jolie and carries her out of the room, shutting the door. Dylan takes that as his opportunity to corner me, and he successfully gets my back to the wall.

"Look, I came to you." He locks me with his hips, and his pants do nothing to hide his hard length. "So I'm wrong then?"

"I don't have us married in my mind. I'm not pregnant, and there's no white picket fence house in my head. I'm in this to see where it goes. I have no preconceived ideas. Okay?" I place my hands on his cheeks, and he nods. "So relax."

He stares at me. "One day at a time sounds good. I am slowly becoming addicted to you."

"Cheesy!" I scream.

But he swallows my yell, and we spend the next twenty minutes making out like teenagers until Lyle tells us the food is here.

Chapter Twenty-Six

DYLAN

THREE WEEKS LATER, I'M ON THE COUCH, WATCHING *SUPERBAD* WITH SETH. MY phone is out and I'm looking at a picture I can't stop staring at—Rian and Jolie asleep on the couch a few weeks earlier. I didn't understand why me holding a baby made Rian so gaga until Frankie and I came home that night and found the scene on my screen.

When Frankie went to the bathroom, I snapped the picture before we woke Rian. After that, my fear of having a family dissipated and I can't stop staring at the picture and thinking what if we do make it long term? A baby on Rian looks like home.

Rian's bedroom door swings open and she raises her hand in victory. "I did it!"

She's holed herself up in that room for two days trying to finish that math problem.

"You solved it?" I tuck my phone away and open my arms.

She runs across the room and throws herself into the chair with me, wrapping her arms around me and kissing my neck. "I think. I won't know until Dr. Giroux looks at my email."

"Way to go." Seth raises his beer.

She kisses me one more time then tries to slide off my lap, but I wrap my right arm—which has become strong in the past weeks—around her to keep her in place. Seth tries to concentrate on the television as though he's not witnessing our affection.

But as always, the more I have of Rian, the more I crave. Is this what all those guys who I made fun of for being pussy whipped felt like? That all they want to do is spend their time with their girl?

I capture her lips and turn us in the chair to block us from Seth, sliding my tongue into her mouth to tide me over until we're alone again. When we're done, Rian gets up and I smack her ass.

"Hey, you should know things are going south with Knox and Leilani," Seth says.

Rian stops walking toward the kitchen and sits down on the arm of my chair. I take the opportunity to slide my hand up her shirt to touch her bare back, my fingers gliding along her skin.

"What happened?" she asks Seth, sounding concerned.

Seth shrugs. "I heard them fighting. Leilani was saying she's going back home to Hawaii. Knox asked when she'd be back."

"And?" Rian asks, much more interested than me.

Knox is a great friend, but I always knew it would end this way. When a girl like Leilani breezes in and out of your life, at some point you have to see her for what she is—temporary. But for some reason, Knox is head over heels and all that rational thinking that's made him a great cop, flies out the window and travels over the Atlantic Ocean when Leilani walks back into his life. After she's gone, I'll be on the bar stool next to him once again, handing him shots to get over her.

"I didn't hear anything else, but when he went to work, she left too," Seth said. "And I haven't seen her yet today."

"She probably bailed again," I say, my hand venturing higher up Rian's back and under her bra strap. How far can I get before Seth notices? I've missed her these past two days as I gave her space to finish the problem. It's not even the sex I miss, as pathetic as I sound. It's just holding her naked body to mine. Making her laugh. And okay, I can't lie—I do miss the sex.

Rian turns to me, her forehead scrunched. "Again?"

Seth raises his eyebrows. I guess he thought all the girls knew. "They've weaved in and out each other's lives more than a crocheted scarf."

Rian's shoulders sag because she believes in happily ever afters. But Knox and Leilani don't have it in them. Rian and I might be different, but Knox and Leilani are on opposite sides of the spectrum. Something neither of them have realized yet.

"I knew they knew each other, but I didn't realize they'd gotten together and apart so many times."

Seth sips his beer. "She's run out on him before. A few years ago when he was drunk one night, he talked about her."

"They're just different," I say, not wanting to get into Knox's business.

"We're different," Rian says, her blue eyes so transparent.

"You don't want to see the world. And I'm not a black-and-white kind of guy. Leilani's a wanderer and Knox is a creature of habit. Explain how those two kinds of people can stay together." My whole hand runs along her skin now. "I believe in opposites attract, but sometimes there can be too much opposite."

Seth nods as though he understands, but Rian's lips tip down.

"I feel bad for him. Do you think she's gone for good?" Rian asks.

As she asks, the door of our apartment opens and Knox walks in, still wearing his uniform. He ignores Rian and me, his sole focus on Seth. "Did she leave a note?"

"Not that I saw," he says.

Knox nods, and his eyes meet mine. His authoritative finger points at me as if I said or did something. "I don't want to fucking hear it."

Knox slams the door behind him, and Rian turns to me.

Seth sips his beer. "Can I stay here tonight?"

"The couch is yours," Rian says.

"Or my bed," I offer.

Rian smiles. I feel bad for Knox. I saw the heartbreak Leilani left behind last time, which was why I wasn't so keen on her reappearance in his life. Still, tonight I'll hold Rian a little tighter.

I wrap my arms around Rian's waist, swiping the chocolate frosting from the bowl and holding my finger in front of her mouth.

"You do know this is taking me twice as long, right?" she says.

I don't move my finger. She puts her mouth over it, twirling her tongue around it. Just like that, my dick pops up in my pants like a timer in a turkey.

"Let's take the bowl to the bedroom," I suggest.

"And leave the cake bare?"

The timer goes off, so she dislodges from my arm to take the cake out of the oven.

"Sure. I say we frost you instead." I swipe another finger of frosting when she's not looking and eat it myself. Damn, she really is a great baker. "Any word from that professor guy?"

"No. I got the receipt that the email went through, but he was out of the office." She puts the cakes on a cooling rack.

"I still think you should do something you love with that money if you're the first one who solved it. Like, I don't know… open up a chocolate-and-chocolate cake shop."

She laughs. "That's the only cake I make?"

I nod and steal another swipe of frosting. "Yeah, because you love your boyfriend so much. But then again, maybe you should serve everything except the chocolate-chocolate because this cake is only for me since I'm the most special person in your life."

"I think I could still sell the chocolate-chocolate cake but give you something no one else gets." She looks coy, like she wants to play.

I've never come across a game I didn't want to conquer. "Like?"

She strips off her shirt and unhooks her bra. "How much frosting can you lick off me?"

"Oh, you have no idea how much I love this frosting and your body. It's like when someone decided to put peanut butter and chocolate together. Perfection." I grab the bowl. "Let's go."

"Your bed though." She places her hand on my chest. "So we can sleep in mine afterward."

I unzip my hoodie, leaving it on the floor, and back her toward my bedroom. "I love that you can be spontaneous but still think of the aftermath."

She giggles and dips her finger into the frosting, then traces a line down her tit and around her nipple. We open my door, she falls to my mattress, and I kick the door shut, my mouth watering and ready to work its way over Rian's body. I bring my mouth to her chest, and with the first swipe of my tongue, she shivers under me.

"Oh, Dylan," she says.

Once I'm done sucking one tit, I swipe the frosting on her other one and mimic my move. Traveling a line from her tits to the top of her waistband with my tongue, I unbutton her jeans and slide the zipper down. I help her get her jeans and panties off. Once she's naked in front of me, I stare at her, still surprised she's mine.

"What are you waiting for?" She props up on her elbows as though something's wrong. "You okay?"

I nod. "Yeah, I'm great."

After dipping my finger into the frosting, I bring my finger to her mouth and she moans around it. Instead of spreading the frosting anywhere else on her body, I fall to my knees and pull her legs over my shoulders.

"I did have plans of licking frosting off you." She watches me slide my tongue up her folds. "But we have time, I suppose."

Her back falls back on the bed.

"That's what I thought." I chuckle into her center, blowing cool air on the flesh I wet with my tongue, and she squirms.

After only the short time we've been together, I know what gets her off. She loves clit play, so I flex my tongue, using only the tip to lick tiny circles around her nub. Her hands go to her sides, gripping the sheets. At least my right hand can widen her, putting light pressure right under her clit, and her back arches off the bed.

I fucking love watching her get off.

The more pressure I use, the more she grinds against my face. My name comes from her mouth, along with praise of how great I am at this, how she never wants me to stop. I watch her chase her orgasm on my tongue, and my dick grows thick and aching between my legs.

I ramp up the speed a touch more. One of her hands grabs my hair, pulling and tugging, as her breathing labors. She's so close, so I up the speed until she unapologetically grinds my face into her pussy. She crests over that threshold and falls back down on her back.

It takes some awkward effort on my part but I remove her legs from my shoulders, ditch my track pants, and nudge her legs open. Her eyes perk up when she feels the tip of my dick at her opening. But she presses her hand to my chest.

"Oh no, you don't," she says, pushing me to sit up.

I sit back on my knees. "What?"

She grabs the bowl of frosting and swipes a smear across my chest. "I get to play too." Her gaze dips to my very erect cock.

I sit back. "By all means."

Her tongue slides along my chest, teasing my nipples. My eyes close, relishing her mouth, until she palms me, rubbing and pulling, her thumb spreading the pre-cum along the tip of my dick. As she slides off the bed and falls to her knees like I did, she urges me to the edge of the mattress. With one hand on the base of my cock, she lowers her mouth, and stars fill my vision.

Damn, is there anything Rian isn't good at? She really is a certified genius.

Chapter Twenty-Seven

RIAN

As I stare at my computer and read the message again, tears well up in my eyes.

"Congratulations, you're the winner. Your check will be issued next week, and your name will be listed in our academic journal next month. Great job, everyone at the association is very impressed. Sincerely, Dr. Giroux, President of the Mathematics Association of America.'" I read the email out loud, still processing that I actually did it.

Jax walks out of his bedroom, spots me, and freezes. "Shit." He turns to go back but then faces me again. "Where's Phillips?"

"He's asleep," I say.

"In which bedroom?" His gaze flickers to Dylan's door then mine.

"Mine," I say, not understanding what's wrong with him.

"Thank fuck." He walks through the living room to the bathroom and shuts the door.

Odd.

I minimize the email, seeing three from my dad waiting in my inbox. Apologies for what he said mostly. I should print out the congratulatory email and go to their house and tape it to every available surface. Maybe then they'd be proud of me. But a part of me doesn't want anyone to know I won.

My phone rings and I jump in my seat.

My eyes zero in on the name. Johann must've gotten word that the problem was solved and the contest closed. Ever since that day I was going to ask him for help and Dylan talked me out of it, he hasn't contacted me. Which suits me fine.

My phone beeps that he left a message, then an email from him pings on my computer. He's probably upset that the contest has been closed and is wondering if I'm the one who solved it.

The bathroom door opens and Jax walks out in a towel. "So you're still together?"

"Yes," I say.

He nods. "Cool." He disappears into his bedroom.

What is up with him?

I look at the box of tissues next to my computer. He thought I was crying over Dylan?

I shut down my computer, walk into my bedroom, and set my phone on the nightstand, then I slide under the covers with Dylan. He stirs, sighs, and wraps his arm around my body.

"Good morning," he murmurs, kissing my forehead.

I run my hand down his chest. "Good morning."

I lay with him as he falls in and out of sleep. Peeking up, I cast small kisses to his chest. "I won," I whisper.

He bolts up and my body falls to the mattress. Looking at me, his eyes widen. "You did?"

I nod.

Then his body is on top of mine "Congratulations! That's awesome."

I nod again but the tears well up even more this time and my throat constricts.

He stares at me in confusion. "Why are you crying?"

I sit up and rest my back on the headboard, shrugging because I have no idea why I'm crying.

Sitting next to me, he pulls me into him. "This is a good thing. A happy moment. You should be on cloud nine."

My tears run down his chest while my fingers follow an intricate tattoo on his thigh. Maybe it's because Dylan and I were friends before we got together, or maybe because Dylan is kind of a private person, but we rarely ever talk about our feelings other than toward one another. I'm not sure how he'll take me opening my heart and laying all my problems out in front of him. This might not be what he signed up for.

"Talk to me," he says.

I sigh. "I'm happy. But I'm upset too. I did it as a big FU to my parents, but I never thought I'd feel this good about doing it."

"Then why the crying?"

I sit up on my knees and face him. "When my parents find out, they're going to be so happy. Like I made their world."

"They are your parents," he says, but he doesn't understand.

"All I've ever done is disappoint them. No matter all the great things I've accomplished, it's never been enough. I think I'm upset because I did this to prove to them I could do it, but all that will happen now is they'll demand more. When will it stop? When will it ever be enough just to be their daughter?"

He takes my hands. "I know you did this for them, but be happy for yourself. And do what you want with that twenty-five grand. I'm not joking that I think you should open a bakery. But do what you want to do. Your parents will always be your parents. I don't have a lot of experiences with parents, but at some point, you have to stop looking for their praise."

"I'm not looking for their praise," I say, sitting down and loosening my hands to lay limp in my lap.

"Truth is, you kind of are. You might've done it with a middle finger, but you did it to prove to them you're smart."

I narrow my eyes. So much for him understanding. "That's not true."

My phone rings with my parents' ringtone.

He brings his knees up to his chest. "They're going to find out, and you're right, they're going to expect more from you. The question is how important is it to you?" His phone goes off on the nightstand and he slides out of bed. Staring at the name, he silences it. "I don't say it to be mean, but you chase their approval. Except for me, I imagine. They probably don't know we're dating, right?"

I sit on the bed, crossing my legs. That balloon I was floating on pops.

He leans over and kisses my cheek. "I'm going to take a shower. Call them and get it over with."

As the door shuts with his departure, I stare at my hands. Is Dylan right? Maybe he is. I slide off the bed, grab my phone, and dial my parents.

They both answer.

"Was it you? We heard that Johann didn't solve it, but someone did." My mom acts as if she's been waiting to find out if a loved one came of surgery okay. This isn't life or death.

I say, "I'd like to set up a dinner. Us and my new boyfriend."

"Sweetheart, did you not hear your mother?" my dad asks.

"Did you not hear me?" I snip.

"Fine. We'll do a dinner, but answer the question," my mom says.

"My boyfriend is Dylan. We've been seeing each other for a few weeks."

"Well, we've met Dylan, sweetheart," my dad says. "And I hoped you were dating him since you were kissing him."

"He's in a different role in my life now. I want you to have dinner with him as my boyfriend."

"This is ridiculous. Answer the question, Rian. Did you solve the problem?" My mom's last ounce of patience runs out.

Part of me wants to tell them no, that it wasn't me, but they won't stop until they find out. Then I'd have a whole other host of problems. "I did."

"You did?" my mom's shocked voice says she didn't have a lot of faith in me.

"Yes."

"Oh, my God. Okay. Okay." My mom can't get a hold of her breath.

"You okay there, honey?" my dad asks. "Are you hyperventilating?"

"I'm good. We'll call you back. I have to call the Fredericksons. Plan the dinner or whatever you want."

"Way to go, sweetheart," my dad says right before the line dies.

I turn off my phone and sit on the edge of the bed.

Dylan is right. I'm allowing them to treat me like this, and I'm the one who needs to make it stop.

Dylan's acting weird. He left to go to work with only a small peck on my lips. Usually I have to push him out the door. As I enter Ink Envy with a dinner for everyone, I'm not sure what I'll be walking into. But I didn't plan on finding Dylan on a table with Lyle holding a tattoo machine to his calf. An array of girls are circled around, asking Dylan a million questions.

"Hey, babe," Frankie says, looking up as she tattoos some guy.

"Forget Phillips. I'm starving," Jax says from behind the table in the front.

I set the boxes of pizza on the counter. Dylan doesn't even notice that I walked in. A redhead on his right paws at his arm, asking questions about his tattoos. He still hasn't seen me, and it probably says something about my trust level that I prefer it that way.

"What are we doing?" Jax leans forward, putting his chin in his palm and staring at the scene.

"Just observing," I say.

Dylan moves his arm so her finger falls off, and he explains nicely about the tattoo.

"Observing if he's flirting?" Jax asks.

I look at him and his eyebrows are raised. I wave Jax off and he chuckles, sitting back down.

"Asking for trouble," he says, picking up the journal thing I've seen him carrying around lately.

The redhead blocks my view again as Dylan lifts his T-shirt to show some tattoo that they're talking about. Her hand reaches out to touch him, but he drops the T-shirt and says something to her that makes her face red. She goes to stand next to her friends.

"And you thought you couldn't trust the guy," Jax says, shaking his head. His feet fall with a thud on the floor. "Lack of trust is the number one killer of a relationship."

"Shut up. I was just..."

He raises those damn eyebrows at me again.

I sigh. "So sue me."

"Hey, Phillips," Jax calls, and Dylan peeks up. "Your girl is here."

"Come here. I'm letting Lyle tattoo me." Dylan waves me over. When I get to the table, he cradles my cheek, kissing me so deep that my knees actually weaken. "I missed you. These are Lyle's fans," Dylan says, winking at me.

I nod. Yeah, right.

After Lyle finishes the small tattoo, the girls—who found out Dylan is off the market—are chatting in the waiting area. He gets up off the table and stands in front of me.

"Can we talk?" I ask.

Dylan tilts his head, but we both know things weren't comfortable this morning. I can't help but think it has to do with my parents. One thing I know about Dylan is that the future scares him. Like when he thought I was ready to walk down the aisle and pop out a bunch of babies. Or when I flippantly made a comment about going on a vacation together next year when a commercial came on. Other than a joke about a nude beach, I got nothing.

"Sure." Dylan grabs one pizza box and nods toward his office.

"Thanks, Rian!" Frankie smiles. "And no little people in there to stop you from doing whatever you want to do."

I laugh.

Once we're behind closed doors, Dylan drops the pizza on his desk and sits, patting his lap. "What's up?"

I sit down and put my arms around his neck. "We're okay?"

"Yeah." He tucks a strand of hair behind my ear. "We're great. Why?"

"Just this morning. When I said you were wrong about my parents… it felt weird after."

He runs a hand up and down my outer thigh. "I shouldn't have given you advice. What do I know about parents?"

"You were right. When I called them and told them about us dating and how I wanted to plan a dinner, all my mom cared about was whether I won. As soon as I told her I had, she hung up to call Johann's parents."

He frowns. "I'm sorry. But I still think you should celebrate for yourself."

I nod.

"Hey." He squeezes my thigh. "I'm taking you out tomorrow. A fancy restaurant where we toast to your accomplishment."

"We don't have to." I look away.

He puts his finger under my chin, bringing my gaze back to him. "Yes, we do."

I smile and rest my head on his shoulder. "Thanks."

"You're my girl. This is boyfriend duties, right?"

I chuckle and kiss the hollow of his neck. I guess it doesn't matter how many small things come up as long as we get through them. That's what makes a strong couple.

Chapter Twenty-Eight

DYLAN

THE DAY HAS FINALLY COME. RIAN AND I SIT IN THE DOCTOR'S OFFICE, WAITING for him to come in and take off this damn cast.

Rian sits in a chair against the wall. "I want you to prepare yourself, because once I have use of both arms, all bets are off. You will be thoroughly fucked tonight."

She giggles and crosses her legs. "You'll hear no complaints from me."

"You might once you see what I can do with two hands." I wink, and she blushes.

Our relationship is going strong. I still can't get enough of her. She received her prize money and her name will be published in that scholar journal, which I know will be a big moment for her. We celebrated her success without talking about what she would do next. She's denied her parents' calls and emails and even told Jax to tell them she wasn't home when they stopped by. I'm trying to stay out of it because I don't know shit about parent issues.

Rian's voice draws me from my thoughts. "I say we ditch the celebratory lunch and head right home then."

"Cool. You are my favorite food," I say as the doctor knocks and then pushes the door open.

Rian purses her lips, and I chuckle. The doctor's cool enough to say a quick hello then wash his hands, pretending he didn't overhear me. The man understands what I'm talking about.

"Okay, let's get this cast off. I will warn you—your arm is going to smell pretty bad. We'll wipe it down before you leave. And you've probably lost some muscle strength that you'll need to build back up." He sits on his chair and wheels it toward me.

The nurse comes in moments later, smiling and putting on a pair of gloves.

Rian stands and comes to my side. Usually this is the type of situation where I'd be alone. Maybe Seth would've tagged along, but it's nice to have someone who cares for me. Not that Seth doesn't care, but he'd laugh his ass off if they sawed into my arm. It's a different kind of caring.

She grabs my right hand, running her free hand up and down my arm. "What do you think your tattoos look like under there?"

Fuck. How did I not think of that? "Let's hope not wrinkly as shit."

The doctor looks up over the rim of his glasses. "You'll gain the strength back right away. We'll give you some exercises to do at home."

I look at Rian and she shakes her head. Amazing how she can read my mind. But she's right—I plan on getting muscle strength back during my workouts with her. Squeezing tits, squeezing ass, finger fucking—it's all on the agenda.

As soon as the cast comes off, I gag, staring at my arm. Where is my awesome forearm with corded muscles and unbelievable ink? This scrawny, pale limb does not belong to me.

"Uh." Rian chokes on the bile that is probably running up her throat when the smell hits her. "That's horrible." But she never lets go of my hand.

"You want to wait outside?" the nurse asks.

I release her fingers because damn, that's worse than when Seth left milk in the fridge for four months.

"No." She swallows and tries to smile but fails miserably. "I'm good." She kisses my cheek then coughs in my ear.

"Man, she's a keeper, huh?" the nurse says, grabbing wipes and running them down my arm.

The doctor holds up the cast. "Do you want to keep it?"

"Hell no."

He laughs and puts it on the counter. "You'll need to head down to the X-ray department so we can have one last look, but I don't expect any issues. It was a clean break. Once you're done there, come back here and let the receptionist know you're here. If there's an issue, we'll call you back into the room. Otherwise, she'll let you know you're free to go."

"These are the instructions," the nurse says, passing Rian a piece of paper. "Like the doctor said, he'll gain strength back quickly. He's young. But in case any of these things occur, he should come back in."

I look at Rian and the nurse. "I am still here, right?"

The nurse laughs. "I've found it better to give the girlfriend the directions."

I shake my head and snatch the instructions out of Rian's hand. But Rian asks a few questions I didn't really think about. Like signs of anything bad and how much pressure I can put on the limb now and of course she's my girl because she asks about sexual activity and what precautions to take. She does it all without one hint of pink in her cheeks.

After I'm done, we all file out. I can't stop flexing my hand open and shut, trying to work some of the stiffness out.

"See you after the X-ray," the receptionist says.

We smile and wave, and it's clear as we walk through the waiting room to the elevators, we're a *we* now. A couple. It should terrify me. I've never liked the idea and responsibility of being a we.

But as Rian reads over the instructions in the elevator, I stare at her. That sliver of tongue rests between her lips when she's reading, and I realize that I kind of like being a we.

Who would have thought? Sure as hell not me.

A couple of weeks later, Rian walks into Ink Envy on a Monday evening. I asked her here under the ruse of helping me with my paperwork, saying I needed her math expertise. But first, I made sure to work the entire weekend—my girlfriend wasn't going to be my first tattoo after my arm finally felt better. I took the full two weeks before I felt confident enough to mark someone's skin.

"What's all this?" she asks staring at the row of candles on either side of the aisle leading to my station.

"Lock the door behind you," I say.

She turns and flicks the lock. I've already shut the blinds so no one can see what's about to transpire.

"I thought we were doing your paperwork?"

"Well, if you'd rather."

She shakes her head. "I look horrible. You should've warned me."

She pulls her ponytail out of her hair and shakes out the strands. But I wanted her in comfortable clothes, so I'm glad she's wearing her yoga pants and T-shirt with a sweatshirt over.

"Warned you about what?" I slide my chair over to her and my hands land on her hips, my lips pressing to her stomach.

"This romantic evening you have planned."

I rest my chin on her stomach and look up at her.

Her fingers weave through my hair. "What did you plan?"

I pat my table. "Sit down."

She smiles and slides up. It's not her first time on my table. Last Saturday night after we closed, she was on the table, and let's just say I had to heavily sanitize it afterward.

"This is not a repeat of last Saturday," I say, and she pouts. I pull out my sketchbook, shielding it from her eyes. "Are you serious about wanting a tattoo?"

Her eyes light up and she stares at the sketchbook, wiggling her ass on the table. "Is that it? My drawing?"

I nod and she squeals, both hands reaching out.

"Gimme," she says like a child. I hand her the sketchbook and her jaw falls open. "But?"

Standing, I cradle her neck with my hand. "I drew this for you. I didn't have the guts to tell you that day, but this is for you. It's always been for you. It's a peony, and it represents wealth and happiness. But it also means beauty and fragility. According to the Japanese, peonies symbolize risk taking. That you don't get big rewards without big risks. So it's you, but it's also a little reminder to spread your wings and take the leap of faith sometimes."

Her eyes glisten with moisture. "I love it," she whispers.

"It's everything I see in you. Everything that makes me more addicted to you every day. But I want you to remember forever to stand out there on your own, out of the shadows, so everyone can see how beautiful, resilient, and strong you are."

Her hand covers mine and I dip my head for a kiss. But I end the kiss because if I don't, we'll never get to the tattooing.

"Do you trust me to put it where I want?" I murmur against her lips.

"I trust you fully." A tear slips from her eye and I wipe it away with my thumb.

How did we get here? How did my life change in a matter of months? She's ingrained herself into my life and my being. There's more transforming between us. I feel it, but I can't describe it.

"Take off your shirt and sweatshirt," I say.

She grabs the hem of both at the same time and tosses them over her head.

I reach across her chest and unhook her bra, kissing her one more time. "Lie on your left side."

She follows my directions and I pull out the transparency I already did because I knew she loved the peony when she saw it weeks ago. I just had to find the balls to tell her I was drawing it for her before we were anything.

"I'm going to try to make this as painless as I can, but it's your ribs, so just tell me if you need a break."

She nods. I hook up my phone to the shop speakers through Bluetooth and hit Play on a playlist I put together. It's sappy and romantic, but I've never been good with expressing my emotions with words, so I picked others to say them for me. "Bad Things" by Machine Gun Kelly comes through the speakers.

After putting on my gloves, I go to work as I would with any client—except her tits, out there on display, are more tempting. Maybe as long as I keep my eyes off of them, I'll be okay.

Once I'm all prepared, I slide the stool over, allowing my body to be closer to her than I would another client. We're not touching, but I'm hyper aware of her proximity. "I'm gonna start."

At the first touch of the needle, she jolts.

"You sure?" I ask.

She nods. "I'm sure. Sorry."

"Don't be sorry. If you—"

"I want it, Dylan. More than I've wanted anything. Well, except for you."

Talk about a line that melts the damn heart. She has to feel what I have the last few weeks. The way her smile makes a shit day exponentially better. Waking up to her every morning fills me with happiness from the second I wake. Every day, all I think about is how to brighten her day. To let her know in a small way how much I care for her.

I press the machine back to her skin, and this time, she relaxes. The songs stream through the speakers as I move the needle along her skin. There might be silence between us, but it's a comfortable silence. I'll never forget this moment until the day I die.

"Don't I have to heal afterward?"

"I'll put some ointment on and cover it."

"So you make this big romantic gesture with candles and a playlist of love songs, not to mention drawing a special tattoo just for me, and you won't be able to have sex with me afterward? Seems a little torturous," she says.

I wipe the tattoo and take the brief break to meet her gaze. "You underestimate my abilities again."

"Oh, so I am getting lucky tonight?" She smiles wide.

I kiss her briefly. "Definitely. There's always doggie."

She chuckles. "I'd say hurry up, but it will be on me forever."

The word forever catches me for a moment. Forever as in for life or eternity. Endless.

I have no idea what will happen with Rian and me. If she'll wake up one day and decide she wants the responsible guy. But she'll look at this artwork I'm inking every day and think of me.

I'm selfish enough to smile because it means I'll be part of Rian *forever*.

Chapter Twenty-Nine

RIAN

I LIFT MY SHIRT FOR THE MILLIONTH TIME IN THE PAST WEEK TO LOOK AT MY tattoo. It's a little crusty, but I can tell it's going to be beautiful once it's healed.

"You're making me jealous. I wish Ethan was a tattoo artist so he could draw on me." Blanca sips her wine.

We're up on the rooftop, waiting for the guys to return from getting stuff for a barbeque. We made all the sides, but for some reason, it's taking them forever to get the meat and alcohol.

"I think we should call the police." Sierra inspects her nails. "I'm starving."

"Knox is the police," I say, dropping my shirt and sitting down at the table with them.

"Do you think Ethan would be jealous if I asked Dylan or Jax to draw me something?" Blanca asks, scrolling through her phone.

Sierra and I exchange a look.

"Um… yeah," I say.

Blanca purses her lips and nods. "I figured."

My phone rings and it's a number I don't recognize, so I send it to voicemail, and we continue talking about Adrian being in Sandsal again. Sierra's worried that it's never going to end and there will always be a reason for him to be out there. Then she'll have to choose to leave her job in order to be with him.

My phone dings to alert me that I have a voicemail, so I excuse myself and walk to the other side of the roof to listen.

"Hello, Miss Wright. This is Dr. Ted Quinton with NASA. I understand from Dr. Giroux that you're the one who solved the problem in the contest his organization hosted. I'm very impressed and wanted to discuss the possibility of you coming to work for NASA. Please give me a call back so we can discuss further. Have a good night."

I hold the phone to my chest for a second then quickly dial back because this has to be a prank. What does NASA want with a math textbook writer?

"Miss Wright," he answers on the first ring.

"Um… hi, Dr. Quinton?"

"Yes, I'm so happy you called me back."

"Are you really with NASA?"

He chuckles. "I am." There's a pause. "I'm a good friend of Dr. Giroux and helped him make up that problem with the hopes we'd find a new recruit. It's an entry-level position, but we're always looking for new talent. I'd love to schedule a video call to talk more about it."

"You don't even know me," I say, still a little stunned that I'm actually talking to someone from NASA.

He chuckles again. "Rarely do we hear people questioning why we might offer them a job."

"I'm just surprised. I thought it was just the monetary prize. I had no idea it had anything to do with NASA."

"It didn't. But I always have my eye out for new talent. I understand you've been working at Pierson since graduation?"

"Exactly, so why would you want me?"

"Well, sometimes you find talent where you least expect to. It's why we like such contests. We find people like you."

"And where exactly is the job?" I ask.

"Houston. Is that a problem?"

My stomach drops and I grip the phone harder. "Um, no." Dylan's face flashes to mind.

"I'll tell you what. I'll have my assistant send you some paperwork that outlines the position and if you're interested we can chat a bit more then arrange a flight and stay for some time next week. I can show you what we have to offer."

"Okay," I agree in a daze.

"Great. It was a pleasure talking to you. Look for that email in your inbox tomorrow morning."

"Okay." I shake my head. "Yes. That's perfect. Thank you."

"Have a great night, Miss Wright."

"You too."

We hang up and I lower the phone, staring into the sun as it's setting. NASA wants to hire me? I remember when I had their posters up on my walls as a kid. When I thought I'd love to work there. My mom's idea, she hung those posters.

I look over the rooftop edge, far down at Ink Envy. Dylan's life is here. We've been together for such a short time; we'd never survive the distance. I'm not even sure we would try. But my heart constricts with the thought of losing him. I lift my shirt and look at my tattoo again. It brings me sadness it hasn't since I got it.

I sit back down at the table, Blanca and Sierra sit up straighter when they see my mood.

"What's up?" Sierra asks. "Who was that?"

I shake my head as the door to the roof opens and the guys file out. I force a smile, which isn't hard because Dylan pulls it from me. Now isn't the time to bring up a potential job that would make me leave Cliffton Heights anyway.

Each guy finds their girl. Ethan places Blanca's favorite wine on the table.

"Hey, babe, can you draw?" she asks him.

Ethan looks at Dylan. "I fucking hate you."

Dylan laughs, his face falling to my neck and kissing the skin there. "Sorry, man."

"I'll totally draw you a tat," Jax offers, starting up the grill.

"Yeah, no, you won't." Ethan cracks open a beer.

"Call Frankie. She'll do something," Dylan says, and Blanca beams.

"Man, you're turning all the girls on to ink now," Ethan says.

Dylan nudges me up, sits down, and pats his lap.

"Is that a no to helping on the grill then, Phillips?" Jax asks.

They've gotten along a lot better recently, even joking around, and Jax's become more comfortable in our group of friends.

"I have my hands full." Dylan whispers in my ear, "I only care about turning one girl on to ink—and all other things."

Shivers run up my spine.

"For the love of God, can we please have one dinner without the two of you making out?"

Dylan laughs. "Jealous, Sierra?"

"She's cranky because Adrian is late coming back," Blanca says.

Seth puts his arm around Sierra. "Want me to be his fill in?"

She shrugs him off and points at us. "Just be prepared—the sex does slow down at some point."

"Maybe Adrian just doesn't have the same insatiable appetite I do." Dylan kisses my neck while his hands massage any body part he can reach.

The man *is* insatiable, and I love it. But I know what Sierra is talking about. I've witnessed it with Ethan and Blanca. Not that they're not still super into PDA, but they've found a routine now—which looks nice too. I like the idea, but I'm not sure how Dylan feels about it.

"Believe me, he does. It's just the distance that sucks." Sierra leans back in her chair and pouts.

"It seems like he's never here," Knox says. "What's up with that?"

She sips her wine. "They're still figuring out how it will all work. His sister taking over, his parents' divorce. Hopefully after next month, he's here more than there."

The whole rooftop quiets except for Jax working the grill.

"Way to kill the mood, Sierra," Seth says.

She kicks him under the table as her phone dings. Fumbling to pick it up, she finally gets a hold of it, reads it, and stands, downing the rest of her wine.

"No burger for me." Sierra leans into Dylan and me. "I'm going to get nailed by my boyfriend."

Dylan laughs.

And she's gone before any of us can say anything else.

"It's like they're in a long distance relationship," Seth says.

"It's just temporary," I say, and Blanca nods in agreement.

Knox leans against the ledge, sipping his beer. From what I know, Leilani left because he said he would never do a long distance relationship. But I'm not even sure Leilani wanted one anyway.

"Fuck that. Never. I couldn't stay away from you that long." Dylan's arms wrap around my waist and he pulls me into him, licking my earlobe.

"Sometimes there's not a choice. Would you rather lose the person than do long distance?" Blanca asks, probably because we both feel the need to defend Sierra and Adrian.

"Believe me, there's no way long distance would work," Seth chimes in. "I mean, sure at first it's probably great sex when you get together, but then week after week, month after month, you're witnessing your friends with their significant others and the longing sets in. Soon fights happen because one of you can't make the trip to see the other. You're spending a fortune on airline tickets. Phone sex becomes dull and unfulfilling. Long distance doesn't work."

We all stare at him.

"You speaking from experience, Andrews?" Jax asks.

"No. Hell, my entire life has been in this town."

"And Evan Erickson lives here, so how do you know all this?" Ethan asks.

Seth throws his beer cap at Ethan. "You guys can stop with the whole 'I love Evan Erickson' thing. I haven't been friends with her since I was nine. I like my relationships smooth as butter. Creamy as vanilla ice cream. No rocky road for me."

Silence commences until Dylan clears his throat. "I'm with Seth. Long distance would never work for me."

I turn to him. I kind of agree, but I won't say anything because of Sierra. If you love the person, maybe you make it work. Their situation is temporary, they have an end date. But some couples don't, and I wonder how they make it work.

"I need sex too much," Dylan says and laughs, most everyone joining in. "And phone sex isn't gonna cut it." He smiles at me.

"What if you actually have strong feelings for the person? You'll throw it all away just because you can't have sex with them?"

Dylan's head rears back when he hears my tone. "Is there something you have to tell me?"

"No. I'm just saying sex isn't the be all end all for a relationship. There are a lot of other things that are more important." I stand, grab a bottle of wine, and pour myself a glass.

Dylan straightens in the chair. Jax eyes me at the cooler. Whatever. All these men who think that sex is the number one thing in a relationship annoy me.

"So you're telling me that you don't enjoy sex?" Dylan asks. "Because I think I have to call bullshit on that one. Being your boyfriend and everything, I'd know."

"Being your roommate, I can second that," Jax says. When I send him a scathing look, he turns back to the grill.

I sip a large portion of my wine. "I'm just saying there's more than sex. There are emotions, and not just the ones when you have sex. It makes me feel like all I am to you is a sex toy."

Dylan's chair slides back along the concrete and he stands.

"Whoa." Jax holds out his hand at Dylan as he makes his way over to me.

"Fuck off, Owens." Dylan takes my hands in his.

They're so warm and welcoming, tears slip from my eyes.

"Rian?" Dylan says in an authoritative voice I've never heard him use with me before.

I swipe my eyes. "It's nothing. I just want to know you're with me for more than a place to put your dick."

He draws back as though I slapped him. "I think you know you're more than that."

"But yet you wouldn't do long distance."

"I think this has gotten way too serious. We're all talking hypothetical. This wine is delicious," Blanca says, trying to save the evening.

"Beer's good too," Seth says.

Knox is staring at us as though he knows something, but he couldn't. Maybe he just sees the demise of a relationship similar to what he went through.

"Let's go downstairs." Dylan takes my hand.

I didn't want this fun night to end like this. When I don't move, Dylan turns back around, his eyes pleading for me to tell him what's going on.

I know Dylan. Sometimes I think I know him better than he does himself. The minute I tell him, he'll shut down. The Dylan I've fallen in love with these past months could disappear forever.

He says my name again like a plea.

"I got offered a job with NASA," I say.

And just like I predicted, Dylan drops my hand. "And where's it at?"

You could hear a pin drop on the roof.

"Houston."

Darkness covers his eyes for a moment, then a smile plasters his face. Not the genuine smile I've been blessed to see every day for months. It's the one he gives customers who annoy the fuck out of him. "You should take it. NASA? Wow, that's amazing."

His arms wrap around me and he pulls me toward him in a hug that holds no emotion. His hands don't linger under the hems of my clothes, and he doesn't kiss my neck or forehead. The hug is not a boyfriend hug; it's a goodbye hug.

Chapter Thirty

DYLAN

Rian has no idea how much I'm struggling not to leave this rooftop right now. My pretending that I want her to go because it's such an amazing opportunity isn't a front. I do want her to go. She's magnificent and she deserves the absolute best in life.

But as she sits on my lap and the breeze wafts her perfume to my nostrils, I want to stop the pain slicing me inside. The only way to do that is get drunk or get the hell out of here and away from her—the reminder of what I'm about to lose.

We finish the dinner that her news did ruin because I'm sour and she's concerned. The others continued bullshit lines of conversation just to fill in the awkward silence.

"Let's go." I nudge her off my lap and take her hand, walking her to the roof door. I need to know where her head is at. I don't stop until we're in our apartment and I flick the lock to give us at least a warning before someone barrels in here.

When I turn from the door, she's in the chair by the couch, her knees pulled up to her chest. "I didn't anticipate this."

I sit on the couch, my arms missing her in them. "You got the call today?"

She nods. "I'm just as surprised as you. I was going to wait to tell you until we were alone, but then all that conversation about a long distance relationship came up and I kind of lost it."

I pace the room, unable to sit still because my mind begs me to grab the keys to my bike and get the hell out of here.

"Are you taking it?" The fact that it takes her longer than a second to speak gives me my answer. I hold up my hand. "You are? So it's just a will I or won't I agree to a long distance relationship? Or do you not even want one?"

"I haven't decided anything yet. He's sending me information. He's flying me down to see what the job entails."

"It sounds to me like you're taking it."

She sits up straighter. "Where do you get that idea?"

"Because it's fucking NASA. Who turns down fucking NASA?" My voice grows louder, and I clench my fists at my sides.

"Who said I want NASA? I never did."

I roll my eyes and stare at her long and hard. Her eyes puddle with tears and my anger shatters. I fall to my knees at her feet, my hands gripping her hips.

"You act like I accepted the job," she says, her voice hiccupping. "Do you really think I want to leave you?"

If she heard my answer, she'd be mad. But doesn't this go along with everything else in my life thus far? Somehow, I'm always the one in the rearview mirror.

I raise my head. "You have to take it. It's a huge opportunity and I won't let you turn it down."

I've never spoken more truth. I'd die a million deaths for her happiness. That's how strongly I feel for her.

She runs her hands through my hair. "I'm not sure it's the opportunity I want."

"You have to consider it. You have to go down there and see what they're offering. You have to."

I lift her shirt, kissing her stomach. The tattoo makes me want to grip her harder. I want to beg her not to go, to stay here with me, but I can't do that. She deserves to be the shooting star.

"Can we please just talk about it later?" She slides down, straddling me on the floor.

Our limbs are as tight as vines around one another, our lips seeking the other's in short kisses as though we're testing if this is where we want this conversation to go. My hands slide up her back and lift off her T-shirt, my mouth exploring her lips, jaw, neck. I unhook her bra and she lets the straps slide down her arms. I toss it to the side.

She bends back, and I run my hand down the middle of her breasts, flicking open the button of her jeans. When I slide my hand under the hem of her panties, she moans and rises on her knees, her lips landing on mine. Our tongues tangle with desperate urgency, as though time is short. And it might be for the future, but not right here and now. I'm going to cherish her body.

I push my finger into her. For a moment, she stops kissing me, pulling back to enjoy the pleasure. Each time her gaze falls to me, my heart turns over.

"Dylan," she whispers.

A shot of electricity zings through me as she says my name like a plea. As though all her pleasure is in my hands and I'm the only one who can push her over the cliff of an orgasm.

Running my finger through her folds, I make small circles along her clit and I manage to ease her body down on the rug. With my other hand, my fingertips skim across her bottom lip. I'm unable to stop staring at her.

An animalistic lack of control comes over me and I need her now. I'm desperate to be buried deep inside her. I fall back on my ankles, bringing her jeans and panties off in one swoop.

Her hands run up my T-shirt. "I need to feel your body."

"Your tattoo."

She gazes down and smiles, climbing up on her knees to help me undress.

As soon as I'm naked, I sit with my back to the couch and she straddles me, sinking down on my length. Her warmth fills me from inside out. How can I live my life without this? I push out all feelings of impending doom and my hand slides to the back of her head, holding her in place as I kiss up her neck to her jaw. I capture her mouth with mine, sliding in my tongue.

Her nipples press against my chest as she rocks back and forth. There's no dirty talk tonight; we're going merely on touch. Feather-light touches leave shivers in their path like waves rolling onto the beach. Each caress has a deeper meaning than any words could describe.

My knuckles skim down her spine to her ass, which I take in my hands, molding and gripping and pulling upward.

"Please don't stop," she whispers. "I want to feel like this forever."

I ignore the hitch in her voice as our tempo increases and her moans turn from a submissive whimper to a groan. Since I love watching her come, I'm relentless on getting her off once I feel the sighs of her impending climax. She rocks harder, chasing the friction of her clit along my pelvic bone.

"That's it, baby."

Her love-filled eyes gaze down at me, her hands tightening on my shoulders, her nails digging in. My hips push up off the couch to get as deep inside her as I can. She cries out and the walls of her pussy tighten around my cock. There's no holding back tonight—my own orgasm comes right after and I spill inside her.

Her body falls to mine and her arms wrap around my neck like a scared child. I run my hands down her back.

I can do this. I can be mature about this because why would I ever chance losing something so good in my life?

Chapter Thirty-One

RIAN

I DIAL UP THE VIDEO CALL TO DR. QUINTON. AFTER HIS ASSISTANT SENT ME THE information on the position, I asked if he and I could talk before I headed down to Houston and she arranged this call. I purposely waited until Dylan was at Ink Envy because things are weird between us. We never talk about the job in Houston. He's quiet and withdrawn except for when we have sex, and then it's like a flood of emotions seep out of him. My heart races when he caresses my body with a longing look in his eyes as though I've already left.

Which is why I felt it was better to schedule this call when I was by myself.

Dr. Quinton answers the call. He's not at all what I pictured. I think I had an image in my head of an older version of Johann, with glasses and a thin frame. This man clearly works out and takes care of himself. Behind him is a framed picture of two blond kids and a woman who I assume is his wife.

"Miss Wright." His smile is bright and welcoming.

"Hi," I say, waving like a moron.

We exchange a few pleasantries about weather and our day. Summer is just on our horizon and I love the change of winter to spring to summer that we get in New York. When I tell him that, he says they get a different change of seasons down there.

"Have you had a chance to review the email?" he asks.

I pull out the paperwork I printed a few days ago. "I did. It's all pretty straight forward."

"Before we begin, I have a question."

"Okay." I look up from the paperwork.

The smile that's been so permanent you'd think it was sewn on his face isn't there anymore. "I wondered why you chose Pierson as your next step after your undergrad? You have some remarkable accomplishments. There are many places you could have gone. Why Pierson?"

"Um…" *Think, Rian.* If I could hit my head, I would. All I can think about is that I wanted to torture my parents, but that won't sound very mature.

"I don't mean to pry. I was just curious. If you'd rather—"

I'm not dumb—I need to answer this question if I want this job. Which I don't even know if I do. "I found Pierson at a job fair my senior year. I was unsure about going to graduate school, so I figured they'd be an interim."

That's the story I told my parents when my mom was appalled that I'd taken the job.

"What made you not pursue your master's? Are you still thinking about further education?" He sits straight with his fingers weaved together before he grabs a pen and poises it to paper.

"I think I got distracted but…" I got distracted by this life I live with Sierra, Dylan, Seth, and Knox. I put more effort into developing recipes than I did looking into graduate programs. "I think I would be interested in continuing my education."

He smiles and checks something off on his paper. "That's great. We do encourage continued education so that you can advance your position within our organization."

"Of course."

We go over some more questions about my education and my ambitions. He explains the job a little more.

"How about you come on out and you can tell me yes in person?" He laughs.

"I have to think about it," I say.

He sobers up and looks me square in the eye. I hold my breath. "Can I be candid, Miss Wright?"

"Please call me Rian," I say.

He nods. "Rian, what's holding you back from accepting this position?" He scans the paperwork in front of him. "You're more than qualified, just from your background. You went to Pierson after college when there were other opportunities for you out there. I see the hesitation in your answers. I don't mean to be arrogant, but we are NASA. Rarely do we hear the word no. Especially when we come to you. I guess what I'm asking is, what am I up against to get you here?"

I blow out a breath and bite my lip. "Truth is, I'm not sure I love math enough."

He sits back in his chair. "Oh. I thought for sure it was a fiancé or boyfriend. I had a speech ready for that. This is a first for me." He chuckles.

"Do you mind if I take a few days to think about it?" I could tell him it's the boyfriend thing too, but that's only a piece of the puzzle.

"Not at all. We'd really like to have you on board, but let me give you some advice. This life is short. Last year I went through some health issues. Before then, I was in the office all the time, never home with my kids for dinner. A typical workaholic. After I became sick and I was forced to slow down, I realized that getting sick was a blessing."

"How so?" I ask.

"Because I got the wake-up call not everyone does. I got to reexamine my life and I found that I love my job, which I'm grateful for, but it's my wife and my kids I love the most. There's truth in the cliché 'you only have one life.' I'd hate to lose the opportunity to bring you on board, but you should do what makes you happy." He smiles, and I nod that I understand. "I'll wait to hear from you, Rian. It was a pleasure talking with you."

"You as well, and thank you for the opportunity," I say.

We say our goodbyes and hang up. I close my laptop and sit in my chair. I need to really consider what I want my life to be moving forward.

The buzzer to my apartment goes off, and I jolt.

I head over to the door and press the intercom button. "Hello?"

"Rian?" It's my dad. "Can we come up?"

I sigh and look around the apartment. No reinforcements. But I need to face them eventually and I've been dodging them for long enough.

"Sure." I allow them in and open the apartment door, grabbing a soda before sitting at the kitchen table.

My mom peeks her head in. "Rian?"

"Come on in."

They each hold a coffee. My dad slides one over for me, also putting a white bakery bag in the middle of the table.

"We heard about NASA," my dad says.

My mom crosses her legs and looks at her lap.

I have no idea how they heard, but it doesn't really matter. "I haven't accepted the position."

My mom opens her mouth, but my dad puts up his hand to stop her. "May we ask why? Does this have to do with Dylan?"

"Yes and no."

My mom sits up straighter, opening her mouth to say something again, but my dad clears his throat. I guess they had a conversation before they came here.

"Can we talk about it?" he asks.

"Sure."

He opens the bag and places a smiley face cookie in front of me. The ones I would get when we went to the grocery store when I was younger. It was my prize if I calculated the groceries with tax correctly.

I smile. "Thanks. What do I need to do to eat it?"

"No conditions," my dad says.

I break off a small piece and eat the sugary goodness.

"So, Dylan… is this serious?" my dad asks.

I'm not sure my dad has started a conversation like this before. It feels odd, but it's a nice change.

"I really like him." I refrain from saying more. Although I think the feelings are there, I've yet to truly accept that I love him.

"Is enough to throw away your entire life?" Mom sneaks her own comment in, and my dad scowls at her.

The frayed thread between us snaps.

"I'm not throwing my life away. Have you ever thought that maybe I threw it away all these years you've forced me into something *you* loved? That I did math only because you forced me into a life of numbers and equations? I'm not you. I don't have the same dreams you do." I push away the cookie that did come with stipulations.

"He has no future. He's great now because you're twenty-eight. But what happens when you're thirty and you're ready for marriage and kids? That guy isn't going to stick around." Her lips purse and she looks at me with disdain.

"How do you know that?"

She shakes her head. "His type is clear as Saran Wrap. I did not bring up a daughter to be this blind. If you don't take this job, you're going to wake up one day as some single mom and saying you wish you would have listened to me."

I roll my eyes and I'm not sure they could get any farther behind my eyelids. "You do this all the time. You don't know him. You're stereotyping him because of his appearance. And regardless, he's not the reason I might not accept the job. It's the fact that I don't want a position that revolves around mathematics."

My mom paces in front of us, looking at my dad as though they're a team and he needs to tag in now.

Dad says, "Sweetheart, you're good at what you do. You're more brilliant than most and you should use that gift you were given. What will you do if you don't take this job?"

I shrug. The bakery idea sounds nice, but I'm not sure I want to put all my eggs in that basket either. "I'm not sure, but some people are lucky and find what they love. I want that."

My mind travels to Dylan and how when he broke his arm, he was depressed because he couldn't work. How many people can say that? Dylan loves what he does.

I shake my head. "You know what? It's time that you face facts. It's my decision now. Time for you to let your baby bird go."

My mom huffs.

"Sweetheart," my dad says.

"No! When will you love me for me? Be happy for me? Everything comes with a stipulation or a condition or a guilt trip if I don't do what you think I should." My fists pound on the table and the smiley cookie cracks into pieces under my right hand. "I'm done. You two can see yourselves out."

My mom swipes her coffee off the table. "The way you speak to us with such disrespect." She shakes her head, heading toward the door.

"Respect earns respect, Mom," I say, but she's gone.

My dad hesitates, but he's just a nicer version of my mom. "I had hopes that we could heal things between us."

"You had hopes that you could convince me. I suggest you stop coming here expecting a different result. Either you both learn to love me for me or stay out of my life." The words are hard to say, but I mean them. I can't be on this merry-go-round anymore.

My dad's shoulders fall and his eyes lock on mine. Probably to figure out if I'm bluffing. But there's no bluffing. I should've had the backbone to say this a long time ago.

He nods and stands, following my mom out the door. The click of the door shutting brings a finality I'm not sure I was prepared for.

Once they're gone, I grab my purse and leave my apartment, needing the security of Dylan's arms. His reassurance that I did the right thing.

I open the doors of Ink Envy with my tears barely held in check. If he's with a client, I'll wait in his office.

Lyle is at the front desk and glances up from his sketchbook like every other time I've been here. Frankie's station is empty, and Jax's tattoo machine is aimed on some woman's pelvis. He nods to me, pausing because he's just as perceptive as Dylan when it comes to people's feelings.

I see no sign of Dylan and ask Lyle, "Where is he?"

Lyle looks to Jax to answer the question and sourness fills my stomach.

"He's in the back doing a discreet tattoo." Jax tips his head toward the back room. I start down the aisle between stations. "Maybe wait in the waiting area or his office."

He's right. I can't very well barge in there.

"Lyle, go tell Dylan that Rian's here," Jax says.

Lyle drops his sketchbook on the table. A minute later, he returns from the back room. "He said he's finishing up. You can wait in his office."

I head to the office, but on my way, the door of the room Dylan's working in opens. When I look in, I spot a girl still straightening her clothes. Whatever they're talking about, they're laughing, and Dylan wipes his mouth with the collar of his shirt.

He sees me and says, "I'll be right with you," as if I'm a customer.

The girl who's flushed from head to toe looks me up and down as though I'm her competition.

Instead of going into his office, I hang out in the hallway, watching him check her out. He allows her to run a fingernail down his bicep. She hands him a piece of paper, and he slides it into his back pocket with a smile.

All those tears that were threatening to come out dry up with the anger twirling around my body like a tornado.

She leaves after kissing him on the cheek and gives him a pat on the ass.

Lyle stares at me in the hallway, and Dylan catches sight of Lyle before turning toward me. I have two choices: get the hell out of here, or stay and demand answers.

Why would I waste a night when I feel so feisty? I open his office door, go in, and slam it shut, preparing for the hurricane that's about to hit landfall.

Chapter Thirty-Two

RIAN

I KNEW HE WOULDN'T DODGE THE CONFRONTATION, SO WHEN HE OPENS THE OFFICE door two minutes later, I'm not surprised.

"What's up?" He nods to me as if I'm an acquaintance.

I cross my arms. "Care to explain?"

He releases a breath. "Explain what? You know it's my job to tattoo people in private places and that means private rooms." He sits at his desk. "I'm actually done early today. Want to go get dinner?"

"Dinner?"

He swivels in his chair. "Yeah. You know, when we put food in our mouths, chew, and swallow. Third meal of the day?"

"Don't."

The smile falls from his face and that hurts worse because he knows what he did out there. What I want to know is if he did it only for my benefit.

"Don't what?" he asks.

"You took her number."

He huffs. "You know how many numbers I get on a nightly basis?" He digs it out of his pocket and tosses it in the trash. "You know this relationship won't work if you don't trust me." He swivels back around, looking something up on his computer. "I could order and we could pick it up and eat at home, or if you want, we can hit up a restaurant."

"*Stop it!*" I yell.

His chair slowly turns, which reminds me of the movie *The Godfather* that Dylan made me watch a few weeks ago. Like I don't want to mess with him right now. But I desperately do. It's time we hash this out.

"What is your problem?" he asks.

"How would you feel if you witnessed what I just did?"

He shrugs, and my hand itches to slap his don't-give-a-shit attitude off him. "I threw it away. I had no intention of calling."

"Let me call Lyle in here so he can pat my ass then. That's okay?"

A condescending laugh erupts out of him. "Lyle wouldn't do that unless he wants to get fired."

"See? There's a problem that you allowed her to."

"She's a client."

I blow out a breath. "You're sabotaging us, aren't you?"

"I have no idea what you're talking about. Now do you want Italian or Mexican? I kind of feel like eating a taco." He waggles his eyebrows.

I throw my hands in the air. "Stop acting like there's nothing wrong. Just stop."

His jaw clenches. "You're seeing things. You can't be insecure if you're my girlfriend."

All that fight in me crumbles. The Dylan I know is gone. "So that's the way we're going to play this? You're going to shut me out?"

"Babe, I have no idea what you're talking about." He stands to approach me, but I put up my arm to stop him.

"*Babe?*" He's never once called me that. He always says my name, or calls me brainiac if he's teasing me. "You want me to break up with you?" I almost whisper, unable to meet his gaze.

He says nothing.

"Just be straight with me, Dylan. If you're done with me, say so. If you don't want to continue this, please don't play games with me. Just be straight. Is this because of the job in Houston? Are you scared? You have to talk to me."

His face softens and his shoulders sag. Finally we're getting somewhere. But then his cell phone rings, and he turns around to grab it.

"Please don't pick it up," I say.

"It could be a client." He answers it.

I have no idea what he even says because my thoughts are on how he's chipping away pieces of my heart. When I leave this office, I have a feeling we'll be done.

He tosses his phone onto his desk. "Are you sure you're not seeing things so you have an excuse to go to Houston?"

Every cell in my body heats with anger. He did not just say that. "Are you sure you're not trying to push me away?"

"Why would I push you away?" His face distorts into a "you're crazy" look.

"Oh, I don't know, look around your office."

He actually scans the room and looks back at me, waiting for me to explain.

I say, "You don't have one personal effect in here."

"You want me to put up a picture of you? Is that what this is about?"

My frustration is so great, I want to scream at the top of my lungs. I settle for digging my nails into the palms of my clenched fists. "You keep everyone at arm's length, and I thought we were over that. I thought you were all in. One roadblock and you're doing everything you can to push me away?"

He scoffs. "You being jealous of a girl whose tits I had to tattoo isn't me pushing you away. It's me paying the bills."

"Come on, you know what you're doing here. I know you do. I'm not even sure I want the job."

Like a cord snaps, his back goes ramrod straight. "I gotta go."

"What?" I run to the door, blocking it. "We're talking this out."

He pockets his cell phone, grabs his jacket off a hook, and puts his hand on my hip, nudging me out of the way. "Take the job."

"Is that what this is about?" I ask. "You think you can force me to leave? Pretend that you made out with some girl in the back room, get me pissed, and I'll go to Houston? And what? It'll prove your theory about life?"

His gaze locks with mine. I shiver at the chill it sets off, but I won't shy away at this point.

"I know you didn't do anything with that girl," I say. "You wiping your mouth with your shirt to pretend like she kissed you isn't the Dylan I've fallen in love with. You did that for your own benefit so you can blame me for leaving."

He tears his eyes away from mine, his hand landing on the doorknob. "You have no idea what the hell you're talking about."

"You're not that guy, and I will not run off to Houston because of some lame attempt to force my hand. I know you would never cheat on me."

A cruel smile crosses his lips and he turns the knob, but I use every muscle in my body to keep the door shut. If he gets out, he'll be gone. "You have no idea the man I am. You think you love me? You love an illusion."

"You have it wrong. That is the man you are. That is the man I'm in love with. You're the one who's scared of him. You created this illusion for yourself so you can always be the victim. It's easier that way, right? It's never your decision, never your fault. Everyone else leaves."

He scowls and turns the knob, pulling forward. My body loses all strength as he opens the door and flees. I slide along the wall and sink to the floor, my face buried in my knees.

The door slowly opens, and when I peek up, Jax is there, eyes closed, shaking his head. He crouches, pulls out his cell phone, types out a message, and puts it back. He doesn't say anything to me, just sits in a similar position, his arms wrapped around his propped up knees.

"I don't understand." I rest my chin on my knee. Jax has known him the longest. Shouldn't he have an answer for me?

He shrugs. "The way we grew up… it comes with a lot of fucked up beliefs."

"But we were doing so well."

He nods. "I thought for sure you were in it for the long haul."

"Were?" My voice cracks. "Past tense?"

He blows out a breath. "Don't listen to me. Phillips isn't one who runs forever. He'll be back, but…"

He doesn't have to finish. I know exactly what he's saying.

I put my forehead to my knees again and tears seep out of me like a faucet. Still Jax sits with me, offering no words of consolation. I prefer it that way. He's not making any promises he knows to he can't keep.

What feels like ten minutes goes by before a soft knock lands on the door. Jax stands. I don't even look up. It's probably Lyle.

Blanca sits down on one side and Sierra on the other side of me. I offer Jax a soft smile before he nods and shuts the door behind him.

"Oh, sweetie," Sierra says, putting her arm around my shoulders.

There's nothing they can say, so I allow them to do what girlfriends are supposed to do in situations like this. Tell me bullshit lines like I'll get through this and he's not worth my time. I see now what Dylan was so scared about. These two have already turned on him. He's right—we were stupid to risk our friendship for something more.

But my heart aches as I walk out of his office with a friend on each arm, knowing I'll probably never be back to Ink Envy. Jax sees us and follows.

"You can't leave me responsible for the place," Lyle frantically says to Jax.

Jax pats him on the shoulder. "Sure, I can. Tell any of my clients I had an emergency." Jax tosses his key to Lyle. "No parties, and don't burn the place down."

Lyle laughs. "You sound just like a dad."

Jax scowls. "Fuck you. That's an insult."

Ethan walks in and gives Blanca a kiss on the cheek.

"Where are you going?" she asks.

"We're going after Dylan."

"Let him rot," Sierra says.

I squeeze her hand for being a protective friend, but I don't want Dylan suffering out there by himself.

"Do you know where he would've gone?" I ask.

Jax eyes Ethan as Knox, Seth, and Adrian join the party in the waiting room.

"You're going too?" Sierra asks Adrian.

"Take me with you," I say, leaving the arms of my friends.

Knox steps in front of me, blocking my way. "Let us talk to him first, okay? We'll text you when we find him."

I nod.

"Who rides with who?" Seth asks.

"What do you mean?" Knox asks, putting on his leather coat.

"Whose bike am I on?" Seth adds.

Knox looks at Jax.

Jax raises his eyebrows. "You are not riding bitch on my bike."

"You three can go in Adrian's fancy car," Knox says.

Seth's shoulders deflate. "You guys get to act all cool on your motorcycles and I ride in the back of a Range Rover?"

Knox nods. "Get your motorcycle license and a bike and you can ride with us."

Seth rolls his eyes. "Whatever."

Adrian and Ethan say goodbye to their girlfriends.

Seth hugs me before they leave. "I'll bring him back to you." He winks.

Jax and Knox roll their eyes because I'm pretty sure they're the ones who know where Dylan might have gone. I mouth a thank you to Jax and he nods like always. A man of few words. We watch them leave.

"Um, Rian, can we call Frankie?" Lyle distracts me as they disappear around a corner.

"I'll run to the liquor store," Sierra says and runs her hand down my arm.

No way we can leave Lyle in charge of Ink Envy even for a half hour. He's clearly not ready.

As I sit on the couch in the waiting room, I remember all the times I came in here and dreamily looked at Dylan. It feels as though we've come so far since those moments, but now I'm lost on where we'll end up. One thing is certain—I don't belong in Texas. Even if Dylan returns and sells Ink Envy and disappears forever, or if we find some new normal for our friendship, or if we work out as a couple, I'm meant to be in Cliffton Heights. It's where everyone I care about lives.

I pull out my phone and email Dr. Quinton my decision to decline the job. Just like math, I'll narrow down my choices one by one. Eventually I'll find the solution to my problem.

Chapter Thirty-Three

DYLAN

THE HEADLIGHT FROM MY BIKE SHINES ON JOYLAND'S CLOSED SIGN; THE S IS tipped upside down. I ride down the long driveway and through the vacant parking lot that's overgrown with weeds and grass.

Once I weave through the opening where I used to witness thousands of families anxiously waiting to get in, I stop at the pool that's now dried up. No one has been here in years. The park was abandoned after they closed their doors due to bankruptcy. I continue on past the merry-go-round that's missing some animals and poles over to the children's area. I park my bike by the bumper cars and game booths, then sit up on a concrete ledge.

Rian's blazing eyes are all I've seen since I left Ink Envy. Truth hurts, and Rian knew what she was talking about. I can't deny it. What she expects from me isn't feasible. I'm not the guy she thinks I am. And I'm sure as hell not gonna be the reason she misses out on a once-in-a-lifetime opportunity.

The sound of two bikes rumbling through the park alerts me that my friends have found me. I had hoped they wouldn't search me out or would overlook this place. I guess our time here meant a lot to them too. They stop near my bike, each cutting the engine and taking off their helmets.

"Funny meeting you here," Jax says, climbing off his bike and hitting the kickstand.

"Why did you follow me?"

Jax sits next to me on the concrete ledge. "Someone has to talk some sense into you."

I desperately want to ask how Rian is. Is she crying? Is she packing her bags? But I leave those questions where they should be—far out of my concern.

Knox leaves his helmet on his bike and joins us. The three of us sit in line, just like when we were younger. We'd come here for an entire day and always end up on this piece of concrete, watching the families wind down for the day as the sun set. I'd see kids fall asleep on their dads' shoulders, or mothers cleaning faces and hands after buckling them up in the stroller. The parents exhausted but with smiles as they looked at each other with happiness in their eyes. I always envied them.

"Remember that time that dad had his son's arm twisted behind his back?" Jax says. "The kid was, like, nine."

I nod. "Knox jumped down and surprised him, told him if he ever saw him do something like that again, he'd find him and cut off his dick." I glance at Knox.

He shakes his head. "I was such a punk, but hopefully nothing else happened to that kid. What about that time a mom hit on Jax?" We all laugh. "And you told her she should be watching her kids and not hitting on a high schooler unless she wanted to be arrested."

"She just left them for anyone to kidnap," Jax says. "What kind of mother is that?"

We saw so many different versions of parents while we sat on our perch, judging. We intervened more than we ever should have.

"Then you have Phillips, always giving his stuffed animals to the kids." Jax's hand clasps the back of my neck and squeezes.

"What was I gonna do with them?" I shrug as though it wasn't a big deal, but I loved the way the kids' eyes would beam and the parents didn't look at me as if I was trash.

"You always were a family man." Knox nudges me with his elbow.

I shake my head.

"Phillips, don't even try to deny it. How many times did you say that you wanted what those people had?" Jax says.

I jump down from the ledge. "Because I was a foster kid. What foster kid doesn't want parents? A family?"

They jump down and join me walking around. It's sad and desolate and depressing here now.

"You wanted your own family," Knox says. "I remember you saying, 'I'd never treat my kid like that,' and 'My wife is going to be smoking hot with a great pair of tits.'"

I huff out a laugh. We really were punks. "I was young and stupid."

"You knew what you wanted, so what changed?" Knox asks. "I see the way you look at her, man."

I clench my teeth. "She's better off in Houston. She has so many possibilities for her life and I want her to realize all of them."

"Bullshit. Come on. Own it, Phillips." Jax's voice echoes through the empty park as we all hang on metal beams from a ride that's half rotted away.

"Own what?"

Jax looks at Knox and shakes his head. "You fell in love with her and you're scared because what happens when you love people?"

"They leave you," Knox fills in for Jax.

"You two are psychologists now, are you?"

"Maybe she doesn't want to leave? Maybe she doesn't want the job." Jax walks up to me. "Maybe she doesn't want to leave you." He jabs me in the chest.

"Do we really have to give you the 'you are worthy' speech?" Knox puts his arm around my neck and rubs his knuckles along my skull. "People have been assholes and yeah, maybe your dickhead parents abandoned you, but that doesn't dictate everyone's actions."

I get out of his hold. "My head is all kinds of fucked up right now. She called me out on all my shit. She figured me out."

Jax laughs echoes in the night. Only the moon lights our path as we continue along. "You're not a Rubik's cube, moron. And I should kick your ass for that stunt with the client."

I nod. He should. It was low. "What if I fuck this up?"

Knox slaps me on the back. "Too late for that."

He's right. I have fucked this all up. When Lyle said she was there, I purposely got Colleen out quickly so she would still be adjusting herself. Wiping my mouth on my T-shirt was playing dirty.

"I guess we're all gonna wait around for her to meet that accountant, huh?" Jax jumps up on a concrete ledge and walks it. "Watch her pop out a few perfect kids. Sit on the sidelines and let some other fucker get the life you want? Just like we used to watch those families here when we were kids." Jax jumps down in front of me and I rear back. "It's time to grow up. You love Rian and she loves you. Shit, I've witnessed so many gooey moments the last few months that I need five root canals."

Knox nudges my shoulder with his. "He's right. It's time you take what's yours and fight what's holding you back. We all have our demons. Everyone grows up with them. You and Jax were dealt a shitty hand, so toss the cards back into the deck and reshuffle. Or better yet, pluck out your cards so that you end up with a royal flush. It's in your hands. You're the one in control, not that jealous boy who used to watch all the families here."

"Man, Whelan, I'm impressed," Jax says.

Jax is right—Knox did good. He's wrong about one thing though. The jealous boy inside me is the one I should be listening to, because he's the one who said fuck this life he was given, he was gonna have the wife and the kids and the whole family. He wasn't scared.

"Where is she?" I ask, my hand digging into my pocket for my keys.

"She's packing for Houston. Leaving on a red-eye, I think," Jax says.

"Fuck." I turn and run back to my bike.

They follow suit.

"I'm not sure you're going to catch her," Knox says.

All three of us climb on our bikes, and with me in the lead, we head out of the park— except we come upon three guys using their cell phones as flashlights when we reach the merry-go-round. I stop the bike, and my friends stop on either side of me.

"Fuck, guys, you knew we couldn't get Adrian's Range Rover through those openings," Seth says.

Jax and Knox shrug.

"Sorry, we weren't thinking," Knox says.

"I gotta go." I rev my engine.

"This is bullshit, I wasn't able to give him his 'come to his senses' speech." Seth holds up a piece of paper. "I wrote down notes on the way here."

Jax inches forward on his bike. "All taken care of. Now we need to stop her from getting on the plane." Jax pats Seth's back.

"Thanks for coming, guys, but my head's on straight again." I wheel by them and out of the park, right to the highway.

I zoom and weave through traffic with confidence and ease. We pull up to the apartment, all of us killing our engines. The guys tell me they'll park my bike.

I run up the stairs of our apartment building, winded when I bust open the door to nothing but darkness. I slam the door and run down the stairs. Jax and Knox are still parking my bike curbside.

"She's gone!" I yell. "Give me back my helmet. I have to go to the airport."

As the words spill out, the door of Ink Envy opens and Rian steps out. Her arms are wrapped around herself in protection.

I know then, more than I've known anything in my whole life, that I'll do whatever I have to in order to fix this. I will not lose the woman I love.

Chapter Thirty-Four

RIAN

WE ALL HEARD THE MOTORCYCLES COMING DOWN THE STREET. SIERRA AND Blanca looked at me. Hell, even Lyle peeked up from his sketchbook.

When a few minutes pass and no one walks in, I figure I'll go outside to save Knox and Jax from having to tell me in front of everyone that Dylan isn't coming back. But as I open the door, Dylan tears out of our apartment building, demanding the guys give him back his helmet. Until he looks up and our eyes lock.

My feet stop. I wait for him to cross the street, holding his hand out for a car to stop.

"Rian," he says.

Just hearing him say my name does things to me. No matter if he's here to tell me it's over or tell me he messed up, I feel better seeing that he's okay.

"Hi," I say.

"I'm an idiot. I didn't do anything with that woman. I swear. I just..." He looks at me, tucking his hands into the pockets of his jacket. "You were right. I was scared. Scared you were going to leave me, because all the people in my life that I love leave me. But I should have trusted you. I should have fought for us. I should have done anything but what I did. And I'm sorry. I'm so sorry."

The truth of his words reflects in his eyes, but the thought of him trying to push me away stings. "I should torment you. Make you grovel."

He falls to his knees and puts his hands in prayer pose.

"I was kidding. Stand up." I don't want him to beg or grovel. I just want him to love me.

He stands. "I was thinking about it, and I could close Ink Envy and open up in Houston. Or do a branch. Maybe Frankie runs this one, I don't know. Or I can tattoo in someone else's shop down there. I can find clients. I'm talented."

"You'd move to Houston?" A warm feeling fills my chest.

He nods. "I can't do long distance. I don't want to be away from you, so if you'll let me, we'll move in together. Or we can get our own places. Whatever you want." He looks around, then down at my hands. "Shit, are you leaving? Let me pack a bag and hopefully I can get a seat on the same plane." He backs up from me and turns to run across the street.

"Dylan!" I yell.

Jax and Knox are hanging on the street corner, Adrian dropping off the guys before going to park his car. Dylan turns around in the middle of the street.

"I'm not going to Houston," I say.

He looks over his shoulder. Jax and Knox laugh so loudly, they startle the people walking by.

Slowly, Dylan crosses back to me. "You have to. You're too smart."

I put my finger on his lips. "My life is here. In Cliffton Heights, with you and all our friends. I'm trying to figure out what will make me happy, and one thing I know for sure is that a big part of that is you and everything else I have here. Maybe part of the fun is figuring it all out, I don't know."

"You can still have me. I'll go with you. We'll make new friends." He takes my hands.

"Hey now!" Seth yells from across the street. "You have free bagels for life. You won't find that in Houston!"

We both laugh.

"I like us here. This is where we fell in—" I stop because I'm fully aware that I told him earlier I loved him and he still ran out on me.

"Love." He cradles my cheeks and steps closer. "We fell in love."

My eyes water and I nod. I inch up on my toes. "Don't ever run away again."

He bends down, bringing his lips closer. "I promise."

Then he seals that promise with a kiss. And like a cheesy romantic comedy movie, all our friends clap and cheer around us.

Problem officially solved.

Epilogue

DYLAN

TODAY IS THE DAY I PROVE TO RIAN HOW SERIOUS I AM ABOUT US. THAT I'M NOT going anywhere unless she's next to me.

"You're being secretive today. What gives?" she asks, coming out of our bedroom wearing a sundress. Although it's early fall, we've been lucky to have an extended summer.

Jax moved in with the guys, so the apartment is officially ours alone. It's weird to have two empty bedrooms, but we turned one into an office with a futon and the other into a guest room.

"It's something we should've done a long time ago, but we've been so busy, I haven't had the time. This is your first weekend without a function to bake for."

Rian finishes putting in her earring and sits on a kitchen chair, sighing. "I never would have thought I'd be in the sweets business."

Rian quit her job at Pierson months ago. It didn't take her long to get her baking business off the ground, and she's doing better than I think she ever expected. She makes anything from cookies to cupcakes, to cakes for people and businesses.

I slide a piece of paper in front of her and massage her shoulders from behind. "You think you're ready to start your own bakery?"

Rian's rents out an industrial kitchen space, where she takes orders online or by word of mouth. She's not ready to put all her eggs in one basket until she knows she'll be happy. Forever the girl with a plan.

She leans back in the chair and her eyes roll shut. "Maybe. I think it would be easier in some regards. I don't much like the hours I have to keep at the industrial kitchen space. But that's a lot to take on. Being an entrepreneur."

I get what she's saying. I'm fortunate that with Jax coming on to Ink Envy, we're back in the black. I'm surprised he's stuck around, but I'm happy he has. It's given us time to rebuild our friendship.

"Take a chance," I say. "I heard there's an open space by this amazing tattoo parlor who will pimp out your goods. Supposedly the owner is really hot."

"Oh, maybe I'll have to check it out, but my boyfriend might get kind of jealous."

"Your boyfriend *is* a little protective when it comes to you. But I get why. He was lucky enough to find a girl like you, so he's right to be afraid to lose you."

She tips her head back and smiles at me.

I lean down and place a kiss on her lips. "Look at the paper."

She picks it up to read it. "What is this?"

"It's my in case of emergency for my insurance," I say.

I take a seat beside her and watch her read the paper. When she's done, she puts it down, comes over to me, and straddles my chair.

"Seth is going to be upset," she says.

"I don't give two shits about his ego." My hands find their way to her ass like they always do. "So what do you say? Will you be my ICE?"

She kisses me. "I say yes."

I squeeze her ass and pull her closer. "I love you." Never have truer words left my lips.

"I love you. Is that what you were planning this whole time? You didn't even have to ask me. I wouldn't say no." She moves to stand, but I hold her to my lap.

"I have another surprise. I think it's definitely get-me-laid material."

She narrows her eyes. "Are you complaining about our sex life?"

Visions of us all over this apartment run through my mind like a movie reel. "Never. Maybe I should say blow job material. Deserving of a swallow." I grin and wink.

"Hmmm… you have my curiosity piqued."

I pat her ass to get her up. "Then let's go."

We leave our apartment, and I walk her down the street toward the gazebo where the event is taking place. How she hasn't already bothered me about coming to this, I have no idea.

She cringes. "You're not planning some surprise with my parents are you?"

"Never."

Her mom didn't talk to her for three months after Rian declined NASA, but last month, we had them over for dinner. I let her mom's ridicule roll off my back, and when we shut the door on them at the end of the night, we agreed that another dinner wouldn't happen for a very long time. Maybe with time things will improve, but since they both act like assholes and make my girl doubt how brilliant she is, I'm not a fan of them being a part of our lives until that changes.

"Good."

We pass Las Tacos and all the activity in the park up ahead is chaotic. Luckily, I already called in our reservation.

"What is this?" she asks.

"It's an adoption fair." Her eyes widen, and I hold up my hand. "Now, I've already reserved one from a litter for us, because God knows I can't see you down again if we got here and all the dogs were gone."

She laughs, but I don't find it funny. I don't want to see her disappointed like that ever.

"We're getting a dog?" Her smile beams like sunlight in my direction.

"We are." I pull her across the street by her hand and walk her over to the booth set up by the no-kill shelter I talked to on the phone. "Hi, I'm Dylan. This is Rian, my girlfriend. We spoke on the phone."

The woman shakes our hands and points at the pen. "Your boyfriend is very persuasive. You get to pick before anyone else."

Rian looks at me as though I just granted her queen for the day. I'll never stop striving for that look on her face.

She bends down and picks up one of the puppies. He has black and white spotted fur and squirms in her arms. She holds him out to me. "What do you think?"

Five other puppies push on the metal fence, eager for attention. A few kids come over and squeal, giving the puppies enough attention that they shift their attention to them.

"Is something wrong with that one?" I point at the one in the back, curled up in a ball on the grass, not interested in the kids, just chilling.

"He's the runt of the litter. Never demands a ton of attention but loves to snuggle." She picks him up and hands him to me.

He curls up in my arms, nuzzling his face between my arm and rib. Rian coos and puts the other dog back down.

I chuckle. "Is this like when I hold Jolie?"

She nods, pulling out her phone and snapping a picture.

"Remember what I said earlier." I wink at Rian.

She turns to the woman. "We'll take him."

"Oh!" Her surprise has me wanting to ask more questions. Maybe people don't normally want the runt? "Let me get the paperwork."

"Are you sure?" I hand him to Rian and he puts his face on her breast, staring up at her. I pet his head. "That's my favorite spot too, buddy."

"I love him. He's so sweet and quiet." She looks at the pen filled with all the high energy dogs. I guess we're on the same wavelength.

"I did this so you can pick one out, not me."

"And I did." She bends down and kisses his head. "Now we need a name."

"And about a million other things."

We fill out the paperwork, now officially co-owners of a dog without a name, and head to a booth that sells everything we'll need.

RIAN

I nuzzle baby Winston in my arms as we leave with all the puppy supplies.

"You will have to put him down eventually." Dylan kisses my cheek, his hands full of bags.

"He can't walk on a leash yet."

"We could try to train him on the way home," he says.

Seth and Knox walk out of Las Tacos, spotting us.

"You got a dog?" Knox asks.

Seth pets Winston and Winston eats up the attention. "What's his name?"

"Winston," I say.

Seth looks at Dylan. "Is that your dog or hers?"

"Ours," Dylan says with a smile.

"You gave your dog an old man name," Seth says.

"It fits him." I shrug. "You not a dog person, Knox?" I ask since he's quiet.

He meets my gaze. The poor guy is still sporting heartbreak, although he's been trying to heal it with an array of women.

"I'll be right back," he says and crosses the street.

We all watch him head over to the gazebo, where there's an open area for the dogs to play.

"Isn't that Evan Erickson?" Dylan asks, nudging Seth.

Seth looks around as though he can't locate her. As if her dark curly hair is hard to miss. With the wind today, it's blowing all over her face. She reaches into her purse and grabs a ponytail holder. The guy she's with pulls it back for her, securing her hair into a low ponytail.

"Who's that?" Dylan asks.

"You guys need to stop. It's probably her boy..." His eyes turn murderous. Not a common look for Seth. "You have to be fucking kidding me."

"What?" I ask, looking at Dylan for some backstory.

"That douchebag she's with is my brother's drug dealer. Fuck." Seth turns away, clenching his fists at his sides.

"Well, that sucks," Dylan says.

"Do you think she knows?" I ask.

"Fucking A. Goddamnit." His hands go behind his head and he weaves his fingers, staring at Evan and the man, blowing out a breath. "To answer your question, no. I'm sure she doesn't. She would never, which means…"

"What?" Dylan bit his lip to stop from laughing because we all know Seth. He's too good of a guy, regardless of their history.

Seth steps off the curb then steps back on. "See. This is why"—he points at Dylan—"I like it smooth as vanilla ice cream. I don't need a bunch of shit to muddle through. And now." He's already in the middle of the street, his hands out to his sides. "I gotta go deal with rocky road."

"Stop making excuses and go save the girl," Dylan yells.

Seth flips him off but continues on his path toward Evan.

My back rests on Dylan's chest, and I turn and look up at him. The love of my life. He bends down and kisses me.

"I fucking love our life," he says.

I giggle and nod. I couldn't agree more.

"Let's go home," he says.

And we do, the three of us, to start a life together that might have a little rocky road. But as long as we charter those peaks and valleys together, that's all we need.

What happens when you fall for the daughter of your family's sworn enemy?

You keep it a secret.

But in a town as small as Cliffton Heights, there are eyes peeking around every corner.

OUR STAR CROSSED KISS

About the Author

Piper Rayne is a *USA Today* Bestselling Author duo who write "heartwarming humor with a side of sizzle" about families, whether that be blood or found. They both have e-readers full of one-clickable books, they're married to husbands who drive them to drink, and they're both chauffeurs to their kids. Most of all, they love hot heroes and quirky heroines who make them laugh, and they hope you do, too!

Blame It On the Pain

ASHLEY JADE

Trigger Warning
This series is not suitable for readers under 18.

Blame It on the Pain
"Only after disaster can we be resurrected. It's only after you've lost everything that you're free to do anything."
—Chuck Palahniuk, Fight Club

Prologue

JACKSON

Pain. It hurts us. It pushes us. It punishes us.

Or, for the few poor souls out there like me…it defines us.

I'm not a good person.

There are no redeeming qualities about me…not anymore.

Any that I had, I'd given to the devil on the night that changed everything.

The night my baby sister died.

The night I murdered her killer.

Yes, I've taken a life…and I would do it again in a heartbeat.

I grew up in Boston. For the most part, I was just an average hard working kid trying to make it into the professional world of MMA fighting.

My mom kicked the bucket when I was 18 from a heroin overdose, and if you know where my father is…well then, give that asshole sperm donor a big *'fuck you'* for me.

It's safe to say that Lilly was the only family I had.

She was four years younger than me, and I spent most of my life either looking out for her or bitching about how annoying she was.

After our mom died, it was just her and I.

Who am I kidding…it was her and I since day one.

My mother's death changed nothing. In fact, Lilly's high school didn't even question when I was the one who stepped up and filled in for all the parental duties.

Here's where I fucked up.

I let my best friend date my little sister.

Mike was training to become a professional MMA fighter as well. We all grew up together, and one day, I caught him making eyes at Lilly…or rather, her making eyes at him.

Obviously, I put an end to that shit as soon as it started.

When she was 14.

The next four years were filled with them making constant googly eyes at one another, but other than that—we were like the three musketeers.

Lilly would even watch us train…she was like our own personal cheerleader.

I'd see her innocent blue eyes and strawberry blonde curls routing for us at every single session.

On her 18 birthday…I caved.

"I'm in love with your sister and I swear to god, I'm going to marry her one day," Mike said as I choked on my beer.

Before I even had time to knock him out or protest…Lilly's 5'1, lanky frame bounced into the room and landed beside Mike.

She grabbed his hand and looked up at me. "I love him, Jackson."

I grunted and downed the rest of my beer before I reached over and grabbed Mike by his shoulders. "Outside…*now*."

He let go of Lilly's hand and followed me out to the porch.

The old wooden swing seat creaked under our weight when we sat down. "You're 22… she's 18."

He laughed. "I know. But it's really not that much of an age difference anymore, especially now that she's legal." He looked down at his feet. "Besides, I've loved her since she was 14."

My stomach knotted and I balled my fists. "That's disgusting."

He rolled his eyes. "Obviously, I didn't do anything about it, asshole," he said. "It's not like that. It's more than sex."

My entire body tensed at those words and I stood up.

I was about two seconds away from knocking his lights out when he shouted, "Which we still haven't had, I swear!"

We both breathed a sigh of relief then. "Look, I know I'm going to spend the rest of my life with her. Now the only question is whether you're going to be happy and support us, or if it's going to come to blows and we're going to ruin a friendship over it. Not to mention, possibly ruining your relationship with your sister."

I shook my head. "You're a fucking prick."

He gave me a wry smile. "No, I'm not, Jackson. If I was, you would have knocked my ass out already. You know I'm a good guy. You know I'll take care of her. I'm *your* best friend for crying out loud."

I crossed my arms over my chest. "You hurt her, I'll kill you. You knock her up before she's 30, I'll kill you. If you cheat on her, I'll kill you. If you ever make her cry…I'll kill you."

He looked me in the eyes. "If I ever do any of those things; then, I wouldn't want to live anyway." He paused. "So, does this mean we have your blessing?" I halfheartedly gave a nod as I heard Lilly come bouncing out the front door.

Her smile was infectious and her eyes were gleaming.

She wrapped her arms around me tighter than she ever had before.

"I love you, big brother…this is the best birthday ever!"

I sighed and returned her hug.

For two years Mike kept his promise.

He treated her like gold and I'd never seen Lilly happier.

Both Mike and I continued to train hard, trying to make it big in the MMA world.

We trained at one of the best gyms and had a coach who swore our big break was right around the corner.

He was right.

Mike was closing in on a deal with a big time sponsor, and I was about to sign a pretty big endorsement deal with a sponsor myself.

My first professional fight was scheduled for one week away.

At almost 24, my dreams were finally coming true.

I was so wrapped up in my own world…I never noticed the signs.

I never noticed when my sister's innocent blue eyes lost their sparkle.

I never noticed when her bubbly personality changed.

I *almost* didn't notice when she stopped showing up to watch us train.

"What's up with my sister? I haven't talked to her in like two weeks. She hasn't shown up here lately…why is that?" I asked Mike as we headed to the locker room after a training session.

Mike shrugged. "I don't know, she's been studying really hard. I think she wanted to go shopping today. She said something about wanting to get a new outfit for the big fight next week."

I laughed. "Yeah, I guess that makes sense. Her boyfriend and big brother are having their first professional fight on the very same night."

I knew that no matter how hard Lilly's intense course load at Harvard was, she wouldn't miss the fight for the world.

He looked down and I watched as he shifted his weight from foot to foot. "Yeah…"

Something was off. I put my hand on his shoulder. "What's going on?"

He shrugged me off and walked toward the showers. "Just a little nervous is all," he called out.

I finished showering before he did.

I walked over to our lockers and proceeded to get dressed. He stupidly left his locker half open…and that's when I noticed it.

A tiny bottle of something that wasn't labeled…along with a needle.

It didn't take a genius to figure out what it was.

Steroids.

I swiped it from his locker and waited for him to come out. "What the fuck are you doing, Mike? Are you trying to ruin your career before it even starts?" I screamed.

He looked around the locker room. "Keep your fucking voice down. What if coach hears you?" he hissed as he reached for the bottle.

I pulled back. "Over my dead body. No way am I letting you ruin everything you've worked so hard for. What the fuck is the matter with you? I never thought you would do something like this!"

He punched the locker beside him. "Everybody in the sports industry uses, Jackson. I'm going to stop after I win the next few fights…it's just enough to put me on the map."

"You're an idiot. You're about to sign a deal with a big sponsor! You don't think they're going to test you for roids? Even more than that, you're ruining the integrity of the sport. *All* sports. Passion is what should be flowing through your body…*not* this shit."

"Look, some of us don't have it like you do. Some of us need a little help from time to time. And I'm not the only athlete to ever try it, most have. It's just a little pick me up."

I shook my head and glared at him. "This isn't a 'pick me up', this shit will send you straight to hell in a hand-basket. Train better, work harder…*don't* do this shit."

He sighed and slumped down on the bench. "You're right. I fucked up, I've just been so nervous and I'm second guessing myself. I don't want to lose."

I sat down next to him. "I understand. What makes you think I'm not feeling the same way? This is a huge deal for us, and it's normal to be nervous. Use that nervous energy as positive fuel. This shit will ruin your life."

He nodded. "Don't tell Lilly about this, please."

"I won't. Besides, if she knew, the fight next week would be the least of your worries. I'm pretty sure she'd kick your ass so bad you wouldn't be able to train for weeks."

He grinned and began changing into his street clothes. "Yup, you're right about that. God, I love that woman."

Blood.

So much blood. Everywhere.

That's one of the things that I remember most about that fateful night.

To this day, I can still close my eyes and recall every single surface marked by blood. The metallic smell of it permeating my nostrils, the way it smeared the walls, the way it pooled on the floor—the large bloody hand print on the wall.

The night my entire world changed, was also the night of the big fight.

I had won. It was a close match and I was definitely swinging for the fences like my life depended on it. My opponent ended up tapping out after a hard uppercut to his jaw that sent him staggering, followed by an axe kick which finished him off.

I looked out into the crowd expecting to see Lilly's smiling face…but I didn't.

Even more alarming…Mike never showed up for his own fight.

Some guy named Tyrone ended up taking his place and won after 3 minutes of conducting an intense ground and pound on his opponent that was brutal enough to make me wince.

Something was definitely wrong…I felt it in my bones. I hightailed it out of the arena while dialing their numbers repeatedly.

I hopped in my truck and headed straight for their apartment.

When I walked in I had to take a step back.

My worst nightmare couldn't have conjured up what was waiting for me on the other side of the door.

Everything seemed to play out in slow motion while I tried to take in and process what I was seeing.

The first thing I noticed was the large bloody hand print against the stark white wall of their small kitchen. My eyes dropped down and my heart squeezed for dear life when I saw the large pool of blood on the floor. It expanded and rounded a corner leading up to the living room.

I didn't want to know where it was coming from…but I knew I had no choice but to find out.

I closed my eyes and took a few tentative steps forward until I rounded the corner.

There on the floor beside the couch…was where my heart turned into dust and my world as I knew it, would cease to exist.

My small, fragile, baby sister's pale, cold, lifeless body was laid out before me.

Her shirt was torn and bruises covered most of her limp, frail, body.

The image still haunts me in my darkest moments.

I dropped down beside her and willed her to wake up.

How could someone do this to her? My innocent baby sister. The greatest person I'd ever known.

I shook her, I shouted her name. I begged and I pleaded harder than I ever had in my life.

"Who would do this to *you*, Lilly?" I whispered, as I held her. "Come on baby sis, wake up. Please," I continued to beg as I felt the first few tears start rolling down.

My thoughts went wild. I thought up dozens of different scenarios in that moment. Everything from a burglar, a secret stalker at the college she attended, to a drug dealer who had the wrong house looking for his money.

Mike. Where the hell was he?

Shit, maybe whoever did this was holding Mike hostage somewhere?

I looked back down at Lilly and my chest felt like it caved in. Something deep within me had severed in that moment. Nothing would ever be the same again.

I looked up to the ceiling and screamed with tears streaming down my face.

I heard some kind of rustling in the distance, near the bedroom down the hallway before a tall shadow loomed before me.

I knew that shadow well. *Almost* as well as I knew my own.

I gently let go of Lilly's body and rose from the ground.

He had the makings of what looked like was going to be a black eye. He also had a fairly large scratch across his cheek.

I quickly looked down at Lilly's pink nails and noticed some dried blood caked under them.

She fought like hell.

I lifted my head and glared at him. I looked him right in the eyes…and I *knew*.

He did this.

He killed her.

He murdered my baby sister…the girl he swore he would love and protect.

Suddenly everything made sense…like why she never showed up to watch us at practice anymore. Why she seemed so distant. Why she didn't seem as happy anymore when I talked to her.

He was abusing her…and *I* ignored all the signs.

I didn't protect my sister…the only person in the world that I loved more than anything.

He bowed his head and teetered back as I advanced toward him. He held up his hands. "Just let me explain. It was an accident. It was her fau—"

Rage filled my blood, and it burned through my veins. I punched him hard. Hard enough that I heard the satisfying snap of his jaw dislocating. "Don't you *dare* try to blame her. Did you give Lilly a chance to talk before you beat the shit out of her and killed her!" I screamed as I punched him again, even harder. This time, sending him to the floor.

He tried to get up but I sent a sharp kick to his ribs. "I told you what I would do to you if you ever hurt her," I sneered before I picked him up by his hair and bashed his head into the nearest wall.

He tried to fight me off, but he didn't stand a chance in hell.

I punched him again and relished when I saw a few teeth fall out. Blood filled his mouth as I dragged him into the kitchen, purposely knocking his head into every hard surface I could find along the way.

We grappled for a few more minutes before I landed on top of him. I continued to punch him letting my rage take over.

"It was the steroids, Jackson. It turned me into a different person. I don't know who I am anymore. Lilly pissed me off and—" he started to sputter through the blood in his mouth.

The fact that he was even attempting to defend himself and still blame Lilly after what he had done only fueled my anger and pain.

"You're a fucking killer," I growled before I dealt another blow to his head.

It was something we were going to have in common real soon.

His eyes opened wide. "Stop. You're really gonna kill me, Jackson."

My fist went flying straight for his chest, effectively silencing him.

His eyes rolled back in his head and a low gurgling sound filled the room.

I reached down and fisted his hair while meeting his stare. "Did *you* listen when my baby sister begged *you* to stop?" I questioned before I sent a karate chop straight to his neck.

Adrenaline mixed with guilt, grief and wrath like I'd never felt before coursed through me as I continued to pummel him.

At some point, I saw life leave his traitorous eyes and heard sirens looming in the distance.

"His blood was *literally* found on your hands, Mr. Reid. You don't stand a chance in hell of walking away from this without doing some serious prison time." My good for nothing attorney informed me.

I glanced down at the cuffs around my wrists. "Did they test his blood for steroids like I told you to have them do?" I asked.

"Yeah. He came back clean."

Fuck. How was that even possible?

That meant that he was in his right state of mind when he murdered her after all.

Rage bubbled in my chest at the thought.

I leaned back in my chair and sighed. "He *killed* my baby sister. It was self-defense."

He matched my sigh. "His attorney is saying otherwise, son."

"*His* attorney. What the fuck are you talking about? He's dead—as he *should* be. Why the fuck does he have an attorney?"

He fixed his tie before he looked at me. "I didn't want to be the one to break it to you, but there's no point in keeping it from you any longer. The big-time sponsor and agent that Mike signed with are going after *you*, Jackson. Not to mention his *very* wealthy parents. They're working with the prosecution and blaming it all on you. They're doing everything that they can to protect their brand. And his parents are doing everything *they* can to protect their family's reputation. They're fighting your story tooth and nail. They're a huge sponsor and combined with Mike's family they have lots of connections and resources. They have the means to take you down."

He paused and looked down. "And the fact is—there were only three people there that night…and two of them are now dead. It's your word against theirs…and it doesn't look good. Especially because you basically admitted to killing him."

He reached into his briefcase and pulled out a folder. "Also, this showed up at my office today. I'm really sorry, Jackson."

I skimmed the letter and pounded my fist on the table. My own sponsor and agent had officially dropped me.

I would no longer be welcomed in the professional MMA world ever again.

"So what are my options?"

He ran a hand over his bald head. "Well, I talked to the prosecutor. I got Man-one off the table." He pulled another stack of papers out and moved his glasses up his nose. "The best they will offer you at this point is Manslaughter-two. 15-25 years. However, here's the clincher—if you *don't* take the deal. Mike's team *will* be teaming up with the prosecution against you." He sighed. "I hate to say it—but this is the only shot you've got."

I pinched the bridge of my nose and snorted. "15-25 years, for killing a piece of shit abuser?"

He visibly swallowed. "And Lilly," he whispered.

I stood up to my full height of 6'3 and got in his face, my shackles straining against me. "What the fuck do you mean *and* Lilly? I didn't kill my sister!" I screamed.

If I wasn't shackled to the heavy metal desk, I would have beat the crap out of him for spewing some shit like that.

He took a step back. "I told you, Mike's team is working with the prosecution. They're not putting the blame on Mike for this, Jackson. They're twisting some horrid tale about you and your sister being super *close* after growing up the way you did…if you catch my drift."

Bile ascended my throat as he continued. "They're going to say that you were jealous of Mike and your sister's relationship. Combined with the fact that he came from wealth and landed a much better sponsor than you did…it all leads to jealousy being the motive."

"But, I was at the fight that night. Hell, I *won* my fight that night. Hundreds of people saw me with their own eyes. Mike and Lilly never even showed up!"

"They're saying that you killed them before the fight because you didn't want him to compete in the first place." He made air quotes with his hands. "Because your jealousy got the best of you and finally came to a head."

I threw up my hands. "And then what? I just decided to attend my fight with his blood on my hands and *then* return to the scene of the crime instead of getting the hell out of dodge? That's insane."

"According to the prosecution's story, you returned to find a way to get rid of the bodies."

"This is bullshit."

"It is," he agreed.

I shook my head. "I'm *not* taking that deal. I'll take my chances in court. I didn't kill Lilly. If they were just accusing me of killing Mike, I would consider folding—because I *did* kill him. But I will not go down for committing the heinous act that *he* did."

He rubbed his scalp again and sat back down in the chair. "Look, I've got to level with you. We won't win this." He motioned toward the papers on the desk. "I'm good at my job. And I fully believe you didn't kill Lilly, even more—I understand what you did to Mike…but I *can't* win this. The system is corrupt as fuck, and we've got everything going against us right now. You're not walking away from this. The only option left is to plead insanity and spend the rest of your life in a straight jacket and a padded room."

I got up and motioned for the guard on the opposite side of the door.

"No," I said gruffly.

Ten days before my trial was supposed to begin, I was informed I had a visitor. Since my lawyer had pretty much all but given up on the case, I was a little surprised.

Maybe he had finally come to his senses and decided to fight for me the way he was supposed to.

I looked around the dreary gray room while I took a seat beside the metal desk. My attention soon focused on the sound of the door opening.

In walked a man wearing an impeccable suit, holding a fairly large briefcase.

He tipped his hat at me before he sat down in front of me.

"Who the hell are you?" I asked.

He gave me a smirk and pulled a pack of cigarettes out of his pocket. "I'm your new lawyer," he said.

I stood up and tilted my head in the direction of the guard, signaling him to let me out so I could go back to my cell. "I think there's been some mistake. I don't recall asking for a new lawyer." I eyed his expensive suit and snorted. "Besides, I'm positive I can't afford you anyway. I have legal aid for crying out loud."

"Sit down, Jackson." His voice boomed throughout the room.

Looking back—I wouldn't say I was scared of him…it was more like intrigued about what he was doing there in the first place.

I begrudgingly sat back down and stared at him. "Okay, let's just cut to the chase then. What's this about? Who are you?"

He cracked his knuckles and leaned back in his seat. "You can just call me your guardian angel, boy," he said smirking.

I had recently turned 24 at that point, and I was practically on death row for killing a man. I was far from a boy and didn't appreciate being told otherwise.

I narrowed my eyes at him. "You have 1 minute before I walk the fuck out of here. I don't give a shit who you are."

He studied me for a beat before he rubbed his chin and laughed. "Alright. Let's just say that I have a proposition for you." He cracked his knuckles again. "Something like a get out of jail free card. You interested?'

I raised an eyebrow at him. "From what I'm told…not even God, himself can get me out of this shithole."

He leaned forward and proceeded to light a cigarette, his eyes gleaming. "No, you're right. God can't…" He flashed me a smile. "But the devil can."

Chills ran up my spine with those words. "I would ask what the catch is, but I'm not sure I want to know," I mumbled.

I heard the click of his briefcase and he handed me what looked to be a contract of some sort.

The first thing that stood out was the name.

"Who's Bruno DeLuca? That you?" I questioned.

He laughed. "No, that is not me. However, I work for him. He's the one who sent me here."

I skimmed the rest of the contract, but I didn't understand it. It just said that I would agree to work for Bruno DeLuca for the next ten years, and failure to uphold my end of the agreement would result in disciplinary action. "What kind of work? And why the fuck would he want me? Who is this guy? And more importantly, what the fuck makes him think he can get me out of serving time for murder?"

He winked and gave me another smirk. "Let's just say that Bruno DeLuca knows a thing or two about murder, kid."

I stood up. "Okay, I've had it with the games. I have a trial in 10 days that I need to pre-pare for and I really don't need this bullshit." I looked at the guard through the plexiglass and signaled for him but he ignored me. I got up and proceeded to bang on the glass when the man's voice halted me.

"Sign that contract and you won't even have to prepare for trial. You'll be out of here within the next 48 hours. You won't go down for your sister's murder, Jackson. And more im-portantly, no one will be making disgusting and untrue accusations about your relationship with her in a court of law and tarnishing her memory."

Needless to say, that got my attention. "What does he want from me?"

"He wants you to do the thing you love the most. Compete and fight."

I spun around and faced him. "That's not going to happen…I'm pretty sure I've been canned from the professional world of MMA fighting. No sponsors or agents will touch me with a 10-foot pole."

He barked out a laugh before his expression turned serious. "This isn't professional fighting. This is underground fighting."

I said the first thing that popped into my head. "That's illegal."

He blew a puff of smoke out and shrugged. "Last time I checked, so was *murder*."

Well, he had me there. Even though I still didn't feel a single ounce of remorse for it.

I sat back down at the table and took a cigarette out of the pack. "Okay, explain to me how he has the means to do this and why he wants me…and I'll consider it."

He smiled and lit my cigarette. "I realize you're from Boston, kid, but Bruno DeLuca is the biggest mob boss to hit New York City since the five families."

I took another drag off my cigarette…I definitely needed it.

"And he runs an underground fighting ring?"

He wiggled his eyebrows. "Amongst other endeavors, yes."

"And he wants *me* because…"

"Because you showed real potential before you got locked up. Not to mention, you beat the shit out of and *murdered* a fellow professional fighter—one who our sources say was even *more* talented than you."

"It was only because of the roids he was on," I muttered.

He waved me off. "Personally, I don't give a shit. The point is that DeLuca wants you, kid. And you're not really in a position to say no to him. You're up shits creek without a paddle."

At least on that fact, I could wholeheartedly agree with him.

"I just don't get how I would be able to walk out of here, though. Look around, I'm in *jail* for Christ's sake. I'm pretty sure the judicial system would have something to say about my release."

He stared at me hard before he rubbed his fingers together. "Money and power, kid. It makes the world go round." His expression turned serious. "For starters, he's going to buy off the judge. He's also having evidence planted that will end up proving your innocence as we speak."

I held up my hands. "Whoa, I'm *not* okay with having an innocent man go down for murders that he didn't commit."

"That's not for you to decide, kid. Let's just say that this guy crossed DeLuca, so he's only getting what's coming to him. You just get to reap the benefits."

I put out my cigarette and went to stand again. "No. I won't do it."

"You don't really have a choice, Jackson."

"What's *that* supposed to mean?"

"If you don't take the deal and work for DeLuca…you will be attacked in your cell, later on, tonight." He looked me in the eyes. "And, kid. I gotta tell ya…the odds aren't in your favor in regards to making it out alive."

I glared at him. Anger pulsing through me. "So, I never had a choice in the first place, did I?"

He shrugged and handed me a pen. "Afraid not, kid. Welcome to the family."

Three years later...

Chapter One

ALYSSA

"YEAH, YOU LIKE THAT, YOU SLUT?" HE SAYS AS HE CONTINUES TO PLOW INTO me from behind.

His words reverberate through my head and I fight back the tears.

Nope. Not even a little bit.

"Yeah," I say, hoping it will all be over soon.

"Who's a little slut?" he asks before I feel his entire body spasm against me.

"I am," I whisper. All while, secretly hating myself for how true it is and for putting myself through this goddamn scenario, yet again.

All in the name of punishment.

That's what I do, though…that's how I cope. If you could even call it that.

A few more slut shaming insults and a loud grunt later…my penance is over.

I leap off the bed and make a beeline for the bathroom.

I force myself to look in the mirror. "You only did it to yourself, Alyssa," I remind myself.

I close my eyes as I run a washcloth under the warm water and proceed to clean myself up.

A moment later the door opens and arms wrap around me like tentacles.

I move my head from side to side, looking for a way out.

"That was great, babe. Huh?" he asks while adjusting his large framed glasses on his face.

I roll my eyes against his preppy, polo shirt and give him a smile that's about as fake as a two dollar bill. "Yup."

I shimmy past him and nod my head toward the front door. "You can go now," I remind him.

He looks puzzled, which only serves to annoy me further.

I swear, every time we have sex…he gets even more attached. I'm going to have to cut him off soon.

I decide to try the nice approach with him one more time. "Look, I have a job interview today and I really need to get ready for it."

He laughs nervously. "Oh, okay. I was getting a little worried there for a second. Thought you were getting sick of me." He takes a step forward. "When can I see you again? I really want to take you out on a date. I was thinking about taking you to the science…"

Ugh…the walls are officially closing in on me.

I cut him off before he has a chance to finish that sentence. "Look, Brock…I think we need to go over the rules of our arrangement again. This…" I gesture between us. "Is just sex. That's it. Once a week—maximum." I walk toward him and cup his face in my hands. "You are a great guy…but I think this needs to end."

Before he has a chance to argue, I continue on with my spiel. "It's not you, it's *totally* me. I just don't think we're looking for the same things anymore." I give him a kiss on the cheek and walk him to the front door. I unlock the door and give him a little nudge. "I'll see you around. Have a safe drive home. Buh-bye."

I slam the door shut and chain lock it behind me.

He's gone…crisis averted.

I fall back against the door…another innocent, harmless nerd prototype bites the dust before he reached stage 5 clinger status.

With a sigh, I walk back into the bathroom and turn on the shower.

I finish the rest of my shower, and study the clothes I laid out for the interview I have later on tonight.

I pull up my favorite tight pair of jeans over my hips and reach for my low-cut white top…made all that more pronounced by my black push-up bra. Then I blow dry my hair and apply a quick coat of lip gloss and mascara.

I shake out my long blonde hair and run my fingers through it a few times.

I glance at the clock and let out a curse.

Given the fact that the city's about two hours away in rush hour traffic, I'm running dangerously close to being late.

And lord knows, I *desperately* need this job.

After throwing on my favorite leather crop jacket, I give myself a once over in the mirror again and decide I'm ready to go.

I can't afford to blow this opportunity.

His dirt brown eyes skim over my body before landing on my chest. He rubs his chin and nods. "Very nice. Now, turn around and bend over for me, sweetheart."

Somewhere very deep inside, my inner feminist wants to claw his eyes out. But then I remind myself that all I've got in the fridge is a container of moldy milk…and cheese that looks like it will make good penicillin soon.

But that fails in comparison to the real reason I need this job.

I turn around and do what he says while he lets out a whistle. After a few moments have passed, I assume it's safe to turn back around and my inspection is over.

He considers me for another minute or so and gives me another nod. "You're easy on the eyes, that's for sure. And you got a rockin' body." He holds up a cue card with a giant number on it. "Think you'll be able to manage holding these up in the cage?" he asks hesitantly.

Seriously…is he kidding?

I maintained a 4.0 for 3 years while studying journalism and news-casting at NYU for crying out loud.

I flash him a strained smile. "Gee, I don't know, Mister. It looks awfully hard."

He cocks an eyebrow at me.

*Shit…*I really need to learn to tone the sarcasm down every once in a while.

He clears his throat. "You and another girl will be trading off. You'll be in the green outfit and she'll be in the red."

Awe, just like Christmas, I think before he continues with his sermon.

"And when you're not working the ring. You'll be eye candy for the elite members. You are to serve them beers, whiskey, whatever their hearts desire in between rounds. Got it?"

I nod my head. "Yes, sir."

He gives me another hard look. "And if you do anything to draw attention to this little operation we got going on here, it will take them a week to clean your brains off the pavement."

I shudder at his choice of words.

"Got it. The first rule of fight club is that you don't talk about fight club."

He shoots me a look of annoyance and mumbles something under his breath that I don't catch.

"So when do I start?" I ask eagerly.

He reaches into his desk drawer and pulls out two scraps of shiny green material. "In two hours. Get ready," he says before throwing them at me.

My mouth hangs open. "You mean, I start tonight?"

He leans his elbows against the desk. "That gonna be a problem for you?"

I quickly shake my head. "No. I would have just come more prepared if I had known is all."

He extends his thumb in the direction of the hallway. "Down the hall and to the left there's a dressing room for the ring girls. There is makeup and all that other girly shit in there." He glances at his watch. "In fact, Lou-Lou should be in there getting ready right now. I suggest you make nice with her. The only fights we like around here are the ones that bring in money. Not no prissy cat fights. Last girl got fired for that," he warns.

"You won't have a problem," I assure him. I make for the door when I abruptly turn around. "Um. So how much does this gig pay anyway?"

He chuckles. "Well, you'll only be working one weekend night, every two weeks," he says. My excitement sinks with those words. "But, you'll be making $800 for the night…plus tips."

I give him a genuine smile this time before I begin walking down the hallway.

Lou-Lou turned out to be nicer than I thought she would be. With her honey-kissed skin, full lips, small stature, and big brown eyes…it was easy to see why she'd been hired.

She flips her long dark hair over her shoulder and studies our reflection in the mirror before she ruffles my hair and winks. "We're like totally salt and peppa," she squeaks. "The guys are totally gonna love us."

Rein in your inner bitch and be nice, Alyssa. I remind myself.

I suck in my stomach and add a bit more bronzer to my mostly pale cheeks.

She gives me another smile before she takes a few steps toward the door. I look at the clock on the wall. "Shit, is it time already?"

She pops her gum and giggles. "No, silly. We need to take care of the fighters before the match."

Say what, now?

"Take care of them…how?" She gives me a wink. "Use your imagination, girlfriend."

Jesus Christ, I knew there was a catch.

Obviously, unfazed by my horrified expression she continues. "You're lucky. You're wearing green. That means you have Jackson…he's like *mega* hot. I mean, I've never been given the chance to try him out, but God, what I'd give to one day." She playfully fans herself. "I'm stuck with some guy who's good looking, but dumb as a box of rocks." She twists her hair around her finger. "See ya in a half hour, babes," she calls out before she leaves.

I spin my chair around to face the mirror again.

Could I actually do…*this?*

I mean…what I do on my own time, is pretty much the same thing. Except I do it with safe nerdy guys. Guys who are into *anime*, and play *dungeons and dragons* in their mother's basements.

Guys who *I* can control. Guys who will say and do whatever I want them to.

Guys who know about my past, but are just so happy to have a real girl to play with, they couldn't care less.

Guys who are really good at hacking computers and taking down certain things that *always* tend to pop up from time to time since that horrible day over two years ago.

I take a deep breath and calm the tremors running through my stomach.

"You only did it to yourself, Alyssa," I remind myself, yet again before I stand up and begin walking down the hallway.

I open the door.

What I'm greeted with, is a sight I'm sure I'll never forget.

Tanned, muscular, flesh—encompassed by the body of an Adonis.

My eyes can't help but stare at the finest ass I have ever seen in my entire life. Two perfect globes…so ripe, I want to bite them.

I bite my lip instead as my gaze spans over his gorgeous back. Broad, sturdy, *powerful.*

I want to scratch my nails down that back, is my last thought…before he starts to turn around.

He briskly runs the towel through his short, dark, hair. "Jesus, Ricardo. Don't you knock anymore?" he barks until he looks at me.

I can't help but look down, but he quickly shifts the towel from his head, over to his package. Doesn't stop me from taking in his large, toned, thighs, though.

Confusion is splashed all over his face. "You're *not* Ricardo," he says in a deep and raspy voice.

I shake my head. Still too transfixed by his body to speak.

My God. His abs. His abs must be made of pure granite. I silently count them in my head. *Yup, he's got an 8-pack.*

He clears his throat, and it's only then that I finally make my way up his body, but not before noticing the name scrawled over his left pectoral muscle in black ink—'*Lilly*.'

Yup, must be the girlfriend…or *wife.*

I swallow my distaste over the fact that he obviously cheats on her, as I lift my gaze and take in his eyes. Wow, they're something else. Mesmerizing, stormy gray swirls that—I'm betting, would almost look dark blue in the right light.

The rest of his face is just as striking. Full, yet masculine lips combined with a strong jawline. Lou-Lou was wrong—'*mega hot*' doesn't even begin to describe how truly handsome he is.

My gaze turns from one of appreciation to annoyance. "So, I'm guessing Ricardo is who you choose to cheat on your wife with then?"

He opens his mouth in either shock, or in an attempt to defend himself, but I don't give him the chance. "Men like you, *disgust* me. There's *no* way in hell, I'm sleeping with you now, asshole. You can forget it."

He takes a step toward me. "*What?*" He looks dumbfounded as I back away from him. "Christ, there are so many things about that statement that's wrong, I don't even know where to start."

I hold up my hands. "Whatever, I don't fuck married men."

"Good thing I'm not married then," he says.

I stare at him wide-eyed.

"Shit, that didn't come out the way it was supposed to. All I meant was that I'm not married. And if I was, I *certainly* wouldn't cheat on her. And furthermore, I wouldn't cheat on her with *Ricardo*—of all people." He smirks. "Let's just say, he's not my type." He looks me up and down, taking in my scantily clad uniform—which only consists of a shiny green bra top and matching booty shorts. "And I don't know who the hell you've been talking to, but you're not expected to fuck the fighters."

"But, Lou-Lou made it seem like—"

He shakes his head. "Whatever you do, don't listen to Lou—Lou. She's very territorial, and likes to steer the new girls in the wrong direction. Just because *she* makes it her mission to fuck the fighters, doesn't mean that *you* have to." He scratches his head. "Besides, if that was the case—*why* would you ever agree to do that anyway? Don't you value yourself at all?" he asks, his tone dripping with both disdain and curiosity.

"I—" I start. I'm at a loss for words. On one hand, I'm appalled at how judgmental he is —but on the other…he's touched on something so personal.

I open my mouth and attempt to answer him again, but instead…I reach for the doorknob behind me and book it the hell out of the room.

I run back down the hall and enter the dressing room. I lock myself inside the small toilet stall and fight back the tears for the second time that day.

His words echo in my head as I look in the mirror. "*Don't you value yourself at all?*"

I draw in a shaky breath and reapply my makeup expertly while I look myself in the eye.

"No, Jackson. Not anymore."

Chapter Two

JACKSON

"**A**ND IN THIS CORNER—WEIGHING IN AT 235LBS OF PURE STEEL. LADIES AND Gentlemen, I present to you—'Jack the Ripperrrrrr,'" the announcer yells, while I inwardly cringe.

There are no words to describe how much I truly hate my stage name.

Needless to say, I didn't choose it.

Just like every other decision for the last 3 years, it was made for me.

I have no control over my own life anymore. And I fucking hate it.

Ricardo, my mob appointed coach; taps my back and whispers words of encouragement. I nod my head as he walks off to sit in the far corner.

I look up at the camera positioned directly above the ring and give another nod. This one's for the devil himself, Bruno DeLuca.

I'd only met him once, but I know for a fact that he watches every single match, without fail.

I search the crowd for Tyrone, yes—*that* Tyrone who fought in Mike's place that horrible night. Funny how the world works. Shortly after I joined the 'DeLuca family', Tyrone ended up joining as well.

Obviously, *not* of his own free will. He got involved with the wrong crowd, in his hometown of Alabama; and ended up going down for some shit that really wasn't his fault, but got put on him anyway.

That's, of course, when DeLuca came in to save the day.

Not only is Tyrone one hell of a fighter, but he's also my good friend and roommate. He's also the only person I talk to about Lilly in my darkest times.

He's not scheduled to fight tonight, but we always show up to support one another.

I lock eyes with him briefly. He gives me a big smile and fist pumps the air. "Give em' hell, J-man! Break bad on em,'" he shouts in his thick Southern accent.

I try not to smirk, and study my opponent instead.

I've got about an inch on him, but he's got a good 10-15lbs on me. From what Ricardo told me about him, he's more of a boxer, rather than an MMA fighter.

This should be an interesting match.

That's the other thing about DeLuca's fight club. It's pretty much anything goes. Even dirty style fighting.

Especially dirty style fighting.

My opponent rolls his shoulders and snorts.

The announcer walks off and I hear the sound of the cage being locked around us.

I assume my stance and the bell rings.

Adrenaline pulses through me as he advances toward me and attempts a right jab to my face.

I deflect and cock my arm at a 90-degree angle and get him with a right hook instead. He grunts and comes at me with another jab and quickly attempts to grab me. He almost had me for a second, but I get him with a sharp uppercut to his jaw.

Blood spews out and he begins to stumble backward.

Then I see it.

Out in the crowd, I can't help but notice her in the second row.

The same girl who entered my dressing room earlier.

Only, it's not her long blonde hair, smokin' body, or beautiful hazel eyes that grab my attention this time.

It's the utter fear I see in them.

I look down and see that some asshole has his fingers wrapped tightly around her wrist…and he's not letting up. It looks like she was trying to serve him a drink, but instead, he's forcing her to sit on his lap.

His movements are only getting more aggressive, and no one's doing a damn thing about it. He then reaches up with his other hand and palms one of her breasts.

That's when I lose my shit.

I run over to the side of the cage. "Let her go! *Now!*"

Both he and the crowd ignore me and begin to chant my name instead. I cock my head to the side and look at Ricardo. "Help her! Get her out of here!" I scream.

He points to his ear and shakes his head.

Fuck, he can't hear me.

I scan the crowd for that asshole, Luke, who's supposed to be in charge of the ring girls. He looks over at her, but instead of helping her, he only shrugs and smiles at me.

I growl and flip him the bird.

I look out into the crowd for Tyrone and begin rattling the cage. The crowd cheers even louder then.

Bastards.

I begin scaling the cage, and finally; Tyrone looks at me. I point in her direction. "Get her out of here, now…" I start to say until I'm quickly yanked back.

Something solid hits my eye with enough force to turn my head and knock my mouth guard out.

I can hear the crowd collectively gasp.

I've never been hit dead on before. I've always been able to deflect it.

My opponent smiles from ear to ear…but little does he know that he just unleashed hell.

Out of the corner of my good eye, I see Tyrone heading in her direction.

At least, she'll be safe now. This is no place for a girl like her, that's for sure.

Visions of Lilly flash through my mind. The pain flows through me and I let my opponent have it.

We start to grapple, but it's a lost cause for him. I'm hitting him with numerous elbow strikes, uppercuts, and jabs. I don't even realize I've already knocked him out until someone bombards the cage and pulls me off of him.

I almost take a swing at them, before I hear Ricardo's voice. "You got him, man. He's out. You did it," he says.

I stare down at my opponent and all I see is Mike…all I see is that night.

Despite the crowds frantic cheers, I run out of there.

After a shower and a brisk visit with one of the mob doc's, it's declared that, although extremely swollen, there's no permanent damage to my eye.

All the fights scheduled for the night are now over, so I grab my bag and head out into the cool late September night air.

As soon as I step out…I'm immediately struck by a tiny fist to the face.

What the hell?

"Thanks a lot, *dick*," a woman's voice yells.

I look down and can hardly believe my eyes. It's the same blonde from earlier. Except this time, she looks beyond pissed.

Not something I was expecting.

I pull my bag up higher over my shoulder and stare at her. "You know, usually, damsel's in distress say 'thank you' after being saved."

She lifts her chin. "Fuck you," she spews. "I really needed this job and now I'm fired." She jabs a finger into my chest. "All because of *you*. Didn't anyone ever teach you how to mind your own business? I was fine in there."

I shake my head and begin walking. "You weren't fine. You were being *assaulted*." I stop walking and look at her. "What the hell is *wrong* with you?"

She tightens her leather jacket around her and crosses her arms over her chest. "I just *told* you. I got fired and I *really* needed that job."

I shrug. "Trust me, you're better off. This is no place for a girl like you."

"You don't even *know* me," she whispers.

Well, she has me there.

I reach into my pocket and pull out a wad of cash. She begins to protest, but I give her no choice. "Here. Sorry for the inconvenience I caused you. Obviously, you really need the money or you wouldn't have punched *me* in the face over it. Word to the wise…not all men would react the same way I would to being punched, so be careful out there."

I continue walking, even though I can hear her footsteps following behind me. "Thanks, but I can't accept this. I like to earn my money."

She tries handing it back to me, but I decline. "Look, Luke owed you money for the night anyway. Consider this your payment from the club."

She begins walking beside me. "How's your eye?"

"Fine. No permanent damage." I cross the street with her still in toe beside me. "Do you live around here or something?" I ask.

She looks at me curiously and I see the corner of her lips twitch. "Well, unlike *you*. Yes, *I'm* a New Yorker."

"What gave it away?"

She smiles and I see the hint of a dimple on the left side of her cheek peek out. "I don't know, but that's a *wicked* cool accent you got there, Boston."

I can't help but smile myself. She's good, I'll give her that much. "So, damsel, what's your name?"

She shoots me an icy cold stare. "I'm not a damsel. And I'll tell you, *if* you promise to never call me that again."

"Deal, but that deals only in effect until the next time I see you." I give her a wink. "Then all bet's are off," I tease.

"Alyssa."

I give her a smirk. "So does that mean you're planning on seeing me again in the future?"

She shakes her head as we cross another street and walk down another block. "No offense, Jackson. But you're not really *my* type."

Not gonna lie, that stung a little. Then, I think about the reality of the situation and know she's right. I already know that this girl deserves a lot better than someone like me. Not to mention the fact that dating isn't exactly my thing. "Yeah, you're probably right. Take care," I say before I begin walking ahead of her.

"Jackson," she calls out and I can't help but turn around. "Thank you," she says before she opens a car door.

I nod my head, but can't help but wonder. "You drive?"

"Yeah, I live on Long Island. Nassau County to be exact," she says.

"I thought you said before that you were a real New Yorker?"

She snorts and her eyes shoot daggers at me. She lets out a slew of curses finally ending with, "I *am* a New Yorker, you Boston prick."

Then she slams her car door and guns the engine.

That's when I notice it. It's a few years old...but she's definitely driving a BMW.

She's obviously not *that* hard up for money after all. And I just gave her everything in my wallet.

Shit, I guess it's true what they say. There really is a sucker born every minute.

Chapter Three

ALYSSA

MOST WOMEN GO TO BARS WHEN THEY'RE LOOKING TO PICK UP MEN FOR A QUICK hookup…not me.

I prefer to pick up my men at libraries, bookstores, and the nearest Starbucks.

I glance at the clock on my dashboard. It's just after 11 pm. Luckily, since I'm still in the city everything is open late, especially on the weekends.

I parallel park into the nearest spot outside the coffee shop and turn my engine off.

The nerve of that bastard. Long Island *is* in New York.

But it's not that statement of his causing me to be in need of seeking out a distraction. It's his *other* statement from earlier still running through my head. "*Don't you value yourself at all?*"

I almost wanted to laugh when he said that the club was no place for a girl like me.

He obviously has no idea who I am. Either that, or he's putting on a really good show.

I walk into the almost empty Starbucks and look around before I spot my target.

Glasses-check. Button-up shirt paired with khakis-check. Not overly attractive by conventional standards, but relatively pleasing to the eye—check. Fingers working furiously on a laptop—check.

I order my favorite—a vanilla chai latte with whipped cream and pull up a seat next to him. "Hey there, handsome. Come here often?" I ask as I lean across the table, giving him a nice view of my cleavage.

He gives me a shy smile and takes a sip of his drink. "Lately, yes. I have a thesis I'm working on."

"Sounds exciting," I say.

He then goes on and *on* for the next fifteen minutes about his thesis which has something to do with acid rain, before I decide I've had enough and interrupt him. I reach across the table for his hand. "It sounds like you're under a lot of stress," I say sympathetically.

He nods his head. "Yes, It's tremendous. I feel like I'm going out of my mind."

I swipe the whipped cream from my drink with my finger and lick. "You know what helps with that?"

He blushes. "Just so you know—I've never, ever, done this before…but I live 15 minutes away from here."

Oh, he's a virgin…that's even better. Perfect even.

"I have a car. We'll be there in five," I say before I stand up and head for the door.

I park in the lot across from his apartment building. I don't usually go to guy's houses and I'm feeling apprehensive about it.

I take a look around the parking lot. It's empty and pretty dark. "You know, I have to be up early. Maybe we can just do it right here?" I offer.

He looks surprised but doesn't protest as we climb in the backseat.

I begin straddling him and grinding against him until I feel his entire body tense. Poor guys nervous. *First-time jitters.*

I cup his face in my hands. "Relax. You don't have to be nervous with me. I'm gonna make this good for you."

I tilt my head to the side and begin kissing him. At first, the kiss is tender…until he bites my lower lip…enough to draw blood.

I pull back. "Whoa, not so hard, sweetie."

In the blink of an eye, he grabs both my wrists in one hand, before he pulls them around my back and secures them with something metal.

My first thought—is that I'm being arrested for prostitution. But the thing is. I'm *not* a prostitute. This is all just some horrible misunderstanding.

Way to go, Alyssa.

"Look, I know what you think. But I assure you, I'm not a prostitute," I begin yelling.

He flips me over so that I'm lying on my stomach. Then he slams a piece of duct tape across my mouth.

This isn't typical police procedure. *Oh, fuck.*

"You may not be charging me for sex, sweetie. But we both know what a slut you really are. I *knew* you looked real familiar. Let's just say that I've seen you before," he sneers against my ear before he begins unbuttoning my pants.

Oh, God.

It's obvious he's not some safe, nerdy virgin after all. Nor is he an undercover cop trying to arrest me.

It's so much worse than that.

And the worst part is…this is *all* my fault.

I struggle against him, but it's no use.

I bash my head against my window in hopes that someone will hear my muffled screams. Or that I'll pass out before the unthinkable happens.

I close my eyes and whimper against the window before the door is ripped open and I feel myself begin to move forward.

I open my eyes and can tell I'm about to hit the concrete, but I'm hauled up just in the nick of time. I'm then shoved out of the way as some massive creature reaches inside the car and yanks my attacker out.

*Wait a minute…*I recognize that broad back.

I open my mouth to scream, but can't due to the tape.

For the next few minutes, Jackson unleashes a plethora of punches and kicks. Blood is dripping from the guy's face, lip, and nose down onto the concrete.

I begin jumping up and down in hopes to get him to stop.

I don't want to be the cause of him murdering some guy…even if a part of me thinks he deserves it.

Finally, he stops punching the guy and looks at me. His features change from concern to disbelief. "Alyssa?"

He quickly rips the tape off my mouth. "He handcuffed me, Jackson."

He looks at my bound hands behind my back. "Yeah, I can see that," he says before he picks the guy up by his collar and searches his pockets. "I can't find the key."

The guy lifts his head and spits blood at him. "That's because there isn't one. Whore's like her don't deserve to be free," he says, before Jackson delivers one final punch and the guy passes out cold.

"Um, is he?" I ask.

"No. Should be, though."

With a grunt, he lifts the guy's body over his head and throws him in the nearest dumpster. "I think it's safe to say that he won't be bothering you anymore."

"Thanks, but it was my fault."

He shakes his head. "Why do most victims feel the need to blame themselves?"

"You don't understand. I was the one who propositioned *him* for sex. I mean, I thought he was a nice, normal guy. Then things got out of hand, but *before* that, I knew exactly what I was getting into."

He gives me an odd look, almost as if he's seeing who I am for the first time. "Still wasn't your fault," he mumbles. "I saw you fighting against him, you clearly didn't want it anymore."

That's when it dawns on me. "What the hell are you doing here, Jackson?"

He points to the apartment building across the street. "I live there."

I blow out a puff of air. "So does he."

"Then you really don't have to worry about him anymore." He looks down appearing uncomfortable. "Alyssa?"

"Yeah?"

"Your pants. I don't know the proper way to say this, but they're way past where they should be."

I look down and curse when I notice my jeans around my knees and I realize that I'm standing there wearing nothing but a bright pink thong. "Well, seeing as I'm a little tied up, you think you can help me out with that, chief?"

"Yeah, no problem."

He bends down and his hands softly brush against my thighs, his touch lighting every nerve ending along the way. He looks up at me from underneath his impossibly long and dark lashes while he gently slides my jeans up past my hips. I let out a breath I wasn't aware I was holding when his fingers graze my lower abdomen before he fastens the button. He swallows hard and my temperature skyrockets when his fingers dip lower and he ever-so-slowly drags my zipper up.

So not the time to be turned on, Alyssa, I remind myself.

He quickly backs away, putting a few feet of distance between us. "I think I have something in my apartment, like a saw or something that should be able to get those off."

I bite my lip. I really do have a thing about going back to guy's places. But Jackson's two for two now. In a single night, no less. And call me crazy, but there's just something about him that makes me feel like I'd be safe with him.

We begin walking across the street to the apartment complex. "I have a roommate. But he shouldn't be home now."

I narrow my eyes at him. "Are you expecting something for your services?"

He looks insulted, which of course, makes me feel like shit. "No. God no. Of course, not. I was just saying that in case you were embarrassed. You know, due to your current situation and all."

No, not embarrassed, but *definitely* feeling like shit now.

Chapter Four

JACKSON

"IF YOU WANT TO GO TO THE POLICE AFTER THIS, I'LL GO WITH YOU," I SAY WHEN I open the door to my apartment building.

Hesitation, discomfort, and finally what looks like resolve flash in her eyes all in the five seconds it takes her to answer. "No."

I say a silent prayer that Tyrone's not home as we ascend the stairs to my apartment. Lord knows, he'll have a lot of questions about this.

Especially since for the last 3 years he's known me, I've never brought a girl back to our apartment before.

Let alone, one who's already in handcuffs. I'd be lying if I said the vision of her bound and standing there in her hot pink thong didn't make my cock twitch.

Until I reminded myself how she ended up that way.

With a sigh I continue leading her to my front door …then I hear it.

Fuck me…this is not good.

"Look, I'm sorry. It turns out my roommate's home after all," I say while trying not to stare into those piercing hazel eyes of hers.

"How do you know? I mean, we're not even inside yet."

"I'm surprised you can't hear it," I mutter as I pull out my key and open the door.

When we walk in, it's even worse than I imagined it would be. He's parading around the living room, *Risky Business* style…in nothing but a pair of green *Hulk* boxers, while Nelly's— *Country Grammar* blasts from the stereo.

Alyssa's mouth drops open and I can't tell if it's because she's impressed by his dance moves, or him in general.

Truth be told, most women are impressed with him.

It's probably the combination of his Southern accent and the fact that he's built like a brick shit house. That, and Tyrone himself has been known to turn on the charm and be a bit of a player when the time calls for it.

And since I've had the liberty of not only being his roommate, but sharing a locker room with the guy for 3 years…I can, *unfortunately*, attest to the fact—that yes—it *is* true what they say about black guys and their equipment.

"From Texas back up to Indiana, Chi-Town, K.C., Motown to Alabamaaaa!" he screams before he spins around and faces us.

Beside me, Alyssa lets out a little giggle.

"Shit, Jackson. I'm sorry. I thought you were still at the club," he says. He flashes Alyssa a coy smile. "And who is this lovely lady?" Before Alyssa can answer, confusion sweeps across his features. "Wait, you're the ring girl. Aren't you?"

Alyssa nods her head while Tyrone holds out his hand to her. "I'm sorry ma'am, where are my manners? We didn't really have a chance to exchange pleasantries at the club, I'm Tyrone."

She clearly can't shake *his* hand, though, seeing as she's still handcuffed and all. She looks down and backs away while uttering a curse. Tyrone immediately and understandably, looks offended, which just makes this whole situation that much worse.

He cocks an eyebrow at me. I know what he's implying and since I'm almost positive that it's not true, I really need to run interference. "She can't shake your hand because she's handcuffed, Tyrone," I offer.

Alyssa begrudgingly turns around to show him.

"Shiiiit, girl. You on the lamb?" he asks.

"No. There was a misunderstanding and I somehow ended up getting handcuffed while in the backseat of my car. But we can't find the key," she says.

She shoots me a glance that I can only interpret as 'please, don't say any more about what happened.'

I nod my head, while Tyrone looks at me, grins, and shakes his head while muttering, "Crazy ass, white boy," under his breath. I take a step behind Alyssa and give him the finger before asking, "Do we have a saw or something around here?"

He rubs his chin and grins. "No Jackson, we're not all freaks like you. But you know who might have one?"

"Fuck," I mumble.

"What? What's the matter?" Alyssa asks.

Tyrone rubs his hands together. "This is gonna be awesome," he says before he opens the front door.

Alyssa quickly follows him even though I try stopping her.

I follow them both out into the hallway. Tyrone pounds on his front door. "Yoo-hoo. Ricky Ricardoooooo, I know you're in there. Open up," he says in his mock Spanish accent.

Alyssa nudges me with her elbow. "Ricardo? You mean—"

"My coach," I finish for her.

The door swiftly opens and out comes a shirtless Ricardo…along with a barely dressed Lou-Lou close behind him. Lou-Lou props a hand on her hip. "Peppa? I thought you got canned?" she sneers.

Tyrone and I exchange a glance, but it's quickly interrupted when Alyssa lunges toward Lou-Lou. "Number one, I have blonde hair, you idiot. Number two—you're a *bitch*. Thanks a lot for lying to me about our '*job description*'. I can't believe I almost slept with *him*!" she screams.

I don't have time to be offended by her statement because Lou-Lou cackles, which only infuriates Alyssa that much more. "I didn't tell you to do anything you didn't want to do in the first place. I know a slut when I see one. Not my fault you fell for the trap and showed your true colors." She motions to the handcuffs and her lips turn up in a snarl. "*Puttana*."

I instinctively stand in front of Alyssa while Ricardo reaches for his shirt. "Whoa, ladies. That's enough," he snaps.

Alyssa proceeds to ignore him, and instead, steps to the side and head-butts Lou-Lou.

Lou-Lou lets out a yelp while I pull Alyssa back to me. "Go home, Lou-Lou," I bark.

Ricardo whispers something in her ear and with a sniffle, she finally, walks down the hallway and into her own apartment.

"You *all* live in the same apartment building?" Alyssa asks when we walk back inside my apartment.

"Yeah," is my only reply because I'm more worried about the red spot forming on her forehead at the moment.

I usher her into the kitchen, pull out an ice pack from the freezer and hold it to her head. She winces, but mumbles a quick "Thanks."

"So, why exactly, do you have the same girl from earlier tonight standing in your apartment, Jackson?" Ricardo asks. His gaze shifts behind her back. "Handcuffed, no less."

He takes a step closer to Alyssa and something flashes across his face.

Alyssa's expression changes from one of annoyance to what I can only interpret as shame… which I'm guessing is due to the handcuffs.

"I've seen you before," Ricardo whispers.

That's odd.

"Yeah," Alyssa says softly while looking down at her feet.

I don't know what the hell's going on, but they exchange another glance and Ricardo clears his throat. "I have a blow torch, I'll be right back."

Alyssa sprouts up from her chair. "A *blow torch*. No. Fuck, no!" she screams.

I run my hand along her cheek in an attempt to calm her down. She shivers at first before she leans into my touch. "Look, I promise, I won't let him hurt you. It's the only way to get those off, though."

"It's gonna hurt, Jackson. What if he ends up burning me?"

I trace my finger down her jaw and she closes her eyes. "He won't. I won't let that happen," I whisper while she nods her head.

Tyrone clears his throat, shakes *his* head, and pulls a bottle of Jack Daniels out of the cabinet.

He pours a glass and walks over to Alyssa. "This should help calm your nerves."

She gives him a smile as he lifts the glass to her lips and she takes a sip.

A moment later Ricardo walks back into the apartment wearing a welder's helmet and a pair of gloves. He's also holding what looks to be a miniature sized blow torch in his hand.

Tyrone tilts the glass to her lips again, but Alyssa declines. "No thank you. I really *don't* like to drink," she says sharply.

She's trying not to show it, but I can see her begin to tremble.

Ricardo pulls out another pair of gloves. "Jackson, see if you can put these on her hands so I don't end up burning her."

I take the gloves from him and make quick work of slipping them on underneath the cuffs.

Alyssa's eyes connect with mine and she swallows hard. "There's going to be sparks," she whispers.

"I'll protect you," I assure her.

Ricardo walks behind her. "Hold still," he says before he pulls the face part to his mask down.

Alyssa glances over her shoulder. "Um, do you have any experience with this?"

"With a blow torch or getting people out of handcuffs?"

"Both."

He jerks a shoulder up. "I'm a Puerto Rican from the Bronx," he says, as if that answers her question.

Her entire body tenses, until I move closer. "Keep your head against my chest," I whisper. "The sparks will hit me, not you."

She shakes her head, her expression turning solemn. "No, I don't want you to get hurt either."

"It's fine," I say as she tucks her head against my chest and I fold my arms around her.

I try not to breathe in the hint of coconut in her silky hair as I continue to hold her.

Tyrone looks at me and makes a "tsk, tsk" sound under his breath. Ricardo starts the blow torch and less than a minute later, Alyssa's hands are free.

"Thank you," she murmurs to both me and Ricardo.

Ricardo nods and heads for the front door. "Training is at 3pm tomorrow, guys," he reminds us before he leaves.

Alyssa stands up and brushes her hands over her pants. "Where's the bathroom?"

I point over my shoulder. "Second door on the right. If you need anything, let me know."

She gives me a smile before she begins walking.

I walk over to the fridge and grab a bottle of water.

Tyrone, who's still in his hulk boxer shorts drums his fingers on the countertop and stares at me. "That girl is trouble with a capital F," he starts.

I roll my eyes. "Last time I checked, trouble begins with a *T*, Tyrone."

"Well, in her case it's F, because she will *fuck* you over and I don't mean in the bedroom. I know you don't date much, but seriously. Take my word for it, that girl is all kinds of trouble that you don't need."

"She's a nice girl…" I start to say.

"I'm not judging, lord knows I've brought home my fair share of crazies…but last time I checked. *Nice girls* don't show up on people's doorsteps in handcuffs. Nor, do they go around headbutting other chicks."

I run a hand through my hair. "She was in trouble. It wasn't her fault."

He gives me a pointed look. "Yeah, it never is." He sighs. "Please, just tell me that she didn't ask you for money already." Apparently my expression must give me away because he lets out another sigh. "In her defense, she didn't ask. I basically gave her no choice but to take what I made from the fight tonight."

He spits out his drink. "You mean to tell me that you handed that girl over 5 *grand*!"

"*What?*" a voice shrieks behind me.

In a flash, Alyssa reaches inside her purse. "What the *hell* is the matter with you? Take your money back, now. I had no idea it was that much."

I begin to protest, but she slams the wad of cash down on the countertop while looking at Tyrone. "You should listen to your friend, Jackson. I'm not a good girl. You don't want to get mixed up with someone like me," she says before she makes her way to the front door.

I instinctively reach for her hand. "Stop. First off, you didn't ask me for the money, I gave it to you. Secondly, you've been drinking—you shouldn't be driving right now. And finally, I can make my own decisions regarding the people I hang out with. So, sit your ass down on the couch…*now*."

She raises an eyebrow at me before she takes a few tentative steps toward the couch in the living room and sits.

Tyrone glances at the money on the counter and shrugs. "Maybe I misjudged you after all," he says in Alyssa's direction before he heads to his bedroom.

I walk out to the living room. "Anything *else* you want me to do?" she asks.

"Yeah, tell me a little bit about yourself, for starters."

She smirks. "Please, like I'm sure you don't already know."

I have no idea what's she talking about, but I'm getting sick of her evasive answers. "You know what? Forget it," I huff before I stand up.

A few moments later I walk back out and hand her a fresh t-shirt and a pair of boxers. "What's this?"

"What does it look like?"

She shakes her head. "I had like one sip of alcohol. I'm fine to drive, really. I don't need to spend the night."

"You live over an hour away. It's already 2:30 in the morning. I'll take the couch, you can take my bedroom."

She stands up. "No, Jackson. You've already helped me way more than I deserve for one night. I can't keep taking advantage of you."

Her entire expression softens, and I can't help but think that maybe, she's finally going to let her guard down with me.

"It's not taking advantage if I offer," I insist.

With a sigh, she holds out her hand and accepts the clothes. "Why are you being so nice to me?" she whispers.

"Why not?" I counter.

Then, to my complete surprise. She stands up on her tiptoes and plants a kiss on my cheek. "Thank you, Jackson."

I watch as she closes the door to the bedroom...and I can't help but think that maybe, Tyrone's right after all.

This girl is trouble...but I still can't help but want to know what her demons are.

A few hours later, I hear the sound of the balcony door close and I'm on my feet.

I scrub a hand down my face and walk outside. The sunrise is coming up over the horizon and Alyssa's curled up on a chair with a blanket draped over her.

"I'm sorry. I didn't mean to wake you," she says.

I take a seat on the chair next to her. "It's fine. Are you okay?"

She twirls her hair into some kind of knot on top of her head. "Yeah, I just kind of have a *thing* when it comes to being at other people's houses. I really don't like it."

Hmm, that's interesting.

"I won't hurt you, Alyssa."

She grips the edge of the chair. "Then what do you want from me, Jackson?"

I decide to be honest with her. "That's the thing. I don't want anything from you." I look at her. "Actually, that's kind of a lie. I would really like to get to know you. Maybe even...if you *let* me. Be your friend."

"My friend? Yeah, right. That's new," she scoffs. "Look, you already know I'll put out...if that's what you're after."

I place my hand on her shoulder. "It's not. Please, don't take offense to this, you're beautiful...but something tells me that you need a real friend much more than you need another guy to fuck right now."

"I don't even know what to say to that," she whispers.

"Say you'll have lunch with me today."

"Lunch?"

"Yeah, lunch. That's all, I swear."

She seems to contemplate this as she stretches out in the chair. "I don't even know your last name. Or anything else about you."

I extend my hand out to her and grin. "I'm Jackson Reid. I turned 27 in August and I'm formerly of Boston, Ma—which gives me my *wicked* cool accent...but now I reside here. "

She takes my hand and smiles. "Alyssa Tanner...I'll be 24 at the end of next month and consider yourself lucky. New York City is the best place in the whole entire world."

"So why do you live just outside the city limits then?"

She closes her eyes. "My parent's house is there."

"Oh, so you still live with your parents?"

She gets up from the chair and walks over to the balcony door. "No, I don't."

I open my mouth to find out more about her, but she interrupts me.

"I'm going to try and get some more sleep. But, I'll join you for lunch, Jackson."

Chapter Five

JACKSON

To my astonishment, Alyssa stayed true to her word and ended up going out to lunch with me.

Since I let her pick the place, we're currently sitting at some hole in the wall diner…seated in a corner booth in the far back.

She looks around the restaurant before she tugs her sunglasses off her face and sticks them in her purse.

I can't help but wonder why she's even wearing them in the first place…given that it's raining out and all.

"Being in public bothers you," I say, making it a statement and not a question.

She folds her hands in front of her before she looks me right in the eye. "How long are you going to go on pretending, Jackson?"

I tilt my head to the side. "I have no idea what you're talking about. I really wish you would just tell me, though."

She studies my face for a few moments. "Tell me, Jackson. Do you have a computer?"

I take a sip of my drink. "Yeah, why?"

"Do you watch porn on your computer?"

I nearly choke on my drink. That was certainly the last thing I was expecting to come out of her mouth. I open my mouth to say something, but luckily, the waitress comes to our table to take our order.

After she's gone, I decide to attempt to break up the now awkward silence between us. "So, you're a porn star. That's the big secret?"

She shoots me an icy cold stare. "Not by choice," she mumbles.

"I don't understand," I say, my confusion growing with every moment that passes between us.

She rubs her temples. "Fine. You really want to know me, Jackson? You really want to know everything?"

"Yes. I won't judge you, I promise."

She leans back against the booth. "I went to NYU a few years ago. If you can believe it, I was on track to become a newscaster. It was my dream, ever since I was a little girl." She closes her eyes for a second before she clears her throat and continues. "Anyway, I was a year away from graduating when my mother decided to get remarried. She ended up marrying a Politician. You've probably heard of him before, John Travine."

The name mildly rings a bell. "Yeah, I've heard of him. I don't remember what he ran for, but the name sounds familiar."

"He ran for mayor of New York City 3 years ago," she tells me.

"So, what happened at NYU?"

She looks down nervously before she begins. "Well, like I said. My mother ended up marrying that piece of shit politician." Her jaw hardens and her entire body becomes rigid. "I hate him, Jackson. The way he exploited my family's tragedy in front of the media. The way he turned my own mother against me. He could drop dead tomorrow, and I honestly don't think I would be able to feel one ounce of sympathy for him."

I reach across the table for her hand. "Family tragedy?"

She pulls back her hand with abrupt force, like my hand is made of lava and I'm about to singe her. There's so much pain in her eyes it almost hurts to look at her. "I can't talk about that. Please."

"I won't force you to tell me anything you don't want to, Alyssa."

She pinches the bridge of her nose. "I was doing really well at NYU. I maintained a 4.0 and everything. I was focused on my goals and kept myself out of trouble. Anyway, my stepfather ran for mayor and my mother and I were thrust into the political spotlight and all that comes with it. Like I said, he exploited my family, he used my mother, and…" She pauses and looks at me. "Just trust me when I say that he's not a good guy, Jackson."

Her expression is filled with so much sorrow, it practically sears me straight to the bone.

"I believe you," I tell her.

She gives me a small smile that fades just as quickly as it appears.

"I wanted to get back at him. It was so unbelievably fucked up, but I decided to do something horrible. Something that I knew would piss him off when he found out. Looking back it was absolutely stupid, and it ended up backfiring big time." She shrugs. "But I had just turned 21 at the time and I was still naive in regards to certain things. Not that it excuses what I did, but…"

I lean forward, my curiosity coming to a peak. "What did you do?"

"Well, my roommate was dating Dean Gaffney, Jr at the time," she starts to say before I interrupt her.

"Wait a minute. You don't mean Mayor Gaffney's son, do you?"

"Yes. That's exactly who I'm referring to."

I know whatever she's about to tell me is going to be bad, real bad.

"Fuck, Alyssa. What happened?"

"I decided that I was going to flirt with him. Maybe even hook up with him. I wanted it to get back to my stepdad. And I thought—what better way to make him upset than having him hear that I was involved with his opponents son." Her eyes become glassy. "I know I broke the girl code. I know, I'm the worst kind of female in the world, but I just wanted to make him angry. I didn't care about the repercussions at the time. I wasn't thinking straight, Jackson. I just wanted him out of our lives. I wanted him to leave my mother and me alone and find another family to terrorize."

"No judgment here, Alyssa. We've all done things we never thought we would in the heat of the moment."

Like murdering your best friend for killing your sister.

"So, one night—he showed up at my dorm room. Melody, my roommate wasn't there at the time. She was busy with her study group. He asked me if I wanted to grab dinner. I thought it was the perfect opportunity. During dinner he said all the right things…and we bonded over our mutual dislike of my stepdad. He also thought it was disgusting how he was using what happened to my fath…" she starts to say before she stops herself.

"Anyway, after dinner, we went back to his dorm. His roommate was out for the evening. We had a few drinks and…"

That's when I decide to stop her. "So he got you drunk?"

She shakes her head. "No. I mean, not exactly. It's hard to explain. I was somewhere between being buzzed but not drunk. It was just enough alcohol to lower my inhibitions, but not to the point where I didn't know what I was doing."

Shit. I really hate where this story's going, but I can't bring myself to stop her.

"So, one thing led to another and we started hooking up." She squeezes her eyes shut. "I was still a virgin, Jackson."

I swallow against the lump forming in my throat. "Did he rape you?"

"No." She takes a deep breath. "He only filmed me having sex without my knowledge and put it out on the Internet for the whole entire world to see."

She scrunches up her nose. "The best part was when Melody burst into the room at the exact moment I lost my virginity. I'll never forget what she said. 'Alyssa, you slut.' Which is conveniently the name of the video."

"Jesus, I'm so sorry, Alyssa."

She shrugs. "Don't be. I only did it to myself. I deserved it. I broke the girl code and hooked up with my roommate's boyfriend. I hurt my mother to the point where she disowns me." She snorts. " The only good thing that came out of it was that my stepdad ended up losing the election…most likely because of me. Besides, milking my family's tragedy…his campaign was built around promoting abstinence for the youth and other Christian family values. Needless to say, my sex tape made quite a mockery of his entire campaign."

Damn.

"I can't believe your mom disowned you after that, though. That's horrible."

"Yeah, well my stepdad didn't really give her much of a choice. After he lost, they moved someplace down south. He became mayor of a really small town down there. She's obviously happy, so again…it is what it is."

"Why didn't you press charges against him?" I ask.

She bites her lip. "I couldn't afford a lawyer. My stepfather's campaign was going down the tubes at that point and he was pissed. He refused to help me in any way. Besides, apparently there's some kind of law in New York that basically states that as long as one party knows about it being filmed it's not illegal. And just to cover his tracks, Dean also told authorities that I knew we were filming it. The asshole even said it was my idea in the first place to make a porno, but it wasn't. Also, he and his father had one of the best defense attorneys lined up to represent them in case I pressed charges and went through with the lawsuit. And technically, Dean didn't distribute the tape for money."

She holds up her hands and makes air quotes. "It got leaked somehow." She rubs her forehead and sighs. "But mostly, I just didn't want to be in the spotlight anymore, Jackson. That tape ruined my life…I didn't have the strength to stand up in court and have my every move scrutinized."

We both stare at one another for a few moments. "So, what happened to your father?" I ask at the same time she asks, "Who's Lilly?"

I stare down at my uneaten food. "Lilly was my sister," I whisper.

Sadness sweeps across her face. "Was?"

"Yeah. She's…um. She's dead."

"God, Jackson. I'm so sorry. What happened?"

I look at her. "What happened to your dad?"

"He's…dead."

"Do you wanna talk about it?"

She chews on her thumbnail. "No, I really, really don't."

"Me either."

She smiles. "Okay, deal. I won't ask you about Lilly and you won't ask me about my dad."

I breathe a sigh of relief. "Deal."

She takes a bite of her bagel. "So, you should probably know the reason I hate spending the night at places other than my own house is because of what happened. It's made me a little paranoid. I always feel like there's a hidden video camera waiting for me in the shadows somewhere."

I take a bite of my now cold burger. "That's understandable."

"And the reason why I go out and have lots of sex with wholesome 'nerdy guys' is because—" She pauses. "Well, originally it was because they're usually good at hacking computers and making the videos disappear." She sighs. "However, it always pops back up. It's gotten to the point where I've stopped trying to track it down. The Internet really is forever."

"I'm sorry," is all I can manage to say because in all honesty her situation sucks.

She looks down. "And since I'm being so candid with you. I guess I have sex with them as a way of punishing myself."

That's...disturbing.

"Why?"

"Do you have any idea what it's like to have millions of people think of you as nothing but a slut, Jackson?"

"No, I can't say that I do."

"Do you have any idea what it's like to know that millions of people saw you at your most vulnerable moment? Completely exposed, raw, naked. And millions of people are judging you...everywhere you go. I can't go to the supermarket without breaking out in a full on panic attack over the fact that the guy at the checkout counter stares at me for a second too long. I can't get a normal job because everyone knows who I am and knows exactly what I look like giving a freakin' blowjob. Hell, I couldn't even finish school because not only did my stepdad stop paying for my tuition after my little stunt, but I just couldn't take the constant scrutiny from everyone."

She then stares at me with those big, hazel eyes of hers...there's so much agony swirling in them it makes my own heart constrict.

"I don't understand why you punish yourself, though, Alyssa. Haven't you already been through enough?"

"Don't you get it? If I didn't put myself in that position it would have never happened. I have no one to blame my pain on but myself. It's not like I enjoy having sex with all the guys that I do. Trust me, I don't. But, I do it to remind myself of everything that I caused."

Tears threaten to spill down her face, but she lifts her chin instead. "Besides, after enough people call you a worthless slut...you can't help but start to believe it."

"I think what you're doing is wrong," I whisper.

"I thought you weren't going to judge me."

"About your past. I just hate the thought of you continuing to punish yourself for something that you've clearly already suffered the consequences from...and then some. It's no way to go through life."

She takes a sip of her drink. "Noted, now can we change the subject, please."

"Sure. What do you want to talk about?"

She gives me a smug smile. "Let's talk about you."

"I thought we made a deal that you wouldn't talk about your dad and I wouldn't talk about Lilly?"

She hikes a shoulder up and takes another bite of her bagel. "Yeah. And that deal is still in full effect. However, I know for a fact that there's got to be more to you than a dead sister."

I narrow my eyes at her. "Sorry," she whispers.

"What do you want to know?" I grit through my teeth.

She appears lost in thought for a second before she answers. "Well, do you have a girl-friend? Or are you just like every other macho fighter and some super male-whore?"

I can't help but laugh. "Wow, look who's judging now."

She purses her lips at me and for a single moment she looks so carefree, it's beautiful. "Hey, the world does nothing but judge me all the time. You have a point, though. I'll try and refrain from making and using judgmental stereotypes in the future."

I give her a smirk. "For your information, I'm not a male-whore."

"So you're in a committed relationship?" She chews on her thumbnail again. "I mean, I didn't see any signs of a female living in your apartment. Is it long distance? What's her name? Will she be mad that I spent the night?"

I roll my eyes. Yeah, news reporter. I can see it clearly now.

"I don't have a girlfriend."

She leans forward. "Oh. So, what about sex?"

Nope…not going there. I can't even imagine what she would think of me if she knew how I got my rocks off.

I remain silent while she continues probing. "You have seen yourself, right? There's no way you're still a virgin."

So she does find me attractive after all. I polish off the rest of my plate and can't help but grin. "I'm not a virgin. Trisha Summer's took care of that when I was 15."

"So, what do you do about sex then?" she whisper-yells.

Since she stopped eating her food and I'm looking for a diversion from this horrible conversation. I reach over her plate and plop one of her grapes in my mouth. "I have it." I pause. "On occasion. But that's as much as you're getting out of me on the subject."

Her nostrils begin flaring, her gaze intense. "Jackson," she says. "I've just admitted the most honest, vulnerable, and embarrassing thing about myself to you. Hell, you can even watch it if you're really curious."

I hold up my hand. "I wouldn't. You have my word."

And I mean it, I have absolutely no desire to watch a video that ruined her life. Something that only added to the emotional scars she's already endured. Something that forced her to put her walls up high, in order to protect herself from the world. So high, she's ensured that no one will be able to get through them.

Why do I suddenly find myself wanting to be the one who makes them come tumbling down?

The intensity in her eyes softens. "That's not the point. The point is, that if we're supposed to be friends…I expect the same amount of truthfulness from you that you expect from me. Now, tell me something heartbreakingly honest about yourself before I reconsider this whole entire friendship for good."

I'm a killer. I murdered my best friend. I don't regret it and I never will.

Instead, what comes out of my mouth is something that not even Tyrone knows about. "About once every 3 months I go to a bdsm club and have sex."

Jesus Christ…I'm a fucking idiot for admitting that to her.

She stares at me wide-eyed. "Like cat-o-nine's and dog collars?"

"No. To be honest—I'm not even into any of the hardcore stuff. I just like having all the control during sex."

Since it's the only aspect of my life that I can still control.

"I'm not a 'Dom' or anything like that. However, for this particular club membership, which is both really exclusive and expensive. They're good about keeping your identity hidden and you get to wear a mask if you want to…which I do."

She crinkles her forehead. "I have a question."

"Shoot."

"Why go through all that? Why not just fuck Lou-Lou or some other girl who offer themselves to you?"

I decide to be honest with her about my other reason for using the club. "Shit like that gets messy. First off, I don't do relationships. Secondly, women in particular; have a really hard time separating feelings from sex. If I hooked up with some girl like Lou-Lou or another ring girl…well, over time they would start to get attached. Shit, poor Ricardo's having a hell of a time keeping her in line as it is. I also know from watching Tyrone go through the gauntlet with various girls over the years…that it never ends well. The girl always gets hurt…and I don't want to be responsible for doing that if I can help it. This way, I just go in. No names or faces are exchanged. We have our moment…and it's done."

I expect her to yell at me. To tell me I'm a pig and a horrible human being. Instead, she nods her head in understanding. "Why every 3 months?"

That's an easy question to answer at least.

"If you don't show up at the club, once every 3 months your membership gets canceled. And once every 3 months is just enough to scratch the itch so to speak. After, I go back to focusing on training and fighting full-time."

"That makes sense, I guess. How long has it been since you've last gone there?"

I look up at the ceiling, hating how this conversation has shifted focus to me. "A little over a month."

She regards me with another nod. "I don't do relationships either."

I feel a twinge of uneasiness with her statement and I have no idea why.

"So, how did you get involved with an underground fight club anyway?" she asks. "Granted, I didn't see much, but from what I did manage to see you're really good. Why not go legit?"

Oh, fuck. I have no idea how to answer this without lying to her.

"Just sort of fell into it," I mumble. "I love MMA fighting, I've studied the craft since I was a kid." I swallow hard purposely dodging her question the best that I can. "Besides, it pays the bills."

She leans forward and presses her palms together, studying my face for a beat. "Who owns the club?"

Her question completely catches me off guard and causes me to pause. The seconds blending into minutes.

Why does she want to know?

And technically, shouldn't she already know that it's DeLuca's club? From what I'm told— not just anyone can work at one of his establishments, even the fight club. You either have to know someone or he specifically scouts you out.

But then again, it might be different for the ring girls. Maybe all it takes is good looks and a nice body to get you in the door.

My expression must be one of concern because she coughs and says, "Never mind. Stupid question. Look at me…already breaking rule number one."

I run a hand along my jaw, focusing on her eyes. Even after today, I don't know much about the girl sitting in front of me, but her magnetic eyes are her tell. I can practically feel every emotion she's experiencing when I look into them.

And right now…she looks nervous. "Are you in some kind of trouble, Alyssa?"

She quickly shakes her head. "No. I mean, why would I be?"

I shrug and lean back against the booth. Her response should put me at ease, but it doesn't. "I have no idea. But if you were, you know you could tell me. Right?"

Fear crosses over her face and before I can stop her…she's hopping out of her seat and running toward the exit.

I quickly track the waitress down and pay the bill before running after her.

When I finally step outside, I find her leaning against the side of the brick building facing the alleyway. She's rubbing her temples and breathing frantically. My chest tightens and I'm struck with the overwhelming feeling of wanting to wrap her in my arms and protect her from the world.

Instead, I gently reach for her arm. "Hey," I say. "It's okay. I won't let anything hurt you, Alyssa."

Her eyes spring open in both surprise and fear and she immediately pulls away from my touch. It's almost like she's a frightened animal and can't comprehend that someone would show her an ounce of kindness.

It's utterly heartbreaking.

She pushes off the building and begins walking down the alley. "I'm sorry, but I have to go. I have to go home, now," she calls out.

I stay a few strides behind her. I'm close enough that I can watch her make it to her car safely, but not so close to cause her to freak out again.

After she reaches her car, she pauses briefly. "Thank you for lunch. I'll find a way to pay you back for it."

I shake my head. "Absolutely not. In fact, I'm going to make sure you get paid from Luke. He should have never let that happen to you in the first place."

She worries her bottom lip between her teeth. "That's not necessary," she whispers. "I don't want you getting into any fights on my behalf, but thank you anyway."

She slips inside her car and puts her key in the ignition.

I jog up to her. "When can I see you again?"

She looks down at the steering wheel. "I don't do relationships, Jackson." I open my mouth to protest but she stops me. "That includes friendships. I've already let you in so much more than anyone else and I haven't even known you for 24 hours."

I stuff my hands in my pockets. "Maybe there's a reason for that, Alyssa."

And there is…I just have no idea what it is yet.

All I know is that I'm so drawn to her.

And it's not just because she's incredibly attractive, either. It's so much more than that. I have this urge to just want to take care of her, and be there for her.

But most of all…I recognize the pain in her soul…because I live with it every day.

She puts the car in reverse and begins backing up. "I'll call you, Jackson," she says before she rolls up her window.

It's only after she's more than halfway down the block that I realize she never gave me her number…and she doesn't have mine.

Chapter Six

ALYSSA

I GRIP THE STEERING WHEEL AND FIGHT BACK THE WAVE OF NAUSEA. I FEEL MY PULSE pounding in my ears and I swallow another big gulp of air.

What the hell is the matter with me?

I mean, besides the obvious panic attack of epic proportions that I'm going through at the moment.

Why in the world did I just tell a guy I hardly know such personal things about myself?

Granted, it was nothing he wouldn't have found out about me sooner or later, but still.

Another round of tremors plague my body and with a curse, I pull over to the side of the expressway. The rain is coming down hard and big droplets splash against my windshield. I close my eyes and listen to the steady rhythm as it continues to fall.

After I'm certain that the worst of the episode is over, I start the car and resume driving.

I wasn't always like this.

Once upon a time, I used to be normal, happy, even.

And up until a few years ago, I had never experienced a true panic attack. In fact, I used to thrive and work best under pressure—something I must have inherited from my father.

My father.

I used to wonder if there was a specific number of tears I could shed that would bring back a missing piece of my heart.

Now, I know, there isn't—because I'm almost positive I must have cried them all during the entire year I was 10. Not a day went by where I didn't wake up to a soggy pillow or fall asleep to one.

Then I turned 11. That's when I learned to stop crying…because tears wouldn't bring him back. Tears were nothing but a complete waste of an emotion and they never solved anything.

I also learned, that sometimes; children are actually the ones to take care of their parents.

Needless to say—My mother didn't handle my father's death well.

Not that there really is a "way" to handle the sudden death of the man you've loved since you turned 16…but I'm certain that becoming an alcoholic isn't the best way to cope.

Especially when you have a child to raise.

However, we made the best of it.

She made sure to put a few bucks aside for food and bills before she blew it all on booze…and I learned to effectively lie to the concerned neighbors and teachers; like when she didn't show up to my recitals, or parent-teacher conferences.

Or even worse—when she *did* show up. Looking like a million bucks, slurring her words, and making an over dramatic spectacle of herself.

Those were the worst. Then after we went home she would apologize profusely for being a horrible mother while crying on my shoulder.

I, of course, being a good daughter—would assure her that she wasn't horrible and that

I wasn't angry with her. Then I would fix her something to eat and snuggle up with her on the couch while watching the news.

For whatever reason, it was her favorite thing to watch and the only thing to calm her down when she became really out of sorts. Probably because she didn't have to feel so horrible about the reality of her own fucked up life while she watched other people's lives falling apart every night.

As crazy as it sounds. I think subconsciously—the reason I wanted to become a newscaster was so that I could find a way to reach her and connect with her, in my own way.

The day my father died destroyed our happy life.

But the day John Travine entered our lives…demolished our shitty one.

I was 15 when he began dating my mother. I have no idea how they met. I can only assume that it must have been at her favorite corner liquor store.

At first, he would only come around in the middle of the night and he was always gone by early morning. It didn't take a genius to figure out the nature of their relationship.

That went on for 2 years.

One day when I was 17—I came home from school to find that he had moved in. Apparently, he was a married man, but he and his wife had just come to a mutual agreement to get a divorce. Either that—or his wife had finally kicked his sorry, cheating ass to the curb.

I didn't know that he was a hotshot attorney or involved in politics when they first started seeing each other, but I soon found out when he began showering my mother with lavish gifts and taking care of all the bills around the house.

Unfortunately, it came at a price. But I'm getting ahead of myself.

Before my mother had to pay the piper…he made sure to get her into rehab first.

For the briefest of moments, John Travine and I had managed to see eye to eye. I was actually grateful to him for coming into our lives back then. I thought he was the answer to all our prayers.

I'd never seen my mother happier than during those first few months when she got out of rehab. Long before my mother became an alcoholic, she had quite expensive tastes and shopping was one of her favorite pastimes. Being with John helped fulfill her desire to live in constant luxury again, not to mention her need for constant attention.

I'll never forget the night that all ended, though.

I was 18 years old and I had just come home from a date with my high school boyfriend, Toby.

There at the kitchen table, clutching a bottle of vodka was my mother.

With a busted lip and a black eye.

At first, I thought that maybe she had gotten drunk and had taken a bad fall.

But then he entered the room.

He glared at the bottle in her hand before he fixed his hard eyes on me.

And I knew.

She had obviously relapsed…and he had obviously felt the need to punish her brutally for it. Or, for all I know, it was the other way around.

My stomach dropped to the floor and the first thing I did was try and get my mother to leave him…but she wouldn't.

A huge screaming match ensued between John and I while my mother sat in that damn chair, clutching the bottle of vodka for dear life.

I threatened to call the cops and he laughed in my face and said they wouldn't believe a whore and a drunk. Especially when my mother would never admit to it.

The next day, when she was sober-ish, I tried again to get her to leave. She adamantly refused, in addition to issuing her own threat that made me back down.

Then she said something I would never forget. She said that if I didn't support their relationship, that *I* was free to leave.

Yup, my very own mother had made it clear that she would choose a man who hit her… over her own daughter.

So I did the only thing I could do. I stayed.

My mother was the only person I had left in my life then and I couldn't bear to lose her.

I stayed….he continued to beat her behind closed doors…and she continued to drink her pain away.

Any time I tried to bring up leaving him to her, she would yell at me and threaten to kick me out.

After hours of non-stop arguing, I would eventually break down and apologize, tell her I loved her, and agree to stop interfering in their relationship.

Then the next day I would have some kind of gift from John waiting for me.

It was a fucked up cycle that I didn't know how to stop because that would mean giving up on my mother…and I couldn't do that.

John's biggest blackmail gift came when he agreed to pay for my tuition for NYU. I had gotten a partial scholarship but was having a hard time figuring out how to pay for my dorm room and other expenses on my part time after school job.

At first, I declined. Unlike my mother, I didn't want any part of his money. Not to mention, I was still undecided about dorming at NYU because I didn't know what would happen to my mother if I wasn't there.

It was when my mom literally broke down and begged me to accept his money and told me that I deserved to live my dream…that I finally caved.

Walking out of that house was one of the hardest things I'd ever done. The pain was excruciating.

The only exception being my father's death and the last time, I saw my mother.

The very last time I saw my mother was after John's campaign for mayor was well underway and my sex tape had just hit the world.

She asked me to come home that weekend. So, of course, I did.

The first thing she did when she saw me was pull me into her arms. She said that we would figure out a way to get through this.

I believed her.

But in the middle of the night…everything changed.

I woke up to the most heart-wrenching scream I had ever heard come out of my mother's mouth. I rushed out of my childhood bed, grabbed a bat from my closet, and ran into the basement where I heard the scream come from.

I ran down the stairs two at a time and came face to face with a sight that sickened me and made my stomach curdle.

There was John…facing a computer screen.

His pants were down around his ankles, and his erect penis was in his hand.

And he was watching the sex tape.

Before I even had time to process everything that was happening…my mother stalked toward me.

John quickly pulled up his pants…and tried to explain himself…but the war raging inside my mother wasn't with him.

It was with me.

She raised her hand and white spots formed in front of my eyes when she struck me, hard. My face stung so bad I had to close my eyes. "You worthless slut! You stupid whore!" she screamed before she dealt another blow to my face.

This one was so bad, blood dripped down my nose.

I tried to protest, tried to stick up for myself...but she wouldn't have it.

"I never want to see you again," she sneered before she ran upstairs.

I turned to go upstairs to collect my things and return to my dorm at NYU, but not before I noticed the sly smile touching the corners of John's lips.

It was a smile that told me that even though he was now in jeopardy of losing the election...he had won the battle when it came to my mother.

She chose him over me.

He found a way to make her hate me.

"I hope you die," I whispered before I continued upstairs, gathered my things, and walked out of my parent's house.

Two months later, John lost the race for mayor...and I was about to be kicked out of school because I couldn't afford to stay—in part, because I stopped attending class and lost my scholarship.

Soon after, I received an e-mail from my mother. She said that her and John were moving away to some small town in the south. She also said that I would be able to keep my father's house...provided that I promise to never speak to her or John again.

I happily agreed.

With a sigh, I open the door to the house, plop down on the sofa and open my laptop.

My head begins throbbing when I pull up the latest search results. Even though the video is a few years old, there are about 20 uploads on various sites in the last three weeks alone.

I quickly press the pause button on one of the video's and immediately scroll down to the comments section of the well-known website.

I scan over the slew of comments containing things like—'she's hot, I'd do her', 'nice tit's', 'girl sure knows how to suck dick', and 'whoever the guy is, he sure is lucky'.

Instead, I focus my attention on the more personal comments.

-Poor John Travine. Too bad his daughter was so much of a slut it ended up ruining his career. If I was her, I'd never show my face in public again.

-I went to school with that girl. Her name is Alyssa Tanner. Always knew she was a whore. I even heard she blew half the football team.

-Bet her snatch is the equivalent of throwing a hot dog down a hallway. If you know what I mean ;)

-Wow, seriously? Could she be any more of a slut!

It's like being trapped on a hamster wheel in the seventh circle of hell. I know I shouldn't, but I just can't help myself.

Finally, I look at the last comment that was posted, this one a mere few hours ago.

-The whore should just do everyone a favor and kill herself.

Little do they know...I'm already dying inside a little bit every day.

Chapter Seven

JACKSON

"**Y**OU SHOULD GET REJECTED MORE OFTEN. IT REALLY MAKES YOU TRAIN BETTER,"
Tyrone says while I slam my fist into the punching bag again.

It's been a little over three weeks since I've last seen or talked to Alyssa, and true to form, I've been taking my frustration out during training.

Ricardo's lips twitch as he holds the punching bag. "That's enough for today, guys. Hit the showers."

I'm about to leave, but I notice movement out of the corner of my eye.

It's that snake, Luke waltzing through the gym; appearing to be without a care in the world.

I'm about to change that real quick.

I hip check him into the wall and enjoy the look of utter shock splashed across his face.

"Can I *help* you?" he sputters.

My 6'3 frame easily towers over him and I relish the way his entire body begins to shake from fear.

I don't give into my anger very often. I tend to bottle everything up and save it for the fights in the cage, but when I do let my fury escape—it sure as fuck makes one hell of an impact. "I believe you still owe money to a certain ring girl," I snarl.

He puffs up his chest. "What are you? Her keeper or something? I don't owe that girl shit. Not my fault she couldn't handle the job."

I launch my fist into his rib cage. "Last time I checked, asshole. Being groped against your will wasn't part of the job description. *You're* supposed to make sure shit like that doesn't happen to the ring girls."

He lets out a big whoosh of air before he collapses against the wall.

I ball my fist again, but he finally reaches into his pocket and pulls out a wad of cash wrapped around a rubber band. "Fine, here. This should cover it. But mark my words, Jackson. If you make a habit of attacking me over the girls I hire, instead of focusing on the fights like *you're* supposed to—Bruno will be hearing about it."

I grab him by the collar. "I really don't give a fuck," I sneer before I let him go.

He fixes his collar and glares at me. "Yeah, we'll see about that," he says before he limps away.

When I turn around Ricardo's eyes are narrowed into tiny slits and Tyrone is shaking his head profusely.

"Locker room, *now*," Ricardo barks.

Shit.

The thing about Ricardo is, he's a great coach—and I'm close enough with him to consider him a friend of sorts...but you never want to piss him off.

He's only 5 years older than Tyrone and I, but rumor has it that he has strong ties to Bruno...hence why it's not only his job to train us, but to look after two of his biggest money making fighters.

It's Ricardo's priority to make sure we stay in top physical form as well as stay out of trouble...in every kind of form it comes in.

The fact that I just went off on one of Bruno's men…doesn't bode well for me.

"What the fuck *was* that?" he snaps when we reach the locker room.

I decide to tell him the truth. "He let Alyssa get attacked during the fight and didn't try to stop it…and if that wasn't bad enough he then fired her for causing trouble. He also didn't pay her."

He rubs his chin, appearing to be lost in thought for a moment. "Alyssa. That's the girl in handcuffs you brought home? Correct?"

I nod. "Look, Jackson. Do yourself a favor and bark up another tree. The only thing that girl's going to do is get you in a shitload of trouble. Trust me. You'll be getting into fights out of the ring left and right the longer you hang around her. If Bruno questions me about you going after Luke, I'll defend you and tell him you were just trying to do the right thing." He pauses. "But you and I both know it's never a good thing to be on Bruno's radar. Don't make a habit out of it."

"Yeah," I agree before he leaves.

After I step out of the shower I find Tyrone standing there waiting for me. "In the last 3 years I've known you; I've never seen you strung out over a girl. What is it about her, man?"

I shrug as I continue getting dressed. "I don't know. She's been dealt a really shitty hand, though. She's not at all what you think, Ty."

"So, she's a lost soul, huh?"

"Something like that," I mumble.

He rubs a hand over his face. "Saving her won't bring back Lilly, Jackson," he says before he heads for the showers.

I instinctively put my hand on the tattoo over my heart.

"I know," I whisper.

"I'm tired as fuck," Tyrone says after we leave the gym. "Training really did a number on me today. I'm gonna grab some coffee."

I look at him and smirk as we continue walking down the street. "Yeah, if that's what you like to call those pumpkin spice froo-froo girly drinks you dig so much."

He turns his head from side to side and grins. "Hey, man. Don't knock it til' you try it."

I roll my eyes and laugh when we approach the Starbucks at the end of the block.

Until I see her.

Looking through the large glass window of the coffee shop, I can't help but notice Alyssa.

She's leaning over the table, her cleavage spilling out of her low-cut top, and flashing a seductive 'come hither' smile to some guy wearing khakis whose typing on a laptop.

How he's still typing with her right in front of him looking like *that* is anyone's guess, but that's beside the point.

I know exactly what she's doing…and it makes me sick.

Sick and pissed.

Tyrone follows my gaze and shakes his head. "Awe, hell. And so it begins," he mutters.

Without taking my eyes off of her, I open the door and walk inside.

Chapter Eight

ALYSSA

I'M AT STARBUCKS, FLIRTING UP A STORM WITH MY NEXT CONQUEST…WHEN A LARGE figure approaches the table and clears their throat.

I glance up and internally wince when I notice Jackson standing there…his eyes never leaving my face. His expression hard and unyielding.

Before I can even say a word, he crosses his arms over his broad chest. "There you are, babe. I was wondering where you wandered off to," his deep voice growls.

Babe? Has he lost his damn mind?

I open my mouth to tell him off, but the guy next to me bolts up from the table like he's been electrocuted. "Crap, man. Sorry. I don't want any trouble," he sputters before he grabs his laptop and literally runs out the door.

I stand up and head for the door, but not before I feel his hand reach for my elbow and pull me back to him. I try not to let his close proximity or his touch effect me, but I fail miserably. My stomach knots up and my mouth goes dry when I get the faintest whiff of his earthy, damn near mouth watering scent.

"Have you learned nothing from the last time you did this shit, damsel?" he asks, momentarily zapping me out of my haze.

I shoot him a look that hopefully conveys how annoyed I am with him using that term and twist out of his grasp.

I run out the door, with his footsteps following close behind me.

I know he's not going to let up, so there's only one thing left to do. Something I've become really good at. I'm going to push him away, for good.

I spin around and face him. "Christ, stop following me, Jackson. Stop showing up when you're not wanted or needed. And stop acting like you actually give a damn. And most of all, stop trying to save me because I'll only end up taking you down with me." I draw in a ragged breath. "Just leave me alone. I want nothing to do with you."

I know my words aren't kind, but I need him out of my life for once and for all.

It's only then that I notice his friend Tyrone is standing there. He narrows his eyes at me before he looks at the ground.

Jackson's nostrils flare and he takes a step toward me. He reaches for my hand and puts something in it. "Take care of yourself, Damsel," he says dismissively before he turns around and begins walking down the street.

I close my eyes and swallow against the lump forming in my throat.

This is what I wanted. So, why does it feel like I just made a huge mistake?

My eyes are glassy when I finally open them and come face to face with Tyrone.

"Wow, you're kind of a bitch," he says.

I shrug because it's not a lie…especially after that encounter. "Yeah well, it had to be done."

I turn to leave but his voice stops me. "Word of advice…the world becomes a dark and cold place after you push everyone who cares about you away. And it really sucks when you have to face your demons all alone."

"I wasn't lying, Tyrone. I'll only end up hurting him in the end. Everything I touch, I wreck somehow."

He laughs. "Have you seen him? Trust me, the man can take a few hits, Alyssa. And believe me when I say that Jackson is a great friend. Just give him a chance to be yours."

"Why is this so important to you? I mean, not for nothing but you weren't exactly rooting for me the last time we saw one another."

He considers my statement for a moment before he answers, "Because he's the greatest guy I've ever met and he deserves to get what he wants...for *once* in his life."

I'm taken back by his statement, but before I have a chance to question him about it, Tyrone turns on his heels and starts walking down the street. My chest squeezes and everything in my body is telling me not to let Jackson walk away.

Before I can stop myself, I call out, "Tell him to meet me for lunch tomorrow around 12. The same diner we went to last time."

Tyrone fist pumps the air and gives me a giant smile. "He'll be there."

I'm walking to my car when I suddenly remember what day tomorrow is.

There's no way I can meet Jackson...I already have a date.

Chapter Nine

JACKSON

THE LAST THING I SHOULD BE DOING RIGHT NOW IS SHOWING UP TO MEET A GIRL who's made it clear that she wants nothing to do with me.

I shouldn't be pursuing this. I shouldn't be hopeful that she'll finally let me in.

I shouldn't be trying to save her from herself. Lord knows, I'm the furthest thing from a hero and there's a good chance I'll only hurt her in the end if she ever finds out the truth about me.

No, I shouldn't be doing any of those things...but...I just can't stop myself.

Another hour goes by and I glance at my watch. Tyrone told me she said 12. Maybe he got the time wrong and she meant 2?

If she meant 2, I'll be cutting it close to training time, but the gyms not that far from here.

I order another water and look out the window. There's no sign of her. I look at my watch again. 2:25pm. It's obvious that she's not coming and I've been stood up.

With a sigh, I stand up and throw some money on the table before I leave.

My muscles ache like no one's business after a grueling workout, all I want to do is go home and fall into bed.

Tyrone's at the bar across from the gym, hoping to strike it lucky with his latest conquest. I considered joining him, but decided against it.

I haven't exactly been in the greatest of moods today. I stick my key in the door and feel a hand tap my shoulder. The touch is light and the hand is soft.

I pinch the bridge of my nose, feeling even more annoyed now that I have to deal with her. "Never gonna happen, Lou-Lou. Try Ricardo's door," I growl.

My statement comes out much harsher than I intended. I briefly consider apologizing but think better of it. Better to just let her think I'm a dick, maybe she'll finally get the picture.

I hear the sound of a throat clearing and I spin around.

A pair of red and puffy hazel eyes meet mine.

"I'm sorry about not showing today, Jackson. I forgot I made other plans and I couldn't get out of them," Alyssa's now raspy voice greets me.

I force myself to ignore the current state she's in. I force myself to look right past the sadness in her eyes, and the fact that she's obviously upset.

I force myself not to think about what those other plans she had may have entailed and the pang of jealousy that snags me.

But mostly, I force myself not to care anymore, because every time I do; she only ends up pushing me away and making me feel like an asshole for wanting to be her friend.

Her friend, right—my inner voice taunts.

"You came a long way for something that could have been done over the phone."

"You know I don't have your number," she whispers when I turn back around and open the door.

"Yeah, well, who's fault is that," I say before I shut the door behind me, with her on the other side of it.

A small knock follows. I pull off my sweatshirt and ignore it.

The knocks increase in both sound and speed. Going from cautious and unsure to impatient and angry now.

And for some reason, *that's* what really sets me off.

I swing the door open so hard the walls vibrate.

She pushes past me with an angry scowl on her face, finally stopping in the living room.

I inhale sharply and continue after her until she does something that entices me, confuses me, and unleashes a fury inside me.

She takes off her shirt.

She's about to start undoing her pants when I reach over and halt her. "What the hell are you doing, Alyssa?"

She looks down and gives me a small shrug. "Well, I tried apologizing to you and you slammed the door in my face," she says, her arms hanging loose in defeat.

I raise an eyebrow, not understanding her thought process. "And you thought stripping for me would accomplish what exactly?"

Her cheeks flush. "I'm not sure. I figured I'd just give you what every other guy always wants from me." She looks down. "Go ahead, Jackson. Take me, use me. Be as rough as you want, just try not to destroy me when it's over."

I don't know what irks me more. The fact that she thinks she's nothing more than a pack of gum to be passed around and enjoyed by all, despite *never* actually enjoying it herself. Or the fact that she just grouped me with every other guy she deals with.

I take a step closer to her and lift her chin. "You're too busy destroying *yourself*, Alyssa. How could anyone else?"

I reach for her arms and lift them above her head. Her chest heaves and I can't help but take in the purple lace of her bra, barely covering her nipples, straining against her breasts and just begging to be released. She sucks in a breath and closes her eyes when my thumb brushes her cheekbone before dipping lower, skimming over that adorable dimple on her left cheek. Which seldom makes an appearance.

She probably thinks I'm about to have my way with her. The goosebumps grazing her delicate flesh and the way her pulse is beating erratically against the pad of my thumb lead me to believe that's what she wants me to do.

And *fuck* if that doesn't make my own heart speed up. *But then I would be like all the others*, I remind myself.

Instead, I pick up her shirt and pull it over her head. Her eyes open, uncertainty etched in her features. "Why?" she asks, her voice barely above a whisper. "Why didn't you?"

I lead her to the couch and drape a blanket over her. "Because I'm not gonna be another notch on your bedpost who takes advantage of your self—destruction." My voice drops down to a whisper, "And because one day I failed to notice when someone else I cared about was in pain …and not a day goes by that I don't regret it."

My hand instinctively lands on my chest and I sigh.

"So, where did you end up going today?" I ask.

I turn my head to look at her when I don't hear a response. Her mouth is parted slightly, her eyelashes fluttering against closed lids, the rise and fall of her chest falling in sync with my own breathing.

I glance at the clock. Tyrone will be home soon…and he might be bringing company.

She looks so peaceful, I don't have the heart to wake her. I gently lift her up, being as careful as I can and carry her into my bedroom. I remove her shoes, flick off the light on the nightstand, and turn to leave.

Her hand reaches for mine. "Stay. Please stay," she whispers before drifting off again.

I crawl into bed and curl up beside her, my hand never leaving hers.

"No! Daddy! Please, no!"

Her screams are the equivalent of waking up to a shotgun going off. She's trembling so hard, I'm convinced she must be having a seizure.

I jump up and flick on the light beside the bed, her screams quickly turning into muffled cries. I gently nudge her, but she doesn't wake. "Alyssa, you're okay. It's just a bad dream," I say. I hold her by the shoulders and try a little harder this time, and finally the shaking stops and her eyes open wide.

She looks around the room, confusion marring her face briefly before she realizes where she is. "Oh god. I'm so sorry." She sits up in the bed. "This is beyond embarrassing."

Her eyes dart to the door and she makes to stand but I gently pull her back to me. I'm all too aware of how much of a flight risk she is and she's not running away from me this time. Especially in this state.

"This happen often?" I ask.

Her head falls against my chest and she lets out a deep breath before whispering, "Not really. Only when I'm exhausted. Usually, I don't allow myself to sleep that soundly because I know what the end result will be."

That's when it sinks in that it wasn't just a random bad dream, but a reoccurring nightmare. I tip her chin up to look at me. "What happened, Alyssa? Trust me enough to let me in." I kiss her forehead. "Please."

She fidgets and squirms out of my arms. Just when I think she's about to bolt, she looks at me and does the one thing I've been waiting for since I met her.

She drops her armor and opens up to me.

Chapter Ten

ALYSSA
Past...

"REALLY, CUPCAKES FOR BREAKFAST, GRAHAM?" MY MOTHER CRIED. "THAT IS not an appropriate breakfast for a 9-year-old."

I grinned around a mouth full of my heavily laden chocolate frosted cupcake. "But I'll be 10 in two days, Mommy," I argued. Before my mother could protest further, I added, "And look, Daddy put goblins on them!"

Since my birthday fell on Halloween, my father's nickname for me had always been 'goblin'. Most little girls would have hated it and wished for a nickname more feminine like 'Princess' or 'Pumpkin', but I loved it.

My mother shook her head and looked at my father. A soft smile spread across his face when he walked over to her and held a cupcake up to her lips. "Come on, honey. Take a bite. No one can resist little goblins." He looked at me and winked. "Isn't that right?"

I nodded my head in excitement. "Do it, Mommy. Please."

She let out a frustrated sigh before she took a haphazard bite. She pursed her lips and looked at me, her expression much softer than it was a moment ago. "Okay," she conceded. "Finish your cupcake, but no more. You need to get ready for school."

My father pulled my mother closer. "You have some frosting right here," he whispered before he kissed her.

I scrunched my nose and made a face. "But it's my *birthday*," I whined, effectively interrupting their moment. "Why can't I stay home with you? Or go to work with Daddy?"

My mother put her hands on her hips and gave me 'the look.' I knew that look well. "Alyssa Ford Tanner. It's not your birthday yet. Now finish the rest of your cupcake and get ready for school."

Yup, she called me by my full name. She meant business.

I scrambled off the counter top and let out a giggle when my father swooped down and picked me up. "I'll tell you what, little goblin. How about I drive you to school today?"

My face lit up. "You mean it?" I asked incredulously.

All my dad did was work non-stop, especially as of late. Sometimes an entire week or two would pass without me ever seeing him.

This time, it had been almost *three* whole weeks. I hated it, but he promised me he would be around for my birthday weekend.

I overheard him telling my mother that him and Ford, his best friend, and partner, were working on their most important case and trying to gather intel, but they were encountering some unforeseen problems.

I didn't really understand it, but I knew my father had a very important job.

He caught the bad guys.

However, he never wore a uniform like some of the other officers I saw. Instead, he mostly wore suits to work and participated in things called 'stakeouts' or 'going undercover.' People at work also referred to him as 'Special Agent.' Whatever that meant.

I knew he traveled to the city a lot. That's where his headquarters and most of his cases were located. It was also his favorite place in the whole entire world.

He only moved to the suburbs because it was what my mother wanted, she thought there was too much crime in the city and it was no place to raise a child.

I, however, loved the city and would beg my dad to take me with him when he left, but he never did.

My dad put me down. "Of course, I mean it. Now go get ready."

I ran up the stairs to my bedroom.

After I was done getting dressed I walked out to the hallway.

That's when I heard it.

"Fuck," my father huffed. "*Now?* This wasn't scheduled to happen for another two weeks." He paused. "The *entire* weekend? You gotta be shitting me."

My stomach dropped. I already knew what was about to happen.

He sighed. "No, it won't be a problem." He cleared his throat. "Yeah, alright. Tell him I'm on my way. I'll be there as soon as I can."

I heard some ruffling and a few more curses erupt from his mouth as I stood outside his bedroom door with tears in my eyes.

He opened the door and glanced down at me. I briefly registered that he wasn't in a suit but wearing black jeans and a t-shirt, which was odd since he was on his way to work.

Hope flickered in my heart.

"Goblin," he began as he kneeled down in front of me.

I lifted my chin, preparing myself for what was to come. "Yes, Daddy?"

His hand reached up and brushed away the few tears that had started to fall. "I'm so sorry, sweetheart. But Daddy has to go to work. I won't be able to take you to school this morning after all."

Disappointment settled in my chest, but that tiny ray of hope refused to leave. "It's okay. I understand," I said. "You'll be here for my actual birthday though, right?"

His hand dropped, the same pain reflecting back at me through his own hazel eyes. "No, baby. Daddy has to take care of something very important at work."

"More important than me?"

"Goblin—" he started, before I cut him off.

I steeled myself, it was the angriest I'd ever been in all of my almost 10 years. "No. I'm *not* your goblin anymore," I said before I turned around and headed for the staircase.

Large arms wrapped around me and held me tight. "*Nothing* is more important to me than you. And you will always be my little goblin."

I turned around and buried my face against his chest.

"I love you so much, Alyssa," he whispered.

"Then stay, Daddy. Please."

"I wish I could. But I can't."

"But you *promised* me!" I shouted through tears.

He closed his eyes and kissed my forehead. "I know. I'm so sorry. I'll make it up to you somehow. I swear I will."

I looked up at him, my resolve firm. "Take me with you."

He gave me another kiss on my forehead and shook his head. "I can't." He pulled something out of his pocket. "I was going to give this to you on Sunday, but I want you to have it now."

I looked down at the white gold chain in wonder. A white gold and diamond encrusted goblin along with a small replica of a police badge containing my father's badge number hung from it.

"But mommy said I'm not old enough to wear real jewelry like hers yet," I whispered as he fiddled with the clasp around my neck.

He smiled and brushed a lock of blond hair from his eyes. "I think we can make an exception for very special birthdays and very special little girls."

I flung my arms around him. "I love the necklace, but I'd still much rather have you for my birthday. I miss you, so much. You're *always* gone, now. I never get to see you anymore. I get so jealous when I see my friends from school with their dad's."

"Jesus, you're ripping my heart out over here, kid," he mumbled.

"Then take me with you. We don't have to tell Mommy."

He chuckled and ruffled my hair. "I can't. I'm sorry. Please try and understand." he said before standing up and walking down the staircase.

Anger burst through me again. Only this time…I had a plan.

I crept down the staircase, being careful to not make any noise as I passed the kitchen and overheard their conversation.

"I have to go to work. We're about to make some major headway. I just got a call from one of his associates that he's doing the drop today. With the way things are going now it looks like we'll be able to nail him for good this weekend," he told my mother.

Her mouth opened in shock. "Really? This soon? That's incredible."

He rubbed the back of his neck. "Yeah, but I won't be back until Monday night, the earliest."

My mother bit her lip and a crease formed between her eyebrows. "But it's her birthday, Graham. Her 10th birthday. This is going to break her heart. You *know* how much she loves you. You're all she ever talks about."

"I know, honey. I know. I don't really have a choice right now, though. Maybe after this case I can take some time off, we'll take a family vacation or something. I'll make it up to her." He bent down and kissed her. "To the both of you." His hand landed on her tummy. "Take care of my girls." He winked. "All three of them."

Three? He always said his *two girls*. What the heck?

She looked down at his hand. "Speaking of which, when are we going to tell her? I'm a little over 3 months already. We can't wait forever."

"Well, I figured we could tell her that she was going to be a big sister on her birthday." He paused. "But, maybe it's for the best that we wait a little longer and let her have this one last birthday as the only child. I don't want to ruin her birthday any more than I already have. She's really upset with me and feels like my job is more important than she is. This certainly won't help matters. We'll tell her when we go on vacation, after I've spent some quality time with her and she's not so angry with me anymore."

Oh no, no, *no*. This couldn't be happening. *Another* kid? A *girl*? I was *never* going to be special to him now. He didn't even have time to spend with *me* anymore…if there's a new baby it will be like I won't even exist.

I recalled what happened to my classmate, Margaret Weiss. She was the only child and her parents showered her in attention, but she said that all stopped after her brother was born.

Now, her parents were always grumpy from being up all hours of the night and they didn't care about her anymore. Which was stupid, she said; because all her new brother did was sleep and cry all the time.

My mother nodded and gave him a kiss. "Sounds like a plan. I guess that means I'll be taking her to school this morning."

"Yeah, I should have left already." He turned to leave and I scrambled to make it to the garage and out to his car before he did.

"Oh and honey," he called out. "Don't make a fuss over the necklace I got her. I know it's a bit much for a 10-year-old, but I wanted to give her something special this year."

My mother huffed before she smiled. "Okay, but you'll have to deal with the fallout if she loses it. She's still upstairs getting ready, right?"

"Yeah. I'll see you on Monday. Love you."

"Love you."

I made my way out to the garage before he did. His SUV was large, shiny, and all black. It even had tinted windows and came equipped with a phone, and special locks.

Problem was…I didn't know how to get inside without him noticing.

I hid underneath the vehicle and watched his feet move as he lifted the hatch in the back and maneuvered some things around, appearing to be looking for something.

He cursed under his breath before his footsteps disappeared and I heard the garage door shut.

Luckily, he left the hatch open granting me the perfect opportunity to climb in and hide under a blanket on the floor in the back seat.

My heart raced when he came back out and climbed in the driver's seat. I thought for sure he would notice me, but he didn't.

We drove for well over two hours at that point and my legs were starting to cramp up.

The vehicle began to slow down and he cursed when his phone rang.

What I didn't count on happening was my mother calling his phone.

"I can't talk right now, honey. I forgot to shut this phone off. I'm just pulling up to the location now."

I heard shouting on the other line before my father's raised voice startled me. "What the hell do you mean she's *missing*, Debra? She was still upstairs when I left. Are you sure you looked everywhere?"

There was some more shouting on the other line.

"Shit. Keep looking. Call the neighbors and check the entire perimeter of the house. I'll put a call into the station. I'm sure she's just hiding somewhere." He paused. "Don't cry, honey. Stay strong. I'm sure she's okay," he said, his own voice beginning to crack. "We will find her. I'm calling the station now. Keep your phone on you."

Oh no. This wasn't supposed to happen. I never wanted to make my mother cry or my dad upset. I just wanted to spend some more time with him and make a point.

He hung up his cell phone and picked up his car phone. "Yeah, Hannah, it's Special Agent Tanner. My wife just reported that our 9-year-old daughter's gone missing. She was last seen inside the house." He paused. "A little over an hour. I want an amber alert issued right away. Blonde hair, hazel eyes…" he started to rattle off.

Panic gripped me. I remembered my father telling me that it was wrong to prank call the police. He told me that it took away from helping actual people who were having real emergencies.

I sprung up from the backseat. "Daddy, stop. I'm here. I'm okay. I'm so sorry."

He clutched his chest and glared at me. "Never mind. I just located her. Please call my wife and let her know. Thank you and I'm sorry for the trouble," he said before hanging up.

He stared at me for another second or so before he reached over and hugged me. "I'm so, *so* angry with you right now." Relief flashed across his face. "But I'm so happy you're okay. Do you have any idea what it would do to me if I ever lost you, goblin?"

I shook my head, tears welling up in my eyes. "You would be fine. You have a replacement on its way anyway," I grumbled.

He looked confused before he sighed. "No one could *ever* replace you, Alyssa. But, how did you find out?"

"I overheard you talking to mommy about it. You're going to have a new little girl and forget all about me."

He moved his seat back and sat me on his lap. "No, baby. That's not going to happen. I promise."

I sniffled and leaned my head against his chest. "I don't believe your promises anymore."

He held up my necklace. "You see this? You're the only girl in the world who will ever have it. I had it made just for you. That's how special you are to me."

"Then why are you having another baby? Am I not enough for you?"

He leaned down and kissed my cheek. "I love you more than all the stars in the sky and water in the oceans. From the very first second I laid eyes on you, that was it, kid. I was a goner." He looked lost in thought as he continued, "I was only 18 when you were born. Your mother and I were barely even out of high school. I was terrified of becoming a father, especially so young. Do you know who gave me strength to overcome that fear?" he asked.

"Who?"

"You did. I will never forget that moment. Your mother was recovering from labor and the nurses left you all alone with me. I started freaking out because I had no idea what I was supposed to do with you and I was sure I was going to screw something up and leave you scarred for life." He paused and smiled. "I remember talking to you and telling you how scared I was. I was about to have a panic attack, but then your little hand wrapped around one of my fingers and held on. You looked up at me with these beautiful eyes full of wonder and a sense of calm washed over me...and I knew I could do it. I knew we were going to be a team for life."

He brushed a strand of hair behind my ear. "That's why I call you goblin. It's not just because you were born on Halloween. It's because goblins are scary and frightening. And you were the scariest thing I'd ever come in contact with...but the best thing that ever happened to me. No one could ever take your place."

He reached for my hand and held it up to his heart. "We have a special bond that can never be broken, goblin. I will love you for all of eternity. You and your mother are the very best parts of my life."

I let out a hiccup. "I'm sorry I made you worry. I'm sorry for upsetting you. I love you."

"It's alright. Let me just make a quick call to Ford and I'll drive you back home."

He picked up the phone. "Hey, Ford. Look, something's come up. It's a long story. But I need you to distract him for an hour or two and buy me some time if he asks about me. I have to drive back home."

He lifted me off his lap and gripped the steering wheel. "What do you mean, what am I talking about? It's happening today. In the next hour to be exact. I heard it from one of his men myself. I tried calling you on your work phone but you didn't answer. I figured you got the same phone call and you were already here." He looked ahead and turned the key in the ignition. "Fuck," he said. "I've just been spotted."

He glanced back at me through the rear-view mirror and gritted his teeth. "No, I can't just drive off. That will only raise their suspicions further. Not to mention, I can't exactly start a high-speed chase with DeLuca's mobsters while my daughter's in the goddamn car!"

"What the fuck is Alyssa doing in the car with you right now? Fuck this. I'm on my way and I'm sending backup." I heard Ford's voice scream on the other line before it went silent.

He swallowed hard and continued to look straight ahead. Nervousness crept up my spine, signaling that something was very wrong.

"Goblin. I really need you to listen to me right now." My father took a deep breath before he continued. "I need you to go back under that blanket and hide. No matter what you see or hear, understand?"

"Wh-why...what's going...on?" I stuttered.

"Remember how Daddy helps to put away the bad guys?"

I gulped. "Y-yeah."

"Well, the bad guys are outside right now. And something very bad will happen if they see you. So, I need you to go back under that blanket and don't come out until I say you can. Okay?"

"Okay. I will. I'm so sorry, Daddy."

"It's okay, Alyssa. I'm not mad at you anymore. Everything will be fine. Ford and some other officers are on their way to come help us. Just do as I say, right now please."

I went back under the blanket in the backseat, my body shaking worse than a tree in the middle of a hurricane.

"Remember what I said. I need you to be quiet and stay under there. No matter what you see or hear."

"Okay. I love you."

"I love you, goblin. Never forget that," he whispered, right before someone tapped on the door.

He got out of the car and slammed the door shut behind him.

"Nice of you to join us, Graham," some deep voice sneered. "Or should I say, Special Agent Tanner."

I heard a few loud bangs and a few more muffled voices in the background.

It wasn't until I heard my father scream in pain, that I lifted my head out from under the blanket.

I scrunched down behind the driver seat but raised my head enough to partially take in my surroundings.

We were at a dock of some sort. There were a few dark SUV's around and big men wearing all black suits.

Then I saw something I would never forget.

My father chained up against a wall. His lip was bleeding, and someone had taken a pair of pliers to one of his fingers. My stomach heaved when I saw the blood dripping down.

I jimmied the door handle in order to go outside to help him, but it was locked.

I crawled over to the console and reached for the phone. I pressed the same button I'd seen my father press many times before.

"Hello Agent Tanner, this is Hannah. Agent Ford Baker has already made me aware of your situation and he's on his way with backup."

"H-hello," I whispered.

"Who is this?" Hannah asked.

"My Daddy's in trouble. The bad men are hurting him. Tell Ford to come, quick."

"Is this Agent Tanner's daughter?" she asked.

"Yes, this is Alyssa. Come quick. He's bleeding and they're doing something to his fingers."

"Alright sweetheart, please hang tight. Help is on the way. Where are you right now?"

"He told me to stay inside the car. I tried to go outside but all the doors are locked."

"Does anyone besides your dad know you're inside the car?"

"No. They can't see me. Their backs are all turned away from me. And the windows are tinted."

"Okay. Listen, I need you to stay away from the big windshield, Alyssa. It's not tinted like the other windows are. You can stay on the phone with me, but I need you to go to the backseat and stay down."

"But then I won't be able to see them," I protested.

Just then another car pulled up. My hopes were soon dashed when the door opened and out walked one of the biggest men I'd ever seen. Even bigger than my own father.

He wore an all black suit, dark sunglasses, and he had on shiny leather shoes with metal tips. There was also a fairly large scar on his face that stretched from his ear to his jaw.

His lips turned up in a snarl, and all the other men around him straightened their spines and lifted their heads.

He circled the men and stopped to narrow his eyes in my father's direction while he took his sunglasses off his face.

His eyes were dark as coal. The scariest eyes I'd ever seen in my life.

And I knew that something very bad was about to happen.

"Hurry. Another man just showed up. He looks big and scary. He has metal tips on his shoes. And his eyes are really dark and there's a scar on his face."

I heard her mumble, "Shit, DeLuca himself just showed up. Where the hell is backup?"

"Wh-who's DeLuca?" I asked.

"Make sure you stay down, sweetheart. Don't let him see you, please."

Tears pooled in my eyes. "Where's Ford?"

"He's on his way, sweetie."

I sniffled and let out a tiny scream when I saw the man take out some kind of metal object and aim it in my father's direction.

"Don't scream, Alyssa," she warned.

"He's about to hurt my Daddy. I want to talk to Ford. Please. I'm begging you. If you don't, I'll scream as loud as I can."

"I'll transfer you over to him right now."

The line went silent for a moment before I heard the sound of his voice. "Agent Baker."

"Ford, help."

"Alyssa?"

The man took another step toward my father. My father had remained strong, but for a single moment, I could see the desperation in his eyes when he saw what was in his hand. And it absolutely terrified me.

"Yeah. He's about to hurt my Daddy. He's wearing all black and he has metal tips on his leather shoes. He has a scar and he's scary and big, like a wrestler. And I'm pretty sure his name is DeLuca something. You need to get here and arrest him."

"Fuck. How do *you* know that?" He paused. "Wait, are you *witnessing* everything that's happening right now?"

"Uh-huh. Where are you?"

"I'm about 5 minutes away. I'll be there shortly. Stay down and do *not* get out of the car."

Three of DeLuca's men approached my father then.

I breathed a sigh of relief when they unchained him.

"They unchained him. I think they're going to let him go."

"Alyssa, listen to me. I need you to put your head down and stop looking at them. Please, sweetheart."

"I don't understand. Wait, another car just pulled up. Is that you?"

"No, that's not me, Alyssa. Now, stop looking."

I ignored his request. "If it's not you then who is it?"

I watched in confusion as four more of DeLuca's men went over to the car and opened the door. They quickly yanked out two males with dark skin. Both men, if you could even call them that—because they looked more like teenagers; wore baggy clothes and had quite a few tattoos. One boy had a blue shirt on, along with a blue bandanna hanging from his back pocket. The other boy was wearing a red shirt and had a red bandanna hanging from his back pocket. They both looked tired and groggy and had bruises and gashes along their faces and arms.

I didn't understand what they were doing there, or what their involvement was.

I held back a gasp when DeLuca stretched a black glove over his large hand and proceeded to wipe down the metal crowbar.

His men then turned both boys to face one another before they shoved what looked to be guns in their hands. However, both boys appeared to be too out of it to be aware of what was happening to them.

Maybe Ford was right. Maybe it was best that I didn't see what was about to happen. I gasped loudly into the phone when I heard two gunshots go off.

My head jerked up and I let out a cry when I saw the two boys slumped over and bleeding.

My father yelled something at DeLuca then, something about them only being teenagers, I think. But I wasn't sure because my ears were still ringing from the shots.

DeLuca backhanded my father and my father, in turn, spit blood at him.

Then he raised the metal crowbar high above his head.

Everything around me stopped when he took the first swing against my father's skull.

"No! Daddy! Please, no!" I screamed out at the top of my lungs while hitting the windshield as hard as I could.

"Stop screaming, Alyssa," Ford pleaded.

But I couldn't.

I watched as DeLuca continued to bash my father's skull in with that crowbar, deforming his once handsome face.

I watched as my father's body went limp, his blood pooling around the pavement.

I watched as DeLuca smirked and relished every second of killing the man I loved most in the world.

Until his eyes connected with mine.

I screamed even louder…and his smirk grew wider.

Finally, I heard the faint sound of sirens in the distance.

DeLuca took one final look at me before he and his men disappeared into their cars and took off quick as lightning.

I was still screaming when Ford pulled me out of the car and I clung to him for dear life, refusing to be anywhere else.

I was still screaming when Ford barked orders to cover my father's body because my eyes couldn't look away.

I was still screaming when the ambulance pulled up and took out three body bags, instead of stretchers.

I was still screaming when Ford pulled up to headquarters and took me inside an interrogation room.

Whenever I close my eyes…I'm still screaming.

"It wasn't those boys, Ford. It was DeLuca. I know it was."

I'd spent almost 48 hours in the same interrogation room at that point. I fell asleep in Ford's arms for a few short hours, only to wake up screaming.

They tried bringing in a child psychiatrist. They tried feeding me.

They tried doing everything they could to get me to believe something that I refused to.

I knew the truth. I saw it with my very own eyes.

I just didn't understand why *they* wanted me to believe otherwise.

Ford dragged a hand through his dark hair. His 5 o'clock shadow looked even more scruffy than usual, not that it dulled his movie star good looks.

Like my father, he was young. Both he and my father were the youngest members of the FBI, still in their late 20's.

I sat up in my seat, my legs swinging because they didn't quite reach the floor yet. "Where's my mom? Why isn't she here with me? Especially when I'm being interrogated. Where's my lawyer?"

Ford threw up his hands in frustration. "I'm not interrogating you, Alyssa. I just need you to understand certain things. And you don't need a lawyer because you're not in any kind of trouble."

"Then why am I still stuck here? Where's my mother!" I screamed.

Fords expression changed from one of frustration to sheer sadness.

He reached for my hand. "She's in the hospital," he said softly.

"Why?"

He rubbed his eyes. "She's not in good shape right now, kiddo. And the doctor's need to look after her for another day or so. She knows you're here, safe with me."

"What happened to her? Give it to me straight, Ford. I'm a big girl now. I'm officially 10 years old today."

A look of pity flashed across his face. "After she found out what happened, she collapsed." He paused, appearing to choose his next words carefully, but I cut right to the chase.

"What happened to the baby?"

"She lost the baby," he whispered.

I pulled my knees up to my chest and began rocking myself. "It's my fault. I didn't want a little sister and now she's dead. Just like it's all my fault that my Daddy died."

Ford immediately stood up, walked over to me and sat me on his lap. "No, sweetheart. None of this is your fault."

I sunk against him and put my arms around his neck. "You're only saying that because I'm a kid."

"Have I ever treated you like a kid, Alyssa?"

I thought about his question for a moment before I answered, "No."

He was right. He never treated me like I was a child. He always talked to me like I was his equal. So much so, that he and my mother got into it a few times. Especially after he let it slip that Santa and the Easter Bunny weren't real, back when I was 8 years old.

I liked that about Ford, though. In a world full of adults trying mold me into what they wanted me to be, he let me decide things for myself. He let me draw my own conclusions after giving me the cold-hard facts.

He never told me I shouldn't do something, or told me I was wrong for feeling a certain way…until now.

"And you trust me, right?" he asked.

"You're the only one I have left now. Of course, I trust you."

He turned us in the seat and hoisted me up on the table. "Then I need you to repeat after me—I saw those two boys kill my father after he broke up a fight brewing between them and a few others."

"But I didn't, Ford. I know exactly who killed my father. I'll never forget his face. I see it every time I close my eyes. It was him. That DeLuca, man. I don't know why you don't believe me. Ask Hannah, she'll tell you."

"Goddammit," he barked. "Listen to me, Alyssa. DeLuca didn't kill your dad. It was two members of rival gangs. He tried to break it up and he got caught in the crossfire. He was at the wrong place at the wrong time."

I shook my head adamantly. "No, it *wasn't*. Ask Hannah! Why won't you believe me?"

He stood up and kicked a chair across the room.

I began trembling. "Ask Hannah," I repeated.

He ran back over to me and grabbed my face between his large hands. "I can't ask Hannah."

I was even more confused by his statement. "Why?"

"Because Hannah's dead. She was found by her car after leaving the station with two bullets in her head."

"W-what?"

His grip tightened around my cheeks. "You heard me. They got to her. I don't know how, but they traced everything. There must have been a mole working for us. A few of them."

He sighed. "And now DeLuca's got all of New York eating out of his pocket. He controls the politician's, the news. Hell, he's about to have *my* department eating out of the palm of his hand soon. Your dad and I were trying to prevent it. We went undercover, without the FBI's knowledge, on our own. Hannah was in on it with us. We were trying to snag him on something and put him away before he became too powerful…but we failed."

His face fell. "We fucked up big time and your father paid the ultimate price for it."

"But he's a bad guy. How is that possible?"

Ford looked at me hard. "Because sometimes in life, sweetheart. The bad guys win."

His grip eased up and I rubbed my cheek. "So put him away for killing my father."

Ford groaned and took a step back. "In order to do that, we need to have something called motive. Not to mention all the evidence points to those two gang members being responsible."

"What's motive?"

"A logical reason behind doing something. Usually in regards to committing a crime."

"So tell them that you and my dad were trying to catch him doing something bad and he got angry."

"I can't do that," he mumbled.

"Why not?"

He leaned his forehead against mine and put my hands on his cheeks. My breathing became uneven and I didn't know why.

Actually, I did.

It was because I always thought Ford was the most handsome man I'd ever seen. Every time my mom would read me a fairytale, I would picture myself as the princess and Ford as my prince.

I never told anyone about that, though. I didn't think my parents would have liked that very much, for some reason I didn't really comprehend.

"Do you think I'm a good guy, Alyssa?" he whispered.

"Yes," I answered without hesitation. "You're one of my favorite people in the whole wide world."

He smiled at me, showcasing his perfectly straight and white teeth.

"You wouldn't ever want to see me behind bars, right?"

My hand flew to my face. "Never. That would kill me."

"Then you can't ever tell anyone about what your father and I did, okay?"

I bit my lip and looked down. "I won't say anything. Ever. I promise."

He tilted my chin up to look at him. "And you'll tell everyone that it was those two gang members who killed your dad, right?"

I shook my head. "No. Because it wasn't them. DeLuca deserves to pay for what he did."

His nostrils flared and he grunted. "If you say it was DeLuca—do you know what will happen, sweetheart?"

"Yeah. He'll go to jail for a very long time. Maybe even forever."

He grabbed my face again and stared into my eyes. "No, he won't. He knows you saw him, Alyssa. And he'll come after you. Along with me, and your mother. And he won't stop until we're all dead." One hand wrapped around the back of my neck. "He'll bash my skull in and spread my brains all over the concrete."

He lowered his voice and whispered in my ear, "And then he'll do it to your mom. And he'll make you watch every single second of it before he does it to you. Just like with your dad."

I couldn't stop myself from dry heaving with those words. Ford reached for a garbage pail and held it out in front of me while he stroked my hair.

After a few moments, my stomach settled and I was able to breathe again. "But that would make me a l-liar. Being a liar is bad. Those two boys were innocent."

He sat on the chair in front of the table I was still sitting on and put my feet on top of his thighs. "I know your mom reads to you a lot. What's your favorite fairy tale?"

I was put off by the change of subject, but I answered anyway. "Beauty and the Beast."

He smiled and tilted his head toward me. "Do you think the beast was bad?"

"No. I mean, at first, maybe. But he changed his ways for Belle."

"And the beast rescued Belle in the end, right?"

"Well, yes…and no. It's complicated, Ford. The beast loved her and Belle loved him. Despite how mean he was in the beginning. She saw past all that."

He lifted my hand to his lips. "Can you see past the wrong I've done?"

I didn't understand what he meant by that. "Of course. I already told you, you're not a bad guy. You're my favorite person."

"I was only trying to put the bad guy away," he whispered.

"I know. I'm not mad at you."

"Will you let me rescue you then?" His thumb grazed my cheek. "Will you let me be your Prince, Alyssa?"

My cheeks flushed and a swarm of butterflies entered my tummy. "I-um." My breathing became shaky. "I'm feeling nervous and weird right now and I don't understand why," I blurted out.

"You never have to be nervous around me. I would do anything in the world for you. You trust me, right?"

"Yeah-yes."

"I would never, ever hurt you."

"I know."

"Who killed your father?"

"You already know."

The pad of his thumb brushed my cheek again and he moved closer. "Who killed your father, Alyssa?"

I stayed silent.

"Better, sweetheart." He planted a kiss on my cheek and I blushed. "Now I'll ask you again. Who did it? Who killed your father?"

He kissed my other cheek right before I answered, "They did. Those…boys. My father tried to stop the fight between them and they attacked him before they shot each other."

He let out a deep breath. "I'm so proud of you."

He kissed the corner of my mouth. "Thank you for letting me rescue and protect you."

"And that's my story, Jackson. You know things that I've never told another soul."

His brows furrow. "Do you still talk to your dad's old partner?"

"Out of everything I just told you, *that's* what you're choosing to focus on?"

I get up off the bed. "Ford protected me from my father's killer."

He runs a hand through his short hair. "Yeah, I know. I get it," he says before mumbling something under his breath that I don't catch. He appears lost in thought before asking, "Is that why you were grilling me about the owner of the fight club? You thought it was this DeLuca guy, didn't you?"

I nod and he stands up. "It's not by the way. He's not the owner. But you realize how dangerous it would be for you if it was, right?"

"Yeah." I stare at him. "I mean, no. If DeLuca wanted me, he would have gotten me by now. Trust me, after the sex tape my identity isn't exactly an issue anymore. Everyone knows who I am now. Besides, the media went with the story about two rival gangs killing a cop. No one knows the truth besides Ford and I...and now you."

"You never answered my question."

"What question?"

"Do you still talk to him?"

"No," I lie.

I might have told Jackson things I've never told another person. But there's no way I can tell him about the exact nature of me and Ford's relationship throughout the years.

Or the moment, or rather, *moments*; it changed.

And the way it broke me.

Chapter Eleven

ALYSSA
Past...

AFTER THAT DAY IN THE INTERROGATION ROOM, FORD REMAINED AN INTEGRAL part of my childhood.

He came around every other weekend and whisked me away for a few hours during another one of my mother's drunken binges.

He tried persuading her to go to rehab, so many times I lost count; but as usual, she insisted that she didn't have a problem and that if he wanted to continue spending time with me he needed to mind his own business.

He attended every recital, every sporting event, and even a few parent—teacher conferences.

At least, he did until I turned 15.

After that, he seldom came around and I didn't understand why.

One time, he mumbled something about it no longer being appropriate for us to spend so much time with one another, and I thought my heart was going to shatter into a million pieces.

Before he drove away from my tear stained face that day, he promised me that he would always be in my life.

I hated that he was purposely distancing himself from me, but to his credit, he did text me a few times a week. And he still made it a point to see me in person during the two days leading up to my birthday.

Those were always the hardest for me for obvious reasons.

I'll never forget the night of my 17th birthday.

I had gotten into another horrible fight with my mother and John. One of the worst ones to date. I found out that he officially moved in with us.

After hours of persuading and guilting Ford into coming to see me, he finally relented.

He pulled up in a shiny new BMW. The color matching his dark blue eyes perfectly.

I let out a whistle when I saw it and those perfect teeth of his flashed me a movie star grin. "You like?"

"I do. It's gorgeous."

He opened the driver side door and threw the keys at me. "Let's go. You drive."

I stared at him, too stunned to speak. "What's with the look? You are 17 now." He winked. "I trust you not to crash my baby. Now get over here."

I bit my lip and walked over to his side of the car.

He got out and stood before me, his large frame towering over me. His eyes briefly scanned over my body before he looked away. "Jesus, what the hell are they putting in the milk these days," he muttered.

"What are you talking about?"

He coughed before looking at me again. "It's just...you look so grown up compared to when I last saw you. I can't believe your mother lets you out of the house looking like that."

I smoothed over the micro denim mini skirt that I wore especially for him.

I didn't usually wear suggestive clothing, but I wanted to look different.

I wanted Ford to see me as a woman, instead of some silly teenager. "Looking like what, Ford? It's been an entire year since I last saw you, of course, I grew up."

His gaze lingered over my legs. "Yeah, I guess you did."

He walked over to the passenger side door. "You gonna be able to drive in those heels, killer?"

I smirked. "I'll manage."

Since I was the driver, and the destination was my choice—I knew exactly where I wanted to take him.

"Out of all the places to go to. You chose *this* place. On your birthday."

The stars lit up the night time sky and the sound of water crashing against the docks hovered in the distance as I parked the car.

I chewed on my thumbnail. "I haven't been back here since it happened. And there's no one in the world I trust to come here with but you."

"I haven't been here since that day either," he confessed.

I leaned against the headrest and pushed my seat back. "Do you think he would be proud of me?"

Ford reached for my hand. "Of course, he would. Why would you think otherwise?"

"Sometimes I think he would be mad that I didn't stop my mother from turning into an alcoholic. That I should have prevented it."

Before Ford could interject I added, "Sometimes I think he blames me for causing his death. All because I pulled that stupid stunt. God, I was such a brat. What the hell was I thinking?"

His fingers linked with mine. "You were a child, Alyssa. It wasn't your fault and he would never blame you. He loved you."

I squeezed my eyes shut and tuned out his words. "She still cries over him. Usually, it's after John has gone to bed and she thinks no one can hear her. But I can. I always can. Hell, sometimes I cry with her."

"Sweetheart—" he started.

I cleared my throat and opened my eyes. "So, anyway. What's new with you?"

He drew back his hand and ran it along his jaw. "Well, I met someone."

"Oh?" I said, hoping my true feelings over his statement wouldn't show.

It felt like he tossed my heart in a blender and pressed 'puree.' Twice.

"Yeah. She's a doll, too. She's a nurse in the ER over at Columbia."

I gritted my teeth. "A nurse, how sweet."

Obviously not picking up on my sarcasm, he continued, "Yeah. She is. Better than the last relationship I had. What a disaster that was. I'm thinking it's time for this old dog to settle down. Make an honest woman out of someone."

"You're not old," I muttered. He laughed. "I'm 35. That's like ancient to most teenagers."

I played with a strand of my hair. "I'm not like most teenagers, Ford."

He stared at me for a beat and swallowed. "No. No, you're not. You've been through more shit than most adults have in an entire lifetime."

"So what's this nurse's name?" I interrupted.

"Penelope."

"That's a stupid name," I said through clenched teeth.

In all honesty, it wouldn't have mattered what her name was, I still would have hated it.

He chuckled. "It's a bit of a mouthful, I suppose."

I glared at him. "Does she put out?"

He looked taken back. "I don't think that's any of your business. You don't hear me ask-ing if you've given it up to Tony, now do you?"

I spun around in my seat. "His name's *Toby*." I crossed my arms. "And for your informa-tion—No, I haven't given it up yet. I want it to be special."

He nodded, relief flashing across his face. "That's good. It should be special—" he started to say before I cut him off.

"But I've given him one hell of a blowjob."

"Christ, Alyssa. What the *hell* is the matter with you?"

"You!" I shouted. "You left me, Ford. I needed you and you weren't there. You were all I had to depend on after mom went off the deep end. You were the only good thing I had left. Especially after John entered our lives."

He sat up straight. "Has that prick touched you? I swear to God, I'll kill him."

I rolled my eyes. "No. I just don't trust him is all. He's not a good guy. Especially now that he's living with us and controlling mom's every move."

"Shit, she let him move in? You know you can tell me if he steps out of line with you or your mother. Right?"

"Yeah."

We stayed silent for what felt like hours before I finally gathered enough strength to ask him. "Why did you leave me? Why did you go away?"

"I told you. Our relationship wasn't appropriate. People were going to talk and assume things about us, about *me*."

I slammed the steering wheel with my hand. "So let them. Who the fuck cares what other people say."

"It's not that simple, Alyssa."

"I don't buy it. We weren't doing anything wrong. And I don't think people would say shit if they knew the way you saved me. If they knew the way you stepped in when no one else did."

He stayed silent, but I continued probing. "What's the real reason, Ford? You've always been honest with me."

He looked down, avoiding my gaze. "I already told you. It wasn't appropriate."

I smacked the steering wheel again. "Bullshit."

"Would you quit doing that!" he shouted. "You're gonna hurt yourself."

"Stop avoiding my question, Ford."

"I already answered the goddamned question," he ground out.

I slammed the steering wheel again, harder this time.

"Stop it!"

"Make me."

He grabbed my wrists. "Stop acting like a child."

"Stop treating me like one then. And tell me the truth!"

"How many times do I have to say it? It wasn't appropriate, Alyssa."

I struggled against him. "Why? You never did anything wrong. So what *exactly* was it about our relationship that wasn't appropriate?"

"Goddammit, Alyssa. *Me*. My thoughts. The way I was starting to look at you, *think* about you. *Feel* about you. Nothing about it was appropriate."

And just like that, the smoke screen was lifted and my heart soared into orbit.

"How could it not be appropriate when I thought the same things?"

"Because you're a child. I'm an adult. I should know better."

"I'm not a child."

"Yeah, well. You're not an adult, either."

"I'm in love with you, Ford. I always have been. I always will be."

He closed his eyes. "Don't say stuff like that."

"Why not? It's the truth."

"You're my best friend's little girl. I was there at the hospital the day you were born for crying out loud. Do you know how *disgusting* that makes me feel? I want to wash my mind out with bleach every single time I think about you. Do you know how *wrong* everything about this is?"

"Then I'll wait." I swallowed hard. "I'll wait until it's not wrong anymore. Hell, I'll wait for you forever."

"That's the thing, Alyssa. I don't know when it would *ever* be right between us."

"Then I might as well do this," I said before I leaned over the center console and kissed him.

I expected him to push me away, to start yelling about how it wasn't appropriate again. Instead, he groaned and pulled me closer to him as his tongue skated over mine.

Heat coursed through me and I reached for his belt buckle.

That's when he stopped me.

"No. You're not ready for that, yet. You deserve more than some cheap fuck in a car with some old man for your first time."

I reached for his belt again. "Okay, so let me take care of you then."

He pulled away. "No." He sighed. "Listen to me and listen good. You are beautiful and special. You're not some *whore*. You're a good girl, you understand me?"

I shrugged. "I thought I'd do something to make you happy. I thought you wanted me."

He tucked a strand of hair behind my ear. "I do." He looked down. "Clearly that isn't the issue here."

"So what's the problem?"

"Gee, I don't know. Where do I begin? Oh, that's right. How about the fact that what we're doing is *illegal*. Use your head. You got accepted into NYU, didn't you?"

"Okay, so when can we take the next step then?" He muttered something under his breath. "How about when you're old enough."

"Can we still do other stuff?"

He raised an eyebrow. "Like what?"

"Like what we were doing before? You know, kissing."

His lips twitched. "Well you can't un-ring a bell, now can you?"

He leaned in so that I was pressed against my seat. "So fucking beautiful," he whispered before his lips landed on mine.

"So does this mean you and Penelope are over?" I asked between kisses. "I'll break up with Toby first thing tomorrow."

His hand stopped moving midway up my thigh. "I can't just break up with her," he said. "I asked her to marry me. The wedding's this summer."

I pushed him off me. "You *what*? How could you? I thought you were in love with *me*?"

He exhaled sharply and adjusted himself. "I am. I just never thought this—" He gestured between us. "Would ever happen."

"Okay, and now that it has you can let her down easy."

He looked at me like I sprouted another head. "And say what? That I'm in love with my deceased partner's daughter? Who by the fucking way isn't even 18 yet."

"Maybe not in those exact words, but yeah. Something along those lines."

He shook his head. "You don't get it, do you?"

"Evidently not. Why don't you catch me up to speed, special agent," I bit out.

"No one can *ever* know about us. It will always be wrong, no matter how we feel about one another. I have a reputation to protect. I'm a trusted *officer* of the law for Pete's sake."

"But, I thought…"

"You thought wrong, sweetheart." He grabbed my face between both of his hands. "Look, if you can't handle this. Then it's best we stop right here, right now."

I swiped at the tears on my face. "I can't stand the thought of you with someone else, Ford."

"That's the way it has to be."

"I don't know if I can deal with that."

"Then after tonight, forget about us. I'll always be there if you ever really need me, but I have to separate myself from you. It's too hard to be around you. You invade my senses until the only thing I see is you."

"But I love you."

He kissed me tenderly. "And I love you. That's why it's so difficult."

I pulled him into another kiss. Our mouths coming together in a rough and needy mess. His hand slipped back down to my thigh. "Goddammit. You have *no* idea how much I want you. How much I've dreamed about this moment. How much I've jerked off to visions of you writhing underneath me."

"Then marry me. Not her."

His hand moved higher, raising the denim of my skirt to the level of my underwear. "I wish I could, sweetheart. Trust me."

"You can. Who cares what other people think and say. We can live in our own little bubble."

"That's not the way the world works," he grumbled.

"So let's make our own world."

"We can't. Now you can either learn to accept it or not. But I'm marrying Penelope. It's happening. Me and *her* make sense together."

I tried to push him off me again but he didn't budge. "Well, I don't accept it. It should be me. She'll never love you the way I do."

I didn't even realize how hard the tears were falling until Ford had stopped kissing me. "Don't you get it now? We can't be together. You can't even handle kissing me without getting hysterical."

His words lit a fury in me and before I could stop myself, I slapped him across the cheek. "Asshole."

He looked as surprised as I felt. He bit my lip and kissed me harder. "That's right. I *am* an asshole. And innocent little girls like you need to stay far away and stop provoking the beast."

"What if I love the beast? What if I accept him for all that he is?"

His fingers grazed over my panties. "Who does this belong to?"

I trailed kisses up his neck. "I think you know the answer to that."

"Say it, Alyssa."

"It's yours."

"Is it?"

I nodded. "You know it is."

"Even after I marry Penelope? Is it still mine then?"

"I don't want to think about that, Ford."

"Well think about it, because it's happening." He slipped a finger inside the material. "Will you still wait for me then? Will you still allow me to be the first? The *only*? No matter how much time has passed between us?"

I held my breath as his finger continued to stroke me. "Answer me."

"Yes. I'll wait for you."

"Promise me."

"I promise."

By the time Ford had dropped me off it was almost 3 in the morning.

I tip-toed inside the house, being as quiet as I could.

Until a voice stopped me in my tracks. "Who was that man that just dropped you off?" John's voice boomed.

I turned to face him. "None of your business. Don't worry about it."

The corner of his lips curled up. "Don't give me any sass, girl. I asked you a question and I expect an answer."

"That controlling tone might work with my mother, for reasons I fail to comprehend; but you're surely mistaken if you think it'll have the same effect on me. I don't answer to you."

I headed in the direction of my room when I was suddenly slammed against the wall. I rubbed the back of my head, trying to thwart off a headache that would be starting soon, thanks to him. "Touch me again and it will be the last thing you ever do, you son of a bitch," I warned.

"Young lady, that is no way to talk to your father."

I saw red at that moment. "You might be screwing my mother, but you are *not* my father."

He looked me up and down, disgust in his eyes. "Yeah, well, maybe if you actually *had* a father you wouldn't be walking in the house at 3 in the morning looking like a tramp."

I was so angry I started shaking. "Yeah, well, maybe if you were half the man *my* father was, you wouldn't have to buy my mother off with gifts to get her to fuck you."

The slap across my face seemed to echo throughout the entire house.

A light turned on in the hallway and my mother stood there in shock.

I took a step forward. "You can try and cover up manure…but at the end of the day, it still reeks like shit."

"What the hell is that supposed to mean?" he barked.

I looked at my mother briefly before focusing my attention back to him. "You might be in her bed now, but trust me when I say that when the booze leaves her system and reality sets in, it's not you that she wants next to her. It will always be him."

My mother gasped but I ignored her and held up my cell phone instead. "And you just made a big mistake by touching me."

I ran out of the house and dialed Ford's number.

A woman's voice picked up on the third ring.

"Hello," she answered.

"Can I speak to Ford?" I heard some shuffling in the background. "It's 3:30 in the morning. Who is this?"

Aggravation coursed through me as it dawned on me. "Why are you picking up his cell phone?"

A giggle erupted, followed by the sound of his low groan. "Because he's a little preoccupied at the moment."

I let out a shaky breath, the impact of her words sinking in.

"Tell him it's important," I whispered.

With a huff, I heard her faintly murmur what I said to him.

"There's nothing more important than you, sweetheart. Just hang up on her," Ford's voice commanded before the line went dead.

I shoved my phone into my pocket and turned back around. I was startled to find John outside on the porch smoking a cigarette.

"Look, I'm sorry about before," he began.

I continued walking, my heart breaking with every step. "Whatever."

"Who was that you were on the phone with?" he asked.

That's when the tears erupted. John stomped out his cigarette, appearing daunted.

"It doesn't matter," I sniffed. "What we had is over, for good. He made that perfectly clear."

He looked pleased. "Listen, I've been thinking, I want your mother to go to rehab."

I laughed and walked past him. "Yeah, good luck with that."

"I'm gonna make it happen, Alyssa. But I'm going to need your help."

He held out his hand. "Truce?"

"Fine," I muttered before heading inside.

An hour later, my phone rang. Ford's name flashed on the screen.

"Leave me alone," I answered.

"Don't be like that, Alyssa."

"Be like what, Ford? Be like you?"

"Stop acting like a child. I told you the way it had to be."

I stayed silent.

"I told you I'll always be there for you when you need me," he said.

"Yeah, except when you're too busy being *there* for her. I won't be the other woman."

He chuckled. "You'd actually have to be a woman for that to happen."

His words stung. There was only one way to make the pain go away. "Have a nice life, Ford."

"Look, I'm sorry. I didn't mean to hurt you like that. You know I love you. I will always love you. But maybe it's best that we don't talk for a while," he said before he hung up.

It was the last time I would speak to Ford for 4 years.

The next time…he would shatter the rest of me.

He stared at me for what felt like forever, finally standing up from his desk after a full 5 minutes had passed.

His gray suit was immaculate, and even though a few lines creased his forehead with age, it only made him better looking.

"You cut your hair," were the first words he uttered. "It suits you. I like it. Makes you look more mature."

I gave him half a smile. "Most newscasters have shoulder length hair. I figured it was time to conform."

He nodded. "Did you get here okay?"

I held up the keys to the BMW. "Yeah. Thanks to a certain special agent I know."

Nothing shocked me more than when I had received the title and a set of keys to his BMW in the mail, along with directions telling me where I could pick it up.

On his wedding day, no less.

Not wanting to acknowledge that statement with words, he gave me another nod.

I wrung my hands and looked around. "I like your office."

"Yeah, I have the promotion to thank for that. It seems the higher up the chain I go, the less field work I do."

I smiled, until I spotted a picture of him and my father on his desk. His eyes followed mine and he looked away.

Figuring this moment couldn't get any more awkward, I decided, to go for the gold. "How's Penelope?"

"Fine," he responded curtly.

He seemed different now. Colder. "Is everything okay?" I asked.

He cleared his throat and walked out from around his desk. "I guess I'm just trying to figure out exactly why you're here, Alyssa."

I stepped back as though I'd been punched. "You really have no idea why I'm here right now?"

The sex tape had gone viral, my stepfather had lost the election, and my mother had officially disowned me.

I had no one else to turn to. All roads led back to him.

"I guess you haven't been on the internet in a while but—"

"I saw the fucking sex tape!" he screamed loud enough to make me jump.

Not waiting for a response, he continued. "Like I said, I'm having trouble figuring out why you're here."

I swallowed hard. "John won't help me and my mother's turned her back on me."

"Okay?"

"Okay?" I scoffed before my voice started cracking. "You're all I have left, Ford."

I took a step toward him and he lifted his chin. "What exactly is it that you want from me, Alyssa?"

"It happened without my consent—"

He cut me off. "Are you insinuating that he raped you? Because it looked like you were a willing participant."

"No. What I meant was that I had no idea he was filming it. I never agreed to that."

He narrowed his eyes. "But you agreed to spread your legs for him?"

Before I could interject he added, "Like some kind of whore."

I heard that word from a lot of people after the sex tape leaked, including my own mother. But hearing it from his mouth made something inside of me snap.

He held me against him. "Shh." He took out a tissue and wiped my face. "Stop crying."

"I c-can't. You promised you would always be there f-for me." I took a deep breath. "I need your help, Ford."

He kissed my forehead. "What are you willing to do for it?" he whispered.

He put a hand on my shoulder and pushed. I backed away from him, closing my eyes in disbelief.

I looked up at him when I heard the sound of a belt buckle being undone. "No." I shook my head. "You can't be serious."

I had always thought about being intimate with Ford, but not this way. Never like this.

He smirked. "What's the matter, Alyssa? You can fuck some guy on video but not me? The man you claimed to love. The one you promised to wait for?"

"I-I. You got married. You chose her. *You* said we shouldn't talk anymore," I stammered.

He leaned into me until I fell against the wall. "I was *trying* to do the right thing," he whispered before he kissed me.

Our mouths tangled and his hands pulled at my clothing. "What are we doing, Ford?" I panted as he kissed my neck.

He pulled back. "You were supposed to be *mine*."

I reached for the buttons on his shirt and he lifted my skirt. "I am yours."

Before I knew it, my legs were wrapped around his waist and he was entering me with a loud grunt as I moaned.

"Yeah, you like that?" he asked before pulling out and slamming into me hard.

I could only nod, my body too far gone to form actual words.

Until his next statement. "Of course, you do. You little slut."

My eyes opened wide and I stopped moving. "Wha—"

His hand slammed over my mouth and his eyes darkened. "You heard me. You lost all your value and appeal the day you became nothing but a worthless slut. You only did it to yourself, Alyssa."

Tears sprung to my eyes with his cruel words as he continued thrusting and taunting me. "I loved you. I was supposed to be your first, your only. Now you're *tainted*…ruined."

He grunted his release and threw me to the ground. "Turns out you weren't that good of a fuck after all. Figure your own way out of this mess, Alyssa. I suggest you continue to whore yourself around because that's all you're good for. Now, get out of my office."

His hands remained clenched at his sides and he took one final look at me. "Your father would be ashamed of you."

I quickly gathered my clothes off the ground and left.

After making my way out to the hallway, I reached up and felt for my necklace. With shaky hands, I tugged on it until it ripped free and fell.

It was then that I realized.

There are a thousand ways to break a girl…but it only takes one to kill her.

Chapter Twelve

ALYSSA

I WAKE UP TO A PAIR OF STRONG ARMS ROCKING ME.

I look up as Jackson peers down at me, concern written all over his striking face.

I don't even realize that I fell asleep again until I glance at the clock, and it reads 3:45am.

For a moment, I'm nervous that I've said something about Ford in my dream state.

I expect him to start questioning me, or ask what I was dreaming about but he doesn't. Instead, his hand drops down to my cheek and brushes across the wetness gathered there. He looks at his fingers, which are now damp with my tears.

Then he pulls me off of his lap and crushes me against him in one of the most powerful embraces I've ever experienced in my life.

My breath leaves my lungs with a big whoosh, and all I can do is breathe him in and succumb to the warmth I feel.

It's been so long since I've been touched like this, I almost recoil.

He must sense this because he pulls back slightly, his thumbs graze over my cheekbones again and for a second; I think he's about to do something crazy—like kiss me.

I find myself wanting him to do just that. I want him to fix me, make me whole again. I want him to erase the past with his purity and kindness.

I wish our circumstances were different, I wish I was the girl he first thought I was. The girl he briefly flirted with on that walk from the fight club. The girl who isn't so damaged she barely even knows how to function anymore.

His lips move closer and my heart stutters in my chest as I close my eyes.

Disappointment hits hard when I feel his lips land on my forehead instead of my mouth.

"Look at me," he whispers. "I won't hurt you."

I've heard those words before…by the one person who swore they never would.

"You don't know that, Jackson. You can't promise me something like that."

His eyes bore into mine before he hugs me again. "You're right. I can't make that promise." He holds my chin between his thumb and his fingers. "But I *can* promise you that I will never intentionally hurt you. No matter what happens between us, just know that I'll always have your best interest at heart."

I stay silent taking in his words, wanting so badly to believe them. I'm so lost in my own thoughts, I almost don't register when he stands up and walks over to his closet.

"Here," Jackson says. He hands me a clean white t-shirt and a pair of flannel boxers. "Change into these. You'll be more comfortable."

I look down at my skin tight jeans and my constricting leopard print tank top and give him a smile. "Thanks."

He returns my smile before he closes the door behind him.

After I change he walks back into his bedroom, this time; carrying a mug. I look down in confusion when I see its contents.

"Hot chocolate with cinnamon and whipped cream?" I question. It's not that I'm not grateful for it, I'm just curious; especially because I never asked for it.

He looks uneasy before he clears his throat and sits on the bed beside me.

"I used to make it for Lilly whenever she was upset." He shrugs. "It was her favorite. It always made her feel better."

I'm touched that he's sharing this part of himself with me.

I take a sip of the chocolate goodness before putting the mug down on the nightstand beside the bed.

Before I can talk myself out of it, I reach for his hand. His hand dwarfs mine in size, but I lay it on top of mine anyway and begin tracing the lines of his palm.

He looks away but continues talking. "My mom was a heroin addict. We barely even survived living in that trailer on her check from government assistance. She made a lot of wrong choices due to her addiction, one of them including the men she brought home." He swallows. "One night, when I was 11, I came home late. I was out playing ball in the park with my friends and lost track of time. My mother was passed out on the couch. She didn't hear Lilly's screams, but I did."

I grip his hand tighter, hoping to give him the strength to continue. He turns his head and finally looks at me. "I ran into her bedroom and saw my mother's poor excuse for a one night stand with his pants around his ankles while he was standing over her bed."

"Oh my god." My hand flies to my mouth. "Please tell me he didn't."

He shakes his head. "He didn't. With strength I didn't even know I possessed, I charged at him. I threw him right out the door and beat the shit out of him. Then I told him if I ever saw his face again I would finish him. When I went back into Lilly's room, she was shaking and refused to speak. Finally, after an hour or so had passed, she told me she was thirsty. It was around Christmas time and we didn't have much."

I look at the mug. "But you had hot chocolate, cinnamon, and whipped cream," I finish for him.

He nods. "Yeah. After that day, it became her favorite. We were all each other had and I promised her that I would always protect her. In addition to taking up mixed martial arts, I slept on the floor in her bedroom at night, every night." He pauses. "Well, up until my mom died and she didn't have to fear her dirtbag boyfriends anymore."

I rest my head against his shoulder, tears prickling my eyes for all that he's endured. "You were an amazing big brother."

"I tried to be. I wanted to be. She deserved that. She was an amazing person. She was brilliant, sweet, compassionate—everything that was right in the world. She was going places. She got into Harvard, she wanted to make a difference." He draws in a shaky breath. "I didn't tell her often, but I was so proud of her."

I grab his hand tighter, mustering up the courage to ask the question that I don't want to ask, but I have to. "What happened to her, Jackson?"

He leans back against the headboard, his face portraying so much grief and agony, I'm about to tell him that he doesn't have to answer.

"She was murdered."

His words hang in the silence between us.

"Did her killer pay?"

He looks at me and his eyes darken. "Not nearly enough."

I fight the involuntary shiver that crawls up my spine.

It's clear that he's not up to talking about this anymore because he turns and flicks off the light.

I lie on the bed beside him, both of us flat on our backs, not saying a word—our fingertips almost touching.

I never knew how comfortable silence could be until now. But as comfortable as it is between us, I need something else.

I turn and position myself on top of him, my legs on either side of him. His eyes open wide at first, but he visibly relaxes when I slide down until my head is flat against his chest.

I can feel every defined muscle his body encompasses. Every ripple of his abs, how hard and broad his chest is. And I'd be lying to myself if I didn't admit that it causes a physical reaction to stir in me, but this closeness is different than any other I've experienced.

"I hate murderers," I mumble with a yawn. "I'll never understand how cruel and inhumane someone's soul must be in order to take another life. It's unforgivable."

His body tenses beneath me and I know it's because he probably feels the same. "I wish everyone could be good like you, Jackson," I whisper before I close my eyes.

His hand skims up the length of my back, hesitantly at first, until I nuzzle against him and he begins drawing slow circles along my spine, lulling me to sleep.

I have no more bad dreams that night.

I do, however, dream about Jackson.

Sunlight peeks in from the corner of the curtain covering the window in his bedroom.

I look down. One heavy and muscular leg is tangled between two of mine.

We must have dislodged ourselves from one another in the middle of the night.

Well, somewhat.

His back is partially turned away from me and my eyes practically pop from their sockets when I notice that he's shirtless, wearing nothing but a pair of boxers.

His broad back is a sight to behold and my breathing hitches in my throat.

When my eyes travel further down, lust crashes into me like a damn tsunami.

A portion of the comforter is draped and bunched up just under that mouthwatering, sculpted V of his, which unfortunately for me…happens to be hiding something that I'm *very* interested in seeing at the moment.

I fight back and forth with my conscience before deciding that if the roles were reversed, I might not like it if he tore back the covers in order to get a better look at my goods.

But then again, I don't look like him.

His body is a work of art. When I look at him, I see the hours of training and discipline, I see the strength he possesses, the well-oiled machine he's molded himself into.

Jesus. Who am I kidding? I definitely wouldn't mind Jackson getting a better look at me. I wouldn't mind Jackson showing any kind of sexual interest in me at all.

The thought surprises me, because although I use sex as a way of coping and punishing myself…the one thing I *don't* use sex for is my desire.

It hits me and I realize how much I've been missing out on.

The question is…does Jackson want me even half as much as I want him?

Like the saying goes, there's only one way to find out.

Since his front isn't facing my back, I'm unable to grind myself against him and feign innocence when he catches on, leaving the ball in his court.

That means I have no choice but to take the initiative and put myself out there.

It's something I've done more times than I care to think about, but for some reason, I've never been so nervous about it before.

And that includes that night in the car with Ford, because I knew deep down that he wanted me.

But with Jackson, I really have no idea. He's so controlled and good at keeping his emotions in check.

I bite my lip and prop myself up on one elbow, my front now pressed up flush against his back. I lift one hand and slowly trail my fingers down his chest. Seeing all those muscles is *nothing* compared to feeling them.

I expect him to wake then, but when I look up his eyes are still closed, his mouth parted slightly.

My fingers find the waistband of his boxers and hover there for a moment. I plant a gentle open-mouthed kiss on his shoulder while I continue tracing the outline of his waistband.

His brows furrow and I think I'm doing something wrong…but then he releases a low and husky groan that goes straight to my core.

Just when I'm about to move the comforter and slip my hand inside the opening of his boxers…I find myself facing the ceiling, with a ginormous weight on top of me.

My wrists are pinned and I'm gasping for air when he settles between my thighs.

The only thought going through my mind is-

Holy. Shit.

When I feel his hardness pressed against my thigh.

"What are you doing, Alyssa?" he asks, his voice raspy with sleep and what I'm hoping is arousal.

I don't answer him because my brain just isn't capable of forming complete sentences right now. Instead, I shift myself so he's exactly where I want him to be and I swear, I die a thousand deaths.

He releases my wrists, grabs a handful of my hair and inhales deeply. "Coconut," he rasps. I don't understand why he's talking about coconuts when all I want to do is lick him from head to toe, but then he groans and flattens his palms against mine. "I fucking love the way you smell." He closes his eyes, appearing to be fighting a war within himself. "I bet you taste as good as you smell."

"Jackson," I whisper. My shorts are bunched up so they resemble underwear and I'm certain that he can feel the wetness between my legs seeping through the material.

And then he thrusts and I feel every single inch of him. Including something I never expected. Something that pushes my own arousal into overdrive.

He lifts his hips and just when I think he's about to end the slow torture and fuck me, he rolls off of me.

I climb on top of him and straddle him, but his hands press down on my thighs rendering me unable to move. "No," he says firmly.

"Why not?"

Then it hits me. Why the hell would Jackson want a girl like me?

I'm used up, washed up and *fucked* up.

"Hey." He lifts my chin to look at him. "Whatever you're thinking right now, cut it out. It's not you, it's me."

"Wow," I scoff. "You won't even fuck me but you're already hitting me with the old 'it's not you, it's me.'"

I move my face away from his touch. "I'd rather you just be honest and tell me you'd rather not stick your dick in a dirty whore." I laugh. "Trust me, I understand."

I raise my thighs and attempt to get off him but he clamps down harder, holding me in place. "And that right there is why this can't happen, Alyssa."

I roll my eyes. "Whatever. Don't bother letting me down easy. I don't blame you for not wanting a slut." He groans and lifts his hips pushing his thick erection into me. "Does this feel like I don't want you?"

He shifts and pulls us into a sitting position. "But the thing is, you're not a whore. That's *not* your identity, no matter what others may say. You're *Alyssa*." His voice drops to a whisper, "But you need to believe it yourself. And I'll only add to your pain if I let you use me as some kind of weapon in order to punish yourself. I don't want to be used by you. I don't want you to put me in the same category as the others. That's why this *can't* happen and I can only offer you friendship."

I nod my head in understanding. I have absolutely no argument for that. He has every right to think that I would only be using him. And I don't want to take advantage of him, no matter how much my own heart, mind, and body are in disagreement when it comes to him.

I need to sort out my feelings and make some serious decisions before I pursue anything with him again.

I climb off of him, wishing the disappointment that fills my chest would stop. I wish that everything was different and that I was a normal almost 24-year-old.

We turn in bed and face one another, studying each other's faces, not sure what to say next.

"Can I ask you something?"

"Sure."

I flush when the thought invades my brain, and before I can stop myself, I utter, "Jackson, do you have a cock piercing?"

He opens his mouth to answer me but starts laughing. My heart constricts because he looks even hotter now. "Wow, that was seriously the *last* thing I expected you to ask me," he says between bouts of laughter.

I hit him with a pillow. "Stop laughing and answer the question, jackass."

"Yes, I have an apadravya."

"How did that happen?"

He raises an eyebrow. "Well, it wasn't some freak accident if that's what you're asking."

I groan. "No. I mean, what made you want to get your dick pierced."

He shrugs. "Tyrone."

It's my turn to raise an eyebrow at him. "Really? Wow, you turning me down makes even more sense now."

I swear he flushes when he catches on to what he said. "Fuck. That didn't come out right."

"Hey, Tyrone's sexy. I can't say that I blame you."

His nostrils flare and for a moment, I see jealousy flash across his face. "What I meant," he says through clenched teeth. "Is that Tyrone was the reason *behind* the piercing."

I give him a wink. "I bet he was."

He groans in frustration and pulls me into his arms. "Do you want to hear the story or not?"

I put my finger to my lips. "Hmm, do I want to hear the story about two hot guys getting their cock's pierced? Yes, please."

He rolls his gorgeous eyes and playfully swats my behind. "Now, you're only getting the cliff notes version. It happened after we both won our first fight at the club. We were at the bar and Tyrone ended up getting drunk when he suddenly announced that he needed to celebrate."

I can't stop myself from giggling. "And he thought getting an apadravya would be the way to go about that?"

He gives me a lopsided grin. "It gets better. He leaped on top of the bar and declared that he was going to do something very alpha male. He ended it with a giant 'I am man, hear me roar, fuckers.'"

I put my hand to my forehead. "Oh god. He didn't."

He shakes his head. "No, he didn't. Because when we got to the shop, he chickened out on the apadravya. He only has a Prince Albert." Jackson laughs so hard he begins shaking. "He kept telling the poor piercer to make it look pretty. Crazy thing is, he doesn't even remember getting it done. He screamed like a girl when he took a piss the next morning."

I can't stop myself from joining in his laughter. "That is an awesome story."

"It is. I'll never forget the look on Ricardo's face when he walked into the tattoo shop and saw what we were doing. He was mad that we fell off the grid on our first night, but he ended up getting his own piercing as a sign of solidarity."

I wipe my eyes and scrunch my face. "Fell off the grid? What is he, your keeper or something?"

Jackson's face falls, but our moment is quickly interrupted when some woman yells, "Tyrone Isaac Davis. That is no way to greet Momma. Now put some damn clothes on and tell your lady friend good luck and Godspeed," in a thick Southern accent.

"Shit. Momma's here."

"Momma?" I question.

He nods before he throws my jeans at me. "Quick, put these on."

I do as he says, but can't help but think—What the hell is going on and who the heck is Momma?

Chapter Thirteen

JACKSON

One second I'm having one of the best mornings I've ever had…and the next I'm hearing the sounds of Tyrone's mother yelling at him from the next room.

I love Momma, I really, really do. The woman is the closest thing to a real mother I've ever had…but her timing couldn't have been worse.

I was enjoying seeing Alyssa laugh, her smile lighting up the entire room…and that dimple.

That fucking dimple.

It gets me—Every. Single. Time.

I would move mountains for that dimple.

I watch as she slides the tight denim over her hips and tucks my t-shirt, which is at least 2 sizes too big on her small frame into the waistband of her jeans.

Fuck, I love seeing her in *my* clothes. I have to bite my tongue when she turns around and I get an eye full of that perfect heart shaped ass.

God, the things I want to do to that ass of hers. The things I *almost* let myself do to that ass of hers.

Fucking hell. Who the fuck was I kidding, thinking that friendship would be enough?

With a grunt, I walk over to my closet and toss on a pair of basketball shorts and a wife beater tank.

Alyssa stands at the door and appears nervous for a moment, but I take her hand in mine and we walk out together.

I'm glad I told her to get dressed. Not that I care what other people think about who I spend my time with…but Momma's opinion has always mattered to me and I don't want her to get the wrong impression of Alyssa.

Lord knows there are enough people in the world who have the wrong impression of her already.

The smell of homemade pancakes, grits, eggs, and bacon make me salivate. There is nothing in the world that beats Momma's cooking.

Alyssa and I are the last to arrive in the kitchen, and when we do…the stares we receive are interesting…to say the least.

Tyrone looks up from his plate and grins at Alyssa before devouring the rest of his biscuit.

Ricardo looks uneasy and a bit angry, until I lift my chin and give him a look. It's a look that lets him know that I'm not ashamed of Alyssa and he should get used to seeing her around. He gives a small nod in my direction before smiling at Alyssa.

And that's when I notice Lou-Lou's expression. She obviously feels threatened by Alyssa's presence. The snarl on her face reminds me of a chihuahua. It's sad because she would be pretty if she wasn't so fucking bitter and miserable all the time.

I guide Alyssa to a stool over at the large oval counter where everyone is gathered.

I hear Momma's throat clear and I look up. Her normally bright ebony eyes are squinted. Her normally smooth, dark and flawless skin wrinkles between her eyebrows and her full lips are in a tight line. She looks like a lion protecting her baby cub, who's about to strike any minute. The spatula in her hand shakes when she glares at Alyssa.

Oh, shit.

Momma's the type who only respects certain people. She's a strong, sassy, Southern woman who takes no crap and expects none to be given. She's also fiercely protective when it comes to her boys…me included. She can be overwhelming at first, but once you get to know her, you end up falling head over heels in love with her.

I make my way to Momma and open my arms wide to give her a hug, but am shocked when I'm lightly pushed to the side instead.

Alyssa raises her chin, holds out her hand and looks Momma right in the eyes. "Hello, Mrs. Davis. I'm Alyssa Tanner and it's a pleasure to meet you, ma'am."

Lou-Lou lets out a small gasp. I look over at her and there's practically smoke coming out of her ears. To this day, I still don't think Lou-Lou's ever greeted Momma properly or looked her in the eye.

The first time she met Momma she cowered behind Ricardo while Momma proceeded to tell her to stop acting like the town cow and givin' the milk away for free. She eased up a little after Ricardo explained that they weren't serious.

The fact that Alyssa just womaned up and didn't let fear hold her back sends a surge of pride through me.

I don't think she realizes how strong she really is.

Momma purses her lips for a moment and looks Alyssa up and down, finally stopping to study her face. Then I see the twinkle in those beautiful ebony eyes of hers. Momma approves, she passed the first test.

She wipes her hand on her apron before shaking Alyssa's hand. "It's nice to meet you too, and please; call me Momma."

I hear the sound of Lou-Lou's glass falling to the floor in the background.

This is fucking great.

Alyssa gives her a smile before stepping to the side. I immediately wrap Momma up in a tight hug. "Hey, Momma. Thanks for making breakfast." She squeezes me tighter. "Nonsense. You know I like to keep my boys fed. How you doin', sugar?" She nods her head in Alyssa's direction. "By the looks of things, I'd say you might have found yourself a keeper over there."

Alyssa returns to her seat, but I don't miss the fact that she smiles at that statement.

I lean into Momma's ear and whisper, "She's definitely a keeper."

"Does that mean you'll settle down and give me some grand babies soon? Because we all know my son, the dip-shit, obviously can't keep it in his pants lately."

I start coughing and Alyssa spits out her drink.

Momma ignores us and continues, "You don't even want to know what I just caught him in bed with. The woman had half her head shaved and tattoo's on her *face* for crying out loud! Not to mention, she was carrying some kind of riding crop when she moseyed on out of the bedroom. And I know she ain't been riding no horse."

Tyrone opens his mouth to say something, but she points a finger at him and shakes her head. "I swear, my boy ain't got the good sense God gave em' sometimes."

I look at Tyrone. I'm not judging, but this is different from his usual modus operandi when it comes to women. But I know he's out screwing anything and everything lately in order to forget the fact that Shelby's wedding is this weekend.

Shelby was his high school sweetheart. Her father was the sheriff in their small town in Alabama, and after Tyrone was hauled off to jail for something that falsely got pinned on him; she was forbidden from ever talking to him again.

He'll always carry a torch for that girl.

He gives me a small shrug and I sit down on the stool next to Alyssa. "Alright Momma, enough," he says.

"Go easy on him, Momma," I say. "He's going through a lot right now."

She flips a pancake and points the spatula at me. "Which is exactly why I'm here right now."

Tyrone shoves another bite of food in his mouth. "I told you, Momma. I'm fine."

She gives him a pensive look. "So, you're saying that you're completely over Shelby, then?"

Ricardo and I groan in unison. Here we go.

"I'm happy for her," he starts before he takes another bite of food. "I wish her all the best with her rich, stuck up, stupid—" He takes a drink. "Ugly, no fun, small dick, stupid—"

"You said stupid already," Ricardo reminds him.

Tyrone tips his drink at him. "Lousy, good for nothing, wanna be cowboy, lying, cheating, mullet haircut, dumb ass, man-boy, soon to be husband." He grips his fork and knife. "Really, guys…I'm *fine*. I hope they have a happy life and have a million mullet-haircut wearing babies."

That went better than expected.

Momma looks at him. "And nothings gonna change your mind about that, buttercup?"

He stabs his eggs. "You got that right."

Momma daintily wipes her mouth with her napkin. "I guess it won't matter then."

Tyrone takes the bait. "What won't matter?"

She smiles from ear to ear. "The fact that last night, our very own Shelby ran right out of her wedding rehearsal in tears. Screaming up a storm about how it should be *you* who should be standing up at that altar waiting for her."

"Fucking shit, man," Ricardo says.

"Well, I'll be damned. Girl's finally come to her senses," I say.

Tyrone shakes his head. "No. There's too much water under the bridge. Too much devastation in our wake."

"Don't be stupid. You better go after her," Alyssa says, much to everyone's surprise.

We all look at her while she looks at Tyrone and continues, "I'm just saying that when you love someone. You don't give up on them. You fight for them. It doesn't matter what obstacles are standing in the way." She takes a breath. "When you love someone, you hold their hand when they're too scared to move forward because all they've ever known is a past that's full of despair and emptiness. When you love someone, you realize that every bit of pain you ever endured is worth it because you found the person who's the very best part of your life." She shrugs. "Or at least, that's how *I* imagine love is supposed to be. Despite whatever bullshit might have happened between you two."

I look at her in awe, but the moment is ruined when Lou-Lou snorts and makes a face at her.

Momma points the spatula in Alyssa's direction. "I knew I had a good feeling about her. She's right, baby. You cain't never could. Which is why I bought you a plane ticket. We leave in a few hours." She pauses and looks at Ricardo. "Don't worry. He'll be back by Monday." She grimaces. "And if he's a little late you tell that no good, son-of-a-bitch De—"

"That's great," I say loudly, cutting Momma off before she says DeLuca's name. "I think you should go," I tell Tyrone.

Momma smiles and Tyrone looks at me. "Yeah, alright. But you know what will happen if it doesn't work out, right?"

"Don't worry. I'll have a bottle of Jack Daniel's ready to go and a copy of Nelly's greatest hits in the CD player. Along with a few Hulk dvd's."

He smiles and reaches over to give me a pound. "My man."

Ricardo laughs. "You better lock that up quick, Alyssa. Looks like you might have some competition on your hands."

She leans forward and crinkles her nose. "I'm not afraid of a little competition." She hikes a thumb in Tyrone's direction. "However, I don't think I can possibly compare to this alpha male with his pretty piercing over here."

The room erupts in laughter…with the exception of Lou-Lou who just crosses her arms and sucks her teeth.

"So," Lou-Lou says while narrowing her eyes at Alyssa. "I take it you spent the night in Jackson's bed? Really giving it the old *college* try with him, huh? Tell me, how was it at NYU?"

Everyone goes silent and Alyssa blinks and looks down, shame all across her face.

I've never wanted to take my temper out on a woman before, until this moment. I absolutely hate that she just did that to her.

Alyssa glances in the direction of the door but I grip her hand under the table and glare at Lou-Lou. "At least she was actually invited to spend the night in my bed. Not just sniffing around me like some dog wanting to get their paws on some scraps." My pupils constrict as I stare down at her. "And despite what you may think, staying up all night and having a meaningful conversation with someone you care about is so much better than being used for sex. But we *all* know *you* wouldn't know about that, Lou-Lou. Now would you?"

Momma claps her hands. "Okay. Who wants seconds?"

Alyssa looks up at me in wonder. "Me. I want more. I would love more."

I search her eyes, feeling the impact of her words hit me right in the center of my chest. I bring her hand to my lips and kiss it. "Me too."

I don't know what I'm doing, but I can't stop myself.

There are a million reasons why I shouldn't be pursuing this. Reasons like the fact that DeLuca basically owns my ass for the next 7 years. Reasons…like what he *did* to her.

There aren't enough words to express how I feel about what he took away from Alyssa.

Not to mention, the fact that I, myself am technically a murderer. And given her own past, I'm sure she won't be so understanding about that.

If I tell her, I could lose her.

And I think I might just be the one person in her life who would be good for her. I would *never* use her.

Which leads me to my next thought.

Something hasn't been sitting well with me since she told me about what happened to her father.

Her strange relationship with her dad's old partner, Ford.

I mean, what the hell *was* that in the interrogation room? That was the very definition of coercion if there ever was one. And on a 10-year-old? I get that he was trying to protect her, but there's a small part of me that feels like he was also out to save his own skin and maybe his intentions weren't as pure as she thinks they were.

However, I *can't* tell her that. When she talks about Ford, it's clear she still holds him in very high regard, even to this day—although she told me that he's no longer in her life.

And if I'm being honest with myself, I'm glad about that.

I've got all these reasons swirling around in my head, but through it all…one thought keeps breaking through the fog.

I want her.

My God, do I *want* her.

But, if I don't slow this thing down...I could lose her.

I meant what I said to her earlier. I *don't* want to be used by her...and I don't want to rock the boat and make things worse for her. I also don't want to stir things up with my *own* sexual desires.

I *have* to slow this down. I have to proceed with caution...not that I should even be proceeding at all. I let go of her hand and move my plate away. "But, I shouldn't. Sometimes too much, too fast can leave you in a lot of pain."

She gives me an inquisitive look before holding her plate out to Momma. "Or sometimes you have to say to hell with it and indulge a little. You might miss out on a good thing and by the time you decide you want it, it's all gone."

Tou-fucking-ché.

Momma fills up her plate with more food. "A girl after my own heart." Her eyes land on Lou-Lou and her barely eaten food. "Men like a little something to hold onto. Can't be all skin and bones with no derriere." She scans the room. "Ain't that right, boys?"

It doesn't take a rocket scientist to figure out that Momma definitely likes Alyssa much more than she does Lou-Lou.

"Yes, Ma'am," we all say in unison while Lou-Lou rolls her eyes and tosses her napkin in her dish.

"I just realized something," Tyrone says in my direction. "If I hop on that plane...I'll miss your fight tomorrow night."

"You have a fight tomorrow night?" Alyssa interjects.

I look down at my plate, hoping with everything that Alyssa doesn't want to come... because she won't like my response.

"Yeah." I rub the back of my neck. "Tyrone. It's okay if you miss my fight. It's not a big deal. There will be *others*."

Shit, I didn't mean for the last part of that sentence to come out so tense.

"I'll come," Alyssa says, excitement in her tone. "Tomorrow is my birthday and I don't have any other plans. I'd love to watch."

How the hell did I overlook that? Fucking hell.

Momma leaps up from the table. "Oh, sugar. I wish I would have known your birthday was tomorrow. I would have whipped you up something special."

"You *can't* come," I whisper.

Alyssa laughs and pats her tummy. "It's okay, Momma. This breakfast was more than enough." She continues talking, obviously not hearing me. "So, do I need to purchase tickets for this thing, or what?"

"No, because you're *not* coming," I grind out softly, hoping she hears me this time.

Momma looks contemplative. "No. I'll admit, I haven't seen many of their fights. I don't much care for the violence, but every time I've ever gone...I just show up with Ricardo and they let me right in the door." She winks. "If that doesn't work, you can always tell them you're Jackson's girl. They'll let you right in."

Motherfucking shit.

Alyssa looks at Ricardo. "Is it okay if I tag along with you?"

Ricardo opens his mouth to answer.

I slam my hand down on the table, startling everyone. "Goddammit, *No*. You're not coming to my fight! I don't *want* you there!"

Alyssa turns to me, her mouth open wide. "O-oh." She looks down. "Okay. Gosh, I'm sorry. I thought..."her voice trails off.

And just like that, I feel like the biggest piece of shit in the world.

Ricardo looks at me, understanding in his eyes before he turns his gaze on her. "You got attacked the last time, remember? And this time, Tyrone won't be there to help. None of us will; because *he'll* be in the cage and *I'll* be stuck on the sidelines. We can't have you sitting in the crowd all alone. It's not safe."

Well, he's not exactly wrong. It's *not* safe for her. Especially when I put a fucking target on her back because I stopped the fight for her the last time she was there.

I *know* DeLuca saw that shit when he went through the footage. I can only *hope* that he didn't recognize her because it's been so long.

Because thinking that he won't care that she showed up at his club would be a rookie mistake. And if she *keeps* showing up and taunting him like a mouse taunts a cobra...well we're fucked.

I just have to make sure she never goes to the club or the gym...ever.

I gesture toward Ricardo. "Exactly. That's *exactly* why I don't want you there. I'm sorry for being an asshole about it."

She pulls on her lip before saying, "Okay. I wish I could be there for you. But, I guess...I get it. Like you said, there will be other fights."

Great...a temporary solution to a permanent problem. Perfect.

I really need to talk to her about this...in private.

A part of me thinks that maybe I should come clean. Tell her that I work for DeLuca.

But then, she'll expect me to quit...not that I blame her. *God* how I want to be free from his chains that bind me.

Then when I *don't* quit...she'll be upset and I'll have no choice but to tell her *why* I work for DeLuca in the first place.

Then I lose her.

And she realizes that yet *another* person she put her trust in...hurt her and fucked her over.

Then she goes back to doing what she was doing before I met her.

The thought of that *kills* me. I can see the real her now. I can feel her opening herself up to me little by little.

And I *want* every single part of it.

I want to be the person she smiles at.

I want to take this burden she carries on her shoulders away for good.

I want her to see herself the way I see her...see how amazing she is...and realize that the horrible past she has doesn't determine her future.

I want her to start living.

I want her to be mine.

No. I can't tell her. I can't.

I fucking can't.

Chapter Fourteen

ALYSSA

AFTER JACKSON'S OUTBURST, THE REST OF BREAKFAST WAS A LITTLE AWKWARD, to say the least.

"You gonna hurt my boy?" I look up from the sink full of dishes that I'm currently washing.

Ebony eyes that seem to pierce right through me hold my gaze.

I almost drop the damn dish.

"No," I tell her honestly. "That is not my intention at all." I can't help the flush that works its way up my cheeks. "Jackson's incredible. I'd be an idiot to mess up a chance with him." I close my eyes. "My past isn't that great. I've made a lot of mistakes. Some my fault, some not my fault…but I'm working on it. I want to be better," I say.

My eyes pop open with my words.

I never thought it was *possible* for me to want something more out of life again. I never thought I was *worth* anything more after that day in Ford's office.

She makes a face. "Sugar, don't get me wrong. Now, Jackson *is* incredible…that heart of his is incomparable to any others. And while he might *look* like one—he is not some mythical creature or a God. At the end of the day, he's *just a* man." She holds me by my shoulders. "All I'm saying is that you're a prize, too. You have to cut a diamond in order to make smaller diamonds, darlin'. But you still have to *cut* the original diamond first. So in the end, it's the imperfections that really make us shine so beautifully. It would do you well to remember that."

And with those words she walks away.

After I finish drying the dishes and put them away, I head out to the hallway. It's almost noon and I need to get home and take a shower. I also have the urge to visit my father's grave again.

Which is odd, because visiting it yesterday afternoon was hard enough for me. I hardly ever go because I always feel like an abomination of some sort. Like I don't deserve to even be there because he'd be so ashamed of the person I've become.

I'll never get Ford's words out of my head.

I'm stopped in my tracks when I see Jackson and Momma hugging. It looks like they're having a moment and I don't want to intrude.

I also can't seem to look away. His big arms are wrapped around her and his eyes are closed while she whispers something to him. I almost wish I had a camera to capture the moment because I love how much *love* he has for the woman standing before him.

When he pulls away, she holds his face in her tiny hands. "You're a good man, Jackson," she whispers with tears in her eyes. "You're a *good* person. Lilly would want you to be happy. You *deserve* to be happy." She gives him a kiss on his cheek. "I love you. You're *my* boy and don't you ever forget it."

"Love you too, Momma," he whispers, his voice cracking slightly.

I have to take a few deep breaths to stop myself from falling apart. Momma's tenderness reminds me of my father and the last conversation I ever had with him. I haven't felt what it's like to be truly loved since that day. My mother didn't know how to love me any-more because she was so consumed by her grief.

I know Ford loved me, for a little while at least. In my own twisted head…I think he still does. And I know I cling to it in my darkest hours because it's all I had after I lost my father.

I turn down the hall and head back to the kitchen. I'm still batting my eyes when I hear their footsteps approach.

Jackson gives me a strange look. "You alright?"

"Yeah." I cough. "Just got something in my eye."

He pulls me gently by my elbow and ushers me into the bedroom. "Can we talk for a minute?"

"Sure. I have to leave, though, can we talk while you walk me to my car?"

He rubs his neck. "I'm not kicking you out or anything. I have to head to the gym for a few hours, but you're more than welcome to stay here and relax. You can even spend the night again if you want."

I grab my jacket. "Thanks. But I have to take care of a few things today."

His jaw tightens and he pulls a sweatshirt over his head. "Okay. I guess I'll walk you out then."

I say a quick goodbye to Momma and the guys, purposely ignoring Lou-Lou on my way out. She's not worth my time anymore. Besides, Jackson more than took care of her anyway.

I realize that we've already made it out the front doors of the apartment complex and he still hasn't said a word to me. For someone who wanted to talk to me, he's being awfully quiet. "Penny for your thoughts?" I ask.

He shuffles his feet and plays with the strings on his sweatshirt. "Look, if I asked you to do something…or rather *not* to do something would you?"

I tip my head back. "It would depend on what it was, I guess. But for the most part, I don't see why not. What's up?"

He winds the string around his finger and it's funny because that's exactly how I'm feel-ing at the moment. Like I'm about to be wrapped right around his finger.

"I don't want you to—" He rubs his face. "Look, I really *need* you to promise me you won't ever show up at the fight club or the gym…ever. It's not safe for you at either of those places. Even if you go with Tyrone. There's no guarantee that something won't happen and he could prevent it."

I don't know how to feel about his request. On one hand, I'm flattered that he's looking out for my safety. On the other, something is a little off. "I guess I can get behind not going to the fight club….but why not the gym? What's so dangerous there?"

His eyes dart to the floor and he shuffles his feet again. "I don't need the distraction when I'm training," he says gruffly.

I don't know whether to be insulted or flattered again.

He lifts his hood. "I can't keep my eyes off of you when you're in the room. I'm liable to get knocked out or something."

"So I'll go to a different room."

He grabs my jacket and tugs me to him. "I'll still feel your presence. I feel you *every-where*, Alyssa."

Butterflies attack poor Momma's breakfast with a vengeance when he utters those words.

I stare at him wide-eyed as he skims the left side of my cheek with his finger. "Promise me, please. It's a hard limit for me. I can't have you at either of those places."

"Okay, fine. But you should know that I'm holding this as leverage. Just in case, I want to drag you to a chick flick or something in the future."

He pulls me even closer to him. "I'll do anything you want. *Anything*. As long as you promise me this."

He's being so serious, it's almost scary. "I promise."

The next words out of his mouth, confuse me. "If you could do anything for your birthday, besides go to my fight, what would it be?"

I have to think about this for a moment because, in all honesty, I have no idea. Between witnessing my father dying and spending the entire weekend in the interrogation room. The night Ford and I had when I was 17. Heck, even the night of the sex tape fell on my birthday.

My birthday has always been bad. I'm convinced it's officially jinxed.

I close my eyes and feel the crisp, cool October air around me.

And for a second, I pretend that I'm someone else. Someone different. Someone, "Normal," I whisper. "I want to be normal and do something a normal 24-year-old would do for her birthday."

"Like what? Go out to a club or something?"

I open my eyes. "Yes! That's *exactly* what I want. I've never been out to a club because I was 21 when the sex tape happened and feared being recognized." My face falls. "I still fear being recognized. I can't go to a club, Jackson."

He tilts my chin up. "I think you're forgetting something, Damsel."

Normally I hate when he calls me that, but he says it so softly and sweetly, I fight back a shiver. "What's that?"

The corners of his mouth tilt up. "Your birthday falls on Halloween. You can be anyone you want to be." He brushes my lower lip with his thumb. "*We* can be anyone we want to be."

I hug him. I hug him so tight because he's right. And I haven't seen the upside to my birthday in such a long, long time. This is a gift in and of itself.

"But what about your fight tomorrow?" I ask, disappointment floating in the air.

He thinks about this for a moment before saying, "Fuck, I'm the last one on because I'm the main event. I won't be done until a little after 10."

For some reason, I refuse to let this get in our way. "Most clubs don't really pick up until after that."

"True. I'll take a quick shower and meet you at the apartment after…if that's okay? I would pick you up but that would cut more time out."

"Don't be silly. It would make sense for me to meet you at your place. In fact, there's a really good club not too far away from here that has some kind of masquerade theme that night. I saw the fliers for it in your apartment complex."

He smiles and pulls me even closer, crushing me to him. "It's a date," he whispers.

Then he touches my ass.

For a moment I'm convinced this whole thing is a dream…but no, he's really sliding his hand into the back pocket of my jeans.

Then he pulls out my phone. "What are you doing?"

"Rectifying a situation," he responds with a wink, before handing it back to me.

I want to tell him to put it back the exact way he got it, but his voice stops me. "I just texted myself from your phone so I have your number. I'll see you tomorrow, but I want you to text me when you make it home safe. And if you need anything between then and tomorrow night, you can always call me."

"I need a back rub and a pedicure. How are you with those?"

He laughs and releases me. "Trust me I'd have no problem giving you a good rub down, but you definitely wouldn't want me polishing your little toes."

"How do *you* know I have little toes? I could have full on Flintstone feet for all you know."

He wiggles his eyebrows. "I have my ways."

"I'll see you tomorrow night, Jackson."

"See you tomorrow night, Alyssa."

I turn around and face my car. "By the way," he whispers in my ear before he backs away. "I *really* like the fact that you're still wearing my t-shirt. Looks good on you."

I blush the whole ride home.

Chapter Fifteen

JACKSON

I JOG UP THE STAIRS TO MY APARTMENT, HAPPIER THAN I'VE BEEN IN AWHILE. She agreed.

She agreed to stay away from the club and she didn't question me about it.

I still have a shot at not royally fucking this up.

I open the door and head for the living room where everyone else is still congregating.

I jerk back when I hear what sounds like Alyssa's voice coming through the surround sound speakers.

My smile plummets when I walk in the room and realize that Alyssa's sex tape is being broadcast on the big screen television while Lou-Lou's standing there with a smirk on her face, holding the remote control.

"Jackson, so glad you came back. We were just getting to the good part."

I fucking lunge at her.

Tyrone and Ricardo try pulling me back, but I'm out for her blood. I have to dig deep and talk myself down from the ledge so I don't actually attack her.

"I swear, man, we had no idea she was gonna play that shit. We didn't see much. I didn't even realize what the hell it was at first," Tyrone yells, holding me back.

"Yeah. What the *fuck* is your deal, Lou-Lou?" Ricardo barks.

Alyssa's voice zaps me. "*What do you want?*"

Then I hear a guy's voice. "*Strip for me. Show me those nice titties of yours.*"

Tyrone and Ricardo lose their grip on me and I lunge forward and get in her face. "Shut it the fuck off *now*, or so help me God. I will tear your head right off your skank infested body," I shout so loud the windows shake.

Lou-Lou's trembling at this point but I literally don't give a fuck. With shaky hands, she presses the pause button.

I want to remind the stupid bitch I said to turn it *off*, but I'm just happy the sounds are gone and it's no longer playing.

Besides, Momma herself decides to get a piece of the action. She reaches for Lou-Lou's arm and begins dragging her toward the front door. "Don't mind me, boys. I'm just taking out the trash." She throws Lou-Lou out the door. "Next time I won't be so kind—" She pauses. "What's that word you like to use again? Oh yeah…*Puttana*," she snarls before slamming the door shut.

She rubs her hands together and looks at Ricardo. "I think it's time for you to find a new distraction."

Ricardo nods. "I still can't believe she pulled that. I always knew she was territorial, but *this*…is going too far."

Tyrone hikes his duffle bag on his shoulder and looks at me. "Maybe I can catch a later flight," he offers.

"No, it's fine." I give him a pound. "Go and get your girl, man. I can't wait to meet her."

He gives me a grin. "Break bad on em' J-man. Call me after you win the fight tomorrow night."

"Will do."

Momma barrels into me and puts her arms around me. "I look forward to seeing more of Alyssa. That girl is something special, I have a sixth sense about these things you know. And my opinion on her hasn't changed one bit. Love you, sugar. There are some leftovers in the fridge for you."

"Thanks. Love you too, Momma. Have a safe flight."

After they leave, I sit down on the couch. I'm *still* reeling from what happened. I force myself to sit on my hands in order to stop myself from putting them through the wall.

"Hey," Ricardo starts. I sit up and glare at him. He blows out a breath. "You want to talk about it?"

"Not really," I bite out.

He holds up his hands. "Okay. I get it, man. I do. That couldn't have been easy to walk in on. Talk about being fucking blindsided. We all were. None of us even knew about that tape or what the hell Lou-Lou was making us sit down and watch. It makes even more sense now why you're so protective when it comes to her. I don't blame you."

I grunt and look away while he continues, "Normally, I'd say this anger would be good for training." He pauses. "But tomorrow is a big fight and I need you to be clear and focused enough to go over strategies." He heads for the door. "So, I'll give you a few hours to cool down before we head to the gym. And I meant what I said, Lou-Lou won't be coming around here anymore."

He stops and taps the wall beside the door. "As your coach, I can't say that I like the idea of you and Alyssa together. You've got one hell of a hero complex and this visceral rage inside you is like *nothing* I've ever seen before. It makes you great in the cage…but it's a liability on the outside. And I'm afraid that she might be the thing to tip the scales in the wrong direction for you." He opens the door. "But as your friend…I think there's something special between you two. I think, in some way that's beyond my understanding; you guys need one another. I think you two get each other in a way that no one else ever will. Anyway, if you change your mind and want to talk about it, I'm here."

"Thanks," I whisper.

I lean back and look at the television. The image on the screen is still paused.

The freeze frame of Alyssa permeates my vision.

I didn't actively go searching for this shit. But right now, this is my very own Pandora's box and I don't know if I can resist the urge to open it.

I know it *won't* change how I feel about her…but maybe it will help me understand her more. At least, that's what I tell myself when I hit the 'play' button on the remote.

The first thing I register is that she looks a little different. Not a whole lot, but there are some subtle distinctions.

For one, her blonde hair is shorter, resting slightly above her shoulders instead of halfway down her back like it is now. She's also wearing less makeup in the video, it makes her appear younger. And the way she's dressed…she's wearing a full sleeved cardigan and her long flowing skirt is almost touching the floor.

It's not a bad look, she's still beautiful…it's just different…innocent.

I can't help but notice that the camera is angled directly behind the guy's head. There's some ridiculously generic tribal tattoo on his lower neck. There's literally *nothing* else giving his own identity away. You wouldn't even know it was the mayor's son filming this.

The camera is *solely* focused and zoomed in on Alyssa. That alone makes my blood boil…because I know this was all a setup.

"*Strip for me. Show me those nice titties of yours.*"

For a moment, I see the hesitation in her eyes before she answers, "*Um. Okay. I can do that.*"

My first instinct is to look down when I see her standing there in her white cotton bra. I'm part enraptured and part disgusted because I can only imagine how many men have ogled what I'm seeing now. How many men just chalked it up to her being some 'whore' and thought they were entitled to watch her like this. Not even caring about the life changing repercussions she suffered from it.

None of those men deserved to be seeing her like this. Hell, I'm not even sure if I do.

"*Have you ever sucked a dick before, hot stuff?*"

I think I'm going to be sick.

"*Yeah. My high school boyfriend,*" she answers.

"*Did you like it?*"

She blushes and nods. "*I did.*"

I can see even more now why the video went viral, not only is she beautiful in a natural way—which alone is appealing. But these personal questions she's answering? It makes it so genuine and real. Like you're right there in the room with her.

"*What did you like about it?*"

She appears to think about this for a second before replying, "*Being able to please him with my mouth. Knowing that I was the one responsible for his pleasure. It's empowering.*"

And now my dick has officially joined the party in the third circle of hell.

"*Yeah? Why don't you finish getting naked and show me how much you like it?*"

I hear the sound of a zipper in the background while Alyssa pulls down her skirt. Then she pauses.

"*No, sweetie. I want you naked, now. Take everything off,*" he commands.

The shame hits me hard when she starts stripping. Not just because my dick's reacting to it...but because I could see myself uttering that very same command to her. The turbulent wave of jealousy that washes over me when she drops to her knees before *him* naked steamrolls over any shame that I felt.

Even my dick decides it's too much of a hassle to compete with my mind and gives up.

My mind wants to conjure up its own alternate version that has her putting her clothes right back on and turning the camera around on *him* before taking a fucking bat to his head.

I can't watch any more. I already know what happens next. I don't need or *want* to see another second of it. I'd rather gouge my own eyes out with a rusty spoon. Disgusted with myself, I rip out the wire connecting my laptop to the television.

It was exactly like Pandora's box. I found no answers by watching it...all it showed me was a different brand of evil in the world.

I wish I never watched it at all.

It *still* doesn't change how I feel about her, though.

Chapter Sixteen

ALYSSA

I'M LEAVING THE CEMETERY WHEN MY PHONE BUZZES WITH A MESSAGE.

Jackson: *I know this is random, but I just wanted to tell you how amazing you are.*

I stare down at my phone and hit the 'reply' button as I continue walking.

I stumble back slightly when I bump into someone.

I look up with an apology ready to leave my lips due to my clumsiness.

Deep blue eyes meet mine and I stifle a gasp.

Ford.

Before I can say anything, he grabs my arm and spins me around until my back hits a large marble statue.

"You haven't been answering my phone calls," he growls.

I swallow down the fear rising in my chest. I'm perfectly aware he's called me a dozen times in the last few weeks…I just haven't really been up to talking to him.

"Sorry. I've been busy," I say.

And then I brace myself. I brace myself for his comment telling me that I'm a whore or something else along those lines, but it never comes.

His gaze locks on Jackson's t-shirt that I never changed out of. "These aren't your clothes. Where have you been?"

"I already told you. *Busy*," I repeat.

He leans in close to my ear. "You're getting a little too big for your britches there, sweetheart. Remember who it is that you're speaking to."

I push my shoulders back and look at him, feeling annoyed now. "You know, lurking around graveyards is a little creepy…even for you."

His eyebrows draw up in surprise. I haven't given him attitude like this in a very long time. Since I was a teenager.

He positions one of his hands on the statue behind my head. "You know why I'm here. I still mourn your father, unlike *you* who tarnishes his memory with your internet antics and whore-like ways."

And there it is.

Ever since that day in his office, I've felt like I was made of glass around him.

But not today.

Today…I feel a little bit stronger. Not a lot, but enough to give him a taste of his own medicine. "Didn't stop you from indulging in my *whore-like* ways in your office that day, now did it? Or when I was 17 for that matter."

To say he looks shocked would be an understatement. He opens his mouth to say something but stops himself and looks down at his feet.

"I'm sorry," he breathes.

I'm certain that I must be hearing things. Ford actually apologizing to me is *not* something I ever expected to hear in this lifetime.

"What?"

This time, when he looks at me, I see a glimpse of the old Ford. The one who was always there for me. The one who actually loved me. The one who saved me.

"I should have been there for you that day. I turned you away and I treated you like gar-bage." He tilts my face up. "I couldn't stand the thought of you giving that part of yourself to someone else. I wanted it to be me that you shared your innocence with." He closes his eyes. "I thought you wanted it to be me."

He cups my cheek and looks at me. "I'm fucked up, Alyssa. You make me that way. I have tunnel vision when it comes to you. But I *know* deep down inside *you* know that no one else will *ever* love you the way I do. They'll only hurt you, sweetheart. And when they do…I'll still be standing here. *I'll* still be loving you when no one else in the world ever will."

I'm at a loss for words. Actually, no. I'm not.

"You hurt me, Ford. That day, you broke something inside of me. I never knew you could hurt me like that."

He pulls me into his arms. "I know, sweetheart. I know. Why do you think I couldn't bring myself to touch you again after that day? I hate myself for doing that to you."

I rub my cheek along the fabric of his suit and fight back tears because it's so familiar and strangely comforting to be held by him again.

"Let me make it up to you, Alyssa."

"How?"

"You know how."

I begin walking away from him, knowing perfectly well why he came here now.

"I told you. I still have to think about it."

Irritation crosses over his handsome features. "It's been almost a *month*. How much time could you possibly need? I already gave you the location and even went as far as to set you up with an interview."

He spins me around. "Don't you want to get vengeance for your father? All I need you to do is go undercover and tell me if DeLuca owns that fight club. We start there and find something we can use. Then we take him and all his other establishments out little by little. I know it's not ideal and it will take awhile. But we need to move stealth-like so he'll never see it coming."

I bite my thumbnail, hating that what I'm about to say will disappoint him. It's the real reason I've been avoiding him. "I went to the club, Ford."

His grip on my arm is so tight I'm sure he's going to leave a bruise. "And? What the fuck happened? Why didn't you tell me?"

I wince in part due to his tight hold and because I know I failed him and my father… once again. "And it turns out that it's *not* his club. I'm sorry. I wanted it to be…but it's not."

He shakes his head. "No. It *is* his club. Stop *lying* to me. Christ, Alyssa…all I needed you to do was go undercover for a week or two—not really all that difficult."

Easy for him to say, he doesn't have the scars that I do. The scars caused by being a 10-year-old who watched their father get brutally murdered in front of them. All while the killer looked right into her eyes and smirked.

But I *still* walked into that club knowing it might be his. I still took the risk.

"I'm telling you, it's *not* his club. Jesus, you think I don't *want* to help you nail DeLuca? You think I would lie to you about something so important?"

He releases my arm. "How good was the source of your intel?"

Guilt hits me when Jackson's face crosses my mind. Luke, the guy who hired me, was actually my original target. And Lou-Lou quickly became my backup. Well, before I found out what a bitch she was.

I *never* intended to make Jackson my source, but in the end, he provided me with the answers I needed. And I have no reason not to believe him. He's never lied to me before.

"Trust me," I say, while digging in my purse for my keys. "I couldn't have found a better source unless it was DeLuca himself."

Ford's eyes narrow while he holds my car door open for me. "What makes you think this source didn't lie to *you?*"

I think about this for a second before replying, "Because I trust this person."

He looks down at my t-shirt and scowls. "Well, I think *he's* wrong. I'll find another way to get you undercover at a different establishment of DeLuca's." I open my mouth to protest but he grabs the back of my neck. "And when I do…don't *fuck* it up again by spreading your goddamn legs for your source this time."

He releases me and slams the door.

It's only when I'm pulling in the driveway that it dawns on me. How does Ford know my source was a *he* in the first place?

My phone rings and Ford's name lights up the screen. I debate not answering it, but decide to just get it over with.

"Yeah?" I answer.

"Listen, I'm sorry. I was a little too hard on you back there. I wasn't very nice to you and you didn't deserve that." He takes a breath. "I'm under a lot of pressure at work, especially with this new promotion."

Two apologies from Ford in one day? It must be a full moon.

"How did you know my source was a he?"

I hear paper rustling in the background. "What?"

"You heard me, Ford. How did you know it was a guy?"

"What exactly is it that you're accusing me of, Alyssa? You act like you don't trust me anymore."

He sighs when I stay silent. "I assumed it was a guy because you're a beautiful young woman walking into a goddamned underground fight club. For crying out loud, you went undercover as a *ring girl*. Not only would it make sense, but it would be smart for your target to have been male. Why do you think I asked *you* to do it in the first place? Trust me, none of my female agents look like you."

I hear the call waiting signal on the other line. I smile when I see Jackson's name.

"Okay fine. I gotta go. Bye, Ford." I go to press the button to hang up but his voice stops me. "Wait a minute, sweetheart."

"What?"

"Are we okay? Because I really don't like that you felt the need to question me. You know I would never do anything to hurt you, right? I love you."

I roll my eyes because he's already hurt me too many times to count in my short 24 years, despite his love for me. "Yeah, I know. We're fine. Look, I have to go. I have another call. It's important."

I hang up without waiting for a response.

"Hey, you," Jackson's voice greets me on the other line.

Wow, do I love the sound of his voice.

I get so lost in that thought, my keys slip out of my hands when I go to open the front door.

"Hey," I respond. "What's up?"

"Just wanted to make sure you made it home okay." He pauses. "I got a little worried when you didn't respond to my text. I hope I didn't freak you out."

I mentally curse myself for never responding to him earlier. "You didn't. I was at the cemetery visiting my dad when I got it, though. I'm actually just walking in the door now."

I don't tell him about Ford...for obvious reasons. There's no way he'll understand our fucked up dynamic. Hell, I've never understood it. Not to mention, he'll probably be upset that I lied to him in the first place.

"Oh." I hear him draw in a breath. "I'm sorry."

Neither of us say a word for what feels like forever.

I plop down on the couch. "Cue the awkward silence that death always ensues."

"You'd think we'd be experts at getting around it, huh?" He clears his throat. "Okay, change of subject. How was the rest of your day? Did you do anything else?"

"Nope, just that."

"That's good." He sounds relieved...which is *interesting*.

"What exactly did you think I'd be doing, Jackson?"

"Nothing," he quickly says. "I'm just happy to hear that you weren't doing anything."

He curses under his breath. "That did *not* come out right."

I decide to cut to the chase. "Is that your weird way of saying you're happy to hear that I wasn't hanging out with another guy today?"

"Yeah," he admits. "Yeah, I guess it is."

"I haven't." I sit up and cradle the phone in my ear. "I haven't been with anyone since before we met."

Since the night he saved me from that guy in the parking lot, I think before his voice interrupts my thoughts. "Is it wrong that it makes me really happy to hear that?"

"That all depends. Have there been any other girls in your bed beside me lately?"

"What?" he says. "No. Not at all."

"Then it's not wrong. Because that makes me really happy as well."

"Good. I guess I'll see you tomorrow."

"See you tomorrow, Jackson. Good luck with your fight."

"Thanks. By the way," he says before we hang up. "My sheets still smell like you. And I fucking love it."

Chapter Seventeen

JACKSON

RICARDO WAS RIGHT, TONIGHT ENDED UP BEING A BIG FIGHT FOR ME. I WON, BUT my opponent was a good 3 inches and 45lbs heavier than me.

He also managed to land not one, but *two*, solid punches straight into my rib cage. Making it the second time I've been hit now during a match. He knocked the wind out of me for a moment.

But then I thought about Alyssa…and how I *needed* to make it out of there in one piece so I could take her out for her birthday tonight.

It was strange because it was the *first* and only time I didn't think about the night Lilly was murdered while in the cage.

I'm not sure how I feel about it. I *need* that pain as my fuel. I need it as a reminder to never forget. A reminder to never *forgive* myself for what happened to Lilly.

I'm standing in the mirror putting tape across my ribs when I hear a knock on the dressing room door. "Yeah," I say.

The door opens and it's the last person I want to see standing there. She's out of her fucking mind if she thinks I want to talk to her. "Get the fuck out," I bark.

"I'm sorry, Jackson," Lou-Lou says.

"Doesn't matter. You crossed a line that never should have been crossed."

"I was hurting."

I spin around and face her. "Hurting? Really? That's the best you got?" I scream. "Hurting," I grit. "*Hurting* is having someone set you up with a sex tape. Hurting is finding out that the night you lost your virginity was posted online without your consent for all the world to see!"

To her credit, she blanches. "I didn't…"

"Yeah, that's just it, Lou-Lou …you didn't. You didn't stop and think about how fucked up it was to play that tape in front of everyone. You didn't stop and think about how it would make *me* feel. Hell, you didn't even stop and think about how Ricardo would react to you pulling some shit like that."

She steps back and looks at me. "Wow, you're really falling for her."

I stop and think about this for a second.

No, I'm not in love with her. Not that I would know because I've never let myself fall in love before. But logically, I know I'm not in love because we've *only* known one another for a month. However, if there's a phase that comes right *before* love. Well, I might just be *there*. And something tells me that I *am* going to end up falling in love with her, whether I want to or not.

"This isn't about me," I argue. "What you did was wrong."

"I know and that's why I'm apologizing to you. I was jealous."

Before I can cut her off and tell her that I've never given her a reason to be jealous because I've turned down every advance she threw my way, she continues, "I've *never* had a guy look at me the way you look at her. I've *never* had someone defend me the way that you defend her. Or protect me, or care about me. I've *never* had someone in my corner…not once. I mean, why the hell do you think I'm *like* this in the first place?"

I push past her. "I'm sorry about that, Lou-Lou. I really am. But, it still doesn't make it right."

"I know, Jackson. Trust me, I know. That's why I came to apologize."

"I can't forgive you," I say and her lower lip trembles. "I'm not saying that I'll never forgive you…just not this second."

She lifts her chin. "Okay. I can understand that." She looks down and shrugs. "It's more than Ricardo's willing to give me."

For a second, I feel bad. But then I remember what she did. I put on my shirt and head for the door. "Jackson," she calls out.

I close my eyes and let out a deep sigh. "Yeah?"

"Word of advice? Since Alyssa and I *are* a lot alike."

I turn around and face her again. "You're nothing alike. *She's* not—"

"Damaged?" Lou-Lou laughs. "Trust me, that girl is as broken as they come. It takes a damaged soul to know one. And just because she's trusting you enough to open up to you…it doesn't mean she's cured. It doesn't mean that her demons are gone. They're only temporarily camouflaged until something causes them to flare up again." She points a finger at me. "Because let me tell you something about the broken people, Jackson. If you hurt us…we hurt deeper than others. If you hurt us…you drudge up every past hurt that we've ever experienced and send us into a tailspin right back down the rabbit hole."

I open my mouth to say something but she cuts me off. "Whether you *mean* to hurt us or not. It doesn't matter, because once we're in that tailspin…how do you think we cope? What do you think our go-to is? It's a vicious cycle and we end up taking down a lot of good people with us. People like you, Jackson. So be careful."

I slam the door behind me.

Lou-Lou's wrong. Alyssa's *not* like her. She's stronger than her fucked up past. And she's got me now to help her get through it.

I stop and pick up a bouquet of roses along the way to my apartment. It's not much, especially considering I'm still on the fence about giving her the other gift I have.

I've never really done the whole dating thing before. Between taking care of Lilly, and training at the gym…there never was much time for girls…just sex. I figured I'd settle down after I spent a few years as a professional MMA fighter, but well, clearly my life didn't go down that road.

I have no idea what to wear to this club. I looked at the flier she was talking about and it said costume optional but mask not.

Mask. Maybe this wasn't such a good idea after all. The only time I wear a mask is at the bdsm club. The club where every sexual fantasy and carnal urge I have come to life. The place where I don't ask for control of my life, *I* take it.

Christ…there's *no* way I'll be able to keep my hands off her tonight. Especially since she's now become the object of every sexual fantasy I have lately.

I decide to go with a black button down and dark jeans. On the bright side, at least my opponent didn't hit my face.

There's a knock on the door and I look at my watch. Alyssa's right on time.

My brain short circuits when I open the door.

She's wearing a cropped black jacket and a short red dress that must be made out of silk because it looks as soft as her skin does. And don't even get me started on her legs. I don't know how a girl who's only 5'3 tops, has legs so shapely and long, but I'm not about to question God's beautiful creation. I'd rather just enjoy it and be thankful.

I force myself to stop staring at those legs, which are showcased by a pair of black heels that I'm secretly wishing were digging into my back as she screams my name.

"Are you okay, Jackson?" she asks, her expression puzzled.

No, I'm not okay. I'm not okay because I told her we could only be friends not even 48 hours ago and every second after that has only made me regret ever saying those words. But then I remind myself of my reasons.

I inwardly groan as I reach over and pick up the flowers and hand them to her.

Her eyes are bright and I see that dimple. "They're beautiful. Thank you so much." She bites her lip. "But I can't take them to the club." She pushes me aside and heads for the kitchen. "We have to put them in water or they'll die." She looks around the kitchen, her expression concerned. "You don't have a vase."

Shit, I didn't really think of that. This is a guy's apartment. Of course, we don't have a vase lying around. I'm about to suggest she stick them in a bowl or something, but I hear another knock on the door.

"Here, take this," Ricardo says, handing me a vase.

I raise an eyebrow. "You could probably give Ms. Cleo a run for her money. How did you know I'd need this?"

"Saw you walking up the stairs with flowers. Figured it would come in handy." He grins. "Although I *am* surprised that you and Tyrone's bromance hasn't reached the level of flowers."

"I wouldn't be one to talk, Ricardo," I tease. "*You're* the one who just happened to have a vase." I point across the hall. "Last time I checked, that was a one bedroom apartment. Tell me, what color flowers do you like to get yourself?"

He looks down. "It's not mine. I had it for…someone."

Hmm, maybe him and Lou-Lou's relationship was more serious than I thought?

"Oh hey, Ricardo. Thanks," Alyssa says while taking the vase.

Ricardo looks at her for a second too long before replying, "No problem. Wow, you look gorgeous."

I fight the urge to slam the door in his face. But then I remind myself that he's my friend and it's not his fault he's got a pair of eyeballs.

She beams. "Thanks. It's my birthday. Jackson's taking me out to a club."

Something flashes across his face. But before I can question it he says, "Well, I hope you have a good night. You really deserve to have a good birthday, Alyssa."

She glances up at him and gives him a weird look, but then shakes her head. "Thanks, Ricardo. I'm um—" She pauses. "I'm gonna go put my flowers in water."

"Have a good night," Ricardo says in my direction before he walks across the hall to his own apartment.

What the heck just happened?

I follow Alyssa into the kitchen where I find her filling the vase with water as she mumbles something under her breath. I put my hands on either side of the sink, caging her in. "Everything okay, Damsel?"

She spins around and looks up at me. I didn't mean to end up so close to her, but like a moth to a fucking flame…here I am.

She waves a hand. "Yeah. I'm fine. The flowers really are beautiful by the way. I love them."

"Good. Makes me feel better about the other thing I got you."

"What thing?"

I back away, feeling like an idiot now for even bringing it up. "It's nothing, Alyssa. Really. I shouldn't have mentioned it."

She makes a face. "It's not nothing." She puts out her hand and pouts. "Now give it to me."

I pull the jewelry box out and place it in her hand. Hoping like hell it won't ruin the night. I didn't intend on getting her jewelry—but it occurred to me that I've *never* seen her wear the necklace she told me about. I can only assume that she must have lost it.

"I know it's not an exact replica or anything. But I tried to match up the goblin the way you described."

She looks down and her mouth opens wide. Her expression is unlike any I've ever seen before and she doesn't say a word.

Shit. I made a mistake.

I'm ready to apologize, but then she literally jumps into my arms, wraps her legs around my waist and hugs me so tight I almost send us both flying backward. "I take it you like it?" I ask. I don't even feel the pain in my ribs because her coconut scent surrounds me. And for the record, I was right. Her dress *is* made out of silk.

I hear a small sniffle. "You have no idea how much," she whispers. I stand there holding her for what feels like hours, not that I'm complaining. I would be more than content to hold her all night without ever venturing to the club. But I know how much she's looking forward to it.

"Are you ready?" I ask after I hear her breathing return back to normal.

She slides down my body and I swallow hard. She turns around, hands me the box, and holds up her hair. "Would you mind?"

My fingertips brush over her collarbone as I fasten the necklace around her neck. My lips hover over her ear. "You look breathtaking," I whisper.

Goosebumps erupt along her soft flesh and she fights a shiver. I meant to aim for her cheek, but before I know what I'm doing, my lips are grazing her neck.

Then she moans and my self-control plummets.

I force myself to back away. "Let's go."

"Okay," she whispers.

Before we leave, she reaches into her purse and pulls out a red and black masquerade mask for herself and hands me a black one.

A black mask that is so fucking similar to the one I already have. My expression must give me away because she asks, "Are you okay, Jackson?" For the second time that night.

No…I'm not okay.

I'm the exact opposite of okay.

Chapter Eighteen

ALYSSA

After Jackson paid the admission and we walked into the club, things got weird.

For the first half hour, he refused to make eye contact with me and practically ignored me.

And since neither of us are big drinkers we didn't spend much time at the bar. Not a whole lot of liquid courage for either of us to rely on.

That only left one thing to do. Dance.

Which Jackson, of course, said he doesn't do.

With only an hour left of my actual birthday, a night that started out so good, was turning out to be a bust.

Which is why I'm currently on the dance floor with some guy wearing a green mask while smoky air and dark sultry music surround us.

I have no interest in my dancing partner other than dancing but even in the almost pitch black room, I can feel Jackson's eyes on me the whole time.

Which is odd, because I swear, it seems like every female's eyes are on him.

And I can't say that I blame them one bit. If only they got a load of how sexy his face is without the mask…I'm pretty sure they'd faint.

My dancing partner grabs my hips and leans in much closer. Through his mask, Jackson's eyes narrow.

The D.J changes the beat up a little and cues up *Meg Myers, Desire*.

The guy presses flush against me and starts getting really into it…until he's suddenly gone and I'm being pressed against a wall instead.

I look up and Jackson's staring down at me, my former dancing partner long gone.

I've never seen Jackson look at me like this before. I don't know if I should be scared or turned on. I choose the latter.

He leans down, his breath tickling my ear. "I've had about as much as I can take, Alyssa. I don't like watching while some other guy puts his hands all over you."

Wow, this sounds a lot like jealousy. Against my better judgment, I decide to provoke him. "Why's that?"

I know exactly what I want. And that's *him*. Now, he needs to decide if he wants me once and for all. This hot and cold business is becoming exhausting.

He closes his eyes. I don't even think he realizes that he's started swaying to the music. And for someone who claims they don't dance, he's awfully good at it.

He raises my hands above my head and slowly grinds himself against me. "I think you know why," he rasps.

I shake my head and bite my lip. "No. Why don't you tell me? Or better yet, show me."

You can cut the sexual tension between us with a knife at this point, but I'm putting the ball in his court. He turned me down when it was in mine.

He leans his forehead against mine, links our fingers together and thrusts against me. "I want to be the *only* one who's allowed to touch your body like this. I want it to be *me* you think about at night when you touch yourself. I want it to be *my* name you're screaming when I'm making you come. I want you to be *mine*, because as far as I'm concerned…I'm already *yours.*"

I'm dizzy with those words. Our lips are so close, we're almost kissing. And my God, do I *need* him to kiss me right now.

"I'm yours. Now kiss me, Jackson."

His thumb brushes over my bottom lip. "Everything will change," he warns.

And he's right. Everything *will* change. But I want it to. I want things with him that I've never wanted with another person before.

I want to give him every single part of me…even the broken parts.

I take off my mask and toss it, not caring where it lands. "Good."

It's *not* a soft and gentle kiss.

It's a kiss that ravages me, consumes me. It's a kiss that claims me…effectively ruining me for anyone else, threatening to haunt me if my lips dare to ever touch another's.

He's putting his mark on me with those lips, branding me with the stroke of his tongue and worshiping me with his every breath.

I've kissed a lot of guys in my lifetime. But I've *never* been kissed like this before.

He nips my lower lip and I let out a groan. His hands are everywhere—in my hair, moving up my spine, lifting and pulling me closer to him.

I feel his hardness against my stomach and taste the hint of whiskey on his tongue, his heart beating faster than the speed of light.

We stay kissing for what feels like forever, neither of us daring to ruin the connection we've forged by coming up for air…until someone clears their throat around us.

I open my eyes and realize that Jackson has me pinned up against the wall, my dress is bunched around my thighs and his own mask has slipped off.

"This is a masquerade themed Halloween party. You both *have* to wear your masks. And stay off the goddamned wall," some big guy in a security t-shirt says gruffly before he walks away.

I unravel my legs from around Jackson's waist and I know my face is probably the color of a tomato. I've never been so happy to be in a dark room.

He cradles my face in his hands. "Do you want to stay? We can if you want to."

I shake my head and Jackson takes my hand and heads toward the exit. "Wait," I say. We stop walking and he looks at me. "I have to go to the bathroom."

He laughs as we walk over to where the bathrooms are, making sure to dodge any security personnel along the way.

"I'll be right outside the door if you need me," he says. He bends down and I think he's going to kiss me again, but he kisses my forehead instead.

I turn around but he reaches for my arm. "Hurry up because I'm not sure how much longer I can keep my lips off of you," he murmurs before he releases me and I enter the bathroom.

For a second, I think I must have walked into the wrong bathroom because I see the back of some guy's head as he leans over the sink, obviously snorting some coke. I look at the bathroom door and sure enough, it *is* a women's bathroom. My bladder doesn't discriminate, though so I slip past him into one of the stalls and take care of business.

The guy's still hovering over the sink when I'm done, but I know Jackson's right outside so I walk to the furthest sink away from him and wash my hands.

It's only when I see his reflection behind me that I jump.

It's the last person I ever expected to see here.

Looks like the mayor's son is the next celebrity rehab star in the making.

The last time I saw him, he and his father were threatening me about going to the authorities after he leaked the sex tape.

"Dean," I whisper.

He wipes off some powder under his nose and sniffs. "Alyssa."

In the mirror, I see his reflection eye my body up and down. "You look incredible," he slurs.

"You look like shit," I counter.

"Yeah. I guess I deserve that," he whispers.

I turn on my heels and face him. "No, what you deserve is to have your testicles ripped off by a piranha while being dragged through hot coals." I shrug. "But hey, not all wishes come true now do they?"

He staggers forward until I'm pressed against the sink. "Look, you have every right to hate me," he whispers. "I'm sorry for what I did to you. I know how fucked up it was." His eyes open wide and he sways. "But there are things that you don't know about. Sometimes there are things that are far beyond our control."

He must be high right now because he's definitely not making *any* sense. I stay silent for a moment because I'm just not sure how to process the words coming from this poor excuse for a pathetic mess standing in front of me.

Finally, he slowly backs away from me.

The door to the bathroom swings open and Jackson walks in.

"You," he sneers.

At first, I think he means *me*. But he's looking right at Dean. Or rather, looking at Dean's back because he's still facing me.

Before I know it, Jackson's yanking Dean by his shirt and bashing his head into a wall.

Dean doesn't fight back for the first minute or so. But then the coke must kick in because he starts struggling against him and attempting to defend himself. Both of them are evenly matched in height, but Jackson's got a solid 30lbs of muscle on Dean. Not to mention, a temper like a raging bull right now.

I'm torn because a big part of me wants to see Dean get what he deserves...but then Jackson bashes Dean's head into the door of the bathroom and I see blood trickle down.

Shit. He's really, *really* hurting him.

Then it hits me...why the *hell* is Jackson fighting Dean anyway? It's not like *he* knows who he is. There's no way he heard our conversation because the door to the bathroom was closed and our voices were barely above a whisper.

The only thing I can come up with is that Jackson's jealousy got the best of him when he walked into the bathroom and saw a guy near me. If that's the case, and it must be; then his reaction is excessive and is quickly crossing over the line to insanity.

"Jackson, stop!" I scream.

It's like he doesn't even hear me. He just continues beating the ever living shit out of Dean.

For a second, I think Dean's down for the count, but he moves and Jackson's next punch misses him.

And that only makes Jackson's temper flare up more. I've never, *ever* seen him like this. He's like a wild animal unhinged.

I scream and chase after them when they both go flying through the bathroom's swinging door. Not before long, Jackson's on top of Dean and a crowd of people have gathered around us. Some even stopping to record the whole encounter on their phones.

Jackson's not missing a beat with his punches and Dean's face is starting to resemble ground beef. His body's starting to resemble a rag doll.

If Jackson keeps this up, he's going to end up killing him.

"Jackson, please stop!" I scream.

"You ruined her life and now I'm gonna ruin yours," Jackson growls between punches.

What?

I don't have time to think about that statement, because some girl starts shrieking, "Someone call the police! I think that's the mayor's son."

My stomach drops to the floor. I try getting between them, but a large arm wraps around my waist and pulls me out of the way.

I look up. *What the hell is Ricardo doing here?*

Ricardo's smart enough to know he can't stop Jackson in this state. Instead, he waits for the split second in between Jackson's next punch and slides Dean's now unconscious body out of the way and hands him over to two big men wearing suits.

That seems to break Jackson out of his haze.

The girl is still shrieking and going on and on about calling the police but Ricardo takes her phone and snaps it in half. "No one is calling the police," he booms.

He quickly turns to the three people who have their phones out recording what happened.

He then proceeds to stomp on each and every one of their phones.

I watch as everyone looks at him with fear in their eyes, including me.

The look in *his* eyes tells me that he'll accept nothing less. He commands power.

My stomach drops for a different reason entirely then…because I've seen that look in someone's eyes before.

I shake my head. *No.* I'm crazy. I'm fucking delusional.

"Alyssa," Jackson says.

I turn my head to look at him, but all I hear are those words that he said to Dean. "*You ruined her life and now I'm gonna ruin yours.*"

It's then that I realize.

Jackson watched the video.

Chapter Nineteen

ALYSSA

WE HEAD BACK TO HIS APARTMENT.

All that's going through my head is—he told me he would never watch the sex tape.

I tell myself to calm down…that maybe, just *maybe* I'm overreacting and Jackson didn't watch my sex tape after all.

I tell myself that *maybe* he just blacked out in the middle of the fight and had a flashback of some kind that caused him to say what he did. He *did* look out of it, like off in another zone completely.

I don't know what to think right now. I feel like I'm grasping at straws because it's better than the alternative I'm faced with.

I mean, *why* would Jackson do that to me? He *knows* how much pain that video caused me.

"I'm gonna go clean up," he whispers before heading for the bathroom.

Those are the first words that either of us have said since we left the club.

I want to ask him…but I don't want him to lie to me.

There's only one way to know for sure if he watched the video.

I have to look at the history on his laptop.

I'm not proud of myself. Jackson's been my boyfriend for all of an hour at this point… but I *need* to know. I have to. Desperate times call for desperate measures.

As luck may have it, I notice his laptop on the couch in the living room.

I flip it open and say a silent prayer.

A silent prayer that turns right around and bites me in the ass when I see that I don't have to go through Jackson's history after all.

Because it's right here in front of me. Still on the fucking screen.

He watched it recently. *Very* recently.

And that makes it even worse. I could forgive him for watching it when he didn't really know me. I could even understand it…he *is* a guy.

But the fact that he watched it *after* I already started opening up to him.

After I told him things I've never told anyone. After I had convinced myself that Jackson was different. That *he* wouldn't hurt me.

That kills me. Wrecks me.

Another thought hits me and I want to fucking cry. No wonder Jackson got physical with me tonight.

Two days ago he was telling me that I wasn't a whore and that it was best to just be friends until I discovered my self-worth.

Then tonight…*after* he watches the video, he's talking about wanting me to scream his name and pushing me up against walls while he kisses me in a club.

I'm so stupid.

I know exactly how Jackson feels about me deep down inside. I *know* how he sees me now.

Just like everyone else in the world does.

And just like that…the scab comes off my wound and I feel it.

I feel all of it in a single rush.

The pain, the heartache, the despair.

There's only one way to cope when I shatter. I go to that place inside myself. The place that screams for me to acknowledge what I truly am and punish myself for it.

I also want to punish Jackson for what he's done. And there's only *one* way I can think of to accomplish both. The only weapon I have in my arsenal.

I slam the laptop and put it back where I found it, feeling myself morph into the person I've come to know so well.

"You only did it to yourself, Alyssa," I whisper to myself.

"I think we should talk," Jackson says.

I stand up and face him, putting on my game face. I throw my purse, not even caring where it lands and take off my jacket. "I don't want to talk."

"But—"

Jackson doesn't get a chance to finish that sentence because I jump on him and start kissing him.

I kiss him so hard I back *him* up against a wall.

It's nothing like our first and last kiss. I don't let myself feel anything. I shut everything off. I only focus on what needs to be done.

"Whoa," Jackson says pulling away from me.

"What?" I question. "Didn't you say something back at the club about not being able to keep your lips off me?"

"Well yeah," he says. "But that was before the fight and—"

I put my finger to his lips silencing him. "I don't want to talk about that, Jackson."

I kiss his neck. "I just want you—" I run my tongue along the shell of his ear. "To get naked for me," I whisper while my hand ventures lower and I grab his package. I smile when I feel him start to thicken in my hand through his jeans.

"Jesus Christ, Alyssa," he groans. "I think we should slow down. Especially since you don't want to talk about what happened. We *need* to talk about what happened."

"Take off your shirt."

He raises an eyebrow. "What?"

I lift my chin. "You heard me. Take off your fucking shirt. I want to see you naked, now."

He gives me a look that I hate. "No. Stop and *talk* to me, Alyssa."

I shake my head. "I don't want to talk. I'd much rather suck your dick instead."

His eyes open wide. "Not like this…not when you're *acting* like—"

I smile because it would be so much better for me if he said it. Like throwing another log into the fire. "Like what, Jackson? Tell me."

"Not like *you*. Not like *Alyssa. My Alyssa*."

I'm going to actually have to work for this. "You're right. I'm sorry." I walk over to him and kiss him sweetly, tenderly.

Then the worst thing of all happens. I start responding to his touch. I start losing myself because it's no longer my kiss…it becomes his kiss.

He cups my face as his tongue parts my mouth and I fall into him. His hands run along my hips before resting on my behind and I can't help but moan.

And just when I think I'm going to float to another dimension…he pulls away and kisses my forehead. "Now let's talk."

I don't want to hear anything he has to say. Nothing will change what I know to be true.

I kiss his neck again before whispering, "I don't want to talk. I just want to be close to you. I need to be close to you right now, please."

He looks contemplative for a moment and I think he's going to reject me. But instead, his thumbs brush over my cheeks and his lips find mine.

I reach for the button on his jeans but his hand lands on top of mine. "Stop, baby. Why are you rushing things?"

The term of endearment sounds so sweet and loving coming from him I have to fight off a shiver. And I have to remind myself why I'm doing this.

My other hand reaches down and starts rubbing along his length. "Let me do it, Jackson."

He bites his lip and closes his eyes. I've seen that expression before. He's fighting a war with himself right now. "Not tonight," he says.

Too bad he chose the wrong side.

"Fine," I say backing away from him.

I know I'm about to go in for the kill. "I'll just find someone else who wants me."

His hands clench at his sides. "Why are you acting like this? You don't have to be this way." He slams the wall beside him. "Tell me what the *fuck* is going through that head of yours, now," he barks.

I lower the straps to my dress. His expression is a combination of both anger and lust. Which I can definitely work with. "Because you keep telling me no and I want you." I slide the top of my dress down revealing my lacy bra. "I want to take you in my mouth so bad. I can't even see straight."

His jaw tightens and he swallows hard. "Prove it."

I begin sinking to my knees but his voice halts me. "No. Not like that."

For a minute…I panic. It feels like he's taking all the control from me. I stand back up. "Then how?"

He looks me in the eye, his expression giving nothing away. "Take off your panties."

It's amusing that he's trying to call me on my bullshit. Lucky for me, I have no problem stripping for him. Besides, he already saw everything when he watched the video.

I give him a sly smile, lift my dress and slip out of my thong. His eyes darken when he looks between my legs before traveling up to meet my eyes.

I twirl my panties around my finger and give him a smirk. "Good enough?"

"No. Come and bring them to me."

"Why?"

His gaze is penetrating. "I want to see how wet they are."

I know I'm blushing.

He knows he's got me.

And it's *not* because my panties are dry. Quite the opposite.

He's playing me at my own game. Twisting it around and turning me on against all odds. Making it so that it doesn't feel like a punishment, but a reward.

I also know that a part of him is hoping I don't take the bait. Hoping I'll back down and reconsider doing whatever it is that I'm doing. Hoping that I'll cool off and hear him out.

Too bad for him that's no longer an option. I'm bringing Jackson into the dark with me and I won't stop until I make him pay. I'll show him my fucked up underworld. He can find his own way out when I'm through with him…unlike me who never will.

Steeling myself, I take the few steps forward until I'm standing directly in front of him.

He takes my panties out of my hand and his eyes blaze when he runs his thumb along the crotch of them. His head rests against the wall and he closes his eyes. I watch his adam's apple bob, straining against his throat as he begins to unbutton his shirt.

For a second, I wince when I see the tape across his ribs, hating the sight of him hurt. I force myself to put it out of my head and focus on the task at hand when he shrugs out of his shirt.

He opens his eyes and his hand reaches out for my cheek. His gray orbs are obscured with both lust and turmoil as his pupil's drill into me. We both know this is the final step before takeoff, the last chance to stop myself.

I slowly drop to my knees. And because I'm more fucked up than I ever realized, I decide to prolong his torture by saying, "Tell me exactly what you want me to do, Jackson."

He groans, his hands tightening at his sides. "Undo my pants and pull me out," he says, low and deep.

I undo his belt buckle and unzip his jeans before sliding them down his hips.

I expect him to be wearing boxers, but he's going commando. My breath catches because his erection is both long and thick. My eyes focus on the glint of metal from the barbell going through the engorged head of his cock. I also can't help but take in the veins and ridges encompassing his shaft and the pure masculine scent radiating off him.

I'm so turned on, I can't find my way into the darkness. I'm completely out of my element now. All I can do is succumb to my own arousal.

I dip my head forward, look up at him and plant a kiss on the small drop of fluid leaking from his tip.

His eyes glaze over and the tight cords of his muscles flex in restraint. I'm struck with the overwhelming feeling of wanting to see him lose control.

I take him in my hand and pump him while I run my tongue along the seam of his balls. My tongue travels back up to his length and I lick the throbbing vein running across his shaft.

"Fuck, Alyssa," he rasps.

I open wide and proceed to fill my mouth with as much of him as I can. I start sucking him with earnest then. His hand wraps around my hair and he thrusts his hips forward. "That's it, baby. Just like that. God, that feels so *fucking* good," he groans, his voice husky.

I don't let up, my mouth bobs up and down, barely stopping for air. I continue even when I begin gagging and his piercing hits the back of my throat. I look up and notice that his eyes are closed, his mouth is parted, and his breathing has become erratic. He's so far gone in the throes of ecstasy, chanting my name like a prayer.

I'd be lying if I said it wasn't the sexiest sight I've ever seen in my life.

"I'm close, baby," he warns. I feel his cock pulse in my mouth and I swallow every last drop of his release while gently tugging on his balls.

"Holy…shit," he grunts.

Before I know what's happening, he's hauling me up to him and crushing his mouth against mine. "That was incredible," he whispers.

I'm brought back down to reality and I give him a menacing smile.

He looks confused for a moment…until I utter my next statement and his face falls.

"Was it better than the blow job you saw me give when you watched the video, Jackson?"

Before he can answer or stop me, I adjust my dress, find my jacket and keys and head straight for the front door.

His hand reaches for my wrist when I touch the doorknob. "Alyssa. It's not what you think."

Anger rips through me. "Oh, so you're going to try and deny it?"

He shakes his head, his expression hurt. "No. I won't lie to you. I…I watched it." He sighs. "Well, part of it before I had to turn it off—"

I didn't think I could feel any worse about the situation. I didn't think there was any more hurt left to experience in my lifetime.

I was wrong.

He's disgusted by me. And why wouldn't he be? He just witnessed who and what I am first hand.

Ford's words from that day echo in my head, shredding my insides. I have no value...no one could or ever will love me.

My hands reach for my necklace and I tug on it until it falls. "Goodbye, Jackson."

Chapter Twenty

JACKSON

"**G**OODBYE, JACKSON."

With those words, she slams the door and takes off. Her necklace tossed on the ground.

I know I fucked up. I know I shouldn't have let her do what she did. Even if it was the best blowjob I'd ever received.

I wanted to wait awhile before we did anything sexual, I didn't want to rush things and screw it all up. But when she uttered those words…about being with another guy…I saw red.

And in all honesty, I *thought* she was into it after I called her on her bullshit. That look in her eye was gone, and her manipulation was replaced by lust. In some fucked up way, I thought it was a good thing.

Clearly, I was wrong.

But I *still don't* regret going after that piece of shit tonight.

She was taking too long in the bathroom and I thought something happened.

Something happened all right…that shit stain was standing right in front of her. How he ended up there in the first place is anyone's guess.

I recognized his tattoo immediately. I was hoping I was mistaken, but deep down I knew it was him. I went into that place inside my head and I blacked out. I barely even remember any of it.

I thought I was in the cage…defending Lilly.

It wasn't until my fist hit the floor and I heard Ricardo's voice that I was brought back to reality.

Then I saw the look on Alyssa's face. She was petrified.

And why wouldn't she be? She just saw her boyfriend for all of two seconds on the verge of killing another person.

And trust me, if Ricardo wasn't there…I would have killed him.

For all I know, I might have.

She didn't utter a word the whole walk home. She just kept her head down and her arms crossed over her chest, shielding herself. I knew we had to talk about it. I knew I had to come clean about watching the video. I knew she would put two and two together and she deserved answers.

I wanted to give her those answers. But when I came out of the bathroom…something happened.

I didn't understand it…but she became someone else. All I knew was that it was because of me.

I tried to talk to her, but she kept telling me she didn't want to talk. Then, she kept throwing herself at me…and kept taking the control away from me. I knew I had to let her have it, within reason…but when I saw it going down a bad road my suspicions were confirmed.

I knew exactly what she was doing.

And the fact that she was doing it with *me*? Even though I made it clear to her time and time again that I didn't want to be used by her....well, I couldn't let it go down like that.

And I sure as hell *wasn't* going to let her go running off to fuck some other dude. That would only make things worse...not to mention, it would kill me.

So, I did the next best thing...I let her have what she was asking for.

Only, I was going to see to it that she wouldn't be punishing herself. That this would be different. It felt like I was fighting against something that was even stronger than me...but I saw the moment the real Alyssa peeked through.

I let her take the control from me...let myself get lost in her, which is something I never, *ever* do. Not that I really had much of a choice in the matter because the things she did to me?

Well, *fuck*.

Porn stars could learn a thing or *several* from her.

Then she looked up at me and gave me a smile that chilled me to the bone. My favorite dimple was nowhere in sight.

I told her the truth about watching the video...I didn't lie. But she never let me explain myself because she took off.

Worst of all? She didn't let me tell her how brave and strong I thought she was for making it through something like that. She didn't let me tell her that I was falling for her. I knew I was a goner the second my lips touched hers in that club.

I want to chase after her, but I know she needs time to cool off. I know that when I push her too far, she doesn't come bouncing back harder and stronger like I wish she would.

We might be similar in some ways, but *unlike* me, my girl's not a fighter...she's a runner. And even though I hate that...I'll accept it because it's who she is and I want all of her.

I hear a knock on the door and I can't get there fast enough.

I'm disappointed when it's Ricardo staring back at me. Not that I'm not thankful for his help.

Although, I still don't know *why* he was there in the first place.

I open the door, gesture for him to come inside and cut to the chase. "Why were you there?"

He looks at me hard and I know I'm not going to like what he's going to say. "No offense, but your girl was dressed to kill tonight. Even I couldn't ignore how hot she looked. That being said, I already told you I was concerned about what would happen on the outside. I was going to tell you not to go. I didn't have a good feeling about it." He shrugs. "But then she mentioned that it was her birthday and I saw how excited she was. It doesn't take a genius to figure out that she must not get out much because of the video. My bad feelings were confirmed, though after you beat the mayor's son to a bloody pulp."

Fuck, DeLuca was not going to be happy about this. Not one bit.

Ricardo must notice my expression because he says, "Don't worry, I took care of everything."

"How?"

"I had a few of DeLuca's men waiting on deck, just in case something happened. Plus, I was in the wings myself. I wish I got to you sooner, but I didn't see you go into the bathroom. I thought you left because I saw you both head out for the exit. I stayed back chatting it up with some hot redhead. Then I heard the commotion."

He runs a hand through his hair. "You fucked him up bad, Jackson. He's got some serious damage. On the bright side, he was so zonked out of his mind he doesn't remember shit before or after. He had no idea he was talking to Alyssa in the bathroom or that he got into a fight."

He smirks. "I had Freddie wreck his car and stage it like he got into an accident because he was too stoned. I also issued him a warning. Not only did I tell him that you were in DeLuca's circle and ran with him. I mentioned that if his memory about tonight were to ever come back, he and his car would be found at the bottom of the Atlantic."

Part of me wishes that the bastard does end up remembering now. It's what he deserves.

"Thanks. I owe you." I pause. "But what about DeLuca's men? What if they say something to him?"

I want to tell him that what I'm *really* worried about is someone mentioning Alyssa being there with me. But, as much as we're friends—I can't.

I'm in a bind because I don't want to reveal Alyssa's past. Partly because it's not my place and partly because I really don't know how strong Ricardo's loyalty is to DeLuca. For all I know, *he* could spill the beans to DeLuca himself.

He jerks a shoulder up. "They won't. They owe me a few favors. But, if DeLuca finds out, I'll handle it. I don't really see him flipping out over some stupid bar fight, anyway. He's got much bigger shit to worry about. It's not like you ended up in jail or on the news."

His words should comfort me but they do the exact opposite. My memory kicks in and I remember that people had their phones out recording the fight.

"Shit. What about the cell phones? It was the mayor's son. You know someone will be more than willing to sell the footage to tmz or post it online."

"Took care of that too," he says.

I vaguely remember him breaking a few cell phones. "What if you missed one? Then what?"

He considers this for a moment. "Then we take care of it."

He looks around. "So where is Alyssa?"

I briefly tell him how I fucked up. I leave *out* the part about her giving me a blowjob… but not about me watching the video.

"Fucking Lou-Lou," he growls. "She doesn't know when enough is enough. Always causing problems."

I don't miss the intensity in his eyes when he says that.

"Yeah, but it was still *me* who watched it. I have no idea how the hell to fix this."

"Maybe it's best to just leave it alone and let it perish. Some things are better that way."

Something tells me that it's not me and Alyssa he's talking about when he utters that statement.

I shake my head. "No. She's special. I can't let it end like this."

He stands up. "Then do what you do best." When I give him a weird look he says, "Fight for her, dummy."

He's right.

I've already tried texting her multiple times, though. I told her how sorry I was and explained what really happened with the sex tape.

I also told her that my feelings for her never changed after watching it. Nor have they changed after tonight…after I saw the other side of her. I told her that if she was willing, we would get through it together because I wasn't giving up on her or us.

Then I told her that I was falling for her.

She still hasn't responded.

I scan the living room and notice that in her rush to leave, she left her purse here.

Maybe *that's* why she never responded to any of my texts.

I pick it up and can feel her phone vibrating through the material.

That's when I realize what an idiot I am. I shouldn't be telling Alyssa those things via text. I should be saying them to her in person. Fighting for her like Ricardo said.

I turn around and face him. "I need another favor."

"What's up?"

"Can I borrow your car?"

After promising Ricardo over and over again that I wouldn't crash his prized Mustang. He handed over the keys.

I got Alyssa's address off her license and plugged it into the gps on my phone. The drive wasn't as bad as I thought it would be.

Her neighborhood is quiet and the houses that line the streets are all large and upscale.

The lawns are green and the streetlights are all in working order. There's no sign of drug dealers or garbage littering the sidewalks.

It's the perfect suburb life. So different from the environment I grew up in.

I decide to park right behind her car in the driveway. I notice another car parked there as well...but from the looks of things, her house is so big, maybe she has a tenant or two living there.

Her driveway is long and her house sits on top of a large hill, meaning I've got a little bit of a walk ahead of me. Dozens of large oak trees line the property. After a solid three minutes of walking, I see a glimmer of light up ahead and I know I must be close.

The light from the porch becomes brighter and after another minute, I'm standing right in front of her house.

Then I see her.

But she's not alone.

I see the back of some other guy, one who's wearing a gray suit.

I can't hear what he's saying, but I watch as he gets down on his knees in front of her and grabs her hips.

His hands are all over her, touching her everywhere...then he leans in and lifts up her dress.

Since her panties are still on the floor in the living room of *my* apartment, she's fully exposed.

I'm less than a second away from charging full speed ahead and pummeling the asshole.

Then I hear her shout something that takes the breath from my lungs. "I love you, Ford."

I quickly turn away and run back down the hill.

I'm running down the hill as fast as I can, so I don't go back and do something stupid... like beat the ever living shit out of an FBI agent.

An FBI agent she specifically told me wasn't in her life anymore.

He sure as *fuck* looked to be *very* much in her life...especially while he was positioning himself to go down on her.

I don't even know what to think at this point. The only thing I feel is betrayed, hurt, and lied to.

And I know...I lied to her, too.

But unlike *her* lie, my lie was to *protect* her from harm.

I've done *nothing* but try and be there for this girl...I didn't use her, intentionally hurt her, or betray her.

The question is...why the fuck did Alyssa feel the need to do *all* of those things to me?

I know she's got her demons...I saw them up close and personal tonight. I also know that she thought the world of her dad's old partner. I guess I know why now.

My chest tightens when I think about what she said. She *loves* him.

I made the mistake of falling for a girl who could never be mine because she already belongs to someone else.

My blood boils at the thought.

But if she loves *him*...why did she lead *me* on?

No. *Fuck*, no.

She wouldn't do that. It would be stupid and *dangerous* to do that.

I force myself to breathe. I have to remind myself that *if* Alyssa was in fact, attempting some undercover shit...then she wouldn't have told me about what DeLuca did to her dad.

Unless she made it up?

No. I saw the agony in her eyes that night when she confided in me. I felt it. There's no way that was false.

At least, that makes one thing she told me true.

Tyrone tried to warn me about her in the beginning. Hell, even *Lou-Lou* warned me about her. I just refused to listen. I didn't want to believe it.

I thought I saw something inside of her that called to me...connected us. Something I wanted to take care of. Something I would have cherished until my dying breath.

I pull the car door open and grab her purse from the passenger seat of the Mustang.

I'm sure as shit not going back up that hill, but I also don't want to have any of her stuff near me. I don't need to be reminded of what a deceitful bitch she is because I'm certain I'll never forget.

And because I'm feeling extra spiteful at the moment, I snatch the necklace I got her. I put them both on the hood of her car. Now, I have absolutely no reason to ever see her again.

Although, if she ever showed up at my place; I'm sure I could have Lou-Lou play along and answer the door for me. I *could* make Alyssa think I was fucking her. I could hurt her the way I'm hurting now, but I'd rather just be done with her for good.

I briefly consider keying her precious BMW, but quite frankly, I don't have the energy to go all Carrie Underwood on her ass. I still have over an hour drive ahead of me.

Besides, I'm sure Mr. Special Agent, *Daddy Warbucks* would just offer to buy her a brand new car. Hell, maybe he's the one who bought her the one she has now.

I *almost* let myself love her. I was right there...on the fucking cliff...already falling... about to land.

I just never knew I was headed for a crash landing.

Chapter Twenty-One

ALYSSA

FUCK, I FORGOT MY PURSE.

I briefly consider turning around. But for what? How the hell can I even begin to explain what goes on inside my mind to Jackson? He'll think I'm a psycho. Hell, I probably am.

A part of me wants to turn the car around, but Jackson will just want to talk about everything. How can I tell him about this place I go to inside myself that causes me to do these things? How can I tell him that when he hurt me…all I thought about was Ford.

How can I tell him about Ford?

I know, deep down inside that Ford is the gatekeeper to this hellhole I'm trapped in. But I *can't* live without him…because he's the *only* one who ever showed me love after that horrible day. He's the one who cared when I had no one else. He's the only tie to my father I have left. And if I sever our relationship…I'll have nothing.

I know our relationship isn't healthy. It hasn't been since that day in his office, maybe even before that if I'm being honest with myself.

But I know *he* loves me. I know he cares…and I know he will always be there for me.

Like now, I think, as I pull into my driveway and see him waiting for me in his car.

As soon as I get out of my own car, his arms are around me.

"What happened, sweetheart? You don't look happy." His blue eyes are piercing tonight and his expression is particularly kind.

I'm immediately uneasy. Ford hasn't treated me like this in a *very* long time. Usually, he's upset with me about something or telling me all that I do wrong. I almost want to ask him when the last time he saw me genuinely happy was…because I'm always miserable when he's around.

I shrug as we begin walking toward the house. I don't really want to tell him about Jackson. Besides, anytime he suspects that I've been out with a guy…wow he gets mad.

I decide to stay silent. Because I know that when it comes to Ford, anything and everything I say will eventually be used against me.

We walk up to the house, but I don't invite him in. I'm too exhausted to deal with whatever it is he came here for tonight. "I'm tired, Ford. I think I'm just going to go to bed. Have a good night."

His hand wraps around my arm and he spins me around. Then I see it. The moment he looks down at my dress and his expression fills with disgust. "I wonder why that is, Alyssa."

When I don't respond, he pushes me further. "I know you've been *seeing* someone."

He says this like the concept of me actually having a relationship with anyone is utterly barbaric.

I let him continue because I'm not sure what I'm supposed to say to that. I don't want to correct him and tell him that we got into a fight and might be over; because I don't want him telling me that he told me so and that no one will ever love me.

"I know you stayed at his apartment in the city the last time I saw you. *He* was also who you hung up on *me* for during our last conversation."

I don't know how he has this information or *why* it matters so much to him. "Yeah… and? What's your point?"

He steps closer to me and I swear his features change right before my eyes. His eyes narrow, his jaw goes rigid and his lips form a tight line. The hand around my arm squeezes so hard I wince. "You said *he* was important, Alyssa."

I laugh, I laugh so hard I must sound like a crazy person. "So? He *is* important. What the hell is your deal?"

"My deal," he grits through his teeth. "Is that there should be *no one* in your life more important than me, do you understand me? You are mine. *My* goddamn whore, you hear me? Not his!"

And then he slaps me. Hard. Right across my left cheek.

And then I'm crying. Because the truth fucking hurts.

All of it hurts.

I want to go numb.

"Goddammit," he screams. "See what you made me do?"

"I'm s-sorry."

"Stop stuttering, Alyssa. I forgive you."

I only stutter like this when I'm terrified or upset.

I'm about to apologize again, but I realize what he said. He forgives *me*? For what? I've done nothing wrong. "I don't forgive *you*, Ford."

He appears confused so I continue, "I don't forgive you for that day in the office. I don't forgive you for the way you treat me. And I definitely don't forgive you for slapping me."

He looks astonished but I'm not done yet. I jab a finger in his chest. "So what? I have a boyfriend. And you know what the best part about Jackson is? He doesn't treat me like *you* do, Ford. He's *nice* to me. He respects me. He doesn't treat me like I'm his property and he certainly doesn't treat me like I'm a whore."

Ford looks at me with so much pain in his eyes…I almost crumble.

He grabs my face. "I'm so sorry, sweetheart." He leans down so we are eye level. "I love you, Alyssa." He kisses my cheek. "Can you forgive the beast?" He kisses my other cheek. "For only trying to save her," he whispers.

I close my eyes because *this* Ford is so familiar. This is the Ford I know in my heart. This is the Ford I love.

His hands find my waist and his thumbs skim over my rib cage. "Please," he pleads.

I open my eyes and look down as he drops to his knees. I've never seen Ford look so sad or desperate before.

He looks up at me. "I know you love me. Don't punish me for loving you back. Please don't punish me for being the only one who could ever love you."

Something about that statement tears at my soul. I can't respond to him, because if I open my mouth…something inside me will crack further. And I won't know how to fix it all by myself.

His hands grip my hips forcefully. "You love *me*, Alyssa. You fucking love me. Let me hear you say it. I *need* to hear you say it."

But I can't. I can't say it. He looks so wounded in this moment, it physically causes me to ache.

But I *still* can't say it.

He fists my dress. "I'll *make* you say it then," he sneers.

What? No. Fear renders me captive and I attempt to shake my head, but I can't move.

He cups my mound through the silk fabric of my dress. "Tell me, does he touch you like this?"

I stay frozen, refusing to answer him. He lifts my dress and the cool breeze hits me, leaving me vulnerable and exposed. "He's never made you come before has he?" He clicks his tongue. "But then again, no one has…have they, sweetheart?"

I don't answer him and he laughs. "You want to know why that is?"

I don't. I really, really don't. Because I think I already know the answer.

I just never wanted to believe it.

His head dips forward and I know there's only one way to make this stop. "I love you, Ford," I shout at the top of my lungs.

But he doesn't stop.

"I own your mind," he whispers, his breath tickling my core. "Because I was the first one to fuck *that* and make it mine."

I crack. My body feels both lighter and heavier at the same time.

He smiles. He's giving me that movie star smile that now makes me feel sick. "I love you, Alyssa."

The tears hit me fast and hard.

What *kind* of man loves like *this*?

That's easy. No man.

Because what Ford feels for me isn't love. "No, you don't."

Something deep inside me snaps with that final realization. I push him off me and open the front door. He chases after me, following me into the kitchen. "Get out, Ford! Get out!" I shove him. I shove him as far as I possibly can and he stumbles back. I need him to *leave*. I never want to see him again.

I scream and pull my hair. Ford looks at me like I'm insane.

Good. Let him see what he's created.

Before I know it, I'm reaching for a knife and aiming it at him. "Get the fuck out!"

His eyes open wide and for a moment, I think he's going to reach for his gun. But he holds his hands up instead. "Put the knife down, sweetheart. Look, I'm sorry for what I said. I didn't mean it. I only wanted to hear you say that you loved me."

"It's your fault!" I scream. His mouth drops open and for a second, I swear, panic flashes across his face.

I'm crying so hard I can barely form words. "It's your fault I'm like *this*. You broke me." I begin shaking. "And the worst part is…in my darkest moments…when I go to that place inside myself. I'm just like *you*."

And it's true. It's so fucking true. I treat others like they're disposable. I treat myself like I'm worth nothing. I manipulate people to get my own way. And I can honestly say, that I don't love myself.

The cold, hard reality is like being thrown outside naked in the middle of a blizzard.

I wipe my nose with my sleeve and fall down to the floor. "You don't love me, Ford."

He begins pacing, looking at me like I'm a mental case. "Of course, I love you!" he screams.

I look him in his eyes for the last time. "No. Because *if* you loved me…you would *never* keep insisting that I go undercover for my father's killer…knowing that he might end up killing *me* if he ever found out."

He opens his mouth to speak but I hold up my hand. "You would want to *protect* me. You would want me to be safe. You wouldn't send me into the eye of the storm. You wouldn't set me up."

A tear falls from Ford's eye. "Alyssa. I—"

"Just leave, Ford. Please, just leave me. That's the only way you can ever make any of this okay."

I hear the sound of the door closing and breathe…actually breathe for the first time in years.

I drop the knife and curl my arms around myself…because I'm all I have left now.

And I have to be okay with that.

Three months later...

Chapter Twenty-Two

ALYSSA

"I NEED A GLASS OF COKE AND A SPLASH OF JACK."

I wink at my customer. "Ah. You take your whiskey like I take my coffee. Cup of cream and sugar and a splash of coffee."

He looks embarrassed. "I guess that makes me sound like less of a man, huh?"

I wave a hand at him and continue fixing his drink. "Nah. You gotta do what's right for you. Don't ever let anyone tell you different."

He leans in. "And what if I told you that getting your number would be what's right for me?"

Somewhere in back of me, someone clears their throat. "I would say that what's right for *me*…is punching you in the face for hitting on my girl."

My customer quickly leaves after that.

I roll my eyes and look up at my friend. "What the hell, Shane?" I nod my head in the direction of the cute musician who hasn't stopped looking at Shane since his shift started. "Your *boyfriend* is sitting right over there watching you."

He flips a bottle in the air. "I know. I'm wearing the jeans that make my ass look great." He begins filling the glass in front of him. "I thought I'd run interference. Besides, I said my *girl*. Not *girlfriend*. If he was really interested in you for more than one night, he would have clarified." He shrugs. "Guy looked like a douche anyway."

I shake my head. "You're crazy."

He purses his lips. "Yeah, but you love me."

I smile because I can honestly say that I do. Shane gave me a job when no one else would. Not only did he hire me, but he also lets me rent the apartment upstairs from the bar.

And when I had a full blown panic attack over possibly being recognized that first night…he wiped my tears away and suggested we dye my hair. He didn't judge me when I told him about the video and he never uses my real name around customers.

I toss my long dark hair over my shoulder and kiss his cheek. "Call me if it gets packed. You know where I'll be."

He laughs. "It won't now that you're off the clock. But I'll call you anyway."

I walk around the bar and head upstairs to my studio apartment.

A lot has changed over the last three months.

For starters…I no longer visit the city. I live here now. I moved out of my father's house two weeks after the last night I saw Ford.

I used the money I got from selling Ford's BMW which was apparently equipped with a hidden gps tracking device to help me move.

That's how he knew I spent the night at Jackson's.

Jackson.

I have to close my eyes at the thought of him.

I went out to my car the next day and found my purse along with the necklace he got for me. I also dug my phone out and wept while I read all of his text messages.

I didn't even think about it, I hopped in my car and went straight to his apartment.

Where he proceeded to ignore me for hours upon hours.

So, I left and came back the next day.

Only to face an angry Tyrone.

He didn't want to speak to me...but after he saw the state I was in...he relented a little. He said that Jackson wouldn't go into much detail about it, but that he saw me with some other guy at my house.

Apparently, he came to my house to talk to me that night and showed up just as Ford got down on his knees and I was screaming that I loved him. He left shortly after that and never looked back.

I never thought it was possible to hate Ford more. But, I really only had myself to blame. I *should* have been honest with Jackson and I *should* have kicked Ford out of my life a long time ago.

I told Tyrone...well, it was more like *begged* Tyrone to talk to Jackson for me and set him straight.

I told Tyrone to tell him that what he saw between Ford and I *wasn't* what he thought it was.

The verdict?

It didn't matter. Jackson was done with me.

I still wasn't done with him yet, so I made one final attempt.

This time, it was Jackson himself who answered the door. He never let *me* get a word in, but I'll never forget what he said—*"I'm all out of fucks to give. Maybe Ford can give you a few."*

Then he slammed the door in my face and locked it.

Yup...I hurt him that much.

And I never, ever got a chance to apologize to him or explain what happened.

I tried for two weeks straight to make things right. But the same thing happened every time. Tyrone would come out and tell me to go home. Nothing was going to change.

It got to the point where even freakin' Lou-Lou was looking at me with pity whenever she saw me in the apartment lobby.

I didn't want to, but I had to let him go.

I can only hope, that our paths will cross again one day.

Chapter Twenty-Three

JACKSON

"I LOVE YOU, SUGARPLUM."

Ricardo and I exchange a glance.

"I promise I'll call you later, sugarplum," Tyrone continues. "I've missed you so much. I can't wait to see you, sugarplum."

"So help me god, if he says *sugarplum* one more time," Ricardo says under his breath.

I pinch the bridge of my nose and lean forward. I don't know how much more of this *sugarplum* shit I can take.

I'm about ready to hand over *my* balls just so he can feel what it's like to have a pair again.

Is this what I would have turned into if things hadn't gone sour with Alyssa?

Nope. Not going there.

Five more sugarplum's and three 'I love you's' later, Tyrone finally gets off the phone.

He turns around and makes a face at Ricardo and I. He's been doing that a lot lately.

Ricardo and I exchange another glance because we both know what's coming, and neither of us are up for it.

"Guys," he starts. "Y'all could be just as happy as I am if you would both stop being so stubborn."

I grunt and Ricardo reaches for his beer.

He points to Ricardo first. "You going out and screwing anything in a skirt night after night isn't helping you. You need to walk down the hall and talk to Lou-Lou. I don't care what you say, man…she meant more to you than you're letting on."

His eyes swivel to me. "And *you*. You haven't been the same since that night you went to Alyssa's house."

My entire body stiffens at the sound of her name.

"You've *changed*, Jackson. You're always in a bad mood these days. All you do is work out and go to the fight club."

I shrug. "That's always what I've done, Tyrone."

He tsks at me. "No. You're different. Even angrier. Like the entire world is your own personal fighting cage now."

He rubs the back of his neck. "I don't think you gave her the benefit of the doubt. I don't understand why you don't just call her up and let—"

"Enough," I warn.

There's absolutely no reason to call her. Why? So she can just lie to me about Ford again. Make me start falling for her and turn myself inside out.

Been there done that.

I rub my temples…trying to push my other thoughts away.

Thoughts like—What if there *is* more to the story? What if she's truly sorry for what she did?

Or worst of all? What if I let myself forgive her?

Then I'll be right back where I started.

Having no choice but to lie to her about working at DeLuca's club and my reason for working there in the first place.

And when she finds out, she'll leave me anyway and it will hurt worse.

No, I'd much rather let my anger and venom for her stew. Let it turn me into a cold, heartless bastard.

He blows out a breath and looks at the both of us. "I'm tired of this, y'all. So, here's what we're gonna do. We're going to *talk* about it."

I rub my hands over my face. I've had enough of this shit. "Oh for fucks sake!" I roar.

Tyrone stops talking and Ricardo laughs.

Tyrone claps his hands. "Okay, this is progress. Let it out. Jackson, why don't you start first. How did it make you *feel* when Alyssa hurt you?"

I look at Ricardo and he smirks. "You gonna answer that?"

I get up from the couch. "Fuck no. Let's grab a drink." I look at Tyrone. "Feel free to stay back and watch some more Doctor Phil."

"And bake some cookies while you're at it, *sugarplum*," Ricardo adds.

Tyrone gives us the finger. "Fuck you both. I was only trying to help."

I toss him his jacket. "If you wanna help you can buy us a round at the bar."

Ricardo looks at his phone. "You guys down to try a new spot? It's kind of a hole in the wall, but rumor has it the bartender is easy on the eyes."

I open the front door. "Fine, but I'm not looking for pussy. I'm just looking to drink."

"Is there something you'd like to tell us, Ricardo?"

Beside me, Tyrone laughs.

Ricardo rolls his eyes. "I guess I just *assumed* the hot bartender was a girl."

The giant bartender with frosted blond tips looks up and gives Ricardo a wink.

That only makes Tyrone laugh harder. "Ah. So you *do* think he's hot?"

The bartender saunters over to us. "What can I get you, boys?"

Ricardo takes a seat at the bar. "Are you the only one who's working tonight? Because there's supposed to be a *hot* bartender who works here."

Frosted blond tips and eyeliner aside, the dude's built like a linebacker who could probably give Ricardo a run for his money.

The guy looks offended, so I clear my throat and cut in. "I think what my rude buddy means is—is there a *female* bartender working here?"

"A hot one," Ricardo interjects.

The guy gives Ricardo a dirty look before focusing his attention back to me and holding out his hand. "I'm Shane."

I shake his hand. "I'm Jackson." I quickly introduce Tyrone and Ricardo.

Shane flips a bottle in the air. "I like you, Jackson."

Well, now this is awkward.

He flips another bottle in the air and winks at me. "So, you know what I'm gonna do for you, sexy?"

Next to me, Tyrone pats me on the back and whispers, "I'm so glad I came here tonight. This is *awesome*."

I'm going to *kill* Ricardo for bringing us here.

Shane slams his hand down on the bar. "I'm going to introduce you to my employee."

I raise an eyebrow. "Come again?"

"The hot female bartender...you're interested right?"

I shake my head. "No." I gesture to Ricardo. "*He* is. The only thing I want is some whiskey if you have it."

He fills up a glass and hands it to me.

Ricardo leans in. "When will she be here?" he asks Shane.

He looks at the clock. "In about 20 minutes. But if you're looking for a quick screw, trust me...she's *not* it," he says before turning to a different set of customers.

"If she's hot, I'll have no problem giving her a long and slow screw," Ricardo says under his breath.

Tyrone looks at him and shakes his head. "I already told you, man. You can screw as many women as you want. It's not going to keep your mind off of Lou-Lou. Just *talk* to her."

"Drop it," Ricardo barks.

I finish my drink and put money on the bar. "Ready to go?"

Ricardo shrugs. "Nah. We're here now. We might as well stay awhile." He swirls the amber liquid around his glass before downing it. "We came here to drink our troubles away anyway."

I click my empty glass against his. "I'll drink to that."

Three games of darts and five rounds later we walk back to the bar for another round.

Or in my case, stumble because I slammed three shots of 151 during the last round that we had and I'm pretty sure I've reached my limit.

It's semi-crowded now, so we're forced to take the last three seats at the end of the bar.

I'm drunk as fuck, but I notice there's a subtle shift in the atmosphere and it seems like everyone's eyes are glued to the same thing.

When I look up, I find out why.

There's some girl bent over a large cooler located at the back of the bar. Her shiny dark hair cascades down her back, but I'm too focused on the way her perfect little ass looks in the skirt she's wearing to notice much else. She leans down even further and I feel myself lean with her as I notice her skirt rising higher...hoping to be rewarded with a glimpse of her cheeks.

I look over and Ricardo bites his knuckle. "Fuck me that's hot."

Tyrone shakes his head and looks down. "My dick belongs to Shelby. This is *Shelby's* dick," he chants to himself.

Ricardo and I burst out laughing.

It feels good to laugh again. Even if it's only because I'm feeling the effects of the alcohol.

I turn to him. "Goddamn, man. How can you ignore *that*? Even *I'm* looking at her," I say. I point in the direction of where she last was and ignore Ricardo's tap on my shoulder. "I mean, she sure as *fuck* is putting it all out there. She's obviously looking for attention and a good time."

I turn to Ricardo, but he's shaking his head at me. I proceed to ignore him. "Looks like you found your quick fuck after all. I bet you won't even have to take her home to get it."

I swipe my hand in the air. "Hey, hot stuff," I call out. "Thanks for the free show. But can I get another glass of whiskey?"

When I turn my head back to the bar, I'm greeted by a pair of gorgeous, but furious hazel eyes.

I must be drunker than I realized, because I swear, I see an exact replica of Alyssa standing before me, only with dark hair.

I turn to Tyrone. "Are you seeing what I'm seeing?"

He puts a hand on my shoulder. "Yeah, brother. And I think it's time to get you home." He casts a sympathetic glance at Alyssa. "Look, he's really drunk right now. He doesn't know what he's saying."

Ricardo nods. "It's true, Alyssa. He's not exactly himself at the moment."

She crosses her arms over those perfect tits of hers and I groan.

But even in my drunken state, I know this woman is poison. I have to get the fuck out of here.

I put one arm around Ricardo and another around Tyrone. "You guys better get me home before her FBI—sugar daddy… and I do mean *daddy* because he's *old* enough to be her daddy…arrests me."

"Fuck," Ricardo mutters.

"Bro…*shut* up," Tyrone yells.

Before I know it, the glass of whiskey I asked for is being thrown in my face and Alyssa's storming off.

Chapter Twenty-Four

JACKSON

From what I'm told, everyone has at least one night in their life where they get too drunk and end up regretting it.

I never had that night.

Until *last* night.

When I was a teenager, I was too busy taking care of Lilly…and when I was 21, I was too focused on MMA training.

For most of my adult life, I avoided getting drunk altogether. Between having an addict for a mother, along with hating the feeling of losing control, I saw no reason to drink to the point of being obliterated.

And this afternoon…I'm adding one more reason to that list.

It makes you act like a dumbass and say stupid fucking things.

Whoever said that a drunk mind speaks sober thoughts…was clearly still drunk off *their* ass.

Tyrone told me everything I said last night…not even bothering to mince words.

I never had any intention of seeing or talking to Alyssa again.

But…I do owe her an apology for how I behaved last night.

Which is why I'm currently making my way *back* to the bar that Alyssa now works at.

If I'm being honest, a small part of me was hoping she wasn't working now so I wouldn't have to go through with this.

But here she is, wiping down the surfaces of the almost empty bar. She's wearing a black t-shirt with the name '*Finnley's*' written across it in white lettering and every time she moves I see a tiny sliver of her toned abdomen.

She's also wearing pants now.

Because I'm a dick.

Shane nudges her and she looks up at me. Her expression tells me that I'm the last person she ever expected to see walk through that door. Shane leans down and whispers something in her ear. She shakes her head and he begrudgingly walks away…but not before giving me a dirty look.

Guess he doesn't like me all that much anymore.

I take a cautious seat at the bar and look around a little. It's not a big place, pretty small actually…but it does have a very laid back vibe going for it. It's definitely not one of those flashy bars that you hear about celebrities going to.

That's when I take another look at her hair.

It's a bit longer now and very dark, almost jet black.

I'm not going to tell her…because then I'd have to acknowledge the fact that I still, somewhere deep inside of me; have feelings for her…but I like it. *Really* like it.

I mean, she looked great as a blonde. But the dark hair?

It makes her hazel eyes pop even more and it complements her ivory skin.

She makes her way over to me after finishing up with the only other customer in the place.

I don't miss the way her smile falls and her full lips form a tight line. Or the way she lifts her chin right before she walks over to me like she's preparing herself, putting on a brave face.

And I definitely don't miss the look of sadness in her eyes before they turn intense. "Whiskey?" she asks.

I detect a hint of snarkiness in her tone and I'm surprised to find that I actually miss her sassy side. Now that she's standing right in front of me, there's a lot of things I find I miss about her.

But I have to force myself not to focus on that because if I do…I'll be reminded of the things I hate about her as well.

Like what she did to me…how she hurt me.

I fucking hate that she hurt me.

Almost as much as I hate that I'm never going to kiss those lips or see that dimple again.

I meet her gaze. "No…I think I had enough to drink for a lifetime last night." I give her a smile. "And if I want more, I can always wring out the clothes I wore last night, right?"

A ghost of a smile touches her lips. I can't tell if it's because she's recalling the memory, or smiling at my lame-ass attempt to break the ice.

A part of me is hoping for the former because a part of me is proud of her for standing up for herself and throwing the whiskey right in my face.

Alyssa's always been finicky when it comes to that sort of thing. Sometimes she defends herself…sometimes she runs.

But she's not running now, which is good. Because I really do owe her that apology. "I'm sorry, Alyssa. There's no excuse for the way I acted or the things I said last night, so I'm not going to waste your time giving you any. I was wrong. Plain and simple."

There, I said it. Now my guard can go back up and I can walk away from her.

She inhales deeply and bites her bottom lip. "I accept your apology. I know it wasn't easy to have to see me again."

She pauses, appearing to be debating the next words out of her mouth. "I wanted to look pretty," she whispers, looking down at the floor.

I have no idea what she's talking about. "Pardon?"

"The reason I was wearing a skirt," she says. "I, um. I wasn't looking for attention or anything. I wasn't trying to put it all out there like you said."

I open my mouth to apologize again, but she continues, "I haven't worn a skirt or a dress in over three months. I didn't want any reminders of the person I used to be…or the things I used to do. But last night, for whatever reason, I wanted to look pretty." She pauses and draws in a shaky breath. "I realized it was a bad idea when a group of guys kept asking me for the bottles of beer that we keep in the cooler instead of what was on tap. Shane had an emergency and it was too late to change since I was by myself and it was getting packed."

Her brow wrinkles. "I heard your voice and it made me happy. But, then I heard the things you were saying about me. And whether I liked it or not, I had to accept that there were people in that bar who might have shared your thoughts. Maybe even some who thought I was a whore."

She looks me in the eyes. "But I'm not a whore, Jackson." She gives me a small shrug. "I just wanted to tell you that."

There are moments in your life that you'll never forget. Some good, some bad, some life-changing.

However, I never thought it was possible to fall in love with a single moment.

Especially a moment with a person who's caused you so much pain.

Especially when the moment puts you in your place for being a monumental asshole.

But this moment right here?

I *love* this moment.

Despite what happened between us in the past, I *still* love this moment.

There's so much strength, growth and beauty in this single moment pouring out from her.... I almost don't want to ruin it by talking.

But I have to, if for nothing else then to say, "You're right, Alyssa. You're not a whore. You never were." I wipe the tear from her cheek with my thumb and stand up. "I was wrong for the things I said last night. And I'm sorry."

I give her one last smile before I walk away.

Then I put my armor up because I *have* to.

I'm stepping out the door when I hear Alyssa's footsteps behind me. "Jackson, wait. Please." I turn around and she grabs my hand and leads me to a small corner of the bar, giving us more privacy.

"I'm sorry," she says.

I open my mouth to stop her, because although the moment we just shared was incredible, it doesn't erase what happened.

And it doesn't change the fact that I'm still irate with her about it.

"Please, I'm begging you to just hear me out," she pleads. I go to turn away, but she tugs on my hand. "Ford was never my boyfriend. I was never with him!" she blurts.

"Although, there was a point in my life when I thought I wanted that," she amends.

I pull my hand away and begin walking again. "I shouldn't have lied to you about him being in my life," she calls out. "But if you knew about the things between us. The things that went on."

I stop mid-stride and turn around. "I don't *want* to know about those things, Alyssa. Keep them to yourself. Trust me, I really *don't* need to hear all about how you loved him and fucked him."

I didn't mean to raise my voice, but I didn't come here for this shit. I came here to apologize and go on with my life. Why can't she just let me?

"But...Jackson. You don't understand."

No, *she's* the one who doesn't understand. "Did you have sex with him?"

She steps back with a guilty expression her face. "Yes. But it was—"

"Did you love him?" I interrupt.

She worries her bottom lip between her teeth before answering, "Yes. But it wasn't—"

I cut her off. "Did you lie to me about the nature of your relationship with him?"

She looks down. "Yes."

I lean in close to her ear. "You see, Alyssa. It really doesn't matter what you think it *was* or what it *wasn't* between you and him. That's none of my business and quite frankly, I don't give a shit. The only thing that matters to me is that you loved him, you fucked him, you *lied* to me about him and all three of those things ended up hurting me."

I walk away from her this time with no hesitation.

The only thing that causes me to pause is when I hear her whisper, "I didn't have sex with him that night. I wouldn't do that to you." But I still force myself to walk right out that door.

Because I don't want to forgive her...I don't want to fall for her. But most of all?

I don't want to have to lie to her about who I really am...again.

Chapter Twenty-Five

ALYSSA

SHANE NUDGES MY HIP AS HE LEANS IN AND WHISPERS, "I THOUGHT YOU SAID HE didn't want to talk to you?"

My eyes scan the bar before landing on Jackson. He's standing in the back playing a game of darts, by himself. Probably wishing it was my face that made up the board. I exhale sharply as I take in the way his gray henley shirt stretches across his broad chest and outlines the muscles of his arms. I force myself not to let my gaze drop to his faded blue jeans, which I have no doubt fit his ass and strong thighs perfectly.

My eyes betray me anyway…and dammit, I was right. They totally do.

"He doesn't." I shrug. "He still hasn't said a word to me."

And it's not like it's because the bar is so crowded or anything. We have a few customers, but there are plenty of seats at the bar.

Which he has yet to walk up to…because he still has yet to order a drink.

Which can only mean one thing. He's here to see me.

And he's been doing plenty of that because, over the last two hours, I've caught him stealing glances at me 32 different times now.

Make that 33.

Those gray eyes of his are burning into me yet again, heating my entire body with a single look.

The corners of his lips twitch. And that's when I know. He totally caught me checking him out just a second ago.

My mouth goes dry when his own eyes drop down, then slowly drag back up my body seductively, finally landing on my face. My brain fizzles. The 'this is your brain on drugs' warning, should also issue a 'this is your brain when Jackson Reid looks at you like *that*,' warning.

"He's been here four nights in a row," Shane says. "I don't understand why he won't speak to you. Want me to kick him out?"

"Absolutely not," I reply.

Jackson might not be talking to me, but the fact that he's been here night after night watching me tells me something.

He still has feelings for me. Feelings that some part of him can't ignore.

Either that, or he wants to see if Ford will show up here. Maybe, see if I was telling him the truth the other day.

I knew I hurt him…but even I wasn't aware of just *how* much I hurt him until his drunken outburst happened and our last conversation took place.

I wish he would just let me explain everything…I know it won't be easy for him to hear, but for some reason, he won't let that happen.

"You gonna be okay to close up by yourself?" Shane asks while casting a look in Jackson's direction.

I glance at the clock, I didn't realize that it was time for last call already. "I'll be fine."

We announce last call and Shane and the last few stragglers leave.

With the exception of Jackson…because I'm certainly not kicking him out. Plus, he'll have no choice but to speak to me if we're the only two people here.

I walk to the door and proceed to lock up and put the alarm on.

I'm wondering why Jackson doesn't leave when he sees me doing this, but he doesn't seem to care that I'm closing the bar. I turn off the lights above the bar but make sure to keep the one on in the back where he is.

I walk over to him, my heart beating like a jackhammer the whole time.

"I like your hair," he murmurs in my direction.

It's such a random statement, but I'll take it. I open my mouth to say thanks, but he gives me a hard look effectively silencing me.

His jaw ticks and he goes back to playing his game of darts. "I hate that you used me that night," he says before throwing a dart at the board.

He hits a bullseye.

"I'm sorry."

He pulls the dart out and takes a step back. "I hate that I watched the video."

He throws another dart, bullseye.

"I know what Lou-Lou did, Jackson. I read your text messages after I found my purse that night. I know you were disgusted with yourself for watching it and I *know* you're sorry."

I tuck a piece of hair behind my ear. "I've had a lot of time to think about it…and I never once asked or told you to not watch the video. You didn't do anything wrong."

He shakes his head. "No. I *was* wrong. *I* told you I wouldn't watch it and I did."

"I forgive you."

"You shouldn't," he says gruffly.

We stay silent after that. I decide to sit on top of the pool table and watch him throw more darts, hoping he'll continue talking to me.

"I hate that his hands were on you, touching your body. Touching what I thought was mine," he finally says.

He throws the dart so hard I think the board's going to come off the wall.

"I didn't want his hands on me."

He snorts. "It didn't look like it from where I was standing. And it certainly didn't sound like you didn't want his hands on you when you told him you loved him." I open my mouth to argue, but he cuts me off. "Don't," he warns. "Because I swear to god, if I hear you say his name again…I'll fucking lose it, Alyssa."

I stay silent. I want to shout everything about my relationship with Ford at the top of my lungs, but I don't want him to walk away from me. Especially now that he's *finally* talking to me.

I desperately want him to give me another chance…because this time around, it won't be tarnished by my past or lies. I feel like I can actually let myself fall in love with Jackson. I can love him the way he deserves to be loved.

He throws another dart, and another, and another. Until he's firing them all at the board like a round of bullets. "I hate that I still want you. Especially when I should know better."

My heart drops with those words.

Then he turns around and the look he gives me, makes the entire world stop. I hold my breath but he steals it from me when his lips land on mine.

The kiss is saturated with need, longing and desire. His tongue probes every inch of my mouth, his teeth crash against mine, and his hands touch my body like it's his possession.

My back hits the surface of the pool table and I moan when I feel Jackson move on top of me. I wrap my legs around his waist and grab onto his shoulders. "My apartment's upstairs," I pant.

Jackson doesn't waste another second, he picks me up and we make our way up the staircase.

He slams me against the door to my apartment and his teeth nip at my neck while his hands dig into my ass. "Hope you have another t-shirt," he growls.

I'm about to ask why, but I soon find out when he shreds the material right down the middle and buries himself between my breasts.

"I need these perfect fucking tits in my mouth," he rasps as he yanks down the cups of my bra and pulls my nipple into his mouth. He lavishes it with his tongue, sucking on it like it's his favorite thing in the entire world.

I whimper when he pauses. But then he moves on to my other breast and pays it the same attention. Bolts of pleasure jolt me when he reaches down and pops open the button on my pants.

He's sliding them down when he stops abruptly and bangs on the wall beside my head. "I can't."

"Can't what?" I ask, still in my delirious fog. He puts me down. "I can't do this to you."

I don't understand how one second he's tearing my clothes off and the next he's walking away. He quickly backs up. "I need to leave."

"Why? I thought…I thought that we were—" I pause because I realize that maybe I misconstrued the situation entirely and this wasn't what I hoped it was after all.

"I thought we were trying again," I say.

He gives me the coldest look I've ever seen. "Well, you thought wrong. I'll stay out of your life for good from now on. I promise."

What the hell is going on with him? None of this makes any sense.

He heads for the exit stairs but I stop him. "No. I don't want you out of my life. I want *you*, Jackson. Talk to me, don't run away."

"Yeah, because you know all about that. Don't you?" he scoffs.

I want to punch him for being so callous right now. With the exception of his drunken episode. He's never been this cruel to me without reason. "Yeah I do. So, take it from me when I tell you that it will only make things worse."

He begins walking down the stairs and I'm right behind him. "I know you. Something is—" I start to say before he cuts me off.

"You don't know me, Alyssa. Trust me."

And with those words he walks away.

Chapter Twenty-Six

JACKSON

"You straight?" Ricardo asks.

I look at myself in the mirror. "As a motherfucking arrow."

"Big fight tonight."

"It's always a big fight."

I know he's on edge because we just got word there was a last-minute change regarding my opponent…but unlike Ricardo, I'm not worried.

Ricardo meets my stare. "The guy fights dirty and he's almost three times your size. He's not a boxer or an MMA fighter. He's a pure street fighter, which means he's a wild card. I don't know how much fucked up shit you have stored in that reserve of yours, but as your coach…I need you to tap in and empty it."

His gaze shifts from one of concern to nervousness. "And as your friend, I'm telling you…I need you to give it everything you got. DeLuca's got a lot of money riding on this tonight."

"He always does."

"Not like this, Jackson," he says before he walks away.

I close my eyes and force myself not to think about Alyssa.

I almost faltered, but I wasn't going to make the same mistake twice.

It's been a week since I pushed her away on purpose.

I was harsh, but I don't regret it one bit.

I knew the best way to get her to stay away for good, was to make her believe that for a fraction of a second we had a chance…then dash all her hopes.

My blood burns for her and I want her every second, of every day. But, you have to be cruel to be kind…and there's nothing kinder than saving her from who I really am.

And of course, the devil himself, DeLuca.

On second thought, maybe it's best that I use the fact that I can't have her as my fuel tonight…because there sure as hell is nothing and no one that I want more than *her*.

I open my eyes, suck in a breath and give myself one last look in the mirror.

Then I punch it, watch it shatter and walk out to the cage.

I turn into the machine.

Chapter Twenty-Seven

ALYSSA

"YOU PUTTING MONEY ON ANY OF THE FIGHTERS TONIGHT, LITTLE LADY?" I look up at the big man and hand him my wages for the past week. "Five-hundred on Jackson Reid."

"You mean Jack the Ripper?"

"Yeah."

"Good pick, he doesn't lose. Go on in."

I smirk. "I know."

I gave Jackson a week. A week to come and find me, a week to make it right. A week to talk to me about whatever it is that's going on with him.

His time is up.

I didn't want to go back on my promise to him, but there was no other way I could track him down. He pulled a complete Houdini act, so I'm pulling one of my own. I know he won't be happy when he finds out I came here, but if I have to provoke him just so I can get some type of response from him, well, then so be it.

I'm not giving up on him and I'm not letting him run away from me.

He's seen all my demons…now it's time to see his.

The large room is full and the crowd is already going crazy by the time I make my way in.

I look up at the steel cage and fight back a shiver. It's monstrous, barbaric and to be honest, it intimidates me a little bit. There's something so unsettling about it. I can understand why Momma doesn't like watching the fights.

Out of the corner of my eye, I spot Tyrone in the crowd. I turn away and flip the hood on my jacket up.

I have every intention of Jackson finding out I'm here, but not until *after* the fight. I already know that he looks to Tyrone before he starts and he'll spot me right away if I walk up to him.

Besides, there's always the chance that Tyrone would kick me out because Jackson told him to.

I study Tyrone's profile for a bit and I can immediately tell that something is wrong. He looks unsettled and he's biting his fingernails while looking up to the sky.

I'm a little worried myself after seeing that now. I mean, what could be so different about *this* particular fight than any other fight?

The crowd's cheering picks up and I focus my attention back on the cage. This time, I see Jackson walking out in his green trunks. I take a moment to admire his 8 pack abs, muscular arms, and the rest of his beautifully toned physique.

I also notice his demeanor. He looks *completely* in the zone. His expression is controlled, his posture resembles that of a brick wall, and well, he looks a little frightening.

Actually, make that a lot frightening. It reminds me of the time he fought Dean in the bathroom.

I can barely even hear the announcer right now because all I hear is the crowd chanting, "Ripper! Ripper!" I'd say the crowd is about 90% male…so the female voices are much easier to pick up on.

I grit my teeth when some woman yells, "You're so hot. I want to have your babies." Followed by another woman screaming, "I'll let you do anything you want to me. You can stick it anywhere!"

On second thought, maybe it's best that I take a page out of Jackson's book and tune out the crowd.

They finally announce Jackson's name and I can't help but let out a few cheers of my own. I know he won't be able to hear me over the frantic cheering that's going on right now.

Like the flip of a switch, the general mood around the room shifts just then and I don't know what to make of it.

But then I see someone else walk out on stage.

My jaw drops and my stomach knots up.

There's no way Jackson's about to fight *this* massive beast.

He looks like some kind of a science experiment gone horrifically wrong. His muscles are way too big to be natural, his veins are bulging and his head looks too small for his massive body. This guy is a tank…he probably eats people *my* size for freaking breakfast.

They announce his opponents stats and I'm sure I must be hearing things, but when I take another look…I know I'm not.

How the hell is Jackson going to fight and *win* against a guy who's 6'7 and 388lbs?

Jackson's 6'3 and 235lbs. This is a completely uneven match.

I know this is an underground fight club and all…but this guy could fucking kill him.

No wonder Tyrone looks so nervous.

Ricardo taps Jackson on the shoulder and says something in his ear.

Jackson then looks out to the crowd to find Tyrone. Tyrone doesn't give him his usual happy musings, instead, he taps the spot over his heart.

Jackson's eyes flash as he pats the tattoo over his own heart where Lilly's name resides and I realize that Tyrone's gesture was much more significant than I thought.

I watch as Lou-Lou walks up with her cue cards, wearing the green flashy costume that I myself once wore, and even *she* looks uncomfortable about what's about to go down.

I don't even have the heart to mentally curse her out when she gives Jackson a small smile and a thumbs up sign before stepping down.

The bell dings and Jackson's off to a good start.

I figured he'd start swinging like a bat out of hell, just like in the bathroom…but he's sidestepping and dodging the beasts punches like a pro.

No wonder he almost never gets hit. Despite his muscular build and the fact that he's in the middle of an underground cage fight, he looks so graceful and poised. He's a natural up there, like his body was made to do this.

He looks so comfortable in his habitat it's amazing to be able to watch him.

Then the big brute he's up against grunts and lunges at Jackson out of nowhere. I'm not sure if Jackson even saw it because it happened so fast.

I hold my breath when the guy punches him straight in the kidney.

The crowd lets out a collective big gasp and even some 'Oh, shit's.'

Jackson stands tall and I feel my entire body relax.

Until the big ogre lunges at him again and his fist connects with Jackson's jaw.

Jackson rebounds, though and gets him with a few quick jabs and a sharp kick. The guy stumbles and teeters, appearing seconds away from keeling over.

I channel my inner *Adrian* and before I can stop myself, I shout, "That's right, baby. The bigger they are the harder they fall."

Some guy next to me apparently agrees with my statement and lets out an, "Oh, yeah! Let him have it, Ripper!"

I'm smiling and laughing...until the beast lunges again and takes another swing at him. He connects with Jackson's face again and blood sprays.

Jackson staggers back and the beast uses the opportunity to send a kick to his ribs.

There are murmurings in the crowd then...things like, "He's never been hit more than twice in the cage, this makes four times in a row now." And, "This is the longest a fight has ever lasted while he's in the cage."

I can't help but look at Tyrone. His palms are drawn together and he's silently whispering something to himself.

Then I realize what he's doing. He's praying for him.

My eyes become glassy and I issue a silent prayer of my own. I'm so worked up I have to take off my jacket and bounce on the balls of my feet to get rid of some of this anxiety.

The guy's about to strike again...but Jackson dodges it and this time, he gives him a menacing smile.

I start screaming along with the crowd when Jackson loses his damn mind and starts unleashing punches and kicks so quick, that if I blink I'm sure I'll miss a few.

Everything is perfect...until the big beast rears his ugly head and deals a hard karate chop to Jackson's neck and headbutts him at the same time. The move is so savage and so ruthless the crowd becomes angry and starts calling for the match to be paused.

Especially now that Jackson's body has gone limp.

My. Heart. Stops.

I realize two things at that moment. One—I swear, I'll go toe to toe with this beast myself if he ever lays another hand on him. And two—that I'm completely in love with Jackson.

I'm soon pushing people out of the way and running toward the cage screaming Jackson's name so loud I think my vocal cords have ruptured.

Tears and screams are ripping right out of me...it feels so similar to the moment I lost my father that it only causes me to scream even harder. "Please, No!"

I feel a pair of strong arms haul me back at the same time Jackson gets back up.

His eyes connect with mine and I'm so relieved I'm about ready to declare my eternal love for him in some massive poetic moment.

Then his eyes narrow and he gives me a look that's so deadly, I immediately know I've made a huge mistake by coming here.

Jackson's not just ticked off or pissed that I'm here. He looks like he wants to annihilate *me* and rip me to actual shreds.

I knew he wouldn't like it. I took that gamble...but I never knew he would get *this* mad about it.

"Jackson's fine, Alyssa. He was just pretending to be down since his opponent was playing dirty," Tyrone whispers in my ear.

I look up and watch Jackson proceed to pummel the giant beast into a bloody pulp, that same look he gave me, now turned on him.

Jackson wins the fight in no time and is declared the victor.

When he scans back over the crowd, his eyes fall on me and he gives me the same death stare as before. Only this time he mouths a word that literally causes me to shake. "Run."

Chills creep up my spine and I hightail it the fuck out of there.

I run back to the bar and try to calm myself down. I'm almost positive that Jackson wouldn't actually hurt me...or at least, I *was* before tonight.

Because I need something to distract myself, I offer to close the bar for Shane who happily takes me up on it.

That's when it hits me…I never collected my winnings. *Dammit.*

I'm just going to have to cut my losses, though because I don't even want to know what Jackson would do to me if I went back there right now…or ever for that matter.

After a few hours, I'm calmer than I was and I proceed to close up the bar.

I'm shutting the door when a large black boot lodges itself in the door frame, preventing me from shutting it all the way.

I look up and stifle a scream when I see a large figure standing before me dressed in a black hoodie and jeans. Their hood is pulled up and since it's dark out, I can't make out their face.

They tilt their face slightly and the light from the streetlight catches illuminating their features.

Jackson's normally gray eyes are the darkest I've ever seen them.

He pushes the door open and I immediately start to back away because I can honestly say, he's scaring the shit out of me.

He doesn't say a word to me, he just slams the door shut behind him and starts dead bolting it. Then he grabs my arm and nudges me toward the alarm.

With shaky fingers, I reach up and set it. I briefly contemplate pressing the panic button and informing the alarm company about a break in because I just don't know what he's playing at or what his deal is right now.

He seems to sense my thoughts because he leans down and whispers, "Go ahead. I dare you," in my ear.

I take a few steps back wishing that I hadn't already turned all the lights in the bar off.

I steel myself and lift my chin. His little game has gone on long enough as far as I'm concerned. "Why are you here, Jackson?"

He takes a step forward and I take a step back. His large frame is looming over me and I've never felt smaller in my whole entire life.

He gives me a smile that reminds me of a crazed killer, albeit a very hot one. "Why am *I* here?" he repeats. "Are you saying that I'm not allowed to be here?"

I fold my arms across my chest and glare at him. "I..um. Y-yeah."

Good job Alyssa, your intimidation level is equivalent to that of a puppy.

Jackson rubs his jaw. "Good thing I don't give a fuck then, huh?"

I open my mouth to say something, but he cuts me off by shouting, "Just like *you* didn't give a fuck when you went down to the fight club tonight, and I specifically told you not to *ever* go there."

He takes another step forward. "You promised me that you wouldn't."

"I'm s-sorry," I stutter. "Look, you're really starting to scare me, Jackson."

He smirks, takes another step forward and removes his belt, which both terrifies and excites me. "I thought you liked danger, Alyssa? You sure put yourself in harms way tonight."

I shake my head. "No one attacked me this time."

"This time," he mocks before his expression turns serious. "Do you remember what I told you to do tonight?"

"Well, yeah but you can't actually be serious—" I start to say until the crack of his belt against the wooden table causes me to jump.

"Oh, I'm *very* serious. As serious as *you* were when you walked into that club tonight. You have 30 seconds," he sneers.

I don't know whether to laugh or cry at this point. Where exactly does he expect me to run to? Especially when he dead bolted the doors?

When I still haven't moved, his eyes narrow. "15 seconds. I suggest you do what I told you to now, Alyssa. You're only making it harder on yourself."

Since it would take me twice as long to run up the stairs to my apartment, I take off in the direction of the bathrooms.

I fly through the swinging doors and fight to catch my breath. I debate hiding in one of the stalls, but mere seconds later Jackson enters the bathroom.

I shouldn't feel so turned on over this little cat and mouse game he started but I am.

I'm nervous too because he's never acted like *this* with me before.

He begins walking toward me and I notice that he's stripped off his hoodie. I also see the few bruises on his face from the fight. I instinctively reach up to touch his face, but he bats away my hand and grips my ponytail while backing me into the stall door.

"What are you doing, Jackson?"

He pulls my hair tighter. "Trying to figure out the proper way to punish you so you don't pull this shit again."

"Look, I'm sorry, okay? I've learned my lesson."

He presses me against the stall. "Not okay. You make me a promise you fucking keep it, understand me?"

"I won't show up at the club again. I promise," I say. My vision gets blurry and I want to kick myself for giving into my emotions right now. But I know there's no point in fighting them.

I draw in a shaky breath. "Believe me, there's nothing you could do to me that would ever be worse than thinking you were seriously hurt in that cage. It was the second worst experience of my entire life." I close my eyes. "So go ahead, Jackson. Do *your* worst. I can take it."

His mouth smashes against mine with so much force I'm certain my lips will be bruised, but I don't care. It's the most violent kiss I've ever had and the passion flowing through us both right now is enough to bring me to my knees. I feel myself drop, but one of Jackson's hands latches onto my hip while the other tugs on my ponytail so hard I yelp.

And when I do, he nips my lower lip hard enough that I taste a hint of copper. He groans and sucks my bottom lip into his mouth until I'm lightheaded and fighting for air. Before I know it, he's dragging me until we're stopped in front of the mirrors and he's directly in back of me.

He lifts my shirt up and his fingers trail down my abdomen before he flicks open the button on my jeans.

I'm about to close my eyes, but he shakes his head and whispers, "Watch," deep and low in my ear. His hand moves inside my jeans, brushing over the damp fabric of my panties.

The sight of his large hand inside my pants as he's stroking me is enough to make me blush. It's such an erotic sight and I'm so wound up I feel like a slingshot that's about to launch into outer space. That feeling only grows when he pushes my jeans down lower, along with my panties, leaving me completely exposed to him.

He positions one of his legs between both of mine until I'm pressed flush against his chest and I can feel the strong effect I'm having on him through his jeans.

Embarrassment courses through me when he slips one of his fingers inside me and we both hear just how wet I am. He curses under his breath as he begins slowly moving deep inside me.

I've never been more turned on in my entire life, but I really need him to know something before we take this any further.

"I didn't sleep with Ford that night. I kicked him out of my life and I haven't seen him since. I only want you."

The sting from his other hand slapping my ass causes me to jump.

"Don't ever and I mean, *ever* utter another man's name while my fingers are inside you."

"I'm sorry," I say frantically. "I just wanted you to know that Ford—" I'm cut off by another sharp *whack* across my ass. This time, it sends a jolt of pleasure up my spine.

"What did I say?" Jackson warns, his voice harsh and rough.

He removes his finger before entering me again, this time adding another finger and stroking me even deeper.

"You want me?" he says, his breath tickling my ear. "Well, you fucking have me. But it comes with contingencies, now."

I open my mouth to find out what he means but he leans down and bites my neck. "I've tried going easy on you. I treated you like you were fragile before. I thought that's what you needed. But not this time, Alyssa. I'm not gonna treat you like you're some sad, broken, and damaged damsel…because you're not, are you?"

"No—" I start to say but it's cut off by my moan when he flicks my clit. "Glad we reached an understanding. Now start riding my fingers until you come like a good girl."

His words light me on fire and I reach up and snake my arm around his neck as I begin doing what he told me to.

But then my pleasure crumbles because although I've been working on myself and changing for the better, there's still some things that haven't completely gone away.

That dark and destructive place inside me taunts me and I feel shame wash over me because I know I won't be able to do what Jackson wants. No matter how much I want to, that place inside me associates my own sexual pleasure as something bad.

I stop responding to his touch. "I won't be able to come, Jackson. I'm sorry." Before he can interrupt me, I continue, "I've never been able to before. It's not a line and I'm not saying it to issue you a challenge. I'm just trying to be honest. So, you can stop and I'll take care of you. I *want* to take care of you. I like being able to turn you on, it makes me feel good. I just don't want you to be disappointed with me for not being able to come and I don't want to fake it with you."

To my surprise, Jackson doesn't stop. He continues fingering me, alternating between shallow and deep strokes. He places a gentle kiss on my temple. "You let *me* worry about your pleasure, Alyssa."

I'm about to protest, but his thumb swirls around my clit and I swear, I see stars. "Give it to me," he demands as his finger plunges into my slickness. "Give me every single ounce of pain you have when you go to that place of yours and trust me enough to take it all away and make it better."

"Okay, I'll try," I whisper.

"Do you like the way my fingers feel inside you? The way I'm stroking your pretty pussy?" he asks.

I blush and shiver at his dirty words. "I do," I respond honestly.

He pinches my clit and I moan. "I know you do, baby. You know how I know?" He pushes his erection into my behind. "Because your juices are dripping down my hand, making me harder than a fucking rock right now."

I mewl and begin moving my hips in time with his touch. He circles my clit again before he submerges his fingers inside me. "Let your pussy grip my fingers, baby. Don't fight it. Just breathe and focus on the way I'm touching you and exploring this tight pussy of yours."

"Oh god, Jackson. Your mouth. It's so dirty."

He licks the shell of my ear. "Trust me, you have no idea how dirty my mouth can get. Just you fucking wait. I'll be tasting every part of you."

I gasp and my hips buck against his erection when the first ripple hits me. I almost want to tell him to stop, because it's too much, but then the second wave happens. It causes such an intense rush of absolute pleasure, I'm screaming my own dirty words and jerking against him.

Jackson holds me while I fall apart in his arms, my movements finally coming to a slow stop as I fall into his chest.

I look up as he brings his fingers to his mouth before sucking on them and closing his eyes.

I'm still catching my breath, trying to gather my bearings when Jackson nudges me forward until I'm bent over the sink. "Spread your legs and hold onto the edges of the sink," he tells me.

I do as he says without protest. I'm expecting him to start fucking me, but he doesn't. He gets down on his knees instead.

Seeing as I just came not even moments ago, I'm confused. "What are you doing?"

He pulls my jeans down all the way and lifts my leg. "That first orgasm was for you. This one's for me," he informs me.

Then faster than I can form my next thought, his mouth is covering my pussy. There are no dainty or teasing little licks, he's eating me like I'm a delicacy that he intends to savor every drop of.

"I was wrong," he rasps while lapping at me. I'm about to ask what he means, but then he says, "You taste even better than you smell."

White blinding light hits me when he sucks my clit into his mouth and I can't help but scream out his name. That only makes him ravish me more with his skillful tongue until I know I'm about to start convulsing again.

If I thought my first orgasm was intense, it has nothing on this one. I'm in a whole other world, so far off the beaten path that all I feel is Jackson. He's permeating every sense of mine. I twitch so hard Jackson has to hold my hips so I don't fall and I scream his name like it's the last word I'll ever say in this lifetime.

All my feelings for him flood through me at that moment, I think about how I felt just hours ago when I saw him in that cage. When I thought I might lose him forever. I need him to know how I feel, I need him to know how much he means to me. "I love you, Jackson," I whisper.

He lifts his head, wipes his chin and stands up. The look on his face is like nothing I've ever seen before and I'm not sure what it means.

My heart is beating so hard, I feel like I'm about to faint, but I know I need to do this.

One of the things I will always remember the most about my father was how much he loved me. He gave me the gift of unconditional love for 10 years, and although I lost my way after he died and it got buried with my shame over the sex tape, and my toxic relationship with Ford, I remember now how special it was to know and feel that.

I look him in the eyes this time. "I love you, Jackson," I repeat.

He just stares at me, not saying a word. I didn't expect him to say it back, but some kind of response would be nice.

I put myself in his place and realize that maybe I've just blindsided him with this weighty statement since it did come out of nowhere. I also probably need to be a little bit more specific with how I feel and what I want.

I move toward him. "I want you, Jackson. I want to try again. I know we've both made some mistakes. I know we crashed and burned right after take off the last time around. But, I also know…there's no one in the world that I want more than you. I honestly don't think there ever will be. No one has made me feel the way you make me feel."

His closes his eyes and his thumb brushes over my bottom lip. "Alyssa," he whispers.

I give his thumb a small kiss. "I'll go all in and give you every single part of me. I'll never, ever lie to you again or break a promise…and I swear, I will do my damnedest not to hurt you." My voice begins cracking, but I continue, "I'll fight for you with every single breath I take, Jackson. And if you're too scared to take the risk and roll the dice with me…don't be… because I'll hold your hand for the rest of my life."

His face contorts in pain so I reach for his hand, hoping to prove it to him, but he rips it away. "No," he says, his voice gravelly. "Get over me and find someone else. Someone that's not me. Someone who can give all of that back to you because I can't."

The impact of his words is like pouring battery acid on a wound. It's tearing me apart, burning me and leaving me scarred. I don't know why he's hurting me like this or saying these things, but my heart pulls when I see the emotion on his face.

He heads for the door and I follow him. "Don't chase me, Alyssa," he shouts. "Let me leave…because if I don't leave right now—I'll *never* be able to stop myself from doing the right thing when it comes to you. And I *have* to do that. Please, just let me give you up."

I try to open my mouth, but the tears are lodged in my throat, clogging my voice. I don't understand any of this.

He pauses right before he leaves. "I'm not who you think I am. But for the very *first* time…I *wish* I was." His voice cracks with his last statement and he slams the door.

Chapter Twenty-Eight

JACKSON

I'M RUNNING THROUGH THE CITY STREETS LIKE A MADMAN AND SCREAMING LILLY'S name…wishing everything was different.

I never once regretted killing him.

I never once regretted taking his life…never had a single ounce of remorse for being a murderer.

I never thought I would.

I never had a reason to.

My soul feels like it's split right down the middle.

Half of it belongs to Lilly—I know that even in the afterlife…we're tied together and our bond will never be broken.

The other half of my soul belongs to Alyssa.

The rest of me is stuck in turmoil because I don't know how to process this new feeling and I don't think I can handle what it must mean. Because if it means, what I think it means…I don't think I can live with myself.

I reach my apartment…at least, I think I do. I'm a complete mess. I don't know how I'm functioning or taking in air.

I must be worse off than I thought because when Lou-Lou finds me on the floor in the lobby. She freaks the fuck out, picks up her phone and dials Tyrone. "I don't know, Tyrone. He just keeps screaming for Lilly. Get your ass down here!" she yells into the phone.

Less than a minute later Tyrone's helping me up the steps. He tells me that it's going to be okay. He also mumbles something about him calling Momma and her taking the next flight out here.

I'm too far gone to be embarrassed by being such a wuss at this point.

He sits me down on the couch and pats my back. "Jackson, please talk to me. I know you hate talking. But right now you're really scaring the fucking shit out of me."

I feel some wet shit on my face and I can't stop myself from screaming Lilly's name again.

I keep imagining what it would be like if she was still here now.…*living*. She would be gearing up for graduation, probably valedictorian because she was so fucking smart…and I would be so proud of her. I would tell her how proud of her I was.

I'd sneak into her first courtroom case and cheer for her in the background. I'd probably be fighting the urge to punch the judge if he ever dared to rule against her. But, I'd make her hot chocolate with cinnamon and whipped cream if she lost the case.

I close my eyes…the wet stuff on my face is getting worse, and my thoughts are firing off like a cannon.

Maybe, she'd be an aunt now. I always wanted to have a family. My kids would adore her…I know they would. She would be the best aunt in the entire world.

Lilly would have liked Alyssa. She would have been concerned at first, like the good sister she was; but I know she ultimately would have ended up loving her, just like I do.

The reality slams into me like a blazing wildfire.

I'll never have any of that now. And neither will she.

There's no graduation, no first courtroom case, no hot chocolate, no family, and no Alyssa.

Because Lilly's tiny body is dead on the floor beside the couch. Her pink nails have blood caked under them…because she fought like hell. Just like her big brother would have wanted her to.

But she lost her fight. Because I didn't protect her like a big brother should.

But I got vengeance for her.

I murdered that son-of-a-bitch for killing my baby sister.

So, how could I have a moment of regret?

I wipe the tears off my face and look at Tyrone. "If I love Alyssa…it will mean that I love Lilly less. It will mean that I accept Lilly's death and that in the end, I'm okay with what happened to her because I had a moment of regret for murdering Mike when Alyssa told me she loved me."

He looks confused but I continue, "So you see, I can't love Alyssa because I can't *not* love Lilly. If I love Alyssa, then I have to regret both loving Lilly in the first place because I have to be fine with her death and regret killing him."

Tyrone shakes his head. "I'm not following you. Did you tell Alyssa the truth about everything?"

I lean forward and put my head in my hands. "No. But let's just say that I'm certain she'll want nothing to do with me if she ever finds out."

He scowls. "You don't know that, Jackson. There are extenuating circumstances and you know it. Again, I think you're not giving her the benefit of the doubt here and just assuming—"

"Her father was murdered. I can't go into any more detail about it because it's not my place, but her father was murdered when she was a kid. Let's just say that she has a very set in stone outlook when it comes to murder in general. Trust me."

He stands up and runs a hand along his jaw. "It's not always black and white or cut and dry." I open my mouth to tell him that for *her* it is, but he cuts me off. "And I think that if you told her, not only would she see that…but you would as well." He holds up a finger. "However, we have a few more things to work out before we come back to that. Starting with you and your feelings. First, I do think you need to accept Lilly's death. It doesn't mean that you loved her any less and it sure as heck doesn't make you a bad brother for accepting it. It simply means that you are aware that her death happened, that you processed it." He sighs. "And you need to process it, Jackson…because she's *not* coming back. No matter how many people you beat up in that cage or how much you blame yourself—it will never bring her back. Her life is over…but yours doesn't have to be. She wouldn't want that…she would want you to go on living. You know I'm right, brother."

I nod my head softly and he continues, "Which brings me to Alyssa. Now, you said before that you can't love her because you felt this moment of regret about killing him."

"Yeah. I've never had that feeling before. I don't know how to explain it. But, I know I don't regret getting vengeance for Lilly. So I don't understand how I had this moment of regret because—" I pause because my heads going around in circles right now and I don't know how to sort out my thoughts.

Tyrone looks at me. "It's because Alyssa loves you…*but* you don't think that she can because, in *your* eyes, she doesn't know who you really are. And because you love *her* and you hate the thought of losing her you wish that you were different. You wish that you were who she thinks you are…correct?"

I think about this for a moment before replying, "Yeah, sounds about right."

He smiles. "Well, you're wrong."

Now I'm completely confused. "But you just said—"

He cuts me off. "I said that in *your* eyes she doesn't know who you really are."

"I don't know where you're going with this, Tyrone."

"You don't have regret about killing Mike and getting vengeance. You regret who you *think* you are. Your own self-identity is tied to being a murderer and all that it entails."

He looks me in the eyes. "You're a good person, Jackson. You're the most loyal person I've ever met. You will fight to the end of this earth and back again for those you love. There's not a thing you won't do for us. Momma's right when she says that you have an incredible heart that's incomparable to others because you lead with it. Your heart is who you are and it's one hell of a good heart. And you know what that means? It means that Alyssa already knows who you are on the inside. You shouldn't wish to be anyone else because it's your heart and you who she loves."

"But I'm a murderer."

"And that brings me to the next point we need to sort out in that head of yours. Remember what I said about it not always being so black and white or cut and dry?"

I nod my head again.

He takes a deep breath. "Would you call a soldier a bad person? Would you think of them as a murderer or a killer?"

"Absolutely not. They're heroes who are defending and protecting others."

He nods. "You're right. They are and they do."

"You've lost me again, Tyrone. Because if you're insinuating that I'm some sort of hero… you're wrong. Heroes *save* people. So, what is it that you're saying?"

"What I'm saying is that it's not always mutually exclusive. There are exceptions to every good thing and every bad thing. Think about it…if a person donates a shit-load of money to a charity, we automatically assume that it makes them a good person." He pauses. "But, if you find out that they only donated to the charity to claim it on their taxes and not from the goodness of their heart. That changes your perception about them a little, huh?"

"Yeah."

"Now, what if a person murders someone? We automatically assume that it makes them a bad person. But, what if you found out that this killer had walked in to find their little sister whom he loved more than life itself brutally murdered?" He draws in a breath. "And in the *very* same moment, his best friend whom he *trusted*, walked out and admitted to killing his baby sister. Which in turn, caused him to black out in a rage that ended in murder. Wouldn't that change your perception about this killer?"

"Yeah."

He gives me a hug. "Let Alyssa decide for herself what her perception of you is. Let her show you that she knows exactly who it is she's giving her heart to. Have some faith and trust in the girl."

I hug him back. "Thanks, Tyrone. I really don't know how I would have figured that all out by myself. I owe you."

"So, you're going to tell her?"

"No. I'm gonna do more than that."

He raises an eyebrow. "How?"

"You still have that camcorder?"

His stares at me wide-eyed. "You sure about this, man? I mean, there's putting your trust in someone and then there's putting your *trust* in someone. She could do anything with that confession, Jackson. In the wrong hands, you could end up right back in jail. And if that happens, dropping the soap will be the least of your worries, brother. DeLuca will have you killed in jail for outing him about staging the cover up."

"You said to have some faith and trust in her, right?"

An hour later I find myself making my way to Alyssa's apartment.

I'm choosing to tell her about what happened on video because, in some way, I'm trying to show her just how much I love her.

I know that the sex tape ruined her life. It left her vulnerable, naked, exposed and judged for the whole entire world to see.

Although this is a different circumstance entirely, this video very much leaves me vulnerable, naked, exposed and open to her judgment.

There's no way to match her love and give her every part of me if she doesn't know my past and what I've done.

Alyssa's video never changed my opinion about her. It only made me fall for her more.

I guess in some way, I'm hoping that she feels the same about me after she watches mine.

I knock on her door with an eerie feeling in the pit of my stomach. On one hand, I'm more nervous than I've ever been in my life. On the other hand, it feels like a giant weight is being lifted off my shoulders.

She opens the door after the second knock and looks up at me.

I shove the disk in her hand. "I need you to watch this. It's everything important you need to know about me."

She opens her mouth to say something, but I guess the look I give her stops her. Instead, she gives me a small nod before closing the door.

I hear her rummaging around briefly on the other side of the door.

Then I hear the words that will change everything.

"My name is Jackson Reid. There are two things you need to know about me. The first—is that I'm in love with Alyssa Tanner. The second—is that I'm a murderer."

With my heart completely in her hands, I walk away.

Chapter Twenty-Nine

ALYSSA

"Now you know, Alyssa. That's my story. He killed Lilly and I don't regret avenging her death. But I do regret not telling you sooner."

I watch as Jackson moves closer to the screen before pausing. "And just in case I never get the chance to say it again. I love you," he says before the camera shuts off.

I wipe my eyes and stand up.

Then I run.

Only this time...I'm not running from anything.

I running toward something.

I'm running as fast as I can to the man I love.

The man that I *still* love. Maybe even more now.

It's almost 4 in the morning and the rain is falling hard outside, It's coming down in buckets, causing me to almost slip on the concrete a few times, but I don't care.

By the time I reach Jackson's apartment, I'm a shivering wet mess. I'm also pretty sure my lips are blue and I'm going to catch pneumonia, but I still don't care.

Tyrone opens the door and I expect him to be surprised that I'm here but he's not. He just gives me a knowing smile and tells me that Jackson is in his room.

He then offers me a blanket but I decline. Instead, I ask him if he would mind if I rummaged around the kitchen for a bit.

He smiles even wider...until I inform him I'm not cooking him anything.

I don't even knock on Jackson's door, I just walk right in.

He's sitting up against the headboard of his bed, he's shirtless, his eyes are closed and the acoustic version of *Shinedown's, Simple Man* is playing on repeat in the background.

I clear my throat and he startles. When he sees me his eyes flicker and his breathing picks up.

He takes in my appearance and opens his mouth to say something, but I put my finger to my lips and hand him what's in my hand.

He looks down at the cup of hot chocolate containing both cinnamon and whipped cream and his breathing becomes shaky.

His eyes are glassy when he looks back up at me and his hand reaches out for mine.

I take his hand and position myself on top him with both my legs on either side of his. I wrap my arms around him tighter than I ever have and my head falls against his chest. Then I plant a kiss over Lilly's name.

We stay like that for a while, neither of us saying a word, which is fine because this moment is too profound to ruin it with words.

He's rubbing slow circles over my back and it feels amazing, but I have to fight off another chill due to my drenched clothes.

Jackson notices this and hauls me upright so that I'm facing him. He motions for me to raise my arms and I do. He starts lifting my shirt, and since I ran out of my apartment wearing nothing but pajamas I'm not wearing a bra. He quickly balls my wet shirt in his hand and throws it across the room causing it to land with a wet thud.

I feel the flush in my cheeks due to being topless in front of him, but it quickly turns to arousal when Jackson leans down and flicks his tongue over my nipple. He does the same to my other nipple and I feel the warmth that he's providing me spread throughout my body.

He lets out a low groan as he begins massaging and kneading my breasts and I can't help myself from sighing his name.

Not before long, my pants are joining my t-shirt on the floor and I'm completely naked before him.

His eyes blaze as he scans over my body and pulls me back to him.

I straddle him and his hands dig into my lower back as he plants gentle kisses along my chest leading up to my neck and finally my lips.

I feel his erection through the flannel of his pants and I grind against it shamelessly, wanting more than anything to feel him inside me.

He runs his fingertips along my hips and blows his breath across my nipples, the sensations causing goosebumps to break out over my skin.

His mouth finds the pulse point on my neck and he drags his tongue along it as his finger dips inside me. The sound of his fingers plunging into my wetness fill the room, but I'm too turned on to feel self-conscious at this point.

I'm on the verge of having an orgasm when Jackson pauses and pulls his pants down. He holds the base of his erection and slips his length between my folds, but doesn't enter me. I look down and lick my lips when I see that my slickness is coating his cock, making it glisten.

He gives me a smirk before he circles the barbell of his piercing directly over my clit causing me to come harder and faster than I ever knew was possible.

He peppers my neck with kisses as the last of my climax trickles out of me and onto him. I'm desperate to have him inside me at this point and I know he feels the same because he reaches into the nightstand drawer and gets out a condom.

He looks at the condom then back to me and I nod my head, letting him know that I want this.

I'm waiting for him to put it on, but instead, he cradles my face in his hands and gives me a look that steals my breath. His eyes penetrate me and I can feel how much he loves me with a single glance.

He puts the condom on and pulls me in for another long and sultry kiss. I think he's going to enter me and start fucking me, but he doesn't.

Instead, he grips my hips and gently lifts me before slowly setting me down on top of his erection. I feel him enter me inch by inch gradually—purposely taking his time to make sure I'm not in any discomfort.

Once he's filled me up to the hilt, I begin bouncing on top of him rapidly, wanting to make it good for him. He groans my name and curses under his breath. Then his hands press down on my thighs causing me to pause my movements while he pulls me in for another slow kiss.

In a single movement, he flips us so that he's the one on top before he begins thrusting inside me. His thrusts are both deep and gentle rendering me breathless. He looks at me as he reaches down and links our fingers together before bringing them above my head.

This concept of going slow and sweet is so new and foreign to me. I'm far from a virgin, but I've never had sex like *this* before. I've never had anyone take their time and worship me or my body. It makes me feel loved and cherished in a way I never knew was possible.

Jackson brushes the tear from my cheek and leans his forehead against mine. "I love you," he whispers. I tell him that I love him too and it's such a tender moment between us, I know I'll never forget it.

I always thought that when Jackson and I had sex it would be a frantic frenzy filled with lust, with him racing to the finish line. I never knew that it would be this passionate and powerful or that it would somehow intensify the connection between us.

Our guards are down and our insides have been stripped, leaving us bare in so many ways. There's something so beautiful and raw about what's happening right now.

My legs start to shake and an all-consuming climax begins to take over my body, heightened by the emotions flowing through me. Jackson stares down at me, watching me with hooded eyes.

His face is strained and I know he's trying to hold off, but I want him to let go at the same time I do. I untangle my hands from his, skim over his broad back and grab hold of his ass while my walls clench around him and I sigh his name. I watch as the muscles in his forearms flex and his mouth parts open before he whispers my name and his release swiftly follows mine.

Chapter Thirty

JACKSON

I PROP MYSELF UP ON ONE ELBOW AND WATCH AS SHE YAWNS AND STRETCHES WHILE sprawled out on my bed.

Her eyes are still closed and she mewls my name in her sleep, which only encourages the morning wood I'm sporting.

Her hair is a perfect combination of bed head and just been fucked hair. I lean in and get a whiff of that coconut scent that I love so much.

She stretches again, only this time the sheet falls and her breasts are fully exposed to me. Her pretty pink nipples are just begging to be sucked on.

A man can only be strong for so long. I don't know where to start first because I want to taste every part of her body. Since her breasts are mere centimeters from my face, I decide I'm gonna start there and work my way down.

I move forward and give her right nipple a little lick and wait for her response. And what a response it is, she moans and arches her back, shoving her breasts into my face.

I suck one nipple into my mouth while kneading the other one with my hand. Her eyes are still closed, but I notice the coy smile on her face. This little minx has been awake the entire time, purposely teasing me with these pretty titties of hers.

In one fell swoop, I dive under the sheet and spread her thighs apart. I loved making love to her last night and baring my entire soul to her…it was the single best moment of my entire life.

But right now? Right now her sex is wet for me and I need to issue my own brand of teasing.

When I look up, I notice her eyes are still closed and she's *still* trying to feign sleep and innocence, even though the little coy smile hasn't left her perfect face. Part of me thinks it's adorable, but the other part of me wants to spank that luscious ass of hers for putting on an act in front of me.

I lift the sheet off her body and throw it on the floor. I position myself between her thighs again and kiss her navel before lavishing it with my tongue. Her hips push up but I grab onto those hipbones of hers that make me lose my mind. "You move and I'll stop," I inform her. "You wanted to be cute and pretend to be sleeping while you teased me with this gorgeous body of yours…didn't you?"

She nods and I bite the inside of her thigh. "I said don't move."

She immediately goes still and I hear a whimper escape. The sound goes right to my cock and I have to suck in a breath.

I inhale the scent of her arousal combined with coconut and I barely suppress my growl. I work my way down her body all while whispering how beautiful she is.

I might be taking the control and teaching her a lesson, but I don't want her to get the wrong idea and think that I'm any less appreciative of her beauty and the gift of her body that she's trusting me with.

I'm very appreciative. I know I'm a lucky man. I've got what most men can only hope and wish to find in their lifetime. I've got a beautiful woman who loves me unconditionally, despite my past. And I'll spend the rest of my life matching that 10 fold.

I draw little circles on the inside of her thighs with my tongue that has her gasping. I see her hands clench at her sides and I bite the inside of her thigh again in warning.

She blows out a breath and I know she's becoming frustrated

I move my head down until I'm directly in front of her pussy. It's pink and smooth, except for the thinnest and tiniest of landing strips, giving away that she is in fact, a natural blonde. I rub my nose against it, inhale sharply, and savor it for a moment. Then I slide up her slit, finishing my slow graze with a flick of my tongue against her clit.

She whimpers again but doesn't move. *Good girl.*

I decide to reward her for being so compliant. If I'm being honest, I'm really rewarding myself because there's nothing like diving face first into her heat.

I eat her and suck her folds into my mouth like they're made out of goddamn candy and I'm the gingerbread man.

That's when she ruins her streak, pivots her pussy into my face and grabs hold of my hair. I let myself enjoy it for a moment because, well—it's fucking awesome.

Then before she knows what hits her, I wrap my arm around her waist, flip her over and prop her up on her knees. Her ass is sticking straight up in the air and I can't help but admire it. More than admire it, I want to build a shrine for that ass of hers and pray to it every day.

I run my finger down the seam of her ass and she jerks up in surprise. I couldn't give a fuck less about her not moving at this point, my desires are now focused elsewhere.

I repeat the gesture and her body tightens. "You've never had anyone play with your ass before…have you, baby?"

She shakes her head and I can't help but thank my lucky stars for being the lucky bastard that's going to bring her pleasure to new heights.

But, I'm not an idiot. I know that this is something that she needs to work up to slowly. Anyone who tells you that first-time anal sex is a 'wham bam thank you ma'am' with no prep—is a fucking moron who has no business participating in the act.

I kiss one of her ass cheeks and slip a finger inside her pussy.

Her back bows and she sighs my name. "At some point," I whisper. "You're going to let me have your ass."

Her entire body goes rigid, so I rub one hand down her back in a calming motion. "But not until you're ready to give it to me."

She visibly relaxes and I plant a kiss on her other cheek. "Do you trust me?"

"You know I do, Jackson," she whispers. My heart swells at the statement.

I slowly slip the finger that's wet with her arousal into her ass. She blows out a shaky breath and goes stiff. "I'm not going to hurt you, baby," I reassure her.

Making sure not to push my way in, I make small circles around the tight bud. With my other hand, I sink a finger back into her pussy and begin playing with her clit.

After a moment, she's calm again and moaning my name. Then she starts bearing down on my finger. I'm not sure if she realizes what she's doing, but it sends my own arousal into overdrive.

"You want me to stick it further in your ass, baby?"

"Yeah. It feels—" She pauses, and I wish I could see her face right now because I know she's blushing.

"It feels what, Alyssa? Tell me, I want to hear you say it."

She pushes down on my finger until it's fully inside her. "It feels good when you play with my ass and my pussy at the same time."

My dick twitches at those words, and I have to remind myself not to pounce because as much as I want to, I'm not taking her ass right now.

She straightens her spine and sits upright. Then she does something that almost makes me come right on the spot.

She partially sits on my lap and begins riding the finger I have in her ass. I move my other hand around to her front so I can trace her clit at the same time. "I need you inside me," she pants. "I want you to fuck me at the same time you're doing this to me."

I'm so turned on with her statement and the fact that she's embracing her own sexual pleasure like this. I eagerly comply and begin to enter her, letting out a groan when I'm all the way in.

"Oh my god," she screams. "It feels even better than I thought it would."

Hell yeah, it does. There's no way I'm going to be able to hold off if she keeps riding my cock like this. I'm going to have to speed things along in order to make sure she gets off before I do. I look down at where our bodies are joined and I quickly realize why it feels exceptionally good.

I'm not wearing a fucking condom. I bring both her and my movements to a rapid halt and slip out. "I have to put a condom on. I'm sorry, I should have been more careful."

She doesn't freak like I assumed she would. Instead, she says the words that every straight man loves to hear when he finds himself in this predicament. "I'm on birth control. I've also been tested and I'm clean—"

She doesn't even get to finish that sentence because I thrust into her. Since one of the membership requirements of the bdsm club—that I won't ever be going back to, was getting tested semi-annually, I know I'm clean as well.

I hold onto to both her breasts while she bounces up and down on my dick. The friction between us is better than any I've ever felt before. "Oh my fucking god, Jackson," she screams so loud I know Tyrone's going to hear, but so be it. Lord knows, I've heard him in the act more times than I can count.

I switch positions then so that I'm thrusting into her doggie style, circling her other hole with my finger, and watching her ass jiggle with my every move. Alyssa's loud moans along with the sound of my balls slapping against her fill the room and it only enhances the act.

A moment later, I get ready for my favorite part. Alyssa's orgasm.

I've never witnessed someone orgasm the way she does. It's truly an experience to watch and if I'm being honest, I really revel in the fact that *I'm* the only one who gets to see her come apart like this. She orgasms with her entire body. She jerks, she pants, her breasts push up into the air, she curses like a sailor, her legs shake, her little toes curl, and her pussy grabs me tighter than a damn vise.

She's on the first wave of her climax, sputtering curses into the air, when she hits her second wave and starts milking my cock, sucking every ounce of come from my balls. It feels so fucking good I begin roaring obscenities over her loud screams until I fall on top of her in a sweaty heap.

I feel her twitch underneath me slightly but I'm too distracted by the sight of my come leaking out of her.

"Momma," she screeches.

"Momma?" I question with a smirk. "You mean like, Whoa, Momma that sure was some amazing sex we just had?"

She leaps up from the bed and her cheeks flush. "I meant *Momma*, Jackson! As in Momma just walked in, did the sign of the cross while saying the Lord's name, covered her eyes, and walked right back out!" she screams.

Oh, *that* Momma. Well, shit.

I forgot that Tyrone had mentioned something about Momma flying out here. If I thought Momma had bad timing the *last* time Alyssa spent the night, it has nothing on *this* time.

I try hard not to laugh at the way Alyssa's freaking out right now. Momma's caught her *own* son in the act quite a few times, I doubt she'll even make a big deal about it. "It's okay," I assure her.

"Easy for *you* to say. Despite who gave birth to you, that woman *is* your mother. And the last memory that woman has of me is watching me strip down for a sex tape. Not to mention, whatever you told her about me when we broke up. This is *so* not okay. This is mortifying."

Guess I didn't think of it like that.

I walk over to where she is and hold her in my arms. "I love you, Alyssa. I will never let anyone talk bad about you. Please, don't feel ashamed or embarrassed. Everything will be fine."

I walk to my closet and throw on a pair of shorts. I hand her a t-shirt and a pair of my sweatpants. "You'll have to roll them up until they fit, but it's the best I can do right now."

She still looks nervous so I pull her into another hug. "It's okay, baby."

She gives me a small smile and I tilt her chin up. "That's my girl."

The corners of her lips twitch. "It was some amazing sex by the way."

I give her a wink. "Oh, I know ."

She begins changing and I head for the door. "I'm gonna go out there first," I say. "But seriously, don't worry. Momma's not judging you. She's the sweetest, least judgmental person I know."

The swipe of the newspaper against my arm almost causes me to laugh. "Jackson Mathew Reid," Momma screams. "You think this is funny, boy?"

This is the first time Momma's ever middle-named me. Heck, I didn't even think she knew what my middle name was.

I ignore the howling of laughter coming from both Tyrone and Ricardo seated at the kitchen counter.

She swipes me again with the paper. "I'm fixin' to lay a real hurtin' on you. I trucked all the way to New York because I thought you were going through a hard time and needed your Momma. Then I come to find you screwing some hussy. *You're* supposed to be the good one!"

"Alyssa's not a hussy," I growl.

She stops mid swipe. "Alyssa? Well, of course, Alyssa ain't no hussy. I'm talkin' bout that two—bit—"

I almost laugh again when I realize. "Momma, that *was* Alyssa. She just has dark hair now."

She puts the newspaper down. "Well, I see. Glad to hear you worked things out with that girl. Bout' time. Now give me a hug."

I pull Momma in for a big hug and Tyrone wiggles his eyebrows at me. "From the sounds that were coming through that bedroom of yours all night *and* this morning. I'd say you two *definitely* worked things out with each other."

I open my mouth to tell him to knock it off, but Alyssa walks out, takes Momma's newspaper and swipes him across the head with it.

Momma claps her hands. "I knew I liked this girl." She lets go of me and pulls Alyssa into a hug. "How you doin', sugar? I like the hair."

Alyssa chuckles. "I'm fine, Momma. Need any help making breakfast?"

She waves a hand and motions for us to sit down. She scans the room and her eyes land on Ricardo. "I reckon I'm gonna be one plate short?"

He gives her a soft nod and she wipes her hands on her apron. "Hmm."

"Hmm?" Ricardo says. "What's hmm?"

"Well, I never thought I'd say this because that Lou-Lou girl really dills my pickle, especially after she pulled that stunt. But maybe you ought to suck it up and talk to her. That sparkle in your eyes is dimmer, Ricardo. That girl had some kinda effect on you whether you're willing to admit it or not."

Tyrone grins. "That's what I've been telling him, Momma."

I take the stack of pancakes from Alyssa. "You know, I have to say. I'm on their side of the fence now. Running into Alyssa again was the best thing that could have happened. Even if I did screw it up by getting drunk at her workplace and saying some really messed up stuff. It led me back to her. Lou-Lou's right across the hall, you guys have been ignoring one another for months now."

To my surprise, Alyssa nods. "It's true. Don't get me wrong, I was pissed at what Jackson did that night. But, I wanted nothing more than to talk to him and work out our issues. I'm sure she feels the same about you. I don't like Lou-Lou…for obvious reasons. But it's obvious that you both have something—" She pauses and makes a face. "Well, you have *something* together. And if she makes you happy that's all that really matters."

Ricardo rolls his eyes, clearly hating that the focus is on his and Lou-Lou's former relationship. Then he looks at me and gives me a wink. Now I know he's going to somehow use me to deflect the attention off of him. "Hey, Jackson. Did you tell Momma how you basically said that Alyssa was nothing but a good time at the bar that night?"

Asshole.

Momma gasps and reaches for the newspaper again.

"He was drunk, Momma. He didn't mean it," Alyssa says, rushing to my defense. I reach for her hand and give it a kiss.

Momma puts the newspaper down and picks up the spatula. Then she turns her gaze on Alyssa. "You work at a bar, young lady?"

Shit, I was hoping Momma wouldn't pick up on that. Fucking Ricardo.

Alyssa crinkles her nose. I squeeze her hand as a signal to deny everything, but she doesn't take the hint. "Well, yeah. I mean, it's nothing crazy or anything. It's low-key and—"

Momma cuts her off. "Do you really think that's safe? You're a pretty young thing…who knows what could happen to you." She points the spatula at me. "I can't believe you're *okay* with this, Jackson."

Alyssa waves a hand. "It's fine, Momma. Trust me, my friend Shane who owns the bar is usually there with me and he would never let anything happen to me. And it's perfectly safe, there is an alarm system and everything. I always make sure to put it on right after I close up and head upstairs to my apartment."

This isn't good.

Momma puts her hand over her heart and takes a step back dramatically. "You *live* at this….this *bar*? What if one of the customers follows you up to this *apartment*? Or even worse hides up there and attacks you? Or attacks you when you're closing one night and this Shane character isn't around?" She shakes her head. "No. This just won't do."

I've never thought about it like that before, but seeing as I pretty much did that to her not even 24 hrs ago…Shit, Momma has a point.

Alyssa opens her mouth to answer, but Momma looks at me. "How can you let this happen?"

I open my mouth to defend myself…but I've got nothing. What Momma's saying makes complete sense.

I look over at Ricardo and he's happily eating his breakfast and humming to himself. I fight the urge to throw my biscuit at his head.

I look at Tyrone and he shrugs.

"Momma," Alyssa starts. "I like it there and even more, I can *afford* the rent there. New York is a ridiculously expensive place to live. What Shane charges me for rent is a steal."

She points the spatula at her. "Until someone steals you away in the middle of the night and you end up on the news."

The thought of that happening makes my stomach knot up.

Alyssa stands up. "You should come there tonight and see it for yourself. It's a safe place. Come and have a few drinks on me and enjoy yourself."

Tyrone snorts. "Momma ain't going to no bar, Alyssa. She can't hang like that."

Momma folds her arms across her chest and glares at him. "I can most certainly *hang* like that. And seeing as I'm here for the next two weeks…it wouldn't hurt to appease Alyssa and see this *bar*." Tyrone chokes on his food, but Momma turns her ebony eyes on me again. "I'll see this bar, but I reckon a few changes will be happening by the time I hop back on that plane."

I give her a subtle nod and finish the rest of my breakfast while answering her questions about the fight and the two bruises on my face.

I stand outside and watch Alyssa through the glass window of the bar. Everyone, including Momma, is there waiting for me to arrive, but I'm enjoying just watching her for a few moments.

After Breakfast, I walked Alyssa home and I went to the gym. After our workout, I told the guys to head to the bar first and said I'd catch up in a little while.

I needed the time to think.

I have no idea how to go about the situation regarding Alyssa and her apartment at the bar.

I would ask her to move in, but that would only make it that much easier for her to find out about DeLuca.

And I don't care how much of an asshole it makes me, there's *no* way I'm telling her about him. Her not knowing will keep her safe.

She's got a bit of a wild streak at times and I don't know how she'll take finding out about everything. But one thing is certain, if she does anything to DeLuca…he will have *no* problem retaliating by having her killed or doing it himself.

I just can't take that chance.

The only reason I'm not more freaked out about her showing up at the club last night is because of her new hair color. I'm hoping that DeLuca won't realize it was her…even though I know it was a big fight for him and he's checking out the footage.

Ironically enough, it was seeing Alyssa there that helped me win that fight in the first place.

My opponent was the toughest one I ever faced at the club. There was a couple of times I thought I was going to lose.

Luckily, I looked out in the crowd and saw Tyrone doing the praying possum. As silly as it sounds, I knew that was his way of giving me advice. When he was a kid and got bullied on the playground by some racist pricks, he used to drop and 'play dead' in the middle of a fight, just like possum's do. It threw the bully off for a moment and Tyrone would use the opportunity to sprout back up and defend himself.

I saw the karate chop at the very last second and tucked my chin. His hand slipped and I swear, he just missed my carotid artery. However, the headbutt that he dealt got me bad. Bad enough where I did go down and I wasn't sure I was going to make it back up again.

I was temporarily knocked out, but I heard Alyssa's guttural cries and I thought someone was hurting her. With strength I didn't even know I possessed, I managed to get back up. I was relieved to see that she was okay, but I was beyond pissed that she was at the fight club. I used that rage as fuel to win the fight. Without her, I don't know if that would have happened.

Just like I don't know what will happen or how to go about her apartment situation.

I could ask her to move in, I'm sure Tyrone would be fine with it…but then I'd have to tell her about DeLuca…and *she* most definitely won't be fine with it.

I could always lease her an apartment. I'm not a millionaire or anything but I do have a decent chunk of change saved up from fighting the past few years. I could put it toward that…but something tells me Alyssa won't go for that.

Not to mention, that somewhere down the road; I figure in the next few years or so… she *will* want to take the next step and move in together. She'll also want to get married and have kids.

I want the same things, but I still have another 6 years and change left in my contract with DeLuca. And that's *only* if I continue to win at least, 99% of my fights, which in and of itself is a whole new set of problems.

The problem isn't that I'll be 33 by the time I'm done. That's still young enough to enjoy the rest my life without feeling like I'll be missing out on anything like having kids and starting a family.

The problem is, and every great fighter and athlete know this…you just can't stay on top forever. You hit your prime and only go down from there. Right now I'm 27…but I'd be an idiot to think there won't be someone younger, tougher and stronger for me to compete against in the next 6 years. Someone who could end up taking me down.

I know that's why DeLuca makes the stipulations that he does and makes the contract for as long as he does. It really *is* making a deal with the devil.

I rub my temples and try to focus my thoughts back on the here and now. I watch through the glass as Alyssa hands Momma a shot and Ricardo and Tyrone start doing a countdown.

I laugh when she tilts her head back and makes a face like it's horrible. Tyrone hugs her and yells, "Roll Tide!" while everyone in the bar cheers.

Alyssa is smiling from ear to ear and I swear, she's absolutely radiant. Her dimple is out and her eyes are gleaming. You wouldn't even know that she barely slept the night before.

"She's beautiful…isn't she?" some deep voice says. I turn around to face the man who's not only interrupting my thoughts but is checking out my girlfriend.

He's about an inch or two shorter than me, he looks about maybe 15 years older than me; and he's wearing a gray suit that looks vaguely familiar.

He looks to be a professional of some sort, so it's kind of odd to see him hanging around some hole in the wall bar.

For once, I decide to remain calm. Of course, I want to punch the guy…but the reality is that he's only admiring how beautiful Alyssa is. As much as I hate it, she's going to catch the eye of other men. I can't go around beating up most of the male population.

"She's gorgeous," I tell him. I silently add *'and all mine'* to the statement. He stands next to me and watches her through the glass. He's got about another 10 seconds to get his fill before I take back my previous thoughts about not punching him.

My hand's ball at my sides when I see that his eyes still haven't moved off of her. Then he says something that makes my insides twist. "You know, I preferred her as a blonde. She looked more innocent that way. But there's something to be said about the darker hair. It really brings out those eyes of hers. I think I like it."

I snarl and shove him against the glass. He gives me a smirk and flips the inside of his suit jacket open, revealing a badge. "Careful, Jackson. You don't want to go to jail for assaulting an officer." The corners of his eyes crinkle. "Not that it would be your first time in a jail cell… now would it?"

I look at the badge and struggle not to lose my shit. *Ford.* Special Agent Ford fucking Baker to be exact…what the fuck kind of name is that, anyway?

I grit my teeth because it's the name belonging to the man who had his hands all over my girl that night. The man who's *fucked* my girl before. The man my girl said she loved.

To hell with it. I'm taking my chances and punching the bastard. One solid punch, that's all I need to feel better.

He seems to sense my thoughts because he holds up his hands and says, "DeLuca wouldn't like it if you ended up in jail. You know that as well as I do, son."

I grab a hold of the hood to my sweatshirt so I have someplace to put my hands for the time being…because being wrapped around his neck…is looking real fucking good right about now. I decide to hit him with a low-blow of my own. "Son," I snort. "*I'm* only 3 years older than her. So tell me, did you call Alyssa your *daughter* when you fucked her, you fucking pervert?"

His nostrils flare before he says, "No, I was too busy calling her a whore instead."

That's. Fucking. It.

I lunge at him and my hands tighten around his throat. I don't give a fuck about DeLuca right now, I'm *never* going to stand by and let some piece of shit call my girl a whore.

He makes a choking sound, and his beady blue eyes begin popping out of his head.

Then it occurs to me. Alyssa might be able to understand and accept the first murder I committed…but I'm not so sure she'll forgive me for this one.

Begrudgingly, I let go of his throat. He collapses on the pavement and gasps for air.

"Fucking asshole," he croaks. "I came here to offer you a deal."

I bend down and laugh hard in his face. "A deal?" I laugh again. "Fuck your deal and fuck you. There's nothing you could offer me that I would want." I gesture toward the window and give him a cocky smile. "Or that I don't already have."

He stands up straight and makes a face. Looks like I'm not the only one trying to restrain myself now. And boy do I want the fucker to hit me. I want him to hit me so I can wipe the fucking pavement with him.

He fixes his tie and looks through the window again. "What about a life with Alyssa," he whispers.

"Already have that," I reply.

I fight the urge to tell him certain details about our life together—like how I was the first one to ever make her come, or how great her ass looked when I took her from behind this morning after licking her sweet pussy. And most important of all; the way her face lights up when she tell me that she loves *me*.

He clears his throat and faces me. "I think you know what I mean."

"Nope."

"Then you've taken one too many hits to the fucking head," he growls. "Do you think you can actually provide a life for her? The kind of life that she deserves?"

I'm not going to let him know how much that comment gets to me so instead I reply, "I can give Alyssa anything that she wants. And if I can't—I'll find a way to make it happen."

"Yeah. But in how many years, Jackson?" he gripes. "If you're even still alive by the time your deal with DeLuca is up. If you even *last* that long in the cage."

The fact that he knows about DeLuca's underground fight club unnerves me. It occurs to me that for all I know, he has a wire on him and I'm sure as fuck not giving DeLuca up.

I roll my shoulders back. "I have no idea what you're talking about. I don't know who this DeLuca is that you're referencing and I know absolutely nothing about this cage you're referring to. Now, if you continue to talk to or question me without a lawyer present there's going to be a problem."

He pinches the bridge of his nose. "I'm not wearing a fucking wire. I'm just trying to help you." He gestures toward the window. "But most of all, help *her*."

"She doesn't need your help. She has me now."

"For how long?"

"Long enough to spend a lifetime with her and grow old with her."

He snorts. "Quite some fairytale you're living in."

I look at him out of the corner of my eye. "I'll do whatever I need to, in order to make sure that happens. I'll make sure I'm around for her."

He folds his hands and touches his pointer fingers to his lips. "I'm sure you will. But, I was referring to her."

I grab his collar and shove him against the glass again. "Is that supposed to be some kind of threat? Because if you hurt her it will be the last thing you ever do."

"I was talking about DeLuca, Jackson. You know, the man who killed her father." He looks at me skeptically. "Unless she didn't trust you enough to tell you the truth about her past."

"I know everything."

I release him and he fixes his collar. "Then you know that she witnessed DeLuca do it. Now, I've done my very best to protect her. I brainwashed her and I manipulated the hell out of her...starting with forcing her to deny to everyone who her father's killer really was. I'm not proud of myself, but it needed to be done."

He looks down at the ground. "I even went so far as to turn her into a broken girl in order to get DeLuca to forget all about her because I hoped he'd see that she was already miserable and suffering enough. That's how much I love her."

I can't help but look at him with disgust. "Sounds like you pretty much tried to kill her yourself then. Good thing she's a hell of a lot tougher and stronger than anyone gives her credit for."

"She is...but she's no match for him. And assuming that you know how he operates, you know that he will get his payback. It's not a matter of if...it's only a matter of when. He likes his revenge best when it's served cold. He likes to watch his prey find happiness and flourish...before he swoops in and snaps their necks." He blanches. "Or bashes their skulls in with a crowbar."

He's got DeLuca pegged right, but I still can't help but wonder. "What makes you think that she's even on his radar in the first place? Trust me, if he was waiting for the perfect opportunity he's had a couple," I say, recalling the two times she's shown up at the fight club.

"She's on his radar because of you, Jackson."

I open my mouth to argue, but I can't.

He takes the opportunity to continue, "She showed up at his fight club on her own a few months ago. She got wind that he might be the owner and she was out for his blood,

Jackson. Luckily, you saved her by denying he was the owner. I'll never be able to thank you enough for that." He pauses. "However, If you know her well enough, you know that she can be reckless at times. She's not always mentally with it. Just look at how the sex tape came to be...*she* actively chose to sleep with her step-father's opponent's son. I'm not saying that it was her fault that he filmed it...but it was still her own thoughts of revenge that put her in the position in the first place. She puts herself right into the eye of the storm without thinking about the consequences."

He looks at me, but I stay silent. I hate what he's saying but a small part of me knows it's true. She did defy me and show up at the fight club when I told her not to.

DeLuca aside, because she has no idea that he runs it ...she *knew* there was a chance that she could get attacked at the fight club by *any* guy because it happened before. And she still showed up there, all by herself. She was so determined to see me and have it out with me...she didn't care about the consequences and took that chance.

"She showed up at the fight club last night...even after I forbid her from going there. Even after she promised me that she never would."

He points at me. "See? You *know* how she is. You're perfectly aware of how stubborn she can be. Now do you see where I'm going with this, Jackson?"

I nod, my heart crashing to the floor with the realization. "So what you're 'deal' really entails is me breaking up with her. And if I don't, you'll bust me for being apart of an underground fight club. And DeLuca will kill me anyway once he finds out that I led the feds to it."

I punch the wall beside his head, hating the fact that no matter what fucking corner I go down, or how much I try...there's always something waiting in the shadows to break Alyssa and me apart.

I just want to be happy with her. I just want to wake up next to her every day of my life with her safe in my arms. I just want her to be my wife and the mother of my future child. I want to have lazy Sunday's in bed, make love to her at night, see that favorite dimple of mine every day, and spend every second of my life loving her.

He gives me a weird look and I'm not sure what to make of it, until he says, "No. That's not my deal. Alyssa's far too much in love with you for that to even be effective. She'll just chase you...and I know all too well how hard it is to resist her. And seeing as you're tied up with DeLuca, the chase will most likely end with her getting killed."

He sighs. "What I'm offering you is an actual chance at a life." He closes his eyes. "With her."

My ears perk up at that. "You mean like witness protection or something?"

His eyes open and narrow into tiny slits. "No, something much better than that. DeLuca would find you eventually in witness protection, and it would only piss him off that much more knowing that you tried to run and hide. Why do you think I never put Alyssa into it?"

On some level, I guess it makes sense. "So what's this deal then?"

"I want you to kill DeLuca."

I must be hearing things. "Yeah, because it's so easy to kill one of the most powerful mob bosses who ever lived." I snort. "Wow, I assumed that you were still way too young for senility to be setting in."

He gives me an eye roll before his expression turns serious again. "I would set it up. It would take a few weeks, but I'll make it happen. There would be no witnesses...other than me."

I push my shoulders back. "If that's the case why don't you just off him yourself?"

He sucks his teeth. "Because I'm an FBI agent, Jackson. If I'm the only one at the murder scene…it will all point back to me. And if it all points back to *me*, I won't be able to get you cleared—"

"And what about *me?*" I interrupt. "I'm tied to DeLuca. And if *I'm* the only one at the murder scene it will all come down on me. Not to mention the fact that his blood will be on my hands. How the fuck can I ever walk away from that alive or without spending the rest of my life in jail?"

He runs a hand through his hair. "Because you won't be the only one there…I'll be there with you. I will protect you and you won't go down for it. It will be pinned on someone else who I'll set up to be there. Someone who I have a special arrangement with. Someone who has more motive than you could ever imagine."

Chills creep up my spine. "If you mean Aly—"

"Are you fucking crazy? Of course, I don't mean her. I love her. I would never put her in the direct line of fire, ever."

"Then who is this person?"

He clicks his tongue. "No. You're not privy to that information until you make this deal with me. And even then, you won't know until you're standing in that room holding that gun. Trust me, it's better that way and it's the only way all the chips will fall into place."

I lean down and rest my forearms on my thighs. This is a lot to think about and take in. There's one hell of a difference between killing someone in a rage because they killed your sister and taking out one of the world's biggest mob bosses. Not mention, trusting a man that you pretty much hate. "I don't know. My gut feeling is telling me not to trust you. And I have no guarantee's that this will go off without a hitch. I have no guarantee that I can trust you."

"Jackson, I'm an FBI agent. Who would know how to commit the perfect murder better than me? And you don't need to trust me, you only need to love Alyssa enough to take care of DeLuca. She'll be safe forever then. But you have my word that you won't end up doing time for it."

I shake my head. "No. I'm sorry, but no. There's too much of a chance for this to backfire. I'll take my chances with DeLuca. He hasn't come after her yet. For all I know, maybe the fact that she's with me is working in her favor. I make DeLuca a lot of money. I'm the best fighter he has. Maybe he knows that if he fucked with Alyssa that he would end up losing me and it would impact his business. He is a businessman first and foremost."

I close my eyes and sigh.

Maybe there's a way I can talk to DeLuca.

I'll have Ricardo set it up for me and I'll put it all out on the table and be honest with him. I'll tell him that I'm loyal to him and I'll continue to be his best fighter…the only thing I ask is that he doesn't retaliate against Alyssa.

I'll tell him to increase the terms of my contract as a sign of good faith…make it 20 years or some shit. I don't know.

All I know, is there's gotta be a better way. Hell, maybe I should tell him that an FBI agent was plotting his murder and trying to enlist me to do so he'll really believe that I'm loyal to him.

Irritation crosses over his features. "I know it's a lot to think about." He pulls his card out of his wallet and hands it to me. "This deal won't be on the table for long. A few weeks at most."

He goes to turn around but pauses. "The only thing I ask is that you don't tell Alyssa I was here or that we spoke about this. She doesn't want me in her life anymore and I don't want to upset her more than I already have."

"Okay," I agree. Not because I want to keep this conversation from her, but because I can't tell her about talking to Ford without giving up my involvement with DeLuca. A part of me wants to tell her about Ford lurking outside her bar, but there's no guarantee that she won't find him to confront him about it. And if she does, I'm sure he'll tell her all about my involvement.

After I watch him go to his car and drive off I head inside the bar.

Momma's got a line up of shots in front of her now. It seems that everyone in the bar is enamored by Momma and wants to see her get drunk.

I shake my head and laugh. Alyssa's eyes catch mine and she lets out a little squeal before running and jumping into my arms.

She gives me a kiss and I begin to lose myself in her, not caring about anything else. Only her.

I pull away and look at her. "I love you."

She gives me a smile and I put her down. "I love you, too," she whispers.

Then she collapses and passes out cold.

I barely even have time to catch her before she hits the ground, taking my entire heart with her.

Chapter Thirty-One

ALYSSA

I HEAR SHOUTING SOMEWHERE IN THE DISTANCE BUT I'M UNABLE TO MOVE.

I'm so cold. My head feels like it's submerged underwater and I'm floating. There's pressure on my chest and chills are raking up and down my spine.

"Did she have anything to drink?" I hear Jackson's voice growl.

There's mumbling in the distance.

"No, I'm not talking about alcohol, Momma," Jackson says. "She doesn't drink alcohol. I'm talking about a regular drink. Water? Juice?"

"I think she had some water," Ricardo says. "I'm not sure, though. We were all paying attention to Momma."

"Well did she leave her cup anywhere? Fuck, maybe someone slipped something into her drink," Jackson barks.

I hear some shuffling before I have the feeling of being lifted in the air. Which only does wonders for the feeling of floating that I have. The chills are getting worse and my body is breaking out in a sweat.

My eyes flutter open, but the weight on my chest feels like it's made out of bricks.

"I swear to god. If any of you fuckers slipped anything in my girls drink," Jackson shouts, addressing the entire bar. "I *will* find you and you'll need a good plastic surgeon by the time I'm through with you."

"We need to get her to the hospital, Jackson," Momma shouts. "She's shaking like a leaf. I think she's sick!"

"What do you mean sick? She was fine this morning and five minutes ago. She's not sick. Someone shithead did something to her," Jackson roars.

"Wait a minute, Jackson. Think about it, she did run to our apartment last night in the pouring *ice* cold rain, wearing nothing but a pair of pajamas. It's still winter outside, she must have been freezing," Tyrone says, worry in his tone.

"Shit. That's right. I should've been paying better attention to her and warmed her up sooner."

I soon feel a wet cloth on my head courtesy of Momma. "Yeah, she's burning up. She feels feverish. I don't think no one slipped anything in her drink, Jackson. But we better take her to the hospital just to be sure."

She runs her hand through my hair. "It's alright, Alyssa. Momma's not gonna leave your side. I'm right here, sugar."

I want to speak, tell her how thankful I am for her, but this feeling is only getting worse. The chills are so bad I feel like I'm going to drop right out of Jackson's arms.

Jackson peers down at me. "Rest if you need to. I've got you. Everything will be okay, baby."

Two hours later, the doctors eyes appraise me over a pair of glasses. He flips open his tablet and scans the rest of the small hospital room, his eyes fall on the three huge men taking up most of the space.

In other words, Jackson, Tyrone, and Ricardo. In addition to Momma, who hasn't stopped holding my hand the entire time.

He clears his throat. "Are *all* these people members of your immediate family, young lady?" Before I can open my mouth, Momma and Jackson shout, "Yes! Now tell us what's wrong."

The doctor's lips twitch. "I see," he says before focusing back on his tablet. "Well, my dear, it seems that you have a touch of bronchitis, a touch of an ear infection, and the beginning stages of what looks to be walking pneumonia."

"Jesus," Jackson says while sitting up in his chair. "Is she going to be okay?"

The doctor waves his hand. "She'll be fine. She collapsed because the ear infection threw off her equilibrium, her chest hurts because of the bronchitis, and she has chills because of the pneumonia. Luckily, we caught the pneumonia in the beginning stages. A course of antibiotics will clear everything up."

The doctor pauses and fixes his eyes on me again. "Young lady, might I suggest that you don't go for a jog again in the middle of the night wearing nothing but pajamas while there is ice and rain falling from the sky during the first week of March."

"Thanks, Tyrone," I mutter.

He holds up his hands. "Don't 'thanks Tyrone' me. If you don't tell the doctor everything, how is he supposed to be able to diagnose and treat you properly?"

I roll my eyes and turn my attention back to the doctor. "So can I go home?"

He shakes his head. "Yes, but not right now. I want to get some fluids in you first. The nurse should be in soon to start an IV. You can go home in the next couple of hours." He looks at Momma. "But I do want to ensure that she has someone to take care of her for the next few days. I don't want her collapsing again." He looks back at his tablet and makes a face. "I see that your address is the same address as the bar called "Finnley's.""

I wonder how he knows that my apartment is at a bar, but before I can ask he says, "My son's a musician who frequents the bar. He's also dating the owner, Shane. Nice guy."

I give him a smile. "That he is."

Momma stands up. "Don't worry, Doctor. I will see to it that she gets the very best care."

She turns to Jackson. "And she won't be staying at no *bar*. She'll be coming back to the apartment with us."

I open my mouth to protest, but Jackson cuts me off by saying, "Yes, of course. And you won't be the one taking care of her, Momma. I will."

Momma smiles and says, "Well, I'm helping. No one makes soup for the soul like I do."

"It's true," Tyrone says. "Momma makes the best chicken soup in the world."

With that, the doctor nods. "Looks like you'll be in good hands. Here's your prescription. But the nurse will be here in a few moments. She'll give you your first dose of antibiotics and she'll start your IV. After that, you're free to go. Take care."

I take my prescription and thank him.

Ricardo and Tyrone stand up. "We can run that over to the pharmacy for you if you want."

"Thanks, guys," I tell them before they leave.

Momma kisses my forehead. "Well, I have to run to the ladies room. You gonna be okay, sugar?"

"I'll be fine, Momma. Thank you."

When she leaves, Jackson envelopes me in his arms. "Don't scare me like that again." He closes his eyes. "I swear, my heart stopped."

I want to kiss him so bad, but I don't want to get him sick. "I'm sorry. I thought I was fine. I hope I don't get you sick."

"Nah, I'm strong like bull."

"Thanks for offering to take care of me. But honestly, I'll be fine. I'm sure Shane will check on me."

"Nope in my bed is where you will be. Where Momma and I can nurse you back to health. Speaking of nurse's...where is she?"

I hear the sound of someone clearing their throat and I look up.

"She's right here," a woman with long blonde hair, who's wearing pink scrubs informs us curtly.

Jackson makes a face and I know what he's thinking because I'm thinking it too. The nurse looks a lot like *me*. She's about 10 years older than me, but she has the same build, similar features, my natural hair color, and even the same eye color; although hers are more of a brown hazel rather than green but still, it's eerily similar to mine.

It's like I jumped into a time machine and pressed 'future.' I'm suddenly struck with the feeling of wanting to apologize for any troubles that she might have endured in her nursing career due to my sex tape.

Then I look at her name tag and see the name staring back at me. I almost pass out again.

"Oh, god," I whisper. Jackson immediately looks concerned.

But I'm too distracted when the nurse gives me a cold smile. "Yup. I'm the woman whose husband you stole. You little adulteress whore."

The brick on my chest practically caves in with that statement.

Jackson stands up and scowls. "First off, don't ever call my girl a whore again. Or I'll be lodging a complaint with the hospital. Secondly, I'm positive that Alyssa isn't responsible for whatever problems you have with your husband."

She puts her hands on her hips and glares at me. "Clearly your new boyfriend knows nothing about who you really are."

My stomach heaves because as much as I don't like it, this woman is right and I do owe her one hell of an apology for my transgressions. I can't put everything on him.

I open my mouth to start, but Jackson takes a step closer to her. "I don't know who you are, lady. But I do know exactly who *she* is. Now I'm only going to tell you this once—leave. Because when the sassy Southern woman, otherwise known as my Momma, comes back in here and hears you speaking to Alyssa this way. Trust me, you're going to wish you had."

I somehow find my voice. "Jackson, stop. She doesn't deserve to be treated like this, she has every right to be furious with me and call me those names. You don't know who she is."

Jackson's eyebrows shoot up. "Who is she?"

"She's Ford's wife."

Chapter Thirty-Two

ALYSSA

"Ex-wife," she informs me. "Well, thanks to *you*."

"I'm sorry."

She frowns and begins setting up the supplies to start my IV. "Save it. You can't apologize for ruining someone's marriage, it's unforgivable."

Jackson points a finger at her. "Look, if you think I'm letting you stick a needle in her arm after you've just verbally attacked her, think again. I want another nurse."

"Jackson, give us a minute."

When he begins to protest, I add, "Please."

He kisses my forehead. "I'll be right outside that door." He looks at Penelope. "And so will my Momma."

I sit up in bed and look at Penelope. "You're right. I can't ever apologize for something like that. It *is* unforgivable. But I will tell you that I'm not proud of myself. And I will tell you that woman to woman, I'm the lowest of the low and I'm ashamed of myself for that."

Her cold demeanor shifts a little and she takes a deep breath. "It wasn't all your fault." She closes her eyes. "In fact, I'd say that a lot of it wasn't your fault. Especially when it started."

She wipes a tear from her eye and looks down. "I don't think you were really old enough to make the adult decision to be involved with a married man back then…were you?"

"I—um," I stall, because being an *actual* adult now, I'm not entirely sure.

"I mean, what were you, like 16?"

I fidget with my hands. "It was within hours of 17th birthday. *I* begged him to see me for my birthday, though. Let's just say that I was with him when the clock struck 12. I felt like Cinderella at that moment. But looking back now, it was never a fairytale. It was a nightmare."

I look her in the eyes and hold out my arm. "But that's still no excuse for my part in hurting you, because I didn't stay 17 forever, Penelope. And although I only had actual sex with him once and hated myself right after. I still wanted it beforehand…and I was 21 years old when it happened."

Another tear falls down her cheek as she puts the tourniquet on and inserts the needle.

"And if I'm really being honest, Ford and I always had an inappropriate relationship. I should have kicked him out of my life a lot sooner than I did. I was too codependent on him…and it was toxic. He was toxic."

She sniffles and I wish I could hug her. I hate that he took down another woman. And I hate that I played a part in it.

She reaches for a tissue and wipes her face. "He is. I realize that now. I think I *finally* got it when our divorce was finalized a little over three months ago. After I discovered everything about the two of you. But he has this way about him, you know? And it's more than just his good looks…it's this way he has of just sucking you in. He tells you what you want to hear. Then he fucks up, you call him on it, and he apologizes and treats you like you're the most important thing in the world again. Until you're not anymore. It's a never ending cycle. Sometimes all in the same night."

She worries her bottom lip between her teeth. "And this whole time...you *know* he's just working his magic. You know he's altering your psyche in some way that you can't explain. But every time you reach to turn that light on...and you get that much closer to realizing it. Bam...he's onto you...and he's ready to strike again and lure you into his trap. The worst part is, you don't even realize how much damage he's caused until it's too late."

I nod my head, knowing all too well what she means. "He's a master manipulator. He's the human version of snake oil. Pretty package, and he'll sell you anything you want...but in the end...you realize that the real snake was him."

"Yeah, that sums it up perfectly. Look, I'm sorry for calling you a whore. I'm a 34-year-old woman. No matter how upset I am, it doesn't give me a right to slut-shame another female. And I should have left him a long time ago. Hell, I should have figured it out right when you called that night. I was so excited to get married to him, though. I thought we would have the picture perfect life. The nurse and FBI agent and our 2.5 beautiful children."

I reach for her hand and she lets me. "Hey. It's not too late to have that. You're nice, sweet, accomplished, and 34 is still young. I would call you beautiful but I'm afraid you would think I'm conceited."

She laughs and I feel a weight lift off my chest. "It *is* a little strange, huh? I mean, even with the dark hair you have now, we still look a lot alike. Obviously, you're younger and your tits don't sag quite like mine yet...but being in the same room with you is like being in the twilight zone."

I think back to all those times when I wished that I was the one Ford chose instead of her.

Oddly enough, I feel relieved because this is like a glimpse into the future of what it would have been like. There's no doubt in my mind now that he would have done the same thing to me and I would have ended up heartbroken like Penelope.

I give her a small smile. "Well, Ford might be the world's biggest asshole, but at least he has good taste." I look down. "And your tits don't sag. You're still rocking it. I can only hope to look as good as you do when I'm 34."

Then she does something that I definitely wasn't expecting. She pulls me in for a hug. "I didn't like you when I first walked in here. But now, I'm really glad we had this conversation."

I hug her tighter and I feel the tears start falling. "Me too. And for the record, I really am sorry. I wish I could take it all back and I wish you never got hurt in any of this."

She pulls away and pats my cheek. "Me too...but I also see now that I wasn't the only one who got hurt. Take care of yourself, Alyssa. Despite what I thought earlier, you're a good person. A good woman."

"Uh. Everything okay here?" Jackson questions, his eyes darting back and forth between us cautiously.

Penelope squeezes my hand. "Yeah, everything's okay. You got a good girl, here. Take care of her." She looks at me. "Maybe one day I'll find my own handsome knight in shining armor like you have."

"I hope so. Because you deserve that, Penelope."

She wipes her eyes and heads for the door. "I'll be back to check on you in a little while."

Jackson stuffs his hands in his pockets. "I'm not sure what I'm supposed to say right now."

"That makes two of us. I never thought I'd say this, but I'm glad I met her. I'm happy I got a chance to have that conversation with her."

"It's fucking weird how much you look alike, though, huh?"

"Can you blame the man for having good taste?"

He walks over to me and puts his arms around me. He looks like he's about to say something, but Tyrone, Ricardo, and Momma walk into the room.

Ricardo whistles. "Did you guys see that smokin' hot nurse walking down the hall."

Jackson grunts but I put a hand on his arm. "You should get her number, Ricardo. I happen to know for a fact that she's single." He looks excited, until I add. "However, she's not a 'hit it and quit it'. So if you pursue her you better be serious. She's been through enough."

"Nah. I already learned my lesson when it comes to broken and damaged girls."

Jackson and Tyrone look at him but he averts his gaze and rubs his neck. "I'll meet you guys in the car."

"I knew he had it bad for Lou-Lou but *damn*," Tyrone declares after Ricardo walks out.

"There's definitely a story there," Momma says. "Poor guy is all kinds of hurtin'."

Jackson nods but turns to look at me. "I'm gonna ask Shane to bring some of your clothes to my apartment, okay?"

"Are you sure? I really don't want to impose."

He lifts my chin. "Alyssa, I take care of what's mine and what I love. Don't you ever forget that."

Almost a week later I'm feeling much better, but since I'm just getting my appetite back, Momma says I'm still not allowed to live at my bar. Those were her words, not mine.

Jackson has been nothing but attentive and caring. He's held me through the night, brought me tissues and magazines, rubbed my feet, and brought me a hot bowl of Momma's soup every hour on the hour, even when I could only stomach a few small bites.

He never *once* made me feel like I was imposing on him and his life. In fact, every time I tried to go back home, he'd sic Momma on me. I learned very quickly that Momma's not a person you want to argue with because I'd be sure to lose every time.

I turn over in the bed and watch Jackson as he sleeps. The mid-morning sun is peeking in through the corner of the curtain giving me just enough light to be able to enjoy the visual of his beautifully sculpted body.

Nothing puts a damper on a couple's sex life like being sick. Needless to say, Jackson and I haven't been able to enjoy one another in that capacity.

But seeing as I'm feeling almost good as new now. I'm thinking it might be time to indulge a little.

I brush my lips against the sexy stubble grazing his jaw before making my way down his neck.

When I look up I notice that Jackson's eyes are still closed, but the boyish lopsided grin on his face tells me that he's very much awake.

I kiss his chest and continue down lower. I run my tongue along both sides of the V of his lower abs and I hear him let out a low groan.

That deep groan of his only fuels me on. When I slip my head beneath the sheet, I see just how much he's awake. I lick the small drop of precome that I see on the fabric of his boxers. Deciding to tease him a little, I place my mouth over the material covering his erection and suck. I find the opening of his boxers and flick my tongue against it, needing to taste him.

Jackson lets out a curse and raises his hips. I eagerly repeat the movement and he reaches down and twirls my hair around his hand before looking down at me. "Are you sure, baby? I mean, are you feeling good enough for this?"

I nod and pull his boxers down all the way. I open my mouth, but Jackson hauls me back up and lays me across his chest.

I frown, until he cups my face in his hands and searches my eyes. "You're so beautiful it hurts sometimes, did you know that?"

My heart soars…until I think about how I must look right now. My hair is in the messiest of messy buns, my eyes are puffy, and my nose is raw from all the tissues I went through in the past week.

This is not just some smudged mascara and chapped lips. Oh, no. This is me looking like a cross between a zombie and a corpse.

I bury my head into his chest and cover my face with my hands.

"Wow, you really know how to take a compliment," Jackson says, his voice light with humor.

"I look like I could audition for *The Walking Dead* right now, Jackson."

He laughs. "Some of those zombie chicks are pretty hot."

I take the pillow from my side of the bed and hit him with it.

He wraps me in his arms and I can feel his heart pounding rapidly against my back causing me to lean into him.

He gives my shoulder a kiss. "Remind me never to tell you how beautiful you are right when you're about to wake me up with a blowjob again."

I turn slightly and raise a brow. "Please, you were definitely awake."

His gaze turns sultry as his fingers begin grazing my upper thigh underneath my shorts. "Maybe," he whispers.

I moan as the pad of his thumb skims the edges of my panties. "I can still give you one, Jackson."

He moves my panties to the side and his pointer finger trails along my outer lips. It takes everything in me not to fall apart and start writhing like a cat in heat. "Rain check," he whispers. "Because right now, I'm too busy loving how wet you get for me when I'm barely even touching you."

He traces my slit with his middle finger. "I love that you're soaking my finger and I'm not even inside you yet." He repeats the teasing motion. "Tell me, baby, how wet are you gonna be for me when I stick my finger in this pretty pussy of yours?"

I'm so worked up I don't care anymore, I grind my ass against his cock and let out a small gasp when he presses his thumb against my clit. "Answer me, Alyssa."

"Why don't you find out?" I tell him. He doesn't waste another second, he pulls my shorts down and two of his fingers dip inside me. "Fuck, baby. You're drenched."

I suck in a breath and swerve my backside against his erection again. He nibbles my earlobe. "You trying to tell me that you want something?"

I nod eagerly and he thrusts into me. "Well, if you want me," he rasps. "Put me inside you."

Desire strong enough to make me dizzy infuses me as I reach behind me, take him in my hand and slowly proceed to slide him inside me.

He lifts one of my legs and rests it on the outside of his before he begins thrusting inside me. This is the sexiest spooning I've ever been apart of—this position is so intimate.

He reaches around and swirls my clit with his fingers. "Oh fuck, don't stop," I scream. His pace picks up and a minute later I'm a cursing, twitching mess around him as my orgasm takes hold of me.

"Fuck, I love the way you come all over my dick, baby," he says. His body tightens, his own breathing is labored and he thrusts into me one last time before I feel the spurt of his release.

He rolls me over until I'm underneath him and kisses my nose. "You're still so beautiful it hurts. Zombie or no zombie."

I fling my arms around his neck and breathe him in. "I'm in love with you, Jackson Reid. You've ruined me for anyone else."

He rubs his nose along my jaw. "I'm in love with you. You're my first, my last and my only love, Alyssa Tanner." He looks up at me and my heart flutters. "I want to grow old with you," he whispers. "I want to let you win at bingo, I want you to help me find my dentures, and I want to spend the evening watching the sunset with you every night from our two rocking chairs." He rests his head on my heart and my eyes fill with tears. "And when I die, you'll be my last thought. When my life flashes before my eyes, I'll see nothing but you. Because you already are the very best part of my life."

"You're mine," I whisper. "Finding you made all the pain I've ever endured worth living through."

I run my fingers through his hair. "We'll have those rocking chairs, Jackson. I know we will."

He wipes the tears from my eyes. "Yeah, baby. We will. I'll find a way to make it happen."

The end of his statement throws me off a little, but I'm soon distracted by the sound of my phone ringing.

"Hey, Shane. What's up?"

"Look, I know you're still probably sick and I know you're moving soon, but do you think you can work at the bar for a few hours tonight?"

"Of, course. It's the least I can do since you've been so cool with me being out this week. Wait a minute—" I pause, unsure if I understood him right. "What do you mean I'm moving soon? Are you kicking me out?"

Beside me, Jackson sits up in bed and puts his boxers back on.

"Kicking you out?" Shane sputters. "No. I'm talking about you moving in with Jackson, silly."

I stare at Jackson then, the way he's avoiding my gaze and the guilty expression on his face tells me everything I need to know. "Yeah," I respond my tone harsher than I intended. "I'll be there at seven."

"Oh, um. Okay, great. See you then," Shane responds before he hangs up.

I crinkle my nose and narrow my eyes. "Something you want to tell me?"

Jackson stands up and opens his arms wide. "Surprise, baby."

I wrap the sheet around me and stand in front of him. "Yeah, *I'll* say. You know, couples usually discuss moving in with one another. Because both parties have to be in agreement. That's the way a relationship works."

I open my arms wide, mocking him. "It's not supposed to be *'surprise, baby'* I've told your landlord / boss that you're moving. Especially when you haven't even discussed it with your actual girlfriend first!" I shout.

He opens his mouth but I cut him off. "I mean, did you even ask *Tyrone* about it? Or is he just as in the dark about all this as I am?"

Jackson holds a finger up and opens the door. "Yoo, Tyrone," he calls out.

I stand there with my mouth open in disbelief.

"Yeah?" Tyrone shouts.

"Is it cool if Alyssa moves in with us?"

"It's cool," Tyrone answers, before adding. "As long as she cooks every once in awhile."

Jackson shuts the door and shrugs. "See? Everything's cool."

I'm so frustrated I begin stomping my feet on the floor like a 2 -year-old. "And what about me? Did you ever think to ask *me?*"

Jackson scratches the back of his head and pouts. "Are you saying that you don't want to live with me?"

I open my mouth to answer but he walks over to me and scoops me in his arms. "I thought we just told one another exactly how we felt about each other?" He kisses my cheek. "Remember? Rocking chairs? Sunsets?" He kisses my chin. "Best part of my life?" He kisses my neck. "Great morning sex?" He moves lower to my breasts and the sheet falls. "Hot zombies?"

I roll my eyes and let out a giggle. "It's a big step, Jackson. We haven't been together long at all."

His expression is sad and it pulls on my heartstrings. "Are you saying no?"

I think about this for a moment. I weigh the pros and cons. Pro's being—waking up next to Jackson, his apartment being in a safer area, kissing Jackson, making love to Jackson, falling asleep next to Jackson. The only con I can come up with is that it's a 20-minute walk away from my job. Unless he expects me to stop working there?

"I'm still working at Finnley's," I tell him.

He looks hopeful. "Of course. I know you like it there. I wouldn't ever expect you to stop. Only now, I'll be walking you home every night. Well, *if* you want me to that is."

"Okay," I say.

"Okay?" he repeats. "Okay, like you'll be moving your stuff in soon? Or, okay you're an asshole and I still can't believe you sprung this on me?"

"Yes. I still hate that you sprung this on me, and I hate that it wasn't discussed and there was no romantic gesture or anything, but okay I'll move in with you."

"Thank you."

Before I can respond he gets down on one knee. I stare at him wide-eyed. "Whoa, too soon. *Way* too soon!" I start. "Don't get me wrong, my gut instinct is telling me to say yes, but we can't get married right now. I need time, Jackson! Like a year or two, at *least*," I begin babbling a mile a minute.

He stares at me like I'm crazy until he looks down and adjusts his position so he's kneeling down on both knees. "Relax. I wasn't asking you to marry me," he says. "Not that I won't be asking you to do that at some point in the future," he quickly says. "But trust me when I do, it will be way more romantic." He grins. "And it's good to know that you'll say yes."

"So, what are you doing then?" I ask, half relieved, half nervous.

"Alyssa," he pauses. "Shit, you never told me your middle name," he whispers.

"Trust me. You don't want to know my middle name," I tell him.

"Of course, I want to know your middle name. I would tell you mine but I'm sure you heard Momma shout it last week."

I bite my bottom lip, wishing I didn't have to tell him.

Jackson stands back up. "What? It can't be *that* bad. Let me guess, Marie? That's a nice name, baby."

I shake my head, not wanting to play this game.

He raises an eyebrow playfully. "Is it Gertrude? Can I call you Gerddy for short?"

"It's Ford," I whisper.

"Huh? What the hell does *he* have—"

"That's my middle name," I say, cutting him off. "He was my dad's best friend. When they were kids they made a pact that the first one to have a son would be named after the other one. Ford doesn't have children and since I ended up being a girl, my mom chose the name Alyssa. But my dad still wanted Ford to be my middle name. I'm sorry, Jackson."

He kisses my hand. "Don't be sorry, Alyssa. I love every part of you. Even the parts I don't always like." He clears his throat and looks at me. "Alyssa Ford Tanner, would you do me the honor of moving in with me?"

"And Tyrone!" Tyrone shouts from the other side of the door.

"And Tyrone," he amends.

My face hurts from smiling so hard. "Yes. I would love to," I say.

I hear Momma and Tyrone cheer from the other side of the door and I can't help but laugh with them. Jackson pulls me into another hug, but I don't miss the strange expression on his face.

"What?" I ask.

He appears to be lost in deep thought before saying, "Your dad really trusted Ford, didn't he?"

"Yeah," I whisper. "Ford's an asshole when it comes to the way he treats women. But that aside, my dad trusted him with his life."

Jackson nods before kissing my forehead. "I'm gonna take a shower."

"Want some company?"

He doesn't respond but he pulls me in for a kiss that answers my question.

Chapter Thirty-Three

JACKSON

Alyssa's father trusted Ford. He was his best friend.

That thought keeps echoing throughout my head.

Not that I'm actually considering taking that deal with him...but it's good to know that *if* I did...he would uphold his end.

I'm not taking *that* deal, but I do have to figure out a way to deal with this whole Alyssa situation. I'm ecstatic to know I'll be waking up beside her every morning, but I still have to work out how I'm going to keep her from finding out about DeLuca.

I figure, the best way to go about it will be to tell Tyrone and Ricardo not to bring up DeLuca's name in front of Alyssa. I'll just tell them it's because I don't want to scare her with the truth regarding who DeLuca is, so it's best we don't mention his name.

Tyrone will probably remind me that he's been completely honest with Shelby about everything, but I'll just tell him I'm not ready to do that with Alyssa.

He'll tell me I'm wrong, then we'll share another Doctor Phil moment...and it will be fine. I hope.

As far as DeLuca himself goes...I'm going to ask Ricardo to set up a meeting with DeLuca for me next week. A face to face sit down.

I'm going to be honest with him and lay everything out on the line. I *was* going to tell him about Ford trying to recruit me to murder him...but after Alyssa told me that her dad trusted him, I don't think I should go that route.

Besides, if anything happened to Ford and Alyssa found out it was my fault...I know a small part of her would be upset.

I won't do that to her.

I'll just take my chances with DeLuca. I've still got the fact that I'm his best fighter as my bargaining chip.

I head into the kitchen and watch Alyssa sitting at the counter while Momma fixes her something to eat. She has her Finnley's t-shirt and a pair of jeans. Tyrone has a fight tonight, so we'll be heading to the club soon. He likes to get there a few hours early in order to center himself.

She gives me a smile when I enter the room. I walk over to her, bend down and kiss her soft lips. "Hey, baby. Going to work soon?"

She stretches her arms above her head and yawns. "Yeah. I'm exhausted but it's the least I can do. Shane's been great about me taking off."

Momma makes a face, and I know she thinks it's too soon for her to be going back.

I honestly hate the fact that she's going in tonight as well, but I can't stop her. I tuck a strand of hair behind her ear. "Drink plenty of juice, and don't leave your cup out anywhere. I'll be by the bar with the guys after Tyrone's fight ends. I can help you man it if you're still exhausted when I get there."

"I'll be fine, but thank you," she says while Momma hands her a sandwich. Alyssa looks up from her grilled cheese and her eyes open wide. "I almost forgot it was Saturday and there's a fight tonight."

Tyrone walks in the kitchen then, his expression tight. "Yup."

His demeanor is a little off right now and I'm not sure what to make of it. He's always a little nervous before a fight, but he usually gets a handle on it by using his sense of humor. Before I have time to call him on it, Alyssa hops off the stool and runs over to him. Then, surprising everyone, she flings her arms around his neck. "Please be careful," she whispers. "Please."

Jesus, watching my fight really did a number on her.

Momma fans her face and Tyrone closes his eyes. "I'll be okay, Alyssa."

The fact that he's not making a joke right now puts me on edge.

"And after I kick his ass, I'll be celebrating by getting another alpha male piercing," he says.

Momma covers her ears and I laugh, feeling the weight in my chest dissipate.

Alyssa smacks him on the chest and chuckles before walking away. "I just don't get it," she says to Momma while rummaging through her purse.

"Get what, sugar?"

"The fighting. It's scary, Momma. If you should be convincing *anyone* to quit their job—" She points at Tyrone and me. "It's *those* two. They're crazy for putting themselves through that."

Momma gives her a weird look. "Trust me, I would if I could. But you know it's all De—"

"Dinero," I shout, as everyone turns to face me. "Cause you know, it's all about the Benjamin's, baby."

Three sets of eyes stare at me like I've lost my mind. Luckily, Tyrone comes to my defense by putting an arm around my neck. "Come on, Biggie. It's almost 7, my fight starts at 9:45."

I give Alyssa a kiss and hug Momma goodbye since she won't be attending the fight tonight.

As soon as Tyrone and I walk out into the hallway his eyes are on me. "Either my music has really started rubbing off on you, or you're hiding something," he says.

"What's the matter?" I deflect. "You don't want to be the Puffy Daddy to my Biggie?"

He snorts. "Uh-uh. Nice try. Something's off with you. And you know I'm not gonna quit until you tell me, so you might as well save me the trouble and spill it."

"I can't."

"Jackson," he insists.

We walk out the apartment complex doors. "Look, I just need you to do me a favor and never mention DeLuca's name in front of Alyssa."

"What? Why? I mean, it's not like we talk about him all that much anyway, but he is the reason our lives are the way they are right now." He pauses. "Shit, she doesn't know you're involved with DeLuca...does she?"

I shake my head and avert my gaze.

"I thought you told her *everything* that night?"

I rub the back of my neck. "I told her that I was a murderer, yes. But I never told her that I'm tied up with DeLuca or that *he's* the reason I'm free."

He looks at me incredulously. "She never asked why or how you're free?"

Oh, she asked. Right before she fell asleep after making love that night. "I told her I got acquitted because of self-defense," I say. "Trust me, Tyrone. I have my reasons. I wish I didn't have to lie. It's just the way it has to be right now."

He thinks about this for a moment. "Can I ask you a few more questions?"

"You can ask, but I might not be able to answer them directly."

He rubs his chin. "First and foremost…does this have to do with *her* safety?"

"Yes."

"Does it have anything to do with the FBI?"

I'm about to ask how he knows that, but then he says, "The night you were drunk, you said something about her having an FBI sugar daddy. So, I assume he's got something to do with it?"

I shake my head. "No. He doesn't. And he was never her sugar daddy, I was just being a drunk ass."

"Oh, I know. I was there, remember? Okay, I have one more question."

"Shoot."

He gives me a look and I know he's about to crack the case. "If you were working for *any* other mob boss…would you tell her the truth about everything then?"

I give him a small nod.

"Shit," he says. "Alyssa's got one hell of a history, doesn't she?"

"I can't tell you, Tyrone. I wish I could. But it's for her own safety that she doesn't find out about DeLuca."

"You don't have to tell me, Jackson. I read you loud and clear, brother. I'm just worried now. I have no clue what her story is—" He pauses and starts listing things on his fingers. "But just knowing that her daddy was murdered, it's got something to do with the feds, and DeLuca himself is involved. Not to mention, the fact that she can't know about us working for him—"

"And he can't know about her," I interject.

"And the plot thickens," he whispers.

"You've got the most important pieces, Tyrone. I just can't be the one to put them together for you because it's not my place to."

He nods. "I understand."

"You still okay with her moving in?"

He waves a hand. "Yeah. She loves you, Jackson. And I know you love her." He closes his eyes. "Sometimes you do whatever you can for the woman you love."

We walk into the club and he looks around. His eyes zero in on the cage. "And to answer your question. I'd be Biggie." He snorts. "Especially tonight."

"Tonight? Why?"

He puts a hand on my shoulder and smiles. "See? Now if you really were a hip-hop fan and liked that song, you would get it."

I raise an eyebrow and he gives me a small laugh. "Don't give me that look, it's nothing. I was just making a crack about the album that song was featured on is all."

Then he pulls me in for a hug, which is rare for him to do here in the middle of the club. "You're my best friend, Jackson."

I hug him back and tell him the same, but an unsettling feeling washes over me. I'm about to question him about why he's acting so weird, but Ricardo shows up and they decide to do some last minute training.

Because apparently….they just got word that Tyrone's opponent for tonight got switched.

That only makes this feeling in the pit of my stomach worse.

One things for sure…I'm finding out the name of that album.

A little over two hours later, I'm standing in the middle of the crowd ready to punch someone.

Tyrone denied me access to the fucking dressing room. I spoke to Ricardo about it but he said that I know the rules before a fight, and since I'm not fighting tonight I have to respect them.

Then I told him that I thought something was wrong. I told him what Tyrone said earlier and I told him what the name of the album was—'Ready to Die.'

What the *fuck* is going on?

Ricardo looked spooked and tried calling DeLuca on his phone to figure out what the hell was going on with this new schedule change, but of course, he didn't answer.

Then he went in and tried talking to Tyrone, but he said he shut down and won't talk to anyone. He's in his own little world right now preparing for the fight.

When I see him walk out and into the cage, I know it's true.

He's not Tyrone right now. He's his own version of the Hulk.

But when I look at him and his eyes connect with mine. He gives me the look. "I got this," he mouths.

I nod my head and pat the space above my heart. To most people, we probably look like two sappy lovers. But fuck those people, I wouldn't have gotten through these past few years without him.

He's been the *only* good thing about making a deal with the Devil.

I look at Ricardo and he gives me the thumbs up sign. "Everything's okay," he mouths.

I breathe a sigh of relief.

Until I see his opponent walk out.

It's the same guy *I* fought last week.

Tyrone and I have a similar build for the most part. He's 6'2 to my 6'3, but unlike my 235lbs, he fluctuates between 230-245lbs, depending on when and how long Momma comes to visit.

I smile because I know he's on the upside of the scale due to Momma being at our apartment this entire week. Then I frown because I know that the extra weight won't make that much of a difference against a guy who weighs 388lbs and is 5 inches taller than him.

But I can't let myself think like that. Tyrone's one tough competitor. We both hold the title of being the best fighter in the club. Which is also why we train together.

He's never even lost a match. Hell, if I'm being honest, he's taken fewer hits than me now. He's only been hit twice, two separate matches.

His secret?

When he gets close to reaching his limit…he becomes fucking psychotic.

I'm not kidding, either. He turns into a full on psychiatric patient. To the point where he begins actually scaring his opponents. It's why his fans call him 'Hulk'. The guy just loses it up there.

In fact, I'd be willing to bet that Tyrone's fights bring in more money than *mine* do. He's way more entertaining to watch than me. If he's not scaring the audience to death with his antics, then he's making them laugh by taunting his opponent.

They announce Tyrone and the crowd goes wild and I join them. "Break bad on em', Hulk," I call out.

He hears me say this and blows me a kiss. Ricardo shakes his head and laughs and the crowd goes even crazier. The first time he did it, I wanted to pummel him, but he thought it was hysterical; and so did the crowd, so he kept doing it.

Then they introduce his shithead opponent. For whatever reason, his eyes lock with mine. I hardly ever do this, since it's not my fight…but this time, I issue my own stare down, letting him know that on a personal level if he plays dirty with Tyrone…he'll be dealing with *me*.

Instead of heeding my warning like I hoped he would. His lifts his pointer finger and traces it across his neck horizontally. Then he gives me a wink.

My stomach coils. Something's not right.

I look at Ricardo, but he's too busy whispering words of encouragement in Tyrone's ear to look at me.

When Lou-Lou walks out on stage, I try getting her attention, but she just gives me a weird look and shrugs before wishing Tyrone luck.

Fuck it. I'm walking up there myself. Maybe I can get Tyrone's attention *that* way. Since I'm standing in the middle of the large crowd, I begin shoving people out of the way.

The match begins but I'm still a good few rows back. That's when I start screaming my head off and pushing people out of the way. When they notice that it's *me* and see how angry I am, they start moving with no hesitation.

I've never acted like this before unless I'm in the cage so they know something's up.

I'm screaming Tyrone's name like a lunatic but I don't care. I look back up at the cage and what I see brings me to my knees.

Everything happens in slow motion.

The beast is sliding a knife down the middle of Tyrone's back. This was supposed to be a fucking fight, not a goddamned stabbing. Ricardo's going off like a motherfucker on the side-lines trying to get to him, but the beast's team of people start throwing punches and kicks, attacking him.

I start scaling the cage, not giving a fuck about anyone or anything, only Tyrone.

I hop on the beast's back and shove my fingers in his eyeballs so hard there's blood dripping down my fingers. He pulls the knife out of Tyrone, grunts and throws me off his back with enough force that I slam into the cage, but I don't care.

I get up, run right back up to him and headbutt him as hard as I can.

He looks woozy and backs up, but at the last second, he starts charging me with the same knife that he stabbed Tyrone with.

That's when Ricardo hops on his back and I hear a cracking sound.

The guy falls limp and I know what's been done…and I'd be lying if I said I wasn't happy about it.

But I have more important things to worry about.

I rush over to Tyrone. He's shaking, and his blood is pooling all around him. I take off my sweatshirt and tie it around his wound tight. He finally looks at me, but when he does, his eyes are glazed over, and I know he's out of it.

I scream his name and tell him to hold on. "I can't lose you, Tyrone," I scream. Hell, I'm probably sobbing, who knows.

I hear Ricardo on the phone calling for the mob doctor to get to the cage.

"Love you, J-man," he whispers.

"I love you, too," I say. "You're gonna be fine. The doctor's on his way."

"Tell Momma I love her and Shelby…tell Shelby I love her," he says. "I did this for her," he whispers.

"What the fuck do you mean?"

He begins nodding off but looks at me. "I made a deal with DeLuca. I asked to be out of the club. I wanted to end my contract." He gulps in a mouthful of air. "I wanted to start my life with Shelby. She didn't know I was doing this, though."

"And what did he say, Tyrone?" I scream, already fearing the answer.

"He told me I had to fight one last opponent…and then I was out."

I shake my head. "No. You had to know it wouldn't be that easy."

He begins nodding off again, but I force him to stay with me. "I know, Jackson. But he promised. His only stipulation was that I had to go a full 10 rounds with the guy you fought last week."

His eyes close but he keeps talking. "I knew it would be a tough fight. I mean, 10 rounds with *that* beast? You only went 3 with him. But DeLuca told me to drag it out to 10 rounds and take my hits and my punishment like a man. But, I never thought it would end up like this. I should have, though, Huh? I mean, it's fucking DeLuca. Still, I didn't anticipate being stabbed."

DeLuca was setting Tyrone up to be killed. There's no way he could have lasted 10 rounds with that guy without defending himself. I barely survived 3 and I did fight back. If Alyssa hadn't screamed, I never would have made it past that.

Weird thing is? That beast looked at me right before Tyrone's fight, like it was some kind of personal message.

Tyrone starts shaking again and I have to hold him down in order to make sure there's pressure on his wound. His eyes flutter and the feeling of dread washes over me. I lower my lips to his ear and whisper, "You're my brother and I love you. You better make it through this because I need you. Don't you fucking bail on me, Tyrone."

The doctor finally shows up, declares he needs to go to a hospital right away and they take him out on a stretcher.

I sit there in shock, my eyes are still wet and Tyrone's blood surrounds me. It feels like my heart just got crushed into dust.

But then venomous rage fills my blood.

And I know exactly who it's for.

The Devil himself.

Fuck sitting down to try and talk to him. *Fuck* laying it all out on the table for him. *Fuck* offering him an ounce of my loyalty in exchange for Alyssa's safety after he pulled this shit.

There's another way to ensure that she's safe.

There's another way to get payback for those I love.

This bastard has now hurt *two* people that I would do anything for.

Fuck this club, fuck his contract, and fuck *him*.

I stare into the camera and narrow my eyes. "I'm coming for you, DeLuca," I sneer, low enough so that only I can hear.

I see the camera move and I know he's watching me.

Good.

Chapter Thirty-Four

ALYSSA

LAST CALL ENDED 20 MINUTES AGO.

Jackson, Tyrone, and Ricardo never showed up after the fight.

I've tried calling Jackson's cell multiple times but he still hasn't picked up or responded to any of my text messages.

I would call Momma, but she doesn't believe in cell phones.

It's obvious that something is *very* wrong. Which is why I locked up the bar and I'm currently standing in front of Jackson's apartment door, pounding on it as hard as I can.

I thought for sure that Momma would be here, but seeing as I'm still not getting a response, that only makes this bad feeling I have worse.

With no options left, I have no choice but to walk down the hall to Lou-Lou's front door.

She answers on the second knock. Her eyes are red and puffy, it's obvious that she's been crying and she's upset about something.

"Look, I'm sorry I'm interrupting whatever it is that you're going through right now, but I can't get a hold of Jackson, and no one is at the apartment—"

"You don't know what happened, do you?" she says, her voice raspy with emotion.

I swallow hard against the lump in my throat and tell myself to breathe before I shake my head.

"There was an accident at the club tonight. Tyrone got stabbed by his opponent when the match started."

My hand flies over my mouth and a sob escapes.

"Everyone's at the hospital because he's having emergency surgery. That's probably why you can't get a hold of anyone."

"Thank you."

I start running down the hall, but to my surprise, I hear Lou-Lou's footsteps behind me.

"It's after 2am, Alyssa. You'll never catch a cab because they're too busy picking up drunk idiots and it will take you an hour to get there on foot. Also, it's not exactly safe to go walking in the city by yourself this time of night. If you want, I can drive you," she offers.

I nod my head, too shaken up to form actual words. My heart is breaking for Jackson… and Momma. Oh, god, poor Momma.

I pray as hard as I can for Tyrone the entire ride to the hospital.

I give Lou-Lou a questioning look when she pulls up to the front of the hospital but makes no move to get out. "You're not coming in?"

She looks down. "I want to, but I don't think anyone really wants to see me."

"Look, don't take this the wrong way, but it's not about you right now. Tyrone needs all the positive thoughts he can get. Plus, I think Ricardo would appreciate you showing up and offering your support."

She gives me an odd look and I can tell she's ready to argue, but instead she gets out with me and hands her keys to a valet attendant. "Do you think they'll give us any information? We're not immediate family and we didn't come in with him. And you already said that Jackson wasn't picking up his phone."

Crap, I didn't really think about that.

I scan the emergency room. The look on both the security guard's face and the nurse at the desk, tells me they're both going to be hard nuts to crack.

Out of the corner of my eye, I see my doppelganger's blonde ponytail and pink scrubs.

"Penelope," I call out, while taking Lou-Lou's hand and rushing over to her.

I quickly explain the situation. She looks sympathetic, and before I know it, she's leading us past the front desk and walking us toward a special section of the intensive care waiting room.

She tells us that Tyrone's still in surgery but she'll keep us updated if she finds out any information. I quickly thank her before Lou-Lou and I round the corner to the small waiting room.

That's where I see Jackson and Ricardo in some kind of standoff, looking like they're about to rip each others faces off.

"You've gotta be kidding me," Lou-Lou mutters. "Stop it!" she screams.

It's no use. In the blink of an eye, Jackson advances toward Ricardo and holds him up against the wall by his throat. "You knew this was going to happen, didn't you?" he sneers.

"You're out of your mind, Jackson. For fucks sake, I snapped that guy's neck. You think I would ever let anything happen to either one of you?"

Jackson shakes his head. "You knew about them switching his opponent before the fight. You *had* to know something was up. You told me everything was okay right before the fight. But, it wasn't fucking okay. You knew about the meeting because he had to go through you to get one! You knew he wanted out and you never fucking told me. And now, my best friend is in surgery fighting for his life."

Jackson slams him up hard against the wall again, but I see Ricardo's eyes flash and that strange feeling washes over me. The very same one I had that night Jackson fought Dean in the bathroom and Ricardo showed up.

"I had no idea that any of this was gonna go down, Jackson. I got him a meeting, yeah. But I wasn't privy to their discussion. It was a closed meeting. Tyrone wouldn't tell me why he wanted the meeting either, he just said it was important. If I had known, I would have talked him out of it," he screams, his voice cracking with emotion.

"You guys are like my brothers. You both are the closest thing to a real family I've ever had. I would never be okay with someone taking either one of you out, ever. I don't care *who* might have issued the order."

Order? Taking them out? What is he talking about?

Jackson eases up on his grip and bangs the wall beside his head. "I swear to god, Ricardo; you better be telling me the truth. Because if I find out that you knew about this…we're fucking done in every way you can think of."

The dangerous intensity in Ricardo's eyes is replaced by sadness. "I didn't know. I swear. I'd let him take *me* out before I'd *ever* let him do it to either one of you."

What should be a somewhat comforting statement, instead forces the hairs on the back of my neck to stand up.

Jackson pulls him into a hug. "I don't know what I'm gonna do if he doesn't pull through this."

My eyes water because the thought of losing Tyrone is heart-wrenching, but the moment turns tense again when Jackson fixes himself and his eyes darken. "Actually, I do."

Ricardo shakes his head. "No, man. Get that thought out of your head right now. He didn't order it. It wasn't him. I'm telling you."

Jackson slams him up against the wall again, but Ricardo deflects it and now he's the one slamming Jackson up against the wall.

"It was. I know it was," Jackson screams. "And you can tell *him* I'm fucking done."

Ricardo's hand wraps around his throat. "Don't be stupid. You'll get yourself killed. You can't be done with him. That ain't the way it works and you know it."

Two thoughts hit me simultaneously at that moment—what else is Jackson keeping from me? And more importantly…what kind of dangerous situation is he involved in?

Jackson lifts his arm and maneuvers out of the choke hold. They face one another again, but this time, it's clear it's not going to end in a hug. Jackson's fist flies out but Ricardo blocks it at the last possible second. Jackson jabs him again, though and gets him right between the eyes.

Lou-Lou and I start screaming our heads off, trying to get them to stop, but they ignore us completely.

"You're not out," Ricardo says before punching Jackson across the face. "I'm not gonna let you kill yourself," he screams before he throws another punch.

Jackson has that wild look in his eyes when he issues a kick straight to Ricardo's side. My hearts in my throat because I know that once Jackson gets started and he's in *this* mindset, the only one who can make him stop is Ricardo, but since he's fighting *Ricardo* right now—I'm terrified of how this is going to end.

Ricardo spits blood on the ground and motions for Jackson to come at him again. If Jackson's eyes are wild, Ricardo's are purely menacing and downright murderous.

My stomach drops and my hands shake because this time, I *know* I've seen that look and I'm not mistaken like before.

And I think I might just know what, or rather *who* Jackson is involved with. But my god, I *hope* I'm wrong.

Before I can focus on that, though, I have to stop this fight. My instincts are taking over and I surge toward them. Lou-Lou tries pulling me back but I twist away. She lets out an ear piercing whistle but it still doesn't stop me or them.

Both of their arms are pulled back and I know it's the last possible second that I have before they both strike each other again.

Lou-Lou screams my name when she sees what I'm about to do, but I do it anyway.

There's no way to describe how it feels to be punched full force by two massive men at the same time.

Well, except one. It really fucking hurts…a lot. Way more than I thought it would. Enough to almost make me regret doing it in the first place. It's literally the complete opposite of 'double your pleasure, double your fun.'

Jackson's fist lands on my cheek, and Ricardo's fist lands somewhere in my stomach region. Seeing as I'm 5'3 they were both obviously going for some low blows.

I let out a sound somewhere between a cry, a yelp, and a scream before hunching over and falling to the floor. That's when I hear Momma's voice. "Oh my god. Look what you boys did! How could you?" she screams.

Both Jackson and Ricardo drop down to the floor, their expressions horrified. "Alyssa? Fuck, baby. I'm sorry. I…god," Jackson says. He cups my face and I wince. "I'm *so* fucking sorry."

"Me too," Ricardo says. "I had no idea you were even here. What the hell were you thinking getting between us?"

"I just wanted you both to stop fighting. I didn't know how else to make you stop."

"*What* is going on here?" another voice calls out. I look up to find Penelope standing over us concern splashed across her pretty face.

"It was an accident," I say. When she raises an eyebrow, I stand up. "Honest, Penelope. I was the one who got in the middle. They didn't even see me."

She crosses her arms over her chest. "I'll get you a few ice packs." Then she looks at Jackson and Ricardo. "Gentlemen," she scoffs that word. "This is the intensive care unit of a *hospital*. This is not a zoo. Keep your hands to yourself. If it happens again I *will* have security escort you out," she snaps, before she turns on her heels and storms out.

"What were you boys thinking?" Momma whispers, her voice shaking.

She looks so heartbroken and devastated right now, I feel myself break.

Jackson and Ricardo stand up. "We're sorry, Momma," they say at the same time. "It will never happen again," they promise.

Then they walk over to her and wrap their arms around her.

I hear her sobbing softly and I lose it. I'm not the only one though, Lou-Lou's also weeping quietly in the corner. I don't miss the look Ricardo gives her. For a moment, I think he's going to walk over to her, but instead, he gives Momma and Jackson one last hug and leaves the waiting room altogether.

I look at Jackson and I want to confront him, but with everything else happening, I don't have the heart to just yet. I don't want to accuse him of lying to me and committing the ultimate betrayal until I have absolute proof and I know for a fact that it's DeLuca he's involved with. I'm going to need a little more to go on than just a gut feeling about Ricardo.

That doesn't mean I'm not still pissed to know that DeLuca or no DeLuca he's obviously been keeping something from me.

He walks over to me and holds out his arms. I take a deep breath and look down before he hugs me. He senses my hesitation and says, "I'm so sorry, Alyssa. I would never hurt you on purpose. Please forgive me."

The tears fall harder then...because if he's lying to me about DeLuca...I'm not sure that I can. Hell, for all I know, Jackson could be the one setting me up for DeLuca.

Oh, god. What if he is?

That thought sends a chill right through me and I have to push myself away from his embrace.

The look he gives me breaks my heart, but I can't stand the thought of being in his arms right now.

I slowly back away from him and he looks both crushed and stunned.

Luckily, Lou-Lou comes to my defense by taking my hand and saying, "I think she's in a lot of pain, Jackson. Probably not the best time to be hugging her. She did just get punched by two huge guys, remember?"

He winces and rubs his face. "I'm gonna go get those ice packs for you."

Momma looks at us. "I'm gonna go see if there's any news." Before she leaves, I run over and throw my arms around her. "I'm so sorry, Momma. I know he'll make it through this. Because he's tough just like his Momma."

She hugs me tight and gives me a kiss on the cheek before leaving the room. That's when Jackson's eyes connect with mine. There are so many emotions in those eyes of his right now, I have to force myself to breathe.

He walks over to me and hands me two ice packs. "Here." Then he turns and walks out the door.

"I'm being a real bitch, aren't I?" I ask Lou-Lou, because let's face it, who would know better than her?

She considers this for a moment before saying, "It's probably not the best time to be so angry with him seeing as Tyrone's still in surgery and we don't know the outcome." She shrugs. "However, you can't really control how you feel when someone you love hurts you. And the fact that you can't even stand being touched by him combined with that look you gave him…tells me that whatever Jackson did to you was unforgivable."

I turn around and face her. "Like what Ricardo did to you?"

She closes her eyes in agony and I feel bad for even asking the question. "No," she says, opening her eyes which are now glassy. "Let's just say that I've been right where Jackson's standing. I know what it's like to be on the receiving end of that look and have the man you…" She pauses and wipes a tear. "The man you love, look at you like the thought of touching you is unbearable and he'd rather die."

She clears her throat. "I'm gonna go grab some coffee. You want anything?"

I *want* to know more about what happened between her and Ricardo, but I know she's not going to tell me. I sit down in one of the chairs. "No, I'm good. Thanks."

She leaves and I curl my arms around myself while saying another prayer for Tyrone.

A moment later, I look up to find one of the most gorgeous women I have ever seen in my life staring at me. Her eyes are bloodshot and there's a look of utter despair on her face, but that does nothing to diminish her beauty. Her skin is smooth and mocha colored, her dark hair falls around her shoulders in soft curls, and her bright green eyes are mesmerizing.

"I'm sorry. The nurse told me this was where everyone was waiting. But I must have been mistaken, seeing as there's hardly anyone in here," she says in a Southern accent.

The accent gives her away and I immediately know who she is. "Shelby?"

She blinks and looks surprised. "Why yes," she says. "I don't believe we've ever met before. I'm not from around these parts. How do you know my name?"

I stand up and hold out my hand. "I'm Alyssa. I'm Jackson's—" I don't have a chance to finish that statement because her arms are around me and she's hugging me so tight I have to force myself not to yelp.

"I've heard so much about you, Alyssa," she says. Then she starts sobbing. "Have you heard anything? Is he still in surgery?"

"The last I heard he was. I know a nurse who works here, she's my—" I pause because I'm not entirely sure what to refer to her as at this point. "Friend and she promised to update me as soon as she can."

"Thank you, tell her I appreciate it. I'm so scared, Alyssa," she sobs. "I won't be able to go on if I lose him."

"He's a fighter, Shelby. He's going to make it."

She pulls away and wipes at her tears with a tissue. "I can't believe this happened." Then her green eyes turn angry. So angry I become alarmed. "I swear, if that son-of-a-bitch DeLuca did this to him. I will raise hell."

My heart constricts and I'm pretty sure I make a choking sound from somewhere deep in my throat.

There's a world of a difference between suspecting something and having it outright confirmed.

Because now I have to face facts, I have no choice but to acknowledge what's happening.

I have no choice but to realize that DeLuca wants his revenge. I have no choice but to accept that Jackson was setting me up.

Somewhere in the back of my mind, I recall Jackson telling me not to go to the club. But before it can hit the surface of my thoughts, I stuff it down. He *has* to be setting me up, this is the only reason I can come up with for him lying to me. Why *else* would he be actively working and fighting for a man who he knows brutally killed my father?

The room spins and I'm struck with the feeling of wanting to call Ford for some kind of protection, but I force myself to stay strong. Despite my father, I already know that I can't trust Ford, he's already shown his true colors to me. There's no way in the world I would ever put myself at his mercy again.

"Alyssa?" Shelby calls out.

Her name sounds so far away now but I don't know why. It's only when Jackson's face appears right in front of me and I let out a scream that I realize I'm on the floor.

"Talk to me, baby. What happened?" Jackson says, searching my face.

I quickly crawl away from him and stand up. I look up just as Lou-Lou walks in the room.

The face Jackson's makes when I walk over to her and reach for *her* hand is unlike any I've seen.

As messed up as it sounds, it's my way of letting him know that I'm on to him. It's my way of telling him that I'd rather hold *Lou-Lou's* hand than ever touch him again, the traitorous motherfucker.

He steps closer to me, but to my surprise, Lou-Lou lifts her chin and glares at him. "Leave her alone, Jackson. I have no clue what you did but she doesn't want you near her for the time being. You need to respect that."

His eyes narrow and he opens his mouth, but the look I give him halts him and he looks taken back.

I thought I'd break down over his betrayal. But I'm not, far from it actually. I'm straight up seething. I'm so outraged I want to put my hands around his neck and strangle the shit out of him. I want to eliminate him and wipe his beautiful face off the planet.

They always say there's a thin line between love and hate and right now, I'm standing on it, planting my fucking flag, ready to build a goddamned house on my newfound land made out of pure wrath. "Touch me again and you'll be in a jail cell," I say deadpan while pointing to my cheek.

Shelby's eyes open wide and she gasps.

Jackson takes a step back and shakes his head. "That was an accident and you know it. I would never, *ever* hurt you on purpose. *You* stepped right in the middle of a full-on fight between two grown men, Alyssa. I didn't even *see* you until it was already too late. You *have* to know that I would never hurt you! I *love* you!" he screams, his voice thick with emotion.

He looks completely wrecked right now and part of me wants to take back what I've said, but then Momma and Ricardo walk into the room and announce that Tyrone's out of surgery and the doctor will be updating us on his condition momentarily.

Any altercation brewing between Jackson and I goes on the back burner as we wait for the doctor to enter the room.

When he finally does, we all hold our breath, until he says, "He made it through surgery."

There's tears, shouts of happiness and smiles.

Until the Doctor's face falls. "He's still not out of the woods quite yet, but we're hopeful about his recovery from the surgery." He pauses and looks at Momma. "But there was extensive damage inflicted to his spinal cord. Specifically his thoracic vertebrae region, and more specifically, his T11 and T12 thoracic nerves."

Momma shakes her head, confused. "I don't understand what that means, Doctor."

Beside me, Jackson closes his eyes. "It means he's paralyzed, Momma."

Momma gasps and Jackson walks over to her and envelopes her in his arms.

The Doctor nods sadly. "Yes. Although we won't know the full extent of the damage or his injury level until he wakes up, recovers from surgery and we can do further testing. And now that the surgery is over, I'll have to ask that only immediate family remain here to see him. The rest of you can come back tomorrow during scheduled visiting hours."

The Doctor leaves after that and no one says a word, but there are sniffles and sobs from both Momma and Shelby.

Jackson and Ricardo look like they're about to lose it but are trying to remain strong. Lou-Lou looks down and her lower lip trembles.

My heart just breaks for poor Tyrone. I'm so happy he's alive, but this is devastating in its own right.

A few moments later Momma and Shelby hug everyone goodbye. Jackson didn't want to leave but when he heard that I was going back to my own apartment and not his, he said he'd be back later.

The four of us walk down the hallways in a clusterfuck of awkwardness. Lou-Lou and I walk side by side huddled up together, the tension between her and Ricardo and Jackson and me is so visible that even the nurses stop and give our group strange looks.

"You need a ride back to your apartment, right?" Lou-Lou says after we walk out of the elevator and make our way toward the parking garage. Fortunately, Ricardo and Jackson went out a different way.

"Yeah, if you wouldn't mind. I'd really appreciate it."

"No problem."

Far behind us, I hear both Ricardo and Jackson's footsteps.

Lou-Lou and I exchange a glance wondering why they're still following us, but we soon find out when we look over our shoulders and Ricardo tosses his keys in the air before Jackson catches them.

"Don't wreck my baby," he warns.

"I won't. I appreciate the favor."

"You owe me," he says before he begins walking closer to Lou-Lou at the same time Jackson walks closer to me.

"Oh, shit," Lou-Lou whispers.

"What?"

"Alyssa, I suggest that if you don't want to be manhandled by Jackson—you start running, now."

She doesn't have to tell me twice. I start running like there's a fire up my ass. I have no idea *where* I'm running, I just know that I'm toast if Jackson gets his hands on me. Especially knowing what I know *now* about him.

I'm not in the least bit turned on like I was during our last cat and mouse game at the bar. My brain and my body are fully aware that this is for survival. I'm sprinting so fast I'm surprising myself.

However, I'm still no match against Jackson. In a flash, his arm wraps around my waist and his large hand covers my mouth so I can't scream as he drags me in the direction of some red Mustang.

In the distance, I see Ricardo doing the same thing to Lou-Lou; only he's shouting, "Give me your fucking keys," in a dark tone that makes me incredibly nervous for her.

Then I have that moment, that moment where I say to myself—'Fuck this shit.'

I'm not letting him manhandle me. He's not taking me out of this parking garage without a fight.

I start kicking my legs and twisting as hard as I can against him. I even go as far as to bite his hand which causes him to curse.

Then I go limp and will my body to become a ferret. This way, I'll be able to slinky myself right out of his hold.

He seems to sense what I'm doing because he gives me a sinister laugh and says, "Nice try, Damsel."

The fact that he's using that name with me again makes me so mad I lift my head and spit in his face.

That's when he lifts me up and puts me right over his shoulder. "Why don't we save the exchange of bodily fluids for after we get home, baby?"

I grunt and smack my hand against his back. "I'm not going to your apartment, Jackson," I scream. "I know who's fight club you work at. I know how you betrayed me." I kick him. "And most of all, I already know that you're either going to kill me yourself or you're handing me right over to DeLuca himself to do it."

At this, he stops moving entirely. "Jesus Christ, you're crazy. You know that!" he roars.

"Tell me, Jackson. How much are you getting paid to be his lackey? To do his dirty work for him?" Then I give him a sinister laugh of my own. "You really had me going with that whole Lilly story. How long did it take you to come up with that? Hell, there probably is *no* Lilly, is there?"

His entire body starts shaking and his hold on me tightens, but I keep going. "Or maybe there *was*. Who knows? Maybe she was a disgruntled ex-girlfriend of yours? Maybe *you* were the one who really killed her. Tell me, Jackson. Where did you bury Lilly's body right after you murdered her, huh!"

"Shut the *fuck* up! You have *no* idea what you're talking about!" he screams so loud I jump.

He opens the door to the Mustang and throws me in the passenger seat. The vein in his neck is bulging and there's sweat pouring down his face. I've never seen him this upset before, not even in the cage.

I open my mouth again, but he opens the dashboard and pulls out a roll of duct tape. Then he slams it across my mouth. I roll my eyes and proceed to peel it off but then he forces the seat all the way back, crawls on top of me and before I know it, both my wrists are being bound behind my back with the duct tape.

This action only further confirms my suspicions regarding his intentions with me.

I kick my feet up and try to kick out the windshield. He sighs and says, "Please, sit still. I know you know about my involvement with DeLuca. But there are some things that you don't know and I would like to explain them to you. Will you let me do that?"

I ignore him and kick the windshield again, until his hand slams down on my thigh and he gets close to my face. "I'm *not* going to hurt you. I'm *not* going to kill you. But I swear on all that is holy, if you don't cut this shit out, I *will* throw your ass in the goddamned trunk, Alyssa."

At this, I finally stop kicking and relax in my seat.

He starts the car but points a finger at me. "I'm warning you right now, do *not* try and do something that will run us off the road."

I want to tell him that since it's New York City, there really would be no point. At most, we'll be going 20 miles per hour before he has to slam on the breaks again. He should worry much more about me making a run for it during one of those stops.

Provided I ever get this duct tape off that is.

He starts driving in the direction of his apartment complex, which throws me for a loop. Doesn't he know that Momma could walk in at any time? Last time I checked, it's bad to have a witness when you commit a murder. It's just one more loose end that you'll be forced to take care of.

Oh god. Would Jackson *actually* kill Momma?

When we reach his apartment, he pulls in the back and parks in a hidden spot I've never seen before. All I can think is. *This* is where he's going to do it.

But to my surprise, he gets out of the car and opens my door. My eyes dart around contemplating where I can run to, but he anticipates this because he picks me up and it's back over his shoulder I go.

On the bright side, at least the surveillance footage will catch him carrying me into his apartment building like this.

My murder will be solved. I'll get my lifetime wish and be headlining the 6 o'clock news after all.

I lift my head as we begin walking and spot Lou-Lou's car parked across the street. Since her windows are tinted, I can't see them…but I definitely hear all sorts of shouting.

The door to the complex shuts behind us and Jackson begins making his way up the staircase.

When we get inside his apartment he heads for the kitchen and sits me on a stool by the counter. He cracks his knuckles and rolls his neck. I can't help but stare at him, that is totally a mob guy move. He notices my face and pinches the bridge of his nose before reaching for the tape across my mouth and tearing it off.

I don't waste the opportunity, I start screaming my head off. *Mariah Carey* has nothing on my vocal chords right now.

Jackson grunts and covers my mouth with tape again. "Fine, I guess I'll go first," he says. "First of all, I love you—despite how batshit crazy you're acting right now. Secondly, I would never hurt you or kill you. It kills *me* that you would ever think that. And lastly, *yes* I do technically work for DeLuca, but it's not because I want to…got it?"

I shrug because I'm not really sure what he means by that. New York is an 'at will' state, if you don't want to work for someone you don't. Not that the mob really adheres to bylaws and regulations, but still. If Jackson didn't want to work for him, he wouldn't. Besides, why would DeLuca want to keep an employee on the payroll that didn't even *want* to work for him in the first place? That's just bad business.

Unless DeLuca is holding something over his head? But what the hell could DeLuca use for leverage?

Jackson begins pacing the floors. "Every single thing I told you about me is the truth, Alyssa. I know a small part of you *has* to know that. I mean, I put it all on video tape for you for crying out loud. You think I would confess to a murder that I didn't commit?"

He has a point, I guess.

I shake my head and he walks back over to me and removes the tape. "Don't scream. Just let me explain. Okay?"

I nod my head because maybe things aren't what they seem after all.

Chapter Thirty-Five

JACKSON

I'VE THOUGHT ABOUT HAVING ALYSSA BOUND AND GAGGED QUITE A LOT SINCE I FIRST met her.

I just never thought I'd be partaking in it to get her to stop screaming such god awful, vile things to me in the middle of a parking garage.

And the fact that she actually thinks I would hurt her? Or worse, *kill* her?

I just don't have the words to express what that does to me.

I wanted to bash my own head through a wall right after I saw what Ricardo and I did to her when she jumped in the middle of our fight. I've never felt like such an asshole but I didn't even see her. Hell, I didn't even know she was standing in the room because I was too worked up about Ricardo and his possible involvement.

And of course, the fact that my best friend was in the middle of surgery and the doctors had just told us there was a chance he wouldn't make it.

Then *that* shit happened.

Then she looked at me the way she did.

I figured she just needed space because of what happened but when I came back, she was different.

I saw her talking with Shelby and then she just collapsed.

I thought she was having a reoccurring symptom due to still being sick. Then she walked over to Lou-Lou and held her hand. Fucking Lou-Lou, the girl she basically hates. She'd rather hold *her* hand than *mine* while I'm going through all this shit.

I knew something wasn't right.

And when she gave me a different look—a look that could have killed me dead right where I stood and threatened to have me hauled off to jail over an accident…I knew I was fucked.

I knew that somehow…she had figured out the truth.

Then I heard the news about Tyrone and although I'm beyond relieved that he's alive…I know that when he wakes up and processes everything, he's going to be inconsolable. I'm inconsolable for him but I'll be there for him and whatever he needs.

The last thing I wanted to do was have it out with Alyssa, I wanted to stay by my best friend's side. Momma told me to go and said he'd probably be out of it until sometime tomorrow, but I still wanted to stay.

Then Alyssa mentioned going back to her own apartment and I knew this shit had to be dealt with tonight. She wasn't cutting me any kind of slack and I sure as hell wasn't losing her without a fight.

However, when she said those things to me in the parking garage? Spewing such *hurtful* things, things like *I* was the one who killed Lilly and she wanted to know where I buried her body. *That* was the closest I'd ever come to wanting to hit a female.

I settled for throwing her in the passenger seat and covering her vicious mouth with duct tape, instead.

Since she had no choice but to remain silent throughout the drive, I took the opportunity to put myself in her place.

That only made me feel like a shithead. Of course, she would think I was setting her up, regardless of the fact that *she* was the one who walked into his club. The fact is, DeLuca's been the metaphorical boogie man to her ever since she was a child. She knows first-hand what he's capable of.

No wonder she didn't push further after I said it wasn't his club. She completely dropped it and never asked me again. A part of me thinks that she didn't *want* it to be his club, because he scares the absolute shit out of her, with good reason. I can't help but think that if she knew without a shadow of a doubt that it was his club, then a big part of her would feel like she'd have no choice but to avenge her father's death…even if it ended up in her murder.

Which let's face it…it most definitely would.

That's one hell of a demand to put on yourself, especially after going through everything that she already has. Not to mention Ford's own method of brainwashing that he did.

She was probably relieved when I told her that DeLuca wasn't the owner. Grateful that she had a few more minutes on the clock before her time was up.

Putting myself in her place puts it into perspective for me.

She's still trembling and I wish that I could hold her, but I know she needs to hear about my involvement with DeLuca before she'll let that happen.

If she'll ever let that happen.

"Everything I told you about Lilly is the truth. With the exception of me getting off on self-defense." She looks confused so I continue, "I was going down for both Mike and Lilly's murder," I say as her eyes open wide.

Maybe *now* she'll realize how much those things she said hurt me. "I didn't kill Lilly, Alyssa."

"I know," she whispers. "I know that now. I just don't know why you would lie to me, Jackson. I loved you. I trusted you. Why would you set me up?"

Her voice is so small and broken my chest squeezes.

"I'm not setting you up, baby. I would never do that to you."

"Tell me why you're working for him then. Tell me why you're continuing to work for him after you know what he did to me."

"Because he's the reason I'm out of jail."

"How?"

"He was my deliverance. He paid off the judge, planted evidence to ensure that I'd walk, and hired the best defense attorney on the East Coast. Hell, DeLuca did such a good job it didn't even make it to trial."

"What was the catch?"

"The catch is that I figured out that the devil doesn't offer you deal's, Alyssa. He only offers you an arrangement with a steep pay off. And he prefers his payment in blood."

She looks down and shivers. "Well, you know what they say—the devil was once an angel."

"I don't think this one ever was."

"What arrangement did you make with him?"

Time to tell her everything.

"Ten years in his *underground* fight club. Which is a load of bull if you ask me, because I've seen law enforcement officials there before. Hell, they place some of the highest bets. Anyway, the terms were one fight every two weeks, to ensure I could recover from any potential injuries."

I grab a stool to sit down on. "I'd be appointed a coach to ensure I never skipped town and to keep me on a leash."

"Ricardo," she whispers.

I nod. "Yup. I'd also have to win at least 99% of my fights."

Her mouth hangs open. "That's impossible. No one's *that* good."

"You are if it's your life on the line."

"You can't be that good for 10 years straight Jackson! Your body will start to deteriorate, it will break down from all the constant wear and tear. There's *no* way you can stay number one for 10 years straight. I've seen the guys you're up against, they're nothing but freak shows on steroids"

Her lower lip trembles and I can see the tears in her eyes. "Oh, god. DeLuca *knows* this. He knows that you'll most likely die in the cage before your contract is up. Hell, he'll probably make sure that it happens."

"Yeah, that's pretty much what happens. The only one who's ever made it through his 10 years alive is Ricardo. The reason Tyrone and I are the best right now is because there's no one else to compare us to. For the most part, guys usually die in the cage around the first year. If he senses you're weak, then he matches you up with an opponent he knows you can't take. If you prove to be worthy, well, then you usually get the honor of dying in the cage around the 7th or 8th year. DeLuca likes to up the stakes by then. Trust me, it's some real fucked up shit."

I look up to the ceiling because I can't look at her when I say this. "And by your 7th or 8th year, it's probably bittersweet because you're so close to being out. You can taste it. But, at the same time, the mentality of being nothing but a machine has gotten to you, so unless you have something on the outside that grounds you, something to go back to…there's really no point in fighting anymore. Sometimes I think the guys don't make it because they just give up. They get tired of feeling the pain that fuels them to survive. I know I am."

"Lilly's murder is how you survive, isn't it? That's the source of all your pain."

"I have to relive every second of it every time I'm in that cage. It's the only way."

I want to tell her that she was the one who grounded me, who made it better for me, and that she was my something to look forward to, but there's something more important that she needs to hear.

"I wanted to protect you, that's why I didn't tell you about DeLuca. I tried to let you go a few times, but I couldn't do it. I need you like I need my pain to win my fights."

"What are we gonna do, Jackson?" A single tear falls down her cheek. "How do we make it through this?"

I don't answer her, instead, I tear the tape off her wrists and hold her in my arms. She buries her face into my chest and sobs her heart out.

"I agree with Ricardo. Don't go after DeLuca. It's too risky and you'll end up dead. We'll have to find another way. There *has* to be another way. I can't and I *won't* lose another man that I love to him."

I stay silent because there *is* another way; the *only* way to stop him. I could care less about my own life, but I'm not letting him take hers.

She tilts her head up and I don't even hesitate to crush her mouth against mine.

There are so many emotions filtering the energy running through us, there's only one way to exert it right now.

I lift her up, place her on the counter and she wraps her legs around my waist. I wish I could be more gentle with her given the fact that I know she's probably feeling sore from what happened earlier, but when she sits up, takes off my shirt and scratches her nails down my back, I lose my composure.

I suck and bite on that plump bottom lip of hers, groaning when I taste the hint of copper because it reminds me that she's alive, that she's safe, and that she's here with me.

I make quick work of unbuttoning of her jeans and pulling them off. Her panties are next and I shred the delicate lace like it's paper while she lifts her t-shirt over her head.

The both of us are so worked up there's no need for foreplay, my own jeans fall at my feet and I'm entering her in a single thrust, pumping into her slickness like it's my salvation, because I know she is.

She falls back and I position her legs on my shoulders so I can get even deeper inside her. I'm so lost in her essence, there are no words. The only sounds are the moans of pleasure and the sounds of our frantic, hot-blooded bodies coming together.

After a moment, she begins to spasm and cries out my name like a lifeline. Her pussy grips me so hard it almost hurts as her come drips down my balls. Before I can stop myself, I'm quickly following her into the pits of euphoria and purging my own release deep inside of her.

I fall on top of her, loving the feeling of her body underneath me, where I can shelter her and see the rise and fall of her chest with every breath she takes.

She kisses me and it's clear that what just happened didn't diminish her feelings, if anything; it only charged them. She pushes her pelvis into mine, purposely enticing me into another round. Her tongue darts out and drags across her bottom lip slowly when she feels my cock twitch against her center. Since she's the puppet master of not only my heartstrings, but my desire—I'm rock hard and inside her again.

I flip her around so that I'm entering her from behind and watching that gorgeous ass of hers shake with my every thrust. I lean down and sink my teeth into her shoulder.

She looks over her shoulder and bites her lip. And fuck *me*, it's the hottest visual I've ever seen.

I don't have to worry about DeLuca killing me, because she's going to.

She moans and I start thrusting harder. The feeling is incredible and I know I won't be able to hold off much longer.

"Jackson, I'm…fuck," she says before she starts jerking and unintelligible screams rip out of her.

Wanting to make it even better for her, I circle her clit and watch as she grabs onto the counter and moans my name. She clenches around me and I get two more pumps in before I'm coming inside her.

"Thank you," she breathes. "You have no idea how much I needed that. How much I needed to lose myself in you."

I almost laugh because I'm pretty sure I should be thanking *her* for that experience. I pick her up and carry her into the bedroom. "You never have to thank me for that. Besides, I needed it just as much, maybe even more."

I pull back the covers and curl up beside her. "I love you," she whispers before she drifts off to sleep.

I kiss the spot over her heart. "I love you," I say before I stand up and reach for my cell phone.

I step out into the hallway and dial Ford's number. He answers on the third ring. "I want to talk about that deal."

Chapter Thirty-Six

ALYSSA

"FORD, IT'S ME AGAIN. I NEED YOU TO CALL ME BACK, PLEASE. IT'S IMPORTANT," I say before I hang up.

I never thought I'd find myself in this position again. However, I know it's the only way. We can't beat DeLuca on our own and he's the only resource I have.

Despite how much of an asshole he is, I know that Ford wants to nail DeLuca. And now that I know for a fact that it's his club...I'm going to help him come up with a plan to do it.

I'm going to have him use me as bait like he originally intended. Then, Ford will take care of him and Jackson and I will be free.

Well, that's what I'm hoping will happen, but Ford has yet to call me back.

It's been almost a week since I first reached out to him. It's strange that he still hasn't contacted me.

I was hoping to see him and finalize a plan before Jackson has to fight again tomorrow night. There's no telling what will happen in that cage after Tyrone's last fight.

Since Jackson's currently at the hospital visiting Tyrone, I'm taking the opportunity to slip out and go to Ford's house myself.

It's too close to Jackson's fight and I can't take the chance of him getting hurt, I'll do whatever I have to in order to protect him.

The cab ride to Ford's is over an hour away, so I take the time to formulate the start of a good plan. I know that going to the club won't work since DeLuca never shows up there himself. Not to mention, setting up some kind of meeting there would harbor too many witnesses. There's no way Ford would take him out with that many people around.

I have to find a way to get DeLuca secluded and completely alone, but I don't know how to go about that.

My mind's on the verge of figuring out a way to do it, but every time I get closer, I hit a mental block and I can't work my way around it.

The cab finally pulls up to Ford's house and what I see causes me to freak the hell out.

There's a red Mustang parked in his driveway.

Ricardo's here.

What the hell is Ricardo doing here?

"Miss, are you getting out or not?" the cab driver grumbles. "Not," I tell him. "Take me back home."

With a curse, he starts to drive away.

I'm more confused than ever now. It's obvious that Ford and Ricardo are doing business together, but what?

I sit up straight in my seat when I realize. They've got to be trying to take down DeLuca? That's the only tie those two have to one another.

My cell phone starts ringing and I almost want to ignore it because I don't want Shane to ask me to work tomorrow night. My life is hectic right now and there's no way I'm going to be able to focus on working at the bar while Jackson could be getting killed in the cage.

I rub my temples and answer the phone anyway. "Hey, Shane."

"Do you have a twin?"

Okay, that's not what I was expecting him to say.

"No, I'm an only child," I say, pushing down sad memories.

"I was joking, Alyssa." He laughs. "Besides, the chick I'm staring at is hot but she looks like an older, more sophisticated version of you, no offense."

"None taken." Then it dawns on me. "Does she have blonde hair?"

"Yup. And she just asked to speak to you. Hold on."

Why is Penelope sitting at Finnley's right now?

"Hey, Penelope. Is everything okay?"

"I don't know. You tell me?" she replies in a snarky tone.

"Um…you're the one sitting at *my* job. What's going on?"

"I thought you learned your lesson when it came to Ford?"

Shit…she must still be checking his phone records.

"I did. I only reached out to Ford because I'm having a personal problem that I need to involve the police with. I figured calling him would speed things along, but he still hasn't called me back."

I can practically smell the wood burning from her thinking so hard on the other line.

"Don't lie to me, Alyssa. Look, I'm not jealous. I don't want him back, but I am concerned about you going back to *him* because you and your current boyfriend are having problems."

I blow out a breath, trying my hardest not to go off on her for sticking her nose in my business. "Penelope, I'm never going back to Ford. I'm in love with Jackson."

"Then why the hell did I find plane tickets and passports with both your names on it?"

Say what?

"I'm sorry. I think I misheard you."

"No, you didn't. I went there to pick up my mail yesterday—since the asshole insisted on keeping the house that *he* bought in the settlement. He wasn't home so I used my key and out on the coffee table were two tickets to Mexico along with two passports. One for you and one for him."

"Oh my god. That's crazy."

"Exactly—" she starts to say.

"I'm *not* leaving the country with Ford. I have no idea what's going on or what he's planning. But I need you to promise me that you won't mention a word of this to him. Don't tell him that you know me and please don't tell him that we had this conversation, okay?"

"Shit, what's going on, Alyssa?"

"I don't know," I answer, before I hang up.

I breathe a sigh of relief when I look out the window and see city buildings.

I quickly take into account all the things I just found out—Ricardo and Ford have some kind of dealings going on together. My guess, is that it involves DeLuca. The only thing that *doesn't* make sense—is why the hell Ford's planning on whisking me off to freaking Mexico.

The only thing I can think of, is that Ford probably doesn't know that I'm with Jackson because we haven't had contact for months. He knows I've never kept boyfriends in the past and he probably just assumed I'm single.

On the plus side, Ricardo and Ford must be gearing up to take DeLuca down. And if my suspicions about Ricardo are correct, who better than *him* to help do it?

On the negative side, Ford's going to attempt to woo me and take me on vacation. Clearly he has another thing coming, but I'll gladly accept him getting rid of DeLuca for me and Jackson.

What I don't understand is why the heck he never picked up his phone for me if he's planning on doing all *this*? But then again, it's Ford. He's about as predictable as a tidal wave.

I pay the cab driver and walk into the apartment. Now that Jackson gave me a key, I don't have to knock on the door anymore.

"Hey," a deep voice says.

I turn around and practically have a heart attack when I see Ricardo standing before me.

How the hell did he make it back here so fast? Then again, he does drive a mustang.

He looks at me and makes a face. "Look, you've been acting a little strange around me ever since that fight. I hope you know that I really didn't mean to punch you. You don't have to be scared of me, Alyssa."

"Yeah," I squeak.

He scratches the back of his neck and it's only then that I notice he's wearing a sweat stained t-shirt and a pair of shorts. His hair is wet and his skin is glistening. He looks like he just finished working out, not driving back from Long Island.

"Where did you just come from?"

"The gym. Why?"

"Are you sure?"

He leans in and gives me a peculiar look. If he wasn't so fucking intimidating, he'd be *ridiculously* good looking. "Am I sure I got back from the gym?" He smirks. "Yeah, I'm positive. So, I'll ask you again. Why?"

"No r-reason." I turn around and attempt to get my key in the door as he walks across the hall to his own apartment.

Then it occurs to me. He could have let someone else borrow his car. Or, maybe it wasn't Ricardo's car in the driveway after all?

There's only one way to find out. "Hey, Ricardo? I was wondering if you would mind giving me a ride."

"I would, but I don't have my car."

Before I can question him further he says, "But you should already know that Jackson's borrowing my car until tomorrow morning because he's going to Boston." He shrugs. "Kind of surprised you didn't go with him actually."

"Going to Boston?" I whisper.

Jackson definitely never mentioned going to Boston this morning.

No. *This can't be fucking happening.*

I open my mouth to cover my fumble but Ricardo says, "He's going to Boston to visit Lilly's grave. Today's her birthday."

He takes a step forward and gives me an odd look. "Did he not tell you?"

"Of course, he did." I laugh nervously. "I just forgot is all." I give him a big smile. "I am naturally a blonde…we do have our moments."

He cocks an eyebrow. "Yeah. Okay, then. I'm gonna take a shower. Talk to you later."

I give him a wave before closing and locking the door behind me. Then I start hyperventilating.

Now it makes sense. It's *not* Ricardo and Ford working together. It's Jackson and Ford.

Which means that Ford *does* know I'm with Jackson.

But those plane tickets and passports…they can only mean one thing.

Ford is setting Jackson up to kill DeLuca and Jackson has no idea.

I wish he didn't shut me out when I tried to tell him everything that happened between Ford and I. Then he would already *know* not to trust him.

I pick up my phone and dial Jackson but it goes straight to voicemail. I leave the longest message I've ever left detailing everything that Ford did to me, including what happened that day in his office.

I also dial Ford, it rings a few times before going to voicemail. I close my eyes. In the back of my mind, I always knew this day would come. I used to be ashamed that I was so terrified about my date with DeLuca.

I mean, who doesn't want vengeance for the death of their father?

I thought I would cry and fall apart when it happened. But surprisingly, I feel like I'm finally thinking rationally.

It's time to have my dance with the Devil.

It's time to protect the man I love and inflict retribution on DeLuca for the one that I lost. Even if it's the last thing I do.

I walk into the bedroom and start going through the boxes that I moved in over the past week.

Covered in a pile of old clothes I find my lock box. I take it out, punch in the combination and open it. I eye my revolver and my semi-automatic pistol. The one good thing that came out of my relationship with Ford was him teaching me how to shoot a gun and taking me to the firing range when I was younger.

I make sure they're both loaded and ready to go before throwing a sweatshirt on and tucking both guns into the waistband of my jeans.

It's funny how a plan formulates itself when you find out the person you love is in danger.

I knock on Lou-Lou's door and wait for her to answer. I know her and Ricardo have some major problems and still haven't worked any of their shit out.

But quite frankly, I don't really give a fuck at this point. I just need someone to use as leverage against Ricardo and that someone is Lou-Lou.

She answers the door and although she looks surprised to see me, she invites me in.

As soon as the door is closed, I take out the revolver and put it to her head. "You crazy bitch!" she screams. "I thought we were friends now? What the fuck are you doing?"

"We are. This is nothing personal, Lou-Lou. I just need a hostage."

I pull her hair and position her in front of me. Given she's so tiny, it's easy to push her around. "However, feel free to think of this as payback for being such a bitch to me."

She starts screaming, but I dig the gun into her head. "Scream and I'll kill you. Trust me, you don't want to fuck with me right now."

She takes a deep breath. "Can you at least tell me why you're doing this?"

"Jackson's in trouble with a certain mob boss."

"Bruno," she whispers.

"Ah, I see you're on a first-name basis with the asshole. Good to know, that might come in handy." I shove her in front of me. "Now open the door and start walking down the hall to Ricardo's. If you run…I swear I'll kill him."

She opens the door with shaky hands and starts walking. She knocks on his door but he doesn't answer. That's when I remember. "Shit, he's in the shower."

"I have a key," Lou-Lou offers. "It's in my back pocket."

"I'm not falling for that."

"Then *you* can get it," she insists.

I dig the gun into her temple as I get her keys out of her back pocket and hand them to her. "You attack me with those and I'll shoot."

"I know."

Part of me is wondering why she's being so cooperative, but I don't have the time to question it.

We walk into Ricardo's apartment and I walk us to the bathroom, with Lou-Lou as my hostage.

Since there's no point in knocking on his bathroom door. I have Lou-Lou open it.

The look on Ricardo's face when he see's that I'm holding a gun up to Lou-Lou's head is one for the record books.

He reaches for a towel and quickly wraps it around his waist before he steps out of the shower.

That's when I silently pat myself on the back because the fact that he's naked as the day he was born means that he has no weapons on him.

However, what bewilders me is why he isn't more freaked out about this. I know he's worried about Lou-Lou, that's more than evident by the way he looks at her. But the fact that he's not puzzled by his current predicament is unnerving.

"How did you find out?" he says, his tone solemn.

I open my mouth, but Lou-Lou cuts me off by screaming, "I didn't tell this bitch shit, Ricky."

I whack her head with the gun. "No talking." I look at Ricardo. "You have his eyes. I'll never forget his eyes. They haunt me in my dreams."

He closes his eyes. "I'm not like my father, Alyssa."

"Doesn't matter. Your father took the most important person in my life from me and he's about to do it again. I want him to *feel* what it's like to lose the most important thing to him."

He sucks in a breath and glances at Lou-Lou. "Yeah. I get that, Alyssa."

His expression quickly changes to nervousness. "Wait, what do you mean he's about to do it again? Where the fuck is Jackson right now?"

"He's working with an FBI agent. An FBI agent that's going to set him up for the murder of your father. I have to get to him before that happens."

"Shit. Can't you just call him and warn him?" Lou-Lou asks, her voice cracking.

"He's not picking up his phone."

"Fuck. *No.* Oh, my god. Shit," she sputters, her breathing erratic.

I yank her hair. "As touched as I am about your sentiments regarding my boyfriend's current circumstance, can you kindly *shut up* so we can get on with the program."

She shakes her head. "I swear, I didn't mean to. I didn't know it was Jackson. Oh, my god," she squeaks.

Suffice it to say, she has both Ricardo's and my attention at this point.

I pull the other gun out of my waistband and put them both up to her head. "You better start making sense, Lou-Lou…or your brains are gonna be all over the carpet. What the fuck did you do?"

"There was this guy. This FBI agent. He started talking to me, you know flirting, all that."

"You talked to the fucking Feds?" Ricardo screams at the same time I scream, "Was his name Ford?"

"H-how did you know?"

"Cut to the chase, Lou-Lou. I know how Ford pulls the females in. Tell me what he wanted you to do. And how Jackson is involved."

"That's the thing. This Ford, guy. He seemed to know everything about me. Things that no one knows."

Ricardo lets out a curse and I scratch my head with one of my guns. "And you didn't find that a little suspicious? You can't be that dumb."

"I'm not dumb. *Of course*, I did. But then he offered me a deal."

"Goddammit, Lucianna! He's a fucking double agent. He's not legit, he works for us!" Ricardo screams at the same time I scream, "What kind of deal!"

I aim one of the guns for Ricardo's head and gasp. "What? What the actual *fuck* did you just say?"

It feels like all the air just got sucked out of the room. The only reason I'm not collapsing right now is because I still have to save Jackson.

Ricardo runs a hand down his face. "Shit," he says. "Look, Alyssa. Trust me when I say that you're better off not knowing the truth. I don't think you can take it and I'm not going to be the one to tell you."

I shoot the wall beside his head. "Tell me. Tell me the fucking truth."

"No. You can shoot me dead, but I will *not* be responsible for putting the same soul-crushing look on your face that my father did the day he killed your dad!" he roars. "My father's eyes haunt you in your dreams? Well, yours fucking haunt *mine*!"

"You—" I pause because my voice is wavering. "You were there that day? The day my father was killed?"

I look at him in disbelief. He's only 5 years older than Jackson. The only young people I remember seeing that day were the teenage gang members.

"I was 18," he says. "In fact, it was my 18th birthday. The day I officially became a man. My father wanted to celebrate by showing me what you do to rats. Or specifically, what you do when you find out that one of your men is an undercover agent."

His face contorts in agony. "You weren't the only one locked in a car that day, Alyssa," he says gruffly before his tone turns somber. "I'm so sorry. I liked your dad. We did some runs together and became close. I looked up to him. Wanted to be like him. He used to talk about how much he loved his little goblin—"

I shoot the wall beside his head again, much closer this time. "Shut the fuck up. You didn't know shit about my dad, you piece of shit! Your father killed him! He *killed* him and I watched every second of it and I saw the look in DeLuca's eyes when he did it. So don't you fucking try and stand there and offer me your condolences or sympathy. Like this is some kind of hallmark moment...when you're literally the spawn of fucking Satan himself!"

His eyes become glassy. "I didn't want to be. That day changed me. You have no idea what that day did to me."

"It will never compare to what it did to me."

"I know," he whispers.

In front of me, Lou-Lou's trembling and I hear her sobbing. "You're the little girl. The little girl in his nightmares."

"Stop, Lou-Lou," Ricardo warns.

Lou-Lou lifts her chin. "No. You need to know, Alyssa. He's not Bruno. Trust me, you don't know what Ricardo's been through. He's not the bad guy. Bruno is."

"I guess it's time to find out then, huh?"

Ricardo's eyes meet mine. "What do you mean?"

"Call your father and find out where he is right now. If you don't, I'll kill her in front of you and give you another nightmare."

Ricardo picks up his shorts off the floor but I click my tongue. "Are you armed?"

"Would it matter? I'm not going to kill you."

"A leopard doesn't change its spots."

"You know, bitch—you're not the only one who watched their parent get murdered by the hands of DeLuca."

"DeLuca killed your parents?" I question.

"Probably," she scoffs. "Who the fuck knows. However, I was referring to Ricardo."

"He killed your mother?" I ask in his direction.

Ricardo closes his eyes and nods. "Yeah. After I told him that I wanted nothing to do with him and said I would never be like him. He tracked my mother down and taught me another lesson."

This time, I see a tear fall down his face and I let mine fall with it. "How are you not more fucked up? How did you save yourself from becoming just like him?"

"Believe me, he's *plenty* fucked up," Lou-Lou whispers.

Ricardo turns around and I read the large tattoo on his back scrawled in black ink. *Sometimes there is absolutely no difference at all between salvation and damnation.*

"It's from the Green Mile," Lou-Lou offers.

I ignore her and wait for him to turn back around. "You going to call him?"

"I don't really have much of a choice. I'm not letting him kill Jackson."

"I swear I didn't know it was him," Lou-Lou whispers again.

I can't believe I almost forgot. "Lou-Lou finish telling me about your involvement with Ford."

She clears her throat. "Like I said, he tried to get in my pants and he knew all this stuff." Ricardo narrows his eyes and she quickly says, "Anyway, he offered me a deal. He said that he would set it up so that I could kill DeLuca. But seeing as he was FBI, *he* would make sure it wouldn't get pinned on me. He said there would be someone else there, someone with more motive than I had to take the fall. I didn't know it was going to be *Jackson* because he refused to tell me who this other person was. He said I wouldn't find out until I got there...but I didn't go through with it. I backed out at the last minute."

Ricardo starts pacing. "Fuck, he was playing you both."

I always knew Ford was manipulative, but even I didn't think he'd take it this far. "I guess that explains why he planned to take me to Mexico. There's really no doubt in my mind that he's setting Jackson up."

When they both look at me I say, "Ford and me...our relationship is...was...complicated. It's really fucked up."

Ricardo looks disgusted. "Trust me, sweetie. You really have no idea *just* how fucked up," he whispers.

My stomach knots with those words but I don't have time to concentrate on that. "Ricardo, I need you to talk to DeLuca. Find out where he is right now. Tell him it's an emergency and you need him to meet you at the docks near Jersey."

"You want to do this *there?*"

"Hell, yes." Not only do I like my revenge served cold too but I need to get him as far away from Jackson as possible and *still* manage to kill him in the next few hours.

I look down at Lou-Lou. "And after that, I need *you* to call Ford. Tell him the fucking jig is up and I'm holding both you and Ricardo hostage. Tell him to meet me at the docks, but *warn* him that if he brings Jackson it will be the last thing that he does."

Ricardo shakes his head. "That's not going to work. He's going to bring Jackson. Especially if he's already targeted him as the fall guy. Also, there's no telling what Jackson will do to Ford if he finds out he set him up. There could be a showdown between them."

Crap, he's right.

"Well then get a hold of Jackson and tell him that something happened to me. Say whatever you have to say to throw him off the course. Don't tell him about Ford just make sure he leaves."

"But you said he wasn't picking up his phone," Ricardo argues.

I smirk. "I'm sure he has a special company phone that you can get a hold of him on."

Chapter Thirty-Seven

JACKSON

RICARDO: *ALYSSA'S GONE CRAZY! SHE HAS A GUN AND IS HOLDING LOU-LOU AND me hostage. Ford's a double agent, don't trust him. It's a set-up. Do not attack him just yet, he might be prepared for that. Get away from him and find a way to sneak to the docks near Jersey. We'll be in the small warehouse-sneak in through the back. Address is in my car gps listed under 10/29/01.*

Make sure you're armed—check the trunk. DeLuca will be there. Stay safe, brother. And when I call you—sound panicked and go with it. Alyssa's fine...well, physically anyway. Erase this text and do not respond to it.

I have to go into Ford's bathroom and read Ricardo's text message three times to make sense of it. Seeing as he texted the burner phone he gave Tyrone and me for emergencies, I know he means business. A minute later, the phone vibrates. "Yeah," I answer. I hear mumbling in the background and what sounds like Lou-Lou and Alyssa arguing.

How the hell did she figure everything out? But even more alarming than that, how the hell am I going to protect her *now* when she's pulling this shit?

"Alyssa's been shot. Come quick," Ricardo shouts before he hangs up.

My heart explodes in my chest, until I remember him telling me to just go with it. I erase his text and walk back out. Ford gives me an odd look. "Everything alright in there?"

"No. Something's come up. I'm leaving," I say, walking toward the door

He steps in front of me and it takes everything in me not to deck him. "What the fuck could ever be more important than *this*? Today's the day. I've set everything in motion."

I bet you did, you lying motherfucker.

I decide to see if his feelings for Alyssa were ever real or if he's been lying about those as well. "Alyssa's been shot." With that, I run out the door and head for the Mustang.

He runs after me. "What?" he shouts. "By who? Where is she?"

"I don't know. She's at the hospital. I have to go."

He's on my heels, but stops to answer his phone when it rings. I open my car door and see his face turn pale. He's so visibly shaken, he has to wipe the sweat from his brow as he whispers something into the phone.

Then he screams Alyssa's name in agony.

His feelings for her are obviously real. You can't fake *that* kind of emotion. However, whatever he feels for her, fails in comparison to what *I* feel for her.

Unfortunately for me...his pain will be cut short soon.

And unfortunately for *him*...it's because he'll be dead.

I peel out of his driveway and head for the docks.

Chapter Thirty-Eight

ALYSSA

"**A**LYSSA'S BEEN SHOT. COME QUICK," RICARDO SHOUTS FROM THE BACKSEAT OF Lou-Lou's car before he hangs up the phone.

I point my gun at his chest. "Really, you couldn't have done better than *that?*"

"It got the message across. He won't be with Ford anymore."

I dig the gun into Lou-Lou's temple. "Now it's your turn."

She pulls up Ford's contact information and hits send. He picks up right away. "Lou-Lou?"

"Hi, Ford. Alyssa's holding me hostage and she knows what you're up to."

"I don't believe you," he snarls.

I grab the phone from her. "Hello, Ford. Or should I say—special *manipulating bastard* agent Ford?"

His breathing becomes uneasy but he stays silent.

"I'm going to make this real easy for you. Meet me down at the docks. Leave Jackson alone. This is between you, me, and DeLuca. If you bring Jackson, I swear on my father's death…it will be the *last* thing you ever do."

"Alyssa, no. Don't do this," he whispers. I don't respond.

"Alyssa," he screams.

That's when I hang up and look at Ricardo.

"You still have one more phone call to make."

I see his adam's apple bob and it's the first time I've ever seen Ricardo look nervous.

He puts the phone up to his ear. "Yeah, it's me."

I hear some murmuring on the other line.

"I know you're busy. But something's come up."

Just knowing that it's DeLuca on the other line makes me want to vomit. I have to force myself to breathe and not pass out.

"I'm being held hostage," Ricardo says before he adds, "I know you don't care."

Uh-oh. This is *not* the way I saw this going. I counted on Ricardo being my advantage.

"Tell him who's holding you hostage and tell him he better be unarmed when he shows up or I'll kill you."

I wish I could see the look on his face when he hears that it's me behind all this.

Ricardo looks at me before he says, "Listen, you need to meet us at the docks near Jersey. Alyssa Tanner's holding a gun to my fucking face."

There's more mumbling on the other line.

Ricardo closes his eyes and lets out a frustrated sigh. When he opens them, he gives me that murderous look before he screams, "I know you don't give a fuck about *me*, Babbo…but she's got Lucianna! And she *will* kill her. Make sure you come unarmed!"

There's silence on the other line and my stomach lurches. My plan is going downhill, fast.

"Okay. I'll be there…unarmed. Make sure that bitch doesn't touch a *hair* on Lucianna's head or I'll be bashing hers in just like her father's," DeLuca's gritty voice shouts before he hangs up.

I look over at Lou-Lou in shock. And to think, I *almost* didn't want to drag her into this. I was only holding her hostage as a way to get *Ricardo* to cooperate. I was going to have her drive us to the docks and let her go.

She's the *last* person I ever expected to be DeLuca's soft spot.

"Damn, Lou-Lou. I sure as fuck underestimated you."

She looks up and gives me a wink. "Yes you did, bitch. And if you want DeLuca brought to his knees, I'll be glad to help you do it. But if you hurt Ricardo; trust me—I'll make your life even more of a living hell than it already was."

I'm not sure if I have a newfound respect for her...or if she's just managed to scare the crap out of me.

"Noted, now start driving."

I adjust myself in the passenger seat of Lou-Lou's car. I have one gun pointed at her head and one gun pointed at Ricardo in the backseat. "Either one of you try and pull something, I'll be reenacting my own version of Romeo and Juliet, got it?"

They both nod and I gesture between them with my guns. "So, what's the story between you two? I gotta hear this."

Ricardo lifts his chin and glares at me. "None of your fucking business," he grits through his teeth.

I crinkle my nose at him. "Well, seeing as I'm the one holding a gun to your face, call me crazy but I'd say it was."

"Oh, I'm calling you *crazy* alright," he mumbles.

"Seriously," Lou-Lou chimes in. "You got a set of cajones, Alyssa. I'm impressed."

"Thanks, I think. But I'm not crazy," I say softly. "I'm just protecting Jackson and getting my revenge."

We stay in silence for the better part of an hour. And all I can think is—what makes *Lou-Lou* so important to DeLuca? Even more important than his own son?

She *can't* be his daughter. That would make Ricardo and Lou-Lou's relationship beyond twisted, especially if it was mostly based on sex.

Unless? Well, I'll be damned.

"Are you guys like step-brother and step-sister or something?" I wiggle my eyebrows. "I'm not judging, that's kinda hot."

"Fuck off," Ricardo barks.

"He's not my step-brother," Lou-Lou whispers.

"Why are *you* so important to DeLuca?" I ask. She grips the steering wheel and winces. "Probably the same reason you're so important to Ford."

I have *no* idea what she means by that, but I have to put it on the back burner because we start pulling up to the docks.

My eyes automatically look at the spot where my father died and I start dry heaving. For a moment, I feel just like that little girl trapped in the car who watched it all happen.

Surprisingly, both Ricardo and Lou-Lou put a hand on my shoulder. "Breathe, Alyssa. DeLuca will be here any minute; if he's not here already and you'll make one hell of an easy target if you're passed out. Then all of this will be for nothing," Ricardo says.

"It's true," Lou-Lou whispers. "It's time to get your payback. DeLuca deserves everything that's coming to him," she says before she gets out of the car.

Ricardo looks in her direction before he closes his eyes and sighs. "Go big or go home, right?"

"I don't think I can do it out here. Not in the same place my father died. It just feels… wrong."

"I get it." He gestures his head to a small run-down building. "There's a warehouse over there."

When we get out of the car he says, "By the way, I'm not letting DeLuca kill you. So, just know that whatever happens, I got your back."

I guess Ricardo's been armed the whole time after all.

We begin walking toward the warehouse and I place both my guns to their heads again and have them walk in front of me.

Seeing as I didn't notice DeLuca's car anywhere, I almost piss my pants when I look down and see a pair of metal tipped shoes.

"Back the fuck up," I command in his direction, surprising myself.

He takes a few steps back and the look he gives me could burn through glass. I take in his jagged scar, which still hasn't faded much over the years and his evil eyes and my stomach recoils.

How can a single person be the source of every nightmare? I can't help it, I start sweating and breathing erratically.

Before I can say another word, he looks at Lou-Lou. "Are you okay, Bambina? Has she hurt you?"

Clearly, he really *doesn't* give a fuck about Ricardo.

"I'm fine," she replies icily.

"Don't take that tone with me," he barks, almost causing me to jump. "You know I worry about you, Lucianna."

Lou-Lou looks up at him and it's like she transforms into a servant right before my very eyes. "I'm so sorry, mio amore. It's been a long day."

I see Ricardo's entire body tense in front of me and I gotta say, my heart goes out to him.

I haven't taken much Italian…but I do know what *'mio amore'* means—'my love.'

It's obvious DeLuca and Lou-Lou are in a relationship of some kind.

Wow. That's just…holy shit balls.

Not to mention…odd and kinda gross.

Lou-Lou's *my* age. DeLuca's in his late 50's, at *least*. Not that *I* should really be one to judge. But now her statement about me and Ford makes perfect sense.

Poor Ricardo.

I can't focus on that right now, though. I have a bastard to kill first.

"Sit over there," I tell them, motioning to the wall.

They do as I say, but I don't miss the look in Ricardo's eye, telling me to get this over with.

I have to take a long deep breath when I realize that it's just DeLuca and I facing one another.

It's surreal. I don't know whether to pinch myself because it's finally happening or scream because a part of me is petrified.

"Alyssa," he says.

I internally shiver because hearing him say my name sounds like nails on a chalkboard. "So we meet again."

He gives me an evil smirk. "Only much closer this time."

"I'm not afraid of you," I say, my voice surprisingly strong.

He puts his hand in his pocket but I point the gun toward Lou-Lou and he pauses.

Dammit, I should have done this earlier. Stupid fucker already showed his cards. "Stand by me, Lou-Lou," I order.

"No!" DeLuca shouts. Ricardo narrows his eyes at me, but I ignore him.

Lou-Lou ignores DeLuca, stands up and walks over to me—staying true to her word. I don't miss the look DeLuca gives her. He's *pissed*.

I pull her in front of me. "It's safe to say that you might not want to make any sudden movements again. I specifically told you to come unarmed."

I glare at him. "Granted, it's not a crowbar, but I swear you'll feel every second of the impact when I kill her."

Lou-Lou's lower lip trembles and I don't know if it's an act or the truth, but either way, it makes DeLuca remove his hand from his pocket.

"You'll never get away with this," he says.

I laugh at him. "I beg to differ."

That's when I hear the sound of someone's footsteps and see a large shadow walking through the back entrance of the warehouse. My heart and my stomach reel when I see a gray suit come into focus and I look up into a pair of blue eyes.

Then I notice the barrel of his gun is pointed at me. "Drop the gun, Alyssa," Ford sneers.

My 10-year old heart breaks all over again. "You gonna kill me, Ford? That's what it's come down to?"

I hate that there's a small part of me that can't kill him because he's the tie to my dad and my dad loved him.

His eyes waver and he sighs. "You know I could never do that. But I can't let you kill DeLuca, either."

"Why not?"

"Because then how would you find out the truth, Alyssa?" DeLuca sneers behind him.

I hear a gun cock and DeLuca laughs and says, "I appreciate you volunteering to be my bodyguard, Ford."

Ford curses under his breath and closes his eyes.

"However, I suggest you stay right where you are, special agent. There's something I've been meaning to tell Alyssa."

Ford moves the gun toward Lou-Lou. "If you do, then I'll take out Lou-Lou."

That's when Ricardo stands up. I breathe easy because I know he's on my side.

Or at least, I *thought* he was.

Ricardo cocks his gun and stands behind me. "And I'll take out Alyssa," he says to Ford.

Over Ford's shoulder, I see DeLuca smile. "Good job, son. I'm proud of you."

"Shit," I mutter as Ricardo jabs the gun into my lower back.

"Sorry, Alyssa," Ricardo says. "But I'm not letting him kill Lou-Lou."

It's safe to say, my plan has officially gone to hell in a hand-basket. Everyone has a gun pointed at them *except* for fucking DeLuca. Everyone's going to die, except the *one* person who should. This situation is completely fucked.

DeLuca claps his hands. "Good. Now that we've got that all sorted out and everyone knows where the other stands. Alyssa, I would like your attention."

Ford's eyes meet mine. "Don't, Alyssa. Whatever he says isn't true. You have to trust me. I love you. I have always loved you."

Behind me, Ricardo coughs. "You are one fucked up person, Ford. And I've seen some shit, but this right here...this takes the cake."

Against my better judgment, I look at DeLuca.

"Please, DeLuca," Ford pleads. "I've never asked you for a single thing, other than sparing her life. If you tell her everything. It will kill her."

"I'm counting on it," DeLuca sneers.

I look back to Ford. "Do you or do you not *work* for DeLuca?"

"Technically, yes. But I didn't always. I am a member of the FBI first and foremost."

Behind me, Ricardo says, "Yeah, he's what we like to call a flipper-flopper. You know, when it suits him."

"Why, Ford? How could you do that after you saw what he did to my father?"

"Because I became too powerful for him to keep trying to take down," DeLuca interjects.

Ford's face pales. "I couldn't beat DeLuca. So, I had to join him. There was no other way."

DeLuca takes a step forward and his face hardens. "Go ahead, Alyssa. Ask him what his *first* job for me was."

Ford's face contorts in pain and I feel so lightheaded white spots form in front of my eyes.

I shake my head and point my gun at him. All thoughts of Lou-Lou as my leverage forgotten. "No," I shout. "You wouldn't do that to my dad. He was your best friend. You grew up together. He loved you. You wouldn't set him up to get killed."

"I'm so sorry," Ford whispers. "I had no choice."

"There's always a choice!"

DeLuca grins and it looks so sickening I have to look away. "And what a choice it was. He obviously chose to save his own ass. He came to me, worked out a deal and gave up your dear old dad in the exchange. You know, he was the one who suggested we do it right here, too. He said your dad liked the water." DeLuca chuckles. "He even set up the two gang members to take the fall for it. I'll admit that was brilliant."

I look at Ford, not even trying to hold back my tears. "You're fucking sick."

Behind me, Ricardo whispers, "Yup."

"I won't deny that," Ford says. "But I love you, Alyssa. You know that I do."

I'm more certain than ever that what he felt for me wasn't love, it was some gruesome combination of guilt, fixation, and control. I look Ford right in the eyes. "No, what I know… is that you were on the phone with me when it happened. You heard me cry my heart out. You heard my screams as DeLuca took my father from me."

I have to put my hand to my chest just to make sure my heart's still beating and it didn't physically crack into a million pieces. "You picked up that scared and destroyed little girl and held her in your arms like she was your own. You held her like you would protect her…all while knowing *you* did this to me. To *him*! How could you?"

A guttural cry rips from my throat and DeLuca laughs like it's the funniest thing in the world. "And that's not even all of it."

"What *else* could there possibly be?" Lou-Lou whispers. Then she gasps.

DeLuca gives me a sinister smirk. "Alyssa? Besides your father dying, can you think of anything *else* that might have ruined your life?"

"Shit," Ricardo mutters.

"*You* were behind the sex tape, Ford?"

He stays silent.

"Answer her, Ford." DeLuca directs. He shakes his head.

"You tell her the truth now. It's the *least* you can do, you fucking scumbag," Ricardo says, low and deadly.

"DeLuca promised Gaffney that he would win the run for mayor if his son Dean did it," Ford says. "However, it was my idea in the first place. I paid the Gaffney's off and promised that Dean would never get busted on a DUI charge if he fucked you and filmed it."

"What the fuck is wrong with you? Why would you do that to me?"

"I needed to do something to—" he pauses like he can't even say it.

DeLuca gives me a shit-eating grin. "To make sure your pretty face would never end up on the evening news. Where you could slip up and tell the whole world what I did to your daddy. Live from New York. You know, you really should have chosen a different major at NYU." His eyes blacken and I take a step back, not even caring that Ricardo's gun is still digging into me.

"I run this city," DeLuca shouts while taking a step forward. "It's *mine*. My greed, my hunger, my money…but most of all *my* control and power. I let you live as a courtesy to Ford; after certain assurances were put in place, of course. But, I *wasn't* going to have your stupid fucking ass mess up what I worked so hard to build. I couldn't take that chance." His lips turn up in a snarl and he winks. "However, I *would* like to thank you for being such a willing participant. Nice tits by the way."

I blink back impending tears…but there aren't *any* left. There's only darkness and pain.

I look at Ford again. "The way you treated me after it happened. I went to you for help and you—"

"Made her believe she was nothing but a whore. Broke her trust in everyone and everything. Hurt her beyond *all* repair. And this was all *after* you had already ripped her heart out. You really are one *despicable* motherfucker," Jackson's voice booms from somewhere in the distance.

"No," I say with my hand on the trigger. "He's one despicable *dead* motherfucker."

"No!" Jackson shouts, coming into view and halting me at the last possible second. "Don't do it, Alyssa."

In my peripheral vision, I see Ricardo aim his gun at DeLuca.

"He deserves it," I argue as Ford's eyes close and he clutches his stomach.

"He does, baby. I know he does," Jackson says. "But you need to let me do it."

"What? No."

"Yes," he insists. "You're not a killer, baby. I am. Your soul is still untarnished and I want it to stay that way. You don't know what it's like to take a life, Alyssa. Mike deserved everything I did to him and I would take his life again in a heartbeat. But, murder is a burden that I never want *you* to bear. I won't let you destroy yourself again because I love you."

He walks behind Ford and lowers his gun to his head. "And you need to let me do this for you. And after this, I'm going to take out DeLuca. I'm going to take every single nightmare away, baby. I promise."

"No," Ricardo barks in DeLuca's direction.

Ricardo moves closer to DeLuca and grabs Lou-Lou right before DeLuca has a chance to shoot Jackson. "Don't you even think about it, Babbo," he says before he puts the gun to her head.

Everyone's attention turns to DeLuca and Ricardo at that moment.

As thankful as I am to Ricardo for not letting DeLuca shoot Jackson, I'm equally petrified for Lou-Lou. I never thought Ricardo would kill *her*. I regret ever bringing her here now.

Then, before anyone's brain can catch up to what's happening. Ricardo leans down and kisses Lou-Lou's tear-stained cheek. "Ti amo. Sii libero," he whispers in her ear.

Lou-Lou reaches behind her and pulls a gun out of her waistband.

She lifts her chin and aims the gun directly at DeLuca's head. He's so caught off guard, he doesn't even have time to aim his gun at her. "Brucia all'inferno. Burn in hell, Bruno," she says as she pulls the trigger, four times.

In slow motion we watch DeLuca's brain splatter all over the warehouse, his body falling to the floor with a heavy thud.

I can't contain the smile on my face. I think it's the brightest it's ever been. I barely even hear the sirens in the distance.

I open my mouth to thank Lou-Lou but she runs out the back door in the blink of an eye.

The sirens get louder and blue and red lights illuminate the warehouse.

"Jackson Reid, put your hands behind your head. You are under arrest," a voice says over a megaphone as the doors burst open.

My heart shatters like glass and I drop to my knees.

That's when Ford lifts his head and smiles at me.

Three weeks later...

Chapter Thirty-Nine

ALYSSA

I LEARNED THE WORLD WAS UNFAIR AT AN EARLY AGE. I KNEW THAT THE BAD GUYS sometimes won and that the good usually paid the price for their sins.

What I don't understand, is why I was forced to learn the harsh lesson twice in my life and why it had to involve the two men I loved the most.

Ford's living his life free as can be while Jackson's sitting in a jail cell.

For murdering Lilly's killer.

Ford attempted to get him for the murder of DeLuca but Ricardo and I vehemently fought those accusations without incriminating Lou-Lou.

Besides, it's not like anyone would be able to find her even if we did give her up. She skipped town right after killing DeLuca and no one's heard from her since. Not even Ricardo.

I have no idea *what* the story is between the three of them, but something tells me that Lou-Lou needed to kill DeLuca way more than I ever did…and that's saying something.

As fucked up luck would have it, the secret wire Ford was wearing in the warehouse didn't support his claims that Jackson killed DeLuca, either.

Ford couldn't pin that on him no matter how hard he tried.

Unfortunately, the tape didn't get any incriminating evidence on Ford himself, the tape just magically happened to 'pick up' right when Jackson walked in and admitted to being a killer. Then it cut off.

And since Ford played both sides of the fence, he claims that he was working under-cover at the warehouse. And since he did call for backup he's not being investigated.

But little did Ford know…I have my own brand of justice that I want to personally serve him.

After tracking down and talking to a few of my dad's old friends who are still members of the FBI, it was finally going to happen.

Jackson was right…I'm not a killer. My soul isn't tarnished, but my childhood was.

I make sure that I have everything in place before I walk into Ford's office. I'm surprisingly feeling calm. The look on his face tells me that he most definitely wasn't expecting me, but he's pleased nonetheless.

"Alyssa," he says.

He stands up from his desk and it's so reminiscent of that day, nausea overwhelms me.

I fight through it, though and take a deep breath.

He walks around his desk and smiles at me. "I knew you would come to your senses. I knew you would realize that I was only protecting you and I *knew* you would forgive me sooner or later. I love you, Alyssa. Everything I did was for you."

I just stare at him, dumbfounded. It's never occurred to me before that Ford might be downright delusional.

Or maybe, he's lied so much that he just can't tell the truth from all of the different worlds he's created.

When I don't say anything, he takes a step closer to me.

I stand there silently urging him to dig his own hole. "I couldn't let you be with Jackson, sweetheart. I had to make him go away. You belong to me, you always have."

He reaches for my hand. "I divorced Penelope for you a few months ago. I wanted to take you on vacation after I got rid of DeLuca and surprise you. We can get married now just like you always wanted. I'm choosing you this time."

I try my hardest not to grin. This is turning out even better than expected.

"You were really going to get rid of him for me?"

He kisses my wrist. "I'd do anything for you."

I reach up and touch his cheek. "I have a question."

"Yes?"

"At what age did I *first* belong to you, Ford?"

He blinks and makes a face. "Come on, Alyssa. Don't be stupid. You remember that night in my car by the docks. You promised to be mine forever."

I lean into him and nuzzle his neck, my nausea getting worse the closer I get to him. "I know it was around my birthday, but I'm having trouble with my exact age. I was hoping you could refresh my memory."

The look on his face is priceless as he pushes me away. "Nice try, sweetheart. Are you really *that* dumb that you don't know the law?"

He walks back to his desk. "Bit of advice, never try to school a federal agent on the law." He crosses his arms over his chest and gives me that movie star smile that makes me want to hurl. "The age of consent in New York is 17."

He sits down and props his elbows on the desk. "And I hate to break it to you, but even if that night was illegal; New York's statute of limitations is only 5 years from the time you turn 18. You're 24, Alyssa. Your time has run out."

He props his feet up on his desk. "In other words, you're screwed. Besides, we never had intercourse when you were 17, anyway. You were 21 the first and only time I fucked you."

I don't know which is worse, how much thought he's obviously put into this, or the smug smirk plastered on his face.

A smirk that I can't wait to wipe off.

I take a step forward and smile sweetly at him. "Hmm. You know what? You're right. I'm sorry, Ford."

He opens his mouth to say something, but I cut him off. "I'm sorry the night you put your hand down my panties and touched me in your car, that I was only 17." I put my finger to my lips. "Or maybe even 16 depending on the exact time."

I take another step forward. "On second thought, No. I'm not sorry. Because I was too young to be making the adult decision to let you touch me like that. And we both know, that as the only *adult* in the car; you should have known better than to touch me like that."

He stabs his finger in the air. "Save your breath because it doesn't matter. You've got *nothing* on me."

He sits up in his chair and snickers. "It doesn't matter that I was the first man to see and stick my fingers in that innocent, virginal, tight little pussy of yours before you became a whore. It doesn't matter, Alyssa…because you're too fucking *late*."

I sharpen my eyes in his direction and reach for the goblin on my necklace. "Does it matter that it was in Jersey, Ford?"

I can see the wheels spinning in his head and I continue, "Because those docks were technically in Jersey territory."

I open my arms wide. "And you know the great thing about Jersey?"

When he doesn't answer I proclaim, "There *is* no statute of limitations for sexual assault. And there is no *deadline* for filing sexual assault charges."

His jaw practically hits the floor. "And just so we're clear here, Special Agent. You did just fully admit to sexually assaulting me and penetrating me with your fingers when I was a teenager. And given your position of power and authority as an officer and the fact that you had a gun on you…do you know what that means?"

He slams the desk with his hand. "Knock this shit *off*, Alyssa. You *wanted* it. You dressed like a little whore and you begged for me that night. It was all *you*."

I ignore him. "It means that it's technically aggravated sexual assault. And do you know what that's punishable by?"

I look up to the heavens and smile. "Up to 20 years in prison."

I start unbuttoning my shirt. "And there's plenty of proof, including phone records. And let's not forget that you gave me a car when I was 17. In addition to your ex-wife who's willing to testify."

I undo the first 3 buttons and I open my shirt. "And there's the fact that I'm wearing a wire and just caught every disgusting thing you said."

He charges after me, but the door opens and in walk a few men in uniform. I wave to my dad's former friend who now lives in Jersey and is an officer there.

"Ford Baker you are under arrest. You have the right to remain silent…" the officer's start to say as they handcuff him.

I walk over to him and put my hands on his cheeks.

"How could you do this to me?" he whispers.

I look at him hard and say, "You only did it to yourself, Ford."

"But why?"

My grip tightens around his cheeks. "Because sometimes in life, sweetheart. The *good* guys win."

I let go of him but he leans his forehead against mine. "Do you know what they do to cops in jail, Alyssa?"

I grab his face again and stare into his eyes. "I'm not sure. I imagine it will be harsh, though. Given they don't take kindly to cops who commit sexual assault on children." I wrap one hand around the back of his neck. "And with that handsome face of yours…you're probably going to be passed around like a little *whore*." I lower my voice and whisper in his ear, "But if I were you, I'd be even more worried…because I hear that you're going to be sharing a cell with Jackson."

When I back away his face pales and he starts trembling.

I kiss the goblin and look at him one last time. "I think my father would be really proud of me right now."

And then I slam the door.

"I knew you could do it, sugar," Momma says as she wraps her arms around me.

I hug her back. "I almost tossed my cookies like five different times in there because he made me so sick."

She gives me a peculiar look but I shift my attention to Tyrone.

It pains me to see him in his wheelchair. Although the damage wasn't as extensive as the doctor's initially thought, he did lose the ability to move his legs. With time, they say he'll be able to drive a car and possibly even walk with special equipment one day. He's adjusting much better than the doctors expected him to…but then again, they don't know Tyrone's perseverance and inner strength.

Shelby's been by his side the whole time and I know that's exactly where she'll always be. I just wish I was able to get Jackson out of jail so he could be here for him too.

"I know you do," Tyrone says, while looking at me. "And I'd be lying if I said I didn't feel the same way."

I didn't realize that I had spoken my last thought out loud.

I sit down next to him. "I'm worried about the trial. His lawyer's good, but he's not the best. Especially since he refuses to spend any of the money in his bank account because he wants me to have it."

Which of course, I adamantly declined.

Tyrone closes his eyes. "Too bad people's perceptions of killers is so black and white. I mean, yeah—he murdered someone…but he's not a bad person. And if everyone knew what actually happened, they would realize that. But even if they did; who knows if the jury or the rest of the world is going to really believe it. They'll probably think it's all some kind of act."

I thumb the goblin on my necklace and think about this for a moment. "I know, I just wish everyone could see the real him."

The idea hits me like a semi-truck.

I stand up and look at Tyrone. "I know how to do that. I think I figured out a way to help Jackson. It's a long shot but it's—" I start to say before everything fades to black.

I wake up to four sets of eyes staring at me: Momma's, Tyrone's, Shelby's, and a man wearing a white lab coat that I vaguely recall seeing once before.

Never mind that though, I have to finish telling them my plan.

I quickly sit up in bed. "We all know how the media affects people's perceptions of things, right?"

They all stare at me like I'm bonkers.

"I think she might have a neurological issue of some kind," Tyrone says while looking up at the doctor.

Momma pats my head. "You do know you're in a hospital, right?"

I roll my eyes. "Yeah, I know; I probably passed out again or something. Maybe I'm sick again. Whatever. This is more important—"

The doctor approaches me and cuts me off. "Young lady, I have *important* rounds to make. So, if you don't mind I'd like to speak with you."

I hold out my hand. "Just fork over the prescription for my antibiotics and I'll be on my way, Doctor. I have important stuff to do."

He sighs "I think we should probably speak in private, this time."

"No. I'm fine," I insist. "I really need to go back home so I can save my boyfriend who's currently in jail."

His eyebrows shoot up. "In that case, I really must *insist* that we speak in private."

He looks at Momma but she shrugs. "I ain't leaving if she doesn't want me to."

I hold out my hand again. "Put it here, Doc."

He pinches the bridge of his nose before he reaches inside his lab coat and hands me a large bottle of pills.

I stare at the bottle of prenatal vitamins and blink while Momma gasps with tears in her eyes. I try handing them back to him. "I think this is a mistake."

He focuses his attention to his tablet. "No mistake. Your HCG levels are consistent with being around 4, maybe 5 weeks pregnant. You'll need to have an ultrasound to confirm this, of course." He moves his glasses up his face and looks at me. "By the way, you're anemic so you really need to start eating more meat in addition to the iron pills I'll be prescribing you. I think that's why you fainted. Either that, or you stood up too quickly and your blood pressure plummeted."

I jump up from the bed, horrified. "I'm not pregnant, Doctor. I'm telling you, there's been a mistake." I lower my voice. "I'm on birth control."

Out of the corner of my eye, I notice that Tyrone appears to be in deep thought before he says, "Did you use a backup method while you were on those antibiotics?"

My hand flies up to my face and I sit back down on the bed.

Fuck a duck. That was an entire two week period of unsafe sex. How could I be so careless?

I look at Tyrone and he smiles. I've never wanted to strangle someone for being so goddamned smart and perceptive. Momma starts jumping around the room acting like she won the lottery. "I'm gonna have a grandbaby."

I can't share in her glee, though. Shelby's eyes meet mine and she gives me a sympathetic look.

At least she understands.

Maybe it's the hormones, but the dark cloud is over my head with a vengeance and I bury my head in my hands and cry. I miss Jackson *so* much. He should be here with me right now.

"Everyone out. Now," Tyrone shouts, causing everyone to startle.

Open mouthed, everyone, including the doctor, leave the room.

He rolls his wheelchair by my bed and reaches for my hand. "I'm not going to sit here and tell you to keep this baby or to get rid of it, Alyssa."

I squeeze his hand. "Thank you. Because right now, I have no idea what to do."

"What I'm going to tell you, is what Jackson would tell you."

"What do you mean?"

"He'd tell you that he'd hold your hand the entire time. And he'd remind you that you're stronger than you think. He'd tell you that he'd respect whatever decision you end up making. He'd also tell you that he loves you." He puts his hand over his heart. "And that's what I'm gonna do, Alyssa. Because no matter what happens…you're not alone and you have me. If you want to cry, if you want to shout, if you want to punch my face in so you feel better. Whether you want to keep this baby or not, I'll still be there."

"Me too."

I look up as Ricardo enters the room.

He looks at Tyrone then back at me. "Tyrone told me you were here. I know I haven't been around much in the last few weeks. I've had to take care of some business. But, I have good news."

"I'd love some good news right about now."

Ricardo smiles. "I've just hired the best lawyer on the East Coast to take Jackson's case."

"How can you afford that?"

"You probably don't want to know. But, I'm going up to the jail this weekend to see Jackson and tell him. I wanted to see if you wanted to go with me but—" his voice drifts off and he looks uncomfortable.

I look down. "Should I tell him?"

Tyrone considers this for a moment before saying, "It's up to you. You don't have to make any decisions right this second. You still have time."

"How good is this lawyer?"

"Excellent."

"I hope so, because I want to put Jackson's video confession out into the world. I want the world to know who Jackson really is."

Tyrone's eyes open wide. "You still *have* that?"

"Yeah. I never intended to use it against him. I just...the video made me fall more in love with him. When he talks about Lilly and how they grew up, how much he loved her and what happened when he found her, you just know that it was raw and honest. Every single word he uttered in that video showed Jackson's soul. He spoke straight from the heart."

Tyrone's eyes are gleaming. "I never thought I'd say this, but we need to use that video. Influence the media, get people to hear what happened. It might not change their minds completely and there will still be people out there wanting him to serve time, but I think a majority will agree that he was justified."

Ricardo snaps his fingers. "I agree. Upload that sucker on youtube right now."

Chapter Forty

JACKSON

YOU WOULD THINK I'D BE UPSET TO FIND MYSELF BACK IN JAIL AGAIN, BUT I'M NOT. I've accepted it.

But it doesn't mean that my heart doesn't ache for Alyssa every second...or Momma, Tyrone, and Ricardo for that matter.

It was ironic that I ended up back here on Lilly's birthday. I chose to kill DeLuca on that day because I thought it would bring me luck. Obviously, fate thought otherwise.

I took it as a sign that Lilly herself obviously wanted me to pay.

But I still don't regret it. Even now.

Just like I wouldn't have regretted taking Ford's life or DeLuca's. Although, after Ricardo visited me and explained what really happened between Lou-Lou, him, and DeLuca; I know that the right to kill DeLuca definitely belonged to Lou-Lou, and I hope that wherever she is now—she's happy.

I was beyond pissed at him for having a gun to my girl's back, though, but I couldn't really argue when he explained that if the roles were reversed I would have done the same.

You see, he trusted Alyssa not to kill Lou-Lou. Hell, he even trusted DeLuca not to kill Lou-Lou due to his sick obsession with her. But he just couldn't trust that Ford wouldn't kill Lou-Lou...because he's a manipulating fucktard.

Those were his exact words.

However, I fully agree.

Especially looking at him right now from across the cafeteria in his orange jumpsuit.

The sight is so spectacular, I wish I could snap a picture and send it to Alyssa.

I thought I needed to protect her and make those who hurt her pay, but as it turns out; she got something even better than payback all on her own.

She got her own brand of *justice*...the way *she* needed to do it. I'm even more in awe of her and the woman she is.

And I know the man who gets the honor and privilege of spending the rest of his life with her, *will* be the luckiest man in the world.

I just wish it could have been me.

But for now, there's one more thing I have to do to settle the score with Ford.

Not only is he serving time for what he did to Alyssa, but he's also the main suspect in the murder of DeLuca now. He, of course, tried to tell them about Lou-Lou, but Alyssa and Ricardo along with me, are refuting his claims.

Which leaves all fingers pointing to him. The fact that he told Alyssa that he was planning on vacationing after taking DeLuca down and she got it on tape, doesn't look good for him.

He keeps insisting that he called for backup and was acting as a member of the FBI, though; so I guess we'll have to see how his defense will pan out in the long run.

And although he could be facing up to 20 years for what he did to Alyssa, the reality is that he most likely won't serve that much time.

For all we know, he could be out in a few months depending on his trial. The only reason he's sitting in jail now is because he's a flight risk and the judge ended up being a friend of Alyssa's dad.

Oddly enough, that's the saddest fact of all to come out in all this.

Alyssa's father really was a stand-up guy...but his worst quality was having Ford as a best friend and partner.

And had Ford not sunk his hooks into Alyssa right after his murder and coerced and scared her into lying about DeLuca...she would have been responsible for bringing him down a long time ago.

That's the way the world works, though, the bad guys win far more often than the good guys do.

But there's days like today. The rare exceptions to the rule.

And that exception is staring at me from across the cafeteria looking like he's about to piss himself.

My guess, would be because rumor amongst us jailers is...that 14 years ago, he pinned the murder of a prestigious officer on two rival gang members.

I look at him and give him a great big smile and he flinches. He was so freaked out about sharing a cell with me, he purposely hit his head against the sink and has been hauled up in the infirmary for the past few days.

But he's out today.

And no matter where Ford turns, he's up shits creek without a paddle.

The rival gangs want a piece of him. Any man with a teenage daughter wants a piece of him. Even DeLuca's inside people want a piece of him, now that Ricardo's taken over.

And then there's the guards.

The guards who heard the latest rumor. The guards who despise the dirty cop who backstabbed their own partner and set up his death. The guards who despise the dirty cop who's in here for sexually assaulting their dead partner's teenage daughter.

That's the funny thing about perception...sometimes, it really is everything.

He's as skittish as a kitten when he makes his way over to me.

I manage to keep my joy in check. "Hi, Ford. How are you doing on this beautiful day here at Rikers?"

"Look, Jackson. I'm going, to be honest with you," he says and I try not to laugh in his face. "I was hoping to bury the hatchet. We're cellmates and—"

"You set me up." I turn to face him. "Why in the world would I ever help you?"

His shoulders slump. "I was only trying to do the right thing for her. You can't blame me for loving her. I know you do, too. And face it, Jackson. You and I aren't really all that different. You're a murderer. And I'm—"

"You're what, Ford?"

He looks away. "I set people up for murders. The point is that we're not good people. So don't act like you're so much better than me. But I think if we work together in here, we might stand a chance."

I almost choke on my barely edible food. "I'm doing just fine on my own."

He makes a sweeping motion with his hands. "Yeah, right *now*. But sooner or later, you're going to need a favor. You're going to need to—"

I stab my food with my fork. "Make a deal?"

He sits closer to me and it takes everything in me not to throw him off his chair. "Yes. You're going to need someone in here who has your back. You're going to need someone in here who will take care of you."

That's when I laugh. "Are you offering to be my boyfriend, Ford?"

He makes a face. "What? No."

"Too bad, that's the way it works in here."

He looks horrified. "You can't be *serious*. For Christ's sake, we were both in love with the same girl."

"A girl that I'm no longer going to see...thanks to you."

He swallows hard. "So, are you saying that you want *me* to—"

I give him a smirk. "Be my bitch. Yeah. That's *exactly* what I'm saying."

He stays silent. I can see him mulling his options and I'm loving every second of this. I push my tray away. "You know, I'm still having trouble figuring out why you're here talking to me. What exactly is it that you want?"

The funny thing is I already know exactly what he wants. He has no control, no power, he's helpless.

Just like how he made Alyssa feel.

He looks around the cafeteria. "I need protection. You know what they'll do to me in here. I need your help, Jackson."

That's when I stand up. "What are you willing to do for it?" I whisper.

He looks up at me and panic flashes across his face. "I'll do a-anything. Just help me. Please."

I adjust myself in front of him and raise an eyebrow. "Then get on your knees."

He looks around the cafeteria again. "Right *here*? Now?" he croaks.

"Yup. I want everyone to know that you're my bitch."

To my absolute delight. He slinks down in his chair until he's on his knees. "Now close your eyes."

After he closes them I back up and another inmate hands me a crowbar. I'll have to thank Ricardo for paying off the guard for me.

"Open your mouth for me, whore."

He winces and opens his mouth.

That's when I thrust the crowbar in his mouth.

His eyes fly open and the look is priceless. Pure fear. I'm pretty sure there's a puddle of his urine on the ground.

He starts choking and trembling. "Yeah, you like that? Of course, you do, you little slut."

He tries to move his mouth away but I don't let up. "Yeah, you heard me. You worthless slut."

There's cheering around the cafeteria and I give him a megawatt smile. "Figure your own way out of this mess, Ford. I suggest you whore yourself around because that's all you're good for. Now, get the fuck away from me."

I take the crowbar out of his mouth and hold it above his head because I want him to know what *that* feels like, too.

He scampers away and cowers.

Just like the vermin he is.

"You have visitors, Reid."

I walk into the visiting room and my eyes immediately connect with Alyssa's.

As happy as I am to see her, I already told her that I didn't want her to visit. Visitation at Rikers is practically an all day event and it's not always safe.

Especially when she comes here looking like that. She's wearing one of my t-shirts and a pair of jeans. Her still dark glossy hair is hanging loose and she's glowing.

She looks so beautiful it hurts to breathe. I'm actually thankful that Ricardo and Tyrone came here with her.

My heart sinks when I look at Tyrone. I can't believe he came all the way here to see me. He has enough of his own problems right now.

Ricardo's the first one to give me a hug. I didn't think it was possible but we've grown even closer after what happened.

In part, due to the three-hour visit that we had when I first got here. He opened up to me and told me the truth about everything. When he left, we both practically had tears in our eyes. He also offered to do what DeLuca did for me. He offered to pay off the judge and have evidence planted again, but I declined.

He said he would figure something else out, but I told him that unless it was legit, I wasn't interested.

I want to be free on my own merits, even though a big part of me knows that won't ever happen.

I hug Tyrone next and seeing him in his wheelchair kills me. He gives me that look that tells me he's doing okay and follows it up with a smile. I smile back because I know that he's going to pull through this.

Finally, I turn and face Alyssa.

Then I force myself to back away. She looks hurt, and I hate myself for doing that to her. But I can't kiss her. I can't hug her. I can't *touch* her because if I do I'm afraid I won't ever stop. I'll unravel and I won't make it through prison if that happens.

We all sit down at the table and Ricardo's the first to speak. "I hired a lawyer for you. He's the best on the East Coast."

My ears start ringing because this whole thing is all too familiar. "I told you I wanted everything to be legit."

"It is," he assures me.

"I wish you wouldn't waste your money. I'm not getting out of here. The prosecutor's going to have a field day with me because they know that I don't regret it. They know that I'm going to accept whatever happens. There's no point in fighting this."

Ricardo lets out a frustrated sigh.

Tyrone looks pissed and opens his mouth to argue, but Alyssa stands up and puts her hands on her hips. "Ricardo, do you think you can distract the guards for a little? I need to speak to Jackson alone."

"You got it," Ricardo says before him and Tyrone leave.

The slap across my face knocks me for a loop. "Snap out of it, Jackson!" Alyssa screams.

I stare at her wide-eyed. "There's nothing to snap out of. I love you but I need you to come to terms with this. I need you to find someone else. Someone who's good. Someone who can take care of you an—"

She sits back down and points a finger at me. "Shut up. There is no one else, there will never be anyone else. I know you're scared because of the first time you were in prison. I get it. I know you've given up all hope of the system working in your favor but you can't. I still believe that good things can happen. I haven't in awhile, but I do now, Jackson."

"I wish you wouldn't because it will only hurt you in the end. And I don't want to hurt you, Alyssa."

She leans forward. "There's still some good in the world." Her brow crinkles. "Now can you do something for me? Please?"

"You know I will."

"I just need you to believe. Believe in me. Believe in yourself."

She stands up and reaches for my hand before placing it over her stomach. "Believe in us. Because I do."

Her stomach feels just like it always has, but for some reason, my heart rate skyrockets and I've never felt more nauseous in my life. "Alyssa, why did you put my hand on your stomach?"

She plays with her necklace. "Because I know deep down that you're scared. And I think you need some extra strength. But I know you can do it. I know you can get through this." She places her hand over mine. "You're not getting rid of us. We're going to be a team for life."

Tears sting my eyes as I remember everything she told me about the last conversation with her father.

And that's when I realize.

She said *us*.

"How? Not that I'm not—" I pause because I really don't know what I am.

Actually, I do. I'm fucking scared out of my mind. This is a different kind of scared that I've never experienced before.

But I'm strangely happy, too. Christ, does that even make any sense?

"I didn't think to use a backup when I was sick and on antibiotics. I'm sorry. I know it's not ideal. I know our situation is completely—" she pauses and exhales.

I place my hands on her hips and move her closer to me. "Scary?" I offer.

She blinks away tears. "Yeah. It is…but I know we can do this. No matter *what* happens. We'll get through this somehow. I don't give a fuck what the rest of the world thinks about you. Our baby will know their daddy is a good man, because they *will* know you."

She runs her hand through my hair and I place a kiss on her belly. "Okay." A sense of calm washes over me. "No matter what happens, I'll still believe in us."

I stand up and give her a hug. Ricardo and Tyrone's eyes meet mine. They both pat the spot over their heart and I smile.

Our visit ends after that but Ricardo walks over to me right before the guards take me away.

"Make sure you go to the recreation room tonight."

"Why?"

He starts walking. "Because there's a television in there."

"And by the way, you have a meeting with your new lawyer tomorrow," he calls out before he walks out the door.

Chapter Forty-One

JACKSON

I WALK INTO THE RECREATION ROOM AND FIND A SEAT. I HAVE NO IDEA WHAT'S GOING on, but Ricardo insisted I come here.

Since there's nothing better to do, I decide to start playing cards with another inmate.

"Hit or Stay?"

I eye my cards. "Hit."

Dammit. I lost. Story of my life.

"Yo, man. That dude on T.V looks just like you," some guy calls out.

I pick the cards up and begin to shuffle them.

"Yo, man," the guy shouts.

My card-mate tilts his head. "I think he's talking to you." I turn my head but get distracted by my image on the screen.

Then I hear the words that I'll never forget. *"My name is Jackson Reid. There are two things you need to know about me. The first—is that I'm in love with Alyssa Tanner. The second—is that I'm a murderer."*

"That *is* me," I tell the guy.

Me and my entire confession. On the fucking news.

What was Alyssa *thinking*? I didn't even realize she still had that.

"A new video has gone viral," the newscaster says after my video ends. "It's sweeping across the nation and has garnered the attention of all social media sites."

My chest tightens. I don't know if this is a good thing or bad.

Every inmate in the room and a few of the guards start watching the television with earnest.

The newscaster's face becomes serious. "We at WKWNY decided to take it to the streets of N.Y with our news correspondent Anne Walley to find out what your opinion is regarding Jackson Reid's leaked confessional tape. Do you think he should stay in prison, America?"

"Shit, man," the inmate across from me says. "If that was my baby sis. You best believe I would have done the same damn thing."

There are a few nods of agreement around the room, but I don't get my hopes up. These are my fellow inmates, after all.

Anne Walley holds the microphone up to a woman with short blonde hair carrying her puppy in one of those big designer purses. She looks nice, maybe this won't be so bad.

"Jackson Reid should spend the rest of his life in a prison cell. What is *wrong* with you people! He's a killer. He shouldn't be allowed to roam free. You don't take the law into your own hands. You do the crime, you do the time," she bellows, before she pets her puppy.

I close my eyes. This is worse than torture. At least, I'll be well prepared for court. I told Ricardo not to waste his money.

I open my eyes as Anne Walley approaches another person and asks their opinion. A male this time. He's about 17 or 18 and he's wearing a baseball cap backwards on his head. "I don't know," he says appearing to be lost in thought. "I mean, I don't really like my little sister all that much." He looks down. "But, if someone ever hurt her or worse, killed her. I can't say that I wouldn't do the same, you know? I guess I can understand where he's coming from."

Anne approaches another bystander. It's another woman. She's in her late 30s and she's holding a crying toddler in her arms. "I'm a Jackson Reid supporter. We need more men like him in the world." She looks down at her child. "I don't want my little girl to live in a world where domestic abusers can get away with hurting or killing others. I want her to live in a world where there's men like Jackson Reid who aren't afraid stand up and get revenge for women like his sister."

Anne approaches another woman. She's in her mid-20's and has a few shopping bags in her hand. "Well, I have a few ex-boyfriends that I'd like Jackson Reid to take care of."

Her face turns sad. "But in all seriousness. Have you seen that video? Ignore the fact that he's good looking and actually listen to the pain he's in, people. The guy lost his sister. She was killed by his best friend. Beaten to *death*. Can you really blame the guy, Anne? I don't think he should be serving any time. It's obvious that he's already suffered enough."

Anne approaches another person. A man in his late 40's this time. He has a beard and a few tattoos. "I don't have a sister," he pauses. "But I *do* have a daughter. And if any—" There's a beep. And another beep. "Put his—" another beep. "Hands on her or *killed* her, you'd better believe I'd find his—" another beep. "and kill him with my bare hands!" he screams into the camera before he briskly walks away.

The recreation room erupts in applause. But then Anne approaches another woman.

Oh, god. It's Momma.

"Jackson Reid is my son," she says in her Southern twang.

Anne Walley looks skeptical. "I'm sorry ma'am, did you say your *son*?" Momma gives her a look and grabs the mic. "That's right. He's my boy. And this—" The camera moves and I see Tyrone, Shelby, Ricardo and Alyssa. My heart squeezes.

"Is his family," Momma continues as they all nod in unison. "We love him. He's a good man, America. He's not perfect, but he's got a heart like no one else and a good soul. Judge not, lest you be judged is all I'm sayin'."

The camera focuses back on Anne. "Well, there you have it, folks."

I walk into the room and I immediately want to turn right back around. This can't be my new lawyer.

She's too young. Younger than me. Maybe even younger than Alyssa, who knows.

The one thing I do know is…there's no way she's the best lawyer on the East Coast.

"I'm sorry. I think there's been a mistake," I say before turning around.

"There's no mistake, Jackson. My name is Michelle. I know you were probably expecting my father."

Needless to say, she's got my attention. "I didn't mean to be rude. I'm just—"

She holds out her hand. "Worried? Scared? Nervous?"

I shake her hand. "All of the above."

She sits down. "My dad is the big wig in the family. The one Ricardo spoke to and hired, actually."

I take a seat, although, I'm not sure why, but for some reason I feel compelled to. "No offense, Michelle. But if your dad is the lawyer. Then why are you here?"

She smiles and tucks a strand of hair behind her ear. "Well, I'm a lawyer too, actually."

"Oh, so I guess you're just taking care of some of the paperwork for him?"

She pulls out a briefcase. "No. I actually asked my father if it would be okay to take on this case myself."

I shift in my seat, trying to think of a polite way to decline and tell her that I need her father. "Look, you seem really nice and—"

"I went to school with Lilly."

I feel the gravitational tug on my heart from hearing her name. *Well, that would explain why she looks so young.*

She folds her hands on the table. "We had a few classes together at Harvard. I'd like to think we were friends. Your sister was an amazing person." •

"I know."

"I saw the subtle change in her, Jackson. She went from being happy-go-lucky and so full of life and happiness to being miserable."

I put my head in my hands. "I should have noticed the signs. I should have—"

"She would have denied it," she says. "I tried talking to her a few times and it was like talking to a brick wall. The only thing that confronting her did was make her distance herself more." She holds my gaze. "Abuse victims leave their abusers on average seven times before they leave for good. It wasn't her fault, but she would have stayed until she found the strength within herself to leave."

I look down. "But if I knew…I could have saved her life."

"No," she says. "And you know why? Because Lilly *already* knew she could go to you, Jackson. She knew how much you loved her. She knew that if she called you and said that she needed you that you would have been right there. She knew that."

I look up. "Why didn't she?"

That's the question that will always haunt me. *Why didn't she?* I would have done anything for her, *anything*.

"Because she blamed herself for the pain," she whispers. "Because he made her. That's what abusers do. They tear you down piece by piece and bit by bit. Until there's nothing left anymore."

She wipes her eyes. "But make no mistake about it. None of this was her fault. It was all him."

"I know." I sit up and look at her. "You know a lot about this."

She nods. "I do."

There's a moment of silence between us before she takes out a manila folder. "It's why I asked my dad if I could take on this case." She bites the cap of her pen nervously. "But you'd really be taking a huge risk with me."

"What do you mean?"

"This would be my very first case by myself."

Oh, *that's* what she means.

I sit back and cross my arms. "Okay, Let's say I hire you. What's the argument?"

"I don't have one."

"Look, I didn't go to law school. And I'm not nearly as smart as Lilly was…but I do know that defense attorneys should present an argument. You know, like self-defense, insanity, or an accidental killing."

She crosses her arms, stares me down and I immediately feel it. "He wasn't attacking you, he attacked Lilly. You're not insane. And you don't regret it, so I'm not sure that going with an accidental killing defense would be the best way to go. So, the way I see it…that only leaves me with one choice."

"Which is?"

"Telling the truth."

I stand up and shake her hand. "You're hired."

She jumps to her feet. "What? Really? You mean it?"

"Yup. That's the only way I want to win this case. And I can't help but think that if it was Lilly herself defending me, she would want the same."

Chapter Forty-Two

JACKSON

FOUR MONTHS LATER, I'M SITTING IN A COURTROOM WATCHING MY LAWYER, Michelle stand before the jury for her closing argument.

As far as juries go, this one is as versatile as it gets.

Out of the 12 jurors made up of my peers…six are female and six are male. They're all difference races, ages, occupations, and they all come from different backgrounds.

But only two of them have sisters.

Seven of them are only children. And the remaining three males have brothers.

Michelle told me not to let it get me down and to let her worry about that.

I turn around and look at my family. Tyrone and Ricardo's eyes find mine. They don't say a word, they just put their hands over their hearts and nod their heads. I look at Momma next. She mouths the words 'I love you,' and I mouth them back to her.

Then I scan the courtroom for Alyssa…but I can't find her.

She's been here every step of the way, so it's disheartening that she wouldn't be here today of all days.

Then it hits me. She won't be able to watch them find me guilty. Her heart won't be able to take it.

Suddenly, I'm glad she didn't come. It would put way too much emotional stress on both her and the baby. I would never forgive myself if something happened to them because of me.

I feel guilty enough for putting her in the position that she's in.

But that's the only regret I feel, still to this day. And the jury knows it because I was honest with them and told them.

Right after Michelle played the video of my confession in court.

That was the only thing that Alyssa and her fought about. Professionally, Michelle was upset because it was going to make finding potential juror's that hadn't seen or watched the video that much harder.

However, personally, she understood why Alyssa did it.

I turn back around in my seat. I don't know whether to face the jury myself or not.

Michelle's not going to like it, but I decide not to. Even though I know that she wants to get their sympathy and she wants them to witness my pain.

But I don't want to look at the jurors because I don't want them to think that I'm purposely trying to intimidate or influence them somehow. And mostly, I don't want them to lose focus on Michelle during her closing speech.

So no, I won't look at the jury. Instead, I close my eyes and feel Lilly's presence around me. I silently tell her that I love her and I tell her that no matter what happens, none of it was ever her fault…because I think *she* needs to hear it much more than *I* ever did.

That's when I hear Michelle start to speak.

"Thank you for your attention ladies and gentlemen of the jury. By now, you've formulated your own personal opinion regarding my client, Mr. Jackson Reid. I know there's nothing that I could say to sway you in either direction at this point."

She pauses. "You also know that by now, my argument has never been about self-defense. Because let's be honest; Mr. Reid was never defending himself against his own abuser. So, I'm not going to stand here and claim self-defense for Mr. Reid. Instead, I'll claim *Lilly's* defense.

"I'll also educate you on some facts regarding the law. To adequately determine the justification of deadly force in defense of a person, in a court of law, one must establish the existence of two main facts, first and foremost. One—you need to determine whether or not my client's use of deadly force was necessary to defend himself or rather, Lilly. Two—you need to determine if Mr. Reid did something that a 'reasonable person' would do in his position.

"And that's where you come in, ladies and gentlemen. You watched the video, you know the facts, you've heard from Jackson Reid yourself. So, knowing what my client knew and being in the same circumstance, would you yourself have had those same beliefs that he did?"

She clears her throat. "But forget all that. I didn't even need to tell you those things in the first place. That's not my real argument, here. Because the only thing I needed to do for this case was let the prosecutor's do their job and let you hear their arguments. The prosecution is required to prove beyond a reasonable doubt that Mr. Reid was not justified in doing what he did. And just so we're clear—*justified* means having done something for a legitimate reason. It's an exception to committing the offense. If the prosecution has failed to prove beyond a reasonable doubt that the defendant was justified, then you the jury must find Mr. Reid not guilty."

She takes a deep breath. "In closing, I just want to leave you with this. If Lilly was someone that you loved. And you found her beaten and murdered like Mr. Reid did. Would you feel justified doing what he did?"

The bailiffs take me away while the jury deliberates. I was told it would be anywhere from a few hours to a few weeks.

To say I was surprised to be called back as soon as I stepped foot outside the courthouse in my shackles would be an understatement.

After we rise for the judge, he calls the court in session and he collects a piece of paper from a member of the jury.

A piece of paper that will determine the rest of my life.

A piece of paper that will determine whether or not I get to spend the rest of my life with Alyssa, my future child, and the rest of my family.

The jury's faces give nothing away.

I wish I could see Alyssa's face *one* more time, I wish I could see my *child* growing in her belly. The thought causes blood to rush in my ears and vertigo plagues me, I want to sit back down because I'm not sure I can stand anymore.

I don't know why Michelle's arms are wrapped around me and she's telling me goodbye, because I'm too distracted by the sound of Momma shouting at the top of her lungs.

Oh, boy. I really hope Momma doesn't try to put a hurtin' on those jurors. Or the judge for that matter, poor guys already frail and old. I turn around to tell her it will be okay, but both Ricardo and Tyrone's arms are around me next. Their hugging me so tight I almost fall over.

"It's okay, guys," I tell them. "I'll be okay. Just promise me that you'll take care of Alyssa and the baby for me. Please."

They pull away and exchange a glance with one another. "Why?" Ricardo says. "You'll be able to do that yourself."

"What—" I start to say, but my breath leaves my lungs as Momma herself plows into me.

I close my eyes and hug her back. "I knew it would all work out in the end," she says.

That's when it hits me.

I look at Tyrone for confirmation. I don't even have to get the words out because he looks at me and says, "Not guilty, brother."

I'm not ashamed to admit, I'm barely holding back tears.

I'm going to be a father to my baby. I'm going to spend my life with Alyssa. I'm going to see my family.

I look at the jury again. And this time, they look at me. "Thank you," I whisper. I get a few small smiles before they start to clear out.

The bailiffs unchain me, and Michelle informs me that I'll need to sign off on some paperwork before I'm free to leave.

This time, I'm the one hugging her because I know what's happening. "Thank you and congratulations on winning your first case."

"You don't need to thank me, Jackson," she says with a grin. "But thank you for being the most memorable client I'll ever have. Thank you for reminding me why I became a defense attorney in the first place."

After I sign the paperwork we walk out to the car. It almost feels unreal. The air is fresher, the grass is greener, and I have a sense of peace.

A light breeze flows through the air and I feel Lilly's presence again. I look up to the sky and blow her a kiss.

Then a bird shits on my head.

Tyrone and Jackson burst out laughing. "Yup, that was definitely Lilly. Totally a little sister move."

I start laughing with them and it's the greatest feeling because I *know* that Lilly would find this highly amusing right now.

Momma hands me a napkin and I clean up before I get in the car.

We head back to the apartment complex and I can't get in the door fast enough.

Apparently, Tyrone and Shelby moved into Lou-Lou's old apartment so that Alyssa and the baby could have this one. Tyrone wanted his little niece or nephew to have his own room.

I'm surprised Alyssa didn't want to move to the suburbs to raise the baby but Ricardo said she wanted to be by her family.

I'm running around the apartment looking for her and my anxiety's through the roof when I can't find her. Then I notice that the door to the balcony is partially open.

I step outside into the warm July evening air.

I find Alyssa standing there with a mug and she gives me her gorgeous smile, complete with her adorable dimple. I don't hesitate to cup her face in my hands and kiss her like it's my last breath.

When I pull away her eyes are still closed and she sighs. "God, I missed that."

"I missed you." I place a kiss on her belly. "The both of you."

She hands me the mug, I take it with one hand and she grabs my other hand. "Come on, you're just in time to watch the sunset."

It's only then that I take a look at the two rocking chairs she has set up on the balcony.

Along with some bingo boards on the table.

"I didn't show up at court today because I knew you'd come home to me," she whispers.

I take a sip of my hot chocolate before I press her hand to my lips and kiss it. "I love you."

She takes a sip of her own hot chocolate. "And I love you."

It's then that I realize.

Without pain, you wouldn't know happiness. If you let the pain take over, you miss out on the good things, the things that really matter...like love and family.

If you don't find a way to make it through the pain...you miss out on the best parts of your life.

Epilogue

P AIN. IT HURTS US. IT PUSHES US. IT PUNISHES US.

Or, for the few poor souls out there like me…it defines us.

Yes, I've taken a life…and I would do it again in a heartbeat.

And one day, I will explain to my son the way the world works.

I will tell him, that the bad guys win far more often than the good guys do.

But I will raise him to know that in a world full of bad…he should do good anyway.

I will tell him that I don't think I'm necessarily a good person, but I'm not a bad person, either.

I will tell him the truth.

I'm flawed. I'm human. I lead with my heart.

And that's okay, because I have a good one.

About the Author

Oh, and if you're wondering if Lou-Lou and Ricardo will have their own story?
You bet they will.
It's available now.
Blame It on the Shame —Trilogy (Parts 1-3)

Want to be notified about my upcoming releases? https://goo.gl/n5Azwv

Ashley Jade craves tackling different genres and tropes within romance. Her first loves are New Adult Romance and Romantic Suspense, but she also writes everything in between including: contemporary romance, erotica, and dark romance.

Her characters are flawed and complex, and chances are you will hate them before you fall head over heels in love with them.

She's a die-hard lover of oxford commas, em dashes, music, coffee, and anything thought provoking…except for math.

Books make her heart beat faster and writing makes her soul come alive. She's always read books growing up and scribbled stories in her journal, and after having a strange dream one night; she decided to just go for it and publish her first series.

It was the best decision she ever made.

If she's not paying off student loan debt, working, or writing a novel—you can usually find her listening to music, hanging out with her readers online, and pondering the meaning of life.

Check out her social media pages for future novels.

She recently became hip and joined Twitter, so you can find her there, too.

She loves connecting with her readers—they make her world go round'.

~Happy Reading~

Feel free to email her with any questions / comments: ashleyjadeauthor@gmail.com

For more news about what I'm working on next: Follow me on my Facebook page:
www.facebook.com/pages/Ashley-Jade/788137781302982

Other Books Written By Ashley Jade

Blame It on the Shame —Trilogy (Parts 1-3)

The Devil's Playground Duet (Books 1 & 2)

Complicated Parts —Series (Books 1 & 2 Out Now)

Complicated Hearts —Duet (Books 1 & 2)

Thanks for Reading!
Please follow me online for more.
<3 Ashley Jade

The National Domestic Violence Hotline
1-800-799-SAFE (7233), or 1-800-787-3224 (TTY).

The National Domestic Violence Hotline
1-800-799-SAFE (7233), or 1-800-787-3224 (TTY).

If you or anyone you know is a victim of *domestic violence,*

I urge and I *beg* you to reach out.

You're *not* alone…and I will pray for you every single day of my life.

Please, don't blame yourself.

And just in case you never hear this…it's *not* your fault. It's **NEVER** your fault!

If you or anyone you know is a victim of *sexual assault,* again;

I urge and I *beg* you to reach out.

It's *not* your fault. It's **NEVER** your fault! Please don't ever blame yourself.

National Sexual Assault Hotline 800-656-HOPE (4673)

National Child Sexual Abuse Helpline (*Darkness to Light*)

1-866-FOR-LIGHT (866-367-5444)

For rape & sexual assault victims call: 212-227-3000

or **email :** help@safehorizon.org

All calls are kept completely confidential.

And if you still can't pick up that phone, you can always email ashleyjadeauthor@gmail.com

I'll never judge you, I'll just listen <3

Acknowledgments

I like to keep these short and sweet.

First and foremost: *Thank you* my amazing fans…seriously, you rock! You'll never know how much you all mean to me.

I can never thank you enough for sticking it out with me and hopefully *now*, I'm starting to make it worth your while and delivering the goods.

Either way, I'll keep trying and giving you everything I've got.

Check out my Facebook page, Twitter account, and page for more updates and new series/ more novels. I *love* connecting with my fans! You guys give me that extra 'push' whenever I feel defeated. (*I also like to give out arcs from time to time.*)

A special thank you to my **Hammie:** You are my love, my muse, my everything. I couldn't have done this without you.

Shielding Gillian

DELTA TEAM TWO, BOOK 1

SUSAN STOKER

As an event planner, Gillian Romano's an expert at rolling with the punches and solving unexpected problems. But her flight getting hijacked while returning from a job is definitely out of her skill set. Passengers are being murdered, and when she's chosen by the terrorists to be their mouthpiece, even more innocent lives rest on Gillian's shoulders. Only the calm, reassuring voice on the other end of the line keeps her sane, forging a bond with a stranger she's never seen but trusts with her life.

Walker "Trigger" Nelson and his Delta Force team have spent years training for close-quarter hostage rescue. When they get called to South America to attempt to save an airplane full of hostages, he doesn't expect to meet a woman who rocks his world in the middle of the op. Gillian's cool head and bravery in the face of certain terror—and possible death—blows him away. Any outcome that doesn't include Gillian leaving that plane alive and well is not an option.

After their safe return to Texas, both Trigger and Gillian are excited to find out if their instant chemistry can survive the real world. Neither realizing that someone isn't happy with the outcome of the hijacking, and is watching, waiting, for a second chance to strike.

** *Shielding Gillian* is the 1st book in the *Delta Team Two* Series. Each book is a stand-alone, with no cliffhanger endings.

Dedication

In January 2018, Mr. Stoker and I filmed an HGTV show called *Mountain Life*. I got into a conversation about my career with the producer, and she was pouting because she'd never seen her name in a book. Well, Gillian, this one's for you!

Chapter One

GILLIAN ROMANO CLOSED HER EYES AND RESTED HER HEAD ON THE SEAT. SHE WAS exhausted…but in a good way. The event that had taken months of her life to plan had gone off without a hitch. She'd been extremely nervous as it had been in Costa Rica, but because everything had gone smoothly, she knew she'd most likely have a lot more business coming her way.

The CEO of Pillar Custom Homes out of Austin, Troy Johnson, had contacted her almost a year ago to inquire about her organizing all aspects of an appreciation trip for the company's most prestigious clients.

She'd said yes—then immediately freaked out. As an event planner, Gillian was used to organizing weddings, birthday parties, and nonprofit galas in the Killeen and Austin areas. Mr. Johnson had gotten her name from the president of a local animal shelter, who'd hired her the year before to throw their annual fundraising dinner. The president had been using Pillar Custom Homes to build his house, and he'd passed her name along.

Mr. Johnson had invited a dozen of his esteemed clients and their families, as well as some of the most influential names in Austin real estate. Gillian had been responsible for all aspects of the trip. From flight and transportation arrangemen gts, to booking the private hotel suites and selecting entertainment options for the four-day trip. It had been the most difficult thing she'd ever done—especially considering the fact she'd done most of her planning remotely—but everything had turned out beautifully, if she did say so herself.

Smiling, Gillian let out a long sigh of contentment. She'd seen the last of the guests off the day before and had spent one day in the beautiful Costa Rican resort soaking in the feeling of a job well done and getting in some well-deserved R&R.

She was now heading home and couldn't wait to tell her best friends—Ann, Wendy, and Clarissa—all about how beautiful Costa Rica was and how well the event had gone.

Her eyes popped open when she heard an odd sound up in the first-class section of the plane. Looking over the seat in front of her, she saw that almost all of the passengers in first class were standing. She wasn't alarmed—until she heard one of the women let out a sound that made the hair on Gillian's arms stand up.

It was a keening mixture of disbelief and terror.

Before she could do more than furrow her brow, a man appeared at the front of the coach cabin. He was holding a rifle. He pointed it up in the air and said something in Spanish, which made people all around Gillian shout out in horror and several began to cry.

Frozen in fear, Gillian couldn't believe what she was hearing when the man switched to English and said, "On behalf of the Cartel of the Suns, my name is Luis Vilchez, and my friends and I have taken over the plane and will be landing in our homeland of Venezuela. Stay calm and don't do anything stupid, and you might live to see another day."

Gillian blinked. Her plane was being *hijacked*? How was this happening? She never in a million years would've thought after 9/11, when airlines had tightened security, that this would happen.

But then again, she wasn't in the United States. Hadn't she been surprised when she realized that she'd forgotten to put the small pocket knife Clarissa had given her for protection into her checked luggage, and she'd made it through the Costa Rican security with the knife in her purse?

But how did he get a *rifle* onboard? Was he a passenger?

Looking closer, Gillian realized he was dressed like one of the flight attendants. Though, now that she thought about it, she figured he could've probably smuggled the weapon onto the plane any number of ways...especially if he had help from someone who worked at the airport.

He nodded at someone in front of him, and when Gillian turned to look behind her, she saw there were three other men standing in the aisles with wicked-looking rifles as well.

Shit, shit, shit.

Swallowing hard, Gillian startled when there was another scream from the first-class area, and she whipped her head back around. The man who'd addressed the plane looked behind him then turned to face the coach passengers again. He pointed his rifle at a woman sitting in the first row. "You. Collect everyone's passports."

The woman stood up and looked visibly shaken.

"Get your passports out now!" the hijacker said loudly. "You will give them to this woman." When everyone remained frozen in fear, he scowled and, without further hesitation, turned to the man sitting in the aisle seat in the bulkhead row and shot him in the head.

The man fell over, and there were more screams and shouts of terror from her fellow passengers.

Gillian knew she was in shock. She couldn't make a sound. Couldn't do anything more than stare wide-eyed at what was happening right in front of her.

"I said, get your passports out...*now!*" the hijacker yelled in both Spanish and English.

The young couple next to her leaned over and immediately began to rummage through their bags, and Gillian did the same. She held out the small blue book as the woman selected to collect them walked down the aisle. Her hand shook as she passed it over, and for just a second, she caught the other woman's gaze. She looked absolutely terrified.

In all the confusion and panic amongst the passengers, Gillian hadn't thought much about what the hijacker had said previously—but now she did. They were going to Venezuela. She wasn't really up on current events, but even she knew the country was in serious turmoil at the moment. And the guy had said he was with a group, "cartel" something or other.

That usually meant drugs.

Too scared to take her eyes off the hijacker, Gillian felt herself breathing fast. This was really happening. The men who'd taken over the plane had already hurt people. Killed someone.

She felt the plane take a hard right, and ridiculously, she put out her hand to brace herself. It wasn't as if she was going to fall out the window or something.

Either the pilots were in on the plot to take over the plane, or the hijackers had gotten to them—they really *were* turning around and heading back toward South America.

She briefly thought about pulling out her cell phone to see if it would work, but Gillian had no idea who she could call. Nine-one-one? No, that wasn't an option. Her friends? What would they be able to do?

"Women in the front, men in the back!" a new voice demanded from behind her.

Gillian turned to look and saw the other hijackers were separating the passengers. The woman next to her whimpered, and her husband whispered something, obviously trying to calm and reassure her.

The man's arm was wrenched upward by one of the hijackers as he was shoved toward the back of the plane. Gillian stood immediately and let herself be pushed forward. She stumbled into the first-class cabin—and froze at the carnage around her.

Almost all of the men and women had been killed. Sometime in the general chaos, perhaps while the passports were being collected, their throats had been slit.

She saw three flight attendants lying motionless as well.

She had one second to be thankful the plane wasn't full before her arm was grabbed in a bruising hold. Looking up in panic, Gillian stared into the stone-cold brown eyes of the hijacker who'd so calmly shot the man in the bulkhead row.

"*You*. You will be our spokesperson with the authorities," he declared.

Gillian shook her head, but no words would come out. She didn't want anything to do with this. She wanted to huddle in a corner and be invisible.

The man leaned into her, and his body odor assaulted Gillian's senses. He smelled like sweat and onions, and she forced herself not to gag. "You have two choices," he said calmly. "Be our spokesperson or die." Then he let go of her arm and stood back. He lifted his rifle and placed the barrel against her forehead. It was hot and felt like it was burning a hole right into her skull.

Swallowing hard, Gillian whispered, "I'd be happy to talk to whoever you want."

His lips quirked upward in an evil, satisfied smile as he lowered his weapon. "I thought you might." Then he grabbed her arm again and shoved his way between terrified women and children and hauled her to the area reserved for flight attendants, where the crew prepared food and drinks for the passengers.

He pushed her down, and Gillian gladly scooted until her back was against the side of the plane. "Might as well get comfortable, we've got a bit of time before we get to Caracas," the hijacker told her.

Gillian closed her eyes—but she couldn't block out the sounds. Women crying, the hijackers threatening passengers, the occasional terrifying shot from one of the guns.

People were dying all around her…and Gillian was utterly helpless. She hated the feeling. But she also knew there was nothing she could do if she was going to live through this, except try to stay calm and do as she was ordered.

Trigger grimly flipped through the folder of information he'd been given before he and the rest of his Delta Force team got onboard the flight to Caracas, Venezuela. Two days ago, a flight heading from Costa Rica to Dallas had been hijacked and flown to the South American country.

Now the plane had been parked on the tarmac for almost forty-two hours, the hijackers waiting for their demands to be met.

The group claimed to be associated with the Cartel of the Suns, who were involved in the international drug trade. It was an organization allegedly headed by high-ranking members of the military forces of Venezuela, as well as some of the most influential government employees as well. Not too long ago, in fact, the nephew of the first lady of the country had been arrested for trying to smuggle eight hundred kilos of cocaine from Venezuela to the United States for the cartel.

Trigger didn't give a fuck about the drugs *or* about the man the hijackers were attempting to free from prison. Hugo Lamas was a border patrol agent in Venezuela who'd been imprisoned earlier that year for taking bribes and allowing millions of dollars' worth of drugs to pass through his checkpoints.

What Trigger *did* give a fuck about was the remaining twenty-four American citizens on the plane. Twelve women, ten men, and two children. He was also worried about the dozen or so citizens from Costa Rica, Mexico, Canada, Japan, Colombia, Panama, Nicaragua, and India onboard.

The entire Delta Force team thought the demands were bullshit. There was no way the

Cartel of the Suns cared about one border patrol agent; not enough to hijack an entire plane. But at the moment, Trigger didn't care what their real agenda was. All he cared about was figuring out how to get onto that plane and take out the assholes who thought it was okay to terrorize innocent civilians.

Reports from Venezuela were that bodies had been dumped out of the plane onto the tarmac. The hijackers weren't fucking around. They weren't just threatening to kill people, they'd already done it. And with every hour that passed, more and more lives were in jeopardy.

The Deltas were called in to assist because they specialized in close-quarter rescue missions. These kinds of rescues weren't exactly Trigger's favorite. The chance of more people getting hurt was extremely high. He hated knowing passengers would most likely die in order for them to get to the hijackers. It was likely the assholes would use men and women as shields to try to survive.

"What are ya thinkin'?" Lefty asked.

Sighing, Trigger turned to his friend and teammate. "I'm thinking this stinks to high heaven."

Nodding, Lefty agreed. "I know. It doesn't add up."

"Nothing adds up," Grover chimed in. "I mean, the Venezuelan government hates the US. And with all the rumors that they're heavily involved in the Cartel of the Suns, why would they call us in to kill their own people?"

"Unless this group *isn't* their own people," Brain said.

Everyone nodded.

"That makes sense," Trigger said. "They could be pissed off that someone hijacked the plane using their name, and they want to send a message."

"But at what cost?" Oz asked.

"They don't give a shit about innocent lives," Doc scoffed. "They don't care about anything but staying in power and making money. Many of them don't care about their *own* countrymen and women starving and suffering, so they certainly won't care about a bunch of foreigners."

"And I have no doubt they invited us in so if things go sideways, they can blame us," Lucky added in disgust.

Trigger ran a hand through his hair and sighed in agitation. "It doesn't matter why we're going, just that we do whatever it takes to get as many people as possible out of this alive."

The rest of the team nodded in agreement.

"What's the latest intel?" Trigger asked Brain.

The other man flipped through his notes and said, "It looks like they've got one of the passengers communicating with the negotiator."

"Smart. So we can't use voice-recognition software," Lucky said.

"Right," Brain agreed. "They also don't seem to be in a huge hurry. They've done the usual thing—bring us food and water or we'll start killing passengers—but otherwise, they just seem to be hunkered down and waiting."

"For what?" Grover asked.

"No clue," Brain replied.

"Who's the passenger doing the talking?" Trigger asked.

Brain shuffled some more papers. "FBI gathered background info on all the US passengers on the manifest. The spokesperson is identified as Gillian Romano. Thirty years old, single, event planner from Georgetown, Texas. She checks out clean. Five-seven, blonde hair, green eyes, a hundred and eighty-five pounds. Got her undergraduate degree from

UT-Austin and worked a series of entry-level jobs before starting her own company about four years ago. Both parents are living and still together; they live in Florida. She was in Costa Rica for seven days, apparently in charge of a big shindig put on by Pillar Custom Homes out of Austin. The guests all left the day before she did."

"You think she's in on this somehow?" Lefty asked.

"No," Brain said immediately. "I've got some of the transcripts of the calls she's had with the negotiator, and she's way out of her league. She's doing as good a job as she knows how, but the ass-wipe she's been talking to definitely hasn't helped."

"We taking over negotiations?" Doc asked.

"Fuck yeah, we are," Trigger answered for Brain. He'd also seen the transcripts. Gillian Romano was clearly scared, but she'd still done what she could to keep the hijackers calm and to get the passengers what they needed to be comfortable. He supposed her skills came from being an event planner.

"We're landing at the same airport, on the one runway they've still got open," Brain informed them. "But we aren't allowed to step foot off the airport property. The government doesn't want us in their country, and especially not out wandering around."

"Assholes," Oz said under his breath.

"So what's the plan?" Doc asked.

Trigger cleared his throat. "Get there. Get the asshole off the phone with Ms. Romano and see if we can't pull as much information from her as possible. Ideally, we'll pose as delivery men for supplies. We'll take out the hijackers and get the passengers to safety."

Grover chuckled. "Well, *that* sounds easy…not."

Trigger didn't even smile. "It won't be. We all know it. Those assholes could get tired of waiting. Most likely this is all a red herring, and they're a diversion from whatever their real agenda is. We have to stay on our toes. Trust no one. They landed in Venezuela for a reason, but whatever that is doesn't matter until those passengers are safe. Understand?"

Everyone immediately agreed. Their mission was hostage rescue. Nothing else. It was up to the CIA, FBI, DEA, and whoever else was involved to figure out the reasons behind the hijacking.

But even as the team fell silent, lost in their own thoughts about the upcoming mission, Trigger couldn't help but feel uneasy. Everything felt off about this op. And getting into an airplane undetected was impossible. Innocent civilians were going to die, there was no getting around that fact.

Trigger's thoughts returned to Gillian Romano, the appointed liaison for the hijackers. Just by reading the transcripts, he could tell she was smart. She was doing her best not to panic, which he admired. Not a lot of hostages he'd dealt with over the years kept as level a head as Gillian. While he hadn't heard her voice, and he couldn't read her emotions through her words, he could still tell she was terrified. And for some reason, that bothered him.

It was ridiculous. Trigger had no idea what she looked like or who she was as a person. She could be a harpy, or some vain chick only concerned about how many selfies she could post on social media. But he didn't think so.

Maybe he'd been hanging out with Ghost and his team for too long. Maybe he'd been wishing a bit too hard that he'd find a woman he could love and cherish as much as the other team cared about their women and families. He couldn't deny he was ready. At thirty-seven, he felt as if his life was passing him by. He wanted what his friends had.

He wanted someone to be there when he got home after a hard mission. Someone he could laugh with, completely let down his tough façade with, and who could make him feel as if the dangerous job he was doing was worth it.

He'd always thought he had plenty of time. But now he was closing in on forty. That wasn't old by any stretch, but Trigger still couldn't help feeling as if a vital part of life was eluding him.

Shaking his head, Trigger tried to get a grip. In the middle of an impossible op, which would most likely end in the deaths of way too many people, was not the time to start thinking about his love life...or lack thereof.

Pushing the inappropriate personal thoughts out of his head, Trigger did his best to formulate a plan. He knew he'd be the one taking over for the negotiator. He was good at it. The rest of the team would scope out the area and glean as many details as possible, so they could figure out the safest way to storm that plane.

We're coming, Gillian, Trigger silently promised. *Hang on just a bit longer, we're comin'.*

GILLIAN TRIED NOT TO HYPERVENTILATE. SHE WANTED TO BE ANYWHERE BUT here. She didn't want to be the negotiator for the monsters who'd taken over the plane. She didn't want to be the person responsible for whether others lived or died. But she didn't have a choice.

The hijacker who seemed to be in charge—the one who'd told everyone his name was Luis—had shoved a cell phone into her hand after they'd landed and told her to talk to the person on the other end.

She'd been speaking with the condescending asshole assigned to communicate with her and the terrorists for almost two days, and he was acting as if she were a stupid little girl who didn't understand the situation.

But Gillian understood more than *he* did. She understood that when he didn't immediately agree to send water and food out to the plane, someone would die. And they had. Another one of the hijackers, Jesus, had shot a man in the temple and shoved him out of the plane. She'd never forget the thud the body made when it hit the concrete below.

The food and water had been delivered not too long after that.

She'd told the man on the other end of the line that the hijackers wanted someone named Hugo Lamas released from prison, and all he would tell her was that they were working on it. Gillian was afraid that soon, "working on it" wouldn't be good enough. Luis was getting impatient and wanted to see proof that the government was doing something to release his friend.

Luis grabbed her upper arm yet again, and Gillian winced. She had bright purple bruises all over her arm because the hijackers liked to manhandle her. He leaned close and once more threatened her. "Tell them we're getting impatient. They need to quit fucking around and release Hugo. We've got eyes on the prison and know they're just stalling. Also, tell them that this plane needs to be refueled. Once Hugo is released, we're out of here. If they keep stalling, more people will die. All of this could be done and over with if they just do what we fucking say!"

Gillian stared up at the man in shock. His beard was growing shaggier by the day, and while she didn't flinch from his stench anymore—everyone on the plane now smelled pretty rank—she couldn't help wincing at the new information.

"You're going to let us all go before you take off though, right?" she asked.

Luis smiled. But it wasn't a nice smile. It was evil and threatening. He ran his fingers down Gillian's cheek and said, "I think I might just take you with us. You've been such an obedient and good girl."

She jerked her head away from his touch, but Luis moved fast, fisting her long blonde hair in his hand and yanking her head backward. He licked up her cheek before moving to whisper in her ear.

"Don't think you're any better than me, girlie. Your blonde hair and tits might get you whatever you want back in America, but you're in *my* world now. And if I want you, I'll have you. If I want to kill you, I will. You'll do *exactly* what I say, when I say it. Got it?"

Gillian's mouth was as dry as cotton. She'd been terrified of the men since they'd taken over the plane, but she hadn't ever been worried that they'd try anything sexual...until now. She nodded as best she could with her head still immobilized by his hand in her hair.

"Good." He untangled his fingers and ran his hand over her head. "You know, if you were nicer to me, then I might be kinder to the others."

Gillian shivered. She definitely didn't want to be "nicer" to him…but if she could free some of the other passengers, it might be worth it.

Deep down, Gillian had a feeling none of them would be getting out of this alive. The hijackers had shown a complete lack of concern for anyone's well-being. They'd killed the flight attendants and the first-class passengers, and had been constantly threatening the rest. They couldn't outright kill them all just yet, they needed them as bargaining chips for the Venezuelan officials, but if they weren't given what they wanted, Gillian knew they wouldn't hesitate to kill more.

Gillian desperately wanted to live. She wanted to save as many of the other passengers as well. In just two days, she'd formed an intense bond with the women around her.

Like Alice, the woman who'd been sitting next to her on the flight. She wasn't dealing very well with the situation at all. She'd been crying for two days straight.

Or Janet and her seven-year-old daughter, Renee.

And especially Andrea. She was about Gillian's age and had been on vacation with some girlfriends in Costa Rica. Her friends had all been on other flights, and she'd ended up on the hijacked plane. Andrea also happened to live in Austin, and despite—or maybe because of— the overwhelming situation they'd found themselves in, she and Gillian had clicked.

Although the women had been separated from the men, Gillian had seen the fear in the men's eyes as well. The group of four guys who looked to be in their early twenties were definitely freaked out. And one older gentleman had a constant look of terror on his face and frequently put his hand on his chest, as if in pain. She didn't know many of the names of the men, but that didn't mean she didn't want to save them if at all possible. No one asked to be in this situation.

The last thing she wanted was Luis, or Alberto, or Henry, or any of the other terrorists killing more passengers when they didn't get what they wanted.

"I'm doing everything I can to make sure the authorities know that you're serious about getting your friend Hugo freed," she said quietly.

"He's not my friend," Luis growled.

Gillian swallowed hard. "Maybe if you give a little, show a little compassion to the other passengers, they'd work faster to get your demands met."

Luis smirked. "You think?"

Gillian nodded.

"So…who do you think I should let go? You?"

She shook her head. "I don't know. Maybe Janet and her daughter. Or Alice. Andrea. One of the men."

Luis laughed. "Why don't I just let them all go?"

She didn't dare agree or disagree. She had a feeling Luis was just fucking with her now. He turned from her without another word, and Gillian sighed in relief—but it was short lived.

He hauled Andrea up from the floor and pulled her in front of Gillian.

"You think I should let her go?" he asked harshly.

Gillian could only stare at him with huge eyes.

"Well? Do you?" he barked.

She nodded slightly.

"No," Luis decided. "She's hot. And much more my type than a spoiled, fat blonde bitch like you."

Before Gillian could get offended that he'd called her fat—she wasn't fat; she preferred the term curvy—Luis had bent Andrea over his arm and lowered his mouth.

Andrea frantically attempted to fight him off. She pushed against his chest and tried to turn her head, but Luis wasn't having it. He used his free hand to roughly grab her chin as he forced his mouth down on hers.

Gillian closed her eyes, but she couldn't escape Andrea's keening whimpers.

She would never get used to the violence the hijackers used against the civilians on the plane. She hated it, and wanted to do whatever she could to make it stop.

How long Luis forced himself on Andrea, Gillian didn't know, but the sudden ringing of the phone in her hand sounded loud in the stifling-hot plane.

Luis straightened, shoved Andrea away from him, and turned back to Gillian.

He flicked open a knife he kept on him at all times and held it to her throat. "Answer it. And make them understand we're serious. You can tell them if they get us food and water within the next two hours, I'll release ten hostages. You can even pick them…as long as it's not your friend Andrea. Or the bitch with the kid. People care a lot more about children than adults. I need her to bargain with. You can choose eight men and two women."

Gillian hated Luis more with every word out of his mouth.

She glanced at Andrea, who was repeatedly wiping her mouth as she quickly moved back to her spot on the floor.

Taking a deep breath, she nodded.

Luis pressed the knife a little harder to her neck. "And we need fuel for this plane. They need to start working on that as soon as possible. But don't say anything that will make me have to kill more people," he warned. Then he took the blade from her neck and pointed it at little Renee. "I'll start with *her*."

Gillian nodded once again and put her back against the door to the cockpit and slid to the floor. Isaac, another hijacker, sat on the flight attendant's seat nearby so he could listen to her side of the conversation as Luis walked toward his fellow hijackers, who were guarding the men huddled in the back.

"Hello?" Gillian said shakily after she brought the phone to her ear.

"Gillian Romano?" a deep voice asked.

Surprised when she didn't hear the nasally, high-pitched voice of the man she'd been talking to for the last two days, Gillian simply said, "Yes."

"My name is Walker Nelson. I'm taking over the negotiations."

Gillian wasn't sure what to think. On one hand, she was glad she didn't have to talk to the other asshole, but on the other hand, she had no desire to start over and explain from scratch what Luis and the others wanted. But as if he could read her mind, Walker reassured her.

"I've been debriefed about what's been going on. Rest assured that we are well aware of the demands the hijackers have made and the Venezuelan government is working on getting Hugo freed. How are you holding up?"

Gillian blinked. "What?"

"How are *you*? I know this can't be easy. And for what it's worth, I think you're doing an amazing job. You just need to hang in there a bit longer."

She wanted to cry. She didn't think the other guy had purposely made her feel as if she was fucking everything up, and yet some of the things he'd said when he was frustrated had done exactly that. The fact that *this* guy had started out their conversation with something positive made her want to curl into a little ball and cry. She'd always considered herself a strong, independent woman, but right now, she'd kill to have someone hold her and tell her things were going to be all right.

"Gillian?"

"I'm here," she said, her voice cracking. "I'm okay."

There was a slight pause, then Walker said, "You're not, but you will be. Are they listening to your side of the conversation?"

Gillian's mind spun with his topic change. "Yes."

"All right, I'm going to need you to get creative. I need as much information as you can tell me about what's going on inside that plane. How many hostages there are. Where they are. Anything you can tell me about the hijackers. I'm sorry that too much time has gone by without someone getting in there and freeing you, but hopefully now things can change. Okay?"

"Okay," she whispered. She felt hope rise within her. This Walker guy sounded like he knew what the hell he was doing, unlike the other guy. "You're American, right?"

He chuckled, and the soothing sound seemed to travel through her body, warming her all the way to the tips of her toes. "Yeah. Currently stationed in Texas."

Stationed. That meant he was military. Which also meant he was probably some sort of special forces guy.

Gillian wasn't an idiot. Living as close to Fort Hood as she did meant she came into contact with a lot of military service members. She knew there were several teams of Delta Force operatives stationed at the base. She closed her eyes and prayed harder than she ever had before that Walker was one of those super-soldiers.

"Gillian?"

"I'm from Texas too," she said softly.

"I know," he returned.

Gillian cried out in pain when Isaac kicked her leg, hard. "Ow!"

"What are you saying?" Isaac barked.

"It's a new negotiator," she told him. "He wants to get to know me."

"Tell him we want more food and need gas. Ask about Hugo," Isaac demanded.

"He already told me they're working on getting Hugo freed. He said there's a lot of red tape and it's taking a while to work with the Venezuelan authorities. But they're working on it," she said quickly when he pulled his leg back to kick her once again. "And I'll tell him about the food, water, and fuel. I haven't had a chance yet," she told the hijacker.

Feeling braver than she had before, just because a kind voice was on the other end of the phone—she already felt safer with him organizing things, than she had with the other guy—she said, "In America, it's customary to get to know someone before you just start demanding things. I'm going to tell him what you want, but letting me talk to him for five minutes isn't going to mess up your timeline."

Not surprisingly, Isaac glared at her. *Very* surprisingly, he nodded. But he leaned forward and dug his fingers into her calf brutally as he said, "Fine, but if we don't have more food soon, it'll be your fault that someone else dies." He squeezed her leg once more, then let go and sat back, his dark brown eyes boring into her.

"Shit, are you all right?" Walker said into her ear. "Did he hurt you?"

"I'm okay," Gillian repeated. She wasn't, but there wasn't anything Walker Nelson could do about the throbbing in her leg or the fear making its way through her bloodstream. She knew she didn't have a lot of time to get information to this guy, and she hoped like hell he'd be able to figure out her clues. She wasn't exactly a pro at spy stuff, but she'd do her best.

"My dad was a pilot," she began. "But he died. My mom worked for the same airline as him, and that's how they met. She was a flight attendant. My dad wooed her by bribing the caterers to deliver her presents. The first gift he got for her was a stuffed animal. Cheesy, but it worked because she agreed to go out with him." Gillian knew Isaac was listening to every word, and she was afraid she was being too vague. But Walker's next words reassured her.

"Right. I know your parents live in Florida and weren't a pilot or flight attendant. So if I'm reading you right, you're saying the pilot's deceased and you think the hijackers got weapons smuggled onboard before the plane took off?" Walker asked calmly.

Gillian relaxed a fraction. He understood. Thank God. "Yeah."

"How many are there?"

"I have six brothers. I'm the youngest," she said.

"Got it," Walker reassured her. "All armed?"

"Yes."

"Guns?"

"Yes."

"Knives?"

"Yes."

"You're doing amazing, Gillian."

"My mom told me stories about how they liked to fool around in the plane after all the passengers had left. This would never happen today, but back then, they had no problem sneaking back on a plane after its flights for the day were over. Mom always wanted to be up front, in first class, but dad preferred the back of the plane."

"Okay…I know you're trying to tell me something, but I'm not understanding," Walker said. "I'm so sorry. Keep going. I'll figure it out."

Gillian refused to get discouraged. She was actually giving the authorities information they could hopefully use, not just getting yelled at by the negotiator and the hijackers. She forced a chuckle, as if Walker had said something funny. "So you know how it is. My brothers were all very protective of me. They always let me have the best seat. I was always in the front in the car, and when we went to shows, they put me in the row ahead of them so they could keep their eye on me."

"So you're in the front of the plane?" Walker asked.

"Uh-huh."

"Got it. They've separated the women and men, putting the women near the front of the plane and the men in the back, right?"

Gillian wanted to cry in relief. He'd understood her lame clues. "Exactly."

"Good job. We knew from the thermal imagers that there were two groups of hostages, one in front and one in back, but we didn't know you were separated by gender."

With every word out of his mouth, Gillian felt better. Heat signatures meant they had some fancy electronics and they could watch what they were doing.

"I'm going to get you out of this," Walker told her.

Gillian closed her eyes. She knew he couldn't promise her that, but she appreciated him saying it anyway. "Okay."

"I am," he said, more firmly now.

"I hope so," she whispered.

Isaac kicked again, and she yelped when his foot made contact with the same part of her leg he'd kicked and dug his fingers into not too long ago. "Get on with it," he hissed.

"That fucker better stop hurting you," he growled. "Are you okay, Gillian?" Walker asked in her ear.

Gillian closed her eyes and soaked in his concern. After the hell she'd been through over the last couple of days, his words were a balm for her battered soul.

In just the few minutes they'd been on the phone, Gillian was already forming an emotional attachment to a man she'd never seen, a man she was relying on to rescue her. But she couldn't help it. His kindness meant everything.

"What happened?" Walker asked urgently.

Snapping out of her thoughts, Gillian blinked.

What the hell was she thinking? The man was doing a *job*. Any attachment she was feeling was because of the situation, nothing more.

"We need more water," she blurted, not taking her eyes from Isaac's foot. She wanted to be prepared next time he decided to kick her. "And food. And they want this plane fueled up."

"Wait—what? They're going to try to fly that plane out of here?" Walker asked.

Gillian ignored him. She didn't know what the hijackers had planned. All she knew was that there were ten people who could escape this nightmare if she played her role correctly. "They said they'd let people go if we got food and water soon, but if we don't, they're going to kill someone else. And they mean it."

"Take a breath, Gillian. I know they mean it."

She ignored him and continued on, talking as fast as she could to make sure she got as much information to him as possible. "

"Gillian," Walker said firmly, "take a breath. There's food and water waiting. It'll be delivered before an hour's up. The deaths are on *them*, not you."

She tried to relax, but she couldn't. Something else occurred to her. "I don't know how it works, but the toilets are all backed up. They're full or something. This isn't one of their demands, but please, if it's possible, can they be cleaned out?"

"I'll see what I can do," Walker reassured her.

"Hang on," she told him, then looked up at Isaac. "He says they have food and water coming."

"And the fuel?"

"Walker?" she asked into the phone. "He also wants this plane fueled."

"Since that's a new demand, it has to go through several layers of approval, but I swear I'll work on it."

It wasn't what Gillian wanted to hear, but she found herself nodding anyway. "All the fuel trucks were moved away from the airport," she told Isaac, making things up as she spoke. "I don't think they have a problem refueling the plane, but it can't happen immediately."

Isaac growled and gestured to Carlos, another hijacker nearby. They spoke in Spanish to each other for a quick moment, then Isaac nodded. "Fine, but tell them that not fueling us up isn't an option. The longer it takes, the more people we'll kill. Ten, fifteen...maybe more...depending on how I feel."

"I heard," Walker said in her ear. "Tell him it'll be done."

"He said okay," Gillian told Isaac shakily. "He'll get the plane refueled."

"Good. Give me the phone," he ordered.

In the past, Gillian hadn't had any issues giving up the cell phone after she'd passed along their demands. But for some reason, this time she hesitated. Walker Nelson felt like a lifeline. Like if she hung up with him, she'd be signing her own death warrant. Her fingers tightened on the cheap plastic.

"Don't give up," Walker said into her ear. "We're here and watching. You're doing an amazing job and you'll be out of there before you know it. I can't wait to meet you face-to-face."

With those words ringing in Gillian's head, Isaac—obviously tired of waiting for her to comply with his order—swung his fist forward, punching her in the side of the head.

She cried out and went flying sideways. In the confined space in front of the cockpit, she didn't have far to fall. Her head bounced off the wall.

Gillian curled into a ball on the floor, holding her head in her hands, both sides throbbed, from Isaac's fist and from smacking against the wall.

The hijacker leaned down and picked up the phone she'd dropped and clicked it off, putting it in his pocket. He turned away from her without another word and headed for Luis, who was standing in the middle of the airplane.

Gillian crawled back over to where the other women were huddled in the first-class cabin and did her best not to cry.

"What'd they say?" Andrea asked. "What's going on?"

"Hopefully they're going to fix the toilets," Gillian informed the others.

"And food and water?" Alice asked.

"That too. The hijacker also said that some of us might be released."

There were gasps of excitement from the women around her, and Gillian wanted to feel happy that some of them would hopefully get out of this horrific situation…but all she could think about in that moment was Walker.

She'd heard his outraged curse when Isaac had hit her, right before she'd lost her grip on the phone. And he'd said he wanted to meet her.

As much as she tried to remind herself she was just connecting with another stranger because of the stress of the situation, she couldn't make herself care. She wanted to live through this awful situation, if only to meet the man who'd somehow made her more determined than ever to survive.

Trigger gripped the table in front of him so hard it felt as if he was going to break it. He'd been impressed by Gillian before, but now that he'd spoken to her, he was even more so. There was no doubt she was afraid, but she was hanging in there. She was clever, and even under the horrible circumstances she'd found herself in, she'd stayed strong, determined to help him as much as she could. He'd expected to have to explain how to give him clues without letting on she was doing so, but she didn't need any explanation.

They'd learned there were six hijackers onboard, and the men and women had been separated, with the women toward the front of the plane and the men at the back. The hijackers had also claimed some hostages might be released, and he had a hunch that was because of Gillian negotiating on their behalf. The request for the plane being refueled was new, but not entirely surprising. However, if the hijackers thought they'd survive their little stunt and be allowed to fly off into the sunset, they were more idiotic than they seemed.

But at the moment, all Trigger's thoughts were on Gillian. He recognized the sounds of someone being hit, and he wasn't happy at all that the woman on the other end of the phone had been the recipient of violence. He wanted her and the other innocent civilians off that plane. *Now.*

"Brain?" he asked his teammate, who'd been sitting next to him listening to his conversation with Gillian. "Did you get anything?"

The other man shook his head. "Not yet. I need to play back the recording and isolate the conversations in the background. It'll take a bit."

Trigger nodded. Brain was a language savant. He was fluent in at least thirty languages and he could pick up new ones without too much difficulty. His job was to listen to the background noise and glean any intel from conversations the hijackers were having with each other.

"The food and water is ready to be delivered," Grover informed him. "And we'll tell the authorities about the request for fuel."

"I've already got the waste people mobilizing," Oz added.

"It's got to feel like hell on earth inside that plane," Lucky muttered. "Between the heat, the toilets, and the fear…" His voice trailed off.

Trigger was more than aware of what the people inside the plane were going through. He hadn't been in their exact situation, but close enough.

He felt a hand on his shoulder and knew Lefty was standing behind him. "She's going to be okay," his friend said quietly.

Trigger shook his head. "We don't know that. I said the same, but I have a feeling she knows as well as we do that there are no guarantees here. This whole thing stinks to high heaven."

"I agree," Doc said. "On one hand, this is a textbook hijacking, but it seems like overkill. The Cartel of the Suns is run by the Venezuelan government. Why would they have to resort to hijacking a plane from Costa Rica?"

"Right?" Lefty asked. "They could just get one of their contacts in the military or prison system to arrange for Lamas to escape."

"Regardless, our job is not to figure that shit out," Trigger told his team. "We were called in strictly to rescue those hostages. Not to solve the world's political issues. We need to concentrate on how we're going to get into that bird and save as many innocents as we can."

Everyone nodded in agreement.

"Gillian said in return for the food and water, they might let some hostages go," Trigger said. "Lefty, you and Grover are with me. We'll put on those overalls the airport staff wear and we'll be the ones to deliver the supplies. Hopefully we'll get a glimpse of some of the hijackers and can assess the situation onboard in the process."

The others nodded.

"Brain, keep working, let us know if you find out anything."

"Will do," the other man confirmed.

"The rest of you will be at the ready, covering our asses out there. I have an itchy feeling at the back of my neck that this is going to move faster than we think," Trigger warned.

"The faster we're out of this country, the better," Oz said. "Ever since we landed, I've felt as if we're being watched."

"Same," Lucky chimed in.

"The US government has arranged a flight for the surviving Americans to get out of here the second this thing is over," Brain added.

"Right. I think it was more the Venezuelan government wanting them gone so there would be no reason for the US to have a presence here for any longer than necessary," Doc said dryly.

Trigger tuned out his teammates. They weren't saying anything he hadn't already thought himself. All he could think about was the way Gillian's voice had trembled with fear—or pain?—as she spoke with him. She was taking more than her fair share of licks from the assholes who were enjoying toying with her…and the negotiators. On the surface, their demands were reasonable and made sense, though he couldn't help but suspect there was something else going on.

But at the moment, his only goal was to rescue the hostages. One blonde in particular.

Chapter Three

TRIGGER DROVE THE SMALL AIRLINE CART TOWARD THE SILENT PLANE SITTING on the tarmac. It loomed large and foreboding. There were no other planes or vehicles around it and no lights on inside the cabin. The sun had gone down and darkness was quickly setting in. The plane was parked well away from the terminal and there was no cover for Trigger and his men as they approached with the requested food and water.

The concrete under the back hatch was stained red with the blood of the men and women they'd dumped outside. The entire first-class cabin had been assassinated, the bodies disposed of after they'd landed. And there had been at least one other passenger murdered and dumped since they'd arrived in Venezuela as well. Trigger wasn't going to let that happen again, not if he could help it.

It was eerily quiet as they approached the airplane, but when they parked under the right side, near the entrance the catering companies used to restock the plane, the hatch slowly opened.

Looking up, Trigger saw a shadowy figure dressed all in black standing near the opening—but he couldn't take his eyes away from the woman who also appeared.

Gillian. He'd bet his life on it.

Her long hair was hanging limp around her pale face. She had on a pair of jeans and a dark blue wispy shirt that fluttered in the slight breeze of the evening. He watched as she took a deep breath, as if enjoying the fresh air, before the man standing next to her shoved the barrel of a rifle into her side.

She flinched away from him and looked down at him, Grover, and Lefty.

The last crew who had delivered supplies had brought a ladder with them and used that to reach the hatch. It wasn't ideal, but since it worked once, Trigger figured they might as well not cause any suspicion by asking for a different delivery method.

"Do you have the food and water?" the woman called down.

Trigger nodded.

"And the toilets?" she asked.

"After these are delivered, they'll start draining the tanks," Trigger said, adding a Spanish accent to his voice.

The man standing next to her said something too low for Trigger to hear, and she nodded. "Just like last time, one of you has to climb up the ladder and hand me the boxes. You can't come onboard, and if you do anything suspicious, you'll be shot. Then they'll kill one of the hostages as well in retaliation."

Her voice trembled slightly, and Trigger's adrenaline poured through his body. He knew he could leap into the plane before the asshole standing guard could kill him, but there were still five more hijackers. They'd certainly take him out before Grover or Lefty could get inside. Not to mention, it would put all of the civilians in danger.

He had to be patient. The moment would come for the hijackers to die, but now wasn't that time.

The woman licked her lips and got down on her knees in front of the opening. "Okay. Just move slow. Don't give him a reason to shoot you or anyone else. Please."

This was definitely Gillian; he recognized her voice. He nodded at her and turned to his teammates. Lefty and Grover met his gaze and they communicated easily without words. They would play this safe, but if the shit hit the fan, they were all ready to act. They had several weapons hidden on their bodies and could draw and shoot in seconds if need be.

Trigger set up the ladder and climbed a few rungs. He reached down and took the box Lefty was holding for him, then stepped up the rest of the way to the opening of the plane.

"I'm Gillian Romano, and that's Andrea Vilmer," the woman said as she reached for the box.

Trigger nodded. He approved of her doing what she could to share the names of the people still inside. She reached for the heavy box and the hijacker next to her backed farther into the plane, so Trigger couldn't get a good view of his face.

Frustrated that Gillian and Andrea had to do the heavy lifting of the boxes, Trigger could only watch as they and the other women nearby struggled to move the boxes from the hatch into the bowels of the plane.

"Thank you, Janet. Maybe there's something sweet in there for your daughter, Renee," Gillian said as she handed another box to a woman behind her. "This one's heavy, Alice," she cautioned as another box was handed to another woman. "Maybe Leyton and Reed will help move the boxes to the back for the men. I know Charles will appreciate getting the water, with his cough and all."

With each box she handed off, Gillian recited names. Maria, Camile, Rebecca, Mateo, Alejandro, Muhammad…she'd done an amazing job of remembering the names of the other hostages on the plane.

Trigger was impressed. Intentional or not, she was doing her best to not only humanize the other captives, but to let him know who was still alive inside the plane. He wished he could reassure her. Tell her that he understood what she was doing, that she was so strong and he admired her. But he couldn't. All he could do was keep handing her the damn boxes filled with food and water.

He wasn't ready for Lefty to hand him the last box. It hadn't taken enough time. He hadn't been able to see enough of the inside of the plane…and he definitely hadn't had enough time with Gillian.

"This is the last one," Gillian told the man in the shadows as she handed it off to someone behind her. "You said if they delivered the supplies within two hours, you'd let ten people go."

Trigger wanted to tell her not to antagonize the hijacker, but he had to keep his mouth shut. It wouldn't be hard for the man with the rifle to realize he wasn't a native Spanish speaker and that something was up. He had a part to play, just as Gillian did. But that didn't mean he liked it.

Refusing to budge from the ladder, he stilled, waiting to see what would happen next.

The man gestured to someone inside the plane and before Trigger knew what was happening, a man in his mid-thirties was standing at the opening of the plane, looking down at him.

"Be careful," Gillian was saying. "Don't fall as you go down the ladder."

With no choice, Trigger had to back down the ladder as the first hostage made his way off the plane.

As each person arrived at the bottom of the ladder, Lefty and Grover pointed them back toward the terminal. Each one took off as if the hounds of hell were at their feet, and Trigger couldn't blame them. It was obvious they were relieved to be away from the plane and from the hijackers.

But something was bothering him about the civilians who'd been chosen to be set free.

Typically in hijackings, the freed were often women, children, or the infirm. Only two of the hostages set free were women, the others all men. Healthy, relatively *young* men.

People who might be able to put up a struggle and possibly overcome the hijackers.

Trigger understood the thought process behind letting the young, healthy, and strong free, and it pissed him off. Looking up at the hatch, he saw Gillian once again come to the edge. For a second, he wanted to encourage her to scramble down the ladder. To get the hell out of there. But somehow he knew, even if it was the right thing to do—which it wasn't— she wouldn't do it. She wouldn't bail and leave the others behind.

For just a moment, their eyes met. Her brows came down, she licked her lips, and he saw her mouth his name in question.

He nodded once—then a black-clad arm reached around Gillian's chest and almost took her off her feet as she was wrenched backward. She let out a small sound of surprise as she was hauled away.

The hatch slammed shut, and Trigger heard the lock engage as it was secured.

"Fuck," Grover swore as he and Lefty grabbed the ladder and secured it back to the utility cart they'd driven out to the plane.

"You couldn't see much, could you?" Lefty asked.

Trigger shook his head. "No. They played it smart. Using the forward door meant the galley blocked the view of the rest of the plane."

"I'm assuming that was Gillian?" Grover asked.

"Yeah," Trigger confirmed.

"I heard some of what she was saying," Lefty said. "She was trying to give us as much information as possible as to who was still alive onboard, wasn't she?"

Trigger nodded. "I think so."

"We've got the passenger manifest," Grover reminded the men. "We've already got the names of everyone onboard."

"Right, but not who was shot and who wasn't," Trigger told his friend. He'd found that people reacted in very different ways to danger. Some froze in terror. Others freaked out. And the very rare few seemed to remain calm and process the situation carefully…like Gillian. She was obviously frightened, but had pushed her feelings to the side to try to help others.

"It was pretty ripe in there," Lefty muttered. "I could smell it even from where I was on that ladder."

For some reason, his friend's words irritated Trigger. "It's not like they can help it," he bit out. "It's fucking hot during the day and they're not running the engine for power. And let's not forget the toilets weren't meant for the number of people using them for days on end."

"Whoa!" Lefty said, holding up his hands. "I wasn't criticizing. Just making an observation."

Trigger took a deep breath and held on as Grover drove them back to the terminal. "I know, sorry."

"Hugo should be freed sometime tonight. We'll stall them by saying the paperwork is still being done or something, but we should be ready to make our move early in the morning," Grover said.

Trigger nodded. That was the timetable he was working toward as well.

The knowledge that by this time tomorrow, the standoff would be over, should've made him feel better. But instead, the unease deep within him continued to grow. For the first time in a very long time, he felt as if the enemy was three steps ahead of them. It wasn't a comfortable feeling…

Especially considering his thoughts about Gillian Romano.

It was crazy. He didn't even know her. Not really. But then again, he knew the important things. That she was smart and considerate. She worried more about her fellow prisoners than she did herself. She was brave...and all he wanted to do was hug her and tell her everything would be all right.

It wasn't like him, but Trigger couldn't get the woman out of his mind. She impressed the hell out of him, and that didn't happen very often. He wanted to get to know her better. Wanted to know every little thing.

But...he was a Delta. Ghost and his team might've found women to spend the rest of their lives with, but they'd been damn lucky. Finding someone who could put up with his job and the danger it brought, and who would be all right with never knowing where he was or what he was doing, was damn near impossible.

No, it wouldn't be fair to Gillian to even ask her to do that.

But damn, did he want to.

Taking a deep breath, Trigger turned his mind back to the task at hand. He was getting way ahead of himself. There was no guarantee he or Gillian would get out of this situation alive. And she probably wouldn't want anything to do with anyone who was even close to this clusterfuck, not that he could blame her. She'd probably want to put it firmly behind her and get on with her life.

Trigger mentally recited the names that Gillian had used so he wouldn't forget them. He needed to talk to Brain and see if he'd been able to isolate any background conversations from his earlier phone call with Gillian. And he and his team had to plan the best way to raid that plane so the least number of innocent civilians were killed in the process.

His head throbbed, but Trigger ignored it and pressed his lips together. He'd get Gillian out of that plane one way or another.

Gillian wanted to cry when the hatch of the plane was secured. The air had been so damn refreshing, she hadn't even minded being forced to haul in all the heavy boxes.

But it had been the man at the top of the ladder that had given her the biggest boost. At first she hadn't paid much attention to him, concentrating more on the slight breeze and fresh air. But when she finally noticed that he was paying *very* close attention to *her*, she took a second glance.

He had dark hair and his biceps strained the fabric of the one-piece jumper he'd had on. His gray eyes were piercing in their intensity, and she swore he was exuding confidence and positivity as if they were pheromones. But the thing that made her truly believe he was the man she'd been talking to on the phone was his lack of fear. The men who'd delivered the last batch of food and water had been falling all over themselves to unload the boxes and get the hell away from the plane.

This man, and his buddies, had given off the opposite vibe. Gillian had a feeling if Luis had made any threatening moves behind her, the man at the top of the ladder would've leaped into the plane and taken him out.

Feeling buoyed by the man's confidence, she'd started using as many names of her fellow hostages as possible. If this was her Walker, she wanted him to know exactly who was onboard.

Her Walker?

Gillian shook her head in exasperation. He wasn't hers. She had to get her shit together. He was just doing a job. Once this was over, and hopefully that would be sooner rather than later, he'd go home and forget she existed.

But a part of her didn't want to believe that. She felt as if she'd connected with the man, but again, that was stupid. He was probably one hundred percent focused on the mission. Namely, rescuing all of the hostages on the plane. She wasn't anyone special, and the sooner she got that through her thick skull, the better.

It was a ridiculous fantasy that he'd felt even a tenth of the emotional pull toward her that she did to him, but it was a hell of a lot better than thinking about her current situation.

She'd actually mouthed his name right before the hatch had shut, needing to know if it was really him. He'd nodded slightly…then Luis had grabbed her and manhandled her back inside the plane.

She sat on the floor with her back against the cockpit door, watching as Alberto and Jesus handed out water and food to the other women. Leyton, a Hispanic man who looked to be in his early thirties, was tasked with schlepping some boxes to the back of the plane for the men being held there.

Turning her attention back to the women, Gillian sighed. She'd hoped they would let Janet and her little girl go. Or even Alice, who hadn't been dealing well since being separated from her husband. But instead, as promised, they'd only freed two of the women. Gillian hadn't known them well; they were older and hadn't said one word to anyone, as far as Gillian knew.

They'd also let eight men go. Mostly young men, who hadn't even looked at the women they'd had to pass on their way out. It made a weird kind of sense to Gillian. The women weren't as strong as the men, and were less likely to plan any kind of revolt.

The hijackers might see Gillian and the others as weaker than they were, but they weren't. They just had to use different weapons than their muscles.

Gillian vowed right then and there to do whatever it took to thwart their plans, whatever they were. If they thought they were going to take off to safety, they were dead wrong. She'd have to find some way to sabotage the plane. She'd watched Luis close the hatch; maybe she could disable the door somehow. They couldn't take off if the door wasn't latched, could they? She didn't know, but it was worth a shot. She'd also work harder to give Walker as much information as she could.

"I need my cock sucked," Luis announced.

Gillian started badly. She'd been lost in her own head, thinking about Walker and how she might be able to fight back, when the hijacker's words interrupted, loud and threatening.

She shrank back against the door and stared at him with wide eyes. He was standing in the middle of the aisle about six rows back, where the first-class cabin ended and the economy seating started.

He was looking at all the women huddled together as if he were shopping and trying to pick out the ripest fruit.

"You," he said, pointing at Andrea, who was sitting on the floor in one of the rows.

She let out a quiet sob and shook her head.

"Get your ass up, now!" Luis ordered.

Ever so slowly, Andrea stood. Her head hung low and she stared at the floor.

"Well? What are you waiting for? Get over here!" Luis said with an evil smirk.

No one said a word. Gillian could hear Janet and the others crying, but no one stood up to the hijacker or came to Andrea's aid.

Gillian's mouth opened—she had no idea what she was going to say; it wasn't as if she was going to volunteer herself—but it was too late. Luis had grabbed Andrea's arm and was roughly towing her back down the aisle.

Luis pulled her into one of the exit rows, probably because it was wider and had more room. He shoved her to her knees in front of him. Gillian couldn't see Andrea any longer, or what she was doing, but she could guess. All she could see was Luis from the chest up. Guilt surged that she was so grateful when the seats blocked her view.

Luis was looking down, and he still had that awful smirk on his face. As Gillian watched, Luis said something to Andrea, and she imagined him holding the other woman's head in his hands as she undid his pants. He stood still for a minute or so—then he threw his head back, as if he was thoroughly enjoying what was happening.

Gillian could tell by his swaying movements that his hips were thrusting forward and back, faster and faster, and she could just imagine what poor Andrea was enduring. Carlos and Jesus were watching raptly from the back of the plane, and she realized Henry was stroking himself as he sat in the jump seat next to her.

Shivering and closing her eyes at last, Gillian couldn't watch anymore.

Luis was horrible. Him *and* his buddies. As if this situation wasn't bad enough, now they were forcing themselves on the hostages? Was she next? Or poor Janet? Alice? What about beautiful Camile? It was too much. Hadn't they all endured enough?

A commotion made her eyes pop open, and she watched as Luis hauled Andrea back up the aisle. His pants were zipped but the button was still undone, and he had a satisfied look on his face. It made Gillian physically sick.

Andrea held a hand over her lips and refused to meet anyone's eyes.

"If you all don't behave and do exactly as you're told, you're next," he said as he threw Andrea back into her spot on the floor. Then he motioned to Alberto and Isaac, and the three of them sauntered down the aisle to have a private conversation in the relative privacy of the middle of the plane, where he'd just forced himself on Andrea.

Henry said something under his breath in Spanish that made the others laugh, and Gillian was glad she couldn't understand him. She had a feeling he'd said something derogatory about Andrea, or maybe about the women in general.

Gillian wanted to go to Andrea. Wanted to ask if she was all right. Reassure her that they'd get out of this alive, that they just had to be strong. But in her mind, the words just sounded hollow. She thought about how *she'd* feel if that had been her Luis had grabbed. She wouldn't want to hear any platitudes from anyone.

Closing her eyes, Gillian tried to dredge up soothing thoughts about Walker once more, but found it was impossible. All her fears and worries were overwhelming her, and she couldn't think about anything other than what Luis and his buddies might have in store for the rest of them.

Eventually, she did her best to get some rest, even if it was filled with nightmares.

It felt as if she'd only been asleep for seconds, but in reality, it had been hours when Gillian was painfully woken up with a kick to her side.

Crying out, she sat up immediately and flinched at the light shining in her eyes.

"Time for another call," Luis told her brusquely. "We need to know when Hugo will be freed and when the plane will be refueled. They're taking too long, and we've been sitting around waiting on them long enough. It's currently one in the morning. They have until five a.m. to have this plane fueled and to set Hugo free."

"What happens at five?" Gillian asked.

Luis smirked and leaned down. "People start dying," he said succinctly. "One every fifteen minutes until we have proof that our comrade is free. Make sure they understand. We're starting with your friends. Maybe with that little girl."

"No!" Gillian exclaimed. "Please!"

Luis grabbed hold of Gillian's hair and jerked backward. He held his knife to her exposed throat and growled, "Then make them understand we're not fucking around! You do that, and everyone lives. You fuck up, and they are all dead! You'll be last. I'll make you watch every person on this plane die. Got it?"

"Yes," Gillian whispered. She had no doubt he'd do exactly as he threatened.

Luis nodded then threw the cell phone into her lap as he stood. "And don't try anything stupid," he warned. "We're listening." And with that, he stood back and stared menacingly down at her.

Gillian's fingers were shaking, but she clicked the phone on and went to the most recent calls. She pressed on the last number received and waited for someone to pick up. Her heart was in her throat, and for a second she thought no one would answer since it was the middle of the night, but finally she heard Walker's voice.

"Yeah?"

"It's Gillian."

"Hey." His voice immediately changed from the gruff, menacing tone he'd used to answer to a gentler timbre. "You all right?"

"Yeah. I'm supposed to give you a message."

"Okay, but first, take a breath."

Gillian frowned. "What?"

"Take a breath, Di. I can tell you're stressed way the hell out. Just breathe."

"Di?"

"Sorry, that just popped out. Diana Prince. You know, Wonder Woman's alter ego? You remind me of her. Staying calm under pressure, looking for ways to help even when the odds are stacked against you. I didn't see a golden lasso earlier, but you might be hiding it somewhere."

Gillian was literally speechless. She couldn't think of a damn thing to say in response.

"Are you breathing? Somehow I don't think you are."

She let out the breath she was holding with an audible whoosh and, amazingly, she heard Walker chuckle on the other end of the line.

"Good. Now, tell me what those assholes want us to know."

And just that quickly, she was sucked back into her current situation. Looking up, Gillian saw Luis and Henry staring down at her with their arms crossed over their chests. She was definitely at a disadvantage sitting at their feet, but she tried not to let that intimidate her.

Hell, who was she kidding? She was way the fuck intimidated.

"They said you have until five in the morning to have the plane refueled and Hugo released. Otherwise they're going to start killing people. One every fifteen minutes." She gave him the message quickly, feeling bile rise in her throat at having to say the words out loud.

"The authorities are waiting for the sun to rise to start refueling," Walker said calmly. "I can tell them they need to start doing it sooner. And I believe Hugo is being released in around two hours. Are they listening?"

Gillian nodded but couldn't get any words out.

"I'm sure they are," Walker said. "Go ahead, tell them what I said."

How Walker could sound so calm and reassured, Gillian had no idea. She cleared her throat and passed along the message.

Luis and Henry immediately began talking to each other in Spanish.

"I don't—"

"Hush," Walker said swiftly through the phone.

Startled that he'd been so abrupt, Gillian swallowed hard and held the phone tightly to her ear. She wasn't sure what to say, or why she was still holding the phone. She should hang up. She'd passed along the message. But no matter how upsetting it was that Walker had been so terse, she couldn't bring herself to break their connection.

She could hear him breathing on the other end of the line, and concentrated on that. She tried to time her own breaths with his. Surprisingly, it calmed her. He wasn't huffing and puffing and wasn't acting nervous or freaked out.

Luis and Henry finally stopped arguing, and Luis stomped away toward the back of the plane. Henry ran an agitated hand through his hair, and he grunted before he too walked away from where Gillian was sitting. He didn't go far, only to where the first-class cabin stopped, but it gave her a bit of privacy.

"Walker?" she whispered.

"Sorry about that, Di."

"What happened?" she asked.

"I needed to hear their conversation," Walker told her.

Then Gillian understood. "What'd they say?"

"I don't know. But my teammate will figure it out. He's on his way, and he'll listen to the recording of our call when he gets here."

"Is that guy really going to be freed soon?"

"Yes," Walker said simply.

"And the plane refueled?"

"I take it no one is listening to you right now?" Walker asked.

"No, Henry's pouting. Oh! Luis, Jesus, Alberto, Carlos, Henry, and Isaac. Those are the hijackers' names."

"Good girl," Walker said, the admiration easy to hear in his tone. "And this is going to be over soon."

"They really *will* start killing people," Gillian warned him. "They said they would start with the women."

"I believe you, but it's not going to come to that."

"Promise?" She knew it wasn't really fair to ask that of him, but she was desperate. Her heart fell when Walker didn't immediately respond. "Sorry. Ignore me, I—"

"I'm not a fortune teller, sweetheart. I wish I was. I wish I could tell you for sure what was going to happen in the next few hours. All I *can* tell you is that I'm doing my very best to get you, and everyone else on that plane, out of there in one piece."

"Please don't let them take off with all of us inside this plane."

"No way in hell," Walker said fervently.

She believed him. "I watched as Luis secured the door. I'm sure I can do something to open it, or to make it not close right. They can't take off without the door being latched, right? Maybe when the plane is refueled, someone can leave a gun or something in a secret compartment that I can get to and take them out. I can—"

"Diana Prince, right down to your toes," Walker interrupted.

"What?"

"We've got this, Di. All you have to do is go with the flow, keep your head down, and not put yourself in the line of fire. Okay?"

"Okay. Walker?"

"Yeah?"

"That *was* you with the food and water, wasn't it?"

"It was."

Gillian felt a little stupid. Of course it was. He'd confirmed it with his nod earlier. But her emotions were all over the place. She was exhausted, stressed, and freaked out. Not to mention, she had a feeling she smelled atrocious…she couldn't really tell, since everyone around her smelled awful too. She hated that Walker had seen her at her worst. She wanted to impress him. Wanted to look like the kick-ass women in the movies who could live through the worst and still manage to seduce the hero.

"I thought so," she said lamely when the silence went on too long.

"What's goin' through your head?" he asked.

Gillian closed her eyes and rested her forehead on her knees. She hurt. All over. She was exhausted and terrified. And she was apparently vain enough to want Walker to like her…when they were in a middle of a freaking *hostage situation.* She was certifiably insane. "Nothing."

"You want to know what I saw when I climbed that ladder?" Walker asked softly.

Gillian shook her head, but said, "Maybe."

He chuckled softly—then blew her mind. "I saw a woman who was at the end of her rope, but who was still holding on. Not only that, but I saw a leader. Someone who everyone on that plane probably looks up to. Someone who might be scared, but was doing her best to power through it for the good of the rest of the team. I saw a woman who I admired, and who I vowed right then and there wouldn't become a statistic or a quick blurb on a news story." And then, after a beat, "I saw a woman I wanted to get to know better."

His words felt good. Damn good. Taking a deep breath, she asked, "You want to know what I saw when I looked at *you?*"

"Sure, Di, tell me."

"Hope."

They were both silent for a moment. "I like that way more than I should. Hang on just a little longer, Gillian. Stay alert, and be as calm as you can. All right?"

"Yeah." Something occurred to her then. Something she should've thought about before. "Walker? You said you're recording when I call you?"

"Yes."

"What if I give them the phone back and pretend to hang up, but don't?"

"No."

"But—"

"No. If they realize what you did, they'll hurt you."

"They're going to hurt me anyway. They've *already* hurt me. So far they've just been toying with me, but I know the second they have the chance, Luis or one of the others will take great pleasure in making me suffer. But if you can hear their conversations, then you might be able to catch them if they fly away."

"You're more important."

Gillian knew she'd replay those three words over and over in her head for the rest of her life…however short it might turn out to be.

She'd had her share of boyfriends, but for the most part, she'd never felt as if they'd put her first. She'd dated a musician who'd moved to LA to pursue his career. She would've gone with him…if he'd asked. He didn't. Then there was the accountant who she hadn't seen for three months around tax time. Also, the guy who loved sports so much he never asked her over when his favorite team was playing because she would distract him.

Walker didn't even know her, and he was putting *her* above capturing six ruthless terrorist hijackers.

"I'm doing it," she told him. "I hope to be able to officially meet you soon, Walker Nelson. Be careful." Then, without waiting for his response—because she had a feeling he'd be able to talk her out of it—she clicked out of the phone app and turned off the screen. As it faded to black, she prayed her plan would actually work and the assholes who were keeping them hostage would actually say something incriminating, and that Walker and his friends would hear them.

She held the phone face up and waited for Henry to realize that he'd left her alone with his cell. Surprisingly, it took another few minutes. When he did, he raced back up the aisle and snatched his phone from her hand. He shoved it in his back pocket and smacked her across the face. "What'd you tell him?" he barked.

"Nothing!" Gillian protested. "I hung up when you left."

"You'd better not be lying," he hissed as he stood over her threateningly.

"I'm not! I swear!"

Kicking her once more, Henry then turned and left. Gillian caught Andrea's eye and tried to smile reassuringly. She wanted to tell her and the others that help was coming. That hopefully this would all be a bad memory soon, but she didn't dare.

She hoped Walker was being honest with her, and that the hijackers' friend would be released. Maybe then they could all get out of here with their lives.

Chapter Four

TRIGGER STOOD ON THE EDGE OF THE TARMAC. EVERY MUSCLE IN HIS BODY WAS tense. He'd heard Gillian get smacked around and hated hearing the fear in her voice. But he couldn't deny what she'd done would be helpful. Maybe not right now, but later, once this was over, the officials could listen to the hijackers talking and learn what their plan had been. From what he could tell, the hijacker who'd taken the phone hadn't realized it was still on, and he prayed the recordings would be audible.

For now, however, they had a plane to storm and hostages to rescue. That was their main objective. Why they were there in the first place.

And they were out of time. It was oh-four-hundred and the deadline the hijackers had given was quickly approaching. Hugo Lamas had been freed, but the second the vehicle had left the prison grounds, it had been hit with a rocket-propelled grenade. Hugo, and everyone else in the vehicle, had been blown to bits.

No one knew who was behind the hit. Was it the Cartel of the Suns taking care of one of their own so he wouldn't talk? Was it someone in the military or government who didn't want him released? A rival drug gang? No one had any answers, and that made Trigger and his team antsy. Whoever was behind the assassination either had inside information about his release or had been watching and waiting. Either way, if Luis and the other hijackers got wind of the fact their friend had been killed, who knew what they might do in retaliation.

There was no more time to stall. The men on the plane were expecting their friend to appear, and when he didn't, they were going to start killing innocent civilians. It was the Deltas' job to prevent that.

"Everyone know their roles?" Trigger asked through their hands-free radios strapped around their necks. When they spoke, it triggered the connection to open.

"Ten-four."

"Yes."

"Gotcha."

The answers were immediate and confident. Trigger's adrenaline was coursing through his veins. They were ready to storm the plane. He and Lefty would go in from the same door the food was delivered through. Grover, Brain, and Oz would breach through the back hatch, Doc would take out the emergency exit door on one side at the wings and Lucky would take the other side. They were hoping the simultaneous breach would cause mass confusion with the hijackers and they'd be able to take enough of them out before they could retaliate by shooting the hostages.

It was risky as hell, but with no other good way onto the plane, it was the best plan of action, and something they'd practiced in training over and over. They were ready. Trigger just hoped Gillian and the others were.

"The refueling truck is about ready to go," Doc said. "Everyone stand by. We'll use it as cover and once we're at the plane, we'll spread out. One, two—Fuck! What the hell?"

Trigger looked toward where the refueling truck sat idling—and saw a twin-engine Beechcraft Queen Air come racing around the corner of the terminal. The propellers were running, and it was clear it wasn't simply a clueless pilot oblivious to the situation. It could hold up to twelve people—and it was headed straight for the hijacked plane with no signs of slowing.

Their carefully constructed plan had just gone to hell.

Trigger's head swung back toward the hijacked plane when he heard the sound of one of the escape slides inflating.

"Fuck, fuck, fuck," Trigger muttered, motioning for his team to move out.

Before they could get to the plane, people started exiting. Two at a time. A man and a woman. The second the first pair made it to the bottom of the slide, they began running toward the small Beechcraft.

They had no idea what the hijackers looked like, so he didn't know if the people running were their targets or not.

Two-by-two, more and more people slid down the escape slide and ran toward the smaller plane now idling nearby.

The first couple swerved around the plane and headed for the terminal behind it.

Parking the plane right in the middle of the path the hostages would take to get to safety was fucking brilliant. It made distinguishing the bad guys from the good guys that much harder.

It was clear the hijackers never had any intention of flying the large plane out of there. They were going to catch a ride on the smaller, more maneuverable aircraft, one that could fly under radar and disappear without a trace into Central America.

Trigger ran next to Lefty as the team headed for the panicked passengers focused on escaping the hell they'd lived through for the last three days.

"They're using the passengers as cover," Trigger told his team. He knew they were already aware, but it still needed to be said. "Shoot to kill, but make sure the person you're shooting is actually a hijacker!"

They had a lot of open ground to cover before they could get to either airplane, and Trigger had never felt more like a sitting duck than in that moment.

A loud gunshot sounded and as one, all seven Deltas hit the deck and rolled. They had no cover, but they wouldn't just stand around waiting to be shot either. Within seconds, they were back up and running for the plane. No one knew who was firing or from where, but they couldn't stop the mission now.

It seemed like it took an hour, but they finally reached the front wheels of the hijacked aircraft. They lined up, using the wheels and each other as cover. Trigger was in front, and he frantically searched for whoever was shooting at them.

The scene was complete chaos. Women were crying, men were shouting, and Trigger knew they needed to figure out who was a hijacker and who was an innocent civilian immediately.

"Grover, take out the pilot in the Beechcraft," Trigger ordered. "Doc, cover him. Lefty, you and Brain need to find a way to reroute the civilians…separate them from our targets. Oz and Lucky, you're on the hijackers with me."

Without a word, the men on his team fanned out. Trigger heard Lefty whistle as loud as he could as Brain began yelling for the hostages to run in the opposite direction from the Beechcraft.

As if the terrified men and women had merely been waiting for someone to tell them what to do, they immediately made a hard right turn and headed for the two men frantically gesturing at them to run toward them.

With the change in the tide of humanity, Trigger could easily make out who was a bad guy and who wasn't. But now there was a new problem—the hijackers were using the women and children as shields.

One man had a small child in his arms. He held a knife at her throat as he bolted for the small plane.

Another had the barrel of a rifle jammed into a woman's side as he forced her to jog toward the Beechcraft.

Then Trigger saw Gillian.

Her blonde hair stood out, even in the low light of the rising sun. A man had an arm around her neck and was attempting to walk backward toward their escape plane while randomly shooting at the retreating hostages and Trigger's team.

Something inside Trigger shifted, and a feeling he'd never experienced while on the job swept over him.

Fear.

Suddenly, he was terrified the man would get on the small plane with Gillian, and he'd never see her again. Never hear her voice.

Not. Happening.

His eyes narrowed and he focused on the man. Tunnel vision. Trigger knew what it was, but he didn't try to snap himself out of it. He had faith in his team. They'd cover him and take care of the other hijackers. The asshole who was hurting Gillian was going to die.

Gillian's head was reeling. When the hijackers had suddenly rounded up all the women and forced them to the back of the plane with the men, she'd thought they were going to let them all go. That the plane had finally been refueled and they were getting ready to take off. When they'd opened a hatch, her conclusions had been confirmed. She couldn't help but smile.

But then Luis had spoken into a handheld radio she hadn't seen before and started pairing up the hostages. One man with one woman. He shoved the first couple out of the door and down a slide, without giving them any warning. Then he did the same with the next. And the next. Then Henry grabbed Alice and jumped out behind one of the pairs of hostages.

What in the world was happening?

She looked out the hatch and saw a small plane coming toward them—fast.

And it clicked.

The hijackers weren't going to leave in the larger aircraft. They had a buddy who was picking them up and taking them away in the twin-engine plane.

Gillian was so stunned, she'd stopped paying attention to what was going on around her, so she wasn't prepared when Alberto grabbed her arm and hauled her against his body. He squeezed her arm so tightly, Gillian couldn't help but cry out in pain.

"You're coming with me," Alberto hissed. "And if you run, I'll shoot you. Understand?"

Gillian could only nod.

He pushed between some of the other hostages waiting anxiously for their chance to escape the plane and hauled her up behind Luis and Andrea. The other hijacker had a small pistol against Andrea's temple and was saying something to her in Spanish. When she and Alberto appeared behind them, Luis straightened but didn't remove the gun from Andrea's head.

"We're having fun, no?" he asked with a malicious smile. Then he leaned into Andrea and licked up the side of her face. "I'm taking this one with me. She sucked my cock so good, how could I not? Me and her are gonna have a lot more fun, aren't we?"

Gillian shuddered as Andrea closed her eyes.

"Come on," Luis ordered. "We don't have much time. Is everyone out?"

"*Si*, Isaac is behind me," Alberto said.

Gillian turned to look and saw Isaac was indeed standing behind them. Next to him was Leyton, the Hispanic man who'd helped with the boxes earlier.

"I'll go with her," he said when their gazes met.

She frowned in confusion.

Leyton reached for her arm. "I'll take her," he repeated.

Gillian had no idea why Leyton offered to go with her when it seemed obvious Alberto planned to use her as a shield. Then she saw Wade, Alice's husband, who'd been sitting in the same row as Gillian when everything had started.

"No, I'll jump with her," Wade said.

Gillian finally realized the men were doing what they could to try to help her. To get her away from the hijacker.

Leyton even reached forward and grabbed hold of her arm. For a short second, he and Alberto had a kind of tug-of-war with Gillian between them.

"You want to come with us too?" Alberto sneered, then put a hand on Leyton's chest and shoved. Hard. The young man fell back, but he didn't take his eyes off the hijacker. "Back off," Alberto said sternly. "And that goes for the rest of you," he continued, talking to the others who were gathered around them. "Do *what* we tell you, *when* we tell you, and you might live through this. Grow a brain, and I'll kill you right here and now!"

"We need to get out of here," Luis interrupted impatiently, before pushing Andrea forward. They both slid down the inflatable slide.

Before she was ready, Alberto jumped onto the slide himself, dragging Gillian with him. The second their feet hit the tarmac, he was yanking her upright and pulling her toward the small plane waiting for them.

People were running around everywhere. Confusion was rampant. The freed hostages didn't know which way to go. Some were heading for the small plane, but others had turned and were running off to the right, toward a man wearing all black. Gunshots rang out, but there was nowhere to find cover.

Alberto wrapped an arm around her neck and pulled her against his chest. Gillian's hands went to his arm and she tried to pull it away from her throat. He was cutting off her air, and the only thing she could concentrate on was getting oxygen into her lungs. As they walked backward, Alberto raised his rifle and shot at the men and women running in the opposite direction, then laughed when screams sounded around them.

"Stop fucking around!" Luis yelled from behind them. "Get to the plane!"

Gillian fought then. She was not going to get on another plane with these heartless assholes. She knew if they got her onboard, no one would ever see her again. Not her parents, not her best friends, no one. They'd abuse her, hurt her, then discard her body deep in a jungle somewhere.

She wasn't just going to let that happen.

Alberto was obviously surprised by her struggles, because he stopped shooting and dropped his rifle. It was slung around his back with a strap, but he needed to use both hands to try to subdue her.

No matter how hard she struggled, though, Gillian couldn't escape Alberto's hold. It wasn't until she heard Luis swearing in Spanish that she realized they'd reached the smaller plane.

Before she could process what was happening, Andrea screamed. Poor little Renee was also crying from somewhere nearby.

Gillian distractedly noticed that Leyton must have followed them off the plane. He was standing nearby. He wasn't helping her, or Andrea, or even Renee. He was just standing there watching, almost as if he was in shock.

She wanted to yell at him to run, to get away from the plane and the hijackers, to save himself, but she didn't get the chance.

One second Gillian was standing, and the next, she and Alberto were on the ground. They'd smacked into Andrea and Luis, hard, and all four of them went down. The other couple was now under them. They were lying at the bottom of the three steps leading into the twin-engine aircraft, Luis yelling in Spanish and trying to get to his feet.

Renee was curled in a ball nearby, crying for her mom.

Everything was chaotic and confusing and happening too quickly for Gillian to process.

A loud gunshot rang out—and everyone seemed to freeze. The sound of glass breaking came immediately on the heels of the gunshot, and shards rained down on the foursome at the bottom of the steps.

"Dammit!" Luis shouted before he finally extracted himself from Andrea and stood. He turned to scramble up the stairs, but another gunshot filled the air, and the leader of the hijackers slumped against the very stairs he was attempting to climb.

Andrea screamed again.

Alberto wrenched Gillian to her knees, but before she could gain her feet, one more shot rang out…

And Alberto slumped against her.

She felt wetness splash against her face before she went down again, Alberto's weight pinning her to the ground.

Andrea continued to scream, Renee continued to cry, and Gillian had the uncharitable thought that she wished they'd just shut up. She could hear more screaming and crying all around her.

Struggling to get out from under Alberto, Gillian heard more gunshots, this time much closer. Flinching with every one, she decided to stay where she was. It was irrational, but somehow she felt safer hiding under Alberto's dead body than standing up and exposing herself to flying bullets.

It might've been two minutes or two seconds, she wasn't sure, but the sound of silence finally registered in her ears.

Then, "Gillian!"

She'd recognize that voice anywhere.

Walker.

Renewing her attempt to get out from under Alberto, Gillian tried her best to wiggle free. She struggled for only seconds before shoving the man's body off herself. Turning her head, Gillian looked into the concerned gray eyes of Walker as he ran toward her.

He looked very different than the last time she'd seen him. Gone were the gray airline coveralls. Now he was dressed in black, even had black makeup smeared on his face. He was holding some sort of rifle and he had something wrapped around his throat.

Reaching down, he hauled her up with one hand, keeping his rifle at the ready, and pulled her toward him.

Gillian went willingly.

He was hard all over, mostly because of the bulletproof vest he was obviously wearing, but even his biceps were as hard as rocks.

She'd never felt so safe in all her life.

She allowed herself a second to close her eyes and relax into him before the sound of Andrea's sobs forced her to open them once more. Looking to her right, she saw a man dressed much like Walker, helping Andrea to her feet. She looked terrified out of her mind. So much so, she couldn't even walk; the man had to pick her up to get her to safety.

Luis's body had been pushed off the stairs and he lie dead on the tarmac, next to the small plane. Another man, obviously with Walker, stood in the doorway of the plane. He was frowning, and he scared Gillian a little bit with his dour expression.

Turning, she saw that Renee was no longer lying on the ground. One of Walker's teammates was pointing her toward the terminal and telling her to run.

Gillian's ears rang. "Is it over?" she whispered, feeling stupid.

"It's over," Walker confirmed.

"Three dead inside, not including the pilot," the man standing in the plane said.

"There's three more out here. Good job, everyone," someone standing behind them said, scaring the hell out of Gillian.

"Easy, Di," Walker murmured, not loosening his hold on her.

It was a good thing, as Gillian knew she would've fallen to the ground without his support.

Looking around, she pointed to Luis. "That's Luis." Then she nodded to Alberto. "And the one who had me was Alberto." Turning, she looked at the dead man behind her. "And that's Jesus."

"We need her to ID the others," the man in the plane said.

"No," Walker replied.

At the same time, Gillian said, "Okay."

"You don't have to do this," Walker told her sternly. "Someone else can figure this goat screw out."

She shook her head. "I need to know they're dead."

Walker pressed his lips together. She could tell he wasn't happy, but he didn't try to talk her out of it. "Oz, drag them to the door. She can ID them from here."

The big man on the plane nodded and ducked out of sight for a moment. Then he was back, dragging Carlos's body by the upper arm.

"Carlos," Gillian said softly.

Oz nodded and repeated the action twice more as she identified Isaac and Henry.

Gillian knew she was in shock. This couldn't be her life. Was she really standing in the middle of a runway in Venezuela identifying dead men? Men bleeding from holes in their heads?

Sirens sounded in the distance, the sound jarring and unwelcome.

Walker kept one arm around her shoulders, but turned her so she was facing him. "Are you hurt?"

"Not really. I mean, I'm alive, I can't ask for much more. What just happened?"

"The hijackers were obviously never planning on leaving via the jet."

Gillian nodded. "The fuel was a decoy." The look of admiration in Walker's eyes was gratifying. She felt raw and off-kilter, but she also felt as if she could do anything if he kept looking at her like she was something special.

"Exactly. They let the hostages go in pairs as a distraction. Since no one had seen what they looked like, we didn't know who was a hijacker and who was an innocent civilian. It was smart. But after Lefty and Brain got the hostages rerouted, it was easy to distinguish who was running for the Beechcraft and who was simply trying to get away."

Gillian nodded.

"The other three made it to their escape plane and let go of the women and children they were using as shields. Looked like Luis was trying to pull Andrea into the plane with him when you and that asshole," he kicked at Alberto at their feet, "ran into them and tripped everyone. It gave us enough time to get to them before they could get inside. Grover killed the pilot, shot him through the window, and Oz went inside and took out the others. And now… here we are."

Gillian's head spun. She was more sure than ever before that Walker and his friends were some sort of special forces operatives. Everything had seemed to happen so fast after three of the longest days of her life. They'd just acted. Thank God.

"Where did Leyton go?"

"Who?"

"Leyton. He was one of the hostages. He followed us to the plane, then he just disappeared."

"I don't know, and right now I don't care. All I care about is that they're dead and you're not," Walker said.

"I think they were going to take me with them," she whispered. "Thank you for making sure that didn't happen."

"No way in hell was I going to let them do that," Walker told her. Then he slowly pulled her into him once again.

Gillian rested her cheek on his chest. He was taller than she was, but they still fit together perfectly. She knew she needed a shower, and she had Alberto's blood in her hair and on her clothes, but she couldn't bring herself to care. All she could focus on was the man holding her.

She'd never felt for *anyone* the way she felt about Walker at this moment.

She was well aware it was because she'd almost died. She was shaking with the adrenaline still coursing through her veins. But some distant, stubborn part of her whispered that this was real. That Walker *felt* something for her, and not just because he was doing his job.

"We need to get gone," one of his friends said gently from next to them.

For a second, Gillian gripped Walker tighter, then she took a deep breath and picked her head up off his chest. He didn't immediately loosen his hold. They stared at each other for a long moment before he reluctantly—at least, she thought it was reluctantly—dropped his arms.

Gillian swayed, and Walker immediately reached out and steadied her with a hand on her biceps. She flinched, and he frowned.

"What's wrong? Are you hurt after all? Let me see."

"I'm okay," Gillian reassured him. "That's just the same place those assholes liked to grab me and haul me around. It's just bruises. They'll heal."

She thought he mumbled something about how he should've killed them slowly, but then he brought his hand up to her face. His thumb rubbed her cheek, and she watched him taking her in slowly. His gaze flicked from the top of her head to her eyes, then her cheeks, and finally her mouth.

She couldn't help but wipe her tongue over her suddenly dry lips, and she loved that his pupils seemed to dilate at seeing the movement.

"What happens now?" she asked quietly.

"The US government has chartered a flight to get you and the other Americans back home as quickly as possible. Venezuela is not a country you want to spend any more time in than necessary right now. Much of the government is corrupt and it's dangerous as hell."

"Yeah, I think I found that out the hard way," Gillian quipped.

His lips quirked up into a smile, but he quickly got serious again. "I'm sure you'll be interviewed about what happened. You should see a doctor to make sure you're all right physically, as well."

"I will," she told him. "What should I say about you and your friends?"

"What do you mean?" he asked with a frown.

"I just…I guess I assumed you'd want your role in what happened here to be downplayed."

"Why would you think that?" Walker asked.

Feeling awkward, like maybe she'd misread the entire situation, Gillian said, "You said you were stationed in Texas, which means you're in the military. And since it's just you guys, and not a whole platoon of men, I'm also guessing you're special forces of some kind? And because of the relationship between the US and Venezuela, I'm further assuming what you did today should be downplayed."

When no one said anything, Gillian looked down at her feet. "Or I'm just a girl who reads too much. Never mind, forget I said anything."

She felt a finger under her chin and looked up into Walker's eyes. "I knew you were a smart cookie. I'm sure the people who interview you will know who we are and what our role was, so you can be honest with them. But once you're home…yeah, it would be good if you didn't talk about us with the media or anyone else."

"What about my best friends? Ann, Wendy, Clarissa, and I tell each other everything. We're more like sisters than friends. I can keep most of the details secret, but they'll know I'm lying if I don't tell them something."

"Use your best judgement," Walker said.

"I like her," one of his friends said from behind them.

"Me too," someone else chimed in.

She saw Walker shake his head in bemusement at his friends, but he didn't take his eyes from hers. He leaned forward and said softly, "You're amazing, Gillian Romano. I'm in awe of your strength."

Then he straightened and took a step away from her.

Gillian shivered, even though it wasn't close to being cold.

She heard yelling, and turned her head to see at least a dozen men headed toward them wearing camouflage uniforms. She looked back at Walker and saw a mask had fallen across his features. He was back in business mode.

"Will I see you again?" she blurted. When he didn't immediately respond, she awkwardly said, "I mean, I live in Austin, and I'm assuming you're stationed at Fort Hood because, you know…it's Army, and really big."

She couldn't interpret the look on his face, but she was relieved to see his expression change. Get softer.

"Go with the Venezuelan officials," he urged. "Be safe, Di. You never know who might just show up on your doorstep someday."

Everything inside Gillian relaxed. He didn't come right out and say that he'd see her again, but he'd insinuated it. She'd take that.

"Thank you all," she told the men standing around her. "I mean it. Thank you."

They all nodded at her.

The last glimpse she had of Walker was him turning around and walking away with his six friends and teammates surrounding him.

Chapter Five

Three Weeks Later

"WHAT IS UP WITH YOU, MAN?" LUCKY ASKED IMPATIENTLY. "YOU'VE BEEN in a funk for weeks now."

It was oh-six-hundred in the morning, and Trigger and his team were doing their customary five-mile warm-up run before starting the rest of their PT exercises.

"He's been that way since Venezuela," Grover added helpfully.

"Ever since he met *her*," Lefty added not so helpfully.

"Fuck off," Trigger muttered. He loved his friends, but they were a pain in the ass.

"Why don't you just call her already?" Doc asked seriously.

"You know why," Trigger said.

"No, I don't," Doc countered.

"Because of what we are," Trigger told him.

"What? Men?"

Trigger stopped running and glared at his friends as they all stopped as well and stared at him in confusion. "We're Delta," he said simply.

"And?" Oz asked when no one else said anything.

Trigger blew out a breath in frustration. "You all know as well as I do what that means. Our lives aren't our own. We could be called away this afternoon for who knows how long. We could be killed in action and no one would ever know how or where we died. We've all dated, and it never works out. Some women just want to screw a Delta. They love the *idea* of what we are and not really who we are as people. Not to mention, a lot of chicks get fed up with all the secrecy and eventually end it. I won't do that to Gillian."

"Ghost and his team have all made it work," Brain said matter-of-factly.

Trigger tried to come up with an argument that would make sense, but he couldn't. The fact of the matter was, he was jealous as hell of Ghost, Fletch, Coach, and the others. They *had* made relationships work. They had women who loved them, who they loved in return, and many of them even had kids now. Like Annie. The firecracker who had him and anyone she came into contact with wrapped around her little finger.

He sighed. "I'm afraid she's too good for me," Trigger said softly, hating to admit the truth. "I took a second look at the information we received from the FBI, and from what I can tell, she's smart, extremely hardworking, and dedicated to her job."

"And those are bad things?" Brain asked.

"Well, no, but you all know what military life is like. It's hard. I'm afraid I'd somehow… contaminate her. She's strong as fuck and independent to boot. She's got a loving family and friends who would do anything for her. I don't want to mess that up. You all know as well as I do that getting involved with us means the possibility of moving, and that means taking her away from her support network."

"Seems to me," Lefty drawled, "that's exactly the kind of woman you *should* want. That we *all* want. We need a partner who won't crumble when we're deployed. Someone who can mow the grass and figure out how to call for a fucking plumber when the toilet overflows. It's a *good* thing that she has a support system. And even if we do get moved out of Texas, she'd make a new support network, with other Delta wives. Besides, no one's saying you have to *marry* this chick. You like her, she obviously likes you. So what's *really* bothering you?"

Trigger hesitated. He knew what he was about to say would sound crazy, but these were his best friends. Men he'd die for, and they'd do the same for him.

"I think she's it," he said, putting a hand on his stomach, which was spinning and rolling.

"She's what?" Grover asked in confusion.

"I don't know how to explain how I know, but we clicked out there. It's stupid, I realize that. Certifiable. We don't even know each other. But something inside knows she could be *it* for me. And if I get to know her better, I'm not going to want to let her go. If she dumps me, it'll kill me."

No one said anything for a long moment, then Brain smiled. Huge. "Congratulations!"

The others chimed in with their own felicitations.

"Hang on, you guys," Trigger complained. "Nothing's happened. She's probably totally forgotten all about me by now."

"There's only one way to find out," Doc said reasonably. "Call her."

"I don't have her number," Trigger backtracked.

"I'll find it for you," Brain volunteered. "And her address too."

"Talk to her, man," Lucky urged. "What can it hurt?"

"Why are you guys pushing this so hard?" Trigger asked. He couldn't deny he was happy for their support, but was a bit confused by it.

"Because none of us are getting any younger," Lefty said reasonably. "You especially."

Trigger punched him in the arm and everyone laughed.

"But seriously, we all love the Army and what we do, but we won't be Deltas forever. There'll come a time when we'll sit up and look around and be alone. And that sucks. I want to find someone smart, independent, and sassy as fuck. Someone who will kiss me and tell me to kick some bad-guy ass when I leave, and be thrilled to see me when I get back. Someone who won't cheat on me and won't decide that she's sick of waiting for me to come home.

"I want her to understand what I do is important to me. In return, I'll treat her like a queen. She'll be the center of my world, and I'll make sure she knows it. Relationships are hard as fuck, even more so for us. So if you feel as if this woman is the one who can be all that for you, I'll do whatever I can to make that happen for you. And I'll fucking kill anyone who tries to come between you and your woman."

Trigger wasn't sure what to say. He was deeply touched.

"What Lefty said," Grover quipped.

Everyone laughed again.

"I'll think about it," Trigger said.

Brain rolled his eyes. "I'll have her info to you this afternoon."

Trigger nodded, then took off running. He turned around and said, "You guys comin' or are you gonna let this old man kick your ass?"

That was all it took for the rest of the guys to dig in their heels and chase after him.

Later that afternoon, Trigger was sitting in his office when a knock sounded at the door. Looking up, he saw it was Brain.

"You know, you didn't *really* have to rush and get Gillian's info to me," he joked.

But Brain didn't crack a smile. "We need to talk," he said instead.

Trigger immediately stiffened. He nodded to a chair in front of his desk.

Brain sat, and he didn't make him wait. "You know how Gillian didn't turn off the phone connection that last time in the hopes that we'd be able to get something from the hijackers when they talked to each other?"

"Yeah," Trigger said.

"We got something."

Trigger leaned forward. "What?"

"As we realized there at the end, they had no intention of flying that big-ass plane out of there. They had a cartel pilot picking them up in the Beechcraft to take them back up to Mexico."

"Mexico?" Trigger asked in surprise.

"Yeah. They were with Sinaloa."

"Fuck," Trigger said, sitting back in his chair with a thump.

"They didn't want Hugo Lamas freed so he could escape with them. They wanted him killed to send a message to the Cartel of the Suns. Essentially, they started a war."

"And like any drug cartel, they didn't care who got caught in the crossfire," Trigger said in disgust. "The people they killed on the plane didn't mean shit to them. All they cared about was sticking it to the Venezuelans. Letting them know they got one over on them right on their own turf."

"Exactly. But there's more," Brain added.

"What?"

"There was talk of a seventh hijacker."

"What are you saying? That we missed a hijacker and he got away?" Trigger asked.

"Yeah, that's exactly what I'm saying. On the tapes, they were arguing about the Beechcraft. Luis was saying they were good because it could hold up to twelve people—and there was seven of them with the pilot, plus two more with the women he and Alberto were taking, leaving room for their 'amigo' and two more, if someone else wanted to bring along a 'plaything.'"

Trigger wanted to kill Luis and the other hijackers all over again. Alberto had planned to take Gillian with him. The thought of what would've happened to her if he'd gotten her deep into the Sinaloa Cartel territory was too disturbing to dwell on.

Brain went on. "But then another said something about how it would be better for their 'amigo' to go with the rest of the hostages, to find out as much information as possible. To find out what the government and the Cartel of the Suns knew about the op. As far as I can tell before the call was abruptly cut off, they were still arguing about that. Half of those assholes wanted to let the mole stay hidden and camouflaged with the other civilians, and the other half wanted to extract him with them."

"So the CIA needs to look into the backgrounds of all the hostages who were on the plane. See who has connections to Sinaloa and Mexico," Trigger said.

"Not that easy," Brain said with a shrug. "Even if we *did* narrow it down, everyone's in the wind. They all went back to their countries and lives. Hell, our target could've used a fake name. But I think we've got bigger problems."

"Bigger?" Trigger asked.

"Whoever was in cahoots with the hijackers knows everything that went down on that plane. *Everything.* They're likely aware of how their friends were killed…and how Gillian was a big factor in giving us time to get to them and take out Luis, Alberto, the pilot, and the others. He or she might not be too happy that Gillian escaped…might even realize that she was giving us intel."

"But why single her out? There's no reason for it," Trigger asked. "There were a lot of other passengers on that plane who interacted with the hijackers."

"I talked to one of the agents who interviewed the hostages. Several said they saw Gillian struggling with Alberto, and saw them go down and trip Luis and Andrea. They also saw you and her hugging. It was the talk of the group. How impressed they were with Gillian and how brave they thought she was…but also how intimate the two of you seemed to be. As if maybe you knew each other before the hijacking, and *Gillian* was the reason the team was sent in. If I was an insider, I'd be pretty pissed off at her right about now. Especially after hearing all my fellow passengers praise her so highly."

Trigger stood so quickly, his chair fell to the floor behind him. "Address?"

Brain didn't quite smile, but his lips twitched as he pulled a piece of paper out of his pocket. "She lives on the north end of Georgetown. Shouldn't take you too long to get there."

"This isn't funny," Trigger said with a scowl.

Brain stood up. "Never said it was. No matter what hang-ups you might have about what you do and who you are, she needs to know that she could be in danger."

"I know."

"The Sinaloa Cartel doesn't fuck around. If they want her dead, it'll take a miracle to make sure that doesn't happen," Brain said solemnly.

Trigger ground his teeth. He turned to leave, but he had one more question. He looked back at his friend. "Did they really hijack an international flight just to kill some border agent who was working with a rival drug cartel?"

Brain sighed and shook his head. "Doubtful. As far as the DEA can tell, it was a distraction from their main goal. Smuggling eight hundred kilos of cocaine and meth out of Venezuela. Sinaloa stole it from the Cartel of the Suns. While the world's attention, and that of the leaders of Venezuela, were on the airport, they loaded up a ship with the drugs and sailed away without so much as a second glance from the authorities."

Trigger could only shake his head. All those deaths because of drugs. Well, more accurately, because of money. He'd never understand it. "Thanks for the heads up," he told Brain.

His friend brushed off his thanks. "Your best bet is to move her up here to Killeen so we can keep an eye on her."

Trigger snorted. "You really think that's gonna happen? You *did* hear me say that she's independent and smart, right?"

Brain smiled fully for the first time. "Yup. You'll just have to convince her. Show her some…leg…or something."

Trigger rolled his eyes and turned to walk out of his office. He knew there wasn't a chance in hell of convincing Gillian to move in with him, even for her own safety. But he couldn't deny the thought of having her in his space was pretty fucking appealing.

Gillian stood in front of her bathroom mirror and stared at her reflection. She looked damn good, if she did say so herself. She was going out with Ann, Wendy, and Clarissa tonight and had dressed for the occasion. She had on a pair of tight jeans that hugged her ass and thighs, high-heel sandals with sparkly crystals, which made them look fancier than they really were. She also picked her favorite black wrap shirt, which hugged her boobs and gave her a ton of cleavage.

She'd used a heavier hand with her makeup than usual and put on her favorite necklace, a two carat—fake—diamond, which rested right in the middle of her chest, bringing attention to the aforementioned cleavage.

Her hair fell in curls around her face, and even though Gillian knew they'd probably come out by the end of the night, at least she'd start out the evening looking good.

Sighing, she leaned on her hands on the counter and bowed her head. Now, if only she *felt* as good as she looked.

Three weeks. It had been three weeks since her ordeal in Venezuela, and in some ways it still seemed like yesterday. Her parents had insisted on flying in to make sure she was all right, and the week they'd stayed had done her a lot of good. She wasn't used to being the center of attention, and talking to the press made her extremely nervous, but her mom had reassured her that the information she'd shared with the reporters was concise and clear without going into too much detail, which was a huge relief. She'd been embarrassed by the way a few of the other passengers had gushed over what a good job she'd done under pressure, but again, her parents being there was a good distraction from everything.

But, ultimately, even the affection and pampering her mom and dad had showered on her couldn't take away all the bad memories of what had happened.

She was still sleeping with the lights on in her apartment and she started at every little sound. She'd fallen back into her old routine, more or less, which was good…but a tiny part of her died inside when she didn't hear from *him*. She'd expected him to be busy right when she'd gotten back home, but with every day that passed without a phone call or even an email, she'd begun to think the connection she'd felt was one-sided.

She'd been so sure they'd connected on a level she'd never felt with anyone else. He said he'd be in touch…hadn't he? She doubted the possibility more and more.

Intellectually, she knew it was unlikely she'd hear from Walker Nelson again. He'd just been doing his job. If he was special forces, he did that kind of thing all the time. Probably rescued hundreds of people. He was probably, even now, on another mission, rescuing someone else. Why would he want to get back in touch with *her*? Just because she'd felt a connection with him didn't mean he felt the same.

She was being stupid.

Gillian knew she was a romantic, and that was why she hoped every day when she got up in the morning that today would be the day. Walker would somehow find her number and call or text her, saying he wanted to see her again. Or he'd be waiting for her outside her apartment complex, leaning casually against the wall, and he'd tilt his chin up in greeting when he saw her.

Huffing out a breath, Gillian stood straight and smoothed her shirt. No, it was obvious that wasn't going to happen. He'd moved on, and she needed to as well.

Her phone dinged with a text, and she grabbed it from the counter and saw she had a few messages she'd missed while she was showering and getting ready.

The first was from Janet. She'd kept in touch after the hijacking, and Gillian loved hearing updates about her daughter Renee. At first the young girl had been traumatized, but after seeing a therapist, Janet reported that she was starting to be more like the girl she'd been before their ordeal. She'd attached a picture of Renee to the text. She was hanging upside down from a set of monkey bars. The smile on her face made Gillian grin. The text accompanying the picture said, *Because of you, I've got my girl back.*

She was uncomfortable with the praise. When all the hostages had been corralled together in a room in the airport in Caracas, waiting to be interviewed individually, they'd talked about everything that had happened. And when the CIA and FBI had arrived to interview them, they'd somehow given the passengers the impression—or maybe it was the hostages who'd given the *Feds* the impression—that Gillian had been their leader, of sorts.

That it was because of *her* that so many people had survived the ordeal.

Shaking her head, Gillian read the next text. It was from Andrea. She lived in Austin as well, but she wasn't ready to meet back up in person yet. Gillian knew she was struggling because of the sexual abuse she'd endured at Luis's hands, and how traumatized she'd been when Luis had tried to force her to go with him.

Earlier, Gillian had sent her a short text letting Andrea know she was thinking about her. Andrea had replied with, *Thanks. I'm doing better and I'll be in touch soon. I really do want to be strong enough to give you a hug in person.*

There was one more text, from Alice, the young woman who'd originally sat next to Gillian on the flight from Costa Rica. She and her husband had both survived and were putting their lives back together in Washington state. They didn't correspond often, but Gillian was glad to hear from her, even if it was only Alice saying that they'd moved into a new apartment complex, one with twenty-four/seven security.

As she was reading her texts, Gillian's phone vibrated with another incoming message. This time from Wendy.

Wendy: Have you left yet? Quit overthinking shit and get your ass to the bar. We've got your first margarita waiting for you!

Smiling, Gillian shot back a quick note letting her friend know she was on her way, then she turned her back on her reflection and headed out of the bathroom. She grabbed her crossbody purse from her unmade bed and put the strap over her head.

She was walking into her living area when there was a knock on her door.

Stopping in her tracks, Gillian made a conscious effort to slow her heart rate. She didn't often get people at her door uninvited, but it happened. There was a buzzer that people were supposed to use to get into the building, but sometimes they slipped behind another resident.

Cautiously, and as quietly as possible, Gillian tiptoed to her door and peered through the peephole.

Shocked beyond belief at the person she saw standing there, Gillian fumbled with the locks as she tried to turn them. Her hands were shaking, and she couldn't get the door open fast enough.

"Hi," she said when she was finally face-to-face with the man she thought she'd never see again.

"Hi," Walker Nelson returned.

Gillian inwardly sighed. If she thought he looked good dressed in his black commando gear with black paint smeared on his face, it was nothing compared to the vision that was standing on her doorstep right that second.

He was wearing a royal-blue short-sleeve shirt, which only emphasized his muscular biceps. His forearms were thick as well, and Gillian had to force herself not to swoon right then and there. She'd always been an arm girl, and Walker's certainly didn't disappoint. He had on a pair of faded blue jeans that hugged his thighs. She tried not to stare at his groin too long, but noticed he filled out that part of his jeans just fine. Finally, he wore a pair of black combat boots that should've looked out of place here in Texas, but somehow seemed to fit him to a tee.

He had a five o'clock shadow that outlined his jaw, chin, and cheekbones. Gillian's fingers twitched with the need to touch it, to see if it was prickly or soft. His gray eyes had flecks of brown in them—and they were looking at her as if she were the only person in the world right that second. She wasn't ever the recipient of that kind of attention from men, and to have *this* man staring at her so intently she thought she would combust was a heady feeling.

They'd been staring at each other so long, Gillian suddenly felt embarrassed. "Um, come in," she said, stepping back and gesturing to her apartment with her hand.

"Thanks," Walker said, crowding her for just a second before passing her in the small foyer.

Telling herself to get a grip, Gillian tried to slow her heartbeat. She was giddy with excitement that Walker was actually here. That he'd tracked her down after all. Excuses to get out of her plans with her friends ran through her mind as she followed Walker deeper into her apartment. She tried to keep her eyes off his ass…without much luck. He filled out the back of his jeans just as well as he did the front.

She inhaled deeply to try to get control over herself and not jump on him, and his woodsy scent filled her nostrils. She didn't remember anything about what he smelled like when she'd last seen him, but that was probably because *she'd* smelled like a fish head that had been sitting out in the sun rotting for a week or more. At the time, she couldn't smell anything other than her own fear and sweat.

He stopped in front of the bar that separated her kitchen from the rest of the apartment and turned to face her. "You look great. Did I interrupt anything?"

Gillian was suddenly very glad she'd planned to go out with her friends that night. Otherwise she would've been wearing her fat pants—large, flowy cotton pants with an elastic waist—and no bra. Her hair would've been thrown up into a messy bun and she would've been mortified. At least now she looked her best.

"Thanks. And I was just heading out to a bar called The Funky Walrus to hang with my friends."

Walker smiled, and Gillian had to lock her knees at the sight. Frowning and serious, he was good-looking. Smiling? He was lethal.

"The Funky Walrus?" Walker asked.

Gillian chuckled. "I know, the name is weird, but then again, a lot of Austin is weird, so it fits. It's not a college bar, and most of the patrons are businessmen and women in their thirties and forties. It's low-key and laid-back, and we try to get together at least once every few weeks to catch up."

Walker nodded, and the ensuing silence between them stretched.

Gillian fidgeted. This was weird…and not at all how she'd imagined this meeting would go. She'd fantasized that she'd be witty and amusing, and Walker would tell her how he'd been thinking about her and he had to come see her.

Taking a deep breath, Gillian decided to make the first move. It seemed unlikely, but maybe Walker was nervous.

"I'm glad to see you."

"We need to talk."

They'd spoken at the same time, and Gillian flushed. Walker didn't sound happy about needing to talk to her, and he certainly didn't sound as if he were flirting, as she was trying to do with him. "Um…okay," she stammered.

He ran a hand over his head and sighed, and Gillian steeled herself for whatever he was about to say.

"I stopped by because we've gotten intel that there was a seventh hijacker on the plane. Using the audio that you managed to record—that last time we talked, and you kept the phone line open when you handed the phone back—it was determined that a hijacker was posing as a passenger. Luis and another hijacker discussed him, but didn't give us any clues as to who he might be."

Gillian blinked—and she felt her heart drop into her stomach.

The only thing she could process was that Walker *hadn't* come to ask her out, or to get to know her better. She'd been dreaming about him for three weeks, hoping against hope that the spark she'd felt between them hadn't been one-sided. With his first sentence, he'd effectively crushed any hope that there might be more between them.

"Oh…" It was all she could say. Her throat was tight and it was hard to swallow.

"I wanted to warn you, let you know that you could be in danger. There's no telling what this seventh person is thinking. We don't know if he might want revenge for his friends dying, or if he might think you heard too much while you were onboard, or might be able to identify him."

Gillian barely heard him. The disappointment and embarrassment she felt was overwhelming. She knew she should be more concerned that there was another hijacker out there, but her disappointment over the reason for Walker's visit had totally overshadowed everything else.

Her shoulders slumped forward unconsciously. "Well…thanks for letting me know," she said awkwardly.

Walker frowned. "Are you okay?"

"Great. Fine. Yeah, I'm good," she said a little too brightly, doing her best to pretend Walker hadn't shattered her fantasy about the two of them getting together. "I appreciate you telling me. I'll be on the lookout."

"I thought we might talk. Go over your memories of the passengers and see if we can't narrow down who the sleeper might be."

Spend more time with him? When all he wanted was information? No, thank you. Maybe later—like a year or two—she'd be able to sit across from him and have a perfectly professional conversation about that time she'd been hijacked and forced to act as a go-between for the hijackers and the negotiators. But today wasn't that day.

She nodded quickly, having a feeling she looked like a spastic rag doll. "Sure. Yeah, fine. But I can't right now. I'm leaving. I have a date…with my friends. My girlfriends."

Walker frowned. "I'm not sure that's the best idea right now. Not when we don't know who the seventh hijacker is or where he might be."

Gillian snorted. "He's not going to care about me. I'm nobody and totally harmless. Besides, I always lock my doors and strangers off the street can't just walk into the building. They have to be buzzed in by a resident. I'll be fine."

"*I* walked in off the street," Walker said flatly.

Gillian was desperate to get rid of him. She wanted to cry. Was *on* the verge of crying. And she'd rather walk over a bed of nails than let Walker see how upset she was. "I'll be careful," she told him firmly. "It was good to see you, but I really need to go now." She turned and walked toward her front door. She opened it and was about to leave when Walker spoke up behind her.

"Um, Gillian?"

She turned. "Yeah?"

"You're going to leave me in your apartment?"

Shit, shit, shit. She tried to play off her blunder. Shaking her head, she said, "No, I was holding the door for you."

He grinned as if he knew she was lying, but he walked toward her without a word. He stopped when he was right in front of her. Gillian didn't dare look up at him. She had a feeling he'd be able to see right through her bravado.

"Gillian?"

"Yeah?" she asked, staring at his Adam's apple as if it was the most fascinating thing she'd ever seen.

"Look at me."

Internally steeling herself, Gillian lifted her chin and let her gaze meet his.

"What's wrong?"

"Nothing," she said quickly—too quickly. "I'm just on my way out and you took me by surprise."

"Are you sure we can't go back inside and talk? I'm not comfortable leaving you like this."

For just a second, Gillian got mad. *He* wasn't comfortable? Of course it was all about him. She was just a stupid, romantic girl who'd foolishly thought they'd connected over an intense situation.

Most of the time she had high self-esteem. She was thirty and owned her own very successful business. She had great friends and people seemed to like her. She had a gift in that she could defuse almost any situation, which came in handy since she had to deal with stressful situations on a daily basis with her job.

But the one thing that eluded her was love. The kind that made a man put her first no matter what else was going on in his life. She was more than willing to reciprocate, and had put her all into each and every serious relationship she'd been in. But when push came to shove, the men she'd thought she loved had proven that she came second.

Taking a deep breath, and trying to ignore how good Walker smelled, she knew she was being irrational. But his words hurt all the same. She shook her head. "I'll be fine. I always am," she said, her voice filled with sadness she couldn't hide. Then she shrugged and slipped away from him into the hall. "Can you get the door?" she asked as evenly as possible.

Walker continued to frown, but he grabbed the knob and pulled the door shut. Gillian made quick work of securing the locks and gripped her keys tightly. "Well, thanks for coming by," she said, not able to be rude, no matter how devastated she felt inside. "Say hello and thanks again to your, um…team for me. I'm running late and really need to get going, or my friends are going to wonder where I am."

"I'll walk you to your car," Walker said firmly.

Pressing her lips together, she nodded. She counted each step as they took the stairs down one flight to the first floor. The silence between them was awkward, or maybe it was just Gillian who felt that way.

Mourning the loss of something she'd never had in the first place, she headed for her RAV4. Clicking the locks, she opened the door and turned to Walker once more. She wanted to ask him what was wrong with her. How it was possible she felt so connected to him when he felt nothing in return. But she merely forced her lips into a smile and said, "Be safe, Walker. It was good to see you."

"You too," he returned, his brow pulled down as if he was trying to figure something out. "I really think—"

"Bye!" Gillian interrupted, needing this to be over. She slipped into the driver's seat and shut the door. Blinking as fast as she could to keep the tears from spilling over, she forced a smile in the general direction where Walker had been standing, put the car in reverse, and backed out of the parking spot. It was a good thing she'd been to The Funky Walrus plenty of times and had the route memorized.

Gillian refused to look in her rearview mirror at the man who, without realizing it, had just broken her heart.

Trigger stared at the taillights of Gillian's SUV as she drove out of the parking lot.

"That didn't go as I imagined it would," he muttered to himself.

He wasn't sure what he'd expected when he'd driven to Georgetown to see Gillian. At first she'd seemed pleased to see him. And Trigger would never forget how his heart had skipped a beat when she'd opened the door.

She was absolutely fucking gorgeous. Not too tall, but not short either. Curvy in all the right places. His eyes had immediately been drawn to her tits. God, they were perfect. He'd wanted to bury his face between the fleshy globes and spend hours worshiping them, but he'd forced himself to be a gentleman and not stare too long.

Her jeans clung to her curves, and it took everything he had not to pop a woody right there in her doorway. She would've slammed the door in his face if she'd looked down and saw his dick pressing against his jeans like that of a prepubescent teenager.

She'd done something with her makeup that made her green eyes stand out, and in her heels, they were almost eye-to-eye. When she'd invited him in, and he'd walked past her, he'd smelled honeysuckle. He had no idea if it was her perfume or shampoo or what, but it made it hard as hell not to grab her and pull her into him and kiss her.

By the time he'd reached her small kitchen area, he'd gotten himself mostly under control, though the smile she'd bestowed on him had left his fingers tingling. He had no idea what he'd even said to her when he'd first entered.

He was more relieved than he cared to admit that she was going out with her friends, and not on a date. He'd been afraid he'd waited too long. Had lost his chance. Not that her going on a date would've kept him from pursuing her. He hadn't been sure about seeing her again, but once he had, he'd been determined to let her know *he* wanted to be the one to take her out. To take her to dinner. To watch her laugh at a funny movie. To hold her hand as they casually strolled down the riverfront in Austin.

He'd wanted to get the business side of why he was there out of the way first, then he could let her know how he hadn't been able to stop thinking about her. How proud he was of her and how she'd handled herself in Venezuela. He wanted to tell her that he'd never felt a connection with a woman like he had with her, and even though it was crazy, he'd wanted to see if she felt the same.

But something had happened. Right after he'd told her about the seventh hijacker, she'd seemed to shut down. He'd seen the light fade from her eyes, and while he knew what he'd said was shocking, her reaction didn't seem to jive with what he knew about her.

Had she been terrified about the possibility of a hidden hijacker? Had merely talking about the incident sent her into a mental downward spiral? He had no clue.

She was polite but distant. The sparks that had been flying between them were suddenly doused, and he wasn't sure why. Then it was more than obvious she'd tried to rush him out of her apartment, that she'd wanted to get away from him.

Trigger hated that. *Hated* it.

Hell, in her hurry to escape, she'd nearly locked him *in* her apartment.

While it was good her apartment complex had rudimentary security, it wasn't going to keep a terrorist out. Trigger only had to wait three minutes for a resident to appear. He'd simply smiled at the man, and the guy hadn't even thought twice about letting him slip in behind him.

No, Gillian definitely wasn't safe here if the hijacker decided for some reason to target her.

But she'd made no secret of the fact that she wasn't all that fired up to see him again.

Sighing in frustration, Trigger wasn't sure what to do. He didn't want to go back to his place in Killeen. He'd spent the last three weeks thinking about nothing but Gillian, and leaving now felt too…final. If he left, he had a feeling he'd never see her again, which wasn't acceptable.

Taking a deep breath, Trigger argued with himself about his next course of action. Follow Gillian and make her tell him what he'd said that had turned her warm welcome cold?

Retreat and try again when he had more information about the hijacker? It would give him a reason to come back and see her.

Wait and make sure she got home all right?

Sighing again, Trigger headed for his car. He didn't know what to do, and for the moment he needed to think. He'd sit in his vehicle and try to work through how the evening had gone from one full of anticipation and excitement to getting the cold shoulder.

Trigger admired Gillian. He hadn't found out one thing about her that turned him off... which was highly unusual.

He liked being alone. Liked not having any responsibilities. But something about Gillian made him *want* to be tied down. *Want* to look after her. *Want* to have someone to worry about other than himself.

It was confusing as hell...and Trigger needed to come to terms with his feelings before he made a decision about what his next step would be.

Chapter Six

"LET ME GET THIS STRAIGHT," WENDY SAID. "HE ONLY CAME TO SEE YOU because he wanted to tell you about this other hijacker?"

Gillian nodded miserably and took another large sip of her margarita. It was amazing how smoothly they went down when she felt like shit. She was on her third one and was definitely feeling the effects of the alcohol. She wasn't a heavy drinker, but she'd had the biggest disappointment of her life earlier and needed to drown her sorrows. "Yup. He said I looked great, and at first he couldn't keep his eyes off my boobs. But it became obvious real quick that he was only there because of business."

Gazing up at her friends, who were looking at her with sympathy, she blurted a little too loudly, "I mean, my boobs *are* on point tonight. My hair actually did what I wanted for once and I squeezed my ass into these jeans. And he didn't even *blink*."

"You said he was eyeballing your boobs," Ann said sympathetically.

"He was!" Gillian exclaimed. "But obviously he wasn't fazed." Her emotions had been swinging from indignation to sorrow all night, and suddenly she was exhausted. Putting her head on her forearm on the table, she said softly, "I thought he was the one."

"Oh, Gilly," Clarissa said sympathetically.

That was all it took for the tears Gillian had held at bay all night to spill over. She lifted her head and impatiently wiped them away. She looked at her best friends. "I love you guys. Clarissa, your husband is amazing. I remember that time you were sick when you were dating, and he took two days off work to be with you. When you didn't make it to the bathroom and puked everywhere, he cleaned it up without even making any kind of gagging sounds."

Clarissa chuckled. "I'm not sure that's the best example of how great Johnathan is."

"It *is*," Gillian insisted. "And *you*, Ann. You're my age and you already have two kids! The two most beautifulist and smart kids on the planet. They're polite and kind and that's because of you and Tom, and how you've raised them."

"They're pains in the asses sometimes, Gillian. They're not always polite and kind."

Gillian ignored her. "And Wendy…" Her eyes filled with tears again, and she closed them to try to control herself. "You and Wyatt are perfect together. Every time he looks at you it's obvious you mean the world to him. Remember that time we were all at that festival in downtown Austin, and that guy started heckling us? We were ignoring him but he wouldn't shut up. Wyatt went right over and told him if he didn't shut the hell up, he was going to find his nuts shoved so far up inside his abdomen it would take a crowbar to find them again. That was so romantic!" The last word came out as a wail, but Gillian couldn't help it.

"Gilly, that guy would've pounded Wyatt. He was half a foot taller and way stronger. Wyatt was being an idiot; it wasn't romantic. We're lucky the other guy thought it was funny and wasn't offended," Wendy reminded her.

Gillian shook her head. "But he did it anyway. Because he loves you," she said softly. "You don't get it. He'd do anything for you. *Anything*."

"I think she's had enough margaritas," Clarissa said dryly, trying to pry the glass out of Gillian's hand.

"No! I know exactly what I'm saying," Gillian protested, keeping hold of her glass. "I'm not you, so I don't know what you felt when you saw your men for the first time, but you've all told me something deep inside felt…*right*. The first time I heard Walker's voice, I knew."

"Knew what, Gilly?" Ann asked.

"That he was mine," she said simply.

Shaking her head at the skepticism she saw on her friends' faces, Gillian tried to explain. "I know it sounds insane. Crazy. Stupid. But I can't deny it. I thought we clicked," she said sadly. "I thought he felt it too. He gave me a nickname. He even told me he would show up on my doorstep."

"He didn't say that exactly, though," Wendy said.

Gillian waved her hand in the air. "Just about. It was more about the underlying meaning of his words. Every day since then, I hoped today would be the day. I hoped he'd show up and tell me that he missed me so much and couldn't stay away anymore. And then there he was! Beautiful. And he smelled sooooo good. But he wasn't there for me. Wasn't there to tell me he couldn't live without me. He only came by because he felt *obligated*."

"You deserve the world," Clarissa said softly. "You deserve a man who will move mountains to be by your side. You're successful, and pretty, and so damn smart."

"If I'm that pretty, smart, and irresistible, then why am I sitting here alone and lonely?" Gillian said sadly.

She hated bringing the group down. Hated that her bad mood had ruined the night for everyone. Taking a deep breath, she took a long swallow of her drink before wiping the last of the tears from her cheeks. "You know what? Fuck him. It doesn't matter. He's probably an asshole anyway. Sure, he's probably really good in bed and we might've had amazing chemistry between the sheets, but he probably has no idea how to be a good boyfriend."

"Gillian—" Ann said, but Gillian spoke over her.

"Like, he'd probably insist we split the bill when we went out to eat, and would make me walk on the outside of the sidewalk so I'd get run over by a car first."

"Gillian, you should—"

It was Wendy who tried to interrupt that time, but Gillian was on a roll. "And he probably has a small dick anyway. That bulge I saw in his pants was probably a sock or something. And it wouldn't surprise me if he wanted blowjobs but refused to recip…resurp…suck on me in return."

"Gillian!" Clarissa hissed sharply.

"*What?*" Gillian asked.

"Was your Walker wearing a blue shirt, jeans, and combat boots when you saw him earlier tonight?"

Gillian's eyes widened. "How did you know? Except his shirt wasn't blue exactly. It was dark blue, kind of a royal blue, and it kinda shone in the light. I don't know what kind of material it was made out of, but it looked silky. I wish I could've touched him…"

"He's standing behind you," Clarissa said with a small grin.

Gillian rolled her eyes. "No, he's not. He's on his way back to his Army fort. He fulfilled his duty by telling me about the hijacker and now he's gone."

Clarissa and Ann both sat back on their side of the booth and smiled. Wendy turned at the waist and looked behind her. "Holy shit," she said softly. "If I wasn't dating Wyatt, you might have a fight on your hands, Gilly."

Gillian froze. She glanced over at Wendy on her left, who was still staring behind them. "Tell me you're kidding," she stage whispered.

"Nope," Wendy said with a grin.

"How long has he been standing there?" she asked Clarissa, thinking she was being quiet during her rant, when in fact, the tables closest to them could probably easily hear her thoughts.

"You're sitting there single and beautiful because you hadn't met *me* yet," a voice Gillian had dreamed about for weeks said from behind her. "When we go out, you'll never pay, and no way in hell will you walk next to the street—or sleep on the side of the bed by the door, for that matter. And just for the record, I don't have a sock in my pants, and I can pretty much guarantee that after I get a taste, one of my favorite things will be going down on you as often as you'll let me."

"Holy shit," Ann said, fanning herself with her hand.

Clarissa merely blushed, but her huge smile said she approved.

And Wendy could only stare with her mouth open.

If she hadn't been drunk, Gillian probably wouldn't have done what she did, but because she was feeling no pain and her inhibitions were down, she turned around and glared at Walker. "What are you doing here?" she blurted defensively. "Are you stalking me?"

He chuckled. "Seeing you again didn't go as I'd imagined it would in my head. I said something wrong and didn't know what. I thought maybe I could try again."

Gillian blinked.

"You came to see her only because of a seventh hijacker," Ann said helpfully.

"She thought you wanted to see *her*, but instead you were there for work," Clarissa added.

"Not cool," Wendy scolded.

"That's what you thought?" Walker asked, gaze locked on Gillian.

She couldn't look away from him, lost in the emotion she saw in his eyes, and nodded.

"I really did fuck up," he muttered. Then he came around the booth and squatted next to where Gillian was sitting. He put a hand on her leg, and she swore she could feel tingles shoot down her thigh. "I didn't come to see you tonight out of obligation, Di. The FBI could've sent someone to inform you about the seventh hijacker. I used it as an excuse to see you again. And I didn't call you before now because I wasn't sure you'd want to be reminded about what you went through. I thought maybe I'd be a bad memory for you."

"You were the *best* memory about that whole situation," Gillian blurted.

"Can we start again?" he asked, not looking away from her eyes for a second.

Gillian wanted to say yes. Wanted to jump at the chance. But she'd had just enough alcohol to be completely honest. She shook her head sadly. "I can't."

"Why not?" he asked.

"Yeah, why not?" Clarissa echoed. "Gilly, you were just sitting here telling us that you had a feeling he was—"

"I know what I told you," she said quickly, cutting Clarissa off then looking back at Walker. "I just…if I hurt *this bad* after a misunderstanding, and I don't even know you, if we start dating and you decide you're tired of me, or I'm too annoying, or too type A, too romantic and needy…it'll kill me." The last three words were whispered.

"I've thought about nothing but you for the last three weeks," Walker told her without hesitation. "I've wondered what you were doing and how you were dealing with what happened. Until I knew for sure you and the others had left Venezuela, I worried that you might get stuck there somehow. You can ask any of my friends; I've been distracted and a huge pain in their asses. And when I heard that you might be in danger, my first thought was getting to you and making sure you were safe. *I'm* the one who has to worry that you'll get sick of dating a soldier like me. You'll get tired of the not knowing where I am or when

I'll be home. Believe me, Di, I know who the lucky one is here, and it's not you. It's me. It's definitely me."

Wendy nudged her shoulder when she didn't say anything.

Gillian looked at her friend, then back to Walker. He hadn't moved. Was still crouched next to her. His eyes hadn't left her face. He was wholly concentrated on her. It felt weird...and good.

"I'm drunk," she informed him.

His lips quirked upward. "I can see."

"I'll worry about you when you're gone, but I'm not going to sit at home and boo-hoo all day and night until you get back. I have a business to run. I have friends."

"Good," he said calmly.

"I haven't had a guy go down on me, so I actually don't know if I'll like it or not."

His smile got bigger. "You'll like it."

Gillian rolled her eyes and looked at Ann and Clarissa. "He's arrogant."

Clarissa shrugged. "Gotta love confidence in a guy."

"You always said you wanted an alpha man," Ann added.

Gillian looked back down at Walker. "Don't hurt me," she pleaded.

"I won't."

The two words were said with such confidence, Gillian couldn't help but believe him. "Okay."

Walker immediately stood and held out his hand. "Come on. I'll take you home."

"But I'm out with my girls."

"Go," Wendy said, pushing at Gillian's shoulder. "I think we can survive the rest of the night without you. Besides, after all this hot talk, I think I'm gonna get home and call Wyatt... see if he wants to come over."

"I'll make sure she gets home all right," Walker told her friends, and Gillian couldn't help but shiver at his tone. It was commanding and warm at the same time...and made her think about what they might do together when they got back to her apartment.

"Oh, but my car is here," she said with a shake of her head.

"You're not driving," Walker growled.

Gillian rolled her eyes again. "Of course I'm not. I'd never drink and drive. That would be the stupidest thing ever. I was gonna take an Uber."

"You're not taking an Uber either," Walker said.

"Why not?"

"One, because I'm here, and I'm taking you home. Two, because it's not safe to go on the internet and arrange to meet with a stranger in their car. Haven't you seen all the crime shows? Once you're in a car with someone who wants to do you harm, the likelihood that you'll end up dead in a cornfield somewhere is ninety percent or more."

Gillian narrowed her eyes at him. "Are you making that up?" Then, not giving him time to answer, she turned to her friends. "Is he making that up?"

"I have no idea," Ann said. "But now I'm going to think twice about getting into an Uber again. I'm not sure there are any cornfields around here, but the next time I see one, the only thing I'm going to be able to think about is whether there are any poor women in there who'd just wanted a ride."

"Good," Walker said. "Are you ladies all right to drive? I can call you a cab, or take you home if you prefer."

Clarissa smiled huge. "We're good. We all had our customary one margarita," she looked at her watch, "two hours ago. And we all ate. It's only Gillian here who decided she needed to get shit-faced and wasn't hungry."

Gillian saw the look of regret cross Walker's face, and she couldn't deny it sent shivers through her.

"Come on, Di. Let's get you home."

"What about my car?"

"We'll figure it out."

We'll. She liked that. A lot.

She stood up from the booth and would've face planted if Walker hadn't been there and put an arm around her waist.

"Walker?" Clarissa said when they were about to leave.

"Yeah?"

"Don't fuck with her. We might be women, and you might be some sort of super-soldier who can kick hijacker ass, but we'll find a way to make your life a living hell if you do anything to hurt Gilly."

Gillian was embarrassed, but when she looked up at Walker, strangely, he was smiling.

"Got it," he said. "And for the record, I'm not going to hurt her. I'm glad she's got friends like you three to have her back."

"Just don't forget it," Ann warned.

He nodded at them then looked down at Gillian. "Ready?"

Wrapping her arm around his waist, and not surprised when she didn't feel an ounce of fat under her hand, Gillian nodded. She stumbled alongside Walker as he led her out of the restaurant and into the parking lot. He helped her into his Chevy Blazer and even reached across her to snap her seat belt into place. But instead of backing up and shutting her door, he stayed in her personal space.

"What's wrong?" she asked nervously.

"Nothing," he said. "I'm just memorizing this moment."

Gillian frowned. "What moment?"

"This one." Then he lifted his hand to the side of her neck, turning her head toward him. He leaned forward, giving her time to reject his advance.

But there was no way in hell Gillian was going to reject anything this man wanted to give her. She leaned toward him, reaching out and grabbing hold of his bicep with her right hand.

Walker's lips brushed against hers gently. Once. Twice. Teasing little touches that made Gillian's toes curl. His tongue came out and licked her bottom lip, before he pressed his lips against hers once more.

As far as kisses went, it was chaste and way too short...but it was the most romantic thing anyone had ever done for her.

Walker rested his forehead against hers, and she could feel his warm breaths against her skin.

"Thank you," he said softly.

"For what?"

"For giving me a second chance," he said simply. Then he brushed his thumb against her cheek once and pulled back. He shut her door and walked around the front of the vehicle. He climbed in on the driver's side and started the engine. Putting one arm on the seat back, he twisted to look behind him before backing out of the parking space and heading out onto the road.

"That kiss was amazing," Gillian told him, her filter obliterated by the amount of alcohol she'd consumed.

"Agreed," Walker said with a smile.

"But I want more."

"Yeah?"

"Yeah."

"I'm happy to give you exactly what you want...when you're not three sheets to the wind."

Gillian frowned. "I know what I'm doing. I've never dranken so much that I can't remember."

"Dranken?" he asked with a laugh.

"Drunken, drunk, drank, whatever," Gillian said.

"Be that as it may," Walker said, "I've never taken advantage of a woman before, and I'm not about to start now."

Gillian pouted. "Not even if she wants you to?"

Walker laughed loud and long. Gillian was fascinated. She never would've guessed that he was a man to let go like that. She found herself smiling in return. Then she sobered. "This is weird. Is this weird?"

"No," Walker said immediately.

"It is," Gillian said. "I mean, we don't know each other, not really. And you saved me from being carted off on a plane to some drug lord's hideaway and being horribly abused and maybe forcibly addicted to drugs. And you *killed* people for me. Shot them! POW! Right in the head. And I got brains and ick on me. I looked like shit when we met. I hadn't showered in forever and smelled horrible. And even though I know it wasn't appropriate at the time, I couldn't help but wonder what you looked like without any clothes on. That's messed up, Walker. And how can I feel like I *know* you, when I really don't?"

"The first time I heard your voice, I got hard," Walker said matter-of-factly.

Gillian stared at him with wide eyes as he went on. "It was so inappropriate. You were a hostage and scared out of your mind. You said, 'I'm here' and 'I'm okay.' And that was that. I fell hard. I volunteered to bring that food out to the plane just so I could get a look at the woman who'd impressed the hell out of me, and who'd made me feel more just with her words than I had in any serious relationship I'd been in before. If this is weird, then I'm okay with that."

"Walker," Gillian whispered.

He reached over and took her hand in his own. "Close your eyes, Di. I'll get you home safe and sound."

"I know," she sighed, and did as he ordered.

The entire car was spinning as if it was in the middle of an F5 tornado. It had been a long time since she'd had as much to drink as she had tonight. She'd started out the night depressed and sad, and somehow here she was...sitting next to Walker, who was taking care of her and making sure she got home all right.

Was this really her life?

Forty-five minutes later, Trigger was staring down at a sleeping—or passed out—Gillian. He'd gotten her into her apartment and shoved a T-shirt he'd found in her drawers in her hands and pointed her to the bathroom. He hoped like hell she'd be able to stay awake long enough to change, because he wasn't sure he'd survive if he had to strip off her jeans and shirt.

He'd been staring at her luscious tits the entire way home; her shirt had gaped just a bit, showing him a slice of creamy, luscious skin that he wanted to lick and taste. But she'd managed to put on the T-shirt, and while it covered her cleavage, it left her long legs bare. He had no idea if she was wearing underwear or not, and he closed his eyes as she climbed under her covers.

"Just push the button on the knob when you leave. It'll lock behind you," she slurred as she closed her eyes and hugged a pillow to her chest.

Trigger hadn't answered. He didn't like the thought of her only defense from someone who wanted to break in being a flimsy lock on a doorknob. Leaning over her, he inhaled deeply, and was rewarded with the smell of honeysuckle once more. Deciding the scent was coming from her hair, he lifted a strand and brought it to his nose. Yup...definitely her shampoo.

Gillian stirred under him, and Trigger dropped her hair and stood. Jesus, he was hovering over her like some kind of pervert. She coughed, and he tensed until she calmed once more.

She was hammered. He couldn't leave her. What if she puked in bed? If she choked? He had to stay for her own safety.

Trigger knew he was being ridiculous, but he couldn't make himself leave. He headed to the front door and threw the deadbolt and engaged the chain, along with twisting the little lock on the doorknob. Then he grabbed a chair from the small table in her kitchen and brought it back into her bedroom. He placed it on the other side of the room from the bed, and sat down slowly. He had a perfect vantage point of both Gillian and the living area of the apartment.

He had no idea if the seventh hijacker would decide to come for Gillian for some reason, but he'd be there if he did...at least for tonight.

Knowing he wasn't going to make it to PT in the morning—for the first time in his career—Trigger pulled out his phone and sent Brain a text.

Trigger: Something came up. I won't be in for PT in the am.

His friend immediately responded.

Brain: You okay?
Trigger: Yeah.
Brain: Gillian?
Trigger: She had too much to drink. I'm making sure she's okay. Will be in later.
Brain: She have any clues about the hijacker?

Trigger frowned. He hadn't even thought to ask her about that. One, she was drunk; she probably couldn't think straight anyway. But two, he realized that he had no desire to talk about the fucked-up situation in which they'd found themselves in Venezuela.

Eventually they'd have to talk about it. He needed to find out if she had any suspicions on who the sleeper terrorist might be. She'd spent more time with her fellow passengers than anyone else and probably had better insights than any kind of report could give him. But for now, all he wanted was to try to understand the crazy feelings spiraling inside him.

Trigger: We didn't talk about it.
Brain: Seriously?
Trigger: Seriously.
Brain: You moving her to your apartment back here? :)

Trigger chortled softly under his breath. That was Brain's advice when they'd first learned about the seventh hijacker. And while it seemed like a better idea than ever right now, he knew Gillian would never agree. She was too independent and she had a life here in Georgetown.

As much as Trigger wanted to wrap her in woolen linen to keep her safe, he also never wanted to clip her wings. He *liked* her independence. He'd just have to find other ways to watch over her, to protect her from the evil in the world. It wouldn't be a hardship.

Trigger: No. I'll talk to you tomorrow.
Brain: Later.

Trigger put the phone back in his pocket and leaned forward, resting his elbows on his knees and staring at Gillian. What was it about her that was so different from anyone else? He wasn't sure, but he was eager to find out.

Chapter Seven

GILLIAN WOKE UP AROUND SIX THE NEXT MORNING, WANTING TO DIE. SHE stumbled into the bathroom and saw her clothes lying in a heap on the floor where she'd tossed them after getting undressed the night before.

She used the bathroom then sat on the edge of the bathtub with her head in her hands. She felt like crap. Not bad enough to puke…she didn't think…but bad enough. She should've known better than to drink all that tequila. But the margaritas had gone down way too smoothly.

She remembered everything about last night.

It was still hard to believe that Walker had come to The Funky Walrus to see her…and that he'd said he felt the same crazy connection to her that she'd felt with him.

Gillian had no idea what to do now. She didn't have a way to contact him—she'd forgotten to get his phone number before he'd left last night. She'd look him up on social media, but she knew that would probably be futile. If he was who she suspected he was, he wouldn't have a Facebook page. And he definitely didn't seem the type to have a freaking Instagram page.

Sighing, Gillian stood and went to the sink. She wasn't up for a shower, but she washed the makeup off her face and threw her now crazy, slept-on-wrong hair up into a bun. She shuffled back into her bedroom and pulled on a pair of black fat pants with huge yellow and orange flowers on them.

Deciding she was going to lie on her couch for a while and try to pretend she wasn't hungover as hell, Gillian headed out of her bedroom.

She froze in the hallway when she heard someone in her kitchen.

All of Walker's concerns immediately sprang into her mind. Maybe he hadn't been so far off the mark when he'd said he was worried about her. Was the mystery hijacker in her apartment right this second, ready to kill her when she showed herself?

For a second, Gillian was paralyzed with fear…then she inhaled.

And smelled coffee?

Would someone hell bent on murdering her stop and make coffee first?

Confused as hell, Gillian walked silently the rest of the way down the hall. She stopped in her tracks when she peeked into her small kitchen.

Walker Nelson was sitting at her kitchen table, drinking a cup of coffee, holding his phone in his other hand and reading something intently. He was wearing the same shirt and jeans as the night before, but now his hair was sticking up in the back, and on his feet were only a pair of white socks.

Gillian's heart lurched. He looked absolutely perfect sitting there in her space. She brought a hand up to her chest and pressed on her heart, feeling it thumping hard under her palm. God, this was so close to the fantasies she'd had over the last three weeks, it was uncanny.

She must've made some sort of noise, because suddenly Walker looked up and saw her lurking in her own hallway, staring at him. He put down his mug and phone and immediately stood. He stalked over to her, and all Gillian could do was watch as he neared.

Craning her head back to keep eye contact with him, she was shocked when he didn't stop as he got close. He invaded her personal space and put his hands on either side of her head.

"Good morning," he said softly, his rumbly voice making Gillian's nipples peak.

She knew if he looked down he'd see the effect he had on her body, but he kept his gaze on hers.

"Hi," she said after a moment. "What are you doing here?"

"There was no way in hell I was going to leave you last night. Not as drunk as you were."

"You never left?" she asked. It was a stupid question. Of course he hadn't. He was wearing the same clothes he'd had on last night, and it wasn't as if he would've left then driven all the way back to Georgetown this morning.

He grinned. "I never left," he confirmed.

"Where did you sleep?"

"On your couch."

Gillian bit her lip. "But it's not that comfortable."

Walker merely shrugged. "It's fine. I've definitely slept in worse places in my life. And it smells like you."

She had absolutely no clue what to say to that, so she just stared up at him. His gaze moved from her eyes to her hair, to her lips, down her body, taking in her shirt and crazy pants.

Gillian wanted to melt into a puddle on the floor in embarrassment. If she'd known he was there, she would've put on some real clothes. A bra. Done something to her hair…like brush it.

Just when she was deciding if it would be weird if she pushed him away and fled to her bedroom to change, he spoke.

"I thought you looked amazing three weeks ago, after everything you'd been through. And last night, you about knocked me off my feet when you answered your door. But this? Right now? I've never seen anything more beautiful in my life."

Gillian's stomached flip-flopped. "I'm hungover, not wearing a bra, just scrubbed the makeup off my face, which I should've done last night, and I think a mouse has taken up residence in my hair," she blurted.

"You're real," Walker countered. "You look mussed and relaxed. Exactly how I've pictured you in my dirty fantasies."

Gillian knew she was blushing, but couldn't help it. "And you look as perfectly put together as you have every time I've seen you. How do you *do* that?"

But he didn't answer her. Instead he asked, "Are you hungry?"

Gillian wrinkled her nose. "I don't know."

"I didn't want to cook anything in case the smell of eggs or bacon made you sick," Walker told her, and Gillian inwardly sighed. Fuck, he was perfect. How in the hell could someone be this perfect?

"A plain bagel," Gillian blurted. "Toasted. Dry. I think maybe I could eat that."

"Okay, Gilly, then that's what you'll have," he told her.

The sound of him using the nickname her best friends called her felt good.

He leaned down and kissed her forehead, his lips lingering for a long moment. Then he dropped his hands from her head and put his arm around her waist as he led her into the living area. He steered her to the couch and urged her to sit. Once she had, he shook out the blanket she always kept on the back of the couch and covered her with it.

"Stay put. I'll make your bagel."

Gillian watched as he strode into her kitchen. He opened her fridge and took out a bottle of water, breaking the seal on the top before walking back toward her. He handed it to her with a smile, then turned and went back into the kitchen.

She took a sip and watched as Walker started making her breakfast…such as it was. He looked completely at ease in her small kitchen. He knew where everything was and acted as if he'd been there hundreds of times before.

Lost in her admiration of Walker's ass as he moved around her space, she blinked in surprise when he sat next to her, a plain toasted bagel on a plate in his hand. She turned in her seat and gave him a small smile of thanks.

She nibbled a piece of the bread cautiously, happy when it settled and she didn't feel the need to puke it back up.

"We need to talk."

His words immediately made her stiffen. It was the same four words he'd used the night before that had sent her into a downward spiral.

"No, don't tense up," Walker said, putting a hand on her thigh and leaning into her. "Listen to me, okay?"

The bite of bagel she'd managed to swallow threatened to come back up after all. It seemed to be stuck in her throat, and she couldn't have said anything if her life depended on it.

"I told you this last night, but I don't know what you remember and what you don't."

"I remember it all," Gillian admitted softly.

"Right, well then, I'll repeat this so you hear it again. Yes, I came down here to Georgetown to let you know about the seventh hijacker. But that was just an excuse. I haven't been able to stop thinking about you. You impressed me three weeks ago. You were level-headed and did everything right. You didn't panic when shit hit the fan. I wanted nothing more than to be there to reassure you and help you navigate the interviews and shit that followed.

"I've missed you, Gillian. Which isn't normal, considering I barely know you. I came down to deliver that message in person hoping that we could talk after. Get to know each other. So I could ask you out and see if you'd go to dinner with me sometime. I wanted to go slow, see if this obsession I seem to have with you is a result of the situation…or more."

Gillian knew her eyes were huge in her face, but she couldn't stop staring at Walker in astonishment.

"I knew I'd fucked up somehow when you left. I saw the light go out of your eyes, and it killed that I had done that. I didn't know how, but it was obvious. So I found out where The Funky Walrus was located and went there with the intention of apologizing for whatever it was I'd said."

Gillian huffed out a small laugh. "Yeah, and then you found me drunk as hell, saying the most embarrassing things."

"They weren't embarrassing," Walker said earnestly. "They were honest. I hate that you thought for even a second that you were just a job to me. You weren't. You *aren't*."

"It's okay," she told him.

"You're way too forgiving," he said with a small head shake, but he didn't give her time to say anything else. "It was probably creepy and wrong of me to stay last night, but I never would've forgiven myself if someone had broken in when you were vulnerable, or if you'd have puked and choked in the middle of the night. But I can't be sorry, because I got to see you like this…" His eyes dropped, and Gillian knew he could see her hard nipples through her T-shirt.

He cleared his throat and went on. "I want to date you, Gillian. Call you and talk into the wee hours of the night. Send you texts to let you know I'm thinking about you. Take you out to dinner and make out in my car in the parking lot when I drop you off. I want to get to know your friends, and to laugh with you. Eventually, when the time is right for us both, I want to hold you all night as you sleep after we've made love. I want to taste every inch of your body and have you explore mine in return. We've had a connection from the start, and as much as I want to get to know you intimately right *now*, I want to savor learning everything about you. Learn who Gillian Romano is. What makes her tick."

Every word out of his mouth made Gillian fall for him more. She wanted to shake her head, tell him no, that she didn't want to go slow. That she wanted to feel his hands and tongue on her right that second. But another part of her wanted what he'd described. Wanted the giddy feeling that came with getting to know a man. Wanted the phone calls and texts. Wanted the sexual tension.

She wanted to be wooed. Mostly because she had a feeling Walker would make her feel just like she longed to feel…as if she was wanted. And she had a hunch he'd never make her feel like she came in second.

"I…I'd like that."

His shoulders dropped as if he'd been afraid she'd turn him down. It was hard to believe that this man, this strong-as-hell, beautiful man, would be worried about *her* turning *him* down.

"But you need to know, I'm not a drama queen," she added.

"What do you mean?" he asked.

"I'm different from most women. I don't do drama. Women in general are really bad about that. They get jealous and bitchy and have to be all dramatic about it. They don't get their way, they cause a scene. They think they should be getting more attention than they are, so some dress more flamboyantly and outrageously. That's not me. I say it like it is, but don't do it for any kind of reaction. I prefer honesty to lies because it's just easier."

"I like that. It's a relief."

"But, Walker, if we do this…don't cheat on me."

He looked shocked at her words. "Why would you even say that? I don't cheat. And I can't imagine, if we get together the way I want to be with you, that I'd ever be stupid enough to fool around."

Gillian shrugged. "Others have."

"Cheated on you? Then they were idiots."

His words were immediate and heartfelt, and they made Gillian relax a fraction. "They wanted something more than me, I guess. One also hit me. You do either of those things, and I'll be done with you faster than you can blink."

Walker sat up straight, and when he spoke, his tone was low and kinda scary. "Someone *hit you?*"

Gillian realized that she was about to have an extremely pissed-off alpha man on her hands if she didn't do damage control. Pronto. "Yeah, one guy. Once. It was the last time I saw him. I left his ass that day and pressed charges. My point is that I don't put up with shit like that. Especially not from someone I'm dating. I'm worth more than that. I'm a damn good girlfriend. Attentive and generous. When I'm with someone, I put them first. If they need me, I'm there, and I want to find someone who feels the same way about me. And cheating, stealing, and knocking me around isn't looking out for my well-being. It's not putting me first."

She could see that Walker was having a hard time letting go of the thought that someone had hit her. She gentled her tone. "It happens, Walker. Unfortunately, all the time. Walking down the street, men feel as if it's okay to whistle and cat call. They don't hesitate to ogle our boobs and tell us how turned on they are. A lot of them feel as if it's okay to smack a woman simply because they're a *man*, stronger and better than a woman because they have more muscles and a dangling piece of flesh between their legs they pee through. It doesn't make it right, but bad things happen to good women all the time."

"Not to you. Not anymore," Walker said in a possessive tone that made goose bumps break out on Gillian's arms.

"Okay," she agreed easily.

Walker took a moment to visibly try to control his extreme reaction to her admission that she'd been hit, then said, "I can't stay much longer as I have to get back up to Fort Hood. My team is gonna give me hell for missing PT this morning. I've never missed it before. Not once."

Gillian blinked. "Really?"

"Really," he confirmed. "You were more important than getting back to run ten miles with my friends."

That felt good. *Really* good.

"But, before I go, there's something else we need to talk about."

"The hijacker," Gillian said somberly. Even though her belly was churning with happiness, she knew they needed to discuss this.

"Yeah," Walker said, his face serious. "No one knows who he is, what he's thinking, or even where he is right now."

"But why would he care about me or any of the other passengers?"

Walker stared at her for a long moment, and Gillian could tell he was weighing what he should and shouldn't say.

"I need you to be honest," she said quietly. "I get that you don't want me hurt, but I need to know everything."

"Right. Everyone's working on this. The FBI, CIA, DEA. The antiterrorist organizations from other countries. Everyone who was on the plane is being scrutinized, even you. Your friends might have people ask them questions about you. Your tax and business records will be combed through looking for inconsistencies. I'm very sorry."

Gillian shrugged. "I don't have anything to hide, Walker. I'm not thrilled, but the sooner they figure out I'm just me, the better."

He smiled briefly, then sobered once more. "There are more questions about this seventh hijacker than answers. Why was he hiding amongst the passengers? How pissed is he that his fellow conspiracists were killed? We know now that the hijackers didn't work for the Cartel of the Suns, but instead were from a rival drug syndicate, the Sinaloa Cartel in Mexico. They didn't want to free Hugo Lamas, they wanted him dead, which they accomplished. They embarrassed the Cartel of the Suns and essentially started one hell of a war."

Holy crap. She was hardly up on all the various cartels and hadn't really paid that much attention to them before she'd been hijacked, but even *she* knew about the Sinaloa Cartel, who occasionally made the local news. What she remembered about them was terrifying. "Why would anyone come after *me*?"

"To find out what you know. Because, when push comes to shove, you were a big reason why Luis and all the others were killed. You stalled them just enough, you put up a fight. Alberto wanted you on that plane, and because he wanted you, someone else might think there was a good reason."

"But Luis was taking Andrea," Gillian pointed out.

"I know. And that means she could be in danger too. She's being checked in on as well."

"Oh," Gillian said, her mind swirling.

"With all that said, I think the chance someone from the Sinaloa Cartel, or the Cartel of the Suns, coming after you is low. But I'm not willing to stake my life on it…or yours. You need to be very careful, Gillian. Don't go anywhere by yourself if you can help it. Don't take any chances. Always lock your door. Get a security system installed, or at least buy those motion-sensor cameras that are so popular nowadays. And for God's sake, don't take an Uber anywhere."

Gillian couldn't help but smile. "You really don't like those rideshare things, do you?"

"No," he growled. "You have no idea who's behind the wheel. What their driving record is, if they've been drinking or on drugs, or if they just got out of jail for sexual assault. Once you get in a car, you're vulnerable. You could be driven anywhere…out into the middle of nowhere and never seen again."

"Okay, Walker," she said, putting her hand atop his on her leg. "I'll be careful. Can I… do the other passengers know about the sleeper guy? I mean, I email and text quite a few of them. I don't know what I'm allowed to say and what I'm not."

"Some will be informed, others won't. The thing is, someone you're talking to could very well be the seventh hijacker, Gillian."

She shook her head. "No. I don't believe it."

She didn't like the look in Walker's eyes.

"No," she said again. "There's no way Janet is a terrorist. Maybe you think it's little Renee? Or Reed? Maybe one of the college boys? Alice, the woman who was so scared she literally peed her pants? Or Andrea, the woman Luis forced to suck his dick? No, *no way*."

"Breathe, Gilly," Walker said gently, turning his hand over so he could intertwine their fingers. "This is something else that you're going to have to do…talk to the authorities about the other passengers. Tell them everything that happened in minute detail. Even the smallest thing could be important, could be a clue as to who the other hijacker was."

Inhaling deeply, Gillian tried to control her panic. It was just now sinking in that someone she'd gotten to know, had bonded with over their horrific experience, might really have been on the side of the hijackers. "I don't know that much, Walker. The men were kept on the other end of the plane, you know that. I only briefly talked to most of them. Mateo, Charles, Muhammad…they all seemed nice. Now, I just don't know. Oh! But now that I think about it, Leyton was a bit strange. When Alberto was trying to pull me onto the plane, Leyton was standing nearby, just watching us. Not helping and not running away like the others. But honestly, I think he was just in shock. Everything happened so fast."

"Okay, Gillian, I'm not the one who needs to know the details, the investigators do."

She frowned at him. "You don't want to know?"

He shrugged. "I want to know whatever you want to tell me. But my job in Venezuela wasn't to solve the mystery of who had hijacked the plane, and why. It was to rescue hostages, and if that meant killing the hijackers, so be it. I'm not involved in the investigation. As of right this moment, my one and only concern is to make sure *you're* safe."

That felt really good.

"If you want to talk to me about what you went through, I'll listen. I've been through some pretty serious shit in my life, and I can help you deal with what happened if you need it. But starting today, I'm the man you're dating, not someone who's with you to pump you for information. Okay?"

Gillian nodded.

"But you have to know that if I think you're being reckless with your safety, or not treating this as seriously as you should, I'm gonna call you on it."

That didn't bother Gillian like it might've if it had been anyone else who'd said it to her.

"If I find out more information, I'll certainly pass it along, especially if it affects your safety. But as far as I'm concerned, we're just a man and a woman who are getting to know each other."

"I like that."

"Me too," Walker said with a smile. "And as a part of this getting-to-know-you shit, you need to know that I work weird hours. I don't have a nine-to-five job."

"I think I got that," Gillian told him with a wry chuckle.

"I don't think you do," he said seriously. "I could be called away on a job at any moment. I'll do my best to let you know, but there might be times I don't get a chance to call you... things can get crazy and intense for me that fast."

Gillian licked her lips and nodded.

"I might be gone for a few days, or a few weeks. I never know how long a deployment is gonna take."

"Okay."

"You think you can handle that?" he asked.

Gillian could hear the worry in his voice, and she hurried to reassure him. "Walker, as I said last night, I'm not going to pine away waiting for you to get back. I'll miss you, but I've got a life. A job that will keep me busy. And when I feel sad, I'll just get together with Ann, Wendy, and Clarissa and have a pity party, then continue on with my life. I've managed on my own for a decade. I'm not going to fall apart when you get deployed. I'm proud that you're serving our country. And..." Her voice lowered, and she couldn't help but glance around her apartment. She wasn't sure what she expected to see; it wasn't as if there were people around to overhear her. "I know that you're not a normal soldier."

"You do?" he asked with a small grin.

"Yeah. I've lived in this area long enough to know that typical deployments from the Army base are for like six months or longer. A team of seven regular infantry soldiers aren't sent to Venezuela to rescue hostages on a huge plane."

"You're right, they're not," Walker said simply.

Gillian nodded. He wasn't going to tell her exactly what he did, and that was all right. "I don't care, Walker," she said earnestly. "I care about you being safe and coming back from your missions safely, but you could be the president's personal bodyguard, and it wouldn't make a difference in how I feel about you."

Walker closed his eyes for a second and took a deep breath. When he opened them again, Gillian saw his pupils had dilated slightly. He leaned into her and nuzzled her hair by her ear.

"Honeysuckle," he murmured. "I'll never be able to smell it again and not get hard." Then, as if he hadn't just said one of the most carnal things she'd ever heard, he pulled back to look into her eyes once more. "Did I say I wanted to go slow?" he asked. "I think I'm an idiot."

Gillian laughed. She could tell he hadn't changed his mind, but it felt good to know he wasn't unaffected by her.

"All I ask is that you be extra careful until the authorities find out who that seventh hijacker is," he said. "It's unlikely that he'd come to Austin to try to do you harm, but until we know his identity, I'm not willing to take any chances."

"Okay."

Walker glanced at his watch. "You feel okay?" he asked.

She nodded, but said, "No. I'm not nauseous, but I don't feel all that good either."

He smiled and ran a hand over her hair. "Poor Gilly. What are you going to do today?"

"Sit here on the couch and binge watch shows that will lower my IQ ten points and try not to even think about ever drinking again."

"Sounds good. Can I call you later?"

"Yes."

"It's Thursday; you have plans for this weekend?"

"I've got a *quinceañera* party Friday night and a golf outing Saturday morning."

"Would you like to go out to dinner on Saturday night?"

"Yes."

He smiled. "How about I pick you up around four? There's a great place up in Killeen I'd like to take you to. We can eat, then I'd love to show you around Fort Hood and where I work."

"I'd love that."

"Good. If it's all right with you, I'm gonna call a taxi and head over to the bar and drive your car back here before I leave."

"You don't have to do that," Gillian told him, shocked that he would even consider it. "I can go get it later."

"I know I don't have to. You feel like crap, and it's not a big deal for me to go get it."

She wasn't sure what to say. She'd already planned to either call one of her friends to pick her up or take a taxi to The Funky Walrus later to get her car. But she couldn't deny that she liked that Walker offered to do it for her. "Thanks. I'd appreciate that."

"Great. I'll take care of it for you then. Gillian?"

"Yeah?"

"I hope you know what you're getting into with me."

"I do," she said simply. And she did. She'd waited a hell of a long time for a man like Walker to find her. She was strong enough to be his woman…if he'd let her.

Chapter Eight

WHEN SATURDAY NIGHT ROLLED AROUND, GILLIAN WAS EXHAUSTED, BUT she also felt as if she'd had way too many shots of espresso. In just a few minutes, Walker would be at her apartment to pick her up for their date.

She'd gotten a bit too much sun at the golf party that afternoon, but she knew the pink would fade in a day or so. Gillian had asked Walker what she should wear, and he'd told her that jeans and a blouse would be perfect. He hadn't told her where they were going, but she trusted him.

It was about a forty-minute drive to Killeen, and Gillian was looking forward to simply talking more with Walker as they drove. True to his word, he'd called on Thursday night. They'd ended up talking for three hours, which surprised Gillian. It was her experience that most guys didn't like to talk on the phone that much. But there hadn't been one lull in their conversation. They'd talked as if they'd known each other their whole lives.

When she'd told Walker that he was the first guy who hadn't seemed to mind talking on the phone for as long as they had, he'd told her that he wasn't like any of the men she'd dated in the past, and that normally he wasn't very chatty, but as far as he was concerned, he could talk to her for hours every night and be perfectly happy.

He always seemed to say the right thing, but Gillian didn't think he was merely saying what he thought she wanted to hear. Their conversation was too smooth, too easy to be faked.

He'd texted on Friday…several times. And each time her phone vibrated, she smiled in anticipation. Then he'd called her briefly that morning to see how the *quinceañera* had gone and to tell her he hoped her golf thing went all right.

It was a new experience for Gillian to have someone be so attuned to her schedule. Walker was enthusiastic and inquisitive about her job. He seemed to be fascinated by how organized she was and how many different kinds of events she arranged. He'd warned her to be safe and they'd finalized plans for the evening.

Since Walker had said jeans were all right, she took a chance and wore her favorite pair of brown and turquoise cowboy boots as well. She wore a turquoise shirt that matched and had braided her hair in two long braids that hung over her chest. She'd also dug some ribbon out of a drawer and tied each braid off with a piece.

She thought she looked cute…but it might be overkill. She definitely looked a little touristy in her cowgirl getup, but she felt good, so decided to go with it.

Gillian had just walked out of her bedroom when the buzzer sounded, letting her know someone was at the doorway downstairs. She pressed on the button. "Hello?"

"It's me," Walker said in his distinctive deep rumble.

Without another word, Gillian pressed the button to open the door and let him inside. She knew she had maybe two minutes before he'd be knocking. She took a deep breath, then another. She was nervous as hell, which was crazy, considering Walker had definitely seen her at her worst…twice.

She'd wanted to look nice for him tonight. To let him know that she was looking forward to spending time with him. The knock on the door came about a minute before she was expecting it. Smiling, happy at how excited Walker seemed to be for their date as well, she peered through the peephole, confirming it was him, before opening the door with a huge smile.

"Hi," she said brightly. "You got up here fast."

She barely got a chance to register what Walker was wearing before he was easing her into her apartment and closing the door. He backed her up against the wall next to her front door then reached out and took her face in his hands, tilting her head up. Gillian grabbed hold of his biceps and looked at him in surprise.

He didn't say anything, which kinda freaked Gillian out. "Walker?"

"Hmmm?" he murmured.

"Are you all right?"

"Good. Great, now that I'm with you."

She smiled uncertainly.

"Shit," he said under his breath. "I'm fucking this up." Then he took a deep breath, grimaced, and took a step away from her.

She shivered at the loss of the heat of his hands on her face. "What's wrong?" she asked, biting her lip.

His hand came up once more and he tugged her lip out of her teeth, then smoothed the pad of his finger across her lower lip. "Nothing's wrong. I just…I almost forgot we were taking things slow for a second. Seeing you almost broke through my restraint."

Gillian frowned. She looked down at her jeans and boots, then back up at him.

"You look amazing," Walker said softly. He picked up one of her braids and fingered it for a moment. "Every time I see you, you surprise me by being prettier than when I saw you last."

"Do I…is this okay for where we're going to dinner tonight? I know it's a bit much, but I love my boots and thought if you said jeans were okay, they'd probably do. And I haven't worn this shirt in a while. And after I'd gotten dressed, it just seemed more appropriate to put my hair up like this than to leave it down." Gillian knew she was babbling, but Walker's reaction had put her off balance.

"It's absolutely perfect," Walker reassured her. "As I said, I almost forgot my vow to take things slow when I saw you and did something I promised myself I wouldn't do."

"What's that?"

"Kiss you the way I've been dreaming about. Put one hand up your shirt and the other down your pants. Take you against the wall as I kept my nose buried in your hair to better inhale your sweet smell."

Gillian froze. *Holy shit.* Walker was way more intense than anyone she'd ever been with before—but she liked it. No, she *loved* that he knew exactly what he wanted and wasn't afraid to admit it.

"Shit, I freaked you out, didn't I?" he asked, taking another step away from her.

"No! I mean, maybe a little, but not in a bad way. I'm just not used to anyone being so honest, but I like it. And…as much as I feel connected to you…I…it's a bit soon for that. But…" She hesitated.

"What?" Walker asked. "You can tell me anything. Tell me to back off, that I'm moving way too fast, that I'm crowding you, that you need space…and I'll respect it."

She shook her head. "I was just going to say that while I might not be ready for all that right now…can I have a raincheck?"

"On the ravaging you against the wall?" Walker asked with a small smile.

"Yeah, that."

"You got it, Di."

They smiled at each other, and Gillian found she missed having his hands on her. She loved that she could make him act without thought. She had a feeling that didn't happen a lot with him. She reached for his hand and intertwined her fingers with his. "Take me to dinner?" she asked softly.

He squeezed her hand and nodded. Together they walked into her living area so she could grab her purse.

"I ordered one of those camera thingies online yesterday," Gillian told him. "It should arrive on Monday."

"Good."

"And I told both my neighbors that a former client was upset with me and if they heard anything weird from my apartment, that they should call the police."

She looked up at Walker and found he was staring down at her with a satisfied look. "Thank you."

"For what?"

"For taking this seriously. I know constantly thinking about your safety is a pain in the ass and can be kinda scary as well. But knowing you're taking this seriously makes me feel a hell of a lot better about being so far away from you."

Gillian had thought about that as well. They lived at least forty minutes from one another. If someone broke in or otherwise tried to hurt her, even if she was able to call him, there wouldn't be anything he could do in the short term. "I might be blonde, but I'm not an idiot," she told him. "The last thing I want is to end up a hostage again. It wasn't fun the first time and I have no desire to repeat it. If you think I might be in danger, I'd be stupid to dismiss your feelings."

"Good. Now, are you hungry?"

"Yeah," she said.

"You gonna be okay for an hour or so, or do you need a snack?"

Gillian chuckled. "I'm not exactly wasting away, Walker. I think I can hold out until we get to the restaurant."

Walker tugged on her hand until she fell against him with an *umph*.

"I *know* you're not disparaging your body, are you?" he asked.

Gillian shook her head. One hand was still in his, trapped behind her back where he was holding her to him. The other she rested on his chest as she looked up at him. "No. But I know what I am and what I'm not. And what I'm not is the size and shape of the women men seem to love to look at on the runways and in magazines. I'm okay with that, because I like to eat. I love chips and salsa, and I won't give up my chocolate."

Walker smiled down at her. "God, you're so refreshing," he said softly. "You really do say it like it is, don't you?"

"Yes."

"Right, well, I don't watch those fancy shows with people wearing ridiculous fashions, and I don't have time to look at magazines like *Maxim* and *Playboy*. What I *do* like is how you feel in my arms. Against me." He pushed harder on the small of her back until she was plastered against his chest. Gillian could feel his erection against her belly, and she swallowed hard.

"I'll be sure to stock up on chocolate so you can have some when you get the hankering for a snack. And chips and salsa is one of my favorite things to eat as well. Spicy or mild?"

"Medium," Gillian whispered, resisting the urge to wiggle against him.

"I like it hot," Walker said suggestively.

Throwing her head back, Gillian couldn't stop herself from laughing. When she had herself under control, she looked back up at him. "Why doesn't that surprise me?"

Walker was grinning down at her. "Because even after such a short time, you know me," he said.

They stayed like that for a long minute. Not speaking, simply enjoying being next to each other. Gillian could feel his heart beating fast under her hand and loved that he wasn't unaffected by their proximity.

Walker took a deep breath, then said, "And now we really need to get going."

"Right, I'm sure you made reservations," she agreed.

"Because of that too," Walker said.

Gillian couldn't stop the giggle that escaped. She loved that he wasn't bashful about letting her know how much he wanted her. She wanted him too, but she wasn't ready to sleep with him yet. She wanted to get to know him better. Her heart said he was the man she could spend the rest of her life with, but her brain was telling her to slow down and make sure.

They walked to her door together and he locked it behind them. They went down the stairs hand in hand and out to his Blazer. Once again, he opened her door and helped her put on her seat belt. Then he shut the door and walked around to the other side.

Gillian felt safe with him. As he pulled out of her apartment complex and headed for the road that led north to Killeen, she relaxed. The night was just starting and it had already been one of the best dates she'd ever had.

Trigger sat across from Gillian at his favorite barbeque restaurant in Killeen and realized he couldn't take his eyes from her. When he'd first seen her in her apartment, he'd acted without thinking. He'd had her pushed inside and up against her wall before his brain had engaged.

She looked adorable. Her braids, the boots, the tight jeans…it all made him want to take her right then and there. Luckily, he'd come to his senses. He never acted impulsively. That would get him killed on a mission, and over the years his common sense had taken over all aspects of his life. He was always methodical and cautious…except when it came to Gillian Romano, apparently.

He'd loved talking to her throughout the week. She was funny and entertaining. She didn't monopolize the conversation, and she asked him questions and had no problem answering his as well. He hadn't even realized they'd been talking for hours until he'd looked at the clock and had been shocked as hell to see the time.

She had a bit of sauce on her chin and, without thinking, Trigger reached over to wipe it off. Instead of being embarrassed, she merely laughed. "Am I covered in the stuff?" she asked with a smile as she brought a napkin up to her face.

"Naw, just a little bit on your chin," he told her with a smile.

The restaurant was crowded, as it was a Saturday night and they had some of the best barbeque in Killeen. Most of the patrons were soldiers from the base, but there were quite a few families there as well. It was an unconventional place to bring Gillian for their first date, but he wanted her to be comfortable. And there was nowhere more comfortable than here.

"Tell me about your team?" she asked as they chowed down on their smoked brisket and chicken. "I mean, I saw them all in Venezuela, but didn't really get to meet them."

"They're some of the best men I've ever known," Trigger said honestly. "They're hard-working, brave, and loyal, and they're also assholes."

Gillian chuckled.

That was another thing Trigger loved about her…she seemed to know when he was joking with her and when he was being serious. He'd once dated a woman who took offense to everything he'd said when he was being sarcastic or just kidding around.

"But seriously, they can be a bit rough around the edges, but I think we all are. We're all single, and have been most of our adult lives. The Army's been our mistress and it can be hard to change our mindset on that."

Gillian was giving him her full attention. "How long have you been in?" she asked.

"I'm thirty-seven. I joined the Army relatively late compared to some others. I graduated from college and started a job, then realized I hated being cooped up in an office all day. There was a recruiting station across the street from where I worked, and one day on my lunch break, I found myself in their office, talking to them about joining. That was about thirteen years ago."

"So you're a lifer then." It wasn't a question.

"Yeah, I haven't thought about when I'll retire, but I'll do at least twenty years," Trigger said. "I met my team in training." He had to be careful about telling her too much, but she'd already pretty much guessed that he was special forces, so he kept going. "Lefty, Grover, and I were in the same recruitment class. We slogged through mud, puked, got rained on, got shot at with rubber bullets, and nearly drowned together. We forged a bond that'll never be broken, no matter what we do in the future or where we go."

"Well, that sounds fun…not," Gillian said with a smile.

"It wasn't, but it was," Trigger said with a smile. "I knew I was going to be doing something that would make a difference in the world. Even if I couldn't talk about it to anyone, I'd know."

"Like rescue hostages from a hijacked plane in Venezuela," she said quietly.

"Exactly," Trigger agreed, reaching across the table for her hand. He caressed the back of it with his thumb and didn't break eye contact with her. "We met Brain, Oz, Doc, and Lucky later, when we were teamed up together. Sometimes I feel as if I've known them all my entire life. We can finish each other's sentences and when they hurt, I hurt, and vice versa. It's a bond I always wished I had growing up. I'm an only child and always wanted a brother or sister."

"And now you have six brothers."

"I do."

Gillian smiled, then she licked her lips and looked down.

"What? What's wrong?" Trigger asked, holding on to her hand when she tried to pull back from him.

"I just…what if they don't like me?"

Trigger couldn't help it. He laughed.

When he got himself under control and looked back at Gillian, she was glaring at him. Once more she tried to pull her hand out of his grasp, but he held on.

"I'm not laughing *at* you," he reassured her. "I'm laughing because if anything, I'm going to have to worry about you deciding you like them better than me. They're going to love you; already do, in fact."

Her brows furrowed. "I haven't really even met them."

"Yeah, but I've talked about you. A lot."

"But we just met a few days ago."

Trigger shook his head. "Wrong. We met a few weeks ago. And the guys saw the kind of person you were *then*, and after me not being able to talk about anything but you for the last few days, they've gotten to know you even better."

Gillian flushed, and Trigger couldn't help but grin. He squeezed her hand. "You have nothing to worry about, Di," he told her softly. "I think I have more to be concerned about. My best friends are all single. They're horn dogs and will probably annoy you to no end.

They're a little uncouth and brash. You might meet them and hate them, and that wouldn't bode well for our relationship."

"I'm not going to hate them," she assured. "They're your friends…how could I?"

They were smiling at each other when someone called from across the restaurant.

"Trigger!"

He turned and smiled as he saw who was approaching. Standing, Trigger shook the man's hand and smiled at the woman at his side. Gillian had also stood, and Trigger introduced everyone.

"Gillian, this is my friend Truck and his wife, Mary. This is Gillian, my girlfriend."

Mary instantly looked like she had a thousand questions, but she managed to keep them inside as she shook Gillian's hand.

"It's good to meet you," Truck said. "We didn't even know Trigger *had* a girlfriend."

Trigger grinned and put his arm around Gillian's waist. "I do," he said firmly. Then he looked down at Gillian. "Truck is with a group of soldiers that we've worked with in the past. His team and mine are all friends. Seems like just yesterday that we were at Truck and Mary's wedding." Then he turned back to his friend and asked, "Are you guys excited to go get your kids?"

"Definitely," Truck said with a smile. "Feels like we've waited forever for the paperwork to go through to be able to pick up Aarav and Deeba. We've sent tapes of our voices and lots of pictures, but who knows how they'll react when they see us for the first time."

"They're adopting two young kids from India," Trigger explained to Gillian.

"Congratulations," she said with a huge smile.

"Thanks," Truck replied. "We're ready to have them home."

"Wait, are you Gillian *Romano?*" Mary asked out of the blue. She'd been smiling and nodding as her husband spoke, but it was obvious Gillian's name had just clicked in her brain.

Trigger tensed. He knew it was a possibility that Gillian could be recognized. Her name and picture had been in newspapers around the country after the hijacking. She hadn't given many interviews, but that didn't matter. She was a weird kind of celebrity.

He felt her tense next to him, but she answered politely enough. "I am."

"You're amazing!" Mary said immediately. "I read about what happened on that plane, and it sounds like it was so horrible. I mean, when I was held captive in the bank I worked at, I was terrified, but that was only for like twenty minutes. I can't imagine being in your situation for over two days!"

Trigger felt Gillian relax against him. "It wasn't fun," she told Mary.

"Understatement of the century," Trigger muttered.

"We can see you're eating, so we'll let you go," Truck told them. "Gillian, it was nice meeting you."

"Same," Gillian said.

Trigger shook Truck's hand again and said, "We still on for that training exercise next week? Your team against mine?"

"Fuck yeah," Truck said with a grin. "May the best team win."

"Which'll be mine," Trigger said. "No way are we letting a bunch of old men beat us."

"We'll see," Truck said. "We'll see."

"Come on, He-Man," Mary teased. "I'm hungry, and if you two stand here beating your chests anymore, I'll never get fed."

Gillian giggled, and Trigger loved the sound. He gave Truck a chin lift and got one in return. Then he waited until Gillian was seated before taking his own once again.

"You guys seem close," she observed when they were eating.

"We are," Trigger agreed.

"I like Mary's hair."

"Don't you dare think of putting any streaks of color in yours," Trigger growled.

Gillian raised surprised eyes to his. "Why?"

"Because it's perfect the way it is. I love the color it is now. It reminds me of fields of wheat that grow in the Midwest."

For a second, Trigger thought he'd overstepped. He couldn't read the look on Gillian's face. But finally she smiled.

"Thanks. I wasn't really thinking about coloring my own hair. I just admire others who can get away with it."

They finished their meal without any further interruptions and Trigger was glad when they left the noisy interior of the restaurant behind and got back into his car. When they were both settled, he turned to her. "Want to see some of the base?"

"Sure," she said eagerly.

So for the next two hours, Trigger drove her around Fort Hood. He showed her where his office was and even walked her around one of the motor pools. When she said she'd never seen the inside of a tank, he arranged for a mechanic working on one to let her peek inside. He took pictures of her sitting inside, and Trigger knew he'd never forget how happy she looked.

"That was fun," she told him when they were leaving the base.

"Yeah," he agreed quietly.

"What's wrong?" she asked, easily reading his mood.

Trigger glanced over at her. He could only see flashes of her face when they passed under streetlights as it had gotten dark outside. He'd done all he could to prolong their time on the base but eventually he'd run out of things to show her.

"I'm not ready to bring you home yet," he blurted, then cringed. He was supposed to be moving slow, and keeping her out all night wasn't exactly doing that.

"I'm not ready to *go* home yet," she said, surprising him. "What do you have in mind?"

"I'm sure there's a late movie we could see," Trigger told her. "Or we could find a bar and hang out. Or…" He let his words trail off.

"Or what?"

Glancing over at her again, Trigger felt the familiar twinge in his belly. She was so pretty. The hair in her braids had started to escape their confines and she looked somewhat mussed after crawling around the tank in the motor pool. But she looked completely relaxed, leaning against his car door with one knee bent and her foot tucked up under her thigh.

"I was going to suggest that maybe we could go back to my apartment and watch a movie there or something. It would be quieter, and we could talk easier…but I'm not sure that's a good idea."

"That sounds really nice, actually," Gillian told him. "Honestly, I have a slight headache from being out in the sun all day today."

Trigger fought an internal war with himself. He wanted to take Gillian to his home. Wanted to see her on his couch, relaxed and happy. But he knew if they went back there, it would be extremely difficult to keep his hands—and lips—off of her. He'd never had a problem controlling himself around women before, but something about Gillian pushed all his buttons. "You're safe with me," he told her.

She looked surprised, but said, "I know. I wouldn't have agreed to let you drive me up here to Killeen if I didn't think I was safe."

"We're taking things slow," he added, a little harsher than he'd meant to.

"I know that too," she agreed.

"Me taking you to my apartment isn't a ploy to get you into my bed." Trigger didn't know why he wasn't letting this go. Probably because a part of him hoped she might push back and tell him it was all right. That she didn't *want* to go slow anymore.

She shifted in her seat and reached over to put her hand on his arm. "If you need to take me home, it's okay," she said quietly.

"No!" he blurted.

After a beat, they both chuckled softly.

"I'm fucking this up—again," Trigger told her, kinda glad he was driving and didn't have to look her in the eyes. "I've enjoyed being with you tonight. There's just something about you that makes me happy. You take such joy in the littlest things, and you don't get all freaked out by a little barbeque sauce on your chin or at having to meet my friends and acquaintances. The more time I spend with you, the more time I *want* to spend with you."

"I feel the same way. I feel comfortable around you, Walker. I don't feel as if I need to pretend to be someone I'm not. And you have no idea how amazing that is. I don't want to go home yet, but if it's going to stress you out to have me come over, then you can take me home."

"How about this," Trigger said. "We go to my place and watch one movie. It'll be after midnight by then, and I'll take you home and we'll figure out when to see each other again."

"Deal," Gillian said immediately. "But I get to pick the movie."

Trigger grinned. "Okay, but you should know I don't have any romantic comedies."

"I'm sure you've got something I'll like."

Trigger wanted to retort that he definitely had something she'd like, but he kept the comment to himself.

Relieved that he didn't have to say goodbye to her just yet, Trigger drove the rest of the way to his apartment with a huge grin on his face.

Two and a half hours later, Trigger lay on his couch with a comatose Gillian in his arms. She'd discarded her boots and had taken her hair out of its braids. It was extremely wavy and fell around her shoulders in disarray. Trigger had wanted to run his hands through it, but refrained.

Gillian had picked *Die Hard* for them to watch, a movie he'd seen countless times. They'd argued about whether it was a Christmas movie or not and within twenty minutes of the first shot being fired on screen, Gillian was sound asleep.

She'd been sitting next to him on the couch and her neck had been leaning sideways at an awkward angle, and Trigger knew it couldn't be comfortable. So he'd pulled her into him and shifted so his head was resting on the armrest, and she was snuggled between him and the back of the couch.

She'd wiggled a bit, then settled. Her cheek was resting on his chest over his heart, an arm and leg slung over his body. She was holding him as tightly as he was holding her.

Trigger was tired—it had been a long day filled with the anticipation of seeing her again—but he couldn't sleep. He'd turned off the DVD and the only sounds in the apartment were Gillian's deep breaths and the occasional shout or car engine revving from outside.

He knew he should wake her up and get her home, but Trigger couldn't bring himself to move. Holding Gillian felt right. It soothed him in a way he'd never experienced before. He wasn't aroused, didn't feel the need to fuck. He was content to simply hold her while she slept.

Shifting so he could put a hand on the back of Gillian's head, Trigger inhaled deeply. The scent of honeysuckle surrounded him as if he were standing in a field of flowers. He'd never be able to smell it again and not think of this moment.

Deciding he'd just close his eyes for a second, then he'd get them both up so he could take her home, Trigger relaxed into the cushions even farther.

He fell into a sleep so deep, so content and comfortable with the woman in his arms, he wouldn't wake up until the sun was breaking over the horizon.

Chapter Nine

GILLIAN WOKE FEELING MORE RESTED THAN SHE HAD IN WHAT SEEMED LIKE AGES. She hadn't had any bad dreams, that she could remember, and actually felt pretty good.

Shifting, she realized immediately that she wasn't alone. Her eyes popped open and she saw she was still on Walker's couch. Was, in fact, sleeping in his arms. Her back was to the cushions and her front was plastered against Walker's side.

When she lifted her head, she found herself staring into Walker's gray eyes. He had a five o'clock shadow, which reminded her of how he'd looked in Venezuela. Except now his guard was down and he seemed somewhat vulnerable.

"Morning," he said softly.

"I didn't mean to fall asleep on you," she said.

"And I didn't mean to fall asleep at all," he returned. "I meant to only close my eyes for a second, then wake you up and take you home."

Gillian gave him a small smile. "I'm glad you didn't. I slept better last night than I have for the last month."

He frowned. "You're not sleeping well?"

Realizing her mistake, Gillian tried to brush off the comment. "I just meant in general."

"No, don't do that. You're not sleeping well?" he repeated.

Gillian pressed her lips together and shook her head slightly.

"Nightmares?"

"Sometimes."

"Flashbacks?"

She nodded.

"You need the lights on?"

Gillian nodded again. "How'd you know?"

"I've been there, Gilly. PTSD isn't fun."

"Oh, this isn't that," she protested. "I'm just having a hard time acclimating back to life from before."

"Which is PTSD," Walker said firmly.

Then he moved so quickly, Gillian didn't have a chance to protest or to do anything except squeak. He was sitting upright and had her straddling his lap before she could think. His hands pushed into her hair on either side of her head and he held her firmly. She should've been concerned over how easily he maneuvered her. How he was holding her and not letting her go…but she wasn't.

"It's nothing to be ashamed of. What you went through was awful, Di. You're strong as hell, but even though I've nicknamed you after Wonder Woman, you *aren't* her. You need to talk to someone, I'll get you some names. It's fine if you need the light on; some of the strongest men I know have nightlights all over their houses. You do what you need to do to cope. Period."

"I didn't dream last night," she told him.

"What?"

"I didn't dream. And didn't even notice the lights weren't on. With you holding me, I think I knew I was safe."

"Fuck," Walker said softly, closing his eyes for a second before opening them again and staring at her with a fire she didn't want to pull away from. "I'm going to kiss you, Gillian," he warned.

"Okay," she whispered.

"But that's all. Just a kiss."

Gillian nodded and licked her lips in anticipation.

One of his hands moved up and over her hair, smoothing it down. Then his fingers went under her chin and tipped her head up gently.

Gillian felt her heart beating out of her chest. She gripped his arms and dug her fingernails into his skin. She wanted him to both hurry up and slow down at the same time. She wanted this moment to last forever, but she also wanted him to kiss her already.

She watched as he licked his own lips, then his head dropped ever so slowly.

Whimpering a little, she leaned forward and met him halfway.

At first the kiss was a bit tentative. Their lips touched once. Twice. Then he growled and the hand at her chin moved to grip the back of her neck. His fingers flexed and his mouth covered hers. He didn't tease, didn't lick her lips to ask for permission to enter.

He plundered.

And Gillian let him. Gladly.

She opened her mouth wider and felt his tongue swipe over hers.

How long they sat there kissing, she had no idea. All she knew was that she'd never felt as excited and treasured as she did in Walker's arms. He held her to him tightly. Pulling a bit on her hair when he wanted to move her head, but it didn't hurt. No, Walker Nelson's kisses didn't hurt in the least.

Gillian sucked on his tongue and felt more than heard the growl he let out. Not too long after that, he pulled back abruptly and forced her forehead to rest on his shoulder. Gillian could feel his chest rising and falling under her and felt some satisfaction that he was breathing as fast as she was.

"Holy hell," he muttered, and Gillian couldn't help it. She giggled.

With his hand still on the back of her neck, Walker pulled her upright. "You laughing at me, woman?"

She tried to stop, but couldn't. By the time she had herself under control and could look Walker in the eyes again, she was surprised to see the gentle way he was staring at her.

Self-conscious, she brought one of her hands to her mouth and wiped at it. "What? Is there something on my face?"

He pushed her hand out of the way tenderly and ran his thumb over her bottom lip. "Your lips are pink and swollen," he told her. "I like knowing that I made them that way."

Gillian licked Walker's thumb, and she saw his pupils dilate.

"No more of that. Or I'll think you're trying to seduce me. I'm not that kind of guy," he teased.

Aware of her position in his lap, how she was straddling him and could feel his erect cock against her, she wiggled and arched a brow. "You're not?"

Without warning, Walker stood, and Gillian was once more made aware of how strong he was and how easily he could move her body around. He put her on her feet, but pulled her into him. They were plastered together from hips to chest and they stood there for a long moment, staring at each other.

"Thank you for the best kiss I've ever had," he told her.

"Thank you," she returned.

"And thank you for not freaking when you woke up on my couch this morning. I swear

I had good intentions. I was going to take you home and give you that kiss on your doorstep, then leave like a gentleman."

"I liked sleeping in your arms better," she said honestly.

"You have plans for today?" he asked.

Gillian shook her head. "Not really. I need to do some work for a sweet sixteen birthday party I'm planning, but otherwise, Sundays are my lazy day."

"How about I make you some coffee? You can drink it while I shower. Then I'll take you home, you can change, and I'll take you out for breakfast. *Then* I'll leave you in peace to have your lazy day."

"That sounds good," Gillian told him. And it did. She wouldn't mind spending the day with him, but she also kinda felt as if she needed some space. She was falling head over heels for this man, fast, and it scared the hell out of her. Yes, she'd thought he was the one for her from the first time she'd heard his voice, but now that she was in the midst of getting to know him, she was freaking out a bit at how perfect he seemed.

Walker leaned forward and kissed her forehead gently. And somehow that kiss felt as intimate as the one they'd just shared.

"There's a half bath down the hall. There's a bunch of extra toiletries under the sink in there…my mom stocked me up the last time she was here. Apparently it doesn't matter that I'm almost forty, she still feels the need to take care of her son."

Gillian grinned. "And you love it."

"Of course I do. I don't think I've ever bought a toothbrush in my life. I use them until they fall apart then I'm damn glad my mommy had the foresight to make sure I had a replacement on hand."

Laughing, Gillian knew at that moment, she was a goner. One date, and one night sleeping in his arms, and hearing him make fun of himself and how he liked his mom fussing over him…and she was in love. Instead of being scary, it simply felt right.

As if he could tell something had changed, Walker ran the backs of his fingers down her cheek. "Go, Di. Before I do something stupid like throw you over my shoulder and drag you into my lair."

Knowing he was only half kidding, Gillian slowly backed away from him. His shirt was wrinkled and he needed to shave, but he was so beautiful, it almost made her heart hurt.

Finally, she turned and headed for the bathroom…making sure to roll her hips just a little more than usual, knowing he was watching her ass as she left.

"I'll call you later if that's okay?" Trigger said as he held Gillian in his arms outside her door. He couldn't remember a better morning. He'd showered while she'd gotten some caffeine in her system, then they'd laughed and joked all the way back to Georgetown. It had taken all he had not to burst into her bathroom when he'd heard her shower turn on.

All he could think about was how she'd look naked as water sluiced over her curvy body. Luckily, it had taken her about twenty minutes to get ready, and that had given him a chance to get his libido under control.

She'd directed him to a small diner near her apartment complex and he'd had the best omelet he'd eaten in ages. Now they were back at her apartment, and he was saying goodbye. He wasn't sure when they'd be able to get together again, but he hoped he could make that happen sooner rather than later.

"It's more than okay," she reassured him.

He looked down at her purse when he heard the sound of another text coming through.

She'd been getting texts all morning, and other than a quick reply to her friends to tell them she was alive and well, she'd been ignoring them.

"You're a popular person," he noted.

"I'm friendly," she said with a shrug. "And I know a lot of people. Both professionally and personally."

"Be careful," Trigger told her. "I don't want to lose you now that I've found you."

Her face gentled. "I will."

"I had a good time," he told her, prolonging their goodbye.

"Me too."

"Okay, before I get too sappy, I'm gonna go." Then he leaned forward, thrilled with how quickly Gillian went up on her tiptoes to meet his mouth. He kissed her, not as hard or as long as he wanted, but long enough for his toes to curl and his cock to harden.

"I'll talk to you soon."

"Okay. See you later."

"Bye, Di."

Trigger backed away, then turned and strode for the stairwell with a purpose. He needed to go before he forgot about his "going slow" edict.

Chapter Ten

GILLIAN SMILED AS SHE HUNG UP THE PHONE. SHE'D JUST FINISHED RESERVING the ballroom at a nearby hotel for a fiftieth anniversary party for a truly wonderful couple. Their daughter wanted to have a huge party for her parents, and Gillian was more than happy to help give the couple an over-the-top celebration.

The last month had been amazing. Even with the hijacking still fresh in her mind two months later, she'd never been happier.

Walker was better than she'd ever imagined a boyfriend could be. Of course she'd dated in the past, but she'd never felt as content with another man as she did with Walker. On the days they didn't see each other, he texted, emailed, and called. She'd communicated more with him in the last month than she did her last boyfriend in all the months they'd been so-called dating.

She knew Walker was very close to his parents, even though they lived up in Maine. They enjoyed their solitude and had no problem with the long, cold winters in the northeastern state they'd made their home. It was funny how different their parents were, since hers moved to Florida because they'd hated the cold. Barbara and Thomas Romano were also very social. They lived on a golf course, and every day her mom drove the golf cart for her dad while he played nine holes. Of course, she did so only so she could see and gossip with the other wives who drove their husbands around.

Gillian had spent every weekend with Walker. Ever since that first night when she'd fallen asleep on his couch, it had been an unspoken agreement that when he took her out, she'd stay overnight with him. He'd been nothing but a gentleman, going no further in their physical relationship than some very intense kisses. She'd wake up in his arms on his couch and couldn't remember ever sleeping better.

Last weekend, Ann, Wendy, and Clarissa had insisted they wanted to spend time with Walker, so, along with their significant others, they'd all gone out to eat. Gillian had been thrilled when Walker had fit in easily with Tom, Wyatt, and Johnathan. By the end of the night, the men had all exchanged numbers, and Walker had somehow gotten the others to all agree to keep their eye on her...just in case.

The seventh hijacker still hadn't been identified, and the next day, she was meeting with a Drug Enforcement Administration employee and someone from the FBI to discuss, in detail, what she could remember about each of the passengers she'd been stranded with.

Gillian wasn't looking forward to the meeting, but Walker had said he'd accompany her, which made her feel ten times better about the whole thing. A part of her felt weak, as if she was no longer the independent business owner she'd spent the majority of her adult life working to make people see her as...but another part didn't care.

She liked being with Walker. And meeting with the two agencies made her nervous as hell. She wasn't a troublemaker. Hadn't even gotten a speeding ticket before. Hell, the first time she'd received a parking ticket she'd nearly had a panic attack because it felt as if she'd broken a major law.

Gillian realized she'd been sitting in her apartment staring off into space as she thought about Walker when her phone vibrated in her hand. Looking down, she saw a text from Andrea.

Over the last few weeks, the other woman had slowly started messaging more frequently, and Gillian was relieved to see that she was starting to heal from her ordeal. Gillian knew she'd gotten off way easier than Andrea had. Luis had taken a liking to the other woman and had forced himself on her. It was hard enough for Gillian to come to terms with what had happened...she wasn't also trying to deal with the aftermath of sexual abuse on top of everything else.

Andrea: Hey. How'd your day go? Did you get the hotel nailed down for that party?
Gillian: Yeah. The Marriott turned out to be too expensive, but The Driskill worked out perfectly.
Andrea: Cool!
Gillian: Any chance you'd want to meet up soon for coffee or something?

Gillian really wanted to see Andrea in person. So far, every time she'd suggested meeting, the other woman had balked, saying she just wasn't ready. That things were still fresh in her mind and she was afraid seeing any of the other hostages would bring back too many unwelcome memories. While Gillian hated that the sight of her could make Andrea unhappy in any way, she totally understood.

Andrea: Soon.
Gillian: Good. I have a meeting with the DEA and FBI tomorrow. I'm not looking forward to it.
Andrea: Can't blame you. They would intimidate the hell out of me.
Gillian: Exactly!
Andrea: What do they want to know?
Gillian: I guess they're still trying to identify the seventh hijacker and they want me to go over everything I can remember about everyone.
Andrea: Jeez, they're not asking much, are they?
Gillian: Right? I keep telling them that I didn't spend much time with the men since they kept us separated, I can't imagine who the other hijacker is. Honestly, I'm trying to put it all behind me, but when the FBI asks you to meet with them it's kinda hard to say no.
Andrea: True. Anyway, glad you got that party worked out. When is it again?
Gillian: Less than two months away.
Andrea: Isn't it late in the game to be reserving the ballroom?
Gillian: lol. Yes! The daughter had a hard time deciding on a venue. She's just lucky The Driskill had a cancellation. If there hadn't been, the party might've had to be held at the Super 8 motel or something.
Andrea: I'm sure if that happened, you still would've made it awesome.
Gillian: Thanks.
Andrea: I'll give you a shout later about getting together.
Gillian: I'd like that. Take care and be kind to yourself, Andrea. What happened wasn't your fault, and you couldn't have done anything differently without putting yourself in great danger.
Andrea: I'll try. Later.
Gillian: Bye.

Gillian sighed and put down her phone. Everything she'd said to Andrea was the truth. She couldn't have done anything differently. If she'd fought Luis, and refused to do what he wanted, he would've killed her. He'd already proven he had no problem using and hurting people to get what he wanted.

She thought about Janet and her daughter. Luis had threatened to hurt the little girl over and over if Gillian didn't do what he wanted, and she knew without a doubt he would've followed through. He'd even let one of his friends use little Renee as a shield when they'd bolted for the Beechcraft airplane. Using women and kids to make their getaway was low. Really low. But Gillian wasn't surprised. They were drug-dealing terrorists, after all.

Trying to shake off her sudden bad mood, Gillian headed into the kitchen to find something to make for dinner. She wasn't really hungry anymore but knew she needed to eat, otherwise she'd feel sick tomorrow when she had to talk about the hell she'd been through two months ago.

She was staring blankly into her pantry trying to decide on what to make when the buzzer for the downstairs door sounded. Frowning because she wasn't expecting anyone, Gillian went over to the wall and pushed the intercom button to see who was there.

"Hello?"

"Hey, it's me."

Immediately, Gillian's mood shifted. "Walker! What are you doing here?"

He chuckled. "Let me up, and I'll tell you."

Gillian immediately pushed the button to unlock the door to the building. She ran a hand over her hair, wondering what the hell she looked like. Walker had made it very clear he liked her exactly how she was—with mussed hair in the morning, or all made up for one of their dates—but she still couldn't help wanting to look her best for him.

She'd never seen Walker look anything but completely put together. Even down in Venezuela. He was dirty and sweaty, but she'd still thought he looked intimidating and *hot* in his black soldier ensemble. Not only that, he had confidence and manliness oozing from every pore at all times.

Gillian had the door open and was waiting impatiently for him when she saw him exit the stairwell and head her way. He was holding a large bouquet of flowers, and inside, she melted a bit. Seeing such a tall, masculine man holding a delicate bunch of flowers made him even more heart-stoppingly gorgeous.

The smile on his face as he approached made her heart rate pick up, and she tipped her chin higher as he got near. The feel of his lips on hers made an electric shock shoot from her lips to her toes. As usual, however, he didn't deepen the kiss, but put his hand on her waist and encouraged her to step back inside her apartment.

When the door shut behind them and he'd locked it, she asked, "What are you doing here?"

"Can't I come visit my girl?"

"Of course," she told him with a smile. "But it's Wednesday."

"I can't come visit in the middle of the week?" he asked.

"You can, but you have work tomorrow. PT early. And it's not like you to just pop in on a random Wednesday."

The small smile that had been on his face disappeared and he put the flowers down on her kitchen counter. Then he leaned in and held her face in his hands.

Gillian loved it when he did that. She stared up at him as he spoke.

"Tomorrow's gonna be hard on you. There's no way I wasn't going to be here to support you through that. *You* don't need me here, but I *need* to be here."

Gillian couldn't remember a time when a man's words felt so good.

"And PT?" she asked.

"The guys know I won't be there."

"That's two," she told him.

"Two what?"

"Two times you've missed PT because of me."

His smile was tender. "And I'd miss a hundred more if you needed me."

"Walker," she sighed.

"Come 'ere," he said and pulled her into him.

Gillian went willingly. Without shoes, she was quite a bit shorter than him, and she could easily bury her nose in the crook of his neck and shoulder. She inhaled deeply, loving the way his woodsy scent made her feel safe and cared for.

They stood like that for several minutes before he pulled back. "Your appointment is at nine, right?"

She nodded against him.

"Austin traffic sucks, so we'll leave at seven-thirty and if we're early, we can stop and get some chocolate doughnuts for you."

Smiling, Gillian raised her head. "What'd I do to get so lucky to find you?"

Walker didn't answer, but his smile said it all for him. "How'd your call for the Howard anniversary shindig go today? You find a venue?"

"Yeah, The Driskill Hotel agreed to my terms. The party's less than two months away."

"That's good they agreed," he told her.

"Next weekend, I've got a corporate event I organized. It's a casual family thing the president is throwing to show his appreciation for his employees. He's rented out the Austin Zoo for four hours, and I have four food trucks parking nearby where everyone can get lunch and drinks for free…do you want to come with me?"

"You want me to?"

"Well…yeah. I wouldn't have asked if I didn't."

"I won't get in your way?"

Gillian chuckled. "Well, if you insist on following me so closely I bump into you every time I turn around, and if you don't let me do my thing, making sure everything is set up and good to go, then yes you will. But I think I know you well enough to know that you'll stand back and watch me from a distance, so no, you won't get in my way."

He smiled. "Then I'd love to come and watch you work."

"Have you been to the zoo before?"

"Di, do I look like a man who spends his time at zoos?"

"No."

"Right."

"So you haven't been before?"

He grinned. "No, Gilly, I haven't been to the zoo before."

"You'll like it."

"No offense, but I don't normally like zoos. Or circuses. I don't like seeing animals penned up for the amusement of humans. But that aside, I can't fucking wait to go to the zoo next weekend, for the simple fact it means that I'll get to hang out with you and see you kick ass at your job. I can't wait to see that. And after you're done corralling food trucks and making sure every man, woman, and child has had an amazing time, I get to stroll around with you, hand in hand, and feel proud and honored that you've chosen *me*, not any of the other men chomping at the bit to have their shot with you."

Gillian rolled her eyes. "No one's 'chomping at the bit' to go out with me, Walker. You seem to have a warped idea of my appeal."

Walker leaned in. One arm went around her waist, pulling her against him, and the other snaked behind her head and gripped her nape. "No, I don't. You're just clueless. You don't see the way the stock boys check out your ass in the grocery store. You ignore the guys who live in this apartment complex who practically drool as you walk by, and you've taken no notice of the scores of soldiers on base who can't keep their eyes off you. I don't give a shit if they look, but as long as you're with me, I'll make sure they know you're off limits."

"Walker," Gillian whispered, overcome with feelings she had no idea how to process. She still thought he was seeing things that just weren't there. She wasn't popular in high school. She didn't get asked out a lot in college. And since she'd graduated, she'd struggled to find men she was attracted to. But the fact that Walker thought she was the kind of woman men couldn't help but stare at felt pretty damn good.

He leaned his forehead against hers as he held her to him, and Gillian lifted his shirt slightly and put her hands on the bare skin of his waist. She felt him shudder, but he didn't move for several minutes.

She knew the second he was going to pull back, and for just a moment, she resisted. She'd been all right with him wanting to take things slow. She'd encouraged it, in fact. But the more time Gillian spent with Walker, the more she wanted him to go a little faster.

She wanted his hands on her. Wanted to know what all the intensity she felt in his gaze and his brief kisses felt like when he let himself go.

She knew he'd be a bit rough and overwhelming, but she *wanted* that. She wanted to get lost in passion for once in her life. Every other time she'd been with a man, she couldn't stop thinking about where she should put her hands. Or if the sounds she was making were weird or not. But Gillian had a feeling when Walker finally lost his restraint, she wouldn't be thinking about anything other than how he was making her feel.

Letting go of her neck and waist, Walker did indeed step back. "You had dinner yet?"

Gillian shook her head.

"What are you hungry for?"

"I don't know. I'm not really all that hungry, to tell you the truth."

"You need to eat," he said.

"I know."

"How about we order something from Uber Eats?"

"Let me get this straight, it's okay to use Uber to deliver dinner, but not for a ride, right?"

"Right," he said with a grin.

"But they could spit in my food. Or contaminate it with rat poison. Or put a roofie in it or something."

She could see Walker digesting her words. Then he said, "You're right. If you want something, we'll call to order it directly and I'll go pick it up."

"I was kidding."

"No, you're exactly right."

"I don't want to order anything," Gillian told him, more because she didn't really want him to leave now that he was there, even if it was just for twenty or thirty minutes to go pick up dinner. "I'm sure I've got something we can make here. There's some chicken in the fridge that I probably need to cook. We can bake it, if that's okay."

"Sounds perfect. I'll help," Walker said.

It took only about fifteen minutes to heat up the oven and prepare the chicken. They watched a cooking show on TV until the chicken was done, then they sat at the table and ate together.

Gillian had lived by herself for almost a decade, and she'd gotten used to eating alone, watching her favorites on the television, and pretty much doing whatever she wanted. But she'd been lonely. Seeing Walker on the weekends had spoiled her. She thought about him all week long and counted down the days until she could see him again.

Yes, she was busy with her work, but that didn't mean she didn't enjoy talking to him and spending time with him. Having him show up on a Wednesday was a surprise. A happy one. And Gillian could feel how much more content she was just having him near.

"You…you're staying the night, right?" she asked after they'd eaten and had gotten the dishes put away.

"I'd planned on it…unless you don't want me to," he told her.

"No! I do. But you don't have a bag or anything with you."

"It's in the car. I didn't want to presume."

Gillian decided to take a chance. She scooted over until her thigh was touching his and put her hand on his knee. "Walker, I don't think it's a secret that I like you. I live for the weekends. You're funny and sweet, and the more I get to know you, the more I enjoy spending time with you. I can't wait to officially meet your friends, and I hope like hell they like me. I know *my* friends have wholeheartedly approved of you, and I'd like to think we're moving forward with our relationship. It's not presumptuous of you to think that you'll be spending the night. I'd probably be offended, or at least really confused, if you didn't. Hell, we don't even talk about me staying over at your place on the weekends anymore. Is *that* presumptuous? Should I feel bad about not even thinking twice about bringing an overnight bag when you pick me up on Fridays?"

"No," he growled, as he leaned over Gillian so abruptly, she fell onto her back on the couch. He braced himself on his hands as he hovered over her. "My friends are going to love you. In fact, this weekend we're going to an event on base with them. It's an event for kids, and one of our friends' little girls is competing. Everyone'll be there, and we'll cheer her on and you can get to know the guys.

"I'm trying really hard not to overwhelm you, Gillian, but it's hard. I think the only thing that's kept me from moving too fast is the fact that you live forty miles away. I'm not a texting kind of guy. Or someone who likes to talk on the phone much, but with you, I find that I can't wait to share the shit that amuses me during the day. I've had to call my cell phone company and get the unlimited texting package for the first time in my life, just so I didn't spend eight hundred dollars on overage fees. It somehow feels different for you to stay with me…as if it's just a given. But I would never want to overstay my welcome or do something that makes you uncomfortable…like invite myself to stay without your permission."

"Permission granted," Gillian told him, running her hands up under his T-shirt to his chest. He couldn't grab her hands and stop her since he was using his arms to hold himself up.

She felt his nipples harden immediately at her touch, but before she could even enjoy the fact that she could turn him on, he was standing next to the couch.

"I'll go get my bag. Lock the door behind me."

Then before Gillian could say anything, he was gone.

There was no doubt Walker was intense and all man. But he was holding back a lot, and it was beginning to concern her.

Taking a deep breath, she tried to get a grip on her out-of-control hormones. She was wet between the legs, as she was most of the time when Walker went all alpha male on her. As much as she wanted his hands on her, she had a feeling if she could just wait until *he* was ready, he'd make it more than worth her while.

Chapter Eleven

A S MUCH AS TRIGGER HAD ENJOYED WAKING UP WITH GILLIAN IN HIS ARMS— she'd refused to go to her bed, opting to stay with him on the couch the night before—he knew they had shit they needed to get done. He had to get her up, get some coffee in her, and get her to the courthouse downtown to meet with the DEA and FBI.

They'd talked about it a little last night, and he knew Gillian still had no idea in her own mind who the seventh hijacker might be. She was leaning toward it being Leyton, but his actions could be explained away by shock over what was happening. She was nervous about the interrogation she was sure she was going to be put through, even though Trigger had tried to tell her it was just a meeting, not an interrogation.

He wouldn't be allowed in the room, even with his level of security clearance; this wasn't his investigation. It was frustrating, but he hadn't expected anything different. The only thing he could do was try to take as much of the stress off Gillian as possible.

She was quiet that morning, and it wasn't normal. He'd spent enough mornings with her now to know that she was naturally chatty and didn't shy away from talking about whatever came to mind after they woke up. But this morning, she wasn't her usual lively self.

Hating that she was worrying about the meeting, but not able to do much about it, Trigger simply held her hand as he drove them into downtown Austin. Traffic sucked, as usual, but because they'd left plenty early, neither of them were stressing about it.

After he'd parked in a garage near the courthouse, he turned to Gillian. "You holding up okay?"

She took a deep breath. "Yeah. I just...I keep trying to figure out who could've been in on it. And it seems impossible that *anyone* could've been in cahoots with those killers. Everyone I saw was crying or acting like zombies because of shock over what was happening. Even the men. Okay, they weren't crying, but it was obvious they weren't happy. They were the ones who had to throw the first-class passengers' bodies out the hatch when we first landed in Venezuela, and it was just awful. It's hard to believe that anyone was that good of an actor. Maybe Brain and the other officials translated the conversation between the other hijackers wrong? Maybe there isn't someone else involved?"

Trigger wanted to agree with her, but he couldn't. He shook his head sadly. "There was no mistaking what they said, Gilly."

"I hate this," she whispered.

Without a word, Trigger let go of her hand and climbed out of his car. He quickly walked around to her door, opened it, and, instead of helping her out, he wrapped his arms around her and pulled her close. She melted into his chest, holding on to him with more desperation than he'd felt in her since he'd first taken her in his arms on the tarmac in Venezuela.

"It's gonna be okay," he murmured.

"I know," she replied.

Trigger gave her another few moments, then pulled back and put his hands on her shoulders. "Your job is not to figure out who the bad guy is here. All you need to do is tell the investigators everything you can remember. Don't analyze anyone's actions. They'll take your information and compare it to the data they've dug up from the other hostage interviews, and hopefully come to a conclusion. It is *not* your responsibility to tell them who you think the seventh hijacker is. They're the experts, not you. Understand?"

Gillian took a deep breath, then nodded. "Thank you. I needed to hear that."

Trigger leaned forward and kissed her gently, then said, "Good. Ready?"

"Ready," she said in a stronger voice.

He couldn't *not* be proud of her. She hopped out of his Blazer and he locked it as they walked hand in hand out of the garage toward the courthouse.

Gillian sat in the chair the DEA investigator gestured to and wiped her sweaty palms on her khaki slacks. She tried not to live her life being intimidated by anyone; she'd met with CEOs, presidents, managers of some of the best-ranked hotels in the world, and politicians without blinking.

But for some reason, sitting down with FBI Special Agent Tucker and Calum Branch, the DEA investigator, was freaking her out.

"Thank you for coming to meet with us today," Gary Tucker said. He was a middle-aged man with a receding hairline and a slight paunch. He was dressed in what she thought a typical FBI agent would wear…black slacks, dark shirt, and a blue tie that didn't match his pants.

"Yes. We're both very glad that you're alive and well," Calum added. He was a bit younger than Gary, and had on a pair of jeans, cowboy boots, and a button-down gray long-sleeve shirt. He even had a cowboy hat sitting on the table next to him. But instead of looking like a Texas cowboy, he looked like a tourist who was trying too hard to emulate a native rancher.

"That makes three of us," Gillian said nervously. She wished Walker was with her, but she understood why he couldn't be. He was sitting right outside the small conference room, looking way too big for the uncomfortable little office chair he'd parked himself in. He'd promised that he wouldn't budge and he'd be right there when she was done, no matter how long the interview took.

"If it's all right with you, I think we should just get right to it," Gary said. "How about you tell us what happened from the moment you realized something was wrong until you were rescued."

Gillian wanted to laugh. They weren't messing around. She took a deep breath and told them everything she could remember. How scared she'd been when she realized what was happening and that the hijackers had actually killed some of the passengers. How terrified she'd been when Luis told her she was going to be the one to talk to the negotiator. She even told the two men how much she'd hated the first negotiator, how he hadn't listened and that she thought it was *his* fault another passenger had been killed.

She praised Walker and said he'd done an amazing job of keeping her calm, decoding her lame clues, and making sure they'd received food and water. He also hadn't gotten anyone else murdered, which was a huge plus in Gillian's mind.

She thought she'd been matter-of-fact in her retelling of what she'd felt, but obviously the men had caught on to her feelings for Walker.

"Did you and Mr. Nelson have a relationship before the hijacking?" Calum asked.

Appalled, Gillian shook her head. "No! I hadn't ever met him before. We don't exactly run in the same circles."

"What do you mean by that?" Gary asked.

"Just what I said. He's in the Army. He lives forty miles away from me. I'm busy with my life and job, just as he is. He was in Venezuela doing his job and I was there…well, being held captive."

"But you and he are dating now," Gary insisted.

"Yes," Gillian said firmly. She wasn't going to be ashamed of Walker.

"Don't you think that's odd?" Calum probed.

She frowned. "What's odd?"

"That the two of you just happen to live near each other and he's the one who was sent to free the hostages from that plane?"

Gillian stared at the DEA agent in disbelief. "Are you insinuating that I somehow arranged for us to meet? That we planned this?"

"Well, no," Calum backpedaled a bit. "But you have to admit it's a bit too coincidental."

"No, I don't," she fired back. "No more coincidental for anyone else on that plane who was headed to Texas. Most of them live here, like I do. And I can't believe you're sitting there accusing me of…what *are* you accusing me of?"

Calum held up his hands in a conciliatory gesture, but Gillian could tell it was a bit condescending. "I'm not accusing you of anything. I'm just thinking out loud."

"Then maybe you can stop, because it's annoying me."

She thought she heard Gary chuckle, but he deftly covered it up with a cough. "We're just doing our jobs, ma'am," he told her. "I know this is hard, but put yourself in our seats. We can't dismiss anything that might lead us to the seventh hijacker. Do you want this person to continue to be free? To possibly participate in other terrorist activities that might result in the deaths of more people next time?"

"Of course not," Gillian said, "but—"

"Right, so we have to ask some uncomfortable questions sometimes," Gary went on deftly. "Not that we think *you're* the unknown hijacker…but you could be. I mean, it would be pretty smart of Luis to put someone he's in cahoots with on the phone to talk with the negotiators."

Gillian could only stare at the other man in astonishment. "I'm not a terrorist," she insisted.

"Isn't that what the seventh hijacker would say?" Gary asked reasonably.

A headache was beginning to form behind her eyes.

"For the record, we don't think you're who we're looking for," Gary said, obviously expecting her to blow off the fact that he'd pretty much accused her of partnering with murderers. "But you can understand where we're coming from, I'm sure."

"We need to go over the passenger manifest person by person. We'd like for you to tell us everything you can remember about each person. What they were wearing, any conversation you might've had with them, and your personal thoughts about them. The smallest thing you recall could be the difference between catching this person and them going free. Understand?"

Yeah, Gillian understood. She understood that this was going to be a hell of a long day. Much longer than she'd anticipated. She had a quick thought about Walker sitting outside the door in that tiny, uncomfortable chair, and she felt bad. Then she had no time to think about anything other than her fellow hostages.

Gary and Calum started off by showing her pictures of the first-class passengers. They wanted to know what she remembered about them during the first part of the flight. Did they ask for a lot of drinks? Did they get up to use the restroom?

Gillian tried to tell the investigators that she hadn't paid any attention to anyone beyond her row, but they kept pressing. They wanted to know about the flight attendants; did any of them look suspicious, had she noticed anything odd with them, were they extra friendly with any of the passengers?

The questions went on and on, and for the most part, Gillian's answers were "I don't know" or "not that I noticed."

Then the interview got harder.

They showed her picture after picture of her fellow coach passengers, and wanted to know her thoughts on each person. They wanted her to talk about their personalities, how they dealt with captivity, and anything she could remember them saying. In detail.

"How about Janet Cagle?" Gary asked, showing Gillian a picture of the young mother.

"She was scared out of her mind," Gillian told them. "The hijackers kept threatening her and her daughter, Renee. Most of the time they sat on the floor between the seats and tried to be invisible."

"Which one of the hijackers used the girl as a shield when they were trying to escape to the Beechcraft?" Calum asked.

"I'm not sure…Isaac? Carlos? In the chaos, I wasn't paying attention. They were forcing pairs of men and women out onto the slide and until Alberto grabbed me, I didn't realize what they were doing."

"What *were* they doing?" Gary asked.

Gillian sighed. She had a feeling he knew the answer to his own question, but wanted to hear what she was going to say. "They were trying to create uncertainty for our rescuers. With one woman and one man paired up, and everyone running toward the smaller plane, it would be hard at first glance to know who was a hijacker and who was a hostage."

Both men nodded. "What about Maria Gomez?" Gary put another picture in front of her.

And so it went. The pictures kept coming, one after another. Camile Millan, Rebecca Crawford, Reed Stonegate, Charles Wayman. Their faces swam as Gillian did her best to recall every little detail about each person. It was hard because most of the men she'd just seen at a distance and hadn't had any real contact with. But of course, Gary and Calum weren't satisfied with that. They pressed for more.

"Leyton Morales," Gary said, putting another picture in front of her.

Taking a sip of water, Gillian stalled a bit. She didn't want to say anything bad about anyone. Didn't want to finger anyone as the hijacker if they weren't. She'd feel terrible if they were unfairly accused. "He…um…I thought he was a bit weird," she said at last.

"Weird how?" Calum asked.

"Just…weird. He stared at the women intently. He also paid a lot of attention to the hijackers. Maybe he was in shock though. I know I was having a hard time processing everything that was happening. He didn't *seem* to be quite as scared as the rest of us. I mean, I don't know him at all, so maybe he had a horrible life and being held at gunpoint and threatened wasn't a big deal for him, and that's why he wasn't as scared." Gillian knew she was talking really fast and making excuses for Leyton, but she couldn't help it.

"Give us an example," Gary ordered.

Sighing, Gillian nodded. "When the hijackers inflated the slide and started pushing people out, he kinda just stood there watching. When Alberto grabbed me, Leyton told him that *he'd* go out the slide with me. But, to be fair, Wade also volunteered to go with me. I think they were both trying to get me away from Alberto, which was really brave of them. Alberto refused, and then Leyton actually reached out and grabbed my free arm. He and Alberto kinda had a tug-of-war with me for a second. Eventually, Alberto shoved him away from me with a hand to his chest, but Leyton didn't back off very far. He just kept staring at us. Then I noticed, when I was struggling and trying not to be pushed inside the smaller plane, that Leyton was once again standing nearby, just watching. Or maybe he was staring off into space."

"Did you see Wade?" Gary asked.

"No."

"Hmmm," Gary said.

He didn't say anything more than that. Just *Hmmm*. It was maddening.

"How about Andrea Vilmer? We understand she had a hard time of it on the plane."

That was the understatement of the century. Gillian nodded.

"What can you tell us about that?"

"What do you want to know?"

"Everything you can remember," Gary said without any emotion.

Her frustration piqued again. "You want to know about her expression of revulsion when Luis licked her neck obscenely? How scared she was when he decided to assault her? How she whimpered in fright when he dragged her down the aisle of the plane? Maybe you want to know how long it took for him to get off as he forced her to suck his dick right there in the exit row? What *exactly* do you want to know?"

She was breathing fast when she was done, but she took a deep breath and continued in a more even tone. "I don't know why Luis decided to single her out. Probably just because she's pretty. I'm ashamed to admit that at the time, I was just relieved it wasn't me…but that didn't mean I wasn't horrified on her behalf. There was nothing anyone could do, and we knew it. If we tried to interfere, he would've killed us without blinking. He was that cold-hearted. I think Luis was the first one to say he was taking her with him, and that's probably why Alberto tried to drag me onto that plane too."

"You've been in touch with Andrea," Gary said. It wasn't a question.

"Yeah. Texts. She's not dealing very well with what happened. She's been in therapy but I'm not sure it's helping yet."

"You've talked to others too, right?" Calum asked.

Gillian nodded again. "Yes, a bunch of us exchange texts and emails regularly. We feel as if we've bonded. We've been through hell and somehow survived."

"How often do you talk to them?"

Gillian shrugged. "I don't know. I talk with some more than others. I text Andrea pretty regularly. And Janet sends me texts and pictures of Renee. We've talked about how best to deal with the angry feelings that we all still seem to have. About how unfair it was that it happened to *us*."

"What about Alice Hicks and her husband Wade?" Calum asked. "You were seated next to them before the plane was taken over. Right?"

"Yes."

"Do you talk to them?"

"I've gotten an email or two. The situation was really hard on Alice. She and Wade are newlyweds. They were asleep when it all started and they were separated. Alice seems to be the kind of woman who doesn't do well at all in stressful situations. She cried a lot, and I saw Wade doing his best to make eye contact with her throughout the entire ordeal."

"What about Muhammad Nassar? He's Muslim. Did you see him have any one-on-one contact with the hijackers?"

"No," Gillian told them. "As I've said over and over, I didn't have much contact with the men at all. I didn't even see most of them. I couldn't tell you what Muhammad did, although I don't think it's fair to think he might be the seventh hijacker simply because of his religious beliefs."

"We weren't accusing him of anything," Calum said smoothly. "We're just trying to find out as much information about everyone as possible."

And so the questioning continued. Alejandro Chavez, Mateo Herrera …they went through every single person, including the passengers from Canada, Japan, Colombia, Panama, India, Nicaragua…

By the time they were done, Gillian could hardly function.

She felt as if she'd taken the world's hardest test…and failed. She didn't think she'd given them anything useful. If she had any suspicions about who the wolf in sheep's clothing might be, she would've told someone before now. The entire interview just seemed so pointless. Did they really care who had stomach problems because of lack of food and water, and who didn't?

"If you think of anything else you didn't tell us today, please contact us as soon as possible," Gary told her. "Anything, no matter how small, could be the difference in taking one more terrorist off the street or letting them continue to ruin lives in the future."

Well, gee, no pressure, Gillian thought. She nodded.

"And you need to be extremely cautious," Calum added. "You were handpicked by Luis to be their voice for some reason. It could be the seventh hijacker was really the one calling the shots, and *he* chose you. Until this person is behind bars, your life could be in danger."

Gillian shivered. Wasn't *that* a fun thought? "Do you really think whoever it is will come after me?"

"That's the thing, we just don't know," Gary told her. "But killing you could be a way to get back at the fact that six of his friends didn't survive their mission."

"They had to know there was a pretty big chance they weren't going to live," Gillian insisted.

Both investigators shrugged.

Great. Just great. "Can I go?" she asked, hating how weak her voice sounded.

Gary and Calum stood, their chairs making obnoxious and ear-splitting screeches as they moved back.

Moving stiffly, Gillian nodded at them, not bothering to shake their hands, and made her way to the door. She knew the men were just doing their jobs, but she needed out of that room.

The second she opened the door, Walker was there. He stood in front of her saying something, but she didn't hear it. She walked to him, then leaned her head against his chest. His arms went around her and held her close.

Gillian didn't even have the energy to put her arms around him in return. She just stood in his embrace with her arms hanging limply by her sides and closed her eyes.

Walker had her. He'd make sure she got home. She didn't have to think about anything but how good he smelled and how thankful she was that he was there.

Trigger wanted to know what the fuck happened behind that closed conference room door more than he wanted his next breath. His woman was fucking exhausted and almost catatonic. He should've tried harder to be allowed in there with her. He would've made sure the two investigators didn't push her too hard.

"What'd you do?" he growled as Gary and Calum exited the room.

They both looked surprised at the venom in his tone. They looked from him to Gillian then back.

"She did good," Gary said quietly. "Much better than we'd expected."

"We might've gone on a little longer than we did with the others, but she had a lot of really useful information," Calum told him.

Again, Trigger mentally kicked himself for not at least forcing them to take a break. Gillian had been in with them for over five hours. She'd missed lunch and had obviously been pushed too far.

Wanting to lambast the investigators, but knowing that would delay getting Gillian home, he turned his back on the two men and leaned down to the exhausted woman in his arms. She was strong as fuck, but even superheroes had their breaking points.

"Ready to go home?" he asked gently.

She nodded against his chest.

"You want me to carry you?"

She shook her head but didn't move.

Trigger couldn't help but smile. He didn't rush her, simply waited for her to gather enough strength to walk out of the building by his side. Within a minute, he felt her take a big breath and pull away from him.

He didn't let her go far, keeping his arm around her waist. She leaned heavily on him and he felt her finger hook into one of the belt loops of his jeans. He wanted to ask her what happened, what was said, but knew that was the last thing she needed. Right now she needed food, and to feel safe.

Gillian didn't need his protection because she was weak. She was far from it. But he needed to give it to her because she was important to him. Over the last month, he'd found himself thinking about her almost every minute of the day. She'd quickly become one of the most important people in his life. And he'd be damned if he did anything to harm her in any way.

He got her to his Blazer and helped her get buckled in. She closed her eyes and rested her head on the back of the seat, exhaustion easy to read in her body language. Before starting the car, Trigger took the time to order food for them from a diner near her apartment. He stopped to pick it up before heading to her place. She didn't even ask what he'd ordered or what he was doing, she was that tired.

The second they entered her apartment, she turned to him. "I'm going to go lie down… is that all right?"

He hated seeing her like this. "You don't have to ask my permission to lie down in your own apartment, Gilly. Go on. I'll be in soon with some lunch."

"I'm not hungry."

"I know, but you need to eat."

For a second, she looked like she was going to argue with him, but in the end, she just nodded and headed down the hall. He hated how her shoulders were slumped and she looked as if she'd just gone ten rounds in a boxing ring.

He gave her twenty minutes—the longest twenty minutes of his life—before following her. He had a bowl of her favorite chicken fajita soup and two of the breadsticks she always raved about. They were soft and buttery, and would give her a needed boost of energy.

She was lying on her side on her bed with her back to the door. Trigger put the food down and sat on the edge of the mattress. He put one hand on her thigh and waited for her to acknowledge him. He knew she was awake because she'd stiffened when he'd sat down so she wouldn't roll into him.

With the patience he'd learned in his Delta training, Trigger waited. Finally, she rolled over and stared up at him.

"You all right?" he asked softly.

She nodded. "Yeah. I just…it was a lot."

"I'm sorry, Di. I should've been there with you."

"You weren't allowed. It's okay."

Trigger shook his head. "It's not okay. If I was there, I could've made them let you take some breaks. Warned them when they were pushing too hard—and don't deny it. They pushed you *hard*."

She gave him a small nod. "But they needed to. If they're going to catch this guy, they need to know—"

"Uh-uh," he said with a shake of his head. "If they're going to catch this guy, then they need to investigate…not push innocent women past their breaking points for information that won't make a lick of difference."

Gillian stared up at him. "So you're saying you think what I told them was pointless?"

"No, not at all," Trigger said firmly. "I know your interview gave them a more well-rounded idea of each and every passenger. You're observant and smart; whatever you told them was absolutely useful. But there was no point in pushing you until you were practically comatose to get it. I'm sure they already have their suspicions about who the seventh hijacker is. They were just using interrogation tricks to see what they could get out of you."

Gillian closed her eyes. "I wish you were there too," she said. Her eyes opened. "But it's done."

"If you want to talk about it, I'm here," Trigger told her.

"Thanks," she whispered. "I mean, I've already told you most of what I told them. I just don't like thinking that someone I thought I'd shared this awful experience with might be in on the whole thing. It makes me sick."

"Come on. Sit up and eat something. It'll make you feel better. Then we can watch TV together the rest of the afternoon. I'll run you a bath tonight and by morning, you'll feel like yourself again."

Gillian smiled at him and scooted up until her back was against the headboard. While she started in on her lunch, Trigger went back out to the other room to get her the present he'd found for her that week.

He held the small box in his hand as he sat back down.

"What's that?"

"Open it and see," he said. "I saw it and thought of you."

Trigger loved seeing the spark of life in her eyes. He hated seeing her so beaten down, and if a little gift was enough to make her smile, he'd make it his goal in life to buy her a million tchotchkes to make that smile permanent.

She opened the box and pulled out the mug that was inside. Grinning, she said, "I like it."

"Told you it reminded me of you," Trigger said. The blue mug had pictures of a cartoon Wonder Woman all over it. She was leaping, running, using her bracelets to deflect bullets, and generally being kick-ass.

"I'm not feeling very Wonder-Woman-like at the moment," she admitted.

"You'll get there," Trigger said without hesitation. "You're human. You're allowed to feel how you feel. You're still one of the strongest people I know."

"Thanks."

"You're welcome. Now, hurry up and finish so we can go out and watch *Luther*."

"You're addicted to that show," she said while chuckling.

"And you aren't?" he asked.

She merely grinned.

Hours later, Gillian already felt more like herself. Lunch had done wonders to elevate her mood, then sitting on the couch being lazy with Walker for the rest of the day had finished the job. Yeah, she'd had a hard morning, mentally, but it was over and done with, and she needed to pull her head out of her ass and get on with her life.

It was Thursday, and Walker was spending the night, and Gillian was determined to have him sleep in the bed with her. In all the nights they'd slept together—*slept*-slept, nothing more—they'd always done it on a couch, his or hers. He'd never moved them to a bedroom. And while Gillian loved waking up in his arms, she wanted to do so in her bed.

After they'd made spaghetti for dinner, laughing throughout the preparation, and before watching more episodes of *Luther*, she'd changed into her sleep shorts and top. It was the first time she'd actually put on a pair of pajamas before snuggling with Walker on the couch. Oh, she'd worn leggings, and a T-shirt without a bra, but this was different. The sleep shorts were *short*, and the top was sleeveless. She felt sexy in the outfit and wanted nothing more than to entice Walker into giving her a few kisses and hold her all night.

He looked like he'd swallowed something sour when she'd come back into the living area after changing, which wasn't exactly encouraging. And when he hadn't immediately pulled her into his side after she sat down, Gillian began to worry that she'd messed up somehow. After he'd been so attentive and concerned about her earlier, she'd thought for sure this was the perfect time to move their relationship forward.

But now Walker sat stiffly on the other end of the couch watching the television screen as if it was the most fascinating thing in the world. It was disheartening.

Wanting to be the brave, kick-ass woman he'd nicknamed her after, Gillian decided to go for what she wanted.

"Walker?"

"Hmmm?" he asked, not looking at her.

"Are you all right?"

"Yeah, why?"

At least he'd turned to look at her. "Because ever since I changed, you've been avoiding looking at me as if you'll get the plague if you even glance over here."

He sighed. "It's not you."

Oh, shit, she didn't like the sound of that. "What do you mean?"

"You've had a hard day...maybe you should turn in early."

Gillian could only stare at Walker in disbelief. Had he really said that?

Yeah, he had.

So much for her feeling good about herself and confident in the relationship they'd been building.

She'd never felt so confused. Walker had pampered her and treated her as if she was the most precious thing in his life all day. And the second she'd changed into something a little more revealing—it wasn't as if she'd put on a sexy teddy or anything; she was wearing shorts and a tank top—he'd frozen solid and was desperately trying to pretend she wasn't even there.

Without another word—what was she going to say? Beg him to look at her? To tell her why he'd suddenly turned into the ice man?—Gillian got up off the couch and headed to her room. She pulled off her cute little sleep set and put on a pair of leggings and a long-sleeve shirt. She had the urge to completely cover up before she went to bed.

Climbing under the covers, she did her best not to cry...but it was no use. The tears fell from her eyes, and she tried to be quiet as she sobbed and wondered what the hell was wrong with her.

Trigger's fists clenched and it took everything he had to stay where he was. He could hear Gillian crying, and it tore at him. When she'd come out of her room wearing that sexy-as-hell sleep set, he'd immediately gotten hard.

He respected Gillian more than she'd ever know, and he'd been doing his best to take things slow. The only way he knew to do that was to keep his dick in his pants. Women didn't like being used for sex, and although that was far from what he'd be doing if he slept with her, he didn't want her to get the wrong idea.

He wanted Gillian. Permanently. But he didn't want to do anything that might make her think this was a short-term relationship. Seeing her silky skin on display and knowing the shorts would give him easy access to the part of her he was getting more and more desperate to touch, to taste, he'd had to distance himself.

He was weak. If he'd pulled her into his side, he wouldn't have been able to keep his hands off her. After the day she'd had, he wanted nothing more than to show her how proud he was. To worship her from the top of her head to the tips of her toes. But it still felt too early. They'd only been dating a month. He had no idea what the rules were for sex in today's world, but he respected Gillian too much to push her into a physical relationship before she was ready. She was vulnerable, and he'd be damned if he did anything to take advantage.

But now she was in her room crying. And *he'd* done that.

He'd fucked up. Instead of respecting her, she'd thought he was *rejecting* her.

Before he registered what he was doing, Trigger was on his feet and headed for her bedroom. It was obvious she was trying to be quiet, but he could still hear her sobs through her closed door. Without knocking, he opened the door and entered.

The entire room smelled like honeysuckle, making his dick once again rise. He ignored his body and walked over to where she was huddled under her covers on the bed. He cringed when he saw she was now wearing a long-sleeve shirt. Seeing the sexy pajamas lying on the floor by the bathroom, he knew she'd probably put on a pair of leggings as well.

He didn't hesitate to climb into her queen-size bed and snuggle up behind her. His arm wrapped around her waist, and he pushed his other arm under her head, so she was now using it as a pillow.

"Go away, Walker," she said quietly.

"Nope."

"I get it. You aren't ready for a relationship. It's fine. I just need some space from you right now."

"And you aren't getting it," Trigger said firmly. "I need you to listen to me."

"I can't," she said, shaking her head. "Don't you get it? You've already said enough tonight."

"When you walked out of this room earlier, it was all I could do not to pull you to the floor, strip you naked, and fuck you until neither of us could walk."

The words came out without thought. They were pure, naked emotion.

Gillian froze in his arms. She hadn't pushed him away in disgust, so Trigger kept going.

"We've only been dating a month. I don't want to rush you into a physical relationship with me. I'm trying to be a gentleman. You had a hard day, and I didn't want to take advantage of that. I knew if I touched you while you were wearing that shorty sleep thing, I wouldn't be able to stop with a little cuddling."

"What if I don't want you to stop?" she asked.

Knowing there was no way she could miss the erection against her ass, since her back was plastered against his front, Trigger didn't even bother trying to hide it from her. "I need to wait," he said simply. "I can't tell you exactly why. I just feel the need to treat you with respect, like the amazing woman you are. To not rush into sex simply because I want you so bad. I want this relationship between us to last. Forever, hopefully…and a part of me feels as if I'm cheapening my feelings for you if I rush us into bed."

Trigger felt stupid voicing his thoughts out loud, but he wouldn't keep them to himself if his silence hurt her. He wanted no misunderstandings between them.

"Make no mistake, I want you, Gilly. But I want to do things right. The last thing I ever want you to think is that I'm using you in any way. I've got good control, but you make me feel as if I'm fifteen again and trying to hide my erection in Miss Noonbreaker's class."

He felt her chuckle against him and relax a fraction.

"I thought you didn't want me."

"I want you," he said immediately. "Don't ever doubt that."

"Will you stay the night with me? Here?"

Trigger winced. "I can't," he whispered.

Gillian turned in his embrace, and Trigger found himself staring into her puffy, red-rimmed eyes, and he wanted to kick himself all over again for hurting her.

"I trust you," she whispered.

"I appreciate that, more than you know, but I can't," he said, praying she'd take his word for it and let it go.

"Why?" she asked.

Closing his eyes, Trigger had known she'd want to know why. He opened his eyes and stared into hers. "Because you feel too good. Being in your bed is too close to what I want for the rest of my life. Everything in here smells like honeysuckle, and there's no way I'd get any sleep. I know I'm not making sense…I can hold you in my arms on the couch and sleep all night because a part of me knows we're not in a bed. The first time we make love, it's not going to be on a fucking sofa. So I can control myself. But if I fall asleep in a bed with you, I don't trust myself not to touch you. To take what my subconscious is screaming is mine."

She stared up at him for a long moment before nodding. "Okay."

"Okay?" Trigger asked. "Are you saying that because you think it's what I want to hear, or because you understand?"

"I get it. I want you too, Walker. I've thought you were mine from the get-go. At least I wanted you to be. I can wait until you're ready."

Trigger chuckled, but it wasn't a humorous sound. "How did I get to be the insecure one in our relationship?"

"I think it's cute. Frustrating, but cute," Gillian told him. Then she got serious. "I'm flattered that you want to respect me. I've never had a man treat me like you do. They were all about themselves and getting what they wanted."

"I'll always put you first, Gillian. Even when it goes against what I want. Understand?"

"I'm beginning to."

"Tell me you understand why I can't sleep in this bed with you. And mean it."

"I understand. Would it be okay if I came out to the living room and slept on the couch with you?"

Trigger stared down at her. He used his thumb to brush away the lingering wetness on her cheeks. "I hate that I made you cry."

Gillian shrugged. "I overreacted."

"No, you didn't. I was an ass and didn't explain myself. I'll try not to let it happen again but…I'm a guy, so it probably will. But in the future, don't let me get away with being all closemouthed and shit. Get in my face and force me to talk to you. Don't slink away and cry because I made you feel bad, okay?"

"I...I'll try."

"Okay. And yes, if you think you'll be comfortable, I'd love to have you sleep in my arms—on the couch."

"I'm comfortable anywhere you are," she reassured him.

Running his hand over her hair gently, he couldn't help but wonder how the hell he'd gotten so lucky. Going down to Venezuela should have been just another mission. Just another opportunity to take out some of the bad guys in the world. Instead, it had changed his life forever. It had brought him Gillian.

He pulled himself from her hold and helped her stand, guilt swamping him once again when he saw she was indeed wearing leggings. That she'd covered herself from head to toe in fabric. Wishing he was strong enough to tell her to put her shorts and tank top back on, Trigger pulled her out of the room toward the couch, and their bed for the night.

He sat and immediately pulled her into his embrace. He swung his feet up onto the soft leather and lay back with her in front of him. They were cramped, and the sofa wasn't overly comfortable, but it was what Trigger needed to keep himself under control. He felt bad that he was putting his own needs above Gillian's, but he didn't change his mind on their sleeping arrangements.

"I'm sorry you had a hard day," he said softly.

"You made it better in the end," she told him.

Trigger kissed the back of her head and inhaled her sweet scent, filling every cell of his body with her honeysuckle smell.

"Sleep well."

"I will now that you're here," she said sleepily.

Trigger stayed awake a long time, thankful that he hadn't fucked things up between them so badly she'd kicked him to the curb. Gillian was always so competent, so take-charge and confident, that he needed to be extra careful not to say or do anything that would take a chunk out of her armor. He loved her just the way she was.

Chapter Twelve

FRIDAY, GILLIAN HAD TO WORK, AND TO HER SURPRISE, WALKER WAS COMPLETELY all right with just hanging around her apartment. He did some work of his own on his laptop, but otherwise spoiled her rotten. He brought her coffee in her new Wonder Woman mug and made her an amazing breakfast of eggs and bacon with homemade biscuits to top it off. For lunch, he went out and grabbed them some sushi. After she'd called a few new clients and got some research done on the events they wanted her to plan, she and Walker had talked more about where he was taking her the next day.

Apparently, the daughter of one of his Army buddies was a tomboy and loved participating in the obstacle course events the base had for kids. She was twelve years old and, according to Walker, one of the cutest kids he'd ever met.

Gillian hadn't spent a lot of time around children, but was looking forward to meeting Annie and spending time with the guys on Walker's team. She'd met them, of course, in Venezuela, but hadn't spent any quality time with them. She was nervous, but looking forward to getting to know everyone.

For dinner, Walker grilled steaks on her cheap outdoor grill—complaining the entire time about how crappy it was, and how he was going to need to get her a new one since he'd be spending a lot of time at her place.

Gillian liked that thought.

That night, they once again fell asleep on her couch, but this time Gillian didn't overthink it. She wanted to move her relationship with Walker forward, but she wanted *him* to want that too. It felt a little weird to be the one pushing for more, but even that made Walker more attractive to her.

Saturday morning, they woke up early and, while Gillian showered, Walker once more got her coffee and breakfast ready.

"You're totally spoiling me," she mock complained when she emerged from her room dressed and ready to head to Fort Hood.

"Good," he said with a smile. "Just buttering you up so when I screw up, you'll find it easier to forgive me."

Gillian knew he was joking but frowned anyway. "Walker, I don't expect you to be perfect all the time. You're going to mess up, just as I am. I'd like to think that, while I might be irritated, I can put it behind me. I like you for who you are."

"Good," he said, pulling her into a hug. "Because I like you just the way you are too. And if you drive me crazy by leaving dirty clothes on the floor, I can look past that too."

She chuckled and playfully hit him in the arm. "I'm guessing that's your way of telling me you're a neat freak?"

He smiled. "Yup. The Army trained me well."

"As long as you don't leave beard trimmings in the sink, I'm okay with that."

He looked horrified. "I don't."

"Good. Can I use your razor in the shower?"

"Nope. I have to draw the line somewhere," he said with a smile. "I'll get you your own razors."

"Deal."

Gillian sighed in contentment. She was enjoying spending time with Walker. She knew next week he'd be back at work and she'd be busy with her own business, but she'd hate not being able to wake up with him and banter like they were right now.

"What's that look for?" he asked with a tilt of his head.

"I like this," she said.

"What?"

"This. Teasing. Chatting. Having you make my coffee and eating breakfast with you. I was just thinking about how I was going to miss it…you…next week, when we went back to our regular lives. Forty miles isn't that far, but when I wake up alone on Monday morning, I have a feeling it'll feel like a thousand."

"I know, Di. I feel the same way. We just have to make the most of the time we do get to spend together," Walker said softly.

She nodded. "I'm looking forward to today."

"Me too. Come on, enough melancholy. Let's concentrate on one day at a time."

"Agreed."

An hour later they were on their way to the Army base and Gillian couldn't wait. They pulled onto the base and, after having their IDs checked, continued to the parking area for the competition. It was packed, and Walker had trouble finding a place to park, which surprised Gillian. She had no idea something like this would be as well attended as it was.

Taking hold of her hand, Walker headed around a building to the field where the obstacle course was located. Gillian had a hard time believing *kids* would be going through the course laid out in front of her.

It had tires and ropes, but there were also wooden boards set up so high, she didn't think any kid would be able to get over them. "Holy cow," she said under her breath.

"Impressive, isn't it?" Walker said with a chuckle.

"Yeah."

"The first time I went to one of these, I didn't think there was any way a kid would be able to complete it, but I was pretty quickly shown the error of my thinking. Over there," he said, pointing off to the side, "is the obstacle course for the kids under six, but everyone from seven and up uses the main one."

"I'm having a hard time imagining anyone being able to complete this…especially a kid."

"Just wait. They're pretty impressive."

"I'm *already* impressed, and I haven't even seen anyone do it yet," Gillian told him.

As if he knew exactly where his friends would be, Walker headed up the bleachers to a section in the top right. There were six men already sitting there when they arrived.

"Hey," Walker said to the group.

A couple of the men gave him a chin lift and the others verbally said hello.

"About time you got here," one of the men ribbed.

"Whatever," Walker said. "We're right on time. Guys, I know you met her before, but this is Gillian Romano. Gillian, this is Lefty, Grover, Brain, Oz, Doc, and Lucky."

She shook each of their hands as they were introduced, and Gillian couldn't stop herself from saying, "I can't wait to find out what your nicknames mean."

Everyone chuckled.

"I think we'll wait another day for that," Walker said with a wink, gesturing to a seat. "I wouldn't want you to think we're all completely nuts."

"Glad to see you looking so good after everything that happened," Doc said.

Gillian smiled. "Thanks. Every day I get better. I still have a bit of trouble at night sometimes, but otherwise I'm good."

"It can take a while for the dreams to stop," Oz told her sympathetically.

"How'd the interview go on Thursday?" Lefty asked.

Gillian shrugged. "As good as it could've, I guess. I told them everything I could remember, they warned me that the seventh hijacker could still come after me, and that I should be careful, and that was that."

Walker frowned at his teammate, and Gillian put her hand on his knee. "It's okay, Walker. I don't mind talking about it."

"*I* mind," he replied. He turned to Lefty. "Can we not talk about that now?"

"Sorry," Lefty said.

"It's fine," Gillian stated firmly. "Walker, I don't want your friends walking on eggshells around me. I want them to feel free to say what they want. It's no secret what happened, duh, you guys were there. It's kinda nice that they're concerned. So back off, okay?"

Brain smirked. "I like her," he said.

"Me too," Grover agreed. "If you decide to dump this asshole, I'll give you my number."

"Shut the fuck up," Walker mumbled, kicking Grover's leg. "She's not dumping me, and even if she was, she wouldn't call you."

Gillian giggled. It was funny how disgruntled Walker sounded. "I appreciate it," she told Grover. "But I'm pretty happy with Walker. But seriously, yeah, the interview wasn't exactly fun. I had to look at every single passenger's photo and tell the investigators what I knew about them. In most cases, it wasn't much, which made them frown a lot and stressed me out. But I told them what I could and that's that. I bought a bunch of those video camera things and I'm being as careful as I can. There's no reason for me to be targeted, and I can't live my life shut up inside my apartment."

"Sounds like you're taking this seriously, which is good," Lucky told her. "We've seen way too many people be stupid when it comes to security or their own well-being."

"Tell me about it," Lefty muttered. "Sometimes we're tasked to be security for dignitaries and other bigwigs. We were in charge of this one guy once who didn't listen to a damn thing we said. It wasn't until he found himself on the wrong side of a picket line, and got caught in a tear gas attack and was almost trampled to death, that he decided to do what we told him."

"Lefty," Walker warned.

Gillian was fascinated. Walker didn't talk about what he and his team did, but she knew he wasn't an ordinary soldier. She put her hand on Walker's knee and squeezed.

"The last thing I want is to end up a sad story on the evening news. While the investigators told me they thought the risk was minimal, they couldn't reassure me that I wasn't in any danger. So, I'm keeping a low profile and going about my business…cautiously."

"Good," Lefty said, nodding. "If you're ever uncomfortable for any reason, get yourself out of the situation, even if you think it makes you look rude. You'd rather be alive than be hurt or killed because you were trying to be polite."

"Has that happened to you before? I mean, to someone you were trying to keep safe?" Gillian asked.

She saw some extreme emotion in Lefty's eyes before he blanked them.

"Sort of," he said with a shrug. "She was an assistant to the bigwig I mentioned earlier. She did everything in her power to get her employer to listen to us, but of course when he didn't, this person was caught up in the danger right along with him. It sucked to realize she understood she was putting her life in danger, but couldn't do anything about it because she had to do what her employer wanted or end up without a job."

"That does suck," Gillian agreed. "Did she quit after that? Find someone else to be an aide to?"

"No," Lefty said flatly. "Not as far as I know."

Gillian wasn't sure what to say to that. It sounded as if Lefty was emotionally tied to this assistant, whoever she was, and she was a bit sad for both the woman *and* Lefty.

"Anyway," Grover said, obviously trying to lighten the mood, "I've got it on good authority that if you want to try out the obstacle course after the competition, you're welcome to."

"Ha. Seriously?" Gillian asked. "That's not happening. Although if you guys want to, be my guest. I mean, you're obviously all in shape, I wouldn't mind ogling if you wanted to strip down to your shorts and have a go."

Walker growled next to her, and Gillian couldn't do anything but laugh.

"The only ogling you're gonna do is of *me*, woman," he said into her ear as his friends all chuckled around them.

A man's voice sounded over a loudspeaker just then, saving Gillian from having to respond to her jealous boyfriend.

"Welcome to another fun-filled day at the races! First up will be our seven-to-ten age group. If heat one could line up behind the starting line, we'll get started soon!"

Gillian eagerly watched as six children, both boys and girls, lined up at the far left side of the field in front of them.

"Man, I can't believe how nervous I am for them," Gillian said with a small laugh. "I don't even know them and my palms are sweaty."

Walker grabbed hold of one of her hands and stroked it. "Not sweaty at all," he declared with a grin.

Gillian rolled her eyes and focused on the field.

Within minutes, the first heat of competitors was off.

Gillian watched in awe as the children raced toward a set of tires. They had to run through them with one foot in the middle of each and get through the entire row without tripping. Then they ran toward low-hanging ropes and fell to their bellies and crawled under them. The next obstacle was a series of stumps at different heights. They had to jump from one to the next, and if they fell off, they had to go back and start from the beginning.

There was obstacle after obstacle, and it seemed with each one, the course got more and more difficult.

By the time the kids got to the end, they had to climb up a rope about fifteen feet to a platform, where they then went hand over hand from one ring to the next, across to a second platform. There, they had to jump up and grab a handhold, using their upper-body strength to pull themselves up and over an eight-foot wall. To get down, they traversed a spider web of ropes to the ground, then leaped over three obstacles before once again getting down on their bellies and crawling in a pit of water and mud under a series of logs, before finally racing to the finish line.

Gillian was exhausted just watching, but every single kid in the first heat finished…and they had huge smiles on their faces to boot.

"They love this, don't they?" Gillian asked Walker.

But it was Brain who answered. "Yup. A lot of the kids practice for months for these kinds of competitions."

"What do they get if they win?" Gillian asked.

"Well, everyone who participates gets a small medal," Brain said. "Usually I'm against any kind of participation trophy, but in this case, it's totally warranted. This isn't some summer club sport where they stand around in an empty field for a few weeks and get a prize for it. They work their butts off. But the winner of each of the six heats goes on to the final round, and the winner of *that* heat gets a hundred-dollar gift certificate to the PX…the post exchange, where they can buy whatever they want."

"Cool," Gillian breathed. "What heat is your friend's kid in?"

"Three," Oz said. "Annie's last year's winner. She beat the time of a bunch of fifteen year olds, and she was only eleven. She wasn't in their competition group, but she would've smoked them if she had been. She's totally gonna win this year too."

"And her dad's okay with her doing this?"

"Fletch? Oh, yeah, he's more than okay with it," Walker answered. "He brings Annie with him when he and his friends practice the adult obstacle course. I've heard her say more than once that the kids' one is too easy."

"Jeez, she must be crazy," Gillian murmured.

"Nope," Walker said. "Only crazy about being just like her dad. Her mom learned pretty early on that the best way to keep her in line was to threaten to take away her obstacle course privileges if she disobeyed. Worked like a charm."

"Are you close with Annie?" Gillian asked.

"Not as close as I'd like. Fletch and his team have been around a bit longer than we have, and they've cut back on missions in the last few years. But mark my words, that kid's gonna be someone special when she grows up. I don't know what she's gonna do, but it's gonna be something pretty damn amazing."

"I'd like to meet her," Gillian said.

"I'll make it happen," Walker told her.

Then their attention was turned back to the field as they watched the second heat of kids run through the obstacle course. It was just as impressive the second time as it was the first.

"Come on, Annie!" Lefty yelled as the third heat got lined up behind the starting line.

"You got this!" Oz called out.

Gillian saw another group of men closer to the field, standing and yelling for Annie as well.

"That's her dad and his team," Walker said into her ear.

Not able to stand the suspense, Gillian stood, as did the rest of the guys around her. Since they were in the back of the stands, they weren't blocking anyone else's view.

"I don't even know her, and I wanna throw up, I'm so nervous," Gillian muttered.

"She's gonna kill it. Don't worry," Walker said.

Then the announcer counted down, and the kids were off and running.

Not only was Annie fast, she was extremely nimble too. She was the first one through the tires, and she practically threw herself on the ground before using her arms and legs like a piston to propel herself under the ropes. She almost seemed as if she were soaring through the air as she leapt over the stumps. Her long hair was in braids so it didn't get in her eyes and they flew up and down in the air as she moved.

Every so often, she'd look behind her at the kids following in her wake. Gillian figured she was checking to see if anyone else was coming up behind her.

Some of the other kids caught up to her as she made her way through the obstacles, and when she got toward the end, where she had to climb to the first high platform, she shimmied up the rope as if she were a little monkey and had done it every day of her life.

"She's gonna win for sure," Doc muttered.

Gillian thought so too—but then the little girl did something surprising.

She was about to start across the rings when she looked behind her again. There was a boy in her heat who was obviously struggling at the rope climb. He'd been behind the older kids the entire course, but was still hanging in there.

But no matter how hard he tried, he couldn't make it all the way to the top of the rope. He'd make it halfway up then slide back down.

Instead of continuing on through the course, and winning and heading to the final round, Annie let go of the first ring and dropped to her knees at the top of the platform above the ropes.

Gillian was too far away to hear what she was saying, but it was obvious she was encouraging the boy. She ignored the fact that the other kids in the heat had passed her and were well on their way across the rings. All of Annie's attention was on the boy trying to climb the rope.

At one point, the boy stopped about halfway up once again, and Annie yelled something to him and reached down to grab the rope herself—then she started pulling it upward. The boy was just hanging on with all his strength, and Annie was bringing him, rope and all, up to the platform. She turned and looped the rope around one of the poles at the top used for safety, which gave her more leverage and allowed her to pull faster.

Gillian turned to Walker. "Is that legal?"

Walker and the other men were all smiling. Huge toothy smiles that went from ear to ear. "No clue. But it's not like she's gonna win the heat, so what does it matter?"

It didn't matter. Not really. Gillian watched with pride as a girl she didn't even know went out of her way to help a fellow competitor. She grabbed hold of his hand when she'd pulled the rope up high enough so she could reach him, and then put her arm around his shoulders when they stood side-by-side on the platform.

They both had some pretty serious obstacles to get through still, and Gillian wasn't sure the boy could make it. But after a short rest, she saw him nod, and both he and little Annie moved to the rings. Annie made it seem so easy to swing to the other platform, but Gillian held her breath as the boy struggled his way across. But he too made it, with Annie cheering on from the other side.

Annie jumped up and grabbed the handhold and pulled herself up to the top of the wall. Then she balanced herself and leaned over, holding an arm downward. The boy was able to jump up and grab the handhold, but Annie was the one who made it possible for him to get up and over the board.

Gillian figured the boy's arms had to be Jell-O by then, but he gamely started down the spider web of ropes, Annie right by his side. They ran together to the mud pit, and Gillian could clearly see the whites of Annie's teeth shining bright as she laughed and smiled at the boy as they shimmied under the last obstacle.

Then, Annie grabbed hold of the boy's hand and they jogged together to the finish line, hand in hand. Dead last in their heat.

But neither kid seemed upset in the least.

A man had run out to the end of the field to meet Annie and the boy, and he pulled her into a huge muddy hug.

"That's her dad," Walker told her. "He's got to be the proudest dad out here today."

"That was amazing," Gillian said in awe. "I mean, it's obvious Annie's competitive, but she didn't even hesitate to stop and help that other kid."

"Told you, she's gonna make a difference in this world," Walker said with pride.

By now, there was an entire group of adults around little Annie. They'd moved off to the side of the field a bit so the next heat could start.

"Come on," Walker said as the others started down the bleachers. "Let's go congratulate her."

Gillian followed Walker and his friends to the field, and she couldn't believe how excited she was to meet a twelve-year-old girl. It had been a long time since she'd been as impressed with someone as she was with Annie. She had a feeling Walker was right. This girl was definitely something special. And no matter what she decided to do with her life, she was going to make a difference in a big way.

They joined the group of men and women surrounding Annie.

"Pretty damn impressive, Fletch," Walker told one of the men, slapping him on the back.

"Thanks. We think so too," Annie's dad said. He had his arm around a woman, and they both looked proud enough to burst.

Gillian waited patiently as Annie's fans congratulated her before she and Walker got to the front of the line.

"Hey, Annie. Pretty impressive out there!" Walker told her.

"Thanks, Trigger," Annie chirped happily.

If she was upset she didn't win the heat and wasn't going to the finals, she sure didn't show it in any way.

"Did you see Rob? That was the first time he finished the obstacle course! He was really nervous before he started, but I told him I'd help him if he needed it. But he didn't *really* need me. He just needed a little hand up on the ropes."

"I saw," Walker said.

"And it's like Dad always says…by lifting someone else up, you're lifting yourself even higher. I pretended I was in the Army and we were on a mission. No one gets left behind."

"That's very true. Are you upset that you don't get to compete in the finals?" Walker asked.

Annie scoffed. "Naw. There's always the next time. Besides, it was better to see Rob's smile when he crossed the finish line."

"Annie, this is my friend, Gillian. She came today just to see you race."

"Hi!" Annie said. "You're really pretty. Are you Trigger's girlfriend? He needs one. He doesn't smile enough."

Gillian did her best not to laugh, but couldn't help it. "I am, and I'm doing my best to make him not be so serious all the time."

"Good." Then Annie turned to her dad. "Dad, did you film that so I can send it to Frankie?"

"Of course, squirt."

"Have you sent it yet?"

"No, jeez. It's only been two seconds since you finished."

"I know, but he's been as excited as I have for the race."

"Frankie's her boyfriend." Walker leaned in to explain. "He's her age and lives in California. He's deaf, and Annie learned sign language just so she can talk to him. They met several years ago and both decided then and there they were going to get married someday."

"Sounds kinda familiar," Gillian said with a smile.

"It was good to meet you," Annie said to Gillian distractedly.

It was obvious she wanted to get on the phone with her friend Frankie and show him her race.

"If you need a flower girl for your wedding to Trigger, I'm available. I've already had a lot of practice and stuff, so you wouldn't have to teach me how to do it," Annie said matter-of-factly.

Gillian almost choked. "Um…I'll keep that in mind."

"Annie Elizabeth!" her mom scolded.

"What?" Annie asked, walking over to her parents.

"Just because someone's dating it doesn't mean they're going to get married."

"But you dated Dad and then got married," Annie said reasonably. "And I'm dating Frankie and I'm going to marry him. And Mary dated Truck and *they* got married."

Fletch's wife rolled her eyes and shook her head. "You're going to have to take my word for it. A man and woman can date and not get married."

"Then what's the point?" Annie grumbled, then was caught up in a hug by Lefty and obviously forgot to be upset at her mom's words.

Gillian hadn't been around Walker when he was with his friends, and was pleasantly surprised when he pulled her back against his chest and put his arm diagonally across her body. He leaned down and spoke directly into her ear, so only she could hear him. "No offense to Annie, but I've heard stories about her mom and dad's wedding. Suffice to say, it involves armed robbers and prosthetic limbs being used as weapons. It's probably safer for us to elope."

Gillian's heart was racing. She liked thinking about running off into the sunset with Walker, but she kept her tone light when she twisted her head around to look up at him. "With my parents hating the cold and yours hating the heat, yeah, it's probably better if we just informed them after the fact."

The smile on Walker's face was something Gillian wanted to preserve for all time.

She heard a click, and she turned around to see Annie's mom smiling down at her phone. "Perfect." Then looking at Walker, she said, "I'll text it to you, Trigger."

"Thanks, Emily," Walker told her, then turned Gillian so she was next to him and started walking off the field. "We're headed out," he informed Doc nonchalantly.

"You're not going to stay for the finals?" he asked.

Walker shrugged. "Now that Annie's out…no. I'll see you Monday morning at PT."

With a smirk, Doc simply nodded.

"That was kind of rude," Gillian informed Walker as they headed off the field toward the parking lot.

"Did you want to stay?" he asked, but didn't slow down.

"What if I said yes?" Gillian asked, curious.

Walker stopped and looked down at her. "Then we'll go back."

"Just like that?" she asked.

"Just like that," Walker said without a trace of annoyance.

"What do *you* want to do?"

"I want to take you back to my apartment and hang out. Talk about the upcoming week, what you have planned. I want to kiss you, but only when we're upright and both fully dressed. I want to know more about the event we're going to next weekend at the zoo, and I want to spend every minute of our time together before I have to take you back to Georgetown. I love my friends, but I see them all the time. I already know them. I'm being selfish, but I want to spend time with *you*, not them. But if you want to stay and watch more heats, I'm okay with that because I'll still be by your side."

Walker didn't look away from her as he spoke, and Gillian couldn't help but fall for him even more.

"I don't care if you leave beard shavings in the sink," she informed him. "You can be as neat as you want and it won't faze me. I'll probably worry that you're doing *too* much for me, that you aren't doing what *you* want, so you're going to have to make sure not to go overboard and spoil me too much, okay?"

"Nope. Now, do you want to stay or go back to my apartment?"

"Your apartment," Gillian said immediately. It wasn't a hard decision.

Walker started walking again, taking her with him. All the way to his apartment, Gillian tried to think what she'd done to be lucky enough to have this man by her side. She couldn't come up with a single thing by the time they'd arrived, so she decided to just go with it. If Walker wasn't freaking out by how well they fit, why should she?

Chapter Thirteen

THE NEXT WEEK WENT BY WAY TOO SLOWLY FOR TRIGGER'S COMFORT. EVER SINCE he'd joined the Delta teams, he'd been single-mindedly focused on his job. He never got distracted, and he spent every day looking forward to training and the possibility of being called for a mission.

But since meeting Gillian, he no longer lived and breathed Delta. He could still focus when he needed to, but in his down time now, he thought about *her*. Wondered what she was doing and if she was having a good day. He was constantly on his phone, texting her just to connect.

It was Friday afternoon, and he and the rest of his team were taking a break from an intense informational meeting they'd been in since nine that morning. It looked like a mission was forthcoming very soon, if the intel they'd been getting was any indication.

"Things seem to be going well with Gillian," Lefty said a little too nonchalantly as he and Trigger stood alone in the Texas heat, trying to thaw out from the frigid air-conditioned room they'd been trapped in all day.

"They are," Trigger agreed.

"She seemed to have a good time last weekend."

Trigger turned to his friend. "What?"

"What, what?"

"Just say what you're thinking before you explode," Trigger said in exasperation.

"I like her," Lefty told his friend. "So before you fly off the handle at what I'm going to say, you have to know that right off the bat."

Trigger nodded, but braced for whatever his friend wanted to tell him.

"I just want to make sure you're not moving too fast with her," Lefty said. "I mean, you met her on an op…that can screw with both your heads."

Trigger waited, knowing Lefty wasn't done. He was right.

"Gillian's pretty, man, so I don't blame you. She's got a good job, she's funny, and all of us like her. She kept her head in Venezuela and seems mature beyond her years. But she also seems like a forever kind of girl. If you're dating her simply to get laid, you're gonna hurt her. Bad. Just be careful, that's all I'm sayin.'"

"You've never stepped into my personal life before. Why now?" Trigger asked, genuinely curious.

"Because it's more than obvious she's in love with you. Or at least she thinks she is. It's obvious by the way she looks at you."

Trigger couldn't help but grin at his friend's words.

"And you like that," Lefty said.

Trigger shrugged. He couldn't deny it. "I haven't slept with her," he said.

Lefty gaped at him. "What?"

"I mean, I've slept with her in my arms, but we haven't had sex," Trigger clarified. "I'm already well aware that we met on an op and that it could be skewing my thinking. I'm extremely protective of her. I'm worried about this seventh hijacker and the fact that no one can figure out which one of the passengers it is. So I'm proceeding with caution. But, Lefty, I've never felt like this about a woman before, and you know I've rescued more than my fair share of damsels in distress over the years."

Lefty nodded. "That's why I can't understand what it is about Gillian that's got you so obsessed."

Trigger couldn't even deny that he was obsessed. He was. "I don't know what it is about her, all I know is that she's gotten under my skin…and I'm perfectly okay with that."

"I hope you're not upset I said something," Lefty said.

"Of course not. I'd be pissed if you didn't. You pick the short straw to talk to me about it?" Trigger asked with a smile.

"Something like that," Lefty admitted. "But seriously, she's cool. We all like her. And you *really* haven't fucked her?"

Trigger had been okay with Lefty's questions, and he knew he'd been the one to bring up the fact that they hadn't slept together, but using the word "fucked" seemed to make the topic ugly. "Careful," Trigger warned. "I'm all right with you questioning my intentions because you're my friend, but I'm not okay with you disrespecting Gillian in the process."

Lefty grinned, not at all intimidated by Trigger. "Sorry."

"And no, I haven't made love with her yet. It's the hardest thing I've ever done in my life."

"I bet it's hard," Lefty said with a sly grin.

Trigger couldn't help it, he laughed. "Shut up, asshole."

Sobering, Lefty said, "I'm happy for you. Seriously. Since seeing Ghost and his entire crew settle down, I think we've all been feeling a bit lonely. I was just worried you'd taken that a step too far and settled for someone."

"I'm not settling," Trigger told him. "Not even fucking close."

"Good."

"You heard anything from Kinley?" Trigger asked.

Lefty frowned and shook his head. "No. She hasn't answered any of my emails or texts, so I stopped trying. I've tried to keep track of the Assistant Secretary for Insular and International Affairs, to see where he's dragging his poor aides, but I stopped after I saw he'd gone to visit Afghanistan to talk about international relations over there."

Trigger shook his head. "He has no clue how much danger he's putting himself in, and everyone who works for him, does he?"

"No," Lefty said with a scowl. "And I doubt he'd care even if he did. I told Kinley when I got her out of that fucked-up situation down in Africa that she needed to find a new job, but she told me it was fine, that *she* was fine. It's infuriating."

"You two clicked," Trigger told his friend. He didn't like the look of frustration and sorrow that passed over Lefty's face before he wiped it clean.

"Wasn't meant to be," he said with a shrug. "You're heading down to Georgetown tonight, right?"

Wanting to press him about Kinley, the first woman he'd seen his friend truly care about since he'd known him, Trigger reluctantly let it go. "Yeah. She's planned a corporate event at the Austin Zoo and invited me to go. I'm looking forward to seeing Gillian in action. She's super organized, and I have a feeling she's like a drill sergeant when it comes to the actual execution of the events she puts together."

"Cool. Tell her we all said hello."

"Will do."

They both saw Doc gesturing to them from the doorway.

"Looks like break time's up," Lefty said. Both men walked back toward the building, and Trigger pulled out his phone to send Gillian a quick text.

Trigger: Just thought I'd say hi and that I might be getting a late start in heading your way tonight.

She responded right away, which she usually did. It was one more thing that he liked about her.

Gillian: Hi. :) And no problem. Take your time and drive safe. I've been putting fires out all day for the event tomorrow. One of the food trucks canceled at the last minute and I've been trying to find a replacement. Can't wait to see you.

Trigger: I'm sure you'll find an even better truck to take its place. Miss you too. Gotta go.

Gillian: Let me know when you're on your way so I don't worry?

Trigger: Of course. Later.

Gillian: Later.

Gillian might not realize it, but the way she always worried about him was pretty special to Trigger. Most women he'd dated seemed to think since he was an alpha soldier, he was invincible. But Gillian was always telling him to be careful and warning him about accidents on the road. She'd even told him about a restaurant in the Killeen area that had been shut down for sanitary reasons and wanted to make sure he hadn't eaten there recently.

Yeah, he had no problem with her worrying about him. It was cute as fuck, and he couldn't deny it felt good.

Taking a breath and putting his phone back in his pocket, Trigger did his best to turn his mind back to the top-secret intel they'd been analyzing before the break. He could think about Gillian all day long, but for now, he needed to be one hundred percent focused because it was very likely they'd be shipped out. Soon.

Later that night, after he'd driven to Georgetown, after he'd kissed the hell out of Gillian when she'd opened her door to him, after they'd eaten the dinner she'd made in anticipation of his arrival, after they'd snuggled on her couch as they watched some random show on TV, and after she'd fallen asleep in his arms, Trigger took the time to deeply analyze his relationship with the woman lightly snoring two inches from his face.

He tried to be objective, to really give Lefty's—and thus, his team's—concerns some thought. But after only a short time, he knew for certain what he felt for Gillian wasn't just because of some hero complex. Wasn't a result of him saving her down in Venezuela. From the first time he'd heard her voice over the phone, he'd been hooked.

Trigger wasn't a particularly religious man. But he'd once read a book about reincarnation, and it had struck a chord within him.

The author explained how souls typically reincarnate together. So those you knew in one life would reappear close to you in another. Your brother in one life might be your mother in another. Or your wife in one life, might end up being your best friend in the next. The author also suggested that in each life, a person had something to learn. Like love, friendship, humility. And if the lesson was learned, then the soul would move on and learn something else in its next life.

Everything about that appealed to Trigger. It made it easy to understand how he and his team were so close. It also explained his instant connection to Gillian.

He knew some people would think he was crazy, that the whole soul thing was a crock of shit, but because of the things he'd experienced and seen in his lifetime, Trigger couldn't dismiss the theory.

Gillian sighed, and the arm around his belly tightened and she nuzzled his chest a bit before settling once more. He knew she was stressed about the next day because she wanted everything to go off smoothly. She'd had one glass of wine and had fallen asleep almost the second he'd settled her against him.

Turning his head, Trigger kissed her forehead gently and stared back up at the ceiling. He wasn't sure what he needed to learn in this lifetime, but he hoped it involved loving unconditionally, and wasn't something about dealing with loss or something equally depressing.

The last thought he had before he fell asleep was that he hoped Gillian was as strong as she seemed. It was inevitable that he and his team would be deployed again. Very soon. In the past, women couldn't deal with not knowing where he was going or how long he'd be gone, and their relationship had ended as a result. He didn't want that to happen with him and Gillian.

Gillian felt as if she were being pulled in a thousand directions at once…but she loved the adrenaline rush she got from seeing all her hard work come together. She'd woken up that morning in Walker's arms and the day had just gotten better from there.

Seeing her man in a pair of jeans and a T-shirt did something to her insides. He was good-looking no matter what he wore, but seeing him dressed so casually was a huge turn-on. He seemed to know; it felt as if he touched her way more often that morning. A brush of his fingertips against her waist as he passed her in the kitchen, a light kiss before she headed to get ready for the day, his arm touching hers as they drove into Austin. He was driving her crazy, but she liked the anticipation.

"Ms. Romano," a man called out as he fast-walked toward her.

She turned away from admiring Walker standing near a group of men, women, and children waiting for the zoo to open its doors to the man coming toward her.

"We need to change the time the food trucks will arrive because I was just informed the monkey demonstration will be starting at eleven."

"It's fine," Gillian informed the harried man who'd been assigned to help her. She thought he was the company president's assistant, but wasn't sure. "Not everyone will want to see the monkeys, and there will be plenty of food for those who do."

"If you're sure…" the man said, his tone indicating that she was wrong.

"I'm sure," Gillian said firmly. "If you can please go tell the employees at the ticket counter that we're all ready out here and it's two minutes past nine. It's time for the doors to open."

"Yes, ma'am," the man told her, then hurried toward the main gate.

Taking a deep breath, Gillian tried to tell herself that she'd done all she could to make sure everything would go off without a hitch.

She felt an arm go around her waist and with one quick inhale, she knew it was Walker.

"Breathe, Di. It's gonna be perfect."

She chuckled. "You're just saying that to calm me down."

"Nope. You've done the work for weeks. Little things might go wrong, but no one's going to care. They're excited about seeing the animals and having a good time. They won't even notice the little shit."

"Thanks," Gillian said, leaning into him for a brief moment. She was used to being on her own at these things. She occasionally might have assistants and people helping her, but ultimately, everything fell on her own shoulders, as it should since it was her business. But still, having Walker there supporting her made everything seem so much easier.

As the day progressed, and Gillian dealt with putting out small issues that kept popping up, she knew that no matter where she was, if she looked around, she'd see Walker. He was giving her space to work, but staying close. He'd brought her water several times, and around twelve-thirty, he'd made her take a short ten-minute break to wolf down one of the tacos he'd gotten from a food truck. Gillian usually skipped eating altogether at events like this, but couldn't deny she felt a hell of a lot better after getting some calories in her.

Around two, when she was standing at the back of one of the auditoriums watching the president of the company give a short speech to his employees about how thankful and proud he was of his work family, Walker came up and bent down to whisper in her ear.

"Can we talk for a second?"

Surprised, she looked up at him. He looked somber and serious, and she knew immediately something was wrong. Nodding, she let him lead her out of the auditorium to a relatively quiet spot nearby. "What's wrong?" she asked anxiously.

"I need to leave," he said.

"Now?"

"Unfortunately, yes."

"Is everything okay? Your friends? They're all right?"

"They're fine. It's a mission. I need to go."

A mission. They hadn't talked much about his job, more because Gillian wasn't sure what she was allowed to ask and what he was allowed to tell her, but now she was kicking herself. "Okay. When will you be back?"

A pained expression crossed his face. "I don't know."

"Can I ask where you're going?"

Walker pressed his lips together and shook his head.

Well, shit. She'd known this time would come, and Gillian did her best to keep everything she was feeling off her face. She had to be strong about this. It wasn't as if she didn't know that Walker and his teammates did some pretty serious shit...look how she'd met him. And she'd known all along that he most likely wouldn't be able to tell her where they were going. She just needed to suck it up.

Giving herself some time, Gillian went up on her tiptoes and hugged him, hiding her face in his shoulder.

His arms banded around her, and she thought he held onto her just a little tighter than usual.

She forced herself to relax her arms, but she kept hold of his shirt at his sides. "Be careful," she whispered.

Walker looked down at her for a long time, his expression inscrutable.

"What?" she asked. "Say something."

"You don't want to ask me anything else?"

"I want to ask you a million questions," Gillian admitted. "But now isn't the time, and you probably couldn't answer them anyway. Just please...come back to me. I can't have found you now, only to lose you."

"You're not losing me," Walker said confidently. "I wish I could tell you everything about where I'm going and what I'm doing, but I can't. I can't *ever* tell you. Even when I get back. You understand that, right?"

She thought she had, but now, faced with his first mission since they'd started dating, it was hitting home exactly how secret Walker's work life was. She nodded. "I admit that this isn't easy for me, but it's harder for someone else out there. Someone who needs a champion. And maybe where you're going isn't a rescue. Maybe you have to go and take out a terrorist or something, but eventually, you'll head to some foreign country to rescue a woman who thinks she's gonna die. And then you and your teammates will be there, giving her another chance at life. I can deal with not knowing because I know what you're doing is important. Maybe not to me, but to someone who might feel just like I did back in Venezuela."

"Fuck," Walker muttered, before leaning down and kissing her as if his life depended on it.

Gillian held on to his shirt and let him take what he needed. She'd give anything to this man; anything he needed from her was his. No questions asked.

The kiss gentled, and Gillian couldn't help the small moan that escaped from deep within her as he nipped her lower lip then pulled back. "Give me your phone," he ordered gently.

Feeling off-kilter from his kiss and the thought that he was leaving, Gillian did as he asked, unlocking it with her thumbprint before handing it over.

He clicked the buttons for a short moment before handing it back to her. "I put Fletch's number in there. He's Annie's dad. He won't tell you where I am or when I'll be back, but he can reassure you if you need it. If too much time goes by and you panic, call him. He'll make some inquiries and let you know what he can. Okay?"

She knew what he was saying. They weren't married. The Army didn't know anything about her. If Walker was hurt or killed on his mission, she'd never know. But his friend Fletch would.

Feeling thankful he'd given her some way to check on him, Gillian could only nod. The lump in her throat threatened to cut off her air along with her words.

Walker took her head in his hands and gently tilted it so she had no choice but to look at him. She loved how he did that all the time. Even more so because it was a very real possibility this might be the last time she'd experience it. She knew more than most how dangerous his job could be.

"I've never regretted anything more in my life than not knowing how it feels to be inside you."

Gillian huffed out a small chuckle. "Then I guess you'd better make sure you come back in one piece so we can get on that, huh?"

He grinned, and Gillian's knees got weak.

"Yeah, I guess so. I'm coming back, Gilly," he said seriously. "I need you to believe that."

"I do."

He stared at her for a long moment before nodding. "Okay. I'm proud of you, you know. Watching you today has given me a new appreciation for what it is you do. You're a jack of all trades and you've handled every crisis that's been brought to your attention with ease. You've come up with creative solutions to issues that would've broken some other people when faced with the same thing. You're able to pivot when needed, and you do it with a smile on your face. I'm fucking impressed, Di. You *are* Wonder Woman."

"Thanks," she whispered.

Walker leaned down and pressed his lips against hers once more. It was a chaste kiss, no tongue involved, but it was just as intimate as if he'd plundered her mouth once more. "Be safe," he warned. "The seventh hijacker is still out there somewhere. I'm not happy that they haven't figured out who it is or what his next move might be. Same rules apply when I'm gone as when I'm here. Don't go out alone if you can help it, don't take a fucking Uber, and let your friends know where you're going if you leave the house."

"And don't go to the grocery store after eleven at night, right?" she teased.

"Exactly. Nothing good happens after that time, and if you need a head of lettuce, you wait until it's light outside."

Gillian grinned up at him and somehow kept the tears she could feel at the back of her eyes from falling. "Got it. I'll be careful."

"I need to go," Walker told her.

Gillian nodded, and he gave her one last long hug.

"Ms. Romano?" someone asked from nearby, and she recognized the voice of the young man who'd been bringing issues to her attention all day.

"Be safe," she whispered to Walker.

"I'll let you know the second I get back," he said with a nod.

Forcing herself to let go and step back, she gave him a lame smile and pantomimed shooing him away. "Go on. Git. Before I latch onto your ankle and make you drag me along the sidewalk as you try to leave."

He smiled, but it didn't reach his eyes. "It's never been this hard to leave before," he admitted.

"What's the saying?" she asked. "The sooner you leave, the sooner you'll get back? Go kick some bad-guy ass, honey."

"Honey," he said quietly. "I like that."

Gillian rolled her eyes. She wanted to tell him she loved him, but felt awkward about it, so she kept quiet.

Walker backed away from her, not taking his eyes from hers until the very last second before he had to go around a corner. One second he was there, and the next he was gone.

Gillian wanted to fall apart, but the man who'd been helping her all day was there with another issue.

"One of the guests' teenage daughters is freaking out in the bathroom because she just got her period and thinks she's dying. The mom isn't dealing well, and…um…do you think—"

"I'm on my way," Gillian said, thankful for the distraction. She'd have time later to break down over Walker leaving. For now, she needed to put her event planner hat on and make sure the rest of the day went off without a hitch.

Chapter Fourteen

TEN DAYS.

Ten of the longest days of her life.

That's how long it had been since Walker had left.

Gillian had coped pretty well the first week, but the night before last, she'd had a nightmare that Walker had been killed somewhere and no one would tell her. She'd caved and called his friend, Fletch, who reassured her that he was still on his mission, and that he wasn't lying dead in some foreign country somewhere.

His deployment wasn't easy, but like Gillian had told him once, she had a busy life that didn't stop just because he was gone. She continued to sign clients for events and was kept occupied by calling hotels and reserving meeting spaces, as well as figuring out other details for the varied events she put together.

At least once a day she heard from one of her fellow hostages. By now, they'd all gotten the news that there was a seventh hijacker, and her phone had been buzzing with texts and emails from everyone she'd gotten close to. Everyone was speculating on who it was and what their next plan would be.

Though, ever since her interview with the FBI and DEA, Gillian had begun distancing herself a little from the others. She felt awful about it, but she couldn't help but wonder if one of her friends could actually be a cold-blooded killer. It seemed unlikely, but if someone like Janet, who'd seemed so scared about her daughter, ended up being a hijacker, Gillian would never trust anyone again.

So she'd spent most of her time with her local friends instead of getting any closer to the women who'd been on the plane with her. She'd gone out for lunch with Ann one day, and then joined Wendy and Clarissa for a movie night at Clarissa's house another evening. She'd cried a little and had a bit too much wine, but overall was pretty proud of how well she'd been holding up.

The biggest hurdle was how much she missed Walker. She missed his texts that let her know he was thinking about her. She missed his laugh. She missed falling asleep with him on her couch, or his. It was as if a part of her was missing.

But the other half of the coin was how proud she was of him. She had no idea what he was doing or where he was, but she'd turned to the internet to do more research on Delta Force. They were one of the most secretive special forces units out there. Walker hadn't been kidding when he'd said he'd never be able to tell her what it was he did when he was gone. Hell, she couldn't find any concrete news stories about any group of Deltas at any event around the world. It was almost eerie how they simply didn't seem to exist as far as the press went.

It had taken a day or so to sink in, but Gillian realized she was all right with the secrecy. As long as Walker returned safe, that was all that mattered. He'd probably seen some horrible things in his life, and she wanted nothing more than to give him happiness when he was home. He needed normal. Not a girlfriend who was hysterical when he left and not someone who brought unnecessary drama to his life. She wanted to be that person for him.

It was late on a Thursday night, eleven days after he'd left, when Gillian's phone rang.

Concerned, because nothing good came from a phone call after ten at night, at least not in her world, and because she didn't recognize the number the call was coming from, Gillian answered it after two rings.

"Hello?"

"It's me."

Two words, but that's all it took for Gillian's entire body to sag in relief. "Walker," she whispered.

"I'm back, but unfortunately I've got about six hours of debriefing meetings to attend before I'm free to go home. Then, as much as I want to see you, I need to sleep. I've been up for about thirty-six hours as it is."

"It's okay. I'm just glad you're home. Are you…is everyone okay?"

"We're good," he said gently. "I just wanted to call as soon as I could to let you know that I'm all right."

"Thank you. I missed you. More than you'll know."

"That's my line," Walker said. "You okay? Anything weird happen since I've been gone?"

"You mean besides me adopting a family of six and moving them into my apartment because they had nowhere else to go? No."

"Gillian," Walker said in a mock threatening tone.

She giggled. "No, nothing weird happened. I've been working, seeing my friends, and locking myself in my apartment by nine o'clock every night."

"Good. Gotten any suspicious texts or emails from the other passengers?"

Gillian thought about a recent text from Andrea, about how she'd given up on therapy because it didn't seem to be helping, and she still felt so angry that she'd been the one singled out by Luis. And the email from Alice, telling Gillian she'd heard Leyton had been detained by Border Patrol when he'd tried to get into Mexico without a passport.

But now wasn't the time to bring all that up. Not when Walker had just gotten home and was exhausted. "Everything's fine," she reassured him. "Go. Do your thing. Maybe I can come up tomorrow evening for the weekend?" she asked tentatively.

"Yes," Walker said without hesitation. "Whenever you can get here in the afternoon will be perfect."

"Okay. Walker?"

"Yeah, Gilly?"

"I'm glad you're home."

"Me too. I'll see you tomorrow. I'll text later when I get back to my apartment before I crash. Okay?"

"Okay. Drive safe. I won't be happy if you made it through whatever you were doing in whatever country you were doing it in, only to get into a car crash your first day back."

He chuckled. "I will. Talk later."

"Bye."

Gillian hung up, but couldn't get Walker out of her mind. Was he really all right? Were Lefty and the others too? He said he hadn't slept in almost two days, so he probably hadn't eaten very well either. Didn't soldiers eat those MRE things when they were deployed?

Springing up from the couch, Gillian headed for the kitchen, a plan formulating in her mind. She knew Walker had meetings he had to attend. Then he had to get some sleep. But he also needed to eat. Something good, and not crappy takeout food or whatever he had in his apartment from before he'd left.

She opened her pantry and contemplated what she could make that would keep until he was done with his meetings. The last thing she wanted to do was push herself on him, especially when he'd just told her he needed to sleep. But she couldn't just sit home and do nothing. She needed to do *something* for him.

Pulling a few ingredients out of the pantry, she nodded in determination. She would make him a casserole that he could easily heat up when he got home and before he slept. Bachelor casserole had always been a favorite of hers, and it was quick and easy to make. She'd just whip up a batch of the noodle and hamburger meal and drop it off for him.

Not caring that it was ten at night and Walker lived forty miles away and it would be close to two in the morning when she got back to Georgetown herself, she got to work.

Trigger was beyond exhausted. He and the team had finished up their job and headed home without catching up on the sleep they'd lost over the last week and a half. Because they hadn't managed to kill the high-value target—the HVT—but instead had taken out half a dozen of his cronies, they'd had to meet with the base general and debrief. There might be blowback because of their failure to kill the head bad guy—as Gillian would call him—but they were all pretty pleased with the terrorists they had managed to take out of commission.

Not every mission was as straightforward as the one he'd found Gillian in the middle of, which was frustrating, but Trigger had learned how to compartmentalize.

He'd borrowed a phone from one of the Army pilots because he and his team always left their personal cells at home when they went on missions, and he called Gillian the second they'd descended low enough to the ground to catch the signal from one of the many cell towers they were flying over.

He might've been embarrassed at how happy he was to hear her voice, if she didn't sound just as relieved to hear from *him*.

Their debrief only took four hours instead of six, which Trigger was thankful for. He and the rest of his team were dead on their feet. He knew they'd need to regroup when they'd gotten some sleep and some decent food, but for now, their best bet was going home and crashing.

Trigger wished he could've seen Gillian when he got back to his apartment, but he smelled to high heaven and could barely keep his eyes open. He wanted to be at least semi-functional when he saw her again.

Unlocking his apartment door, Trigger froze.

Something was wrong.

It smelled…homey.

He'd been gone for eleven days. The air in his place should've been stale, but instead, the scent of food surrounded him and made his stomach growl.

It was three-thirty in the morning. What the fuck was happening?

Pulling out the K-BAR knife he kept on his person at all times when he was on a mission, Trigger eased his door shut and put down his duffle bag. He crept into his apartment and noticed a light on in the kitchen. A light he definitely hadn't left on when he'd departed twelve days ago. For a moment, he was a little frustrated, thinking that perhaps Gillian had decided to come up to his place even though he'd said he needed some sleep. It was a shitty thought, but he was exhausted and in no mood to entertain anyone. Not even Gillian.

But the kitchen was empty. Trigger saw a piece of paper on the counter, but ignored it for the moment. He needed to clear the rest of his apartment, make sure no one was lurking in the shadows or Gillian wasn't sleeping somewhere. As irritated as he was at the thought she might've ignored his request to come up the next afternoon, after he'd had a chance to unwind from his intense mission, he didn't want to scare the shit out of her by pulling out a knife if she'd decided to surprise him.

But after a quick search, Trigger found his apartment empty.

Putting his knife away, he walked back into his kitchen. Pulling open his stove, he found a glass dish covered in aluminum foil. He felt the dish and realized it was still warm.

Even more baffled now—had someone broken in and cooked dinner? Of course they hadn't. That was just stupid—he picked up the piece of paper and opened it. Glancing at the end, he saw it was a note from Gillian. He read quickly.

Welcome home!

I know you're tired and I didn't want to bother you. It's not the same thing at all, but I know sometimes after a major event that I've spent weeks planning, I don't want to talk to anyone. I need to go home and decompress without having to think about anyone or anything for a while.

Anyway, I started thinking about how if you were tired, you were probably hungry too. I'm sure they didn't have our favorite takeout place wherever you were.

So I made you a casserole. It's nothing fancy, just noodles, hamburger, cream of mushroom soup, sour cream, and cheese. But I thought maybe it might hit the spot. I didn't want to leave your oven on, because I had no idea when you'd get home, so it might be cold. But you can always warm it up in the microwave.

I'm glad you're back. I've thought about your job a lot since you were gone, and for the record…I can handle it. I don't like not knowing where you are or if you're okay, but I'm one hundred percent sure that wherever you are, you're keeping our country safe from men and women who want to do it harm, or you're helping someone like me…a normal person who somehow got stuck in a situation they never thought they'd find themselves in.

Before I met you, I never really thought much about men like you and your teammates, but now that I've experienced a situation where I've needed help firsthand, I'm as proud of you as I can possibly be.

Eat something. Get some sleep. I'll see you soon.
Xoxo, Gillian

PS. I didn't break into your apartment. I knocked on the manager's door. I don't think he was very happy to be woken up at one in the morning, but after I told him what I wanted and how amazing you were, he begrudgingly agreed to let me into your apartment. He glared at me the entire time, and I think he thought I was going to steal something, but I was only in here for like ten seconds, long enough to put the casserole in your oven, turn on a light so you wouldn't come home to a dark apartment, scribble this note, then leave.

How long Trigger stood in his kitchen, reading and re-reading the note from Gillian, he had no idea. He'd never, in all his adult life, had someone do for him what she'd just done.

When he'd called, it had been after ten. She'd cooked the meal for him, driven up to his apartment, woken up the manager of the apartment complex to get into his place, then driven back home.

She understood that he needed to decompress. She'd *heard* him when he'd said he had to get some sleep. But she'd gone even further, understanding that he probably hadn't eaten very well recently either.

He wasn't happy that she was out driving at night as late as she had been, but he loved that she'd been thinking about him.

Eventually, he turned and took the casserole out of the oven. He scooped some onto a plate and ate it standing up right there in his kitchen.

The meal was delicious. It was lukewarm, but he was too tired and impatient to wait for it to heat up, even if it only took a minute or two in the microwave. He ate way too much, his stomach protesting after the lean rations it had gotten over the last week and a half, but Trigger didn't care. That meal was made with love, for him, and he appreciated it more than he'd ever be able to put into words.

He put the leftovers into the refrigerator and headed to his bedroom. He took a ten-minute shower to wash the rest of the dust and dirt from his mission off his body, then dropped into bed. Right before he fell asleep, dead to the world, he reached for his phone and typed out a quick text.

Trigger: I'm not thrilled that you came up here in the middle of the night, because it's not safe, but that casserole was literally the best thing I've eaten in my life. Thank you, Di. You really are Wonder Woman. MY Wonder Woman. Be ready, we're both sleeping in my bed this weekend. I'm done waiting. You're mine, and I intend to show you how much you mean to me over and over, until we're both so exhausted we can't move.

Knowing that Gillian was asleep, he didn't wait for a response. He put his phone face down on his bedside table and fell into the sleep of the exhausted.

Chapter Fifteen

GILLIAN COULDN'T BELIEVE HOW NERVOUS SHE WAS. IT WAS RIDICULOUS because she'd been ready to make love with Walker for weeks now, but reading the text he'd left her last night had knocked her for a loop.

She was thrilled that he wasn't really mad she'd essentially broken into his apartment, but was a bit surprised about his change in demeanor when it came to moving their physical relationship forward.

He'd been adamant about moving slow, making sure they were both on the same page, but that text she'd received had been the opposite of tiptoeing into a physical relationship. She knew exactly what Trigger wanting her in his bed meant.

And while Gillian had been chomping at the bit to move their relationship to a more physical level, now she was freaking out.

She stood in front of the mirror in her bathroom and tried to objectively evaluate herself. She'd put on a matching cream bra and panty set that made her feel good. But now that she was looking at herself in it, she wasn't so sure. Walker was the epitome of hot. He had muscles on top of muscles, and even though she hadn't seen his stomach, she'd felt it. She was guessing he had at least a six-pack, and probably those V-muscles that pointed down to his groin.

Gillian wasn't anywhere near his league when it came to physical attributes. She had a nice set of boobs, but her stomach was a bit too poofy and her thighs touched when she walked. She burned a bit too easily and hadn't ever found joy in lying in the sun and baking, so she was very pale.

She fluffed out her hair and had to admit that it was one of her best features. She also liked her green eyes.

Blowing out a breath, she turned away from the mirror. She was who she was. Just because she carried more weight than was deemed acceptable didn't mean she wasn't attractive. Walker certainly didn't seem to see what *she* did when he looked at her.

She pulled on a pair of jeans and a cute ruffled cold-shoulder pink shirt. She went a little heavier on her makeup, simply because she hadn't seen Walker in almost two weeks and she wanted him to see her at her best. He'd certainly seen her at her worst in Venezuela, and in her "I'm lying around the house not expecting company" clothes as well.

Still feeling nervous, she packed an overnight bag and got ready to leave her apartment. She'd spent the morning working on the anniversary party for the Howards. She'd talked to the staff at The Driskill and finalized some small details about the food that was going to be served and how to set up the ballroom. It was good to keep busy as it kept her mind off Walker…mostly.

For some reason, as she left her apartment, Gillian had the fantastical thought that when she returned, her life would be different. Which was insane. Having sex with a man wasn't exactly life-changing. Women did it all the time. But she had a feeling that sex with Walker would definitely not be run-of-the-mill.

The drive to his apartment seemed to take forever, and it didn't help that there was an accident on the road that slowed things down as well. She called him when she got into town.

"Hey, Gilly. You close?"

"Yeah. Finally. There was a wreck and it took forever for me to get past it."

"It's okay. I'm just glad you're almost here."

"Me too," Gillian told him, feeling shy.

"Drive safe and I'll see you soon."

"I will. Bye."

Walker hung up without another word, and Gillian couldn't help but feel nervous all over again. This was crazy. She was just going to see Walker. He was the same man he was two weeks ago when she'd last seen him.

But was he? Just from the text he'd sent the night before, Gillian had a feeling he was different, and she had no idea what to expect from him.

She pulled into his parking lot and grabbed her bag before she headed for his apartment. To her surprise, he was standing outside waiting for her. Without thinking, Gillian started to jog toward him. Talking and texting with him wasn't the same as seeing him in person.

He looked good, the same as he had before he'd left. No bandages, no black eyes, no sign of any kind of injury. A part of Gillian had wondered if he'd been hurt and just didn't want to tell her. But he looked tall and strong, and it was such a relief, she threw herself into his arms as soon as she got close.

"You're really okay," she mumbled as she buried her face in his neck.

His strong arms wrapped around her, taking her off her feet as he hugged her back. "I told you I was fine," he said with a laugh.

He put her on her feet and stared down at her with a look so hot, Gillian had to force herself to swallow. "Hi," she said awkwardly.

Walker huffed out another chuckle. "Hi," he returned.

Gillian put one hand on his cheek. "You look good."

"Did you expect me to come back with green skin and all my hair shaved off or something?"

She grinned. "No, but I don't know you well enough to know if you saying that you were fine *really* meant that you were fine, or if it was manspeak for 'I took a couple bullets but they didn't kill me so I'm good.'"

He stared at her for a heartbeat before throwing his head back and laughing so hard, she could feel his body shake against her own. The sound was beautiful. All the more because she was witnessing it in person, and he really was all right after his mysterious mission.

When he'd gotten himself under control, Walker leaned down until his lips were almost brushing hers when he spoke. "I might downplay how I feel when I talk to you, but I won't lie. If I get shot, I'll tell you I got shot. But you have to understand that unfortunately, getting injured kind of comes with my job. You can't freak if I come back to you with a few scrapes and bruises."

"I can and will," Gillian retorted. "*You* have to understand that the thought of you being hurt turns my stomach and makes me want to march out into the world and beat the crap out of anyone who dared lay a hand on you. I'll do my best to control myself, but you're just going to have to work extra hard to be careful so I don't lose my mind when you come home."

She couldn't interpret the look on his face. But when he said, "Okay, Di. I can do that," she relaxed in his arms.

Walker stared down at her for so long, she started to get concerned. But just when she was about to ask him what was wrong, he moved. He bent and picked up her bag with one hand, keeping his other arm around her waist. He moved them toward the building without another word.

He didn't let go of her for even a second as they made their way to his second-floor apartment. He unlocked the door and led her inside.

The second the door shut behind them, he dropped her bag and Gillian found herself backed up against the wall in the foyer with Walker looming over her.

"Thank you for the dinner last night…well, this morning."

"You're welcome," she said, holding onto his forearms as she stared up at him.

"What time did you get home?" he asked.

Gillian shrugged. "Around two."

"While it was appreciated, don't do that shit again. It's not safe to be driving and walking around at that hour."

"I wanted to make sure you ate," she said softly.

Walker put his hand in one of his front pockets and pulled something out.

Looking down, Gillian saw a shiny silver key in his palm. She looked back up at him in confusion.

"I had a talk with my manager this morning. Told him that you were always allowed in my apartment, and he shouldn't give you a hard time about letting you in no matter what time it is. But I figured it would be easier if I just gave you a key, that way you won't have to wake him up again and deal with his attitude."

"You're giving me a key to your place?" she asked, her brows furrowed.

"Yeah."

She didn't reach to take it. This seemed like a huge deal, and she was having a hard time processing it.

Walker had a small smile on his face and he moved his hand, tucking the key inside the front pocket of her jeans. Then he leaned in closer, forcing Gillian's head back farther.

"You get the text I sent early this morning?"

She nodded.

"Anything about what I said that you don't understand or want?"

Gillian licked her lips nervously. "No, it was pretty clear," she told him. "But…I'm not sure what happened in the last two weeks to make you change your mind from the whole 'going slow' thing and 'I can't sleep in a bed with you' to now."

"I finally got my head out of my ass," Walker said with no hesitation. "I suppose I wasn't being fair to you, but I've seen too many relationships with my friends crash and burn when their girlfriend couldn't handle the uncertainty that comes with our kind of job."

Gillian was a little disappointed with his answer, but she couldn't really blame him. He went on before she could say anything.

"And everything I told you before was true. I was afraid to get tied any closer to you because if you decided you couldn't handle what I do, it would've killed me. As far as I'm concerned, you're perfect. You have your own friends, you're smart, funny, employed, and you've got an innocent soul. And I want all that for myself. I don't want to corrupt you, or change you in any way, but I know that if you're with me, I'll end up doing just that. I guess that's why I was holding back. But when I got home last night, dead on my feet and completely exhausted, and I saw that you'd gone out of your way to respect my need for space to clear my head after the mission *and* to feed me, it hit me."

When he didn't go on, Gillian asked, "What did?"

"That I've been an idiot," Walker said gently. "I was keeping you at arm's length when I should've been doing everything in my power to tie you closer to me. I know it's only been one deployment, and it was a relatively short one at that, but do you think you can handle what I do? Being left on your own for unknown periods of time without having any idea when I might be back or what I'm doing?"

"Yes," Gillian said simply. She wasn't fond of being left in the dark, but if that was the only way she could have Walker, she'd deal. He was hers. She felt it in her bones.

"Fuck, I don't deserve you," Walker muttered before his head dropped.

Gillian didn't have time to think about anything other than how his lips felt on hers. He physically tilted her head with his hands and the second she opened to him, he was there.

How long they kissed against the wall just inside his apartment, Gillian didn't know, but when she felt his hands at her waist, pulling her shirt up, she gasped and pulled back.

"Arms up," he ordered.

Bemused, she did as he requested and within seconds, she was standing in front of him in her bra. His gaze immediately dropped, and she heard him groan before his hand came up, pulling one of the cups of her bra down, exposing her rock-hard nipple. Then his mouth was there, sucking hard, making her back arch and her fingers spear into his hair, holding him against her.

One of her legs came up and Walker caught it in the hand that wasn't at her chest. He pulled her into him, throwing her off balance. But she knew she wasn't going to fall. No way would Walker let that happen.

His mouth moved up and he sucked on the fleshy part of her breast as his fingers pinched and rolled the nipple he'd just had in his mouth. She looked down and inhaled sharply at the eroticism of what she saw.

Walker's slightly stubbled jaw was working as he sucked on her flesh. "Are you giving me a hickey?" she managed to get out between pants.

He lifted his head and grinned. "Yup."

"How old are you?" she teased.

"Thirty-seven," he answered as if she'd asked a serious question. "And I want to see my mark all over you. I'm claiming you right here and now, Gillian. Tell me to stop if you don't want this. I'm a possessive and protective bastard. If we do this, you're going to have to be all right with that."

His eyes were serious and piercing in their intensity.

"Do I get to claim you right back?" she asked. "You won't get upset if I put handsy bitches in their place when they try to touch you? Or have a stare-down with a pushy chick in a bar? Because I don't share. If you cheat on me, I'm done. You'll get no second chances."

Instead of being concerned over what she'd said, Walker grinned. "I can't *wait* for you to get all possessive on me in public. And as I told you before, I don't cheat. Why the fuck would I when I've got this?" he asked, but it was a rhetorical question, because he once again lowered his head to her chest and ate at her nipple as if he were starving.

Gillian's head fell backward against the wall with a loud thump.

"Ow," she whispered, not really feeling the slight pain, but it was enough for Walker to move. He immediately brought his hand up to the back of her head and turned them so they were walking—more like stumbling—down the hall toward his bedroom.

The second they entered, Gillian inhaled deeply, smelling Walker's unique scent, and she knew her nipples had just gotten harder. She'd fantasized about being in here with him.

At the edge of his bed, he stopped her and reached around for her bra clasp. Within seconds, it was undone and falling to the floor. He didn't stop there; he undid the button of her jeans and lowered her zipper. Then he put his hands against her sides and pushed both her panties and jeans down at the same time.

"Step out," he whispered when they fell to her ankles.

Gillian managed to toe off her sandals and kick off her clothes without falling on her face. But then she realized that she was completely naked, and Walker still had on all his clothes. It was uncomfortable, but also kind of hot.

He stood a foot in front of her, completely immobile. His eyes ran down her body, from her head to her toes, then back up again. His chest was heaving with his breaths, as if he'd just run five miles.

Forcing herself to stand still, Gillian waited for him to say or do something. When he didn't move, she began to feel self-conscious.

"Walker?" she whispered. "What's wrong?"

"Nothing," he said with a croak. "Not a damn thing. You're beautiful. Way too pretty for the likes of me."

Gillian rolled her eyes. "Please," she said. "If anything, the opposite is true."

He put a finger over her lips and his gaze met hers. "Don't put yourself down," he ordered. "I won't tolerate anyone saying anything unfavorable about you, and that goes for yourself as well." His finger dropped from her lips, but didn't break contact with her body. He drew it over her chin, down her collarbone to her left breast. He swirled the digit around her hard nipple then down her side, where she squirmed away from him a bit when it tickled.

His lips quirked up, but he didn't stop. His finger traced her hip bone, then he brushed the curls between her legs. Gillian locked her knees but couldn't stop herself from inhaling sharply as he brushed against her clit. She wasn't sure if he'd done it on purpose or not, but when his smile grew and he did it again, she realized he knew exactly what he was doing.

Gillian reached for him and frowned when her hands touched his T-shirt instead of his skin. "If I'm naked, you should be too," she complained.

His finger continued its teasing, and he used his other hand to reach behind his head to remove his shirt. One quick movement and the cloth was on the floor at their feet, forgotten.

Gillian was having a hard time concentrating as Walker's finger had dipped lower between her folds, but she couldn't help sighing at the sight of his chest. He was ripped, and had both the six pack and those sexy-as-hell V-muscles she'd fantasized about—but it was the large bruise on his side that caught her attention. It was in the ugly green and yellow stage, but it was obvious something had hit him hard.

Without words, she ran her thumb over it gently.

"I'm okay," he said quietly.

Gillian nodded.

"Look at me," Walker ordered.

But she couldn't tear her eyes away from the mark on his side. She kept trying to imagine what in the world could've happened to bruise him so badly, but couldn't come up with anything.

One hand gripped her hip, and the other went under her chin to force her gaze away from his side.

"I'm okay," he said firmly.

Inhaling deeply through her nose, Gillian nodded. This was what he was talking about earlier. "Okay. You're good," she said. "But that doesn't mean that I'm happy. It doesn't mean that I don't want to inspect every inch of you to see where else you're hurt. To kiss every bruise. Every scrape to make it better."

He smiled. "I'm okay with that," he told her. "In fact, I think we should make it tradition. Whenever I come back from deployment, my own nurse has to do a very personal inspection of my body from head to toe."

"Deal," Gillian agreed immediately. "But I can't do that if you're wearing clothes. Strip, Army Boy."

Walker barked out a laugh and Gillian smiled. This was what had been missing from her relationships in the past. Laughter. The few times she'd had sex, it had been quiet and serious the entire time. Being with Walker was fun. It was exciting and nerve-wracking, but she'd never made a man laugh like this in bed.

Walker leaned over and pulled back the covers. Once again, his woodsy scent rose from the linens, and Gillian practically dove onto the mattress. She wanted to roll herself all over the sheets, imprinting his smell onto her body as if she were a wild animal, but she restrained herself. Barely.

Trying to figure out the best way to lie to appear the most seductive, she soon forgot all about positioning herself as Walker made quick work of his pants and stood by the bed, naked as the day he was born.

Inhaling sharply yet again, Gillian squirmed on the bed. She could feel her body readying itself to take him. She was so wet between her legs, and she wanted nothing more than to feel him inside her…finally.

"Walker," she breathed.

He smiled, then slowly joined her on the bed. Instead of lying next to her, he straddled her legs and hovered over her, his weight on his forearms on either side of her head. She could feel his hard cock brush against the curls between her legs, and she immediately tried to shift, to open her legs wider, but his knees prevented her from moving like she wanted.

Whimpering, she ran her hands up and down his sides, wanting to touch him everywhere at once.

"Last chance," Walker told her.

In response, Gillian moved one hand between their bodies and grasped his hard-as-nails cock. She realized that her hand barely closed all the way around it, and she only managed one quick up and down stroke before Walker had grabbed her hand and moved it away from his dick.

Gillian pouted. "Hey, not fair," she complained.

He chuckled, and once again Gillian realized how much she liked hearing him laugh.

"There'll be time for that later. If you touch me right now, I'm going to go off like an untried boy. It's been thirteen long days for me, sweetheart. Cut me some slack."

"I guess you can't really masturbate while you're on a mission, huh?" she asked.

"No. And I was too tired last night to do more than eat, shower, and fall into bed."

"I suppose you're right," she told him with a smile. "I mean, I was able to take care of myself last night when I got home, so it's only fair."

Walker groaned. "Seriously, woman? That was just cruel."

Gillian smiled. "Hey, a girl's gotta do what a girl's gotta do."

"You think about me while you got yourself off?" he asked.

"Of course."

"Was I touching you?"

"Yes."

"Tell me," he ordered.

Gillian blushed. She wasn't afraid to admit that she masturbated, but telling him about it was a bit daunting.

"Was I touching you here?" he asked, seeing that she was shy. He shifted above her and one hand cupped her breast.

"To start with," she said breathlessly.

For a moment, he teased her nipple, then his fingers brushed down her belly. "Here?" he asked.

Gillian nodded as his fingers brushed her clit. She saw that Walker's head was lowered and he was watching his own fingers as they played with her soaking-wet slit. She sighed and put her head back down on his pillow. She gripped one of his arms tightly as her hips began to undulate under his ministrations.

Then he moved down, until he was on his belly between her legs. He pushed her thighs apart, using his broad shoulders to keep her spread open for him.

Any conversation they'd been having about what she'd been thinking when she'd masturbated had stopped. He was concentrating too hard on what he was doing—and Gillian was too lost in the pleasure he was giving her.

Using one hand to spread her lower lips, Walker leaned down and inhaled deeply. Gillian blushed but didn't have time to complain as the man between her legs groaned then licked her from bottom to top.

"Fucking heaven," he muttered before he did it again. Then again.

Gillian writhed and put her hands on his head.

"*Mmmm,*" she murmured as he closed his mouth around her labia and used his tongue to give her the most intimate kiss she'd ever received.

Walker took his time. Kissing, sucking, and licking every inch of her pussy. By the time he slowly inserted one finger into her tight sheath, Gillian thought she was going to die. She lifted her hips off the mattress to try to take him deeper.

"You are so sexy," Walker said as he lowered his mouth once more. But this time, instead of licking her, he latched onto her clit. He sucked at it like he'd done to the flesh of her breast.

"Walker!" she exclaimed, and tried to buck him off. But he put his free arm across her belly and held her down as he continued his assault on her extremely sensitive bundle of nerves.

Gillian felt her orgasm rising hard and fast. It felt different from any that she'd given to herself. She wasn't in charge. She had to lie there and take what Walker was giving her. When she felt herself getting close to the edge, she usually backed off the speed of her vibrator and eased into the orgasm.

But Walker wasn't backing off. He was sending her hurtling toward the edge with no parachute. She was going to fall, and fall hard.

Gripping his short hair, Gillian tried once again to pull away from his mouth. But he wasn't letting her go. In fact, he eased another finger inside her body and began to thrust them in and out. The sounds his fingers made were loud in the quiet of the room. Gillian knew she was soaking wet but wasn't feeling any kind of embarrassment at that moment.

Just when she thought she was going to explode, Walker stopped sucking. He didn't lift his head, or remove his fingers, he just went still between her legs.

Gillian hung on the precipice, torn between being glad he'd stopped and pissed way the hell off.

"Walker?" she croaked.

Then, just as she thought she'd lose the orgasm she'd been climbing toward, he moved. He sucked harder than he had before and used his tongue to lash her clit at the same time he turned his fingers inside her and pressed against her G-spot. His pinky finger also brushed against her anus, stimulating the nerves back there.

She was stunned by the simultaneous assault on her senses, and immediately was lost in the throes of the most intense orgasm she'd ever experienced. She bucked and thrust her hips up toward Walker and threw her head back, screaming out his name. Her muscles shook as the mind-blowing pleasure went on and on.

Gillian had no idea when Walker had changed position. He was now on his knees, putting on a condom he'd produced out of thin air. Thankful that he was coherent enough to use protection, she could only moan when he lifted one of her legs and hooked it over his shoulder. He then put his arm under her other knee and leaned over her.

She was spread wide open beneath him, and she inhaled deeply when she felt the head of his cock brush against her still very sensitive folds. Looking up into his eyes, she saw his pupils were dilated and his nostrils were flaring with every breath he took.

"Tell me you're mine," he ordered in a low, gruff voice.

"After that mind-blowing orgasm? I'm totally yours," she told him.

He grinned briefly, then groaned when he pushed inside her.

It had been a while for her, and because he was so big, she winced as he entered her body.

He noticed, but didn't stop until they were fused together so tightly, she had no idea where she stopped and he started. Then he reached under her and palmed her ass, pulling her butt cheeks apart and pushing inside her even farther.

At first, she felt as if she were being torn apart, but after a second of adjustment, the pain morphed into complete ecstasy. Gillian clenched her inner muscles and was rewarded with a groan from Walker.

"I know I hurt you, but I couldn't stop," he said after a moment. He hadn't moved once since getting inside her, letting her adapt to his entry.

"It's okay."

"It's not," he countered. "But you were so fucking beautiful. Tasted so good, I couldn't stop myself. I'm sorry."

"Stop apologizing," Gillian scolded. She reached down and grabbed hold of his butt and kneaded the rock-hard flesh there. Then she tightened her stomach muscles and leaned up so she could reach his head. She nipped at his ear, then sucked the lobe into her mouth.

She felt him lurch inside her, and it gave her such a feeling of power, she did it again. "You like that," she said.

"I like every fucking thing about you," he returned.

Then he moved his hand farther up on the mattress, taking her leg with him since it was resting on his arm, which opened her even more. Gillian felt her inner thighs protest at the stretching, but she didn't care. She felt sexy as hell all spread out under him with his cock deep inside her.

"Move," she ordered.

"Are you sure? I don't want to hurt you, and I don't think I can go slow."

"Walker, I just came harder than I've ever come in my life. I'm wetter than I've ever been as well. I'm good. Fuck me."

That was all the permission he needed, apparently, because before the last syllable was out of her mouth, his hips were moving. Slow at first, as if he didn't really believe that she wasn't in pain anymore. But with every slow slide into her body, he got more and more confident, until he was hammering against her so hard, the sound of their bodies slapping together was loud as it echoed around the room.

At first, Walker stared into her eyes as he made love with her, but after a while, he looked down between their bodies. Gillian's eyes dropped too, and the sight of his cock disappearing into her body, then reappearing, shining with her juices, was erotic as hell. He must've thought so too, because a muscle in his jaw tightened and he groaned.

Gillian did her best to participate, to lift her hips into each thrust, but it was awkward with the way her ankle was resting on his shoulder and her other leg was in the crook of his elbow.

But her hands were free. So she brought them up and pinched one of Walker's nipples as he fucked her.

"Damn," he said as he thrust harder into her.

Smiling at his reaction, she did it again, played with his nipples much as he'd done to hers earlier. When she noticed he was staring at her chest, she looked down to see her tits bouncing with every thrust he made inside her.

Gillian had never felt this powerful. Yeah, he was on top of her, and she couldn't move much, but she knew with a bone-deep conviction that she was in control. All it would take was one word from her and he'd stop.

She brought a hand to his nape and tugged him down toward her. His rhythm stuttered as he did as she requested. Aware that it wouldn't be good for him to go back to work with a big ol' hickey on his neck, she settled for latching her mouth onto one of his pecs. In about the same spot as he'd marked her earlier. She didn't mess around, sucking on his skin as hard as she could. He wasn't thrusting into her now at all. His entire body had gone still, allowing her to do as she wanted.

When she was sure she'd broken enough blood vessels under his skin to leave a hickey, she playfully nipped at him before pulling back. She stared at the mark on his chest with a satisfied smile.

"You did say you were possessive," Walker remarked with a chuckle.

"If I'm yours, you're mine," Gillian told him.

Without a word, Walker pulled out of her body.

"Walker! No!" Gillian complained. But he had her turned and on her hands and knees before she could blink.

Then he was pushing back inside her. He felt even bigger like this, if that was possible. She fell to her forearms, her ass in the air, and Walker groaned.

"You have no idea how good you feel," he said.

Gillian couldn't answer as he fucked her hard from behind.

"I can't stop," he said apologetically.

"Good," she breathed out.

He awkwardly reached around and tried to manipulate her clit once more, but Gillian moved her arm down, shoving his fingers out of the way as she began to finger herself.

She liked this position because she could reach her clit without any issue, and she could also use her other hand to caress Walker every time he pulled out of her soaking sheath.

"Fuck, that's so sexy, make yourself come, Gilly," he croaked. "I want to feel you explode around my cock."

More turned on than she'd ever been in her life, Gillian buried her head into the mattress and inhaled Walker's scent into her lungs as she frantically worked herself up to another orgasm.

"That's it. I can feel you tightening around me. Fuck, I'm not going to last much longer. Hurry, sweetheart."

Feeling his urgency, Gillian did her best to obey. She was on the edge when she felt him spread her cheeks and press his thumb against her ass. He didn't penetrate her there, but the carnality of his touch had her hurtling over the edge before she had time to prepare.

"Yessss," Walker hissed as every muscle in her body clenched.

He thrust into her twice more, then pulled her hips hard against his and grunted and groaned as he finally orgasmed.

For a second, Gillian thought she'd gone blind, but eventually her sight returned and she realized she still had her face buried into the mattress. She turned her head and took a deep breath. Her chest was heaving in and out and her ass was still up in the air. Walker's cock was still deep inside her body, and he was holding her so tightly she had a feeling she'd have little finger-size bruises on her hips in the morning.

"Fuck," Walker whispered. "You killed me."

Gillian couldn't help it. She giggled. The movement made Walker's now soft cock slip out of her body, and they both moaned.

He helped her roll onto her side then pulled the sheet up and over her. "Stay right there. Don't move," he ordered.

"I couldn't even if I wanted to," she mumbled.

Walker's weight left the bed and she figured he was going to take care of the condom. He was back within seconds, climbing under the sheet with her and pulling her against him. Gillian rested her cheek against his chest and lifted one thigh to rest over his.

"I meant it," Walker said after a long moment.

"Meant what?"

"You're mine now. I'm not going back to sleeping chastely on the couch anymore."

"Okay."

"And if you thought I was protective and annoying before with my warnings to be careful, you're probably going to be unpleasantly surprised at how intense I can be about your safety from here on out."

Gillian didn't even tense. "Okay."

"I'm serious, Di. You're strong as fuck and independent to boot, but no more driving up here in the middle of the night. I want you to text me whenever you leave your apartment and when you get home."

"Are you going to start telling me who I can spend my time with and what I'm allowed to do when I'm not with you?" Gillian asked.

"No."

"Then I'm okay with you wanting to know I'm safe."

She felt him let out a long breath. Picking up her head, she looked him in the eyes. "I won't let you take control of my life. I'm still going to hang out with Ann, Wendy, and Clarissa. I'm still going to run my business the way I see fit. But I've waited forever to find you, Walker. I don't mind that you want me safe. That you worry about me. I'm okay with you coming to the events I plan when you can. I like having you by my side. You being concerned about me feels good. Just don't turn it into a controlling thing, and I'm okay with it."

"I don't want to control you," Walker said immediately, running his hand over her head. "But I know the evil that's out there. And the thought of it touching you makes me crazy. Somehow you still have this innocence about you, despite what happened in Venezuela, that I want to protect. I don't want anything else to happen to you. Ever."

Gillian put her head back on his chest. "Okay."

"Okay," Walker agreed.

Gillian knew it was only like four-thirty in the afternoon, but she was exhausted. She hadn't slept well last night after her impromptu trip up to Walker's apartment. And the two orgasms she'd just experienced had blown any desire to get up and do anything to smithereens.

"Tired," she whispered.

"Then sleep," Walker told her.

"Do we need to do anything?"

"No."

"Walker?"

"Yeah, sweetheart?"

"I'm glad you're home."

She felt him smile against her head. "Me too. Now shut up and take a nap. I haven't had nearly enough of you, and you still need to examine me from head to toe to make sure I'm not injured anywhere besides my side."

Gillian huffed out a breath. "I'm going to regret agreeing to that, aren't I?"

"Never," Walker promised.

Gillian wanted to talk some more. Wanted to ask how the other guys were and if they had been hurt as well. She wanted to ask what came next with them, how they were going to make this semi-long-distance relationship work, but she was too tired.

One second she was thinking that it didn't feel weird at all to be completely naked in bed with Walker, and the next she was fast asleep.

"She knows, and she's talking to the Feds," the mysterious seventh hijacker told Alfredo Salazar.

Salazar was the son of one of the leaders of the Sinaloa Cartel. His father had sent him to Texas when he was ten years old to learn the business and to eventually run the operation from the other side of the border. He was now twenty-five, and one of the most feared men in the Austin area. Salazar was in charge of millions of dollars' worth of meth and cocaine that was delivered from Mexico. It was his job to distribute it around Texas, and up into the rest of the country as well. He was as ruthless as his father and didn't tolerate any threat to his business.

He was at the top of the pile when it came to the US operations. He also kept a close eye on the lieutenants, hitmen, and falcons under him. He had lieutenants who were ultimately responsible for supervising the hitmen and falcons, who could also carry out some low-profile executions without his permission, but *nothing* happened in his organization without Salazar's knowledge.

The hitmen were important to the operation because they were the security for the cartel. Their main task was to defend their turf from rival groups, police, and the military. They stole, kidnapped, extorted, and assassinated where necessary to keep the cartel running smoothly.

The falcons were at the bottom of the cartel hierarchy. They were the eyes and ears for the gang and reported back to the hitmen and lieutenants the activities of their rivals, police, and others who were actively working against them.

Salazar didn't usually communicate with falcons directly, he had lieutenants who listened to their grievances and dealt with their issues. But today, he'd agreed to meet with this particular falcon because of what had happened a few months ago in Venezuela.

"Are you sure?" Salazar asked.

"Positive. She had a meeting in Austin with that pain-in-our-ass DEA asshole Calum Branch, and some FBI shithead as well. She was there at least four hours. They're already trying to crack down on our operation here in Austin because of what happened in Venezuela. The last thing we need is that bitch telling them anything else."

Salazar leaned back in his chair and eyed the low-level minion in front of him. He hadn't been opposed to the hijacking scheme because it was a means to an end. Namely, getting rid of Hugo Lamas, who'd been a pain in his father's ass way before he'd been thrown in jail. The

Sinaloa Cartel hated the Cartel of the Suns. And anytime they could take out one of those assholes was a good day.

It was unfortunate that they'd lost six of their own in the process, but he'd had a hand in personally picking the men who'd carried out the hijacking. He'd chosen them because they were expendable. He didn't mourn their deaths, but he didn't want any more of their brethren to die as a result either. Their deaths were honorable, but their sacrifice shouldn't bring negative attention to the cartel.

If Sinaloa had additional pressure put on their operation here in Austin, it wouldn't be good. They were already losing too much product because of crackdowns at the border, and he couldn't afford to lose any more.

"Bring her to me," Salazar told the only member of the group to survive the hijacking. "I'll figure out what she knows…and if she needs to die."

"But I can take her out easily. One tap to the head and she won't be an issue anymore," the falcon protested.

Salazar raised one eyebrow. "Are you disagreeing with my order?" he asked in a deadly even tone.

"No, of course not."

"Good. Then go get her and bring her here. I want to talk to this bitch myself. I'll find out what she told the Feds. If she needs to disappear for good, *I'll* make the order for that to happen." He leaned forward and pinned the falcon with a deadly gaze. "You aren't a hitman. I'm giving you this task as a reward for your loyalty, and because of the good job you did in fooling everyone in Venezuela. But when Gillian Romano is standing in front of me, I expect her to be unharmed. Understand me?" His threat was clear.

The falcon grimaced, but nodded. "*Si, Senor.*"

"Good. Now get the fuck out."

Salazar had forgotten about the falcon as soon as the door to his office closed. He had more important things to worry about than one fucking woman. Like the twenty-five-million-dollar shipment of cocaine that was supposed to arrive that afternoon.

Chapter Sixteen

THE LAST TWO WEEKS HAD BEEN IDYLLIC FOR GILLIAN. THE ONLY THING THAT would've made them better was if she'd been able to see Walker during the week. They spent the weekend he'd returned from his mission together, and it had been harder than she'd thought it would be to leave to go back to Georgetown on Sunday night.

But they both had work they had to get done. Their phone calls and texts were much more intimate after they'd spent the weekend making love, and Gillian loved the change.

Walker hadn't been kidding, he was very protective and concerned about her. But it hadn't been a hardship to send him quick notes letting him know when she left her apartment and when she returned.

He didn't care where she was, as long as she returned home safely afterward. It had actually been Gillian who'd suggested that maybe they could both download a tracker app on their phones. He'd agreed in a heartbeat.

So now at any time of day, she could click on the app and see exactly where Walker was, and vice versa. It felt a little stalkerish, but Gillian couldn't deny that it made her feel safe that he knew where she was at all times.

The Howard anniversary party was quickly approaching and because it involved over three hundred guests, it was taking up most of her time and energy. She had a few small parties and gatherings that she was also planning and executing, but those were pretty straightforward and didn't take much effort.

Today, Gillian was meeting the Howards' daughter downtown at a catering company so she could taste different kinds of cakes and make the final decision on what she wanted at the anniversary party.

Since the meeting was at ten, Gillian hoped the Austin traffic wouldn't be too bad getting into the city. She'd already scoped out the area and there was a parking garage within a block of where they were meeting, which was a relief. She hated trying to find parking downtown.

Gillian knew Walker was busy that morning with meetings, but she decided to give him a quick call just to say good morning. He'd told her that she could call whenever she wanted, he'd always pick up as long as he wasn't busy.

"Hey," he said after only two rings.

"Hi," Gillian said happily. She didn't always get to talk to him in the mornings, so she was pleased when she'd been able to catch him.

"Did you have a good morning?" he asked.

"No."

"No? Why not? What happened?" Walker asked worriedly.

"I didn't get to shower with my boyfriend," she said with a pout. "And I had to get my own coffee, and my Wonder Woman coffee mug was dirty."

"Oh, you poor thing," Walker said, the relief that she'd been kidding easy to hear in his tone. "Sounds like your boyfriend is being a slacker."

Loving their banter, Gillian beamed. "I don't know, he more than makes up for not being around during the week when we get together on the weekends."

"Yeah?"

"Oh, yeah," Gillian said with feeling. "How was your morning? How'd PT go? Did you run a marathon this morning for fun?"

He chuckled. "Only six miles. Then we hit the obstacle course and ran through that a few times."

"A few?" Gillian asked. She knew he and his friends had probably done it at least twenty times in a row. And had probably put on their rucksacks for half of those rotations. Walker and the others were serious about staying in top physical shape. She knew it wasn't easy for Walker, since he was getting close to forty, but she'd seen him work out...there wasn't a doubt in her mind that he was just as fit as his friends who were years younger.

"You on your way to Austin?" Walker asked, turning the conversation from him.

He did that a lot, and at first it irritated Gillian, because she thought he was trying to avoid talking about himself. But eventually she realized that he wasn't trying to dodge her questions, he just wasn't self-centered in any way, shape, or form. He told her once that he asked her a lot of questions because he was more interested in *her*. If he couldn't be with her, he wanted to know everything about what she was doing and thinking. It made him feel closer to her. How could she argue about that?

"Yeah. I left about ten minutes ago. There's a bit of traffic, but it's not too bad."

"You can't wait to eat cake this early in the day, can you?" Walker asked with a chuckle.

Gillian smiled. Walker had found out all about her sweet tooth during the weekends they'd spent together. Her ideal breakfast was coffee and a sticky-sweet doughnut. "Hey, it's a tough job, but someone has to do it," she told him.

"True."

"What's on your plate for today?" she asked.

"Meetings this morning, then me and the guys are headed over to one of the elementary schools on base to volunteer. We're reading to the kids, things like that."

Imagining Walker sitting on a too-small chair reading to a bunch of kids who would be enthralled by whatever story he chose to read to them made Gillian's panties damp. She wasn't ready to have kids, but she couldn't deny the thought of Walker holding a small baby made her ovaries go into overdrive. "Sounds fun," she told him.

He huffed out a laugh. "Kids scare the crap out of me," he admitted.

It was Gillian's turn to laugh. "Why?"

"Because I'm afraid I'm gonna say the wrong thing and they'll go home saying some bad word they learned from me and will be scarred for life. They're like little sponges, absorbing everything around them, and I know I'm too intense. The last thing I want is them learning any bad habits from me."

"Walker," Gillian scolded. "You're intense, yes, but not in a bad way. I'm sure they see you watching out for them. Being friendly with your guys. Being respectful to their teachers. Not tolerating bullying. Greeting the smallest kid in the class with a special handshake. They're not stupid, they know when adults are bullshitting them, and you're the last person to do that."

"Thanks, Di," he said softly.

Gillian heard someone say something to him in the background, and he told them he'd be right there. She wasn't surprised when he came back on the phone and said, "I have to go."

"I heard."

"Thanks for calling. I needed to hear your voice this morning. I might be busy, but you'll let me know how the taste test went this morning and when you're on your way home?"

"Of course. I'm leaning toward the double chocolate cake, it should appeal to the greatest amount of people, but we'll see how everything tastes when we get there," Gillian said. "You're still coming down this afternoon, right?"

"Wouldn't miss it. If possible, I'll see if I can leave a bit early and get there in time for dinner. That okay?"

"Of course. You're always welcome here." Gillian had given him a key to her apartment the weekend after he'd gifted her with the one to his place. Since he'd returned from being deployed, their relationship had moved forward at warp speed, but Gillian wasn't complaining. She just hated having to be apart from him during the week. They hadn't talked about moving in together, but every Sunday night when she had to say goodbye, it got harder and harder.

She knew it wasn't feasible for him to move to Georgetown to live with her, so if they were going to move their relationship to the next level, she'd have to be the one to go to him. It would be difficult for her business, and she'd have to put a lot of miles on her car, but if Walker asked, she'd move in with him tomorrow.

She'd had a long conversation with Ann about her relationship with Walker and even though she'd been afraid her friend was going to tell her she was crazy, and that she was moving way too fast, Ann had asked her one question.

"If you got a phone call with the best news you'd ever heard in your life, who would be the first person you'd want to tell?"

The answer was easy. Walker. Gillian felt bad about that since she'd been friends with Ann for so long, but the other woman simply chuckled. "That's the way it's supposed to be when you love someone. They're the first person you should want to turn to when something good happens, *and* something bad. You know I love you, as do Clarissa and Wendy, but you told us from almost the second you got back from Venezuela that you thought he was it for you. Moving in with him, being in a relationship with him or anyone else, doesn't mean you love us less, it just means we have more to gossip about when we get together."

"Gillian?"

She blinked and realized that she'd been daydreaming and not paying attention to Walker on the phone. "Sorry, I'm here."

"Drive safe, and be careful walking to and from the caterer."

"I will," Gillian said. "I've got the pepper spray you got me, and I'll make sure it's out and ready."

"Good."

"Although it's not even ten in the morning. I'm sure the homicidal maniacs are still sleeping from being up and causing mayhem until the wee hours of the morning."

Walker didn't even chuckle. "There's no timeline for bad shit happening."

"But you always tell me nothing good happens after midnight."

"Which is true. But that doesn't mean that assholes can't be drunk at nine in the morning, or looking for an easy mark to get some cash for the drugs they need to get them through the day."

"Okay, okay, okay. I get it. I'll be careful, Walker. Promise."

"Good."

"Say hi to your friends for me."

"I will. I'll talk to you later."

"Walker?"

"Yeah?"

He sounded distracted and Gillian knew he needed to go, that he had to get into a meeting. She'd wanted to tell him how much she missed him and how important he was to her, but while he was rushed didn't seem like the best time. "Have a good day," she said somewhat lamely.

"You too. Bye."

"Bye."

Gillian clicked off the phone connection and sighed. She loved talking to Walker. They never seemed to run out of things to say to each other. But now she needed to concentrate on the other cars around her and finding her way to the right address downtown. With all the one-way streets, she frequently got turned around.

But this time, she was able to figure out where she was going without any issues and she pulled into the parking garage with plenty of time to spare before her appointment. Gillian chose to park at the top of the garage, near the elevator doors. There were fewer cars at the top of the structure, but that was all right with her. Gillian had seen a documentary once on how shoddy architects had designed a parking garage and it had collapsed, trapping and squishing people on the lower levels. It seemed safer to park at the top. Yeah, it was a longer fall down, but at least she'd be on the top of all the debris.

Her friends gave her shit about being so paranoid, but Gillian didn't care. She'd get the last laugh when she was standing on top of the pile of rubble that used to be a parking garage.

She took the elevator down to the first floor and headed for the caterer.

An hour and a half later, and full of sugar from all the cakes she'd tasted, Gillian headed back to her car. They'd settled on two cakes for the party, one the double chocolate cake Gillian had guessed would be a favorite choice, and a simpler vanilla cake with chocolate frosting for the other.

Gillian was thinking about all the things she still needed to do to finalize everything for the Howards' anniversary party as she stepped out of the elevator on the top floor of the parking garage—and didn't see the two men in masks running toward her until it was too late to do anything.

The pepper spray Walker had given her was inside her purse, but even if it had been in her hand, she wouldn't have had time to do anything other than brace.

One of the men grabbed her around the waist and clamped his hand over her mouth.

Gillian screamed, but the sound barely traveled further than the next car over.

The second man grabbed her legs when she began to kick and fight. They shuffled her over to a white panel van—how cliché—and stuffed her inside when the door was opened.

There were no seats in the back of the van and it was full of all sorts of tools. Gillian had watched enough crime shows to know if the men managed to take her out of the garage, she was as good as dead. They could bring her to the middle of nowhere. Lord knew there were plenty of places in Texas that were totally isolated, even around Austin, that she didn't have a hope in hell of escaping.

Panicked, she fought as hard as she could. She knew she'd made contact with her kidnappers because there was a lot of grunting and swearing.

"Hold her down!" one man said.

"I'm trying!" the other answered.

"Hit her!" a third voice ordered.

The third voice registered in her consciousness as being female, which was a shock, and for a second, Gillian thought it sounded familiar, but then she couldn't think about anything other than the pain as a fist landed on her cheekbone.

Momentarily stunned, she stopped fighting. The door slid shut and she heard the engine rumble as it started.

No!

She tried to fight some more, but because of her momentary lapse, the men had gotten the upper hand. One grabbed her wrists and the other zip-tied them together. He tightened them so much, she squeaked in pain.

"Shut up," one of her kidnappers growled into her face.

She spit on him.

He swore, and the last thing Gillian remembered was his fist coming toward her face.

Trigger couldn't concentrate on the book he was reading to the group of second-graders gathered around him. He'd been set up in a corner of the classroom with five kids, and he loved their enthusiasm and the way they hung on his every word. But he couldn't stop thinking about Gillian.

It was two o'clock, and she should've been done with her appointment at the caterer and back home well before now.

But every time he checked the app on his phone, it indicated she was still in the parking garage near the caterer. He figured she'd forgotten her phone in her car and maybe she'd taken her client to lunch after they'd chosen which dessert to offer at the anniversary party in a couple weeks.

But that didn't really make sense. Gillian *always* had her phone with her. As a small-business owner, she relied on email and phone to talk to new and current clients. She might silence it when she was in a meeting, but she never left it behind. And seeing that blinking icon on the app that said her phone hadn't moved—long *after* her meeting should have ended—made no sense to him.

He hadn't even been able to check in on her until noon, when he and the team had been released to grab a quick bite before heading over to the elementary school. At first he hadn't thought much about where her phone was pinging, until he'd zoomed in and realized her phone was in the parking garage.

It wasn't fair to the kids, but Trigger read the book in his hands as fast as he could. He couldn't let this go. When he was finished, he stood and spent a moment praising each of the kids around him, then he strode toward the door. He flashed the "danger" sign to Lefty before he slipped out of the classroom.

He didn't bother with texting; he clicked on Gillian's name and brought the phone up to his ear. With the way his skin was crawling, he didn't really expect her to answer. And he was right, she didn't. Her voice mail kicked on after five rings. He left a quick message telling her that he was worried about her and asked her to please call him as soon as possible. He then sent a text telling her the same thing.

By the time he was done, Lefty and Grover had joined him in the hallway.

"What's wrong?" Lefty asked, all business.

"I don't know. It's Gillian. She had an appointment downtown this morning and she should've been done by now. The tracking app shows she's in the parking garage nearby. At least her phone is."

"You tried calling her?" Grover asked.

Trigger nodded. "No answer."

"Cops?" Lucky asked.

"You know as well as I do that they'll just tell me she's an adult and she doesn't have to report her every move to me. She'll have to be missing for twenty-four hours before they'll consider taking my report," Trigger said.

"But they could do a welfare check, right?" Grover asked.

"Maybe. I'm headed down there now."

"You want us to come with?" Lefty asked.

Trigger nodded. "If nothing's wrong and I'm overreacting, we can all have dinner or some-thing. I've got my bag in my car already, since I was headed down there later anyway."

"But if something *is* wrong, we'll be there to have your back," Grover said. He then opened the classroom door and signaled to the rest of the team that they needed to move out. Within five minutes, Trigger was surrounded by men who hadn't thought twice about coming to his aid, even if they didn't know what the issue was.

Lefty explained the situation and within five minutes, they'd all piled into both Trigger's and Doc's vehicles to make the trip down to Austin.

Trigger knew he was driving too fast but didn't care. The closer they got to Austin, and with every call that went unanswered by Gillian, he knew deep in his gut that something was very wrong.

She'd been very good about letting him know her whereabouts. The situation in Venezuela had scared her, but Trigger didn't think it had fundamentally changed the way she looked at the world. It was one of the many things he loved about her.

Fuck. He loved her.

From the first moment he'd pushed inside her body, she'd been his in a way no woman had ever been before.

Gillian still saw the good in people. In the world. She had an intrinsically positive outlook on life and felt as if everyone had good in them, that everyone was redeemable. Trigger knew differently, but he found her innocence refreshing.

He just hoped it hadn't gotten her killed.

Gillian regained consciousness in a blink. She wasn't confused, knew exactly what had hap-pened, but couldn't understand *why*.

Squinting, she looked around her—and her blood froze.

She was in some kind of rundown house. She had no idea where. There was trash and debris all around her, along with some shabby furniture. She was sitting in a very uncomfort-able wooden chair with her arms secured behind her back. Her ankles were also tied to the legs of the chair.

But the most frightening thing about her situation was the plastic tarp under her feet.

She wasn't an idiot. She'd seen *Dexter*, she knew what that meant. They were doing their best to contain her DNA so there would be no trace she'd been here.

Her limbs started shaking but Gillian couldn't stop. She whimpered in fear.

Just then the door opened, and she stared at the men who entered and felt herself shake even harder. With just a look, she knew the man in front wasn't someone who felt any sympathy for her. He was Hispanic, with dark hair and bottomless dark eyes. It was if they looked right through her. He didn't see Gillian Romano, he saw an enemy.

Being so loathed and hated wasn't a feeling Gillian was familiar with. She was a nice person. She went out of her way to make others comfortable and to make them like her. What she could've done to this man to make him hate her so much, she had no idea.

"So you're Gillian," the man said after he'd stopped in front of her.

Licking her lips, she nodded. Feeling thankful that she hadn't been gagged, Gillian couldn't seem to make her voice work.

"I hear you've been chatting with the Feds and DEA."

She blinked in surprise. She'd had no idea why she'd been snatched out of the garage, but that wasn't what she thought the man would say.

When she didn't respond, the man tilted his head and studied her. After a moment, he asked, "You have no idea who I am, do you?"

Gillian shook her head.

"Does the name Salazar mean anything to you?"

Gillian wracked her brain, but couldn't think of anyone she'd ever met with that last name, and she eventually shook her head once more.

The man chuckled, but it wasn't exactly a humorous sound. "I think you're the only person living within a thousand miles of Austin who hasn't heard of me," he said.

Gillian hated feeling at a disadvantage.

"I'm sorry, Mr. Salazar, I'm usually very good with names and faces. If we've met before, I've forgotten the circumstances."

If anything, her apology seemed to amuse him more.

"My name is Alfredo Salazar." He paused as if gauging whether knowing his first name would jog her memory. When she didn't say anything, he continued. "I'm the leader of the Sinaloa Cartel here in Texas…and really, all of the southern US."

Gillian's eyes widened. *Oh shit. Shit, shit, shit.* She didn't watch the news much, it was too depressing. But she'd recently had a very thorough education on the Sinaloa drug cartel, thanks to her plane being hijacked and a few internet searches.

"I see that's ringing some bells," Salazar said. "Let's start again. I have it on good authority you've been talking to the Feds and the DEA about us."

Gillian tried to swallow, but her mouth was too dry.

"I want to know what you told them. What you know. And if I think you're not being honest with me, then I'll have to have my friend here," he nodded to one of the men who had walked behind her to stand at her right shoulder, "remove one of your fingers. Then if I think you're still holding back, maybe I'll take an ear. Or a toe. I can play this game all day," he said, and Gillian had no doubt he'd do what he threatened. "So…what did you tell them about us?"

"No-Nothing," Gillian stammered. "I mean, they didn't really ask about you, about your organization."

Salazar nodded at the man standing behind her and before she could blink, he'd grabbed her hand and had a huge knife pressed against the base of her thumb.

"I'm told it hurts like a son of a bitch," Salazar said matter-of-factly.

"I swear, they didn't ask about the cartel at all!" she cried. "They wanted to talk to me about the passengers on the plane. That's it! I had to look at pictures of every single passenger and tell them what I remembered about them. They're trying to figure out who the seventh hijacker is. That's all!"

The man with the knife still held it against her thumb; he hadn't cut her yet, but Gillian knew she was only one second from losing a digit. The cold steel against her flesh was tricking her brain into thinking he *was* cutting her, especially since she couldn't see her hands where they were bound behind her.

"And who do you think it is?" Salazar asked.

"I don't know," Gillian wailed, scared out of her skull. "Maybe Leyton. He acted really weird and gave me the creeps. But as I told *them*, I didn't spend any time with the men so I couldn't tell them much."

"But you spent a lot of time with the women, didn't you?" Salazar asked.

Gillian nodded. "Of course. They kept us separated."

"You think maybe it's Alice? Or Janet? Maybe Maria Gomez?"

Gillian had no idea how this man knew who the other passengers were, but it shouldn't have surprised her. Whoever the seventh hijacker was had obviously passed along the information about what went on inside the plane.

"I don't know," she said again. "I'm just an event planner. Not an investigator."

Salazar studied her for so long, Gillian was afraid to even breathe. The man holding her hand had an iron grip, and she knew she couldn't do a damn thing if Salazar decided to cut off her thumb.

"What were you doing in Austin today?" Salazar finally asked.

"I had a meeting with a client to decide what kind of cake to serve at her parents' anniversary party."

"You weren't meeting with the Feds again?"

"No! I haven't heard from them since I met with them a month or so ago," Gillian said.

"And I suppose you don't know that the caterer you visited is located smack-dab in the middle of drug central, downtown Austin?" Salazar drawled.

Gillian blinked in surprise. She *hadn't* known that. She had no reason *to* know that little fact.

"Christ," Salazar said with a shake of his head. "You're like the epitome of white privilege, aren't you?"

Gillian had no idea what he was talking about, so she didn't agree or disagree, feeling that was the safer thing to do at the moment.

"You live in your lily-white world, never worrying about being shot at because of the color of your skin. Never having to bother your little head about finding yourself in the wrong part of town because your blonde hair and green eyes will save you somehow. Even in the middle of a fucking hijacking, you came out on top, being picked as the chosen one to talk to the authorities." He shook his head. "You ever done drugs, Ms. Romano?"

Gillian shook her head.

"Not even smoked a little pot?" Salazar insisted.

She shook her head again.

"Ever been tempted?"

Again, she silently answered in the negative.

"There's always a first time," Salazar said smoothly. He crouched down a few feet in front of her, not touching the plastic sheeting that had been laid at her feet. "Everyone says that drugs make you feel like shit. That they're bad. But what you don't know is how fucking *amazing* a little cocaine can make you feel. It's the best feeling, euphoric. There's nothing like that first high. You'll spend the rest of your life chasing the feeling you got the first time you shot up. You don't want to feel good, Gillian?"

She hated the way her name sounded on his lips. On the outside, Alfredo Salazar was good-looking. But she could feel that he was evil through and through. He wouldn't hesitate to have her killed. He loved money and power, that was it. All she could do was stare at him in terror. She didn't want him to force cocaine on her. Or any other kind of drug. She didn't want to be addicted. Not when everything in her life was going so well.

"Look at you, your heart is beating out of your chest. You're like a feral dog, too scared to move, but terrified to stay where you are as well. You honestly have no clue who the bad guy was on that plane, do you? Out of all the people you befriended, you have no idea who wants to see you and everyone else dead."

"No," Gillian whispered.

"And you told the authorities that too, right?"

She nodded.

"Bet that pissed them off," he muttered.

"They weren't thrilled," Gillian said hesitantly. She'd hated letting them down, but she'd told them everything she could think of. She knew nothing she'd said had helped in the slightest. They'd been polite and thanked her for her insights, but deep down, she was aware she'd disappointed them.

Salazar shook his head and muttered more to himself than her, "Fucking bitches and their drama." Then he lifted his chin at the man holding the knife to her hand and he let go. Gillian breathed a sigh of relief. But it only lasted a heartbeat, because the man behind her then wrapped his hands around her head and tilted it backward.

Gillian lost sight of Salazar and struggled in the man's grip. But with her hands tied behind her and her legs immobilized, she had no leverage. No way to protect herself.

"Relax, *chica*," Salazar said. "I believe you. I apologize that you were inconvenienced today. I should've done a bit more looking into the situation before believing one of my falcons. But that doesn't change the fact that I can't simply drop you back into your world of ignorance."

"Please, don't kill me," Gillian whispered as she stared up at the ceiling. "I won't say anything about what happened. Hell, I don't even *know* what happened, or why."

She heard Salazar chuckle. "I'm sorry, but I don't believe you. You'll tell someone. A friend, a boyfriend, the cops, someone, then I'll have to worry about that shit, along with all the other crap piled up on my plate at the moment. But…I can't help but be intrigued by the innocence and goodness you wear like a fucking cloak."

Gillian shivered as she felt a finger trace along her vulnerable throat. Salazar had obviously gotten up and approached her. With her head forced back like it was, she was completely at the mercy of this man. "I was like you…once. But that ended on my ninth birthday when I was introduced to the way my life was going to be. I saw my first man killed that day. He deserved it for snitching on the Sinaloa, but it was…jarring, to see a man's blood spurt out of him and watch as he writhed on the floor, begging for mercy."

Gillian couldn't stop the tears that fell out of her eyes. She wanted to be brave. Wanted to be the kind of person who could kick ass like the ones in the books she read. But she wasn't. She was tied up and helpless. She had no idea if Walker or anyone even knew she was missing at this point.

"In a second, you're going to be offered a drink. You're going to drink it without fuss. All of it. Every drop. Understand?"

She didn't want to. She knew whatever was in the cup was probably poisoned and this was literally her last seconds to live.

"I can see your mind working overtime. It won't kill you. It's Rohypnol. It'll relax you. In fifteen or twenty minutes, you'll fall asleep. You won't remember what happened here. You won't be able to tell the cops anything about me or what we talked about. It'll be as if it never happened. This is in your best interest. It's this…or my lieutenant slicing your throat and you bleeding out."

Salazar leaned over her until Gillian was looking up into his steely brown eyes. "But this is your only free pass, Ms. Romano. If I hear you've somehow remembered our little talk today, and you've snitched, it won't go as well for you a second time. And I understand you have some good friends in the area too, right? You wouldn't want your friends—Ms. Pierce, Ms. Reed, or Ms. Thomas—to have an accident, would you?"

The thought of Ann, Wendy, or Clarissa being in the hands of this cold-hearted monster made her physically sick. Gillian shook her head as best she could.

"Good. So we're on the same page. Now, drink up."

Before she could agree or not agree, a plastic cup was pressed against her lips and the goon who held her head pressed on an area of her jaw that made her cry out in pain. With her mouth open, the second man tipped the glass and she had no choice but to drink.

It tasted horrible and burned as it went down her throat. For a second, Gillian thought they'd forced her to drink acid or antifreeze or something, but when she inhaled through her nose as she swallowed, she knew it was some kind of alcohol. Tequila maybe.

She sputtered and choked, but the men didn't relent. By the time they let go of her, she was soaked from her chin to her belly button. She tried to breathe, but gagged instead.

A huge hand covered her mouth from behind and she stared up at Salazar as he said, "If you throw it up, you'll have to swallow it back down. Can't let good roofies go to waste."

Forcing herself to take a big breath through her nose, Gillian tried to tamp down the need to puke. When the man finally let go of her, she immediately inhaled and asked, "What now?"

"Now? We wait for you to go to sleep. Then my men will find a nice quiet place to drop you off. Wouldn't want any big bad drug dealers to find you passed out now, would we? They might not be as nice to you as I've been."

Gillian wanted to scratch his eyes out, but she couldn't do anything but sit there and listen.

"Just because I made a mistake in believing my falcon and having you brought in doesn't mean I'm not keeping an eye on you. Be a good girl, go back to your white world of privilege and stay there. Understand?"

Gillian had no idea what he was talking about with a falcon, but she nodded anyway. She was still terrified of what was going to happen to her when she went unconscious. The alcohol was going straight to her head, but it was the drug he'd forced her to ingest that worried her the most.

She knew all about women being roofied at clubs. It was an infamous date-rape drug. She didn't want to forget what happened here. It seemed very, *very* important that she not forget.

As the minutes ticked by, she repeated the words over and over in her head in the slight hope that maybe when she woke up, her unconscious mind would be able to recall them.

Salazar, falcon, Salazar, falcon, Falazar, salcon…

The room was beginning to spin.

"That's it, Gillian. Close your eyes and go to sleep. When you wake up, this will all be a bad dream."

She did as ordered, feeling as if her body belonged to someone else. *Salafar, fanzar…*

Gillian tried to hang on, tried to memorize what she needed to before she lost it completely, but it was too late.

Salazar waited until he was sure the bitch was out before motioning to his lieutenants. "Bring Vilchez to me as soon as she can be found. First, I told her to bring Gillian to me unharmed. Those bruises on her face are gonna piss her man off, and that's the *last* thing we need. Secondly, this meeting was unnecessary and potentially dangerous to our organization. She's already on the Feds' radar, and her new boyfriend is one of the men who took out Luis and the others. I've done as much damage control as I can do here, but there's still a chance she'll remember something and talk. Vilchez has a *lot* to answer for."

"*Si, Senor,*" the men said in unison.

"Where do you want us to put her?" the man who'd forced the roofied drink down Gillian's throat asked.

"Don't care. Somewhere without cameras," Salazar said impatiently, then turned and left the room. He was pissed he'd wasted his time on this shit today. He had more important things to do—namely, distributing the millions of street dollars' worth of cocaine he'd just had delivered the day before.

Vilchez would be dealt with one way or another. Making sure his falcons knew their place was imperative, and disciplining Vilchez would serve as a reminder of how they were supposed to be serving Sinaloa. Watching and reporting so they could stay under the radar. Not lying about what they'd seen or heard to serve their own vendettas.

Sinaloa came first, period. When a falcon agreed to work for Salazar, he or she was putting their own needs second to those of the cartel. A reminder of that would be good for everyone.

The falcons would be scared into thinking before they acted.

The hitmen would have a chance to practice their interrogation techniques.

And the lieutenants would learn to think twice before bringing stupid shit to his door.

Shaking his head, Salazar strode confidently to the car that was waiting at the curb. His Mercedes was out of place in the rundown neighborhood, but no one would say a word, he was sure of that. He owned this part of town. Half the residents were working for him and the other half needed the drugs he supplied.

Putting thoughts of Gillian Romano out of his head, Salazar settled onto the leather seat of his car and nodded at his driver. This little meeting might've been an amusing break from his normal routine, but it was also annoying, because now it meant he had to deal with the reason it had come about in the first place.

"Fucking bitches and their drama," he murmured for the second time that afternoon, before picking up one of his many untraceable cell phones and dialing another one of his lieutenants. Time to get back to work making money and selling drugs.

Chapter Seventeen

FIVE HOURS.

That's how long it had been since Trigger figured Gillian had gone missing.

He and his team had gone straight to the parking garage where her phone was pinging and, after driving through it, had found her car on the top level. Her purse, with her phone and pepper spray inside, was also there, kicked underneath a car near the elevators.

The app had said the phone had been there since eleven thirty-three and it was now four-thirty. He felt sick and at the moment had no idea what to do next to try to find her. They'd called the police as soon as they'd found her purse and realized she was missing, but searching for someone took time. Time Gillian might not have.

He'd told the cops as much as he could about Gillian being a hostage a couple months ago and how the seventh hijacker hadn't been identified, but knew none of that was any help. Lucky had called the DEA agent who'd interviewed Gillian, and he'd been in contact with the FBI, but again, nothing happened fast with those bureaucracies, and the thought of Gillian being in the hands of the drug cartel who'd had no problem killing innocent civilians on the plane ate away at his soul.

"We're gonna find her," Grover said quietly as he stood next to Trigger on the top level of the garage. Trigger hadn't wanted to leave since it was the last place Gillian had been. The surveillance cameras were on a timer, and at the exact moment his woman had been taken, the fucking things had been pointed at the other end of the garage. By the time they'd swung back around, Gillian was gone.

He'd promised to keep her safe, but how the hell could he do that when he had no idea who to keep her safe *from*?

"Trigger? Did you hear me?" Grover asked.

He nodded. The words were merely platitudes. They both knew there was no way Grover could promise that they'd find her. Thousands of people disappeared off the face of the earth every day. Killed by strangers, or even by people they knew and loved, their bodies buried or dismembered and thrown away like trash.

The thought of his Gillian being discarded like that hurt like hell.

"Holy shit, Trigger!" Lefty exclaimed, running toward him and Grover at a dead sprint from the other end of the garage, where he'd been looking for clues.

Trigger's heart stopped.

"A woman's been found on the other side of the city," Lefty told him excitedly. "She was lying unconscious in a parking lot between two cars. They think it's Gillian!"

"Is she alive?" Trigger forced himself to ask.

"Yes. She's being transferred to St. David's, north of here."

Trigger was on the move before Lefty had finished talking.

Gillian was alive. That was the only thing that mattered to him at the moment.

Brain got behind the wheel of Trigger's Blazer and drove like a bat out of hell to St. David's. He didn't bother to park, but pulled up outside the emergency room entrance to let everyone out.

Trigger made a mental note to thank him later, but for now, all his attention was focused on getting to Gillian.

He strode up to the desk and noticed that the woman's eyes widened in alarm at his approach, but he didn't slow down.

"Gillian Romano," he barked. "She should've just been brought in. She was found unconscious in a parking lot. Where is she?"

The woman cleared her throat and said, "I'm sorry, sir, if you'll just take a seat, I'll see what I can find out about her. Are you family?"

"Yes." The lie came out without hesitation. "I'm her fiancé."

She looked skeptical, but didn't call him on it. "Okay, as I said, if you'll take a seat, I'll be with you as soon as I can."

"No," Trigger said with a shake of his head. "I need to be with her now. She has to be scared out of her mind."

The woman opened her mouth, probably to deny him once again, when a commotion sounded behind them.

Turning, Trigger immediately recognized Gillian lying on the stretcher that was being wheeled into the emergency room. Somehow they'd beaten the ambulance to the hospital.

Without hesitation, Trigger headed for the woman who held his heart in her hand.

"Step back, sir." He heard someone say, but he didn't. He couldn't.

"Gillian?" he called when he got close.

Her head turned—and the second he caught sight of her, Trigger wanted to fucking kill someone. She had the beginnings of a black eye and her cheekbone was bruised.

But it was the clear finger marks on her neck that had him seeing red.

"Walker?" she croaked and held out a hand to him.

Both the paramedics' heads swung toward him at the same time security closed in on the group. Trigger knew his team had been at his back the entire time, and they probably made quite an imposing sight to the employees in reception.

But before he could be hauled away from Gillian, one of the paramedics held out his hand. "He's fine," the man barked, stopping the security officers in their tracks. "She hasn't said much since she came to in the ambulance. But she recognizes him. Let him through."

Grateful for the reprieve, Trigger didn't hesitate, he went right up to Gillian's side and gripped her hand in his. He tried to assess her, but when she whimpered, he couldn't look anywhere but into her eyes. "I'm here, Di," he told her softly. "You're okay. I'm here."

"Walker," she said again.

"Move with us," the paramedic ordered, and without looking away from Gillian's dilated pupils, Trigger nodded.

"You're okay," he repeated as he walked alongside the gurney with Gillian's hand in his. They didn't get a chance to say anything else as the paramedics wheeled her into a room and got to work transferring her from their gurney to the bed. The grip Gillian had on his hand was almost painful, but there was no way Trigger was going to complain.

She looked okay, beyond the bruises on her face and throat. He turned to listen to a paramedic as he briefed the doctor who appeared inside the room.

"Patient's name is Gillian Romano, age unknown, as she didn't tell us anything other than her name. She was found unconscious in a parking lot on the south end of town. Other than the superficial bruising, we haven't found any other obvious injuries. No broken bones and no pain anywhere that we can tell. Her heart rate and blood pressure are high, but that's most likely because she didn't seem to know where she was or what was happening when she regained consciousness. We started an IV, but we suspect she's high or has ingested some sort of drug within the last few hours because of her dilated pupils."

Trigger listened with a bizarre mixture of horror and relief.

The doctor nodded. "Nurse, please do a complete blood panel and we'll see if we can get her to tell us what she's taken. I'd also like a rape kit done, just in case. She might need an MRI to make sure she didn't hit her head at any point. Gillian, can you look at me? What happened?"

Instead of looking at the doctor, Gillian kept her eyes glued to Trigger's. He hated, *hated*, the look of terror in her eyes. "It's okay, sweetheart. You're safe now. Can you tell us what happened?"

She shook her head.

"You're safe," he reiterated.

"I don't remember," she whispered. "I'd tell you if I could, but I don't remember anything. All I know is that I woke up in an ambulance and my head hurt."

Trigger's stomach rolled. "What's the last thing you remember?"

Gillian swallowed hard and closed her eyes. After a moment, she opened them and said, "Talking to you on the phone in my car."

"You were going to the caterer to taste cakes for the Howards' anniversary party," he prompted.

She blinked. "I don't remember anything about that. Did I make it there?"

"Yes. You parked in the garage nearby and met with the Howards' daughter. You guys picked out two different cakes." Trigger knew all this because he'd talked to the caterer himself to verify that Gillian had actually made it there.

"I can't remember," she whimpered.

Trigger touched the backs of his fingers lightly to her face. "Does this hurt?"

She shook her head, but winced when she pressed against his fingers. "My throat hurts though, and I feel as if I'm hungover."

"If you'd please step back, we need to examine her," the nurse said impatiently.

Trigger reluctantly let go of Gillian's hand and stepped to the side.

The second he let go of her hand, Gillian started to shake. Trigger wanted to go right back to her, but he forced himself to stay where he was. He knew he was lucky to be allowed to remain in the room, and he didn't want to do anything to force the doctor to kick him out.

He watched as Gillian's clothes were removed and placed into a bag for the police to collect later.

"Damp," the nurse said as she cut Gillian's shirt off. "Smells like alcohol too. Were you drinking earlier?" she asked.

Gillian shook her head, but kept her eyes closed as her body was manipulated by the medical personnel.

"She's got ligature marks around her wrists and ankles," the nurse added. "Looks like they're bruising, but the skin's not broken."

"We'll need pictures for the detective assigned to her case," the doctor said.

They were talking as if Gillian wasn't there. As if she couldn't hear every word they said. It infuriated Trigger, but he kept quiet.

That was, he was silent until it came time for the nurse to do the rape kit, and she tried to kick him out of the room. "You'll need to step outside, sir," she told him firmly.

Doing his best not to lose his shit, Trigger stepped up to the bed and took hold of Gillian's hand once more. "Do you want me to leave, Gilly?" he asked quietly.

Her eyes popped open and she shook her head frantically. "No! Don't go! Please!"

"I'm staying," Trigger told the nurse firmly.

She pressed her lips together but didn't force the issue.

"I was raped?" Gillian asked fearfully as she looked up into Trigger's eyes.

He eased himself into a chair near her head and put his hand on the uninjured side of her face. "It's just a precaution."

"But was I?" she asked. "I can't remember anything. I don't hurt…down there. Did someone touch me when I was unconscious? I don't think I would've gotten drunk in the middle of the day…but I guess I did?"

"*Shhh*, sweetheart. Don't get yourself all worked up."

"I can't remember!" she repeated in a tone full of agony.

"They took blood. They'll find out what you were given. Until then, you can't panic, Di."

Gillian squeezed her eyes shut and did her best to control her breathing as the nurse put her legs in stirrups and began the rape test.

"I'm not Wonder Woman," Gillian whispered. "I'm scared to death. My head and neck hurt, and apparently I was tied up. How come I can't remember any of it? That makes no sense!"

"You being scared doesn't make you any less amazing or kick-ass, Gillian. And not remembering makes sense if you were given something to help you forget," Trigger soothed.

"But why?"

"Why what?"

"Why didn't they kill me?"

Trigger had been wondering the same thing, but he didn't let on. "Maybe because whoever took you realized how amazing you are, and killing you would put a black mark on his soul he'd never recover from."

For the first time since he'd caught her eye as she was being wheeled in, Trigger saw something in her expression other than absolute abject terror. "Yeah, I'm sure that was it. Must've been my wicked sense of humor."

Trigger was overwhelmed with gratitude that his woman had managed to break free of the tight hold fear had on her.

"We're going to figure this out," he told her, looking intently into her eyes as he said it, so she'd believe him. "Brain and the rest of the team is on this. I want you to come and stay with me until whoever did this is caught."

"And if they can't catch him? It's not as if I can give any information about what happened," she said.

"Then you'll just have to stay with me forever." Nothing felt as right as the thought of going to sleep every night with Gillian by his side and waking up to the same.

"If you're feeling responsible for whatever happened to me, and that's why you're asking, then my answer is no," she told him.

Trigger opened his mouth to protest, but she went on before he could.

"But if you're asking because you truly want me there, if you might think you could someday love me as much as I love you, then my answer is yes."

They were in the middle of an emergency room. A nurse had just put Gillian's legs down after doing a rape test, and Trigger was overwhelmed with her bravery.

"I love you. When I realized you were missing, it felt as if my heart had been ripped out of my chest. It only started beating again when we got word that you'd been found and were alive. I want you to live with me so I can see your smiling face every day. So I can feed you coffee and doughnuts every morning and hear your sigh of contentment. I want to laugh with you and argue as well…simply so we can make up afterward. And yes, I want to keep you safe, but eventually this hard time will pass, and I'll still want to wake up to your gorgeous face every morning."

"Damn, that was beautiful," the nurse mumbled as she busied herself off to the side, preparing slides for the labs.

Gillian huffed out a laugh. "I'm not quitting my job. I've still got events to organize and finalize."

Trigger frowned, but nodded.

"How about this—I finish with the events I've got planned right now, then I switch my focus to the Killeen area. That doesn't mean I'm going to stop working in Austin, because I have a lot of contacts here already and repeat clients, but I'll do my best to stay closer to home."

"I'd move if I could," Trigger told her honestly.

"I know. But what you do is important, and you have to be as close to the base as possible."

She hadn't said anything that wasn't true, but it still smarted. He nodded.

The doctor came back into the room. "How do you feel, Ms. Romano?"

Gillian shrugged. "I'm okay."

"On a scale of one to ten, where ten is the most pain you've ever felt in your entire life and one is no pain whatsoever, where would you put yourself right now?"

"Three?" Gillian said with a shrug. "My head and throat hurt, but that's about it."

The doctor nodded approvingly. "You'll need to talk to the detective when he arrives, but I don't think there's any need to keep you overnight. Your pupils are still a bit dilated, but other than not remembering what happened, you don't seem confused or disoriented."

"I'm not," Gillian told him.

"Do you have someone who can stay with you?"

"Yes, she does," Trigger said immediately. "She's going to be staying with me. I'm in the Army and have enough medical knowledge to watch over her. I can bring her to the hospital if her condition or pain level changes."

The doctor nodded again. "Good. I hope they find whoever did this to you."

"Me too," Gillian said.

Then the doctor smiled distractedly and spun on his heels and left the room, his attention already on his next patient.

Trigger knew they needed to wait for the police detective to get there, but he wanted nothing more than to wrap Gillian up and take her home. He was well aware that he'd almost lost her. He had no idea what happened, but he had a gut feeling it had to do with the hijacking. Someone wanted information, and they'd decided to snatch one of the people who might have it. He made a mental note to call the FBI agent and make sure the other passengers were on high alert.

Gillian had been kidnapped, probably questioned, then given something to make sure she didn't remember anything before being dropped off at a random location, largely unhurt and unmolested. It was more than odd, and it didn't make sense…which made it all the more worrisome.

The rest of the afternoon and early evening was spent talking with Gillian's friends and making sure they knew she was all right and where she'd be living for the foreseeable future. The detective also arrived, and it was painful and frustrating—on all their parts—to have to listen to Gillian say over and over again that she didn't remember anything about her abduction.

The detective left with no more information than they'd had before. He'd also confirmed Trigger's suspicion that if they didn't get any DNA from her clothes, and if she hadn't been assaulted, there wouldn't be much the police could do to find the perpetrators unless Gillian remembered something.

Trigger knew she was frustrated and exhausted, and when the doctor finally signed her discharge papers, he couldn't get her out of there fast enough. She was wearing a pair of scrubs a nurse had scrounged up and she fell asleep almost the second he started driving north.

His teammates had been there with him the entire time. Bringing them food for dinner and doing their best to keep Gillian's spirits up.

Lefty and Brain were with Trigger. The others had left with Doc, back to the parking garage to retrieve Gillian's car, which they'd drop off at Trigger's apartment complex.

"I've been researching," Brain said after they'd been driving for fifteen minutes and they were all sure Gillian was asleep. "The doctor suspects Rohypnol, and I agree. In some cases, people are able to remember bits and pieces of the time right before they were dosed."

Trigger grunted. It would be helpful if Gillian remembered something, but it wouldn't change what had happened to her.

"Who do you think is behind this?" Lefty asked.

"Honestly?" Trigger asked.

"Of course," Lefty said.

"Sinaloa," Trigger replied with no doubt in his voice.

"Yeah, that's what I was thinking too," Lefty confirmed. "Roofies are easy to get in Mexico. They're legal down there, so it wouldn't be hard to put some into a drink and force her to ingest it."

"But kidnapping her doesn't make a lot of sense," Brain added. "Why now? I mean, they've had months to make their move and take her out if they wanted. And why release her without any real harm?"

"I'm guessing they heard about her visit with the FBI. Maybe they wanted to know what she told them. If she knows who the seventh hijacker was," Lefty mused.

"And when they found out she had no clue, they decided it wasn't worth the risk to kill her," Brain concluded.

Trigger's jaw ticked in frustration. Everything his teammates were saying made sense, but he hated that it was *Gillian* they were talking about so unemotionally. This was what they did with every mission. They talked it through…but it felt wrong this time.

"Guys?" he asked.

"Yeah?"

"What's up?"

"Can we please drop it for now? The last thing Gillian needs is to subconsciously hear us talking about her," Trigger said tightly.

"You're right, sorry," Brain apologized.

"Yeah, sorry, we should've waited," Lefty added.

Trigger took a deep breath and tried to relax, which was impossible.

"So…you're moving her in, huh?" Lefty asked, and Trigger could hear the smirk in his voice even if he couldn't see him from the driver's seat.

"Yup."

"She realize that she's never going back to her apartment in Georgetown?"

Trigger smiled for the first time in hours. "Don't know. Don't care."

His friends chuckled.

"You need help moving her stuff from her place to yours?"

"Would appreciate that," Trigger said gratefully.

"She gonna lose her mind when we show up with her shit?" Brain asked.

"Don't know," Trigger said again. "But in the long run, she'll be okay with it. I love her, she loves me back. She was meant to be mine. There's no way she's living anywhere other than by my side until I know for sure she's safe from whatever is threatening her. And afterward, I'm hoping she'll be so comfortable, she won't even think about leaving."

"Your place is pretty small," Brain observed. "I bet you could find something bigger. Maybe a three- or four-bedroom condo or something."

"It's on my radar," Trigger admitted. Just last week, he'd perused the internet looking for places to rent around the base that were bigger than his apartment. "But for now, my place will do. It's small but safe. And I'd rather not worry about being distracted with moving until the threat to her is over and done."

"Agreed. Happy for you, Trigger," Lucky said.

"Thanks."

"I'd complain about things not being the same, now that you've found a woman, but after seeing Ghost and his team fall—and fall *hard*—and how their relationships have all weathered the changes, I don't mind so much," Brain said.

Trigger agreed. The other Delta team had proven that, with the right women, having a family and a life as a Delta soldier could go hand in hand. He hadn't been looking for love, but it had fallen into his lap, and he'd be damned if he'd give up Gillian because of fear of making a relationship work.

His and Gillian's souls were linked and nothing was going to take her from him. Nothing and nobody. He'd do everything in his power to make sure of it.

Chapter Eighteen

A WEEK LATER, GILLIAN WAS FEELING MUCH MORE LIKE HERSELF. THE FIRST FEW days had been rough. She'd been sore and she felt extremely vulnerable. She hated not being able to remember what had happened to her. She'd finally been able to recall being at the caterer and tasting the different kinds of cake, but everything after she'd left the building until she'd woken up in the hospital was still a blank.

It felt good to be able to hole up in Walker's apartment and hide from the world. She knew without a doubt that he'd keep her safe. She hadn't even been upset when his team had shown up with a whole hell of a lot of her stuff from her apartment. Things were cramped in Walker's place now, with her stuff comingled with his, but he'd never complained.

For the first two nights, he'd held her all night long, reassuring her when she woke up with nightmares. But after that, she'd gotten tired of him treating her like a fragile piece of glass. She wanted to be Diana Prince for him again. Be the tough woman he'd nicknamed her after.

So the third night, she'd made her move before they'd climbed into bed. He wanted to continue to coddle her, but she knew she'd get her way when she got down on her knees in front of him, and he didn't protest. Her face had still been sore, but that didn't mean she couldn't show him without words how much she loved him.

He hadn't let her linger too long, much to her disappointment, but he'd more than made up for it when he picked her up, placed her on her back on his bed, and proceeded to give her two of the most intense orgasms she'd ever had. Then he'd made love to her…there was no other word for it. He was tender and gentle, and he looked her in the eyes the entire time he moved inside her.

Her third orgasm had been less intense than the previous two, but just as earthshattering. When he'd finally let himself go, she couldn't take her eyes away from the pulse pounding in his neck as he'd thrown his head back and groaned through his orgasm.

She'd thought their lovemaking would be a turning point, that things would go back to normal and he'd loosen up a bit on his protectiveness. But she'd been wrong.

Now Gillian was torn. While she loved the fact he was so concerned, he refused to let her go anywhere by herself. She quickly felt as if she was losing her independence.

Ann, Wendy, and Clarissa had visited once, and Walker had only left when her friends had promised not to leave her alone. Of course, her friends had thought it was romantic and sweet, but Gillian was starting to get frustrated.

Yes, she'd been kidnapped and roofied.

Yes, she was still freaked about the whole thing.

But that didn't mean she'd suddenly turned into a five-year-old who had to be supervised at all times.

As the first week rolled into the next, Gillian became more and more irritated. Walker was being *too* protective. It was stifling, and even though she knew he loved her and *why* he was loath to have her out of his sight, it had to stop.

His latest decree was the last straw. He'd overheard her talking to the Howards' daughter and reassuring her that the party would go on as planned the upcoming weekend. As soon as she hung up, he'd started in.

"I don't think it's a good idea for you to go to Austin this weekend."

Gillian did her best to control her temper before she turned to face him. "Walker, I have to. This is my livelihood. I've spent nearly three months working on this party. I'm not missing it."

"You've done all the leg work, it'll happen just fine if you're there or if you aren't," he said in a maddeningly calm tone.

"You have no clue," she said a little harsher than she'd intended. "You were there at the zoo. You saw what I do. There are a million little details that need to be dealt with. Things go wrong and someone has to be there to redirect everyone."

"You can hire someone to do that. You should probably hire an assistant anyway," Walker said reasonably.

"Are you serious right now?" she asked, putting her hands on her hips.

"Yeah. I am. *You* can't seriously be thinking about going back to Austin already? Your face is still bruised and you were kidnapped a little over a week ago. Why would you think it's a good idea to go back there?"

Gillian had been holding back her frustration for a few days—and she couldn't do it anymore. "I love you, Walker. I do. But I can't be the kind of woman who's happy sitting at home waiting for her man to come back from deployment. I need to work. I love what I do. I thought you understood that?"

"I do," he said immediately, stepping toward her.

Gillian wasn't ready to be placated, so she backed up so he couldn't touch her. They both knew that was her weakness. That when he put his hands on her, she melted like a piece of chocolate on a hot day.

Walker straightened and his lips pressed together before he spoke again. "Fine. We haven't talked about this, so now's as good a time as any. When I realized you were missing, it was the worst day of my life. Worse than any mission I'd been on. My world stopped. I didn't know what to do or where to even start looking for you. Even worse was the fact that you'd already been missing for a couple hours. I know better than anyone how easy it is to kill someone. You might've already been dead before I knew you were missing. I wasn't there for you when I'd promised you'd be safe, and it almost destroyed me."

Gillian's defenses began to crumble at the evidence of his heartbreak. "Walker," she whispered.

He shook his head and spoke before she could continue.

"We'd done everything we could and it wasn't enough. The Feds had no idea where you might be, the surveillance cameras hadn't caught anything. Your phone, purse, and car were still there in the parking garage. We literally had no clues. *Nothing.* You could've been in Mexico already for all we knew. Then, by some miracle, we got the call that you'd been found alive. My heart started beating again at that moment, and I swore that I'd *never* let you down again."

"You didn't let me down," Gillian insisted. "There was nothing you could've done. Walker, I could get hurt or die walking down the street outside your apartment. Or driving to the grocery store. Or I could have a heart attack."

"Can you please stop talking about you dying?" he begged. "I can't take it. Not with you standing there with the bruises still on your face and you not letting me touch you."

"Okay, Walker."

"I'm not sure you realize how much of a miracle it is that you're standing in front of me right now. Every day, hundreds of people go missing, never to be seen again. And from everything Agent Tucker has found out, and what me and the team suspect as well, you were taken by the Sinaloa. The most ruthless and dangerous drug cartel the world has ever known. They hijacked a plane, for God's sake, in order to get back at a rival drug gang.

"Not only were you left alive, but they didn't sexually abuse you, they didn't break any bones, they didn't send body parts to me in the mail, threatening to do more if I didn't do what they wanted. You should *not* be standing in front of me right now. It makes no sense. None.

"I know I've been overbearing and an ass for the last week, but it's because I love you so damn much, and the thought of someone deciding they made a mistake and you shouldn't have been set free, and recapturing you, makes me absolutely crazy. I can't go through that again. I can't! It's unfair for you, and it makes me look like a domineering boyfriend when I can't leave your side for two minutes without making sure someone is watching over you, but I literally *can't* do anything else.

"I'll get better, I promise. But all I want is for you to be safe. I want to marry you. Have a family. Grow old with you. I know you're independent. I love that you have your own life, that you don't need me to be happy. If you ever decided you didn't love me anymore and you left me, it would suck, but ultimately, I'd be okay…because I'd know you were alive and well. But if you were killed, I wouldn't be able to survive.

"You were meant to be mine, Gillian. I need you like I need air to breathe. You've changed my life in such a short time it's almost unbelievable. I used to live for the Army. For my teammates. But now I live for *you*. Now that I've had a taste of what my life can be with you, I can't go back. Please tell me you understand."

Gillian's eyes were filled with tears. She'd known Walker was on edge and worried about her, but she hadn't realized to what extent. She took a step toward him, and before she realized that he'd moved, she was in his arms.

"I love you, Walker. I understand, I do. I'm not saying I want to jaunt off to Austin by myself. I don't think I'll be able to go there by myself ever again. I assumed you'd be *with* me." She looked up at him. "I swear I'll be careful. I won't complain if you dog my every step during the party. I just…I've worked hard to build up my business. If I flake out on this event, it'll hurt. Clients will lose confidence in me. It doesn't matter that I was possibly kidnapped by a drug cartel; people are selfish. They want what they want. They might be sympathetic toward me and what happened, but they still want their party."

"I'll want the rest of the team to be there as well," Walker said after a moment.

Gillian nodded. "I have no problem with that."

"And you aren't to go *anywhere* without one of us with you."

"Even to the bathroom?" she teased.

Walker didn't crack a smile. "One of us will scope it out before you go in, and no one else will be allowed in while you're in there."

Gillian took a breath. She wanted to protest. Tell Walker that he was being paranoid. But then she remembered how scared she'd been when she'd woken up and realized she had no idea what she was doing in an ambulance, and why she was hurting so bad. "Okay," she told her boyfriend solemnly.

Walker put his hand on the back of her head and brought it to his shoulder. "Okay," he whispered.

They stood like that in his kitchen for quite a while, Gillian staring out the window that led to his balcony, watching the birds flying from tree to tree outside.

Falcon.

She abruptly pulled back and looked up at Walker. "Falcon!" she said urgently.

"What?"

"Falcon. I don't know what it means, but it has to do with my kidnapping."

He raised an eyebrow, but his expression hardened. "You sure?"

Gillian nodded. "Yeah. I don't know why, but...yes."

Walker ran a hand over her hair, then brushed the backs of his fingers over her healing cheekbone. "I'm proud of you, Di. You are every inch a Wonder Woman."

"But it makes no sense."

Walker shook his head. "Doesn't matter. I'll call Agent Tucker and let him know. He can research and see if he can figure out what it means."

Gillian closed her eyes and willed her brain to recall something else.

Falcon, falcon, falcon. She repeated the word over and over in her head.

Then another word popped into her brain.

"Salazar!" she blurted.

This time, he looked shocked.

"What?" Gillian asked. "Who is that?"

"Alfredo Salazar is the head of the Sinaloa Cartel here in Texas. Calum Branch, the DEA agent you talked to, claims he's headquartered right in Austin. I don't know why you're remembering that name, but if he was the one who took you, or had you taken, then it's even *more* of a fucking miracle you're standing here in my arms right now."

"Why?" Gillian asked, not sure she wanted to hear the answer.

"He's ruthless. He started as a part of the gang when he was still in elementary school. Killed his first man around age ten. Everyone knows that if they cross him, they're dead. It's said he has no mercy. That he killed his own *sister* when he thought she'd betrayed the cartel."

Gillian's eyes widened with every word from Walker.

"I need to call Tucker," he said.

Gillian nodded. "I know."

"Maybe I'll see if Ghost and his crew can come to Austin with us as well," he muttered.

As scared as Gillian was, she thought that was a bit overkill. Having fourteen men following her around during an anniversary party would be a bit much. But she'd fight that battle later. Maybe when they were both replete after a few orgasms.

"Walker?"

"Yeah, sweetheart?" he asked distractedly.

"I trust you."

That got his attention. He raised an eyebrow.

"If something else ever happens to me, I trust you to get there in time. You've changed my life too. I always felt as if something was missing, even though I have great parents, amazing friends, and a job I love. Now I know it was you. *You* were missing."

He leaned down and kissed her gently.

"We're going to get through this," she told him. "Neither of us is used to living with someone else. Throw in close quarters, me being hurt, and you dealing with the fact that you couldn't help me...we're bound to fight. Thank you for not shutting me out or storming off. It's not easy to talk about what's bothering us, but I appreciate you doing just that."

"I've been a bachelor for a very long time, but nothing feels as right as waking up with you in my arms, Gilly. I can't promise to always be happy and in a good mood, but I do promise to never take what's bothering me out on you. I'll do my best to talk things through before we go to bed. I never want to go to bed mad."

"Me either. And, Walker?"

"Right here, sweetheart," he said with a smile.

"I haven't missed that your friends moved practically my entire apartment here this week."
He smiled. "Wasn't keeping it a secret."

"So now that I'm better, I'm assuming you don't want me to go back to Georgetown?"

"Absolutely not," he said immediately. "And not just because I'm worried about your safety.
I like you hogging the covers at night. I like watching you brush your teeth in my bathroom…
our bathroom. My sheets and towels smell like honeysuckle, and I freaking *love* it. I like bringing you coffee while you get ready in the morning, and I love looking up from whatever I'm
doing and seeing you. I love *you*, Gillian."

She practically melted in his arms. "I love you too, Walker."

"You're okay with moving in…permanently?"

"Do I have a choice?" she asked cheekily.

"You always have a choice," he said without cracking even the smallest smile. "I'd never
force you to do anything you don't want to do."

"I want to live with you," she told him.

"Good. Eventually, we'll get a bigger place. We're stuffed in here like sardines. I don't
mind it, but after a while it might get to be a bit much. Now, as much as I hate to let you go,
I really do need to call Tucker. You remembering even those two small words is a good thing.
It might not mean anything to us right now, but the fact that you're strong enough to break
through the chemicals that fucked with your memories just reinforces my thought that you
are fucking Diana Prince."

And with that, Walker kissed her on the forehead and turned to grab his phone.

Gillian gave him some space, heading into their bedroom. She didn't need to hear his conversation. She had no idea what falcon and Salazar meant, and she could admit that she kinda
didn't *want* to know. She had a few more last-minute details to work out for the Howard party,
and she needed to talk to their daughter and reassure her that she'd be there on Saturday night.

"It's not much," Gary Tucker told Trigger.

"I know, but I wanted to let you know as soon as possible that Gillian had remembered
something."

"Hmmm. All right, I agree with you about the name Salazar. Although it's probably unlikely that she actually saw him in person. He's elusive and doesn't get involved with extortion
and kidnappings."

"I might not be an expert on drug kingpins," Trigger said, "but I'm guessing he's more
involved than everyone thinks. I mean, I know there's a hierarchy in organizations like that,
but wouldn't he be aware of everything that's happening? Who's targeted and why?"

"Holy shit," Agent Tucker said suddenly.

"What?" Trigger asked in alarm.

"Hang on…I'm calling Calum. As DEA, he knows a lot more about the Sinaloa than I
do."

Trigger waited impatiently as the FBI agent patched in the other man.

"You here, Branch?" Tucker asked after a minute or so.

"Yeah," the other man answered.

"Trigger?" Tucker asked.

"Also here," he confirmed.

"Right, so, Calum, Trigger called to tell me Gillian remembered two things from her
kidnapping."

"That's great," the DEA agent said.

Trigger was glad to hear the sincerity in his voice.

"The first was the name Salazar."

Calum whistled long and low.

"Yeah. Trigger and I were having a conversation about him when something occurred to me."

"What's that?" Calum asked.

"We were talking about how unlikely it was that Salazar himself had any direct contact with Ms. Romano. I told Trigger that he probably left the kidnappings and assassinations to the lower members of his organization."

"That's probably true. Drug lords usually don't bother themselves with that sort of thing. They've got highly trained and trusted members of their organizations who do the dirty work."

"Exactly. Which brings us to the other thing Gillian remembered."

"Well? What was it?" Calum asked, when Gary hesitated.

"She remembered the word 'falcon.'"

"Wow. Okay, that makes sense. I just wish we knew what the context was," Calum said after a moment.

"Would one of you please fill me in?" Trigger asked impatiently. He had no clue what falcon could possibly mean, but obviously it had some relevance, based on what the two men were saying.

"So, in cartels like the Sinaloa, there are different levels of players," Calum explained. "At the top are people like Salazar, the drug lords. They're the ones ultimately in charge. The head of the snake, if you will. Under them are lieutenants. The people at that level are in direct contact with the drug lord and are highly trusted and valuable, as they supervise a lot of the lower-level people in the organization. Next come the hitmen; I think their job is self-explanatory. But under *them* are the members known as falcons. It's the lowest position in the gang, and most of them work hard to gain the trust and favor of the hitmen and lieutenants with the goal of moving up the ladder someday."

"So, what does Gillian remembering the word falcon mean in this context?" Trigger asked.

"Normally, I'd say we're not sure. It could be that whoever had her kidnapped referred to a falcon in one way or another. Or it could mean that she saw a bird flying overhead after she was dumped and her brain simply conjured up the word 'falcon.'"

"Then why was Tucker all fired up to bring you in on this call?" Walker asked.

"Because remembering the word falcon all by itself means nothing. But remembering it in conjunction with the name *Salazar* means she was definitely in the hands of the Sinaloa Cartel. There was a reason she was taken, but there was probably a bigger reason she was let go relatively unharmed...which I don't have to tell you is very, *very* rare. I can count on one hand the number of people who've escaped the Sinaloa Cartel's clutches after being kidnapped," Calum said.

"Of the people you know who have escaped...how many have been retaken by the cartel?" Trigger asked.

"None," Calum told him without hesitation. "There's only been one situation where we know for sure what happened. We had a UC—sorry, an undercover—imbedded with the cartel, and he reported that the hitmen had kidnapped someone who they'd thought was snitching. Turns out they grabbed the wrong man. They had the same name, but the poor schmuck who ended up in front of Salazar was a guy who happened to be in the wrong place at the wrong time. He was let go after a severe beating and a warning not to say a word about what had happened to him. The guy ended up moving to Canada with his family, and he still lives there to this day."

Trigger let out a long breath. "So what are your thoughts on all this in reference to Gillian?" he asked. "And give it to me straight. Why was she taken, what are the odds she's still in danger, and do we have to look over our shoulders for the rest of our lives? Do I need to request a PCS move to Alaska?"

"Honestly, I'm not sure what to think," Calum said, and Trigger tensed once more. "I mean, the fact that she was let go unharmed is a good thing."

Trigger wanted to argue the "unharmed" thing, but let it go.

"But nothing about this is normal. The hijacking was an extreme and bold move, and the fact that we still don't know who the seventh hijacker was means there are a lot of loose ends. Ms. Romano had a very active role in that whole thing, she was picked out of all the passengers to be the spokesperson between the hijackers and the negotiators. She was also right there when the hijackers were killed as well. So it could be the Sinaloa was just trying to find out what she knows about who the other hijacker might be."

"We're headed into Austin this weekend for an event she's planning," Trigger told the men.

"Do you think that's a good idea?" Tucker asked.

"No," Trigger said emphatically. "But I can't keep her locked up forever. If she's brave enough to get back on the horse after she was bucked off, then I'll be right there by her side. Me and my friends."

Trigger knew the two men understood what he was saying when they both murmured their approval. They knew he was Delta Force, and that he'd be on security duty.

"Let us know if you notice anything that looks off," the FBI agent said.

"I will," Trigger reassured them.

"Thanks for letting us know what Gillian remembered," Calum added. "I know it doesn't seem like much in the scheme of things, but the fact she remembered anything at all is pretty damn amazing."

"That's what I told her," Trigger agreed. "I'll stay in touch."

The three men hung up, and Trigger stood in his living room, staring outside for a long moment. In some ways, the phone call made him feel better about Gillian's safety, but he was also still uneasy. He figured he'd be nervous about her for a long time coming.

When she'd been missing, and he'd realized they had absolutely no clues as to where she might be, he'd almost lost his mind. It wasn't often he felt helpless, and he hated the feeling.

He wanted to keep her locked in his apartment safe and sound forever, but knew that wasn't feasible. Besides, with his luck, someone in a nearby apartment would start a grease fire and the damn building would burn down. He'd learned throughout his career that sometimes the safest place was actually the most dangerous.

He had to let Gillian fly, but that didn't mean he couldn't be there to catch her if she fell.

He looked down at his phone and clicked a button to call Lefty. He needed to let his team know they'd be going to Austin for a party on Saturday.

Chapter Nineteen

GILLIAN LOOKED AROUND THE LARGE BALLROOM AT THE DRISKILL WITH satisfaction. Everything looked absolutely beautiful and the event was running incredibly smoothly so far. She'd arrived at the hotel earlier that afternoon to make sure everything was set up to her specifications. She'd put on the only dress Walker's teammates had brought over from her apartment; luckily it was dressy and appropriate for the event. She'd bought the light green dress one day while shopping with Ann. Her friend had said it made the color of her eyes pop, and in a moment of weakness, Gillian had bought it.

When she'd come out of the bedroom with it on, she'd thought for a second Walker was going to bend her over the sofa and take her right then and there. She wouldn't have been opposed, although it would've meant she'd have been late getting to the hotel.

Instead, he'd restrained himself, whispering in her ear that when they got home later that night, he was going to fuck her so hard she'd feel him inside her for at least a week.

Gillian's knees had gone weak, but she'd merely replied that she couldn't wait.

Walker had followed her around the hotel as she'd met with the various members of the staff to make sure everything was ready for the party. He hadn't been intrusive, standing off to the side, but he refused to let her out of his sight. She'd had several people ask about him and his friends, and she'd explained them away as being security. He and his teammates looked like models in their dark suits. None of them wore a tie, but their white shirts under black suits made them look like they were straight off the set of *Men in Black* or something. She'd gotten a few weird looks at her "security" explanation, but no one had questioned her further.

Lefty and Brain had studied the guest list she'd received from the Howards' daughter and hadn't found any names that had caused alarm. Two hours ago, the couple of the night had arrived for what they'd thought was an intimate dinner for two arranged by their daughter, and had been pleasantly surprised at the huge party being thrown in their honor.

The cakes had been well received and devoured within an hour. The drinks were flowing from the open bar and the DJ was playing music that everyone, no matter their age, could appreciate and dance to.

Overall, the evening had been a success, and Gillian was relieved it was finally winding down.

"Ms. Romano?" a staff member of The Driskill said from behind her.

Gillian turned. "Yes?"

"*Erhm*…there's been a problem with the credit card used to pay for the Howards' room for the night."

"Oh, I'm sure it's just a misunderstanding. I'll come with you and take care of it and make everything right with my client later. Walker," Gillian said, turning to him. "I'll be right back. I'm just going to go to the front desk real quick."

"I'm coming too," Walker said.

Gillian wanted to roll her eyes and insist she could probably make it to the front desk and back without him watching over her, but since she truly didn't mind, she simply nodded.

She followed the employee through the throng of people in the ballroom and out into a hallway. The hotel was older, and the hallways were narrow. Because there were so many people, and it was a Saturday night, it felt as if they had to fight their way to the front desk.

The front desk staff was slammed with all the people checking in and needing this or that, so she handed her card over to the employee and stood off to the side, waiting for her to return. Walker was standing across the room, against the wall. She caught his eye and smiled, loving how his face gentled as he smiled back at her.

A ruckus at the other end of the lobby made him turn his head, and Gillian looked in that direction. A man and a woman were yelling at each other, and the man reached out and shoved the woman's shoulder. Gillian watched as Walker pushed off the wall and headed for the couple.

Of course he would. There was no way he'd stand by and watch as someone assaulted a woman.

"Gillian!"

Hearing her name, Gillian turned her head—and gaped at who was standing there.

It was Andrea. And she looked absolutely horrible.

She had makeup on, but it couldn't hide the deep bruises on her face. One arm was in a sling, and she had a huge bandage on that hand as well.

"Holy shit, Andrea, are you all right?" Gillian asked, rushing over to the woman she hadn't seen since they'd been rescued in Venezuela.

Andrea grimaced and nodded. Then winced at the movement.

"What happened?"

"I had to come warn you. I didn't know where you lived but remembered you talking about this party when we were texting. The cartel kidnapped me and wanted to know all about the hijacking. They said they were going to come after you too."

"They already did," Gillian admitted.

Andrea's eyes widened. "They did?"

"Yeah."

Andrea seemed to sway on her feet. "Oh, shit, I don't feel so good," she moaned.

"Come on, let's find you somewhere to sit," Gillian said, putting her arm around the other woman's waist.

"I shouldn't have come. I found a place to park in the first row of the lot. Can you believe that? Just help me out there, and I'll get out of your hair."

"Should you be driving?" Gillian asked in concern as Andrea turned them toward one of the many hallways off of the lobby.

"Probably not, but I had to come see you. I didn't want to say anything over the phone in case they were listening."

Gillian looked back into the lobby for Walker. She wanted to make sure he saw where she was going, but he was busy trying to control the inebriated man at the other end of the large room. The woman wasn't helping the situation, as she kept trying to hit her husband or boyfriend or whoever he was.

Thinking she'd just be gone for a minute or two, and Walker wouldn't even know she was missing, Gillian helped Andrea limp down the hallway toward the exit. They went outside, and Andrea pointed at the far end of a line of cars. "It's in the first row, down at the end," she said.

"I'm so sorry this happened to you," Gillian said.

"Me too," Andrea agreed.

When they got to her car, Gillian kept her arm around Andrea's waist as she led them to the door. "Give me your purse, I'll open the door for you."

"Thanks."

Gillian let go and dug into the small purse for the keys.

She'd just clicked the door locks when she felt something push into her side.

"Get in," Andrea said in a tone Gillian hadn't ever heard from her before.

She looked down in confusion—and was shocked to see a gun in Andrea's hand. She'd shoved it against her side and was pressing it into her flesh aggressively.

It took a second for Gillian to comprehend what was happening. "What?" she asked in disbelief.

"Get in the car," Andrea repeated. "Do it. Or I'll fucking blow a hole in your side."

"Why are you doing this? Did they put you up to it?"

"They? The cartel? Fuck them! I did *everything* they wanted. And for what? Nothing, that's what! I urged Luis to volunteer for the job in Costa Rica. Salazar told us it would be a piece of cake. Sinaloa supporters would deliver weapons to the plane and it would be easy to take it over. And it was. That asshole Lamas was killed, just as we planned…but then *you* fucked everything up!"

Gillian was still trying to wrap her mind around what she was hearing. "Luis? The hijacker? You *knew* him?"

"He was my husband!" Andrea spat.

"But…you have different last names."

"Which doesn't mean a damn thing. It wasn't hard to get false documents. Let me introduce myself properly—my name is Andrea *Vilchez*, not Vilmer. Luis Vilchez was my husband. The love of my life. And you got him killed!"

Gillian's mind was spinning. "Me?"

"Yes, you bitch! We were home free, almost in the getaway plane. We would've taken off and flown under the radar back to Mexico, and we all would've been promoted from our flunky positions in the cartel. But no, *you* had to go and trip Alberto. I don't know why that asshole broke from the plan and decided to take you with us. Then you tripped and gave those assholes a chance to shoot my Luis! You ruined *everything*!"

"But—"

"Get in the car, Gillian, and I'll make your death as painless as possible. If you don't, I'll shoot you in the gut, which means you'll bleed out nice and slow. Then I'll go inside and start shooting the guests at your precious party. I'll save that asshole who killed Luis for last. Before I kill him, I'll make sure he knows that his death is *your* fault."

Gillian wasn't an idiot. There was no way Andrea would be able to kill Walker. Not with her being as beaten up as she was right now.

She *was* an idiot for leaving the hotel, even though she'd thought Andrea was a friend. But the very last thing Gillian was going to do was get in that car. If she did, she knew without a doubt she'd die a horrible, painful death, no matter what Andrea promised.

And suddenly, a phrase popped into her head.

Fucking bitches and their drama.

Gillian knew she'd heard that when she'd been kidnapped.

"You told Salazar that I knew more than I did, didn't you?" she asked.

Andrea smirked. "Of course I did. And he did just what I wanted—he approved your kidnapping." Her face contorted with rage. "But then you had to go and make him believe you didn't know shit!"

"I *didn't* know shit," Gillian insisted.

"He was supposed to fuck you up! Take off a few fingers. Torture you the way *I've* been tortured every day since my Luis was shot!" Andrea hissed.

"Is that what happened to you?" Gillian asked, looking down at Andrea's bandaged hand.

"He didn't like that I'd lied," Andrea said in a way-too-calm tone. "Told me he was making an example of me. Took three of my fingers and beat the shit out of me. Then he threw me into the basement of one of his trap houses. Hoped I would bleed to death, but if I didn't, he was sending another falcon—a fucking newbie at that—the next day to finish what he'd started. I was to be her first kill. But I got the fuck out of there. I've been in hiding for the last week, just waiting for tonight and the chance to get my revenge."

Gillian wanted to feel remorse that Andrea had been beaten so badly, but she couldn't. Not when she was there to kill her.

Then something else occurred to Gillian—and she felt like the most gullible person ever. "Luis didn't assault you on that plane," she said flatly.

Andrea smirked again. "Nope. I gladly sucked him off. And it was *awesome*."

Gillian felt sick. She shook her head. "I'm not going with you," she told Andrea.

"Yes, you are. Get in," Andrea demanded.

"No," Gillian said, taking a step back. She had no idea how many minutes had passed, but Walker had to have realized she wasn't standing by the front desk anymore. He'd find her. She just had to give him enough time.

Andrea lifted the gun and aimed it right between Gillian's eyes. "Get. In. The. Car."

Gillian was tired of being scared. Tired of looking down the barrel of a gun.

She had no idea what came over her—but she was done being a victim.

"I cried for you," Gillian said in a steely tone. "I felt horrible that you had been treated so badly on that plane…or what I *thought* was badly. I even talked to the other passengers about doing something to help you out. And the entire time you were probably laughing at us. You didn't care about those passengers who were killed. You were cheering on those monsters the whole time! I have more respect for Alfredo Salazar right now than I do for *you*."

Andrea didn't even flinch. "I don't give a shit about anyone but myself. I cared about Luis, but now he's gone. Because of *you*. One more chance. Get in the fucking car!"

Gillian stared into the eyes of a woman she'd thought she knew. A woman who'd witnessed the most traumatic experience of Gillian's life.

Andrea wasn't who she'd thought. She was a cold-blooded killer.

At the same time she heard a shout from her right, Gillian moved.

Instead of reaching for the gun aimed between her eyes, she swung her fist and hit Andrea's bandaged hand as hard as she could.

The gun in Andrea's hand went off, and Gillian felt an immediate rush of fire in her upper arm. She dropped to the ground even as something went flying over her head. She caught a flash of black, and then someone pulled her backward and threw himself over her.

Struggling under the heavy weight, Gillian did her best to fight.

"Easy, Gillian, it's me," Lefty said into her ear.

She immediately stopped moving, and instead gripped his sleeve with the hand on the arm that didn't hurt.

"Just give him a second, and then we'll move," Lefty said.

His words didn't make much sense, but Gillian remained still, trusting him.

Trigger was more irritated with the fighting couple in the lobby than anything else. He stepped in when the man shoved his girlfriend, but the woman didn't back off, even when her man had been subdued. It had taken way too long for hotel security to get there and take over, separating the couple and calling the police to straighten everything out.

It had only been minutes, actually—but it seemed like longer when Trigger looked back to where he'd last seen Gillian, only to find the space near the front desk was empty.

For the second time that month, his heart stopped beating in his chest.

"Where's Gillian?" he asked Lefty when his friend came up beside him.

Within moments, his entire team was in the lobby, trying to figure out where she might've gone.

It didn't take long for one of the guests milling in the lobby to tell them she'd seen someone in a knee-length green dress with her arm around another woman—who looked as if she'd recently been beaten up—heading down a hallway toward a back door.

Trigger had no idea who the woman was, but the hair on the back of his neck was standing straight up. He'd never ignored his instincts before and wasn't going to start now.

He and the rest of his team headed down the hall. They couldn't draw their weapons, not in the middle of a crowded hotel, but they were just as lethal without them.

The second they exited the hotel into the parking lot at the back of the building, Trigger saw Gillian. She and another woman were standing face-to-face at the far left side of the first row of vehicles. It looked like they were simply talking, which made the butterflies in his stomach relax.

But then the mystery woman raised a gun and pointed it at Gillian's face.

Trigger was moving before he'd even thought about it.

His team was well trained, and they immediately fanned out. Doc, Oz, and Lucky split off to the right to come up behind Gillian and the woman, and Lefty, Grover, and Brain followed Trigger.

He couldn't hear what was being said, but it didn't matter. No one pointed a gun at his woman. *No fucking one.*

As he got closer, he heard the other woman say, "One more chance. Get in the fucking car."

He opened his mouth and let out an almighty roar that he hoped would shock the woman into turning and looking at him. Gillian seemed to move at the same time. He didn't see what she did, but the other woman screamed and a gunshot sounded in the quiet Texas night.

Trigger leapt over a now crouched Gillian and tackled the woman. She fell backward, her head hitting the pavement with a loud thump. He wanted to turn and check on Gillian, but he trusted his team to pull her away to safety and administer first aid if needed.

The sound of the gunshot still ringing in his ears, Trigger's adrenaline was flowing through his veins as he subdued the woman under him. She struggled weakly in his grasp, and as he stared down into her bruised and battered face, he realized that he recognized her.

"Andrea Vilmer?" he asked in shock.

"It's *Vilchez*," she hissed, then tried to spit in his face.

It all clicked then. She was the seventh hijacker.

Vilchez was Luis's last name, and she was obviously related to him. Sister, wife…it didn't matter.

Blood was seeping through the bandage on her hand, and Trigger spared only a brief thought as to what might've happened to her. He was more concerned about making sure she never got a chance to hurt Gillian again. She'd done enough. More than enough.

He hauled her upright and quickly secured her hands behind her back with a zip-tie. He had a feeling Gillian might make fun of him later for having the damn things on his person, but he'd learned the hard way on a mission to always have a way of securing the enemy.

It was only then that he looked back at Gillian. Lefty was on top of her, looking back at him. Lucky and Doc come up next to Trigger, and he immediately let them take control of the spitting-mad woman he'd tackled.

"The police are on their way. And Brain's calling Branch and Tucker," Lucky told him.

Trigger heard his friend's words, but he couldn't look away from Gillian as Lefty slowly moved off her.

Blood. It was staining the ground under her, but he couldn't tell where it was coming from. Feeling as if he was moving in slow motion, he went toward her. Gillian blinked. Then blinked again. But this time it took a moment for her eyes to re-open.

Everything in Trigger's world stopped. "No," he said in a choked whisper as he went to his knees next to Gillian.

"I'm sorry," she said in a rasp he could barely hear. "I shouldn't have left the lobby with her."

"Don't talk," he ordered, terrified out of his mind, any and all medical knowledge he had going straight out the window. This was his woman lying there bleeding—and he couldn't think of one damn thing to do about it!

"It's Andrea."

"I know," he said. "Please, don't talk."

Her eyes closed again. "Salazar beat her up because she lied and told him I knew who she was, and was telling the authorities."

"Don't leave me!" Trigger begged. "I can't live without you."

Her eyes opened again, and she looked up at him in confusion.

"Save your strength. The ambulance will be here any second. Just hang on."

"Walker—" she began, her brow drawing into a frown.

"*Shhh*," he ordered.

"I'm not dying, Walker," she told him firmly.

He looked at the blood under her and pressed his lips together.

"I'm not," she insisted. "My arm hurts like hell, and I think Lefty squished all the air out of my body when he jumped on me to protect me from stray bullets, but I'm not dying. At least…I don't think I am."

Trigger blinked, took a breath—and everything suddenly came into focus. The blood under her was only on one side. Her pupils were reacting to light, and her breathing was a little fast but even.

"Fuck," he said, sitting back on his heels. "Fuck, fuck, *fuck!*"

He heard Lefty and Grover chuckling from next to him.

"Shit, man, you seriously thought she was dying?" Lefty asked.

"Shut up," Trigger grumbled.

"You did!" Grover crowed. "Hey guys, Trigger saw a little blood and freaked out!"

He tuned-out the ribbing his team was giving him when he felt Gillian touch his arm. He immediately leaned closer and grabbed hold of her hand.

"I'm okay," she told him quietly.

Trigger nodded. "Now that I can think straight, it looks like it's just a graze. But you're still going to the hospital," he said sternly.

"Okay, but only long enough for them to sew me up. I'm exhausted. I've worked my ass off today, and you promised to do dirty things to me when we got home."

He barked out a laugh and closed his eyes as he shook his head. When he opened them again, he saw tears in Gillian's eyes. "I'm sorry about Andrea."

"Me too," she agreed.

Trigger knew Gillian would have some hard days ahead of her. They'd both known the seventh hijacker was one of the passengers, but to have been betrayed by someone she'd thought was her friend had to hurt. He'd do whatever it took to erase the pain and betrayal from her eyes. He also knew spending time with her true friends—Ann, Wendy, and Clarissa—would help as well.

But he had no doubt his Wonder Woman would straighten her shoulders and be back to her usual brave self sooner rather than later. As sirens sounded in the distance, Trigger vowed to be by her side every step of the way.

Epilogue

GILLIAN HELD ON TO THE COUCH WITH FINGERS THAT HAD TURNED WHITE WITH strain as Walker took her from behind.

It had been three months since Andrea had tried to kidnap and kill her behind The Driskill. She'd had to throw away the green dress Walker had liked so much, but she'd gone shopping with Wendy and Clarissa, and had found the dress she'd worn tonight.

It was shorter than the one she'd worn all those weeks ago. Cut low, showing off her cleavage, and she'd hoped after Walker had seen her in it that *this* was how their night would end.

She'd met him at the restaurant for dinner, since he'd had to work late, and his reaction to the dress, and her in it, had been everything she'd hoped for. His eyes had widened, then his pupils had expanded, and he swore low under his breath.

Throughout dinner, he couldn't keep his hands off her, his fingers frequently straying into indecent territory on her leg as they sat next to each other on the same side of the booth in the steak restaurant. He wasn't as chatty as usual either.

It was probably a good thing they both had their cars and had to drive separately to their apartment, because otherwise, Gillian had a feeling she would've been naked and he would've been on her in the car.

As it was, the second the apartment door was shut behind them, Walker had grabbed her, pulled her into him, and kissed her as if he hadn't just that morning had his wicked way with her.

Now she was bent over the side of the couch as he took her from behind, just as she'd imagined he'd do after the Howard party when they'd arrived home.

She was still fully dressed, except for the white silk panties he'd ripped off her right before he'd entered her from behind. They'd stopped using condoms a couple weeks ago, and Gillian still couldn't believe how amazing Walker felt inside her.

His hips sped up as he neared his climax. One of his hands pushed under her belly and down, and he roughly strummed her clit as his cock slammed in and out of her.

"Come for me, Di," he ordered.

Gillian had tried to explain to him once that just because he ordered her to orgasm, didn't mean it was going to happen, but tonight she was right there with him. She'd been soaking wet and ready for him before they'd gotten home, and seeing him completely lose it, unable to hold back, had pushed her close to the edge.

As usual, he didn't back off manipulating her clit when she got close. One second his touch almost hurt, and the next, she closed her eyes, arched her back, thrust her ass against him and came. Hard.

She felt him slam inside her once more then hold himself as far inside her as he could as he came, as well. His groan echoed around them, but his fingers didn't let up on her clit. Gillian tried to squirm away from him, but it was no use.

"One more," he croaked. "Let me feel you squeeze my cock."

That did it. Another, smaller orgasm ripped through her, every muscle in her body tightening. She swore she could feel him still throbbing inside her.

They stayed like that for just a moment, their hearts beating out of their chests, sweat dripping from their brows.

"Holy crap," she muttered when she could get her brain to work.

Walker chuckled and slowly pulled out of her soaking folds. Gillian felt a rush of his come slide down her inner thigh.

"I know it's inconvenient for you, but I'll never get sick of seeing that. It's sexy as fuck," Walker told her. "Come on, I'll help you get cleaned up."

He helped bring her upright and kissed her gently before putting his arm around her waist and walking her down the hall to their bedroom.

Cleaning the evidence of their lovemaking away and changing for bed didn't take that long, and within ten minutes, they were snuggled together in their bed.

"In case I forgot to tell you, which I think I did, you looked beautiful tonight," Walker told her.

"Thanks. I'm glad we finally got to do the whole bent-over-the-couch thing," she told him honestly. "I was beginning to think you'd treat me like a fragile piece of glass for the rest of our lives."

She felt Walker shudder, and even though she knew he didn't like talking about that night, she needed to.

"You're the strongest person I know, Di. Seriously. But I just…that night…fuck."

Gillian smoothed a hand over his chest. "I know."

"No, you don't. When I saw her lift that gun and point it at your head, my life flashed in front of my eyes. I don't get scared a lot, just ask the guys, but at that moment, I was terrified."

Gillian got up on an elbow so she could look him in the eyes. "I *know*. I think I was more scared that night than on the hijacked plane. Maybe because of the hatred I saw in Andrea's eyes. She legit despised me. It was a hard thing to reconcile in my brain because of how nice she'd been to me since the hijacking, and how bad I felt because of what I'd thought had happened to her while we were on that plane."

"How do you feel about what happened to her?"

"About her being killed in prison?"

"Yeah."

Gillian tried to sort through her feelings before she answered. "Relieved," she said after a beat. "I know that's bad, but—"

"It's not bad. I celebrated with the team today when I heard," Walker admitted. "I was so damn glad she was dead, and you wouldn't have to testify, and that hopefully any threat her connection with the Sinaloa Cartel might've caused you is now over and done with for good. It's not as if the authorities don't already have the cartel on their radar, and since it's not a secret that Andrea was the seventh hijacker anymore, there's no real need to be concerned about Salazar coming for you."

Gillian lay back down, her head resting on his shoulder once more. "The news said she was targeted at the prison?"

"Yeah," Walker said. "She'd been in isolation, but someone fucked up, or maybe they did it on purpose, and she was let out into the yard with the general population. My guess is that someone connected to Sinaloa took the opportunity to take her out. She wasn't exactly on their good list. They have long memories and a certain code they live by."

"I *do* feel bad for her," Gillian said on a sigh.

"Uh-uh," Walker said, shaking his head. "She gets none of your goodness. None of your sympathy."

"But her husband was killed," Gillian protested.

"They *chose* that life," Walker said as he rolled her onto her back and loomed over her.

His eyes were intense as they stared down into hers. "No one forced them to get involved with the cartel. No one forced them to be drug dealers. Luis was a murderer. It's not like he was on an innocent business trip and was killed in a car wreck. She doesn't deserve one ounce of your goodness."

"Okay, Walker."

"I mean it, Gillian. She got what was coming to her."

"I said, okay."

She watched as he took a deep breath and relaxed when he rolled back over and pulled her back into his side.

"I'm proud of you, Di," Walker told her. "I wasn't thrilled to have to leave you a month after it happened, but you were tough as hell through that deployment."

"I wasn't thrilled either, but I hung out with my girls and got a lot of work done on the few upcoming events I was planning."

"I almost begged my commander to let me stay back stateside, before I figured it would be just as hard to leave you the next time we got called out, so I bit the bullet and went. But I thought about you every second."

"Which isn't safe," Gillian scolded.

Walker chuckled. "The guys knew I wasn't one hundred percent and made sure I didn't take point on anything."

Gillian wasn't sure what that meant, and she didn't really want to know. "They're good guys," she murmured.

"They are." Walker moved then, reaching over her to a drawer in the small table next to the bed.

She grunted as she was mushed against his chest for a second before he lay back down. "What the hell?" she grumbled. "Sniffing armpits is not sexy, Walker."

Before she could shift and get comfortable again, Walker had taken hold of her hand, which had been resting on his chest. Her eyes got huge as he slid a beautiful, perfect princess-cut diamond ring onto her ring finger.

"Wha—"

"I love you, Gillian Romano. I can't imagine spending my life without you. Will you marry me?"

The proposal came out of nowhere...but then again, it didn't. They'd settled into living together so easily it was as if she'd lived with him forever. She'd officially canceled her lease for her apartment in Georgetown, and the stuff that wouldn't fit into his apartment was sitting in storage, waiting for them to find a bigger place to live. Walker told her, and showed her, every day how much he loved her, and they'd had a long conversation one night about souls and how he truly believed they'd known each other in another lifetime, and that was why they'd clicked so immediately.

"Of course I will," she told him with a huge smile. "On one condition."

"Name it," Walker said.

Gillian loved the carnal look in his eyes and knew she was about to get thoroughly ravished...again. "I'm not planning our wedding. I don't want something big. I have to think logistics and plan parties every day of my life. I want something low-key and stress-free. I just want to get it done, hang with our friends, and get on with the rest of our life."

"Will your parents freak if they don't get to participate in a huge wedding for their only daughter?" he asked.

Gillian loved how respectful he was of her parents. They'd once again flown out to Texas when they'd learned she'd been shot, and although it wasn't how she would've wanted

Walker to meet them, she couldn't have been happier with how that had turned out. Her parents loved Walker immediately, which wasn't surprising.

"No," she told him. "Will *your* parents be upset?"

"No. I think they're just happy I finally found someone to put up with me. So whatever kind of ceremony you want, you'll get," he said. He picked up her hand, kissed the ring he'd just put there, then gently pushed her onto her back. "Anything else you want to talk about before you can't think anymore?" he asked as he slowly inched his way down her body, pushing the covers down as he went, exposing her to his burning gaze.

Gillian eagerly spread her thighs, giving him room as she shook her head. "No, I think I'm good."

"Oh, you're gonna be good, sweetheart," Walker said with a gleam in his eye.

It was at least an hour and a half later—and three orgasms; two for her and one for him—before Gillian could think once again. Walker was curled up against her back, holding her, and Gillian gazed down at the beautiful diamond on her finger. She thought about her friends, and Walker's team, about how lucky she was to have escaped death not once, but twice, and vowed right then and there to be happy.

No matter what happened in her life from here on out, she had a man who loved her, good friends, and a job she enjoyed. Life wasn't perfect, but hers seemed pretty damn close at the moment.

"These babysitting jobs are my least favorite," Doc grumbled as part of the team stood outside a room in a nondescript building in Paris, France. Doc, Trigger, and Lefty were on duty at the moment, and Grover, Oz, and Lucky would take over later. Brain was on patrol duty, hanging around outside, listening to the chatter of the people gathering near the building and watching for anything that might compromise the safety of the officials inside.

Normally, Lefty would agree with Doc about babysitting, but earlier that day he'd seen the Assistant Secretary for Insular and International Affairs, Walter Brown, arrive—and he knew that meant his aide was probably around somewhere.

Kinley Taylor. He'd met her the last time they'd been tasked with bodyguard duty in Africa. Her boss had been there, and he hadn't given even the littlest shit about his assistant. He'd sent her back to his hotel to pick up something he'd forgotten—in the middle of a fucking protest. She'd almost died, and if it hadn't been for Lefty slipping out, following her, and making sure the asshole protestor who had his hands on her regretted picking her out of the crowd to mess with, she would've been killed.

He and Kinley had spent the rest of the trip meeting on the sly whenever they could. She was funny. And petite, which appealed to his masculine side. He'd always been drawn to smaller women. He'd wanted to wrap his hands in her long black hair and pull her close every time he saw her, but they'd kept things professional and aboveboard.

They'd had a lot of fun on that trip. Laughing and joking with each other, but even as she teased him, he'd sensed an underlying sadness in her. It made each smile she shared with him even more rewarding.

When that summit had ended, and thus Lefty's bodyguard job, she'd promised to keep in touch, but he hadn't heard from her again.

It had taken him quite a while to get over her. He didn't know what he might've done that made her change her mind about keeping in touch, and that bothered him.

But now they were once again in the same place at the same time, and Lefty wanted answers. Wanted to know why she'd so coldly ghosted him when he'd thought they were actually friends.

Delta Force was used every now and then to watch the backs of high-ranking government officials when they went overseas. This time, their job was covering the Deputy Secretary of Agriculture. Important political members from countries all over the world had been invited to Paris, and like usual, having that much power in one place attracted the crazy, the unhappy, and the people who just wanted to protest against something.

Kinley's boss was being protected by another Delta team out of Fort McNair in Washington, DC. Lefty had met the men a couple of times on other ops, and he knew they were good operatives and would do whatever they could to protect not only the Assistant Secretary for Insular and International Affairs, but his assistant as well.

But that wasn't good enough for Lefty. He wanted to watch over Kinley personally.

"What's wrong?" Trigger asked.

Lefty mentally swore. He knew one of his friends would notice his odd behavior sooner or later.

"She's here," he told Trigger.

"Kinley?" his friend asked, knowing exactly who he was talking about.

Lefty nodded.

"She still working for that asshole?"

"As far as I know."

"You talked to her yet?" Trigger asked.

Lefty shook his head.

"We'll make sure you've got time to make that happen," Trigger said.

"'Preciate that," Lefty told him. And he did. They were here for a job. There wasn't time for fun. No romantic dinners at a charming café and no visits to the Eiffel Tower. But everyone knew how upset he'd been when Kinley hadn't responded to any of his emails or texts. His team would do what they could to make sure he got the closure he needed.

Lefty could remember his last conversation with Kinley as if it were yesterday.

"Thanks for being a stalker and following me into that mob of people."

"You're welcome. I hope this isn't goodbye for good. I like you, Kinley. I'd like to keep in touch…if that's okay."

"It's more than okay. I'd really like that. I don't have a lot of friends. Living in DC is… tough. People are always using others to try to climb the political ladder."

"And you don't want to do that?"

"No way! If I had my choice, I'd be living on a farm in the middle of nowhere with only animals to keep me company. They're honest. They don't lie or try to hurt you."

"Who's hurt you?"

"Oh…I was just saying. But yes, I'd love to keep in touch."

He'd thought about that exchange again and again for over a year, since he'd last seen her, and it bothered him more and more, especially after he'd never heard back from her. He'd tried to blow it off and tell himself she was just being polite when she said she'd keep in touch, but he didn't think so. Something about the entire situation seemed off.

And now Lefty had another chance to get to the bottom of the mystery that was Kinley Taylor. He couldn't wait. If she thought she could blow him off again, she was insane. No one had fascinated Lefty as much as she had. A part of him wanted to know what he'd done that had made her ghost him, but another part was worried.

They'd clicked. That never happened to Lefty. Ever. Something had scared Kinley away from talking to him, he was sure of it. He wanted to know what it was.

For the first time in his life, he was grateful for bodyguard duty.

I hope you're ready to give me some answers, Lefty thought to himself, his eyes constantly roaming the hall for potential threats to the men and women inside the room behind him. *Because I'm not willing to let you go so easily this time. I want to know everything about what's behind the sorrow I saw in your eyes...and fix it.*

I hope you LOVED Gillian and Trigger's story. Next up is *Shielding Kinley*. Find out what Kinley's hiding and if Lefty can break through her protective walls!

Want to talk to other Susan Stoker fans? Join my reader group, Susan Stoker's Stalkers, on Facebook!

About the Author

New York Times, *USA Today* and *Wall Street Journal* Bestselling Author Susan Stoker has a heart as big as the state of Tennessee where she lives, but this all American girl has also spent the last fourteen years living in Missouri, California, Colorado, Indiana, and Texas. She's married to a retired Army man who now gets to follow *her* around the country.

She debuted her first series in 2014 and quickly followed that up with the SEAL of Protection Series, which solidified her love of writing and creating stories readers can get lost in.

If you enjoyed this book, or any book, please consider leaving a review. It's appreciated by authors more than you'll know.

www.stokeraces.com
www.AcesPress.com
susan@stokeraces.com

Also by Susan Stoker:

Delta Team Two Series
Shielding Gillian
Shielding Kinley
Shielding Aspen
Shielding Jayme
Shielding Riley
Shielding Devyn (May 2021)
Shielding Ember (Sep 2021)
Shielding Sierra (Jan 2022)

SEAL of Protection Series
Protecting Caroline
Protecting Alabama
Protecting Fiona
Marrying Caroline (novella)
Protecting Summer
Protecting Cheyenne
Protecting Jessyka
Protecting Julie (novella)
Protecting Melody
Protecting the Future
Protecting Kiera (novella)
Protecting Alabama's Kids (novella)
Protecting Dakota

SEAL of Protection: Legacy Series
Securing Caite
Securing Brenae (novella)
Securing Sidney
Securing Piper
Securing Zoey
Securing Avery
Securing Kalee
Securing Jane

SEAL Team Hawaii Series
Finding Elodie (Apr 2021)
Finding Lexie (Aug 2021)
Finding Kenna (Oct 2021)
Finding Monica (TBA)
Finding Carly (TBA)
Finding Ashlyn (TBA)
Finding Jodelle (TBA)

Delta Force Heroes Series

Rescuing Rayne
Rescuing Aimee (novella)
Rescuing Emily
Rescuing Harley
Marrying Emily (novella)
Rescuing Kassie
Rescuing Bryn
Rescuing Casey
Rescuing Sadie (novella)
Rescuing Wendy
Rescuing Mary
Rescuing Macie (novella)
Rescuing Annie (Feb 2022)

Badge of Honor: Texas Heroes Series

Justice for Mackenzie
Justice for Mickie
Justice for Corrie
Justice for Laine (novella)
Shelter for Elizabeth
Justice for Boone
Shelter for Adeline
Shelter for Sophie
Justice for Erin
Justice for Milena
Shelter for Blythe
Justice for Hope
Shelter for Quinn
Shelter for Koren
Shelter for Penelope

Ace Security Series

Claiming Grace
Claiming Alexis
Claiming Bailey
Claiming Felicity
Claiming Sarah

Mountain Mercenaries Series
Defending Allye
Defending Chloe
Defending Morgan
Defending Harlow
Defending Everly
Defending Zara
Defending Raven

Silverstone Series
Trusting Skylar
Trusting Taylor (Mar 2021)
Trusting Molly (July 2021)
Trusting Cassidy (Dec 2021)

Stand Alone
The Guardian Mist
Nature's Rift
A Princess for Cale
A Moment in Time- A Collection of Short Stories
Another Moment in Time- A Collection of Short Stories
Lambert's Lady

Special Operations Fan Fiction
http://www.AcesPress.com

Steal You

KD ROBICHAUX & CC MONROE

$$Prologue$$

LIZITH

"**B**ROKEN UNDER ME LIKE A LITTLE BIRD. YOU WOULD DO ANYTHING FOR ME, wouldn't you, Lizith?"

I peer up from under my heavy lashes at the man I have grown to love as he looms over me like the devil himself. His blue eyes pierce me, and the blood in my veins drains. He smirks with the change in my breathing, his cock jutting against his briefs, his chest thick and taut and bare for my eyes to consume.

"What do you want me to do to prove I'm worthy enough for you?" I cry, because for the past few months, I have felt more love and experienced the greatest sex, even my first time, with my separated—albeit still married—Human Anatomy professor. At nineteen, I have learned more about myself and how deep the darkness inside me goes, all so Xander will love me back in the way I love him. Unconditionally.

"Just give it time, little bird."

My green eyes are still blurred as the unstoppable tears soak into the skin of my cheeks. I try to look around his dark classroom, all the windows too high for anyone to see us. Only the night sky and moon are shining through; the Artscape glass on his locked door never shows a shadow on the other side. But why would it, when no one is left on campus this late at night?

Licking my swollen lips, still tender from all his rough kisses and not so gentle bites, I blink away some tears. "What if I found someone else to preoccupy my time until then?"

I know what I'm doing, and I know just what kind of beast I am provoking when I ask this, but I want him to feel what I do. I want that storm of anger yet desirable jealousy I chase daily to spark a fire in him. I want him to feel even an ounce of what I do right now, on my knees, naked with my hands bound behind me with his tie. A captured victim of lust, love, and taboo I have been for him since I was eighteen.

"You wouldn't do that, and do you know why?" he asks, but it's not a question he wants me to answer. He brings his cock from its confines and he traces the wet tip along my lips, marking me with his cum. "Because, little bird, you belong to me, and hurting others to protect my sacred belongings isn't something I'm opposed to. You don't want to see anyone get hurt because of you, do you?"

His words are dark, and it makes my love for him run deeper when it should make me run farther.

"Look at me. I would do anything," I confess, and he growls, grabbing my chin and opening my mouth wide to fit his cock inside.

Without warning, he goes deep, hitting the back of my throat, and I nearly gag. But it feels so right. "You look heavenly taking my cock with all that mascara running down your cheeks. You're a mess. My mess."

My insides flutter, butterflies taking a hold of me. Because I'm the one to make him lose his control. I am the one he wants, and he takes everything from me. He captured my innocence, locked it away in his chambers, and filled me with lust, passion, and danger.

He keeps fucking my mouth and I relax, looking up at him and letting him fuck me like he wants to. I am his little bird tonight, and just like every other night, I fall deeper in love with him. Like sap slowly rolling down a tree, my blood does the same, filling with him and seeping through my entire body, making me his completely.

Xander growls above me, watching his cock own my mouth, and if I could, I would rip my hands free to touch him. I want to hold those hips and help him possess me more. I want to lick up that small drop of sweat beading and rolling down the ridges of his abs.

Every other night, we meet here and fuck for hours, make love on end without ever stopping. Sometimes, the sun rises before we even get a second to breathe. When we are apart, I can still smell him, feel him, and taste him. He's imprinted on me like a physical and emotional memory that never fades, only growing more vibrant with time. The kind you obsess over in hopes you never forget a single second or let it dull in your mind.

My brunette hair is caught up in his tan hands laced with experience. At thirty-two, he's had over a decade more than me to hone his skills as a lover. They are traced in thick veins that scream power, control, lust. His thick thighs brace as the powerhouse to his calculated and controlled strokes into my tight, warm mouth.

"I'm going to fuck you hard, Lizith, and you will feel it for days. It will make you crazy to ache from me but not have me."

Dropping from my mouth, he steps back, and I get a second to breathe. I gulp for the cold air—thick with sex but still chilly—and I cough when I take in too much.

"Easy, baby." Bending down, he grabs me by the elbows and helps me up. His touches are rough but still have a slight undertone of care and adoration.

He loves me.

He has to.

I feel it in everything he does.

He has to.

"Untie me," I moan while he guides us to his desk.

"No." His tone is sharp and sure, unyielding.

"Please, untie me and make love to me. I need it!" I cry, turning with effort against his steady hands to look him in the eye.

"I don't have time for this, Lizith. Don't do this again tonight." His eyes dilate and there is a tic in his jaw as he grows frustrated.

"Why can't you just show me you love me like I show you? Don't you love me as much as I love you?"

"Is that what you want?"

He unties me as he asks his question. Once my hands are free, I pounce, jumping into his arms and wrapping my legs around him. Xander catches me, gripping my ass while my hands fight to touch anywhere they can.

"You want me to tell you I love you? Is that it? Tell you I can't fucking sleep at night, because you are always on my fucking mind?" He moves quickly, lying my back against his cool wooden desk.

"Yes. Tell me what you feel." I watch him, nothing but a mess of breath and emotions. Deprived and desperate for his words.

Before he speaks again, he grabs his cock and lines himself up with my entrance, and I watch with him, mesmerized as he slowly slides inside. An audible gasp of relief leaves us both. He's thick, an expanse of power, danger, and pleasure inside me.

"I look at you and I see my demise. I see the end of me," he confesses. "I see the power I have over you and how far I'm willing to go to fucking ruin you. I want to be the man who breaks your heart and fucking destroys you. Because, little bird…" He pauses, thrusting into me hard. My eyes roll back as I arch off the desk. I lose my surroundings for a moment, but he brings me back before I can catch up.

With a tight grip on my chin, he immobilizes my jaw and my eyes focus on him. "The man who destroys you, forever owns you."

I choke, a sound of welcomed torture leaving me. I don't have anything else to say as I come just from pure obsession. I want him to break me, because I plan to do the same. He sees the end because I am the end of anything that was before me.

"Fuck!" he growls, as my core tightens like a vise.

My toes curl and my body feels like lava as my orgasm consumes me. He keeps pounding, chasing his own. The dark hair he wears slicked back is now falling around his forehead. His blue eyes have nearly gone black, and those veins in his neck begin to bulge. I watch silently, my mouth in an O and my words stuck inside.

The second he comes, he howls into the empty room. "Your blood is now mine as mine is yours. I will love you without boundaries and I will own every part of you. You are my obsession."

"Xander, I love you!" I cry out with him, consuming his orgasm as mine peaks again, hitting me for a second time.

I've become Xander's, and in no time or universe will he ever be rid of me.

Chapter One

LIZITH
Eight years later

WISHING I COULD SHOVE IT IN DEEP, STABBING HER WITH THE METAL PIECE OF equipment I could so easily turn into a torture device, I gently pull the speculum out of my patient's vagina. I set it on the rolling tray before pulling my gloves off and throwing them in the hazardous waste bin as I imagine her screams of pain.

"You know I'm not allowed to say anything official. But from your internal exam, you seem perfectly healthy to me, Jacqueline. I don't feel anything out of the ordinary, but the doctor may want to conduct his own exam to be sure." I see the sliver of excitement flash over the slut's face, and I keep my own expression schooled, not revealing my disgust in the vile woman. "You've been trying to conceive for several years now, and according to your chart, you've never attempted any form of fertility treatment. And I know you hate it when I bring it up, but your age—"

"I know, I know. Forty is entirely too old to be trying to have a baby. But I'm a firm believer in if it's supposed to happen, then it will," she cuts me off, sitting up and smoothing her perfect waist-length white-blonde ponytail.

Long enough to strangle her with.

The thought puts me in a happy place, so I easily make my voice pleasant. "As your PA, I'm giving you my professional opinion. If you truly want to have a baby, and you've been trying for this long, tracking your cycles like you say you have, then there is probably something keeping that from happening. Your ultrasound last time was clear. No cysts on your ovaries, no uterine fibroids." I let out a breath. "The problem could lie in your husband's sperm. Do you think he would be willing to come in for a semen analysis?"

She chuckles, crossing her legs beneath the examination sheet, placing her perfectly manicured hand beside her knees, and leaning to the side prissily as she touts, "That man would do anything I ask him to. I'll set up an appointment for him on my way out."

Her cockiness makes me want to slap her. If only her husband knew she wasn't really a hypochondriac who came in to the gynecologist once a month for checkups, but to fuck her doctor. In the two years I've worked here at Dr. Curtis's office, I've seen Jacqueline Stine no less than twenty times. After the sixth time in as many months, when I first acquired my dream job I'd worked so hard for, I asked Dr. Curtis why she required so many appointments. Especially when her charts indicated she was perfectly healthy and not receiving any type of monthly treatment. He briskly explained she had an uncontrollable fear of STDs, borderline obsessive, so she came in regularly to be tested for peace of mind.

A married woman with an obsessive fear of sexually transmitted diseases? Was she worried her husband was cheating on her? Her ever-present attitude and surety in his giving in to her every request would indicate no. Plus, why would she be trying to have a baby with a man who she suspected was unfaithful? But considering the fact she was the only patient who had a signed consent form in her file stating a nurse or physician's assistant is not required to be present in the examination room with her doctor indicated something else entirely. So did the locked door I discovered soon after my suspicions were birthed.

As always, I pick up my iPad off the counter and let her know the doctor will be in to see her as soon as he's finished with his current patient, closing the door gently behind me. As calmly as I can manage with the rage still boiling through my veins, knowing what would be happening in Exam Room 3 in the next few minutes, I make my way to the checkout desk and let Aria know that Mrs. Stine needs to schedule a semen analysis for her husband before she leaves.

Shuffling to my desk, feeling discouraged, I think about all the reasons why I'd wanted so badly to work at this office, one of the most highly acclaimed OBGYN/Fertility Treatment Facilities in the state of Texas. I'd grown up an only child, my parents trying for countless years to have a second child. I witnessed all the struggles, the pain—both emotional and physical—while my mom tried everything, including in vitro fertilization, as she and Dad did their best to give me a sibling. But nothing ever worked. My parents made a few close friends throughout their treatments, in support groups for people going through the same thing. As I got older, I realized it was one thing for a couple who had never had a baby to struggle with infertility. Their dream of creating a life together through their love of each other something they wanted to experience. It was something entirely different for people like my parents. My mom already knew how wonderful it was to feel a new life growing inside her belly. They already knew what it was like to look into a baby's eyes and feel love like they never thought possible. I remember her telling me about the sensations of my kicks. The way she felt this sense of completion when she knew a part of her heart beat inside me. I'm weak in my heart for women who can't have kids, but I feel most connected to the ones who lost something they already greatly knew. It wasn't *more* unfair than the couple who were denied the gift of a child, but an entirely different form of torture. It was when my mom and dad finally gave up trying, on her fortieth birthday, that I decided I wanted to become a fertility specialist.

Several minutes later, I keep my back turned toward the door as my boss and his patient leave the exam room, and I ignore their goodbyes, waiting to hear Mrs. Stine make her way to the checkout desk. My skin always crawls when she's near, knowing what she does behind her husband's back. So when she sets the appointment for her husband, and then her next visit, I breathe a sigh of relief when she finally leaves.

I log in to the office network with my employee number and passcode, typing in my last patient's name. When Jacqueline's file pops up, I scroll to see when the appointments were set.

"Wow, you wasted no time, did you?" I murmur under my breath. "The perfect cover up."

Mr. Stine is now set to come in tomorrow morning for his semen analysis. So now the cheating skank can go home and tell him she got him the earliest available appointment so they can get the baby train rolling.

I shake my head, logging out of the program before grabbing my lunch kit and purse and heading home for the day.

I remove my shoes as soon as I walk in my apartment's front door, putting them neatly in their designated place with calculated effort. Setting my bag on my couch as I pass behind it and into the kitchen, I place my lunch kit on the counter. I strip as I make my way toward my bedroom, tossing my scrubs into the washer as I go. My bra and panties follow suit, leaving me naked as a jaybird as I enter my room. I smile at the old saying as I promptly sit in my computer chair, wiggling the mouse to wake up the monitor. In the top right corner of the split screen, I watch Aria and Dr. Curtis leaving through the front door of the office, him turning to lock up for the evening as her short, round figure waddles toward her Ford Focus. The other eight squares on my monitor are still, no one else inside the building.

Choosing the surveillance camera for Exam Room 3, I rewind through the last hour, only catching the tail end of the doctor and Mrs. Stine's sexcapade before he helps her back into her clothes. And as she turns back around to him after he zips her into her dress, I see the exchange like I do every month—him pulling out a round packet of birth control pills from the pocket of his white coat, her taking it from him with a sly grin and bat of her fake eyelashes, and then she slips them into her expensive-looking purse. I save the clip into the file I've kept since I placed the microscopic hidden cameras throughout the building, stretch my arms high above my head with a groan, and spin the seat around, prancing my way into my en suite to take a blistering shower.

Chapter Two

LIZITH

I LOCK THE DOOR OF THE EMPLOYEE BATHROOM BLINDLY, KEEPING THE LIGHT OFF AS my eyes stay glued to my phone. Surveillance Camera 7 is pulled up on my app, and I watch as he locks the door behind him after entering the room reserved for men.

My breath catches as I take him in. So tall, so muscular. Age has done nothing to soften the hardness of his features, of his body. His thick black hair is styled atop his head effortlessly, and I nearly swoon at the gray near his temples and throughout his sideburns.

My back hits the wall as he makes a circle around the room, and I slide down until my ass hits the floor when he passes by the hidden camera and I get a close-up view of that perfect face. It hurts to look at him he's so fucking handsome. And even though the screen is black-and-white, I swear the blue in his eyes catches the fluorescent lights perfectly and calls to me like a siren through the camera. A cluster of a million emotions, desires, and cravings crash into me. My owner has returned.

Professor Xander Stine.

My Xander.

He takes hold of the brown paper bag he picked up at the front desk before being directed to this room, and he pulls out the plastic sample cup, twisting the lid to break the seal. He places them beside him, where he now sits on the leather couch we disinfect after every patient. His demeanor makes it seem like he owns that couch, turning it into a throne with his masterful and natural authority.

I bite my lip as he undoes his belt and unfastens his flat-front khakis, pulling down the zipper and opening enough to reveal the front of his briefs. I swear I can hear the noises from his actions in this room, as if he were beside me, or better yet, as if I were the one undressing him. And when he pulls the elastic over his already erect shaft and leans back to relax against the cushion, I nearly jump out of my skin as my whimper echoes throughout the empty bathroom. My heart thumps as his head falls back against the top of the couch, and when he takes hold of his thick length, my core clenches and begins to ache. I feel his imprint even years after he left me. I remember its throb and the way it owned me, pulsing wildly as he released a thick stream of cum each time we made love.

With his first full stroke up and down his cock, the only one that's ever been inside me, I can stand it no longer. One hand finds its way between my stomach and my scrub bottoms as I hold my phone with the other one, and as I watch him fist his long, rigid dick, his nostrils flaring as his brow furrows, his eyes closed in concentration, my fingers find my drenched heat. My panties are soaked through from watching him and remembering our time together. I can feel the wetness on the back of my knuckles, even as I circle my clit with my index finger, dipping my middle one inside my tight entrance.

He pumps his cock over and over, his hips moving ever so slightly as if on instinct. I rub the bundle of nerves faster, knowing that look on his face, the one that always told me he was close. Is he thinking of me? Is that my name dripping from his snarled lip? I think these thoughts right when he reaches to grab the sample cup, and quickly add a second finger inside my channel. I bite my lip hard to keep myself from calling out his name as we explode together. Him inside the cup, where he sits on the other side of the wall my back is pressed against, and me all over my own hand, as I pant, trying to catch my breath while my eyes never leave him on my little screen. He was thinking of me as I watched him, I just know it. I can feel it in my soul. We fucked each other mentally, and one day soon, he will fuck his little bird physically once again.

It's not until he tucks himself away and is rebuckling his belt that I finally lumber off of the floor, my legs trembling from both my orgasm and knowing only mere inches of sheetrock separate me from the man who owns my soul.

I set my phone behind the faucet so I can keep watching him as I wash my hands in the sink while he does the same in the next room. My motions mimic his purposefully, wanting to feel close to him, feel like I'm trickling my way into his bloodstream. I see him reach out and snatch two paper towels from the metal holder attached to the wall, tossing them in the trash when he's finished. He goes back over to the couch, twists the lid back onto the plastic cup, and places it inside the brown paper bag as instructed. Finally, he opens the metal door on the opposite wall and sets the bag inside the cubby, which opens on the other side as well, inside the lab. We keep everything discreet when it comes to semen analysis, to make the men as comfortable as possible in such an awkward situation. The only person he would've seen was Aria when he first checked in, where she would've handed him the paper bag along with a sheet of simple instructions for him to follow, which he'd sign before heading to Room 7. And he won't have to see or speak to anyone else on his way out. His follow up appointment will be set for the exact same time five days from now, when he will get the results.

My heart aches as I see him reach for the handle and leave, and I close my eyes and listen to his footsteps as he walks in front of the employee bathroom where I hide, on his way out the front door. And just as quickly as he appeared, he's gone.

I gather myself, slipping my phone into my pocket and leaving the dark bathroom to hurry into the lab. I stop just inside the brightly lit room, allowing my eyes to adjust before they land on the small metal door to my right. I approach it slowly, as if there's something inside the cubby that might suddenly jump out and bite me if I don't tread carefully enough. I reach up, take hold of the small handle protruding from the left side, and tug, the metal squeaking as the door opens, revealing the brown paper bag. The brown paper bag my Xander was just holding.

The brown paper bag that holds the contents of all my hopes and dreams he made me believe would come true all those years ago.

And then an idea hits me so hard I can't believe it never dawned on me before this very moment. My gut clenches at its genius.

Before all this, I had only planned to get him here so I could show him the evidence of his wife's infidelity. I wanted to stand inside the room with Xander, Jacqueline, and Dr. Curtis, and present him with everything going on behind his deliciously muscular back. And in my mind, I imagined him leaving her right then and there, taking hold of my hand and leading me out of the office, petting me—his good, well behaved, and solicitous little bird. From there, we'd get into his car, leaving everything behind, and we'd live happily ever after. But the moment I saw him enter the clinic alone, I flew away, flew away like the wounded little bird I am, and hid in the dark bathroom. Too afraid to upset my love. He never did like surprises anyway.

But now, a different plan forms inside my head, and instead of taking the sample over to the equipment to run the usual tests, which would gage the number, shape, and motility of the sperm, I move to the sperm washing station.

"Premium wash," I whisper, knowing it's the best of the three techniques—basic, premium, and swim-up technique—to gather the most of the healthy and viable sperm. Professor Xander Stine would only have the best and most virile ejaculation, I'm sure. There is nothing less than perfect about the man. But I want to take no chances. I only have one shot at this.

I snatch a pair of rubber gloves from the box on the wall then sit on the rolling stool in front of the microscope, pulling the plastic sample container out of the paper bag. This bag holds the key to my happiness, the promise I was given from him that was then stolen away. But now I will take it back. Gold, treasure, and any riches in this world pale to the virile man and his cum inside this cup. Even when he unloaded into the plastic container, it was perfectly done—no spills, no need for cleanup. Because Xander, my keeper, is perfect, and I will make sure that his perfection would only belong to me. I will give him a child of great worth. I will carry his life inside me and intertwine us permanently, just like he always wanted.

"Little bird, you do as I say and you only spread your wings for me. I want to own that perfection, little thing, and I promise I will take it if you don't give it. We are intertwined, and my promise is to keep you forever. So, you do best to always give me you. You are mine."

Like a catapult, his words slam into my memory, dousing me in what I deem as the holiest of grails. I am doing exactly what he demanded. And he's going to praise and pet my wings when he sees what I have done for us.

Regaining my bearings, I focus back on the important task at hand. I close my eyes and murmur to myself the instructions of how to do this, almost superstitiously—something I do every time, knowing it is in my hands to make a couple's dream of having a baby come true. And that's our dream, and I know better than to mess up my keeper's wants.

"This method uses density gradient centrifugation to isolate and purify the motile sperm in order to obtain a sperm sample with a motility of at least 90%, depending on the initial quality of the sample." I take a breath, forcing myself to relax my shoulders, even as the adrenaline courses through my every vein. "Different concentrations of isolate—extremely dense fluid—are layered in a test tube in an ascending order of density, the heaviest layer at the bottom." I pull a sterile test tube from its packaging, grabbing the different bottles of fluid I will need from the temperature regulated cabinet above my head. "When a semen sample is placed upon the uppermost isolate layer and centrifuged, any debris, round cells, non-motile and poor quality sperm remain in the top layers. Only the motile sperm are able to get through to the bottom layer and are then concentrated for use in artificial insemination. This procedure takes one hour."

And for the next hour, I work diligently, handling Xander's sperm like the treasure it is. Reaching the final step, I gather all of the separated sperm into a syringe and cap the open end, slipping it down the front of my scrub top between my breasts to keep it as close to body temperature as possible. I smirk, thinking of the many times Xander's cum had been all over my tits, marking them as his, as I clean up my work station. Moving over to the computer, I make up results for the semen analysis I never conducted, saving them to his file.

Grabbing a glass container of gonadotropin and a bottle of clomiphene citrate, I hurry into one of the exam rooms and pull open the bottom drawer where we keep all the necessary tools we use during different OBGYN appointments. I gather a packet containing a sterilized speculum, another one that holds a catheter, and some lidded syringes, then make haste toward my desk, thankfully passing no one on my way. I'm usually the first PA here every morning, the other two and the nurses usually not arriving until around 10:30 a.m. I glance at the clock. Perfect timing.

I toss everything into my bag and throw it over my shoulder, then force myself to calmly walk to the front of the office.

"Hey, Aria. I'm not feeling too well. Ginger and Lashelle should be here any minute, so I'm going to take a sick day," I tell her, making a show of rubbing my lower stomach.

"Lizith Morrison taking a sick day? I thought the day would never come. First time in two years." She chuckles. "Feel better, hun."

"Thanks," I reply, relief filling me when she doesn't ask me a million questions as I hurry to the door.

"Hey!" she calls.

My heart stops, and then takes off at lightning speed. Fuck. Did she see the smuggled equipment in my purse? Did she see the syringe peeking out from my cleavage? Do I make a break for it and just run out the door?

I pause with my fingers wrapped around the handle, waiting to shove the door open, and peek over my shoulder at her behind the reception desk. "Yeah?"

She smiles saucily then speaks in a quiet tone. "Did you see the guy who went into the Strokin' Room? Holy bejeezus. No wonder crazy ol' Mrs. Stine wants to have his babies. I mean damn!"

I fight back the urge to pull the scissors out of the penholder on her desk and stab her in the throat, instead forcing a smile to my lips I hope doesn't favor a sneer as I shake my head. "No, I must've been in the bathroom," I say, and then push out the door.

Xander is mine, and the idea of any woman standing in the way of us, like his wife once did, makes me murderous. Once I'm pregnant with his child, I'll never be able to part from my love ever again, and even a brief whisper of a joke about coming close to what I lost all those years ago will send me over the edge of my very steep, dark cliff of insanity.

My knees weaken and my skin grows hot as my heart plummets into my stomach at the memory. Red-hot and fresh in my mind, I stumble into the car, slipping back to that night.

"Little bird. Please don't cry." He attempts to soothe me, but I can't find a ledge to grab as I slip from his hold.

Dropping to my knees at his feet, I sob, kissing the bare skin and soaking it with my tears. "You promised me forever. You said you would leave her and make me your good little bird for forever." I stay naked, my chest caving in on me and my spine protruding out of my back from my bent frame, begging at his feet like Judas. Tonight when we made love, it was different. It wasn't another night of promise.

It was my fucking goodbye.

"I have no choice and you must remember that. Stop crying at my feet, Lizith. You are making me angry."

"Then get angry!" I seethe, rapidly rising to my feet, my dark hair cascading around my face in my abrupt movement. My teeth grit, my tears salting my tongue as they fall messily. He doesn't budge from his outburst and I react, slamming my closed fist down on his tight chest.

"Stop it, Lizith, or I will punish you." Xander's jaw flexes repeatedly, seizing my wrist in an attempt to stop me. I drop my head again, sobbing harder, my breathing coming out in short spats, leading me closer to hyperventilation.

"Oh, Xander, my love, you're already punishing me enough. Nothing else could destroy me as badly as you leaving," I admit, my legs and arms going numb as I drop once again to the floor in front of my fireplace. This time, I land on my side and curl up into a ball, one hand against the skin of my chest, trying to relieve the ache, as the other pets his perfect, large, masculine feet.

"I have to stay with her, little bird. I don't have an option. She is the one who has taken us apart. But don't forget, I told you this would happen. The man who destroys you, owns you. Never forget I will always own you." He stays standing over me, his naked glory glowing over me as if I'm a fallen angel at her creator's feet.

Peering up once more, I see he looks down on me, the lust still there as he watches me weaken at his altar, my wings burned to ash. "So you will always be mine?"

"Oh, little bird, always is not long enough. You are mine infinitely. No matter what, I will love you and always want you. But we end here. Go on and lick the wounds clean where I hurt you. But just know you will never heal completely, because I won't let you. I am unforgettable."

And as unforgettable as he was, he is attainable now. I licked my wounds clean, admiring the scars he left behind. Now he will be mine forever, and healing me will be his first job after I steal back what was mine.

Chapter Three

XANDER

JACQUELINE'S SMOKE PERMEATES THROUGH OUR PENTHOUSE APARTMENT ON THE UPPER side of downtown, her family's money and ours evident all over the place. My nostrils flare as I prepare to meet her at the end of our entry hall. I suspect she will have a glass of red wine pressed against her lips, the red of her lipstick staining the glass and causing me to find one more thing that makes me detest her even more. She's as bitter as the dry wine she drinks nightly.

Before I make it to the end of the hall, I remember the bitterest taste she left in my mouth to this day, and that was when she ripped me away from my tiny thing, my aphrodisiac, my perfect obsession—my little bird. Today I came in that plastic cup with the image of my small, dainty yet womanly little pet underneath me, and I swear my body felt her as if she were there with me. Even closer than I could imagine. But I left her broken and alone years ago, and now I am stuck with a wife who I despise and who loathes me even more.

As I step into the kitchen, her eyes penetrate me, boring into me and spewing hate before words have even left her crimson lips. She was once beautiful, young, and vibrant, the life of the party, a showstopper in her youth. Then one day, she snapped. She left me for another man, and when she came crawling back, her eyes lost their life, her hands that warm touch, and her soul was sucked dry. I went back to her, because I didn't have a choice. I was going to be with Lizith, but when Jac found out about my love affair with a student, she took me by the throat and threatened to sic her father—the dean of my university—on me and my name. She also swore she would find the one I was with and ruin her as well.

Charlie Aimworth is one of the most well-known and respected deans in academia, and he would've had my fucking balls in a vice and I'd be dead to the world. My reputation would've been destroyed, and God knows what my little bird would have gone through. Jacqueline's ruthless, and I wouldn't let my pet suffer at her fucking hands. I sacrificed my life with Lizith for hell with Jacqueline.

I agreed to stay married and walk away from Lizith as long as Jacqueline agreed to give me a child. I've always wanted a family, even though one wouldn't peg me for a family man. I may be dark and my desires even more cryptic, but deep inside me there is still that normal human desire. The darkness surrenders to that light, and if I am going to stay in this unhappy marriage, then I need something to bring me to the surface when I begin to drown in Jacqueline's rip-roaring river.

"How was your chump in a cup? Did you get enough in their to prove how weak your shitty little swimmers are?" Her eyes narrow in on my cock behind my jeans.

I scoff, dropping my keys and traveling to the fridge to get myself started on a drinking bender to prepare for the fight of the night. "Baby, insulting me won't make me insecure. Don't be so childish. It only ages you." I throw the lid of my beer in the trash and scorn her with a look over the bottom of my bottle after I raise it to my lips.

Seething, she hisses her response. "God, I fucking hate you."

"There is a door, babe." I nudge my shoulder in the direction of the door, hoping this will be the time she walks away without a fight. But I would be foolish to think her leaving, even on her own freewill, would be clean. Jacqueline would never let me be happy.

"I plan to make this worse for you. Don't you know that?" she asks, standing and rounding the counter to stand in front of me. Her dragon nails still wrapped around the rim of the wine glass, she stops just inches in front of me.

"You and I both. You think you stand a chance of outdoing me, Jac, but you don't. Take as long as you want making me wait for my child, but just know the longer you keep up this cruel, miserable bitch act, I will stand on the sidelines laughing." I step in closer, within an inch or two of her Botoxed face.

"You sick bastard, I fucking hate you!" She loses the glass, throwing it behind me and letting it shatter against the kitchen wall, her wine staining the wall and hardwood floor. I don't even flinch, my cares fucking gone. She storms out to the foyer, kicking the metal suit of armor some of my students gifted me with three years ago, as she screams, "And get rid of this ugly goddamn thing!" like she does almost daily before leaving the apartment with her bag and keys. Off to complain to her fucking father, I'm sure, but better for me to have the rest of the night off from her and her mind games.

Grabbing another beer, I head for my study, ready to blow off some steam. My red-blooded desire to mate has hit me. I'm angry and pent up, and her attitude just reminds me of a certain darker-haired beauty who used to defy me just to rile me up. Lizith loved my heavy hand on her pert ass, my grip wrapped around her throat while I fucked her wildly, and goddamn it if she were here, I would do it. I would go to my little bird and fuck her mercilessly, filling her with my cum.

The dark wooden floors and my floor-to-ceiling windows invite me in, setting the dark mood to match my rage. I take a seat at my desk and close my eyes, letting my breathing mellow out, repeatedly inhaling and exhaling deep and loud. My veins are on fire with hot blood pumping like lava inside me, and my mind is spinning with the images of my possession.

"Lizith. What a beautiful name. Exotic tasting." I look over the brunette siren with green eyes standing in front of me. She's my student, this is taboo, and it's everything I want. I've never fucked a student, but I want to fuck her, mark her crudely with my cum on those pouty lips. My bite marks would decorate her already luscious tits even more. And hidden behind that tiny denim skirt, I know in my very bones there is a virgin pussy waiting to be fucked by a real man.

Her cheeks have flushed red, and the bridge of her button nose and the tops of her cheeks have also darkened a shade. Everything about her screams virgin.

"Um, I'm sorry, what?" Lizith's eyes sparkle, damp with aroused tears. I see the crazy in her waiting to be discovered. I want that crazy, and it's just sitting inside her, dormant, and I plan to be the one to set it free. Technically still married to a woman I hate will not hold me back. Because the second I saw that innocent little thing step into my classroom, I knew hell had handed over my wild little bird. The devil danced inside me, and Lizith answered to her master's call for a waltz.

"I know you didn't really come up here to my desk on your first day to ask me if I prefer papers to be typed or handwritten," I respond cockily, my brow quirked. I take note in the way her breath hitches and the veins in her neck move with her swallow.

"Professor, I… I don't think I understand. I really just want to know which you prefer." She bats her lashes and bites her lip, and I see it then. Little bird is asking for her wings to spread.

"Fine, pretend you didn't come up here to tempt me." I stand, knowing I am playing with fire. This is the first conversation we have ever had, seeing as she stepped into my classroom barely an hour ago. Yet, little does she know I've been anxiously waiting for her, Lizith Morrison, to arrive. Checking the door of my classroom to make sure it is closed, I see shadows pass outside the tapered glass as I step up to her. Her front touches mine and I smirk. Without a second longer, reading her willingness to stay and tiptoe into the water of the unknown, I wrap my hand around her throat forcefully, and she gulps, her eyes widening, but a little smirk tugs at her lips.

This crazy fucking temptress. She is nothing like I expected.

"I like my papers in pen when you are the one behind the ink. But make sure you don't draw outside the lines, Lizith. I don't like to be disobeyed."

A lone tear leaves her eye and her cheeks color, a beautiful shade of fucking rose. "Yes, Professor. I promise to stay inside the lines."

And just like that, she becomes mine. I will be her keeper, and I will train her to obey all I want her to. I know this woman has the power to change me just like I have the power to ruin her. And I can't wait to see just how much she can take.

I come to, leaving the memory on repeat in my mind. I miss Lizith, and if I could I would find her, touch her, fuck her, and steal her back from whatever fool is probably occupying her time in a poor attempt to replace me. But if my heart is as in tune with hers as I believe it is, I know out there I am still ruling her mind, her fucking soul.

I need my little bird.

Chapter Four

LIZITH

"**P**LEASE REMOVE YOUR CLOTHING FROM THE WAIST DOWN. THERE IS A SHEET for you there on the examination table to cover yourself with. Press the green button on the wall when you are ready for the doctor to come in," I say into my full-length mirror that stands next to my closet door, giggling as I pull the string on my scrub bottoms. It's the usual spiel we give our patients at the beginning of their appointments.

The blue fabric falls to my feet and I step out of them, reaching for the hem of my top and lifting it over my head before letting it fall to the floor. Seeing myself standing there in nothing but my colorful lace lingerie—the only thing I wear because Xander always loved his little bird's feathers to be bright and lovely, the opposite of the whore he was married to—my eye twitches, seeing the pool of clothing at my feet.

"Nothing but perfection, Lizith. You must not disobey," I whisper as I gather up the scrubs and rush them out to the hallway, tossing them into the washer. My strict routine had been thrown off by coming home from work early. The anxiety lessens as I make my way back into my bedroom, perching upon the edge of my mattress as I reach for my phone.

Sliding my finger across the glass, I open Glow, my period tracking app, on my phone. The calendar pops up, and I see my last menstrual cycle began nine days ago. I gasp, closing my eyes as I hold the cell to my chest, careful not to disturb the syringe still hugged between my breasts as I fall backward onto my bed.

"Please, God, let this work," I whisper, and then my eyes snap open as I recite to the ceiling. "Depending on the number of days in a woman's cycle, which is an average of twenty-eight days, she will normally ovulate on day fourteen, counting the day her period starts as day one. Sperm have an average life span of seventy-two hours. Most die off in the acidic vaginal canal after twelve. But once they are in the right cervical fluid, they can be found with weak motility but still alive for up to seven days inside a woman's body."

Five days. I don't ovulate for five more days. So there will be no taking the easy way into this.

I sit up, pulling my purse over to me, my jaw ticking at the fact I hadn't placed it in its proper spot on my couch even as I pull the glass container, pill bottle, and syringe out of its depths. I stand, lining all the items up on my nightstand, before pulling the catheter and speculum out of my bag, setting them on the foot of my bed as I take my purse out to the living room and put it in its rightful place on the couch cushion closest to my front door.

I breathe a sigh of relief as my body relaxes, knowing my master's good little bird fixed her mistake. I prance back into my bedroom on my toes before stopping in front of my nightstand once more.

Pulling the cap off of a syringe, I stick it into the glass container, all the while narrating, "Gonadotropins are hormones—luteinizing hormone, also known as LH, and follicle-stimulating hormone, also known as FSH—that can be given in an injection to stimulate a woman's ovaries to produce follicles, which contain an oocyte, better known as an egg." I take the prepared shot and walk over to my full-length mirror, tracing my fingers over my stomach, below my belly button. In a trance, remembering Professor Stine's speech word for word,

I continue, "Gonadotropins may be given to women as a fertility treatment if she does not ovulate, or if she ovulates irregularly, in order to stimulate development of a single follicle and ovulation of a single egg. It may also be given to women who ovulate normally. The injection may improve the chances of becoming pregnant by stimulating the ovaries to produce more than one follicle."

And with that, I stab the needle into my stomach, pressing the plunger with my thumb, biting my lip as I savor the sting. I dispensed way more than what would normally be prescribed to a woman for fertility treatment, and I'm not entirely sure this will work to bring on my ovulation faster, but it can't hurt.

I walk into my bathroom and properly dispose of the syringe before flouncing back to my nightstand. I pull open the top drawer and grab one of the mini bottles of water I keep there for when I get thirsty in the middle of the night, twisting the top off and placing it on the table. I open the pill bottle there, pouring a number of the pills into my palm. "Clomiphene citrate is a synthetic medication that is available in pill form. It is often used as a first-line therapy for women who do not ovulate and exerts its effect on the ovaries indirectly by stimulating the body's own hormones."

I toss back the medication and swallow them with my water, replacing the caps on each of the bottles. I take the pills, the glass container of hormones, and empty water bottle into my bathroom, carefully lining the prescriptions up in my medicine cabinet attached to the wall, and throw my trash away, smiling at what a tidy and perfect little bird I am for my master. I think back to a time when I wasn't so neat, just a messy freshman in college with her things strung around her off-campus apartment.

"My pet's cage is filthy. When I return, I want your shit cleaned up and your nest perfectly straightened. Do you understand, little bird? I will not tolerate anything other than your space being as bright and lovely as you. If not, I will not hesitate to punish you."

My punishment always equaled the severity of my indiscretion, so occasionally I'd leave my shoes outside their place next to the front door just to provoke a light spanking. But the pleasure I received when I was his perfect little pet far outweighed the dark indulgence of pain. So I did my best to keep everything obsessively clean.

Giggling at the memory, I twirl back into the bedroom and over to the mirror. Grasping both sides of the curved stand, I carefully slide it across my lush, perfectly white carpet, wincing as the feet of the mirror mess up the triangles made by the vacuum moving back and forth across its fibers. I will fix them later, because right now, the most important thing is lining the mirror up with the bed so I can see how to do what I've only watched trained medical doctors perform on other people.

When I have the mirror butted up against the mattress, I skip over to the opposite side of the bed, tilting my head to the side to take in my setup, and grin. "Very good," I chirp, and then pull the pillows from beneath my colorful comforter, stacking them in front of my hips. Taking hold of my panties, I slide them down my legs then place them flat atop my dresser. I leave my bra on, as it holds the syringe full of Xander's semen to my body, against my heart. Climbing up onto my bed, careful not to disturb the instruments at the foot of the mattress, I lie back, propped up with my pillows in order to see my reflection. I spread my legs, seeing my pussy lips glisten with arousal knowing I will soon be once again full of my master's cum.

I reach for the speculum and, watching in the mirror, I insert it inside myself. "The doctor will use a speculum to hold open the patient's vagina in order to get a clear view of the cervix. Depending on the tilt of the uterus, this can determine whether it will need to be manually readjusted in order to reach the opening. The catheter will then be inserted through the cervix, and using an X-ray, will be fed into the uterus until it is lined up with the fallopian tube expected to drop the follicle for that cycle. The washed semen will then be injected through the catheter."

Carefully, I get the speculum adjusted, cranking it open as far as I can stand so I can see what I'm doing. It's uncomfortable, almost to the point of pain, being spread so wide, but I know my effort will be worth it if this works. It takes me a few tries, but I'm finally able to insert the catheter through the tiny opening of my cervix, but without an X-Ray machine, I have to just pray for the best when it comes to the placement deep inside me.

I let go of the thin, clear tube and grasp hold of the syringe between my breasts, feeling its warmth in my cool palm. I tug the cap off and close my eyes, pressing the plastic filled with Xander's cum to my lips in an emotional kiss. "I'll give you what she won't, my love. I'll make your dreams come true and give you the child you always wanted. It's up to me to help you keep all your promises she forced you to break," I breathe.

Attaching the syringe to the open end of the catheter, I take a deep breath before letting it out and completely relaxing, and press the plunger. I melt into my pillows propping me up, my body going dead weight as I imagine the clear liquid swirling inside my womb. I feel my heart explode with love for Xander Stine, and through that overwhelming onslaught of emotion, I plead with my organs. "Please. Let this work. Give the man who owns you everything he's ever dreamed of."

I remove the catheter and speculum, and carefully lie perfectly flat on the bed, not wanting to take the chance of expelling any of the liquid gold from my uterus. I have to fight with all my might not to properly dispose of the instruments, knowing I can't rise from my horizontal position just yet. So to distract myself, I remember back to Xander's and my first time making love, when I gave him my most precious gift.

My eyes water after my third spanking for tempting my keeper. I shouldn't talk to boys just to get attention from Xander when he isn't spoiling me. He has played me like a fiddle, bouncing me back and forth like a stress ball between his heavy hands, making my mind go crazy and my heart rattle loose.

I love him.

I have loved him since the first day he tempted me with the hiss of his tongue and the cruel enticing words that dripped from those lips. The lips that have only ever kissed me, nothing more. Lips that have never touched me past where I speak of all the ways I would love him and worship him if he would just let me.

I've begged him to be my first touch, but he keeps pushing it off, telling me I'm not ready to break yet, not ready to be numb inside. "I'm not ready to watch the light leave your eyes or the sanity leave your mind. I will destroy your heart, Lizith. But first I need to make sure my bird can handle her wings being broken."

I am ready, and today I tempted the beast, poked him with a stick, and now he's angry. He's fuming, and hell is wreathed in a cloud of smoke around him.

"Dominic, stop!" I giggle louder, just a few minutes until class starts. My classmate, who has drooled at my feet since the first day of class, is sadly the pawn in my twisted and petty little girl games.

My keeper hates games.

I'm not sure what Dominic said, but when he laughed, I joined along, using this as a way to get Xander's attention. I bite my lip and take the tip of my finger, trailing it up the length Dominic's decent-sized bicep. It is a hot dog against a slab of succulent meat compared to Xander's. He is nothing compared to my owner.

I peer over and he isn't looking up from his desk. My entire body erupts in goose bumps, both an indication of my annoyance and arousal. I'm turned on that he isn't giving me the attention I'm looking for. He's made me crazy.

I used to be such a nice girl. A normal girl. Now I'm stumbling foot over foot to gain attention from the man with enough danger in the tips of his fingers that it should make me run. I used to spend every night playing violin, or drawing in my notepad. But now I spend it naked, in the middle of my bed, reading poems of a dark nature with words of dangers in love and ownership.

He towers over me those nights, touching himself while I softly whimper the words of wishes that I desperately want to feel and not just hear and wonder. Before he leaves at night, he bounds my hands behind my back and kisses me from the top of my head, down between my strained shoulder blades, along the thin trail of my spine, and over my wrists and fingers. Xander whispers praise against my butt, biting the skin and bruising it.

"I couldn't write enough words of perfection about your body. I couldn't even scratch the surface on the art that is your faultlessness."

Whenever he says those words, I melt, cry out, and whimper in my agony. I want him to show me what he means. I want actions that substantiate what he says. He's killing me, and I just need him to stop tormenting me in daylight and in the darkest parts of my desperate dreams.

"Lizith?" Dominic calls out to me and regains my attention. Turning back to him, I give him a fake flirtatious grin. That grin is my keeper's favorite, and I think he felt the shift in the air, because from the corner of my eye, I see his head slowly lift. The static in the room that is our connection awoke him. The kinetic energy told him that his little bird shared something that is only his.

Finally.

The perks of sitting just a few feet away in the front row—and today, I wore no panties under my skirt—is Xander will not be happy when he notices this. I bat my lashes and bite my lip, repositioning my legs, making sure he gets a glimpse. I lean in closer to Dominic and hear Xander growl.

"Class is cancelled. Everyone out!" He stands, owning the room with his booming presence. Xander's fist balls and slams down on the desk, and I jolt with the thundering sound.

I have upset him, and now instead of gaining his attention, he is making us leave. I scold myself, slapping the inside of my thigh. No one sees this gesture as they all pile out, and are excited that they don't have to stay. Dominic is busy packing up his bag as I stand on wobbly legs, my heart racing and my face reddening with shame.

"I don't have another class after this. How about we grab some lunch?" Dominic asks.

"I can't. I need to um… I need to study." I look over and watch Xander breathe deeply, his eyes penetrating me. He's daring me to say yes; he is challenging me to let another man entertain his bird.

"We can study together, maybe over dinner?" he attempts again, looking over to where my eyes are traveling. My head is down and I already feel my knees going weak, ready to apologize. I went way too far.

"Lizith. I would like to speak to you about your recent paper." Xander takes charge, and if I don't get Dominic out of here, our secret may be revealed. Dominic looks him over suspiciously.

"Rain check?" I know that will never happen, but getting him out of here is my sole focus.

"Yeah, sure. You gonna be okay?" He rubs my shoulder and my eyes squeeze shut. Touch, physical touch, is off limits.

"Yes, thank you. I will see you tomorrow."

He leaves and the second he shuts the door, I fall to my knees and crawl to Xander, rounding his desk in tears. I feel awful that I punished him and broke our rules just for his attention.

"Xander, I'm sorry." I get to his feet and keep my eyes down, looking at the shiny material of his expensive Prada dress shoes. Rounded at the tip, long and sleek, thick and powerful. Just like his cock.

"You did a bad thing. You want me to leave you?"

I peer up fast, my head whipping and nearly cracking, my heart rate speeding through all the red lights. "No! Please, sir. I promise I will never do that again. Don't leave me." I lay my head against his shin and wrap my arms around him.

"I wouldn't leave you. I would be ripped from you—in cuffs. You can cause me to hurt people, Lizith. You played with fate today, and you awoke the devil. You naughty little bird," he scolds, leaning then to grab a fistful of my hair.

When his grip is firm, he tilts my head back and I enjoy the sting. It's my apology. With calculated and stoic movement, he drops to his haunches and assesses my now red and tearstained face. I choke on my breath, aware of his presence and scared from his threats. I know Xander would break the hands of any man who touched what was his.

"How could you let someone touch you, bird? How could you let another man have the delicate feel of my belonging on their fingers?" he asks, his cock now bulging in his pants. I drop my head to steal a glance, but his grip tightens. "Answer me!"

The stark difference from his calm demeanor to his furious tone is daunting. I don't know what to say anymore.

"I'm a mess." It's all I can muster, all that makes sense.

"The prettiest fucking mess. Goddamn it. I want you at my place when I get home. Naked on the bed, Lizith."

My stomach flips. It worked! I went against him, did everything that would upset him in order to get him, and I know it worked. Sometimes I just have to steal his attention if I want it. Because I know he will always reward me with thanks when I give him exactly what he wants—even if he didn't ask for it.

"Yes, my keeper. I promise. I will be a good broken thing and will take my punishment willingly." I try to lean and give him a kiss, but he turns me down.

Grabbing my chin in his hand, he paralyzes me. "I will kiss you when you learn how angry you have made me. Don't ever do anything like that again to get my fucking attention, Lizith. Next time, I will break a man's arms."

I gulp, letting more of my tears fall. I hurt him, and now I am consumed with guilt. How could I hurt my love? "The apartment, or your condo?" I whimper. I much prefer the small, cozy apartment he has close to campus. The condo he used to share with his whore wife just feels so... cold.

"Condo. Now." Silencing me, he stands, pulling our bodies apart. With shaking legs, I stumble to a pathetic stance and grab my bag, no longer looking back at him, because I caused waves and put a wedge between my love and me. I shouldn't have been such a bad little bird.

Hours pass, and I sit on his bed naked and cold, afraid and alone. My body shivers, my skin raised with a thousand goose bumps, as every noise I hear, I assume it's him. I look over at the clock on his nightstand and see it's nearing 7:00 p.m. Xander should have been home hours ago. My hands leave my lap in a slow trail to the black silk sheets adorning his bed. The sheets that wrap him up gently every night, encase his body, and shield it from the night air.

I've never wanted to be both a sheet and a nocturnal breeze before. Fighting for the ownership of my love, I would lace myself in satin and silk, and then I would lie under my keeper and wrap him in my arms. The effect of a cocoon protecting Xander, letting him know I am here forever, even if it were only as an object.

I see small figments of his wife, Jacqueline, in this room and my blood boils to a full-on raging volcano. I know they separated before we started this and she is no longer living here; she left him for another man. And if I wasn't insanely crazy about him and completely possessive, I would slap the stupidity out of her. How could she leave Xander? How could any woman? If I ever lost him, I would spend a lifetime searching the depths of the oceans, the most frightening forests, and the darkest of shadows to find him once more.

I look over to the fireplace and see his wife's picture sitting in the frame, and my eye twitches, my palms shaking a bit. I stand and scurry across the room like a cat and grab the frame in a rough grip. I look at her face, fake and despondent, a crossroads demon vying to steal my keeper's soul. Xander isn't in the picture and I'm glad, because I would never damage anything that holds a piece of him. I begin to hum a slow, drawn out version of "Every Breath You Take."

With great precision, I flip it over and slowly move the small black pieces holding in the back of the frame. When the picture finds my hands, I look closer, trailing my finger over the shape of her face. I wonder what would happen if I placed her perfume against the column of my neck, or if I traced my lips in the same red lipstick she wears. Would Xander like it? Is this the type of woman he desires? Does he miss her? I never ask questions. I only hear phone conversations when she is calling to bitch about something.

Does the defiance and the domineering behavior turn him on? Because she is a vile woman and it makes no sense. Am I just a pawn in their marriage? A form of foreplay? Will he take her back one day? She doesn't know me, but if she did, would jealousy bring her back?

"No, shut up, shut up. You're his bird. His love." I shake my head violently, trying not to let the voice in my head that only started coming around when I fell in love with Xander take over. I snap, ripping the picture in half and dropping it to the ground with the frame. I walk back to the bed and curl into a ball. Xander is mad at me and he still isn't here. What if he's with her?

"Lizith, what is this mess?" My keeper opens the gates of my self-imposed hell and pulls me back in, yanking me from my fit. I sit up and my hair falls messily over one shoulder.

"Xander, you came." I swallow past the lump in my throat, tasting a bit of salt from the tears my mouth caught.

"I told you I would. Why are you crying? And why did you do this, Lizith?" He picks up the picture and I whimper, dropping my head in pain. I hate that he is coming to her aid, that he is bringing Jacqueline into our nest of sacred, tortured, disturbingly sick love.

"Don't touch the picture. Don't touch her," I whisper, and before I get a chance to look, he's standing in front of the bed, where I am miserably waiting.

"Someone's feeling what I felt earlier. A touch can sometimes be deeper than emotions and words. You touched someone else and it's hurting you, because I've broken you enough to own you. Finally, you learn, little bird."

His warm, calloused hand touches me, and I feel what he means. His touch could tell me what a thousand words can't. He loves me and I know it. He owns me and he knows it. We are each other's jugular vein, Achilles's heel, and the heartbeat of our survival.

"Why are you holding yourself from me? It hurts, Xander. I love you. Don't you love me?" I ask, crawling to the end of the bed to get closer.

"I don't believe in love when it comes to you. Love is weak compared to what I feel for you, Lizith. I own you. I'm sick over you. You fucking got inside me, and I should push you away and do far worse than what I have already."

I don't care if it's only been a few weeks in his world. I have fallen in love with Xander, gone mad—completely insane—in a matter of days, and it is exactly where I want to be. And no one and nothing can ever slow me down or bring me back to reality. I'm in Xander's world now.

"Make love to me. Till dawn. Ruin me, Xander," I whisper, my lips drawing nearer to his neck.

"Until the dawn rises, the stars and the moon will witness the hours we'll spend stealing each other's breath." Leaning in, he kisses my cheek, biting the dimple that appears from my thankful smile. He always knows when to dig deeper into himself in order to bring me back to the brink. He's smart, so smart. Handsome and irresistible. "The night will watch two people become one. She will fall silent as she loses her breath, a dark voyeur peeking in while I make you a woman and take what is mine."

I crumble to nothing and fall deeper under his spell. He wiped away my insecurities with his poetic words and intimate touches. Xander is a man of great power and has complete influence over me. I have never been more sure of what my wants are, and in this life, Xander will be that want.

Placing his palm flat against my collarbone, he pushes me back onto the bed, my breasts lightly jostling with the motion, but his eyes never waver from mine. I watch him tower over me, eating me up with his heavy, dominant presence. I bite my lip and feel the jumble of butterflies dancing in my stomach. I'm going to become his. Right here and right now.

"You are fucking stunning. I've never fucked a body so goddamn perfect, never touched a woman so beautiful. You're in control of me right now, Lizith," he admits.

"Teach me how to be the perfect lover, Professor."

"I can do that, but are you sure you know what this will mean?"

"Yes," I whimper when his thumb grazes my nipple.

"Focus, little bird. I'm serious. Do you understand what happens after I take you?"

I gulp, suddenly afraid, my arousal dissipating. Am I ready? "No, sir. What will it mean?" I force my demeanor to turn sharp, matching him, trying to convince him, and myself, that I am up for the challenge. I cannot look weak in front of him. I must appear strong.

"You can't ever run from me." He leans in to bite the shell of my ear, his breath whispering against my neck and making me shiver. "You run to me when I call, and you understand my ownership over you."

I nod, unsure—not of him, but of myself. I don't think he understands what I am willing to do to keep him. "Are you sure you are ready, Xander? You may not understand the water you have tainted under my feet. You didn't calm my storm; you wreaked havoc on me like a hurricane," I implore, and for a moment I think I see my defeat mirrored in his dilated blue irises.

"You're coloring outside the lines, Lizith. Don't try and overrule me," he growls, but before I can whisper another provocation, his hand grasps my throat with purpose. I squeak out a sound barely above a whisper and he smirks, a low laugh leaving the depths of his wide chest. "Now I'll show you what it's like to be ruled, owned, and destroyed by love. Because you love me, don't you, little bird?"

I nod, my airways seemingly restricted from the awareness of my love for this man, not just from his unshakeable grip. I am choking on my obsession and wringed lifeless by my insanity. The insanity this man caused.

"No more words now. You just listen." As he drops his large hand from my neck, I gasp for air, trying to regain control over myself, but the moment I do, he takes me over once again. "Sucking cock isn't easy, pretty little baby. You have to be gentle with your keeper, and patient."

I sit at the edge of the bed, my body following the gravitational pull that is Xander. It's like it knows what it has to do. My feet touch the cold wood of his bedroom floor, a shiver moving up from my pink toes to the rest of my body, escaping at the tips of my hair follicles.

I watch him look down on me as he reaches behind his head and grips his shirt to remove it in one swift motion. His abs electrify my blood, sending a crackle through my veins. They are defined, so defined I'm scared I'll cut myself on the rigid borders. They match his strong jaw—all his edges sharp.

"Remove my belt and release my cock, beautiful." He pets me, running his curved hand over my head, through my hair, then down my cheek.

I nod, my shaking hands reaching up for the first time as a woman discovering her lover. The sound of the metal on his belt is deafening and it seems to echo against the silent room louder than my labored breathing.

"Like that, just like that."

Finally, after what felt like a small eternity, but was really seconds, I have his erect length, thick and alive, in my hand. Xander is smooth, hard, warm, and everything a man with power should be.

"You look like a goddess holding me in your hands. The image of lust. Kiss the tip and taste my need for you, bird."

I gulp again, this time blinking up at him, looking to him with unease. I don't know what to do, because I have never done this type of thing before. "I'm scared," I admit, coiling in on myself. I want him to love what we are about to do as much as I will. I don't want this to be a chore for him—the breaking in of an inexperienced virgin.

"You're scared? Of what?" He grabs my hand and brings it to his lips, kissing each finger with purpose.

"I've never been touched by anyone like you. By anyone at all. What if I'm bad at it?"

"Oh, Lizith, I hope you are terrible at it. I want to teach you how to give pleasure, but only to me. So the worse off you are, the more fucking pleasure I will take from it."

"Does it turn you on?"

"You? Yes, Lizith, you turn me on." I shake my head, dropping it against his palm cradling my cheek.

"No, does it turn you on to see me so broken? To hurt me? To demean me?"

His face grows stoic, his stare locking in on mine. "I will never demean you. Know the difference between that and wanting to make you mine, perfectly mine. As if I made you for me, directly from my fucking rib. I glorify you, bird. I. Fucking. Love. You." He executes each word with a slow drawl, deep sounding, as if it were leaving his soul and floating from between his lips.

"Freedom," I whisper. I can see he understands me by that one word as he nods. His declaration has set my soul apart from reality. I feel free to now love him the way he loves me. To be unafraid of who we are, to understand this love has no boundaries. We will never be like Prince Charming and his princess, or a queen and king. Better yet, we are the darker side of love, the kind you are told to run from. We are Bonnie and Clyde, or more accurate, Joker and Harley.

Xander removes all restrictions from between us, baring his body to my now naked form. I watch every muscle move, each tic of his jaw as he strips down for me. I lick my lips and bow my head like a broken bird waiting for her wing to be put back together.

"Give me those lips. Fuck me, those pouty little lips." Starting with his fingers at my forehead, he drags them through my hair, gripping a handful at the top of my head, bringing me forward with whispers of love for me. And in a moment, I learn the real taste of my keeper.

The head of his cock touches my lips, the wet tip salty and powerful. I whimper, my eager mouth and even more fervent heart lurches forward as I suck the crown, my eyes lulling back as I do.

He hisses, and I open my eyes to see the first look of pleasure being taken versus given, and I now know what he has felt only ever giving pleasure the past few weeks.

Xander's sudden expression of gluttonous desire spearheads my suddenly confident approach. Slowly, I relax my mouth and throat, my eyes watering and collecting tears in the corners as I take in a few inches. When I feel his shaft hitting the back of my throat, I gag.

"Slow and easy, bird!" he barks, turning back into the dominant. I back up slowly and hum my apology. "I didn't mean to yell. I just want you to go slow." He pets me again, and if my mouth weren't rammed full with cock, I would have bowed my head and blushed under his sweet praise. "Flatten your tongue, massage it against the bottom of my shaft while you suck, but give me your eyes, Lizith."

I peer up and adjust my mouth to his liking. When I get a steady pace going and he has given in to his pleasure, he starts thrusting forward with tiny, calculated movements, fucking my mouth like I have only ever read about in the naughty books I own. I am living the fantasy of all those paperbacks that were once gripped in my hands, except Xander is real and better than any fantasy.

"So pretty, so strong and brave taking me for the first time." He keeps going, his head slanted and looking down on me as if admiring a work of art. "I need to fuck you," Xander growls, changing position without warning.

He drops from my mouth and suddenly moves me up the bed by my ass. His hands grip the skin of my plush, toned skin, and his face is within inches of mine when he settles me beneath him as he towers over me. I grab hold of his face and watch his eyes as they consume me.

Reaching between us, he finds my core, checking me, it seems, as he moves his fingers in circles around my clit then my opening. I cry out, the feeling incredible and the sensations heightening.

"You respond so fucking perfectly to me. Wet, warm, and ready. Do you like it when I play with your little clit?" he asks, and I nod, moaning louder when he pinches. "Fuck yes, you do. Taste yourself, baby." He brings his fingers up from my pussy and I open my mouth to take in the taste. I never thought this was something sexy or appealing, but the look on Xander's face when he feels my tongue touch his fingertip proves I was wrong.

"You're ripe and fertile. I can taste it, sweet bird. Are you on the pill?" He licks the rest of me from his fingers, even as they're still in my mouth. Our tongues touch around them, and I nearly orgasm from the eroticism.

"No, I'm not."

"Fuck."

I panic, thinking he is going to push me away and end this before we can really begin. "No, please, it's okay. I'm not afraid. I can give you a life—I want to give you me. Everything."

"Oh, sweet baby, you're too young right now to have a family, and I'm too selfish to share you with a child just yet. Maybe one day." My stomach coils, the feeling of rejection closing in on me. "Don't look so sad. I have protection." Standing, he goes to his nightstand, and I smirk inwardly knowing I get to have him. I admire his backside, which is strong and defined.

He slides on the condom and drops to his knees. I prop up on my elbows to look at him, wondering where he is going.

"Easy, eager one. You need to learn patience. I'm just stealing a kiss from your lips."

And with that, he closes his mouth around my pussy and my hips leave the bed, the room filling with my loud scream. "Xander!" I grip the sheets, praying they will have mercy on me, unlike Xander, and they will release my pleasure. It's so much. Too much.

"Come here. Please!"

Moving back between my legs, he balances his weight on his knees and pulls me up to him, to straddle his waist. I do as he asks and I band my arms around his shoulders to brace myself for whatever he plans to do.

Dropping my forehead to his, I whisper his name one last time. "Xander." And with slow measure, he takes my hips and slides me onto his cock. I feel it then, when he reaches my barrier, breaching me and breaking through. I cry, losing myself in the pain, aware I was nowhere near ready for this agony.

"Breathe me in and breathe me out." Our foreheads stay connected, as do our eyes, while he leads me, breathing in and out with him as he goes deeper, inch by inch.

"And just like that, I'm in your blood, your soul." He places his hand above my heart and slides all the way home, ending the pain so I can find pleasure.

Lying me back down, he thrusts into me hard this time, the pain still slightly present. It's masked when he takes my nipple between his teeth and pulls, releasing it and giving me two fast thrusts.

"Oh, Xander. Never stop."

"I won't. Until dawn, remember?" Leaning back, he pushes into me, stationing his hand spread out over my waist and my stomach. I can see how small I look next to his large frame. He slides in and out of me, and I wish it was his cock pumping against me, skin on skin.

"Take off the condom. Please."

He fucks me harder, ignoring me with purpose, because I see him fighting the urge. It's insane, the thought of us having a child, but as far as I'm concerned, that is just semantics when it comes to our desire and my love for him. I would do anything to have him soul to soul, skin on skin.

"Xander, please, I want you to come inside me. Don't ruin my first time." I bite my lip as he grabs my breast hard.

"You don't know what you are taunting me with. I want a family, Lizith, and you're dangling that dream in front of me like steak in front of a fucking dog."

"Good. Take a bite, my keeper," I moan against his mouth, sitting up trying to ride him despite my inexperience. I clench down when his cock hits my cervix, and that feeling is his cue.

"Goddamn it." Just like that, he lifts me off him, flipping me on my knees, and I hear him remove the condom. Looking over my shoulder, I watch as he lines himself up and slowly enters me.

"Oh!" We both gasp in unison, euphoria hitting us instantly. I've never been this close to anyone before. I have never known who I am as a woman more than I do now, skin against skin with the man who I feel is part of my soul. I was made for Xander, and Xander was made for me.

"Xander, I feel it coming. Please come with me," I beg, his thrusts increasing in speed. His abs hit my back and I reach back to grip his hair, tilting my head so our lips can touch. With a dance of our tongues and one of his hands grasping my breast for leverage as his other reaches around to thrum my clit, we hit our peaks together.

"You're my broken bird, my life, Lizith. Promise that I have you forever."

"Yes! I am yours, Xander. My keeper."

Dawn came that morning and even then we never stopped. He kept making love to me bare. I didn't become pregnant that night, but maybe now I will. I am keeping my promise and giving Xander the life he always wanted.

After a few more minutes, I leave the bed and clean up, ready to meet my keeper again and share our news. What a sweet homecoming it will be.

Chapter Five

XANDER

SINCE JACQUELINE AND I FOUGHT, I HAVE AVOIDED HER LIKE THE BLACK PLAGUE. Secretly, I've been praying all week, waiting for our results, hoping my shit isn't working or that my seed is poisoned. Because having children and passing on my legacy has lost its appeal. And if I'm the broken one, maybe Jacqueline will leave me.

I fucking pray she will.

I loathe her now, years of disdain turning me black inside and creating a deeper core filled with putrid hate. I am ashamed of the man I let her control. I am a man of dominance, and she belittled me, stripped me bare, and dragged me by the fucking balls. And last night, in my tossing and turning state, I remembered the one woman who latched on and dragged me by my throat.

Lizith. Her long fucking hair, dark and cascading down her shoulders. Fuck, I bet she's grown up so much. Matured, but still seemingly innocent in the wideness of her eyes and the swell of her doll-like lips. Her skin still creamy, always looking untouched, except under her panties and bra, where I would bite to bruise her with my mark. Our little secret.

I step on the throttle when I hit the highway, her image fueling the alpha beast inside. I miss my mate that I made the mistake of letting go. I bet she is married now with that white picket fence. A man with cufflinks and a cheap tie, working a nine-to-five before coming home to dissatisfy her. He can't touch Lizith like I can, and I hope—fucking beg God—that at night when she closes those pretty greens, she sees my eyes piercing into her, my hands breaking her in underneath me. Because even if she settled down in a life of lies, hiding the damaged little bird she is, I know I still haunt her nightmares. Because she still haunts my dreams.

I will always own Lizith, even in the air and space between us, in her mind and in her fucking beating heart.

I arrive at the fertility clinic and park my sleek black Model S Tesla next to the white Mercedes Jacqueline drives. I take a deep breath and look at my distant eyes in the rearview mirror. My peppered hair is styled to perfection without a strand out of place. The slight wrinkles around my eyes show years and years of torture. I may be getting older, but my body doesn't show it. I've stayed fit and as youthful-looking as I could.

"Here we go, Xander," I rumble low in my chest, taking one last look before climbing out of the car. I went with a casual look today, dark denim against my brown distressed boots and lightweight gray top. They complement my rugged features well. The sun beams down, and in a brief moment, I close my eyes and see Lizith grasping my shirt. She always did that when I came to her after being away for so long. Opening my eyes, I take notice that my hand is gripping my shirt in reaction.

Shaking my head and getting myself in the game, I compose myself and walk into the building. I'm greeted by the overly flirtatious blonde at the front desk, "Good morning, Mr. Stine."

"Morning. Has Jacqueline checked in yet?" I ask, signing in and checking over the list.

"Um, yes. She did. But she went back to talk to Dr. Curtis. Said she had some questions for him."

She seems off, a little uneasy with her answer, and I quirk my brow. "Hmm. Sounds important. I guess I will just wait for her to come out."

"Perfect, you will be seeing his PA today. I'll let her know you're here, and I'll let Jacqueline know as well."

With a subtle nod, I decide I will let it go for now, and watch her disappear. Taking a seat, I pull out my phone and check the online boards to see if any of my students have submitted their thesis paper. A few minutes later, I hear that nails on a chalkboard sound. Jacqueline's heels click harshly against the tile floor and her fake laugh echoes as she ends a phone call. I refrain from subjecting myself to the adolescent behavior of rolling my eyes at her.

Standing when she gets close as the receptionist waits beside the front desk with a manila folder in her hand, I greet my wife with forced effort. "Hello, is everything all right? You had to see the doctor?"

Instantly, she rolls her eyes and pulls out her lipstick, the same damn color she's worn every day for the past twenty years. Fiery, devil red. "Xander, don't act like you care. I just had some fertility questions. Don't pretend like you're the perfect, concerned husband when we both know it's a waste of time." I tighten my lips and my jaw flexes as my hands grow white under the extreme pressure of me squeezing them into fists.

Lizith would never disrespect me like that. She would thank me and fall to my fucking feet for making sure she was okay. Though Jacqueline is right—I don't give a shit. But she said it loud enough for the others in the room to hear. And I, Xander Stine, do not like to be disrespected in front of anyone.

"You're right. I don't. Don't forget to add some cover up. Your fucking age is showing, *baby*," I sneer, dragging out the last word with disdain. She scoffs, and I walk past her, meeting the receptionist with an unaffected smirk, as if everything is normal and the exchange she witnessed was nothing but pleasant. "After you, dear."

She gulps then sets into a scurrying pace. Jacqueline catches up as I take a seat in what I assume is the physician's assistant's office. I haven't met him yet, having only come in to give my sample, but from what I can see, he is pristine—like me. Everything is hung evenly, the desk is clean, and everything is in its rightful place. Nothing is out of the ordinary or scattered like many offices are. It's as if I was the one who resided here.

The colors are black and white with gold accents—my personal preference—and I look at every detail. The bookshelf just behind the PA's chair catches my eye, and I see multiple books, more than half I've read and own, some of my favorites. What in the actual fuck? It's as if I stepped into my own office.

Jacqueline sits next to me, and as I go to comment about it and ask her who the PA is, I hear a voice that steals my breath and snaps all my male arousal into overdrive. The dreams she haunted are now given a reality.

"Mr. and Mrs. Stine, I'm glad you could make it in today."

I don't turn around. Instead, my eyes stay focused in front of me as each step she takes closes in on me and I wait for her to assault my vision. Is this a dream? A fucking flashback? I answer that when she finally rounds the desk and Jacqueline says hello.

"Xander?" Jacqueline's voice pulls me from myself, and when I focus my eyes on the goddess in the chair on the other side of the desk, my cock goes hard and my heart seizes in my chest. Green eyes and long, straight brown hair and still the flawless face of my goddamn visions—in both my beautiful heaven and darkened hell. My fucking lifeline.

"Xander! What the hell is wrong with you?" Jacqueline snaps at me, and I sit up, finding myself suddenly.

"Sorry, I forgot I had to do something for work. Hello, I'm Xander." I look her over, taking a moment to peruse her beautiful body behind the clear glass of her smudge-less desk. Good little bird, keeping everything clean like her keeper likes it.

She is wearing a short purple dress under her white coat, and her lean legs are crossed at her ankle like I trained her to do. Her tits are still as luscious and mouthwatering as they always were, but it's those fucking eyes that steal my breath. She challenges me with a smirk on her pouty lips and a knowing glint in her green orbs.

"I know who you are." She pauses, and I look to Jacqueline, panicked at the way she said that. "I mean your wife has told me about you, and you are both here to start a family." Jacqueline doesn't catch on and makes work of looking at her phone, and my eyes find Lizith's when she rolls "family" off her tongue in a jealous tone. I'm the only one who notices, because I know her invidious tone of voice.

I shake my head as my eyes zero in on her, and hers drop submissively. I watch her body slowly coil in and she places both her palms on the desk, facing them up. She waits a few seconds before looking up to me from under her thick lashes, her head still drawn down. My fists in my lap turn white as my jaw tics. I shake my head again and watch her eyes well with tears. I give her a stern look without saying anything, and she knows what to do. She takes a deep breath and keeps her tears at bay as she falls back into a normal posture.

Jacqueline finally looks up when she picks up on the silence. "Sorry, it was work. All right, what are we looking at here? Was he…" She tilts her head to me, the mention of me distasteful in her mouth. But it doesn't distract me from my little bird. Fuck, I missed her. "Broken?"

Lizith's eyes pinch as she looks at Jacqueline. I clear my throat, and she jumps a little, her glare turning into a soft smile, faking it like she knows she better or her little ass will be what's broken. "No, Xander, you are not the problem. You had one hundred and twenty million for your sperm count per your ejaculation. Placing you far above average." Jacqueline misses the way Lizith's lip lifts and her legs tighten under the table, her thighs clenching together.

Fuck. I smell her. The second she relaxes, I smell her feminine scent, my poison.

"Well, maybe we should do it a second time, because if it isn't me, then it must be him," Jacqueline insists next to me in annoyance. But she is a fly in this room because I just metaphorically whipped out my cock and showed the woman of my dreams what a real man I am.

That's right, little bird. The second she leaves this room, that fertile body and warm pussy is going to get all that seed, and you will take it like a good little pet.

"We can do that. I can schedule it, but I think we should also run another test on you as well, Jacqueline." Lifting her hand, she tucks her hair perfectly behind her ear, and seeing the first set of pearls I ever gave her adorn her lobes, I swallow thickly. Lizith is playing with me, and I'm about to fucking burn her. She should have known what she was doing would earn her the worst punishment.

And as she tries to convince Jacqueline to retest, I realize this is no coincidence. This isn't happenstance. This was done on purpose. She knew this from day one. But for how long? How long did my little bird plan this, and how the fuck did she pull this off? I left her behind and didn't give her a chance to find or follow me, but she fucking did.

What a psychotic, dangerous, insanely fucking gorgeous, bad little bird she is. But fuck me, what a good girl my baby is. I should run, and most men would, but this just makes me want to reward her with punishment. How dare she be this close and know this was her plan all along without telling me and fucking waiting years to make herself known again? How dare she stay away, yet be so close without coming to me?

What the fuck are you up to, my broken little psycho?

LIZITH

"Fine. But I will only let Dr. Curtis do it. He is very thorough and I trust him to make sure it is done safely," Jacqueline speaks at me, not to me, or so she thinks. Little does she know that while Xander thinks she is talking about trust, she is really talking about climbing higher on her throne of lies and deceit.

"That's fine, Mrs. Stine, if that is what you would like. I will have you make an appointment with him at his earliest convenience. Other than that, I have nothing else to add unless you two have any questions for me." I look at Xander when I say this, and my eyes nearly water when I see the shadow of hurt under his scowl of disappointment. He's mad at me, and I know it from the way his lip curls when he speaks. That and the way his knuckles grip the chair and his taut shoulders go stiff in that perfect gray tee that is lucky to be against his flesh.

I didn't want to hurt him. I thought this would have made him happy, but it seems to be the complete opposite. I just want Jacqueline out of here so he can come barreling back in and punish me with his hands, and lash the whip of his harsh, hurt words against my heart. I will take it in order to make him feel better after the pain I caused him.

"No. We don't," he speaks. It's a gravelly smooth sound, like whiskey on rocks, and it melts my core. That's his Dominant voice, the keeper in him coming out.

I stumble on my words, coughing to wake my throat from its slumber. "Okay. Please schedule your next appointment, and I will see you both *very* soon." I enunciate the word, my eyes looking him over with my brows drawn in sorrow. I hurt my keeper, and my wings are tucked and bent from shame and pain. I lost a feather when he looked at me like I crushed his heart in my hands.

He nods and stands, and with a few heavy, calculated, and unfaltering steps, he disappears from my office with Jacqueline in tow. Immediately, the tears fall and I break character like I shouldn't. My shoulders slump and my knees cave in and bang together as I cry into my palms. I did this all wrong, and now I feel like I made a mistake.

I hurry and stand, losing my clothes, because I can sense him still near, I feel his presence, and I don't want to upset him more.

Stripping to nothing and falling bare on my knees just to the side of my desk, I drop my butt to my feet and lay my palms face up, lowering my head in surrender. Then I wait. Doing my best to stop the tears and breathe in and out calmly, I'm unable to. I hurt him. I hurt Xander. I did to him what I promised I would never do. Even after he crushed me and left me with wounded wings, I promised I would never hurt him.

I must have gotten lost in my thoughts, because I didn't hear him reenter my office until he speaks.

"Lizith," he says sternly. It's like a crack in the foundation when he calls me by my name. His voices crawls into my skin and bruises me with punishment. I'm his little psycho, his broken bird, his good little girl when he is proud of me. But Lizith is reserved for the few times I have hurt him beyond what he can control.

I don't look up, but I speak, desperate to share a conversation with him after years of being starved of it. "Xander, my love. I am so sorry. I wanted you to be happy, and I didn't do that. Break me. Please, pluck my feathers and bruise me. Just don't hurt anymore, my keeper." I choke out the last part with a pained sob. And before he can speak, I crawl to him, naked, bared to him completely, vulnerable, and stripped of any identity of my own. I am his now. I belong to Xander.

The carpet scratches my knees, and I do it purposely to punish myself. When his brown boots come into view, I bring the peaks of my knees to the tips of his shoes and slowly, looking up, my eyes assess every inch of him, especially his cock outlined in his fitted jeans. My heart cracks deeper in my chest. He is my home and he has been gone for so long. The image of seeing him or the dream of touching him again was never as good as this reality.

When our eyes meet, he is still stone-faced, and I shake my head back and forth, my silky hair rubbing against my hot, sensitive skin. "Please, touch me. Forgive me. Do whatever, but please fucking touch me, Xander." Suddenly, he bends enough to grab hold of me under my chin and around my neck with authority and barely lifts, but I set into motion and come to stand.

"Watch your mouth, little girl. I don't like hearing nasty things fall from my bird's cherry lips." My knees buckle at his power. My core tightens and I begin to grow wet. God, I have missed his strong, aggressive control over me. "You hid from me. You knew about me being here all along. You have been here and you waited. You fucking kept yourself from me, and that isn't like you, Lizith. I trained you better than to challenge me. But here I am at your fucking mercy, mad as hell, and ready to punish you. You have me by the fucking throat, you bad girl."

I choke when his grip tightens on my throat as he spins me around and pushes me against the wall. "I wanted to wait until you were ready. You told me you couldn't have me anymore, keeper. That's why you left. You really hurt me when you left me, Xander." My eyes drop, and those tears return with a vengeance, falling fast.

"Leaving you was the only choice I had, but coming back to you was always an option."

"But… her." I don't call her his wife, because I refuse to give him claim over anyone but me. "You left me with nothing but a goodbye and a kiss from death, Xander. You left me to start a family with her instead of me!" I snap. The years of controlled behavior that he instilled in me left, and I fucking snapped, taking him by surprise and spinning in his grip. Banging on his chest and slapping his face over and over again, I start to scream, not caring if anyone can hear. But he is stronger.

"No!" Covering my mouth, his hand leaves my neck and he spins me around, and within seconds, his free hand comes down hard on my ass. The sting is so deep I feel it in my very blood, causing a pulse at the place of his assault.

"Uh!" I muffle a yell into his palm he clamps over my mouth.

"You calm down and tell me why you did this. You tell me what you wanted from this." He has somehow not broken demeanor. Xander maintains control and exudes his authority.

I wait a few moments and take deep breaths through my nose, and once I calm, I nod against the wall.

"Good, now sit on the desk and spread your legs while you tell me." I do as he orders and move to the desk. Scooting back on it, I spread my legs and watch him take a seat in the chair in front of me. He places his ankle on top of his opposite knee and stares at me. His cheek rests against two long, thick fingers and his other hand is placed, beautiful and stoic, against the arm of the white chair.

His look is impassive as he peruses my body, his eyes assaulting my breasts then my little stomach, and all the way to my wet, bare core. I moan and move my hips in a circular motion, wanting some friction, but he stays seated and it drives me mad.

"Speak. Touch yourself while you do, Lizith."

I gulp and tentatively move my hand along my stomach until my dainty finger makes contact with my clit. "Oh, Xander," I whisper, a breathy moan in the closed office.

"Now, little bird, or I will leave and make you follow me again," he threatens, and I nearly come, the thought of him leaving so I can chase him again sickeningly arousing.

"I wanted you. I wanted to be what you needed, and I knew I could be, but I had to do it so you wouldn't be able to leave again."

"Fucking eyes. Now."

My head snaps up at his demand I meet his hungry, pissed eyes. "I… I… God, I wanted to do something so dangerous and wrong and sick, because it was a way for me to make you proud. You always loved me most when I was your bad little psycho."

"And? Spit it out, sweet girl," he coos, playing good cop, coercing it out of me.

"I followed you and waited until she slipped up. Waited until I could find a way to keep her from hurting you anymore. So when I found a way, I took it."

He places his foot on the ground and leans forward, looking at me with interest and lust. "What did you do, little bird?" he challenges, knowing that isn't all I did.

I rub my clit faster with my secret on the tip of my tongue, and the minute he quirks his brow and his tongue brushes against his lip, I explode. "I had to steal you, Xander!" I orgasm hard, feeling every part of my body as if I were standing outside it and watching myself reach euphoria.

He growls and stands above me as I'm still coming down from my orgasm, my breath heavy. Grabbing my throat again and bringing my lips just inches from his, he whispers, "Stole me? What did you do, Lizith?"

I try to breathe, but between the orgasm and his grip, I can't get my control back. "I… stole your sperm! I injected myself with your seed so I could give you what your foul, cheating wife can't!" I yell out when I finally can, and I watch his face go stony again as he lets me go. I go to claw at him, but he steps back before I can pull him in to comfort him.

"How do you know she's cheating?"

It hurts that this is what he asks about first.

I almost say something, but decide against upsetting him more. "I have videos, surveillance of her having sex with Dr. Curtis, and she's been lying. Taking birth control from him so she can't get pregnant. She hurt you, and I have proof. So I took your sperm. I wanted to give you what you wanted. I wanted to please you. I wanted to show you how much I love you."

He keeps his back to me and plants his hands firmly on his hips. I stand on shaky legs and bring my arms around my chest to shield myself from the cold air.

"Xander. Please don't be mad at me. I thought you would be happy. Aren't you happy with me for bringing us together again?" I wait, and when he says nothing, my heart breaks all over again. He isn't happy. He is going to say goodbye and go back to her, isn't he?

"Send me the tapes. Now. I expect them in my inbox by the time I get home." And with that, he leaves me cold, alone, broken, and naked for the second time. And just like the first time, I lose my sanity a bit more. But I make a promise to win him back. I will chase him again if he leaves.

I will.

Chapter Six

XANDER

HOW DARE SHE HOLD THIS FROM ME FOR LONGER THAN MOMENTS? FUCK, EVEN seconds? She knew Jacqueline was a manipulative bitch, and yet she waited to tell me. I wanted to smack that ass beet-red and make her sleep at the foot of the bed like my little servant, begging for forgiveness. And trust me when I say—I will. Because Lizith, my little bird, not only put my life in sudden disarray, but she knocked me on my ass and pissed me off.

I should be incomprehensively upset, with no ounce of desire or understanding in my mind, but I'm not. I'm knocked over and fucking in love with my sweet psycho. She came back and claimed me, in the only way she knew how, and I may be ready to reclaim what was once mine—shit, has always been mine. But I will make sure she licks my wounds and aids the bruises I will leave on that ripe ass of hers. The bite marks I will ruin her dainty little thighs with. Shit. I want her.

Once home, I get to work on making sure Jacqueline receives the homecoming of a lifetime. Am I pissed? Yes. Hurt? No. And the only reason I am disgusted and manic over Jacqueline isn't for the loss of the marriage I am about to end, but over the fact that she manipulated me. She thought she could win at making me out to be the fool. Oh, but this serpent is vile, and I will make sure the tables will flip on her.

For years, she dangled her power over my head like a thorny crown, and now I have all the power to give it back tenfold, and she better believe I will. I wait at my desk, staring at my inbox, knowing damn well Lizith has my email address. She knows where I live, having access to private information in my medical files, and she knows my life and more. A fucking email isn't hard to find with her long list of obsessive skills.

When her name pops up, I immediately open it and see the attached videos and pictures with a note.

Master,

I am beyond sorry for what I've done. I shouldn't have gone through with this without consulting you first. I should be sitting at your feet, begging you to take me back and forgive me. Please don't leave again. I don't want to waste more time trying to make you mine again when we could just be together.

Please, Master, my keeper… Xander. My love for you is bursting from me, and I'm not afraid to take this even further just to have you.

I read it over again, and a smug, proud smile tugs at my lips as my cock hardens. I love how she has always been mine. Always willing to apologize when she fucked up, and always willing to do something to be sorry just to let me have a reason to turn that ass pink.

I slowly type the next sentence out as if I were looking her deep in the eye.

Send me your address. Have your ass bare and face up when I get there. Don't make me have more than one reason to destroy you tonight, little bird.

I wait, and within fifteen seconds, she responds. Another twitch in my dick, knowing she is on the other end hungrily waiting for a drop of water in her drought for me.

What time, my love?

I laugh low in my throat, knowing she is probably rocking with joy in her seat.

Does it fucking matter? Your punishment begins now. Ass up and waiting for me. Don't you dare let your ass touch the bed. I hope your legs and knees fucking burn with exhaustion by the time I get there. I will know that you disobeyed me if they are not sore and you aren't trembling when I walk in. Leave the key under the mat. My key.

A brief moment passes as I stand to pour myself a drink. Amber liquid in an expensive glass tumbler. Putting one hand against my side in a balled fist, the veins straining, I stand over my desk and see her response waiting. I open it and read the crisp black letters.

Yes, Master.

And just like that, I am reminded that in just a few short hours, I will be with my other half again. My broken one.

"Little bird, you didn't show up after my final class today," I growl into the phone at Lizith, my cock hard and ready for what was supposed to be our end-of-day rendezvous. I've been seeing her now for a month and a half, and every day, I have spent my afternoon and nights with her.

"I'm so sorry. I slept through my alarm. I'm not feeling well, my love," she whispers the last bit, sounding so damn fragile, and it takes a hold of my chest. I'm falling for her fast. Even though this started as nothing, it has grown into everything to me. I would break bones and end the life of anyone who'd try to take her away from me. Lizith was innocent and untouched before me, soft and gentle, reserved just for my hands. But in the time since I've first taken her innocence, her adoration and love for me grew and she molded herself into the perfect woman that I dreamed of since I knew what wanting someone was.

But back then, even before she became that person, I wanted the girl she was then, and more so as the woman she is now. She obsesses my thoughts, haunts them day in and day out. I crave her like the blood in my body craves its survival. I want her even when she is being her worst self. Selfish, jealous, and even a little bit psychotic. In fact, I want her even more then. She is the physical being of an injected drug. Lizith isn't a woman you start something with and then slowly weed out when you get bored. You don't get tired of Lizith; you fucking chase her to the ends of the earth and then hope, fucking pray, that she keeps you. Because if she let me go, I would not just chase. I would crawl on burning ash and bleed for her. Bleed for her to take me back.

The keeper is kept by his little bird.

Suddenly, I lower my voice as the alpha in me wants to get to her and take care of her. She isn't capable of taking care of herself, because only I can do that for her—because I am her strength when she needs it. "What's wrong, baby?" It's rare for me to call her such a thing, but I feel possessive and itch to cure her.

I can practically see her flushed cheeks and innocent little smile, coming alive like a child who's been praised. "I think I have a terrible cold. I can barely keep my eyes open." She sounds vulnerable, all alone and waiting for me.

"I have just the remedy for you. I'll be there shortly. Leave a key under the mat in case you fall asleep. Lock the door, baby. I don't want anyone getting to you before I do. I'll be your knight in shining armor," I joke lightly as I stand, grabbing my closed briefcase and keys from my desk.

"Oh, Xander, that is so unlike you. You are usually the scary dragon." She giggles first then sniffs. Fuck, she's my kryptonite.

"Call me a jack of all trades."

"I think more a man of decadence and chivalry."

"Nah, just a beast caged for the night so I can tend to my sick queen. I am far from all things good, baby," I growl with a smirk as I lock my office.

"Not true, 'cause I wouldn't do the things I shouldn't do if I didn't believe there's a great man underneath all the danger and thorny tendencies." Her voice is hushed and gentle, setting the tone

for me to be tame and in control of my rough side. I hurry to the car, picturing her in her bed, wrapped in my clothes she steals, thinking I have no clue that she does it. Silly girl.

"So what are you saying?" I prompt.

"I think you aren't a monster or a beast. I just think you are a king with darker desires that speak to those same parts of me. That's what I'm saying, Xander," she purrs, my name erotic sounding on her lips.

"Call me your keeper, and I promise to be only the gentle king tonight," I challenge.

"You are always my keeper, and I could never go for too soft, maybe a little more gentle. But never go soft on me completely."

"Never. I will be there soon, little bird."

I hear her soft hum as she takes my praise. "See you, not soon enough."

Within fifteen minutes, I am at her apartment door with my hands full with soup from the local bakery and some fizzy drink—like a real chump. I never even did things like this for my soon-to-be ex-wife. Not even close. And though this started out as something that was suppose to be nothing, I can't help but see it's beyond that now. Nothing has turned into everything to me.

She doesn't answer within seconds of my fist rapping against the door, so I let myself in with the key she left, impatient and determined to get in to see her. When I open the door, which gives a clear view of her small apartment's hall where her room sits at the end, it frames her dainty little body. Her willowy legs are peeking out of one of my Harvard shirts she stole like a sneaky little pixie. Her long brown hair is thrown up on top of her head. And the part that makes a grip around my heart is the small amount of red blushing her cheeks and just under her upturned nose, where she has used a tissue over and over again to wipe away her sickness.

Lizith is my sick little bird, and this is the first time I will be able to tend to her like a real keeper would. She's so fucking glorious in her weakness.

"Helping yourself through the door, I see," she teases, stopping halfway to me in the middle of the hall.

"I was going to wait, but then I realized I'm not a man who can idly stand by and wait patiently to see his lady." I start toward her slowly, my lip tugging in the corner as I watch her with deep intent.

She waits a second, her smile broadening until her dimples blossom and with barely a whisper, she remarks, "Chivalry. Told you, you still had it." Her left knee bends slowly, swaying back and forth as her teeth catch hold of her lip. My growl comes from deep within my chest.

"It will be dead if you do not stop tempting the ungentlemanly side of me." My stalking still stays steady, each of my steps carrying me slowly toward her.

"Maybe I like tempting th—" She stops when she coughs, her hand automatically going to her lips. And like that, I am on her, wrapping her up in my arms and taking her back to her room.

"You poor thing. How long have you felt like this?" I ask, laying her on the pristine, perfectly made bed covered in a silky gray duvet. I love her on a bed of silk. Her skin is like porcelain, and it should be treated as fucking such.

"Last night after I left your place, I started to feel a little uneasy. Then this morning, I woke up and my fever was out of control. 102.2 to be exact."

I growl again. "Lizith, you should have called me. Whenever your body changes or needs attention, you tell me. I don't like not knowing what is going on with you." I stand back and start to undress, losing my vest and tie, and then my white shirt and jeans come next.

"You had a busy day. I didn't want to disturb you by being an inconvenience," she responds, turning on her side to look up at me, her hands acting as her pillow under the side of her cheek.

Now stripped to my black boxer briefs, she lets out a soft gasp as she takes in my entire form. I tower over her, and with a soft caress, I raise the back of my hand and stroke her cheek. "What kind of life is worth living if my little bird isn't always inconveniencing me? I welcome the fucking distraction, baby." Closing her eyes like a pet being rewarded for good behavior, she slips into my submissive.

"Will you bring whatever is in that bag into bed please, my keeper?" As she bats those long fucking lashes at me, I feel myself stiffening, but I silence that beast for now. Tonight is a night of bonding and connecting, building something more dangerous, destructive, and all encompassing.

"Anything, little one." I move around the room and get her soup.

"Sit up," I say firmly, yet with a gentle caress. She follows suit and sits up straight, leaving room for me to climb behind her. Once I settle with each of my legs on each side of her, I wrap my free arm around her ribs, just under her breasts, and I pull her back to lean against my chest.

"Talk to me before I feed you," I whisper into the shell of her ear, her honeysuckle and peppermint oils mingling and making me ravenous.

A brief pause passes, and then her soft voice fills the silence of the afternoon. "Have you felt loved, Xander?" Her question is not one I was expecting. My skin prickles as I think back to as far as my childhood, and a chill rumbles like thunder up my spine.

"No." My parents never showed affection toward me or each other. I can count on one hand how many times they said 'I love you' to me. They died when I was just a teenager, and after that, I didn't fall in love; I fell in line. I went to a pristine college, met a pristine—or so I thought—woman, married her in a pristine church, and lived a life of forced 'I love yous' and infidelity.

"You never loved her?" She never says Jacqueline's name, refusing to give her any ties to me.

"No. I loved the idea of her, the status she could bring me. It's all a part of the world I was exposed to, Lizith." I dip the spoon into the still steaming soup and bring it slowly to her lips. "Blow." She follows orders then opens up for me. Humming appreciation for the warm, potent taste.

"How do I fit into the lifestyle? Do I serve a purpose for you?"

I don't know what to say, how to respond to feelings outside of sex, because that is not who I am. In a relationship where she wants to talk and where I badly want to give, it's hard for me. It's a foreign taste in my mouth. I wait a moment, using another spoonful of soup to suspend my time.

When we stay silent, she doesn't fill the void with words, but her actions try to exert influence. She gently rubs her hand in circles on my thigh. "Xander. I know I shouldn't ask, but I really want you to tell me things. I want you to trust me beyond intimacy. I want you to tell me who you are." Those words trespass beyond my walls of safeguarded secrets. Lizith is a siren, and she knows how to use it.

"You serve a purpose by adding value to my life. I am not a man of many words and hearts and flowers, but know that you are the most precious thing in my life. And I may not show you much past the touching and the possessive behavior I latch on to, but I value you beyond the life that I thought was meant for me. You broke through the barricade of darkness in me. You tapped into the cold parts of my heart, little bird, and it's fucking me up."

Before I can gain an ounce of control, she takes the soup from my hand and places it on the nightstand next to her bed. She moves to straddle me and, closing the space between us, we both breathe heavily, her shoulders lifted and her head slowly tilting from left to right as she inhales me, taking my scent, and assesses my face. "Xander, how can I show you love? How can I make you feel it for the first time?" A little tear slips from those green eyes, and I just grip her tighter around the waist.

"In every fucking way only you can," I growl, dropping my forehead to hers. "Every way. The crazy way, the way that will drive me up-the-wall insane. The kind that will test my patience, all while making me so fucking proud to call you mine. Obsess over me, breathe me in like oxygen. Let me in this body and do whatever I need to feel that love." I bite her lip and she whimpers.

"Can I say it? Please?" she begs, wounded and pathetic and beautiful-sounding all at once.

"*Those words are insignificant. They don't even touch the feelings I have for you.*"

"*Say it. Please, I need to hear it.*"

"*Why?*"

She cries harder, and I love those tears. They fuel me on. I want her to beg.

"*Because, Xander, I want to love you in all the ways they couldn't. I want to hurt you in the ways you hurt me. You say it, and that means I have power over you, and that means you have power over me. It's madness, my keeper.*" *She waits on the edge, her lips a whisper of a touch against mine. I smirk briefly then my lips fall straight. A pregnant pause later, and all the air in the room sucks dry and my words echo.*

"*I fucking love you.*"

I hear those words echo in my mind, remembering the day I fell in love with Lizith, and that feeling is just as strong, if not stronger, and it's choking me. I want to get to her, and as I sit at my desk, I see her email with all the documents and videos I needed. I grow impatient as I view them and find myself laughing sinisterly in my throat. I should be jealous, or at least have a bruised ego, but I don't, because in just a few short hours, I will be Lizith's for good and she will be *fucking mine.*

I respond to her email when I finish converting them.

Send me your address, and do not fucking test me tonight, Lizith. Be ready for me.

I wait a moment, taking a sip of my freshly poured scotch, the burn crisp in my throat. Within a minute, there is a response, and I smugly smile. She has been waiting like a good little submissive for me to respond.

Yes, my keeper. I'm sorry—so sorry, my love.

She leaves her address, and I see she is only a few blocks away from me. That bad girl just added another slap to her punishment. I go to exit my email, when another one from her pops up. I open it and eye over the typed black words, crisp, daunting, promising, and everything I have craved for the years I spent without hearing them.

I love you.

Without response, I stand and take my scotch and evidence to the living room. Setting up my vengeful homecoming for Jacqueline, I finish up and make quick work of prepping to leave. The entire time, I hear Lizith whispering "I love you" like she did every night after that first time.

"I'm coming home, little bird. I hope you're ready," I murmur into the empty apartment, my bag packed and ready by the door.

Going to the living room, I wait for what feels like hours. Because I know the wealth waiting for me once I end this with Jacqueline.

Chapter Seven

XANDER

I HEAR THE FRONT DOOR OPEN AND SHUT BEFORE THE SOUND OF HER KEYS HITTING the glass dish in the foyer echoes throughout the room. The *click clack* of her heels gets louder, but it no longer annoys me, knowing I'll soon never have to hear it again. As she enters the living room, scrolling on her phone, she doesn't pay attention to the bodies slapping together on the giant TV screen. I take a sip from my tumbler of scotch, the ice clinking together and bringing her eyes to me.

That's when Jacqueline finally looks up to find the video footage of Dr. Curtis fucking her as she's bent over the examination table at the clinic.

Suddenly, it's not the sound of her keys, or her heels, or the ice in my glass filling the room. It's her phone falling out of her grasp and shattering on the hardwood floor. I smirk, my eyes going from her to the TV just as Dr. Curtis rears back and slaps her ass, causing my wife to throw her head back, her face contorting in pleasurable pain. My cock doesn't even twitch as she begins to fuck back into him, her nostrils flaring and her lips snarling, begging for more.

But then the screen goes black and I look up to see Jacqueline holding the remote to her chest, her eyes staring but not seeing as she appears to search her mind.

"What is it, *wife?* Don't want to spice up our sex life a little, watch a little porn to get our engines revving? I believe this one is titled '*Cheating Cunt Gets Fucked Like a Whore by Her Doctor.*'" I take a final sip of my scotch, emptying the glass, leaving behind only the ice.

"How...?"

"How... what? Did I get ahold of a tape of you fucking our fertility doctor? The security footage of the clinic just magically appeared. What does it even matter?" I ask, my voice an eerie calm.

"Security cameras in an exam room?" she whispers, her lip trembling.

"I think the last thing you should be worried about is the how. You should be much more worried about the repercussions of your actions. We are no longer *even,* you bitch. We're over, and there's nothing you can do or say or hold over me anymore." I smile wickedly.

"Xan—"

"*Nothing!*" I roar, and her hesitant step toward me halts as fear fills her eyes. My mind drifts back to the time that same look was shared in this very same room, only it was me who felt such dread.

"What are you doing here?" I bark, seeing Jacqueline sitting on the couch. We've been separated for months without a fucking word. Blissful silence. Yet here she sits, legs crossed, her stiletto dangling from her toes and her arms crossed beneath her breasts.

"I know about her," she says simply, and my eyebrow quirks.

"Know about who, exactly?" I prompt, my gut sinking, but I manage to keep my voice calm.

"I know about your little whore, Xander! Don't act fucking coy!" she screeches.

My stance widens, and I square my shoulders. "You know nothing."

She gets to her feet, toeing her heels off as her hands ball into fists. "I may not know who she is, but I know she fucking exists! I found your little trophy collection," she yells, throwing the wooden box of Lizith's panties at me, but my reflexes are good with my instincts on high alert, and I catch it before it hits the ground.

"What the fuck does it even matter to you, Jacqueline? We're separated, remember? You left me for another man," I remind her, and then it dawns on me and I can't help but throw my head back and laugh. When I calm, I look her dead in the eyes. "He broke it off, didn't he? He left your skank ass high and dry. Or did he ride you hard and put you away wet?" I sneer, looking down and then up her body with disgust plain on my face.

Fire flashes in her eyes as she glares at me with pure hatred. "He couldn't get over his stupid dead wife. Didn't want to be in a committed relationship."

"So now you have no one to take care of you, and you came crawling back to me?" I scoff.

"To start. But then I found that." She gestures at the box in my hands. "And I had just enough time before you got home to do a little digging. A student, Xander? Really? Could you be any more cliché?"

"How—"

"The fucking love note she left you on the fridge, Professor Stine," she says nasally. "Unfortunately, it's signed with some stupid nickname. Whoever the fuck your 'little bird' is better be glad I don't know who she is, or her college career would be over!" she yells, wildness entering her features.

"We're separated, Jac. Again, what does it fucking matter?"

"About that," she snaps. "This separation is officially over. You're ending everything with your little whore, or I'm going to take all of this to my father." She holds up the letter Lizith had left me a few weeks ago. "And what do you think Daddy, the dean of the university you teach at, will have to say about you fucking a student? Your life will be over. You will never be able to find work as a professor ever again. You will be blacklisted, shamed, and humiliated."

Just then, Lizith's perfect face flashes through my mind. She's worth it. Having her would be worth giving up everything—my tenure, my respect, my wealth. Everything.

But what about her? She's so young, so vibrant, only on the cusp of starting her adult life. She has so much ahead of her, and if this comes out, if all this is made public, it will ruin everything for her.

Suddenly, Jacqueline's mood swings like a boomerang, and if I wasn't so numb, it would've given me whiplash. Her voice is sugary sweet. "Xander, baby. Let's just put the last few months behind us. We're even now. We both got it out of our systems. Let's be happy together, clean slate. We'll start over. And…" She shifts her weight from one barefoot to the other but doesn't continue.

"And?" I prompt, even as my heart is breaking.

"And… I'll give you that baby you always begged me for."

Chapter Eight

LIZITH

TEARS LEAK FROM THE CORNER OF MY LEFT EYE, OVER THE TOP OF MY NOSE, THEN mingle with the ones forming in my right as the side of my face presses into my comforter. My entire body aches, having been in this position for at least an hour now. My back hurts with every breath I take, so I try to time them with the movements of my arms. My keeper told me I had to stay up on my knees, my naked bottom up in the air, but he didn't give me specifics on how to position my arms. So I alternate between having them above my head and stretched out behind me.

Every time I believe I can't stay like this any longer, I remember the hurt in Xander's eyes, the pain I caused him with my deception. And my resolve to please him regains strength. If this is what it will take to make him come back, then this is what I must do. I will allow myself no other choice.

To pass the time, I think about what could be going on inside my body at the moment. And to distract myself from the pain, I begin to recite the stages of human embryogenesis. "Day one, fertilization. Day two, cleavage. Day three, compaction. Day four, differentiation. Day five, cavitation. Day six, zona hatching. Day seven, implantation. Day nine, cell mass differentiation. Day twelve, bilaminar disc formation. Also day twelve, mesoderm formation. Day eighteen, mesoderm spreading. Day twenty-three, embryonic sack enlargemen—"

"And what stage of development could you be, my broken little bird?"

His deep voice inside my bedroom makes me jolt, but I keep my position, my heart pounding with both excitement and overwhelming love. He came! My keeper truly came!

I take a deep breath and close my eyes, counting the days since I inseminated myself. "Implantation, Master," I respond clearly.

"And what does that entail?" he prompts, making my soul soar. How many times had we done this in the past, him quizzing me, rewarding me for correct answers, punishing me when I would be wrong? Sometimes I'd give the incorrect answers, even when I knew the chapter by heart, just to feel his heavy hand against the raw flesh of my backside.

I smile through my flowing tears, the pain in my body all but forgotten. "After ovulation, the endometrial lining transforms, preparing to accept an embryo. The lining thickens, the secretory glands elongating, and it increases in vascularity. After its transformation, the lining is then known as the decidua. Then it splits into an inner and outer layer. The fertilized egg, also known as a blastocyst at this stage, implants in the inner layer, and then the placenta forms around it."

"Now, tell your Master. Were you in your fertile window when you filled yourself with my seed?" His voice is much closer, and I squeeze my eyes closed, trying to absorb him with all my other senses. I hadn't heard him enter my apartment; I was focused too much on the agony of my immobile position and my recitation.

"I was a few days earlier than my window," I breathe, "but I took precautions."

"Precautions? What did you do, little bird?" I feel his heat behind me, my skin prickling at his nearness.

"Clomiphene citrate and gonadotropins."

"Ah, you cunning little thing. But without blood tests and ultrasounds, there is no way to tell if your attempt at forcing an egg to release early worked. Yet... if my calculations are correct, that means today"—his hand glides over one of my upturned globes, and I could sob I'm so overwhelmed with happiness—"would be your ovulation day."

"You're astoundingly accurate, as always, my love." I barely get out the words before my world spins on its axis as Xander's steely arms scoop me up before laying me on my back. But I've been in that position for so long that I can't unfold my limbs, the ache almost unbearable, and I can't hold back the whimper that escapes me, along with a few tears.

"There's my broken little bird," he coos, taking his wide, searing palms and placing them around where my thigh meets my hip. He begins to massage the muscles there before working his way down to my knee, and I moan at the glorious feeling of his hands on my flesh. He moves to the other side, showing it the same attention before pulling my legs straight, forcing me to stretch out. As circulation returns, pins and needles shoot down my calves and into my feet, but most of the pain is gone.

I stay perfectly still, not knowing what his next move will be. I have no idea what went on in the past hours, while he was home, after he saw my task of getting the videos into his mailbox before he got to his house was complete. Will I be rewarded or punished? Can he see I've been punished enough? I've learned my lesson. There is nothing in this world that would ever make me hurt my Master ever again.

My eyes never leave his devastatingly handsome face, the new lines at the corners of his eyes and the deep trenches between his brows only adding to his perfection. Finally, he crawls over me, his knees and hands pressing into the mattress at my sides. I lie completely still, taking long, slow breaths to keep from launching myself upward and latching onto him.

His eyes move over my breasts and down to my stomach, his brow furrowing as he takes in the faded bruise. "Clomiphene and gonadotropins. You pierced yourself, took a needle to your beautiful flesh," he murmurs, and I can't tell by his tone if he's angry, or sad.

"For you, my love. I would do it again and again if it meant I could give you what you've always wanted. What *we* have always wanted. I'd do it again, and much more. Whatever it takes," I vow, and my breath catches in my throat as he leans down, pressing his lips to the mark. And then he moves, trailing kisses over to my belly button then down before laying his stubbled cheek to the skin directly over my womb.

"Are you in there, little love?"

I barely make out his whispered words, but as they circle around in my spinning mind, they do something to my heart. He's never spoken so softly, never shown such a crack in his armor. Those words weren't meant for me. They were meant to be between a man and the child he's always dreamed of.

After a moment, he rises above me, his mesmerizing eyes staring down into mine. "That's not the way I wanted my baby to have its beginning inside you. But I understand why you did it, bird. And if you hadn't gone through all of this, biding your time until the opportune moment... only the universe knows what would've happened. I would've wasted my life with a woman I despise while she continued to lie to me, never giving me the one thing I want out of this existence." He bends his elbows to whisper in my ear, "But you, little bird, *you* took matters into your own hands, knew what would make me happiest, even though you took that control away from me. And I forgive you."

All the air leaves my lungs with his final words, and I let out a sob. "Thank you, Xander" is all I can say.

"I need to take you, little bird. I need to fill you with my cum, just in case it didn't work," he tells me, his tone desperate.

"Yes. Yes, Master. Please," I beg, and finally reach for him.

"You are such a good girl. What if I would have been upset and not forgiven you? What would you have done?" He leaves open-mouthed kisses all over my stomach, misleading me with his question.

I gulp. "I would have understood and taken any kind of punishment you wanted to give me. I would take a year's worth of lashings, if it meant you would forgive me." In that instant, he bites the bruise on my stomach. I jolt upward, and little pain-filled yet aroused tears drop from my eyes. I'm filled with so much remorse, sorrow, and bittersweet feelings from our homecoming that I can't control my emotions. I am an absolute wreck.

"I'm in love with you, and we both know I couldn't hurt you for that long."

I peer down at him and whimper. "You did when you left. I've been in constant pain and desolation since you walked away." He stops his torture when my words hit him, and he slowly takes in what I said, giving me time to continue. "And if I wouldn't have conceived this plan, I would have spent the rest of my seconds, minutes, hours, years on this earth in pain."

"Stop it now. Do not dwell on the past. I did what I had to do." I see something pass in his eyes. A quick look of regret? Yet it seems far deeper than that. It's the look of guilt layered with remorse. I almost call him on it, but I decide against it. I assume it's the realization that I am right. He destroyed me. Brought me back to life. And then destroyed me again.

"I had to do things that way, because it was my only option, but fate and the universe had other plans. All the evils in this world sparked a dark desire in you, and you gave in and latched onto it, and it brought you back to me. Now lie back and let me make it up to you. Let me kiss away those years of pain." He silences me before I can speak, his lips descending on mine, licking, biting, controlling, and taking what's his.

Usually, I would fight to take it all from him after years of deprivation, but I'm dying to be spoiled with his affection, stroked deep with his apologies. He's being too damn good to me, his touches so intimate. I've dreamed of this homecoming for so long. Touched myself so many nights to the image of him.

He trails his hand down to my thighs, and in a quick move, he pushes my knees toward the mattress, spreading me open for him. Our lips part and he stands at his full height again, and like déjà vu, I watch him undress like I watched him do so many times all those years ago. It takes me a moment to notice my own breathing has begun coming out as sad sobs.

He removes his shirt and pauses. Reaching out, the tip of his finger touches the pout of my bottom lip, and I pucker to leave a kiss, my face becoming stained with tears. "You have no reason to cry, little bird. I am here now, and I will never leave your side again."

"I love you. Xander, I love you. Please, take it." I shiver under his harsh, lusty gaze.

"I love you too, pretty baby. Remember that as I take you tonight, because there will be moments when you might think I hate you, and you won't remember anything but my fucking name."

I gulp once again, and he removes the rest of his clothes, his cock already standing full-mast. Licking my lips, I feel my clit throb and I swear to the high heavens or the pits of hell that if I don't feel him inside me soon I will completely fall apart.

His cock gains my full attention, and a thousand and one memories of times I was beneath him and taking each thrust, each delicate touch, and each ravishing fuck come rushing in like a hurricane's wave. I whimper looking at his hard shaft, knowing that, finally, it's all mine and we will never part again. Ever. Because if the sperm didn't take before, it will now. He will own me, and he will be trapped.

I will have imprisoned my love in cage like he has ensnared me all these years, and I yearn for that knowledge.

I feel like my body is submerged in ice water, and when I rise from it, I am thrust straight into desert heat. My body is alive with two opposing forces, desire and fear. I have wanted him so long I fear I may shatter into nothing upon his claiming, yet I desire him so much that I hope he never stops.

"I'm fucking hungry. I want to eat you alive. Make your body shiver and your skin prickle with desire," he whispers, coming down onto his knees between my spread legs. He makes first contact, his thumb kneading the inside of my knees, his cock heavy and throbbing between us. The head angry, just like he feels inside. Xander isn't mad at what I've done. He's mad because he wants me too much and he can't stop the resentment stirring in his brain after years of leaving us both empty inside until our reunion.

"You look so different, little bird. God, you're more of a woman now. Still fragile, but a woman. Look at these delicious legs." Xander leans down and nips at my thigh, and I shudder, my back arching from the bed and hands gripping the sheets under me.

"Oh, Master! Please tell me I haven't changed too much," I sob, as he tilts his head to the other thigh to nip at it.

"Never. I still smell and see the young woman I fell in love with all those years ago. Your pussy is potent and begging to be tasted. What do you think, little one? Should…" He pauses, moving his lips up my thigh with an open-mouth kiss. "I…" Another kiss, only higher this time. "Fucking…" He is two breaths away from my wet center, which is desperately trying to get his attention. "Taste it?" And with his eyes looking up over my shaved mound, he unleashes a whip of his tongue against my clit, and I unravel. I come on his tongue, unprepared but so wound up that I couldn't stop myself. That was euphoria.

"Xander!"

"Mm-hm. Still the same sweet, devilish taste. Still as responsive as ever. You fucking siren." He keeps at me, eating me and swallowing down my juices, feasting on me as if I were being served up on a silver platter.

"Don't you ever try to leave me, Lizith. You let me go so easily before. But know that if you ever try to leave me," he whispers against my skin, leaving my core and moving up my body, caging me in. When we are face-to-face, our lips but inches apart, his strong, dominant hand finds my neck and he squeezes with enough force to momentarily steal my breath. "I won't be so quick to let you leave. I would hunt you down and lock you away. Now, answer me honestly and I won't be forced to do so, sweet baby." Pausing, I nod, my eyes heavy from lack of oxygen.

"Has another man touched this exquisite little pussy in my absence?" he asks, and I shake my head rapidly, without pause. And when I try to speak, with no luck from lack of oxygen, he releases my neck from his grasp. "Speak now."

Xander is content with my answer, but I want him to be pleased. "Little birds only belong to their masters. My pussy is yours. My creamy, soft skin is yours. My dangerous, psychotic heart is yours." I recite, word for word, what he told me when he made me his the first time, and I watch his eyes glimmer and his lips tug in pride.

Xander speaks, recounting that night so perfectly, repeating what he said after he told me that. "Now what do you tell me, little bird?" He knows what is coming and he is on edge waiting for it, giving me momentary power.

I pause, eyeing his face. When enough time passes, I smirk darkly, sinisterly, fucking crazily. "I am your little bird now, Master. So fuck me like Masters fuck their pretty little psychos." And with a dark look in his eyes and a proud, tempting smile on my face, he thrust into me fully, nearly splitting me in two.

"My kingdom. I'm back in my world," he growls, his eyes turning a darker shade, a slight mist glazing them.

"I kept it just how you wanted it. But better. God, Master, you make me feel alive. I haven't breathed since you left," I moan as he keeps his weight stable on his extended muscular arms. That's when I see it; how I missed it before, I don't know. Just to the left of me, on the underside of his bicep, he has a black bird tattooed there. Shadows and gray hues surround it to make it masculine and forbidding. Edgar Allen Poe would appreciate the darkness of the intricate ink.

"X… Xander," I say through a sob, my lips reaching to kiss the skin where it lays.

"That's right. You think you were the only one living in pain without our love? You think you are the only crazy one here? Wrong. You marked me deep too, baby." He breaks from his role as Master and slips into my soft lover.

His crystal blues and faint lines around those beautiful orbs pierce me, and my eyes water. "I love you. I love you so much." I kiss the skin each time he slides from me, and when he slams back in, I scream out my sorrow and bittersweet happiness. He's home. My keeper is home again.

I find relief and feel justified when I see the tattoo. Xander never forgot me. He never let me go.

He keeps at me, taking and giving, stealing and returning. The thrusts are deep and pronounced and done with purpose.

"I love you, baby," Xander whispers, kissing my neck. He has one hand on the underside of my knee just up beside his rib; his other is above me, lost in a grip of my hair. My hands scratch at his broad shoulders, and my lips are locked on his tattoo. "Come now. Relax and come knowing you are with me again and forever."

I clench and scream out, his name a plea on my lips, and with a bite on my shoulder, he causes me to erupt.

"Fuck. I missed you," he growls once again, and follows me over the edge. My insides fill with him, and it is the perfect completion on the day of our reunion.

"I love you."

"I love *you*."

"I'm home," he whispers.

"Forever."

Chapter Nine

XANDER

TWO PERFECT, BLISSFUL WEEKS HAVE PASSED SINCE THE NIGHT I CLAIMED LIZITH as mine once more. We've alternated between her apartment, and the one I kept for the past seven years, from the first time Jacqueline and I separated. I could never get rid of it; too many memories of the beautiful girl who brought me to life haunted the walls like ghosts clinging to this realm. Every time I entered the place, I could still feel her presence.

Jacqueline never went there. I never bothered to tell her where it was, and she never cared enough to find out on her own. She'd disappear for numerous days at a time, staying with her family—or so I believed. And that's when I'd spend time in my secret domain, a shrine to the only woman I ever loved.

It was surreal having Lizith there again. On one hand, it was like she came home after too long away, but on the other, I didn't like that the place had bad memories attached to it as well. It was in that apartment when I'd told her we couldn't see each other anymore. It was there I broke not only my little bird's heart, but mine as well.

"I'll die without you, my love. Please! You can't do this! You promised. You promised you'd leave her, that I was the one you desired. Please! Master!"

Her heart-wrenching sobs still echo through these walls, along with my cold responses as she wailed at my feet.

"This can't go on, little thing. It was never meant to be. I have to go back to my wife."

I had to hurt her. It was the only way to keep Jacqueline from figuring out who Lizith was and ruining her life. I didn't care about my own. I could've found something else to do with my life besides teaching. But Lizith… she was still so young, so new at adulthood. She didn't have anything else to fall back on if my cunt of an ex marred her name. And Jacqueline could be a vengeful bitch. It didn't matter that she was the one who left me for another man. I could never let her find out who Lizith is. Because she'd then have the power to completely destroy me. A reason Lizith would never forgive me for.

I shake out of my darkening thoughts, refocusing on how good life has been for the last two weeks. Because my apartment held those bad memories, and since Lizith's is so small, I decided it was time for us to start anew. In the hours after teaching class and before my bird gets off from work, I've been scouring the city for the perfect fresh start. Somewhere Lizith and I can fill with only good memories, never to be scarred by our past. And I've finally found the perfect place.

I meet her at her apartment when she gets off, pulling in right behind her as she parks. Her face morphs with happiness when she sees me, and that look never gets old.

"Evening, handsome," she purrs her usual casual greeting I've grown to love. It was strange at first, my now mature woman having an adult mind of her own. Before, she'd been my toy that I molded to be exactly what I wanted. She lived and breathed for my attention and affection, completely selfless, almost as if she was a robot I'd programmed myself. But now, after living by herself for all these years, she has opinions, desires of her own. She's still my little bird, perfectly submissive to what I want, but when we aren't in the bedroom and she isn't under my thumb, I've learned I love to hear whatever is on her mind.

When I had her all those years ago, if we weren't in the bedroom—or any other room I decided to fuck her in—the only time I saw her was in my class. She was a very busy student, and I kept myself occupied with consulting jobs between lectures. There was no time for affectionate banter and shared meals. The closest we'd ever gotten to that was that one time when she was sick. Any other time, she was either naked beneath me, or sitting in the front row of my classroom. Now, we have a real relationship, one between a man and a woman who love each other equally. And I want to show her how much I love the new us.

"I have a surprise for you, my sweet," I tell her, my voice soft as she comes to stand before me, wrapping her thin arms around my neck to pull me down for a kiss.

She smiles in response, not asking for any hints, because she already knows I won't give her any. She's my well-behaved little thing, who occasionally disobeys on purpose in order to receive welcomed pain with her pleasure. But for the most part, she sticks to the rules to make me happy, my love growing even stronger with the control she lets me have over her.

I open the passenger side door of my Tesla, and she slips inside. "Buckle up," I order, before shutting the door and circling to the driver side.

She sits quietly with her hands in her lap as I pull out of the parking lot and onto the main road, never once asking where we are going. She's content just to be with me, anywhere I decide to take her. We've kept a low-key existence in these two weeks, not going out but a couple times to dinner, making sure to keep to places Jacqueline would never go. I can't risk running into her, can't allow her to find out who my little bird is.

Pulling up to the gated community, the wrought iron fence separates as soon as the scanner detects the tiny barcode in the top corner of my windshield. A few more minutes of driving leads us to the back, the newest addition to the neighborhood, and finally, I pull up in front of the brand new, just finished two-story brick house.

Still, she sits quietly, waiting for a cue from me. She won't ask why we're here, in this strange place we've never visited before. And I believe it's just as much because she loves surprises, as she wants to please me.

I turn off the car and get out, walking around the front to open her door. She places her tiny hand in the center of mine as she stands, her eyes twinkling at me before she faces the beautiful house.

Suddenly, an overwhelming sense of joy fills me, a giddiness I can't remember ever feeling before. I suppose this is what it feels like for children on Christmas morning, who have parents who actually make a big deal of the holiday and get them presents, yet it's strange, because I'm the one who's giving the gift. I've never been so excited to give anyone something before, and in this moment, my heart races with eagerness. I can't hold it in any longer. I pull her close as she takes in the house, and I lean down to whisper in her ear, "Welcome home, Lizith."

Her face snaps toward me, her eyes wide, her lips parted. "Home?"

I grin, my face just now getting used to the unfamiliar expression. I hadn't smiled much in the last seven years, but in these past two weeks, it's been hard for me to stop. "Come inside."

I take her up the front porch steps and unlock the door, opening it to reveal the exquisite foyer and beyond, where a wide staircase leads to the second floor. It's completely empty, but the walls are freshly painted with the neutral color scheme I picked out, giving Lizith a blank canvas to decorate any way she likes. We're so like-minded I know I'll love whatever she decides on. Her office at work could've been my own.

She takes a tentative step inside, her eyes unable to land on one single thing as she tries to take it all in at once. But the look of wonder on her exquisite face lets me know she likes what she sees. She lets go of my hand to walk up to the staircase, placing her palm on the dark stained banister, gliding it up the smooth, shiny wood. Tilting her head back to look up, she turns in a slow circle, trying to see what's behind the second floor railing, but she decides to save that for later as she spins toward the right. She shoots me an excited grin before hurrying in that direction.

Her movements are no longer slow and uncertain. They're now animated and eager as she skips through the gourmet kitchen with its giant island in the center. She opens and shuts all the cabinets and drawers, laughing gleefully when she turns on the sink and the faucet immediately runs with filtered water. My heart thuds with love as I continue to watch her, taking in her beauty and her delight as she flits through the kitchen, and when she's finished in here, I follow her, chuckling, as she dances back into the foyer and then through to the living room.

She stops in the middle of the room and gasps, turning her amazed expression toward me before hurrying over to the wall lined with floor-to-ceiling built in bookcases. She runs her hand along one of the empty shelves and beams over at me. "Oh, Xander. How beautiful these will be filled with all our books!" She circles the room then, opening the walk-in closet near the staircase to peek inside then making her way to the other side, where the giant bay windows take up the entire far wall. "We could put cushioned window seats here," she murmurs, more to herself than to me, and I love that she's already making plans to turn this house into our home.

She walks through the arched entrance and into the formal dining room, the space wide enough to fill with a huge table with as many seats as she wants. This is what I had in my head when I first toured the model of this house, because that's how they set it up, so it surprises me when she says, "This would make a wonderful office for you, my love. We can fill it with dark wood and leather furniture, with a big desk right in the center." She spreads her arms, indicating where she'd put it.

"You wouldn't want this to be our dining room?" I ask, looking around with new eyes, picturing the space as my own study.

She giggles. "What in the world would we need a fancy big dining room for? Neither of us has any friends, unless you count your work colleagues. I certainly wouldn't invite anyone from my work over. I'd end up stabbing our receptionist if she looked at you the way she did when you came in for your appointments."

I lift a brow at that. "Yeah, not quite ready for your coworkers to know about us being together, seeing how I was just there last month leaving a sample…." I halt that thought, not wanting to speak of anything negative in our new house. Only good memories inside these walls.

Her face goes soft as she glides over to me, wrapping her arms around my waist and looking up at me. "I have no problem keeping you all to myself, Xander."

My heart skips a beat at the overwhelming sense of love I feel rolling off of her in droves. "Good, because I am as much yours as you are mine now, little bird," I rumble, watching her eyes fill with tears as she smiles. She shakes her head and lets out a gentle laugh, before stepping back once more.

She leaves the room and moves into the next, one that is set up to be the laundry room. On one side are the hook-ups for the washer and dryer, and on the other are shelves, rails for hanging things, and a wide tabletop with a sink on one end. "Oh my God, Xander. This is wonderful! This will be much better than what I have now!" she exclaims, spinning and putting her palms to the table, before lifting herself to sit on top of it. She swings her legs back and forth like a giddy child.

I saunter over to her, parting her knees and maneuvering my body to stand between them. "I taught my little bird how to keep her cage nice and clean, and after all these years of abiding by my rules on order, even without me there to praise you for your efforts, you deserve only the best of the best."

She crosses her ankles behind me, using the muscles of her legs to pull me tightly against her. "You're too good to me, my keeper," she breathes, leaning in to press her lips to mine.

"My actions are justified, believe me. Now, would you like to look upstairs?" I nuzzle her nose with mine.

"Yes!" she squeals, and I step back, helping her down.

She takes off out of the utility room and runs around the house to the bottom of the steps, and I chuckle, chasing her as my little bird takes flight up the steps. I keep myself alert in case she slips in her hurry to reach the top, ready to catch her if she were to stumble, forcing myself to keep my hands off her perfect ass as it bounces in front of my face But we make it to the second floor without a single hitch, and when she stops in the center of the landing, I nearly run into her.

From where we've halted, you can see into all four bedrooms as they make a circle, the staircase coming up through the center. But instead of looking inside the empty rooms, she makes her way to one of two hallways between two of the doors. I smile when she gets to the end and sees that it opens up into a room I pictured as an entertainment area, a place to sprawl on overstuffed couches and watch television.

"This wall would be perfect to project movies on!" she exclaims, and my smile turns into a grin when her mind goes in the same direction mine did.

"Yes it would," I murmur, my eyes following her as she peeks into the half-bath off to one side, and then I trail behind her as she makes her way to the second hallway. This one leads to a door at the end, a bedroom set off from the other four on this floor. It was a selling point of this house. I saw a glimpse into the future, of being able to take Lizith as loud and wild as I want, even as our children slept, none the wiser, just right down the hall. I had seen many models where the master bedroom was on a separate floor than the rest, but I didn't like the idea of sleeping that far away from my kids, unable to hear them if they called out in the middle of the night.

She places her hand on the doorknob but hesitates, her eyes downcast as I stand beside her, waiting for her to enter. After a moment, I hear her shuddered breath, and my heart plummets to my stomach.

"What is it, little one?" I whisper, placing my finger under her chin and tilting her face up so I can look into her shimmering eyes.

"There's... there's only one room this could be... and... and I'm"—she lets out a sob, even as her lips form a smile—"just s-so happy, my love. I've dreamed for so long... to be yours, really yours, where we'd live together, sharing a bedroom. And I just can't believe that dream is finally coming true."

Without another thought, I lunge, and the force I kiss her with sends her stumbling until I have her pressed against the wall. My hands dive into her hair at the back of her head, and I use my grip to turn her head how I want it, plundering her mouth with my tongue. By the time I release her, we're both panting for breath, unable to speak at the intensity of our love for one another.

Instead, I step away and allow her back to the door, and this time when her hand meets the knob, she spins it and pushes inward. It opens to a massive room with vaulted ceilings. Over in the far right corner is a wide platform, two steps up, where our king size bed will go. My little bird deserves to sleep on a pedestal.

I step to the side and lean my back against the wall to watch her take everything in. I can practically see her imagination running wild with the way she'd like to decorate it, where all the furniture will go. When she reaches the two doors on the left wall, I hear her sharp intake of air when she opens one and sees the gargantuan closet, with its rows upon rows of railings, shelves, and glass drawers. There is an island in the middle, with small drawers surrounding it for jewelry and lingerie. And one entire wall is sectioned off into cubbies, each with their own individual light, to showcase shoes and handbags. Things I plan on spoiling her with for years and years to come. My little bird has lived modestly for nearly a decade. It's time she lives in the lap of luxury like she deserves.

"Everything I own will only fill up one of these rails." She giggles, and then she moves on to the wall of cubbies, sticking her hand in and wiggling her fingers under the light. "And I certainly don't own any shoes that would merit being displayed in a spotlight," she adds, turning her gaze at me. "We'll put all your fancy Italian loafers in here." She nods to herself.

"Oh, little thing. If you think for one second that this house is the last thing I'll ever spoil you with, you are so very wrong." I smirk.

She doesn't respond. She just smiles at me coyly as she passes back through the door and opens the next one. This time, she lets out a squeal that makes me chuckle. I knew she'd love the en suite. There's a giant Jacuzzi tub, a glass enclosed shower that takes up the entire back third of the room, and a double sink vanity, with heated floors and towel racks, and the toilet is behind its own frosted glass door.

As she opens the little private room containing the toilet, she glances back at me shyly. "Give me a minute, my love. Nature calls. I have a pack of tissues in my purse."

I nod and step backward into the bedroom, closing the door. After several minutes, right when I'm about to go back in to check on her, the door finally opens, and Lizith stands in the frame with something in her hand, her eyes brimming with tears. Her lower lip trembles, and I take a step forward to embrace her. "What is it, little bird?"

She holds out her hand, her fingers trembling, and when she places the small object in my palm, she lets out a sound that's a cross between a sob and laugh. I pull my eyes away from her emotional state and look down at what she's given me.

A pregnancy test.

With two pink lines.

My widened eyes shoot up to her now overflowing ones, and the beauty of her face is so striking it knocks me back a step, and without realizing what's happened until I feel her soft stomach against my cheek, I fall to my knees at her feet and wrap my arms around her hips.

Chapter Ten

LIZITH

THE PAST WEEK HAS BEEN AN ABSOLUTE DREAM. I TOOK TIME OFF WORK AT Xander's suggestion, so I could go shopping for everything to fill our new home. He handed me his black credit card and told me to spare no expense, get anything my heart desires.

We both decided we wanted all brand new furniture. We wanted our home to be a fresh start, somewhere with none of our past attached to it. And as anxious as I was to fill the house with a beautiful bedroom suite and overstuffed couches and all matching kitchen appliances, there was one room I couldn't possibly wait to complete.

The nursery.

It was finished before the painted details even dried in any other room. I'd had a vision of my dream nursery since the moment Xander professed his desire to have children someday, back when I was still his student. And as I look inside our baby's bedroom from where I lean against the doorjamb, I beam with pride at how perfectly my vision came to fruition.

The dark cherry circular crib is the focal point of the room, with a white canopy hanging above it, framing it like a throne awaiting its ruler. Would it be a little prince or princess to fill the spot? I have no preference; the only thing that matters to me is that our baby is healthy. I have more hopes of them looking like their father than I care whether it's a boy or girl.

The nursery also contains a changing table, a rocking chair, and a wardrobe, all in the same dark cherry wood as the crib. I kept everything else gender-neutral, with cream bedding. There are decorations here and there, using a houndstooth pattern and little Scottie dogs wearing red collars. I've always loved the look of houndstooth, but never felt I was classy enough to pull it off. After all, I spend my days in scrubs. But this child will be treated like royalty, a future king or queen, so I finally felt I could fill a space with my favorite pattern.

I also enjoyed working on our living room downstairs. Xander had wasted no time hiring movers to pack up all of our belongings that wasn't furniture and having it all delivered here. It was so relaxing, almost meditative, opening each box of our books and filling the built-ins with the titles. We had duplicates of several, and it made me smile knowing we could've been reading identical books at the same time throughout the years of our separation.

I didn't want a TV in the living room. We so very rarely watched it anyways, so I decided to have the only one in the house upstairs in the space I'd made into the entertainment room. Instead, I filled the rest of the living room with two giant, cream-colored L-shape couches put together to make a U, with a huge ottoman in the center. I covered it in tons of colorful throw pillows.

On the one wall without windows or shelves, I painted my favorite quote, Emily Brontë's *"Whatever our souls are made of, his and mine are the same."* And on the one-foot tall space between the top of the bookcases and ceiling, I scrawled, George R. R. Martin's *"A mind needs books as a sword needs a whetstone, if it is to keep its edge."* Xander had practically tackled me to the fluffy couch when I'd uncovered his eyes with my hands and he took in the elegant calligraphy, kissing me over and over and telling me how absolutely perfect it was.

Finally, something I absolutely adored because it was all Xander, just outside the living room, by the staircase leading to the second floor, was a metal suit of armor. It stood there, tall and proud, looking like a guard ready to defend our castle. Unfortunately, with it being an antique, it had been slightly damaged in the move from Xander's old place to here. Nothing major, it could be easily fixed. The little screw that held the knight's staff in place was now loose inside its hole. A couple times now, the staff has fallen. I have been meaning to get a new screw, one that isn't stripped, to replace the old one, but with all the other things to worry about, it hasn't been high on my priority list. Already, I'm having to jot things down in order to remember them. Pregnancy brain is already in full effect.

One thing I don't have to write down is my lunch date with my dad. I haven't seen him in quite some time, both of us always working. He's an English professor on Xander's campus. Soon after I took the pregnancy test, I expressed to Xander that we needed to tell my dad the happy news. His face had lost all its color, and I'd giggled and told him it would be fine. We were all adults now, so my dad certainly wouldn't hurt Xander for impregnating his daughter, even if it is out of wedlock.

Hurrying out the door and locking it behind me, I hop in my car and make my way to where I'm meeting my dad. I wait in the downtown café, staring dreamily out the window I'm seated beside. It's a rainy day, but that's the best kind. Darkness consumed me since the day I met Xander at eighteen, and it is where I always find myself wanting to be.

When I asked my father to meet me here, he'd been surprised, asking me what was wrong. I'd laughed his worry away, telling him I had some good news I wanted to tell him in person. But now, as I touch my still flat stomach, knowing our baby is growing inside, I find myself slipping into a bit of nervous jitters. No one in my life ever knew about Xander. I never made friends after I fell in love, because I was consumed with Xander. I didn't need nor did I desire to make any. They wouldn't have understood. No one will, and I suppose my father won't either.

It's not just Xander's mature age; it's also the fact that he and Dad were colleagues before he retired. My knee twitches under the table. I wore jeans and boots today; my cream, loose-fitting sweater hangs off my right shoulder, and the thin strap of my tank shows. My hair is slicked back into a tight ponytail cascading down my back in loose curls. I take a small sip of my hot tea when I see my father appear at the entrance. He looks around a little and I wave when his eyes find me.

His hair is all gray now, even his mustache he recently started sporting in his retirement. As he gets closer, his warm brown eyes lift with his gentle smile. My dad and mom were the only friends I truly had. When my mother died of ovarian cancer, he and I relied heavily on one another, because we both lost our prized best friend.

"Baby girl. How are you?" We exchange kisses on the cheek and I take a seat, watching him adjust into his before I respond.

"I'm good, Daddy. Just busy with work. How are you? How's retirement?" I smirk, sliding him his black coffee I ordered.

Smiling, he nods, taking two sugar packets from the bowl on the table and ripping them open. "Still new. I am adjusting to it, though."

"That's good. It feels like the year went by fast," I respond, lifting the tea to my lips and taking a sip.

"I always thought it was just a stereotype, but its not. I do, in fact, golf a lot." He chuckles, and the sound is warm. I truly love my father. I laugh along with him, but it dies down as I remember what I'm here for. I don't want to upset him.

"What is it, baby girl?" He notices my worry, and that may be the one thing my father, Dennis, has always been the best at.

"Dad, I—"

"Dad? That's a little formal for us. What's going on, little one?" He reaches across the table and places his slightly wrinkled yet strong hand over mine. I wait a moment and watch the scene in front of me. I say a silent prayer to my mother above and ask that she guides me through this. "Daddy, I have wanted to tell you about this for years, but it didn't seem right. I don't want to hurt you, and I want your acceptance." I close my eyes and see Xander in my head, his defined face giving me courage. It's as if he is here in front of me. His face is stoic, but there is a slight smirk playing at his lips, and his blue eyes are piercing. Everything behind him is gone and it's just white. I drown in that for a moment, submerse myself in him, before opening my eyes again. Met with my father's worried face, I know I need to confess everything and stop the waiting.

"Daddy, I'm pregnant. I'm in love."

His hand flexes on mine and his face is a mix of happiness and hurt. "Wow. Well, I am happy for you, sweetie, but a little confused that you didn't tell me that you're seeing anyone. Aren't we closer than that?"

It's my turn to comfort him. That was by far more painful to hear than what I thought his disapproval would have been. "Oh, Daddy, yes, of course we are. We are close; it's just… you knew him, and the way we started and *when* we started is something I knew you wouldn't be okay with." He swallows and tilts his head, urging me to continue with his gaze. "I was eighteen when we met, and I fell in love. But we ended after a few short months. I won't go into detail, but we recently reconnected, and it happened so fast. I really didn't know when to tell you without upsetting you." I leave out the details about why we ended and how we reunited. There is a side of me that I will never let anyone see—anyone but my Xander.

"Who is he then, sweetie?" he pushes.

"Please don't be upset with me," I whisper, dropping my head.

"Tell me, Lizith Morrison," he demands, suddenly less patient.

"I have been in love with Xander Stine for some years now, Daddy. I'm so sorry, but please don't be upset." And just like that, I watch the color drain from his face. Mortification. He is mortified. "Daddy?"

"Um." He coughs and clears his throat, trying to regain his composure. "Lizith. How? When? I mean, baby, this is not good." My body shudders and my eye twitches. I feel my Master's favorite side of me trying to break free, and I fear she may if my dad says that again. Xander and I are all things that are better than "good." We are all that is right in the world.

"I love him. Nothing you say will change that or stop me. Nothing," I say with a chilling tone, and pulling my hand free from his on the table, I regain my posture and I stand tall, defending what's mine. My love, my Xander.

I watch my father shake his head in disbelief, and I see something in his eyes that I can't place, but it looks like pure fear. "I need to go. We will talk later. I need a minute to think about this." And with that, I let him leave, not ready to explain Xander further. This is the bubble I never wanted anyone inside, and this is one of the main reasons. No one will understand Xander. No one but my mother, because I know in the afterlife, those we love can feel everything we do from love, all the way to pain, and I'm sure my mother can feel inside my heart exactly what I feel for Xander.

I close my eyes and sit up straight. Breathing deep through my nostrils, my eyes open and I focus on centering myself again. I cannot break character in front of people. It wouldn't end well. Do I feel remorse and regret for hiding this from my father? Yes. But at the same time, I'm a woman now. A successful woman who can make a life of her own without having to ask permission or approval from anyone.

I grab my jacket and throw it on before taking my tea and heading out to the Tesla. Xander let me have it to play with today, and I plan to take it for a short joyride. I need a second to collect myself. I don't know what I will tell Xander about my father, but for now, I know I will do whatever is needed to stay loyal and by my keeper's side. My father will forgive me; he has to, and with the time he has requested, I will let him come to terms with our relationship on his own.

Speeding onto the highway, I get lost. I drive farther out of the city and deeper into my mind. I am losing control of my own body. Right then, I see a deserted grassy field on the side of the road on the outskirts of town and decide to stop there. I need a minute to breathe, and no matter how deep my foot digs the pedal and the notch on the dash rises with the speed, I can't control myself.

I don't want to hurt my father, but I also hate that he just left without even asking me more. Even worse, he ran out of there as if he were on fire. I take a few long breaths when the phone rings through the car speakers. I see Xander's name on the dash and my heart rate kicks into overdrive. I debate ignoring it, but the last thing I want to do is upset my master.

"Hello, handsome."

"And where would my little bird be going in the opposite direction of me, and so goddamn fast?" he growls.

"How do you know where I'm going? How do you know I was speeding?" I look around outside the car, seeing the cars sporadically pass by me.

"Do not answer my questions with a question, little one. You trying to leave me? Did your daddy tell you to leave me? I thought I told you I would always know where you are and I would never let you leave me."

I smirk, my wings extending. I love when he gets this way over me. "Is that why you let me drive your nice toy, Master? So you could keep watch over me? I would never leave you, Xander. Only if I had a death wish by my own hands," I whisper, bringing my hand up to my neck, where I feel it dampening from the arousal coming over me. My Xander was tracking me, hunting me, and his deep, smooth voice telling me so has my body lit on fire with renewed desire.

"You are breathing deep, Lizith. I know you aren't touching yourself without me. Don't you remember the rules? Are you fucking begging for a punishment, little bird?" he bites, and I grin. I want that punishment, because he hasn't given me one in weeks.

"Oh, Xander," I moan, my hand trailing into my jeans and past my lacy panties. I find my clit, my hand restrained in the confines of my tight jeans, but the friction is incredible.

"Lizith. You better not touch yourself without me. You are being very bad, little thing. Very fucking bad."

I bite my lip and circle my clit harder. "Oh, fuck. It feels so good," I groan louder.

"Goddammit. Enough." In my mind's eye, I see the veins protruding in his neck.

"You aren't here to stop me, keeper," I entice him, pushing him past angry. I want him enraged and untamed. I want him to punish me tonight, and maybe then I can settle back down, because right now, I can't seem to forget the pain in my father's eyes and what I fear is waiting around the corner. What that is, I don't know.

I hear him slam his fist on something in the background, and I can't tell what it is. But I do know it fuels me on. "I can't stop. Because I know its upsetting you and I want you mad. But you are too far to get to me," I tease him.

"Oh, little bird, you are going to regret this."

I start to add more pressure and listen to him growl under his heavy breath, and all it makes me do is try harder and my moans thunder through the car. Then I hear the line go dead without another word, but I can't stop. I am in the thick of it, on the cusp of coming to the idea of my Xander mad with a belt in his vascular, twitching hand.

"Xander!" I scream, and right as I'm about to explode, there is a loud, demanding rap on my window. I hurry and pull my hand from my jeans and look out the tinted window, and that's when I see hell above me. The dark shadow of my Master.

"Xander?" He looks angry, and suddenly my blood drains from my face. I gulp, my body heat simmering and fear setting in. I roll down the window, and with smooth, calculated, and slow movements, he leans in. "How did you get here?" I look in the rearview mirror and see his personal driver he uses on rare occasions drive away. I swallow, answering my own question.

He doesn't say anything. Instead, he looks completely collected and held together. Eyeing me over, he stops when he reaches my eyes, and his are far darker than I have ever seen. I know that look. I feared it at first.

My jaw goes slack and I open my mouth to speak, but fear grips onto my tongue and renders me speechless.

Xander laughs deep in his chest, a sound so frightening I feel it in my bones and goose-bumps erupt over my skin. When he stands back finally, I watch in slow motion as he removes his expensive Italian black leather belt with a simple sleek silver buckle. When he pulls it from the belt loops, he steps back and makes room.

"Get out. Now." Shaking my head, I stare up at him in fear. I have seen him go black, but never this intensely.

"Out of the car. Now!" That vein in his neck becomes noticeable, and the heat in his veins shades the skin red and I jump into action. Stepping out of the car with my tail between my legs, I do what he says. "Don't play with me, Lizith. You know what to fucking do."

I nod, knowing what to do, but unsure if he will do what he usually does—a little spanking then a lot of hard fucking.

I turn and drop the back of my hands to the curve of my ass, touch my wrists together in a light kiss, and wait. When it's clear of cars and the highway goes quiet for a moment, he binds me with his belt, his thick fingers making quick work of his task.

I breath heavily, my chest rising and falling as my heart beats so rapidly I feel it may leave my body and run away. "Xan—"

"Quiet." Taking my elbow roughly, he walks me around the front of the car, my steps wobbly and uneven as I trip a few times. If it weren't for Xander holding me so tight to his side, I would have fallen on my face, unable to catch myself with my arms trapped behind me.

Opening the door on the passenger side, he puts me in the car and buckles me in, my hands still bound and digging into my back, wedged lightly between me and the white leather of the seat.

I watch as he slams the door, walks around the front of the car, and then sits in the place I occupied moments ago. I keep my head down, knowing I have no right nor room to speak, because I awoke the keeper and he is not happy with my games.

"You got what you wanted, Lizith. I am going to take you home and fucking ruin you. Hope you enjoy your next thirty minutes of sitting comfortably, because in a few short hours, you will be lucky if you can walk. Hell, you will be sleeping on that fucking stomach for a week."

With that, my eyes water at the fear inside me, still scared, but his little bird is flourishing inside and coming alive. I haven't been ruined in our special way since we came back together, and now I'm overwhelmed with knowing what's about to happen.

"Don't cry, little bird. I broke you enough to prepare you for this," Xander murmurs, and I stay silent, watching the minutes on the screen of his car slowly tick by and draw me closer to what I need most.

My keeper to bring me back to my beautiful, unstable psychosis.

Chapter Eleven

XANDER

THE DRIVE IS SILENT, AND MY COCK IS ROCK-HARD FOR HER. SHE TESTED ME today, and hell if that didn't bring me to life after the dull hours in class all day. I tracked her on my Tesla and got to her as quick as my driver could. I was weakened for a moment when I saw her driving so fast and far away from me. Afraid she told her father everything and he spilled the secret that I have yet to tell Lizith. A dark secret that has the power to have her slipping from my fingers.

When I finally got to her, I was wound tight but thankful when I realized she's still not aware of all the secrets I hold. I know I need to tell her, but now is not the time. Not when I just got her back.

Peering over at her, I see she hasn't lifted her head, and I warm, knowing she is under my power now. We are nearing the outskirts of downtown close to where our home is when my phone rings. I see the name Claire pop up and I answer, taking note when Lizith shifts and whimpers when she sees the female's name.

"Claire, what can I help you with?" I ask.

"Sorry, Professor Stine. I know you said we are allowed to call you regarding our assignments, and I was just wondering." She pauses, her voice shaky yet flirtatious, and I smirk. I can practically feel my little bird raging from here. Her eyes are glued to the dash's screen, her mouth in a tight slit and her eyes narrowed. "Sorry, sir, I was a bit nervous to call." She giggles like a schoolgirl, and I look to Lizith, daring her to sass me or say something to my student.

I would be lying if I said I wasn't in some way trying to rile her up. I know how much she needs me, and throwing jealousy in with her need will create one hell of a bad little thing in my hands tonight.

"That's fine, Claire, but I am a bit busy. What can *I help you with?*" I draw out with a low rumble, and Lizith hisses at me, her eyes going mad.

"Well, I have been having trouble with my recent thesis, and I would love to meet with you after class tomorrow, maybe have a little private session," she purrs, and I see Lizith's eyes water and her lips fall into a broken frown.

"I can meet with you in an open-door appointment." I finally let my bird have some relief and shut down my student.

"Oh, okay. That's fine too. I guess I'll see you tomorrow." She sounds let down, but I don't care. I can't take my eyes off my girl, the red light we are stopped at making that possible.

"Goodnight, Claire." I end the call before she can say her goodbyes, and I expect Lizith to set off into a rage, but she doesn't. She stays still with her head low and tears falling down her rose-colored cheeks.

After a few moments of silence, she whispers into the car, "Since when do you give students your number? I thought I was the only one who ever got that special treatment." Her jealousy is coming through, rearing its ugly head, and I welcome it. Our lovemaking is always more ravishing when we are on fire with jealousy. But this time, I may have hurt her, and that knowledge becomes apparent when she whimpers softly.

I love when she fucking whimpers.

"All professors do it now. She isn't special. She doesn't make house calls," I respond as I pull up to our home.

"Don't make what we had then sound like it was nothing. Don't think so carelessly of me. You make me sound cheap." She turns her body from me, drawing as close to the window and door of the car as she can.

I want to respond, but I know better. I leave the car and come around to her side, and with gentle yet sturdy force, I grab her neck and set her into motion. She struggles a bit to get out, but once her feet hit the ground, I move us toward the house. Lizith's back faces our home, and she walks backward as I slowly walk forward, guiding her.

"You are really pissing me off, little bird. You better tell me what has got you acting so crazy and disobedient tonight." She shakes her head, denying me what I want. "Tsk, tsk, little thing. You are pregnant and I can't get too rough, so the only way I'll understand is if you willingly tell me, or I will fuck you so thoroughly—so fucking deep and hard—until you are about to come, and then I will stop. You only got me to that point once before, baby, and I remember how much you hated it. Want another night wound tight and throbbing? Soaking wet and fucking empty with only the imprint of my cock inside you?" I squeeze her neck tighter, and her chin lifts and her jaw goes lax.

"Or do you want my cum deep inside you and your pulse beating rapidly while you clench around me when you come? You pick, baby." With that, I sweep her up and carry her through the door, up the stairs, and into our room. I throw her down on the mattress of our four-poster bed draped in white canopy curtains. She bounces and shakes, her entire body afraid of me.

I stalk her, pacing around the bed, and she watches me in silence.

Lizith tries to move, but my belt keeps her partially disabled from doing so. I undo my nicely pressed suit pants and release my cock. "On your knees, bird. Suck my cock." She stays in her place on the bed and doesn't attempt to slide to the floor. "On the fucking floor!" She jolts and sets into motion. I stroke my cock as I watch her move, her eyes and body giving her away. She is desperate for this side of me. I haven't given her this since we found our way back to each other, and it might have been years, but it all feels like yesterday. So right. So natural. And I know she feels that too.

"Do it exactly how I like it. Do you remember, my pretty mess?" I look at her mascara-stained face and my spine curls, the beast inside me almost breaking from my skin. Lizith nods, and I reward her by petting her hair. "Good girl."

Leaning in slowly, she brings her lips to the head of my cock, and I thrust gently, breaching her mouth and granting myself entrance.

"Fuck!" I grunt, as I grab her ponytail at the base and gain stability to start pumping. I love fucking her mouth. "More spit, get fucking dirty." She peers up at me, and I watch as I slide in and out of her mouth, getting more and more wet as my precum and her saliva mingle. "Just like that." I tilt my head and really watch her take me. I know I am pushing her gag reflex when her eyes water and she makes little noises around my cock, making it vibrate against my shaft and driving me wild.

"You gonna tell me now, little thing?" I ask, and she drops me from her mouth.

"No," she says with surety, and I snap. Leaning down, I grab her by her throat and pull her to her feet. Spinning her around, I undo my belt from around her wrists and smack her hard on her ass with my bare palm. She yelps and cries out. "Xander!"

"I'm your fucking keeper. Undress! Now!" And she does, no hesitation in her movements. I keep stroking my cock, gripping harder when I see her round tits, perky and full. When she removes her shoes and bottoms, I growl as I choke my cock to the sight of her in little black, sinful panties. All lace and leaving nothing to the imagination.

"On your knees on the bed," I bite out, and she does so slowly, taunting me with graceful movements. When she is in the position I want, her ass beckons to me. Lizith lays the side of her face on the bed and flattens her palms next to it. Her ass rises in the air, and I stand just to the side of her. I admire the view for a moment while I steady my emotions and my movements. I have to be in control completely, nowhere else in my mind or heart but in the place of her Dominant.

She waits for me, and in two little moves, my belt is folded in my hand, each end clasped in my hand as it falls into a teardrop shape, and as she whispers my name, I rear my hand back and bring the belt down hard. Lizbeth screams and it echoes in the room. She curls her spine as she tries to get her ass away from me, and I move. With my free hand, I splay my palm in the center of her smooth back and push down, making her ass rise back up.

"Two more, baby. Don't try and move again."

Lizith is crying, but she begs me, "Yes, Master. Please, do it again, my keeper."

I bring it down again, leaving a red welt on her perfect globe. "Tell me why you are being so fucking defiant tonight!" I demand, and I look at her face, which is contorted with both pain and pleasure.

"No!"

I swing it a third time without warning. "Yes, Lizith, or you won't fucking like what I will do to you tonight," I speak low, through gritted teeth. "Now!"

"I just need you to remind me who I belong to! Make me remember how fucking crazy you are over me! You never punish me anymore, Master!" she screams out as I bring down my belt for a fourth smack that she wasn't expecting.

"Oh, my good girl. There it is." Dropping the belt at my feet on the floor, I grab the lace fabric covering her pussy and pull, ripping it clean from her body. And like everything else, I give no warning when I thrust deep into her snug heat. I'm still dressed in my suit pants and pressed button-down shirt and vest as I peer down at the graphic scene in front of me.

Lizith grips the sheet and tries her best to look back at me as I slide in and out of her viciously—violent and delicious. She bares down on me every time, trying to get me to stay in, and I smile like the devil. My greedy little thing.

"Xander! Do you want her? Do you have another little bird?" she cries, peering back at me. I shake my head and move her fast. Pulling out and grabbing her hips, I flip her on her back and lift her hips from the bed, her top half the only thing left on the mattress as I grip her thighs and slam back into her.

"Don't you dare fucking ask me such a foolish question. Look at my cock wet from your juices. You think I have something better? Look at this, baby. Fucking look at it!" I demand, my eyes looking at our connection. When her hazy, hooded eyes follow mine, her jaw drops as she looks at her hungry pussy lips clinging to my cock as I slide in and out harshly. "Does it fucking look like I want anything else? Like I could find anything better, my psycho little bird. Now shut your pretty mouth and let Master take care of you." I let go of one hip, bring my hand back, and slap the part of her ass I can reach from this position, the loud smack echoing and causing her to hit her peak.

Lizith comes hard, going crazy. Her little stomach spasms and tightens, her legs shivering around my hips, and her chest turning a deep shade of red. Her eyes never leave our connection, and that sight alone makes me come hard. So much so that it leaks from her within seconds.

"Fuck," we say in unison, not sure how we will come down from that.

Chapter Twelve

XANDER

ALL MY STUDENTS' HEADS ARE DROPPED LOW AS THEY TAKE THEIR FINAL. THIS IS my last class of this semester, and I am more than thrilled to take some time off work to spend it in my home with Lizith, petting her stomach, still so small but full of life.

I check my black and stainless steel Sea Dweller watch and see I still have ten minutes left before I can call time on the exam and send the students away for winter break. I peer up when I hear someone making a loud entrance, disturbing me and my class.

I stand abruptly when I see a heavily intoxicated and disheveled Jacqueline. I growl and restrain from rolling my eyes at her, a behavior I seem to want to resort to whenever I am in her presence. I can't believe I loved her at one point.

I thought we were done. She has nothing over me anymore.

"Xander!" she announces on a slur. I button my coat and lift my hand to my class, signaling for them to not pay any mind and get back to their test.

"Jacqueline. In the hallway. Now," I demand with a crisp, tight bark.

"Don't tell me what to do, you old sick fuck. Any other girls in this classroom you are fu—"

I cut her off before she can finish that statement. I grasp her by her elbow and thrust her into the hall. One passerby looks at us funny, and I give them a quick nod and smirk, playing it off, as Jacqueline is barely able to contain herself, flailing about and struggling to stand on solid ground. I can smell the cigarettes and whiskey on her breath, and I nearly choke on the pungent scent. She reeks.

"You're a damn mess, Jacqueline. What the fuck are you doing here?" I grit out, pacing back and forth in front of her, my palms twitching to release my anger the best way I know how. But my little bird isn't here to help settle me.

"You. You are fucking Dennis's daughter. You sick man, I didn't know you had it in you."

I stop abruptly. A bone-chilling shiver runs up my spine as my eyes find the tiled floor of the hall. I feel like the wind was knocked from me.

"Excuse me?" How the fuck did she find out about Lizith and her connection to Dennis?

She laughs, and it reminds me of a scarecrow. A tall, gangly thing possessing the power to put fear in me.

"You fucked her all those years ago, because you wanted to get back at Dennis and me," she slurs, standing straight from her leaning position against the wall. Slowly, my eyes draw up and my body pivots.

"You have no idea what you are talking about, Jacqueline." Her name drips like poison from my lips as I grasp at straws.

"I left you for Dennis. And that upset you. So you took the opportunity to seek payback because you still loved me." She takes the tip of her long white-tipped nails and drags them down the V-shape where my jacket parts over my chest. "So when that little play thing, that slut, Lizith, was on your roster, you put two and two together and made her your little slave."

"Don't you fucking call her that, and don't you dare say her name, Jacqueline," I hiss, closing my hand around hers and thrusting it away from me. "You are wrong. You know nothing," I remark, but inside, I'm a mess, because she's fucking right.

When I met Lizith on the first day of class, I had it all planned out in my head. Claim her, break her, and leave her a mess for Dennis to pick up, because he fucked what was mine, and I wanted him to know that I could take from him what I thought he took from me.

But then I broke Lizith. I broke her so bad that I fucking fell in love with her and wanted only her. Joke was on me; my plan had backfired. But I never wanted Lizith to know. I didn't want to hurt her in a way that I couldn't heal her or subdue her into seeing that while it may have been the wrong start, it was the greatest beginning, because we had each other. My fucking soul mate became mine, all because of false and vile beginnings.

"What do you fucking want, Jacqueline?" I'm at her mercy, and usually, I would laugh in her face and tell her to go to hell, but I will do anything to make sure this secret is only told to my little bird by my lips.

"You blackmail, and I will blackmail you. You come back to me, leave behind that tramp."

"Watch your fucking tongue, Jacqueline. You don't understand what I am capable of when it comes to her," I threaten.

"You delete the tapes, come back to me, and I won't tell her why you took such an interest in her."

"She's my life, Jacqueline, and no matter what, she always will be. I'm not coming back to you. You don't love me, and I sure as fuck don't love you."

"You're a man of control and power, Xander. Don't act so foolish. It's not about love; it's about status, and divorce doesn't make anyone look good," she sneers, blinking slowly. I'm sure she doesn't even know if she's awake or asleep. She is that inebriated.

"You see, Xander, when I made you come back to me, you should have left her in the past but you didn't. So when daddy dearest, Dennis, called me the other day to scold me, I knew I had regained control. She's fair game. Collateral damage, if you will." She shrugs carelessly, and I bite the inside of my cheek, my palms gripped in tight fists at my sides. I can feel my jaws burning from the gnawing tension, and I don't know what to do to gain the upper hand.

"Stay the fuck away from my woman or you won't have a chance to look bad in front of anyone. I won't let you do this to me again, you pathetic bottom feeder." I get close to her with gritted teeth, when my door opens beside us and one of my students leaves.

"Sorry, Professor Stine. I left my completed test on your desk."

"Thanks, Jonathan. Have a good winter break." I stand straight and give him a stoic, controlled farewell, and he scurries off. Looking back, I see Jacqueline's eyes beginning to sober up, but what I don't see is fear. I threatened her, and she knows I make good on my threats, but that still does not faze her. Jacqueline is out for blood, and knowing I cause her no fear makes her the deadliest of threats in mine and Lizith's life.

More students start piling out, and I look to the end of the hall, just to the left, and see class is over by the time on the clock. Under my breath, I try to stay as reserved and collected under her thumb as I can, and I let out a solid warning.

"You stay away, Jacqueline, because no matter what you do"—I step closer and my breath whispers across her face—"I will do it ten times worse, and I will fucking haunt you."

I pull back and enter my room again, leaving her cursing behind me. "Don't threaten me, Xander! That little plaything will fucking know what you did to her! So help me, God!" Students look at me with curious shock, and I just wave them off and say goodbye, wishing them luck in their endeavors.

Once Jacqueline makes her hasty retreat and my classroom is empty, I slam the door shut, the frosted glass rattling with it. I come to my desk and take a seat, dropping my head in my hands and thrusting them through my hair.

I try to think of something—anything—to control the situation, and the only solution is to lock away my bird and give her no way to run from me, because if I give her an out, she may take it. This will be sure to break her fragile, kind, and all-mine heart. It will make her hate me, and I know this. No matter how much she belongs to me or how psychotic she can be with her obsession over me, this may be the one thing that stands to abolish everything we built.

I open my MacBook Air and hit Google Search, looking up the current weather in Aspen, Colorado. The forecast shows blizzards with guaranteed snow-ins, and that is my out. I start searching for remote cabins, cabins fucking lost in the hills where we will get the most snow, and I start making calls. I finally find a luxury cabin that guarantees us privacy, and after listening to the owner warn me about how we will be cut off from the real world and stuck in the snow for a few days, I take it.

We leave tonight.

I am still fuming just a mere ten minutes after Jacqueline's departure, when there is a light rap on my classroom door.

"What?" I snap, forgetting where I am for a moment. I stand and wait for whoever is bothering me at this moment of panic. But when the door opens slowly and my little bird stands there so patiently and submissive, with her head down and her long brown hair tucked behind one ear and the rest falling behind her, I feel a small semblance of control for the first time in the last thirty minutes.

"My love, I'm sorry to bother you. I just wanted to surprise you with lunch on your last day." Dressed in a beautiful blush-pink sundress, which is peeking out from behind her stylish long black trench coat, her feet are covered in little ballet flats, and she holds a picnic basket with a meal that smells divine even from this distance, and a thermos.

Lizith doesn't look up, nor does she take a step forward as she waits for my approval, and I thank her beautiful soul, which told her to come to me when I needed her. I feel heartache and guilt inside my chest, and I fight back the prickling behind my eyes at the sight of my beautiful little bird being so true to me, when I have only fucking deceived her.

"Step in, my darling. I didn't mean to yell at you."

She finally peers up, and her pink cheeks and pale, striking green eyes pierce me as she collects her things before stepping into the room and shutting the door. She locks it as I stand waiting for her.

"I saw her. Was she here harassing my keeper? Did she say something to you that has upset you?" Placing the basket on my desk, she comes to stand in the small space between the desk and me. Her scent fills my lungs, lavender and a hint of my cologne. My knees nearly buckle in her presence.

"Are you wearing my cologne?" I question, finally gifting myself with physical contact as I lay my hand on the lowest point of her back and my other at the nape of her neck, where I squeeze and release repeatedly.

"Yes, I wanted to smell you on me all day." She drops her head shyly and blushes.

"You don't deserve me," I whisper.

"I know, but I try really hard to be worthy of you."

My heart cracks as she misunderstands what I mean. "No, my love, you don't deserve a monster like me. You deserve rivers of decadence, surrounded by mountains of gold, framed by a sea full of waves made of diamonds." I lean in, my lips a whisper against hers.

Lizith's eyes haze over, shutting and opening slowly as she perches on her tip-toes to try and get closer. I need her so fucking bad, and I know I don't deserve her. I don't even deserve to breathe the same air she does.

"No, I need rivers of soft whispers, mountains of love kept between us, and waves of infinite touches from you, my keeper. I don't want anything else but you. Not even all the riches in the world. Just you."

And just like that, I anticipate the heartache this weekend away with her will bring. Lizith may just fucking bend, snap, and fucking crumble to ashes under me after she learns about the truth of how we came to be.

"Xander, I know she wasn't right. She looked mad leaving here. Does she know about me?" she asks, reaching her hands under the flaps of my jacket and around to my back, rubbing soft circles on my lower back just above my belt.

"Don't worry, little bird. She's just a deranged woman loose from her padded room," I say, digging the knife of guilt deeper. But I have to hold off. I have to wait to get her locked away, like the beast in his castle. But the selfish, egomaniacal, lovesick fool in me knows no bounds, and I need to ensure that she understands how we started may have been wrong but not who we are; it isn't what matters. Even if how we began is sick, I don't want her to lose sight of where it brought us and how much I truly fucking love her.

I see it then, the rush of fear coming in like a tidal wave in her eyes. Her body goes rigid under me, and I see her left eye twitch a little.

"You can't leave me again. I won't let you leave again, Xander. Whatever she is threatening you with, I don't care. I won't let her take you away again."

She begins to tremble under me, the fire in her eyes raging, and I calm her then. "Little bird, enough. Get on your knees and settle." I let my secret slip away for now, because my girl needs reassurance that I will not break her heart again—by leaving her, at least. I scold myself mentally and release her as she does what she's told, her body still shaking.

When she is on her knees and her thighs rest against her calves, I take a seat in my chair and look into her eyes, mine silently guiding her. She nods knowingly, and she crawls between my legs, laying her head on my thigh. I bring my hand to her head and start petting her hair gently.

"Beautiful bird, my love. So elegant and exquisite. I am not going anywhere, Lizith. Just relax." My hand travels from her hair and meets her thin neck, where I squeeze once before moving to her shoulder to message the soft skin. Her eyes never leave mine as we share soft touches.

"I am taking you away for a long weekend. Four days. To the mountains. Have you ever seen snow, pretty baby?"

She blinks twice, a giddy smile taking over her face, and I grin at her enthusiasm.

"No, I haven't. I have always wanted to." She nuzzles into my thigh, closing her eyes and thanking me with a gentle touch to the back of my calf. "You don't have to take me away though. I can stay here with you and be just as happy. And what's better is I took a few days off of work so I could spend some of your winter break at your feet," Lizith purrs, and my cock twitches.

"I'm taking you away, and I am going to spoil you fucking rotten, my little thing."

"You already do—everyday." With that, she slowly climbs to her feet and into my lap, curling into me as best she can. "How about I take the time to spoil you? Maybe against this desk." She pecks me on the lips once and parts from me before I can prolong it.

"Bird," I warn, knowing exactly what's coming.

"I know you loved fucking me hard against this cherry wood. I remember you liked it in my ass the most when I was here." She bends over, lifting her dress as she goes. Those creamy cheeks beckoning me as if I were a sailor lost at sea, looking for something to guide him home.

"Fuck," is all I can manage to say.

"You would leave me wet and leaking with your seed while I tried hard to pay attention to you teach. My scent still in the air." I think back to the times I fucked her before class when we first got together, and I swear it's so potent I can almost fucking smell it. "Please, professor, teach me how to take it like a good little bird," she coos, and I nearly break the chair when I stand abruptly and push it back against the wall. My hand comes thundering down on her globe, which ripples until I stop it with a firm grip.

"You are so fucking vile today. Are those my lady's hormones speaking?"

She giggles. "No, Master, that's my insatiable desire for you."

"Damn it, you bad girl." I snap her panties to the side and slide my finger from her clit all the way to her puckered hole. As I breach it, she jolts forward and nearly howls my name. "Xander!"

"Shh! I don't need the dean hearing about the fuck session I had during lunch. Now, hold still. I'm just starting. Seeing some grapes in the picnic basket on the desk, I pluck one free. Bringing it between us to her clit, my finger lightly thrusting in her ass, I rub her juices all over the grape, and when I feel its good and wet, I bring it to my mouth and fucking savor her taste.

"So ripe. You taste so damn delicious."

"I want a taste," she begs, her green eyes darkening over her shoulder.

"I don't want you to. That's all mine, and I'm so selfish I don't want to share it with you." I bring another grape from the basket, and she shakes her head.

"No, I want *your* taste."

I understand what she's asking and I'm more than happy to oblige. "Turn over and lie on my desk. Spread your legs." She does it willingly and quickly.

I unbuckle my pants, every move slow and methodical, so she can anticipate my touch. I want her quivering, weak, and a fucking mess before I take her away. That makes me selfish and fucked up, but when it comes to her, I always have been, and I will do anything to keep her, even if it's in the most fucked up way.

"This what you want?" I ask when I release my cock from my pants, and I take the grape to the tip and collect some of my precum.

Lizith whimpers, "Yes, Master."

Smirking deviously, I feed it to her. My insides fucking burn with my need to be with her. She savors the taste, before swallowing and humming her appreciation.

"Good girl. Now lie back, 'cause I am going to fuck you hard, fast, and dirty, so we can eat before my final class." Nodding, she waits, and I take her just like I promised I would. I ruin her for the rest of the day, and by the time our red-eye takes off, she sleeps on my shoulder nearly the entire flight.

I however can't sleep, too worried for what is about to transpire between us in the next few days. And I just hope she will see the past as something that started our beautiful journey to forever.

I look down at her as she smiles softly in her sleep and whisper with my lips on a top her head. "Please, forgive me, little bird. Please understand how much I love you."

She stirs a bit then settles again.

Chapter Thirteen

LIZITH

I HAVE ALWAYS WANTED A SECLUDED WEEKEND AWAY WITH XANDER. HE WANTS TO hide me away and hold me captive at his mercy, and I want nothing more this Christmas than to be his. We haven't really celebrated the discovery of our little bean growing inside me, and I plan to let him ravish and captivate me, and then lay like a pet at his perfect feet all week.

He's been on edge the past few days, and I wonder if it's me or the divorce, or what I truly hope it is—school drawing to an end. I don't want him to be angry with me in any way, and I don't believe he would have any reason to be, since I have behaved better than he could ever want me to. And I sure as hell do not want Jacqueline to arouse any kind of emotion from him, because that is *my* time, energy, and emotions I want him drowning in. I will not share, and I will not let her come take away my keeper again.

I love him so much.

My eyes flutter open, my REM cycle breaking, and that dizzy state I come in and out of leaves me.

"Good morning, pretty little thing," Xander greets me in my post-slumber haze. The handsome perfection before me is a sight that warms me to my very core, and I get that shiver down my spine and goose bumps on my arms that arouse me. The reaction I get now is the same one I got all those years ago. Blue eyes sizzle, creating a slow burn inside me, and I take a deep breath. My eyes flitter like an excited fairy under his calloused hands touching my cheek as if I'm made of glass.

"Don't you mean goodnight?" I gesture with a side-eye to the window next to me in First Class. We took a later flight, because I was feeling the waves of severe morning sickness.

"Ever wise." He pauses, bringing his lips to my forehead resting on his shoulder, and his strong hand grips my upper thigh. "And ever fucking sassy," he growls, and I giggle when he squeezes the pressure point on my knee. A pool of arousal collects in my core, and if we weren't sharing First Class with a bunch of strangers, I would go ahead and start our weekend of ravishing.

"It keeps you young, and we all know you need it." I give it right back, knowing that comment will land me an open palm to my bare bottom.

Xander didn't make a sound, and I peer up and see him looking forward, his tight jaw flexing and his hand on my thigh tightening. "Master?"

I gulp when he slowly peers down at me with a steady movement. Maybe it isn't as humorous now as it was when we used to use it as foreplay.

"*One lash for being so fucking sassy. My age only controls you more. My age only fucks you better than any age after me.*"

"Xander, I was… j… just teasing," I stutter, suddenly afraid.

Burning a hole into me with his eyes, he speaks. "I'm only getting older, and I won't let you trade me in for something younger."

Oh, the rarely seen insecure side of Xander. He pets my wings when I fall short of confident, and on the rare—so very rare—occasions that he lets me return the favor, I thrive on it.

"Xander, don't ever say that. I don't want anything different. *Ever.*" The last word comes out more dark and belligerent than I planned. "Please, never think of me wanting another man. There is no one I'd allow to own me like a perfect little bird other than you," I whisper, nuzzling my face into his neck while my hand cups his chiseled jaw.

"Don't be so sure."

Part of my tough exterior crumbles and I'm thrown into the abyss. "Keeper, please don't say that. I don't want anyone else!" I holler, gaining the stares from others, but I don't care.

"Bird!" Xander barks, gripping my chin between his fingers. He holds me in place with no room to move and I feel tears building—from hormones and the pain in my heart.

"No. I don't want you feeling this way, my love. You are my everything, and when you speak like that, it seems like you are looking for an out. Please tell me you aren't going back to her and this trip is just a final goodbye." A tear slips and I reveal my ugly truths.

"I'm never leaving you. Now hush and kiss what you hurt." Releasing my chin finally, he takes my hand from where I have it placed against his abs and brings it to his heart. I nod and drop my head to his chest then pepper it with sorrowful kisses.

We have an audience, and I'm sure they all think the worst. Either I'm his daughter, or I am a woman he's paid to take away to cheat on his wife with in a lap of luxury. But it doesn't hinder me. I am his, as he is mine.

We spend the rest of the flight touching gently and sometimes eagerly. We speak few words, but powerful ones with passion, fire, and promise.

He has a driver, and our luggage is already collected by the time we step out into the crisp night air, snow hiding inside heavy clouds, just waiting to fall. Those clouds are promising me a weekend of no escape from my love and our dirty, dangerous bubble.

How captivating it has yet to be.

We pull up to the cabin around 9:00 p.m. and the porch light is welcoming, already setting the stage for a romantic, cozy getaway. The two-story, dark wood cabin is haloed by tall trees with the heavy scent of pine. I take a deep breath as he pulls me into his side and the driver unloads the bags.

"Welcome to your cage, pretty bird." He caresses my lower back as my eyes jump all around the cabin, looking at all the windows and details. And it becomes even more breathtaking when we step inside. Right in the entryway, there is a brightly lit crystal chandelier with three tiers. It centers the stairs, which you can take up to the left or the right, and down the center is a path that leads to the kitchen and living area. My breath catches, because I truly feel spoiled. Just like he did with our home, he even takes me on vacations that are beyond my wildest dreams.

"Professor Xander Stine, you have truly outdone yourself, and I can't even begin to think of how to repay you for this gift you have bestowed upon me. Really, you have done so much to bring us back together, and I don't have enough in my possession to give you what you truly deserve." I blink up at him, my cheeks flushed.

"Your life in my fucking hands," he responds quickly, almost brash, as if he is hanging on to something that could easily slip away. It has my skin raising with little bumps from the sudden rushing cold air of uncertainty. What has gotten into my love? I haven't let on that I know he is… off, as I wait in my cage for him to come to me and lay his burdens at my feet. But he still hasn't, and it's becoming decisively harder to keep my mouth and heart separate. I want to help him, no matter the situation. I have him, and he has me; whatever falls outside of that realm will not part our entwined souls.

"You already have that. I gave it to you the day your eyes met mine and your lips touched my skin. And yet I still don't think it's enough." I moan against him when he pulls me in tighter and leans his head to bite the side of my neck. My keeper is lost and seeking refuge, and I am here to give him shelter from whatever is plaguing him. Tonight, he will not touch gently. No, tonight, he will stroke me with fire and douse me in gasoline to feel his burning touch more harshly, because he needs me to forgive him for something I feel like I already know but somehow don't.

We are linked on a whole other level, so much so that I know when something is bound to fall apart. And he may not realize it, but I am already prepared to rebuild wherever falls around us, even without knowing a thing of what haunts him.

"Take me to bed first. We can explore tomorrow," I whisper into the cabin, my breath heavy and needy. I run my hands up and under his jacket and shirt, finding the warm skin and his trail of hair tempting me past the point of return. The deep V at his hips meets my spread fingertips and I whimper, moving them slowly up his abs. Still so tight and warm and exotic, even with age. "Xander, please," I beg, while errant tears of the almost unbearable need for my love, fall. It's as if we could never get close enough, like I may never be able to imprint him into my heart deep enough—to where I won't feel like I'm missing a part of me. I am no longer my own person. I no longer belong to myself. I was born and raised with a heart pumping blood through me that all belongs to him.

I am of his rib, of his soul, of his sum. I love Xander Stine, and I would lose all pride, dignity, or human rights to submit to him completely. I'm sick and twisted, and I truly lose no sleep over knowing how psychotic I can be for him.

"Tomorrow won't come for an eternity when I get you alone. You're going to regret those words, my warped little bird." He grasps my jaw with his fingers and my eyes flare. His blue eyes turn a smoky gray, as if the storm in him is overtaking, and I shiver, fucking shake to my core, when he does this to me. "Crawl," he demands, and for a moment, I stand before him unsure.

"But the bedrooms are upstairs." I stare at the twenty steps of the staircase to the left, the one closest to where we stand, and he doesn't flinch or reassess his demand.

"Yes they are. Crawl. All the way to the bed."

I peer up at him and, after a brief pause, I finally nod in understanding.

"Yes, Master." Just like that, I get on my hands and knees, jutting my ass out as I do. That way, he gets a view of what is his. When my hand hits the first step and I lift up, I peer back at him over my shoulder, my wavy locks covering half my face, and I drop my eyes just the way he likes—submissively. His cock tents his faded jeans that he wears better than men half his age.

"The longer you take to get up those stairs, the longer I will go without fucking you till your pussy screams for me to stop. Now fucking crawl, my lovely tease."

I giggle adolescently, like a kid on Christmas. Xander leans and slaps my ass hard, and I jolt into motion, crawling with ease and stability to make it safe for me and our little one inside me. That's Xander's and my hearts beating as one inside me, and I must protect it at all costs.

Finally getting to the top of the stairs, I feel and hear him behind me, his feet heavy and his breathing deep and dominating.

"Which way, my keeper?"

"To the left, little bird. First door." I follow his directions, and when I breach the door, the hardwood floor is darker than the rest of the house, a deep cherry. The bed is a large, black sleigh bed with all black silk blankets and one white, fluffy throw blanket draped on the left corner. All the walls are painted white, with the exception of the one behind the headboard of the bed; that one is black. There is a beautiful abstract artwork of silver, gray, and black streaks on a glossy canvas, and my heart pitter-patters.

"You found something made just for you, it seems," I whisper, now in position at the end of the bed, the backs of my thighs pressed against my calves and my hands face up on top of my legs.

"I like all my things to be how I demand them to be." He lifts a masculine brow, indicating I am one of those things.

My stomach flips. I love when he talks so crass, like I'm his possession. There are days I love feeling like his person, but mostly, I like to feel as if I'm his property. It fuels the darkness inside of me.

"Oh." It's all I can say, because I feel him in my blood and I can't get him out; it's too much. I love him so much, and suddenly I'm overcome with trying to find out what is going on with him. My docile, meek, submissive side is starting to close up. I want to fix him. I want to release him of his worries.

"Face down," he barks, and I almost do it on instinct, but something else inside me builds and I break the rules, fall out of line, knowing it will cost me.

"Xander." I slowly stand, pushing up from the ground with my fingertips and tiptoes until I stand in front of him. I watch his eyes widen and his nostrils flare. I see the rage that accompanies my disobedience in his entire stature. He's wound tight, and his stiff shoulders and balled fist at his sides scream louder than his harsh words could.

I was ready to make love, but no matter how much I try to ignore that telltale sign flashing red warning lights, I can't.

"Xander," I say again, reaching out for him, but before my hand can touch his arm, he takes a steady step back and hisses.

"On your knees, little bird. Did I tell you that you could move?" he yells, and I see the loss of control he submits to and my heart aches—truly *aches*. I feel whatever my keeper does. Down to my very bones, I *feel* it.

"My love, please." I bring my hand to my slightly rounded belly and caress it while I drop my eyes to the floor. Xander makes no noise or movement, and as I look up to see his reaction, his demeanor has changed. With a hand ruffling through his salt and peppered hair, he has the other on his hip and his eyes are wild, moving back and forth between mine with a sheen of tears threatening to spill over. I break my stance, needing to feel him, touch him, break him open in my hands.

"Keeper, what is haunting you? Tell me, please." My arms wrap around his waist and under his shirt to touch his warm skin. My bare chest is against his, my warm wall of safety almost crumbling under me as he lets a tear fall and his body trembles.

Xander Stine never cries. Not even on the day we first said goodbye and he walked away from me. To see him so damaged and broken over something I have yet to discover devastates and alarms me.

"I can't do it when you are naked. You are too bare and vulnerable, and I am about to strip your fucking soul, baby. My sweet little baby." He cups my face and kisses me wherever he can. My nose, my cheek, my forehead, just under my eyes.

I start to panic, and the natural response that comes with that is my tears. I grip his biceps and whimper. "What did you do? Xander, what did you do? Please." I pause, and he drops his forehead to mine, and the night he left me broken with clipped wings on his floor comes rushing back.

I push back from him abruptly, causing his hands to rip from my face as I twitch. "You're leaving again, aren't you? Just say it!" I scream, the tears now falling faster. I don't care that they make me ugly and vulnerable. I am breaking all over again, and my keeper is the wrecking ball.

"No, Lizith, I am not leaving you. But you may fucking run from me when I tell you this."

"I told you I would never run. You can't get rid of me, Xander! You can't." The psychotic side of me starts to rear her twisted head. The side that never existed until I fell in love with him.

"What did you do then? Just please, tell me," I beg, stepping only one foot closer, leaving a gap between us.

"I won't do it in here. Go downstairs. I'm going to pour myself a drink and meet you in the living room downstairs." And faster than the speed of light, he's gone, leaving a trail of fear in his absence. I feel terrified, unsure and so scared that I can't trigger myself into motion. I feel glued to this damn floor.

Finally, after a few breaths and a moment of surreal realization that something bad is happening, I move. Covering myself in the fluffy white throw blanket, I make my way downstairs. I hear him in the kitchen, making his scotch on the rocks, and I hurry my steps, wanting to get this over with.

I walk into the living room and take a seat at the edge of the couch, doing everything within me not to start chomping on my nails like a bad habit. Finally, he appears, and I look up at him.

It's been just minutes, and somehow it looks as if days of worry have gone by and his heart has become more devastated than before.

Xander makes a home in front of me, sitting on the coffee table. He doesn't look at me as he settles himself. Placing the scotch beside him and then resting his elbows on his knees, he runs his hands over his face before they end in mock prayer at his lips. Our eyes lock, and he speaks.

"I love you, Lizith, and you need to know something. What I've done is going to hurt you, but never doubt that I fucking love you."

I lean in closer, hanging on his words. "I love you, too, Xander."

With one last draw of a deep breath, he begins. "We were not happenstance. You and I were a sick game, and I was the one holding the dice." I shake my head, not sure what he means. "Let me speak. Do not interrupt."

I nod and bite at my lip nervously.

"I didn't want to go with you to see your dad, not because I was worried about the fact that we used to work together. It was because he fucked Jacqueline." I shake my head bewildered, almost certain I didn't hear him right. "Your father was the man she left me for, right before we met."

My eyes close and I almost laugh. He can't be serious. This isn't real. This is all part of some sick game, right?

"Don't look at me as if I'm fucking with you. I'm not, Lizith. Your dad is the reason I picked you. You were a pawn in my game to get back at my wife."

"Jacqueline," I say in a bone-chilling whisper, correcting him as my heart snaps in half and I start to spiral. I was a pawn?

"With Jacqueline. I wanted to hurt her and get revenge on your father. I wanted him to know I was fucking his little girl and destroying her from the inside out."

And just like he promised, his words strip me bare and rip me to shreds. My love didn't pick me because he saw me and knew I was meant to be his. I was just trash on a puppet string to him. I feel an army's worth of rage muster then boil inside me, and I try to breathe through it. But how can I?

"Then I fell in love with you, because I realized you were always meant to be mine. I couldn't tell you then, because I was in too deep and I didn't want to hurt you. You were too young and still so fragile."

"And now I'm just washed up and used to taking beatings from you? Used to having a broken heart at your hands?" I stand and he jolts back, surprised by my reaction. But I can't help it. This is betrayal in the highest form. This is treachery wrapped inside deceit, and I feel as if I just lost a part of myself.

"Lizith, listen to me." He stands and stalks toward my retreating back. He reaches me and grabs my arm, but I rip it from him, spinning on him fast.

"No! I don't want to hear more! You used me! Took everything from me!" I grab the glass vase on the table next to me in the foyer and smash it to the ground, screaming as I do. It's violent and heartbreaking, and if we were back home, our neighbors would have heard it.

How could he do this to me? How?

"Little bird, please."

"No! You can never call me that again! I hate you, Xander Stine! I despise you!" I turn to leave the cabin, uncaring that I have no shoes or my belongings. I am out of my mind and need to get away. The pain that flashes in his eyes is nothing compared to the pain I'm feeling. *Nothing.*

But the door doesn't open. No matter how hard I pull, and I try it over and over again.

"It's an automatic lock. It can only be opened with the code."

I stop, my spine tingling as my heavy breath becomes the only thing I hear.

"What is the code, Xander?" I turn slowly, my back hitting the door and my chest caving. I already know the answer. It's all coming together.

"I'm not giving you the code. And before you break any windows, you won't be able to. They are all double-paned—weatherproof—and cannot be broken." He has his hands in his pockets as he stands stoic, proud, unfazed and not one bit remorseful for locking me away.

"You did this so I couldn't run from you," I whisper, my eyes widening as tears stream down my red cheeks.

"I knew you would try, and I refuse to let you leave me, Lizith. You don't ever get to leave me."

Like that, I slide down the door until my ass hits the ground. I bring my knees to my chest and drop my head in defeat. Trapped and brokenhearted, all by the same man.

"Lizith—"

"Leave me alone. Please, just leave me alone," I whimper, keeping my head low.

He kneels in front of me on his haunches and pets my hair, and I nearly cringe. "Fine. But you can't leave, little bird. I will tell you everything when you are ready, but you are mine to keep here until you forgive me." I sob with his words, and he stands. I watch his feet as he moves to where my bag and purse are. I lift my eyes slightly to watch him when I see him grab my phone.

"Dinner will be ready soon, and I will be keeping your phone, so you won't be able to call for someone to come get you."

I sob harder. Never did I think he would do this to me. Ever. Now, I really am a broken bird inside a cage. I am not connected to my love anymore, and that alone feels like death. I've lost my heart.

XANDER

There never came a point in my time loving Lizith that I thought I would ever hurt her like I did tonight. I had planned to keep that secret buried as long as I lived this life with her, but Jacqueline didn't give me a fucking choice. I had to tell her, and I had to do it this way. There's something dark inside both of us, and if we don't handle this without a way to escape, we will never make it out together. I have to lock my love up until she is ready to fight for us, ready to forgive me and everything I have done.

I take a sip of my scotch, stirring the gravy for the mashed potatoes and grilled chicken I've prepared for us. I have been in here for a half hour and have not heard her move from her place at the front door. I move the chicken onto the glass dish and begin to prepare our plates. When I set the table, I go to collect her off the ground. As I step into the foyer, I see she lies at the door, glass inches from her, circling her in all directions. Broken things surrounding my broken love.

I don't say anything as I go to tower over her. She doesn't look up, but her face has gone stony, emotionless, devoid of anything. Her cheeks are stained red and her eyes are a darker color. I bend and pick her up in my arms to cradle her. She doesn't budge, just curls into a ball and digs her face into my chest.

I set her down on the bar stool at the marble counter then sit beside her and begin to eat, waiting for her to join me. She stares at her food for a moment, like she's going to refuse, but her stomach provokes her. It growls at the scent of the tender meat, and she knows she needs to eat for our little one. Slowly, she begins to take small bites, never looking at me. I, however, watch her like a hawk as I eat everything on my plate. She's so damn sad, and I hate that it's all at my hands.

She leaves maybe a bite or two of her portions, and I decide that's enough. Without another word, I pick her up once again and carry her up the stairs. She lets me bring her into the bathroom, and I set her on the counter so I can start her bath. I get it going, and when I turn to undress her, she is already standing there naked.

"Leave," Lizith tells me, but I ignore her. I begin to undress, and as I drop one item of clothing, she does something that knocks me for a loop. Grabbing my shirt, she places it over her body and covers her skin.

"Undress, Lizith," I warn her, but she shakes her head as she leaves the room. I drop my head and growl, growing frustrated, because I don't know what the hell to do. We are like ghosts of ourselves, strangers even, and it's not something I know how to handle. I've never been in love with someone the way I am with her, and I have never had to fight for it.

"Lizith!" I yell, still in my jeans as I leave the bathroom to follow her. I catch up to her once she makes it into the other bedroom, and I pull her to me. "What are you doing?" I spin her around to look at me.

"I'm getting away from you. It's my turn."

I scoff, shaking my head. "Your turn for what?"

She tucks her hair behind her ear and looks at me with no emotion. "My turn to treat you like you are nothing but a piece of garbage for me to dispose of."

I instantly twitch, and just like she did earlier, it's my turn to snap. "I never treated you like garbage, Lizith. I treated you like fucking gold!" I turn and punch the door as I exit. I need a minute; *we* need a fucking minute, because I'm feeling lethal and not opposed to making her submit to me, willing to use dangerous measures.

As I walk down the hall, I hear her scream. It echoes in the house, and you would think my hands were wrapped around her fucking neck and draining her life with the kind of noise she makes. I ignore it though, going into our room and slamming the door.

There are too many emotions coursing through me, and I don't know how to settle myself. Do I go to her and force her into forgiveness, or do I give her the damn silent treatment and the absence of me until she comes crawling for my attention?

I don't know, and I'm starting to think I should just tell her it was all a lie and then threaten Jac to stay away.

I shower in scalding water, taking on the pain in hopes of relieving the anger in me, but nothing happens. And for hours, I lie in bed listening to the sound of my broken bird's sobs. But I stay planted in bed, knowing I can't tell her everything until she comes to me. I can't fuck this up more.

LIZITH

Betrayal often comes disguised in the form of love. Loved ones hurt you most, because they have the biggest parts of you and know the power they possess over you. And power is the true root of all evil. Not only do I feel like Xander betrayed me, but also my father. How could he not tell me the moment he found out? How could he have moved on with a woman like Jacqueline, just a few years after my mother's death?

My mother was a beautiful, kind, humble woman, and Jacqueline is none of those things. But no matter how much I try to latch onto that for my own sanity tonight, I can't help but come back to the way Xander played a part in this. The day we first met, I was hooked and knocked over with the idea it was all fate. I felt my soul intertwine with his. The whole time I looked at him with adoration and love, he looked at me like a challenge, a pawn to hurt those who wronged him.

I feel used. I feel ashamed and embarrassed, because I have spent the past several years fawning at his feet and doing everything I can to prove my love for him, even when he was nowhere in sight. All to keep him. What was it all for?

I lie atop the blankets, my body overheated from my rage. I stare out the window, watching the thick snowflakes fall slowly, and I know right away that come morning, we will most likely be snowed in. His plan all along. Xander wanted to trap me so I couldn't run, and an unfamiliar feeling rises within me. This is the first time I am not turned on by his need to claim me and keep me as his. Usually, his possessive actions would fuel my love for him, but I have nowhere to run at a time I want to hide the most.

I didn't give him more than a minute or two to explain anything, because once he laid out the basics, I was shaken to my core. I don't know if there's anything else he could say that would possibly fix this. Xander Stine may have spearheaded his own demise, and I'm collateral damage.

I finally let my clustered mind take me under, and I close my heavy eyes.

Just mere hours after my eyes shut, I am awoken to the strange feeling of being watched. And sure enough, when my eyes flutter open, Xander is sitting adjacent to my bed, in the corner of the room on the lounge chair.

His eyes are dark, and it looks as if he hasn't slept all night. He changed into black jeans and a light button up. The top three buttons are undone, and a glimpse of his tan chest with a sprinkling of hair is showing as he holds a tumbler of dark liquid in his hand.

"Good morning." He is the first to speak, and as he does, I peer out the window, seeing there is no sun in the sky, just heavy snow clouds. Checking the clock, I see it's 7:00 a.m.

"You're drinking this early?" I don't know why I ask, or even care for that matter.

"The love of my life said such foul things to me last night. I've found it necessary to drink in order to drown out the sound of it on replay." My heart cracks just a little bit deeper. No matter how hurt I am by all that I discovered last night, I do not hate Xander. I could never hate him, and I shouldn't have used those words against him.

"You didn't deserve that," I admit, sitting up in bed.

"You don't know what that did to me, Lizith."

"And you don't know what you have done to me… for years. That was a brief moment of weakness leaving me. You have had years of lies between us. Do not try to play the victim," I scold, standing and moving to the en suite bathroom. I need a shower. The air is cold now that my body heat has resumed its normal temperature.

"Lizith, stop being so damn hostile with me. We have to fix this, and you need to let me explain everything. This isn't fair." He stands behind me now, his large frame crowding me as I start the bath and add the honeysuckle bath salts.

"You know, before you, I was normal. I had a beautiful childhood. I did normal things. Then I met you, and I changed for you. I started loving the normal less and less. My young adulthood became anything but simple. I spent years obsessing and losing sleep over you. I lost all my sanity to be with you. Because I believed from the moment that you touched me that I was the love you always wanted." I bring my closed fist down on his chest. "You made me a hopeless lover, and then you stripped me of any hope I had left. I can't look at you, Xander, and it absolutely kills me." I back away again, so exhausted from crying.

I sink down to the floor at his feet and begin to nuzzle into him. "I broke over and over again until I was molded into what you wanted, because I had faith in you. And you lied. Since the moment I met you, you've lied." I grow weak and tired, and I believe I'm falling into some kind of depression. I'm alone, and right now, he's the only one I can cry to, and he so happens to be the very reason for my heartbreak.

"I did, but I had no fucking idea that the person I was deceiving was meant to be my fucking soul mate, little bird. You are my lifeline, and had I not picked you as revenge—and I know that is twisted, but had I not—you and I wouldn't have found each other."

He pets my head, and I can see some sort of logic behind that, but that doesn't excuse everything else.

"Then why not tell me sooner? You could have told me that everything in our relationship was a lie far sooner than now."

"Would it have made a difference?"

"Yes! It would have, Xander! I wouldn't have been so in love with you that I couldn't see past the deceit. Time builds more love and intimacy. It builds our foundation, and that was built on lies! You could have told me before you brainwashed me into this weak psycho!" I scream, sliding away from him and clinging to the claw-footed bathtub.

"I didn't brainwash you. I found you and set you free. You were always made to be this way for me. You think I've ever loved a woman the way I love you? Do you?" he leans over and screams in my face, and I take it, shuddering. "Do you think I ever loved someone enough that I would lock them away to force them to stay with me?" He crouches more, getting closer and closer. "Do you think I would ever let you fucking get inside my head and soul if I didn't love you? You fucked me up just as badly, little bird, and you can be mad at me right now, but I do not regret the fucking lie, because it made you mine. And I will steal you with lies and deceit, if that is how I get to keep you. Just like you stole me back! We are both sick and twisted, but don't ever tell me that I made you that way, when we both made each other absolutely fucking savage."

Xander leaves again, and like the past three times we've spoken, I scream. I'm spiraling down the deep depths of hell and I can't control the downfall. I'm going insane. Cabin fever has sunk in, and it's only day one.

Chapter Fourteen

XANDER

FOR TWENTY-FOUR HOURS, WE DIDN'T TALK. SHE LOCKED HERSELF IN THE bedroom and spent time screaming, crying, and sleeping. I checked on her when she finally slept, just to make sure she and our child were still okay. But finally, I forfeited the battle and decided to let her have some space, because whenever we go in calm like a couple of lambs, we leave roaring like furious lions in a battle over prey. I need to let her come to me when she is ready.

I have stationed myself downstairs in the study, drinking and planning my lessons for the following semester. But to say I got more than one lesson plan finished would be a lie, because I keep watching the clock, counting down the hours to the day we will have to leave. I swear I will extend the trip until the day she forgives me, even if that takes fucking years.

My phone buzzes in the drawer to the left of me, and I take it out. Seeing a message from Jacqueline, I grit my teeth, my once calm exterior bursting at the seams.

Tell her, or I will. Simple as that. Come back, or I will ruin everything you love. Including her.

"Damn it!" I grab the entire glass bottle of scotch and throw it across the room. Glass ricochets off the wall, and a piece clips my bicep. I don't even flinch, and it isn't a light scratch. Blood starts to ooze out, and I let it.

I stand and start pacing in front of the cherry oak desk, the smell of liquor now permeating thickly in the air.

"Xander, you're bleeding," Lizith says from the doorway, appearing out of nowhere. I look down at the gash and see a small sliver of glass still embedded in my skin.

"I'm fine." I try to remove it and it burns so much, I hiss through my gritted teeth.

"Please, Xander, let me help get it out, and I can stitch it up. I brought my first aid kit."

I nod, letting her leave to grab it. Why am I not shocked she came to the cabin prepared? The traits of a good physician's assistant, I guess.

"Sit down, right here." She guides me to the couch next to the desk, and I sit on the edge as she sits on her knees, bringing my wound to her eye level.

"What happened?" she asks, taking a pair of tweezers and, with great precision, removing the glass. I don't flinch away, but my face scrunches up in discomfort.

"Nothing, it's nothing."

"Another lie." She peers up at me with a look of pain.

"It's Jacqueline. She is messaging me. And it's not a lie, I just don't want to get worked up and talk about it. I am already at my wit's end here, Lizith."

She doesn't respond. Instead, she goes to work cleaning up the blood and sterilizing my arm. The first stitch goes through and I grit my teeth. This shit hurts.

"Xander?"

"Fuck. Yeah?" I hiss, twitching under her steady hands.

"Did you ever plan to tell me?"

I hesitate for a moment. Knowing she is ready to talk, I just hope this ends with us locked in a room and between silk sheets.

"No, I didn't. I thought about it, and so many times I almost did, but in the end, I didn't. Because it wasn't going to change anything. I love you, and I know you love me, despite how you feel right now."

"But those are secrets, and it says more about who you are if you are willing to hide secrets, more than what the secret itself is."

"Lizith. I can't apologize enough or put into words how sorry I am that I hurt you. But I know that you were made for me. Day one, before I met you, having only seen your name on my roster, I started it as a game. But by day two, when I actually met and spoke to you, I knew I didn't stand a chance. Day three, I knew I needed to keep you. I knew I was going to be with you, and everything before you meant nothing." A quick moment of relief floods her eyes and she smiles bashfully. I almost reach out to touch her, but I know my little one better; she isn't completely there.

"Start from day one, please. Tell me everything, and damn it, Xander, please do not lie anymore." Lizith finishes then, placing a bandage over the stitches, and then she surprises me. Scooting closer, she rests her head on my thigh and practically purrs as she falls into her safe place, ready to hear the truth.

"Okay." I take a deep breath and tell her everything, no details left out. "When she left me for your father, I was so bitter. So angry, baby. Not because I loved her, but because I was being played. And honestly, my ego was bruised, and I am a man."

She nods, letting me continue without interruption.

"At first, I planned to out her to her family, but then I knew it would be 'he said, she said' and a nasty game I didn't stand a chance at winning. Then a few days later, just as I was on the cusp of letting it go, my attendance roster came across my desk, and there, like a sore thumb, your last name stood out. I did some research, and sure enough, you were the daughter of Dennis Morrison, and I came up with my plan. You were eighteen, legal, and the perfect pawn to use to mess with the man who got in the way of my reputation." I look down and see delicate tears swelling in her eyes, and I know my words are hard to hear, because they are surely hard to say. It's as if I am swallowing nails.

"Then you walked in, and I saw the innocence in you, but I could practically smell the crazy inside you, waiting to be released. I searched for my soul mate in the darkness and never found her, and then there you were, mine for the taking. I knew I wasn't going to let you go, even after I broke your father's heart."

"What was your plan? What would you have done to hurt him?" she whispers, wiping away the lone tear that escapes.

"I was going to let him see his perfect angel grow black wings, and then I was going to make you crazy over me. And when the moment was right, I was going to clip those wings and break your heart—send you running back to him. Then he would have known the reason his daughter had gone mad was because of me."

"So why didn't you?" She moves a little, lifting her head just a bit to look at me with her wide green eyes. I don't know what she will do when this is over, but if I lose that look, it will be the end me. I promise that.

"I kissed you, and you whispered how afraid you were of my kiss because of how alive it made you feel. Remember that?"

She smiles and her eyes sparkle as she whispers what she'd told me that night. "You kiss like the devil, but it's laced with heaven, and I want to find you in the in-between, keeper mine."

Lizith claimed me as her keeper before I even asked her to. "That is how I knew I loved you."

"Xander," she whimpers, and I move. Lifting her up, I bring her to my lap, so that her thighs bracket mine, and bury my hands in her hair.

"You have to forgive me, little bird. I know this is hard and it may never be forgotten, but know that it isn't who we are, and I won't let you go another day letting it define us."

"It's hard. You talked about me like I was nothing. I used to feel like my very existence was because of you, Xander. I used to feel so connected, and now I feel like I am all mine again. Alone. I don't feel you here anymore." She touches above her heart, and it's my turn to whimper. Like a fool.

"I'm there, more than ever, baby. I am there." I touch her stomach and drop my forehead to hers. "You are my soul, my existence, my everything. Please don't think you aren't in every cell inside me." Our baby joins us as a family, and I will pull every stop I can to make her understand she has never been more wrong about anything in her life. Lizith Morrison is mine.

"Even when you left me to go back to her, I didn't feel like I'd lost our connection. That's why I stalked Jacqueline. Trying to find out what power she held over you, because there had to be a reason you were going back to her. Surely, you didn't love her. The semester before I graduated, I followed her to the fertility clinic, and that's when I applied there for an internship. As soon as I got my degree, I became Dr. Curtis's PA, gaining access to her personal records. It killed me to think she was trying to have your baby, but at the same time, I knew something was… off. That's why I installed the cameras, and that's how I found out everything she was doing. Yet, through all of that, I never once felt this disconnection from you, even going seven years without allowing myself to see you." A tear slides out the corner of her eye and travels down her cheek.

"She was going to ruin you, my love," I confess, and she lifts her shimmering eyes to mine. "When your father left her, she came crawling back to me, and she discovered clues that made her realize that not only was I moving on, but I was moving on with one of my students. She didn't know who it was, but if she were to find out, she had the power to completely ruin your life. Her father was your dean. I had to leave you the way I did to protect you. I couldn't let her find out who you were, because she would have destroyed your career before you even got started. I knew how important your work was to you, how it was your way of staying connected to your mother after you lost her, your hope to one day help women who were in her same situation, unable to have babies on their own. I couldn't let her do that, little bird."

She stays silent, visibly absorbing everything I just relayed. And as her eyes fill with tears once more, I realize I need to distract her, pull her out of this misery. "Dance with me?"

"Dancing won't make this stop hurting." She moves her hand and places it on her heart. I feel it breaking, and I am not even touching her.

"No, but it could start the healing." There's a pregnant pause while she decides what to do before conceding. She stands and moves to the middle of the room, waiting for me. I move around the room, locating the Bluetooth speakers and connecting my phone.

"Hurricane" by Thirty Seconds to Mars starts to play. "Let me lead you?" I stand in front of her now.

"You are always leading me."

Another nudge to my heart, knocking it out of rhythm. "I'll be so damn careful with your heart this time. Trust me like you always have."

She nods, this time without words.

I pull her against me and make her bare feet rest atop mine. I don't want her to step on any glass, and I want her as close as possible. The music surrounds us, and we stay quiet, our eyes searching one another's as our souls try their damnedest to find each other again.

"Tell me you still love me," I beg.

"I love you, Xander. You know that."

"I don't. Because I betrayed my love, and she's hurting beyond what my hands or words can fix. How can I gain your forgiveness?"

"Time. Answers. I don't know. I still have so much to ask," she admits.

"Ask me something else."

"Not yet. Give me these few minutes to just take it in. To feel you." Lizith lays her head against my shoulder, and the music plays on. I bring my lips to her hair and take it all in. She smells like honeysuckle and grief. I can smell her regretting us, and as it travels through my senses, I know I don't stand a chance at fixing this on my own. I might lose my little bird.

The song ends, and the second it does, she leaves me. I watch her walk away like a ghost. I don't go after her, because it's the way it needs to be. Lizith has to come to terms without me to force the issue.

When am I going to wake up from this nightmare?

LIZITH

I tried to put all the pieces together in my mind to reach a solution and wave a white flag of surrender, but it is still too much and I still have so many questions.

Xander is being patient and not following me around or tying me to a bed until he gets my forgiveness, and I appreciate that. I start to think about the idea of my father and Jacqueline together, and I nearly lose my lunch. How could he go from my mother to that devil in human flesh?

Why didn't my father just tell me? And how come this woman is always weaseling her way into Xander's and my relationship? Will she always insert herself back into his life? I don't want to give her victory, but she is on the very edge of succeeding, because I cannot live a life with Xander when Jacqueline is doing her best to break us apart. We are having a child, and maybe that is why my sensibility is kicking in, because I need to protect my offspring.

Jacqueline may always hold the gauntlet of victory.

I sit in the bathroom, looking myself over and taking in my appearance. My eyes are sunken in and my hair is a wild mess on my head. I'm makeup-free with blotchy red spots from all my crying.

Deciding I need to make myself presentable, I work my curly hair into loose waves. I part it down the middle and let it fall like old Hollywood glam. Next, I do my makeup. My eyes are smoky and my lips red by the time I finish. Why I'm getting ready with nowhere to go as the day is drawing close to an end, I don't know, but I need to feel human.

"You look beautiful, my little bird." Xander appears in the doorway. I'm all done up, except for my short silk white robe.

"I just needed to do something. All this fighting and being locked in a house has made me stir-crazy."

He waits then extends an olive branch. "They came and shoveled the snow in the driveway. I can order a car and take us to dinner."

"Really?" I perk up, taking slight joy in his kind gesture.

"Yes, as long as you don't run," he says, looking down at me. He looks larger than usual, leaning in the doorway, his shoulder against the frame and his foot crossed over the other.

He looks… normal. Not *his* normal pristine professor persona. More like a dominant alpha dressed in simplicity.

"I'm not eighteen anymore, Xander. I am a woman growing with child." I tuck my neat waves behind one ear. "Besides, I still have questions."

"And hope?" He clings onto my confession.

"I don't know. I want to, but I don't know. May I get dressed now?" I sidestep him, but his hand reaches down to rest softly on my stomach, his warm palm feeling strong against the cool silk fabric on my skin.

"Can I watch you dress? See you pick your clothes?" Most would find his request odd. But we are odd, and I don't tell him no.

I nod, and he releases me. I drop my robe at my feet then glance over my shoulder to find him looking me up and down, over and over again. Opening the suitcase, I feel his eyes on my backside as I rummage through my new panty sets I brought for what I thought was our romantic getaway.

I pick all lace. Black, like my wings. I slide on my panties and hear him growl, but I don't face him. I torture him longer. When I hook my bra on, I turn and stand still, popping one knee and hip, showing off my young and nearly flawless body to him. I spent years keeping my body in shape, so when we reunited, he would have a perfect little bird to praise.

"It's fifteen degrees outside, Lizith. You have to dress accordingly." I watch his Adam's apple bob.

"I have stockings and a warm jacket. So, I should be just fine." I pull out my all lace black dress with a nude underlay and two cutouts just above the breasts. The neckline is like a choker, going all the way up to the underside of my chin. I slide it on. "Can you zip me please, Mr. Stine?"

He is on me in three strides, his knuckle moving from the dip in my lower back all the way up my spine. "Punishment worked. This is killing me, baby. You're crushing me under your thumb." He leans in and kisses the spot between my shoulder blades and I shudder.

"Good. I plan to make it worse every second, Xander."

With that, he zips me up and steps away, heated and pissed—right where I want him.

"I'm getting dressed. I will meet you downstairs." He leaves with a huff, and I smirk and finish putting on my outfit.

Within ten minutes, I am ready and meet him at the door. He looks good, and it makes me a little bitter. He has on his nice dark jeans and a pullover sweater with a hoodie and his black jacket. He styled his hair atop his head, and he cleaned up his growing beard, leaving a smattering of salt-and-pepper five o'clock shadow.

"Put your coat on. The car is ready."

I slide on my heavy black peacoat, and he silently escorts us out. We climb into the large, four-door, sleek black SUV. The driver tips his hat, and Xander gives him a location.

"Jordan's Steakhouse, Downtown Aspen."

"Yes, sir."

I look out the window in wonderment, watching the snow on the trees and the ground pass us by. I have never seen snow before, and even if I am still watching from closed confinements, it's truly breathtaking.

Xander grabs my thigh hard and drags me to him suddenly, and I lose my train of thought when I look up and see him glaring at me.

"What is wrong with you?" I ask, trying to move his hand.

He leans in close, his lips whispering against my ear. "You aren't paying enough attention to me, and I don't appreciate it."

I gawk at him, shocked that he thinks he has the right to hold all of my attention. "I'm still upset with you, Xander, so deal with it."

He tightens his grip and I yelp, my hand flying up to his chest as he wraps his arm around my neck and pulls my face to his.

"Stop with the whiplash. You make me fucking crazy. One minute, you want to forgive me, and the next, you are back to treating me like you despise me," he accuses.

I'm about to break free from his touch, when I see sadness morphing his face. His brows crease inward and his jaw tightens.

"Don't look like that. It hurts," I whisper.

"That's because I am hurting," he admits, and I exhale and drop my head against his.

"We both are, and there isn't anything I can do to make that stop, Xander. So stop expecting me to forget everything." I let him down as gently as I can, because I know the feeling of heartbreak.

"I don't expect you to forget everything. I expect you to just touch me or kiss me or just fucking need me."

The driver peers back at us, and I choose to ignore him.

"If I do that, it will make things worse." I finally break free from him and scoot across the seat again. His hand finds my thigh immediately, and he keeps it there. Xander doesn't speak, but he breathes in and out deeply, his eyes forward and face tight.

I let him keep his hand there, but my upper body turns away from him. We finally pull up to the restaurant, and the car is filled with palpable tension. He tips the driver and helps me out, making sure I don't slip on the ice in my heels. Walking into the swanky, upscale steakhouse, I take note of all the black and red accents that give this place a romantic vibe. Xander would pick this place in an attempt to woo me and sweep me away, but I have other plans, and they don't include me cuddling close.

There is a wait, but of course, we are whisked away to a private booth in the corner, under a warmly lit chandelier that gives us more privacy.

Looking over the menu, I feel his eyes boring into me, but I give no indication that I feel his wallowing all the way from here.

"Good evening, sir, ma'am," the waiter greets us. He is handsome, well built at six feet tall, with wide shoulders and blue eye behind thick lashes. He's no Xander, but I can see him being the cup of tea for many women.

Xander gives him a curt nod, barely acknowledging him before he looks to me. I give him a sweet smile and warm greeting. "Hello." This gets Xander's eyes off the menu and onto the man standing just to the side of him. His eyes go dark and then he looks to me quickly, sneering and gritting his teeth at me with agitation. I ignore it and listen emphatically to the waiter's selection of specials and options.

"We will take two medium-well 10-ounce steaks with a house salad and a side of red mashed potatoes. Water for us both. Sparkling," Xander orders, and I rush to stop the waiter from leaving.

"Actually, I don't want any of that. I will have a fresh squeezed lemonade and baked salmon with brown rice and quinoa salad. Thank you, sir." That earns me a full-on growl in front of our server, and I see his eyes go wide as Xander turns in on me.

"Yes, uh... right away." And like a scared puppy, he scurries away and leaves me with the beast.

"Do not act like a childish fool. I won't tolerate it."

"I'm not acting. I didn't want what you ordered. You don't have to be such a high-handed caveman all the time, Xander."

"It's what you always order at steakhouses. Don't play this game. Call another man any kind of name like 'sir' again and I will spank you right in front of everyone here."

I scoff. "You wouldn't dare."

"Try me. Better yet, fucking test me, little bird."

I turn my head and curse the tears that well, doing my best to not let them surface all the way to edge. Maybe I am in over my head. This is something I have never done before—done things to purposefully hurt or fight with my love. I'd once done something stupid to gain his attention, but I had never intentionally wounded him. This isn't like other times he hurt me. When he left to go back to Jacqueline, he did it for reasons that didn't purposely destroy me. But now I know how we met and fell in love was all a game, and I just can't get past it.

We don't speak anymore. And each time the waiter comes back to us, he lets his eyes linger on me a little longer than what he should, and Xander takes notice. I opened a door I shouldn't have, and now this poor young man has no idea what kind of lion he has prowling and circling around him.

"You like that?" he asks as we start to eat.

"What?" I prompt after I swallow a bite of my savory salmon.

"You teased him. You made him desire you, and now I am seconds away from laying my fist into him repeatedly." He doesn't look at me as he says this, and he says it so nonchalantly it's frightening. Xander has always been jealous over me. Especially when men my age take notice or grab my attention.

I wait to respond, because I know I have to be careful with my choice of words. "As much as I would like to, I don't. I don't want attention from anyone."

Xander once again goes quiet. This seems to be the soundtrack of the past forty-eight hours together. Cat and mouse.

As we finished up our meal, Xander's attention was on his phone, checking emails and such. I wish I had my phone so I could distract myself. But instead, I play devil's advocate and decide to attempt another round of talking through my recent revelation.

"Did you love her when you and I first met?"

Instantly, his phone becomes a lost item on the table. Without hesitation or asking for further explanation, he answers, "I never loved her. Ever."

"So you really did all this for revenge on her for making you look bad?"

"My reputation is pristine, and my ego knows no bounds. You know that, Lizith," he says matter-of-factly. "Call it one of my many character flaws."

"I know. So I was just another way of proving how big your ego was. You knew you could conquer me, and you did."

"That's how it began, but as I said, that quickly became untrue. But I'll take that jab."

We remain quiet for a moment. "My mother was my best friend. The day I met you, I wanted to call her to tell her about you. It was all I wanted to do, but I couldn't, because she was gone." He doesn't move, barely even releasing a breath as he gives me the floor. "She had this amazing laugh. It was almost breathtaking. I remember stopping everything I was doing whenever she was laughing just to listen to her, because I loved the sound of it. My father and I both were enamored by her grace and carefree ways."

"She's not the only woman who could make people fall at her feet, completely smitten."

I don't respond, but I feel his compliment down to my bones. It feels nice being compared to my mom.

"She was so selfless. She did charity work and found any way she could to help others who needed it. And she was classic, timeless, beautiful. I wanted to be her."

"Why are you saying this, little one?"

"Because even though I am gut-wrenchingly hurt and upset with you, I am disgusted over the fact that just a year after I lost my mother, Jacqueline was the woman my dad fell for. A vile, ruthless woman took the place next to my father where my mother stood. She was still fresh in her grave, Xander. How could he do that to her?"

"Lust and manipulation."

My brows draw in when he says this, our eyes connecting. "What?"

"I don't want to upset you more, bird."

"No, say it. I didn't just tell you all that for you to harbor more secrets."

Xander takes a deep breath. "I never loved her. I lusted after her. When we met in college, she roped me in with lies and lust. I swear she used her body as a weapon and manifested a belief in me that she could be kind and lovable. But she was just a serpent in the bedroom, and once the preacher at our wedding closed his Bible, she changed."

I cringe. Knowing that sex with her was good enough to blind him into marriage makes me nauseous.

"You have to have met my mother. If you had, you would understand. I don't think Jacqueline at her best could touch my mother at her worst."

"I believe you. I do, because I am in love with her protégé. There isn't anyone or anything that could talk me out of loving you, or push me away."

That is no false confession. "I know."

"I am sorry your father and I have hurt you." His first real apology since he told me.

I dip my head and pick at the lace of my dress, uncaring if I snag the fabric. "Thank you." I tuck my hair behind my ear, and in that moment, I realize this is the first time I have told him this much about my mother.

Her Lizith seems so out of reach, like another woman from a different world. I am no longer that innocent naïve girl she once knew, but now a woman possessed by love for a man she should have never met. But I am too far gone and too much in love with Xander to keep up this charade. I can't go another day without forgiving him and loving him.

"Will that be all for you both this evening?" our waiter interrupts us, his eyes falling on me, smoldering and curious. He is undressing me with his eyes, and with my forgiveness just on the tip of my tongue, I do not like the way it feels. I feel as if I betrayed my love by welcoming attention to get him jealous. Now, I am filled with regret.

"That is all. Lizith, let's go." Xander leaves two one-hundred-dollar bills. Doubling the amount of our actual tab. He does it as a show of power, and it fills my stomach with the soft beginnings of desire. A slow, steady burn.

He stands and puts on his jacket as I slide gracefully from the booth and stand just to the side of him. Not wanting another second of attention from the server, I place my hand in Xander's after we both finish putting on our coats, and I stand behind him, using him as my shield. The server stares me down as he begins to walk away, when Xander grabs him firmly by the elbow.

"A man should know better than to fawn over a woman already so obviously claimed. You never know the lengths some men are willing to go to when they find another gawking at their woman. Run along, little boy, and pray we never cross paths again."

I watch as the color drains from the young man's face, and it's as if he tucks his tail between his legs as he breaks free from Xander and scurries away.

Xander doesn't even look back at me as he leads us out, poised and collected as if he didn't just dole out a threat. I officially lose my sense and become putty in my keeper's hands.

Chapter Fifteen

XANDER

I LET THE HOT WATER RUN OVER MY BODY AFTER A NIGHT OUT WITH LIZITH. I DIDN'T speak to her at all on the way back. Instead, my hands twitched as I itched to go back and put a fist through that fucker's face. He practically drooled and touched her with his eyes, imagining the things he would do to her.

He was Lizith's age. Young, untainted by years of life behind him that would make him hard to love. He would touch her in a way I cannot—with youthful hands lacking the roughness of age. I'm so much older than Lizith, and she has decades left of beauty, and one day, she may not want me anymore.

Before my little bird, I never questioned my looks and charm. Now, with a beautiful angel-like creature like Lizith, I fear time like a plague chasing after me. I can't outrun it. Then, when she tempted him out of revenge, I was reminded that I am by far living a nightmare that gets closer with each passing day.

My muscles bunch under the water and soap cascading down my skin. The room is spinning, and I feel sudden anxiety that I can't slow down.

"Xander?" Her voice revives me, bringing my head out from under the water. I keep my hands braced on the shower wall in front of me.

"Yes, my love?" I try to seem controlled. My blood may be rushing with insecurities, but I don't dare voice it to her.

"I was wondering if we could talk."

I take a deep breath and watch her body outlined on the other side of the fogged glass. "I'm in the shower, little bird. Wait on the bed for me and I will be out in a moment." I deflect and show dominance. Control the situation, and I can keep some sanity.

"Okay." She leaves, and I spend a second or two reining back in my emotions and putting on my game face. I climb out and towel off, wrapping it tight around my waist, low on my hips. Stepping out, I am met with a surprise.

"Lizith?"

"Little bird. Call me by my name, my keeper." She sits in the middle of the bed, naked. On her knees, she perches with her hand extended out with a tumbler filled with scotch on the rocks.

"What are you doing, little bird?" I question, stepping closer. I'm shocked by the turn of events.

She has her head down, but when I whisper this question, she slowly brings her eyes up. "I forgive you, my keeper. I don't ever want to go another day telling lies or spewing hate. I can't do it, my love. I just can't." Her lip trembles and thousands of goose bumps break out over her skin as she starts to shiver and the ice clinks against the glass.

Just like that, I move. Taking the drink from her hand, I place it on the desk and replace her hand with mine.

"Stand up. You're my equal." I pull her flush against me, her barely there bump touching my stomach.

"Look at me." I grip her chin in my hand.

"Do not apologize for what *I* did. I shouldn't have hidden this secret. This is my fault."

She nods, her beautiful eyes locked on mine. I can see deep into her soul. "I thought about it and realized how much your lie changed my life. If you didn't pick me that day, Xander, I wouldn't be with you, and our love wouldn't exist." I watch her eye twitch—my stunning, neurotic woman. "Our miracle wouldn't exist. And we both did things wrong. I lied for years, planning to win you back and start a family I promised you. You were hurt, but you forgave me. I owe you."

"You do not owe me anything. I thrive off knowing you did everything to win me back, just the way I like it." I tighten my grip on her chin. "Crazed and possessive. You would do anything I ask, and I wouldn't have it any other way."

Lizith trembles, knees buckling as I catch her before they go out completely. "I think your little wings just grew back."

"Because we are mending each other."

"No, it's because we thrive on the damned and broken inside us. You can never do that again, Lizith. We can never turn on one another. We have no one but each other. This world is against us already, so we cannot be at odds."

She blushes, nodding and letting those tears fall without reservation. "Kiss me, Xander. Make this all better."

With apologies on our lips, I decide to change the mood. "Now that we are both on the same page, you do owe me."

She shakes her head, confused. "What do you mean?" She reaches between us and releases the towel from my hips, leaving us both naked, and my cock goes full-mast.

"You flirted to upset me, and bad little birds get punished. You owe me a thousand apologies, starting now. On all fours, on the bed. Ass in the air and lips on my cock. I want you to choke on me until I flood your mouth with my seed, little bird."

Her nipples could cut me as they pebble against my abs. "Xander, I didn't want him. I wasn't flirting. I promise." She drags her nails up my abs and I growl.

"Your eyes sparkled when he reacted to your charm. You wanted to make me boil and it worked. I don't take kindly to you fucking with me like that. You are mine." I move my hands from her jaw to her neck, and I squeeze with just enough force that her breath catches. She is so fucking painstakingly beautiful it nearly squeezes the very life out of me. Her green eyes and pale skin are my undoing.

"Are you going to hurt me?" Her lashes bat up at me and those eyes penetrate me. Lizith looks afraid but excited, hopeful yet petrified.

"Do you want me to? Just ask, little thing, and I will give you what you and I both want."

That snarky, smug smirk tugs at her lips, and I watch the fire dance across her hazy eyes. "Don't let me come till you see fit. Fuck your sorries into me, and then when you think you have found my forgiveness, fuck me so hard I don't remember anything but the feel of you."

I growl, my cock now leaking heavy beads of need all over her stomach. How could she be so beautiful and forgiving and selfless after everything that transpired over the weekend? I don't mistake it as submission. I identify it for what it is—control over me. This porcelain beauty was made for me. Lizith Morrison has me by the neck, heart, and fucking balls. I would take a life for her if she asked.

"On. The. Fucking. Bed. Don't think I won't punish you even worse for letting foul words fall from your perfect mouth, little bird. Suck my dick; choke on it. Make me praise you. Got it?"

She nods, her neck moving along the inside of my hands.

When she turns, I can't control myself. She's one step away from me when I reach around and roughly grab her tit in my hand, the other hand grasping her ass and squeezing before I spank it. "Mine." *Fuck.* "My fuck doll, my queen, my siren. You don't understand what I will do for you. You have no damn idea." I release Lizith, going to my knees on the end of the mattress, and she gets into the position I ordered.

She licks those full lips and opens to speak, but I shut her up with my cock. I shove it to the back of her throat and her eyes squeeze shut, water escaping the corners. She gags on me, and it's like a symphony.

"Fuck. Do it, beautiful." I lean and slap her ass again, and she starts bobbing her head the best she can from her position. Grabbing all her hair and knotting it in my fist, I move her back and forth, watching the violence of my princess sucking my cock.

Lizith is everything to me. My plaything, my heart, my goddamn lifeline. My most precious possession. I'm a thousand lifetimes of unworthiness for her. I do not deserve this classic beauty.

Her green eyes have darkened and she looks up at me under thick lashes. I bite my lip, my entire body flexed and tight. The veins in my arms are thick as I steer her head. The veins that line my hips between my V are pronounced, alive, and pumping with alpha blood.

"You are so damn beautiful. I love you like hell loves tortured souls." I grit through my teeth, throwing my head back when she moans. It vibrates against my shaft as it's deep in her throat. That's when it hits me. What the fuck am I doing? My lady deserves the spoiling; she deserves her one thousand apologies in the way of intimate pleasure.

My nostrils flare, and every ounce of restraint I have is tested as I leave her mouth. She peers up, confused, somehow wiping away the spit around her lips with grace.

"Keeper? I wasn't done. Was I not doing it the way you wanted?" Lizith sits back, her ass meeting her calves. Embarrassment floods her body and her cheeks and neck go red.

"No, you were doing it perfectly. Too good for what I deserve. You deserve the pleasure. On your back, pretty thing." I turn on the cool and collected part of me.

"But—"

I hush her and gently touch her cheek. "No, on your back. I want to feast. I want to spoil. I want to ravage you." I hear and see her gulp.

"Xander," she practically pleas, asking for something we both don't know or understand. Their is a deep ache and a palpable need to mate and be so damn connected that we could crawl inside one another, become the same soul, the same body, the same heartbeat.

"I know, little bird. I'm trying to scratch that itch. Let me inside you, and I promise I can mend everything I broke."

"Promise?"

"What did I say?"

She smiles, and this one reaches her eyes. And with that, she relinquishes her trust and lets me take everything from her. I lay her back slowly, her body surrendering to the silk sheets. I spread her legs and kneel between them. Her pointed knees graze against my ribcage as she smiles innocently up at me, the tip of her finger between her teeth.

I tilt my head, and my lip catches between my teeth, mimicking her action. I take in her body, looking down the slim column of her neck to the sleek, smooth skin over her collarbone. Her pink nipples are hard and rosy, beckoning me. I lean a little and grab a hold of her breast, pinching the nipple between my long, thick fingers. My other hand finds my cock somewhere in my venture, and I squeeze tight, trying to imitate the tightness of her smooth slit, but it's not enough.

If it isn't her, it's not enough.

"Suck these fingers, baby." My hand leaves her nipple, my other still going strong on my cock. Placing three stiff fingers to her lips, Lizith sucks them in and wets them. My jaw unhinges as she moans around them, her eyes eating up my working hand on my shaft.

"Deadly."

She giggles. "Then fuck me like it, my keeper."

With that, I take my three wet fingers and slam them into her. She screams, her back leaving the bed and her arms seizing as her hands grip the sheets. "Xander!" I start out rough, showing her how fucking much she needs a man like me. Not a man her own age. Lizith would never be worshipped or pleased in the way only I can. It isn't possible.

"Yeah, you're ready. Give me your orgasm, and then I will give you real pain. Real euphoria." I curl my finger upward and hit her spot. She detonates around my hand, her eyes never closing, staying focused on mine. For a split second, I swear her soul leaves her body and slams into me.

Before she even has a moment to collect her existence again, I replace my fingers with my cock and she is back at it, screaming, clawing, and reaching for me. I drag her hips up and balance her weight on her shoulders as I pound into her, ready for my release. She has me wound so tight I plan to go over and over again. This is just the beginning of a never-ending night where I will be inside her. Apologizing and stealing back what she took from me.

"Don't stop. Please, Xander, never stop loving me like this." Reaching up, she grabs her hair in her hands and cries out into the night.

And with a slap to her hip, I make a vow to her. "I will never stop. Ever."

For the next four days, we apologize to each other. Nonstop. Through fucking, through lovemaking, through late-night talks about her beginnings and mine. I truly learn who my little bird is. And for the blizzards that kept us locked up tight, I am forever in their debts.

Chapter Sixteen

LIZITH

IT'S BEEN TWO MONTHS SINCE OUR TRIP TO ASPEN, AND THINGS HAVE BEEN UTTERLY blissful. Our home has come together slowly but beautifully, since I'm still working. Xander knows how much my work means to me, so after asking me only once if I'd like to quit and stay home during my pregnancy—my response being an emphatic no—he hasn't brought it up again. I'm not quite sure what I'll do after our little one arrives, but for right now, I'm content working while I'm pregnant.

I did, however, get a job at a different fertility clinic. Both Xander and I decided it would be best if I quit working for Dr. Curtis, and I made sure to gather all of my hidden cameras before my last day. As far as I knew, Jacqueline hadn't confronted Dr. Curtis about the surveillance footage Xander had access to. She hadn't come into the clinic since that last day, when I'd given her and Xander the fake results to his semen analysis.

She had, however, been threatening my keeper, and for that, I was not happy. But even as my rage built toward her, putting thoughts of painful revenge inside my head for upsetting my love, I tried to keep myself calm. I had to protect our baby growing within me, make sure nothing happened to our little miracle, so I couldn't let something as insignificant as that wretched woman give me undo stress.

At first, the threats were about him telling me the truth. He ignored the texts for a while, but finally, I told him to respond, letting her know I knew everything about our beginning and that we were still happily together. I figured if she didn't have that ammunition, then she would give up and sign the divorce papers Xander's lawyer had sent her.

But alas.

Her harassment continued, with promises of destroying my keeper's reputation. With her father being the dean of Xander's campus, those threats put fear inside my heart. His reputation meant everything to him. It's what fueled his vengeful plan toward Jacqueline and my father in the first place.

But then Xander calmed that fear by reminding me—and Jacqueline—of the surveillance footage of her fucking another man. And so things had been pretty quiet this past week.

I got off at noon today; the new clinic I work for is only open half a day on Fridays. It's been really nice, because it gives me a little more time to do housework before Xander gets home from teaching his Friday classes. He usually arrives around 5:00 p.m.

Glancing at the clock on the kitchen wall, I see it's 1:26 p.m. I need to run to the grocery store to pick up a couple of ingredients I forgot for dinner. Damn pregnancy brain. I swear, even when I write myself a list, I'll just end up forgetting it at home. With that thought, I shove my new list into my handbag, grab my keys from the hook on the wall in the foyer, put in the code to our security system Xander insisted on having installed, and hurry out the door, locking it behind me.

I'm a little winded as I walk the aisles of the grocery store. Only last week did I have to move into actual maternity jeans. I had nausea off and on during my first trimester. I could only keep down a couple different starchy foods for a while, and I haven't quite gotten all of my strength back yet.

I look into my shopping cart, mentally checking off everything on my list as I read each item. Seeing I've got everything I need to make our favorite baked potato soup for dinner, I make my way to the register.

Bending down to grab a king size package of Reese's Peanut Butter Cups—the very first craving I ever had with our little one, and something I continue to *need* every night for dessert—I glance over my shoulder, getting the distinct feeling someone is watching me. Figuring someone is just in line behind me, I'm surprised to discover no one is there.

Thinking nothing of it, I begin loading all of my items onto the conveyor belt, and when I'm finished, I wheel the cart to the end of the register for the teenager to fill after bagging all my groceries. I grab onto the side of the cash wrap, feeling a little dizzy for the tiny bit of exertion, a couple of spots showing up in my vision.

"You all right, ma'am?" the cashier asks worriedly.

"I'm fine." I smile. "It'll pass. Just a little dizzy. The joys of pregnancy."

"Oh, I totally remember that. Congratulations," she tells me, and I see her warm smile as my vision clears.

Nearby, I hear something glass shatter, making me jump. And then soon after, a woman's voice comes over the store's intercom. "Clean up at Register 6, please. Clean up at Register 6."

My eyes automatically look up, seeing I'm at Register 4, before the cashier steals my attention. "That'll be $46.21." And when I go to swipe my card, she reminds me, "Insert the chip, dear."

I chuckle. "Thanks. I still forget to do that after years of swiping."

"You're not the only one. I can't tell you how many times a day I say that," she says kindly. She rips off the receipt from her register and hands it to me. "You have a good evening. Get home and put your feet up. Make your hubby cook tonight. You deserve it."

I don't correct her about being married. Instead, I give her a grin and tell her to have a good night as well, pushing my cart toward the automatic doors. I quickly put everything into my trunk and roll my buggy into the closest cart return, getting that same weird feeling of being watched as I hurry back to my car. I glance out my window as I lock my doors the instant I sit down in the driver seat, but I see no one.

Maybe I'm just overly tired. I might do what the cashier suggested and just take a nap when I get back home. But I'll set an alarm to wake me up in time to cook Xander dinner. It's one of my many joys in life now, receiving his praise over every meal I cook for him in our amazing kitchen. As my belly grows rounder, Xander has grown softer, unwilling to dole out punishments. And for once, I don't mind. Having our baby inside me has turned on a light in me, casting out my love of the darkness and replacing shadowy corners with sunbeams. I work hard to earn the gifts and pleasure he spoils me with, the thought of purposely doing something wrong in order to earn a punishment never crossing my mind anymore. Maybe it's just instinct, wanting to protect our child. At first, I was worried Xander would grow bored with our sweet yet passionate lovemaking and would miss our more brutal fucking. But every time I see him watching me as I undress, I can tell our baby's light has filled him too.

Pulling up to the gate at the head of our neighborhood, I reach into my cup holder for my card. There's no one in the brick security hut at this time of day during the workweek, so I roll down my window and wave my card at the sensor. The gate slowly rolls open, letting me through. Hearing an engine rev behind me, I glance in my rearview mirror to see someone speed through before the gate closes. A common occurrence when there's no security guard on duty. Even I've done it a couple times before, in too much of a hurry to wait for the gate to close before I can scan my card to wait for it to roll back open once again.

My attention returns in front of me, and I slow down when I see there are children playing on the sidewalk up ahead. I give them a wide berth as they wave at me when I pass by. I still haven't made an effort to get to know anyone in the neighborhood, but everyone is always super friendly, waving at each other on their jogs, pleasant exchanges if you happen to be outside doing yard work at the same time. It might be nice to make some friends who are close by, especially with a baby on the way. I remember my mom being really close to some of our neighbors who also had kids. People she could rely on when she needed any kind of help, or even just to come over for nice conversations on our back porch while us children played in the yard. I have so many fond memories of looking up to find her laughing with one of her mom friends.

God, I miss that laugh.

Pulling into our driveway, I don't park in the garage, remembering Xander wants to start getting some of his tools organized in the new cabinets we had installed when he gets home from work today. I smile, remembering how excited he was when we went to the hardware store last weekend to pick out everything he wanted. He'd had a small toolkit when he lived in his condo, but now he could spread out and have any equipment his heart desires.

I gather the few bags out of my trunk, make my way up the front steps, and let myself into the house, punching in our code before the security system goes off. I kick the door closed, and take all of the bags into the kitchen. Glancing at the clock, I see it's now 3:07. Just enough time to put the groceries away and catch a decent nap before I need to wake up to fix dinner and have it ready by the time Xander gets home at five.

Heading into the foyer, I stop at the bottom of the staircase, shaking my head at the metal suit of armor standing guard at the steps. I bend down and pick up the staff that had fallen once again across the bottom stair, putting it back in place and making a mental note to remind Xander to use his new tools to fix it. But then I chuckle, knowing my pregnancy brain will probably forget yet again.

Holding onto the banister, I lumber up the stairs, making my way down the hallway until I finally collapse onto our king-sized bed. I don't even bother getting under the covers. My eyes close and I immediately fall asleep.

B-b-b-beep! B-b-b-beep! B-b-b-beep!

I feel around my body, my eyes still closed, trying to grab a hold of my phone to turn off the alarm. But I can't find it. Growling in frustration, I open my lids to peer around my still-made bed, my cell nowhere in sight. That's when I remember—I never set an alarm before I laid down. So what is that annoying sound?

It takes me only another moment to realize it's the security alarm going off. Since it's linked to our smoke detectors, my first thought is that I left something cooking in the kitchen that's now smoking up the first floor. But I remember I didn't start cooking when I got home from the grocery shopping. I came up here to take a nap instead. So what the hell is going on?

I roll out of bed, rubbing my eyes, and then walk out of the bedroom, heading down the hall toward the stairs. I've taken two steps down the staircase when I notice the light is on in the nursery. What the hell? I know for a fact I didn't leave the light on. My keeper taught me many things back when I wasn't neat and tidy, and one of those things was to always turn the lights off when leaving a room.

The incessant beeping continues, tugging half of me down the steps to go turn off the alarm, but the other half of me is being pulled toward my baby's room. Is Xander home early? Surely it can't be him allowing the alarm to continue to sound.

I slowly take the two steps back up onto the landing, rounding the banister to creep toward the nursery. Peeking inside, my heart plummets to my stomach.

"Ah, there's Sleeping Beauty."

Her voice sends a chill down my spine.

As she sits in my rocking chair, her long, thin legs crossed as she dangles a stiletto from her toes, Jacqueline takes a drag from her cigarette. She blows the smoke up toward the ceiling, and it swirls around the smoke detector before dissipating. My eye twitches seeing and smelling this vile woman defiling Xander's and my little one's room. How dare she?

Suddenly, I find my voice. "Get out of my home, Jacqueline."

She purses her red lips and then shakes her head. "No, I think I'll stay for a while. Have a little chat. Just us girls." She takes another pull from her cigarette. "You really should be more careful about locking your doors when you're home alone."

I step farther into the room until I can rest my back against the crib, continuing to face her head on. "What do you want? Why won't you leave us alone? You don't even love Xander," I ask, my voice steady, even though I'm trembling on the inside with a mix of rage and trepidation.

"Silly girl," she says, her eyes lowering to my stomach. My arms automatically cover it. "Who cares about love? Love doesn't get you anything. It's his power."

My brow furrows.

She looks delighted at my confusion, throwing her blonde head back and laughing. "Surely you don't think all the nice, expensive things Xander buys for you comes from a professor's salary? The fucker drives a Tesla for God's sake."

I never cared about anything but the man. My thoughts never wandered in the direction of Xander's money. He was a professor at a very prominent school. I knew public school teachers didn't make much, but I always figured a college professor made a decent amount. I know my dad did. We were always well off, and I know my mom's fertility treatments were super expensive, and they never blinked an eye at paying the cost. Of course, my dad never splurged on anything like a Tesla.

Her face grows bored while I stay silent, and she rolls her eyes. "He was a trust fund kid. His parents died when he was a teenager, and they left him their whole fortune. Millions of dollars. The stipulation was he had to earn a master's degree before the funds were transferred to him."

Her words don't have the effect on me I'm sure she was hoping for. Xander is a millionaire. Okay. So what? It's not like he was hiding it from me. He spoiled me every chance he got, buying me this incredible house, everything I could possibly want inside it, gave me gift after gift, filling the lit cubbies in our closet with designer handbags and expensive shoes.

No, her words don't make me angry at my keeper for not telling me about his trust fund. They make me even prouder to call Xander my love. The money would've been transferred long ago, and yet he still continued to teach at the college. He was passionate about his job, taught in a way that made his students passionate about his subject as well. No one ever had anything bad to say about Professor Stine's class, except for the fact he was very strict when it came to term papers. Everything else said about him was voiced with excitement and interest.

She must see her information doesn't have the outcome she was wanting, because her face morphs into a mask of pure rage. "Love doesn't get you anything!" she repeats in a screech. "I left Xander to be with your asshole father for love. But that fucker broke up with me, spouting some bullshit about it not being fair to me because he was still in love with your stupid dead mother!"

With those words, the piece of my heart my father had broken locks back into its proper place. But I only have a moment to enjoy the feeling. With my back to the crib, I have nowhere to go as she comes at me. And before I can even lift my arms from around my stomach to protect myself, she jerks the Scottie-shaped lamp off of the side table and out of the wall and brings it down on my head.

Everything goes black.

XANDER

I'm at the end of a lesson on fallopian tubes when my cell starts going off in my pocket. I have it on silent, but the vibration is long and continuous, unlike the patterns I have set for texts and phone calls.

Immediately, my heart thunders, knowing something is wrong as I pull my phone out and see it's the security system's app going off. As I slide my finger across the bottom to open it, nausea fills my gut as a clipart illustration of a flame fills the screen.

"You okay, Professor Stine?" a student calls from the theatre-style seating.

"Class dismissed," I murmur, rushing over to my desk, grabbing my briefcase, and running out the door.

My phone goes off again as I jump in my car, and I answer over the Bluetooth, "This is Stine."

"This is Garrett with Parkside Security. The smoke detector in the room you nicknamed 'Nursery' set off the alarm, sir. Is this a false alarm, or would you like us to call the fire department?" he asks.

Realizing it'll take me at least fifteen minutes to get home and not knowing what is going on, I give him the go-ahead. "Yes, send them," I reply, trying my best to keep calm as I speed down the highway.

"Fire department has been notified. They will be there within three minutes. Is there anyone currently in the home? We tried calling the other two phone numbers on the account, the home phone and one belonging to…" He drags out the word like he's searching for something. "Lizith Morrison. But neither call connected."

My hands grow clammy around my steering wheel. *Oh God. Where are you, little bird?*

"Lizith should be home. I saw her come home from the grocery store on our surveillance cameras about an hour ago." The cameras! God, I'm obviously not thinking clearly or I would've just looked to see if she's safe.

"All right, sir. Just drive safely. The fire department will be there shortly," Garrett says, but I ignore his suggestion, reaching for my cell and pulling up the surveillance camera app.

"Mother *fuck*!" I shout, absently hearing Garrett's voice fill my car as an all-out rage fills my very soul. "Contact the police. Lizith is being attacked! She's fucking pregnant!" I watch helplessly as the black-and-white image of Jacqueline smashing a lamp on my bird's head fills the screen. Like a man possessed, my foot slams the pedal to the floorboard, using my car for what it was designed to do. To get me somewhere *fast*.

I vaguely absorb Garrett informing me the police are on their way as I make it to our gated community. I come to a stop and roll down my window, when what I really feel like doing is smashing through the godforsaken wrought iron fence. I wave my card at the sensor, and then I pound my fists against the steering wheel as I watch the gate slide open at an agonizingly slow pace.

When it's barely wide enough to fit my car through, I stomp my foot down once again, and the Tesla shoots forward like a bullet. I pay no mind to the enraged people on the sidewalk, shaking their fists at me and yelling for me to slow down. The only thing I care about is getting to my little bird before Jacqueline hurts her even worse than she already has.

I don't even bother turning the car off as I screech into our driveway and bolt out, running as fast as I can up the steps and through the front door. I slam against the wall of the stairway in my panic to get to Lizith, hearing something behind me. Thinking Jac might be trying to get away, I turn slightly as I continue up the stairs two at a time, but when I look over my shoulder, no one is there. I urge myself to calm down so I'll be able to take care of Lizith when I get to her. I have to get to her, make sure she and our little one will be all right.

When I enter the nursery, Lizith is lying in a heap on the floor, her head surrounded by a halo of blood on the otherwise pristine white carpet. I fall to my knees at her side, a strangled sound coming out of my chest as I reach to feel for her pulse. Tears instantly spring to my eyes as I feel it there, strong and steady. And with all of my knowledge of human anatomy, I know head wounds bleed profusely, but can also look much worse than they actually are. With her pulse beating against my fingers, I know she'll be okay, and suddenly, nothing but the urge to kill consumes me.

I stand and turn toward the door, finding Jacqueline standing there with a knife from my kitchen. When she sees the look on my face, every muscle in my body tense, ready to attack, her face changes from her usual ugly sneer to pure panic as she takes off running toward the stairs.

I stalk after her, reaching to grab for her long, blond ponytail trailing out behind her, but I miss, following her down the stairs as she runs as fast as she can in her high heels.

And that's when it happens.

It's as if the whole thing plays out in slow motion.

She reaches the bottom step, ready to bolt toward the door just as the sound of sirens fills the foyer. But there, lying across the last stair, is the suit of armor's staff I had never taken the time to fix. Her foot catches it before she sees it there, and she falls forward with a scream.

The front door bursts open right as a red puddle starts to expand out from under Jacqueline's body.

"Freeze! Police!" an officer orders, raising his gun to where I stand on the staircase as his eyes move from Jac's sprawled figure on the floor up to me.

I lift my hands in surrender, keeping my voice calm. "I'm Xander Stine. This is my house. My security company called you because my woman was being attacked. She's upstairs, unconscious."

He keeps his gun aimed at me as I see an ambulance pull up in front of the house.

"Please, sir. I have surveillance cameras. You can watch the footage and see I did not touch this woman. She was the one attacking Lizith," I urge.

Three EMTs hurry through the front door, forcing the policeman to move to the side. When they stop at Jacqueline, getting ready to care for her, I stop them. "No! She's the assailant! My woman is upstairs unconscious from a head wound. You have to hurry. She's pregnant!"

The EMTs glance from me to the officer, and I breathe out a sigh of relief as two of the three men jog up the stairs at his nod. The other stays, kneeling down at Jacqueline's side before rolling her over.

The sight is absolutely horrifying. Blood gurgles from her mouth, the same color as she always wore on her lips like a sign of her future. From my distance, I see the knife sticking out of her chest as her bloody mouth opens and closes like a fish out of water. She reaches up toward the EMT, before her arm falls to the red-stained floor, her eyes never blinking again.

Chapter Seventeen

XANDER

I DON'T RECALL ANYTHING FROM THE PAST TWO HOURS, OTHER THAN WATCHING MY little bird fight the dawn. She won't open her pretty green eyes for me, still unconscious and far away, yet so close. The police let me ride in the ambulance, and then they took my statement as the doctor whisked my lady away from me. I growled through clenched teeth, having to let the cops and doctors separate us. But I gave them access to my security footage and the contact through the security company without a blink.

The only thing I am laser-focused on is being wrapped up in Lizith and nursing her back to health. My stomach ties in knots as I stare down at her angelic face lost in the slumber of her subconscious, and for the first time in a long time, the spiritual man inside me comes forth as I beg the gods, the heavens, and the universe, whoever the hell will listen, to heal my girl. I would even beg the devil and sell him my soul if he would breathe life back into my only reason for existing.

"Xander," a voice I wasn't expecting calls me from my lost thoughts, and I turn toward the door of Lizith's private room.

"Dennis. I'm glad you came." I stand and button my coat jacket. My hair is a disheveled mess, but I still try my best to look like a guardian over my broken angel. Even though I am anything but. I am a man gone, fucking lost, dying internally because the woman I would lay my life down for is fighting to come back to me. I bet in that mind of hers she is chasing me, trying to catch that fading light I stand in the center of. And I have faith in our love, and even more faith in my little bird. She wouldn't leave this earth before me. She'll likely leave it the day after me. Because she's my very blood, bones, and flesh. Our souls are intertwined, and not even death can part us.

Fight, little bird. Fight, and I will reward you with a lifetime of everything you've ever dreamed of and more.

"I will be honest, Stine. I'm surprised you called me at all." He looks over my shoulder, and I watch the tortured expression overtake him as he watches the most precious thing that graced this earth lie there helpless.

"I'll always do what my Lizith would want, and that means calling you and bringing you here." He nods in understanding. I'm nothing but clear—this was not for him; this is for her.

"My little girl," he whispers, walking around me to stand at her bedside.

I watch carefully, making sure he doesn't move her in the slightest. In my mind, any movement could hurt her. She looks so fragile.

"Baby," he exhales, his eyes welling with tears. He leans over and kisses her forehead, and I resume my seat at her side, taking her thin hand gently in mine. I bring her fingertips to my lips, kissing each one repeatedly. She still tastes like my bird, and I'm even more eager for her to wake.

Feel me, bird. Keep running to me, and I will lick your wounds after days and days of rest.

"I'm really sorry, baby. I let you down. My choices put you here."

I don't say anything, knowing he needs this. This wasn't all his fault; this was both of us. His poor choices and my lack of protection put my queen in this position. Lizith has been a martyr for us since the moment she fell under my spell, and I should have known one day that would put her in danger. I owe her all the riches in this world.

"Her mother must be so disappointed with me," he murmurs, and even though he is looking at her, I know he's speaking to us both. "When I met Jacqueline, I didn't fall in love with her. I was blinded by the idea of her. The hope that she could stop the pain I felt from losing Briana, but she never did. Within months, I knew she was never going to be able to fill that hole in me. No one will ever take her place."

Dennis peers up at me, and I nod knowingly. Lizith is a product of Briana; she has told me that multiple times since we fell in love. And I would never be able to replace Lizith. Not even in death, nor thereafter.

"She threatened to find whatever I loved most and destroy it in the palm of her hand. Turn it to ashes," he confesses.

I growl, her threat broad but hitting me right where my jugular is. I hate that woman.

"But with time, she forgot about me. Years went by, and I knew I could finally breathe. But then I found out about you two, and so did she. When she called me and told me she found a way to hurt me, I started planning. I watched her, followed her for days, and the moment I slipped up, she got to my daughter—my life."

"Mine," I growl, reclaiming my woman within seconds.

"Easy there. She was mine first, and I may be opening up to you, but I still don't think you're good enough for my little girl," he says with no trace of deception. He is serious.

"I'm not. No one is, but if she is going to settle, I will gladly be that placeholder."

"I love her, Xander. I know my presence has been nonexistent since her mother passed, but we all cope in our own ways. And unfortunately, I did it wrong, and it nearly cost me the only part of Briana I have left. Our daughter."

"Then be in her life," I mutter, not wanting to share her, but knowing she needs him. Lizith claims I am all she will ever need, but I know better what my little bird needs.

"I want to. I just didn't know how to before. I do now, seeing her like this."

"You should see what it is doing to me. It's dark and hollow in there." I don't look at him, but I feel his eyes burning into me as I place my hand over my heart.

"You love her, don't you?"

"What kind of foolish question is that? I don't just love her, Dennis. I fucking live and exist only for her. You will never understand the ties we have or the way she and I were born as two parts of a whole. We walked this earth with the same soul. Only in our meeting did I feel like I had finally lived." I hear his gulp and I don't even bat a lash. I will let everyone who crosses paths with Lizith know what she means to me, no matter the consequences.

"Don't let her go. Don't ruin my little girl, all right?" he pleas.

Finally, I tear my eyes from Lizith, and with no expression, I release with surety, "I already ruined her."

He blinks a couple times, and I swear I feel the shiver up his spine all the way from here.

"Xander? Daddy?"

Angels sing in my ear. I stand, and the chair goes flying back, but Lizith's hand stays in mine. Her soft green eyes open and close slowly, lazily, squinting in pain.

I push the button beside her bed and signal for the nurse. Grabbing her ice water from the side table, I bring it to her lips, nursing her already. My heart is in my throat. I can feel it pulsing through me at an uncharted rate. She takes a few little sips, smiling up at me as best she can in her barely conscious state.

"What happened? Did you stop her?" Her eyes suddenly grow wild, and I see fear etched in every part of her body. Her tense shoulders, her wide eyes, and her tight lips.

"She's dead. She tripped and impaled herself on the knife she was going to attack me with—"

"Stop," she interrupts. "I can't hear anymore. She's gone, and I can't bear to know the details. She could have killed me, Xander. She could have killed our child." She takes her IV-connected hand and rubs circles on her stomach. I watch her eyes fill with pools of tears.

"No, no, our little one is fine. They did a test earlier and said everything looked good."

"Yes, your little girl is doing just fine. Her heartbeat is as strong as ever," the doctor announces, and we both freeze, our eyes locked. I reach for her hand and bring it to my lips as a soft whimper leaves hers. Dennis takes her other hand and gives it a squeeze, and I sneak a glimpse at him to see him watching her adoringly.

"It's a girl?" Lizith asks, and the doctor rolls a seat up to the foot of her bed.

"Yes, she's a healthy baby girl."

"Xander!" she cries, pulling my hand to her lips this time and peppering it with soft kisses. I feel my chest puff out and my lion mane ruffle with pride. She's made me a father, and she is now worshipping me at my altar.

"You gave me a little girl, huh?"

She stops, and uncaring that others are in the room, she looks remorseful, her eyes dropping. "Is that not okay? Did you want a son, my keeper?"

I growl and lean in suddenly, everyone in the room fading away. "Do not say such terrible things, little bird. I want whatever you will give me. A little one just like you is more than enough. My perfect family." I brush my lips against hers, and she tries to pull me in deeper, but I stop, not wanting to share too much of our passion with others around us.

"Your mother would be so proud." Dennis steals her attention and I let him, reluctantly stepping away and freeing her hand from mine while I stand to speak to the doctor after he checks over the monitor and all her vitals.

I listen in closely though.

"I heard everything. I could hear you and Xander talking. Daddy, this wasn't your fault, and I may have been mad at you, but I understand the pain of losing what you love, losing your everything." I know she's referring to the day I left her.

"But I still shouldn't have let you down. You needed me after your mother died, and I grew selfish and let you walk around alone and broken. I was the worst father."

I do my best not to agree or say anything, letting them have this moment.

"I forgive you, Daddy. Just, please, be in my life more. I want our daughter to have a grandfather. I want her to know about Mom, and I can't do that if you aren't there sharing all the stories and giving her love. I don't have many people in my life, Daddy. It's just you and Xander, and I am okay with that, but I want her to have an abundance of love."

Oh, my little bird, so gentle and nurturing. I peer over my shoulder at her, and in that split second, I want to flip the roles, crawl to her on my hands and knees, and beg for her love and fucking affection.

"I will be there. We will mend what I broke, and I will be there." He makes this promise to her, and I store it away for a day when he may try to forget it, but I will never let him. You make a promise to my queen and I will see that it is followed through.

"All right, her vitals are normal. We want to keep watch on her for the next couple hours, and then we will release her later this afternoon. Do you have any questions?" Her doctor snaps me from my eavesdropping, and I shake my head. Giving him a curt nod and thank you, I shake his hand and let him leave.

"I would like to let our girl sleep. She needs her rest, Dennis."

He nods in agreement, giving her a soft kiss on the forehead and saying a gentle good-bye. "Call me when she is awake and doing better."

This whole sharing thing is going to be the death of me. "I will call you when she's had a couple days of rest, and then you can stop by and have dinner with us."

His eyes glint, hope sparking in them, and I almost tell him to not get too excited, but when I look to Lizith, I see the softest, most thankful smile she has ever worn on that delicate face, and I puff up my chest. I would give her anything.

"Thank you. Sounds good. Call me if you need anything, sweetie," he says to her one last time before disappearing and leaving me alone with her.

"You were so kind to him, Mr. Stine. What ever did I do to deserve such niceties?"

I grin and climb onto the small, stiff bed, and then I move her gently, making sure not to hurt her. "You just fought our biggest battle yet, and I think you deserve much more than me being kind to your father." I place her chin between my thumb and pointer finger and tilt her head up to me carefully. "Do you want to talk about it, my love?" I change the subject, and I watch terror and pain pass through her eyes.

"I never want to talk about her again. Not this day, not the past, and I certainly don't want her tainting our future," she whispers.

"Anything you want, baby. I will never utter her name again."

I leave out the part that, while trying to occupy myself, waiting for Lizith to gain consciousness again, I'd sent my lawyer an email asking what would happen with my filed divorce paperwork. I received a response stating Jacqueline's and my marriage ended upon her death. Instead, I keep that to myself and make my own plans. I will marry Lizith soon, while she is still pregnant with our daughter, growing our life and starting ours.

"Xander, we are going to make it out of this, right?" she asks, looking around.

"We always do. I promise to never let another day go by with pain or secrets or regrets. I will protect you from here on out, little bird. Trust in me." I kiss her lips softly. They are dry from her being unconscious and dehydrated, but instead of offering her more water, I wet her lips with my tongue. She moans into my mouth, and we spend minutes kissing with a softness I am growing to love. I want to be gentle with her when she is heavy with our child. I want to safeguard her and spoil her with things she has never had before me.

"I love you so much. Thank you for being pleased with a little girl." She blushes, her lip catching between her teeth.

I nearly take her on this bed right here when she does this. "I believe you know what it means when you get pregnant with a girl."

My smart girl smirks knowingly. "Why yes, my keeper. They say men with higher testosterone create girls." Her hand travels down my abs, and she plays with the belt around my expensive suit pants. I growl and feel her feeding my ego, and it starts to boil out of control.

"You know how to bring me to my knees. You know my weaknesses, little bird."

"The tables have turned, and that terrifies you." Lizith grows bold and grabs my cock over my slacks, and I react.

Grabbing her wrist with force, I lean in and bite the soft skin of her blushed cheek. "Do not mistake my gentleness for loss of power. I still own you."

She whimpers. "But the only difference now is I own you too. We own one another, Xander."

I smirk at her wit. "Yes, we do. Now shut those eyes, Lizith, because you need rest. Do not make me tell you twice."

"Yes, my love." She does as told, and for the next few hours, I hear those steady breaths and feel that strong heartbeat against my side where she is curled into me.

I love you, Lizith, and soon you will be tied to me.

Chapter Eighteen

LIZITH

IT'S BEEN TWO WEEKS SINCE THE ACCIDENT WITH THE WOMAN I WILL NEVER SPEAK of again. It's tragic the way she went, but her death is on her own hands, and I have to learn to accept that. I blamed myself for a few days, but Xander made it a personal mission to see that I stop that, and with just a few words from him, I did.

Learning to let go and let what is, be, I have come to feel safe. I don't worry about her and the threat she caused my keeper and my family. She is no longer here to hurt all the things that I love.

"Good morning, sweet baby," Xander whispers across the skin of my shoulder. I lay bare in the early morning light seeping in through the window of our bedroom, and I smile.

"Good morning, my love," I respond, warmth filling my stomach. I turn in his arms, and my bare chest grazes his. My heavens, he is still so beautiful. Day by day, he grows older and wiser and more handsome than the last. He will destroy me.

"What will this Saturday bring us?" I kiss his chest from one side of his collarbone to other, his abs bunching under my fingers as they dance over them.

"I have a lot of things to show you, but I can never start my day without the touch of my little bird."

"Do you want me, Xander?" I play coy and tease him.

"Every second. How does the lady of the house want it?"

"I want you to make love without inhibition. Touch me and say things to me that you wouldn't say before." I'm in the mood to mate with my keeper. I want to be ravished by him.

His cock is hard and he is already undressed. "I want you on top, pretty thing." He rubs my cheek with his thumb.

"Anything for you."

He roles to his back, placing his arms behind his head as he watches me. Letting me take control while he enjoys the show. He catches his lip between his teeth, and my core tightens in anticipation. I straddle him, sitting up on my knees, and still his cock graces my clit. Xander is a real man, his cock long and thick, smooth and rock-hard. I've never wanted anything else. His abs are tight, his chest peppered with hair only adding to my attraction to him.

"Pinch your little nipples, sweet thing." He doesn't move his hands from behind his head yet, and I swear this whole scenario is going to be my undoing. I follow his orders, squeaking as I pinch the tight buds. "Good girl, now slide down my cock, slowly, little bird. Don't get greedy."

I nod, my lips pouting naturally and my eyes round. I balance my hands on his chest and slowly glide myself down his shaft.

"Oh!" I cry, his cock still stretching me almost painfully, even after months of being with him again.

"Fuck. So tight and wet. Fucking hot. Your pussy is so greedy." I nod, biting my lip knowingly. He wants me to play the innocent girl who doesn't know what she's doing. I like to act the part, since it was who I was when he first had me. Nostalgia fills me.

"Fuck me, sweet girl. Move those sinful hips up and down. Come on, little bird, don't be shy." We roleplay.

"Oh, oh!" I scream when he sets me into motion by bucking up into me with what looks like little effort. Xander is so strong and experienced. He doesn't just fuck me; he owns me.

He still hasn't moved his hands and I take advantage, controlling the motions as I start to ride him. Leaning back, I grab onto his shins and glide my pussy up and down his girth as he watches our connection with fire in his eyes.

"Fuck, that's a slutty cunt. *My* slutty cunt."

I whimper like a wounded animal when he talks like that. I love when he speaks to me in such a crass manner, so much different than his usual collected and educated demeanor.

"Choke me," I beg, needing that dark and demanding touch. I ride him faster, my walls squeezing tighter with each thrust. My body doesn't want to let him go, my pussy just as eager as my heart.

"Easy, baby. Don't go so fast. We have all morning." He moves one hand from behind his head, the other one keeping its place. Bringing his hand to the side of my upper thigh, he slaps it then soothes it with a hard squeeze and massage.

I bear down on him. "Xander!" I scream, and he leaves my thigh, bringing two fingers to my mouth. Shoving them deep in my mouth, I suck on them as if it were his cock, and I keep a steady pace.

I moan around his fingers, aroused tears flooding my eyes. It feels too good. It's overwhelming.

"That's right. Take the pleasure, baby. Let those tears fall against your pretty tits. Let them slide down your growing stomach and then over that perfect pussy."

I groan around his fingers as my tears fall, hitting my chest as I start to ride him faster, chasing my orgasm, or better yet, running far away from it.

"There it is. I feel it coming, baby. Let go, relax your mind, and give your master what he wants."

He can feel my orgasm, and I know it because it's pumping through my veins, beating out of my chest, and consuming my entire body.

"I can't until you take control, keeper. I can't do it," I admit on a cry, and that's when it happens. Little bird gets what she's wanted all along.

Xander moves quickly, flipping us so he's on top, hovering over me, with his weight on his fists beside my head.

"Take it, baby. Fucking soak me." He pounds into me recklessly, yet still gentle enough to not hurt me or our baby. That turns me on even more. He is so kind, gentle, and aware of me. I treasure his honor and protection.

"I want us to come at the same time, baby. Please," I beg.

"Fuck, say it then." He pushes in harder, hitting my cervix.

"My keeper you are, and my keeper you will always be," I rush out, my eyes rolling back and my soul leaving my body. I come then, my juices leaving me like he asked and my soul floating above my body.

"Goddamn it," he roars, coming inside me, our orgasms becoming one. I don't know when mine stops, because his goes on and on. I become nearly paralyzed.

"Xander, what are you doing?" I ask when he starts up again, his cock hard inside me still.

"I'm not done with you, woman. Not even close, my love."

My heart dissolves into mush. Xander takes what he wants for the next three hours, and I nearly lose full function of my legs by the time he is done with me.

"Sparrow," he whispers into the quiet room, our lovemaking finally settled.

"What?" I ask, drawing patterns along his abs as I stay snuggled into his side.

"I want to name our little one Sparrow."

I smile wide, my dimples showing. I get the reference. "Because she is our baby bird," I whisper back.

"Yes. I keep seeing sparrows in my dreams, so I looked up the meaning and it felt right."

"What does it mean?" I lay my head on his chest and he plays with my long, dark locks.

"They say when you see sparrows in your dreams it's a sign of freedom. It represents joy and happiness. It marks the symbol of innocence. Our daughter was the start of us. If you didn't take it upon yourself to create her, we wouldn't have *us*."

I feel my heart bloom in my chest. How in the world could a man so dangerous and dark be so kind and warm and already a perfect father?

"Xander—"

"You did this. You gave me a life."

I turn a little so he can fully rub his calloused hand against my six-month belly. "We did this. Xander, I wouldn't have done such a thing if you didn't love me. I knew we were meant to be, because you made me feel it here." I touch his heart with my lips as my free hand touches mine.

"You know if this were a story, we would be the bad guys, the ones you should despise."

"I would be the bad guy, the dangerous one, the one to despise over and over again, in any realm. I am crazy, Xander, and I would go through great lengths to keep you." My eye twitches a little, my body heating at the thought of ever losing him again. I feel the inner psycho in me coming out to play.

"And I would be your keeper, awakening that dark side in you, over and over again."

"Promise me this," I start, moving from my laid-out position to straddling his stomach. I wrap my hand tightly around his neck and breathe heavily, needing to hear him say it. "Tell me that you'll never leave me, but that you'll always stay and keep me crazy."

His lip curl in a sinister grin, and he reaches up to mimic me. Grabbing my neck, he squeezes enough to solidify his stance, but not enough to cause me harm or leave a mark.

"You belong to me, little bird, my crazy girl. Now, don't play with fire. Tell me you're mine," he demands, tightening his grip.

A brief moment passes, and I smile wickedly as we sit with each other's hands at our throats. "I am always yours, Professor Stine. I'm a good little bird for my keeper."

He growls approvingly. "Good, now get on your knees and say sorry for ever thinking otherwise."

I don't say I word. I just follow his orders, climbing from him and dropping to my knees beside the bed. He sits up and places both his feet on each side of my knees.

"Sorry, my keeper," I tell him with sincerity. I scoot back a little and kiss the tops of his feet, and he rewards me with a soft petting. And just like that, my wings spread wide, the black feathers shiny and full, healed and beautiful.

"Stand up and let's go bathe. I have a surprise for you this evening. I need you clean and ready by five." With that, he stands and grabs his sweatpants from the floor, leading the way to the bathroom to start my bath. Instead of standing, I crawl proudly, satisfied and blissful inside.

Chapter Nineteen

XANDER

S HE IS READY, HER LONG, THICK DARK HAIR CURLED LIKE A STARLET FROM THE '50S, classic and stunning. Her makeup is soft and not dark, just the way I like it. She doesn't see me watching her from the entryway of our room as she sits at the vanity I made just right for her—a place for my beautiful creature to sit and admire her perfection.

"Close your eyes and do not open them."

She jumps a little when I surprise her with my presence. Lizith doesn't hesitate, not even to look back at me. I smile proudly. She is so good.

I walk to her in a few steady steps and cover her eyes with a long strip of white satin.

"Xander, why are you blindfolding me?" she asks, but it's pure curiosity that fills her voice, not fear.

"You will see, eager little thing. Now stand." I guide her, and she stands effortlessly, letting me help her and giving me her full trust. I remove the silk nightie she wears by dusting the thin straps off her shoulder. As she stands naked, I appreciate the view of her swollen belly; it's truly magnificent. My life growing me another. Beautiful.

I leave her standing and move to the closet to grab her white strapless bra. I don't need to ask for its location, because she keeps her bras in color-coordinated order in the top two drawers of our walk-in closet island. I hook it into place, and she stays quiet and content, trusting me fully.

"Good girl," I praise when I slide on her white lace panties.

She nods sweetly, a small smile gracing her face. Moving to the bed where the white dress bag lays, I unzip it, removing the beautiful handmade dress I designed for my lady. It's a strapless wedding dress, fitted tightly around the breasts, then loose and flowing to the ground from the bodice. The entire bottom half of the back is covered in white feathers, representing her nickname. Little bird. Innocent and pure.

"Arms up." I resume dressing her. She follows the order and I slip the dress on her.

"A new dress? Oh, I bet it's beautiful," she comments, as I zip it up. It fits her perfectly. I stand back and admire the vision. Lizith is a work of art. I swear there is a light haloing her entire frame, and I grasp my chest, trying to keep my heart from stopping.

She has no idea she's wearing the dress I will marry her in. She thinks it's just another dress for another day. I buy her dresses often, but never one so elegant and beautiful. But it is not the ensemble that makes her shine; it is all her. No other woman could make this dress look as stunning as Lizith does.

"Let's go, my love." I pick her up then, carrying her bridal-style from our bedroom suite. I go carefully down the stairs and then out the front door. There is a car waiting for us, and I slide her inside, climbing in after and shutting us in.

"I can't wait to see the dress and where you are taking me, my love." She doesn't ask where we are going, once again trusting me and just happy to be going anywhere with me.

Little does she know, she is officially going to start her life with me. She and I will finally be whole. My wife, my love, my little bird.

"You will be pleased. I promise." I kiss the tip of her exposed shoulder, watching goose bumps overtake her skin.

"I know I will, because I am with you, my keeper," she responds, leaning into me. Her hands touch the feathers on the dress and she smiles, whispering between us, "Feathers for me."

"They match your wings, little bird," I respond, kissing the tip of her nose then her lips.

"You spoil me," she giggles.

"Forever."

We fall silent as we drive farther out of town and closer to the farm. Today, I will marry Lizith under a willow tree.

We pull up and she smirks, staying reserved yet giddy.

"We're here." I move to exit the car, my driver opening the door. I help her out and once again carry her to where the pastor is standing. My last surprise pulls up, Dennis and another man, who I paid to make the end of our vows even more special. "Ready, beautiful?"

She nods eagerly, and I slowly untie the satin and release it from her eyes. She blinks a few times and adjusts to the setting sunlight. The sky is a mixture of oranges and purples, and still, she shines vibrantly as if it were the middle of the day. She is the sun.

When she looks me over and then notices her father approaching, I watch the knowing light in her eyes ignite as she peers down at her dress.

"Oh my…. Xander, I…." she stutters, unable to complete her sentence.

"Let's make this unbreakable. Give me yourself completely, Lizith, and be my wife." I pull her into me tightly, without space between us, her bump pushing into me and giving me comfort.

"I want nothing more than to be your wife." She leans up and kisses me under my jaw. Her father comes to stand next to her, and she reaches out to grab his hand. He brings her knuckles to his lips and gives it a soft kiss.

"You look beautiful, my sweet girl," he tells her, and Lizith's eyes tear up. I hurry to catch the one that gets away, bringing it to my lips to kiss it off the tip of my thumb. Her father and her share a short moment, and then her attention falls back on me.

"Go ahead." I don't look at the pastor as I signal his beginning, my eyes staying glued to my life. The entire time he speaks, she and I share gazes filled with love. It's nearly too much for me. I have never felt emotions this strong, a connection so deep, and I don't want to ever lose this feeling. Ever.

"Lizith, you can share your vows first, per Xander's request," the pastor says.

"Xander, I don't have anything prepared, or course, which is fine. Because I don't need time or preparation to convey my love and promises to you. I feel them every day, every hour, every minute. I fell deeply in love with you before I even heard you speak a word. My eyes met yours all those years ago, and I felt myself come alive. I felt a purpose. I felt my soul awakening inside me. You were the first man I loved, the first man I would do anything for, and I want you and only you to be my last. I give you all of me. I am yours to keep forever, Xander, and I would steal every single part of you in order to keep you."

"Baby." I lose it. I cry, feeling every emotion. I cry because I'm at her mercy.

"Little bird, you are no longer Lizith Morrison. You are Lizith Stine. You are now mine to protect and hold and love. I cherish the very ground you walk on, and I live for all the crazy in you that calls to me like a siren. I belong in your soul, as you belong in mine." I have to stop, because I can't control the immense amount of love I have for her. I've tapped into a side of me I never knew existed.

"Hey, it's okay. Look at me." She wipes my tears and pulls me through, leaving her hand on my cheek. I rub my lips together and clench my jaw, reigning myself in. Once I am there, she nods and encourages me to continue.

"I only breathe because you walk this earth. I only live because your existence keeps my heart beating. Without you, I would be a broken man. You are my very purpose on this earth, Lizith, and the life hereafter, I plan to make sure you are my purpose there too. I love you, my sweet, perfect little thing." I squeeze her small, delicate frame closer to me once more and drop my forehead to hers.

Our tears fall and collect on the fabric of her dress covering her baby bump.

"And you, little Sparrow. You are the product of our love. You are the solidification of us. You are the concrete foundation and tangible proof of our two souls being one." I back away a little and kiss her stomach, praising my daughter who I already love so deeply. Lizith gave me the one thing I wanted in life and then some. She gave me a child and her unconditional, devoted love.

The pastor announces us man and wife, and I kiss her with gusto. I give her everything in me. Our lips touch, our tongues grazing one another, our tastes mixing and igniting a fire. We are one. We are forever.

The man with her father opens his box when we part, and three sparrows release and fly above us. Lizith smiles wide and her tears trail over her rounded cheeks, her happiness so apparent it touches me, and I grin adoringly at her.

"A sparrow represents our freedom. We are free to be nothing but each other's, Lizith Stine." As I pull her into me, she smiles up at me wickedly.

"All because I stole you."

"No, all because you found me." I place my hand on her stomach and her lips against mine, and I take a mental snapshot of this moment to keep for all of time.

Two darks souls, twisted and alike, somehow created something innocent and haloed in light. Lizith and I were fated, created by the dark and not the light. We were the things you run from in the shadows. I am hers and she is mine, never to part and always intertwined. She stole me like I stole her soul, and we will never give each other back.

The End

Breaking Without You

CARRIE ANN RYAN

Praise for Carrie Ann Ryan....

"Count on Carrie Ann Ryan for emotional, sexy, character driven stories that capture your heart!"—Carly Phillips, *NY Times* bestselling author

"Carrie Ann Ryan's romances are my newest addiction! The emotion in her books captures me from the very beginning. The hope and healing hold me close until the end. These love stories will simply sweep you away."—*NYT* Bestselling Author Devney Perry

"Carrie Ann Ryan writes the perfect balance of sweet and heat ensuring every story feeds the soul." —Audrey Carlan, #1 *New York Times* Bestselling Author

"Carrie Ann Ryan never fails to draw readers in with passion, raw sensuality, and characters that pop off the page. Any book by Carrie Ann is an absolute treat."—*New York Times* Bestselling Author J. Kenner

"Carrie Ann Ryan knows how to pull your heartstrings and make your pulse pound! Her wonderful Redwood Pack series will draw you in and keep you reading long into the night. I can't wait to see what comes next with the new generation, the Talons. Keep them coming, Carrie Ann!"—Lara Adrian, *New York Times* bestselling author of CRAVE THE NIGHT

"With snarky humor, sizzling love scenes, and brilliant, imaginative worldbuilding, The Dante's Circle series reads as if Carrie Ann Ryan peeked at my personal wish list!"—*NYT* Bestselling Author, Larissa Ione

"Carrie Ann Ryan writes sexy shifters in a world full of passionate happily-ever-afters."— *New York Times* Bestselling Author Vivian Arend

"Carrie Ann's books are sexy with characters you can't help but love from page one. They are heat and heart blended to perfection."—*New York Times* Bestselling Author Jayne Rylon

Carrie Ann Ryan's books are wickedly funny and deliciously hot, with plenty of twists to keep you guessing. They'll keep you up all night!"—*USA Today* Bestselling Author Cari Quinn

"Once again, Carrie Ann Ryan knocks the Dante's Circle series out of the park. The queen of hot, sexy, enthralling paranormal romance, Carrie Ann is an author not to miss!"—*New York Times* bestselling Author Marie Harte

To those who were left behind.
Like me.
Like my family.
Like so many others.

Breaking Without You

From *NYT* bestselling author Carrie Ann Ryan, comes a brand new series where second chances don't come often, and overcoming an unexpected loss means breaking everything you knew.

Violet Knight fell for Cameron at the wrong time. And when he left, she thought her life was over. But then, after the worst happened, she truly understood what that phrase meant. Now, he's not ready for a second chance, and she's not offering one. Though given that their families have been forced together after losing one of their own, she knows there's no turning back. Not this time. Not again. Not when it comes to Cameron.

Cameron Connolly never wanted to hurt Violet, but there were reasons he had to leave all those years ago—not that she'd believe him if he told her what they were. He not only left her, he also left his foster brothers. Honestly, Cam didn't want to come back to Denver to help run his father's failing brewery. But when it comes to his brothers, he knows he'll find a way to make it work. Perhaps he'll even earn Violet's forgiveness and face the connection they both thought long forgotten in the process. Because he wanted her then, but now he knows he needs her. He just hope she needs me.

Author's Note

I've suffered from depression and anxiety for over half of my life, perhaps longer at this point. I'm a survivor like many of my readers and friends. I lost two close friends to depression when they took their own lives. So, I have been on both ends of the pain that comes from this disease.

The Fractured Connections series is what happens after you lose someone. I've had the idea for this series for a couple of years now, but after I lost my husband suddenly to a brain bleed, I *needed* to write about what happened after. What happens when you have to live on without those you love.

Allison, a character you will not meet but who is on each page by just her memory, lost her battle with depression and anxiety. She was a fantastic person, one who smiled and held parties, who lifted up her friends and always had a joke for those who needed it.

Her suicide is not on-page, is not detailed, and is not glorified. I talked to other survivors, had them read this book as well as help me with certain scenes before I even wrote a word. But there still could be some difficult topics for some.

If you need help, please reach out to someone. We do not need to suffer in silence. We do not need to suffer alone.

Prologue

I'LL ALWAYS REMEMBER.

They say that some points in time will stay with you no matter what happens. But they also say that you can ignore those times, that you can bury them and move on.

Those people don't know anything.

Because I'll always remember.

Of all the people who could have walked through that door, of the numerous individuals who had keys to that home, it had been me.

I was the one to see.

I was the one to find her.

And I'll always remember.

Because you never forget when you see the end.

Even when it's not yours.

Chapter One

VIOLET

I T DIDN'T SEEM RIGHT THAT THE SUN WAS SHINING, AND THAT BIRDS WERE CHIRPING in the air. It didn't seem appropriate that the sky was free of clouds, or that the world seemed to scream of beauty and peace.

I didn't find it fitting at all.

Because I was outside this afternoon instead of working or being with my family. I was watching strangers lower my best friend into the ground.

My best friend wasn't supposed to be dead. We weren't even thirty yet. No, *I* wasn't even thirty yet. She would never reach it.

I watched as they lowered the casket inch by inch—ashes to ashes, dust to dust, as the saying goes. I watched it all and didn't shed a tear. I'd done my crying. I had lost so many tears, so much of myself with each crying jag and hiccupping sob.

I couldn't cry just then.

I was surrounded by my family, my friends, Allison's family, and everyone who had known my best friend throughout her life.

She had been such a joy, such a bright spot in this sometimes-dark world. She'd made me laugh, made me smile. And she had done so for countless others, as well. She was the happiness we all craved.

But all of it was a lie.

I knew that now. I'd discovered that the Allison I thought I knew hadn't been the Allison she'd hidden deep inside.

That shamed me. It made me want to leave, made me want to throw myself to the ground and curl up into a ball. It made me want to switch between pitching a fit and just weeping and praying that something could be changed.

It made me angry, it made me sad, but mostly…*mostly*, I just felt ashamed.

Because Allison was lying in that casket, wearing a blue dress that made her pretty blue eyes stand out.

No, that wasn't right either. Because Allison's pretty blue eyes were closed, and they wouldn't be looking at anything anymore. No more searching for the next best thing, no more looking for anything.

Allison's parents had decided not to do organ donation, even though I knew that Allison had wanted to do it. She hadn't put it on her driver's license, though, and since we were not old enough in our minds to finish our wills, there hadn't been instructions for burying my best friend.

I was going to make a will as soon as I could. Because I did not want my friends mourning for me while wondering what I had wanted, and then watching it slip through their fingers when they realized that my parents were the ones in control.

Allison hadn't been married, hadn't had a power of attorney.

When she died, her parents had been the ones to make all the decisions, and that should have been fine. But I knew Allison—at least I thought I had. And so had my sister, Sienna, and our other best friend, Harmony.

The three of us thought we knew what Allison would have wanted.

We figured she would have wanted to be cremated, her ashes scattered to the wind in the different places that we had known and loved together. That was something I wanted, as well. I vividly remembered my conversation with Allison about it one night when we all got a little too drunk and started talking about death. It was something that a lot of people talked about, at least that's what I thought. It was part of everyone's future—the end, the idea that you wouldn't be around to make your own plans unless you wrote them down ahead of time.

But I didn't think that any of us had written them down. Well…maybe Harmony. Harmony had been through her own heartbreak. She probably had a full list of what she wanted when her end came.

But now, I was going to make sure that I had my list. Because Allison had not been cremated. Her organs had not been donated. She was going into a hole in the earth, and her parents had every right to make that decision.

I wasn't going to hold onto any bitterness when it came to that. I had enough for everything else that had happened. I didn't want to hold onto that and only remember watching my best friend being lowered into the ground and the darkness that came with that.

Hell, I didn't want to remember any of this at all.

But it wasn't like I had a choice. This day would be in my memory until the day I died. Until somebody tossed my ashes to the wind.

I closed my eyes and held back a groan. *No, Violet, it will be before that, won't it?* Before ashes and dust. I honestly wasn't really thinking clearly.

I almost jumped when Sienna reached out and squeezed my hand. My little sister—not quite so little since we were both nearly thirty—leaned into me, resting her head on my shoulder.

We were almost the same height, but I was wearing taller heels, and that meant she could easily place her head on my shoulder. I wanted to turn around and just pull her into my arms, tell her that everything would be okay. And knowing Sienna, she wished she could do the same for me.

I tore my gaze away from the hole in the ground where Allison lay and would forever stay until she was no more, dust to dust and all of that. When I turned, my gaze met Harmony's where she stood stoically on the other side of Sienna.

Harmony had her dark red hair pulled back into a bun, and I didn't really understand why she had done that. She usually wore it down. All of us generally had our hair in long waves or straightened. The four of us had decided to see who could grow their hair the longest and the fastest. Harmony had won, but for some reason, her hair was back today.

Then I remembered.

It was how she had worn her hair at her husband's funeral.

She hadn't wanted to look the same as she had every day when she had known and loved her husband. She'd wanted to appear different than when he had seen her, the times when he had played with her hair with his fingers.

So, she had worn it back.

It seemed we each had a special way to wear our hair, our makeup, and ourselves for funerals.

I wasn't even thirty yet, but I had been to enough funerals for a lifetime.

I didn't want to go to any more.

I didn't want to be here at Allison's. She shouldn't be dead. She had been alive and healthy and whole just a few days ago. But now I knew that maybe she hadn't been. Perhaps she hadn't been healthy or whole at all.

Maybe that's why she'd ended her life at the age of twenty-seven. Just a year younger than me.

The four of us had been friends since high school, Sienna and I being close for far longer since we were sisters. We were all in the same two grades and became fast friends. We had even gone to the same college, and all stayed in Denver to retain our friendship.

I knew that not everybody had that ability. With the way everybody kept moving for their careers and the way the world seemed to become a smaller place, most people didn't have their childhood friends in their lives. But I was lucky. I had been able to keep my three best friends by my side throughout my pain—and theirs. We had grown together, lived together.

But now, there was only three.

We had lost our fourth.

And I didn't know what the next step was.

Whispers brought me out of my thoughts, and I tried not to feel selfish. I was so busy worrying about myself and how I was going to feel that I couldn't really think about the world without Allison in it.

Every single person around me had been connected to her.

My brother, Mace, was here, standing right behind me with his fiancée, Adrienne, at his side. He hadn't brought their little girl Daisy with them, as they hadn't known how she would react at a funeral, being so young. I understood that, though Daisy had known Allison.

I had been in the room when Mace explained to his daughter that Allison wouldn't be able to come back for another tea party. That she wasn't going to attend another Thanksgiving like she had the past couple of years.

I didn't cry as I remembered these things, although my eyes did burn.

Why couldn't I cry? I should be crying.

Sienna was crying. Harmony was crying. Adrienne was crying.

My mom was sniffling on Mace's other side, my dad putting his arm around her shoulders as he held her close. I had witnessed that as I turned to look before, but I knew he would still be there, comforting her.

My parents were sweet, amazing, and they had loved Allison like their own daughter.

And now, Allison wouldn't be coming home.

She wouldn't be doing anything.

Allison's parents stood on the other side of the casket, crying into their handkerchiefs. They were poised, prim, and a little separate from the rest of the world. They had been that way long before they heard that their daughter wasn't going to wake up again. I remembered going over to spend the night at Allison's house when we were in high school. Her parents were nice but very reserved. Though that didn't mean they were bad parents. They were wonderful, and Allison had loved them. I just didn't think they had known their daughter as well as maybe my parents knew me.

But, then again, I hadn't known Allison the way I probably should have either.

Maybe I would have seen it if I had. Maybe I would have been able to stop it. Or, maybe, I was being selfish again and just needed to stop and breathe.

Others began talking, and I knew we would soon be moving from the cemetery to the wake at Allison's parent's home. They had a large house that could hold everybody so we could eat, drink, and maybe laugh at some memories.

I didn't know if I could do any of that, though.

I had only been to one funeral before—Harmony's husband, Moyer.

I didn't even know if I remembered that as clearly as I should. And I never asked Harmony if she did. I always felt like I shouldn't. There were some things you just didn't talk about until the time was right. I just didn't know when that time would be.

My gaze traveled over the rest of the mourners, and then I sucked in a breath.

I should have known they would be here.

Of course, they would be here.

The Connolly brothers had known Allison almost as well as the Knight siblings and Harmony did. Even if they hadn't been in our lives for a few years, the Connolly brothers had been part of our crew when we were in college and were very much part of Allison's life back in high school.

I let out a shaky breath, willing the guys not to look up and meet my eyes. I knew I shouldn't study them, shouldn't look at them. But I hadn't seen them in so long, even though I knew they had moved back to Denver.

Everybody in our circle had known.

There was Brendon, the eldest, and the one in a neatly cut suit. I knew he grieved. He had been friends with Allison just like his brothers. But I didn't really know him all that well. I didn't know how he felt, but I was glad he was here just the same.

Because that meant Allison wasn't alone.

None of us were.

Next to Brendon stood Aiden, his hair a little messy, grief clear on his face.

I finally felt a tear fall and quickly wiped it away as Sienna squeezed my hand, letting out a sob of her own.

Aiden and Allison had been *the* couple in high school and into college. They had eventually broken up, not because they hated each other, but because they hadn't been right for each other. That was what Allison had always told me anyway, and I believed it. Aiden had moved on, maybe not to other women, but to other parts of his life. I knew he had gone to culinary school and was a chef somewhere now, but I hadn't really heard much about him since he and Allison broke up.

But now he was here, watching the first love of his life fade away into the darkness.

Another boy was standing on his other side, an older teenager. He had the look of the Connollys, but I had never seen him before.

After the Connollys' father had passed away, I hadn't known there were more foster brothers added to the family. The other three had been adopted in high school, though Aiden and his twin, Cameron, were biological brothers, as well. Maybe the boy I didn't recognize wasn't a brother at all. Perhaps he was just a friend. And maybe it was none of my business since I had no idea what they were all up to these days.

My gaze traveled to the right of the young man, and my jaw tightened.

The final brother.

Cameron. *That* Cameron.

The one that had broken my heart and walked away as if he hadn't known that he held it at all. He still looked as sexy as ever with his dark hair brushed back from his face and his beard just past scruff. Today, he wore a suit just like his brothers, but I had never known Cameron to live in one like Brendon did. Even Aiden wore suits more than Cameron.

Cameron was rough. Edgy. Dangerous.

He was a man that I hated, the first man I had ever loved, the first for a lot of things. And he was *here*. In my presence. I wasn't going to be selfish and make this all about me, but I hated that he was here. I didn't like that I had to see him today of all days.

But I would push that thought out of my head because today was not about me. It was all about Allison. Today was about my best friend.

I pulled my gaze away from the Connollys and focused on what came next. We made our way to the cars and then to Allison's parents' house. All the while, a drum beat behind my eyes started, telling me that a migraine was coming on. I quickly popped a pill and then chugged the water that Sienna handed over to me without asking. I knew that I would be incapacitated later, but maybe it was something I deserved.

I hadn't had a migraine in over two weeks, but this one was coming for me soon. That much I knew. Though with everything that had happened, I was surprised that it hadn't come on sooner.

It was going to hurt, but maybe I needed that pain.

We walked through the halls of the home that Allison had grown up in, the house we had all slept in a time or two. We had gotten ready for our junior prom here, although my sister had been in the grade below us and was only allowed to attend because she was going with a junior boy. Somehow, we had made it work so we could go to almost every dance together, even when we left Sienna behind in high school.

Today I walked through these halls again, looking at the photos of a young Allison on the walls.

My fingers traced the edge of one of the frames, and I let out a deep breath.

Everything was going to be okay. Because it had to be. Life would move on. It always did.

I just didn't want it to move on without my best friend.

I walked to where the food was, where everybody was gathered and talking. It wasn't that the whispers had gotten any louder, but maybe it was just that I was finally listening.

"*I heard she took pills,*" a voice said from far off in the distance.

"*Yes, then drowned herself in the bathtub,*" another voice said, equally as vicious but still almost sickly sweet.

"*You know, I heard the police found no note. They don't know how she did it. We don't know exactly how she did it. And nobody knows why. Maybe her friends do.*"

I ignored that last voice, or at least I tried to.

Then there was another.

"*You know, it does seem out of the blue. But maybe if we keep looking, we'll see what happened. I mean, no one just does this.*"

I swallowed hard and then took a few steps away. My hands were shaking, and I tried not to listen to any more of the murmurs.

Of course, there would be speculation. Of course, there would be whispers. Allison was bright and cheery and far more energetic than any of them or us.

Gossip had run rampant when Harmony's young husband died, but we had pulled through. We stood together as a team, the four of us, and made sure that Harmony knew that she was never alone.

And I was going to do the same thing now. So, I took a few steps towards Sienna and Harmony. The three of us grabbed hands, standing in a circle that was one shy of what it used to be. It was odd. I could actually feel the distance between us growing because there wasn't that fourth person in the circle, clasping hands as we always had.

The actual physical representation of what we were now hit me a little too hard, and I blinked quickly. I had only shed that single tear, and I knew I couldn't do any more.

Not with all the eyes watching me. Not with all the whispers.

Mace and Adrienne had gone home, not being able to stay for the wake because they still had to drive over an hour back to Daisy. My parents had gone as well, my father battling a cold. He would be fine, but I knew that the day had taken a lot out of him.

All of them would have stayed for me and Sienna and Harmony if we needed it.

But we had each other.

We had each other.

"They're all talking about it," Sienna murmured.

"Just ignore it. It's always best just to ignore it." Harmony's voice was a little shaky, but she held her chin high.

"I hate it. I just want it to go away. I just want to go sit up in Allison's old room and play a stupid board game like we used to." I closed my eyes, the headache starting to push its way into my brain. I knew it would likely transform into something more soon, the lights getting a little too bright, the tastes in my mouth going bitter.

"We need to get you home soon," Sienna said. "I can tell a migraine is coming on."

"Yes, it's going to suck. Let's just stay for Allison's parents for a little longer, see if there's anything we can do for them. Then, I'll go home and lick my wounds."

"I love you guys," Harmony said, bringing both Sienna and me in for a hug. So I leaned on my friend and held my sister close. This wasn't right. It wasn't supposed to be just the three of us. I mean, I knew that it would be eventually, but when we were older—far older when we were watching over our grandchildren, maybe even our great-grandchildren if things worked out.

We weren't supposed to be doing this at such a young age.

It wasn't fair.

But, as they say, life isn't fair.

Death shouldn't be either.

Allison's mom called out for Harmony, and she squeezed my hand before walking off to join the other woman. One of the caterers needed help with something, and Sienna charged in to assist, not even bothering to see if anyone else would offer to help. That was my sister. Always there.

That was my friends, we were always there for each other. Even if not all of us were here anymore.

The headache was coming on strong, and my hands had started to shake. I knew I needed to leave soon. The others would understand if I left, even if I had been the one to say that I needed to stay. Because I knew that I wouldn't be able to drive home soon if I didn't go now. So, I went over to the coats, slid mine on, and ignored more of the whispers as people tried to catch my eye. They wanted to talk to the girl who had found Allison.

I knew that much. But I had talked to the police, I had discussed things with Allison's parents. I had shared with my friends. I had talked to everybody about what I had seen, detailing it so much that I knew I could probably say the words by rote without even showing a single emotion.

Maybe that was for the best.

Because I didn't want to feel anything.

Didn't know if I really could.

So, as I turned away from the whispers and the knowing looks, I told myself that I needed to go home. Of course, just as I thought that, I slammed into a large chest.

A hard, *familiar* chest.

Of course.

"Violet," Cameron whispered, his voice rough, that low, deep growl that I remembered vividly.

"I—" I couldn't finish the sentence.

Because as soon as he wrapped his arms around me, the dam broke. Tears slid from my eyes, and I let out a low groan that I knew others might hear. Cameron surely did.

In response, he let out a low curse that vibrated through my body and held me close. And I broke.

The others might not be able to see me, but Cameron could. And, of all the people I could have broken in front of, of all the individuals that could have held me when I shattered into a thousand pieces, it just had to be him.

He was the one who was there for me when I fractured.

Of course, he was.

Chapter Two

CAMERON

I HAD EXPECTED SOME REACTION THE FIRST TIME I TRULY SAW VIOLET AT THE FUNERAL, the first time that I spoke to her in what seemed like forever. I didn't expect the reaction I got. My arms were around her, holding her close as she quietly wept against my chest. I hated when she cried. I'd hated it when we were younger, and I damned well sure hated it now.

It didn't matter that we were at a funeral and crying was sort of expected, I didn't like to see her with tears in her eyes. I sure as hell didn't like it when those tears seeped through the shirt of my suit. It all felt too real, and I didn't want to feel anything real just then.

"Come with me," I whispered, pulling her towards the other end of the hallway.

There was nobody near, but I knew that other people could probably hear. Violet was being pretty quiet, and I was doing my best to do the same, but some people probably knew that she was crying—on my chest. And the fact that they were already gossiping about numerous other things having to do with Allison meant that they would easily add something else to talk about.

When people were hurting, when they were at a loss for what to do, they sometimes just talked. I understood that. Didn't mean I liked it.

I tugged Violet, lightly so she wouldn't think I was manhandling her, and she thankfully started to move. Of course, if needed, I probably would've forcefully hustled her into another room just so she could breathe. Yes, I was an asshole, but it was for good reason.

At least that's what I told myself sometimes.

"You can let it all out. I'm here." I knew it was the wrong thing to say as soon as I said it. She froze in my arms, so I closed the door behind us and gave her some space. She took a step back, blinking wildly.

Her mascara and eyeliner had run down her cheeks, her nose was red, her face was splotchy. Violet had never been a pretty crier. That was something we both knew. Not that what I thought about her really meant anything anymore. After all, I had left. It didn't matter that I'd had a good reason. I took off without a fucking word. So, I probably deserved the anger in her eyes now, and the fact that her hands were fisted by her sides. I probably deserved all of that and more.

If her brother were here, Mace probably would've kicked my ass. Not only because of what I did in the past but because she'd been crying in my arms. Mace would've likely thought it was my fault.

Because it was always my fault, it seemed. Though I deserved that.

"I…I didn't realize you were right there. I'm sorry for bumping into you. Thanks for getting me out of view of everyone else." Her voice was cold, even though there was a bit of scratchiness to it that told me her crying was far from over.

"I just happened to be the guy you ran into. Is there anything I can do?" She shook her head and wiped her face, looking as put-together and sexy as she always did. Damn sexy. She had been stunning and gorgeous when we were younger. Now, she was a fucking bombshell. It was really hard to remember that we were no longer a couple. And we wouldn't ever be again. That was my fault, though. I knew that.

Violet shook her head and pinched the bridge of her nose. It looked as if she might have a headache, but I couldn't be sure. "I made a scene. I hate making scenes."

"You didn't make a scene."

She rolled her eyes, finally looking more like herself than the red-eyed, crying girl that she had been just moments before. "Of course, I did. They all heard. They've been talking shit about Allison already. And probably about me, too. But I'm done. I need to go. Thank you for being there. Of course, it was you who was there. Of course, it had to be you, Cameron."

I didn't know why, but as soon as she said my name, I straightened, swallowing hard. She'd said my name countless ways before, sometimes in anger, sometimes in lust, sometimes just with happiness.

But, hearing it right then, I knew that I had missed it. Oh, I had known long before this, but with Violet right in front of me, it was easy to remember what life was like with her in it.

And that was a damned shame because, from the look in her eyes, this was as close as we would ever get. But that's all I wanted anyway. I had enough going on around me. I didn't need to deal with Violet Knight and everything that we had dealt with in the past.

"Do you need me to find your sister?"

"I'm fine. Just fine. Go back to your brothers. Go back to your brewery. Just go back to the life that you so desperately craved. Because you're not in mine, Cameron. I hope you remember that."

And then she walked out, slamming the door behind her. Okay, it wasn't quite a slam because she obviously didn't want to make a scene, but it was close. My head hurt. I was such a damned idiot. But I always had been, so there was nothing new about that.

I followed Violet out of the room, wincing when I realized that we'd actually gone into the guest bedroom where people would have gotten the wrong idea if they'd seen us. Because they always jumped to conclusions when it came to us. Really, everything about me. Nobody trusted the Connolly brothers. They never had. And they probably never would. It didn't matter that all of us had our own businesses, or at least we had at one point. It didn't matter that we had all made something of ourselves and weren't the same kids and teenagers we were when we first moved into the area.

No, back then, we were just three kids who had been forced into a new family. We were just kids from the wrong side of the tracks. And it didn't matter that most of us had money now, we were still trying to figure out how to leave a legacy that wasn't ours to give.

And now I was thinking way too hard about something that really had nothing to do with me anymore.

Because while I might be back in Denver, it didn't mean I'd be back forever.

Well, maybe I would be. I didn't really know, and that was probably why I had a headache. That and the fact that I had just watched a girl I'd known, one that had fallen in love with my twin brother back in high school, being lowered into the ground. She was dead, and I didn't even remember the last thing I'd said to her. It wasn't like she and I were friends, at least not recently. We hadn't really seen each other at all since I walked out of Violet's life—and out of my brothers' lives for that matter.

I'd seen Allison once or twice, maybe at the grocery store or the bar. But we hadn't really spoken. I hadn't been her friend over the past few years. But she hadn't been mine either.

I didn't know why I felt shame crawling up my neck at that or when I thought about the fact that I hadn't really thought about Allison much at all since I left. I had enough crap to deal with. I also had much more on my mind than I once had.

My brothers were waiting by the door for me, giving me odd looks. When Aiden handed my coat to me, I shoved it on. We said our goodbyes and paid our respects to Allison's family before jumping into Brendon's SUV.

Brendon had driven because he was more of a control freak than the rest of us. Not that that was saying much since we were all a bit controlling. It just hadn't made sense to take more than one car when we were all coming from and going back to the same place.

Aiden sat in front with Brendon, not even looking at me. My own twin brother, my flesh and blood, not even giving a damn. Maybe he cared too much, and it hurt to look. It was hard to confront a person that was your mirror-image and yet not know them at all.

We'd been close as hell when we were really young. And then we'd been pulled apart because the system hadn't worked well enough to get both of us in one place. I hadn't seen my twin for years, hadn't known if he was okay, hadn't even been able to write.

It wasn't as if they gave foster kids the addresses of where their relatives went. It didn't matter that Aiden and I were twins, they'd split us up anyway.

It wasn't until Jack and Rose Connolly came into our lives that Aiden had come back into mine. Jack and Rose, yes, just like the couple from *Titanic*. They had adopted three boys all at once. We'd started off as fosters, but then we'd taken their name. Brendon was the oldest, though not by much. And then came me, and then Aiden. I remembered joking that I was the older twin, therefore, the wisest one.

Yet I was the one who'd made the stupidest mistakes when we were younger, so maybe Aiden was the wise one.

We were brothers, the three fosters of the Connollys who'd become the three Connolly brothers.

We'd been everything to each other, and then Rose passed away, and things didn't seem as important anymore. Rose died, and some part of Jack faded with her. She was the only mother I'd ever known—in reality anyway. Oh, I remembered my birth mother, had seen her more than a few times, even after the adoption. But she didn't have custody of us, had lost it because she preferred the needle or whatever she could stuff up her nose to the two twin boys that she had given birth to. Oh, yeah, Aiden and I came from great stock, products of a junkie and some John who knocked her up. It was something the kids on the playground always liked to make fun of us for.

Snapping myself back to the present, I realized that I wasn't alone in the backseat. It wasn't something I could ignore, at least not over the past seven years. Or rather, *he* wasn't something I could ignore.

Dillon sat beside me, scowling at his phone as he played some game where he tried to milk cows or something. Yes, the eighteen-year-old who thought he was a master guitar player and who was now currently still staying with me because of obstacles out of my control was playing a farm game. Yes, it was one that I played when I was bored, but I wasn't going to really think about that right then.

"Did you finish your chores?" I asked, nudging Dillon with my arm.

I didn't fail to notice that Aiden stiffened in his seat, and Brendon's hand tightened on the wheel.

Dillon was the elephant in the room, the eighteen-year-old that hadn't been a surprise to me but was a surprise to them.

Yes, I was an asshole.

But when your drug-addled mother comes to you and says she needs your help—and you go—you have to deal with the consequences. Aiden hadn't gone. He hadn't wanted anything to do with our birth mother. And I understood that. Even if I was pissed off at him and hated myself because I hated *him* sometimes, I got it. Our mother was a bitch, a liar, and a thief. I didn't ever want to call her a whore, but others did.

She had never been a good person. She had beat us, used us, and probably would have tried to sell us one day if she could.

But she had needed help with another son.

Dillon.

My brother. *Aiden's* brother.

And while not by blood, maybe Brendon's brother, too.

And so, the elephant in the room, the boy who thought he was a man, currently sitting beside me. He looked up and nodded, even as his eyes narrowed, and he glared.

He was such a little asshole sometimes, but then again, so was I. And I didn't have the excuse of being a teenager.

"I did. I wanted to get it done before we went. I didn't know Allison, but she seemed like a nice lady from what others said. I'm sorry she's gone."

And that was why I liked this kid. Maybe I even loved him, but I'd done a really good job of burying all of my emotions and feelings for the past seven years. But Dillon was good. Even if we'd both fucked up with the whole college thing.

I wasn't a dad, I'd never claimed to be, but I had failed when it came to Dillon. And he had failed himself, as well. The little shit had lied about planning for college, about submitting his applications and wanting to do everything himself.

Instead, he had decided to move to LA, even though we were on the outskirts of it anyway when we lived in California. No, Dillon wanted to be the next big rock star in the greatest rock band of his generation. Though it wasn't like I actually knew the names of current music groups anymore, so I couldn't even say where Dillon got his influences.

Then my kid brother's little friends had decided that they were going to college because their parents had actually forced them to do their applications. Maybe if I had done the same, Dillon wouldn't be forced to take a gap year. Or, perhaps, if Dillon hadn't been a little liar, he wouldn't be in the situation he was.

"Allison's a great woman," Aiden said, his voice gruff. Dillon met my gaze, and I gave him a slight nod. Aiden coughed. "*Was* a great woman."

Aiden didn't speak to Dillon often, and I didn't blame him for that.

When I went out to California to check on our mom, I'd found this kid—a boy who wasn't quite as little as I thought. An eleven-year-old full of temper and hatred. So, I moved there to try and help. I'd tried to get in contact with Aiden during that time, attempted to tell him that we had a brother.

But Aiden didn't accept a single call. Not for a year.

And I'd stopped trying.

Because I had chosen our mother over Aiden—at least that's how he saw it. So, I guess I deserved the fact that Aiden hated me.

But Dillon didn't deserve it. And so, the family drama that was the Connolly family was never-ending. Because Jack died too, damn it. Old Jack died and left the family business to us.

A failing brewery that brought the Connolly brothers back together.

And while Dillon might not be a Connolly, at least not in name and even though Jack and Rose had never met him, he was my brother. And I would just have to reconcile the fact that things were different now. And that I had no idea how to clean it up.

We pulled up behind the brewery, and I winced at the fact that there were still a few spots open. It was early evening, it should be the start to the rush. There should be more cars in the parking lot. When we walked in, I held back another curse. There sure as hell should be more people sitting and having a brew. It was right about the time of the evening that the early people would come in for their beers. At least that's how it'd always been for Jack and Rose.

But not anymore.

The place wasn't actually a brewery anymore, it was a bar. It'd used to run craft brews before craft beer was a thing and I came into the family. The bar, however, had kept the name and the label, still selling their microbrews as well as some crafts and domestics that were the mainstay of most bars.

The four of us went to the back, Dillon having already taken off his tie, Aiden and I pulling at ours. Corporate Brendon kept his on as if he'd been born in a suit. It was kind of funny considering that, as a kid, he'd never worn a suit and sometimes didn't even wear two shoes. But I knew that Brendon sure as hell had a lot of shoes now.

"So, what are we going to do now?" Brendon asked, sitting on one of the chairs in the private, back room.

Aiden flipped the chair around and sat in it backwards before speaking. "Well, if we're going to finally fucking talk, I guess we should try and fix this place. Because we can't let Jack and Rose's place go. The Connolly Brewery has always been part of this neighborhood. We're not going to lose it."

I narrowed my eyes. "You say the 'neighborhood' as if it isn't downtown Denver. Breweries come and go." I knew that better than my brothers did since I'd owned my own with a partner back in California.

"Shut the fuck up, Cameron."

Dillon's wide gaze moved from me to Aiden and then to Brendon before going back to his game. Dillon was here because I was his guardian. It didn't matter that the kid was eighteen now and didn't technically *need* a guardian. He lived with me, and I wasn't about to let him go home alone where I couldn't watch him. So, that meant Dillon was part of these family discussions. Because, damn it, Dillon was my family. I'd just have to figure out how to put all of the rest of it back together again.

"The bar is failing, it's in the red, and we're going to have to change that. I know the three of us moved back because Jack asked us to in the will, and so we're here, but it's been a few months now, and we haven't done anything. We'll have to start doing it. Cameron, I know that you sold your half of the brewery back in California to move out here, so what are you going to do now?"

"What I've been doing. Working behind the bar." I'd moved back after Jack's death, and I'd done my best to keep the bar running since. Then Brendon returned. It had taken him a little longer to wrap up everything with his personal life.

Aiden had just arrived, finally leaving the restaurant he so desperately craved to be a part of. I didn't know the story behind it and, damn it, I wished I did. Because that would mean Aiden was actually fucking talking to me.

"There needs to be some changes," Brendon said quietly. "We can't keep it open like this."

"Just shut up," I said, running my hand through my hair. "Just…not now. Not the day we buried Allison."

Aiden narrowed his eyes. "Really? You're going to be the one to bring her up?"

"Because you haven't yet. But I know it's on your mind. Let's just take today. We just need today."

"You're the one who said that when we lost Jack. You're the one who said we needed that day, needed some time. Well, enough time has passed." Brendon stood up, shaking his head. "And, you're right, I'll give you today. But, tomorrow? Tomorrow, we're going to figure out what the fuck we're doing. Because tomorrow might be the beginning of the end when it comes to this place. And I don't want that to happen. You may think I do because I wear a suit and I have a different job than you. But I love this place. It's our home. And we left that. We left Jack behind. So, now, we have to fix it."

Brendon stormed out, and Aiden left right on his tail. I looked over at Dillon, who was doing his best to just stare at his phone. There weren't any games on it this time. Just a blank screen.

"Let's go home."

"It's weird calling it *home*. We're not even out of boxes yet."

"You're right, kid. I guess we should fix that."

"I'm not a kid."

I shrugged. "Jack always called me 'kid.' Even when I was in college." I winced, but Dillon didn't say anything. I probably shouldn't bring up the college thing, but now that it was out there, I continued. "We'll get on that, too. We'll get on everything. I guess our time of mourning Jack and what we all had is over. Probably has been since we walked into the place. You know? We'll get it done. We have to."

And I knew we would.

I'd save the brewery.

I'd save Dillon.

As thoughts of Violet's wide eyes brimming with tears filled my mind, I hesitated. It wasn't my place to save her, but maybe if I weren't such an idiot, I could fix what I broke there, as well.

Maybe it was time. Maybe it was past time.

Chapter Three

People are the worst. But you're still my person
—*Allison in a text to Violet*

VIOLET

I LOVED MY JOB. I TRULY DID. BUT ON DAYS WHERE ALL I HAD WAS HEADACHES, FALSE starts, and the inability to focus, I didn't know if I actually liked it.

No, that wasn't really the case. I just didn't like my life at the moment. I didn't hate my job, I just really hated this day.

I was exhausted, mostly because I hadn't slept the night before and because it took so much extra energy to remain happy and appear whole these days. My brain still ached just thinking about Allison and everything that had come with that. My heart hurt, my body hurt…everything hurt just thinking about my best friend.

Coming home after crying on Cameron's shoulder, or rather his entire chest hadn't helped things. I came home after practically running from him and had fallen into my migraine spiral. I was used to them, and they came often. No amount of hormones or Botox or drugs could help my migraines. They were just a part of me and something that even my boss knew about. Thankfully, his wife suffered from debilitating migraines as well, so he understood, and we worked around my illness when it came to my job. I wasn't really sure how it would have worked if he weren't so accommodating. What wasn't helpful was the fact that not everybody understood my migraines, and some—mostly the woman who sometimes shared my lab bench—thought me being home and having extra time was because of something else.

She thought the fact that I sometimes needed to stay at home, trying not to throw up all day because I couldn't see straight, had to do with her. Yes, I came in and worked on weekends. I worked long hours when needed. I got my work done, no matter the cost or the time.

But Lynn *always* thought it was about her. After all, we had been friends for a few years before we ended up not being friends anymore. But it wasn't really my fault. She was currently married to my ex-husband and had been with him before he was my ex.

Yes, I had somehow become a cliché. I'd married someone who I thought was a decent guy, a man I thought I loved. And maybe I *did* love him. But he didn't love me the way he should. We were married for eight months. Eight freaking months where I'd thought I was doing okay. But everything had changed over a year ago. Everything fell apart.

Kent Broadway had cheated on me. I should have known a man named Kent would do something like that. I tried to go with the whole Superman/Clark Kent thing, but, every Kent in every book and TV show I'd ever seen or read other than Superman was an asshole. Maybe there were good Kents in the world, but not mine. I know I shouldn't call him *my Kent*. There was nothing *my* about that Kent.

So now, Kent and Lynn were together. Married. And good for them. Because I didn't have to think about him anymore. Ever.

Okay, I had to think about him every day I was at work because I was an environmental chemist and worked my ass off alongside another in the field. Lynn.

I had been the one to introduce Kent and Lynn, and they'd hit it off. I'd been so happy that my work friend and my husband were friendly. Because that didn't always work out. I really hadn't been friends with any of Kent's coworkers or their wives. We just hadn't meshed. But that was fine. You were allowed not to get along with everybody in your life. But, apparently, the two people I introduced had gotten along a little too well. And that made me a little sick. I hated the idea that I had to work alongside the woman who'd taken the man I didn't even love anymore. I wasn't even sure I ever truly loved Kent. And maybe that was on me. But, mostly, it was just the whole situation. It made me feel weird and like I was messing things up.

But I was getting used to it. Kent and Lynn had been married a month, and Lynn was finally back to work after her long honeymoon and vacation. The two of them had taken a three-week trip all over Europe. While there, she had posted all sorts of photos on social media, and even though she had unfriended me, our mutual coworkers were constantly commenting on the pictures. Therefore, I saw them. It wasn't like I tried to run away from it, but it was hard to pretend that I was okay. I really wasn't anymore. Everything was falling apart around me, and yet it had nothing to do with Lynn or Kent.

That was in the past. I had been divorced for a year now, and that really wasn't what was on my mind.

No, what was constantly on my mind was the fact that Allison was dead, and there was nothing I could do about it. And the fact that I had felt more of a connection with Cameron after I yelled at and cried on him than I had ever felt with Kent.

And what did that say about me?

How self-centered was I, that those were the two things on my mind? And not because of what they were, but because of how they revolved around me.

Why didn't I see that Allison needed help? Why couldn't I see that she was drowning?

Why couldn't I foresee that she wasn't going to be here anymore because of something inside of her? I hadn't seen any of that. What did that say about me?

No, it wasn't truly about me, but maybe I'd been selfish enough that I missed the warning signs. Or maybe there hadn't been any warning signs at all, and I was just reaching for answers to something I couldn't change.

And then, added to all of that, I was worried that Kent had cheated on me because it was my fault.

God, there was something truly wrong with me today if that was where my mind had gone.

Because it didn't matter that I'd had a connection with Cameron when we were younger. It didn't matter that I had loved him with all my heart. I had fallen out of love with him when he broke me into a million pieces. When he shattered me like glass against stone.

I was dust in the wind when it came to my relationship with Cameron. It didn't matter that he was still sexy as hell and had no right to be. It didn't matter that I still felt that little pulse inside my gut when he held me. It didn't matter at all.

Because I was not with him, and I was never going to *be* with him. He didn't fucking matter.

Yes, I had loved Kent. No, I wasn't in love with him, and yes, I had fallen *out* of love with him faster than I had with Cameron, but maybe that was for a reason. People loved others differently. Every relationship was different. Maybe I had the most the first time, so I wasn't going to hurt as much the second time. Or maybe I was just tired and needed to stop whining to myself. It was stupid.

I was feeling stupid.

"Violet, darling? Is everything okay?"

That set my teeth on edge. *Darling*. Lynn calling me darling. She hadn't called me that when we were just friends before she became a two-timing tramp.

Oh, God, why did I think that?

It didn't matter that she had cheated. It didn't matter that she had helped my husband commit adultery. I should not call her a tramp. Calling other women names was wrong.

And yet, I still hated her.

Even if I didn't want to. Even if I didn't really feel that deep of an emotion and was more just *blah* when it came to Lynn. I honestly didn't really feel anything about her. Maybe I should be more ragey. Or perhaps I was losing my freaking mind.

"What was that?"

I tried not to say her name, mostly because when I did, she gave me this sad, puppy-dog look like she was worried about me. Why should she be worried? She was the one who had to sleep with Kent for the rest of her life. She was the one who would have to go down on him because that's how he liked to orgasm. He never liked to come during intercourse.

Oh, God, why was I thinking about things like that? Bile rose in my mouth, and I tried to shake away the horrific thoughts. Maybe I needed to have sex again.

It had been over a year, after all. Maybe sex would help things. Or perhaps drinking. Wine would help. Yes, wine.

I didn't have a migraine, wine would definitely help.

"I just wanted to make sure that you were doing okay. You've been staring off into the distance rather than at your paperwork for a while. I did want to say that Kent and I are so sorry about your friend, Allison. The few times that we met her, she seemed so nice."

We. All of those we's. Kent had known Allison better than Lynn because I was married to the man. But as was the way with overlapping friendships, she had known Allison, as well. But they hadn't come to the funeral, and for that, I was grateful. Not because it had to be about me, but because I didn't want it to be about me. I hadn't wanted the additional whispers about the girl who had found Allison dealing with the fact that her ex-husband and his new wife were there.

It was all so exhausting—putting all these labels on everything. It just made me tired.

And it made me realize that I was once again staring off into the distance, and Lynn was giving me that sad, puppy-dog look that I hated.

"I'm just thinking, no worries about me."

"Well, if there's anything I can do, just know that I'm here." She squeezed my shoulder again and smiled at me. I ignored the touch.

I just nodded, giving her a smile. See? Everything was okay. Or it would be. I was a professional, and I got my work done, even if my brain sometimes decided to go off on a tangent. No, it wasn't easy working with the woman my ex-husband had married, but it wasn't the end of the world either. I had seen the equivalent of that. I had watched that end happen as they lowered Allison into the ground. Working with Lynn seemed like a small drop in the bucket.

That oddly calmed me.

So, I rolled my shoulders back and went back to looking at my data as Lynn walked back to her own paperwork, texting as she did. No doubt messaging Kent, but that was fine with me. I honestly didn't care.

Truly.

I was an environmental chemist who worked at the University of Colorado at Denver. I was listed as an associate professor on the tenure track, but I wasn't actually teaching this year. They'd dropped one of the classes that I normally taught, so now I just put in more hours in the lab. I worked under one of the tenured professors, but I had my own research team of grad students and undergrads that wanted to follow the grad-student track.

I really loved what I did, even if it stressed me out sometimes. Lynn worked under the same professor, but she was actually teaching two classes this year—one with the undergrads, and one of the small set of grad students we actually got at the university. We weren't the main University of Colorado campus, but we were growing bigger on the Auraria campus each year. As soon as they built the new science building and added more dorm rooms downtown, everything had changed just a little. It was far different than it was when I had gone here.

I hadn't actually decided to come back and work here until the position opened up and one of the professors that I'd had when I was an undergrad offered me the job.

I didn't make beaucoup money, but I didn't need to. I got to study the ways the city of Denver and its suburbs affected the environment. Because we were surrounded by mountains and lush greens, yet we were still in a desert period. I enjoyed going down to Cherry Creek and running samples, then going up into the mountains to take samples there. It just depended on what area of study I was focusing on for the semester. There was just so much to the way Colorado's environment impacted the city and vice versa. It made for a rich study.

It would be easier if I could actually get more funding, though.

I snorted, shaking my head. Since I wasn't teaching this semester, I was on a federal grant, which was actually harder to come by these days than it had ever been before. And with the way things were turning out, I was afraid that it would be impossible come next year. A lot of my friends were having to either work on new areas of study or get second jobs not focused on research.

Things were shifting dramatically, and I knew that I couldn't just keep my head down and focus on my work. Not entirely. I had to be aware that, one day, I might not be able to do the research I was doing, despite the fact that it was desperately needed with the way our environment and climate were changing.

But, right then, my focus had to be on the numbers in front of me. It was all about pH and other data for now.

The information I worked with today would help me tomorrow, and maybe help someone else a few years from now.

See? I loved what I did. Even if the lack of funding, the fact that I worked with my ex-husband's current wife, and my migraines that came out of nowhere, sometimes made me not want to work at all. But I really liked shoes, and I liked a roof over my head. And, occasionally, I actually liked a good meal that wasn't frozen or a can of green beans.

My stomach rumbled at that thought, and I snorted. Apparently, it was lunchtime, even though I should probably keep working. So, I noted the time and worked for another twenty minutes, making sure I stopped at a place I could come back to later. Then I locked up all my stuff and went down to the break room to eat my lunch. We were chemists, so it wasn't like I could just eat at my desk. My work area was surrounded by things I really didn't want my food near or vice versa. I really didn't want chemicals in my food as it was.

Then again, my brother was a tattoo artist, and I knew he didn't work while he was eating either. Yes, he may be able to have a drink when I couldn't, but he still didn't eat a sandwich with one hand as he tattooed someone with the other. The thought actually made me smile.

I sat in the break room, looking out the window towards the mountains. Today was a pretty clear day, and I was grateful for that. We'd had a few horrible fires during fire season, and the haze from that had been ridiculous. When the rain finally came, it had cast a pall over the Rockies so even though the smoke was finally gone, there were so many clouds it was hard to see the mountains at all. It wasn't until recently that I had been home one day as the sun was setting and I could see the sun from behind the mountains, turning them a dark purple. The effect was so vivid, I knew that I would actually be able to see the mountains the next day.

Now, I looked out at what I studied, what I loved. With my job, there were a few places that I could live, but this was the best for me. This was what called to me. This was my home. My parents lived here, and the rest of my family. Yes, Mace was about an hour south, but I saw him often. Even more so now that we were making sure we didn't lose touch.

I loved Denver. It was a part of me. I would never leave my friends or my family.

I looked down at my packaged salad and frowned.

Allison had left us. She had left, and I didn't know why.

It was the idea that I had to come to terms with that, which scared me more than it probably should.

I was a scientist. I needed answers. And there weren't going to be any of those for me. Not for any of us.

I let out a shuddering breath and wiped at a tear, grateful that there was no one else in the room. Sienna, Harmony, and I would have to go through Allison's things soon, something that her parents had asked us to do.

Although they had taken care of all the funeral arrangements and made decisions that I might not have agreed with at the time but understood, they were letting us deal with her apartment and her things. I wasn't sure that they would have been able to do it themselves. And, one day soon, I would be grateful for that. But right now, the idea of going through things with Harmony and Sienna hurt me. It was like a sharp, stabbing pain that ebbed to a constant, dull ache.

But I would do it because it's what Allison deserved. I missed her with every breath, but I couldn't bring her back just by missing her.

I couldn't do a lot of things.

For some reason, the memory of Cameron holding me when I broke filled my mind again.

I knew that I would be forever grateful that he had been there to keep me away from prying eyes, but I truly wished it hadn't been him.

Because he'd brought back all sorts of feelings.

So many memories and emotions that I shouldn't feel.

My life wasn't as complicated as I was making it seem, at least to myself. But right then, with everything going on, I sometimes wished I could just go back to the way things were in college. When there was laughter before there was heartbreak. Before there had been loss.

But there was no going back to that.

This was my life now.

And if losing Allison had taught me anything, it was that I would have to learn to live it. Even if it hurt.

Chapter Four

CAMERON

I worked at a bar, needed a damn drink, and wasn't going to get one anytime soon. I should be used to it by now though, because I didn't really get what I wanted often.

And that made me sound like a petulant child, but sitting here listening to my brothers who didn't really feel like brothers anymore, trying to change everything that had once brought us together didn't make me feel like I was winning.

But maybe there was no winning in this. Maybe there couldn't *be* any winning in this.

"There needs to be more changes, Cameron." Brendon paced the office floor, pinching the bridge of his nose. He had been sitting behind the desk at first, pouring over accounts and paperwork. The ledgers might be mostly electronic, but my brother had wanted to look at all of them in hard copy again so he could focus. That meant they appeared to be piled almost to the ceiling at this point. The fact that my brother was probably the best tech wiz out of all of us was a non sequitur. Brendon just needed something tactile when he was stressed.

I was also stressed out, and that meant *I* needed a damn drink. "I know we need to make changes, but that doesn't mean we have to change *everything*. Next, you'll want to take down that prop from *Titanic* and remove everything that was Jack and Rose."

Above the arch to the hallway that led to the restrooms was an old, carved, wooden sign that said, *I'll never let you go…unless you need to.* I loved that damn sign.

Aiden let out a grunt and shook his head. I glared at my twin. "You have something to say?"

"You know, I think you're saying enough for both of us, don't you?"

"Stop it," Brendon snapped. "We don't have time for bickering."

"We always have time for bickering," I said casually. "It's what we're good at."

"Now you're just being a dick," Brendon said, looking down at his papers again.

"Why don't you say that to my face, asshole?" I stood up, clenching a hand into a fist. I needed to punch something. Needed to do anything but sit here and listen as everything changed, while I felt completely out of sorts. I wasn't an idiot. I knew that we needed to do some things to help the business. But going in and changing the entire menu, the atmosphere, and most of the things that were done for years seemed like a lot all at once.

And maybe it was because I was stressed out about Dillon and my own life, but the fact that I was back here at all when I didn't know if I would ever come back didn't help.

But it didn't matter.

Nothing mattered.

And maybe that was the problem.

Brendon looked up then and clenched his jaw before he spoke. "Stop it. Just stop it. We're not going to fight. We're not going to act like we're teenagers again. You came here knowing that there would be some changes. You came here with Dillon for us to figure out what we needed to do next. We don't want to lose the bar. Hell, I know it sucked when the brewery shut down, and we weren't even here then. We're not going to lose this part, Jack's legacy. But we're going to have to make some changes. Something you damn well know. We're in the red. Jack was in the red for long enough that we may lose the place unless we get some steady business."

"I know all of that. I looked over the numbers just like you did. I'm the one who used to run bars and breweries in California."

"I know. That's why I'm so confused that you're pressing back so hard."

I sighed into my hands and then ran my fingers through my hair. "I know it doesn't make any sense, and I *know* that I'm being unreasonable about some things. But can't we just go slow?"

"We can go slow and still change the food options. We don't need to have the same bar food that's on all the menus around us that nobody wants to eat anymore since they're clearly not doing it here. People are only coming in for the beer, which is great. But we make more money with food." Aiden folded his arms over his chest and glared at me. My twin was really good at that, but I couldn't really fight back. I had moved away, and Aiden hadn't followed.

Maybe we needed to deal with that, too. Just not now.

"But what are you going to do? Make something pretentious and froufrou?"

Aiden flipped me off. I kind of deserved it, I was being an asshole. "Shut the fuck up. I left my job at a Michelin-starred restaurant to come work at a pub. So, yeah, I'm going to implement some changes. I'm going to add tapas and different things that will make us stand out. You can fight all you want, but that kitchen is mine. So, you better back the fuck off."

Aiden stood up then. Looked like I might be getting my fight, after all.

Brendon stood in between us, shaking his head. "I can't right now. I seriously cannot with the two of you. Yes, Aiden, we are going to use some of your new food. But you aren't going to take away all of the bar food. Because we are a bar and grill."

"We don't actually have *grill* in the name," I said, knowing that both of my brothers would glare at me.

Aiden turned, his hands on his hips. "I'm not going to take away your precious wings or anything like that, but I'm going to add some things. We are in foodie nation. People like to try new things. We can have the normal fare, and then we can have a dash of something different. Let me do what I need to do in my kitchen. I'm good at my job. There's a reason I was the top sous chef at my restaurant."

I didn't add that my brother never would have made it to the head chef position because the owner of the restaurant had let his son take the job. Aiden wouldn't have made it to the next step in his career because the new head chef and the owner would have made it impossible for him. I didn't know everything that had gone on, but I knew enough. Aiden might have left everything behind when he came back to work at Jack's place, but he also needed a new start. We all did.

"I have a few other ideas, but I need to work them out before I bring them to the table." Brendon played with the cuffs on his shirt, rolling them up on his forearms. The man always wore a button-down, even when he was in jeans and trying to be casual. I never really understood it, but I knew it's what made my brother feel comfortable, so whatever.

"Fine. Do what you want. I'm going back to the bar to help Beckham because I know we're going to get our one rush of the day soon."

"We'll have more rushes." Brendon sounded so earnest, I wanted to believe him. I truly didn't want to think about the fact that this could be the last few months that we worked at this place. Maybe it would have been easier to shut it all down and start over somewhere else, but that was only in the numbers. That didn't take into account the memories, or the sweat and tears. This was Jack and Rose's place. We weren't going to fuck it up.

Apparently, we *were* going to change it.

"I'm heading back to the kitchen to see what I can do. I don't want to change everything, Cameron." Aiden glanced at me then, and I froze. He looked so honest, so much like me when I was lost. It startled me sometimes to remember that we were twins. We had been best friends, brothers by blood, and foster brothers. And then we walked away from each other.

It was hard coming back, but it was even harder to face the fact that I had left at all.

"Just don't add an *amuse-bouche* or something that takes dry ice or requires changing states of matter."

Aiden snorted. "Molecular gastronomy is not my favorite thing. I know it works in some restaurants, but I've always been more of a meat and potatoes guy."

That made us all laugh, considering that Aiden had tried to be a vegetarian at one point for Allison, though neither of them had ended up remaining so for longer than a month. Aiden might like meat and potatoes, but he also made it fancy as fuck. That's what made my brother so good at what he did. But that didn't mean I had to enjoy all the changes coming at me. And maybe it was because I was feeling a little lost about not being able to help Dillon and being back in town with all of these memories slammed into me, but it all made me feel on edge. Or maybe it was the fact that I kept thinking about Violet and how she'd felt against me when I held her.

Damn it, I really needed to stop thinking about Violet.

"Seriously, though, I'm going to work at the bar. Let me know if you need me."

"Is Dillon busing tables?" Brendon asked, his voice deceptively calm.

"He is. He's not old enough to work behind the bar yet, but he can bus tables and, eventually, if he's not a brat, he can be a waiter."

"And is that what he wants to do? Be a waiter?" Aiden asked, his voice emotionless. Damn it. I needed to figure out what to do about Aiden and Dillon since I wasn't sure the two had actually spoken a complete sentence to each other, but tonight wasn't that time.

"No, he wanted to be in the next big band. But that didn't work out all that well. So, we're working on figuring out college forms. And don't even get me started on the student aid. FASFA is the devil."

Brendon snorted. "It really is." He paused and then looked up at me. "If, uh, you need help with that, let me know. Numbers are sort of my thing. And I'm pretty good at paperwork." He held out his hands, gesturing at the papers on the desk. I nodded, a lump in my throat.

"I might take you up on that. I mean, I'm good with the paperwork for the bar, but going to college was not really my thing. At least the paperwork wasn't."

Aiden sighed. "We all went to college, but I think Jack and Rose took care of all the paperwork for us."

"And I will always be grateful for that," I said, laughing. "I know Dillon and I are working on what college he needs to go to. We'll figure it out."

Aiden stuffed his hands into his pockets and rocked back on his heels. "You know, I hear Violet works at UCD. I mean, she's pretty close to here and probably knows all about colleges."

"Don't go there," I said, shaking my head. "We can't go there."

"Sometimes, I don't think we have a choice." Brendon said the words softly, not looking at either of us.

No, sometimes we didn't have a choice in what happened around us. But, sometimes, we needed to make that choice for ourselves.

I gave each of them a nod and went down to the bar where, thankfully, a nice, late-evening rush was coming in. I had opened, and I would probably end up closing with Beckham.

We couldn't afford more than the two of us as bartenders right now, but both of us needed the work. Beckham was about my age, had a big beard, and long hair tied behind his head. He looked almost hipster, but I had a feeling he had been like that even before it was a thing.

That thought made me laugh, and Beckham raised a brow. "What's so funny?" he asked, his voice low. Beckham rarely smiled, and he didn't laugh. At least not since I'd known him.

Jack had hired him on when we were all out of town living our own lives. Beckham and some of the waitstaff were the only ones that stayed on after Jack's death. It made sense to me. Food service wasn't an industry where everyone stayed at the same job for years. We could pay them, so that wasn't the issue. It was more that they hadn't wanted to work with anyone but Jack, or they had moved on because it was their time.

Now, we had new staff in the kitchen—people that Aiden was dealing with, thankfully, not me. And we had a few new waitresses. And one new busboy.

Dillon.

"I'm just thinking about stupid shit," I said quickly, finally answering Beckham's question. "What can I do to help?"

Beckham just shrugged, pulling two drafts before going down to get a couple more mugs. "I'm filling up some pints for the guys at the end. I think Tracy's going to come by with an order for some mixed drinks, though." He tilted his head towards the redheaded waitress who was at a table with five women. "Pretty sure they're not the beer type."

I narrowed my eyes at the group of ladies and nodded. They were all dressed to the nines and giggling. Probably starting their evening before they did a Denver bar crawl. "That happen often? People coming in here dressed to the nines?" I'd been working here for a couple of months but still hadn't gotten used to the clientele since I was usually in the back—or had been before Brendon came to work here full-time on top of his other job.

Beckham just shrugged, sliding the beers down the bar into the waiting hands of the men at the end. Then he went back to pulling more drafts, not even looking at what he was doing. He just knew where everything was. He had been doing it for years, apparently.

"Not often. We have a decent happy hour on vodka, so sometimes people start here, mainly because they came here to eat lunch with their parents or something and know the place. It's familiar. The girl in the black, the one with all the sequins or whatever glitter crap that is? Her dad comes here often. So, it's not like we're a big place that college girls come to for drinks. But we do okay. People like us. They remember us. It's just making sure that new people can find us, I guess."

I blinked, wondering where all the words had come from. Beckham didn't speak often, but when he did, what he did say seemed to be important.

Beckham had been right, Tracy slid over five orders of various vodka drinks that would be a pain in the ass to make. But I didn't mind. This was my job, after all. I might like owning businesses, but I also liked working with my hands and mixing drinks. There was chemistry to it, making sure that everything was just right. Because when you worked with fresh ingredients, the recipe wasn't exactly perfect. You had to alter it depending on what you were using. That's what I liked. So, I went back to work, quickly mixing the five drinks. Dillon came by to help as a barback.

"Anything else?" Dillon asked, glaring. I knew my little brother didn't like working behind the bar cleaning up, and he sure as hell didn't like busing tables. But Dillon needed a job, and I needed the help. The kid got paid, and I could also keep an eye on him.

"We're good back here. But it's getting busier, so I guess you working over in that section is probably good."

"Is Brian coming in tonight?" Dillon asked, mentioning the other busser we had.

"No, you're by yourself here. Do you think you can handle it?"

Dillon just snorted. "I think I can handle busing a few tables. It's not brain surgery."

"Is that what you want to do? Be a brain surgeon?" I didn't know what Dillon wanted to do with his life, but then again, I didn't think Dillon knew either. I also didn't think that at eighteen you could really make decisions about what you wanted to be when you grew up. You were still growing up, so taking some gen-ed classes and figuring out what your major could be, seemed like the best course of action. The whole idea that you had to figure out your entire life at age fifteen while you picked out where you wanted to go to college seemed ridiculous. Not that I actually told Dillon any of this because I was still pissed off that he had lied to me.

And I was still mad at myself that I hadn't noticed.

"I don't want to be a brain surgeon. I don't really like blood," Dillon said, and I laughed.

"I'm not a huge fan of blood either. We shouldn't be talking about blood and other bodily functions while we're working anyway."

"True. Okay, I'm off to go clean up after those guys. I think they threw half their wing bones on the floor."

"Damn. Do you need some help?" While Dillon needed to work, and I needed to make sure that he was keeping on the right track, I didn't want him cleaning up after assholes.

"I said, I have it." Then he stomped off, and I just shook my head, watching him go. Beckham gave me a look that I couldn't read, and we both went back to work.

A couple of hours later, I felt the hairs on the back of my neck stand up.

I knew it was her before I heard her voice.

Violet was here. And so were the others.

I hadn't known that they came to this bar. I hadn't seen them since I came back to town, but here they were, in my place.

"I got this," I said to Beckham as I went over to where Violet, Sienna, and Harmony were sitting.

"Hey." I stuffed my hands into my pockets, wondering if I could be more of an idiot. Probably.

"Hi," Sienna said, kind of smiling. The expression didn't really reach her eyes, but I didn't blame her. Everything was still so raw and emotional for them. Violet's little sister felt things strongly. She always had, even when we were younger. I didn't know how she felt about Allison. I didn't know how any of them were feeling. Hell, I didn't know how I was feeling about Allison.

But I was glad that they were here, even if it confused me.

"It's good to see you, Cameron," Harmony said softly. She grinned, but like Sienna, it didn't reach her eyes. Damn it. I wished I could help these three, but I was already out of my depth with so many other things, this would just make it worse for everyone.

I looked over at Violet, clearing my throat. "Can I get you ladies something to drink? To eat?"

"We're here to make sure that the Connolly brothers know that we're supporting the bar," Sienna said when Violet didn't reply.

I turned to Violet's sister. "Really?"

"Of course. We've come in on and off over the years, but it's been more off since we've been so busy with our lives. But that's going to change. We need a new place to actually sit and drink that's not our house with a bottle of wine. Because while that's good, sometimes, you just need to get out. So you're stuck with us. And we need booze. We need lots of fucking booze."

Her eyes filled, and Harmony reached out and grabbed her friend's hand. I cleared my throat and nodded.

"So, what are we having?"

"Beer and shots," Violet said.

My brows rose. "Really?"

"Do you think we can't handle it?"

I met Violet's gaze and shook my head. "I think you can handle just about anything, Violet." I regretted the words as soon as they left my lips. "I know what you guys like. I'll be right back."

Then I walked away, wondering if I really knew anything at all.

Because, right now, it felt like I *was* nothing.

Chapter Five

That's next level hotness right there
—*Allison in a text to Violet about George Clooney*

VIOLET

I watched Cameron walk back to the bar and wondered what the hell I was doing. There were many ways to be a masochist, but apparently, watching my ex-boyfriend walk away while we were in his family establishment was a new way to have it happen. Maybe I liked pain, perhaps I enjoyed that burning sensation around my heart that had nothing to do with heartburn or any actual vascular disease, and everything to do with the fact that I was an idiot.

"The more you watch him, the more I'm afraid that we made the wrong choice." Harmony leaned forward and gripped my hand.

She was always doing that, making sure Sienna and I knew that we were loved and taken care of. I hated the fact that Harmony was actually getting used to the idea that this was her lot in life now. Apparently, one of my best friends in the entire world thought it was her job to make sure others knew that they were loved and cared for when the rest of the world was burning down around them. I hated it so much for her, but I didn't know how to make it better. I didn't know how to make anything better. I knew the three of us really needed to talk, we needed to make sure that not only were we there for each other but were also open about talking about Allison. I just didn't know when that time would come. Because it sure as hell wasn't now.

"I love this place." I shook my head as I squeezed Harmony's hand back and looked over at Sienna so my sister knew that I was telling the truth. "I really do love this place. Yes, it holds a lot of memories, and the current bartender who's not the sexy, bearded Beckham currently makes me want to pull out my hair, but that doesn't mean that I don't love this place."

For some reason, that sentence made Harmony and Sienna both laugh.

"What?" I asked, frowning.

"You just called Beckham sexy?" Sienna asked, looking over at the man who wasn't really our friend, mostly because we didn't know him all that well. But he was someone that I considered a pleasant acquaintance.

"Is he not?"

"Oh, he's sexy as hell. But I didn't think you would actually say that when there's another bartender at the bar that I would assume you would think is sexier."

"We are not going to compare bartenders. Plus, Beckham has this whole I-have-secrets-and-I'm-not-going-to-tell-you vibe."

"Oh, he totally has secrets, but don't you think Cameron does, too?" Sienna asked, giving me a weird look.

"Let's get off this subject, shall we?" I asked, keeping my voice pleasant. I felt anything but congenial just then, but it was my fault for coming here and daring to call someone sexy. Just because I thought Beckham was hot didn't mean I didn't think Cameron was sexy, too.

"Before he comes back, quick question," Sienna said quickly. "I never asked, did you ever find Aiden sexy? Because if you find Cameron sexy, then his twin has to be sexy too, right?"

There was something in my sister's eyes when she said that, and it kind of worried me, but now we were going way off track from any conversation that I wanted to have right then, and it wasn't like I could really figure out what was going on.

"Of course. But I was never truly attracted to Aiden the way I was to Cameron. I don't know why. But you know they are different people. Hell, I used to think Brendon was sexy, too."

Harmony snorted. "Oh, I used to think Brendon was cute, as well. Moyer told him once, I think. Mostly because he knew it would make me blush."

I smiled. "I forgot that the two of them used to work together." As soon as I said the words, I wanted to take them back. Because the reason that Harmony knew Brendon as well as she did was because Brendon used to work with Moyer, Harmony's late-husband. Everything was so convoluted and connected that it sometimes hurt to think about it. Especially because it wasn't supposed to be like this. I wasn't supposed to lose so much all at once. And Harmony sure as hell wasn't supposed to lose everything either.

"So, what do you think he's really bringing us?" Harmony asked, thankfully moving on and away from the subject of Brendon and any other conversation that could be awkward. Of course, everything that we were talking about today would likely be strange. We were sitting in my ex-boyfriend's bar, a place he owned now with at least his twin, someone who happened to be the love of Allison's life at one point. And the other brother in the place was a former friend of Harmony's late-husband. To say that everything was awkward would be an understatement. Of course, it was all strange. Because that was how we lived now. This was our life. Thankfully, before I could put my foot in my mouth again or wonder what the hell we were all going to talk about, Cameron showed up with a tray of pints of beer and six shots.

"Now, this is good Irish whiskey, but I'm going to hope that you all took a car service here. Because, if not, you're not getting a shot." He held up the tray and did indeed hold them back from us.

"Of course, we took a car service here. We want to get drunk. Being drunk is helpful."

Sienna smiled, and I wished I could be happy like that. I would have loved to act like everything was okay, as if I didn't feel like I was dying inside. It was all just too much. Being here with my friends and trying to act like we weren't missing our fourth, being here where I knew we would end up seeing Cameron, it was just hard. But I had put it out of my mind because we were trying to support the family who had always supported us. Jack and Rose had been part of our lives ever since we met the Connolly brothers. They had been an amazing couple who had taken on three foster brothers and brought them back together. They had even made sure to put Cameron and Aiden in the same home because they knew that the twins had been split up when they were younger.

When Cameron and I were dating, we had talked about how he felt about that, at least in a sense. We'd never gotten too deep, never dove beneath the fragile surface that was his pain. I had understood at the time that it would take longer. And I loved him. So, I would have waited.

But that time never came. Cameron had walked away.

"Well, now I can give you your shots."

"Well, we were going to pay for them anyway," I said and then groaned. "Never mind, ignore I said that. Of course, you're going to make sure we're not going to be drunk and getting behind the wheel. It's been a long day."

It had been a long week. A long month. But I had a feeling Cameron knew that.

"Of course, I'm going to make sure you guys are okay. I'm not going to let you guys get hurt."

I knew he hadn't meant to say that because his jaw suddenly went tight, and my belly clenched. Harmony and Sienna looked between us, slowly moving their beers and shots towards them as Cameron set them on the table. Nobody was talking. It had been awkward before, but now it was even worse. I swear I could feel every single eye on me like their literal eyeballs were sliming down my body as I tried to figure out what to say next. Why was I so awkward? Why was this so awkward? Why was my life so awkward?

"Do you want me to start a tab for you guys? Or is this going to be all for the table?"

Sienna was the one who answered. "Just a normal tab for the table. You might want to send out some wings or whatever Aiden's making, though."

"I'm sure Aiden will make you something fancy." Cameron didn't sound like he was too happy about that, and it had me wondering if Cameron liked any of the changes that I knew were probably coming to the pub.

I knew the bar was in trouble, only I didn't know exactly what was going on. But the fact that all three brothers were back in town trying to take care of it meant that something else was going on. Aiden was like a Michelin-star chef or something close to that, and that meant that he probably wouldn't be happy making bar food all the time. I knew that Brendon worked with fancy companies and dealt in all the money—not that I actually knew anything about that since I made barely any money in my job. I might like shoes, but I also liked them gently used.

"How about wings and something that Aiden wants to make for the table." Harmony said it with a smile, but I still watched as Cameron's jaw clenched once again.

"I'll let him know you're out here." Cameron glared over at the teenager I'd seen at the funeral. "Hey, what are you doing?"

The boy looked up guiltily from his phone that he had pulled out of his apron pocket. "Nothing."

"What did I say about your phone?"

Cameron grumbled something under his breath and then nodded at the table before going off to join whoever that was. His brother? No, I knew all the Connolly brothers. Maybe his son? I froze at that thought. No, that wasn't possible. That kid had to be in his late teens. There was no way that he was Cameron's son. He did look like he was related to him, though.

"Who is that?" I asked, my voice low, not wanting others outside of our table to overhear.

Sienna leaned closer. "Dillon? I think Aiden said that's their brother. I don't know the story, he sort of mumbled it to me when I saw him at the funeral, and I asked point-blank. Like I said, I don't know the story behind it, but he looks an awful lot like Aiden and Cameron. And because he didn't live here with Jack and Rose, he's not a foster brother. I know it seemed to hurt Aiden to even talk about it, though, so I didn't ask any more questions."

I sat back in my chair, blinking. Another brother?

That was different, but it was all a little too much for me to think about just then. I'd figure out what it all meant later. For now, I held up my shot towards the other ladies, who did the same. We clinked glasses, slugged them back, and then slammed the glasses on the table.

We each chugged half of our beers and then did the other shots before finishing the other half of our ales like we were younger than we were.

My stomach grumbled, and I knew that drinking on an empty stomach was probably stupid, but we were here to not only support the bar and the Connollys but also make the plans that we needed to for the next time we met up.

We needed to clean out Allison's apartment, and we needed to go through every single one of her things. And it was going to kill me, day by day.

No, I couldn't say that phrase. I couldn't say "kill me," or "I just want to die." All of those phrases that we use in the vernacular. Like "I could just kill myself" or stupid things like that. Because those were real words. And they really meant something.

Death was real. Allison was gone. And I needed to not be an idiot and use words that hurt, even if I was only saying them to myself. Cameron came over with a plate of wings and three glasses of water, as well as three more beers. He held back the shots, and for that I was grateful. Two shots and chugging a beer was probably too much for me already. I would likely feel it in the morning. But maybe I needed to feel it. Perhaps I just needed to feel period.

"Thanks," Harmony said as she handed out the plates that Cameron had given us. "They look great."

Cameron nodded. "We were always good with wings, Aiden makes the sauce even better. But don't tell him I said that."

"I heard you anyway," Aiden said, elbowing his brother out of the way. "Now, these are nachos, but not just any nachos. I added some shredded chicken and a little bit of better cheese than what you can squeeze out of a bottle."

He went on to explain the nachos in every single detail, and they did look fabulous. They may have sounded a little pretentious as he described them, but even then, the smell wafting up made my stomach grumble and my mouth salivate. Sienna was practically hanging off every word Aiden said, but then again, maybe I was just seeing things. Sienna and Aiden had always been friends, and we had hung out with Allison and Aiden often when they were dating. Or perhaps I was just trying to put a new spin on things so I wouldn't have to think about Cameron and the fact that he was still standing there, watching us.

"They smell amazing," I said as I reached for one. I took a bite and almost groaned aloud. It was only the fact that Cameron was still glaring that I didn't. Maybe if I really hated the fact that he was still there, I would have made more of a scene about it. But I didn't want to hurt him. The whole point of my pain was that I didn't want to hurt at all. So, lashing out wouldn't help. He had left years ago. I stayed. He hadn't given me a reasonable explanation, so I could be pissed at that. But I wasn't going to be petty and try to hurt him over nachos.

Delicious, amazing nachos. The best I'd ever had.

Oh my God, I wasn't going to make it much longer. I wanted to shove my face into the appetizer and eat them all.

Some look must have crossed my face because Cameron just snorted. "Well, apparently, the nachos are a hit. Aiden, I guess you win."

Aiden just grinned. "Of course, I win. And this is just the start. Just wait until you see what I can do with mushrooms."

"Like deep-frying them?" Cameron asked, and I knew he was just fucking with his brother.

But Aiden fell for the bait because he narrowed his eyes and opened his mouth, probably to yell. But before that could happen, Brendon walked in, a smooth smile on his face.

Brendon was always smooth. Sometimes, I thought he was *too* smooth, but I had seen the rough edges and knew there was more beneath the surface. He slid between the twins and put his arms around their shoulders. "I see that we have special guests tonight."

"Yes, but your brothers seem to have already noticed." Harmony laughed as she said it, and Brendon rolled his eyes.

It was nice seeing Harmony laugh, I didn't see it often enough. I would have thought that seeing Brendon would hurt her because whenever I thought of him now, I always thought of Moyer. But that wasn't really how Harmony felt. And maybe that was good. Maybe it was good that she would be okay, and that she wasn't stressing out like I was. Or maybe I was just going crazy.

"Why don't you join us?" Sienna asked, gesturing to the larger table that we were at. The rush seemed to be over, and I held back a twinge that it seemed to be over quite quickly. But with the food I was tasting, I had a feeling that maybe the bar would do better soon, especially if this was one of the changes the brothers were making. I hoped it would turn around because I didn't want to lose Connollys.

The bar. Not just the Connollys. I had already lost them, right?

"I think that could be arranged," Brendon said, taking a chair beside Sienna. Aiden took the chair nearest him so he was sitting beside me. Cameron just shook his head. I tried not to feel disappointed. There was no reason to feel that way. I didn't know this Cameron, wasn't sure I even liked him. But I sure as hell didn't like the fact that he reminded me of all the pain he'd caused when he walked away.

"I need to make sure Beckham isn't alone up there. I know we're not too busy,"—he paused, and the brothers looked at each other before looking away—"but he needs to take his break soon. Let me know if you need anything, I'll be sure to send Dillon over."

And with that, he walked away, and I wondered what the hell I was going to do. Because Cameron Connolly wasn't supposed to be in my life. Not anymore.

Yes, I had walked into his damn bar, but that didn't mean that I really wanted him in my life. I didn't want to have these feelings where I wanted to make sure that he was okay and comfort him. I wasn't supposed to want any of that. But, apparently, I was losing my mind.

Aiden brought out another dish, this time with pork belly and some other sauces that I hadn't really heard of before. That second beer after those shots had really hit me, and now I was drinking water. I didn't want to get drunk, I just wanted to stop feeling.

It was nice catching up with the guys, finding out what they had been up to and what they were doing now. But in reality, I just wanted to know more about Cameron. Because I'd missed him. I couldn't lie to myself and say I didn't. Because I did. He made me happy. Or at least he *had*. And, yes, I was probably setting myself up for more heartbreak even having him in my life, though it wasn't like I wanted anything more than him serving me booze and talking to his brothers. But it would probably happen. It usually did.

Aiden and Brendon didn't really talk about Cameron or Dillon, but they were the two giant gorillas in the room. It was evident that Dillon was related to them, at least to the twins, but Aiden didn't talk about him at all. Didn't even look at him. And I had no idea what that was about.

All I knew was that Cameron was apparently hurt, and my stupid, emotional soul wanted to reach out and make sure that he was okay.

Maybe I did need more beer.

"Yeah, we're thinking about doing it maybe tomorrow or the next day. We don't have as much time as we should because of her landlord, but we'll get it done." I pulled my thoughts from my self-pity and looked up as Harmony casually mentioned the fact that we needed to clean out Allison's apartment. Sienna wiped away a tear, and Aiden leaned closer to my sister and gripped her shoulder before quickly letting go. Sienna didn't move towards him, but then I wasn't sure if she had noticed the touch at all. She was closing in on herself, much like I did. We were far too alike sometimes.

"We can help if you want," Brendon said then cleared his throat. "I know I helped when, well…you know."

I had forgotten that. I hadn't been able to help Harmony as much as I wanted to when she had to clean out some of her house after Moyer's death. Harmony had decided to move to a smaller place after her husband died. The couple had bought a larger home because they had been planning on having a family, and I didn't think that Harmony had wanted to live there once her husband was gone.

I didn't blame her for moving, but I hadn't been able to help with the move as much as I wanted to. My grant had been up, and I had been working practically twenty-hour days trying to make sure that I still had a job and that those under me could keep their jobs, as well. I knew Harmony understood, but I had never forgiven myself. But, apparently, Brendon had been there for her. He had been friends with Moyer, so it made sense.

"You don't have to help," I said quickly. "I mean, we might need some help with the heavy lifting, and I know that my brother wanted to come up from the Springs, but I don't know if he'll be able to." Mace and Adrienne were working harder than ever because their shop had made the national news and they now had to turn clients away at this point. So, it wasn't like he could really take time away from his family to come and help me out. He would if I asked, but if others closer could help, maybe we should take them up on it.

"Of course, we'll help," Aiden said. "You just tell us when you need us, and we'll be there."

Something warmed inside me, and it felt weird. I knew that my friends and I weren't alone. We had each other. We'd always had each other. But with my family so far away—even if only an hour—sometimes, I felt like it was just the three of us. The three of us against the world—when it should have been four.

So, maybe having help even in the form of friends that I had thought long gone, maybe that was good for us.

"I think that's exactly what we need," Harmony said, nodding.

Cameron didn't come back to the table. Instead, he sent Beckham. I didn't know if that was about the brothers or me, or if maybe he really did have to deal with the broken tap that Beckham mentioned. It didn't really matter, though, because we were leaving. And Cameron wasn't mine. He hadn't been for a very long time.

I made sure that I picked up all my stuff, still a little buzzed even with all the water that I drank and food in my belly. We said goodbye to the others, promising that we'd let them know when we decided to clean Allison's place, and then we made our way to the car service area and then home.

As soon as I walked through my door, I locked it behind me then slid to the floor, tears sliding down my cheeks.

Everything hurt so much.

Allison was supposed to be out with us. She would have been the one to make us laugh and bring the boys over so we could get over whatever issues we might have had with them. She would have been the one to make everything okay. But she was gone.

And I was left behind.

And it just hurt.

I hoped it wouldn't always hurt. But I was afraid. I was so afraid that it would.

Chapter Six

CAMERON

"Hey, bro, I think your girl left this."

I turned around at the sound of Dillon's voice and frowned. "My girl?"

Dillon rolled his eyes like the eighteen-year-old he was. At least that had gotten better over the past few years. When the little brat had been younger, the eye rolling had never ceased. Ever. It was like a constant state of eye rolling. I wasn't quite sure how Dillon had been able to see anything when he was doing that constantly. But then again, I was pretty much the same way when I was his age.

"Your girl, the one who came with her friends that you were talking to. She sat with her friends that Brendon and Aiden seemed to know. You know, the ones from the funeral?"

"I know who you're talking about, but why do you think she's my girl?" I didn't know why I was continuing this odd conversation, but for some reason, I wanted to know why Dillon thought that Violet was my girl. Because she was definitely not mine. Not anymore. The way she could barely look at me was proof of that.

"Brendon mentioned it." The fact that the kid was talking to Brendon at all was a good sign. If only he could do the same with Aiden. Dillon continued. "He said that you used to date or something. I don't know. But she was there, and you guys had this whole like explosive chemistry thing going on—not that I know anything about that," he added as he held up his hands in a surrendering gesture.

Apparently, I looked slightly menacing or something, but I couldn't really help it. I hated the fact that my brothers talked about me behind my back, but then again, I sort of did the same with them when I was worried. Brendon wasn't technically Dillon's brother, but of the two of them, at least between Brendon and Aiden, Brendon was getting closer to Dillon.

Aiden was keeping his distance, and I understood that, after all, there was a lot of baggage when it came to the three of us and how we were related.

"She's not my girl anymore."

"Because you left?" A pause. "You left her because of me, right?"

I pinched the bridge of my nose, not really wanting to have this conversation but knowing that this one—as well as many others—were long overdue. Thankfully, we were in the back where it was just the two of us and Beckham coming in and out so we wouldn't be overheard too much. Because I really didn't want to have this conversation while I was with the rest of the staff or any customers.

"We broke up because I was an idiot."

"You cheated?"

I shook my head. "No, nothing like that. But I like the fact that you think cheating makes you an idiot. Because…don't cheat. That makes you more than an idiot. It makes you worse than the scum that you find on the bottom of your shoe. Just make sure you remember that."

Dillon rolled his eyes again. "Of course. I'm not a dork."

"Okay, then."

"But you still didn't answer my question. What happened?"

I shook my head. "That's something I really need to talk with Violet about first." I let out a sigh. "But I'll never regret finding you. I'll never regret being your big brother and having you in my life. I hope you know that." I stuffed my hands into my pockets, and Dillon did the same. I didn't even think he realized he had done it, or that it mirrored my movement and said that we were related in more than just DNA.

"Yeah, well, I guess you don't suck."

"Thanks for that. But you really think this is her scarf?" I asked, holding the silky, blue thing up close to my face. I could smell her on it, that sweet scent that was just Violet. Oh, I had seen her wearing it, and I knew it was hers. I just needed Dillon to say it too, just to make sure that I wasn't imagining things. Or seeing things that I wanted to be true.

"It's hers. So, do you want me to put it in the lost and found, or do you want to go to her house and give it to her? That way, it's that whole, 'hey, you left this. Here,' thing."

"Really? What kind of movies have you been watching? I thought they all had things blowing up, not those romantic comedies you seem to want me in."

Dillon just grinned. "I watch things. I know things."

"Yeah, you sure do know a lot. Now, go finish taking out the trash, and I'll figure out what to do with this scarf."

"Just don't be all gross with it and like, jerk off into it or something. Okay? Because she seemed like a really nice lady, and you doing that…kind of creepy."

I let out a groan and pinched the bridge of my nose. "I'm going to pretend you didn't just say that. Because that is disgusting. And if I ever hear you doing any of that, well, I really hope I never hear about it. But if I do, I'm going to kick your ass."

"That sounds like a plan. Because I'm not some creepy jerk. I just really hope you aren't either. Now, off to the dregs. Yay for taking out the trash."

Dillon grunted and growled and went back to his work. I just rolled my eyes much like my little brother had done earlier.

"I'm losing my damn mind." And the fact that I was talking to myself just told me that I'd probably already lost it instead of just started to lose it.

I looked down at the blue scarf in my hand and squeezed it just a little bit so I could feel the softness between my fingers. I knew where Violet lived thanks to Brendon, who seemed to know everything. I wouldn't have to ask anyone or even look her up.

Knowing it was probably a bad idea, I told Beckham that I was heading out for the night, well aware that the other man would be able to easily close alone since it was his job, and got into my car. I was probably making a huge mistake, but then again, I made a lot of those. More so recently than ever before.

And I wanted to see her. I wanted to make sure that she was okay. Because I knew she really wasn't, not after losing Allison. Aiden wasn't okay, how could Violet be?

She lived in a small house in one of the suburban neighborhoods close to downtown Denver. I knew she worked at the old university that we had all gone to, but it was kind of nice seeing her in a house that she owned, being a grownup. I'd just recently bought a small house that I shared with Dillon. I guess signing the papers meant that I was staying, even more so than me trying to fit in at a pub that wasn't really mine. Or one that didn't feel like mine anyway. I had made good money when I was in California, and selling off my old place had made me even more. So, I could send Dillon to college and not even have to worry about saving for it. Because I already had. I just hadn't been paying close enough attention to make sure the kid actually got in. But that was changing. I wasn't going to remain the idiot I had been, thinking that we had it all figured out and handled.

And now I was just stalling. I pulled into the driveway since Violet was either not home at all, or her car was in the small, attached garage. I really hoped she was home. I didn't know what I was going to do once I saw her, but maybe it would come to me by the time I made it to the door.

I gathered up her scarf and wondered why I was here at all. Maybe I missed her. Or maybe I just needed to atone for my sins.

Because there was sure a hell of a lot of them.

I knocked on the door, not wanting to ring the doorbell in case she was asleep. Not that I thought she would be, but I wanted to give her the opportunity to ignore me. Because she was allowed to do that. She was allowed to forget that I even existed. I had been an asshole, I had left, and I deserved whatever came to me.

But all those thoughts fled as soon as Violet opened the door, and I saw her wide eyes filled with tears, her cheeks red from crying.

"What's wrong?" I asked, instinctively reaching forward before pulling my hand back. She wouldn't want me touching her, and I would do well to remember that.

"I just had a tough day. What are you doing here? Is everything okay?"

I shook my head before moving my hand forward so she could see her scarf. "Everything's fine. My brother just found your scarf, and I figured I'd bring it to you. And now that I'm here, I realize that this was actually a really stupid thing to do. You could've remembered your scarf at any point and come back for it. Or maybe this isn't even yours, and I should just be going now."

I took a step back, grateful that she didn't have stairs on her front porch, when she suddenly moved forward and took my hand. I froze, wondering when I would stop reacting this way every time we touched. We used to touch all the time, used to do more than that. Now, just the feel of her made everything seem different. It was as if I was coming home. Not that I was actually doing so.

"Thank you for bringing my scarf back. I didn't realize I even left it. I guess I'm not quite all there right now."

I handed over her scarf, reluctant to let it go, and then stood there with my hands once again in my pockets, rocking back on my heels. "I'm glad that Dillon found it."

"Oh, it was Dillon? You said your brother and I thought it was one of the other two. Not that Dillon isn't your brother...I'm just rambling now. Do you want to come in?" She paused as if she hadn't really meant to say that, and I was a little surprised she had. "If you want. You don't have to. I just...I was just sitting here awkwardly in the dark, crying. So, maybe I could use some company."

I nodded and then took a few steps in as she gestured for me to enter. I liked the inside of her house—the warm colors, and soothing tones. Her couch was big enough that I could probably lay on it and not have to scrunch up. And that was saying something since most couches these days seemed to be too small for any man my size.

Not that I was actually thinking of myself on her couch. Not at all.

"Can I get you something to drink?"

"No, I'm okay. But are you? Why were you crying?"

She turned on more lights so I could see more of her, and I noticed that her eyes were clearing up a bit, her cheeks not as red as they had been when she first opened the door. "I'm just thinking about Allison. And the fact that she wasn't out with us tonight. And that your brothers are going to come help us clean out her apartment. It just sucks. And I hate that there're no answers."

"I hate that there are no answers for you either. For any of us. I know Aiden loved her back in the day, and I figured that they were still in contact with one another, but that was a long time ago. I hadn't really seen her since I left." I held back a cringe, not meaning to bring that subject up.

"I assumed you didn't talk to a lot of people after you left," she said, a bit icily.

I deserved that.

"I should probably apologize. Probably should have done that a long time ago." My words were soft, but they still felt like barbs.

"Apologize for what? Walking away without saying goodbye? Or leaving the rest of your family in a lurch just like you left me?"

"I deserve that," I said, my voice rough.

"Yeah, but maybe I deserve something, too. Why did you leave, Cameron? I figure it had to do with Dillon now that I know a bit more, but that doesn't make any sense to me. Why couldn't you tell me? Why did you just walk away as if I was nothing?"

I swallowed hard, my hands clenched at my sides. "That couldn't be further from the truth. You meant everything to me."

"Don't lie to me. If I meant so much to you, you wouldn't have left like you did."

This wasn't how I had wanted this conversation to go. Hell, this wasn't how I wanted anything to go. I hadn't come here to talk about this, but it was time. Everything was past time.

"Seven years ago, my mom contacted me. Not Rose, the one who birthed Aiden and me and threw us out on the streets after she overdosed. Aiden and I are twins, the same birth mom, same birth father. And you know I don't know who my dad is." I didn't know why I was repeating the obvious, but I needed to collect my thoughts.

"I know," Violet said, her voice soft. We were standing in her living room, facing off with one another as if this had been waiting for us this entire time. And maybe it had. I should have told her this before. I shouldn't have hurt her like I did. But I was young, stupid, and didn't know what to do with my own emotions, let alone hers.

But that was all on me. And I knew it.

"Mom was doing drugs, and Aiden and I were the result of one of her Johns. She needed money for the drugs she loved, and so she sold her body. And while I will never judge anyone for the choices they make if they want to be a sex worker, I will always judge my mother for making the choice so she could shoot up again. I will always judge her for taking Aiden and I with her down that rat hole."

"Cameron, you don't have to start there if you don't want to. You just have to tell me why you left, not how you came here in the first place."

"But I have to. You have to know why it's all connected. And why I'm such a fucking screw-up."

"You're not a screw-up. Yeah, you screwed up, but you're not one."

"I sure as hell feel like it sometimes. But, anyway, Aiden and I were finishing college, and Mom contacted me. She left us before because she OD'd. She almost died, and the state took her away. I was born and raised here in Colorado but in the system most of the time. And then Jack and Rose took me in, and then they found Aiden."

"I had forgotten that, the fact that you and Aiden didn't grow up together."

Thankfully, Violet sat down on the edge of the chair and let me do the same. My knees were weak just talking about this. I wasn't a big fan of it. But she needed to hear it all. And maybe I needed to say the words.

"After Mom OD'd the first time when we were really young, they put Aiden and me into the system. Brendon was in the system too at that point, but we didn't know each other then. We were all just young boys who were split up into homes because no one wanted to take two twin one-year-old boys that may or may not have learning disabilities since their mom was on drugs when we were born."

"That's just cruel," Violet said on a whisper.

"That's life. Nobody wants to adopt grown kids. They all want little babies, and they sure as hell don't want kids that may have to deal with withdrawal at some point in their lives. Not that I remember any of that. Anyway, Jack and Rose adopted both Aiden and me, making sure we were in the same home, and then they got Brendon. And that's when you met us. In high school and college. The seven of us were all a big unit."

"I know. I was part of it. That's why I don't really get why you just left like that."

"Because while we may have been a unit, and while I loved you—"

"Don't say that. Not now."

"But I did. I loved you."

"Not enough. Obviously."

I held back a wince, knowing I deserved it. "My mom called me, saying that she had OD'd again and needed my help. I hadn't planned on going down there until I thought she was really going to die. So I left, only for a weekend I thought, and found out she was going to lose custody of her other baby if she wasn't careful. That boy was Dillon. It was with a different John, and no, I don't know who Dillon's birth father is. I'm not sure she does. Regardless, even though I hated my mother, I didn't want her to die. I don't know what that says about me, but I just didn't want her to die. And I didn't want her to take Dillon down with her once I found out about him."

I looked up, and Violet was wiping away tears, but I continued. "She was out in California, had been there for a while, I guess. I lost track of her after everything happened when I was a kid, and it wasn't like I could just look her up on Facebook or some shit like that. Apparently, she kept track of me, though. She didn't ask for money, didn't ask for anything, really. She just didn't know what to do with this other kid that she had. This eleven-year-old. Eleven years old, and I didn't even know he existed. Aiden and Brendon didn't know either, not that Brendon was actually related to the kid, but sometimes, I forget that Brendon's not my biological brother. You know?" Violet nodded in answer, and I continued.

"Aiden wanted nothing to do with my mom at the time. He told me if I left, I deserved whatever I got. He said we were making a life out here, and to go back to Mom would just fuck everything up. Because you see, I didn't know that she had a kid when I went out there. All I knew was that she needed me. And in some self-righteous, bullshit part of myself, I wanted to make sure she was okay. I didn't want her to die alone, you see. And so, Aiden said that if I walked out, that was it. That I would be choosing her over the family we had made. I didn't think about it like that, I just thought about the fact that I wanted that part of our past not to die alone. And so, I left."

Violet's eyes widened. "So, you're saying Aiden didn't know about Dillon at all? I find that hard to believe."

"As soon as I found out about Dillon, I tried to contact Aiden, even Brendon. But they wouldn't answer my calls. And I was too busy trying to figure out how to raise this eleven-year-old while feeling like a kid myself. And I didn't really keep trying to contact them after about a year." I paused. "I told Jack and Rose, though. At least over the phone. They understood, but then I was selfish and made them promise that they wouldn't tell Aiden. I was so pissed at him for not helping me when I needed it, and I didn't want to hurt him. Or maybe I wanted to hurt myself. I don't know, but Aiden never answered my calls, he pushed me away just like I pushed him away. And so, in the end, I was out in California, trying to start a new life and raise this kid."

I paused, swallowing hard. "Mom died about a year and a half after I moved out there. OD'd again, but that was the final time. I barely scraped enough money together to cremate her because it was cheaper than a burial out there. Dillon still has her ashes. I wanted nothing to do with them. I don't even know if Aiden knows about the ashes. Hell, that's probably something else I should tell him." I let out a sigh and rubbed my temple. "Everything's really fucked up. And it has been fucked up for a long time. And so, I left. I left Denver, and I left you. Because I couldn't say goodbye to you. I didn't know how."

"Cameron."

Violet's voice was soft, and I could see her shaking. I didn't know if it was sympathy or rage. Or maybe it was a mixture of both.

Her shoulders lifted and fell as she took deep, gulping breaths, and then she looked at me, and I knew that there was just rage there.

"Really? Really? You could've just said it. You could've just told me. I wasn't going to break because you needed to leave for your family. No, I broke because you didn't have the decency to say goodbye. That's why it hurts to look at you. That's why every time I see you, I remember everything we once had, and how you threw it all away. I'm not going to hold taking care of your family against you. I'll never hate you for wanting to make sure that little boy was okay. But I can hate you a little for how you did it all. I can hate you a bit for how it broke me into a million pieces and left me shattered on the floor.

"And that's why you need to go. Because I don't think you can be here right now. And I think I need to breathe."

There was nothing else to say right then. I had told Violet why I left, which, in retrospect, was a stupid decision. But I hadn't known what else to do at the time, and I had messed everything up. There was no amount of atonement that would make that okay.

So, I stood up and left, closing the door softly behind me. I just hoped that she would lock it and keep herself safe. But then again, it wasn't my responsibility to keep her safe. I had nothing to do with Violet. Our lives might have been tangled once, but it didn't mean they had to continue being so.

I didn't know what direction I was headed—not physically or emotionally. But no matter what, it wasn't going to be with Violet.

It couldn't be.

Chapter Seven

VIOLET

To say I was not ready for today would be an understatement. But there was no getting away from this. There was no running from anything. Allison needed us, even if I wasn't sure exactly what that meant anymore.

Harmony stood on one side of me, Sienna on the other, and I wondered how it had all come to this.

Death wasn't supposed to be easy, life was hard, after all. But what was left behind seemed to be the hardest, at least in my recent experience.

Allison was gone, her life cut far too short by her own hands. And I still didn't know why she had done what she did. Maybe there wouldn't be any answers. Perhaps there didn't need to be. Maybe those answers were only for her, and even though I was the one left behind, it didn't mean that it was all about me.

Because it wasn't. Of course, it wasn't.

And today wasn't about me either. It wasn't about the fact that my chest felt too tight, or that my palms were clammy. It wasn't about the fact that I knew a migraine would come on eventually, or that I felt like I was going to throw up if I didn't focus.

It wasn't about any of that.

No, today was about saying goodbye to Allison once more and cleaning out everything that she had once loved and owned.

It still shocked me a little that Allison didn't have a will. But because of that, her parents had been in charge of everything, though they had left this part up to me and my friends and family. Allison's parents were already dealing with enough, compartmentalizing the fact that their daughter was gone and they had no answers. They had handled the funeral, the casket, dealt with watching their daughter be laid to rest, inch by inch as she was put into the ground.

They'd held the wake at their own house. They had fielded the questions, confronted being strong in the face of insurmountable pain.

And though I didn't agree with exactly how they had handled everything, it wasn't my place to say anything. But what *was* my place, was making sure that they didn't have to deal with any more than they already had. Because while I lost my friend, they had lost their daughter.

They had lost their only child, their baby girl. And I would do anything to make sure they didn't feel any more pain from that.

So, Sienna, Harmony, and I were going to clean every inch of Allison's place and make it ready for the next tenant.

Somehow, we were going to make this place that still smelled of Allison no longer have even a single inch of her. There would be no remnants of the woman that I loved, no remnants of the best friend who had held me when I cried, who'd helped me through my migraines, and through college when I thought that I was making a mistake in my chosen field.

Allison was always the strong one, but I hadn't been able to see beneath the surface. I hadn't been able to see that something else was going on with her.

And I'd never forgive myself for that.

"Where do we begin?" Sienna asked, her voice hesitant.

"We start where we need to. So, we have boxes, and we'll put things into piles." Harmony clasped her hands in front of herself, her voice sounding far stronger than I thought it could. After all, Harmony had done this with her husband's things. Apparently, she was an expert at this now.

The fact that there was that much knowledge while dealing with loss at our ages just pissed me off.

"So, what kind of piles are you thinking?" I hadn't really done this before, not really. And I really wasn't in the mood to think about it now. But we didn't have a choice.

"Well, there're things that we'll want to keep for ourselves, there're things that her parents may like, there're things to donate, things to sell. And, obviously, there may be some things to throw away. There'll also probably be a pile that we have no idea what to do with, but we'll come back to that later. It really just depends on what there is. I know it's going to be hard, and it'll suck. But that's why we have wine for later, and that's why we don't have to do it all right now. We can do a little bit, and then a little bit later. As long as we do it in steps, we'll be okay." She took a deep breath. "We're going to be okay."

I inhaled deeply just as she had and then wrapped my arm around Harmony's shoulders. I kissed her head and closed my eyes, resting my temple against hers. Sienna wrapped her arms around both of us, and we just stood there, the three of us as a unit. A troop against what was coming next, and the fact that we weren't four. We would never be four again. And it sucked.

"I guess we should get started?" I asked, my voice low. I really didn't want to start. I just wanted to go home and wrap myself in a blanket and forget that any of this ever happened. But there was no ignoring this. There would never be any forgetting this. How could that actually be when every single time I looked in the mirror, I remembered that I had walked in to see my best friend in the entire world no longer with us.

Because there was no turning back from that.

"Like I said, piles. Maybe we should start with the living room? I don't know if we're ready for the bedroom yet. That might be too personal."

"Everything's going to be personal here," Sienna said wisely. "Even the bathroom's going to have stuff that she used every day. Like her lotions and everything that reminds me of her. I just hate this. I want to know…I want to know why. I want to know why she's gone. And I know we'll probably never find out, and I hate it. It just makes me so angry." Sienna threw her hands into the air. I reached out to my little sister but stopped when she glared at me.

"Sienna." I didn't know what else to say. There were no words for this.

"No, just don't. Just let me be angry and a little whiny right now. I think I need that. I'll let you do the same when you reach this part of the grief. Because I still think that you're in that numb part right now, Violet. The part that hurts. I was there for a while. But I keep moving around from each set to another."

"Stages of grief are crap," Harmony said, her voice low.

"What?" I asked, confused.

"There aren't just stages you randomly move through. No, you feel it all. You feel every single little part at all times, at every single point of the day. Sometimes, you move forward, sometimes, you move two steps back. It's not a gradual progression, so everything is perfectly fine eventually. Because it's not going to be fine. You're never going to be fine. But, eventually, you might be okay with who you are as you find your way to breathe again. But there are no stages of grief. There's just grief. Plain and simple. And there's nothing simple about it. There is grief. There is loss. And there is you, finding a way to live through it and knowing that everything hurts around you. So, everything's going to hurt. You're going to be angry. You're going to be sad. You're going to be numb. You're going to be all of it. And that's okay. It's okay to feel all of that. Or nothing. It's just okay."

I stared at my friend, wondering why she hadn't said any of this before. But, then again, when would she have been able to? We hadn't understood what she felt when she lost her husband. I still didn't. I would never be able to feel that, and I swore I never wanted to. We had lost Allison, and it was a different kind of grief, but it was still grief. We were just trying to find our way.

Someone cleared their throat from the doorway, and we all turned to see the Connolly brothers standing there, looking awkward as if they had heard Harmony's entire speech.

From the way Brendon was looking at her, I figured that they had heard every single word.

And I had no idea what we were going to do about it.

Not that I really knew about anything anymore. But that was enough of those self-pitying thoughts. There were important things to get done today, and feeling bad about myself wasn't one of them.

And, speaking of feeling bad, I noticed exactly who was here. Brendon, Aiden, *and* Cameron were standing there. The only one missing was Dillon, but then again, he wasn't a Connolly, was he? I didn't even know Dillon's last name.

I hadn't asked many questions, or how old exactly Dillon was—though I figured he was eighteen if I did the math right about Cameron's story. I hadn't asked what Dillon's plans were, or what Cameron's plans were when it came to the kid. I hadn't asked any of it because I'd been too hurt about having to remember exactly how I had felt when Cameron left all those years ago. Yes, maybe that made me selfish for those few moments, but I needed that. Because he had been selfish, and I hadn't really wanted to lash out at him, but I needed those few moments to regain a bit of the person I had become when I put myself back together after losing him. I might not like every part of myself, but I had enough respect for myself to be okay.

"You guys showed up," Sienna said quickly, moving forward. "I know you said you were, but I was afraid that you would get busy or decide that it was just going to be too hard. But, thanks for coming." Sienna reached out and hugged Brendon and then Cameron and then Aiden. And because Sienna had done it, Harmony moved forward and did the same, saying something soft to each of the brothers that I couldn't really hear.

"We're here for you if you need us. We like you guys. Just wanted to make sure you knew that."

"Thank you for coming," I said softly. I guess we're going to need help with the heavy lifting, after all.

"Do you have a moving truck or anything?" Aiden asked, frowning as he looked around the space. He had once loved Allison, and I didn't know how he felt standing in the place where she had once lived that had nothing to do with him. Everything was just so complicated and connected, it was hard for me to truly understand what anyone was feeling when I didn't even know what *I* was feeling.

"No moving truck today," I said, trying to keep my voice strong. It wasn't easy when all

I wanted to do was break down. But I had done that enough recently. Today, I would work, and then I would get drunk. Really fucking drunk.

"So, it's just packing up? When are you planning on the moving truck?" Cameron asked, looking at me and then pointedly looking away. I knew it wasn't anger that I saw in his eyes. He was just trying to give me space. But I really didn't have time to deal with any extra feelings right now.

"We have some time, and I don't want to do too much at once," Harmony said. "Today's all about piles, maybe packing some things up. We brought some boxes."

Brendon cleared his throat. "I did too, just in case. But you don't have to use them if you don't want to." He added that last part almost as an afterthought, and I wondered why Brendon was acting so weird. Then again, I didn't really know him anymore. Maybe he was always this way.

"I'm sure we'll need them. We always need a lot more boxes than we think at first. Anyway, we were thinking about starting in the living room." Harmony looked sad and confused as she looked around. "And I don't really think we can split up on this, because I think it's something that we need to work on together to make decisions. I know what everyone thinks, and I know what I'm doing here because I have some experience, but I really am out of my depth. If anyone else has any ideas, I would really appreciate hearing them."

I moved forward and hugged my friend close. "I'm here for you. Always. And, don't worry, we'll figure it out. How about everybody take one corner of the living room, maybe work in pairs, and we'll just go through everything piece by piece. Some things are going to be easier than others, some things might take some discussion. And we don't have to do it all today. We just have to get started. We just have to get started." I repeated the last part, knowing it was for me. It sucked, it all just sucked. There really wasn't another word for it.

Somehow, I ended up working with Cameron, and I didn't know if my friends and sister had meant to do that or if it was just by happenstance. Brendon knew Harmony the best, so he worked with her and was so gentle with how he helped her. I figured that he knew that every single moment she was thinking about losing Allison, she was probably thinking about her late-husband, too. I knew I was.

Aiden and Sienna worked together, the pair quiet yet the only two laughing softly as they looked at things. They had known Allison the best, even though Allison was also my best friend. It was sometimes hard to remember that. Hard to remember that Allison had touched more than just one person. She had affected the lives of so many, and yet here we were, without her.

A hand grazed my shoulder, and I didn't move away. I couldn't. "These are her picture albums," Cameron said softly. "Why don't we stack these, and you guys can look at them later?"

I shook my head quickly. "Box them, and then we can take them to my house or something. I'll look at them later. *Way* later. I don't think any of us are ready for that right now."

The others had been listening and agreed quickly, and Cameron boxed them up so I didn't have to touch them, so I wouldn't have to look at them. Maybe it made me weak, perhaps it made me shallow, but it hurt to think about everything, and I just needed some space. Just needed time to breathe.

We worked for three hours, slowly putting things into piles.

It was weird to think about putting someone's life into a pile. I didn't even know if I could do that for myself.

What was the pile of old bills that were already paid?

What about the stack of DVDs that she had watched at one time, but no one really needed anymore?

There were the CDs that hadn't been thrown away when she went fully to digital. There were random knickknacks that people had given to her over time, or those I knew she had gotten from friends, or when she traveled. There were picture frames all over, Allison's smiling face looking down at us as if she had held a secret that I didn't know.

But I guess that was the case, after all.

There was so much we had missed, and I didn't want to miss anything anymore. I didn't want to miss any of it.

There was the TV, of course, and all her electronics. I had no idea what to do with some of the stuff. But Aiden, Brendon, and Cameron figured out where she kept her old boxes in the back and packaged those up. We would likely either sell or donate them since none of us really needed or wanted them.

"Would Dillon need any of this?" I asked, my voice soft. "I mean after we talk to Allison's parents. I don't know what Dillon's plans are, but maybe he would like something to start out?" I didn't realize I'd said the words out loud, or that I'd even thought them until they were already out for everyone to hear. Harmony and Sienna both gave me soft smiles as if they were happy with what I had asked. But I really wasn't sure I'd done the right thing. Aiden glared and then turned away, not answering. Brendon gave me a similar smile to the girls' as if he'd been thinking along the same lines but hadn't spoken up. But it was Cameron who spoke first.

"Eventually, he's going off to college," he said quickly. "This is just a gap year for reasons I can get into later." He sounded a bit angry about that, but I didn't press. Not yet. "But, maybe? Let's see what Allison's parents say first, and then we can talk about it. I think that's really generous. Really generous."

"Allison's parents said that we could have anything we wanted in here, that they wanted nothing to do with it. But I'll double-check. I kind of like the idea of something that she enjoyed being used with something that a friend might like. I don't know, maybe I'm just getting sentimental." I sighed, stacking up the greeting cards from the latest holiday that Allison hadn't tossed yet.

"You're allowed to be sentimental. You're allowed to feel whatever you need to," Cameron whispered, and I ignored him. Or, at least I tried to. I was a little too confused to make any decisions right then. But at least I was trying to think of the future, trying to think of someone other than myself.

"I don't understand why there wasn't a note," Sienna said quickly, anger back in her voice. "Why didn't she tell us? Why didn't we see it?" Aiden wrapped his arm around her shoulders, and Brendon looked at them both as I tried to find the words. I just didn't have any. How could I?

Because I'd been thinking the same questions this whole time.

"Sometimes, there are notes. Sometimes, we don't get the answers in life. Sometimes, we just don't know."

I wiped the tears from my face and didn't pull back when Cameron leaned into me, giving me as much comfort as I would allow.

"And that's a really crappy thing to say. And I really need a drink. Does anyone need a drink? I could really use a drink."

Everyone was silent for a moment before they all got up and looked ready to go.

"How about we drive back to our places, and I'll set up some ride shares to get us back to the bar? That way, we can drink to our hearts' content and not worry about driving." Brendon was already looking down at his phone at something, and I just nodded, knowing that was probably the best answer to everything.

"Usually, I just drink alone at home," I said quickly and then laughed. "But that makes me sound sad."

Brendon snorted. "No, that makes you sound like any other American who lives alone. We just happen to own a bar so we can make drinking in public feel like you're drinking alone. But we'll have a drink in Allison's honor, and we'll try to make it to the next day. How does that sound?"

I looked at Cameron, wondering why we were always in each other's presence when I knew that we should stay away. But it wasn't as easy as just walking away like he had before. And yet, it hadn't exactly been easy then either.

"Let's go, then. Let's go see what we can do so we can make it to the next day."

And maybe that would be our new slogan for the rest of this period. What could we do to make it to the next day? Because Allison hadn't made it to her next day.

And, somehow, I would have to make it for the both of us.

Chapter Eight

CAMERON

I T WAS PROBABLY AROUND THE SECOND DRINK OF THE NIGHT THAT I REALIZED THAT we shouldn't be here. That drinking away our worries wasn't going to help anything in the long-run. But considering that I was already a little numb where it counted, I knew the others had to be way further down the rabbit hole.

Because, yes, I had known Allison, and I missed her. Going through her things was hard, and I'd hated every bit of it, but watching Violet and the others deal with it, each of their emotions playing out on their faces so bright and vivid that it hurt to even think about…that was harder.

There wasn't anything I could do about it though, except to keep drinking and make sure that the others didn't drink too much. We had each taken a car service so we could get home safely, but I knew none of us wanted to deal with the aftereffects of a hangover. We weren't in our early twenties anymore, and drinking too much and feeling bad the next day wasn't really something that any of us needed to put ourselves through.

But nobody really seemed to mind just then.

Thankfully, we were in the back room next to the pool tables so others wouldn't be able to witness our drunken debauchery unless they came back here. And they never seemed to since we weren't busy.

Brendon brought by some shots, probably making our third drink of the night, even though I think we might've been on our fourth at this point. I wasn't really sure. Maybe our fifth.

It was tequila, my arch-nemesis because I was usually an Irish whiskey kind of guy. But since we started with tequila, that meant I couldn't add any more liquor. Just beer and tequila. I'd probably throw up later, but it'd be better than adding whiskey on top of it. Or even something stronger or sweeter.

My stomach rolled. Yeah, best not to remember that night when I was barely twenty-one and drank way too many fruity drinks alongside Violet. She hadn't wanted to drink alone, so I had been stupid and said that I would drink the same thing she was.

We both ended up lying on the bathroom floor, sick, pale, and not wanting to touch each other, even though we had both promised to have the hottest sex of our lives.

That'd taken another three days to get to, considering that we had both been hungover for more than forty hours.

Jesus, I'd been young. Too young.

"Okay, this shot is for us. For the fact that we're here. Together." Brendon held up his shot, and I did the same, doing my best not to remember that sweet-tasting drunk night as I looked at my brother and then the rest of them. Aiden had his arm around the back of Sienna's chair as the two of them laughed, telling some joke that none of us heard, but was apparently hilarious to the two of them. Sienna held up her other arm, grinning. And, for the first time, I thought the expression might just reach her eyes. Though not fully. I didn't know when that would happen, but I hoped it did soon.

Harmony sat between Brendon and Violet, rolling her eyes as she held up her shot. For some reason, I didn't think she was going to be as drunk as the rest of us. Either she wasn't finishing her drinks, or she had a higher tolerance for liquor than any of us did. Considering that the Connolly brothers could drink almost anybody under the table, that was saying something.

Violet sat by me and gave me a look that went straight to my balls. Yes, I was an idiot for even thinking that, and I knew she was drunk—I was on my way to being drunk, too. But she was so damn sexy. Always had been. And I could never resist her. So, I was going to do my best tonight to just keep drinking and do that whole resisting thing that I wasn't very good at.

"Yes, I'll drink to that." And then we all took the shots and banged our glasses on the table, though not too hard, thankfully. After all, this was our bar, and I didn't want to break shit.

Considering that it was a Saturday night, it should have been busier than it was, but it wasn't, and that worried me. I knew that all of us were working on ideas for how to increase the bar's presence and keep it afloat, but right then, with a couple of empty chairs at the bar, and the fact that it should've been filled to the rafters with people, it worried me. So, I sipped at my beer and tried not to worry. That could be left for tomorrow. God knew I stewed enough for everybody here.

As did Brendon. And Aiden.

Aiden took a bite of the nachos that Beckham had brought to the table earlier and frowned.

"They aren't using my recipe," Aiden grumbled. "What's the point of me telling them what to do when they won't fucking do it?"

"Maybe you shouldn't curse at them and growl?" Sienna asked, batting her eyelashes like she was so sweet.

"I am fucking nice. And a damn good boss," Aiden said before he took another bite of the nachos and scowled.

"I think they taste just fine, Aiden," Harmony said, dipping her chip into some sour cream. "I mean, yours are better, we all know that because you are a god of cooking, but these aren't bad."

"Yes, because whenever you want to think about good food that brings people in, you want the phrase 'not bad' as part of that." Aiden let out a sigh and stood up, a little wobbly. Okay, apparently, we might've been on drink six. I wasn't really sure anymore. "I should go back there and tell them what they're doing wrong."

I reached out over Sienna and tugged on my twin's arm. "No, you can do that tomorrow. When we're sober, probably hungover, and not acting like assholes. Don't go back there when you're drunk and start yelling at people. Number one, it's probably not the best thing for our staff to see us like this when they're working and we're not, and number two, it's probably going to break like thirty health laws. So, don't fuck up and just sit down."

Aiden glowered at me before doing as I suggested. "Well, that's all nice and dandy for you, but at least you have someone running the bar when you're not there, someone who actually knows what the fuck he's doing."

I turned as Aiden lifted his beer in cheers toward Beckham. The bearded bartender just rolled his eyes and toasted with his bottle of water. Thankfully, Beckham didn't drink when he was on duty. The bartender who worked with Beckham before I came back had done a few too many taste-tests throughout the evening. So much, in fact, that he was basically a drunk loser who spent all his time trying to get wasted with the college co-eds instead of actually working.

I had fired him quickly, and Beckham had done his best to pick up the slack when I was trying to figure out my way in the new place. I knew Jack hadn't wanted things to go downhill, but he had been sick, and there was only so much he could do on his own after Rose died.

And my brothers and I hadn't been here to help.

So, it was my fault that everything was like it was now. And we were going to fix it. I just hated the fact that we were changing everything to make it happen. Because there had to be some things that Jack loved that had worked out. No, the food wasn't as good as it used to be, and that was because of the old cooks that we used to have. And maybe one of the current ones we still had if the nachos were anything to go by tonight.

And, no, we didn't have some of the new craft beers that I wanted. But I was getting some of them in and using some of my connections back in California to get it done. A lot of the local bars had the Denver local brews because it was Colorado and we were sort of at the center of the whole thing. But I wanted something different. So, I would try to get some of the Colorado brews, and some of the California ones. It was harder than it sounded, but I was making it happen.

Brendon, however, was doing his best to try and get people here in snazzy ways. Ways I really wasn't in the mood for. But it wasn't my place to say anything. It was never my place to say.

"You know, that wing night I'm working on, that's going to be good for us. We just need to get the word out." Brendon chugged the rest of his beer and then stood up. "Speaking of wing night, let's go play pool."

I snorted, finishing the last of my beer. "How the hell do those two things go together?"

"They do because I say they do." Brendon raised his chin and held out his arm as if he were a duke in the Regency era. "My lady, does thou want to play pool?"

Dear God, my brother was an idiot. A very big idiot.

"You're drunk," Harmony said, laughing as she stood up. But she put her hand on his arm anyway and did a little curtsy as if she were wearing one of those long dresses, even though she was in jeans. "I would love to beat your ass at pool."

"Those are fighting words, my lady."

"My lady?" Aiden asked. "Seriously?" He looked down at Sienna and glowered. "You want to go beat their asses, short stack?"

Sienna blinked. "Seriously? Harmony gets *my lady*, and I get short stack? Why don't you just call me the lovely troll or the court jester at this point?" Sienna tossed her hair back from her shoulders and stood up, pushing past Aiden to get to the pool area.

I looked over at Violet, who was laughing behind her beer at the four of them. "So, you want to play?"

"What? I'm not a fair lady or even a court jester? I'm just a whatever?" She finished her beer and set the glass down.

"Well, you're Violet. Figured us going over there and kicking their asses as a duo was probably better than watching them fall all over each other because they're too drunk to actually see where the ball is."

"I don't think Harmony is drunk. In fact, I think that's her first beer from earlier, and she's just doing tequila shots."

I looked over at the table, noticing that, yes indeed, that was Harmony's first beer from earlier. It was probably all warm and disgusting now, but I didn't think that Harmony minded since she wasn't really drinking it.

"Well, she can beat us all, but I can't just let my brothers go in there and be idiots alone."

She snorted. "So, you have to be an idiot with them?"

I scooted my chair back and stood up, holding out my hand. "Pretty much. Let's go, Violet."

"I guess." She slid her hand into mine, and it was as if she'd always been there, as if there hadn't been a time where she wasn't in my life. But I knew that wasn't the case. I knew I had hurt her. I'd even hurt her recently. I was the asshole here, and I always would be.

"We have to make sure that at least Brendon doesn't win. Because he always gets the most arrogant when he does." I whispered the words, knowing the others would be able to hear.

"Oh, I remember. You and Aiden are pretty arrogant yourselves, though." Violet looked down at our clasped hands, and I realized that I hadn't let go of her yet. "I thought I said that we wouldn't be near each other. That you needed to go." She murmured the words, but I still heard them.

"I'm not good at doing what I'm supposed to."

"I guess I'm pretty much the same."

I let go of her hand as we entered the pool room and went for our cues. Somehow, we were just drunk enough to make a game with six people. Considering that there were only stripes and solids, it didn't make any sense, and Harmony had declared herself the winner even though Sienna was the one who had taken to standing on a chair, raising her arms, and fisting her hands in the air.

And that's when I knew that we were beyond drunk and probably needed to go home.

Thankfully, Beckham saw us and laughed as he held up his hands for our phones.

"Okay, folks, I'm going to call you guys some ride shares, and then you are going home. Don't forget to drink a glass of water while you're waiting, and then another before you go to bed. And some aspirin then and when you wake up. Because I do not want to hear you all grumbling tomorrow that you're all hungover and bitchy." He looked over at the girls. "I'm actually talking about the men, not you."

"I assumed when you said bitchy, you were talking about Aiden," Sienna said very seriously.

Aiden, for some reason, found that hysterically funny and couldn't stop laughing. I looked over at my twin, wondering when I'd actually heard him laugh last. It had to have been years ago. But, maybe, if I'd actually lived in the same state as he did, I would've heard it before this. Damn, I missed it. I'd missed so much. I'd stayed away because Dillon needed me, but I hadn't wanted to leave. And, frankly, I'd been scared to come home. I'd fucked up more than once, and I didn't want to do it again.

So, just hanging out with my friends and my brothers, maybe that was the first step—or at least a step in the right direction.

I helped clean up the pool area and went back to the front of the bar, making sure everything was cleaned up. We were the last ones in the place, and Beckham just shook his head as he shooed everyone out.

"I got it, boss. You never get drunk or actually have fun these days. You're allowed to do it now. Nobody else really saw you like that, only me."

I nodded, holding out my hand for the other man. "Thanks, Beck. No one really needs to see us like this."

Beckham shook my hand and gave me a tight nod. "Well, sometimes, you just need a day where you can breathe. I know today must've been hard for the girls, and you guys. I didn't know Allison, but I can see from the way you guys are grieving for her that she must've been a good person."

I swallowed hard, my throat tight. "She was one of the best." I hadn't been here to know who she had become these past years, but it still didn't make any sense that the smiling girl that I had known wasn't here anymore.

But that was the thing with death, nothing made sense.

Beckham got cars for everybody, and somehow, Violet ended up in mine. I didn't really know how that had happened, but Beckham had a way about him. Either he was an idiot, or he was trying to get on my good side. Not that I actually knew if this would be good. For all I knew, this would mess everything up even more.

"Why am I at your house?" Violet asked as we got out of the ride share's car. I did my best to focus on giving the man a tip before helping Violet into the house. "I think Beckham's weird."

"Or you and Beckham have serious plans that did not involve telling me about them." She raised her chin and sauntered into my living room.

I did my best to keep my gaze off her ass, but it was very hard when she was wearing tight leggings that just seemed to mold to her butt. I really, really liked her curves, had liked them before, and I liked them even more now.

I looked around my living room, hoping I had cleaned it up at least a little bit, and then looked down at Dillon's shoes in the entryway. Shit. I had forgotten. I forgot that I wasn't alone in this house.

"Uh, we need to be quiet, Dillon's here."

She rolled her eyes and glared. "What do we have to be quiet about? Am I here for nefarious purposes?"

I snorted. And then I went up to Violet and framed her face with my hands. "We're too drunk. Way too drunk."

"Of course, we are. I think being drunk's the only way I can actually think."

And because I knew it was a mistake, I let it happen anyway. I lowered my head and brushed my lips across hers, just a caress, for just a moment.

I had missed this. Missed this more than anything.

And when she didn't move away, I kissed her again.

This is what I'd been missing. Violet.

It'd always been her.

And I knew there was no way that she would let me continue doing this. Knew that there was no way that this was the right decision.

So I kissed her.

Because I had to.

Chapter Nine

Don't make any mistakes. Unless they're with me. Then that's fine.
—Allison in a text to Violet

VIOLET

MY HEAD WAS FUZZY, AND IT WASN'T JUST BECAUSE OF THE LIQUOR IN MY system. No, it was because of the man in front of me, the one who currently had his lips pressed to mine. This was such a mistake. This was beyond a mistake. I should have found a way to get into my own ride share and gone home on my own.

But when Beckham asked me on the way back to the pool room if I wanted to get into Cameron's car or go home alone, I had said that, of course, I wanted to go with Cameron.

Yes, I was drunk, and I was making poor decisions. But, apparently, Beckham thought he was a matchmaker. And he hadn't wanted me to be forced into a situation I wasn't comfortable with.

So, yes, while he was a nice man, I was still going to beat him up. Just like I was going to hurt Cameron.

But all thoughts of that fled my mind when Cameron's hand slid through my hair to cup the back of my head and pull me closer to him. I wrapped my arms around his waist, pressing my body against his as I kissed him even harder. I had forgotten what his kisses felt like. I had forgotten what he felt like. Yes, he was larger than he had been even seven years ago, more muscular, a little sharper-edged. But he still felt like Cameron.

My Cameron.

Yes, I was drunk, but I wasn't drunk enough to actually think that he was mine.

Yet I couldn't stop kissing him.

I just wanted to feel. I just wanted to be. I didn't want to think about Allison, I didn't want to think about work, I didn't want to think about my ex-husband and his new wife, I didn't want to think about the fact that I still had to worry about the rest of Allison's stuff.

I didn't want to think about what life would be like without her.

So, I just kissed Cameron. I knew it was selfish, knew this was all a mistake.

But I didn't stop.

He was the one that pulled away first. And then he leaned his forehead against mine and let out a ragged breath.

"What are we doing?" he asked, his voice rough.

"I don't know, but I want to keep doing it."

He pulled back, his brows lowered as he frowned.

"If we do this, it's going to change everything. We're not kids anymore."

"It meant something when we were kids too, though. And I just want to feel. I know it's all complicated, and I know that this is wrong and stupid. But I have just enough liquor in me to make me brave enough to say it, though not enough where I'll be taking advantage of you, or you'll be taking advantage of me."

He studied my face. "I would say that that's just the right amount of liquor, the right amount of drunk. But I can't take advantage of you."

I moved closer, impossibly close, so we were pressed against one another and I could feel the hard ridge of him on my thigh. "Personal advantage here. It's just you and me. And you're helping me feel. I miss feeling. Can you do that? We can deal with the tomorrows tomorrow. We can deal with everything that's going to hurt. But I just miss people. I miss being held. I just miss it all."

I miss you.

I didn't say that. I couldn't. Because I was afraid if I did, Cameron would see too much. Because I still loved him, and I hated that. Maybe it was a different kind of love, maybe it wasn't the part that meant I was *in* love with him. I had moved on from that and pieced myself back together after he left. And though he'd apologized and groveled, I didn't know if that was enough yet.

But it was just enough that I could want to lean into him, and I needed to be held. And maybe I was taking advantage of him, but from the way his eyes darkened and the way he let out a slow growl, I knew that he wanted me as much as I wanted him. Hell, I could feel how hard he was, yes, he wanted me just as much as I wanted him.

I didn't say anything else just then, and I knew it was because, if we spoke, we would just break the bubble that meant everything would be okay, and that this was just for right now. Because it wasn't going to be. There would be ramifications, but we would deal with them tomorrow.

My head was swimming, the mixture of the booze and Cameron filling me up, so I just closed my eyes and leaned into him as he took my lips again. He tasted of beer, a little tequila, and even some nachos. He just tasted of Cameron. I loved it. Or at least I *had* loved it. Maybe I just missed it.

Maybe I just missed touching.

I had been married since I was last with Cameron, I'd been in other relationships. Cameron wasn't my only, far from it, but he had been my first love, my first everything.

So, having him hold me right then felt like coming home a bit.

There was a reason that taking advantage was something that happened.

Sometimes, you just needed.

So, I kissed him back, wanting more, *needing* more.

"If we're going to do this, we can't do it out here. Dillon could walk in at any moment."

This. He was talking about sex. Something that I was also talking about. Okay, I could do this. I'd had sex before. I'd had lots of sex. I'd had lots of sex with *Cameron* before. This wouldn't be anything new. It wasn't going to be scary. It would be exactly what I needed.

And I was going to thank God that I had just enough booze in my system just then so I could make this happen. Because it's what I needed. What I wanted.

"I forgot about Dillon."

Cameron let out a rough chuckle. "You make me forget about a lot of things." And then he leaned down, put his arm under my legs, and lifted me up to his chest. I let out a little screech and put my hand over my mouth so I wouldn't get any louder. I didn't want to wake up Dillon, an eighteen-year-old boy who would know exactly what his brother and I were doing. I did not need to deal with that embarrassment anytime soon.

Cameron grinned, and he looked just like his younger self. No worries. And that's what we both needed. Just us.

I knew that the word *us* held baggage far beyond just two letters put together to make a word. But I was going to ignore all of that. And because I had enough alcohol in my system, I could.

And so, I let my hand go and brushed the back of my fingers along his bearded cheek.

His jaw was defined, square and a little angular. It had been that way before, but now it looked even more masculine.

And while he and Aiden might be twins, I had always loved the way Cameron looked more. Maybe because he smiled more. Perhaps because I loved the way Cameron looked at *me*. He had always looked at me as if I were the best thing that had ever happened to him. I had never really believed that. Never really thought that I could ever be that for anybody. But it had been true, even in the short time that we were together.

Cameron wasn't looking at me exactly like that now, but I understood that he would never do that. Because we weren't who we were before. We were who we were now, and I was just going to live in the moment, just be with him with his arms around me. He carried me down the hallway, both of us quiet and looking at each other. Neither of us wanted to wake up his brother and ruin the moment. Neither of us wanted to say anything or think too hard and ruin the moment that way either.

When we got into the bedroom, he set me down and kissed me again, this time a little rougher, a little harder. I could feel the need in that kiss, the desire in his touch.

His hands trailed over my body, and I arched into him, pulling my mouth back and moving my head to the side. His lips latched on to my skin, licking and biting and sucking along my neck and down to my shoulder. He tugged at my jacket, and I did the same to his, both of the garments pooling to the floor. I was only wearing flats and could easily slip out of my shoes, and that made it easier for me to go up onto my tiptoes and bring his mouth down for another searing kiss.

His hands moved to my butt, and he molded me with his large grip. Then he pulled me closer, pelvis to pelvis so I could feel the hard ridge of him against the heat of myself. I wanted him inside of me, wanted him on top of me, below me, anywhere near me. I needed this, craved it.

It had been so long since I had been with anyone, far longer since I had been with Cameron. And I didn't want to wait any longer. I slid my fingers under his shirt, reveling in the hard ridges of his abdomen. He was sculpted, easily had an eight pack, and it made me want to giggle. He was like one of those cover models in the books I loved, but he was all real. There was nothing fantastical about him. He was real, and all mine for the night.

I scraped my fingernails down his skin, and he let out a slight groan, shivering under my touch. And when I put my hand on the hem of his shirt and tugged. He let me slide it over his head, lifting his arms for me.

"Wow," I whispered, my voice a little shaky with awe.

"You like?" he asked, flexing for me. I laughed, unable to hold myself back.

I loved laughing when I had sex. I just loved being. I loved the fact that Cameron could make me smile and do stupid things to make me feel like there were no worries in the world even when we were on the verge of something more.

The booze in my system seemed to rev me up, and I leaned forward, licking his nipple. He let out a shuddering sigh, and I bit down before going to his other pec. He was tattooed, a few down his side and one over his shoulder. He didn't have too many, and I knew his brothers had more, at least they had back when we were younger. When I moved behind him to look at his back, I noticed that he had a couple more that he didn't have back then.

There were no women's names, no female faces. And for that, I was grateful. But there were a few jagged-looking tears along his side, and I wondered who they were for. For him? For his family? For his mom?

I didn't ask. Instead, I kissed his spine all the way down to the top of his jeans. And then I stood back up and leaned around to kiss his lips. He kept kissing me, and I fell into him, loving the way we were going slow, feeling one another. He had his hands under my shirt, undoing my bra even as I still wore my blouse, and I just grinned. He had always been very good at that.

Soon, I was naked from the top up, my breasts in his hands as he sucked one nipple into his mouth, using his fingers to play with the other.

Each suck and little bite went straight to my core, and I knew my panties were wet for him. I knew I needed him.

"I need you," I whispered, not meaning to actually say the words. Cameron could know that I needed him, could know that I wanted him. But just in body, not in soul.

I needed to remember that.

Cameron leaned back and winked before going to his knees. My eyes widened when he kissed his way down my chest, my belly, to right above the waistband of my pants.

With one hand, he slowly slid his finger along the elastic, not quite lowering them. He used the other to untie one of his shoes, then the other. And then he was barefoot, his pants undone, and slowly sliding mine down my body. He cupped my butt as he did it, and then kissed my core over my panties before stripping me completely out of my pants.

And then I stood there in my underwear, looking down at him and sliding my hand through his hair.

Cameron had always been good with oral sex, and while I liked giving him head, I knew he enjoyed eating me out even more.

To say I had been a lucky girl would be an understatement.

And, no, I was not going to remember everything that came after when he left—the pain, the breaking. Because that wasn't going to happen again. This was just one time. This was just Cameron and me. No promises, no memories.

Cameron kissed me over the top of my panties again and then slowly pushed them back so he could kiss me where I wanted him most.

I let out a groan, throwing my head back and almost falling right down on my butt because there was nothing to hold me up except for his very strong arm. Thank God for Cameron and those strong arms.

"I'm going to fall if you keep doing that," I panted.

"I'll catch you."

And he would, but then I remembered the time he hadn't. But I pushed that out of my mind. Instead of relying on him, though, I took a few steps back and leaned against the edge of the bed, spreading my legs so he could see me.

He grinned and then crawled towards me. Crawling was a good step. Almost like groveling. I'd take it.

And then he kissed me again, this time lower. I groaned, my head rolling back, my eyes closing. He sucked and licked and then he used his fingers. And when I came, my legs were wrapped around his head, and I was groaning, hearing his name on my lips as I tried to keep quiet so Dillon wouldn't overhear.

Soon, Cameron was above me, stripping off his pants as he gripped the base of his cock in his hand.

"You look so fucking beautiful." He groaned. He was growling his words, a glare on his face, his eyes narrowed. For some reason, that was really sexy. He probably shouldn't have looked sexy, should have looked very scary, but I couldn't help my reaction. This was Cameron. And I was always far too weak when it came to him.

"Well, what are you going to do now?" I asked, my voice low and kind of sultry. I hadn't meant to sound like that, but it was Cameron. Again, I couldn't help myself. Before he could answer, though, I sat up. I was on my knees, shaking, and I pulled at his thighs so he could come closer. His eyes widened, and then he smirked. Oh, I loved that smirk. Because he didn't always mean it, but I knew it meant naughty things.

And speaking of naughty, I opened my mouth and swallowed him whole. He groaned, his hands sliding through my hair as he slowly worked his way in and out of my mouth. I used one palm to cup his balls, the other to wrap around the base of him because I couldn't actually swallow all of him.

I flattened my tongue and hummed, knowing exactly what he liked, or at least how he used to enjoy it. And from the way he groaned, the way he shook, I knew he still did. And then he pulled out and kissed me again, his whole body quaking.

"If you keep doing that, I'm not going to last. I'm not as young as I once was."

"Neither am I, but I don't mind."

And then I leaned back and spread myself for him.

He groaned and then went to the nightstand, slipping a condom down his shaft. Thank God he had remembered because I had forgotten.

I had always used condoms with my exes, except for my ex-husband and Cameron. My ex-husband and I never used condoms once we got married because I had thought we were trying to have a baby. Cameron and I had stopped using condoms after we were both tested and I had gone on birth control.

We were not those people anymore. We were not in a committed relationship, and I didn't know if he had been tested or not. I had, but I still wanted to be careful. It didn't matter that I was on birth control, I needed that barrier. I needed far more than just that barrier if I were honest.

And then he was over me, sliding into me as he met my gaze.

I groaned, my entire body shivering as he filled me up. His mouth was on me just for a moment before he pulled back to look at me.

And when I looked into his eyes, I felt barer than I could ever remember, even when I was naked. It didn't matter that I was still wearing my panties and he had just moved them off to the side, it didn't matter that we had been intimate like this before.

Because this was different, this was new. This was nothing like it had been before.

Yet it felt like it should have been.

And that scared me. That scared me more than anything I could have possibly felt just then. And then he moved. He moved slowly and so sweetly that I could almost forget that I was supposed to be scared, forget that I wasn't supposed to be here. He moved, and I moved with him, and when we both came, I called his name, his mouth on mine, taking my shout.

Everything felt like it had before, only different. Like time had passed and we weren't exactly the same people that we had once been. Because we weren't.

We fell into each other twice that night, exhausted and no longer drunk. But it was like we both knew if we stopped, if we pulled away, that would be it. That it would be the end again. I was afraid to know what would happen when we did.

I fell asleep on his chest, holding him close as he held me so tightly, I knew I would likely be a little bruised in the morning. But I didn't care because I needed this night, even if it scared me.

When I woke up the next morning, my head pounded, and I knew a migraine might be coming on a little bit later and not just from the drinks. I knew I had made a mistake.

There was no more booze in my system, no more shots of tequila to help me make this better.

I was in bed, completely naked, and completely sated by Cameron Connolly.

I had promised myself that I wouldn't let this happen, but I had because I'd needed someone, and he had been there. Because he had always been there, except for the one time when it had truly mattered.

I hated this, and I hated how I felt. Because I blamed myself for this. I was the one who'd said that everything would be okay, even though I knew it would hurt.

What the hell was I going to do?

Cameron was still sleeping, out of it, and I knew if I moved, he wouldn't actually wake up.

Thankfully, he was still a hard-sleeper, so I rolled out of bed and pulled on my panties, remembering how he had pulled them off the second time we made love. No, not making love. It was just sex. There was nothing about love. We were not in love. We were not in a relationship. Everything would be fine.

I pulled on the rest of my clothes and tried to put my hair back into a bun even though I knew I looked like it was the morning after. It was, after all.

I didn't know if I was supposed to leave a note or pretend that everything was okay, but Cameron knew where I was, knew where I lived. And I knew that this wasn't the end. I knew that we would have to talk about it. But not this morning. Not when my head hurt, and I was afraid that I was going to throw up. Not because of the hangover, but because of an oncoming migraine.

I quickly tiptoed out of his room and called a ride service so I'd be able to get back to my house. I picked up my purse from the front entryway table, having forgotten that I'd left it there, and then I looked up at the sound of someone clearing their throat.

Oh, of course. *Of course.*

"Oh, hi, Dillon."

Dillon took a bite of his cereal and lifted a brow. Then he swallowed and smiled. "Hey there, Violet. Need a ride?"

He was very subtly trying to let me get out of this quickly, but I still had no idea what to say to him. "No, my driver should be here soon. Um, bye." I scurried out of the house and waited on the side of the road for my driver to pick me up.

Last night had been one of the best and worst times of my life. And I knew it was only the beginning. Because there was no going back to the way things were.

Though I didn't know where they were going from now on either.

Chapter Ten

CAMERON

Waking up in the morning all alone because the woman you'd been sleeping next to most of the night had tiptoed her way out without waking you wasn't the best way to start your day. And it had all gone downhill from there.

I pinched the bridge of my nose, trying to calmly let out a breath, but I couldn't help it. I was just so fucking tired.

I'd rolled over that morning and put out my hand so I could touch Violet, so I could make sure that everything that had happened the night before was real, but Violet wasn't there. She had left.

Maybe I should have expected it, and somewhere deep down I had, but it was still a bit of a shock to open my eyes and realize that she wasn't there.

I'd stumbled out of bed myself, rubbing my eyes with the heel of my hand as I shoved myself back into my jeans, at least doing up the zipper if not the button. I had thought that maybe she was still in the house, maybe getting coffee or just sitting on the couch, wondering what the hell we had done.

As soon as I'd gone out there, Dillon had raised one brow at me as he finished up his cereal and then shook his head.

Apparently, I had just missed her. By literal minutes.

She had run out of the bedroom, grabbed all her clothes, had an awkward run-in with Dillon in the living room, and then had found her ride share so she could leave me without a word.

Not unlike what I'd done to her all those years ago.

Damn it.

I still couldn't quite believe what we had done.

Yes, we had done it before, we had been with each other before, but it was still a little shocking to me that we actually did it again. I had loved being with Violet before, had enjoyed every single part of us. But I had truly thought that what we had was gone. Then, somehow, last night, she had turned to me, and I had done the same with her. I wouldn't regret it, because if I did, it would make what we did wrong. And it wasn't.

But it still made me want to punch something.

Because I knew it was all a mistake. I had known it was a mistake going in, not because anything with Violet would be bad, but because it wasn't the right time. She had said that she was taking advantage of me, but I still felt like I was the one taking advantage of her.

Maybe I deserved everything I got, because I seemed to be making one mistake after another—just like I had before.

But I couldn't focus on that, couldn't concentrate on Violet right then. Because I had to focus on the issue that was the bar.

I was starting to hate Connollys, little by little, day by day. It had been a touchstone for Jack and Rose. It had been their place. Something that had kept a roof over their heads and kept them together. They had loved working here, and they had brought us in when we were just kids, freshly out of whatever other foster home or street we had been in or on at the time.

They hadn't cared that, yes, they worked at a bar and owned one, and had brought in children during working hours. We had never gone behind the bar, at least not then, but we had still seen how the business worked.

We had seen how it ran correctly. The place had been thriving back then, with constant regulars coming in and out. There had been other bars around, but this place had been the hopping one. Maybe that was because of Jack and Rose. They had been that good, that amazing.

Or maybe it was because the other places around here weren't quite as good and they closed before Jack's did.

I let out a breath, trying not to focus on that last thought. Because I didn't want this place to close. It was mine, Aiden's, and Brendon's. And as I looked over at my youngest brother, I thought it might be Dillon's, too. No, Dillon's name wasn't on the deed, and he wasn't going to lose anything if this place closed, but he was still my brother, our brother, and trying to figure out how all of that worked within these walls was a whole other matter.

"What's up with you?" Brendon asked, his brows lowered. "You're not even out there working, yet you're glowering."

"You only think I should glower when I'm out there?" I asked, annoyed that Brendon had walked in on me in the back office. I just needed time to get my thoughts in order, and the fact that that's what I kept doing these days was starting to piss me off.

"I don't even get you. But we have a problem."

I leveled my gaze at him, really hating that statement. "That's not the first time you said that. What the fuck's going on now?"

"Well, the printer that we used to get the word out, as well as the publicity team that I hired to help with the online stuff got the date wrong.

I shook my head. "Huh?"

"For wing night. You know, the whole day that was supposed to bring in new people and new flair with Aiden's wings and his other new stuff on the menu? It's not going to happen today."

I froze, trying to comprehend what my brother was saying. "What do you mean it's not going to happen today? We've been working on getting this ready for the past month. I had to make sure that the place looked nice, but it always does because Beckham and I know what the fuck we're doing. Aiden has been working on getting that new menu ready, including two new types of wings. We've been getting *everything* ready for today. Your job was to get people in. And you're saying you didn't get it done?"

Brendon raked his hands through his hair, looking the angriest I had ever seen him. And I had seen Brendon looking pretty mad.

"I don't fucking understand it. I've used these people before, but they totally fucked up this time. If it weren't for the fact that I know they're not working with another bar, I would assume they were trying to sabotage us. But it's simple human error. I just didn't catch it."

I pinched the bridge of my nose. "And why didn't you catch it?"

Brendon turned on his heel and threw his hands up into the air. "Because I have another job. Because I'm doing this on the side of what's actually bringing in money. And because I'm stupid. I don't know. I'm sorry. We're just going to have to figure out what to do with tonight because it's just not going to happen the way we want it to."

"We're going to lose a lot of money on this. You get that, don't you?"

"I am the money man. Yeah, I get that. And you can yell at me, punch me, do whatever the fuck you want. But don't worry about it, because anything you do, I'm going to want to do more to myself. I'm never working with that company again. I'll just have to do that all on my own from now on."

I folded my hands over my chest, anger coursing through me. Not directly at Brendon, but he was in front of me, and that meant he got the brunt of it. "You say that, but I'm thinking that maybe we should be helping you out there because you doing it on your own clearly isn't working."

Brendon froze and stared at me. "Seriously? You're just going to kick me out, just like that?"

"Didn't say that. But you had one job and, apparently, you're not doing it right."

"That's the problem. I have more than one job. We're all floundering here, and I don't know what to do with this place. Nothing that works for my other businesses is working on this."

"Because that's the food service industry," Aiden said as he stormed into the office. "And you know how the food service industry is. Yes, you're a brilliant businessman, but you know that food service is completely different than anything else."

"Yeah, that's why I try not to dip my toes into those waters."

"Well, you're already dipped. You've done a whole dunk into the damn thing. We grew up here, Brendon." I started pacing the office, anger rising in my chest. "Why can't we get this right? We're not fucking idiots."

"Yeah, well, doesn't seem the case right now," Aiden muttered under his breath, and I turned on him.

"Just stop it. This is getting frustrating. We're trying little things, trying to bring this place up, but the problem is that people just don't come in here anymore. They go to the other four hundred places that are within walking distance."

"Maybe we can get one of those apps and do takeout orders or something?" Brendon muttered under his breath, starting to take notes on his phone. "Or try different ways to get people coming in like another wing night."

I knew Brendon wasn't talking to me, just brainstorming ideas off the top of his head, but it was still frustrating. "I don't want to close this place, but we're not working together, and it's fucking us over. Don't you get that?" I rubbed my hand on my shoulder and continued to pace.

"Well, of course, we're not working together. We don't even like each other." Aiden shook his head and leaned against the door frame.

"I don't *not* like you guys," I said, my voice low.

"Yeah, that's not really a ringing endorsement," Brendon said, smoothly. "I happen to like both of you, you're my fucking brothers. I'm the only one out of the three of us, no, make that four of us, who's not blood-related to you guys, but I actually like you. I want to make sure that this family doesn't blow up. We are a fucking family, and we're not doing anything about it. Yeah, you ran away, Cameron, because you had things to do, but you didn't come back until now. You didn't come to us when you needed us."

I stared at Brendon, wondering where this had come from, and at the same time knowing it was probably overdue.

"I tried to come to both of you. You ignored me."

"Because I was angry with you, but then you never answered my calls either."

"I just can't, I can't with either of you," I grumbled and tried to catch my breath.

"Then why don't you just leave?" Aiden snapped. "You're very good at that. That much I can remember. So just leave. Go home and find another place to work. If you hate it here so much, then just go."

I rolled on my twin, wondering what the fuck had happened. Because this wasn't just me. This wasn't about me leaving to go take care of Dillon. This was something more, and

I didn't get it. But I didn't know how to ask Aiden because I knew that my twin wouldn't answer anyway.

Maybe there were just some things that blood couldn't fix.

"I can go," Dillon said from the doorway. I hadn't even known the little asshole was there, and now I was afraid that somehow Dillon had heard too much, even though we hadn't even mentioned him. Not really.

"What?" I asked, confused.

"If me being here is screwing everything up, I can go. I have friends. I can find somewhere to stay." The kid raised his chin, and I knew that it was taking everything within him to actually say the words.

"You're not going anywhere. You're part of this, too."

Aiden flinched ever so slightly, and I wanted to punch the asshole. Didn't Aiden see that Dillon needed people? That Dillon was one of us?

Then I paused, wondering if I saw it. Because none of us were actually talking to one another. We were talking over each other, fighting about what we couldn't fix. Arguing over something that wasn't there anymore.

Brendon started yelling, saying something about numbers that made no sense to me. Oh, it probably would have made sense if I were actually listening, but I was focused on looking at Aiden and the way he was *not* looking at Dillon.

What the fuck were we doing?

Why couldn't we just talk and work this out?

Then I remembered living on the street when we were younger, holding Aiden close because we were so scared and didn't know where we were going to get our next meal. I remembered going from one home to another, trying not to get beat up by one of the foster dads, or touched by one of the foster moms—or another foster dad.

I remembered being stripped from Aiden's arms, screaming and reaching out to him even as he reached out to me.

I remembered wondering when I would see my brother again—if at all.

I remembered eating a worm out of the dirt one day when I was so hungry I couldn't stand it, and that was the only thing I could think of to do.

I remembered finally seeing my brother again after so long, when really it had only been about a year or so—maybe even less. I hadn't been able to count the days because I wasn't able to go to school like I should have.

I hadn't seen a calendar or known exactly how many hours had passed since I last saw my brother.

But over the years I was away from him again, I knew exactly how many days had passed. How many months.

I knew because I had helped put that distance between us.

And I didn't know how to put us back together again.

Because it wasn't just me anymore. It was Dillon. Dillon deserved to know Aiden. He deserved to have a future. Yes, both of us had screwed up because we didn't know what we were doing in terms of this whole growing-up thing. But we were learning it together. I just never thought that I would be learning it with only the two of us and not with my other brothers.

I needed to fix that. Because this was fracturing. It wasn't the walls of the bar cracking, it wasn't the fact that the business was failing.

It was us. We were.

And we wouldn't be able to fix anything else until we fixed ourselves.

But with the way Aiden's jaw was set, and the way Brendon kept pacing back to his phone as if he were doing two thousand things at once and not able to focus on what was in front of him, I knew that today wasn't going to be that day. So, I let out a breath and nodded at Dillon so the two of us could leave.

"You always leave," Aiden shouted at my back. "That's what you're good at."

I stopped where I was, knowing that if I said anything in the mood I was in, I would fuck things up again. But I couldn't help it. Fucking things up is what I was good at.

"At least I was fucking there for him. You weren't. You didn't have the balls to even try."

Aiden looked like I had punched him. And maybe I had in a way.

Brendon finally looked up from his phone, his eyes wide, his jaw a little slack.

And then I turned on my heel and walked away again, putting my hand on Dillon's shoulder so he knew that he wasn't alone.

I'd come back to the bar later and work my shift, but that's all it was. A job. I didn't feel like this place was mine. Didn't feel like this place was anyone's, really.

We were going to lose it because we couldn't figure out what to do with each other, let alone the business.

And, yes, that was ignorant and probably stupid.

But there were some wounds you couldn't heal. There were some things you just couldn't fix. And as I thought about the woman who had been in my bed this morning, I realized that maybe that was true for more than just my family, more than just this business.

Maybe it was true for everything I touched.

Maybe I just couldn't fix anything because I wasn't worth fixing.

Chapter Eleven

I wish I could strangle your brain sometimes. Out of love. Because screw migraines.
—Allison in a text to Violet

VIOLET

THERE WAS A SPECIAL PLACE IN HELL FOR OVERHEAD LIGHTING, THE SUNLIGHT that was streaming through my open curtains, and any form of light on any electronic device I owned.

Yes, I was slowly losing my mind because of everyday things, such as light.

Let there be light, my ass.

Bile rose in my throat, and I staggered my way around my living room, doing my best to keep my eyes shut as I drew my curtains closed.

When I decorated this house, I had known that I had a migraine issue. I'd had it since I was a teenager, and no amount of Botox shots or any other meds seemed to help. Oh, they would help for the short-term, but it was like my body got used to them, and then I would get another migraine the next month that would set me back even more.

So, I had made sure that I had beautiful curtains that looked decorative but were also able to block out any form of light that could come at me.

So, while sunlight was the thing of the devil, my blackout curtains were peace.

At least, part of that peace.

I rummaged around, trying to ignore every single sound that I was making since it seemed amplified right then, and found the scarves and other sheets that I used to cover my lampshades and other things around my house.

I still needed some light to function, but I could mute it as much as possible.

In the end, my house would resemble a den of iniquity, but I didn't care because, somehow, it gave me comfort.

Not that I was anywhere near comfortable just then, but I could at least try to improve my mood.

My stomach grumbled, and then I almost threw up, knowing that while I was hungry since I hadn't eaten in over a day, there was no way I could swallow anything. Just the idea of anything more than water—and water was a lot at this point—would be too much for me.

I had gotten home from Cameron's the day before and had fallen face-first onto the couch, groaning as my head started to ache.

I didn't even have time to think about the fact that my heart ached or that anything else a little lower ached, as well. I was too busy trying not to throw up on myself because everything hurt. Thankfully, I had fallen asleep, but I had done so with the curtains open and a single lamp on. That first burst of light into my eyes when I opened them after my very horrible rest had been too much for me, and I had thrown up right on my carpet.

I was usually better at preparing myself, but I was so out of sorts from everything that had happened, that I was clearly too many steps behind on this migraine.

"I just want to go to bed," I whispered to myself, but then I winced because I had been far too loud. Even a whisper was too much.

Everything seemed like it was too much.

I staggered around my house again, finishing up the clean-up on my rug. I had started it before and then had gotten nauseous and had to take care of my stomach again before I could finish cleaning.

Doing anything while suffering from a migraine hurt, and it was almost too much to bear, but cleaning up after yourself because you got sick because you were in pain? That was one of the worst things.

Thankfully, it was still the weekend, and I didn't have to work until tomorrow. But I really didn't know if I was going to be up for even that. Though it wasn't like I could just call in sick and say that I would try to catch up.

I already had to catch up on work that I had been a little slow on because I was so in my head when it came to Allison.

And Cameron. But I wasn't going to think about him.

I couldn't.

Regardless, I felt like I was losing my wits and everything else because I was just not up to being the Violet that I needed to be.

Just thinking about the fact that I had to work tomorrow not only made me nauseous again but also reminded me that I didn't know when or if I was going to get my next set of grants. With the random shutdowns that kept happening in the government, I knew that my funding was going to come to a close soon.

So, I was making sure that I had backup plans in place when it came to working with the university. Though I didn't want to only teach. Yes, I liked it while I was doing it, but I really enjoyed the research side more.

But there wasn't a lot of money for me to keep doing it these days. There wasn't enough money for any of us.

And on that depressing thought, I put my hands over my eyes and laid down on the couch again.

The house smelled of cleaning products and my own stench that I really didn't want to think about. But I didn't even want to take a shower, just the thought of the action was too much for me. My skin hurt. Everything hurt. My *hair* hurt.

I didn't even know that it was possible for someone's hair to hurt this much, but here I was.

Everything just hurt.

And because I needed to be in the middle of the house just in case I had to get water or rush to the restroom or do just about anything other than sleep and pretend that everything was fine, that meant I had to stay in the living room.

I hated whining, but that's all I could really do with a migraine.

It wasn't just a simple little headache like the media might have you think. People that said, "oh, no, I'm getting a migraine. This really hurts," really didn't understand that sometimes that was just a headache.

And, yes, headaches were horrible, and they sucked, but they were nothing like a debilitating migraine.

I'd had them for most of my life, and I was still trying to figure out exactly how to get through them.

I remembered the last time I'd had one of the worst ones ever. I had been down in Colorado Springs, supposed to be watching my brother's daughter, Daisy. Daisy had gotten sick herself, and my brother hadn't been answering his phone. That meant that I had to call his—at the time—ex-girlfriend to come and pick Daisy up and take her to the hospital.

Thankfully, Adrienne had rushed to help, and she had been on all the call sheets for Daisy at the doctor already.

And, even more thankfully, Adrienne and Mace were now together, happy, and getting married.

At one point, I used to think that I maybe helped in that a little, but I didn't really want to rely on my migraines to keep my family happily in love.

And now I was losing my mind because that's where my thoughts had gone.

I was just about to fall asleep again when there was a soft tap at the door. I wanted to groan.

Maybe it was the UPS man with my latest Amazon shipment. It didn't matter that I had a Prime addiction, Amazon was my everything. Of course, I didn't remember Prime shopping, but that was the deal with Amazon. Sometimes, you just opened your door and there was a package that you had forgotten you ordered.

I just lay there, hoping that whoever it was would go away, but then there was the sound of a key in the door and the lock turning.

There were only a few people with keys to my house—my parents, Mace, Sienna, Harmony, and my neighbor, Meadow.

The latter, it seemed, was who it was, because she walked in, tiptoeing inside the house with a frown on her face. I forced one eye open so I could get a good look at her, wondering why she was here.

"I'm sorry, I watched you staggering into the house yesterday, and I haven't actually seen anyone moving inside since," Meadow said softly as she came closer. And it was then that I realized that she had a whole box of things with her, and it wasn't from Amazon.

No, Meadow wasn't a good friend, but she was a friend nonetheless. I didn't really know her all that well, other than the fact that she was always there for me when I was having a bad migraine. Meadow worked from home, and her office window faced my house. And because she actually liked light—while I hated it today—that meant that, sometimes, she couldn't help but notice when I came home or left.

I remembered that Meadow wrote textbooks or something, or maybe she edited them. She also tutored when she wasn't working on those. I couldn't imagine reading right now, all I wanted to do was go back to bed. Or throw up. Or maybe try for some water. Nope. That just made me want to vomit again.

"Hi," I croaked. Keeping my eyes closed.

"I just wanted to drop off some things in case you're ready to eat later. And I figured I'd clean up around here as quietly as I could if you needed me. Then, if you need to wash your hair or do anything else, I'm here for you."

Meadow started puttering around, and I held back a smile. Not because I didn't want to smile, but because that action would probably hurt. Everything hurt.

Meadow was about my age, gorgeous, and single. I didn't know why she didn't have someone special, other than the fact that maybe she just didn't meet many people because she never left her house.

Of course, not leaving the house would probably be a nice thing because I didn't want to leave my house just then. Every time I did, I had to deal with more drama. Situations that I put myself into, I remembered.

No, my work drama really wasn't my fault. Neither was the fact that Lynn was there and had been texting me all weekend.

I'd ignored most of them because I had been sleeping, but she kept wanting to check in on me, making sure that everything was fine with our working relationship.

It was all a little too much, and I couldn't focus on anything. So, I wasn't going to focus on any of it at all.

I was just going to pray that this migraine would be over soon.

I felt someone move closer to me, and I opened my eyes to see Meadow sitting on the coffee table, looking at me.

"This is a bad one?" she asked, keeping her voice low. I was grateful for that.

"Yeah," I whispered. I used to try to nod or shake my head and answer so I wouldn't have to talk, but I figured out that doing that hurt more than just the whisper.

Migraines were the work of the devil, that much I was sure.

"Is there anything you need?"

"I don't know. Death?" I froze as soon as I said the words, and Meadow did, too.

Meadow didn't really know my other friends, but she had met them a few times over the past few years. She hadn't been at Allison's funeral because she had been out of town for something, but she had sent flowers. She also knew exactly how Allison had died, and she had been by my house to help me after the migraine that had come from me reliving exactly how I found Allison.

I didn't realize how much I used the word *death* in random conversation. Didn't comprehend that I said stupid things in the vernacular that hurt even more.

But it wasn't like I could apologize to Meadow for making myself hurt.

So, I just let out a sigh and wrapped my fingers around the edge of the blanket, pulling it closer to me.

"I'm going to get a cool washrag so you can wash your face. You're sweating a bit, and I know that you don't like that on your skin."

"Everything hurts," I said. I wasn't just talking about my physical body either.

There was something in Meadow's eyes that told me that she understood exactly what I was saying. "I know."

She tucked me in a little bit more and then went back to my guest bathroom to get a washrag.

As soon as she came back and wiped my face, I let out a groan. It felt so good, as if maybe she could wipe away some of the migraine itself.

I knew it didn't make any sense because the rubbing, even as softly as she was doing it, started to hurt my skin, but the coolness made me feel like maybe I had a fever. I knew that wasn't the case, but migraines just knocked all of my senses out of whack.

"I know you're not going to want to eat and the idea of it probably makes you want to get sick right now, but I'm going to put something in the Crock-Pot for you, and then I'm going to come by and check it later. I'm only doing that because you have nothing in your fridge.

"Shopping hurts." I paused. "That's not what I meant to say, but words hurt." She snorted, and I held back a smile only because that, indeed, would not be the least painful thing I could do just then.

"I know everything hurts. But you're going to have something to eat later for yourself that will last the whole week, or I can freeze it for you. Either way, it will be food. For later. But for now, just try to keep down some water and go to bed. I'm here if you need me."

"Thank you, Meadow."

"You'd do the same for me."

I really wished that was the truth. And maybe it was. Because I knew I would do this for Harmony and Sienna. And, yes, I would probably do the same for Meadow, she just never seemed to need me. I was always the needy one. But all of that just reminded me that

I had not been there for Allison when she needed me. Needed us. She hadn't asked for help, but I hadn't seen that she needed help either.

Was this survivor's guilt? Or was this just the idea that nothing was under my control and everything was just crumbling into pieces.

I didn't know how long Meadow had been there, but when the doorbell rang, I let out a scream. Well, at least a silent scream. I put my hands over my ears and rocked back and forth.

Who was the evil person on the other side of that door? Who would dare ring the doorbell on today of all days?

Meadow was still apparently in my house because she padded towards the front door then opened it and whispered something fiercely.

I couldn't make out the words, but as soon as I heard the deep tones of a whisper on the other side of the door, I knew exactly who was at my house.

Of course, he was here.

Meadow, ironically, knew everything about Cameron because we had gotten drunk on wine and cheese one night when we first started hanging out at my house, and I had told her everything. From the fact that I had loved him, to the fact that he had left me.

Then, we had held each other's hair back as we threw up because we'd had one too many bottles of wine and one too many bites of really stinky but amazing cheese.

So that meant that Meadow knew exactly who Cameron was as he walked into the house.

Then, the traitorous bitch left me.

Okay, that was uncalled for, but I was in pain, and she was out of the house after quickly waving goodbye and leaving me alone with him.

Cameron.

What was I supposed to do? I was helpless here, and all I wanted to do was crawl under the blanket and never find my way out.

"Those damn migraines," Cameron whispered, his voice low. Cameron had seen me during a migraine or two back when we were dating, but I'd hidden most of them from him, mostly because it hurt too much to deal with human beings.

But he had helped me through a few of them, and he apparently remembered exactly what to do. He went and got another cool washrag, the best thing ever in the history of the world, and then somehow got himself onto the couch with my head on his lap.

He ran his hands through my hair, softly petting me back to sleep.

Nothing had ever felt so good.

And nothing would ever feel this good again.

This was perfection.

I slowly drifted off to sleep, without him even saying a word. Because, honestly, there was nothing he could say to make this better. There was nothing he could say that I would want to hear.

All I wanted was to get better. Somehow, with my head on Cameron's lap and his hands in my hair, I knew that just might happen.

That probably should've scared me, but I was so warm and comfortable right then, it didn't.

Nothing else mattered.

Chapter Twelve

CAMERON

Violet was on my dick.

That was the only thing that kept going through my mind as I watched her finally fall asleep as she lay on my lap, my fingers playing with her hair.

Violet was on my dick.

And not in a good way.

I let out a soft breath, trying not to shift because I knew that might hurt her, and then she would wake up and feel like crap even more.

I hated seeing her in pain, and these migraines were no joke. They had always been debilitating and seemed to knock her back a few steps. I hadn't known how to help her back when we were younger, and I still felt so far out of my depth that it wasn't even funny.

I remembered back when we were first dating, and she'd gotten the start of a migraine in front of me. She had tried to hide it. At first, I didn't know if it was because someone had made fun of her for them, or if she was just embarrassed or proud, but I'd been really confused.

I had always thought that migraines were just more painful headaches where you could just pop a few pills and get through it.

I had been wrong. Seriously wrong.

I'd held back her hair when she threw up, and I had learned how to take care of her using cold compresses and by just lightly running my hands through her hair.

She'd always told me that she hated being touched when she was in pain, but me running my fingers over her scalp had always felt good.

So, I did my thing. I massaged Violet's scalp, and she didn't back away. Finally, she slept.

It was odd that even after all this time, I could do these things, and she could just relax in my arms. So, here she was again, asleep on my lap, very close to my dick, and finally looking like maybe she was at peace.

And, yes, there was something deeply wrong with me for thinking about my dick at a time like this, but I couldn't help it, she was Violet, and my thoughts tended to stray there more often than not with her.

It was late in the day, and I had worked the afternoon shift at the bar. I didn't have to go in tonight because Beckham was working. I could have if I wanted to, just to check things out and maybe actually have a conversation with my brothers, but I had come to Violet's instead because I had texted her and she hadn't responded.

That might make me needy, but I had actually started to get worried. Because even when we were angry with each other back in the day, she'd always texted me back. She always let me know that she was okay. And she hadn't this time. I hadn't heard from her at all since she left my house, and Dillon had been the last person I knew that had spoken to her at all. For all I knew, she hadn't gotten home safely, and something was wrong. I had even texted Sienna to ask if she knew whether Violet was okay, and she had said that she hadn't heard from her sister all day either.

I had not only worried Sienna and therefore Harmony, but I had started to worry even more myself.

So, I had driven over here to make sure that she was okay, only to find that she was anything but.

I was grateful that her neighbor Meadow had been here for her, and from the scents coming from the kitchen, the other woman had made dinner for if and when Violet woke up and was actually in the mood to eat.

I didn't know Meadow, but she had let me into the house just fine, so I guess she trusted me or had at least heard of me. Or Meadow was a serial killer, and I had just let her out of the house after she had tried to murder Violet but had gotten interrupted.

I pinched the bridge of my nose. I really needed some sleep if I was going on about that in my head. Yep, I was losing my damn mind. But that wasn't anything new.

Violet shifted ever so slightly, her hand under the blanket I'd pulled over both of us slowly rubbing along my inner thigh. I froze, making sure she was still asleep before shifting myself so she wouldn't accidentally touch something that would probably make both of us uncomfortable.

Thankfully, she went right back to sleep, and I just lay there, making sure I kept my fingers on her scalp, trying to ease away the tension of the migraine.

I had no idea what it felt like to actually have one, but I was glad about that. From the way they literally took Violet down to the ground and made it so she couldn't do anything but try to breathe, I knew I would probably react even worse than she did.

Because she had an inner strength that I was a little jealous of. And because I was one of those guys who actually reacted like the joke of a guy with a man-cold said we did, I probably wouldn't do well with a migraine.

With the temperature in the room, and the sweet smells of whatever Meadow had put in that Crock-Pot drifting over me, my eyes slowly closed, and I found myself falling asleep even though I hadn't meant to.

Violet was out on my lap, and I laid my head on the back of the couch, telling myself that I wouldn't sleep, that I would just rest for a little bit.

I snored myself awake at the sound of my phone buzzing.

I held back a curse and slowly reached into my pocket to pull it out, very thankful that it hadn't woken Violet.

She was hopefully on the other side of her migraine if the vibrations against her head hadn't sent her into another tizzy.

Hell, that probably wouldn't have felt good at all if she were awake.

But she was still sleeping, snoring slightly.

I thought it was pretty damn cute, and then I realized that there was no more light coming from behind the blackout curtains. The tiny sliver that I could sometimes see that told me exactly what time of day it was no longer there at all.

I cursed again, this time a little bit louder as I looked at the clock.

Yeah, it was almost midnight, and that meant that I had stayed here for far longer than I wanted to.

I hadn't been sleeping well, thinking about Violet, the kid, my brothers, and the bar. Apparently, I just needed to pass out. It seemed Violet was the same way from the way she hadn't moved an inch from my lap.

The buzz of my phone was a text from Dillon, asking where the hell I was.

I couldn't really blame him, considering that I hadn't told anyone where I was going, and I sort of just lit out of the bar after my shift was over. I knew that Dillon was supposed to work the dinner shift busing tables and working on possibly starting to wait tables too, but I didn't even know what time he was getting off that day. That was Beckham's choice.

I let out a breath, then quickly texted Dillon back, telling him that I wouldn't be home but that I was okay.

Dillon: *You at Violet's?*

Me: *Yeah, she's not feeling well. You okay?*

Dillon: *I'm fine. Sorry she's sick. You need anything?*

And this is why I loved that kid. Not just because he was my brother, but because he actually cared about others. Yeah, he had that veneer of a perpetual teenager that was just on the cusp of adulthood, and he still acted like a brat sometimes, but he was a good kid. Somehow, Mom hadn't fucked him up completely. Hell, somehow our mother hadn't fucked Aiden or me up either.

I ignored the little clutch I felt at the thought of Aiden's name, knowing that I needed to fix things with my twin. Because my brothers were worth more than me walking away when things got tough.

But that was something for another day.

Today was about making sure that I didn't fuck things up with Violet. After all, she was the one still in my lap.

Me: *Everything's good here. I'm just going to make sure she's fine. I'll be home in the morning. Do you need anything?*

Dillon: *I'm fine. Worked. Going to play games. Eat. Sleep.*

I snorted. Yep, that sounded like any other night. Dillon hadn't made a bunch of friends yet in Denver, though I hoped that would change soon. I didn't really know how adults made friends, so I wasn't very good at it other than work friends and my brothers. But maybe Dillon needed to find a group of people to hang out with. Or he would do better once he was in school and could actually make friends among his classmates.

I knew when Dillon had said that he would just leave and go hang out with his friends so as not to bother my brothers and me, that he was talking about his friends from California. Those friends were off in college, and we weren't in California anymore.

I needed to do better about my little brother. Hell, I needed to do better about all my brothers.

And I would. Just as soon as I figured out what the fuck the right decision was.

Me: *Don't stay up too late. We have a morning shift.*

Dillon: *Well, I guess you do too. Don't stay up too late with your girl.*

I didn't say she wasn't my girl because it wasn't like I could actually say that now, was it? We weren't going to be able to ignore each other. Not anymore. And I didn't want to ignore her. Maybe that made me a masochist, knowing that it would hurt more in the end if things went to shit, but I didn't want to walk away. Not again. I just hoped that she would be able to forgive me. Because I missed her. I missed her so damn much.

Me: *Get some sleep. Thanks for checking in.*

Dillon: *I was just worried I'd have to go live with Brendon or Aiden or something if you croaked on me.*

I laughed this time, trying to quiet myself so I wouldn't wake up Violet.

Me: *Yes, that's what I'm going to do from now on. Every time you annoy me, I'll just threaten you with having to live with one of them. I've done it, it's not pretty.*

Dillon: *Yeah, cause living with you is such a joy.*

I could practically hear Dillon rolling his eyes. But I still smiled.

Me: *Well, I guess I need to threaten Brendon and Aiden with you then, don't I?*

Dillon: *** (middle finger emoji) ***

Me: *Goodnight, loser.*

I paused.

Me: *Love you, kid.*

There was no answer for so long, I figured he'd either not seen it yet or was just sitting there wondering what the fuck was going on. I didn't really talk about my feelings all that much, and I knew I needed to do better about that.

Dillon: *You too, bro.*

Something warmed inside me, and I hoped that maybe we were going down the right track. I loved that kid. He wasn't my actual son, but I had raised him, at least these last few years.

I didn't know exactly what Dillon had gone through, but I figured it was enough to connect us in some ways.

Now I just needed to find a way to connect Dillon and Aiden. I had a feeling that Dillon and Brendon would be just fine. I had watched them over the past month or so as they circled around each other. They didn't have the animosity towards one another as Aiden had for Dillon, even though Brendon hadn't known that Dillon existed either. It was more that Brendon and Dillon didn't really know how to act around one another and were being cautious. But there was no hatred.

I was really afraid that there *was* hatred when it came to Aiden and Dillon.

But that was on me. And I was going to fix it.

As soon as I fixed everything with the woman currently lying on my dick.

And on that thought, I slowly slid out from under her, grateful that she was still sleeping. I leaned down and ran my thumb along her cheekbone. And then I kissed her forehead. When she didn't wake up, I knew that she needed the sleep. I also knew that she probably needed a better place to sleep than her couch. Because, yeah, I loved this damn couch and how deep it was so it could fit both of us quite nicely, but I knew that she might like to wake up in her bed.

I slid my hand under her neck, and then my other arm under her legs and picked her up.

She snuggled into me, letting out a soft moan, and I willed my dick not to get hard. Because I loved that moan. She moaned like that often for me. At least she used to.

I tucked her into bed, wiping her hair from her face. And then I put a glass of water by the bed, her migraine meds that I found in the bathroom right by it. I didn't know if she would need them or if we had missed the window for it, but I also didn't want to wake her up. Because when she was sleeping, she wasn't in pain, and I was going to count that as a win. And then I went and cleaned up the living room just a bit before putting away the dinner in the Crock-Pot. Thankfully, Meadow had kept it on warm, and everything seemed just fine. But I still found some Tupperware in one of the cabinets and as quietly as I could, put everything away and did the dishes. I didn't know if the Crock-Pot was Meadow's or Violet's, but I figured that leaving the ceramic part in the drying rack with the rest of it on the counter was just fine.

I was exhausted, but I wasn't about to go sleep in bed next to Violet without her knowing that I was really there. Nor was I going into the guest room because that just felt weird.

I looked at the couch that I actually liked, took one of the throw blankets from the other end, and laid down, knowing that tonight might be slightly uncomfortable, but I'd be just fine.

I didn't want to leave her all alone. Didn't want to leave her at all. I had to figure out what exactly that meant, though.

I woke up to the feeling that I was being watched. And when I opened my eyes, I smiled up at a very groggy-looking Violet.

She narrowed her eyes and pouted just a little. "Did you tuck me in?"

I stretched but kept my head firmly on the little throw pillow she had. "A couple times. You doing okay? What do you need?"

"I don't know. I just didn't expect to actually see you here. I kind of thought that you were just like part of my imagination and I had just wished you here or something."

I smiled. "You wished me here? Like you wanted me here?"

I didn't know why I sounded so needy, other than the fact that I was indeed a little needy.

"I don't know. But, I'm glad you're here. Thanks for taking care of me." She rubbed her temples, and I sat up quickly.

"What's wrong? Do you need anything?"

"I'm fine. I think. It's just coming out of a migraine. It hits me hard. It's sort of like waking up after a very long cold or when you sleep so hard that everything seems just…off. You know, like when you take a nap in the middle of the afternoon, and you wake up and realize that it's like that time right before dinner, but you feel like you've already slept and you don't really know if it's light or dark outside and you're a little off? That's how it feels, but like a little bit harder and a little bit longer."

I snorted.

"Seriously? Hard and long is going to make you think of a dick?" She paused and then laughed. "Okay, now that I'm saying it again, totally a dick."

I laughed, still keeping my voice pretty low. "Sorry, apparently, I resort to being a teenage boy when I first wake up."

She looked down at my crotch, and I snorted. Yes, I did indeed have morning wood. "Apparently, in more ways than one."

She rolled her eyes, but not as much as she might normally have, and I figured she was still probably right on the edge of feeling better from the migraine.

"Want me to make you some breakfast?"

She froze. "Really? You want to make me breakfast?"

I shrugged and then twisted on the couch so my feet were on the floor and she was standing in between my legs. I ran my hand along her hip, and she didn't pull back. I counted that as a win.

"If that's what you need. If you want something like toast, I can do that pretty easily. But I'm pretty good at breakfast. Or we can heat up some of that stroganoff that your friend made for you. Though I think you have to add the cream at the end. Which would make sense if she didn't want to overheat that."

"Meadow made stroganoff? I knew she said she made something in the Crock-Pot and I could smell something delicious, but I couldn't really put two things together and form an idea of what it could be."

"You always did like stroganoff."

"It's like one of my favorite things ever. Maybe I'll do that for lunch or dinner. And I need to thank Meadow for making it. And I'll thank you, too."

She leaned forward and kissed me softly. I didn't move or pull back. I just let it happen, worried that I'd scare her.

"Thank you," she said softly.

"You're welcome. I'm here for you, Violet. Always. Anything you need."

"I'm starting to really believe that."

She let out a shaky breath and then sat down on the coffee table in front of me. She rested her hands on my knees as if she needed to touch me but wasn't exactly sure what to do. So, I put my hands on the couch, gripping the edge slightly so I didn't move forward and scare her too much.

"Thank you for taking care of me. Thanks for just being here. I had forgotten what it felt like to have your fingers in my hair. It always made me feel safe. So, thank you for that. And just thank you in general."

"You're welcome."

"What are we doing?" she asked, and I blinked.

"I thought I was going to make you breakfast."

"No, I meant what are we doing. Everything is so complicated, Cameron. I'm afraid that if we continue to do this, we're just going to make it worse. Our lives are already so connected with how much time we're all spending together these days. What if we mess it up?"

"What if we don't?" I hadn't meant to ask that, but it really honestly seemed like the best thing to say.

"I don't know how I survived losing you the first time, and I don't want to do it again. So, we have to take this slow, or at least as slow as we're doing now." She winced, and I kind of winced along with her. "Yes, we've already had sex, and we might have sex again."

"Well, I'm going to be honest and say that I hope we do."

"Yeah, I kind of like the sex, too."

"Kind of?"

"Fine, it's the best sex ever. But let's get to the actual subject."

I tabled that, but I really liked the fact that she'd said, "best sex ever." Not going to lie, that also made my dick hard. "Okay. So, what are we going to do?"

"I don't know," she said softly.

"I didn't want to leave you before. But I did. And I can't take that back. But I'm here now. And we keep finding ourselves in each other's circles. I keep coming right back to you. And I think it's always been you. I'd like to spend more time with you. I just want to know what happens next. And I want to know what you think. And I want to just…I just want to know I'm not making a mistake. I like being with you. And I hope you like being with me."

I hated talking about feelings. Hated opening myself up like that. I wasn't really sure what else I could do right then, though. I just had to be honest. Because lying and walking away when things got tough is why everything got all messed up to begin with.

"I guess it's pretty complicated, but it makes sense. And I hated that you left. It hurt. But I'm not that person anymore. We're not that young. So, if this doesn't work out, we both have to tell each other. You can't walk away again. And I can't walk away just to hurt you."

She paused, and I just sat there, waiting to see what she would say next.

"I'm going to have to forgive you. And I guess I have to forgive myself for thinking that was the end, too. That it was the only thing that made me who I was."

"You were always more than just me, Violet. I hope you know that."

"It took me a while to figure that out. But I did. And I guess…I guess this means we try."

I nodded hesitantly. "We try. And I'd like to take you out sometime. A real date. Where we get to know the Violet and Cameron we are now. And we try to figure out what the next step is. Because I wanna take that step with you, it's just figuring out what that is that's the hard part."

She laughed. "Figuring out the next step is the hardest part of every phase of life. But I guess I'm going to figure that out with you. Because I can't stay away from you, Cameron. Even if it might not be the best thing for me."

I leaned forward and kissed her hard, surprising both of us. "I guess it's my job then to make you see that it's not a mistake."

And then I kissed her again, hoping that we weren't making that mistake. Because I wanted her in my life. And that meant I had to be a better man than I was and make sure that she saw that I wasn't the guy that would walk away again.

And that meant I had to fix everything else in my life, as well.

Because Violet deserved more than a man with a failing business and a family that was falling apart. And hell, so did I.

I guess that meant that this conversation was going to be the first of many for me.

But now, I had Violet in my arms, and that was a pretty good way to start the morning.

Chapter Thirteen

The outdoors are evil. Why must you love them?
—Allison in a text to Violet

VIOLET

GOING ON A DATE WAS SUPPOSED TO BE NICE. GOING ON A HIKING DATE COULD be very cute. Going on a hiking date where I actually had to work and collect some samples wasn't really my best idea, but between both of our jobs, Cameron and I had been a little too busy to do anything about this new relationship of ours.

I pressed my hand to my stomach, trying to keep my breath steady.

New relationship. I still didn't know exactly how that had come to be. One moment, I was having a headache of a lifetime and trying not to throw up again, and the next, I was sitting in front of Cameron, and we were discussing who we were as one and the fact that we could actually try and make this work.

I had been so hurt when he left, felt so broken, but he knew that. He knew that, and he had apologized. He'd apologized, explained, and even groveled.

I couldn't hate him anymore for what he had done. Because we all made mistakes, some of us more than others, but there had to be a reason for forgiveness. If not, what was the point of an apology at all?

"Are you regretting asking me to come?" Cameron asked as we walked to the back of the SUV where all of my equipment was.

"What?"

He leaned forward, cupped my face with his hand, and ran his thumb along my jaw. I loved it when he touched me. And he was doing it more often lately. In the past week since we both decided to try this whole romance thing, and even though we hadn't seen each other much, he kept touching me. It was as if some new switch had been flipped in both of us and we were just trying to figure out who we were. But he wasn't holding anything back. At least it didn't feel like it. He had even kissed me right in front of his brothers when I stopped by the bar after work a couple of days ago. I'd only been able to stay for ten minutes, but he had still kissed me. Much to the pleasure of his brothers, who had hooted and hollered.

"I asked you if it's really okay that I'm here. I was a little worried that you were going to regret that I came along."

I blinked, trying to focus on the here and now rather than the eight hundred thoughts twirling in my head. Sometimes, it felt like more than that, and sometimes, all I could do was look at Cameron and just think of one thing.

Him.

Yes, I was officially losing it.

"I'm sorry, just thinking. But I am glad you're here. Even though this is a very weird date."

His eyes narrowed even though I could see the laughter in them. "Are you saying that I'm the weird date? I mean, you are the one dating me. So, I guess that makes you weird, too."

"Oh, shush. And yes, you are weird. Very, very weird. But I like you anyway. Despite all of that."

With one hand still on my face, he wrapped the other arm around my body and patted me on the ass. "Okay, I'll be your weird date. But only because you're weird, too."

"Yes, because that makes total sense."

"I try. Now, I'm here, and I'm the one with the big muscles." He paused, using his hand that had been on my face to flex his muscles for me. That meant he still had his other hand on my ass, but I didn't think he minded. I didn't. Remember that part where I was losing my mind? Still doing it.

"Yes, you are all muscly and pretty. But I am still very muscly myself." I flexed both of my arms and waggled my brows

"I know. I've seen you naked.

"Okay, we're going way off track here." I rubbed my temples, trying to force my mind to focus on what I actually had to do today. Technically, I was working, but it was for the project that I'd already been paid for, and it was side-work. I had already collected most of my samples, but I wanted to gather one more. I didn't really need Cameron here to lift anything since I could do it on my own just fine, but it was nice not to be alone. Plus, the whole idea of being alone in the woods after listening to way too many true crime podcasts where a woman alone in the woods ended up murdered didn't seem like a great idea.

"You don't have to lift anything. I can handle it."

"I know you can handle it, but I'm here. That means you don't have to handle everything on your own."

For some reason, I had a feeling that those words had more to do with everything about the two of us and not just what I needed to get out of the back of the SUV. But I wasn't going to touch that, not then.

"Okay, then you take the really heavy bag with all my equipment in it. But that stuff is more expensive than anything you own most likely, so if you break it, you buy it. And since I don't think you can actually buy it, I'll have to take your soul." I lowered my voice. "And it's been a while since I've had a soul."

Cameron started laughing just like I wanted him to, and I grinned. I wasn't usually this dorky, this weird. But Cameron seemed to bring it out of me. It was like I could just be myself in strange ways like I had been before everything changed.

Yes, I was still worried about work and the fact that Lynn hadn't even wanted to be on this trip with me today. I was still worried about how my sister and Harmony were doing because none of us were truly finding ways to heal. And I was still worried about Allison. No, worried wasn't a good word for that. I was just broken over it.

But I was going to figure it all out.

"Tell me where you want me," Cameron said, and I smiled.

"You have to stop saying things like that, or I'm going to get all nervous and say something stupid. Or more stupid. Or is it stupider? You know, for someone who has a Ph.D., I really suck at grammar sometimes."

Cameron shrugged and picked up the bag that I knew was heavy, but with those muscles of his, he could handle it. "I think the English language just makes it hard for anyone to actually know. The I before E, except after C thing. Totally a crock. Because there's a whole list of words that make that a lie."

"You know, it's kind of sexy when you talk about grammar and the ways that it sucks."

"Don't get me started on those letters that don't actually say anything. I mean, this is how you spell it, but the P is silent? Never made any sense to me."

"Well, I'm sure we could rant about it on social media, but that's probably already been done. Like a thousand times."

"True." He paused, then took a deep breath. I looked at him, wondering how this had happened. How the two of us had actually come to be here after everything changed. But then again, time passed, and people changed. And that meant that who we were to each other was changing, as well. Hopefully, it would be for the better. "It's gorgeous out here," he said, his voice sounding a bit odd.

"And it's my job to try and protect it."

"I know, it can't be easy. Humans are kind of the worst thing that's ever happened to Earth."

"Don't even get me started. I literally wrote my dissertation on that."

"But you'll find a way. All of you. Because that's what you do. You find a way to protect all of us. But, damn, I've missed this place. Yes, California was gorgeous, and I loved the ocean, but apparently, I'm a mountain man. Because look at this."

He moved his free hand around to gesture at the big mountains and plains all around us. "This is stunning. And, somehow, this is real. I mean, you look at pictures of it, and it looks beautiful, but then you sit here, and it doesn't even look real. It looks more real in photos than it does when you're actually focusing on it in real life. Like I could put my hand on that tree right now, and it wouldn't feel like it was truly here." He paused. "Okay, now it sounds like I'm eating some of those mushrooms that are probably around this forest."

I laughed, shaking my head as the two of us went down the trail. "No, it sounds like you're in awe of this place. I am, too. That's why I'm here to save it. Or at least try. I'm focusing more on the streams and tributaries right now than the rest of it. The others on my team are focusing on the other types of eco-life. But my grant was for water, so I'm going to take a few samples, and then we should be done. It shouldn't take too long."

"Just tell me what to do so I don't fuck up your science." He brushed his free hand down my arm, and I looked up at him, smiling. "I love when you get all science-y. You're brilliant, Violet. Just hope I remember to say that more often."

I blushed, ducking my head. "You're not so bad yourself."

I knew I was smart. I always had been, and I was never really ashamed of it. But it was still a little hard to call myself that. And it was really hard to sit there and not act like a schoolgirl and giggle when Cameron said it to me as plainly as he had. It was just one of those things. Maybe it was part of my self-consciousness, but I would find a way to deal with it. I always did.

We walked down the trail, talking about things that didn't matter, and some things that did. The sun was shining, and there was a slight breeze. It was always a little colder when you got closer to the mountains so, thankfully, we were both wearing light jackets. It didn't take long to collect the samples, and I knew I could have done this on my own, but it was kind of nice spending the day with Cameron.

"The guys don't mind that you're out here today?" I asked as we made our way back.

He shrugged. "I'm working tonight, and this way, it gives the three of us a little more breathing room."

I winced. "Things aren't working out all that well right now?"

"Things are pretty much sucking, but we'll figure it out."

"Are you talking about the bar itself or your brothers?" I had waited to ask more about this because I wasn't sure I would be privy to the knowledge. After all, Cameron and I hadn't really been dating all that long, and I didn't want to pry when it wasn't my business. But now we were a couple. Now, we were trying to figure out what exactly we were to each other and move in a new direction that neither of us really knew anything about. And that meant I needed to know his fears, his wants, and his desires. I needed to know if he was dealing with anything in his life that was hurting him. Because, somehow, I wanted to find a way to fix it. Or at least be there for him. He had been there for me so many times since he came back from California. Now, it was my turn to try and help. Hopefully.

"A little bit of both." He shook his head as I reached to help him with the bag when we got back to the SUV. We were the only people in the small lot that really wasn't a lot. It was behind a gate for no trespassing, but I was allowed in here with my grant. Meaning, no one would be around if we wanted to talk about something that Cameron didn't want to be overheard saying. "I've got it."

"Okay. Now, do you want to tell me exactly what you mean by that?"

"The fact that I've got it? Yeah, let's talk about the bag itself." He put my equipment in the back of the SUV and shook his head. "Do I have anything else? Not really. Yes, well, I'm not really going to touch on the fact that you and I are trying to figure out who we are. Because that…that's something that we're working on together. As for my brothers and the bar? I have no idea. We're trying to save Jack's place. It's just not easy when I don't think the three of us really know what we want to do with it. And a lot of it's out of our hands. A lot of it has to do with the fact that it is the food service industry and it's not easy."

"And I guess you have to deal with the fact that you guys really haven't been in the same place for long, at least not at the same time." I was trying to dip my toes into the waters and not cause waves, but I wanted to help. I really loved the Connolly brothers, and I hated seeing them hurting.

"I'm not a hundred percent sure what we're doing. But that's pretty much been the case for a while now. The three of us—four of us if you include Dillon and, frankly, we need to include Dillon—are trying to figure it out. I'm just not good about doing that all the time."

I reached out and squeezed his hand, and he gave me a small smile before continuing.

"Aiden and I fucked each other up. But we were always like that. It was mostly to do with our mom at first, and the fact that I went to Mom because of some misguided notion that she needed me. That hurt him. And I know it's not the case, but I have a feeling that he thought I chose her over him. Hell, it's not just a feeling, he told me straight to my face that's how he felt. I was an asshole, a real big asshole."

"But you also wanted to help your mom. And then you had Dillon."

"I did. And I'm never going to regret going out to California. I can't." He looked at me, and I nodded, swallowing hard. "I will always regret how I handled getting there. Hurting you? Dumbest mistake of my fucking life. And I'm never going to truly forgive myself for that. And I shouldn't."

"But we're moving on from that," I said firmly. "Because we have to."

"And that's something I know that you are far too gracious about. But, thank you." He kissed me hard and then continued. "But I fucked it up with Aiden, and Brendon, too. That much I know. I'm trying to fix it, I just don't know exactly how to do it. We need to sit down and talk, but we're too busy yelling at each other most times to actually get it done. And then there's the whole elephant in the room. Dillon himself."

"Because he's not a little kid anymore. He's a man, even if eighteen doesn't feel old enough to be a man."

Cameron snorted. "Don't I know it. That kid can vote and fight and die for our country, but I still want to wrap him up in bubble wrap and make sure that nothing harms him. And at the same time, I want to kick his ass because we keep making stupid mistakes."

"You sound like a big brother, maybe even a little bit like a dad." I whispered that last part, having not really meant to say it.

"We do have this weird relationship. And we're working it out. Dillon's a good kid. Or man, I guess. But we're figuring it out. It's just not easy sometimes when we're constantly butting heads with each other, yet still trying to be on the same side when it comes to Aiden and Brendon. Because I hate the fact that there are sides at all."

"If there's anything I can do, just let me know. I hate seeing you guys hurting like this."

"I hate seeing it, too. And we're going to fix it. Because there's no other option, damn it. Dillon's my brother, but so are Aiden and Brendon. The four of us will just have to find a way to be a happy fucking family. And if I knew how to do that, we would already have it in the bag. So, just one thing at a fucking time." He shook his head, and I smiled at him, going on my tiptoes to kiss his jaw.

"You're pretty amazing, Cameron Connolly. I just hope you know that."

"Yeah? How amazing am I?"

His hands reached around and grabbed my ass again, bringing me close to him. So close, in fact, I could feel the hard line of his erection pressing into my belly through his jeans and my shirt.

"Cameron Connolly, are you thinking what I think you're thinking?"

"You know it could probably ease all my hurts if you just kept kissing me. You know, kiss me to make it better."

"First, that's a low blow. Second, I have a feeling that you're not actually talking about kissing your lips."

He grinned and looked down at his crotch. I laughed. "Cameron."

"You told me yourself that no one would be here. Why don't we steam up the windows like we used to?"

"Really? That's your line? Steaming up the windows?" I pressed my thighs together because it was indeed a very damn good line.

"What?" he asked, acting all innocent. There was nothing innocent about him, and that's how I liked it.

"Fine. I will have sex with you in the car. But we're using the back seat and not the front one like we did that one time because I hit the horn with my back, remember? And then we woke up that dog that started barking, and then we were afraid that the cops were going to come. It was a whole thing."

He started laughing and then picked me up quickly. I wrapped my legs around his waist and kissed him.

"I was kidding. We don't actually have to have sex out here."

I smacked him on the back of the head softly. "No, no, I want you right now. And you're the one who teased me. So, we're going to be very gentle so that we don't hurt the car."

"Hurt the car?"

"Or anything inside the car. We're not kids anymore."

"Yeah, I am pretty old. I don't think my back's going to be able to take it."

"So, I'll be gentle. Now, get me into that car and let's do it."

"Ah, yes, so sweet. Very innocent."

"You're the one who started all of this."

"No, you did. Just by being you."

I ignored the way that my heart clutched just a little. I still didn't know exactly what the two of us were doing, but I was really enjoying this part. I enjoyed how it made me feel all warm like there wasn't anything hard in the world that we couldn't handle.

Because it wasn't easy, and it never had been. Cameron had always had shadows, and I hadn't always known how to help. Sleeping with Cameron wasn't going to fix everything, it wasn't going to make everything better, but sex was never easy either. It was a connection, and it meant something to us.

Plus, I had missed him. And I liked the way we were now. So, even though I was looking into the past, I was also looking at the present and to the future.

And then I let all of those thoughts move out of my brain as he kissed me, this time deeply, and seriously.

"If you're sure," he whispered against my lips.

"With you? Totally."

He smiled and kissed me again. Somehow, the two of us got into the back of the car, my jeans down to my knees, his as well, though it hadn't been easy to get there. His mouth was on my breast, my shirt completely off, and my bra on the floor behind the driver's seat. He hovered over me, his dick covered in a condom, slowly working in and out of me as we moaned. It was soft, sweet, and still a little awkward since we were indeed in the back of an SUV, and Cameron was not a small man.

I couldn't exactly wrap my legs around him since we hadn't bothered to take off our shoes, but I still arched into him, running my hands down his back, sweat making it slick and easy for me to pull him closer.

And when I came, he came with me, and everything felt like maybe this could work.

Because, yes, we had made mistakes, and we would probably make more of them, but we were learning more about each other every day. Learning who we were. And we were taking those steps together. It was hard to trust, hard to truly believe that nothing was going to happen again in the future that might hurt me, hurt us. But I didn't think he'd leave me again, not like he had. We had both made promises that if this didn't work out, we would walk away together, but both of our eyes would be wide-open the whole time.

And I had to trust in that. Because if I didn't, then what was the point of this?

As he kissed me again, slowly working me to my peak once more even though he had already finished, I knew that this was a different Cameron than the one I had fallen in love with before. Then again, I was a different Violet.

We weren't the people we were, and maybe that was good. Because those people had been unsure, and they had been hurt. I just hoped that the people we had become didn't hurt each other in the end.

When he kissed me again, and we cleaned each other up, I smiled at him, hoping against all hope that this could work. Because I had fallen in love with Cameron Connolly once before, and he had shattered me into a million pieces.

And I knew if I let myself love him again, it would hurt worse to lose him.

Then again, it could feel even better while I had him.

And that was the hope I clung to.

That was the hope that made me think that this could actually work.

Chapter Fourteen

CAMERON

T ONIGHT WAS NOT GOING TO SUCK. AND IF I KEPT TELLING MYSELF THAT, IT would actually go well. It was wing night part *deux*.

At least that's what Brendon kept calling it. I just kept thinking it was everything that we had hoped for all thrown into a bucket of doom.

Or maybe something a little more poetic, but I kind of sucked at the whole poetry thing.

That reminded me, I should probably send flowers or something to Violet. What did one do after you had some of the best sex of your life in the back of an SUV like you were teenagers rather than heading into your thirties?

There had to be a hallmark card for that. There was a card for everything, maybe even a special flower. Nothing like red roses or anything. Maybe something purple. Was purple the color for car sex?

Oh, good. Come on, let's find me officially losing my damn mind.

Because there was no way my thoughts should be on random colors for car sex when tonight was wing night part *deux*, and I was afraid I was going to fuck everything up again.

Okay, not just me. The Connolly brothers were really good at fucking things up as a group. But I wasn't going to let that happen. I was not going to let our lack of communication and our issues with wanting to deal with the things that were actually right in front of us be a problem.

We were going to talk it out. We were going to make wing night work. And I was going to actually eat some bar food and enjoy life.

I was not going to let the business fail.

None of us were.

"You're looking a little green over there," Dillon said, his voice soft. Soft and yet there was still humor in it. That just made me smile, and I shook my head.

"Green?"

Dillon shrugged. "You know, nervous. I guess green's envious. Or maybe you ate the wings and are feeling a little nauseous?" He grinned as he said it, and we looked around the office, making sure no random customer had come to the back for some reason to overhear that.

"Shut your mouth. Don't let anyone else hear you joke about the food. The last thing we need is people not wanting the wings because of what you just said. And I'm not going to repeat what you just said because we're not going to let that happen."

"You really just confused me. But, anyway, you doing okay? Can I help?"

See? That was why I liked this kid. He may be slightly immature, may still need to figure out what he wanted to do with the rest of his life, but he was caring. He was not the product of our mother. He was just Dillon. And for that, I was grateful. I just wished that Aiden and Brendon could see it.

"Just nervous. Like always."

"Well, isn't your girl and the others coming? That should make you feel better." Dillon waggled his brows, and I just shook my head.

"Having Violet here will be nice, but three extra people eating wings won't really tip the bank scales. So, let's just cross our fingers that everything works out okay."

Dillon shrugged again. "There's a few people in, at least more than usual. I'm not quite sure since I haven't been here that long. Beckham's working, and I figured you'd be out there. They have me waiting tables tonight. Apparently, I'm training or something." He used his fingers to make air quotes when he said the word *training*, and I just shook my head.

"Yes, training. You need to learn how to work every part of the bar and restaurant."

I looked at him, frowning. "You're family, Dillon. When we were younger, we all learned every single part of this place. I always sucked at the cooking, but Aiden was damn good at it. Aiden hated working with people at the bar, but I liked that part. Brendon didn't like either but really liked working things from behind the scenes. So, let's see where you fit in." I paused. "That's if you want to. Fit in, that is."

Dillon shoved his hands into his pockets. "I don't know, man. It's not easy trying to figure out where I fit in, or if I will. And you know I hate actually talking about my feelings, so let's not actually talk about them, okay?"

I shook my head. "Today, we will not talk about your feelings if you don't want to. Mostly because you've got a thousand other things to do. But, soon, we'll be talking about it. Because, yes, we filled out the college forms, and hopefully you're going to get in, and everything'll be fine. But that's just gen-ed classes. What do you love to do? What's your passion?"

"If I knew that, I wouldn't be busing tables and possibly waiting on them."

"So, figure it out while you're in school. You have a couple of years or so of gen-ed classes, I would assume. Maybe start off in like the business sector or something? That should maybe give you the broadest options." And then I shook my head. "Brendon would probably know more about that, but he's helping you, right?" I knew that Brendon and Dillon had been talking more. I just didn't know what about since neither of them told me anything, and I didn't want to push. Well, now I was pushing.

"Yeah, he's helping. He read over my essays after you did and added a few more notes for me." Dillon held up his hands. "Not that you didn't help me out completely but, apparently, Brendon has a way with words or something."

I just smiled. "No, Brendon helped me with my school papers, too. He's a year older, remember? So, he had already gotten into college when Aiden and I were applying. He helped Jack and Rose and me figure out exactly what I needed to say. I'm glad he's helping you. He knows what he's doing." I paused again. "At least, usually. I think this bar is just stressing all of us the fuck out so much that we've all lost the ability to know exactly what we're supposed to be doing."

"You'll figure it out. You always do. You were really good at the place you owned back in California. And I know you made a shit-ton of money off it so you could come out here."

The kid grinned, and I rolled my eyes much like he did.

"It was not a shit-ton. But it was comfortable enough that I could help you with school. So, just don't fuck up. That way, I won't waste my money."

"I'll do my best. But no pressure or anything."

"Yeah. No pressure at all." I ruffled his hair like I had done when he was a little kid, and he pulled back, laughing. That was when Aiden and Brendon walked into the office, their brows raised. Brendon looked like he was smiling, but Aiden looked like he had no idea what to do. That was something I would have to fix. I just didn't know how to do it.

"We ready?" I asked, rubbing the back of my neck. "At least, I hope we're ready, right?"

"We're ready. The printer and the publicity people that I worked with this time got the word out. And I know I said I was going to work on all of it myself, but that's just not feasible. I trusted different people this time, people that actually worked directly with me rather than against me. So, there are people coming in, and there better be some amazing wings."

Aiden shrugged. "Of course, there're good wings. And tapas. Because I don't really give a flying shit if you say tapas are too fancy. We're changing this place for the better, and yes, it's wing night, but we are not just some sports bar with no name and no ability to actually draw people in. It's going to be damn good food, and they're going to like it. They're going to come in for the gimmick, and then they're going to like the damn food, and then they'll come back. Because it's the only way we're going to make this happen."

My eyes widened at Aiden's words as much as the tone. "Okay, then. I guess I'd better get behind the bar."

Brendon shook his head quickly. "Before you do, there's a few things I want to go over."

"There're always a few things you want to go over," Aiden said, growling.

I noticed that Aiden glanced over at Dillon but didn't say anything. Dillon didn't say anything either. This wasn't a mess. This was a total fucking mess. But we were going to fix it one little wing and tapa at a time.

"Okay, I think the next step needs to be the pool league that we talked about."

I frowned. "Pool league? When did we talk about that?"

"He said it like on the second meeting you guys had," Dillon said, shoving his hands into his pockets just like Aiden had just done.

I looked over at the kid and nodded. "You really should be taking notes for us, like an executive assistant or something."

"Good thing you didn't call me a secretary, or I'd have to kick you in the shin," Dillon said.

I looked over at my other brothers, all of us with laughter in our eyes. Yes, this kid was pretty amazing. "Okay, so what is this about a pool league?" I asked, trying to remember exactly what we had talked about when I first moved back. I didn't really remember much since everything had been thrown at me all at once and it was a little confusing.

"It's a co-ed pool league. I've started talking with a few other bars about it. What it does, is we bring in teams from the surrounding bars and bring in a shitload of people, and you do about four couples per night playing pool. It brings in money for watching it, brings in money for the actual league itself. And we can make it a whole thing. We just need to make sure that we have the right people playing from our bar."

I nodded, going around the desk to make some notes. I pulled up my phone and started typing. "I remember now. I think we did something similar to this back in one of the bars I first worked at when I moved to California. My bar didn't actually have a pool table so we couldn't do that. But this could work. It could really work."

"Of course, it'll work. I've thought about it a lot. I ran all the numbers, and it can at least put us in the black for this quarter and into the next. Then, we can figure out the next step. But as soon as they come in and eat Aiden's food and taste our beer? It's going to work."

"Of course, my food's going to bring people in. I'm amazing." I knew Aiden was joking, but still, it was kind of nice having my twin actually like what he did for a living.

"And, Beck and I've been working with bringing in different beers for people to try. The ones from California, and maybe some others that may not be as famous but taste amazing. So, between what we have on tap and the food, we should be able to keep them here once we get them through the doors."

"Okay, let's make tonight work. The special starts for sure in about thirty minutes, but people are already starting to come in and order."

"Let's make it happen," I said, reaching out and putting my hand on Brendon's shoulder. "We're going to make this work. We're not going to let Jack's place die."

I reached out and put my other hand on Aiden's shoulder. I knew this blocked out Dillon slightly, but I needed these two guys to understand what I needed them to do. "This place is part of us. We can't lose it. And we're going to make this work." I gave them both a squeeze and turned so I could let Dillon back into the circle. "The four of us can make this work."

I emphasized the word *four*, while Brendon nodded, smiling, Aiden jerked a bit.

I knew it had been minute, and probably hadn't even been intended as mean, but Dillon had seen it.

"Yeah, the four of us," Aiden said quickly, and that made me sigh. The knot of anger or frustration that always filled me released slightly because Aiden hadn't sounded worried or anxious about me adding Dillon to it. We just didn't know how to make this work. I had never heard of a family situation quite like ours, and making these kinds of connections wasn't easy. But we were going to do it. Because I wasn't going to let it happen any other way.

Brendon cleared his throat and then nodded to Dillon before the two of them walked out. I didn't know if they had planned it or if it was just that the two understood each other, but soon, Aiden and I were alone in the office, and things were about to get even more awkward.

"Thanks for including Dillon," I said quickly.

"Yeah, I can't really exclude him, can I?"

"Aiden."

"We have to work. Let me just deal with that first. I'm trying, Cameron. I just feel like everything came out of the blue, even though it shouldn't have. And that's not just on you, it's on me, too. But I just need a moment to breathe. So, just let it happen, okay? I don't hate the kid. I just don't know him."

"That's my fault."

"No, it's Mom's. And both of ours. But it's mostly Mom's. And that's what I have to deal with. So, let's just work tonight and make sure we don't lose this place. Because I think if we do, I think that's it. You know? There's no coming back from that."

"I know. I love this place. It saved us."

"So, I guess we should save it back. And I'll try not to be an asshole to the kid. Mostly because I don't like acting like an asshole. It just keeps coming out naturally, and it's starting to bother me."

I laughed. "We're twins. I'm an asshole, too."

"Yeah, but at least you're getting laid regularly. I'm an asshole with just my hand."

"You know you could fix that. I saw the way that you were looking at—"

"Nope. Not going there. Your girl, though, she walked in as soon as I came back to the office. She was just taking a seat with her other girls. So, go say hello to Violet, and then get back behind the bar, and serve everybody some really expensive beer."

"You know that's not how this works."

"Well, it's how it should. Just make us some money. Now, I'm going to go make the most amazing food in the history of food."

"You are weird."

"I know. But it's what draws in the ladies."

"You just said you weren't getting any."

"Stop throwing my words back in my face."

I laughed. Loving this. We sounded like we had in the past, like the brothers that we used to be before we quit talking because we were too afraid of what the answers would be if we asked too many questions.

Aiden seemed to come to the same realization, and he stopped laughing, his eyes growing slightly cooler but not as icy as they had been for the past few months.

Things weren't completely better, but they weren't worse either. They were going to change. We were going to find what we once had, even if it was a little banged up.

I had to believe in that.

Aiden lifted his chin, not in anger but as a goodbye, and then went back toward the kitchen.

I let out a breath, rolled my shoulders back, and went out to the front.

There were indeed more people here than usual.

I almost wept in relief.

Dillon was out training while he was busing, doing more things at once than I thought possible.

The tables were full, the bar was packed, and while I knew that Beckham needed my help, he waved me off for a minute, and I knew that he was giving me some time to say hello to Violet.

So, I went over to the table, kissed her hard on the mouth, waved at the other girls, and then left her blinking at me without even saying a word.

Hey, maybe this whole figuring myself out thing was working.

Because I had a girl that I had once loved and knew that I was falling in love with again, brothers who might be confusing as all get out but who were trying to find our connection again, and customers who wanted beer, wings, and even some of Aiden's tapas.

I worked harder than I had in years, and I loved it. The back of my shirt was sweaty, my feet hurt, and I had a slight headache from the noise in the bar, but it was amazing. We hadn't run out of wings, but we had come close. I only think that we stopped from running out because everything else on the menu was ordered to its full extent, as well. And that stuff hadn't been on sale or anything.

It was pretty amazing.

Violet and the others left pretty quickly after eating, not wanting to take the table. And while I was grateful they had done that, I missed her. She had leaned against the bar and kissed me goodbye as her sister and Harmony laughed and waved on their way out.

It was just like it used to be, where we were a unit. Yet it was completely different at the same time.

Things were finally starting to die down, and Beckham waved me off, wanting to close part of the bar down like he always did. The man was super particular, even though he didn't own the place. He had his ways, and I wasn't going to stop him because they worked. Beckham was the best person we had, and I wasn't about to lose him.

I was just walking back to the office to see if there was anything I could do before I went back out to the front when I saw Brendon leaning against the doorway heading into the kitchen. I went up to him, about to ask what was wrong, when he held out a hand, quieting me.

"What?" I asked, my voice a whisper.

"Look," he said, his voice almost inaudible. He pointed over at Aiden, who was at the workstation fixing up a couple of tapas plates, and lo and behold, he wasn't alone.

Dillon stood next to him, wearing an apron with his hair back and gloves on.

"See, this is how you roll it," Aiden said, showing Dillon how to plate one of the appetizers.

I blinked, looking over at Brendon.

Well, then.

"Come on," Brendon said, pulling me back.

"How did that happen?" I asked as soon as we were out of earshot.

"I walked by, and Dillon went right up to Aiden and asked if he could show him how to do something back there."

"No shit?"

"No shit. Apparently, Dillon has bigger balls than any of us thought. Anyway, Aiden stood there for a second frowning with that normal glowering look that he gets and then he gave Dillon a tight nod and moved over so he could show him how to plate something. Never saw the kid's eyes light up the way they did at that."

"Yeah, I saw those eyes. I saw them once before when he was playing in that band of his. But even then, I don't think they were as bright as they were tonight. Shit. Maybe I should be looking into culinary school for the kid."

Brendon rubbed his chin, nodding. "Maybe. Let's get him into a couple of gen-ed classes first while he figures things out, and Aiden can help train him a bit to get his feet wet and see if that's what he likes. That is, as long as Aiden keeps playing nice. But I think he will."

"I think he will, too. I think we all have to."

"Let's just give him some time. I think time is what we all need, we just didn't really know what to do when we were waiting for that next step. You know?"

"I know. I miss you guys. Sorry I was a fucking idiot."

Brendon ran his hand through his hair, looking more disheveled than usual. The man never used to, but tonight may have been a busy night, and it meant more to all of us than just numbers.

"Aiden should have called. I should have called back. It's on us just like it was you. We were all just so angry with each other that it was easier to walk away than pretend that we had anything important to say. And so, yeah, I think Aiden and I lost out on a lot of time with a kid who's pretty amazing. But we aren't now. And I'm not going to take that for granted. And from what I just saw in there with Aiden? I don't think he's going to take it for granted either. So, let's just give him some time."

I swallowed hard, my throat feeling oddly full. I cleared it. "Time works." I paused again. "We'll work it out."

"We will. Because we're Connollys. And that kid in there? He's a Connolly too, even without the name. I don't have the blood, and I'm one. You and Aiden don't have the blood, and you're Connollys. So, Dillon is, too. He's one of us. And we're not going to fail him. We're not going to fail each other. Not again."

I didn't reach out and hug Brendon, even though some part of me wanted to. I just stood there awkwardly in the hallway, my throat thick as I waited for any shouts from the kitchen in case Dillon and Aiden stabbed each other or something.

I figured this was a good step in the right direction. We had worked hard. We had plans to get more people in, the food was amazing, the beer was fantastic, and I had my brothers back.

I just needed to keep them.

And along the way, I just needed to make sure I didn't fuck up. Because I was good at that, and I was afraid that if I messed up again, that would be it. There'd be no coming back.

So, it was on me not to be the reason we lost it all.

And it was on me not to be the reason I lost Violet.

So, I would just have to do it. But the thing was, I wanted this. I wanted it all to be right. And I was going to do my best not to be the man I was before.

Chapter Fifteen

Shot! Shot! Shot!
—*Allison in a text to Violet*

VIOLET

"I THINK THIS WAS THE BEST IDEA WE EVER HAD," SIENNA SAID. I LOOKED OVER AT my sister.

Sienna had her head back on the chair, her eyes closed and covered by cucumber slices. I hadn't realized that some spas actually used cucumbers, but Sienna had apparently asked for them specifically.

I loved my sister, even if she was a dork. But then again, I was just as much of a dork as she was.

I didn't have the cucumbers on because they had slid off.

"It really was a great idea, Harmony," I added, sinking back into my chair.

My friend smiled, her eyes closed. "I occasionally have them. I knew we needed a day that was just us. We've been so busy with our various jobs and other household issues. Not to mention the fact that a certain friend of ours has a boyfriend, but I figured it would be nice to have some girl time."

"And thank you for inviting me, too," Meadow said, her voice soft.

"I'm glad you were able to come." I had invited Meadow to a couple of girl-time things, but this was the first time she had come to hang out with the three of us. I wasn't sure if it was because she actually wanted to hang out with us, or if it was the fact that she knew we were missing our fourth. Meadow wasn't replacing Allison, not in the slightest. Because we had always invited Meadow along with us even when we tried to do girl-time things with Allison. Meadow hadn't been able to come, but today, she was here.

And so, the four of us were enjoying our spa day, each of us in the middle of a different treatment. We were all completely clean, scrubbed, and massaged. I was going to get a facial soon, and I was contemplating getting a hair mask since the ends were getting a little dry these days. I had dyed it blond recently, and it was a little unhappy with me at the moment. But I liked the color, and so did Cameron.

A small smile played on my face, and I felt more than saw Harmony sit up and smile back.

"You're thinking of Cameron."

I looked up at her. "How on earth did you know that?"

"I see you didn't deny it."

"Of course, she's not going to deny it," Sienna said, her eyes still behind those cucumber slices. "Why would she deny it when she's getting laid?"

We all laughed, even Meadow.

"I think you're very lucky that we're behind closed doors right now or we'd probably get kicked out," Meadow said, a smile in her voice.

"As if they aren't used to a group of women talking about getting laid or random male body parts," Sienna said smoothly.

"Speaking of male body parts…" Harmony said, acting all too innocent.

"Hey, we're not talking about that. And, Harmony, I am truly shocked. *Shocked.* You are the sensible one of us."

"Hey!" Sienna said, finally pulling off her cucumber slices and setting them down on the table next to her. "I resemble that remark."

"I am the sensible one," Harmony said, throwing her hair back and looking very mysterious and classy. "However, I would also like to know about the size of your boyfriend's penis."

She said it so pompously that I couldn't help but snort. Thankfully, I had already finished drinking my water, or I probably would've sprayed it all over everybody.

"You did not just ask that."

"I believe I did," Harmony said smugly.

"I too would like to hear about the size of Cameron's penis," Sienna added, not sounding quite as pompous but doing pretty well.

I scowled at both of them and then looked over at Meadow, who sat on my other side. "So? I take it you want to know, as well?"

Meadow raised her chin and then plucked at a non-existent spot on her robe. "I would never dare ask such a sensitive question. However, if that information was just casually mentioned, I would indeed take in any type of gossip you may have about a certain appendage of a man I might've just met."

I just looked at her, laughing. "You guys are sick. Sick, sick, sick."

They all laughed, and I just shook my head. I had missed this. Harmony had been right. We had been so focused on our jobs and just trying to heal after Allison that we hadn't taken time to just be together. It felt weird that Allison wasn't here with us, but it also felt strange that we weren't talking about her.

So, I needed to change that. Even if it hurt.

"You know who the first person would've been to ask about his penis?" I said, keeping my voice casual. We hadn't broached the subject of Allison, not in any real detail, but I didn't want to *not* talk about her. The more we pushed her down into our memories, the more I was afraid we were going to forget her. Or forget what she meant to us.

"Allison would've already known the size of his penis," Sienna said.

My brows rose. "Huh? Are you saying that she would've already seen it? Because I have questions about that."

Sienna shook her head, smiling, and this time I thought it actually reached her eyes. And we were talking about Allison. That was progress. Even if just a little. "No, I'm saying she would've already gotten it out of you. In fact, I'm a bit surprised that we don't actually know about the size and girth of this penis since you've already bounced on it a few times. In fact, you bounced on it a lot before. So, why didn't we ever ask before now? I feel like we're missing out on this whole friend thing."

"I agree. You didn't tell us about his penis at all before. Is there something we should know? Is his penis okay?" Harmony sounded so serious that I couldn't help but laugh, tears rolling down my face.

"I don't think we've ever actually used the word *penis* in conversation as much as we did just now."

"Oh, I think at my bachelorette party we said penis a lot. But we were drunk, and Allison kept saying 'shot, shot, shot.'"

Harmony laughed as she said it, and for that, I was grateful. We were learning, healing, and trying to figure out how to have conversations about the people who were no longer with us. We were not only talking about Allison, we were also talking about somebody's bachelorette party. A bachelorette party for a wedding to a husband that was no longer with us. That was progress. I hated that we had to have this kind of progress at all, but I didn't want to hide. I didn't want to be scared anymore. And I didn't want to feel this pain when I thought about the people who weren't here.

"Cameron's penis is just fine."

"I'm so sorry," Meadow said, deadpan.

"That's not what I meant."

"So, his penis isn't fine?" Sienna asked, leaning forward. "Is there anything you can do? Wait, he has to be really great at oral if his penis sucks. Because if he isn't good at any of that, I don't know why you're with him."

"Oh, stop it, all of you. Cameron's penis is amazing. It's long, it's thick, he knows exactly what to do with it. Oh, and he's really good at oral. He was really good at oral before, and he's even better now. I can come like three to eight times a night, just with that mouth of his. But his penis? Best penis ever. Now, I never want to have this conversation again because I think I'm beet-red. And I'm about to get some skincare that might be completely negated because we keep talking about the word *penis*."

They were all silent for a moment before everybody dissolved into fits of laughter. Soon, we were each wiping tears from our faces and shaking our heads.

"I'm so proud of you," Harmony said. "And so happy for you. I mean, a man that's good with his mouth and his cock? It's like the holy grail." She paused. "Well, maybe not the holy grail, that seems kind of sacrilegious right there. But you know, it's like a unicorn. Yes, Cameron is a unicorn."

"Oh my God. Now I'm going to picture him with like a horn on his head. Or like one of those...remember that photo we saw of the guy in all purple with like his mane of random-colored hair, and he had the hooves on his hands so he was like cosplaying a unicorn?"

"Oh God, now I'm going to just picture Cameron like that all the time," Sienna said. "I mean, we're going to the bar later tonight, right? Or is that tomorrow? Why can I never remember what my schedule is without my phone in hand?"

"The pool league starts tomorrow," I answered.

"Okay, good. Because now that gives me time to find something with a unicorn for him to wear for us. He can be our mascot."

"You've officially lost your damned mind," I said, laughing again. "And now, if I picture Cameron dressed as a unicorn while having sex with him, I'm going to blame all of you. If that happens, a curse on your sex lives. A curse."

Meadow patted my leg. "You know, it's kind of mean to curse our sex lives when you're the only one having one."

"You know, Meadow," Harmony said, leaning forward again so she could meet Meadow's eyes. "I think you're my new best friend. Because I totally agree. You're not allowed to put a pox on all our sex houses."

"I cannot believe you just tried to use a Shakespeare quote. About sex."

"It's Shakespeare. There's always weird sex in Shakespeare." Sienna frowned. "Right? I actually don't remember reading Shakespeare. I mostly remember that movie with Leonardo DiCaprio. He was so young then."

I shook my head and leaned back, closing my eyes as my friends talked about Leonardo DiCaprio then versus now. We were all in agreement that we really didn't like him now but had had such a crush on him in *The Man in the Iron Mask*. What was it with that sweet baby face of his and that long hair? It made no sense.

"Seriously, though, you're smiling again," Sienna said softly, and the others quieted down.

I looked down at my hands, wondering if that was true. It could be, I didn't really know how to explain happiness. I had been so stressed about so many things and focused on try-ing to just keep my head above water, that the idea of joy seemed almost farfetched.

"I feel like I could be happy," I said softly. "Mostly because I feel like I'm me again, just not the same me as I was before."

"You're never going to be the same person you were a week ago, even a day ago. So, you're definitely not the same person you were when you were with Cameron the first time," Harmony said softly. "And that's okay. You're not supposed to be the same person after things happen."

"He broke me." I hadn't meant to say the words, but then again, my friends knew. Meadow might not know as much, but she knew a lot. And she was here now, so I wasn't go-ing to hide how I felt from her. There was no use in doing that. Plus, I knew she had secrets of her own, and I never wanted to pry. "He broke me into a million pieces. He made me feel like I wasn't good enough. That I did something wrong that made him run away."

"I never did get to throat-punch him," Sienna said softly.

That made me smile, but only for a moment. "He apologized, though. He explained, and I forgave him. I do forgive him. And, yes, while I can't forget—we're not supposed to forget what hurts us—it does make me more cautious. But I also can't walk into every part of our relationship wondering when he's going to leave me again. That's not healthy, and it would make being with him completely idiotic. You know?"

"I think he realized what he did wrong. You can tell that he's not the same person he was. And from what you said, and from how he acts, he never left to be malicious. He didn't leave because he didn't love you."

I rubbed at my chest, frowning. "No, he didn't love me enough. Or I didn't love what we had enough. Maybe he didn't trust me at all. But I can honestly say it doesn't matter now. Because that's done with. He's back. He apologized. He groveled."

"But did he grovel enough?" Sienna asked.

"I don't know. I don't know if it would be enough for anyone else, but I think he grov-eled enough for me, for us. Because I see the way he is with Dillon. I see how his relation-ship with Aiden and Brendon is forever changed and how he was forced into a situation that he doesn't understand. He doesn't know how to fix it. His relationships or the bar. And every time I tried to pull away from him after he came back, I found myself coming right back to where I was. In his life, and in his circle. Someone else might think that I'm stupid for believing I can trust him again, but if I don't let myself fall, even just for a moment, I'm afraid I'll be standing on the outside looking in at my life forever. I'm afraid I won't be able to feel again."

"I'm going to ask you something, and I want you to be honest. And I want you to not hate me for asking," Harmony said quickly.

"Okay," I said, a little worried.

"Are you with him because of what happened with Allison?"

I froze, wondering where that had come from. But since it was from Harmony, I knew there had to be a reason. Harmony had done her best not to make any major life decisions after losing her husband, and she more than anyone knew how the pain of losing someone you loved affected your decision-making skills. And she had done it twofold.

"I'm not going to say it didn't play a part in it. But I'm not with Cameron to feel. I know I didn't say that right. I'm feeling with him, but he's not the only reason I am. I have you guys, and I have a career that I love even though it stresses me the fuck out."

"Even with Lynn and douchebag?" Sienna asked.

"Even with Lynn and douchebag. And, honestly, they literally mean nothing to me. They annoy me because I have to deal with Lynn on a daily basis at work, but I can avoid her, and I can still love my job. I can still be stressed out about funding and the fact that sometimes my research just doesn't work out the way I want it to. All of that is just normal daily life. Lynn and douchebag mean nothing to me. But Cameron means something. He always has."

"And being with him makes you happy. I know it's hard to quantify what happiness means, but he is." Harmony looked down at her hands before shaking her head. "And I see the way he is around you. He's always loved you, and he always looked at you like you helped raise the sun and let it set again in the evening. And I know he hurt you, and you can forgive him and not forget, and that is perfectly fine. You guys are both different people now, and I know you're in a different relationship than you were before. Neither of you is going into this blind. And I'm so happy that you found that. Because you deserve it. You deserve so much happiness." She paused. "And I know that Allison would feel the same. Because we all deserve happiness. Even if we don't think we do."

I wiped away tears, leaning forward to grip her hand. Sienna scrambled from her chair to come and sit on the edge of Harmony's seat to get closer. I moved slightly and opened up my left hand and gestured Meadow forward. Meadow looked a little hesitant at first, but then came and sat on the edge of my chair. Then it was the four of us, just sitting in silence.

I didn't want Meadow to feel left out, but I knew she might be uncomfortable. However, this was the future. This was where we were.

And we had to figure out what to do with that.

"I'm never going to understand what happened. With Allison, I mean," I said quickly. "I'm never going to understand, but I don't think we're supposed to. But she's gone, and it changed us. And I still think those changes are evolving. And I know that we're going to find ourselves in situations where it hurts again, and we won't know what to do. So, I want you to know that I'm here. I wish that Allison had known I was there for her, or maybe it didn't matter because she couldn't reach out anyway. I don't know what went through her mind, but I want you to know that I love you guys." I squeezed Meadow's hand. "And I know you're new to us, Meadow, but we're here for you, too."

"Allison seemed like such a bright person. I'm sorry she's gone. But I'm really glad that you three are here. You're such a cohesive unit. And I'm glad that you have each other to lean on." Meadow squeezed my hand back, and I held back a sigh of relief.

The four of us sat there, talking about Allison, and then our conversation led into other things—our work, our lives. Even Cameron again.

And when we cleaned up and made our way back to our homes, I felt a little heavier and yet lighter at the same time. It was good to talk about Allison, to have her in our lives even though she wasn't really here. I didn't want to forget her. I didn't want to not feel that pain when I thought of her. Because feeling those emotions reminded me that she had been in pain. That she had needed someone. And that maybe she'd just needed an answer that we didn't have.

The tears fell again, and I brushed them away as I walked into my home. Crying was fine. It meant that I was feeling something. And I knew I couldn't be numb anymore.

It wasn't fair to anyone for me to stay numb.

When the doorbell rang, and I answered it, I knew it would be him. Not just because we had made plans for him to come over after my spa day, but because I knew I could rely on him. And maybe that was silly. Perhaps I was in for heartache. But I needed this. I needed to feel.

And so, I kissed Cameron. I leaned into him as he held me.

Because this was just one step, one breath. We were figuring out who we were with each moment and with each passing day. Yes, I missed my best friend. I missed her with everything that I had. And I hated that she wasn't here.

But I was here.

And so was Cameron.

And I couldn't add the quantifier that he was here *for now*. Because that wasn't fair to either of us. So, I was going to live in what we had and be part of this relationship.

I knew I was in love with him. Again. I was in love with Cameron Connolly, and I prayed I wouldn't break again.

Because I was afraid of what would be left over if I did.

Chapter Sixteen

CAMERON

"THIS IS TOTALLY GOING TO WORK," DILLON SAID, PACING IN FRONT OF ME.

I smiled. "Really? I'm so glad that you have all this confidence."

Dillon rolled his eyes. "Of course, I have confidence. I think I'm the only one that has any confidence in this family."

We both froze at that, and my eyes widened. Family. I was pretty sure that was the first time Dillon had ever said the word when it had to do with any of us.

"I mean…you know what I mean. I'll just go work or something."

I stood up from behind the desk where I was going over some last-minute details and went to reach out for him. Thankfully, Dillon quit moving and just stood there, looking down at his shoes.

"Family works. We were a family before, Dillon, the two of us."

"Yeah. I guess."

I closed my eyes and let out a breath before squeezing Dillon's shoulder. "No, we weren't. We really, really weren't. We weren't really a family when Mom was there, but that wasn't just you. She lost custody of Aiden and me, too. She just wasn't really good at being a mom."

"I never really thought of her as one anyway."

Dillon's words hurt, and I knew the kid was in pain. But they weren't untrue, so I kept going. "Yeah, I never really did either. I don't know why I even called her Mom, I guess mostly because it was just habit."

I usually called Jack and Rose by their names these days, even though I sometimes slipped up and called them Mom and Dad. Or maybe it was the other way around. It was always just a mix of the two for me. Dad and Jack. Mom and Rose. They were both. And they were so much more.

"Didn't you call Jack and Rose, Mom and Dad? They adopted you, right?"

I nodded and pulled my hand back to stuff it into my pocket. "Yeah. I was better about calling them Mom and Dad when they were alive. I think when I left, I kind of just went back to calling them what I had when I first moved in. I don't really get it. But you know, family's complicated."

"No shit."

"I'd say watch your language, but I guess you're an adult now."

That made Dillon smile. "Fuck, yeah."

"Hey. I'm still your elder."

"Yeah, really old. Like super-elder. Like Gandalf."

"Call me that again, and I'll kick your ass."

"Well, that means you'd have to actually catch me. You're old and feeble."

"That's it, I'm going to kick your ass." I reached for him, but Dillon slid out of the way and ducked before running right into Brendon.

My suited-up brother raised his brows before shaking his head. And then he reached up to undo his tie. "Sorry I'm running late, work got in the way. But I'm here to play pool and kick ass and take names."

"Yeah, totally not happening. I'm going to win."

"I still don't know why I can't play," Dillon said, sounding a little bit like he was pouting but not as much as he used to.

"First, Cameron, there's no way you can beat me," Brendon said, smiling.

"Second, you need to work, Dillon. Plus, there's no way that you have the skills the rest of the Connolly brothers have."

"The rest?" Dillon asked quietly and then seemed to shake it off. "Anyway, I should go back to work."

Brendon winced, and Dillon scurried off to go and get his stuff ready for busing. I met Brendon's gaze.

"Too much, too soon?" I asked, my voice deceptively casual.

"Apparently. We'll get it right someday. I kind of like the kid. But there's no way he can beat us at pool."

"Damn straight."

"There's also no way that you can beat me at pool." Brendon took off his suit jacket and hung it up on the hanger that we kept on the back of the door.

"I have Violet on my side, and she's a pool shark. The two of us are going to kick ass."

"No, Harmony and I are going to win. We're going to beat all of you."

"You know what's going to end up happening, don't you?" I asked, clearing my throat.

"Aiden and Sienna are going to end up wiping the table with all of us. Yeah. That sounds likely."

"So, tonight though, we're all set up?" I asked as Brendon rolled up his shirt sleeves.

"I hope so. I just walked in, but the scents coming from Aiden's kitchen smell amazing. My mouth is watering. I know it could be the fact that I haven't really eaten since lunch and even then, that was a really shitty salad, but I digress. When are the girls getting here?"

I looked down at my phone. "They should be here any minute. I'm really glad they agreed to do this with us."

"I don't know if they're going to do the whole pool league, though, they do have lives outside of this bar."

"Don't I know it," I said, only grumbling slightly. I hadn't really seen Violet much this week between my hours at the bar—we were actually starting to hop a little bit better—and the fact that she was just working longer hours, finishing up her research grant material. That, and she had spent more time with the girls than she had before, and I didn't fault her for that. I still didn't know how I could help her heal when it came to Allison, but I figured she and Sienna and Harmony were working it out some way.

"So, four teams are coming?" Brendon asked, looking down at his phone for his notes.

"Yeah, we're going to do the three of us this time because you're starting it off, and then another couple or duo from one of the other bars. We'll have another night here where it won't be all of us but more of the other bars, and then we'll move on to other venues. I think in three weeks we come back here. We have it all written out, right?"

"Yup, I've been working with the other bar owners, and they're excited about this, too. Anything that brings more money to all of us."

"It's sort of working with the enemy of my enemy thing," I said, only slightly teasing.

"These guys really aren't enemies. As much as I'd like to think so. We don't have a group clientele, at least they do. We're the ones on the lower end of the totem pole here. But it should bring in more money for all of us in the end. At least, that's what I hope."

"Okay, I guess it should get done. It is kind of weird that we're selling our skills in order to get people to come in." I rubbed the back of my head as I said that.

"Yeah, but hopefully it will get more people in for the next set we host. We're just going to be ourselves, sell this bar, sell our souls a bit most likely, and then get what we need to get done."

"So, I guess you'd better get down there and do it," I said quickly.

Soon, Violet and I were walking past the kitchen, bringing Aiden with us as my brother grinned, holding a plate of tapas.

It was nice to see him smile.

"Are these for us?" I asked, reaching for one of the small, bite-sized things that looked like it had cauliflower on it. Maybe?

Aiden smacked my hand, and I winced.

"Do not touch that. That is not for you, that is for the girls. Well, at least Sienna."

"Ooh, really?" I made sure to overexaggerate my words, and Aiden rolled his eyes.

"Not like that. Sienna likes to munch on things while she plays, that way she can beat all of your asses. So, don't touch. These are not for you," he repeated.

"But they're for Sienna? Interesting." Brendon leered as he said it, and I grinned.

"You guys have way too much time on your hands if you're thinking about Sienna and me. That is so not going to happen, ever."

Aiden froze for a moment as he said it, and I looked up, only to see Sienna in the hallway, both she and Violet looking at the two of us with their eyes narrowed. Sienna, however, widened her eyes for a fraction of a second before she shrugged and walked over to us.

"Good to know, Connolly. I was worried you were going to fall in love with me and things would get awkward. But as long as you feed me, I will be fine." She popped whatever that cauliflower thing was into her mouth, grinned, and then sauntered her way back to the pool area.

"Food," Harmony said, clapping her hands in front of herself. "That wasn't awkward at all. Brendon? Let's go claim a cue because I refuse to lose to these girls. You cannot make me out to be the loser here. Okay?"

I was grateful that Harmony was the one to speak first because, yes, that had been awkward. Brendon held out his arm, and Harmony pushed him out of the way, laughing as the two of them walked side-by-side back to where the two pool tables were.

I just looked over at Aiden and then Violet and then let out a breath. "Okay, then. Game on."

I took a few steps forward, kissed Violet on the mouth, and smiled again. "It's good to see you. I missed your face."

"You say the sweetest things. I missed your face, too." And then she patted my cheek and reached around to pat my ass. "I also missed other things." We walked into the pool area, and the others looked over at us.

"Unicorn!" Sienna called out, and I stared at Violet.

"Unicorn?"

Her cheeks were bright red as she shook her head. "Don't ask. For the love of God, don't ask."

"Well, now I'm kind of worried. Unicorn? Is that some kinky thing you want me to do?"

All three girls started giggling, and I thought I'd lost my damn mind. I did not understand women, even if I loved them.

The way the pool tournament worked was that each of the couples played each other, at least for the night, and then there would be points tallied for the winner. The tournament would last for eight weeks, and then at the end, there would be a big pool of money for the winners, and hopefully a lot of money for the bars that hosted the matches. Since we were starting it and it had been our idea, or at least Brendon's, we had most of our people up and stacked at the front. Two of the bartenders from Sandy's down the street had offered to take part, too.

One was a man named Samson who glowered and didn't talk to anyone, and the other was Charlotte, who apparently liked to talk to everyone. She draped herself over Brendon and then Harmony, and then she flung herself at Aiden before coming over to me. I really, really didn't know what she was up to. Was she just this flirtatious because she wanted to be? That was fine, but I was very taken and wasn't about to get involved in that. But I had a feeling she was using her flirtations as a distraction.

Too bad we were better at ignoring her than she thought.

I wrapped my arms around Violet's waist and kissed her hard. "You ready for this?" I asked, my voice low.

"Of course, I am. We're going to kick their behinds."

"Behinds?"

"Asses. Sorry. I'll add more curses to my daily life."

I rolled my eyes, and then we went to it, first playing against Brendon and Harmony.

Somehow, we ended up stripes, even though I had a feeling Violet had been going for solids when she broke. But it didn't really matter. We were going to do this. We were going to win.

We did not win.

Brendon and Harmony kicked our asses, but it was fine, we could still end up third for the evening and rack up some points for ourselves. That meant we had to go against Samson and Charlotte, who had lost to Aiden and Sienna.

"I'm going to head to the bathroom before we start again, okay?" Violet kissed me hard and then ran off towards the restroom. I watched her walk, my eyes on her ass before I pulled them away and tried to focus on the fact that tonight was fun. Beckham and the waitresses and one of our spare bartenders were working their asses off with the full crowd. People came to watch and then would move in and out of the area to go eat something, watch something on TV, or just have a few drinks. I'd never seen the pub this busy, and if we kept this up with new ideas and really good people, beer, and food, we would make it.

I was just going to rack the balls when Charlotte came over to me, rubbing herself along my side. I narrowed my eyes and took a step back.

"What's up, Charlotte?"

She smiled at me, a seductive grin that did nothing for me other than sound about a thousand warning bells.

"Oh, just wondering what a big man like you is doing all alone with his balls."

Dear God. That had to be one of the worst lines I had ever heard, and I had said some pretty bad lines myself throughout my life. Recently, in fact.

"I'm sure you and Samson are going to be hard to beat. But Violet and I...we're a team."

Was that subtle enough? Maybe I should just rub myself all over Violet so Charlotte got the message. Charlotte moved even closer, and I took a step back. But she moved faster, rubbing herself all along my side again before going up on her tiptoes to bite my ear.

Oh, hell no.

"Oh, I'm going to have fun with you tonight," she whispered, her warm breath sending revulsion through me rather than shudders.

I pushed her away, but even as I did so, I looked up to see Violet standing there, her eyes wide. She didn't look hurt so much as angry. No, there was hurt there mixed with the anger. She looked between Charlotte and me and then just shook her head before spinning on her heel and storming out of the place.

Everything had moved so fast, I wasn't even sure that anyone else had seen it. No one else had been in the room other than Charlotte and me, but I hadn't realized that until it was too late.

It didn't matter that I had pushed Charlotte away, it didn't matter that I hadn't done anything wrong. To someone who already had trust issues when it came to me and how I had treated her in the past, this looked bad, seriously fucking bad.

"Why did Violet leave?" Brendon asked, worry on his face.

I shook my head in answer. "I'm out, Violet and I call it. I have to go back to her."

Harmony stepped in front of me, though, her hand out.

"Harmony, get out of my way," I growled.

"Don't bark at her like that," Brendon snapped.

I glared over at him before trying to move past Harmony again.

"I can handle it myself, Brendon. And you cannot handle Violet right now. She's angry and hurt."

"What?" I hadn't realized Harmony had seen what happened. Not that anything had happened, but still.

"I just saw the tail-end of it, and while I'm sure you thought nothing was wrong, Violet is allowed to react how she wants to. She's already a little tender. So, I'm going to go and help her figure this out. You join Brendon and figure out how to work things out between the two of you and finish the game. Do it for your bar. I will help Violet." Harmony cleared her throat. "And don't tell Sienna until she's done. Let her win. She needs this happiness." Then Harmony picked up her stuff and walked away, leaving me with Brendon.

What the hell?

What. The. Hell?

Chapter Seventeen

You're my person
—Allison in a text to Violet

VIOLET

I SHOULD HAVE DONE SOMETHING OTHER THAN WALKING AWAY. I SHOULD HAVE screamed, I should have asked him something. I should have gone to that woman and tugged on her hair and beat the shit out of her.

I should have done anything other than walking away.

But that wasn't me. I wasn't good at confrontation. I walked away and thought through my options before I figured out what I needed to do next. I went through every scenario, and then I reacted. I hid inside myself, and I let the reactions come.

That was how I operated. I wasn't someone who could just go up to someone else and scream at them how I was feeling. The fact that I had ever done that with Cameron meant that he got under my skin in ways that no one else had or could.

I rubbed my chest, at the same time trying to will away the migraine that I knew was coming on.

It hurt so much.

Should I have left them like that, knowing that it could have been more if I hadn't been there? Or knowing that it could have been more even if I had been there the whole time.

None of it made any sense to me, but it wasn't like I knew what I was doing.

I walked away because I was scared. Scared of what I had seen. Scared by the fact that I had trusted, and it had screwed me over.

I should have stayed. I should have talked it out. I should have answered my damn phone when he called later.

But now it was the next morning, and I had done nothing. I had done nothing because I needed to think.

And that had been a mistake.

Because now I was alone, breaking all over again, and wondering if I had trusted too quickly. It didn't matter that Cameron probably hadn't done anything wrong. That wasn't the point.

It was the fact that I had trusted too quickly.

The fact that, for a brief moment, I had *known* that I had made a mistake in trusting.

And because of that, I didn't know if I could truly trust *myself*.

It was like I was peering through the fog, trying to figure out exactly what hurt and why I couldn't react the way I needed to. I knew there were things I needed to do. I knew that I needed to talk to Cameron. I needed to realize that everything had just been blown out of proportion and it was all just stupid. I knew all that.

It didn't make it easy to do. It was like I was two steps behind, watching my life fall apart before me and seeing the decisions that I needed to make yet wasn't able to make.

And this time, I knew it wasn't just a headache, it wasn't just a migraine.

My heart hurt, and my palms turned sweaty, and I felt like something was constricting my chest. As if there was a two-ton elephant—or however much they weighed—on my chest right then, making it hard to breathe. Everything hurt, and I felt like if I didn't make a decision, I was going to mess everything up. But if I *made* a decision, it might just get worse. I couldn't focus, couldn't take everything in. I couldn't breathe, couldn't do *anything*.

Was this anxiety? Was this an actual panic attack?

I tried to suck in a breath, only it didn't work, so I sat down in the middle of the floor of my living room and forced myself to breathe, forced myself to focus.

Sweat dripped down my temples, and I tried to just be. I needed to focus on my breathing, if I did, everything would be okay. It had to be.

Nothing was out of my hands completely. Nothing was entirely scary. Everything was going to be all right.

Cameron wasn't cheating on me, that much I knew. But it was just seeing him there, having that split-second moment of insecurity that had sent me into a tailspin. Because I was so afraid that if I was wrong, I would break, and I couldn't be like that anymore. I couldn't be that person.

And then I thought of Allison. And I thought of why. And I just…I couldn't think anymore.

Because I didn't know why Allison had done it. I didn't understand why she had left us all, and why we were all still here wondering why she wasn't with us. It didn't make any sense.

I had gone through a divorce, faced the fact that my husband had cheated on me, and I hadn't reacted like this. I knew I hadn't loved Kent the way I should, and that was on me. I had still been broken over Cameron, and yet I had gotten with Kent because I thought it was the only thing that I could do to try and heal.

And then he had proposed to me, and I said yes. It had been too fast and too wrong. I'd thought I'd gone down the right path, that I was doing what was expected of me even though my family didn't know him and I wasn't sure I loved him. And when he left me for Lynn, I had been angry, but I hadn't been broken.

Cameron had been the one to do that to me.

And I had been the one to do that to myself because I had trusted him back then.

So, trusting him now was hard, and yet seeing that woman all over him changed something inside of me. Something I didn't want to think about.

Because Cameron had never once cheated on me. That thought shouldn't have ever come into my mind, and yet when he left me before, when he walked away without a second glance, I had thought that maybe there was someone else.

And maybe there was. Perhaps there had been the idea of another woman. His mother.

Not in a creepy, weird way, but in the fact that he had left me for a connection that he hadn't been able to fix.

And I had forgiven him for that. But I didn't know how to put everything back together again.

Why had Allison done this?

I asked myself that question again, I knew it was all connected.

Because how was I supposed to know when enough was enough and when the pain was too much? What had I missed with my best friend? If she was hurting, why didn't we realize it, why couldn't we find the answers? Were there any answers? Why was she gone, while I was still here? Why was the pain inside of me so bright, and why did it burn so much when I was still here, and she wasn't?

I stood up on shaky legs and went to the bathroom, looking at my reflection in the mirror.

All of my makeup had run down my face, my black raccoon eyes staring back at me. I looked like I was dying inside. I had bright red cheeks and even brighter eyes, and I didn't recognize myself.

Was it because I missed my best friend? Or was it because I didn't know why she was gone? How could I be okay with being here, with being alive, when I didn't know why she was gone?

My head started to pound, and I knew I just needed to take my meds so I could function. It didn't feel like a full-on migraine, but even a partial one could incapacitate me for a time.

I opened my medicine cabinet door, pulled out my pills, and looked at the bottle. I looked at the number that was left. Shaking my head, I quickly took one and drank my glass of water before putting the bottle away.

Every time I looked at my pills, at *any* medicine, I thought of Allison. And that worried me. Not because I feared for my life, but because I hadn't seen the signs in her. And I didn't like the idea that we'd never get any answers.

I didn't like the idea that the answers were never going to be there. That I would never know if I could have changed something. Done something.

I was being selfish again, but right then, where everything felt as if it were falling apart again, maybe I needed to be a little selfish.

"I need help," I whispered.

That was the gist of it all. I needed help. I needed help, and I wasn't going to get it. Not standing here looking in the mirror, or even talking to my friends. I wasn't going to get it by worrying if Cameron was going to come after me, or if he was going to call again. I needed to talk to someone who could actually help me with trying to figure out what I had overlooked, and what was wrong with me. Why I missed Allison so much.

I just needed help.

So, I took a deep breath and went to get my phone.

I needed help.

And so, I called my brother. Mace would help. He would know who to call.

Because I missed my best friend. And I didn't want to lose Cameron or myself because I didn't know how to deal with all of that.

So, I asked for help.

Chapter Eighteen

CAMERON

VIOLET WOULDN'T ANSWER MY CALLS. DID SHE NOT TRUST ME? I CURSED. Then again, I didn't know why I was even asking myself that question. Did I even deserve Violet's trust? That was the question that needed an answer. I sure as hell hoped the answer was yes, but what if I was wrong? What if I was so fucking wrong?

"Hey, Brendon and I wanted to talk to you. You okay, bro?" I shook myself out of my thoughts, knowing that I needed to call Violet again, that is if she would answer her fucking phone. Or I could go there. Everything would be okay. I just needed to talk to her.

"I'm fine. Let's go," I said, getting up from the desk. I'd been going over the numbers from the night before, even though Brendon had already done them, and I liked what I saw. I just wished everything else in my life was working out. So far, only the bar was doing well. Considering that was the one thing that hadn't been doing well recently, maybe I should count my blessings.

I didn't want to count those blessings. Well, not just them. I wanted to count Violet among them, too. And that meant I needed to talk with her.

I followed Dillon out of the office and into the bar. We hadn't opened yet, so it was just my brothers and Beckham behind the bar, cleaning glasses.

"What's up?" I asked, knowing my voice sounded a little on edge. Hell, I was on edge.

"You want to talk about it?" Brendon asked, playing with the condensation on his water glass.

"I'm fine." I ran my hand over my face, knowing I needed to shave soon but not caring. I just didn't care about anything right now except for fixing what I'd messed up.

"You're not fine. Just go talk with Violet." Aiden glowered at me, and I sighed.

"I'm going to. As soon as she answers her damn phone."

"Go to her house," Aiden said quickly.

"Doesn't that border on stalking?" I was only partly joking.

"Not if you just do it the once, and you guys are already dating," Dillon said quickly. We all looked at him, and he held up his hands. "I mean, don't break into her house or crawl in through her bedroom to stare at her when she's sleeping or anything."

"What the hell are you watching these days?" I asked. Dillon shook his head.

"It doesn't matter. All I'm saying is you're allowed to go to her house. Don't force your way in, but ask her what is going on. If she tells you that she never wants to speak to you again, after that, well, then you have your answer."

I looked at my little brother and frowned. "You're suddenly a font of knowledge. I'm a little worried about you."

Dillon blushed a bit, ducking his head, and I leaned forward, a little concerned. "Well, since you're all here, I should tell you that I'm going to be a font of more knowledge soon." He grinned and held up a piece of paper like he was showing off a good grade, and then I realized exactly what it was.

All thoughts of my other worries slid out of my head, and I couldn't help but smile widely, elation filling my veins, even if only for a moment. "You got in? You fucking got in?"

Brendon cheered with his water glass, and Aiden looked between all of us, smiling. Smiling was good. Smiling was not scowling.

"Yep, I got in to the University of Colorado at Denver for the spring. Which is great because I have no idea what I want to be when I grow up, but at least I'm going to be spending a lot of money to take classes."

"Don't worry about the money. Just get good grades and pass. Then we can figure out what you want to be when you grow up later. Which is really weird to say because it took me a really long time to realize what I wanted to be when I grew up." I went around the bar and hugged the kid, and Beckham poured sodas for everyone except for Brendon, who stuck with his water.

"Aiden?" Dillon asked, his voice soft.

I froze, not wanting to interrupt the moment, but if Aiden hurt Dillon's feelings, I was going to get really pissy. I was already on edge, and I didn't want to hurt anybody because I was so pissed off at everything.

"What's up, Dillon?" Aiden asked, his voice calm. Calm was good. It wasn't being an asshole.

"Will you still help me with the whole food thing? Because I'd like to do it, I just don't want to get in your way, but I also don't want to try out for culinary school when I know next to nothing, and then realize I don't actually want to do it and waste everyone's time, you know?" Dillon had stuffed his hands into his pockets and said the words so quickly that I barely understood exactly what he was saying as he spoke.

Aiden was silent for a moment as he studied Dillon, and I held my breath, hoping that they weren't going to come to blows—if even verbally.

"Of course, I'm going to help you. You're my brother."

I swallowed hard, emotion clogging my throat. I wasn't going to cry, but it was damn close. Hell, I didn't think Aiden had ever used those words when it came to Dillon before, and from the look on the kid's face, he realized it, too.

Aiden cleared his throat and looked around at all of us. Brendon leaned back as if he had a feeling he knew what our brother was going to say. I had no fucking clue and was a little worried. Then again, I was always worried these days.

"Since we're getting everything out in the open here, I'm sorry, Dillon. I was an asshole. I'm an asshole for many reasons, but mainly because I made you feel like you weren't wanted. That was never the case. I just didn't know how to deal with the fact that I had this long-lost brother on top of the fact that Jack and Rose were gone, and Cameron was back. We'll figure things out. If you want to go to culinary school, I'll help you there too because I am probably the best chef in Denver." He winked when he said it, and I laughed, all my emotions warring with each other. Holy hell. "Shut the fuck up, Cameron. I am the best. However, if you want to be second-best, Dillon, I can help you."

"And when the student surpasses the master?" Dillon asked, and I snorted, glancing at Brendon, who grinned widely.

"He has you there, Aiden. Make sure you don't teach him too well."

Aiden flipped us all off. "If he ends up being the best chef in Denver, it'll be because I've retired, but then everyone will know that I *taught* the best chef in Denver. Anyway, you need help, I'm here for you. And I think I'm a little done with the whole brotherly love thing, but just know that I'm going to stick here. I'm not leaving and going to another place. I like this bar. I loved what Jack and Rose did with it, and I love what we're doing with it. So, you're stuck with me for the time being."

"Good to hear, because the bar's doing fucking fantastic, at least for that one night. We're not out of the woods yet, but I can actually see the light at the end of the tunnel."

Brendon cleared his throat and looked at all of us, and I leaned against the bar, waiting. Beckham was there, part of our conversation. He might not be family, but he was close enough now. He was helping keep the bar in the black, and that was all that mattered.

"We need to keep at it. We need to keep working our asses off, but we're going to be able to keep Jack and Rose's place, at least for the time being. So, let's keep at it, and let's just not fuck up."

"Hear, hear," I said, raising my soda glass. We all clinked glasses and took sips, and I shook my head.

"I don't want to lose this place. I *can't* lose this place. So, I'm here. For the long haul."

Aiden nodded. "All of us are. But the kid's going to be in school soon, so I guess we're going to have to deal with a new busser."

"Hey, I need spending money."

I nodded. "True, but you're still not getting a raise."

"But I may be a server soon. I mean, my training did go well." Dillon grinned, and I rolled my eyes just like he had a habit of doing. I had been doing it often. No wonder teenagers did it incessantly.

"Okay, so we're all in agreement," Brendon began. "We're going to make this place work, and we're going to kick ass. Dillon is going to school to take at least some gen-ed courses until he decides what direction he wants to take. He'll figure it out, and we'll be there for him. And, Cameron? You don't have to pay for all of it. We are Connollys. We take care of each other."

"I'm not really a Connolly, though," Dillon said quietly.

I cleared my throat again, meeting Dillon's gaze. I hoped he understood that I was being completely serious now. "Yeah, you are. If you want the name, we can get you the name, but no matter what, you're a Connolly. You're our brother."

Dillon looked like he was on the verge of crying, but then again, I thought the rest of us were, too. At some point during the conversation, Beckham had quietly walked out. While I appreciated it, I kind of felt like we were all in need of a beer or something, even if the kid wasn't old enough to drink and it was still a little bit early.

"While we're on the subject of brothers…" Aiden said softly. I stiffened and looked over. "Yeah?"

My twin let out a breath. "Don't ever walk away again. We're brothers. I walked away, too. That much I know. Not answering your call for a fucking year? That's on me. I didn't deserve for you to ever call me again after that. You tried. You even came here to my house to try and tell me about Dillon, and I didn't even bother answering the door because I was so pissed at you for going off to Mom. That's on me."

I nodded, remembering that cold night that I had stood out on Aiden's porch, banging my hand on the door, willing him to come out so we could just talk. But Aiden had been so pissed off, and then I had been so livid that nothing had happened at all. We lost so many years.

"I won't let that happen. I'm not leaving. We're going to talk shit out."

"Good," Aiden said. "Because if we don't, I'm going to kick your fucking ass. Because you're my fucking brother. You don't get to leave like that. You don't just get to say things are too hard."

"Same goes for you," I said, this time growling just a little bit. "And I don't know what's going on with you, but if you need us, we're here."

"I'm fine. You're the one who seems to be in the doghouse, though," Aiden said quickly.

"That much is true," Brendon put in. "Go get your girl."

"I'm going to. Because I'm a fucking asshole, but I love her."

"Yes, use those words. It's very sweet. Very romantic." Aiden lifted his glass up in cheers, and I rolled my eyes.

"Fine. I'm going to be a little late for my shift then, most likely. I have to go get my girl."

Dillon hooted, and Aiden shook his head, but Brendon was the one to reach out and stop me.

I frowned. "What? I'm not on until later tonight."

Brendon sighed. "Oh, that's fine, and I can work behind the bar if you end up not showing up at all."

"Please don't do that," Beckham called from the back, and we all laughed.

Brendon scowled. "I'm just fine as a bartender."

"No, you're not," Beckham called again.

My brother just stared, the tick at the corner of his mouth in full force. "Anyway, if we ignore that asshole—"

"Not an asshole. Just a better bartender!"

"Shut up, Beckham!"

"You're not my boss."

"Yes, I am. We all are. Anyway," Brendon continued, "I know we just talked about the whole not being a stalker thing and going to her house, but you really don't want to go to her house."

"Why?" I asked.

"Yeah, why?" Dillon added.

Brendon shrugged. "Because she's not there."

I narrowed my eyes. "And you would know this why?"

"Because I was talking to Harmony about it, and it seems that she, along with Sienna and Violet, are off in Colorado Springs visiting Mace for the day. They're having a nice family meal even though the Knight parents are out of town."

"You were talking with Harmony?" Aiden asked.

"Off-subject."

"No," I said softly, "that might not be off topic at all." I sighed. "I guess I'm driving down to Colorado Springs."

"You're going to go grovel in front of her entire family?" Dillon asked. "That's actually pretty good. Groveling in front of others accentuates the groveling I think. It probably adds more points for later grovels, too. So, yes, do that."

I threw my hands up into the air. "Where are you finding these things? Is there a special book I should be reading about groveling and how to deal with women?" I asked, but I wasn't actually joking just then.

Aiden and Brendon laughed, but Dillon just grinned. "My ex-girlfriend really liked romance novels, so I started reading them with her. You learn a lot about women by reading romance. You should pick up a book. They're interesting, and there's some hot sex in there, so that's a plus. Don't worry, they use condoms, so I get extra safe sex lessons. Plus, whenever one of the heroes is an asshole, he still gets the girl because he grovels. And he actually means it. So, do it. Mean it. Get down on your knees if you have to, but just do it well."

I looked at my little brother in an all-new light and blinked. "Romance novels?"

"I have a few on my phone that I can send you links to after you beg for forgiveness. Because no matter what happens, you're going to end up having to apologize again later for something that you do. It's what we do. We're men."

"Aren't you eighteen?" Aiden asked.

Dillon smiled wide. "Yes, but I know all."

"Yeah, not so much," Brendon said but pulled out his phone anyway. "So, where should I start?"

As Aiden also had his phone out, I just laughed, then shook my head and walked out of the bar, knowing I had a place to be.

The drive wasn't going to be fun on my way to Colorado Springs to go see my girl, but I needed to grovel. If my little brother was on the right track, I needed to bow and scrape well.

Chapter Nineteen

VIOLET

I WAS OKAY. I WAS BETTER THAN OKAY. MOSTLY BECAUSE I WAS OUT OF MY HOUSE with people that I loved, and I knew that with just a few more breaths, I would be fine.

I had called Mace the night before, and he had told me that he was going to come and get me and that I wasn't going to sleep alone in my house. That I was going to be just fine, and that I was going to find a therapist that worked for me, and we were going to get through this.

My big brother was a lot of things, and amazing was just one of them.

He was a little older than Sienna and me, so there'd always been some distance between us, but no matter what, he was there for us. And he was there for me today.

I ended up driving myself to Colorado Springs after letting Sienna know that I was going to spend the night at Mace's. I didn't have to work until Monday, so I planned to take some time for myself. I might even take Monday and Tuesday off, too, because I was allowed to when I had the vacation time. I might as well use it for my mental health.

I wasn't depressed, at least I didn't think so. I did not have thoughts of ending my life or doing anything to harm myself. But I needed to work out my feelings about Allison, and I needed to get through my grief. And to do that, I needed to talk to someone beyond my friends and family.

I was aware of that, and I was going to lean on my friends while I did it.

So now, I was at Mace's house, his fiancée leaning into him as their daughter Daisy danced around the kitchen.

Sienna and Harmony were with me in the living room, laughing as we ate some appetizers and waited for dinner. We were doing an early meal since it was the afternoon and Daisy wanted to play, but I didn't mind. I was surrounded by people I loved who loved me.

And, yes, we all needed to work through our emotions and our feelings, but we were doing it. And I wasn't afraid to ask for help. I'd always been a little bit scared to ask for help because I had to deal with my migraines and then the fact that I was worried about school and then my divorce and Cameron and all of that. It was hard for me to want to ask, knowing that I might ask too much.

But I was going to get over that, even if it annoyed me sometimes.

"Okay, so we have cheese. Lots of cheese." Adrienne grinned from the kitchen, and I looked over at her.

"What is it with you Montgomerys and cheese? It's like every time we come over here, it's cheese this and cheese that."

"One does not mock the cheese," Adrienne said serenely.

"Cheese, it's good!" Daisy exclaimed, and we all laughed.

"Seriously, though," Mace said quickly. "Don't mess with cheese with the Montgomerys. At least the Colorado Springs ones. Thea, Adrienne's sister? She's insane with the cheese."

"Hey, I'm going to tell her you said that. And then you're not going to get the brie with the pepper jelly on top. You know, the stuff made from the gods. It's like ambrosia."

"Okay, I retract my statement. I will never, ever mention anything bad about cheese."

My brother looked me directly in the eyes with a very somber expression. "Because that cheese is the best thing I've ever had in my life, and I will not risk it. Never. Not even for a joke."

"Mace got weird," Sienna said, not quite whispering in my ear.

"Very, very weird," I agreed.

"I don't know," Harmony said, shrugging. "I kind of agree with him about the cheese. I've had some of that pepper jelly. It's pretty amazing."

"No, you had pepper jelly," Mace said, "but you've never had *Thea's* pepper jelly." He kissed his fingertips like a chef. "The best thing in the world."

"And yet we're not going to have any tonight?" I asked, my stomach suddenly rumbling. "Because I feel the more we talk about it, the more we should actually have it."

"It's not like Beetlejuice where you say it three times, and it just shows up," Adrienne said dryly as she set a cheese platter down on the table. "But I have three types of cheeses for you. Only three because I get a little overwhelmed by more than that. Now, if we were at Thea's table, we'd have like seven. But that's just her and Dimitri, they're kind of special like that."

I shook my head, laughing, and put a piece of Havarti on a cracker. I really liked cheese, apparently not as much as some people, but to each their own.

"I love you, Auntie Violet," Daisy said softly, hugging me.

Daisy had hugged me more in the past twelve hours than I thought she had for the past month. Maybe she assumed I needed it, or perhaps she just needed it, too. I knew Daisy missed Allison, all of us did. And holding onto the little girl, the bit of my brother that was all the best parts rolled into one—daisies and unicorns and puppies—just told me that I had made the right decision in making sure that I was okay. All of us were hurting in little and different ways, and it was okay. It was okay to talk about it, it was okay to miss Allison. It was okay to be completely confused about why we were where we were.

We were just finishing up the cheese course and getting ready to head into the dining room for the rest of the meal when my phone buzzed.

"Is it Cameron?" Sienna asked quickly.

"Do I need to kick his ass?" Mace asked. "Because I wasn't allowed to do it before. I deserve an ass-kicking."

"Yes, you do deserve an ass-kicking." Adrienne grinned.

Mace scowled. "I meant I deserve to kick his ass. I misspoke. Shut up."

"Don't tell your fiancée to shut up," Sienna snapped. "Violet, is it Cameron?"

I looked down at my phone and groaned. "No, it's the end of the world."

"Is it Kent or is it Lynn?" Harmony asked.

"I never liked Uncle Kent," Daisy said. "He was a butthead."

"Daisy!" Adrienne said quickly. Of course, there were little red splotches on her cheekbones, so I had a feeling that Daisy had learned that phrase about Kent from someone in the family, and it wasn't me.

I just shook my head. "Oh, he is a butthead. But I'm going to answer this. Who knows, maybe Lynn is hurt or something and can't come into work."

I waved off their looks, knowing that I probably shouldn't answer, but I wasn't a mean person, and my goal in life at least for now was to face my demons, even if one of them was named Kent.

I figured the call was about to drop soon since it took so long for me to answer. When I did, Kent's very chiseled and boring face came on the screen, his eyes narrowed.

"Hi, Kent. How can I help you?"

"I thought you weren't going to answer." He paused. I saw him frown, and I wondered what the hell this could be about. "But I'm glad you did."

"Good. How can I help?"

"Lynn and I just wanted to ask you something. No, we wanted to say something."

"Okay." I had a really bad feeling about this, but it wasn't like I could hang up. And, frankly, Kent hadn't called me since the divorce was final, so I was kind of wondering what exactly he had to say. It wasn't like Lynn had been the one to call me. And we worked together. It would make sense if she called me. Maybe not on a Sunday, but you never know.

"Well," Kent cleared his throat. The phone rustled, and then it moved to landscape mode, so both he and Lynn were in the frame.

Great. This was going to help me. Totally.

"We just wanted to let you know that we're expecting. A baby. We're having a baby."

I waited for the shock, waited for it to hurt. I was expecting the pain that had come when I saw Cameron standing there with a woman next to him. I was waiting for that infinitesimal amount of time to pass where I thought that my trust in Cameron wasn't good enough.

That never came.

And honestly, I didn't think it would come at all.

"And?"

Kent cleared his throat, and Lynn gave me that sickly sweet little smile of hers. The one that said she pitied me.

I really hated her. Not because she used to be my friend and was now married to my ex-husband. Not because of the cheating. Because of those looks.

"Well, we know it's been really hard at work with how things are."

I held up my hand and realized that they couldn't actually see that, so I just shook my head. "No, you're going to stop right there. Live your life. Love your life. I'm doing the best to live mine. I've learned the hard way that others can't always live their lives."

They gave me a strange look, and I swallowed back some tears. Not because of them, but because of those who I had lost because they couldn't live the life they wanted. Or some other reason that I just didn't know.

"I'm happy for you. Happy that you're moving on. But it's not my business. It never was." And so I hung up and really hoped that they wouldn't call again. Because, frankly, I wasn't in the mood to keep hitting ignore.

My ex-husband and his wife were having a baby. That was great. Seriously great for them. Kent had always wanted kids, and while I wanted some in the future, the two of us having kids had never really been a big part of my plan. Yes, that was probably on me. I hadn't really felt when I was with him. But I did feel when I was with Cameron. And so, the next time Cameron called, I was going to answer. I wasn't going to be so far into my head that I would run away again.

I was just walking back to the dining room when the doorbell rang. I frowned.

"Can you get that, Violet?" Mace asked from the kitchen. "My hands are full, and you're closer."

"Sure. But you're lazy," I called out and then laughed when I knew my brother was trying to flip me off from beneath the pot holder.

I opened the door and then froze.

"Cameron."

"You're here. Oh, thank God. I had Brendon text me the address, though I don't know exactly how he got it, and I'm not going to ask. But I was really afraid that I read it wrong and would end up at the wrong door. But you're here."

I swallowed hard and looked at him. "Yeah, I'm here. And you're here."

"I'm here to say I'm sorry."

I shook my head and then moved forward to put my hands on his chest. Damn, I missed him. "No, you don't have to be sorry. That was so not on you. I think I just got overwhelmed and I walked away, and then I couldn't answer my phone. Couldn't because it was too much, not because I didn't want to. And I'm sorry."

He blinked. "Really? Wait, no, I'm supposed to be the one groveling here. I'm the one who let that woman touch me."

I shook my head and bit my lip. "Let's never talk about that again because that was so not on you. I'm the one who walked away because I got overwhelmed. I did exactly what you did. We really suck at communicating." I said quickly. "I'm so sorry."

"No, that's my line. Seriously. I'm the one who sucks at communicating. I'm sorry." He was almost growling the words now, and I had a feeling that he had practiced a whole speech and I was ruining it for him.

"I love you." His eyes widened, and I continued. "I love you so damn much. I loved you when you left, and I loved you even more when you came back. I just didn't realize it. There are a lot of things that we need to talk about, but first…first you need to know something. I love you and I'm sorry for walking away like I did. I'm sorry for it being too much and me not knowing how to handle it. I did exactly what you did, and now that I'm thinking about it in retrospect, I'm really ashamed."

Cameron shook his head and cupped my face, kissing me hard. "I came here to apologize to you. To grovel as Dillon said. He said a good grovel is exactly what was needed."

"He told me he was reading those romance books and learning about women." I laughed when Cameron rolled his eyes. "No, really. He mentioned it. I guess that's where he learned the word."

"That's what he tells me. But I love you so fucking much, Violet. We need to do this better. We need to be better at this. We're older now, we have more experience. We can't be stupid at this."

I kissed him then and fell into him. "I love you so much."

"And I love you so fucking much." I sighed at his words, let them sink into me. "I've loved you for so long, and I made so many bad decisions that broke everything that I had with the people I loved. With people who loved me. And I'm never going to do that again. Yes, I'm going to make mistakes, but I'm never going to make this mistake again. So, anytime there's an issue where it gets to be too much, we need to talk it out. Or we need a sign or something to say that we need some space. Something so we don't end up in this situation again. Because, Violet? I can't live my life the way that I know I need to if you're not in it. I need you by my side. I need you." He let out a breath. "You're the one who talked about breaking before, but I know I'd be broken without you, I was already breaking without you before. So, let's do this thing. Let's figure this out together. Because I love you so much."

"I don't want to ever break again. Not like that. And I do trust you. I'm the one that walked away this time. But I'm not going to do it again. So, come on inside, Cameron. Let's have dinner with the Knights, let's take it one step at a time. Because I love you. And I want you in my life just like you said. And we'll come up with that sign when things get to be too much. We'll come up with everything."

And so, I took his hand and led him into the living room.

I knew we had more to talk about, that there would be more emotions and feelings that we needed to deal with as time passed. I knew I wasn't completely over losing Allison, and I never would be.

But that was just one part of my life, a part that I would get through by talking with good friends, with family, and with my man by my side.

The man I loved with all of my heart.

We'd ended up apart for too long because of mistakes we couldn't erase, but now we were together in spite of those. And that meant more than anything.

That was a promise.

A promise worth keeping.

Epilogue

CAMERON

THE BEER WAS POURING, THE TAPAS WERE POPPING, AND PEOPLE WERE laughing, spending money, and having a good time. The fact that we were on week eight of the pool tournament, and I was in second place along with my girl meant that we were doing pretty damn well for ourselves.

The bar was doing great, and I knew we would be just fine, no matter what happened next. The Connolly brothers and Jack's place, The Connolly Brewery, were going to thrive.

And as I wrapped my arms around my woman, kissing her hard before she bent over so she could take her shot, I knew that my girl and I would be just fine. Plus, as I took a few steps back to watch her ass as she moved, I knew I was a very, very lucky man.

"You know, you're making it very hard for me to concentrate when you keep looking at me like that," Violet said, shaking her hips.

I just grinned, keeping my eyes on her ass. "Well, I can't help it. I kind of like it."

She looked over her shoulder and mock glared. "Kind of like it? I don't think so. You're supposed to love it."

"If you two could stop discussing Violet's ass and everything you'd like to do with it and get to actually playing pool, that would be wonderful," Brendon said, chalking up his cue. He met Harmony's gaze, and both of them started laughing at a joke I probably wasn't privy to. Didn't really understand what was so funny about the fact that I liked watching Violet's ass, but...whatever.

There was shouting from the kitchen, and I winced. "Damn it," Brendon muttered under his breath. "You want me to go handle that?"

"I've got it," Dillon said quickly before running back there. The fact that the shouting was between Aiden and Sienna was not lost on anyone. They had been disqualified the previous week at another bar because they had been fighting and hadn't actually finished the game. So, they weren't even in the tournament tonight. I didn't know why they were fighting, but I figured we'd learn eventually. We were all too close these days for us not to figure it out. Dillon was a brave soul for going back to the kitchen. But Sienna liked him, and Aiden and Dillon had created a bond over the past couple of months and seemed to understand each other better than they had before.

Things were looking good, and I was damn happy.

Violet missed her shot, cursed under her breath, and Brendon and Harmony smiled at each other before Brendon went for his own shot.

"Sorry about that," Violet said.

"No worries, this is just fun at this point. The next tournament is getting set, we have another special going on, people are crowding the bar. I'm happy." I kissed her temple, and she leaned into me, so I wrapped my arms around her.

Things hadn't been easy for the past two months, and I knew they wouldn't be completely easy going forward either. But that was fine. All three of the girls had started going to therapy, and I had even gone with Violet a couple of times. I'd had a therapist when I was younger, but then I quit going, but I actually liked going and talking with Violet's so I might end up getting one of my own. That was if I didn't just keep talking with Beckham or my brothers behind the bar. They said a bartender was like a therapist sometimes, and most of the time, Beckham usually ended up feeling like he was qualified for both jobs—or so he said.

Therapy or not, I loved the woman in my arms, and one day I would ask her to marry me. Not yet, not when everything was just a little too fresh, a little too raw. I wanted to make sure that she was settled and ready for what we faced.

She had grant money coming in for work, and Lynn was no longer working at the school because she was pregnant and didn't want to be near some of the chemicals and had decided to be a stay-at-home mom. That meant that Violet didn't have to deal with her ex-husband or anything having to do with him, and she could actually do what she loved and focus on it.

I knew she was still dealing with grief over Allison. That would likely be never-ending even as it changed.

But we had each other, and we trusted each other.

And maybe Dillon was right, and reading romance novels had helped just a little. It felt like I could get into Violet's head just by reading someone else's words regarding what a woman might actually want. Of course, it was fun reading it to each other, and especially when we got to the dirty bits and could try and act out some of the scenes to see if it was physically possible. It was research, after all.

Brendon missed his shot, so I went for mine. I made two balls and then missed the third.

I cursed at myself, but Harmony looked like she was on cloud nine. She sauntered over to the table, pulled her hair back from her face, and sank their last two balls and then the eight ball in quick succession.

I felt like we had been hustled, even though I'd been watching her get better over the last two months.

"That's my girl," Brendon called out, spinning Harmony around. She pushed at his shoulder, and the two of them separated, not looking at each other but still smiling.

I rolled my eyes at them as they started doing an actual synchronized dance that I had no idea when they'd had the time to practice, but apparently, they were competitive when it came to pool.

Violet pouted for a second before laughing at the spectacle that was the dance before turning around in my arms and kissing me on the chin.

"Well, we got second place. We still get money, right?"

"Yeah, a few bucks. Kind of pissed off that Mr. Moneybags over there got most of it, but whatever."

Violet kissed my chin again. "How about I use some of my winnings to buy you a beer."

"So you can give more money back to the bar? I think I like this."

"Sounds like a plan to me. Because I plan on hanging out with you here for a long time to come, Cameron Connolly. So, you better keep that sign above the door and the Connollys within these walls. Because I love it here. And I love you."

"I love you, too, Violet Knight." And I kissed her, ignoring the catcalls from around us. People were coming in to congratulate the other team and then taking the pool table for their own, enjoying the time, having fun, drinking and just being.

But I only had eyes for the woman in my arms. I knew that everything was going to be all right, just like she'd said. Because I had Violet. I had my family. I had this bar.

And I didn't need to keep running away from things.

Finally.

Next in the Fractured Connections Series:
Harmony and Brendon in Shouldn't Have You.

A Note from Carrie Ann Ryan

Thank you so much for reading **BREAKING WITHOUT YOU.**

This story wasn't easy to write. But it was one that I needed to get on paper. This series is heavy, I know that, but in the end, there is hope, there is that happily ever after. I wanted to write a series where there is love even when it doesn't feel like there can be.

I'm honored you're reading this series and I do hope you continue on. This is possibly one of my most personal series and I'm blessed in the fact I get to write it.

Next up is Harmony and Brendon in *Shouldn't Have You*, and if you know my personal story, you know this book will be hard, but then again, there is a reason we all love reading HEAs.

After that, Sienna and Aiden have some explaining to do. And Meadow and Beckham surprised me and screamed that they needed their stories as well.

BTW, in case you didn't know, Mace and Adrienne had their story in *Fallen Ink* as the Fractured Series is part of the Montgomery Ink world!

And if you're new to my books, you can start anywhere within the my interconnected series and catch up! Each book is a stand alone, so jump around!

Don't miss out on the Montgomery Ink World!

- *Montgomery Ink (The Denver Montgomerys)*
- *Montgomery Ink: Colorado Springs (The Colorado Springs Montgomery Cousins)*
- *Montgomery Ink: Boulder (The Boulder Montgomery Cousins)*
- *Gallagher Brothers (Jake's Brothers from Ink Enduring)*
- *Whiskey and Lies (Tabby's Brothers from Ink Exposed)*
- *Fractured Connections (Mace's sisters from Fallen Ink)*
- *Less Than (Dimitri's siblings from Restless Ink)*

If you want to make sure you know what's coming next from me, you can sign up for my newsletter at www.CarrieAnnRyan.com; follow me on twitter at @CarrieAnnRyan, or like my Facebook page. I also have a Facebook Fan Club where we have trivia, chats, and other goodies. You guys are the reason I get to do what I do and I thank you.

Make sure you're signed up for my MAILING LIST so you can know when the next releases are available as well as find giveaways and FREE READS.

Happy Reading!

The Fractured Connections Series:
A Montgomery Ink Spin Off Series
Book 1: Breaking Without You
Book 2: Shouldn't Have You
Book 3: Falling With You
Book 4: Taken With You

Want to keep up to date with the next Carrie Ann Ryan Release?
Receive Text Alerts easily!
Text CARRIE to 24587

About the Author

Carrie Ann Ryan is the *New York Times* and *USA Today* bestselling author of contemporary, paranormal, and young adult romance. Her works include the Montgomery Ink, Redwood Pack, Fractured Connections, and Elements of Five series, which have sold over 3.0 million books worldwide. She started writing while in graduate school for her advanced degree in chemistry and hasn't stopped since. Carrie Ann has written over seventy-five novels and novellas with more in the works. When she's not losing herself in her emotional and action-packed worlds, she's reading as much as she can while wrangling her clowder of cats who have more followers than she does.

www.CarrieAnnRyan.com

Also from Carrie Ann Ryan

The *Montgomery Ink: Boulder* Series:
Book 1: Wrapped in Ink
Book 2: Sated in Ink
Book 3: Embraced in Ink
Book 3.5: Moments in Ink
Book 4: Seduced in Ink
Book 4.5: Captured in Ink

The Montgomery Ink: Fort Collins Series:
Book 1: Inked Persuasion
Book 2: Inked Obsession

The Promise Me Series:
Book 1: Forever Only Once
Book 2: From That Moment
Book 3: Far From Destined
Book 4: From Our First

The On My Own Series:
Book 1: My One Night
Book 2: My Rebound
Book 3: My Next Play

The Tattered Royals Series:
Book 1: Royal Line

The Ravenwood Coven Series:
Book 1: Dawn Unearthed

Montgomery Ink:
Book 0.5: Ink Inspired
Book 0.6: Ink Reunited
Book 1: Delicate Ink
Book 1.5: Forever Ink
Book 2: Tempting Boundaries
Book 3: Harder than Words
Book 4: Written in Ink
Book 4.5: Hidden Ink
Book 5: Ink Enduring
Book 6: Ink Exposed
Book 6.5: Adoring Ink
Book 6.6: Love, Honor, & Ink
Book 7: Inked Expressions
Book 7.3: Dropout
Book 7.5: Executive Ink
Book 8: Inked Memories
Book 8.5: Inked Nights
Book 8.7: Second Chance Ink

Montgomery Ink: Colorado Springs
Book 1: Fallen Ink
Book 2: Restless Ink
Book 2.5: Ashes to Ink
Book 3: Jagged Ink
Book 3.5: Ink by Numbers

The Gallagher Brothers Series:
Book 1: Love Restored
Book 2: Passion Restored
Book 3: Hope Restored

The Whiskey and Lies Series:
Book 1: Whiskey Secrets
Book 2: Whiskey Reveals
Book 3: Whiskey Undone

The Fractured Connections Series:
Book 1: Breaking Without You
Book 2: Shouldn't Have You
Book 3: Falling With You
Book 4: Taken With You

The Less Than Series:
Book 1: Breathless With Her
Book 2: Reckless With You
Book 3: Shameless With Him

Redwood Pack Series:
Book 1: An Alpha's Path
Book 2: A Taste for a Mate
Book 3: Trinity Bound
Book 3.5: A Night Away
Book 4: Enforcer's Redemption
Book 4.5: Blurred Expectations
Book 4.7: Forgiveness
Book 5: Shattered Emotions
Book 6: Hidden Destiny
Book 6.5: A Beta's Haven
Book 7: Fighting Fate
Book 7.5: Loving the Omega
Book 7.7: The Hunted Heart
Book 8: Wicked Wolf

The Talon Pack:
Book 1: Tattered Loyalties
Book 2: An Alpha's Choice
Book 3: Mated in Mist
Book 4: Wolf Betrayed
Book 5: Fractured Silence
Book 6: Destiny Disgraced
Book 7: Eternal Mourning
Book 8: Strength Enduring
Book 9: Forever Broken

The Elements of Five Series:
Book 1: From Breath and Ruin
Book 2: From Flame and Ash
Book 3: From Spirit and Binding
Book 4: From Shadow and Silence

The Branded Pack Series:
(Written with Alexandra Ivy)
Book 1: Stolen and Forgiven
Book 2: Abandoned and Unseen
Book 3: Buried and Shadowed

Dante's Circle Series:
Book 1: Dust of My Wings
Book 2: Her Warriors' Three Wishes
Book 3: An Unlucky Moon
Book 3.5: His Choice
Book 4: Tangled Innocence
Book 5: Fierce Enchantment
Book 6: An Immortal's Song
Book 7: Prowled Darkness
Book 8: Dante's Circle Reborn

Holiday, Montana Series:
Book 1: Charmed Spirits
Book 2: Santa's Executive
Book 3: Finding Abigail
Book 4: Her Lucky Love
Book 5: Dreams of Ivory

The Happy Ever After Series:
Flame and Ink
Ink Ever After

Single Title:
Finally Found You